Critical acclaim for *Penny Vincenzi*

'Penny Vincenzi has delivered an unputdownable family saga in her latest novel . . . A cross betwen Barbara Taylor Bradford's *A Woman of Substance* and Anthony Powell's *A Dance to the Music of Time*, this is volume one in Vincenzi's series, *The Spoils of Time*' *The Lady*

'Packed with passion, pain, pace and palaver . . . it's high-class, well-structured . . . with enough juicy sub-plots and interesting minor characters to keep you gripped through many a chilly evening . . . Fans are in for a feast' Val Hennessy, *Daily Mail*

'Deliciously readable. Penny Vincenzi's novels are rollicking contemporary fantasies' *Mail on Sunday*

'The literary equivalent of a huge box of beautiful hand-made chocolate truffles – a total indulgence' *Ideal Home*

'This is another of Penny Vincenzi's unputdownable block-busters – with a rattling good plot and a feisty heroine'
Woman and Home

'Like an illicit lover, I have been sloping off all week to snatch another hour's pleasure with *Almost A Crime*, Penny Vincenzi's terrific new novel' Jilly Cooper, *Daily Mail*

'A rampantly riveting read . . . This one's the business' *She*

'A super read that will keep you guessing right until the end'
Company

'A turbulent novel of epic proportions spanning three decades and two continents . . . A powerful, sexy read' *Options*

'A wickedly good read' *Sunday Express*

'Seductively readable . . . I carried on reading late into the night'
The Times

Penny Vincenzi began her career as a junior secretary for *Vogue* and *Tatler*. She later worked as Fashion and Beauty Editor on magazines such as *Woman's Own*, before becoming a contributing editor for *Cosmopolitan*. She is the author of two humorous books and ten previous novels. Her latest novel in Orion paperback is *Into Temptation*, the third in the trilogy 'The Spoils of Time'.

By Penny Vincenzi

Old Sins
Wicked Pleasures
An Outrageous Affair
Another Woman
Forbidden Places
The Dilemma
The Glimpses (short stories)
Windfall
Almost A Crime
No Angel
Something Dangerous
Into Temptation

Another Woman
Forbidden Places

PENNY VINCENZI
Two Great Novels

ORION

An Orion paperback

Another Woman
First published in Great Britain in 1994 by Orion
First published in Orion paperback in 1995

Firbidden Places
First published in Great Britain in 1995 by Orion
First published in Orion paperback in 1996

This paperback edition published in 2003
by Orion Books Ltd,
Orion House, 5 Upper St Martin's Lane,
London WC2H 9EA

A CIP catalogue record for this book is available
from the British Library.

ISBN 0 75284 251 X

Printed and bound in Great Britain by
Clays Ltd, St Ives plc

Another Woman

For my family, all of it,
with much love

Acknowledgements

As always there are people without whose help this book could not have been written.

In no particular order, but with equal gratitude, for their knowledge, expertise and patience in the face of my interminable questioning I would like to thank Felicity Green, Caroline Baker, Karen McCartney, Sian Banks, Sandra Lane, Robert Carrier, Stephen Jones, Mary Anne Champy, Ursula Lloyd, Tony Rossi, and Dr David Storer.

Nobody could enjoy more inspired publishing; could I thank in particular Susan Lamb for constant emotional as well as practical support; Katie Pope and Caroleen Conquest for exemplary patience and attention to the nuts and bolts which would otherwise surely all have fallen out; and Rosie Cheetham, who is everything an editor should be: patient as well as hard-headed, inspiring as much as truthful, and above all optimistic in the face of such considerable odds from her author such as ever later delivery, much noisy anguish and a complete inability to predict even in the vaguest terms how the book might finish.

And as always, a special thanks to my agent Desmond Elliott, who is also the wisest, funniest and most wonderfully encouraging friend.

It was going to be the perfect wedding.

Of course everybody always said that about weddings, but nobody sitting round the great pine kitchen table of the bride's home that perfect July evening doubted it for a single moment. How could they? When the couple themselves were so patently and blissfully happy, sitting together, holding hands, smiling round at their families, at indulgent fathers, proud mothers and assorted friends smiling back at them. When the sun was finally setting on a perfect day, night drifting over the deep Oxfordshire valley, with just a touch of mist promising another still more perfect one tomorrow, the thick, rich scent of the roses drifting in through the open door? When Maggie Forrest, mother of the bride, could finally relax, knowing that everything was in order, the pink and white marquee up and decked with flowers, the tables half set, the champagne (vintage) delivered and in crates in the utility room off the kitchen, the food in the process of being transformed from dozens of pounds of salmon, chicken, beef, mountains of strawberries, raspberries, eggs and cream into the most splended wedding feast by the caterers, and the cake, four exquisitely iced tiers, standing on the dining-room table?

What could possibly go wrong now? they might have asked one another. For such a perfect match, between Cressida, younger daughter of the immensely successful and distinguished gynaecologist James Forrest, and Dr Oliver Bergin, also a gynaecologist, only son of Mr and Mrs Josh Bergin of New York City. Cressida, so pretty, with her fair English-rose beauty, so enchantingly mannered, so extremely well suited to the life and husband she had chosen; and Oliver, so dashingly handsome, and almost too charming for his own good, as Maggie Forrest had remarked, laughing, to Julia Bergin on the first occasion they had met. The guest list was long, but not too long, just 300, for Cressida had insisted on being married in the little stone church in Wedbourne where she had been christened. All over England the women on the list had been buying dresses, choosing hats, mulling over the wedding lists (the General Trading company and Peter Jones), and checking on their husband's morning suits; and the chosen eight whose small children were to be attendants had been trekking up and down to the London studio from where Harriet Forrest, Cressida's older sister, ran her fashion empire, and where the dresses had been made – not Harriet's usual sort of thing, but charming nonetheless, sprigged muslin Kate Greenaway style for the girls, white linen sailor suits for the boys. Cressida's dress had been made at the Chelsea Design Company, a wonderful creation in heavy cream silk, studded with pearls and with the palest, tiniest pink silk roses drifting down the train. It hung upstairs now in the attic room that Maggie used for sewing, swathed in its muslin cover, the veil beside it in a box, waiting for its tiara of fresh flowers to arrive in the morning, along with her bouquet (cream and pink roses) and the baskets of daisies and scabius that the attendants were to carry into the church. In the dining room of the Court House the presents were stacked, ready to be shipped over to New York, when young Dr and Mrs Oliver Bergin settled into their new home in East 80th. Marvellous presents: glasses, china, linen, silver, all listed, the thankyou letters long since written.

A few miles away in Oxford the string quartet that was to play at the wedding was practising a rather difficult Mozart piece which the bride had specially requested; the vicar of St Stephen's, Wedbourne was running through the few wise if predictable words he always spoke at weddings and the organist was rehearsing the choir, and in particular the dazzling-voiced small boy he had just discovered in the neighbouring council estate, in 'Love Divine'. A few miles away in the garage of the Royal Hotel, Woodstock, the cream vintage Rolls belonging to the bride's godfather, the famously powerful and rich Theodore Buchan, was being given a final and quite unnecessary polish.

Everything ready; everything perfect. For a perfect wedding for a perfect bride.

And who could possibly have thought, on that golden scented evening, entertained a suspicion even for a moment, that the perfect wedding was never to take place at all?

The Evening Before

Chapter One

Harriet

Late, she was going to be late, for the bloody pre-wedding supper. God, her mother would never forgive her. She could see her now, carefully serene smile growing tense as she looked ever more frequently at the clock, could hear the barbed comments, about how she, Harriet, was always late, always had so much, so many terribly important things to do; and her father would be trying to calm her, to make light of her lateness, and Cressida would be saying of course it didn't matter, it didn't matter at all, everyone else was there, telling her mother not to fuss, but making in fact the lateness more noticeable, more important. Well, it was all very well for her mother and for Cressida. They didn't really have immense claims on their time. They didn't have to worry about leaving London mid week for a Thursday wedding. Thursday! Why not a Saturday like everyone else? Of course her mother had worked very hard on the wedding, but it had been the only thing she had had to think about, and Cressida's job with her Harley Street doctor was hardly stressful, she could take time off whenever she needed to, at the bat of her long eyelashes. They didn't have a business to run, collections to design, stock to deliver, books to balance. Or not balance. Harriet suddenly felt so sick, so frightened that she braked violently and pulled over onto the hard shoulder. She sat there, breathing deeply and slowly, hauling herself together. Don't panic, Harriet, don't; don't look down even. It'll be all right. Well, it probably won't, but you'll be all right. It's not a hanging offence, going bust, going bankrupt. It may be the end of a dream, but she could survive that. She'd survived the end of others after all.

Her head ached, and her throat felt dry, scratchy; it was a bit like a hangover. Only she hadn't had a drink. She'd wanted to have a drink all day, several drinks, but she hadn't. She'd had to keep her head clear for the endless phone calls, the faxes, the decisions. All to no avail, it seemed. She was almost certainly done for: stymied; defeated. She needed more money than she could possibly even imagine getting hold of, within twenty-four hours, and the one person who might be able to supply it was the one person she couldn't possibly ask. So that was that really. She just had to face it, and rethink the rest of her life. Harriet looked at herself briefly in the rear-view mirror; the events of the day showed with awful clarity on her face. It wasn't just that she was pale, most of her make-up gone, her hair uncombed, not even that she looked tired; her dark eyes were heavy, her skin somehow dull, her mouth drawn and taut (rather like her mother's, she thought with horror, consciously relaxing it, forcing a fake smile into the mirror). Her mascara had smudged, adding to the shadows under her eyes, and the collar of her white linen shirt was crumpled. Her earrings were hurting her; she pulled them off and felt her ears throb painfully, and for some reason that was the last straw and she felt hot tears stinging behind her eyes.

'Oh for God's sake, Harriet Forrest,' she said aloud, wiping them irritably away, 'don't start crying now, just because your ears hurt.' And she turned on the engine again, pulled back onto the road and put her foot down, forcing her mind away from the day behind her and on to the one ahead. Her sister was getting married, and she had serious responsibilities, not the least of which was to get to the Court House as soon as ever she could. Sitting on the M40 feeling sorry for herself wasn't going to solve anything. Against all logic she felt suddenly better, more in order, better in control; she was even able to appreciate the beauty of the evening, the darkness settling onto the shadowy Chiltern hills. It would be nice to see everyone, especially Rufus and Mungo, and Merlin would be there, bless him, she hadn't seen him since he got back from Peru, although she'd heard him talking on *Start the Week* or something, his wonderfully strong voice sounding more as if it belonged to a twenty- than an eighty-year-old. And then she switched on the radio, and Pavarotti was singing 'Un bel di vedremo' from *Madame Butterfly* and that really was too awful, too cruel, and although she did not stop again, she saw the last twenty miles of her journey through a dreadful haze of pain.

'That was mean of You, God,' she said aloud again, as she finally turned the Peugeot into the gravel drive of the Court House. 'You really had it in for me today, didn't You?'

James

James felt a rush of intense relief as the lights of Harriet's Peugeot beamed into the darkness. It wasn't just that he had been, as always, worried about her, for she drove so much too fast (and in that way, as in many others, she was very much his daughter, the carrier of his genes), it was

6

that her arrival would create a stir in the room, a regrouping, would make it possible for him to leave it, to escape briefly from its claustrophobic perfection. He was finding it almost physically stifling, having enormous difficulty in sitting still; indeed had got up so often to refill the glasses, to offer more coffee, to pass fruit, cheese, biscuits, that Maggie had finally said sweetly, but with a just discernible touch of irritation, that he was making everyone feel exhausted, and that he should relax and let people help themselves. As if she of all people knew about relaxing, with her overcontrolled calm, her near-manic, all-encompassing smiles. Susie, for all her energy, her eager vitality, had a well of calm within her that was truly restful. He looked at her now, as she sat chatting easily, happily to Josh Bergin, to Cressida, to Oliver, and wondered resentfully as he had a hundred, a thousand times if Alistair recognized his intense good fortune in having her as his wife. She had taken that marriage in all its distinct lack of promise and turned it into something happy, constructive, strong. He had never in all the years heard her complain about, even belittle it; it was her job, her career and she had been hugely successful at it. And now, by some extraordinary, almost evil quirk of fate, it was threatened. She had come over to him in the garden where they'd been having drinks in the scented early evening, before supper, her dark eyes just a little wary, and said, 'Jamie, we have to talk.' And a little later, while Maggie was putting the final touches to her supper, and Alistair was, in his beautifully mannered way, helping to carry glasses in from the garden, he walked with Susie through the rose garden and she said, her voice half amused, half anxious, 'Jamie, you're not going to believe this, but Rufus tells me he wants to get married.' And he said, 'Well, is there any great problem in that?' And she said, 'Just possibly, yes, there is. He wants to marry Tilly Mills. I'm not sure quite why, but I think it might very well open a rather large can of worms, don't you?'

And ever since he had been so afraid, so deeply uneasy, that he had had trouble swallowing Maggie's perfect supper, and had been more consumed with longing for a drink than he could remember in the whole of the – what? – twenty years that had passed since Tilly Mills had been born.

It was the forced inactivity that was so frightful, his absolute powerlessness to do anything about it. Any other night, he would have perhaps have talked to Rufus, questioned him casually, gently about his life, about his plans, would have been able to form at least some impression of how serious things really were. But not tonight, with all the family gathered for his daughter's wedding, when he had so many other worries and concerns, slight in absolute terms, but of immense importance in the immediate future, and so he had simply had to sit and watch Rufus, as he sat at the table, displaying the slightly old-fashioned charm that was his trademark, talking with huge and courteous interest to his mother, (he was famously devoted to Susie), to Julia Bergin, to Maggie, to Janine Bleche, Cressida's French godmother (amazingly glamorous still, even if she was over seventy), and know that before he could explore the matter any further, at the very least twenty-four hours would have to elapse. It was almost unendurable.

He looked with intense envy at his godfather, slumbering sweetly in the corner by the Aga: Sir Merlin Reid, famously eccentric explorer (and making discoveries still, even in his ninth decade, with the world so much smaller, so much more familiar than when he had begun his travels, sixty-five years earlier). Merlin had cut short his last expedition (travelling the Central Cordillera by mule) in order to be at the wedding. He had never married himself, had said no woman would stand for him, nor he for any woman, but James was a son to him, and Cressida and Harriet granddaughters: he would not have missed being in the family, he said, at this time for the world. He was still, in his mid-eighties, wonderfully erect and youthful, his white hair thick, his blue eyes brilliant; he was much given to bargaining for everything, not only in the souks and casbahs and bazaars of the world, but in Harrods and Sainsbury's and even on British Rail.

'Give you five guineas for that tie and that's my last word,' he would say to some flustered young salesman, or, 'If you think I'm paying twenty quid to travel twenty miles you can think again, fifteen's my last offer,' and just occasionally someone would give in to him, either to humour him, or to amuse themselves, would sell him a shirt for half price or give him two pounds of apples for the price of one. He had never managed to persuade British Rail or London Transport to drop their rates for him, but London cabbies occasionally would, especially if he had regaled them with some story of his travels, a journey into the unknown or a brush with a hostile tribe which they could pass on to other customers.

The passionate envy James felt as he looked at Merlin now was not only for the sweet sleep he was so patently enjoying, but for the long peaceful life, devoid of any complexity or wrongdoing, that lay behind him. Merlin might have risked acute danger at the hands of hostile tribes, deadly wildlife and savage environments, but he knew nothing of guilt, of remorse, of wrecked relationships, of ruined lives.

And then James thought that there was at least one thing he could do, that would make him feel a little better. He could tell Theo. As he had done in every other crisis of his life. He would call Theo at his hotel – the bugger should have been here anyway, what was he doing for Christ's

8

sake, spending this important evening alone with his new little bimbo of a wife? Despite everything James grinned to himself at the thought of what Theo was almost certainly doing with the new little bimbo – and talk to him. Not now, of course not now. But first thing in the morning while everyone was busying about, occupied with things like hair and flowers and dresses and hats, he would go and talk to Theo, lay his troubles before him, and ask him what he thought he should do. Theo would have an idea. Theo always did.

Tilly

Far away in Paris, Tilly Mills, despite every resolution to the contrary, heard herself saying that yes, she would like to go to Les Bains Douches with the new big screen hotshot, Jack Menzies, who might have a face like an angel with a past as *Arena* had put it last week, but also had a serious personal hygiene problem. She knew it was crazy, that she had an early call, that it had been a tough day, that if Mick McGrath should be there he would kill her, that she had been late the night before, that it might hit the papers and upset Rufus, but she had to do something to distract herself from the thought of what was going on in England. The frenetic atmosphere of what was still considered one of the chicest discos in Paris would surely take her mind off the twin spectres of a self-congratulatory James Forrest leading his younger daughter down the aisle, watched by roughly 300 adulatory friends and family (Rufus Headleigh Drayton amongst them), and the colour and added interest she might have brought to the occasion had she yielded to temptation and Rufus's fairly intense pressure and attended the wedding. She could have been there right now, in England, a few miles (or not even a few miles) from the heart of the Forrest home, casting a six-foot-one-and-a-half-inch shadow over James Forrest's happiness.

'Shit,' she said aloud, 'shit, shit, shit,' then she stood up, tugged her Lycra dress down so that so long as she stood absolutely straight it just covered her buttocks, and sashayed across the room towards the exit, feeling rather than seeing every pair of male eyes (and a good few female ones as well) fixed upon her, and sensing rather than hearing her name being passed from mouth to mouth, table to table, and then as she hit the street, walked through the door of the restaurant followed by Menzies and his minder (Christ, what was she doing with this Hollywood riffraff when she could be with Rufus?), met the inevitable wall of flashbulbs, went into further automatic pilot, and in one swift movement smiled at them, made some crack about giving them a flash and slid into the Menzies limo. And wondered as it shot off into the night, not for the first time, how she imagined she could possibly move with any degree of permanence from this world into the sweetly ordered, old-fashioned one inhabited by Rufus Headleigh Drayton.

Theo

Theodore Buchan, sitting alone in the bar of the Royal Hotel, Woodstock, embarking on his fourth Armagnac, and waiting with a fair degree of impatience for his fifth and fairly new wife Sasha to return from what she still insisted on calling the girls' room – he must have a little chat with Sasha about the things which were begining quite seriously to irritate him – was also concentrating his formidable energies on not thinking about the wedding at which he was to play a considerable part the next day.

'Of course you must come,' James had said, when Theo had first tried to make excuses, offering perfectly genuine-sounding alibis in the form of conferences, company launches, merger announcements, a long-postponed and promised honeymoon with the new Mrs Buchan. 'Of course you must come. Cressida is your goddaughter for Christ's sake, and you're my oldest friend, and how could you even think we could do any of it without you? How could I get through the day even? Besides you love weddings – even when they're not your own. And since when, Theo, could a conference, let alone a honeymoon, not be put off?'

He had been genuinely and deeply hurt; Theo had recognized the fact, promised to come and spent the following months preparing himself for the ordeal.

The wedding itself of course would be wonderful: the daughter of one of his oldest friends marrying the son of another. Dear old Josh, who'd been at the International School with him, with whom he'd gone on sexual rampages in Geneva, whose best man he had been at his wedding to Julia. That marriage had lasted. Only Josh's second, and the first had been very swiftly over. And Julia was a good wife to him, of course. That helped. Intelligent, (whatever the Forrests thought), gracious, a little intense – but then she was an American – and very sexy. Very very sexy. There'd been that rather strange incident one night when Josh was away – Theo wrenched his mind away from the incident: one of the few times he felt he had behaved really well – and she had been a terrific mother to Oliver. Although she did rather over-love him, Theo felt. But the boy had survived her spoiling, was really very nice indeed. A perfect husband for Cressida. The whole thing was nearly perfect. The only thing that could have improved on it would have been Cressida marrying his own son, his beloved Mungo, named by his doting parents after an obscure Scottish spirit in honour of the country of his conception, but that would have seemed almost incestuous, so closely had they grown up together. Worse still, if she'd fallen in love with – Theo switched his mind away from the one unthinkable, the one he and James never even spoke about, and concentrated instead on Oliver. Charming, brilliant, good-looking Oliver. A little lacking in humour perhaps, but still a golden, blue-eyed boy. Literally as well as metaphorically. Not only graduated summa cum laude out of Harvard medical school, not only winner of a research scholarship to the Mount Sinai, but a superb sportsman too, played tennis for Harvard; wasted, in a way, on the medical profession, but he would no doubt make a fortune out of his specialty, as they called it out there. He was already doing brilliantly.

Funny how history repeated itself. The gynaecologist's daughter marrying the gynaecologist – and this was third generation. Well, at least Cressida was Oliver's first choice, the love of his life. Not entirely predictable, perhaps, gentle, sweet little Cressida – several people had remarked that Harriet seemed more his style: hopelessly wrong there of course, but then people were usually wrong about such things and few people knew and understood Harriet. But certainly he needed a Cressida, a loving supportive wife, someone who could run his home, entertain for him, back him up, raise his children perfectly. And Cressida was extremely socially accomplished: despite her gentleness, she wasn't shy, and she was very efficient – although undeniably impractical: it was a family joke, Cressida's physical incompetence, it wasn't just that she couldn't change a plug or thread up a sewing machine, she could never even get the right station on the radio, or fill up the windscreen wash on her car. But she was superb at persuading people to do things for her, at delegating; she would be a perfect wife. For a rich man. Not so good for a poor one, maybe. Well, that was all right. She wasn't marrying a poor man.

Funny, how marriage as an institution went on and on. People said it had had its day, that everyone simply lived together these days and so on and so forth, but the fact remained that in the end they usually wanted to formalize things. He'd read somewhere that statistically there were more marriages than ever. Well, thought Theo, waving at the barman – Christ what was Sasha doing in the lavatory, giving herself a blowjob? – he certainly kept up the batting average. Five was quite a good total. It was his compulsion to own things, of course, that had led him to it: companies, houses, paintings, cars, horses, all neatly packaged up and labelled 'property of Theodore Buchan'. And women. He'd tried not owning them, tried just having mistresses, but it never worked. Most recently and most terribly it hadn't worked. He was too possessive, too distrustful to love and let go, in that awful modern phsychobabble phrase. It was fine, having a mistress as well as a wife, you could love her and let go, although even then he found that painful, when he was very involved with them, with the mistresses, and they started having other relationships. That was how he'd arrived at marriages three and four: both wives had originally been mistresses that he hadn't been able to face losing. Then somehow there'd still been something missing in the relationship, risk, intensity, and he'd had to find a mistress as well . . . and so it had gone on. Until – well, until. And then there'd been Sasha and she'd gone straight to ranking as wife. He'd met her at a race meeting in Longchamps, she'd been with someone he'd been trying to do a deal with, and he'd taken one look at her, so edibly delicious, so perfect, with her peaches-and-cream skin, her tumbling hair, and a body that he could see would soothe and ease him out of the considerable pain he was in, and he'd had to have her. She was lonely, she told Theo, her blue eyes wide with innocent distress (and so was he, rawly, desperately lonely), and she didn't like being on her own, she was no good at it, she really needed someone to care for. And Theo had offered himself up to be cared for, and that had been that. And without looking too far forward and by sheer force of will refusing to so much as glance backwards, he had married her. And it had worked to a surprising degree. Theo was still slightly shocked at how well it had worked. And he'd managed to avoid thinking too much about what had happened before until tonight. And tomorrow. When he had to confront it, face it, face – well, face the whole damn thing. He didn't know how he was going to handle it. He felt, if the truth was to be told, shit-scared. Which was a situation Theo wasn't used to at all.

He waved at the waiter again, asked for a cigar; he was just drawing it into life when Sasha came hurrying across the room, slightly flushed, freshly made-up, hair reshaped, a cloud of that heavy sexy smell she wore – what was it called? Obsession, great name – hanging about her. She sat down beside him, kissed him, took his hand, smiled into his eyes. Theo looked at her, at her swelling breasts in her black dress, at her perfect thighs, disappearing into her short skirt, at the delicately rounded stomach, and felt his erection beginning to form, to stir with its profoundly powerful precision. He didn't say a word, just stared at her for a moment, stood up quickly, pulled her up almost brutally, and then dropped her hand and stalked out of the bar and into the lift. She followed him, half anxious, half excited; he stood aside to let her past, then shut the door and pushed her against the back of the lift. His face must have been easy to read, for she smiled at him, very slowly and confidently, and pushed up her dress; she was wearing no pants, no tights.

Slowly, gracefully, like a dancer, she raised one of her golden legs and wrapped it round his waist; Theo felt her hand unzipping his fly, reaching for his penis. His blood sang, his entire energy focused on her, on reaching into her; and as he felt her, sank into her wetness, stood there braced against her, feeling the glorious pulling pleasure so intense it was near to pain, holding her small buttocks, kneading them, reaching for release, he was able for a brief but timeless time to forget, even to care about, what he had to face the next day.

Susie

Susie felt terribly tired. Like James, she looked enviously at Merlin sleeping so very soundly in his corner. The day seemed to have gone on forever. Normally she never felt tired, certainly not in social situations; she tried to ignore the fact now, afraid of its implications, concentrated even harder on Josh and the stories of his youth. She liked Josh; he was so uncomplicated, so charming – and so very good-looking. Susie could never understand why women said they didn't like good-looking men. In her experience, they were no less interesting and no more conceited (which was the charge women tended to set against them) than plain men, and at least you could enjoy the looks if they were being boring.

Alistair was good-looking; it had been a factor certainly in her decision to marry him. She really couldn't see why that was so terrible. If you were going to live for the rest of your life with someone, you wanted them to be the kind of person you'd be happy with; Susie would not have been happy with a physically unattractive man.

She looked at him now, being charmingly attentive to Maggie, and thought how good he was. He found Maggie something of a trial, she knew, although he greatly enjoyed her cooking, and had had two helpings of her salmon en croûte that evening, and one and a half (mindful of Susie's watchful eyes) of the chocolate mousse. He was always telling her how wonderful it was to be given things like cream and pastry and roast potatoes, after the food he got at home: it was one of his jokes that

13

even the water in Susie's kitchen was low-fat. Just the same, he looked wonderful on the low-fat water, ten years younger than his fifty-nine years, his dark brown hair still thick and hardly grey, his lean body muscley and strong, his blue eyes brilliant and amusedly alive. In fact she had to admit he actually looked a lot better than James these days. James had put on a lot of weight lately, and he often looked terribly worn. He did now; well, that was partly her fault. Perhaps she shouldn't have told him. But if she hadn't, Rufus might have said something; not the kind of thing James would be able to handle in the middle of his daughter's wedding day. And he had other things on his mind as well, poor Jamie: Maggie increasingly – what? – difficult, his practice increasingly demanding, and shorter term, there was tomorrow to worry about. Not that anything major would, could possibly, go wrong, but he had a speech to make, hundreds of guests to receive, a strung-up wife to steady, a daughter to lead down the aisle. Not easy, any of it.

She saw Janine looking at her, smiling, and smiled back. Dear Janine; how lovely she was still, and how very Parisienne, with her jet-black bob, her pale face and dark eyes, and her tiny, trim figure. She was dressed in a plain linen shift, made Maggie look very gross; Susie wondered, as she so often had, if Maggie had any idea that Janine had been Jamie's first love, had schooled him in sexual matters when he'd been a raw boy of eighteen and she a sophisticated woman of thirty-three. And then decided she couldn't possibly. Maggie was a darling, but she wasn't overburdened with intuition. Thank God . . . Susie looked at her watch: almost half past ten. It was getting late. The bride should be getting her beauty sleep. She looked as if she needed it; beneath her happiness was a heavy shadow of tiredness.

Although Harriet looked a lot worse. God, she was thin. Even to Susie, who saw thinness, not cleanliness, as next to godliness, Harriet looked thin. And pale and exhausted. Poor little thing. She had a lot to carry in that business of hers, and no help from anyone really. Of course she wanted it that way, had turned down a lot of offers of partnership (including a very generous one from Theo), had a seeming obsession about making it on her own, (and you didn't need to be a psychoanalyst to work out that one, Susie thought), but when things got tough she must surely yearn for an arm to lean on.

Thinking of arms made Susie suddenly sharply aware of her own, aching dully (probably it wasn't, probably entirely pyschological) and the phone call she had to make in the morning. She'd almost decided to leave it until the day was over, but she liked to face things, did Susie, liked to know what she was up against. If the news was there, she needed to hear it: for better or for worse.

The phrase, singing through her head, made her think again of the morning, of Cressida's wedding day, of the need for them all to go, to leave the family in peace. She stood up, held her hand out to Alistair.

'Darling, come along. We should get over to the Beaumonts. And Cressida should go to bed. Maggie darling, wonderful meal as always. You really are marvellous, feeding us all, tonight of all nights, when you've so much else to do. Thank you. Cressida, sweetheart, sleep well. And you too, Harriet, you look exhausted. Maggie, send her up to bed. Goodnight, everyone, see you in the morning. Merlin, darling, don't get up, you've been having such a lovely sleep. I'm so glad you got back in time, from – where was it? Ecuador?'

'Peru,' said Merlin. 'Think I'd have missed this? Told the pilot chappie I'd give him a bit of a bonus if he got us down ahead of time.'

'And did he?' asked Harriet, taking the glass of wine her father had handed her, sitting down between Susie and Alistair in an attitude of profound weariness.

'No. Useless these commercial chaps. No fire in their bellies. No incentive I suppose. Still, at least we got here. Susie, you're not going, are you? Night's still young. Hoping to get that husband of yours to play chess with me. What do you say, Alistair?'

'I'm sorry, Merlin, I'd have loved to, but Susie has other plans for me,' said Alistair. 'Rufus, are you coming with us or what?'

'I'm – not sure – Mungo, what do you think?'

'I think we should get Oliver safely back to his hotel,' said Mungo. God, he was delicious, thought Susie, looking at him, smiling at him (few people could look at Mungo without smiling), trying to analyse for the hundredth time what made him so extraordinarily attractive: the nearest she had ever got was to express it as a kind of messed-up perfection, as if something had got hold of the genes that had given him his straight, heavy dark hair, his deep brown eyes, his square jaw, his aquiline nose, his classic mouth and shaken them vigorously so that they fell back not exactly true, the hair determinedly untidy, the eyes just slightly too deep-set under the winging brows, the nose a trifle flaring, the mouth a millimetre fuller (and therefore infinitely sexier). He was, she had to admit, in a different league of looks altogether from her own beloved Rufus; Rufus, who might have been sent from Central Casting to play the archetypal Englishman, blond, tall, slightly languid, not overtly sexy at all. Mungo was all about sex; Janine had once remarked laughing that he made the simple act of handing you a cup of tea into an invitation to bed. And yet it was apparently so unstudied, so unself-conscious, as undeliberate as breathing or blinking (while at the same time of course you knew he was aware of it, knew what he could do to you, should he so choose); that was its greatest charm. Lucky boy, she thought: dangerous boy. As dangerous as his father. He saw her smiling at him now, smiled back, just at her, for a brief, intensely attentive moment, then at all of them again, around the room. 'I'm taking my best-manly duties very seriously, you see,' he said.

'Mungo dear, we can take Oliver back to our hotel,' said Julia Bergin, smiling her neat, well-ironed smile.

'No, Mother, let them. I'd like that.' Oliver stood up, kissing Cressida briefly. 'Now you do realize, don't you, this is the last time I'll see you, Miss Forrest.'

'What on earth do you mean?' said Maggie. She sounded genuinely alarmed.

'Mummy, don't look like that,' said Cressida laughing. 'He means tomorrow I'll be Mrs Bergin. Goodnight, Oliver darling. Sweet dreams. Harriet, come up with me, will you? And Mummy, come and kiss me goodnight. Promise. And you, Daddy.'

'May I come up too?' said Julia. 'Or would I be intruding on this very special occasion? I'm just so excited to think I very nearly have a daughter.'

'Of course,' said Cressida. 'Just give me ten minutes to get into bed and then you can all file in one by one and pay your respects.'

What a perfect daughter, thought Susie fondly, watching her leave the kitchen, arm in arm with Harriet. And what an absolutely perfect bride she was going to be.

Mungo

All Mungo had wanted to do all evening was get to a phone. A private, quiet phone, not one of the Forrest extensions, with people picking them up and putting them down all over the house. He could hear one ringing even now, adding to his anguish. He'd tried twice to make an excuse to go out and use the phone in Rufus's car, but he'd been stymied. For some reason he hadn't actually wanted to tell Rufus: which was seriously stupid, actually, Rufus was such a gent, would never have asked him who he wanted to call or why. It was just that somehow, against all possible odds, nobody had the faintest idea that he was so desperately in love, not even that he was having a serious relationship, and he wanted to keep it that way as long as he possibly could, a quiet, gentle secret. Like his quiet, gentle Alice. Of course he could have pretended he was calling his banker, or his lawyer (faintly unbelievable on such an occasion, and at such a time, although he could always have said the call was to New York). Anyway, in the end he'd decided to leave it, until he got back to the hotel. It wouldn't be too late. Alice never went to bed until well after midnight, and then they could talk for hours, undisturbed. God, he was missing her. All this family togetherness and lovey-doveyness was making his balls ache, he missed her so much. Well, maybe in a few months it would be his wedding everyone would be turning up for. Only of course he didn't want a big affair like this one. Weddings were a bit devalued in Mungo's currency. When your father had just got married for the fifth time, in a huge haze of publicity, you wanted something a bit alternative for yourself. Maybe a beach wedding, or perhaps they could dash up to Gretna Green. That would be very romantic. And then spend a few days in the Scottish Highlands. Mungo had never seen the Scottish Highlands. Like most immensely wealthy, overindulged people, he was more familiar with places the other side of the world than those near to his own doorstep. Anyway, he was sure they were very beautiful and, even if they weren't, seeing them with Alice would surely make them so.

God, he loved her. He felt sick, he loved her so much. He'd spent the whole evening thinking how wonderful it would have been for her to be there, how well she would have fitted in, how much everyone would have liked her, and wondered how he could stand not having her there. Well, it wasn't for much longer. He would tell his father tomorrow, he had decided, after the wedding, and then once he'd done that, he would tell everyone else. And then they could be together for the rest of their lives.

Surely, surely his father would be pleased, surely he wouldn't put up any resistance. He would just be delighted that Alice was going to – what was his phrase on these occasions? – take Mungo on. That was what he'd said when he married Sasha. Thanked her for taking him on. And it would be such a perfect day to tell him: Cressida's wedding day. When everything else was going to be absolutely right.

The Wedding Day

Chapter Two

Harriet 6am

Cressida must have gone for a walk. Of course, thought Harriet, looking into the empty room early, very early, only just after six, on this perfect morning, misty, golden, gathering its beauty about it for the day ahead. Obviously. It would have been exactly like her. She would have gone down to the stream to sit on the little bridge (*her* little bridge as she liked to call it, so irritatingly, it was no more hers than anyone else's), to be still and calm, to savour what lay ahead. She'd always done that, ever since she was tiny, before some important event (her first day at a new school, the presentation of some great new love to the family, the announcement of her own engagement); taken herself off, wanting to be alone. There was nothing, nothing at all odd about it, that she wasn't there; nor in the fact that her room was so tidy, that her bed was made up, apparently unslept in. Cressida was the neatest of people, had been so right through adolescence even. While Harriet's room was permanently shell-shocked, Cressida's, whether she was using it or not, was pretty, charming, sweetly ordered, and there was no change that morning. There were rather more flowers in the room than usual, grand flowers, roses and freesias and lilies, as well as the blue and white jugful of more homely varieties that stood on the pine chest of drawers; and her going-away hat, jauntily red and befeathered, stood on the 1940s hatstand she had been given for an engagement present (she had a passion for hats). And of course there was a rather larger pile of letters than usual on her little desk, already neatly stamped, waiting to be posted, late thankyous for late presents, but otherwise it was exactly, completely as usual. A perfect room for a perfect daughter. No wonder, thought Harriet, Cressida was their mother's favourite: the apparent embodiment of all Maggie's ideal virtues. Cressida even looked like Maggie, with her English-rose skin, her fair, just curly hair, her wide blue eyes, her sweetly curving mouth. Harriet, with her die-straight mink-brown hair, her faintly olive skin, her grey eyes, her sculptured cheekbones, looked, as her mother often told her slightly edgily, exactly like her grandmother – James's adored, wonderfully vibrant mother Rose. Rose who until her death had given Maggie such an inferiority complex. No wonder Harriet's resemblance to Rose distressed her.

Harriet hardly minded any more about Cressida's first place in her mother's heart, it was a fact of her life, like always being late, the one in trouble, the one everyone thought of as plain. The nagging lifelong anxiety that their father also favoured Cressida was harder to endure. Harriet adored her father; he had always seemed to her, even since she had been grown-up, exactly what a father, a husband, a doctor for that matter, should be: loving, caring, conscientious.

She hoped he would enjoy today: it was a special thing for a father, to lead his daughter down the aisle, and the way she was going, it would be a long time before it happened again. Well, the weather was doing its bit for them: it was perfect. It might be nice, Harriet thought, looking at the dew-spangled meadow beyond the house, to go for a walk herself. She certainly wasn't going to go back to sleep now; the anxieties which had invaded her sleep, made her dreams fitful and wearying – all night long she seemed to have heard voices, phones ringing, faxes bleeping – were crowding back in upon her, making her feel panicky. She might even go and find Cressida; the kind of conversation they would have would guarantee at least a degree of distraction. Just as long as her mother hadn't got there first. The thought of having to listen to the two of them discussing the guest list made her feel suddenly worse. She looked at Maggie's bedroom door: firmly shut. She was obviously still fast asleep. Good. The longer she slept the better. For all of them, thought Harriet, and then hastily crushed the thought. Her mother wasn't that bad. Just a panic machine.

She was just closing the door again on Cressida's room when she realized suddenly that yes, there was something not just, not quite as usual; the window, which Cressida kept always open at night, a crack in the winter, wide in the summer, was closed, and the room was slightly hotter, just a little less fresh-smelling than usual, and the curtains hung unusually lifeless and still. Now why . . .

'Harriet, *mon ange*, is Cressida all right?' It was Janine's voice, very quiet; she had come out of her own room looked concerned, pulling her silk wrap round her.

'Yes, of course. Well I think so, she's not there. Why shouldn't she be all right? said Harriet.

'Oh – I heard her earlier. She was – vomiting. I got up to see if she needed help, but the bathroom door was locked. Nerves, of course, *la pauvre petite*, but still – '

'Are you sure it was Cressida?' said Harriet, anxiously. Cressida's delicate stomach was a nightmare. 'Daddy said he was going to give her something in case.'

'Oh, but of course. Her door was open, the cover thrown back. And then I heard her go back to her room.'

22

'Poor old Cress. Well, I suppose it is pretty traumatic. Anyway, she's obviously all right now, room shipshape as usual, and she's gone for a walk. To the bridge I expect.'

'Ah, The bridge. What would you all do without that bridge?' said Janine, smiling. 'Harriet, I would so like a cup of tea. Would you make me one?'

'Yes of course. I was going down anyway. You go back to bed, Janine, and I'll bring it up.'

'No, I would rather come down with you.' She followed Harriet quietly down the stairs into the kitchen, then shut the door, smiled at her again. 'Now we can speak more easily. We do not wish to awaken your mother, do we?'

'We certainly don't,' said Harriet. 'Hallo, Purdey, I'll take you out in a minute, you'll need a walk.' She bent to stroke the old labrador, who was fast asleep in her basket. 'She'll have to be shut in the utility room later, poor darling. That's funny – '

'What is that?'

'She's wet. And her paws are muddy. She must have gone out with Cress. But then she'd have stayed with her surely. Purdey, what have you been up to so early? Rabbiting I suppose.'

Purdey raised one weary eyebrow, lowered it again and sank back into her slumbers. She seemed exhausted. Harriet looked at her and smiled tenderly.

'She's getting so old, poor darling. There, Janine, one cup of lemon tea. I'll just drink mine and then I think I'll go and find Cress, make sure she's all right – '

'You are worried, my darling, are you not?' said Janine. 'About other things than your sister. I could see it last night.'

'No, really Janine, I'm fine,' said Harriet, forcing a smile, fighting down the awful realization that Janine would suffer from her incompetence along with, more than, the rest. 'Just the usual traumas, you know? But nothing serious, I promise. Nothing that's going to spoil today anyway – ' Her voice trailed away and Janine said of course, she quite understood, and smiled at Harriet, and as she met her brilliant dark eyes Harriet could see that, as always, Janine was not remotely fooled by any of it, and she was suddenly a small girl again, crying behind her bedroom door, and she could hear Janine's voice, quietly reasoning with her father at the foot of the stairs . . .

★

'Jamie, don't be angry with her. Don't. It is not right.'

'Janine, I'm sorry, but this is none of your business. Harriet is my daughter and I have to be firm with her. She has to learn she can't behave like this.'

'Like what? James, Harriet is only nine years of age. And she is terribly upset at the moment. She needs discipline, yes, I agree, but she also needs kindness and sympathy.'

'Oh Janine, really.' Her father's voice sounded almost amused. 'I thought the French were supposed to be tough on their kids. You sound like one of those American softies. It was only a puppy, for God's sake. She hasn't suffered a major bereavement.'

'Only a puppy! Jamie, how can you say such things! That is being very, very tough, as you put it. To her *of course* it is a major bereavement. And since we are discussing the French attitude, I think there is much to be said for it. I would say we are not so much tough as demanding. We expect much of them. We treat them in a mature way. But we do try to understand them. And at this moment, I think Harriet needs much understanding.'

'Well, I suppose so. I'm not very good at being understanding, I'm afraid. These days. All right. We'll try a bit harder. But she's so – awkward. It's difficult, when – '

'When the other little one is so easy and so good. Yes, yes I can see that. But – ' There was a fraction of a pause.

'Yes?' said James, his voice wary.

'Well, it is no business of mine, of course. But I don't think sending her away to this school is a good idea. That is certainly one thing we would never do in France. She is so young, Jamie, so tiny. She should be at home.'

'Janine, forgive me, but it is none of your business. Maggie is finding her impossible, she's disruptive, both here and at school, and this place we've found specializes in difficult children.'

'Well I suppose you know what you are doing.' Janine's voice was cool, then she said, 'I am going up to my room now. I am a little tired. Goodnight, Jamie.'

'Goodnight, Janine. Sorry to have involved you in all this.'

'Oh, don't be foolish. I am family – nearly. I like being involved. In the rough and the smooth as well. I only wish I could help.'

''Fraid you can't,' said Jamie and his voice was heavy. 'It's – oh Christ, there's my phone. Not the hospital, not tonight, please God.'

'I will ask Him for you too. Goodnight, my dear.'

Harriet heard steps on the stairs, coming down the corridor, hid under her duvet, screwing her eyes up tight. There was a gentle tap on the door, then she heard the handle turn.

'Harriet? Are you all right, *mon ange*.' The voice, the voice she loved so much, so pretty, so much more interesting than her mother's, was concerned, gentle. She lay silent: determinedly, deadly still.

'Darling, I'm sure you must be awake. Do you want to talk to me?'

'No,' said Harriet, sniffily and reluctantly.

'All right. But if you change your mind, I am going to bed, but I do not expect to sleep. I plan to read for quite a long while.' Janine bent to kiss Harriet, her perfume, expensive, rich, seeming to surround her. Harriet put her arms out suddenly and gripped her neck.

'You're my favourite grown-up,' she said. 'My favourite grown-up of all.'

'Darling! What a nice compliment. But – '

'It's true. Daddy's so cross all the time, and Mummy – well, Mummy hates me.'

'Harriet, of course she doesn't hate you. You must not say such a thing.'

'I do say it, because she does.' She pulled a tissue from the box by her bed and blew her nose. 'You'd hate me too, if you had to live with me. Anyway, they're not going to have to live with me any more, are they, they're sending me to this boarding-school place, getting rid of me – '

She was crying again now, harder than ever. Janine reached forward, drew her into her arms. It was funny, Harriet thought, that she was so small and thin, not cuddly and cosy-looking like her mother, and yet her arms were gentler, more comforting. She snuggled into the arms now, rested her head on Janine's breast. 'You should have been a mummy,' she said.

'Well, I would have liked that. But it didn't work out so well. And I have you and your sister and – '

'I wish you were my godmother. Not hers.'

'I will tell you a little secret,' said Janine, brushing her lips across Harriet's head. 'I wish I was your godmother too. I love Cressida very much of course, but I feel you are more like me. Not so perfect, not so good.'

'She's not perfect,' said Harriet, her voice muffled again in Janine's soft jumper. 'She's not perfect at all.'

'Of course not,' said Janine. 'Nobody is perfect. But she is nearer to it than I, I think.'

'No she isn't. I hate her. I've always hated her.'

'But why?'

'Because she's so pretty and goody-goody and she's always being sickly sweet to everyone, and she's mean to me so often, and nobody ever realizes.'

'Harriet, you exaggerate I think.'

'I don't, I don't. Once she threw my lovely baby doll, the one that cries you know, out of the window, and she got stuck on the flat roof and she

25

was there for days in the rain, and another time she took my new pen that Grandpa Merlin had given me and lost it, and she told my best friend at school that I didn't really like her and was always saying mean things about her and – oh I know you won't believe me either, grown-ups never do.'

'I believe you,' said Janine unexpectedly, 'of course I do. But all sisters squabble, Harriet, I certainly used to with mine. And I am sure you are not perfect either. And,' she added with a spark of amusement in her dark eyes, 'it certainly was not a good idea to throw your soup at her this evening.'

'I know. I know it wasn't. But she was giving me her look, you know? Her horrible goody-goody look, while Mummy was telling me not to be rude. And I thought – well I knew – it would make me feel better. And it did for a bit,' she added with a sheepish, tearstained grin.

'But now you are in terrible trouble, and not allowed to go to the party tomorrow, and your mother is very upset, and your father is angry. Do you still feel better?'

'Yes,' said Harriet, surprising herself with her own certainty. 'Yes, I do. It was still worth it. Seeing her face change.'

'You might have changed it forever. If the soup had been hotter.'

'I know. And I know it was wrong. But she's oh – oh I don't know. And they both love her so much. And – '

'And her puppy hasn't just been run over, and she's not being sent away to school. Is that it?'

'Yes,' said Harriet. 'Yes, that's it.' And she started to cry again.

'Harriet, listen. It was dreadfully sad about Biggles. Even I cried, and I do not greatly like dogs. Although I'm sure Biggles was a very special one. I still have the photograph of him you sent me. But you can have another puppy. Your parents have said so and – '

'And what's the point of that,' said Harriet, 'when I'm not going to be here with it? Oh Janine, it was so awful. The worst bad dream you ever had, only much much worse than that. I can't stop thinking about it, it just goes on and on over and over again, in my head, like something on TV. I see it happening, I look out of the window and the gate's open and I know I've shut it and I'm running and running down the drive and calling and calling him, and I can see him there, looking at me from the opposite side of the lane, sitting in the long grass, and then the lorry coming and him suddenly starting to pad over the lane towards me, rather slowly, wagging his tail, and then – and then the lorry on him, on him, Janine, tons of lorry, what do you think he felt like, can you imagine, and all my fault, all of it – oh Janine, how could I have done such an awful thing? I didn't deserve him, did I, I didn't deserve to have him. I wish I'd been under the lorry with him – '

'Oh Harriet, my darling, *chut, chut*, please, don't say such dreadful things. That would be no better, it would be a million times worse.'

'Well I do. And then Mummy appeared, and she just led me back into the house, wouldn't let me see him, wouldn't let me near him, and Cressida was on the stairs, and do you know what she said?'

'No, I don't.'

'She said, "Well it was your fault, you know, Harriet, you should have shut the gate." Even Mummy was cross with her. And her horrible kitten was fine, sitting there on her bed washing itself. I'll never forgive her for that, never. Of course she said she was sorry, Mummy made her, but she didn't mean it, and she was holding her kitten at the time, stroking it. It's all right for her, she's still got something to love. Anyway, I don't want another puppy, I want Biggles.'

'Well,' said Janine, 'well, my darling, it is all very sad of course. But the pain will get better, I promise you. That is the first important lesson you are going to learn in life, Harriet. That pain gets better. All pain. And when it gets better, you will find you do want another puppy, and you won't forget Biggles, but you will love the new one, a little bit differently of course, and –'

'But I've told you,' said Harriet, 'I'm not going to be here. I'm going to this stupid school. So I can't love anything, differently or not.'

'Well,' said Janine with a sigh, 'perhaps you will like the school and perhaps it will not be stupid. Now then, would you like me to stay here and read you a story until you are feeling a little bit more like sleeping?'

'I'm frightened to sleep,' said Harriet, 'I dream about it all. What happened. Every night. I try to stay awake, but I can't. In the end I go to sleep and the dream comes.'

'*Allons, allons, mignonne,*' said Janine, taking her in her arms again, stroking her hair. 'You shall come to my room, if you would like that, and sleep in my bed with me tonight. And if I think you are dreaming badly, I will waken you. All right? And very possibly, I think, once you have slept one night without the dream, it will not trouble you again.'

'I think it will,' said Harriet, 'but that would be lovely, yes. I'd like that. Thank you.'

Janine held out her hand. It was such a beautiful hand, very white, with long slender fingers and brilliant red nails. Not the sort of hand you'd think would be comforting, but it was, warm and soft; Harriet closed her own round it and followed Janine along the corridor and into her room. And in the morning, she was still in Janine's bed, and she realized she had slept all night without having the dream at all.

★

All the same she didn't get another puppy; she said she didn't want one. If they thought they could make her less upset about sending her away, just by doing something easy like buying her another puppy, they could think again. She still couldn't believe it was all happening. She watched the trunk that had been her mother's filling up slowly with her new uniform, she was bought new shoes, a lacrosse stick, a rather formal-looking watch, she had a medical check at the doctor's, she was taken to the dentist, she had her hair cut, all in readiness for this dreadful event and she was taken to tea with another little girl who was already there, at St Madeleine's, who told her it was lovely, great fun, much better than being at home, and she counted the time that was left until she had to go, first in weeks, then in days, finally in hours, and right up to the last minute when she was dressed in her new uniform, all brown and blue, she really expected her father to come into the room and say, 'OK, darling, it's all right, you don't have to go if you really don't want to,' but he didn't; it was all coming true, the nightmare.

She behaved, in her rage and terror, even worse than usual; she shouted at everyone, she refused to eat at mealtimes, (raiding the larder when no one was around for cakes and biscuits so she wasn't hungry), she was rude to any of her mother's friends who asked her kindly if she was looking forward to going to her new school; and she fought endlessly with Cressida, on one dreadful occasion pushing her from the top to the bottom of the stairs and knocking two of her front teeth out. They'd been loose anyway, so she couldn't really see what all the fuss was about, and she said as much to her parents when they sat her down and asked her if she wasn't ashamed of herself.

'Harriet, darling,' said her father (for he was more tolerant, tried to be more understanding of her behaviour than her mother was), 'why did you do it? I don't understand,' and she said nothing, nothing at all, knowing that he wouldn't believe her if she told him the reason, that Cressida had told her she couldn't wait for her to go away.

The night before she went she lay in bed so frightened she thought she would die, her heart beating in great painful thudding bursts, her hands clammy with fear, determined not to cry, struggling not to cry; and there was a gentle knock at the door and Cressida came in, looking so sweet, so concerned. 'I shall miss you,' she said, 'I don't really want you to go,' and she climbed into bed with her. To her great astonishment Harriet discovered that that made her feel better, all her hostility suddenly vanished, and they fell asleep in one another's arms. She woke later, much later, to hear her parents whispering in the doorway.

'Look,' her mother was saying, 'isn't that sweet? Would you have believed it possible?'

And 'No,' her father said, 'but it's very encouraging. Maybe the separation really is going to be the best thing for them.'

'I hope so. I'm so glad they've made it up, that they're parting friends. Cressida's had to take such a lot from Harriet these past few weeks. If she wasn't such a sweet, forgiving little thing . . .'

Go on, Daddy, go on, say something nice about me, say something that shows you don't think it's all me, thought Harriet, feeling quite weak with the huge effort of keeping still, breathing quietly and steadily when she wanted to leap out of bed into their arms, beg them, for the last time, not to send her, promise to be good.

But 'Yes I know,' he said, 'let's hope this school can really do something for Harriet, make her a little bit sweeter too. Come on, we don't want to wake them, all hell will be let loose.'

And they went out, closing the door with infinite care behind them, and Harriet lay awake for hours, seething, aching with misery, and when she finally went to sleep she dreamed for the first time in ages about Biggles and his tiny golden velvet body settled into the long grass by the side of the road, the last look of adoration he gave her as he set off towards her on his fat paws, and the hideous sound of the lorry's brakes screeching and then the dead silence that settled on everything, and nothing to be seen of Biggles but a small trickle of blood leaking out from under one of the lorry's front wheels.

The school was horrible. She could never remember feeling so lonely, so permanently, utterly unhappy, so literally sick with longing for home. They all wrote, even Cressida, but she wasn't allowed to phone because the staff said it would be unsettling for her, and new girls weren't allowed even a Sunday exeat for the first half of the term because that was supposed to be unsettling too. Harriet couldn't imagine being any more unsettled than she was already; she felt permanently sick, she had terrible diarrhoea almost all the time, she couldn't sleep, and she seemed to hear and see everything from the end of a long tunnel. She watched herself getting up in the morning, getting dressed, picking up the awful breakfast, trudging from the house over to the school; going to lessons, playing games, doing prep, and then going to bed again, and lying awake hour after hour, unable to sleep. The other girls began by trying to be kind, but they gave up in the face of her awful, blank-faced hostility and started teasing her instead, calling her Po Features and Farty Pants, imitating her as she ran endlessly, doubled up, to the loo.

She did badly at everything, made dense by misery, her considerable facility for games wrecked by increasingly poor health. When they came for her at half term, she fell into her father's arms, sobbing helplessly; she was even pleased to see Cressida, and held her hand in the back of the car all the way home.

When it was time to go back, she locked herself in the lavatory and refused to come out; it was only when they promised that if she wasn't feeling better by the end of term she could leave that she agreed to return. Then Cressida wrote to her, warning her not to believe them, that she had heard them saying the school was doing her good, that she was bound to settle down in time, and she realized that if she was ever to escape she would have to take some action herself.

The best thing, indeed the only thing, she decided, was to get expelled; once she had thought of it, she was excited at the sheer simplicity of the notion. She embarked upon her plan with the nearest to enjoyment she had felt for a long time, and started stealing the other girls' things, over a period of a few weeks: a watch, a bracelet, a transistor radio, and some money from the lost property fines box, left unattended one day on the secretary's desk. She left everything in her locker, which was duly searched when the alarm went up. Harriet stood in the headmistress's study, looking at all the things on the large desk, and waited to hear the wonderful words, 'We've asked your parents to come and take you home again.' She had even begun to pack a few things in her attaché case before she was sent for, so confident was she.

Only the wonderful words didn't come; instead the headmistress went droning on for hours about letting herself and her parents down and instead of being expelled, she was taken to the school psychiatrist, a droopy woman with greasy hair who said things like 'Nobody is angry with you, Harriet, just very upset' and 'You must learn to understand yourself better, Harriet, and then you will know why you do these things.'

She had to spend an hour three days a week, learning to understand herself; the psychiatrist, who dressed in sagging beige garments and whose name was Dr Ormerod, asked her endless questions about her family, whether she felt they loved her, how she felt about her sister and whether she was angry about being sent away to school. Harriet certainly wasn't going to make Dr Omerod's job easy for her and give her the satisfaction of telling her she hated her sister, that she knew her family didn't love her and she was extremely angry at being sent away to school; and besides she knew that if she did that, she would be labelled disturbed and unhappy, rather than bad, and crush any hopes of getting expelled. She said she loved her family and especially her sister, and she loved school, but she had lost her watch, she didn't like the girl the bracelet belonged to and she'd needed money to buy the new David Cassidy LP.

She'd confidently expected this to do the trick and that her parents would be finally phoned and told to come and collect her immediately, but Dr Omerod who had sat listening to her very carefully, clutching her beige cardigan tightly around herself, her crumpled beige face very solemn, had suddenly smiled and said, 'Well done, Harriet. You've made some very big progress. You've learnt to confront yourself, be honest about yourself. A lot of grown-ups can't do that, you know. I'm proud of you. I'm going to talk to Miss Edmundson again, and see what she thinks, but I would like to see this whole thing set behind you. We need some more sessions of course, but I think we're very well on our way.'

Harriet gave up, resigned herself to a life sentence.

And then Sir Merlin turned up.

She had always adored Sir Merlin. Even when she was tiny, only two or three, his visits were wonderful occasions, exciting, unpredictable; he brought her extraordinary presents, a stuffed monkey, a real shrunken head, a baby python. She loved the python and slept with it for a few weeks, but it began to grow rather large and feeding it was a problem. Sir Merlin came to an arrangement with the local abattoir where it was let loose on the large rat population, but Maggie, finally driven beyond endurance when it rose up at her one morning from the depths of the airing cupboard where it liked to sleep, insisted slightly hysterically on it going to the zoo. When Harriet was only six, he took her on a four-day camping expedition in a remote part of the Pyrenees; she returned exhausted, sunburnt, covered in mosquito bites and blissfully happy. Since then he had taken her on a trip every two or three years to all manner of marvellous places, as once he had taken her father. Together they had travelled to India, Morocco, Egypt, and had driven the length of America in a boneshaking truck; Harriet, while loving every trip more than the last, had come to associate travel with acute physical discomfort. And the best thing of all about her journeyings was that Cressida had shared none of this enchantment, had never shown the slightest desire to go. Even as a child she had liked her comforts.

'Bit of a softie, your sister,' Sir Merlin had remarked one night as they lay together in the confines of the truck, gazing at the glories of the Arizona night sky. It was the nearest he had ever come to criticizing Cressida, but Harriet knew he didn't like her, and it made her happier still.

Cressida did not miss out altogether, because Theo, who thought she was wonderful, took her on long, exotic, sanitized holidays, staying in five-star hotels, flying in private planes, sailing on luxury yachts: all very far removed from the wondrous, vast, magical experiences that Harriet shared with Sir Merlin. The unique bond between them, forged by their first shared adventures, was strong and powerful; and Merlin had fought hard alongside Janine, Harriet knew, to spare her the miseries of St Madeleine's. But he had not won.

She was sitting on a bench in the playground playing cat's cradle with herself when she heard the familiar poop-poop of his beloved dark green Lagonda; hardly able to believe she wasn't dreaming, she looked up and flew across the tarmac to him, flinging herself into his arms.

'You're looking very thin,' he said, picking her up and setting her down again on the running board, and his brilliant blue eyes were concerned. 'Don't they feed you here?'

'They try to,' said Harriet with a shrug, 'but I can't eat it.'

'Damnfool idea, the whole thing,' he said. 'I've come to take you out for lunch. Just got back from Java. Wonderful place. Tell you all about it. Come along. I suppose we should warn someone.'

'Grandpa Merlin, they won't let me out for lunch,' said Harriet, her eyes round with horror. 'We're not even allowed out on Sundays and this is Tuesday.'

'Oh rubbish. I'll just tell 'em. Come on, Harriet, where's your spirit gone?'

'Dr Omerod's busy killing it off,' said Harriet with a sigh.

'Who's she? Never mind, tell me later. Hey, you!' He waved his stick at one of the staff who was walking towards him.

'Grandpa Merlin, you can't do that,' said Harriet, 'you have to be polite to staff.'

'What for? If they can't look after you properly they don't deserve politeness.'

'I'm so sorry.' Miss Foxted, the Latin teacher, as beige and droopy as Dr Omerod, her bosom hanging almost to her waist, with plaits coiled over her rather large ears, was hurrying over to them, out of breath with anxiety, 'You really can't park that car there.'

'Why not?' said Sir Merlin, looking at her in genuine puzzlement. 'What harm's it doing? I don't see any precious plants beneath it, anything like that.'

'Well, it's . . . it's the playground. It's dangerous.'

'Stuff and nonsense. Girls aren't blind, are they? Can see a car when it's moving, I imagine. Now look here, I'm taking Harriet out for the day. Have her back by bedtime if you like.'

'You can't do that, I'm afraid,' said Miss Foxted, her beige face strained with anxiety and disapproval. 'It's a working school day, you know. And we insist on formal appointments, even for day exeats. Besides, I'm afraid I don't even know who you are. It would be irresponsible of me to allow Harriet off the premises.'

'Well, I can see that,' said Sir Merlin, suddenly reasonable, holding out his hand, 'I'm her father's godfather. Sir Merlin Reid. How do you do. Want to phone I expect. We'll wait here for you.'

'Sir Merlin, I really can't – '

'Look,' said Sir Merlin, 'look, go and talk to your boss, whoever she is, will you? We haven't got all day.'

'But – I really don't see – that is – ' Miss Foxted's voice trailed into helplessness.

'Tell you what,' said Sir Merlin. 'We'll come with you.'

They followed Miss Foxted across the playground towards the headmistress's study, stood outside while she went in; they could hear her voice, and Miss Edmundson's voice, slowly rising. Finally Miss Edmundson came out. She smiled her gracious, understanding smile at Sir Merlin, held out her hand.

'Sir Merlin! How nice to meet you. Now then, I understand you want to take Harriet out for the day. I'm afraid that will be quite impossible, against all our rules. Later in the term, one Sunday perhaps – '

'Have you phoned her father?'

'Certainly not. There is no question of her going out, therefore no question of phoning him.'

'Look, woman – ' said Sir Merlin, and his white bushy eyebrows began to bristle; it was a sign to those who knew him that he was losing his temper. Miss Edmundson did not know that; she stood her ground, flushed.

'Sir Merlin, I really don't like – '

'I don't care what you like. I don't like what I see of this child. She's shockingly thin, she looks as if she hasn't had any fresh air for months. What have you been doing to her?'

'Sir Merlin, I assure you – '

'I'm not interested in your assurances, I'm interested in Harriet. And I'm taking her out.'

'But – '

Sir Merlin took Harriet's hand, went to move away, then turned back. 'Incidentally,' he said, 'what are the fees in this establishment?'

'I'm afraid I don't – '

'They must be at least a thousand a term. That's about – let's see – ' He pulled a calculator from his pocket, and beamed at her over it. 'Wonderful things these. You should get one if you haven't already. Pay for themselves time and time again. Now then, thousand a term, let's say twelve weeks, that's eighty-four days, eleven pounds point 9047 pence a day. That's a lot of money, wouldn't you say? That you're saving on Harriet today. I'll tell my godson to dock it off the fees next term. Good day to you. Can't wait any longer for you to make some damnfool phone call. I'll have her back for bedtime, don't fret.'

'Sir Merlin – '

The Lagonda was halfway down the school drive before Harriet dared even to breathe.

Sir Merlin accomplished what the stealing, the illness, the misery, the tears, the begging letters to her parents, had not. Harriet was removed from St Madeleine's; she first heard of this decision not from her parents, or even Miss Edmundson, but from Cressida. 'I'm so excited, they've said you can come home,' she had written in her neat, careful handwriting, 'but I heard them say if you're at all naughty you've got to go again.'

★

'I think I'll go down to the bridge and find Cressida,' said Harriet, putting down her mug of tea. 'She's obviously feeling more nervous than we all thought. Funny, she was so amazingly calm last night. I'll be back in a minute, Janine. Purdey, walk?'

But Purdey raised one weary eyebrow and sank back into her dreams.

Harriet went into the utility room, pulled on her mother's old Barbour over the long T-shirt that was the nearest thing she possessed to a nightdress, stuck her feet into a pair of the long line of wellies that stood there and went out into the golden morning. The air was fresh, almost tangibly sweet; it was like breathing champagne, she thought, surprised at herself for thinking it. She was not greatly given to poetic observations. She walked across the small brick-paved courtyard outside the back door, through the walled rose garden that was her father's pride and joy, and across the lawn. In the far corner was a small gate and beyond that a field leading to the stream and the little double-arched bridge. It was an absurdly pretty spot: the setting for countless family photographs, both formal and informal. A weeping willow trailed into the water, and on the other side of the bridge was a stone seat, set into a small grassy mound, with ferns growing round it.

Harriet had half expected to see Cressida standing on the bridge playing Pooh-sticks with herself, as she had done all her life at times of emotional turmoil – good or bad. She would stand there, leaning over, staring intently into the water, waiting for her stick to come through, a bundle more of them in her hands (Cressida never did anything without being carefully prepared), and usually Purdey would be sitting beside her, watching the water with the same concentrated gaze. Only this morning Purdey wasn't there, and Cressida wasn't there either; nor was

34

she in the little spinney beyond the bridge, or at the top of the meadow opposite. She was nowhere to be seen.

Frowning slightly, Harriet turned and walked – quickly, anxiously, while telling herself that of course there was no need for anxiety – back across the grass, towards the house. And noticed, as she should have done earlier, she told herself, that there was only one set of footprints in the thick dew and they were her own; and no doggy prints either. So where had Cressida gone, with Purdey, and where was she now? Back in the house of course, Harriet told herself, she must have missed her, she would have gone down the lane, maybe towards the bridlepath, she liked that walk (but so early in the morning? so far on such a day?).

She walked across the courtyard and into the kitchen, her heart pounding just a little too hard, smiled, carefully casual, at Janine, said (her voice just slightly strained), 'Cress back?'

And 'No,' said Janine, sounding surprised, 'no, she is not back, was she not at the bridge?'

'No,' said Harriet, 'no, hadn't been there actually. Well, I expect she wanted to go a bit further, calm her nerves. I'll – I'll get dressed and go down to the shop in the car and get a paper, I think, probably pass her in the lane. If she's not back already.'

'Yes of course,' said Janine, 'and *chérie*, I will go and take a bath and we can all meet again here in a little while. I expect your mother will be down soon.'

''Fraid so,' said Harriet, with a grin.

It was still very quiet upstairs; her mother must have taken a sleeping pill. Otherwise she would have been pacing the house by now. Harriet looked at her watch: quarter to seven. That meant Cressida had been gone for at least an hour. A long time for a wedding morning. Or maybe she'd come back, through the front door, and Harriet had missed her. She knocked gently on Cressida's bedroom door: no answer. She opened it, looked in: the room was exactly the same – still, lifeless, neat. It was almost as if – Harriet shut the door again, stood very still for a moment and then, feeling slightly sick, her heart thudding uncomfortably in her throat went to her own room, pulled on some leggings and a clean T-shirt and ran downstairs again. Bloody Cressida, she thought, feeling suddenly angry: this was playing the drama queen just a bit too thoroughly. She must have realized they'd all be getting up by now and would start worrying: shit, where had she put her car keys? Probably on one of the hooks on the dresser, where they all hung their keys. Yes, she remembered now, she'd put them next to Cressida's – hung on that irritating key ring of hers, with the naff 'First Class Toilet' sign – the night before. Harriet reached for them, and then saw that Cressida's weren't there: not on the hook, not on any hook, she thought, her eyes racing over the dresser. She ran out to the drive: no red mini there as it had been last night. Well, of course not, she said to herself, hanging onto calm with great effort. James had told her to put it away, said they must clear the drive, either he or Cressida must have put it in the garage. Harriet went over to the garage, stood looking at the big white double doors, taking deep breaths, confronting what she was afraid of; then put out her hand to turn the knob. and noticed that her hand was shaking, her palm slippery with sweat. She pulled the door back and looked cautiously, almost fearfully in.

And what she saw was precisely what she had been afraid of seeing: the only car in the garage was Maggie's little Renault; Cressida's car was gone.

Chapter Three

Theo 6am

Theo woke up feeling, as he so often did, in serious need of sex. He could never understand why people didn't want sex in the morning; after a night of close proximity to someone, curled, wrapped round them, the smell of them, the shape of them, the feel of them, what else could a normal person desire? It was the logical, natural sequence of events: first the foreplay, then the act. One of the main reasons he had made Sasha (apart from her blonde hair, wide blue eyes, impressive breasts and extremely good legs) the fifth Mrs Buchan was that she was wonderfully responsive in the mornings. 'Oh, Theo,' she would say, laughing, turning to him, kissing him, feeling for his penis, stroking it, fondling it, 'Oh Theo, you are so wonderful.' It was the best possible way to start the day; he would rise, after it, refreshed, as sleep alone could never make him feel, and stand in the shower, singing in his curiously tuneless voice, before heading for the gym and his religious-like progress round it. After that, and another shower, he would make his way through glass after glass of orange juice, bowl after bowl of coffee (wherever he was Theodore liked coffee in the French way) and a proper breakfast too, two very lightly boiled eggs followed by a great pile of croissants and pains au chocolat and tartine, and then he would take his great six-foot-five, 100-kilo frame into his dressing room and clothe it, and finally, still feeling wonderful, would pronounce himself ready for the day.

Only today, little of this progress through pleasure was to be granted to him. The Royal Hotel at Woodstock was extremely good, but there was no gym, no indoor pool even, nowhere for him to exercise. God, he should have told Jamie to check on that. So it would have to be jogging which he didn't enjoy these days, now that he'd got so heavy, and what they called a Continental breakfast was no doubt a piddling little glass of orange juice and a couple of chewy croissants. He could have the English, which was clearly excellent, he'd studied the menu the night before, bacon, eggs, sausages, mushrooms and black pudding – God, it was years since he'd had black pudding – maybe that would see him through to the wedding luncheon which would not be until nearly teatime.

James had asked him if he and Sasha would have supper at the house that night, after everyone had gone; he was still trying to get out of that one, an emotional evening in the bosom of the Forrest family, with its own particular attendant torture, think of an excuse, but so far he'd failed. James had been quite hurt enough that he'd stayed at the hotel the night before, and . . . Theo wrenched his mind from the problem and decided to have a shower; but the thought was not tempting, an English shower, feeble, trickling, he'd spent half an hour the night before trying to get the soap out of his hair. God, where was Sasha?

It was only just on six, she couldn't possibly have got up yet. Sasha liked to sleep late, usually slumbering peacefully (after satisfying his demands so deliciously) while he exercised, occasionally sitting up sleepily to be fed morsels of breakfast and sips of orange juice and then often dozing again until he got dressed and made the half-dozen or so phone calls that heralded the begining of his working day.

'Sasha?' he called fretfully in the direction of the bathroom. 'Sasha, where are you?'

No answer; Theo felt a rush of something close to real rage. She didn't have to do much, for Christ's sake, just be there for him. That was what women were for, in his opinion: to be there for men. When he had first met Sasha, she was actually working in a public relations company, and she'd told him she wanted to carry on with her work: her insistence that she was in some way important, contributing to the running of the company, amused and almost touched him, indeed he had enjoyed teasing her about it at the time, especially in front of his friends. 'How was the board meeting today, Sasha?' he would say, or 'Tell us about that big deal you've got going through, Sasha, the one with that bank,' and she would blush prettily and say, 'Oh Theo, I can't, you know it isn't like that,' and he would say, 'No, no, if it's important to you, then we're all interested, I'd like you to tell us all about it.' And he'd listen, smiling indulgently as she stammered through some story of a decision to take on two extra account executives, or a new contract with a client in the City, and then he would ask everyone their views on whatever it was, and she would sit only slightly discomfited, looking at him adoringly. But once they were married, he'd insisted on her severing every connection with the company; he was her partner now, he said, with just the merest shadow of menace in his voice, and the only deal she need concern herself with was the one with him. Yes of course she'd said, she completely agreed and understood, and she could quite see that looking after him was going to be not only much more important than anything else she might be involved in, but a great deal more interesting and fun. And she had tried, she had tried very hard, and in the nine months they had been married had made him very nearly happy. Not quite, but that wasn't her fault. She was only thirty-one years old (to his fifty-nine), loving, thoughtful, charming to his friends and associates, a surprisingly talented housekeeper, a good cook (a talent she didn't often get a chance to display) – and if she wasn't exactly clever (a fact which he gently reminded her of from time to time, when she showed any real interest in his business affairs) she was bright enough to chatter away amusingly in any company. She was also extremely good at spending money. Theo had told her he wanted her to look the part of the wife of an international businessman and she'd taken her duties seriously, becoming a personal customer at such disparate places as Chanel, Valentino, Ralph Lauren, Jasper Conran and Jean-Paul Gaultier. Theo raided the jewellers of the world for her, and was said to be seeking a knighthood, simply so that Sasha could have a tiara; meanwhile her collection of gems was dazzling, although mostly stored in the vaults of various banks, her preferred jewellery chosen from Cobra and Bellamy and Butler and Wilson.

Theo's five children, with the exception of Mungo, detested her, seeing her as a totally unscrupulous gold-digger, and his two elder daughters by wife three no longer spoke to him, since he refused to have them in the house unless they could be genuinely friendly to Sasha. His eldest son, Michael, by wife one, was distantly courteous to her, since his life and personal fortune were too caught up in the business to be otherwise, but Mungo, by wife two (always said to have been Theo's one great true love, and who had died tragically of cancer after five very good years), made his father very happy by being patently fond of Sasha, said she was gorgeous, that it was nice to have someone his own age around, and that from where he was sitting, anyone who would take his father on deserved any little rewards that happened along her way.

What he meant also, Theo knew, was that anyone who could distract his attention from Mungo's misdemeanours, or make excuses for them, was extremely welcome; wife number four in particular had been less than fond of Mungo, feeling, perhaps with some justification, that never having done what anyone would actually consider a day's work in his life, and having lost at least a million at the poker table, a little discipline was called for, albeit somewhat late in the day, and had urged Theo to cut Mungo's allowance, stop giving him the run of the Buchan homes, and make him at least consider the possibility of casting his mind in the direction of doing something in the way of gainful employment.

Well, she had been right, had number four, Jayne by name: Mungo's behaviour was a great deal less than exemplary; but Theodore was hard-pressed to upbraid him on it, having led an almost identical life up to the age of thirty himself, when he managed to find the rush of adrenalin, hitherto only experienced at the poker game, in the business world and had trebled the fortune his father had left him by the age of thirty-five.

'Business is just like poker,' he was fond of saying, 'it has nothing to do with chance or luck, or the cards you are dealt, and everything to do with how you read the situation. You can turn a terrible hand to a good one, simply by patience, and watchfulness.'

This maxim was much quoted in the business press. There was, as the financial journalists argued, a little more than patience and watchfulness to making a couple of billion pounds, which was what Theo was currently said to be worth, via his various companies (mostly food, oil and timber), but he would smile charmingly and say no, no, not at all, and if they ever cared to play poker with him, he would prove it to them.

He lived in one of three homes: a fine London house in The Boltons, a large apartment of breathtaking beauty in Paris, on the Ile St Louis, on the Quai Bethune, a chateau in the hills above Nice. He also owned a small island near Mustique, and another even smaller off the west coast of Scotland, a castle in County Cork, and an apartment in Trump Tower, New York – but they were for occasional visits, he explained, they were not homes. His favourite was undoubtedly Paris; Paris was where he had grown up, he said, where he had spent his happiest times, where he had his closest friends.

'Paris is a sexy city,' he liked to say, 'people know how to enjoy themselves, how to please themselves.'

Sasha, on the other hand, preferred London.

Theo got out of bed, pulled on his bathrobe and went over to the window. It overlooked a quiet courtyard at the back of the hotel; in the distance he could see the glorious lyrical parkland of Blenheim. It was a perfect day; well, that was good. Probably be too hot, but the sun would shine on the bride, and they would all be able to wander about in the garden, drinking the champagne that he knew would be excellent because it had been his wedding present to James (not Cressida, to whom he had given a bed of considerable splendour, a late eighteenth-century French four-poster, with exquisitely painted and fluted posts and wonderful cream brocade curtains). 'I don't want any bloody nonsense,' he'd said firmly, when he called to say twenty cases of Veuve Clicquot were being delivered to the Court House, 'expensive business getting married, Christ, I should know, and you're not a rich man.'

'I'm quite rich enough thank you,' James had said with a touch of irritation, and Theo had said it was impossible to be rich enough and that James wasn't rich at all by his standards, which was true, and couldn't he give an old friend a little something to launch his daughter into married life?

As he looked down into the courtyard, frowning, increasingly displeased at Sasha's absence, he suddenly realized that his car was missing. It was his favourite car: the silver Bentley Continental, immensely valuable. He kept it garaged in London through the winter and drove it with great pleasure down to the South of France every spring; he had driven it back up this summer, so that Cressida Forrest could have it for her wedding, and Theo's chauffeur, who had sat wretchedly in the back of the Bentley for most of the journey up from Nice, was due to drive it over to the Court House at 1.30 to take first Maggie and the bridesmaids and then Cressida and James to the village church. And the last thing Theo had done last night before getting into bed was look fondly out of the window at it; now it had gone.

He turned to the phone and called reception: where was his chauffeur?

'In his room, Mr Buchan. Shall I call him for you?'

'Yes please. Tell him to get up here fast. and send up some tea, would you?'

'Certainly, Mr Buchan.'

'And have you seen my wife?'

'Yes, Mr Buchan. She went out about half an hour ago. She said she was going for a walk.'

A walk? Sasha's idea of a walk was from one department of a shop to another. What the hell was going on?

There was a knock at the door; it was Brian, the driver. He looked nervous; he was wearing his dressing gown.

'Yes, Mr Buchan?'

'Brian, where the hell is my car?'

'Your car, Mr Buchan?'

'Yes, Brian. You know what a car is? Motorized vehicle, four wheels, engine, that sort of thing. I have a few. Special favourite parked in the courtyard here last night. Any suggestions, Brian?'

'Well, Mr Buchan, I do have one.'

'Well, one is better than none, Brian. Come along, let's have it.'

'I think Mr Mungo might have it, Mr Buchan.'

'Mungo? Took the Bentley? Brian, I do hope not. For both your sakes.'

'I'm afraid that is what has happened, Mr Buchan. I'm sorry.'

'But why did you let him, for Christ's sake? And when did he take it and where?'

'Well – he took it last night, Mr Buchan. Very late.'

'Brian, for Christ's sake why did you let him? You know that car is priceless. And that Mungo drives everything as if it was his Maserati. What was he doing taking it, late at night? He'd had at least a bottle of champagne and God knows how much wine at dinner. Sweet Jesus, if anything's happened to that car I shall personally drive what is left of it over first him and then you.'

'Yes, Mr Buchan.' Brian looked as if such a course of action would be welcome.

'OK. Let's get some sense here. Why did you give him the key?'

'I – didn't. Well, not at first. He'd had rather a lot to drink as you say, and he said he felt like a drive. I told him he couldn't have it, no matter what, and he said he'd win it off me. At poker.'

'Oh really? You embarked on a game of poker, with my car as stake. Brian, you are fired. As of this moment.'

'Mr Buchan, of course I didn't. I said he couldn't have the car whatever he did. And then he said quite right, Brian, spoken like a man. Let's have a game anyway. He said he couldn't sleep. So I said all right, and he went off and came back with some cards and a bottle of Scotch and young Mr Headleigh Drayton.'

'Rufus? So he's in on this as well.'

'Yes, Mr Buchan. Well, we started and we played for – oh a couple of hours. Then the phone rang. It was reception. They said was Mr Mungo here, and I said yes. He took the call, and he seemed very upset. Genuinely upset. He was very white. He asked me to excuse him and Mr Headleigh Drayton for a moment, and they went outside the door. When they came back, he said "Look, Brian, I absolutely have to go somewhere. It's a real crisis, I swear. Let me have the car." He'd left his in London, as you know, and came down with Mr Headleigh Drayton. I said he couldn't and that I didn't trust him, told him to get a taxi. He said how was he going to get a taxi at two thirty in the morning in the middle of the country. He did seem terribly upset, Mr Buchan, they both did.'

'Dear me. I suppose they were in tears.'

'Mr Headleigh Drayton was very near tears, sir.'

'Good God,' said Theo, concerned for the first time at something other than his car. 'And they wouldn't tell you what it was about?'

'Well – not really. They said they couldn't, but they had to get over to see someone, that it was literally life or death. I said they should call an ambulance, but they said they would do less damage by dealing with it themselves. "I swear to you, Brian," Mr Mungo said, "I swear on my mother's grave I'm telling you the truth." Well you know as well as I do, Mr Buchan, he just wouldn't lie in such a way.'

'No, no, I daresay he wouldn't,' said Theo impatiently. 'All right. So did they say where they were going? Give you any clue? Or say when they'd be back?'

'They said whatever happened, they'd have the car back by this morning, Mr Buchan. But that was all. And I believed them. So I – I let them have it. I'm very sorry, sir. But I felt it was worth the risk.'

'Well I hope for your sake, Brian, that it was. I very much hope so. Oh, incidentally, have you seen Mrs Buchan this morning?'

'Yes, sir. About an hour ago. I saw her going out of the front of the hotel. She had low-heeled shoes on, sir, she looked as if she was going for a walk.'

'The world's going mad,' said Theo, 'that's what they told me in reception. I'm going back to my room. Let me know the moment they return, Brian.'

'Yes, Mr Buchan.'

Theo went back to his room, and was about to get in the shower when the phone rang. 'Brian? What – '

'No, Theo, not Brian. It's me. James. How are you?'

'I'm about as all right as could be expected under the circumstances. My car, my son and my wife have gone missing, but otherwise everything is normal. They're not there, are they? Any of them?'

'No,' said James, 'no, not as far as I know.'

He sounded very odd; strained, his voice under tight control. Nerves, Theo supposed; he'd seemed all right last night at dinner.

'Jamie, are you OK?'

'No, not really,' said James. There was a silence, then he said, 'Theo, I've got to talk to you. Could I come over?'

Theo had heard those words, in that desperate overcontrolled tone, twice before. 'Sure,' he said, trying to sound reassuring.

'I'll be there in ten minutes.'

'Fine. I'll put the kettle on. Suite 2. First floor. Come straight up.'

That was an old joke of theirs about the kettle. He ordered some more tea and coffee and sat back to wait, remembering, remembering the first time, thirty years, a whole lifetime ago.

★

James had walked in the door, looking terrible. His face was white, drawn, as if he was bleeding internally. He looked a lot older than his twenty-nine years.

'I've got to do something terrible,' he said.

'What do you mean, you've got to? If it's upsetting you that much, don't do it.'

'I do have to. I don't have any choice.'

'What sort of something?'

'Finish with Susie.'

'I'll have her,' said Theo cheerfully.

'Theo, don't. Don't joke about it. It's not funny.'

'No, I can see that. I'm sorry. Tell me about it.'

'Well – it's quite simple really. I have to finish with her.'

'But why? I thought you and she were finally getting it together. After all these years.'

'Christ Almighty, Theo, don't make it worse.'

'Well, why are you going to finish with her when it's clearly making you so extremely unhappy?'

'Because I'm getting married.'

'Good God, Jamie, who to?'

'Maggie Nicolson.'

'Oh Jamie, Jamie, no.' Theo was surprised at the depth of emotion in his own voice. 'Don't do it. Please. I'm deadly serious, you can't do that. You can't.'

'Of course I can, Theo,' said James. His voice was calmer: it was as if Theo's reaction had steadied him. 'I'm going to.'

'But why?'

'Because – because I want to. Because I love her.'

'Bollocks.'

'Theo, don't be offensive. Maggie is a great girl. I'm very lucky.'

'Uh-huh. So great you've hardly been near her for weeks. Hardly out of Susie's bed.'

'Don't be filthy,' said James wearily.

'I feel filthy. It's filthy news. What are you up to, for God's sake?'

'I'm not up to anything. I'm getting married. Christ, Theo, give me a drink. A very big, very strong one. Then I'll go and see Susie.'

'Not if I can help it you won't. This is suicide, Jamie. Suicide of the soul.'

'Yes,' said James, suddenly. 'I know. Christ I'm a shit, Theo.'

And he sat, drinking Scotch after Scotch, turning the glass in his hand, his voice increasingly blurred; and Theo sat listening to him, also drinking hard, trying to grasp what James was saying, what he was going to do, and to work out what he could do to help him.

In the end, all he could do was support him. James's mind was made up, irrevocably; he had asked Maggie Nicolson to marry him and she had accepted. Plump, sweet-natured, dull little Maggie, whom he had known for a couple of years now, whose father was the senior consultant gynaecologist at St Edmund's Hospital (where James was a registrar), who had an undoubted crush on him, whom he had taken out from time to time, flirted with, danced with, and even (James now confessed to Theo) had taken to bed a few months earlier – 'Don't look at me like that, Theo, she's a lovely girl, and actually quite – how can I put it – '

'James, don't tell me she's sexy. I can't bear it.'

'She is. She's potentially very sexy. I'm – very lucky.'

'So you proposed, did you?' said Theo. 'Just like that? Swept off your feet?'

And 'Yes,' said James, 'yes I did.' And went on to say that the Nicolsons were delighted, were cracking champagne all over the place, the announcement was going in *The Times* and the *Telegraph* in a matter of days, and that Maggie was a lovely girl, she would make a marvellous wife, he was a lucky sod, and Theo had to be happy for him.

'And what's in this for you?' asked Theo, in a pause in this soliloquy. 'Apart from gaining a wonderful wife, I mean?'

'I don't know what you mean,' said James.

'Of course you bloody well do. Old man Nicolson's bought you, hasn't he? Look at me, Forrest, and tell me he hasn't. You can't. Come on. What's he offered you?'

Jamie was silent. He stared at the floor for a long time. Then he suddenly got up and rushed to the bathroom. Theo heard him vomiting. He went in after him, and sat with him, proffering him tissues, towels, glasses of water.

'You silly bastard,' he said equably, 'here, come on, come back into the other room. Look, I don't give a shit what you do, Jamie, as long as you're happy. But you're not going to be.'

'I might be,' said Jamie.

'No, Jamie, you won't.'

'Well I have to try to be. That's all.'

'What exactly is it? That he's giving you?'

Jamie walked into the sitting room again and sat down heavily on the sofa. He didn't look at Theo. Finally he said 'His full support, as he puts it, for Senior Registrar at St Christopher's Cambridge. That means a hell of a lot. Almost a guarantee, you could actually say. The medical profession is just as open to politics as any other. And the same thing for junior consultancy at Teddy's when he retires from the NHS in three years' time. Honestly, Theo, I listened to him, and it was like Christ in the wilderness. Temptation beyond endurance. My whole life set up for me. Success, money, status – guaranteed. I'm getting bloody nowhere, Theo. And all I have to do is marry a sweet girl I'm terribly, terribly fond of. Who will make in any case the perfect consultant's wife. Which Susie wouldn't.'

'Of course she would. She'd be very good at it, chatting up all the patients.'

'No she wouldn't. Too frivolous. And she is so appallingly extravagant, she needs a seriously rich husband. Which I'm never going to be. It just can't work, Theo. Not ever. And she's putting a lot of pressure on me. We had a terrifc row about it only two days ago.'

'How convenient for you. Or rather for Maggie.'

'Oh, go screw yourself, Theo. I really can't even think about marrying Susie. Ever. Anyway, sitting there, at the table at Simpsons, with a lot of claret poured down my throat, I was suddenly looking at a golden future. And I just couldn't turn it down. Of course it was all very subtly done. I mean not like I've made it sound at all. But it was made very clear that none of it would happen if I didn't marry Maggie.'

'And you want it that much?'

'Yes,' said James, sounding slightly surprised. 'Yes, I suppose I must do. Bloody hell, Theo, you've no idea what a jungle the medical profession is. Everyone thinks it's all so gentlemanly, but it's just as corrupt as everything else. Jobs for the boys, all fixed long before you go for interviews, the boards going through the farce of talking to you, pretending to consider you. Six senior registrarships I've applied for in the past nine months, and sixty-six ahead I'd say. I want to be a consultant; to earn some money, to have some status before I'm an old man, Theo. And without a helping hand I'm not going to get any of it.'

'I still can't believe it,' said Theo, looking at him morosely. 'It's disgusting. And I can't believe any man would sell his daughter like that. They must both be desperate. She's not in the pudding club is she?'

'No, of course she's not,' said James wearily. 'And neither of them are desperate, as you put it. But Maggie and I are very fond of each other and I think he can see I'll be the sort of son-in-law he wants. Shit, Theo, half the world runs on arranged marriages. Look at the French even. They work very well. You ask Janine.'

'Oh for Christ's sake,' said Theo. 'Jamie, you're crazy. I just hope you know what you're really doing, that's all. And I hope Maggie doesn't. Poor cow.'

'Maggie is very happy,' said James slightly pompously. 'Very.'

'At the moment, I daresay she is,' said Theo. 'It's all the other moments I'm worrying about. All the rest of her life. I hope she never gets to find out about Susie.'

'She won't because there'll be nothing to find out,' said James. 'I'm going to finish with Susie. Completely. Obviously.'

'Oh yeah?' said Theo.

About three weeks before the wedding, he had dinner with Maggie. James had been going to join them, but got caught up at the hospital. Theo sat and became extremely drunk as he listened for what seemed an extremely long time to Maggie telling him how wonderful James was, how happy she was, how perfect their life was going to be. She really didn't deserve what was coming to her, he thought; she was such a sweet, pretty girl, so extremely naive, so desperately in love. Well James was right about one thing: she would make the perfect consultant's wife. She was a well-bred English rose, twenty-four years old, she did all the right things, knew all the right people. She had been a deb, done a history of art course, (and a cookery course) and worked at a gallery in Bond Street. She shared a flat in Kensington with four other girls, and was busy decorating and furnishing the charming little Fulham cottage she and James were going to move into after the wedding. Her father had put down a very large deposit on it as a wedding present. 'I still can't believe it all, Theo,' she said, helping herself to a second dollop of whipped cream to go on her trifle. 'It's all too good to be true. Of course I always knew Jamie liked me, and we'd had some lovely times together, but I thought he'd gone off me actually, until a few weeks before he proposed. I mean I did think there was someone else. But it was just that he was so busy. They work the most horrendous hours and days at that hospital, you know.'

'Oh I know,' said Theo. He kept his eyes firmly on his plate.

'Theo,' said Maggie suddenly, 'I want to ask you something.'

Christ Almighty, she's going to come out with it, thought Theo; what on earth am I going to say?

'Yes, Maggie,' he said.

'Theo, look at me.'

He raised his eyes reluctantly, met her candid blue ones, anxious in the candlelight. 'I hope it's not serious,' he said lightly.

'It is. Well, it is to me.'

'Ask away.' He poured himself another glass of wine. Maggie was on water.

'It's just that you know Jamie better than anyone in the world, I should think. And so I thought you'd know.'

'Know what, Maggie?'

'Well – if he minds about my father.'

Jesus Christ, this is getting worse every minute. 'What about your father, Maggie?'

'Well, the thing is, Theo – oh dear, this is so difficult, so embarrassing – '

'Maggie, I'm not easily embarrassed.'

'It's just that – well, there are some things we never talk about. And – '

'Maggie, maybe I'm not the person to talk to about this.'

'Oh Theo, I think you are.'

She leant forward suddenly, her hands clasped. Her face was flushed, her eyes brilliant. Her fair hair with its loose curls was tumbled on her shoulders; her dress was quite low-cut and a very pretty full white bosom swelled up from it. He could smell her, feel her warmth; for the first time he understood how James could be marrying her. She was, in her own way, very attractive, quite sexy even. He smiled at her.

'Go on then.'

'Well, you see my father is quite – dominating. He likes to control things. And people.'

She had guessed. She knew. Not so stupid after all. And very brave. Theo put his spoon down, took both her hands in his. 'Maggie, I can't tell you how – '

'Let me finish, Theo. Please. Then you can have your say. It's hard enough anyway. Now the thing is, Jamie's parents are quite hard-up. They're lovely people, but they really haven't got any money. Well, you know that. And my father has a lot. And he's just throwing it about all over the place, buying the house, paying for the honeymoon. He's so tactless. And I just wondered if Jamie minded. He's never said anything about it – in fact if I try and ask him he changes the subject.'

I bet he does, thought Theo, I bet he bloody does.

'And I don't want him to feel – well, humiliated. Or his parents, come to that. It's all so delicate, Theo, don't you think?'

Theo felt as if he had suddenly surfaced after a rather long spell under-water. He smiled at her, released her hands, sat back with his glass of wine. 'I really don't think you should worry too much about Jamie,' he said finally. 'He's not really the sensitive little plant you seem to imagine. He can look after himself, old Jamie can. I don't think he'd mind any of that in the very least.'

And 'Oh Theo, thank you,' said Maggie, 'that is such a relief. What a good friend you are.'

Afterwards, after dropping her off at her flat, he wondered if he should actually have told her the truth, and knew that in fact he had not been a friend to her at all.

★

It was a measure of Theo's anxiety about James that he had forgotten about his beloved car as he sat and waited for him. It was also a measure of his faith in his son – which was both considerable and oddly justified. Mungo might have been expelled from two schools (once for smoking cannabis, once for what the headmaster had described as fornication), he might not yet have shown a great interest in anything remotely resembling a career, (although he was currently masquerading as an estate agent and had an office in Carlos Place, whose earnings were, Theo was forced to recognize, just beginning to balance out with its costs); he consistently lost large sums of money at the poker table, consumed awe-inspiring quantities of alcohol, and his idea of being faithful was not being in bed with one woman while another was actually under the same roof; but he was fundamentally honest, loyal and, when the occasion demanded, sensible. And Theo knew that this occasion demanded sense. Mungo would be back, and he would bring the car back; things just might be a little tense in the meantime. He wished he could feel as certain about Sasha. He wasn't going to stand for this sort of thing from her. He was lighting the first cigar of the day, as a comment on his uncertainty, when the phone rang.

'Theo, good morning.'

'Yes, Mark?' Mark Protheroe was his personal assistant; he ran the London office with a towering efficiency that at times awed Theo himself. He also had considerable power. He had a watching brief on the companies worldwide, handled all Theo's charitable ventures, and dealt, together with Theo's personal secretary, with his diary, a work of some complexity. Mark was on paper an unlikely candidate for the job, a Wykehamist, with a double first in mathematics; he was tall, stooping, and extremely thin, with a hawklike nose, huge bony hands and very faded blue eyes which could absorb the contents of a company report, a balance sheet or a computer screen faster than most people could note the date at the top of it. He reported directly to Theo rather than to George Harding, managing director of Buchan International, a fact which caused Harding to complain vociferously that the swift path he liked to tread was often obstructed by the need to involve Mark Protheroe in considerable and absurd detail. Theo shrugged off the complaints, saying that it was his company, his system and if George didn't like it he knew what he could do, and that Mark's brief was simply to receive and transmit information which should in no way affect any decision-making Harding was involved in. This was not strictly true and Theo knew it and Harding knew it, but generally speaking the arrangement worked, mainly by virtue of Mark's ability to sift through information at a rate which at times seemed almost instantaneous and decide which of it needed Theo's urgent involvement and which did not. It was a dangerous brief that he held; 95 per cent of the time he got it right. Theo had met him at a business convention Mark was attending in his capacity as lecturer in economics at the Manchester Business School, had made him an offer that quadrupled his salary as well as putting the use of his private plane and the company apartments in New York and Tokyo at his disposal, and was still surprised when Protheroe accepted.

Mark's voice, level, calm as always, came over the phone now. 'Morning, Theo. Just an update. London market's steady, Japan looks slightly unsettled, New York closed well up.'

'Fascinating,' said Theo.

'Yes indeed,' Protheroe earned his salary as much for unruffled good natured fielding of Theo's quixotic responses as for any of his more technical skills. 'Only two other things to watch at this stage. Tokyo Electron have dropped for some reason, only three points but they dropped four yesterday; and I'm afraid we've missed out on Tealing Mills.'

'How for Christ's sake?' said Theo scowling into the phone through his cigar smoke. Tealing Mills was a timber company, family owned and in trouble; he had been watching it obsessively, convinced he could buy into it and turn it round, had instructed Mark and George Harding to pounce. It was such obsessions, such convictions that had made Theodore Buchan into a billionaire.

'They've – well they've sold a 20% share apparently,' said Mark, his nervousness just detectable. 'Twenty four hours ago.'

'How the hell did we miss it?'

'We blinked,' said Mark. 'It happened that quickly.'

'I pay you not to blink,' said Theo furiously. He groped for the lighter; his cigar had gone out. Christ, this was turning into a bad day. 'Can't I leave anything to you guys to see to? You know how much I wanted that company. Timber's going through the roof. What the hell are you doing Mark? And who's bought the bloody thing anyway?'

'Private individual. New York based. I've got the New York people on it. They're getting back to me.'

'Private individual! Shit a brick. Can we get hold of any more?'

'Difficult at the moment I'd say. They've got enough money to see them through a bit.'

'Bloody brilliant. So we've totally goofed.'

'Well – yes. If you regard this company as really important. George and I don't. It's doing OK, but that's all. You have interests in far more profitable timber companies.'

'Yes, but not ones I can get a hold of. I can turn Tealing white-hot. Correction. Could have done. Stay on it, Mark. Ring me when New York opens at the very least. Tell them to find out who this person is. And keep trying to get hold of some more of the shares. Someone must be offering them.'

'Sure. Er – '

'Yes?'

'Won't you be in the church?'

'Ring me on the mobile. It'll be with Brian.'

'Yes, all right. Oh, and Exmoor phoned, want to check you'll still be going on Saturday.'

'Of course I will. What a bloody silly question.'

'Yes indeed.'

The Exmoor Foundation was a small community for the mentally handicapped Theo had financed and built from nothing on the edge of Exmoor; it was one of his favourite projects, and he took a personal and oddly tender interest in it.

'All right, Mark. Speak to you later.'

He put the phone down scowling and poured himelf another coffee. God, it was filthy. He dialled room service, complained about it, ordered some more, and was trying once again to relight his cigar when Sasha walked in. She looked gorgeous; she was flushed, her hair was in a tangled blonde cloud and she was barefoot. Her blue eyes as she looked at him were innocently wide, but just slightly wary. Theo looked back at her without smiling.

'Where the hell have you been? And where are your shoes, for Christ's sake?'

'They're outside the door, Theo. They're muddy. I've been for a walk.'

'Sasha, since when did you like going for walks?'

'Since this morning,' said Sasha. 'It was lovely. I really enjoyed it. I think I might take it up as a regular thing.' She spoke as if walking was a rather unusual occupation like scuba diving or rock climbing.

'Well, next time, you might tell me where and when you're going. I've been worried out of my head about you. Come over here.'

He held out his arms; Sasha went over to him and put her arms round his neck, kissed first his cheek, then his lips, very gently. He slid his hand into her raincoat and met a bare breast.

'Mrs Buchan! What is this?'

'A breast. I think.'

'Sasha, most people wear clothes before going for country walks. If you're going to make it a regular activity, you'd better get the equipment for it. Stand up.'

She stood up. He undid the belt of her raincoat; it swung open. Underneath she was stark naked. Theo caught his breath, sat staring at her, feeling his skin prickle, his balls stir, his breathing deepen. Shit, she was gorgeous.

'You're gorgeous,' he said simply. 'Take that raincoat off.'

Sasha took it off. She was smiling gently now, clearly assured of his benevolence, his trust. She leant towards him gently; Theo put out his hand and pushed her upright again.

'A moment, my darling. I'm not yet absolutely into my dotage. Would you mind telling me exactly why you developed this sudden urge for early country walking after – what? thirty-one years of sleeping late? Well, maybe only thirty. I daresay you woke early as an infant.'

Sasha looked at him slightly less confidently. She shivered slightly and reached for her raincoat. Theo put out his arm and held hers.

'No, don't put it back on. I like the slight sense of disadvantage you're at, and besides it's very nice for me. Just tell me, Sasha, I'm not going to beat you up.'

'Oh, Theo – '

'Don't Oh Theo me. I don't like being lied to. Or prevaricated with.'

'Theo, I would like to get dressed.'

'And I would prefer you didn't. Why did you go out?'

'Theo, for God's sake, I told you – '

There was a knock on the door. 'Yes,' shouted Theo.

'It's me,' said James's voice and he walked in.

'Christ I'm sorry,' said James. 'You did tell me to come straight up.'

'Don't worry about it,' said Theo expansively. 'We're pleased to see you, aren't we, Sasha?'

'Yes of course,' said Sasha, smiling automatically. She had put her raincoat back on. 'How are you, James? Er – would you both excuse me? I have to have a bath.'

'Sure,' said Theo. 'Close the door, darling, won't you? This is a private conversation about to be held. Very private.'

Sasha looked at him, her blue eyes suddenly dark with hostility. Theo was surprised; she was normally totally acquiescent. She turned and walked through to the bathroom and slammed the door. Taps started running very hard.

'You're a bastard,' said James. He managed to smile rather weakly. 'You really can't talk to your wife like that.'

'On the contrary, I can, and frequently do,' said Theo calmly. 'Coffee, Jamie?'

'Yes please,' said James. He sat down and took a cup. His hand was shaking visibly. He drained the cup, held it out for more.

'You look as if you need a brandy,' said Theo. 'Want one?'

James shook his head. 'Of course not.'

'Sorry. One of these days I'll crack that resolve of yours.'

'Of course you won't, said James irritably. 'Never.'

'OK,' said Theo, refilling the cup. 'What is it? What's wrong?'

'It's Rufus.'

'Rufus! What on earth has Rufus been doing? Nothing in my car I hope. You haven't heard from them I suppose?'

'No. Sorry.' James looked at him, tried to smile and then suddenly put his head in his hands. Theo looked at him in alarm.

'Jamie, come on. It can't be that bad.'

'It's quite bad,' said James. 'Rufus is in love. Says he's going to get married. Susie told me last night.'

'So?'

'So it's with – with someone he has no business to be in love with.'

'Oh for God's sake, Jamie, do stop talking in riddles,' said Theo wearily. 'Who's the boy in love with? And what's it to you? Apart from the little matter of – well we won't go into that now.'

'We might have to,' said James. 'He's in love with Ottoline Mills.'

'Shit,' said Theo, 'shit a brick.'

Chapter Four

Tilly 6am

'Fuck off,' said Tilly politely, slamming down the phone on the well-spoken robot who had just informed her that it was *six heures*. She tried to open her eyes, but they felt raw and scratchy, and her head throbbed horribly. 'Shit, shit,' she said aloud, she shouldn't have had all that red wine last night, she should never have gone to that bloody place with that little nerd, it always always had this effect on her, she really should have learnt by now. It would show too, on her face, on her skin, she would look terrible, and she only had – what? Three-quarters of an hour, not long enough to go for a run, maybe the hotel sauna – yes, that would help. God, it had better be open; of course it would be, this might be Paris, but she was in a small piece of America, that's why she had chosen to be here rather than somewhere more romantically French – who needed that on a trip? Tilly unwound her long legs from the foetal position they liked to spend the night in, sat on the edge of the bed, her head in her hands, her long red nails pushed into her short cropped black hair, trying to force the pain out.

'Come along, Ottoline,' she said, 'pull yourself together,' and she stood up, fighting the nausea, the pain, wrapped herself into the thick white bathrobe that the Intercontinental Hotel had loaned to her, and padded along the corridor to the elevator.

The Fitness Centre was not only open, it was busy. Complacently lean, tanned Americans and earnest Japanese walked, jogged, stepped, rowed: every machine was in action. Tilly looked round the room, swept it the half-inviting, half-contemptuous smile that accompanied her down the catwalks on the most prestigious fashion shows in the world, and walked into the sauna, ignoring the pile of towels on her way in. It was empty, thank Christ; she took off her robe and sat down naked, as wearily as if it had been night-time (if only, if only it was), on the wooden slatted seat, drew her knees up, sat hugging them, her head thrown back, waiting for, feeling already, the hard dry heat take possession of her, reaching inwards for her aching bones, her sore stomach. Trickles of sweat were forming between her breasts, her thighs, on her forehead, it was good, so good this, healing, soothing, and she felt suddenly she could cope with it, the long awful day ahead, the heat of the city, the bad temper she was going to encounter, from French fashion editors, hairdressers, make-up artists, and that bastard of a photographer McGrath. God, she hated him, with his bald head and his ponytail, and those dreadful glittering, evil eyes. The real Evil Eye, maybe he had that even, and maybe he could – Tilly realized suddenly that her thoughts were drifting dangerously free, she would be asleep again in a minute, and she stood up, feeling the room swim nastily, nauseously. Outside the sauna she breathed the suddenly fresh air, and without daring even to pause, jumped into the ice-cold plunge pool, feeling its shock on her skin, her veins, her lungs. Christ Almighty, she was going to faint, she was going to die. She hung onto the rail, her eyes closed, counting; get up to sixty, Tilly, and you can get out. But could she stay there deathly, mortally cold for so long? Yes, she could, she must . . . forty-nine, fifty . . . fifty-five, nearly there, now, fifty-nine, sixty. Thank Christ. She opened her eyes, started to climb out, realized she had left her robe in the sauna, realized there was a smiling, cocky bastard – French, he had to be, in those grey jersey shorts – standing at the top of the steps to the plunge pool watching her climb out, realized her breasts – the nipples hard and stiff with the cold – were already out of the water, and that the rest of her must surely follow. Well, OK, fine, if that was how he wanted to start his day, getting his rocks off on a bit of voyeurism, let him. She continued to climb, enjoying the moment as she finally stepped right out when he saw that she was taller than him, by two, maybe three inches, looked down at him, first at his face and then, pointedly, consideringly, down at his crotch, and walked slowly, gracefully past him, retrieved her robe and made for the elevator.

Back in her room she did feel much better: tired, but at least likely to stay alive. She stood in front of the bathroom mirror, drenching herself in Opium body lotion, looking at herself dispassionately as she was able easily to do (indeed it was one of the essential qualities, one that separated a good model from a great one, Felicity her agent had told her once), at the small head set on the long proud stalklike neck, the great slanting brown eyes, the chiselled lips above the tiny pointed chin, and the great slender height of her, six foot one and a half inches, the breasts that managed to be full on her wraithlike torso, the awesomely narrow hips, the flat stomach, the high, taut buttocks – slightly darker than the rest of her body, which was what the arty-farty girl from *Vogue* had labelled cocoa-butter brown in her copy – and then the legs, forty-five inches from hip to floor, legs that fashion editors at once loved and loathed, necessitating trousers specially made for sessions, false hems on skirts, legs that propelled her along without seeming (as another arty-farty journalist had said) to make any true contact with the ground. She brushed what there was of her hair: it was good, the short cut, very good. After ten days she still liked it. It had been the right thing to do. Tough, like the plunge pool, but right. Nicky Clarke had been telling her to cut it for months and she had resisted him, saying there were too many black girls around with short crops. 'Not the way I'll crop it,' he'd said, and had spent a whole afternoon working round and round her head, caressing it tenderly, sensously with his scissors, getting it exactly, exactly, the right shortness, a perfect carved cap with a lick of length over the nape of her neck. Clever boy, Nicky: very clever.

She hauled on a pair of leggings and a big T-shirt, heard her stomach rumble ominously; she should eat. Otherwise that row would be going on all day. She'd pick up a baguette on the way down to the studio, eat it in the taxi. She might throw up, but it was worth the risk.

In the taxi, blind to the golden beauties of early-morning Paris, going towards the Marais, to Mick McGrath's studio, munching the baguette, feeling steadily better, she looked at the real people – as opposed to the fantasy folk, like herself, like Susie Verge the fashion editor from *Sept Jours* she would be working with today, like Laurent the make-up artist, like McGrath – and felt sharply ashamed of regarding her day with foreboding. What she did, what they all did, was, as Nöel Coward had so memorably said, better than working; and as her mother had also said, slightly less memorably, 'Ottoline, you don't know what the word work means.'

Her mother certainly knew what work meant: it meant sewing, eight, nine, ten hours a day, in a sweatshop in Brixton, putting sequins, pearls, diamanté, frills, onto the bodices of the sort of evening dresses that still sold on great bushy rails in street markets. Sewing with an aching head and sore eyes, and for years and years a gnawing anxiety about her child, first with the childminder (all right, but not good – too many children, too few facilities), then at school (poor, not even all right – far too many children, hardly any facilities), and finally not at school at all, but bunking off, hanging around with her friends at McDonald's and Burger King, making a milk shake and a cigarette last all day. She had tried so hard, her mother had, to persuade her to get her GCSEs, to get something behind her: 'You'll never get anywhere, Tilly, not without qualifications. I got my school cert and it made all the difference.' And she had looked at her mother's poor, weary, pale face, and been too kind, loved her too much to say what nonsense, it had got her nowhere. And of course she, Tilly, had got everywhere without them, both literally and figuratively, had travelled all over the world, in the company of the world's most famous photographers and fashion editors, and appeared on the cover of every glossy magazine, had been, at only eighteen, signed by the Deep Blue jeans label company, for a rumoured half million to promote their new perfume, d'Accord, had been the star of fashion shows in London, in Paris, in Milan, in New York, with an annual income that ran easily into six figures. She owned a Ferrari (which she couldn't drive), a large flat in Kensington, (which she seldom saw), a small roomful of designer clothes (which she rarely wore); was admired, pampered, quoted, sought after: all on the strength of (as she often said, laughing, in interviews, to the despair of parents of teenage girls everywhere) straight Es in third year; after which she had been spotted by Felicity Livesey of Models Plus in Ken Market one day, as she sat on the floor, endless legs stuck out in front of her, sharing a strawberry shake with her friend Mo, watching the world go by.

★

'Excuse me, but I wonder if I could have a word with you?'

'Pardon?' said Tilly. 'What've I done now?'

She was, at fourteen, constantly expecting trouble; she often found it. The woman looking down at her thoughtfully was young – well, youngish, probably a good twenty-five actually, and dressed a bit too trendy. People that age should stop trying so hard, thought Tilly, licking the straw with relish.

'Nothing,' said the woman. 'Except look rather interesting.'

'Oh puh-leeze,' said Tilly. 'What is this, a pick-up or something? Look, lady, I'm not interested.'

'It's not a pick-up,' said the woman, looking at her calmly. 'Well, not in the sense you mean. I'm from Models Plus. I thought maybe you'd like to come and see us.'

'Oh sure,' said Tilly, 'and my name's Cindy Crawford. Listen, I don't want to be rude, but I really have got places to go, things to see.'

'OK,' said the woman, shrugging. 'That's fine by me. But take my card. Discuss it with your mother. And if you're interested come and see me, preferably with her. I won't tell her you were quite clearly bunking off school,' she added, with the glimmer of a smile, and turned away and walked off in the direction of Kensington High Street.

'Cheek!' said Mo.

'Gross,' said Tilly.

'Let's see the card.'

They looked at it. Felicity Livesey, it said. 'Director. Models Plus. 748 Old Brompton Road. 071-467-0873.'

'Wow!' said Mo. 'Hey, Tilly, do you think – '

'Nah,' said Tilly, her voice very firm. 'It's a fake. I know she's some dyke.'

'Yeah, probably. Still, you could ring.'

'Mo, do me a favour. This is the oldest trick in the book. I wouldn't even think about it. Got any money left? I could do with a ciggy.'

'Hi,' she said, noticing with some anguish that she had only two units left on her phone card. 'Is Felicity Livesey there, please?'

'I'll see. Who is it calling please?'

'Oh she won't know me. She spoke to me in Ken Market yesterday. Tell her the black girl. Outside the jewellery store.'

'Just hold on please . . .'

Shit, thought Tilly, snooty cow. She watched her two units dissolve into one, and listened to the chatter on the other end. It didn't sound like a put-up job, she had to admit. Come on, you bitch, get a move on . . .

'Hallo? Can you ring back in half an hour please? Miss Livesey is interviewing at the moment.'

'Oh – yeah, OK,' said Tilly, and put the phone down. Bugger. Phone card dead, no more money, now what did she do? Reverse the charges? No, they'd never take a call from her. Shit. It'd have to be Ron. She hadn't asked him for a while. Well, not for two days. But it'd have to be lunchtime, so he'd think she was actually at school – better go home and put her uniform on – so she couldn't ring back in half an hour. Well, if this Felicity person was on the level she could wait for her. She had better things to do than run around after her.

'Hi, Ron. How're you doing?'

'Fine thanks, love. How about you? I hope you've been at school this morning.'

'Ron, course I have. What do you take me for? I'll tell you what I did if you like, biology, we did the digestive system of the rat, it was gross, first we – '

'OK, OK, girl, that'll do. Why aren't you there now?'

'Because it's lunchtime. I came out for a sarnie.'

'Ciggy more like it,' said Ron tartly.

'Ron! Would I? Well-brought-up girl like me.'

'Well brought-up, yes, but something went wrong along the way.' He grinned at her over his stall, over the military-straight rows of vegetables, crisp white cauliflowers, gleaming peppers, shining glossy tomatoes, set out to tempt the customers, who were then given slightly less white, gleaming, glossy produce from behind the counter. 'How's Mum? Got over that cold yet? Here, have an apple.' He handed her a big, golden russet; Tilly hated russets, but she bit into it obediently, to please him.

'Yeah, she's better. Tired though.'

'Course she's tired. She works too hard. Here, darling, mind the shop for me one minute, would you? Call of nature.'

Tilly ducked under the stall, took up position behind it, gazing out at the market; it looked so different from this standpoint. She loved doing this: she'd begged Ron for a regular Saturday job, but he said he couldn't afford her, and he wouldn't exploit her, make her work for nothing. So she did the odd hour when he was really busy in the middle of the day, earned a couple of quid – 'Now that's not for fags, Tilly, understand?'

'Course not, Ron, what do you think I am?'

He was back very quickly, grinning up at her with his little monkey face. He was at least nine inches shorter than she was.

'OK, my love. Thanks. I needed that. You all right then?'

'I'm fine. I must get back to school though. Ron, you couldn't – well – '

'Lend you a quid? Tilly, I've lent you five this month already. I'll have to start keeping a slate. What do you do with them all?'

'Buy chips. The school dinners are gross. And I get so hungry. Please, Ron, I'll pay you back.'

'Yeah, and pigs'll fly. Oh – all right. But it's the last one. For a long time. OK?'

'Sure. Thanks, Ron.'

She pushed the pound coin into her blazer pocket. It was about three sizes too small for her, the sleeves way up her wrists, the bottom hardly skimming her waist.

'And bring your mum round Sunday, OK? I'll do you a Chinese.'

'Great,' said Tilly. She dreaded Ron's Chineses, greasy, slimy stir fries, usually ducked out of them, but she might have to eat this one. She'd pushed her luck with him lately.

'Hi, this is Tilly Mills again. Is Felicity Livesey there?' Now come on, you stupid cow, put me through.

'No, I'm sorry, but Felicity asked me to tell you to come in and see us. With your mother.'

'Well – I don't know. When?'

She could hear the girl shrug. 'Doesn't matter.'

'Tomorrow morning?'

'Yeah, sure.'

'OK. Thanks.'

Tilly walked up and down the Old Brompton Road several times before she finally plucked up the courage to go through the door marked Models Plus. She had spent hours getting ready, washing and blow-drying her hair – God, it needed straightening again, already – ironing her only skirt and the blouse her mum had brought her home from the workshop, making up her face with great care, sticking on her false eyelashes. She had expected number 748 to be rather glamorous, some huge building like a film studio; it was actually a small entrance by a sweet shop. A sign told her to go to the second floor; she went up, feeling slightly sick, still half expecting the whole thing to be some awful hoax.

It wasn't. She found herself in a large room filled with an extraordinary number of people. A girl sat by the door, manning a switchboard; beyond her there was a big round table, seating about four more girls and two men, each with a telephone and a Rolladex; beyond them was a pair of sofas, each containing at least three girls with a couple of boys perched on the arms, all talking; and beyond that a desk, on its own, with its back to the window. It was empty.

Tilly looked uncertainly at the girl by the door; she looked back, her eyes blank and slightly hostile.

'Hi,' said Tilly. 'I've come to see – '

'Sorry,' said the girl. 'We're not seeing anyone at the moment. Books full. Got any pictures? You can leave them with me.'

'No, I haven't got any pictures,' said Tilly, trying not to sound rude, 'and I'm here because you told me to come.'

'What's your name?' asked the girl, sounding more bored still.

'Tilly. Tilly Mills.'

The girl looked at her diary, shook her head. 'Sorry. Must be a mistake.'

'Look,' said Tilly, 'there isn't a mistake, and I rang yesterday. Felicity Livesey told me to come and see her.'

'Oh,' said the girl, looking slightly less bored. 'Well – I'll ask. She's not here anyway. You can sit down over there.'

'I'll stand, thanks,' said Tilly. She wasn't going to be told what to do by this stroppy cow. She saw the girl raising her eyebrows impercep-tibly towards the round table; another girl got up and walked over to her.

'Hi,' she said, 'you want to be a model? We're not taking anyone on at the moment, but you can leave your pictures, if you like, and we'll get in touch if – '

'Look,' said Tilly, 'I don't really want to be a model, but Felicity Livesey told me to come in and see her. If she's not here and you're not taking anyone on, that's fine by me, but I'm going.'

60

'Sure,' said the girl, smiling at her, rather patronizingly, 'fine. But it would be better to leave some pictures. You never know . . .'

'I know, thanks,' said Tilly and walked very swiftly, propelled by disappointment and hurt pride, towards the door. As she reached it, it opened and Felicity walked in.

'Hi,' she said, 'nice to see you. How are you? Where's your mum?'

'At work,' said Tilly firmly. Well, it was true.

'No school today?'

'No. It's a half-day. For – for study leave.'

'Oh I see,' said Felicity, smiling at her slightly conspiratorially. 'Well look, I've just got a couple of calls to make, and I'll be with you. Mary Anne, would you make two coffees please? One for this lady; could you wait there?' she added, indicating one of the sofas. Mary Anne had the grace to look just slightly shamefaced.

Tilly sat down, looked around, tried to pretend she felt all right. She felt terrible, dressed in her neat little skirt and blouse, as if she was naked and they were all dressed, as if they spoke a language she didn't understand. The girl next to her on the sofa, a fragile whey-faced blonde in army trousers and DM boots, was saying to one of the boys, 'I've been down at Petty France all morning, bastards won't give me a passport till tomorrow and I have to leave tonight, or I'll lose the booking.'

'They suck,' said the boy agreeably, retying his ponytail. 'I lost mine last year, you should have heard the fuss. You got any gum?'

'Yeah, sure.' She offered him a stick and then one to Tilly; Tilly took it gratefully.

'Thanks.'

'You new?'

'Yeah. Well, maybe.'

'You have a great look,' said the boy, smiling at her. His eyes were very blue, his eyelashes very long. Tilly blushed.

'Thanks.'

The girl from the round table who had told her to go away came over; she looked just slightly awkward.

'I'm Jackie. Could I just take a couple of Polaroids?'

'A couple of what?' said Tilly.

'Polaroids. Photographs.'

'Look, I told you, I don't have any,' said Tilly irritably. 'I'm waiting to see Felicity.'

'I know that,' said Jackie, with immense, bad-tempered patience. 'I'm going to take the pictures. With this camera. See?' She waved it at Tilly.

'You're a bully, Jack,' said the boy with the blue eyes. 'Can't you see she's scared? Go on,' he said to Tilly, 'it really doesn't hurt much.'

'Oh, – OK,' said Tilly, trying to look cool.

Jackie took her onto the landing, told her to look into the camera, took one full-length photograph and one close-up, then walked back into the room without a word. Tilly followed her, slightly uncertainly. She longed to see the pictures, but didn't like to ask.

Felicity was waving to her from her desk. 'Come over here. Sit down, and drink that coffee. Or don't you like it? Sorry, I should have asked.'

'What? Oh, yeah, thanks,' said Tilly. She looked at the Polaroids which were in Felicity's hand.

'Right,' said Felicity. She had a form, which she started to fill in. 'What's your name?'

'Tilly. Tilly Mills.'

'Just Tilly? What were you christened?'

'Ottoline,' said Tilly, embarrassed.

'Ottoline. That's a great name. I love it.'

'You can't. It's a crazy name.'

'It's great. How old are you – Ottoline?'

'Fourteen,' said Tilly.

'Uh-huh. Address?'

'Sixteen, Gareth Road, Brixton.'

'Right. And how tall are you?'

'Five eleven,' said Tilly.

'Still growing?'

'Yeah, I think so.'

'Stand up,' said Felicity, 'and turn round slowly. Mm. Yes. Yes, that's fine. Let me look at your hands. Oh, nice hands. It's unusual, you know, in a girl your age. You obviously take care of them. I'd be a bit worried about that scar on your cheek. How did you get that?'

'Fell off the swing,' said Tilly.

'Well – maybe it wouldn't matter.' She leant back in her chair again. 'Sit down again, Tilly. Have you ever thought about modelling?'

'No. Not really,' said Tilly.

'I think possibly you should. But I do need to see your parents. When could they come in?'

'I haven't got a dad,' said Tilly, 'and my mum works. Like all the time. She couldn't come in here.'

'Not even on a Saturday?'

'Well – maybe. I'd have to ask.'

'Of course. Because, you see, I can't go ahead without her permission. I presume you do go to school sometimes? Or at least you're supposed to?' She grinned at Tilly.

'Yeah, course I do. I'm coming up to my GCSEs.'

'Good. Because we don't like taking girls away from their studies. Until you were sixteen you'd only work after school or in the holidays.'

'And you really think I could make it?' said Tilly. She felt slightly dizzy suddenly as if the room was whirling, very slowly; she put her hand out onto Felicity's desk to steady it.

'Well, Tilly, I really don't know. I never, ever make any promises. This is a funny fickle business, fashions change all the time. All I can tell you is you look pretty OK for now. And I can tell from these Polaroids you're photogenic. But you may be awkward in front of the camera, you may hate the whole thing – and that shows – you may just not catch on. And it's a long hard haul, Tilly, be warned. It's not glamorous and it's not easy. But I'll say all this to your mum. Try and persuade her to come in next Saturday for a chat. I'd so much like to meet her.'

'Yeah, OK,' said Tilly, trying to stay sounding cool. 'Yeah, I'll try. Can't promise anything though. Thanks,' she added, standing up. Outside she had to resist a strong temptation to do cartwheels right down the street.

Her mother was very unhappy about even going to see Felicity Livesey.

'It'll never come to anything, Tilly, and it's an awful world. I wouldn't want that sort of thing for you.'

'Oh Mum,' said Tilly, 'don't start on that sex and drugs and rock'n'roll thing. Listen, you should meet this woman. She's cool. I liked her. You'd like her.'

'I wouldn't like her,' said Rosemary Mills firmly. 'Filling your head with all that nonsense. It's immoral.'

'Mum, she was not immoral. She won't even let me have my test shots done without talking to you.' This was true; Tilly had tried to get away with telling Felicity her mother was going away.

'What are test shots?'

'The pictures they take to see if you're going to be any good. Then they go towards making up your portfolio and your model card,' said Tilly. She felt rather pleased with her mastery of all this technical jargon.

'But Tilly, I can't afford to have expensive photographs taken.'

'You don't have to afford it. The agency pay. They reckon to get it back later.'

'You seem to have had a very long conversation with them,' said Rosemary wearily.

'Mum, that's the whole point. She's nice. She's careful. I swear you'd like her. And think. If I make it I'll make lots of money, and we can get a smart house up West somewhere, and you can leave that foul job.'

'Oh Tilly,' said Rosemary with another heavy sigh. 'Don't start daydreaming too soon. You're just going to be more and more disappointed. When – when could we see this woman?'

'Saturday,' said Tilly, sensing victory. 'She said she'd come in any time. We could go just before teatime and then we could go round Uncle Ron's for a Chinese. He asked us the other day, I forgot to tell you.'

'Oh – well, I suppose there's no harm talkng to her,' said Rosemary.

'Oh Mum, thanks!' Tilly flung her arms round her mother's neck. 'You're ace, Mum. Listen, do you want a cup of tea or something?'

'Yes please. Something. Camomile. There are some leaves in the jar.'

Tilly sighed. Her mother loved all that herbal rubbish. It was a hangover from her seventies youth. Tilly hated the smell of it even, it turned her up. But she'd have gone out and grown the leaves herself, she was so happy. She went over to the kitchenette, made the tea, singing.

'You won't regret this, Mum. Honest. I'm gonna change our lives.'

Rosemary took the cup, smiling slightly anxiously at her. 'Tilly, please don't get too hopeful. It's a fairy story really.'

Tilly looked at her mother sitting on the saggy old sofa, at her pale worn face, her long, rippling, faded blonde hair, her still beautiful hands, oddly graceful in her long flowing skirt, and thought how much she loved her. It wasn't cool to love your mum, most of her friends hated theirs, never spoke to them from one week's end to the next except to row with them or ask for money. But then she and her mum were different, battling away alone against the world, just the two of them, fighting for their corner and their place in it, no dad to come between them, no brothers or sisters to claim attention – and then, as she so often did on such an occasion, at some important point in her life, Tilly thought about her, about the other one, the other one who should have been there, sitting with them. Would she have been part of this adventure, would Felicity have approached her too, seen the two of them? Maybe she would – if she had been an identical, as much like her as, say, Gary Redburn was like Garth, with the teachers not able to tell which of them was in the lesson and which wasn't and who was fighting and who had bunked off and not knowing who to punish.

Well, no use even wondering. She wasn't here, she wasn't anything, never had been, not for a minute, not even for a moment probably, and that was that, thanks to that bastard. Bastard. One day, thought Tilly, settling into the familiar, outraged contemplation that was almost meditative, one day she'd get him. She'd get him as her mother, too gentle, too sick at heart, too overawed by him had finally failed to do, she'd get him and tell everyone and make sure he suffered for it.

Her thoughts clearly showed, for Rosemary suddenly said, very softly, 'Tilly, I know what you're thinking, and don't. Sometimes, I wish I'd never told you.'

'I'm just so glad you did,' said Tilly, hauling herself back to reality. 'I'd still feel there was something of me missing and I wouldn't know why. More tea, Mum?'

It was history now: a short sweet history of almost instant recognition, of a too tall, awkward, rebellious schoolgirl become a superstar, a top model, sought after, at only fifteen years old, by the haut monde of the fashion business; of photographers, fashion editors, art directors fighting to book her from the moment Felicity had released her first upon London, then Paris and New York; of dozens, hundreds of fawning articles about her, interviews with her, of her face on television, on hoardings, on buses. Famous she became, known simply as Ottoline, swiftly, suddenly famous, gazing with her raw, rich, gawky sensuality out of the pages of every magazine in the world, stalking down the catwalks with her light, arrogant tread, photographed at airports as she arrived for collections, at charity shows, and soon, surprisingly soon, in the gossip columns, for like all creatures famous for their beauty she was required to bring that beauty to grace all number of occasions: parties, premieres, charity openings. Right through the latter part of the eighties she queened it, an icon for her time, smoothly rough, sharp, flashy, newly rich, outrageously sexy; there were famous affairs, with the glitzy superstars of the eighties, with photographers, rock stars, designers, and she took to it with delighted ease, loving it, laughing with patent, infectious pleasure at it all.

By the time the decade had drawn to its painful Armageddon-like end, lurched into the frugality of the nineties, she was safe – rich, famous, still hugely in demand. She had bought her mother not the smart house up West, which Rosemary had in any case not wanted, but a pretty little cottage in Peckham Rye, from which Rosemary ran her own business as an aromatherapist. It had been Tilly's idea that; she had done a beauty photograph for *Vogue*, and the make-up artist was studying aromatherapy.

'You'd love it, Mum, right up your street, all herbs and God knows what. I've brought you a pamphlet, you should do a course and get going on it.'

'Don't be silly, Tilly, how can I do a course at my age and who'd pay for it?'

'I'd pay for it,' said Tilly, carelessly happy at her new power to give. 'It's nothing, only a few hundred quid, and you could do it from home, it'd be great.'

And Rosemary had first remonstrated with her daughter for speaking of 'only' hundreds of pounds, had warned her of seven-day wonders and houses built on sand, and then had sat down to read about aromatherapy and at the end of the evening had said to Tilly, smiling, that she did think it sounded very nice, very interesting and she'd certainly like to consider it as an option.

'Bloody hell, Mother, you'll be pushing the daisies up before you've done anything at this rate,' said Tilly impatiently and made inquiries herself, and before she knew what was happening Rosemary was studying aromatherapy and loving it as Tilly had predicted.

Tilly had started out living in Peckham with her, but on her eighteenth birthday had moved out to Kensington: 'We're going to start fighting otherwise, and you're going to get upset and I'm going to get awkward and I don't want that, and nor do you. I'll be round to you lots and lots, but not all the time. OK?'

'OK, Tilly,' said Rosemary.

★

She got to the studio at seven. Mick McGrath, looking even more seedy than usual, was sitting drinking coffee, reeking of garlic, reading the London *Times*.

'Hi, babe.'

'Hallo, Mick,' said Tilly coolly.

'Good day. The light's really nice. I've told that group of freeloaders in there to pull their fingers out and get you ready fast. I want to be out by eight o'clock latest. In the Place des Vosges, in your wedding frock.'

'OK, OK,' said Tilly, rummaging in her bag for her Gauloises. 'But don't blame me if they don't deliver. You know what Laurent's like, he starts out slow and gets slower as he warms up.'

'Hey, that's good,' said McGrath, smiling at her. 'I like that. You're getting witty in your old age, Til. Yeah, well I'll keep on his tail. Oh, and you have to call your agency. Soonest. Felicity's at her desk waiting for you now. Keep it brief, for Christ's sake, though. Coffee?'

'What do you think? Black.'

She called the agency. Felicity's calm voice came down the line: 'Tilly, hi.'

'Hi, Felicity.'

'I know I've got to be quick. Mick told me so in his inimitably charming way. But it's important. Tilly, I've had a call from Meg Rosenthal.'

'Yeah?' said Tilly. She was struggling to find her cigarettes, and couldn't; she dropped her bag, everything spilled out on the floor. 'Shit.'

'Not quite the reaction I was expecting.'

'Sorry. Spilt all my make-up. Including that gorgeous powder she gave me.'

'Who, Meg? Have you tried the foundation yet? It's all gorgeous, I must say. And the colours – '

Rosenthal was the new word in cosmetics: more haute couture than Lauder, more brilliantly fashionable than Saint-Laurent, more expensive than Chanel. Launched simultaneously in Britain, America, France and Italy, sales were soaring after only nine months, and rich women everywhere were filling their dressing tables and make-up purses with it.

'Yeah, they're great. Love it all.'

'They want you, Tilly.'

'You mean – really want me?'

'I mean really want you. A two million-dollar contract and that's just for starters.'

'Shit,' said Tilly again. Mick's tiny office spun slightly. It wasn't just the money, nor was it the thought of the fame; it was that a top-of-the-range cosmetics company should decide to stake everything on her. A black girl. Not Christy, not Cindy, not Linda, not your archetypal WASP glamour babe, but her. She knew what it meant, and it was quite literally breathtaking. It meant they saw her as twice as beautiful, twice as inspirational, twice as desirable, as all of them: simply because she was black. It was that simple. For a black girl to sell beauty to rich white women, she had to be twice everything. Probably three times. She had to be perceived not as black, not as white, not as anything – except absolutely, one hundred per cent beautifully, glossily, stylishly perfect. No messing. That was the only way it wasn't a gamble, wasn't a political gesture, wasn't a statement. These guys were only interested in one thing and it wasn't statements. Well, except financial ones. 'Shit,' she said, for a third time, and then, 'What's it mean?'

'Most relevantly, money apart, it means you have to move to New York almost at once . . .'

'Why?' asked Tilly.

'They're in a hurry. They want to announce it, promote you, start touting you around absolutely straight away. They really do need you, Tilly. It's just huge.'

'Yeah,' said Tilly. She was trying to take it in, to work out what it might mean to her, today, tomorrow, next week, next year. Belonging to someone else, that's what it meant, becoming a piece of property, her every move mapped and studied and ordered. The one thing she most hated, most dreaded. On the other hand – well, on the other hand, it was a lot of what Tilly called the fuck-off factor. It would turn her into a very powerful force. Very powerful indeed. Which meant – 'Oh God, Felicity,' she said, 'Felicity, I don't know. What do you – '

'For fuck's sake, Tilly, I told you to be quick. Get off that phone.' Mick McGrath's black eyes were snapping dangerously.

'Felicity, I have to go. I'm sorry. And I have to think. I'll – I'll call you tonight. Promise. With an answer.'

'OK, I think that's fair. I'll tell them. Bye, Tilly.'

'Bye Felicity.'

Tilly put down the phone, stood there briefly concentrating on what she had just heard, what she was feeling, and then almost visibly shook herself back into the present. She would think about it later, maybe tonight: not now. One of the reasons she was so successful, so sought after, was the way she gave herself entirely to the job in hand, whether it was a milllion–dollar deal or a one-off editorial shoot. She went into the dressing room; a small pale creature, with a wild mop of black hair, dressed in black T-shirt, black trousers and black plimsolls sat playing cat's cradle with a very long hair ribbon.

'Hi, Laurent.'

'Hi, Tilly.' He looked at her, dropped the ribbon. 'Who cut your hair? It look like sheet.'

'Thanks, Laurent. I'll tell Nicky.'

' 'Oo is Nicky?'

'Laurent, you know perfectly well who is Nicky. Nicky Clarke. Très famous.'

'Très terrible as well. Oh well, I must try. Let us start with the make-up. You are to be a bride, *n'est-ce pas?*'

'Yeah, that's right,' said Tilly absently. Suddenly, sharply she properly realized what day it was. Cressida's wedding day. Of far more importance than any job, any deal, any contract. And what was she doing? Leaving them to enjoy it in peace, leaving Cressida to mince down the aisle on her father's arm, and him to smile complacently upon her and the congregation as she did so.

'You're crazy,' said Tilly aloud, 'fucking crazy.'

'*Comment?*' said Laurent, distracted from a deep study of whether navy or purple mascara woud suit Tilly's surprisingly long eyelashes better. '*Qu'est ce que tu as dit?*'

'Nothing,' said Tilly, 'just thinking aloud. Christ, Laurent, you're not putting that filth on my mouth? And if you are I want another coffee first.'

'Tilly, you cannot have another coffee,' said Laurent, his rather small mouth setting petulantly. 'Mick wants you all done by eight and is already ten off eight now.'

'Oh – all right,' said Tilly. 'Where's the frock?'

'Here,' said Mick's assistant and stylist, a rather fierce Sloaney girl called Emma. She had got the job against fierce competition purely by virtue of her background; Mick, who had been raised in a council block in Tower Hamlets, was famous for his ferocious snobbery and while being foul-mouthed and deeply unpleasant to almost everybody he ever came in contact with, could be unctuously charming in pursuit of an invitation to a charity ball, a weekend at a country house, a society wedding. He liked to hear Emma's clipped bossy tones on the phone, arranging bookings, demanding things, telling people he was too busy to speak to them; it made him constantly, gloriously aware of how far he had come.

'It's going to be a bit too short, even if you don't wear any shoes,' said Emma, 'so we'll have to shoot a bit carefully. They just refused to let it down.'

'I expect they did,' said Tilly. 'What's it cost, a million francs?'

'More I should think,' said Emma. 'Pretty, though.'

Tilly looked at the clouds of cream slubbed silk, studded with pearls, and sighed. It did seem doubly ironic that she should be modelling wedding dresses today of all days.

'Best get going then,' said Emma. 'Mick's having a baby out there. You'll have to put it on there, Tilly, no way you can walk along in it, and we certainly can't get you into a car. It's only a five-minute walk and you can change in a shop doorway. OK?'

'OK,' said Tilly equably. She was famous for her unfailing good humour. She had once posed naked in a rainstorm on the top of Beachy Head and, while everybody else shivered and complained, had got the giggles and stood there shrieking with laughter for a full five minutes. The pictures had made headlines round the world.

They walked along the narrow, still quiet streets; the Place des Vosges, the sun shafting through its vaulted arcades, had a cathedral-like quality. It had been worth the effort, the early start. Tilly looked at her watch: still not eight, not quite seven in England. She was standing in the doorway of a shop that sold outrageously expensive bric-à-brac, dressed only in her pants, the dress supported by Emma and Laurent poised over her head, when Mick's portable phone rang.

'Yeah,' she heard him say, as the dress settled around her, 'yeah, she's here and, no, of course she can't come to the phone. She's working for fuck's sake. You heard of work, mate? It's what she gets paid ten thousand a day for. Yeah, well, it is a lot of money. Tell me about it. What? Is it really urgent? Oh, all right. But make it quick, OK?' He handed the phone to Tilly. 'It's for you,' he said. 'I wish you'd tell your boyfriends not to call you on the job.'

'Oh go fuck yourself,' said Tilly equably, fiddling with the silk roses on the neckline of her dress. 'Who is it?'

'It's Rufus somebody something. Very upmarket, darling.'

'Yeah?' said Tilly sharply, freezing in her task. 'Give me the phone, Mick. Rufus? Yeah, it's me. What's the matter?'

Rufus's light, public-school voice, high with anxiety, cut into the peaceful, golden morning.

'Tilly, I'm sorry to ring you there, but I simply had to speak to you. Something awful's happened, it's an absolute nightmare. Mungo and I've been up with Oliver most of the night. He says – well, he says he can't go through with it. It was Mungo's idea to call you. Tilly, what the hell do we do?'

Chapter Five

Susie 8am

Susie liked waking up. Being an intrinsically happy person, she enjoyed surfacing slowly into the day: reflecting upon it and its content, the shape she had planned for it, the people she would see. She would lie there, smiling, going through the gentle stretching and relaxing programme that her body trainer had taught her (for Susie did not like to waste so much as a moment), and then reach out for the thermos jug that contained her hot water, pour it into the cup on her bedside table, add two pieces of lemon from the covered container at its side, and leaning on one elbow would sip it slowly, consideringly, before getting up and pulling on a swimsuit, tracksuit and trainers and running down the stairs and out into the street where her silver Mercedes convertible was parked. She lived with her husband and her two younger children (Annabel, aged seventeen and Tom fifteen) in a house of extraordinary beauty on Chiswick Mall; it was a short drive therefore to the Riverside Health Club, where she swam thirty brisk lengths. She was back in the house, bathed and dressed by 7.30, listening to Annabel's complaints that her alarm hadn't gone off, that her head/stomach/back hurt, that someone had taken her tights, that there was no orange juice, that the spot on her chin was worse, and to Tom's desperate groans as he sat at the kitchen table trying to do two hours' prep in fifteen minutes. And then, when they were finally gone (Annabel to St Paul's, Tom to Westminster), she would take a large cup of strong tea, with two sugars, up to her husband, wake him with a tender kiss and tell him his bath was running. Susie was exceptionally nice to her husband; she felt it was the least she could do after marrying him when she did not love him in the least. She had made him very happy, and he had provided her with a very pleasant life; it seemed to her a perfectly fair exchange. The fact that she had conducted an adulterous liaison with another man for most of the twenty-nine years of her marriage seemed to her neither here nor there. Susie was not given to introspection; what mattered was what lay on the surface of life, and the surface of hers was calm and charming.

But today was a little different. In more ways than one. Today was threatening, the waking less gentle than usual, the thoughts and memories that came into her head troubling. There was no question of her shaping the day ahead, that was all done for her, and for the other 299 guests at the wedding of Cressida Forrest and Oliver Bergin. There was the phone call to make; and there was no pool within reach, no comforting, happy routine in which to hide herself, to slough off the disturbing thoughts. She wished fervently she had insisted after all that they shoud drive down from London that morning, instead of staying with the Beaumonts, near neighbours of the Forrests, it would in every way be easier, more comfortable for her; but Alistair had said he'd rather they started the day down there, he didn't want to be worried about traffic, and Annabel had said if they did drive down from London her outfit would get creased and Tom had said at least if he had to go to the horrible wedding he would be able to play tennis before and after it. (She thanked God that Lucy, her eldest, was in New York and needed no consideration in the matter). And so she had given in, as she always tried to, for the sake of ease, of greater pleasantness. Only Rufus had expressed no preference, had given her his sweet smile and said it didn't matter where he began the day, he didn't care, as long as he could end it with Mungo in London.

'Darling,' Susie had said, 'darling, as long as you both get Oliver to the church on time, I don't care either.'

And Rufus had kissed her and said he would, of course he would, but it was hardly a danger, Oliver being so exemplary a citizen; their responsibilities were likely to begin and end with making sure he didn't get to the church too early. 'His stag night was the shortest I can ever remember, Mum, all over by midnight, and we had to send the stripper home. He's a great guy and I'm very fond of him, but a lot of the time I do feel he's another generation.' Susie had laughed and said in that case she could relax and stop worrying about it all. In any case there seemed no excuse for them to stay in London, and so it came to pass that they travelled down and she was waking this morning in the Beaumonts' large, indisputably charming but extremely uncomfortable house, with its even more uncomfortable guest room. One of the worst things about staying with friends, of course, was that she and Alistair had to share a room and in this case a bed; they had had separate bedrooms for years, not as a reflection upon their sex life, which was modest, though pleasant, but on the erratic hours Alistair kept as an international lawyer, and his insomnia. Well, the insomnia hadn't been too much of a problem the night before, Susie reflected, since she hadn't been able to sleep either, and had been quite grateful to be able to pretend to be reading, but the night had been a torture nonetheless. She had finally fallen asleep at four and dreamed of Jamie's anguished face, exactly as she had last seen it in the garden of the Court House the evening before; and now it was – what? – after eight. God, she hated waking up late – and she felt wretched, thick-headed, slightly sick, and with this general sense of unease. And no swimming pool to work it off in.

She got up, looked out of the window. What she saw lifted her spirits. The sky was clear; there was just a very slight trace of mist drifting still in the small valley below the house. The Beaumonts' two hunters were grazing in the paddock; Janet Beaumont, smiling peacefully beneath the brim of her large straw hat, was in the rose garden clipping the huge white roses, some of which Susie knew would adorn the breakfast table. On the tennis court, just beyond the rose garden, Tom was playing tennis with Mike Beaumont, his normally cheerful face contorted into ferocious concentration, his heavy dark hair flopping into his eyes. Susie looked at him, and her heart tumbled over with love. Mothers weren't supposed to have favourites and of course she didn't; it was just that Tom was her baby, her last-born, and she felt more protective, closer towards him than the others. When Rufus had been fifteen, he had seemed almost grown-up, but then the way she felt about Rufus had never seemed to have much to do with the way she felt about her other children. It was a love that was differently shaped, differently experienced – scarcely recognizable as mother-love at all. But Tom – Tom was still to her a small boy. All mothers said that of course, that the baby stayed the baby; but there was something different, special about Tom. He still needed her, needed her a lot; and oh Christ, she thought, the ugly fear rising in her throat, hitting her hard, how would he be if – 'Oh shut up,' she said aloud, 'don't be negative, Susie, it'll be all right, and you'll know for sure in an hour or so.' She forced her mind back (Susie's mind was in general very biddable) to the day and to admiring Tom's service, which was impressive; indeed she spontanously clapped an ace, winging down the line past Mike Beaumont.

Tom looked up at the house, saw her and waved; she waved back, and decided to go and join them on the court. Susie was never troubled by self-doubt, by the thought that she might not be welcome anywhere: she knew with a sweet certainty that she was. And sure enough, as she left the court, three-quarters of an hour later, hot, happy, her ill-ease worked away, she heard Mike Beaumont say, 'Your mum's top of the range, Tom.'

Susie rewarded him with one of her most dazzling smiles.

She was lying in the stained roll-top bath in what had once been the nursery bathroom, idly soaping herself, anxiety creeping back into her head, when she heard the phone ringing in the hall downstairs. Janet answered it.

73

'Maggie!' Susie heard her say, in her low, headgirl voice. 'Hallo, dear. Lovely day for you. All set I – what, dear? No, no of course not. Well, how extraordinary. I can't imagine – oh, look, Maggie, of course she can't be far away. I expect she's gone for a walk, calming her nerves a bit. Or a little drive. I – oh I see. Well, dear, I wish I could – yes, Maggie, of course I will. At once. Yes, of course. Can I phone anyone for you? Yes, all right, my dear. Don't worry, I'm sure it's perfectly all right.'

Susie sat up, dropped the soap in the bath. The sense of foreboding had suddenly increased, and it had nothing to do with Jamie. She climbed out of the bath, put on her robe and padded down the stairs. Janet was standing at the kitchen window, staring out.

'Janet, what did Maggie want? What's wrong? I heard you on the phone.'

'Oh – nothing's really wrong I'm sure,' said Janet, turning with a quick, rather stiff smile. 'It's just that Cressida's gone walkabouts. I'm sure that's all it is. But I can see why Maggie would be worried. That she's not there, I mean.'

'Well I can't,' said Susie. 'And we all know how Maggie worries. Poor darling,' she added hastily, anxious as always that not a breath of criticism might drift from her in Maggie's direction. 'I mean, it's not even nine yet. I expect she's gone to find some peace and quiet.'

'Susie, dear, I think there must be a little more to it than that,' said Janet, a touch of reproof in her voice. 'Apparently she's been missing for well over an hour, Maggie said. It does seem very strange. I would be beside myself, if it was my daughter. She'd have to be feeling very upset, surely, to disappear for so long. Without saying a word. And you said she seemed so calm last night, not nervous at all. What on earth could have happened to her?'

'I can't imagine,' said Susie. 'And yes, she did seem very calm. But maybe it was all an act. She's a very good actress, Cressida, always was. I honestly think the most likely thing is she's just gone off to be by herself for a bit. Such an ordeal, one's wedding day. However lovely.'

And she was back vividly, clearly, at her own, twenty-nine years earlier, alone in the house with her father, waiting to leave for the church. He had handed her a glass of champagne, and she'd caught sight of her face in the drawing-room mirror, so pale it was almost corpselike, her dark eyes huge, and she'd seen her hand tremble as she took the glass.

★

Neil Carrington came over to her, gave her a bear hug.

'Darling, there's no need to be quite so frightened. It's not like you. Where's the girl who was calmly playing tennis an hour before her coming-out ball?'

74

'A bit older and a bit more thoughtful,' said Susie with a rather shaky smile.

'You're not – doubtful are you? Because if you are, it's still not – '

'Oh Daddy,' said Susie, hugging him back, a great rush of love filling her for a man who could genuinely contemplate cancelling a wedding for which a church was already filled, a lunch prepared, champagne iced, ten bridesmaids dressed, and a huge amount of money spent. 'Daddy, you're an angel and of course I'm not doubtful, Alistair is an absolute darling and the perfect husband, and I'm a lucky girl.'

'All right. As long as you mean it. I've never actually heard you say you love him – '

'Haven't you?' said Susie, draining the glass quickly. 'Well, you must have missed all the occasions when I did. Of course I do, who couldn't? He's sweet and kind and good and – '

The phone rang suddenly, shrilly, through the house. She knew who it was; she froze, hesitated just for a moment, then said, 'I'll get it. It'll be Bunty calling from LA, she promised she would.'

'Bad timing,' said her father. 'The car's just arrived. Be quick, poppet.'

'They can't start without me,' said Susie, going out into the hall.

'Susie?'

'Bunty! Hallo.'

'Who the hell is Bunty? It's Jamie.'

'You're sweet to ring, Bunt. Really lovely. Perfect timing! Daddy says I have to be quick.'

'Susie, don't, please don't. I can't bear it. I love you. You know I do.'

'I don't know actually,' she said, hearing her voice, cold and controlled. 'And as you couldn't be with me, I've had to do it without you. Very sadly. I know you'll be thinking of me though. Look, the car's here, I have to go. Sweet of you to call. Bye, Bunty.'

She put the phone down, very carefully, as if it might shatter, and stood there quite still for a moment, staring at it; then she lifted her hand and pulled down the short veil over her face. A tiny tendril of dark hair had escaped from the crown of lily of the valley on her head; she left it, falling onto her forehead, symbolizing, she felt, a last-minute, last-moment bid for freedom, a last look at love. Then she walked back into the drawing room, took her father's hand. 'Come on, Daddy,' she said, 'time to go.'

She smiled and she smiled and she smiled until she felt that her face would never ease into any other expression. She smiled at the guests and she smiled at Alistair and she smiled at the best man and the bridesmaids, and she smiled at her mother; she smiled at the cameras, she smiled at the manager of the Dorchester, she smiled at the maître d', and she smiled most determinedly and blindly at Serena Hammond, her best friend and chief bridesmaid, as she helped her to change out of her dress, her exquisite wild silk, rose-strewn Belinda Belville dress, so suited to her dark beauty, and into the cream silk Ossie Clark suit in which she was to embark on her first journey as Mrs Alistair Headleigh Drayton.

'It was wonderful, wasn't it?' she said, setting down her bouquet, looking at it, pulling one single pink rose out of it, handing it to Serena. 'Would you be terribly sweet and press that for me, give it to me when I get back?'

'Of course,' said Serena, 'of course I will. Are you – OK, Susie? I mean really OK.'

'Serena, I feel wonderful,' said Susie. 'Absolutely wonderful,' and then quite suddenly her heart, her aching, tender heart, which had through the long day grown physically heavier, until she felt she must hold with her hand the area beneath which it lay, to support it, to keep it from falling, crushed, somewhere deep and desolate within her body, it stirred, that heart; and the pain was sharp, uncontrollable suddenly, and she winced, heard a faint strange whimpering sound escape her, so faint she wondered if it had indeed been real, and then she saw Serena staring at her alarmed, and she sat down on the bed, and buried her head in her hands and wished she could stay there forever in the quiet darkness and never move again.

'Susie,' said Serena, 'Susie, what is it, are you ill?' And she could not answer, dared not move even, in case the tears came, broke free, alongside the grief. She sat for what seemed a long time, was indeed a long time, on such a day, such an occasion. She heard first the phone ringing, then a knock at the door, heard Serena say, in an anxious whisper, that she was all right, but had a sudden headache, needed five minutes to recover, that they must all wait, Alistair, the guests, everyone, was that so much to ask?

She sat there, thinking of Jamie with such longing, such love that he seemed to be physically beside her; she saw him, saw his slightly untidy face, with its wide, laughing blue eyes, his wild fair hair, heard his voice, his slightly husky voice, saying 'Christ, Susie, I love you, I love you,' and then, harsher, colder, filled with brutality, saying, 'I'm going to marry Maggie Nicolson, I'm sorry, Susie, but that's what I'm going to do.' And she saw him again, no longer laughing, his face no longer untidy but neat, controlled, forbidding; and she felt him now, felt his hands on her, felt her body rising, throbbing with desire for him, heard her own voice, her own laughing exulting voice saying, 'Jamie, Jamie, this is heaven, this is so good' and then that same voice, dead, leaden, saying, 'Fine, absolutely fine, I understand, I hope it works for you, Jamie.'

And then because she was well disciplined, well behaved, because she had chosen this day and what it was to do to her and her life, she finally lifted her head and said, still dry-eyed, still somehow smiling, 'Sorry, Serena, I'm so sorry. Just a bit faint, that's all. Give me my hat, there's a love, and I must go down quickly, they'll think I've done a runner.' And she stood up, seized her flowers, and almost ran to the door and out to the landing where Alistair waited, anxious, and she smiled at him too, and said, 'Darling, I'm so sorry, bit of a hiccup with the buttons,' and together they went down the stairs where she paused and threw her bouquet and was careful that Serena, whom she loved, would not be able to catch it, for she felt that anything associated with pain could not possibly bring anything near to happiness.

★

'Mummy!' It was Annabel, appearing in the doorway, the great fall of dark hair so like her mother's, half covering her face. 'Mummy, I've forgotten to bring any tights. Can I borrow some of yours?'

'Yes,' said Susie, endeavouring to hide the irritation in her voice, smiling determinedly at Annabel, 'well, yes, you can, but I've only brought a couple of pairs myself. So – '

'Well, I can't see why you need more than one,' said Annabel. 'So that means there's a pair for me.'

'I like to have a spare pair,' said Susie mildly, 'in case of accidents.'

'Yes, well, this is an accident. In a way. Honestly, Mummy, I'm only asking for a pair of tights. Not to borrow your entire outfit. Oh, and can I use your make-up, it's so much nicer than mine?'

'It's nicer than yours because I don't leave everything open all over the dressing table,' said Susie.

'I don't actually and anyway, yours is obviously nicer because it's better. I can't afford Estée Lauder and Chanel.'

'All right,' said Susie with a sigh, 'but please put everything back when you've finished with it. How are you feeling, darling, anyway? Sleep well?'

'No, not terribly, I had awful dreams and I've got a really bad headache.'

'Too much wine at supper, dare I suggest?'

'I hardly had any wine, that's not fair, about a quarter of what you were drinking. Honestly, Mum, you're turning into a real alkie.'

'Thanks,' said Susie.

'Well it's true. Oh and by the way, Rufus has gone missing.'

'Dear God,' said Susie cheerfully. 'I hope he hasn't run off with Cressida.'

It was a flip, thoughtless remark; she regretted it instantly, seeing

Janet's face set into reproach, Annabel's into intense curiosity. 'Sorry!' she said. 'Sorry, Janet. Bad form. Sorry, Annabel. Bad joke. Do you mean Rufus is not in his room as of now, or he hasn't slept in it?'

'Hasn't slept in it,' said Annabel, clearly enjoying the potential drama.

'Well that's all right, darling. He went off with Mungo Buchan after dinner last night, he's probably at the hotel with him still.'

'If he was with Mungo, I should think they're pissed as newts in some gambling den somewhere,' said Annabel prissily. Susie sighed: if Tom was the nearest thing she had to a favourite, Annabel was the furthest from it.

'Darling, that's not fair. Rufus is quite sensible really, and he certainly wouldn't let Mungo do anything awful on quite such an important occasion.'

'Rufus isn't sensible at all,' said Annabel irritably. 'And anyway, you know he just follows where Mungo leads. They're a lethal combination, and we really should have kept them under lock and key last night.'

'Oh rubbish,' said Susie, realizing that Janet Beaumont was looking increasingly uncomfortable, 'you're being overdramatic, darling. Go and have a bath or something and I bet you anything you like Rufus and quite possibly Mungo too will be here to join you for breakfast.'

'Anything?' said Annabel.

'Anything.'

'Peugeot 205 then. When I pass my test.'

'Well, darling, I didn't mean quite – '

'Mummy! That is so exactly like you. Backing down when the going gets tough and – '

'I'm not backing down,' said Susie, almost crossly, 'and all right, Annabel, if they – '

There was a scrunch of tyres in the drive and Theo Buchan's silver Bentley appeared; Rufus jumped out of it and it reversed sharply again, vanished down the lane.

'Thank God,' said Susie, as he walked into the kitchen. 'Rufus, I am particularly pleased to see you. You've just saved me about eight thousand pounds and your father's wrath.'

'Oh,' said Rufus, 'how come?'

His voice was oddly expressionless, his voice heavy. Susie looked at him sharply. 'What's the matter?

'Oh – nothing. Nothing really. I think I'll go and have a shower. If that's OK. Sorry if you were worried.'

'Is – is everything all right?' said Janet, 'With – Oliver, I mean?'

'Oh – yes. Yes, he's fine. Nothing to worry about.' He walked out of the room in silence.

'Well really,' said Annabel, 'talk about the spectre at the feast.'

'What feast?' said Janet darkly.

'Oh, there'll be a feast,' said Susie. 'Of course there will.' She glanced at her watch, felt her heart thud, fiercely, uncomfortably. 'Janet, could I make myself a cup of coffee and then a phone call? To London? I promise to be quick.'

'Yes of course,' said Janet Beaumont, 'use the phone in my room, dear, it'll be quieter. I'll make you a coffee, we could all do with one I should think.'

'Thank you,' said Susie, and stood there watching while Janet with agonizing, awful slowness plugged in the kettle, searched for the coffee pot, cut open a fresh bag of coffee, discovered all the cups were in the dishwasher, washed out four by hand, poured the coffee, fetched some milk from the doorstep, asked everyone if they wanted sugar, and all the time she thought of Mr Hobson arriving at his consulting rooms, drinking his own coffee, putting in the phone call to the lab, making a note of it, setting it aside, and then waiting for her to phone as she had said she would. He'd wanted her to go in for the result, said he didn't like giving these things over the phone, but she'd said she had to know, she couldn't wait another day, that there were reasons besides her own impatience, her own anxiety, that he knew how sensible, how steady she was, she would be fine, and he had given in, saying very well, as long as she promised to come in the following day, with her husband if possible, so that they could discuss the next steps – if indeed next steps had to be taken. And finally she had the coffee and sat on Janet's bed, looking at the phone and feeling very sick; she took a large swig of it, as if it was something much stronger, and quickly, almost feverishly, dialled the number.

'Mrs Briggs? Mrs Headleigh Drayton. Is Mr Hobson in? I've arranged to ring at this time.'

'Ah, Mrs Headleigh Drayton – good morning. Yes, he's here, I'll put you through.' And was she imagining it, or was Mrs Briggs's voice slightly lower, gentler, more carefully concerned?

Mr Hobson's voice, smoothly easy, came on the line. 'Mrs Headleigh Drayton. Good morning. What a lovely one for the wedding. All well down there?'

'Yes, yes, fine,' said Suzie (for what was a vanished bride, set against what she might be about to hear?). 'Thank you. Mr Hobson, do you have the results of the mammogram?'

'Yes, I do,' he said, and his voice had changed, she knew it had now, this was not imagined. 'Mrs Headleigh Drayton, I – well, there's no point beating about the bush. I know you've no time for that sort of thing anyway. Now I've had a look at your ultrasound as well as the mammogram, and I'm not entirely happy, I'm afraid. It isn't just the lump, there's a bit of microcalcification as well – close by it.'

'Oh.' She felt odd: not upset, hardly touched by it even, but just very distant, as if she was sitting, very small and still, in the middle of a large empty space. She knew Mr Hobson was still talking, but she couldn't really hear the words; she sat there, trying to make sense of it all, trying to get herself back to reality.

'. . . so I'd like you in as soon as possible,' she heard finally. 'Later today if that's feasible.'

'It isn't,' said Susie. 'It really isn't. But – well, I suppose – I suppose tomorrow, if – ' To her horror she heard her voice, or rather the voice of the small still creature, shaky, trembling strangely, felt something on her hand, looked down, saw a splash of wetness – how absurd, was she crying? She never cried, certainly not easily, like this. She hauled herself together, smiled into the phone.

'Yes, tomorrow, that would be fine. Of course I have to talk to my husband – '

'Of course. I'm so sorry, Mrs Headleigh Drayton, and especially to be breaking the news to you on the phone on such a day, but that was – '

'I know, that was my idea.' She smiled again, brightly, as if he could see her.

'What you have to bear very much in mind is that even the worst possible scenario is nothing like it was. There are many treatments, the prognosis is good – '

'Yes. Yes of course,' said Susie, thinking of a friend who had had that treatment, who had undergone chemotherapy and its attendant tortures, the nausea, the weakness, the weariness, the baldness – and still died. 'Yes, I understand.'

'So – tomorrow then. You can arrive any time, but the earlier the better. I'll tell Mrs Briggs to make the arrangements. Nothing by mouth after midnight. Now would you like me to speak to your husband? Explain things to him?'

'Oh no, no that's fine,' said Susie. 'I'll talk to him. He'll be fine. He's very – supportive.'

'Good. Exactly what you need. I'm so sorry to have cast a shadow over your day.'

'It's all right,' she said, smiling again determinedly. 'It really isn't your fault.'

'No, but I do always feel somehow responsible. Goodbye.'

'Goodbye,' said Susie.

She put the phone down and sat there, staring out of the window; she realized she was cradling the breast in her hand, the left breast, that had been invaded so swiftly and silently by this obscene, all-consuming monster.

Cancer. There was no doubt in her mind as to Mr Hobson's conclusions. She had known anyway, for a while. Apart from the lump, discovered as she tenderly, lovingly massaged her Chanel body lotion into her breast, it had been one of her days for meeting James. She had been excited, happy, and there it was, small, sinister, predatory. She hadn't said anything to James, of course; had waited indeed for two weeks, telling herself it was probably just a purely temporary thing, that it would disappear after her next period. It hadn't. She'd lost weight, too, had been aware of it for a little while; not a lot, but enough to notice. She had stopped having to be careful; she'd tested herself in fact, had eaten all the things she always refused, for over a week, chocolates, puddings, potatoes, cheese, and at the end of it, stubbornly, defiantly the scales had shown a drop of almost two pounds.

'So,' she said aloud, 'so, Susie, what to do?'

And as she sat there, trying to digest the news, to face the fact of her possible, probable death in – what? – six months? a year? a painful, ugly, hideous death, when she was still young, still beautiful, still happy, she knew exactly what she was going to do. She was going to have James, all to herself, for as much of that time as she possibly could. He owed her that much; they all did. She had earned it.

Chapter Six

James 10.30am

He knew there must be something wrong as he pulled into the drive: Maggie was standing by the back door, her plump face tense, white, and Janine beside her, holding her arm. His first thought was of course that Cressida must be ill, and he wondered briefly, almost idly, what he could give her, what shot might settle a stomach, ease panic, cure the migraine that occasionally plagued her. And then Harriet, her face as white as theirs, eyes wide and frightened, came running out to the car, and he stared at her through the open window. 'What is it?' he asked. 'What on earth's going on?'

'It's Cressida,' said Harriet, quite quietly but with an undertow of panic in her voice. 'She's gone.'

'Gone?' said James, getting out of the car, looking towards Maggie and Janine and then back at Harriet, aware even as he spoke the words how stupid, how dense, how unhelpful he must sound. 'What do you mean gone? Of course she's not gone.'

'Daddy, she's gone,' said Harriet. 'And her car's gone, she's been missing for ages – probably hours – '

James had once been in a car that had skidded and turned over twice; he had felt then a chilled, blind terror, a sickness that had consumed all his senses. He leaned against the car to steady himself; Harriet's face and voice seemed to be very far away, her voice echoing and odd, rather slow. 'Three hours?' he said, and was aware how foolish he must sound. 'Cressida's been missing for hours, but that's absurd, she was here when I left about – what was it, seven o'clock?'

'How do you know she was here then?' asked Harriet quickly. 'How do you know, did you see her?'

'Well, no – but her door was closed, everything seemed calm – '

'Where on earth have you been anyway?' said Maggie. She had walked over to the car; her voice was high, shaky with tension. 'What have you been doing all this time?'

'I went for a run, as usual,' said James easily, blessing his infinite capacity for deceit, 'and then I realized I hadn't got enough cash for the waiters today, so I drove into Woodstock to the cash machine. I'm sorry.

Anyway, Harriet, where were you at seven? Why on earth weren't you raising the alarm then rather than waiting three hours?'

'Daddy, I was looking for her,' said Harriet, quietly, patiently, her dark eyes nevertheless angry, 'and trying not to raise a panic. I felt sure she'd turn up. Anyway, we've been looking for her for ages now, making phone calls – '

'Who have you phoned?'

'Well, Mummy phoned the Beaumonts, I tried to get hold of Mungo, only he's not at the hotel, and Theo's line is constantly engaged – '

'What about the Bergins? Does Oliver know anything?'

'We haven't phoned them,' said Harriet.

'Why on earth not, for Christ's sake?' Careful, James, you're sounding hysterical now; don't add to this panic. He made a huge effort to level his voice. It was surprisingly difficult; there was a fierce, hot sensation behind his eyes, a constriction in his throat. 'If she really is – well, missing, then surely he is above all the person who has to know. He also might very well know where she is. She might be there, with him.'

'Oh of course she's not with him,' said Maggie. 'That's absurd.'

'I don't see why. It seems at least a possible explanation to me.'

'James, of course she's not with Oliver,' said Maggie. 'She was so insistent she didn't see him after midnight even, don't you remember last night, it's absurd to talk about – '

'Oh for God's sake,' said Harriet, 'don't start arguing about it. You phone them if you think it's a good idea, Daddy. We weren't prepared to, that's all, not yet . . .'

'I'll phone them,' said Janine quietly. 'It would be more discreet, I think. Can I use the phone in your study, Jamie?'

'Yes of course. Thank you, Janine.' She disappeared into the house; they all stood looking after her, staring at her small back as if in some way she was carrying with her the answer to the mystery.

'Well, we may as well go in,' said James finally. He was beginning to feel slightly steadier, able to think. 'No point standing here. What about her flat in town? Have you phoned there?'

'Yes, of course. We keep ringing it. No answer.'

'And – I suppose you haven't – that is, should we phone the – the police?'

Maggie had reached the doorway; she turned to look at him, her face puzzled.

'No,' she said, 'no of course not, why should we phone the police?'

'Well, because there might have been – Cressida might have had – well, you know – an accident.'

'Oh don't be absurd,' she said, 'of course she hasn't. Of course we

83

shouldn't bother the police with it. Harriet, make some tea, would you? I feel – I feel – '

She looked terrible suddenly; no longer just pale, but grey with fright, her eyes huge, the pupils dilated. She walked forward and staggered slightly; James caught her arm and helped her to a chair in the kitchen. She was very hot, he noticed, almost with distaste, sweating heavily; but her hands were cold, her lips white. She was about to go into shock, he thought. He turned to Harriet, said, 'Darling, make that tea quickly, would you, lots of sugar for Mummy,' and pushed Maggie's head down between her knees. Her neck was wet with sweat, her hair clinging to it, and there was a damp patch on the back of her velour tracksuit top. What on earth was she doing dressed in something so warm on such a day? he wondered, and then knew: she was covering herself up as much as possible, as always hiding the heavy body she was so ashamed of, hated so much and yet seemed incapable of doing anything about.

Harriet came over with the tea; Maggie sat back, took the mug with a hand that shook.

'Better?' asked James. He watched her as she sipped at it, saw a slight colour seep back into her face.

'A bit.'

'Good. Don't worry, darling, she'll be – '

'Look Jamie,' said Maggie, and there was an edge to her voice that he found almost comforting in its normality, 'I'll try to keep calm, I'll do whatever is necessary. But don't tell me not to worry and don't say any more you're sure she'll be back. I can't stand it.'

Janine came into the kitchen; she smiled quickly, carefully at them.

'What did Oliver say?' asked James. 'Did he – '

'I didn't speak to him,' said Janine. 'I was put through to Josh and then to Julia, unfortunately. I said I wanted to talk to him about a little present I had for Cressida which I was going to ask him to give her on the plane.'

'That was clever,' said Harriet.

'Well, she seemed to accept it. Anyway, Oliver was asleep.'

'So late? How odd.'

'He was up playing poker with the boys until three, Julia said. She sounded a little disapproving. She is absurd, that woman, she behaves as if the boy was two, not thirty-two. She was very reluctant to wake him up. I couldn't really – well, I didn't want to force her. At this stage.'

'No – no, I suppose not. I must say that doesn't sound like Oliver. He's not a poker player at the best of times. Bridge is more his style. But maybe he couldn't sleep, and those two can be very persuasive. But anyway, did Julia sound – well – quite normal?'

84

'Oh yes. Very normal. She said what a wonderful day it was, and she hoped we were all feeling as great as she and Josh were.'

'Dear God. Well, it certainly doesn't sound as if there are any clues there. You were right, Mummy,' said Harriet. 'Daddy, should we phone the police do you think? And – and the hospitals?'

James stood by the window, constantly expecting, hoping, praying, that Cressida's little car would pull into the drive, that she would jump out, run in, full of apologies; he was afraid himself of ringing the police, of what it meant, that they were making it official, the disappearance, that they needed help. He felt very sick himself suddenly; he forced himself to smile at Harriet.

'I think maybe we – ' he said, and then the phone rang. Maggie jumped up, moving with extraordinary speed across the kitchen, snatched it up.

'Cress – oh – oh Mary.' There was a sharp intake of breath, and she handed it to James, shaking her head.

'Hallo, Mary? Yes, this is James. Yes, she's fine. A bit panicky. Busy morning here as you can imagine. What can I do for you? Oh really? Well, yes of course you can. We'll see you then. Bye, Mary.'

He put down the phone. 'That was Mary Fortescue. She wants to drop Belinda off a quarter of an hour early, and then get down to the church and check the flowers in the porch. Apparently that's her bag.'

'James,' said Maggie, and her voice was only just under control, 'James, I don't want Belinda Fortescue here early, rushing around in her bridesmaid's dress. The child is a nightmare at the best of times, I never wanted her as a bridesmaid anyway and – '

Tyres scrunched onto the drive; they all stiffened. It was the florist's van. He knocked at the open back door, loudly, stood there whistling. Harriet went to the door.

'Oh! Mr Spragg,' she said, 'good morning.'

'Morning, Miss Forrest. Got some lovely things for you here. One bouquet and eight posies. And the coronets. Now do you want them or shall I take them away, try and find someone else who can use them?'

They all stood there, staring at him, frozen. His words seemed horribly prophetic, his bonhomie hideously misplaced. He looked at them, and his smile slowly faded.

'Nothing wrong is there?'

'No,' said Harriet, smiling quickly, 'no of course not. How lovely, Mr Spragg, do bring them in. Maybe if you put them in the utility room, it's cooler in there.'

Mr Spragg's face eased out of anxiousness; he turned and went to his van, carried first one and then a second box of bouquets. He was whistling again, loudly and tunelessly – 'Here Comes the Bride'. James felt as if barbed wire was slowly tightening round his heart.

'Right, and there's the buttonholes. Sign here, Miss Forrest. Beautiful they are. Now you all have a lovely day and give your sister a kiss from me. I can remember making up her first bridesmaid's posy, pink sweetheart roses, I can see them as if they were here now. Well, I expect you're all very busy so I'll be getting along. Mrs Spragg's going to pop down to the church at two, if that's all right, just to see the bride. I would but I've got a very busy day. I hope all goes well.'

'Oh – yes, thank you, Mr Spragg.' James forced his voice into action; it was extremely difficult. 'I'm sure we will.'

The van disappeared down the drive. Maggie looked at James as if for comfort and then suddenly started to cry, tears rolling down her face. She started drumming her hands on her knees; Harriet stepped forward. 'Mummy, don't – '

'Stop it!' Maggie's voice was loud, raw. 'Don't touch me. Just find her, go and find her.'

'Maggie, pull yourself together,' said James, aware of the desperate edge to his voice. 'This won't help anyone.'

'I can't, I can't,' cried Maggie, her voice a wail. 'She's gone, she's gone, and we shall never find her, never, she's run away, and the whole day will – '

Yet again the phone rang. Christ, James thought, it was like some ghastly persistent torture, he felt the ringing physically, like a probe entering his brain, somewhere behind his ears. He picked it up.

'Yes? Oh, Julia, good morning.' He looked at them, over the phone, his eyes asking for guidance. They all stared at him, helpless. 'How are you?' he said. 'Sleep well, I hope? In spite of everything. Good. Yes, indeed, a lovely day. I'm sorry? No, she's not here just at the moment. She's – in the bath. Can I get her to – yes, of course I will, Julia. How kind. How very kind. Goodbye. Yes, just before one we said, didn't we? For a glass of champagne. Excellent. See you then, Julia.'

He put the phone down again. 'She rang to speak to you,' he said to Maggie, his face carefully expressionless, 'to say she was sorry she missed you earlier when Janine rang, but she had just got out of the tub, as she calls it, and to – I quote – to tell you good morning, wish you the happiest of days. That's all.'

'She is very American that one,' said Janine lightly.

'Well she would be,' said Maggie. 'She *is* American. Nothing else? Nothing about Oliver?'

'No. Nothing. He's obviously still asleep.'

'James, what do you think we should do?' Her eyes were on him, strained, frightened.

'I think,' he said rather heavily, 'I think, quite honestly, we should phone the police.'

'So do I,' said Harriet.

A small pained cry escaped Maggie.

James braced himself to confront the truth. He phoned first the vicar, then the police, and he phoned all the hospitals in the area; there had been no accidents, not even minor ones. The Chief Constable, whose daughter had been delivered of a fine strapping son in her own front room by James Forrest one December a few years earlier when all the roads for miles around had been closed by freak weather – James had trudged on foot through the snow to get to the house – made half a dozen calls to all the major units in the country. There were no serious accidents on record. 'And I've had the hospitals checked out too. Nothing. I wouldn't worry too much, Mr Forrest. She's probably just – well, there is one thing you could do – ' He hesitated.

'What's that?' asked James.

'You could phone the Missing Persons' Bureau. Very good people they are, very experienced in this sort of thing.'

'Well I might. A little later,' said James, shrinking from further phone calls, explanations, forms, details, red tape, further confirmation that Cressida was precisely that: a missing person. 'Thank you.'

He looked at his watch: moving towards eleven. Christ, this was getting out of hand. They'd have to start notifying people soon, couldn't go on like this. It was madness. But it seemed crazy, irresponsible, not to tell Oliver first: they should have done it hours before.

He phoned the Bergins' hotel. While the number rang interminably, he stood staring out of the window, thinking inconsequentially that the white roses would actually be at their best next week and what a pity that was, what a waste, and it was several seconds later, when the hotel switchboard answered, before he forced himself to the realization that of all the possible, indeed almost certain, waste of today, the roses constituted the very least.

'Lambourne Park Hotel,' said the girl's breathy voice, 'how may I help you?' And again James found himself distracted by minutiae, by how much he hated that phrase, so awkward in its syntax, so redolent of learnt-late rather than instilled good manners; then he pulled himself together, back to reality, and said, 'Dr Bergin, please, Dr Oliver Bergin.'

'One moment please,' said the voice and there was the abstract clicking of computer keys and a long pause; then 'Dr Bergin doesn't appear to be answering at the moment, sir, can anyone else help you?'

'No,' said James irritably, 'no they can't, I'm afraid,' and then suddenly Julia's voice came on the line, just slightly less well modulated, marginally quicker than usual: 'Julia Bergin speaking.'

'Oh,' said James, thrown into total confusion, 'oh – Julia. this is James Forrest. I – I was actually hoping to speak to Oliver.'

'Why?' said Julia, and again this was not the rather fey, carefully flirtatious woman he normally spoke to, it was someone businesslike, quick, almost sharp. 'First Janine, now you. Why do you all want to speak to Oliver, James?'

'Well – I wanted to check something with him.'

'And what was that, James? Maybe I can help?'

'I don't think so Julia. It was about the – the best man's speech. I wondered how – how long it might be.'

'I would have thought you should have spoken to Mungo. He would surely have more idea.' She sounded more herself, the voice softer again.

'Yes, but he's on the tennis court.'

'I see. Well, Oliver isn't here right now.'

'He isn't?' Dear God, had the entire world gone mad, disappeared?

'No, he's in the tub. No doubt reflecting on his future as a married man. A very fortunate married man, of course. Will I have him call you?'

'Oh – yes, Julia, yes please. As soon as he's out of the – er – tub. Thank you. I'll be by the phone.'

'All right, James. Goodbye for now. My, it's getting late, isn't it?'

'Yes,' said James, looking helplessly at his watch and the clock on his desk: another ten minutes had passed, it was indeed getting late, after eleven now, after five past. 'Yes it is. Well – thank you, Julia.'

'And there's nothing else?'

'No, no, nothing. Thank you again.'

Silly woman. Fussing over her little thirty-two-year-old boy, hanging around in his bedroom on the morning of his wedding. What on earth was she doing in there, and would she be soaping his neck for him in a minute, checking he'd rinsed his hair properly? God, Cressida had a tough row to hoe with Julia for a mother-in-law.

'Only maybe you won't,' he said aloud, and sat down at the desk, buried his head in his hands, his eyes tightly closed, his thumbs pushed into his ears as if to shut out as much as possible of the world, willing it away. As he always did, always had, in moments of appalling crisis. As he had, almost exactly twenty-five years ago, as he finally left the delivery room at St Edmund's Hospital at five in the morning and stumbled exhaustedly into his room, wondering how, how in the name of God, he was ever to recover from the sheer awfulness of what he had done.

★

'Mr Forrest? Staff Nurse Jackson here. We've got an admission into the labour ward, and I'd really like you to come over and have a look at her.'

'Ah,' said James, playing for time, 'ah, yes, Staff. Yes, yes, I see.'

'She's very small, the baby seems to be quite big, and she doesn't seem to be getting anywhere. And she hasn't been coming to antenatal clinics.'

'Isn't Dr Meadows there?'

'No, it's young Tim Davies on duty, and I really don't think he's got the experience, and we've got three others in labour anyway – '

'Ah', said James again. He looked at his watch: one thirty, dear God, and he was in no condition to look at anything, except possibly another stiff whisky; he'd already had a great deal of wine, he'd known it was foolish, that he was on call, but he still found entertaining the Headleigh Draytons a strain. He wished Maggie would stop insisting on being quite such close friends with them, asking them for dinner and so on. He'd promised himself just one drink before dinner, but somehow the one had led to another and then he'd had to listen to bloody Alistair banging on about his bloody career and his bloody family and how he'd put his bloody son down for Eton already. If only, James had thought, if only he knew; he had sat there, glass after glass of claret going down, (surreptitiously because they all knew he was on call, well diluted with a great many glasses of water), looking at Alistair's handsomely good-natured face, and then at Susie's beautiful one, listening to her lovely husky voice as she regaled them with some amusing story, not hearing a word of it, wondering with the old, sick, illogical jealousy how she could possibly have married Alistair.

'Yes, all right, Staff,' he heard himself saying, quite clearly, quite coherently. At least it would get him away from this filthy evening. 'I'll come over. Be about fifteen minutes. All right?'

'Thank you, Mr Forrest.'

He had drunk almost a whole bottle of water and two mugs of strong coffee and gone; they had all looked at him anxiously and asked was he really all right, but he said yes, fine, he'd only had a couple of glasses, and that was hours ago (hoping no one had been counting). And went out to his car, and drove the few miles to St Edmund's where Rosemary Mills was lying in the labour ward.

She seemed incredibly young, but then most of the mothers did these days. She was nineteen, she told him, her eyes resting trustingly on his, large blue eyes in a small pale face. She was very small; James looked at

89

her narrow hips, small, childlike legs, either side of the huge stomach as he examined her, and sighed silently. Then he smiled his careful consultant's smile, patted her hand gently.

'Right,' he said, 'everything looks all right. Your cervix *is* dilating although it's slow. But there's nothing to worry about.'

'It doesn't feel all right,' she said, her face contorting as a contraction hit her. She panted heavily, fiercely, her eyes fixed on him, clinging to the hand of the student nurse who was with her; he could see what she was doing, desperately trying to relax her body. One hand was clenched, the other flexed open.

'Been to classes?' he asked carefully, when she was finished, had swallowed, drawn breath, the midwife had wiped her dry mouth.

'Well – not here.' Her voice was pretty: slightly husky, with – what was it? – a West Country accent. 'But to yoga classes. I – know what to do.'

'Hmm. I'd advise some pethidine. Help a lot, you know.'

'Oh no,' she said quickly. 'No, I don't want drugs.'

Oh God. This was going to be tough.

'Well – it could be a long night. Think about it at least.'

'I have thought about it,' she said, 'and I know I don't want any. I want to have my baby naturally.'

She sounded fierce; very fierce for such a gentle creature. She had been brainwashed by some bloody natural-childbirth freak. James would have them all bound and gagged and made to watch a long, tough breech birth, without benefit of pain relief.

'Well, we'll see how you get on. Of course,' he added carefully, anxious not to alienate her, 'that's best if you can manage it, and if everything is straightforward. Now according to Staff Nurse, you haven't been coming very often for your antenatal care. In fact, the last time we saw you was three months ago. That was silly, you know.'

'I know,' she said humbly. 'I'm sorry. I hate hospitals.'

'Well you're here now. With your husband?'

'No,' she said quickly, 'with my yoga teacher and my mum. Can they come in – later?'

'I don't know. We allow husbands, but not – '

'Oh God, it's starting again,' she said and started panting.

Staff Nurse Jackson patted her hand briskly. 'Good girl. That's right. You sure you wouldn't like some pethidine?'

Rosemary Mills shook her head. Her teeth were gritted. The student nurse looked as white and exhausted as she did.

★

'She's very large,' said Nurse Jackson. She had asked him to come into the corridor. 'Don't you think? Especially for a primagravida?'

'Not really,' said James curtly. He turned away from her, afraid his breath must smell of drink. It was too late: she knew, and she could see he knew she knew.

'Dr Forrest, are you all right? You look very – tired. Would you like me to try and find someone else? Even now.'

'No,' said James. He found a packet of peppermints in his pocket, started chewing them. 'I absolutely would not. This is a perfectly routine case. She's already 5 cm dilated. She may have a tough time, but that's all. Still, I'll stay and see her through.'

'How was the heartbeat?'

'The heartbeat was fine.'

Staff Nurse Jackson met his eyes. 'I'm sorry, Mr Forrest, but I just don't like the look of it. Her waters broke over an hour ago, she's been going hard for almost six hours as far as I can make out. And in mild labour for much longer than that. And she's only thirty-six weeks. And as I say very big.'

'Thirty-six weeks. Yes of course,' said James quickly. He hadn't noticed that. Shit. Did she know he hadn't noticed?

'Mr Forrest.' The eyes were more contemptuous still. 'I do think this one might be a Caesar. Should we tell theatre, have them on standby?'

'Staff, I'll make my own decisions, thank you. Now you can get me a coffee, I've had a very long day, I'd only been home a couple of hours, and then you can try and persuade that stupid girl to have some pethidine. All right?'

'Yes, Mr Forrest.'

He drank the coffee, sent for some more. He still felt odd, slightly distanced from reality, but not drunk any more. Of course not drunk. God, what was – well, maybe three glasses of wine? And a gin and tonic of course, but that had been many hours ago. He had frequently drunk much more than that in the past and gone on to beat Theo at poker. He was just tired. Terribly tired. And upset. That was all. Maybe he could get a few minutes' sleep before he had to deliver the baby. He closed his eyes; the room swirled briefly. He drank some water, tried again, hung on through the swirling, and dozed for a while. His phone woke him. It was Staff Nurse Jackson. 'Mr Forrest, she's been pushing for almost half an hour, not getting anywhere. Could you come down please?'

'Yes of course.'

He stood up; he felt sick, still slightly odd, but much more sober. Good, the coffee had worked. He sook another slug of water, hurried along to the delivery room. Rosemary Mills was wide-eyed with terror and pain; her face was white and contorted.

'Ah,' he said. 'How are you? Pushing I hear. That's good. How about some gas and air?'

'No. No, I really don't want any. Please don't make me.'

James struggled to sound patient. The slight sense of unreality he was feeling, the sense of physical distancing from the room, from the girl, from her pain, helped. He managed to smile at her, to pat her hand. 'No, not as long as you're coping. And you're pushing now, Staff Nurse tells me. That's the good part. It will soon be over, and the baby will be here. Now I'm just going to have another look at you. Tell you how you're getting on.'

He examined her; the tummy was very big. Staff was right. He did an internal. The head needed turning. That was it, that was what was holding things up. The heartbeat was absolutely fine, nothing serious there. Just a bad hour ahead for the poor girl; well, she should have some pain control. Silly bloody nonsense, all of it.

'Right,' he said, 'now everything's fine and you're doing well, but the baby's head is in slightly the wrong position.'

'What does that mean?' Her white face was panicked. 'Is it dangerous?'

'Not at all, no. It's facing the wrong way – just slightly. That slows things down. But it may turn as it comes into the birth canal. All right?'

She nodded dully. Then a contraction came; she pushed. Another; she pushed again. And again. After twenty minutes, nothing had happened; the baby hadn't budged. She was yelling now, her courage finally deserted her, her face contorted with fear as much as pain. 'Get it out,' she kept crying, 'get it out, get it out. Please, for God's sake, just get it out.'

'All right,' said James gently, 'all right. I'm going to use forceps and give you a local anaesthetic, something called a pudendal block. And you'll have to have an episiotomy. It will help us turn the baby's head and get it out. Do you understand?'

Rosemary Mills moaned helplessly as her legs were placed in the stirrups. She looked like a small animal in a large trap. James looked at her. He had not known many births as bad before. He still felt sick and his head ached horribly. Christ, this was a nightmare. 'Get me another glass of water,' he said curtly to Janet Adams, the student nurse, 'and call the paediatrician.'

He put the blades on the baby's head – turned it and began to tug, gently. The baby proceeded, smoothly, easily now down the birth canal. He manipulated the head between contractions. Released from some of her pain Rosemary Mills was quieter, biddable. He felt better: in control, excited almost, as he often did before a birth. The baby was face downwards now; he did the episiotomy, gave a final pull and the head delivered. It was a very dark head, the hair very black. A pair of small brown shoulders followed, he gave an injection of syntometrine and the rest of the body emerged. A little coffee brown female body. He lifted the baby, slapped her gently, heard her cry, handed her into her mother's pale, shaking arms.

'She's lovely,' he said.

'Yes,' said Rosemary Mills, her voice little more than a croak. 'Yes, she is. Really lovely. I can't believe it.' She looked up at him, gave him her trusting, childlike smile. James smiled back just slightly awkwardly. He felt he could have served her better. But: 'All well then,' he said to Staff Nurse Jackson.

'Just as well,' she said, 'there's a crisis in the theatre, baby with a heart problem.'

'Ah,' he said. 'Well, we were lucky.'

'Thank you,' said Rosemary, 'thank you for everything.' She was high now, with pleasure and relief, smiling, laughing almost, stroking the baby's black head, her small pudgy nose, looking at her dark blue eyes.

'What are you going to call her?' he asked as he delivered the placenta and prepared to stitch her up.

'Ottoline,' she said.

'That's a fine name.'

'I know. After Lady Ottoline Morell. She's a great heroine of mine. And her daddy's.'

'And where is her daddy?' asked Staff Nurse.

'Oh – he's off working,' she said quickly, bravely. 'He's in a band.'

It all made sense suddenly. She wasn't going to see a great deal of the daddy. Probably after a while she wouldn't see him at all. She had a tough time ahead. But meanwhile, the miracle had been worked again, a baby had been born, given life, love, tenderness; and it was all worth it.

James smiled at her. She smiled back at him. Staff Nurse Jackson smiled at them both. And then Rosemary Mills was sick. That was quite normal. It was the syntometrine. As she vomited, as Staff Nurse rushed for a bowl, James patted her hand, took the baby from her. And saw a bulge in her vagina, a nightmare sight, a second bag of membranes making their way out of the birth canal.

'Staff,' he said, his voice light, shaky with urgency, 'Staff, take this baby. There's another one in there.'

'Ah,' said Staff Nurse quietly. She laid the baby in a cradle, told the junior midwife to take her away.

'Right,' she said, her calmness icy, reproachful. 'I'll try the paediatrician again. You – '

'It was a singleton,' he said, 'I know it was a singleton. There was no other heartbeat, no sign – '

Nurse Jackson looked at him, and her eyes were very contemptuous. 'I did say – '

There was a great gush of water over the bed, and a small foot appeared. Rosemary Mills groaned; James with difficulty stopped himself from doing the same. Twins, and this one a breech. God Almighty.

'I'm sorry,' he said to Rosemary. 'I didn't – didn't realize. It was very high up, you see, it's very often difficult to tell in those circumstances. Nothing to worry about though, soon get this one out.' God, if only he felt clearer-headed, less exhausted. 'Now you're going to start pushing again, and I'm going to deliver your baby.'

She tried; she tried desperately. But she was very tired. Progress was terribly slow. 'What's the heartbeat, Staff?'

'Still a hundred.'

'Good. Thank God. Now come on, there's a good girl. Push, Rosemary, push.'

He was fumbling now; his hands, normally so skilful, seemed awkward, undeft. He hurt her; she cried out. 'Sorry, Rosemary. Sorry. Won't be long.' Right. He eased the buttocks out; progress. And then there was a trickle of fresh blood. Shit. That was the second placenta separating. Keep calm, James you still have time. 'Heartbeat, Staff?'

'Seventy.' She sounded stern, amost angry.

'Right. Good. Another push. Good girl. Well done. Ah, you have another daughter. That's something to keep you going. And now the shoulders. Soon be over.'

'Mr Forrest, this is too slow. Much too slow.'

Stupid bitch. How was that going to make the girl feel? Anyway, it wasn't. The baby was coming. Although the head seemed to be very large. Never mind. It would be all right. Perfectly all right. Only – Christ, now the cervix was begining to close down. That was the syntometrine at work.

'Mr Forrest, it's been almost half an hour. We have to get her to theatre.'

'No, no, it's too late for that.'

'Mr Forrest, the heartbeat's down to fifty.'

'Shut up,' he said. 'Shut up and help me.' He was sweating, everything was very hot and strange. He had the forceps on the head now, and was tugging, tugging really hard, with all his weight. Get it out. Get it out.

'Ah. Here she is. All's well, Rosemary. Well done.'

Only it wasn't. The baby was a strange colour: paler than the other

94

one, almost chalky, and blotchy. And it wasn't all right. There was no heartbeat.

He intubated the baby, ventilated it on the Resuscitaine. Still no heartbeat.

'I'm so, so sorry,' he said to Rosemary Mills, as the second baby was handed over to Staff Nurse, to be taken away to the mortuary, 'so terribly sorry. There was nothing, nothing more we could do. The baby was so big, you see, and you were so tired, and it was a breech. We did all we could.'

'Yes,' she said, dully, 'yes. I see.'

Her eyes were almost closed, her body seemed to have collapsed. Her face was grey, drawn with pain and grief; she was not properly conscious of anything. Ottoline had been taken away to the nursery, to be checked, monitored, just in case there were any complications, but Rosemary Mills seemed scarcely aware of it.

'Well,' he said, 'I think we should get you stitched up now. Then you can have a nice sleep. And have your Ottoline with you, if you like, if there's no need for her to stay in the nursery.'

'I don't see,' she said suddenly, 'I don't understand why you didn't know. Surely you could have felt it. The other one.'

'Oh no,' he said, and felt a rush of fear in his bowels, 'Oh, no, not possibly. I assure you, Rosemary. The other baby was very high up, you see, and the heart was under your own ribs, so it was quite undetectable. All I could feel, hear, was a normal singleton – that's what we call a single foetus.'

She sighed. 'It sounds so much less important when you say foetus, doesn't it? Not a baby, not a twin baby, not a dead baby.'

'Perhaps to you. Not to us.'

Clever little line that. It sounded caring, properly concerned.

'But I still don't see why you couldn't – '

'Look, Rosemary,' said James, gently firm. 'I hate to say this. I really do, but if you'd come in regularly to antenatal for check-ups we would have – '

'Oh no! No, no.' The cry was a wail of agony, fiercer, keener than anything she had uttered in childbirth. 'Is that really true? Do you mean it was my fault, that I could have saved the baby myself . . . ?'

James took a deep breath. He hated himself for doing this, but he had to start covering himself now. If there was trouble over this, if it ever emerged he'd been negligent, drinking for Christ's sake, he'd be done for. He had to force the fact home, that she was actually responsible; and anyway, she was, dammit, she was.

'I'm sorry,' he said, quietly, steadily, 'but that's exactly what I do mean, Rosemary. If only we had been able to look after you – '

She suddenly started to cry, with a new frantic energy; her sobs rose, became hysteria. Staff Nurse Jackson came hurrying in from the corridor where she had been trying to get hold of Jason Benjamin, Rosemary Mills's boyfriend.

'Don't,' she said, 'don't upset yourself. Please, Mrs Mills. It's all right. And Ottoline is doing beautifully. You can have her with you very soon now.'

Rosemary stared at her. 'Sorry,' she said, between rasping gulps for breath, 'I'm sorry. I know I'm lucky, I have one lovely baby. But Dr Forrest was just explaining how it was my fault, how I should have come to antenatal. I just didn't think, didn't know – '

'Of course not,' said Nurse Jackson soothingly, and the look she shot at James across the bed was white-hot fury, total disgust. 'Of course not. You mustn't allow yourself to think that way. Really you mustn't.'

'But I have to. It's true, isn't it? It's my fault. All my fault. Oh God, I wish I was dead too.'

'Now what good would that do?' said Nurse Jackson, sternly kind. 'Then who would care for little Ottoline? And as you say, you do have one very lovely baby. Mr Forrest, could I have a word with you?'

'Not just now,' said James, settling down at the foot of Rosemary Mills's bed, preparing to complete his sutures. 'I'm busy, looking after my patient. As you see. Perhaps later.'

He forced himself to look at her and saw what he had feared. She knew exactly why the twin had been undetected, and why it had consequently died; and exactly why, moreover, he had told Rosemary Mills that the blame lay actually with her.

He visited Rosemary each day, on his ward round, and was always kindly, courteous and sympathetic towards her (although careful not to seem excessively so, lest that might be in some way interpreted as displaying guilt); she was a sweet girl, anxious not to be a trouble and even apologizing for her frequent weeping.

'I know I shouldn't,' she said to him on the fourth morning after the birth, dabbing her eyes rather helplessly with a very soggy tissue, 'and I know how lucky I am that Ottoline is alive and doing so well but I just can't stop thinking about the other one. And feeling bad about her.'

'I know, I know,' he said, handing a clean tissue, 'and that's natural, indeed you *should* grieve for her. It would be wrong not to. But you're right, and you do have a lovely baby, and she is doing beautifully, and you should be very proud of her. What does her daddy think about her?'

'Oh – ' She flushed, looked down at her hands. 'Oh, well, he's very proud of course. He hasn't actually seen her yet, because he's away on this tour you know, but he sent me those flowers, look, and he's rung twice. He'll be back for when I get home, he's promised me that.'

'I should hope so,' said James lightly, smiling at her, going along with the soothing fiction that Mr Benjamin was indeed such a very busy man he couldn't possibly be expected to take time off to visit his baby daughter and traumatized girlfriend, and torn between a sense of outrage on Rosemary Mills's behalf and an unbidden sense of relief at the realization that she was going to be very poor, very under-resourced and highly unlikely even to consider taking any action against him and the hospital.

'Oh,' she added, looking up at him rather nervously, 'Tamsin, that's my yoga teacher, I hope you don't mind, she'd like to have a word with you. About – about everything. Would that be all right?'

'Yes of course.' said James easily, 'perfectly all right.'

He thought that Tamsin was one of the most frightful women he had ever met. She had long plaits, steaked with grey, falling from a centre parting, a high, lined forehead, and an earnest pale face with unpleasantly small eyes. She wore long flapping Indian skirts, and although it was October, open sandals showing very unsavoury feet. She had a large number of beads around her neck and bangles virtually up to her elbows. She smiled at James, but her small eyes were cold.

'Dr Forrest. I'm Tamsin Smith.'

'How do you do – Miss? – Smith.'

'Ms please, Dr Forrest. How is Rosemary coming along?'

'She's fine, Ms Smith. Recovering well.'

'She seems very emotionally labile to me.'

'Most women are emotionally labile after childbirth, Ms Smith.'

'The women I work with are not. They tend to be on a very high emotional plane.'

'I don't understand,' said James, looking at her coldly. 'In what way do you work with these women?'

'I bring them through their childbirth, Dr Forrest. Lead them into motherhood.'

'And how do you do that exactly? By the way, it's Mr Forrest. I am a consultant, an obstetric surgeon.' He knew that was silly, that it would antagonize her further, but he couldn't resist it. 'You were saying, you brought these women through childbirth? I don't quite – '

'By being with them. By using the yoga method, relaxation, visualization, acceptance of pain, the opening to the birth experience. Sharing women's emotions, helping them to overcome their fears, to reach the final exaltation of birth. I feel Rosemary was robbed of much of that, Dr Forrest.'

'I see. I have to tell you, Miss Smith, that left to accept her pain Miss Mills would have experienced a great deal more and there would have been no exaltation of birth whatsoever.'

'Just the same, one of her babies died.'

It came swiftly, that lash, catching him unawares. He managed to meet her eyes; he hoped his own were steady.

'There was nothing that could have saved that baby.'

'Indeed? I have reason to doubt that. I believe there was negligence.'

'That is a very serious statement, Miss Smith. I would not advise you to repeat it. And whatever reasons you have, no doctor here would accept them.'

'No doctor, no. Of course not. But I happen to know there has been – gossip. To the efect that you could have saved the baby, had you been more – competent.'

'Oh really?' He took a deep breath. Steady, James, don't let her rattle you. Keep cool. 'Miss Smith, I would like you to leave. I find your remarks offensive and I am really not prepared to discuss this with you. There will be an inquest on the baby, an inquiry into my handling of the birth. There is nothing more to say for now.' He stood up, hoping she would do the same; she didn't, just sat there, staring up at him, oddly in command.

'I will leave, Dr Forrest. But I wouldn't like you to think you have heard the last of this. I intend to take legal advice on Rosemary's behalf and to see justice done.'

'I shall wait with interest. Good afternoon, Miss Smith.'

He went over to the door, held it for her; finally she stood up, walked slowly out. She didn't say goodbye, didn't say anything. It was very unnerving. James watched her walk down the corridor, her bracelets jangling, and then went back to his desk and sat down again. God, what he'd give for a drink.

He reached for his phone, rang the labour ward, asked for Staff Nurse Jackson. She was just coming off duty; he asked if she would come and see him.

'Yes of course,' she said. 'I'll be along in a minute. Any problem?' She sounded slightly disdainful. Christ, was this a further mistake? Too late now if it was.

'No. Not at all. Thank you, Staff.'

She came in, looking tired. 'Tough birth. Prem. Saved it though.'

'Good. It's a tough business. Nobody really understands that.'

Why did everything sound like a justification suddenly?

'Oh I think they do. What's the problem?'

'Oh – nothing really. Just had a visit from that dreadful friend of Rosemary Mills. The yoga woman.'

'Oh – her. And?'

'She threatened me with legal action. Silly bitch.' He smiled cheerfully.

'Well, the committee will find you whiter than white,' said Staff Nurse Jackson. Her face was politely blank. 'So I'm sure you shouldn't worry.'

'Oh I'm not worried. There was just one thing though. She said she'd heard gossip. I wondered if you – '

'Said anything? Mr Forrest, what about? Of course not. But you know, there always is talk on these occasions. And the little student – what's her name, Adams, was very upset.'

'But she hasn't said anything to you?'

'No. Although she did ask me something.'

'Which was?'

'How I thought you could have missed the twin. She said she just couldn't understand it.'

'And? Why didn't you tell me?'

She shrugged. 'Nothing to tell. I said it wasn't always easy. That the heartbeat was muffled by the ribs.'

'I see. Well – thank you for that. Was there anything else?'

She hesitated. Then she said 'Well – she did say you'd seemed very tired.'

'I was, dammit,' said James. He could feel the sweat breaking out on his forehead. 'Terribly tired. It was four in the morning for Christ's sake.'

'Yes of course,' said Jackson.

'So did you – '

'I told her you were fine. And that it was nothing to do with her. But she's a silly little thing. She may have – chatted a bit. To her friends. These things always escalate.'

'Do they?' said James. 'Oh God. Should I say anything to her?'

'Of course not. That would look very –' She paused. 'Well, anyway – don't. If I pick up any gossip, I'll stop it. To the best of my ability. And, as I said, I very much doubt if the medical inquiry will find against you. I wouldn't worry too much Mr Forrest, if I were you. These things happen. Unfortunately. Just the same – '

'Yes?'

'You were very tired.' The real meaning was plain. James looked down at his hands. He remembered how useless they'd been that night, awkward, unsure, feeble. Christ, what a mess. What a bloody awful mess.

★

Later, much later, the matter was dealt with in the usual way: with bland reassurances, with carefully worded justifications on behalf of the hospital and a carefully coded conversation between James and Mr Nicolson, who asked exactly what had happened, and when told nodded and said that if a patient refused antenatal care, then in his book that amounted to criminal negligence, and assured James that the medical union would back him to the hilt, especially as he intended to write a personal expression of confidence in his medical judgment and skills. There was, naturally, an official investigation: the post-mortem had shown that the baby's death had been due to separation of the placenta and lack of oxygen supply to the brain, and the verdict of the official inquiry was that every effort had been made by the hospital staff to save it in an untenable situation.

Staff Nurse Jackson had still been a considerable source of anxiety to James, but, as he pointed out in another carefully coded conversation, she too had failed to establish the presence of a second foetus; she was also about to be promoted to Sister, and she told the inquiry committee that both she and Mr Forrest had done everything possible, given the very difficult circumstances – an uncooperative patient, a large baby in the breech position, and a separating placenta. Rosemary Mills, discharged from hospital, still experiencing considerable emotional trauma as she struggled to come to terms with the death of one baby while rejoicing over the birth of another, was told in a coldly formal letter that while the hospital naturally regretted very deeply what had happened, there was nothing more they could possibly have done, and had she only come for regular antenatal checks then there might have been a better chance for twin two.

At no time was the slightest breath of criticism directed towards Mr James Forrest.

There was just one thing he could do, one act of contrition he could make, that just might help at another time, another crisis, another birth, and he did it. He gave up alcohol forever.

★

'May I come in?'

He was so lost in the past, in the nightmare of it, that he half expected Staff Nurse Jackson, Rosemary, even little SRN Adams to walk in the door; he turned and the relief as he saw Janine was so intense he forgot the terrors of the present.

'Janine! Come in.'

'You look better, *chérie*. Is there good news from the Bergin household?'

'I'm afraid not. No news. Unless you could regard Oliver being in the bath as news.'

'I fear not. Does he – '

'Couldn't speak to him. Only mama.'

'*Tiens!* How I dislike that woman. Terrible clothes, terrible hair, terrible perfume.'

In spite of himself James laughed. 'Really, Janine! You can't dislike a woman because of her perfume and her hair.'

'I can. Very easily. And besides, I don't trust her. There is something about her that is – two-headed.'

'Two-faced,' said James, smiling tenderly at her. Janine's occasional lapses into less than perfect English never failed to enchant him. 'Janine, we are all two-headed at times. I don't think we can condemn poor Julia on that basis.'

Janine shrugged. 'Perhaps. But she is not to be trusted. Believe me. She likes to appear so sweet and charming, but when the mask drops, just for a moment, she is very very different. There was a little incident last night, and I did not like it.'

'What was that?' said James, intrigued.

'Oh, Cressida came in from the garden with a bunch of sweet peas, and she gave them to Julia, in the kitchen. It was a pretty gesture. Julia took them and smiled and kissed her, and said how very lovely of her, all those little things she does, and then Cressida went to change and I said I must go too, and we left Julia. But I had left my spectacles, and when I came back, Julia did not hear me, she had her back to me and she was pulling the flowers to pieces, taking their heads off and putting them one by one into the dustbin. Then she saw me and tried to pretend she was simply sorting them out – she said some of them were half dead.'

'Well, that doesn't sound too dreadful to me,' said James lightly. 'Maybe she just doesn't like sweet peas. I don't think you'd get very far in a court of law with that one, Janine.'

Janine shrugged. 'Maybe not. But I have observed other things. Anyway, the fact remains, I do not trust the belle Julia. Now then, what I really wanted to say was that I think you should try to give poor Maggie a little something. She is becoming hysterical, she will make herself ill, and that will not help anyone. What do you think?'

'Oh God,' said James, 'inevitable I suppose. She's increasingly hysterical these days anyway. I'm worried about her. Yes, all right, Janine. I'll get her something.'

'Will she take it?'

'Oh yes,' said James with a sigh. 'She'll take it. She'll take anything, any pill, any potion. Grabbing at straws.'

'What for? Why should she be grabbing at straws? In what is she drowning?'

'Her own sense of inadequacy,' said James. 'Poor woman. I should never – ' The phone rang. 'James Forrest.'

'James, it's Oliver. Mother said you called. About Mungo's speech. What – '

'Oh – Oliver. Yes. Look, it wasn't about Mungo's speech. I'm afraid I told your mama a small fib.'

'She tells plenty of those herself,' said Oliver cheerfully, 'so don't worry about it. What did you want to talk to me about?'

'Well, it was – you see – oh God, Oliver, there's no way of dressing this up. It's Cressida. She – '

There was a very long silence; the room seemed stifling, claustrophobic. James could hear the blood pounding in his head, was suddenly aware of the clock ticking on his desk, of Janine's light breathing close beside him. Then: 'She hasn't gone, has she?' said Oliver, and his voice was very quiet and totally without emotion. 'She hasn't actually gone?'

Chapter Seven

Harriet 11.30am

'Harriet, you got a minute?'

It was Merlin, in the corridor outside her room (where she had retreated briefly, with a bottle of iced lemonade, to take a break from the telephoning), his weather-beaten old face with its brilliant blue eyes, its shock of white hair, looking suprisingly cheerful, a touch of normality in this nightmarish day.

'Yes. Yes, I suppose so,' said Harriet.

'Could I use that computer of yours? Got an article to write, promised I'd send it off this morning if I could. Might as well put all this time to good use. Janine suggested I ask you. Damned attractive woman that. Sort of woman who makes me think of settling down.'

'Merlin darling,' said Harriet, laughing, 'What are you saying? Have you finally sown all your wild oats?'

'Well, I don't want to end my days a lonely old bachelor,' said Merlin. 'Been thinking about it for some time as a matter of fact. Never met the right girl, you know, that's been the trouble.'

'Well, maybe she's been here all along,' said Harriet. 'And yes, of course you can use my machine. Only you won't find much peace anywhere, I'm afraid, Merlin. Mummy keeps coming in here, and – '

'Good Lord,' said Merlin. 'Can't face that. Maybe I won't – '

'No,' said Harriet, 'you certainly should. I tell you what, we'll take it up to the big attic. No one ever goes up there, except Mummy, to sew, and she won't be doing that today. You'll be perfectly quiet up there. Hang on a minute, I'll unplug it. It's very portable.'

They went down the corridor silently, tiptoeing like two guilty children, and up the back stairs to the attic. It was very hot; Harriet pushed open the big skylight window, and the sweet fresh air rushed in, full of birdsong, cooling the room.

'It's such a lovely day,' she said, staring upwards at the perfectly blue sky, 'It seems so terrible . . .'

'Oh, I don't know,' said Merlin briskly. 'Be even worse if it was raining. Can I move this sewing machine of your mother's, use the table?'

'Yes, of course you can. And I've got the extension lead, look, we can set you up in no time.'

Merlin sat down at the table, started tapping his way into the computer. 'Lovely things these,' he said happily, 'transformed my life, I can tell you. Should have brought my own, but I didn't think I'd get a chance to use it. Bloody silly really, you never know what's going to happen, do you? Right, then, here we are, bless you, Harriet, that's marvellous. I'll just sit here quietly, won't be a bother to anyone. Not like that sister of yours,' he added darkly. 'Causing all this anxiety. Very selfish if you ask me – '

'Oh Merlin, don't,' said Harriet quickly. 'Something must have been terribly wrong for her. Poor Cress. Oh God, Merlin, there's her dress, I'd forgotten just for a moment this is where they'd put it. Such a lovely, lovely dress too.' She shook herself. 'Listen to me. As if a dress mattered.'

She went over to the dressmaker's rail, where Cressida's dress had been hanging for over two weeks now, swathed in its muslin wrap and gently, tenderly, without knowing why, stroked it, as if it was Cressida herself, Cressida in distress, in need of comforting. And the room suddenly felt stifling again, and her head felt as if it was being crushed, crushed in some kind of vice, and she stood there staring at it, trying to make sense of what she saw. For as she touched the dress, the wrap, which was not fastened in any way but was simply draped loosely over it, started to slither off and what Harriet was looking at was not Cressida's wedding dress at all, but an old ballgown of their mother's.

And the wedding dress, like the bride it had been made for, had gone.

Chapter Eight

James Midday

He was walking along the first-floor landing when he heard the sobs coming from Cressida's room: soft, muffled, desperate. Christ, she was back, back for help, for comfort: afraid to face them all, hiding, rather as Harriet used to do when she was little. What had happened to Cressida, what could possibly have gone wrong in those few hours, to change her from radiant bride to desperate runaway? He was almost afraid to go in, to face all her pain; stood outside the room for an absurdly long moment before knocking gently and opening the door.

'Cress?' he said. 'Cress darling?'

And the figure lying on the bed, weeping into the lace cushion, turned to him slowly, turned a ravaged face: only of course it wasn't Cressida at all, it was Harriet, and she had clearly been crying for some time.

'Daddy,' she said, reaching out for his hand, 'Daddy, I'm so sorry, it's only me.'

He took her in his arms, rocking her gently, kissing her, smoothing her hair, hushing her, trying to ease her pain away. After a while she stopped crying and said, 'There's something new. I was – going to come and tell you. I haven't told anyone else.'

'What?' he said. 'Have the police – ?'

'No, no,' she said, 'not the police, or the hospitals, no news. But Daddy, I just went up to the attic, and – it's so weird, so spooky, I just can't think – ' Her voice trailed away, silent tears began again, rolling down her face. James set her away from him, stared at her.

'What, Harriet, what is it? For Christ's sake, Harriet, you've got to tell me.'

'Yes of course. I'm sorry.' She swallowed, took a deep breath. 'Daddy, her wedding dress has gone.'

'Her wedding dress? What on earth do you mean? How can it be gone, why, what could she – ' His own voice trailed away, he sat staring at her, equally shocked.

'I don't know. I don't understand it. I just can't think why she should have taken it. But it's gone. And not just ripped of the stand, there's another dress where it was, under the wrap you know? She obviously wanted to take it, didn't want us to know.'

'Oh for God's sake,' said James. He felt very tired suddenly; he couldn't take much more of this. 'Harriet, has she run off with someone else? To get married to – oh it's preposterous. It makes no sense at all.'

'I know. I know it doesn't. But she obviously did plan it. The disappearance I mean. She must have done. Well at least we know now she hasn't been abducted, which was one of Mummy's wilder fears.'

'No. I suppose we should tell her. Or shouldn't we?' They stared at each other, visualizing the fresh trauma this news would inflict upon Maggie, wondering if it was worth it.

'Yes, I think we should. I think it's better.'

'I'll go down then. In a minute.' He sighed, sat very still, staring out at the day. 'Harriet, has she ever said anything to you, anything at all that might indicate she wasn't happy about marrying Oliver?'

'No,' said Harriet, 'no. Nothing. But then I haven't seen much of her lately. What with – well, work and everything. I kept thinking we ought to spend some time together, but somehow – oh God.'

'Well,' he said, 'if she'd told anyone she'd have told you.'

'No, she wouldn't,' said Harriet flatly.

'What do you mean? Of course she would. You're so close.'

'Daddy, we're not close. Everyone thinks we are, but we're not at all. I really don't know what goes on in Cressida's head, never have. She's always been very – self-contained – with me. Since we were tiny. And I – well, anyway, she hasn't.'

James stared at her; if she had announced she was working for MI5 or had signed up for the next space project he could hardly have been more astonished.

'Well,' he said finally, 'who do you think she might have talked to?'

'I have no idea,' said Harriet and her voice was oddly blank, cool. 'No idea at all. I really don't know who her friends were, who she might have confided in. She was a mystery to me. More than I realized,' she added with the shadow of a smile.

'But darling – you were fond of each other, weren't you?' He could hear the pleading note in his own voice; it seemed very important somehow.

'Yes, we were,' said Harriet quickly, 'very fond. Of course we were.' James chose to believe her. For the time being. It was simpler that way.

'Do you think,' he said, looking rather helplessly round the room, 'we should look through her things? For addresses, contacts? Would it be – '

'I have,' said Harriet, with a slightly apologetic grin. 'I've been right through her desk. Very neat, very tidy, nothing in the least helpful or – incriminating. No address book though – '

'What about bank statements? They might give us a clue – '

'No bank statements. Nothing like that at all. I did think that was interesting. It all points to her covering her tracks.'

'Well, I don't know. She'd probably keep that sort of thing in her flat, wouldn't she?'

Harriet sighed. 'I suppose so. Yes of course. I hardly ever went to that flat, you know.'

'None of us did,' said James. 'She always told me, when I suggested I come to see her there during the week, that it was horrid and she hated it, and she'd rather come to me. I don't think I've been there since – oh, before last Christmas. We don't have a key for it, I suppose?'

'No. All her keys are gone.'

'I wonder if we ought to go up there anyway, have a look round?'

'Daddy, you can't go. Not today. I will if you like – '

'No,' he said with a sigh, 'no, let's leave it for now. Maybe this evening if – oh God, Harriet, this is a mess. A bloody awful mess. I feel so guilty, as if it's all my fault somehow.'

'Well it isn't,' said Harriet. 'Of course it isn't. You've been a wonderful father to Cressida.'

'Not wonderful enough it seems.' He sat looking round Cressida's painfully neat, perfectly pretty room, and his heart ached physically with the pain of her loss. The cancelled wedding, the trauma of the day seemed nothing; he just wanted her back, safe, so that he could comfort her, find what the trouble was. His lovely, gentle, sweet daughter: where was she, where had she gone, what had distressed her so dreadfully, that she would do such a thing?

'Do you think we should actually ring the bank? Her account is still here in Woodstock, isn't it? It might give us a clue. What do you think?'

'Well – I suppose I could. Oh God, I hate sitting here in her room prying into her life.'

'Come into my room, you silly old thing. I've got my mobile in there anyway.' She smiled at him; James felt tears sting his eyes.

'All right. Thank God for you, Harriet.'

'Oh,' she said, 'you won't get rid of me so easily.'

He shuddered. 'Don't joke about it.'

He phoned the bank. The manager, Tony Bacon, with whom he played golf occasionally, was out until late afternoon, his assistant was pompously unhelpful. 'This is extremely confidential information, Mr Forrest. We would never disclose any details of a customer's affairs.'

'Not even under exceptional circumstances? We are extremely worried about her.'

'I'm afraid not.'

'But my daughter does still have an account with you? She hasn't closed it in the last few days or made any large withdrawals?'

'I'm sorry, Mr Forrest, I really can't help you.'

'Oh all right, all right. Would you get Mr Bacon to get in touch with me please? As soon as he gets in.'

'I will certainly ask him to ring you, Mr Forrest.'

'Self-satisfied jumped-up little creep,' said James, switching off the phone with unnecessary violence. 'Any other good ideas, Harriet?'

'Doctor?'

'She saw someone in London. Haven't the faintest idea who. Oh, this is hopeless.'

'What about having another word with the vicar? See if Cressida might have talked to him? She was so good about doing the flowers in church and everything, they chatted a lot – you never know – '

'Well, we could try,' said James, 'but I'm sure his code of practice or whatever would forbid him telling us anything. Aren't priests suppose to take secrets to their grave?'

'Yes, but it might not be a secret,' said Harriet. 'She might have said something quite openly to him. Like she was worrying about going to live in New York or something – '

'Yes, I suppose so. Yes, all right.'

'Daddy, try not to worry. The police were so reassuring.'

'Yes, well, she's not their daughter,' said James. He voice sounded very unsteady even to himself. He dialled the Vicarage.

'Mrs Hodges? James Forrest again.'

Sylvia Hodges' careworn voice came down the telephone: it suited her perfectly that voice, he thought: if a voice could be lined, pale, scrubbed, then Sylvia's was.

'Oh, Mr Forrest. We've been so anxious. Has she – '

'No, I'm afaid not,' said James, cutting her off. He couldn't stand anyone thinking, even for a moment, that Cressida had returned. 'No news yet.'

'You mustn't despair,' said Sylvia Hodges, 'you must have faith. Not a sparrow falls, you know, – '

'Mrs Hodges,' said James, perversely irritated by her concern, 'I am nowhere near despair. I assure you of that.'

'We're praying for you here,' she said, 'and thinking of you so much. Such a wonderful, sweet girl. We're both so fond of her. I was saying to

Alan only last night, oh for a daughter like that – oh dear – ' Her voice trailed away, as she realized her tactlessness.

'Well, thank you. Is your husband there? I just wanted another word with him.'

'He's out in the garden. Hoeing. And working on the compost. He always does that when he's upset. He finds it healing.'

'Well, I might try it,' said James with an attempt at cheerfulness. He winked at Harriet. She smiled back.

'Alan Hodges here, Mr Forrest. No news, I gather?'

'No news,' said James. 'But – well, we're turning over every stone here, Mr Hodges. As I'm sure you can imagine. Talking to everyone who just might have some ideas to toss into the equation. Now of course I'm not asking you to breach any confidences, but did Cressida ever say anything to you about – well, express any doubts at all about her marriage?'

'I quite understand what you're saying. And I'd like to help. Now let me see. Well, let me begin by saying I can honestly tell you she certainly never told me anything that would be classified as confidential. That any help to you?'

'Yes, I suppose it's comforting in a way. You mean she never told you she was planning to take the veil or anything like that?' He winked at Harriet again; she had looked at him sharply. God, maybe that had crossed her mind; maybe it should have crossed all their minds.

'Oh no, Mr Forrest. Most definitely not. Not the veil.' The voice, as earnest as his wife's, sounded shocked. James smiled into the phone in spite of his misery. Alan Hodges had not so much been in the back row when senses of humour were handed out, he hadn't even been in the room.

'Well, I didn't really think that. But – well, she never talked about her plans – '

There was a silence. James's flesh began to creep. There was something; he could feel it.

Then, 'No. No, absolutely not. She seemed very calm and settled. Except – well – '

'Yes? Except what?'

'The other afternoon. Good gracious, it must have been only the day before yesterday. The panic about her passport, you know?'

'No,' said James sharply. 'What passport?'

'Her new one. Didn't she tell you about it? Oh, maybe she didn't want to worry you. She certainly didn't want Mr Bergin to know. She'd left renewing it until terribly late. She was afraid she wouldn't be able to get away on her honeymoon.'

'I didn't know, no,' said James, carefully.

'Well, obviously, she was keeping her worries to herself. It was only by chance I met her, in the post office in Oxford, she was getting one of those short-term passports you know, that do for a year. It was all she had time for, I suppose. Nasty little cardboard things.'

'Yes, but that wouldn't have been any use anyway,' said James. 'She – they were going to New York. It wouldn't have got her there.'

'Indeed not. I hadn't thought of that. Well, she seemed very upset, distraught almost, I would say. Quite out of character. Although of course brides often do get into a bit of a state. Anyway, if I think of anything else, Mr Forrest, I'll certainly ring you. And I'll ask my wife if she has any thoughts as well. And try to keep your spirits up. I'm sure she's all right. We're praying for you all. Please know that. And if there's anything more I can do . . .'

'Thank you,' said James. 'Thank you very much, Mr Hodges.'

He put the phone down and stared at Harriet. 'Did you know anything about Cressida's forgetting to renew her passport?' he asked. 'I mean just in the past few days?'

'No of course not. In fact I know it was all right, because she had to get her visa, don't you remember? About a month ago. So there can't have been a problem surely. And Oliver's got it anyway, because of the honeymoon being a surprise and everything. Why?'

'Well, for whatever reason, she was applying for a new one the day before yesterday. Alan Hodges met her in the post office in Oxford. Oh God, Harriet, this is getting worse and worse.'

Chapter Nine

Mungo Lunchtime

He had the worst job of all, it seemed to him: standing at the church, missing out on all the drama, in order to head off any arrivals. It would be a while yet of course: surely nobody was going to get there before one, not even the most neurotically punctual guests, but all the same, maybe some of the bridesmaids' parents – anyway, James Forrest had said that someone should be there, just in case, and Rufus had volunteered, saying that he, Mungo, should stay with Oliver. Mungo had studied the two options and hastily opted for lychgate duty; Rufus would be far better doing his support number, it was just his sort of thing. Bit of a goody-goody, old Rufus. Mungo was very fond of him, but he longed just once to hear he had done something truly horrendous, like getting two girls pregnant at the same time, or embezzling some of the bank's funds, or just running up a humungous debt somewhere and being unable to pay it. It was highly unlikely, of course. Rufus was upright, charming, and self-disciplined; Mungo had only seen him properly drunk once, and that had been to celebrate getting a first at Cambridge. What on God's earth Tilly could see in him, he couldn't even begin to imagine: Tilly, with her wonderfully outrageous approach to life, her overt sexuality, her staggering beauty, her interestingly individual morality; but she certainly saw something.

It was the most extraordinary relationship: sweet, tender, defying any kind of logic. Mungo watched them sometimes, caught together in a charged, almost tangible stillness, not even touching, excluding everything and everyone around them, and knew he was looking at love. It charmed him, even while it baffled him, made him happy, gave him pleasure. It had probably, he thought, been the inspiration for his own passionate, all-consuming love affair. The one he had to speak to his father about, that he could hardly believe in himself (so unpredictable, so unexpected it had been), the one he hadn't shared with anyone, not even Oliver, not even Harriet, the two people he probably felt closer to than anyone in the world. Now there was compatibility. Stange, so strange, he thought even now, that Oliver had chosen Cressida, sweet, gentle, softly spoken Cressida, when he could have had Harriet. Harriet who was so original and clever and go-for-it and successful, who had always seemed to know what Oliver was thinking before he knew it himself, who loved doing all the things that he did, sailing and riding and rock music and travelling. They had once gone on a trip together with Merlin, when they were both about fifteen, had gone down the Amazon in a small boat, just the three of them and a guide, and had disappeared for days, come back charged with excitement, with wonderful tales of crocodiles (stunned at night by shining a light in their eyes) and sweetly smiling friendly dolphins and great shoals of fish, and monkeys and the brilliantly coloured parrots they had seen on a trek through the steaming jungle, so thick that their guide had often had to chop a way through it for them; the chattering, screaming noise by day and the deathly silence at night, the feeling that they had travelled back thousands, maybe tens of thousands of years. Cressida had listened to their stories, her eyes wide with horror, and said she couldn't imagine anything more horrible and Oliver, reacting to her with barely disguised scorn, had said that he and Harriet were going to set off on their own as soon as they were allowed. They planned the trip for years, right up to the age when they both left school and no longer spent family holidays together. The adults teased them about it, asking them when they were off, how much money they had saved, whether it was to be China or India or the Arctic Circle this year, and Merlin would defend them, saying they were a fine pair of travellers, he was proud of them. But they had never gone, and Oliver went backpacking on his own in his college vacations and Harriet threw all her energies into building up her fashion business and wanted only to lie on a beach and recover in the short weeks available to her, and now of course it was quite forgotten and their wonderful joyous closeness had gradually disintegrated. Oliver had changed, naturally, had become grown-up, seriously grown-up and fiercely ambitious – and maybe that was a factor in choosing Cressida, so much more suitable these days, more – well, more wifely than Harriet, more the person he needed to be married to.

Only it was beginning to look like she wasn't. Mungo wrenched his thoughts back to the present, and his task, refusing to allow himself to contemplate for more than the briefest wildest moment the glorious prospect of climbing into the car and just driving away, and wondered if there was anything he could do for Oliver, apart from getting him so hammered he wouldn't even know his own name. He decided there wasn't.

The Forrest women, as he thought of them, and especially today, Maggie, Janine, Susie, Harriet, were all at work on different telephones, Maggie in her bedroom, Janine in the study on James's line, Harriet on her portable phone, and Susie at the Beaumonts', all working through sections of the guest list, telling people that Cressida was ill, that the wedding was postponed, that they were desperately sorry, that they would be in touch just as soon as it was possible to rearrange, refusing offers of help with the notifications (lest wires should be crossed, messages overlaid, lists muddled).

Christ, thought Mungo, what an incredible, filthy mess. The whole thing. Not just Cressida's disappearance either, it had started hours before that, the nightmare; and he relived sharply, suddenly, the terrible scene at two that morning, when he and Rufus had driven over to the Bergins' hotel, gone up to Oliver's suite and found Oliver head in hands, horribly drunk, tears pouring down his unshaven face, saying he couldn't go through with it, couldn't marry Cressida, that even now, even at this late stage, they had somehow to get him away, get him out of it, that if they didn't he would kill himself.

★

'But why, Oliver, why?' Rufus said over and over again, and Oliver just looked at them, his blue eyes almost black with pain, his fair hair wild where he had been pushing his hands through it endlessly, hopelessly, and said he couldn't tell them, it was all too horrible, they just had to do something, help him, save him. He was extremely drunk, but there was a kind of quiet sanity about him as well. Mungo found the combination strangely terrifying.

'If you don't, I'll do something desperate, I swear I will,' he said, and as they tried to calm him, tried to find out what the trouble was, what had happened, he suddenly got up, walked almost calmly into the bathroom and locked the door. They looked at each other, Rufus and Mungo, thinking, hoping even, that it was over, that it had been simply a rather extreme case of last-minute nerves; then he'd walked out again, and smiled at them, with a sweet serenity, and said, 'That should settle it, then.'

'What should?' Mungo said rather stupidly, and Oliver smiled again, more serenely still, and said, his voice slurring, 'Taken something for it.'

Rufus looked at him thoughtfully and then got up and went into the bathroom himself; he came out with an empty half bottle of aspirin in his hand. 'Ollie, did you take these?' he said gently, and Oliver nodded and said, 'Yes. Had to do something.' And sat down, picked up a copy of *Sporting Life* and started reading the Goodwood report. To the end of his life Mungo was to associate horse racing with personal tragedy.

Rufus was wonderful. He went very quietly down to the hotel dining room and found several salt cellars, which he emptied into a jug of water

113

and made Oliver drink. Then he took him into the bathroom. Mungo who was squeamish sat outside, trying not to listen and wondering if he should go and get Julia or Josh Bergin. After ten minutes Rufus, came out with Oliver and laid him down tenderly on his bed.

'Ring room service for some coffee, and some bottles of still mineral water,' he said, 'and ask them to leave it outside the door.'

'Should I tell the Bergins?'

'Christ no. He'll be fine now. We caught it in plenty of time. Poor old boy.'

They both looked at Oliver who lay glassy pale, his eyes closed, half asleep.

'How did you know what to do?' said Mungo.

'Girl I knew at Cambridge did exactly the same thing. She lived with a medic. He got me to help. As long as you're really quick, there's no lasting damage done. But we have to keep pumping fluids into him.'

'What on earth do you think it's about?'

'Can't imagine. Just nerves I expect,' said Rufus, his voice rather determinedly easy. 'They seemed perfectly OK at supper.'

'Yeah. I wonder if Cressida's been over, if something's happened since.'

'It hasn't,' said Oliver's voice, very quiet, rather hoarse, from the bed. 'Haven't seen her since I left the house. Don't worry. I'll be fine now.' His eyes closed; Rufus took his pulse.

'He really is fine,' he said quietly. 'Don't look so scared, Mungo.'

'Sorry,' said Mungo . He was feeling rather sick himself. 'It's just so terribly unlike him. He's usually so calm, so steady. He never even gets drunk.'

'I know. I know.'

The coffee and water arrived; they fed it to him alternately, tenderly, as if he was a sick child. It was a long night; he had to be helped into the bathroom quite frequently. He slept a lot, fitfully at first, then more soundly. At around five, he woke and seemed almost himself.

'Must have a pee,' he said, standing up, smiling at them. 'Don't worry, Rufus, I won't do it again. Can't think what came over me. I'm so sorry.'

He came out again, walking rather slowly and painfully. 'I guess this is what old age feels like,' he said, 'bloody awful. Every joint aches.'

'It's dehydration,' said Rufus. 'Drink some more water.'

'I'm full of bloody water. I'll start leaking in a minute.'

He drank another tumblerful, lay down again with a groan. 'You are such good friends,' he said simply. 'I owe you my life, don't I?'

'Doubt it,' said Rufus with a grin. 'You'd have called someone else, if we hadn't been here. You weren't doing it for real.'

'No,' said Oliver, pulling himself together with a clear effort. 'No, of course not. Panic, that's all. Awful thing to do though.' There was another silence; then he said, 'I'm so sorry' again, and closed his eyes.

'Oliver,' said Rufus gently, 'Oliver, is it really all right? The wedding? Because it's not – '

'What? Oh God, I expect so. Maybe. I don't know.' And then was asleep, deeply and sweetly, in minutes. They sat looking down at him.

'I think we should stay with him,' said Mungo quietly. 'I don't like the thought of leaving him alone.'

'Yes, of course we should. Poor old sod. What a nightmare. What do you think we ought to do? About it, I mean.'

'Christ knows. Should we talk to someone, do you think? Try and find out if there really is a problem?'

'Well yes, probably, but I can't think who,' said Rufus. 'Cressida? Harriet? His mother? I mean think of them all last night. They all looked like a commercial for soupy happiness.'

'I think we should talk to Tilly,' said Mungo suddenly. 'She's very close to Oliver. And uninvolved enough to maybe have picked something up from him. Didn't they have dinner two nights ago?'

'Yes, they did,' said Rufus. 'I was furious because she wouldn't let me join them. She wanted to give him a present, apologize for not coming to the wedding.'

'Why wasn't she coming, actually?' said Mungo. 'She was going to come. She told me she was looking forward to it.'

'She suddenly had to work,' said Rufus. He sounded defensive. 'You know how in demand she is.'

'Yes, but – '

'Well it doesn't matter why. She just couldn't come. But she did see Oliver. You're right. It's a good idea. She might have picked up something. I'll call her. Very soon.' He looked at his watch. 'Six thirty in France. I'll get hold of her in an hour or so. Christ, what a night. Let's try and get a bit of sleep. Shall we toss for the other bed?'

'Not me,' said Mungo with a weak grin, heading for the door. 'I'd honestly rather take the floor in his sitting room.'

They were woken by Julia Bergin; she came in, without knocking – well, she was his mother, thought Mungo, but it still seemed odd – and practically tripped over him. She stood there, looking down at him, her face white with shock – and that was strange too, he thought, for she was fully made-up already, at – what? seven in the morning, and neatly dressed in trousers and a sweater.

'What the hell are you doing here?' he said, and her voice was harsh, angry, and 'We thought we should stay with Oliver, he wasn't well last night' Mungo said, sitting up, feeling slightly sick again.

'What do you mean not well?' she said, and Rufus came out of Oliver's bedroom, pushing his hair back, closing the door gently behind him.

'He was – very drunk,' he said carefully, 'and – well, we were worried about him. Taking care of him. That's all.'

'And why was he so drunk?' asked Julia Bergin, and Mungo thought how strange it was that the graciously charming woman – over-gracious indeed, absurdly charming – he had always known had become this hostile, harsh creature. 'Were you drinking with him? I thought you were going to go back to your hotel last night, when we left the Forrests, not come over here causing trouble – '

'Yes, we were,' said Rufus gently. 'But Oliver phoned and asked us over. He said he was – nervous. He wanted company.'

'I was here,' said Julia, and the expression in her eyes was heavily antagonistic. 'He could have talked to me.'

'Yes of course,' said Rufus, 'but I – well, I expect you were asleep. It was quite late.'

'Well you can leave him to me now,' said Julia. 'And I'd like you to go, get out. Immediately. I still don't quite understand what you're trying to tell me. Was there some problem that I should know about?'

'I – don't think so,' said Rufus. He still sounded calm and quiet. Mungo was impressed. 'But he was quite – sick. Perhaps you could keep an eye on him.'

'Rufus,' said Julia Bergin, and her voice shook a little, 'Rufus, I am Oliver's mother. I have looked after him for thirty-two years now. I don't need to be told what to do with him in any situation.' She went through to the bedroom, looked down at her sleeping son. They couldn't see her face. 'He looks perfectly all right to me. I have to tell you I find your story a little hard to believe. I would suggest that what really happened was that you both wanted a drinking partner and came over here of your own volition.'

'Well, you can suggest whatever you like, Mrs Bergin,' said Rufus, more determinedly equable than ever. 'My only concern is for Oliver.'

'Mine also,' said Julia Bergin. 'Now please leave.'

They left, too exhausted to argue.

'Weird,' said Mungo, as he started up the Bentley. 'Seriously weird.'

★

Well, even this boredom, waiting for guests who clearly weren't going to come, was better than being back in that nightmare room. Mungo wondered how, in fact, Oliver would be taking the news of Cressida's disappearance; it was not something he would like to have to predict with any accuracy. But however it was, things were going to be difficult. Mungo was not too familiar with difficulty; if he saw it coming he moved swiftly and determinedly in the other direction. Certain things he had had to face, had had to deal with: his mother's death, his father's marriage to his next wife – and the next one, bitches both of them (but he approved of Sasha, she was a peach, pretty, fun, not too bright, kept his father permanently in a good mood; and he'd been so terribly down, so wretched in the time just before he'd met her, really not himself at all, Mungo often wondered if something had happened he hadn't heard about).

A couple of the schools he'd been sent to had been a bit grim, especially that awful English prep school stepmother one had insisted on, but when she went, so did the school. Since then life had been pretty much all right, he'd loved the school in Geneva, enjoyed the Sorbonne, and hadn't even minded too much his father's efforts to initiate him into the business. It had been boring and, he could see, frustrating for his father, but distressing it hadn't been. He had tried most of its facets, the super-markets, the foodbroking, the hotels, the chemical division, before sitting the old buzzard down and making him face the fact that none of it was for him. His father had been angry and bawled him out, but he was used to that; the rages, the threats of disinheritance (also uttered when he had some particularly large gambling debt to settle) meant no more than the ones he'd had to listen to when he had been naughty as a small boy: threats to beat him with a leather strap, to cancel his birthday or Christmas, to send his pony back, to confine him to his room for a week. None of them ever carried out: just a few hours of mild anxiety and then his father would come up to his room or out to the stables when he was sitting with his pony, and look slightly shamefaced and say 'I hope you're sorry, Mungo' and Mungo would say, his eyes filled with the great tears he could summon at will, 'Yes, I'm really sorry, Dad' and he would get first a playful cuff round the head, then a hug, and his father would say, 'Well, we'll let it go this time. But never again, all right, never again?' And he would hug him back, and say 'Course not, Dad, never again,' and there would be no more talk of punishment until the next time – and never any actual punishment at all.

Looking back now, he could see he had got away with murder; he could also see why wives three and four had hated him so much. His father loved him best, and they knew it, better than them, better than the poisonous little sisters they foisted upon Mungo, Careena and Dido by wife number three, Christina by wife number four (still very young, Christina was, an overripe, overweight thirteen-year old, sanctimonious and spotty, thank God her mother would hardly let her near any of them). He wondered if Sasha would have a baby: that would be good – Mungo liked babies. He had always imagined having lots of children. It was one of the things that just slightly troubled him about Alice . . .

★

'I love your kids,' he said to her, lying beside her on the pillow, looking at her beautiful face, her streaky blonde hair, her clear blue eyes with just a very few lines round them. 'I think they're great. Honestly. How do they feel about me?'

'Oh Mungo,' she said, putting out her hand, stroking his cheek, 'they love you. Of course they do. You're such fun for them. Like – well, like a big brother.'

'Yes, well, that's fine,' he said, 'but it isn't quite the same as being a dad, is it?'

'No, it's not, but you're not their dad.'

'If we get married, I will be.'

'Mungo, darling, can we not talk about getting married? It so – '

'So what?' he said, sitting up suddenly, 'Alice, so what? I keep telling you I want to marry you.'

'I know, I know you do.'

'And you say you love me.'

'I do love you, Mungo. Very much. But – '

'But what? But you don't love me enough? But you don't want to marry me? But I'm not good enough for you?'

'Mungo, maybe I love you too much. To marry you.'

'But why, why? I don't understand.'

'Mungo,' she said with a gentle smile, 'Mungo, I'm thirty-nine. You're twenty-seven. That is a great many years' difference.'

'No it's not. It's twelve years. It's nothing, nothing at all.'

'It isn't nothing. I'm a middle-aged woman. You're a very young man. If you were thirty-seven, and I forty-nine, that might be different.'

'I don't see why,' he said, and panic rose in him, panic and fear of losing her, of not being able to keep her forever.

'Then I'll tell you,' she said, her voice enragingly patient, reasonable. 'You're young and you have a right to a young wife.'

'I don't want a young wife. I don't like young women.'

'Mungo, that's ridiculous. Of course you do. You want a young wife, who can give you children – '

'You can give me children.'

'Well – maybe, maybe not.'

'I thought you were getting all that checked out.'

'I have.'

'And?'

118

'Well, in theory I can still have babies. Or at least one baby.'

'Well then.'

'But in practice, it may not be quite so easy.'

'Then,' he said, leaning over and kissing her, 'then we shall have to put in lots of practice. To make it easier.'

'Oh Mungo. Darling Mungo. What can I say?'

'Nothing. Just that you love me.'

'I love you, Mungo.'

'Now don't say anything else.'

And he slithered down in the bed again and began to make love to her. Making love to Alice was quite unlike making love to anyone else he had ever known. She was at once so gentle and so strong; she would lie, apparently passive, as he aroused her (and she was so deliciously, swiftly easy to arouse, fluid, soft, sweet), and so gloriously yielding as he entered her, unfolding to him in all her warm tender depth; and then suddenly she would change, would grow fierce, almost violent, would turn him on his back and mount him, plunging down on him again and again, using him, working at him. 'Don't,' she would say, 'don't come, not yet, don't, don't,' and he would lie beneath her, trying to wait, to distance himself from the leaping, desperate climax that grew, thrust, forced itself within him, up to her. 'Wait' she would say, command him, 'wait,' and would climb from him, kneel above him, tantalizing him with her wetness, her heat; and then finally she would fall onto him again, yelling, crying out with hunger, and come, over and over again, great unfoldings of tension, he would feel them, pulling, clutching at him, and then she would slowly fall again into stillness, and was the old Alice again, no longer predatory, no longer fierce, but the still, calm woman he loved. He loved them both, both his Alices, loved them with a binding love. She was beautiful and desirable and desiring; she was also fun and clever and wise. She was perfect; he loved her. And he wanted to marry her.

He had met her over the New Year skiing in Val d'Isère; she was there with her children, staying with friends in their apartment. She was waiting in the queue for the ski lift, and the first thing he noticed about her was her perfume, which was one he knew and loved: strong, sexy, and very potent.

They got talking: he liked her. He bought her a hot chocolate at the café at the top of the mountain; she was coolly, amusedly friendly. They did the long tough run down to the town together, and he was impressed by her courage and her skill, bought her a hot wine as the dusk fell, arranged to meet her for lunch the next day. She had a superb figure, and an extremely sexy voice, husky and low. They went over to Tignes for lunch, skied back into Val d'Isère together, met for dinner that night. By the end of the week, he was quite sure he was in love with her.

She was divorced and lived in London with her three children; she worked as a secretary to a children's charity, not for the money, but to amuse and interest herself. 'My husband is very generous, but I'm easily bored.'

She had been divorced for three years; her husband was an investment banker, now married to a girl younger than Mungo. The children (two girls and a boy, aged fifteen, twelve and nine) were remarkably nice and well adjusted: testimony, Mungo felt, to Alice's skills as a mother. The eldest, Jemima, was at boarding school, Katy and William still at home. They lived in a pretty little mews house in Chelsea, just off the Kings Road; Alice had decorated it charmingly, and it had an enchanting tiny walled garden which was her pride and joy. Mungo went there very often for Sunday lunch, which was invariably delicious, always bearing expensive presents for everybody, and they would all go for a walk in Richmond Park or Kew Gardens in the afternoon with Lottie, the King Charles spaniel. It all seemed wonderful to him; he had never known ordinary family life. It became a tradition that he took them all out to tea somewhere afterwards; occasionally somewhere very special like the Savoy or the Ritz, but often somewhere quite ordinary, even occasionally McDonald's. Jemima, who had her mother's blonde beauty and was rather sophisticated for her age, liked the posh Sundays, and so did Alice, but the others preferred the more modest ones. Mungo liked going to McDonald's best of all. The children had no idea how extraordinarily rich his father was, or indeed how serious he was about their mother; they just all enjoyed him, although Jemima had a rather half-hearted crush on him, which he encouraged, and when they got back on the Sundays she was home, he would give her what he called flirting lessons. She didn't actually need them. And then, much much later, they would sit alone in the tiny garden, he and Alice, surrounded with the lush scents of her roses and lavender and stock, and drink the bottle of extremely good champagne he also always brought with him, and sometimes talk and sometimes be quite easily and peacefully quiet. To Mungo who had spent his entire life in a rather frenetic pursuit of pleasure those Sundays seemed almost magically sweet.

He saw Alice in the week as well of course; he would take her to dinner or the theatre, and then they would go back to his flat in Sloane Street and experience some extremely joyful sex. She had refused to go to bed with him for quite a long time, telling him that it was foolish, dangerous even, that she did not want him reading more into their relationship than he should; but one night, after a particularly happy evening, when she was sitting on his small balcony, smiling at him, her lovely face soft in the dusk, he suddenly said, 'I love you, Alice. I really do.'

And she had said, 'Oh Mungo, don't.'

'Don't what, Alice? Don't love you? Or don't say it?'

'Don't even think it.'

'But why?' he said, hurt, shocked almost. 'Why can't I think it, when I know it?'

'Because you don't. You are a young, young man, free to do whatever you choose; you have no business to be thinking you're in love with someone almost old enough to be your mother.'

'Oh for Christ's sake,' he said, 'you're not, and anyway, what I choose to do is be in love with you. I don't want anything else. Please believe me.'

He heard almost to his own surprise a catch in his voice as he spoke; looking at her, he saw her face soften into tenderness, concern, saw her almost speak, then hesitate. Mungo was a past master at manipulation; the years he had spent working on his father's emotions had been a superb training. He found that the easy tears were still at his command; he looked at her, knowing his eyes, his dark brown eyes, were huge and dark with them, felt one even roll over and splash down his cheek.

'Oh Mungo,' she said, putting out her hand, wiping the tear away with her finger, 'darling Mungo, don't cry.'

'I can't help it,' he said, 'it hurts me so when you talk like that. Don't you feel anything for me at all? Am I just someone to fill your lonely evenings?' He wondered briefly if he had gone a little far there, moved into Act Two of the melodrama when Act One was not even complete; but 'Of course you're not,' she said and her voice was at once also hurt, but full of tenderness. 'I love being with you, spending time with you. But – '

'But you don't love me? Not in the least?' Another tear, another splash.

'Well – oh Mungo, don't. I can't bear it. Yes, yes all right, I do love you. Quite a lot. There now, I've said it, I'm afraid.'

'Why afraid? Alice, why afraid?'

'Because I have no right to be telling you. Involving you.'

'Alice,' said Mungo, kneeling in front of her, taking both her hands in his. 'I am involved. We're both involved. We can't help it. We're in love with each other. And it's wonderful. Nothing to be afraid of. Now, can we please do the sensible thing, and go inside and go to bed?'

And 'Yes, Mungo,' she said finally, after an endless silence. 'Yes, Mungo, of course we can.'

She had been from the beginning appalled by his idleness, his willingness to live off his father; it was entirely due to her influence that he took the office in Carlos Place, started his estate agency only a month after their meeting. He knew very little about the business, but he had at least an instinct, a sympathy for it, and he hired a small but excellent team and bluffed his way along. There was after all no great hurry to get into profit; his father was so delighted by the whole thing, Mungo knew he would back him for five years if necessary. It was also due to Alice that he gave up gambling, apart from the occasional poker game, started drinking less and completely gave up even soft drugs. Alice felt very strongly on that subject; she said that apart from her own distaste for anything to do with drugs, she had the children to worry about, and any bad example they might be exposed to.

'You've reformed me,' he said to her one night, early in May, soon after they had first gone to bed together. 'My father won't recognize me when he next gets back.'

'Where is he at the moment?'

'Mexico. With Sasha.'

'On holiday?'

'Good God no. My father doesn't believe in holidays. Sasha's honeymoon was twenty-four hours at the Bel Air, en route to San Francisco and a conference he was chairing on AIDS research.'

'It doesn't sound very romantic. Poor Sasha.'

'Oh, she's all right,' said Mungo easily. 'She has a great time. She just shops. She's very good at that.'

'And what else?'

'I don't think anything else. Well, you know, the usual things my father wants, looking great, being nice to him, sex, I suppose.'

'I see,' said Alice.

She had known about his father of course; her husband had even, she thought, met him once or twice.

'He must be quite a hard act to follow,' she said sympathetically.

'Oh, not really,' said Mungo, vaguely, 'I've never really seen myelf as following him. Up to now.'

He had started asking her to marry him in late May; initially she had assumed he was joking, then as she realized he wasn't, had refused, resolutely at first, then slightly more half-heartedly.

'It's ridiculous,' she kept saying, 'I can't even let you think about it.'

Mungo told her she was in no position to tell him what or what not to think and continued to ask her. He asked her by phone, letter, motorbike messenger (cards accompanied by bottles of champagne, jewellery and the perfume he loved so much) and even by singing telegram. And in person on every possible occasion, and in every conceivable situation, in bed, over dinner, in the car, while they were out riding with the children (the children well out of earshot), at concerts and theatres, and once, most romantically, in his father's box at Covent Garden. They were watching *La Bohème* at the time; Mungo did not greatly like opera, but Alice loved it and it seemed to him a most appropriate situation. He ordered a bottle of champagne for the interval and it was brought in by one of the uniformed lackeys, together with a dozen red roses and a note which he handed to Alice.

'Oh my God,' she said laughing, kissing him, 'oh God, Mungo, what am I to say to you? I can't cope with this very much longer.'

'Say yes,' he said, 'it isn't very difficult,' but she managed not to, managed to keep saying it wasn't a good idea, that she really couldn't, until finally one night he lost his temper at yet another refusal, stormed out of her house and walked very fast back to Sloane Street.

When he got in, there was a message from her on his answering machine.

'I love you,' it said, 'and yes, perhaps I will.'

Now all he had to do was tell his father.

★

Mungo moved into the shade of the lychgate. He was terribly hot, and thirsty as well. This was ridiculous. Nobody was going to come yet, nobody at all. He wondered if he could sneak into the pub for a quick beer. It would only take ten minutes. He was severely tempted. He looked up and down the lane: no sign of anybody, let alone wedding guests. It was as if the nightmare had stopped the whole world, held time still; there was a tiny drifting breeze ruffling the long grass just inside the churchyard, a bird sang half-heartedly in the hedge, the noise of a thousand bees at work in the perfect flower garden of the little cottage opposite the church: those were the only sounds, the only movements. It was almost spooky, the silence; the whole thing had somehow shades of a ghost story. It seemed as reasonable an explanation as any suddenly, something supernatural, Cressida spirited away perhaps, into some strange half-world. For want of anything better to do, Mungo moved into the churchyard, started reading the gravestones. He had never done such a thing before, was startled, instantly saddened by them, by the brutally brief lives ended there: a young couple dying in 1601 within days of one another, a young mother (twenty-four years old) 'taken at Christmas-time 1797, mourned by her five beloved children', of countless babies dead in the first year of their lives. A shadow covered the sun for Mungo; he sat down abruptly in the grass, thinking of Alice. Life suddenly seemed very fragile, happiness brief. They must be together quickly, he thought, must waste no more time. And then he heard a car coming down the lane and looked over the wall and it was Harriet's with Sasha driving it; she pulled up by the lychgate, got out, leant on the wall.

'Hallo, Mungo. I thought you should know what's happened. And I've brought you some beer. You must be terribly hot.'

'Glad someone thinks of me,' said Mungo, standing up, taking the cans gratefully. 'You're a doll, Sasha. What has happened? They haven't found her, have they?'

'No. Not her. But they've found her car.'

'Oh shit.' Mungo sat down abruptly again, feeling sick. 'Crashed? Is she – '

'No, not crashed at all. The car was fine. Parked neatly in a country lane. Somewhere in Essex.'

'Essex? What on earth was she doing in Essex?'

'Picking up her plane.'

'Her plane? Sasha, this is purest fantasy. Cressida can hardly handle the lawnmower.'

'Well, maybe not, but she can handle a plane. She has a pilot's licence. What's more, Theo has been paying for her lessons. He didn't know about the licence, though. She swore him to secrecy. Mungo, what the hell do you think is going on?'

Chapter Ten

Theo 2pm

Theo felt terrible; guilt suffused him. He shrank from what James might have to say to him about Cressida's flying lessons; he would see it as an appalling betrayal of friendship, of trust. Theo set aside as determinedly as he could the remembrance of another, greater betrayal – or what James would certainly see as one – and concentrated on this one, the part he had played, however unwittingly, in Cressida's disappearance. It was ridiculous, he told himself, to feel so bad, he had only paid for the bloody flying lessons (and promised Cressida not to tell anyone about it), but the fact remained that if he hadn't done it, she couldn't have taken off quite literally into the blue. OK, if she'd been desperate enough to vanish, she would no doubt have gone anyway; but he had certainly made it easier for her. And he'd kept his promise not to mention it to anyone: 'Please, please don't tell them, Theo,' she'd said, her blue eyes wide with anxiety. 'You know how hopeless I am, I'll have such trouble with it, probably never master it at all, and then they'll all laugh at me. I'll tell them when I've finally cracked it and it'll be wonderful.'

And he had agreed, unable to refuse her as always, had kissed her and told her to tell the flying school to send their bills to him. 'On one condition. You take me up on your first solo flight.'

'Of course I will. Of course. I promise.'

That had been over eighteen months ago, and she never had taken him up: had confessed to him, ruefully, whenever they were alone together that it was exactly as she had feared, that she was indeed completely hopeless, still hadn't got the hang even of keeping the nose steady, although she did love it, loved her lessons, and hoped he wouldn't mind if she went on, and no, he had said, of course he didn't mind, it was fine by him, she should go on for just as long as it took. He did wonder (as she'd been having so much trouble) if she was actually at the best flying school, but she assured him they were wonderful, terribly kind and patient. She'd told him it was somewhere in Wiltshire; quite what she was doing flying out of Essex he couldn't imagine. Maybe she'd just had a few lessons there. It had never occurred to him to check on the school; he had rung his secretary and she had confirmed that yes, all the bills had come from some place in Essex, a very intensive course, several hours a week, but that they had ceased in April that year. 'Apparently she got her licence last September. Just went on flying with them once a fortnight. They said she was very good. Very good indeed.'

'And she took one of their planes?'

'Yes. They're very upset. They want to speak to you.'

He had called them, spoken to the owner of the school, Richard Crooke, who had personally instructed Cressida. She had turned up that morning apparently, at eight thirty, asked if she could take one of the planes up and not returned. No said Crooke, she hadn't seemed at all upset, she was her usual steady, highly competent self. She'd said she'd be back in an hour. There was enough fuel on board for about five hundred miles. Had Mr Buchan any idea where she might have gone and when she might be back?

Theo said he had no idea, no idea at all, but of course he would contact the school immediately they heard from her, and trusted that they would do the same. Crooke asked if, in the event of the plane not being returned, Mr Buchan would be underwriting the cost. Theo said there was no question of the plane not being returned, and asked if Cressida was really a good pilot.

She was excellent, Crooke said; from the very first lesson she'd been a natural, shown a complete grasp of the whole thing. No nerves, no mechanical problems. 'And she loved it. She was laughing with pleasure from the moment the plane started taxiing down the runway. All the things that people usually don't like at first, banking, landing, she just took in her stride. Her first solo flight, she was off, straight over the sea.' He hesitated. 'She didn't mention to you that she had asked me to look out for a plane for her?'

'No,' said Theo. 'No, of course not.'

'Well, she did. In fact I'd found one. Just a tiny one, a Cessna, two-seater. That was what she liked best. Said the four-seaters were too cumbersome. She said she was going to come over and see it last weekend. But she never did.'

'But that's not the plane she's gone off in now?'

'No. That's one of ours. The one she flew most. Got her licence in. She said it felt like a pair of running shoes to her, that plane, she was so comfortable, at ease in it. She was a lovely girl, Mr Buchan. I hope to God nothing's happened to her.'

'Yes, well, I hope so too,' said Theo. He'd put the phone down feeling rather sick.

He wished Sasha was with him, but she had gone to see Mungo with some beer, and to tell him the news. He needed her, he needed her very badly. To distract him. What he should have done, he thought, staring morosely into his glass of whisky, was gone to meet Tilly at Heathrow, instead of letting Merlin go. She was coming over, had managed to catch a lunchtime flight. That would have cheered him up, distracted him from his guilt. His marriage to Sasha had not dulled a response to a sexuality as raw, as uncompromising as Tilly's. But he could see that he couldn't have left his post; and besides, her imminent arrival was probably causing James as much anguish as the disappearance of his daughter. Bloody silly idea getting Tilly over really; he had tried very hard to dissuade Mungo and Rufus from doing it. But Mungo had said her presence would help, she was so full of common sense and Oliver was so fond of her, and anyway things could hardly be worse. Theo had said shortly that they could be worse, much much worse actually, and Mungo had asked why; and short of giving him a full explanation (which was really not his to give) Theo had been forced to let things run their course. In any case, maybe it was better that she came, that the confrontation between her and James was finally forced; the drama of the aborted wedding might take the edge off it. And there was no doubt that Tilly would cheer things up.

Extraordinary set of coincidences that had brought things thus far, almost unbelievable. That this girl should not only have met Harriet, but become a friend, quite a close friend indeed, and then to all of them, their tight little circle, and finally that Rufus should have fallen in love with her – it was bizarre, nightmarish. The only thing that saved the situation was Tilly herself. She was superb. In every way. He'd known she would be beautiful, sexily, raunchily beautiful: he'd seen dozens, hundreds probably, of pictures of her. But he had expected her to be tough, self-seeking, and quite possibly extremely stupid. He'd waited to meet her the first time, expecting to dislike her intensely. And she had walked into the room like some graceful, rangy black lioness, smiling her impossibly wide, glorious smile, and had taken his hand and shaken it, and it had been like a man's handshake, so firm and strong, and said, 'Hi, Mr Buchan. I'm Ottoline Mills.' And he'd looked at her, at the slanting eyes, the wild mass of hair, at the long narrow body (dressed in a long slither of a black dress under a black leather jacket), and had not just responded to her, been charmed by her; he'd liked her. It was nothing to do with her beauty or her sexuality or the fact that, yes, she was tough, but humorously so, and that, no, she was not stupid, quite the reverse indeed, coolly, sharply clever; it was the fact that she was plainly extremely nice. He could see it was a little early to reach such a conclusion, that he could be accused of being overwhelmed by her, but he was sure of it nonetheless. And everything that had happened since had reinforced that view.

He could scarcely blame Rufus for falling in love with her, in spite of the appalling complications of the thing. What was less clear was why she should reciprocate that love: Rufus, however sweet, was patently not the sort of man with whom Ottoline Mills had spent much time or indeed would have been expected to enjoy spending time. Himself certainly (Christ, if only), Mungo perhaps (God forbid, especially now the boy seemed to be settling down finally – something was having a good effect on him). But Rufus, with his gentle manner, his tender heart, his old-fashioned charm – very unlikely. But love him she plainly did; further proof, Theo felt, of her niceness, that she should value such old-world, intangible virtues. Rufus was not rich, he was not particularly witty, he was not stylish, he was not even chic, he cultivated an almost deliberate shabbiness. If you looked at him and Mungo together, Theo had once remarked to Janine, Rufus looked like some slightly well-worn classical building and Mungo like some stark, perfectly conceived piece of modern architecture. But Rufus was clever, articulate, cultured, original. Of all those qualities, Theo supposed, it was the last that had won Tilly's heart. She was certainly something of an original herself . . .

Josh Bergin had rung suggesting a walk, had come into his room looking grey with strain, and Theo had been unable to refuse. He hated walking, it seemed to him the most dreary of physical activities, if indeed it could be dignified with such a name; but he couldn't think of an alternative. Josh was hardly in a state (nor did it seem suited to the situation) to swim, or to play golf; walking was at least sober, respectable.

Well, at least there was good news about Tealing Mills. The New York individual, whoever they were, had put their shares – at a huge profit incidentally, they were obviously extremely canny – back on the market. Theo had instructed Mark to buy. 'And while you're about it, tell George I think it might be time to get on with buying some more of those CalVin shares. I know I said softly softly, but that was my policy with Tealing. That is one baby I don't want to lose. Or rather have you guys lose it for me.'

'Sure,' said Mark. 'I'll get back to you.'

Theo put the phone down; he wished to hell all he had to worry about today were his companies and their conduct. His pleasure over the Tealing business was intense, almost sexual in nature. Theo could never quite decide which gave him the greater buzz, women or deals. He thought probably deals; certainly the pleasure was longer-lasting. And now if he could just wrap up CalVin, the day would at least have had something in its favour.

Theo poured himself another large whisky (God, why wasn't it working, why couldn't he get drunk?) and sat reflecting upon CalVin: not a Scottish company this time, but an extremely profitable little wine-producing company in the Napa Valley, California (hence the name). Not only was it profitable, it was an exquisite place; he rather fancied making a home there, building a house. Not as a major home, more of a refuge; he might not even tell Sasha about it, he thought, smiling into his glass. It could be extremely useful, in the just-possible event of his wanting to be on his own, or almost on his own, for a few days: secluded, peaceful, utterly private.

Well, that was for the future: meanwhile there was Josh to be taken care of. He couldn't put that off any longer. He picked up the phone again. 'When my wife gets back, tell her I've gone for a walk with Mr Bergin, would you?'

'Certainly, Mr Buchan.'

God, she'd been a long time. Disappearing seemed to be the order of the day altogether.

Josh didn't say anything for a long time; he led the way rather determinedly through the hotel grounds, over a stile and into some woods in total silence. Theo, who disliked any silence that lasted for more than twenty seconds, stuck it out for as long as he could and then said, 'I suppose in twenty years or so we'll all be laughing about this.'

'Maybe,' said Josh. 'I certainly hope so.' He looked at Theo. 'It really is one's worst nightmare, isn't it?'

'Oh, I can think of much worse,' said Theo carefully, thinking how Josh really did look more English than the English, tall, blond, quietly dressed; he even talked like an upper-class Englishman. Well, that old-money New York crowd prided itself on its cosmopolitan character; he had been to banking dinners there with Josh and wondered at times whether he was actually back in London. Especially now that the London financial scene was so overrun with barrow boys. Wall Street seemed better.

'I can't,' said Josh. 'I really can't think of anything much worse. Poor Oliver. Poor old boy.'

'Yes,' said Theo, 'poor old boy.'

'He's so upset. He's much more easily hurt than anyone realizes, you know. He comes on very controlled and upbeat, but he's actually extremely sensitive. And he adored Cressida. Really adored her.'

'Yes, well, we all did,' said Theo. 'Mustn't speak of her in the past tense, Josh. She'll be back.'

'Yes. Yes of course she will,' said Josh. He didn't sound terribly certain.

'Definitely,' said Theo. There was another long silence.

'We didn't all actually,' said Josh suddenly. He sounded rather strained.

'I'm sorry?'

'We didn't all adore Cressida.'

'Really? Who didn't? You?'

'Oh – yes. Yes of course I did.' He sounded even more tense. Theo looked at him curiously.

'So – who? Who didn't?'

'Julia didn't.' The words came out almost defiantly.

'Oh really?'

'No. In fact I would go so far as to say she didn't like her. Christ, Theo, I've been keeping this to myself for months now.'

'Well, old chap, mothers of sons don't often like their daughters-in-law. Jealousy you know. Freud at work. Thought you Yanks were heavily into all this psychiatric stuff.'

'Oh yes, of course, I know all that. And I'm the first to admit that Julia is – what should I say – highly strung. She virtually lives with her analyst. She seems very cool and in control, but she's a hotbed of emotions underneath. Rather like that crazy old father of hers.'

'How is dear Vernon?' asked Theo, laughing at Josh's contorted face.

'Well, I fear,' said Josh, relaxing suddenly and laughing back. Vernon Coleridge, Julia's father, lived as a virtual recluse in Palm Beach; Julia, the focus of his life, was now almost his only visitor.

'Anyway, this was rather more than just jealousy, I think. She often said she – didn't trust her.'

'Really? Why? Whatever made her feel that way?'

'She said Cressida had – lied to her.'

'What on earth about?'

'Oh – this and that. Small things mostly, that didn't really matter, I suppose.'

'Go on, like what?'

'Well, for instance, she told her that she'd had a bad riding accident as a child and had completely lost her nerve. When Julia asked Maggie about it, Maggie told her she certainly couldn't remember it. And she said she'd always wanted to go to boarding school, and that because Harriet hadn't liked it, she wasn't even allowed to try. Again it turned out that she'd always said she didn't want to go, had become hysterical at the very suggestion. Oh yes, and she said she'd always desperately wanted a puppy, and because Harriet had had one and it had been run over, that was that.'

'None of it sounds very serious to me,' said Theo lightly. 'Typical rewriting of childhood history. Sympathy bids. I expect she was just trying to get Julia on her side. She probably sensed she didn't like her.'

'Well – maybe. And I expect you're right. There was a lot of jealousy. Oliver being not just the only son, but the only child. Julia does – what shall I say? – like to mother him still. But there was something rather more serious. That I never discussed with her as a matter of fact.' He looked at Theo. 'Are you sure you want to hear all this? Maybe this isn't the time.'

'I think it's exactly the time,' said Theo. 'And I do want to hear it.'

'Well – she'd been staying with us in New York for a week or so. Earlier this year. Julia was away, gone to see her father, he had a chill or something. Cressida had been out shopping all day and arrived home at around six thirty, terribly upset, said some man had been following her. She hadn't been able to get a cab and she'd been walking the few blocks home up Madison. As she turned into our street, there's a small florist on the corner, he'd pushed her into the doorway, started trying to kiss her, and got his hand into her blouse. She only got away by kneeing him in the crotch. She certainly looked a bit roughed up, she had a bruise on her face and another on her arm, and she was very shaky and tearful. I wanted to call the police, but she begged me not to, said everyone would fuss and she just wanted to forget about it. She especially didn't want Oliver knowing about it, he'd freak out, as she put it, and she couldn't face going over and over it.'

'Where was Oliver?' said Theo.

'He was with a patient. Delivering a baby. Anyway, rather reluctantly I agreed. I sent her to bed, told Oliver when he came in that she wasn't well, and not to disturb her. She didn't appear again until the morning, and then she seemed better. We talked after Oliver had gone. She insisted no real harm had been done to her, and she wasn't hurt at all, although she was still upset and a bit subdued. She said she just wanted to try and forget the whole thing – she really didn't want any more fuss. She said, quite rightly, that both Julia and Oliver would berate her for walking up the street, not getting a cab, and I had to agree that they would. I said they'd be right moreover and she said she was very sorry, she knew it was stupid of her. But she was going the next day and she didn't want her last evening with Oliver spoiled. So I said I wouldn't say anything. She told him she'd hit her face on a door, when he noticed the bruise, and I tried to tell myself no great harm had been done.

'A couple of days later, the hall porter rang up. He had a limo driver with him, and he'd brought in a pair of Cressida's gloves. Said she'd left them in the limo, the night before last, that they looked expensive and he thought he should bring them back. Well that was the night of the alleged attack. I asked him if he was sure it had been then and he said sure he was sure, the next two nights he'd had off, his wife was in hospital or something. I asked him where he'd brought Cressida from and he said up from Brooklyn. That she'd hired him for the day, and he'd taken her down there at lunchtime, dropped her by some subway station and been told to pick her up three hours later. He'd brought her right to the door. I – well I don't know what you make of it, but it sounded pretty odd to me.'

'Very odd,' said Theo. 'Bizarre. And you never – taxed Cressida with it?'

'No. Well, I told you, she'd gone back to England.'

'And you didn't mention it to Oliver?'

'No. No I didn't. It was an almost impossible conversation to have. I'm sure you can see that. And then we didn't hear from her for weeks, by which time the wedding plans were in full swing. It didn't seem – appropriate to start implying she was a liar.'

'I'm sure she wasn't,' said Theo. 'I mean isn't. What about Julia, what did she say?'

Josh looked awkward. 'I – well, I didn't tell Julia either. Now of course I think perhaps I should have done. But it was all so inconclusive, so insubstantial, and Julia would have made such a terrible performance of it. Used it to prove her feelings against Cressida. And I thought – well, it seemed better, more positive, to believe Cressida. So I kept quiet. Until now.'

'I see,' said Theo. He felt outraged, defensive on Cressida's behalf. The sensation he had been struggling with all day, that he was in a nightmare and was about to wake up suddenly, revived with great force. 'Josh, I've known that child all her life. Really really well. She's been like a daughter to me. A sweet, adorable daughter. She just doesn't tell lies. Well, maybe white ones, to spare people's feelings or whatever, but nothing major – '

His voice faded slowly. Was persuading him to pay for her flying lessons and making him swear not to tell anyone about it really a small white lie? Harmless, perhaps, but quite substantial actually: involving someone else in a deception as well as herself. He suddenly didn't feel quite so sure about Cressida Forrest.

Chapter Eleven

Tilly 2pm

She made it. Sweet-talking the cab driver, jumping the queue at the check-in, haring up those fucking awful travelators at Charles de Gaulle, waving her passport and ticket wildly at the departure gate, she had fallen into the cabin of the plane with one minute to spare, had stood there, gasping for breath, laughing, dressed just in a vest T and her cut-offs, still with all the make-up on; had walked through, more slowly now, into the first-class cabin, enjoying the stares – some hostile, mostly appreciative – of the businessmen self-importantly stacking up their laptops, files, organizers for the journey, and slumped into her seat, next to a particularly oyster-eyed old geezer, smiled at him, fumbled in her bag for her cigarettes, started to light up, been reprimanded by the steward and offered a peppermint in return (a peppermint, for God's sake, what use was that in a crisis?) and sat watching Paris slowly shrinking beneath her.

'Champagne, madam?' It was the peppermint-bearing steward.

'What do you think?' said Tilly, grinning at him, taking the glass from the tray. She could never understand the mealy-mouthed crowd who survived transatlantic flights on distilled water and a couple of mouthfuls of celery; she took everything she was offered and enjoyed it.

'Lovely day,' she said cheerfully to her companion.

'Indeed,' he said slightly coolly, and opened the *Herald Tribune*.

Tilly shrugged and drained her glass, waved it at the steward. 'Could I have another? Maybe with a little orange juice?'

She had scarcely finished that and the plate of smoked salmon they brought her when the pilot announced they were begining their descent. She looked out of the window, and saw the orderly green patchwork of England below her. God, it was always so nice to get back; she'd only been away ten days, but it still felt like forever. She enjoyed travelling – for around forty-eight hours. After that homesickness set in. Tilly was famous for her homesickness; she had even declared herself hungry for England in the middle of winter from a beach in Barbados. If she did this thing with Rosenthal, she'd never be home. Oh God . . .

She wondered who might meet her. Rufus had said it probably

wouldn't be him. She'd promised to get a cab if there was no one there for her. It really was time she passed her test. Bloody thing. She didn't know anyone, anyone at all who'd failed three times. And there was her car, her beautiful Ferrari – 'Bit like you,' Mungo had said when she showed it to him, 'long and sleek and fast and black.' He was a great guy, Mungo. Much more her style with those amazing, dramatic dark looks, the sexy chat, the instant easiness with her world. Mungo had spent most of his life kicking around with the sort of people she worked and lived with, international, glamorous people, moving with ease from country to country, continent to continent, intensely fashionable, individual and, OK superficial, but amusing, interesting, fun. Rufus's world, measured by such things as schools, accents, career structures, and the still stately pattern of upper-middle-class English life, was far stranger and more difficult for her to enter. If she didn't love Rufus she'd be off with Mungo before you could say fuck. Or alternatively his gorgeous great bear of a father. But she did love Rufus, she loved him to pieces and it was having a strange effect on her.

Tilly had not known love before. She had known sex and desire and pleasure and bed-based friendship but not, most assuredly not, love. Love had come creeping up on her, sly, unexpected, with a sweet smile and a pair of soft brown eyes under a heavy blond fringe and the sort of voice that had always sent her into fits of mirth. Love had spoken to her politely, held doors open for her, pulled back chairs for her, asked her how she was, waited patiently outside photographers' studios for hours while jobs overran. Love had sat in fashion shows, watching her, smiling in appreciative wonder at her, and had cheerfully cancelled tables for dinner afterwards because she had to be up at five, four even, the next day. Love had read her poetry, and taken her to romantic films, to concerts and to High Mass at Notre-Dame and Sacré-Coeur, to Versailles, studying enraptured her myriad reflections in the Hall of Mirrors, to Giverny to take her wandering through the tumbling, dreamlike colours of Monet's gardens. Love had taken her to bed and pleasured her to an astonishing degree, and finally, only a week ago, had lain on the pillow beside her and asked her to marry him.

'Marry!' she'd said. 'Marry you!' and 'Yes,' he'd said, his brown eyes hurt at the reaction, 'marry me, Tilly, please. I love you. I love you so much.'

'Yeah, and I love you too, but people like me don't marry people like you. Why do we have to get married anyway? Risk spoiling everything. This is great.'

'I want to make you mine,' he said simply. 'I want to live with you, and grow old with you, and have babies with you – '

'Oh no,' she said swiftly, sitting up, reaching for her cigarettes, lighting one, 'no babies. Absolutely no babies. Sorry Rufus. No way.'

'Oh not now,' he said, misunderstanding, 'of course not now while you're working, but when you've finished, when your figure doesn't matter so much – '

'Fuck my figure,' she said, 'my figure has nothing to do with it. I just will never ever have a baby, OK? I couldn't face it, couldn't go through with it.'

'But why?'

'Because it scares the shit out of me, that's why. All that pain, all that danger – '

'Darling Tilly, there isn't any danger, not now – '

'Oh really?' she said, and noticed that the hand holding her cigarette was shaking, feeling rare tears behind her eyes. 'You tell that to my mum, Rufus Headleigh Drayton, you tell her there was no danger. I'll – oh shit, can we stop this please? No babies, that's all, Rufus, no babies.'

And he had held her and comforted her and said of course no babies if she minded that much, if she was that afraid, but she had to tell him why. She ducked the issue (of course, because she had to, she had still not decided what to do), said maybe she had seen too many horrific childbirth scenes in films or something, but anyway, she was phobic about it and that was that.

'In any case,' she said finally, 'I don't see how I can marry you. I mean, think what sort of wife I'd be to you. How many lawyers have wives like me?'

'Not many, poor things,' said Rufus, kissing her gently. 'I'll be the envy of every court in the world.'

'Don't be stupid,' said Tilly irritably. 'I know the sort of wife you need and she isn't black and she doesn't come from Brixton. And she's very happy to spend her time doing the flowers and having the house done out and being on charity committees and inviting important people to dinner.'

'You do know, don't you?' said Rufus, surprised.

'Rufus, I know lots of things. I've been around. I've been to a few of those power dinners, I've seen those women at work. I'd be a total disaster. I have a much better idea. You get a suitable wife and we'll meet once a week for a fantastic fuck.'

'No,' he said, and his brown eyes were very tender, very honest, 'no, I'm sorry, I couldn't do that. I'm like my dad. A one-woman man.'

'And is your mother a one-man woman?'

'Yes of course she is,' said Rufus, half indignant. 'You'd love my mum, Tilly. And she'd love you. She's the best. She's so pretty and she's such fun and when she's there everyone always has a good time.'

'And a good lawyer's wife?'

'A great lawyer's wife, yes.'

'And I suppose she went to the best schools and all that garbage?'

'Well yes, she did, but that doesn't mean – '

'Rufus, I know what it means. I love you, but I'm not going to marry you. I'm not going to marry anyone. I never want to belong to anyone that much.'

'But Tilly, love is about belonging,' said Rufus, looking hurt. 'I feel I belong to you anyway.'

'Yeah, I know, and I kind of feel the same thing, but that's a different sort of belonging from being married.'

'I don't understand,' said Rufus.

'Rufus, all my life – '

'Such a long life – '

'I thought you wanted me to explain.'

'Sorry.'

'All my life, and I mean all, since I was really really tiny, I've wanted things to be down to me. Independent, you know? Not having to ask for things, not having to be grateful. To be in charge. My mum spent most of her life being grateful for lousy jobs she should have thrown back at people, for the odd bit of money she could persuade my dad to give her, for droppings from those self-important turds that call themselves the social services. Christ! And she's worth so much more than any of them. I hated it so much, Rufus, watching it, watching her. And I decided I was going to do it all my way, stay free, stay clear. Not have to take, from anyone, not put myself at risk.'

'That seems to cut out me altogether,' said Rufus. He sounded very sad. 'You won't be at risk from me, Tilly, I'll never ever leave you, let you down. And isn't it worth it, taking, if you really love someone? I would.'

'You say that,' said Tilly, 'but you don't know. You've always had so much you don't know you're taking. Anyway, of course it doesn't cut you out. It doesn't cut out anything we have. It doesn't cut out love or fun or sex or being together.'

'It cuts out giving,' said Rufus. 'Tilly, won't you even think about it, marrying me? Not even one day? I want it so much, I want to know you're mine, I want everyone to know you're mine.'

He looked so wretched Tilly was shocked. She leant over and kissed him tenderly.

'Rufus, I *am* yours. And everyone does know. I'm not going to leave you. I love you much too much. I just don't want to marry you. I don't want to marry anyone. And like I keep saying, I'd be the most terrible wife for you anyway. You need someone like – well, like Cressida. An English rose in frilly blouses.'

'I don't want an English rose in frilly blouses,' said Rufus irritably. 'I want you.'

'You've got me.'

'I mean married to me.'

'Rufus, I can't. You haven't been listening. But I tell you what. You're lovely to ask me. Thank you. Maybe we should get to sleep now.'

'I shan't be able to sleep,' said Rufus.

But he did, curled around her, his head buried in the nape of her neck. It was Tilly who couldn't sleep, lying awake for hours, thinking not about Rufus and marriage, but about her mother's anxious, troubled life, and her inability to do anything about it, and childbirth and its attendant terrors, and the tiny plaque in the Crematorium Garden of Rememberance that read 'Beatrice Mills. Sister to Ottoline. Born and died, 20 October 1974'.

'Miss Mills?' The voice was charming, courteous. Tilly looked at its owner, tall, taller than she was, and very erect, despite what was clearly considerable age. He was dressed in a manner that seemed slightly eccentric even to her, a white shirt, very baggy khaki shorts and a morning coat; but the legs beneath the shorts were not spindly old men's legs, they were strong and very tanned, as was the rest of him, and the hand he held out to her was large and firm.

'Yes,' she said, grinning at him, shaking his hand, 'yes, I'm Tilly Mills. Hi.'

'How do you do. I'm Merlin Reid.' Tilly had heard about Sir Merlin, and had longed to meet him; he'd sounded like her kind of person.

'Young Rufus asked me to meet you. Said he thought we'd get on. I can see we will,' he added. 'Got any luggage?'

'No,' said Tilly, 'only this' – indicating the leather rucksack on her back.

'Good girl. I only ever take a rucksack myself. Most people take far too much luggage. Follow me, then.'

He led the way out of the airport; a stout, ferret-faced female traffic warden stood by what was clearly his car (1930-ish, Tilly thought, dark green, with a running board, brown hood folded down), writing out a ticket.

'Oh wow,' said Tilly, walking round the car, stroking it, totally ignoring the warden. 'This is some car. What is it?'

'I'm glad you like it. I'm very fond of it. It's a Lagonda. We've been together for about thirty years. Driven her all over Europe.'

'Really. It really is f – very beautiful.'

'You can't park here.' said the warden, clearly as enraged by being ignored as by the flagrant disregard for parking restrictions. 'I have to give you a ticket.'

'I think you should brush up on your grammar,' said Merlin. 'Quite incorrect, that sentence. Clearly I can park here, or I wouldn't have been able to do so. What you mean, I imagine, is that it is against your horrible rules for me to park here, You should make yourself plainer, madam. Now please remove that piece of paper from my windscreen.'

'I can't do that I'm afraid.'

'Wrong grammar again. Of course you can. By raising your arm and lifting the ticket with your hands. I can do it too. Look. Now take it back and get out of my way. I'm very busy.'

'I have to warn you you are still in breach of the law,' said the warden, groping on the ground for the ticket which she had dropped. 'I have your car number and I shall issue a duplicate ticket which you will receive through the mail. There could be an additional penalty, moreover, for trying to obstruct the course of justice.'

'Oh get out of my way, you ridiculous woman,' said Merlin. 'It's you who are causing the obstruction. Pity you weren't born fifty years earlier. You'd have been of great value to the Third Reich. Good afternoon to you.'

He opened the passenger door for Tilly, cranked up the car and drove off in a cloud of smoke; the warden stood staring after them, her mouth a wide O.

'Dreadful people,' said Merlin cheerfully. 'Should be put away. Are you comfortable, my dear? Good. We have a little drive ahead of us, so we can get to know one another. Like an apple?' He produced one from the pocket of his morning coat. 'They were selling them in the village shop. Awful little things, I told the woman I'd take them off her hands. She tried to make me pay, we had a bit of a barney, but in the end I beat her down to half price. Anyway, they're better than nothing.'

'They certainly are,' said Tilly, biting into the classic country-shop apple, small, soft, slightly withered. 'Do you want a beer? In exchange. I have a couple here, in my bag. It's travelled from Paris, but it's probably all right.'

'Oh yes, rather,' said Sir Merlin. 'That would be fine. As long as it's not that German stuff you all drink now. Buddy something or other.'

'Do you mean Budweiser?' said Tilly. 'That's American. But this is Dutch. Would that be all right?'

'Yes, fine. Some of our finest allies, the Dutch. Thank you very much. Take the top off for me, would you?'

'It's really kind of you to come and meet me,' said Tilly, handing him the beer.

'Oh, not at all. Relief to get away as a matter of fact. God, there's a to-do going on at the house. Poor old Jamie.'

'Well, I suppose it is worth a bit of a to-do,' said Tilly, grinning at him. 'I mean it is Cressida's wedding day and – '

'Lot of fuss about nothing if you ask me,' said Sir Merlin.

'Oh Sir Merlin, you can't say that, surely.'

'Indeed I can. I can and I do. Your grammar is a little at fault as well. Look, my dear, when you've lived as long as I have, you'll know nothing is really very important. Twenty years after some event that you thought catastrophic, you're wondering what it was all about. Or you can see it wasn't catastrophic at all.' He took another swig of beer, looked at Tilly thoughtfully. 'Give you an example. All my young life dreamed of going in the army. My grandfather was a field-marshal, Father was a general; place all ready for me at Sandhurst. Got turned down at the medical. Dicky ticker, they said. Although I can't say it's ever bothered me since. Well, I was very upset at the time. I'd have fallen on my sword if I had one. But now I can't think of anything worse. I'd never have really travelled, never have learnt what I've learnt, carried on seeing the native as fuzzy-wuzzies instead of fine, civilized chaps. More civilized than we are, most of them. Well, I don't know why I'm telling you that. Where are you from? Somalia by the look of you.'

'Brixton really,' said Tilly, 'but yes, my dad was from Somalia.'

'Thought so. Fine people. Anyway, you mark my words, Miss Mills, in a few years you'll be wondering why on earth there was such a fuss over this. Oliver's a tough young nut. He'll get over it.'

'Well – I suppose so,' said Tilly slightly doubtfully. 'And please call me Tilly.'

'Right you are. You haven't got another of those beers, have you? It was jolly good. Excellent people, the Dutch. Excellent. Lived in an attic in Amsterdam for a year or so with six of them. Never a cross word.'

'Why did you do that?'

'Well, it was in the war. Had a little sailing boat, made a few trips over to Dunkirk, you'll know about that I trust. Picked up some chappie who had a Dutch wife. Jewish. She was with her parents just outside Amsterdam, he was desperate to get her home to England. Well, I pulled a few strings you know, managed to get over there and went to see her. Nice girl. Wonderful people, put me up. Just leaving with the girl when the Gestapo started on the village. Local baker let us hide in a little attic, above his grain store. Had a hidden door. Just for a few days, we thought. Well the few days turned into a few months. Pretty exciting. I have to tell you I enjoyed it. Got a bit restless, but we made out. Wonderful fellow the baker. They – well, they shot him in the end. And his wife. And found the attic, dragged the family out, put them on a train to Bergen-Belsen. All dead, I'm afraid. Well, when you've seen things like that some damn silly girl running off in her wedding frock doesn't seem very important.'

'No,' said Tilly. 'No, I can see that.' She was completely engrossed in the story. 'Why didn't they take you as well?'

'I was out on the roof. We'd made a sort of trapdoor, took it in turns to climb out each day, get some fresh air. It was my turn. Felt terrible about it, but giving myself up wasn't going to help anybody. After that I made my way to the border, got out. I had a very good German passport some johnny at the Foreign Office had done for me. And I speak their filthy language of course. Anyway, where was I? Oh yes, the Dutch. Lovely people. Survived that terrible winter, never broke. How did you meet young Rufus then?'

'Through Harriet,' said Tilly. 'And Mungo and Oliver. In Paris. Um – did you say Cressida had run off in her wedding dress?'

'Well, she took it with her. Don't suppose she was actually wearing it.'

'Why on earth should she have done that, I wonder?'

'God knows. Dreadful behaviour altogether. Always thought she was spoilt. Harriet's worth ten of her. Work for Harriet, do you? Bit of sewing I suppose?'

'Um – not exactly,' said Tilly carefully. 'I'm a model.'

'Oh are you? What, walk up and down on the – what's it called – catwalk, that sort of thing?'

'Yes, that's right.'

'Had a girlfriend who was a model once. In London, just before the war. Worked for the chappie who makes clothes for the Queen. Norman Hartnell. Never let me near her, in case I creased her frock. You don't strike me too much like that. What do you think of Harriet?'

'I think she's great,' said Tilly. 'Really great. And clever too. She's going to be really big.'

'You mean successful? I think so too. Gave her a bit of money, you know, helped get her going.'

'That was kind.'

'Yes, well, haven't got any nippers of my own. Always had time for Harriet. Took her travelling with me a bit. Wouldn't have taken Cressida. Not in a million years. Not surprised she's done this between you and me. Not surprised at all.'

Tilly looked at him thoughtfully. 'Really? I don't know her very well. I only met her once or twice.'

'Not worth meeting much more often. Not for a girl like you anyway.

Only thing that ever impressed me was that she played a fine game of poker.'

'Poker!' said Tilly. She thought about Cressida, with her soft sweet manner, her slightly helpless charm, and tried to imagine her at a poker game. It was almost impossible. 'That's amazing. When did you discover that?'

'Oh – a couple of years ago. We were stuck in Charles de Gaulle Airport. I was on my way back from somewhere or other, stopped over to see Harriet and Cressida was there staying with her, said she'd travel back with me. Well, you know what the French are like, go on strike as soon as look at you. We were there all night, made friends with a couple of young chaps and one of them suggested a game. I expected Cressida to say she couldn't play, but she was very good. Didn't win of course, I always do that, but – '

'You do?' said Tilly, grinning at him. 'You played with Mungo Buchan?'

'Of course I have. Many times. He did beat me once, I think. Anyway, she asked me not to mention to the family she could play. She said she'd been learning and was planning to surprise them at Christmas or some such nonsense. What do you think of Mungo then?'

'He's cool,' said Tilly.

'I take it that's a compliment. I agree with you. A most interesting young man.'

'Yeah, I suppose,' said Tilly slowly. She was still trying to imagine Cressida playing poker. 'Yeah, he is.'

'So how do you fit into all this?'

'I told you. I know Harry.'

Careful, Ottoline, don't even think about the other connection; not now.

'Rufus seems very fond of you.'

'Yeah, he is. And I'm very fond of him,' she added with just a touch of defensiveness.

'Good,' said Sir Merlin. 'Wouldn't want him hurt. Very fond of his mother,' he added slightly unexpectedly.

It was an exhausting drive. The novelty of being in an open 1930s convertible rather than an air-conditioned limo very soon wore off. The fumes and the noise on the M4 were appalling, and as the car never went above 45mph, the journey took a long time. Tilly drifted into a confused agitated sleep, and woke to hear Sir Merlin singing 'It's a Long Way to Tipperary' very loudly. 'Have to sing,' he explained. 'Only way I can keep awake. Sing with me, won't you?'

Tilly didn't know many of the songs in his repertoire, so they settled for 'London's Burning' and 'Ten Green Bottles'. She was inordinately relieved when they turned off the motorway and he announced they were almost there. She was to be taken, Sir Merlin told her, to where Rufus was staying, at the Beaumonts', old friends of both the Forrests and the Headleigh Draytons. 'And after that I think I'll head over to the hotel where young Theo's staying. Get a bit of peace and quiet.'

'I'd much rather go there,' said Tilly. 'Can't get along with these country types.'

'Nor me, my dear. Can't stand them. But Rufus has told me to take you there, so I have to, I'm afraid. You'll like Susie, though. Lovely girl. Lots of guts. Ah, here we are, our turning. Hasn't she done well, the old darling?'

It took Tilly a few moments to realize he was referring to the Lagonda rather than Rufus's mother.

Rufus was standing in the Beaumonts' drive. He looked rather pale, but cheerful.

'Tilly! It's so wonderful to see you. You seem to have got here very quickly.'

'Sir Merlin and I made good time,' said Tilly tactfully, getting out of the car and kissing him briefly, feeling her heart lurch as always at the sight and sense of him and marvelling as always that she could feel such tenderness and such passion for someone who was so patently a product of everything she disliked and disapproved of. And thinking, too, that if she went to New York they would be forcibly separated for a great deal of the time, and that would be at one and the same time almost unbearable and a very neat way out of her dilemma. 'It was very kind of you to bring me,' she said, hauling herself back to the present, holding out her hand to Sir Merlin. 'Thank you. I enjoyed it. I hope we meet again.'

'Oh, I shall make sure we do. I enjoyed it too. Good afternoon, my dear. Everything all right, Rufus?'

'Oh – well, you know, sir. As well as can be expected. Everyone's a bit hysterical.'

'Lot of silly fuss,' said Sir Merlin, turning back to his car. 'I'm off to have a stiff drink and a nap. See you later, boy. Give my love to your mother.'

'Yes, I will, sir. And thank you again.'

'Pleasure. You've got a good one there,' he said, indicating Tilly.

'I know,' said Rufus, giving Merlin his oddly sweet smile. He took Tilly's hand and led her towards the house.

'Do we have to go in?'

'Well – just for a bit. Mum's here. I'd really like you to meet her. And I can tell you what's been happening. After that, we can go and see Oliver. He was so pleased you were coming.'

'OK.'

They went into the house. Tilly having admired the exterior, which was large and modestly grand, was amazed by what she found inside, an extraordinary blend of ripped sofa covers, kicked-about paintwork and what were clearly extremely expensive bits of furniture dotted about. A great many silver-framed photographs of children in various stages of development stood on a large table in the hall and what was obviously a valuable oil painting of a woman in a red crinoline hung above the stairs. The stairs themselves were covered in extremely theadbare carpeting, the floor of the hall was stone, and of the drawing room very unpolished wood. A woman with wild grey hair held back from a pleasantly plain face by a velvet Alice band came down the stairs. She was wearing wellingtons, a floral, full-skirted Laura Ashley dress and a sleeveless quilted jacket. She held out a very rough hand with rather dirty nails to Tilly.

'How do you do. You must be Tilly. Jolly nice to meet you. So good of you to come all this way.'

Tilly looked at her in horror. If this was Rufus's idea of a pretty, fun person, then they really did have no future together. She smiled slightly nervously and said, 'No problem.' The heat, the long journey and her anxiety made her suddenly feel rather dizzy.

'Now what about a cup of tea? My goodness, I've made a lot today. Rufus dear, bring Tilly into the kitchen – you don't mind a kitchen tea do you, Tilly? Careful, dear, of that dog, she's blind and deaf and gets a bit snappy if she's startled. Now then, I expect you're hungry, that drive with Merlin must have been jolly tough, I've got some cake or would you prefer a sandwich or something? – William, darling, I've told you not to bring bridles into the house, take it out to the tackroom.'

'But Mum – '

That was funny, thought Tilly, she could have sworn Rufus's small brother was called Tom.

'Take it out at once. Now, Tilly, would you like China or Indian?'

'Indian please,' said Tilly, 'with lots of sugar.' She sat down thankfully at the huge wooden table, which was covered in newspapers, mugs, letters, a pile of snapshots, a dog's lead and a lot of crumbs, removing something excruciatingly unfriendly from beneath her buttocks which proved to be what looked like a cross between a metal brush and a comb.

'Great,' said William, swooping on it. 'My curry comb. It's all right, Mum, I'm going.'

'I'm glad to hear it. Dreadful child,' she added, smiling at his disappearing back. 'Seems to have been home forever already and we're only three weeks into the holidays. Rufus dear, tea for you? Now – ah, Susie, there you are.'

And into the room, smiling, came a woman who Tilly could indeed recognize as extremely pretty and who could quite clearly be tremendous fun: a woman with dark brown hair, tied back loosely from a perfect oval face, large dark eyes, perfect, almost unlined skin. She was wearing beige shorts (revealing very tanned, very good legs) and a white T-shirt and she looked about thirty.

'I'm Susie Headleigh Drayton,' she said, holding out her hand to Tilly. 'How do you do? It's lovely to meet you and it's so nice of you to rush over from Paris. All the boys seemed to think you would make them feel better. I can quite see why.'

Tilly smiled back at her, took her hand, knew she was going to like her immensely, knew also at once why Rufus was as he was. 'I can't really,' she said, 'but I'll do my best.'

'What were you doing over there? The shows?'

'No, they're over. It was a photographic session for *Sept Jours*. Wedding dresses,' she added, after a pause.

'How ironic,' said Susie lightly. 'On such a day. One of my favourite magazines that. Do you enjoy modelling?'

'Yeah, I love it,' said Tilly briefly.

'I did a bit when I was young. I was with an agency that's gone now, called Peter Hope Lumley. I never really got going because I wasn't tall enough, but I did a few shows and lots of head shots. Mostly with Barry Lategan, does that mean anything to you?'

'Yes, but he doesn't work much now,' said Tilly, both impressed and irritated that Rufus hadn't mentioned this crucial piece of information about his mother. 'He was great, though. The guy I was working with today, Mick McGrath, he has a kind of shrine to Lategan in his studio in Paris.'

'Really? He was such a sweet man. I loved him. Anyway, I never got very far. But it taught me all kinds of useful things, like how to do my hair and put on false eyelashes, and I developed huge muscles in my arms, carrying my bags around, all those shoes, my goodness – '

'You don't have to do any of that these days,' said Tilly. 'They have hairdressers and make-up artists and the fashion editors bring everything, down to the last pair of tights.'

'So I understand. Aren't you lucky! Well, I'm sure they make a much better job of it than we did.'

144

God, she was nice, thought Tilly. Really really nice. She wanted to get to know her: properly know her. She sat there trying not to stare at Susie, at her lovely, fine features, her curvy mouth, her slender, young girl's body, and as she looked, Susie looked back at her, and Tilly saw within the depths of the velvety dark eyes an odd expression, something close to wariness, to anxiety. And she noticed something else too: a heavy shadowing beneath the eyes, a tautness to the jaw when the smile relaxed. There was something going on here, Tilly thought, some unhappiness beyond the disappearance of a close friend's daughter. She was intrigued, and more than intrigued – concerned. She smiled at Susie, and Susie smiled back, warmly, sweetly, and Tilly thought, in recognition of her concern.

'Mum, unless there's anything you want me to do, I thought we'd go over and see Mungo and Oliver,' said Rufus. 'Mungo's running out of positive thinking and wants to talk to Tilly and Oliver's in a very weird state apparently. His mother's totally freaked out and his dad's gone for a long walk.'

'How extremely sensible,' said Susie. 'About the best thing he could have done, I would think. If I was Josh I'd spend my whole life going for long walks. That woman is exceedingly irritating.'

'Fearfully glam though,' said Janet Beaumont, coming over to the table with four cracked mugs, a milk bottle and an exquisite silver teapot. 'Wish I had a figure like that. You have of course, Susie. Lucky you. How about some cake? Tilly, what about you?'

'Mustn't,' said Tilly, 'it looks delicious, though,' she added politely, eyeing the wonderfully solid, large iced chocolate cake on the dresser. 'Is Harry around? I'd love to see her.'

'Who?' said Susie. 'Oh, you mean Harriet. Yes, she's on her way over. So please wait for her, Rufus. Poor girl, she's worn out, trying to console her mother and keep calm herself. She's so fond of Cressida, of course.'

There was something about the 'of course' that struck Tilly rather forcibly; she looked at Susie sharply. But Susie was relaxed as she looked back at her, smiled her lovely, radiant smile.

'How well do you know Cressida?' she asked.

'Oh, not very well,' said Tilly. 'Harry's my friend. She was how I met Rufus.'

'Well, bully for Harry,' said Susie lightly. 'I have to say she is my favourite of those two girls, although of course one shouldn't be saying any such thing. Not that Cress isn't adorable, but Harriet has so much gumption. The way she's built up that business of hers, almost single-handed, I really do admire her. And she had a tough childhood – '

'Really?' said Tilly. She thought of her own childhood and wondered what tough meant to Susie Headleigh Drayton.

'Yes. Very tough. Sent off to that awful school when she was only nine – Janet dear, this is wonderful cake – '

'Glad you like it. I thought everyone would be hungry when we got back after the wedding. Oh dear – '

'Yes, well, we're all hungry before it,' said Rufus cheefully. 'So it hasn't been wasted. Yes, I'd forgotten Harriet was sent away. Didn't last long though, did it? Merlin rescued her, like a real wizard.'

'Yes, but if he hadn't . . . And I always thought it was so unfair that Cressida was allowed to stay at home. Still, Harriet always says now it was the making of her – '

'It probably was,' said Rufus. 'Look at all of us. Stuff the British Empire was made of – ' He winked at Tilly.

'Rufus darling, you know perfectly well none of you went away until you were thirteen. And Tom hasn't gone at all.'

'Yes, well, you spoil him. Your baby.'

'I do not,' said Susie serenely. 'I don't spoil any of you. Never have.'

'Maggie says you always spoiled me,' said Rufus. 'She said it at lunch yesterday, didn't you hear her?'

'Oh really?' For the first time she seemed less relaxed. 'I don't see that Maggie is in any position to know such a thing. Or to make such a judgment.'

'You know Maggie,' said Janet Beaumont, taking a second slice of cake. 'So tactless. Always speaks her mind. I do feel rather sorry for her though,' she added. 'She doesn't have an easy time.'

'She seems to have quite an easy time to me,' said Susie briskly. 'Neither of the girls at home, Jamie in London half the week, plenty of help – oh I know she's had the wedding to do, but – '

'Well I wouldn't like to be married to James Forrest,' said Janet.

'Really? Why not specially?' Susie's dark eyes were very brilliant suddenly. Now why should that be, thought Tilly, what is he to her? (feeling her own flesh crawl, her pulse quicken at the name).

'He's such a demanding creature. Everything in the house has to be perfect. Maggie was telling me he threw a terrific wobbly a couple of weeks ago because she still hadn't got the drawing-room carpet and curtains cleaned.'

'Doesn't sound too unreasonable to me,' said Susie lightly.

'I know, but there's always something. She has to run around after him, seeing to his clothes like some sort of valet. And you know how vain he is – '

'Is he?' said Rufus. 'I didn't know that.'

'Oh terribly. Mike teases him about it sometimes. That's my husband,' she added to Tilly.

'Yes, well no one could call Mike vain,' said Susie laughing. 'I doubt if he even knows where a single mirror is in this house. Alistair's quite vain as a matter of fact. If you call fussing about clothes vain. Still, I don't think Jamie's all that bad to live with. He's very good and supportive to Maggie, and frightfully good-tempered really – '

'Yes, well, you always see the best in people, and anyway he's got a bit of a soft spot for you,' said Janet winking at her.

'Rubbish!' said Susie cheerfully. 'No more than for any other pretty lady. Oh, there's Harriet's car now. Rufus, go and bring her in, give her a cup of tea.'

Tilly was sorry Harriet had arrived so soon; she could have sat listening to stories about James Forrest for a very long time.

Harriet came into the kitchen looking tired; she smiled round the table at them, and then went over and hugged Tilly.

'It's lovely to see you,' she said, 'thank you so much for coming.'

'Lovely to see you too,' said Tilly. She hadn't seen Harriet for three or four weeks; she looked terrible.

'How's your mother, Harriet dear?' asked Janet Beaumont, passing Harriet another cracked mug.

'Pretty bad,' said Harriet carefully. 'But Janine is doing wonders with her. I've told you about Janine, haven't I?' she said to Tilly. 'My wonderful French fairy godmother.'

'I thought she was Cressida's godmother,' said Janet.

'She is, her real one. But she and I have this secret code. She's always been so good to me. Don't tell Mummy for heaven's sake,' she added.

'No of course not.'

Maggie Forrest seemed to need a great deal of protection from life, Tilly thought; she wondered why.

'Anyway, there's some news about Cressida. Extraordinary news. No, she hasn't been found, but her car has. Somewhere in Essex, of all places. And, even more peculiar, she's got a pilot's licence. Nobody had the faintest idea. And she took a little plane from her flying school this morning, really early, and hasn't come back – '

'Good God,' said Susie, staring at her. 'Cressida! I can't believe she's capable of it. Not just learning to fly, but doing something like this. It's so calculated and – and tough, somehow. She's always seemed so sweet and – well, helpless. And what on earth is she doing taking flying lessons in Essex? it's such a long way away.'

'I know, I know,' said Harriet wearily. 'Anyway, Daddy's phoning round every little airport, and big one for that matter, in the country . . . '

'And abroad, presumably?' said Rufus.

'Yes. We thought at first she couldn't have gone abroad.'

'Why not?'

'Because Oliver's got her passport. Ready for going to Mexico today. But apparently she's got one of those post office jobs – the vicar saw her getting it.'

'Good God,' said Rufus. 'How absolutely extraordinary. You've spoken to Oliver presumably about this?'

'Yes. Yes of course. He had no idea she could fly. No idea at all. He's – well, he's very shocked.'

'Let's get over there,' said Rufus, standing up, taking Tilly's hand. 'Are you coming, Harriet?'

'Oh – are you going already? I was hoping to talk to Tilly.'

'You can talk to Tilly later,' said Rufus. 'I honestly think we should go and support poor old Mungo. And we both thought Tilly would be able to help.'

'I would have thought it was Oliver who needed the support,' said Susie. 'But anyway, yes, I'm sure they'll welcome you.'

'I – I think I'll stay here for a bit – if that would be all right, Janet,' said Harriet. Her voice was almost deathly quiet. 'I don't think I can face any more scenes.'

'Oh Harriet, please come,' said Rufus. 'I know it would help, and I'm sure Tilly would – '

'Rufus, leave poor Harriet alone, for heaven's sake,' said Susie. 'She's absolutely worn out. Harriet darling, you're very pale. I bet you haven't eaten anything all day. Why don't you have a sandwich or something?'

'No – really, I'm not hungry,' said Harriet. 'But thank you anyway. Lovely tea, Janet. I'll see you later, Tilly. Maybe back here or something. I'd ask you over to the Court House, but – ' Her voice trailed away.

'Oh I don't think that's a very good idea,' said Tilly quickly. 'Rufus can sort something out. You stay here, Harry, you look rotten. We can talk later. Come on, Rufus, let's go.'.

They drove over to Woodstock in Rufus's rather uncharacteristically flashy Porsche. Tilly suddenly felt desperately tired and slightly surreal; she had planned to talk to Rufus about the offer from Rosenthal amongst other things, but she drifted off instead into a strange half-waking, half-sleeping state. She woke in the courtyard of the Royal Hotel to see Sir Merlin's car parked next to an extremely large and beautiful Bentley. 'My

God,' she said, unwinding herself with difficulty from the confines of the Porsche. 'You lot do have a corner in good cars.'

'Yours isn't so bad,' said Rufus. 'Oh Tilly, it's nice to see you. I hope I've said that.'

'You haven't,' said Tilly, grinning at him, 'but I kind of took it for granted.'

'Good. I love you.'

'I love you too,' said Tilly, kissing him on the mouth, putting her arm through his.

'Have you thought any more about marrying me?'

'I've thought about it, yes.'

'And? What are you thinking?'

'Nothing very different,' said Tilly, kissing him gently again, 'just that I love you. But I have something else to talk to you about.' She smiled at him. 'Is Mr Buchan here? I hope so. He's really wild.'

'Theo? I'd forgotten you knew him. Now I feel jealous. Yes, I think so. He certainly was. Anyway, Mungo will know. What's the something else like?'

'Oh – business,' said Tilly. 'It can wait.'

Mungo and Oliver were in Mungo's room. Oliver was extremely drunk. He was still in his striped trousers and his white shirt; his fair hair was wild and his blue eyes were bleary, dark shadows etched heavily underneath them. A half-empty bottle of bourbon stood on the table by him.

'Hi,' he said, 'so good of you to come. Welcome to my bridal feast. Hallo, Tilly. Specially good of you. Long way from Paris.' He got up and went over to her, gave her a hug. She hugged him back. He smelt very strongly of bourbon and the extremely expensive aftershave he always wore. The mix wasn't exactly good, but it was very sexy. Oliver wasn't conventionally, overtly sexy, but there was a tension, a tautness about him that was very attractive, almost challenging, Tilly had thought the first time she met him. She had danced with him once, and felt that tension, felt it right through him, a physical thing, and she imagined then that once released it would have a power of its own, strong, possibly dangerous. She had considered (not having then met Rufus, fallen in love with him) working on it, on him, exploring him, the challenge had been as arousing as Oliver himself, and she'd stood still on the dance floor briefly, just looking at him, contemplating him and what his rather awkwardly moving body might do for her, and he had recognized it and stood still himself, looking back at her, and then pulled her to him, quite abruptly, and she felt his erection rising against her, felt his face against her neck, his lips on her ear, and a flood of quite extraordinary warmth had filled her, and she'd slithered one hand slowly down his back, towards his buttocks, and as it moved she felt the tension beneath it leaving him, easing, and his hand joined hers, echoing the charge in him, and he'd said, 'Tilly, you are just – just – ' and then the music had changed, grown faster, and she'd said laughing, 'What am I, Oliver, what am I?' And he'd stood back, and she'd watched him gather himself together again, look over at where Harriet was dancing with Mungo, and he said 'Gorgeous,' lightly, but carefully, and then 'Come on, let's get a drink.' And the others saw them going to the bar and joined them, and she had never been in a situation to explore him again. Now sharply she remembered and standing there, close to him, felt confused, almost embarrassed. She smiled at him, kissed him on the cheek.

'It was a long way,' she said, 'but it was worth it.'

'You haven't got Harriet with you?'

'No. She's at the Beaumonts'.'

'Ah. Well, do have a drink, all of you. Help yourselves. Mungo old chap, you do the honours. Tilly, what'll you have?'

'Diet Pepsi please,' said Tilly.

'Rufus, old man?'

'Oh – the same.'

'So she's up in the sky somewhere, then,' said Oliver. 'My bride. My beautiful bride. Oh God.'

'Yes,' said Rufus. 'Yes, so it seems. You had no idea she could fly?'

'None.'

'How odd. So unlike Cressida to have a secret like that.'

'Oh yes. Very unlike her.' He sounded bitter suddenly, angry. It was hardly surprising, Tilly supposed. Poor Oliver. Grief apart, the humiliation of this was fairly heavy. And he had one hell of an ego, Oliver. He was nice, he was clever, but he did have an attitude.

'Mind you,' said Rufus, 'she did surprise one now and again. Didn't she?'

They all looked at him.

'Did she?' said Mungo. 'I always thought you could read Cressida like a book.'

'Yes. A mystery book,' said Oliver and laughed shortly.

'What do you mean, Rufus?' said Mungo.

'Oh – nothing much. She just wasn't quite as straightforward as she seemed.'

'In what way? Give us a for-instance. You never know, it might help.'

'I'm sure it won't, but – well, for instance I never knew she could speak such perfect French.'

Mungo stared at him. 'She can't.'

'Yes she can.'

'Rufus, she can't. When she came to stay with my dad and me in Paris quite recently, it was embarrassing. She insisted on trying out some very schoolgirly stuff one night in a restaurant.'

'Well I'm sorry but she can. I've heard her.'

'When?'

'Well,' said Rufus, clearly enjoying the mild furore he was causing, 'she was in Paris visiting Harriet once, and I arrived in Harriet's flat and she was on the phone, I don't know who to, but it was about some money she was having transferred into a French bank or something. And she was absolutely fluent. A lot better than me.'

'Did you ask her about it?'

'Yes. She didn't know I was there at first – she was a bit embarrassed. Not about speaking French but about the conversation. I told her I hadn't taken any of it in, which was true really. I said I was impressed by her French and she said she'd just done a crash course, she'd always regretted not going on with it at school.'

'I see.' Mungo looked at him thoughtfully. 'How odd. Did you – did you mention it to Harriet?'

'No, Cress asked me not to. She said it was a bit of a sore subject, Harriet had always had trouble with the language and she'd cracked it so easily.'

'Oliver, did you know she could speak perfect French?'

'Not really. It wasn't the sort of thing we discussed,' said Oliver blearily.

'Oh well. You must have got things muddled, Mungo. Must have had dinner with her before she did the course.'

'Rufus, we had dinner with her about a month ago.'

'Well, she was obviusly fooling around. I can't think it's very important.'

'No. No, of course not. Tilly, do you know anything surprising about Cressida?'

'I don't know her well enough to be surprised by her. If you see what I mean,' said Tilly. 'I've only met her about three times. Twice in London and once in New York.'

'Oh yes, last Christmas? When she was staying with Oliver and we all had dinner?'

'Yeah. The only thing that ever surprised me was how different she was from Harriet. Not to look at so much, there was some kind of family look, but their personalities. It was hard to believe they were sisters.

Harry's so positive and independent and ambitious, and Cressida's so – gentle and feminine and all that stuff.'

'Everyone said that. Says that,' Rufus corrected himself. 'We mustn't start talking in the past. I'm sure she'll be back. Soon.'

'Yeah,' said Mungo. 'Of couse she will.'

'Oh yes, and there was something else,' said Tilly, 'something really surprising. I only learnt today. Sir Merlin told me. Did you know, I suppose you did, that she was really good at poker?'

'Poker! Cressida! Oh that's ridiculous,' said Mungo. 'I tried to teach her once. She gives everything away all the time, can't remember anything, doesn't concentrate – '

'Merlin said she was great. That she's planning to surprise. you.'

'Well she certainly will,' said Mungo. 'I'll believe it when I – '

Oliver suddenly stood up. 'Oh God,' he said, 'going to throw up,' and he rushed into the bathroom. They waited for a long time; in the end Tilly stood up and went in after him. He was sitting on the lavatory, his head in his hands. She sat on the edge of the bath, and stroked his hair gently.

'Oh Til,' he said, 'oh Tilly, what a frightful bloody mess.'

He looked up at her and his eyes were red; a tear rolled down one cheek. She reached out and stroked it away.

'Oliver, I'm not going to say anything stupid, like you mustn't worry. But you have to hang on in there. She'll be all right. I know she will.'

He shook his head, took both her hands, clung onto them. His eyes as he looked at her were tortured, agonized.

'No. No, I don't think she will be. And even if – oh God, Tilly, this is so terrible. So much more terrible than you can imagine even. I – '

He stopped, bit his lip. Tilly looked at him, waited.

'Yes? You what, Oliver?'

'Oh – nothing. Shit, I'm going to be sick again.'

Tilly stayed with him, held his head, fetched him some water. He sat down on the bath beside her, put his arm round her. 'You're a great girl, Tilly, he said, 'the best. Should be marrying you really. Only Rufus wouldn't like it.'

'Not too much,' said Tilly lightly. 'And anyway, it would be a terrible idea.'

'Well, thanks. You really know how to make a man feel better.'

'You know what I mean.'

'Yes, I suppose I do. I bet we'd have a good time in bed though.' He smiled at her, distracted just momentarily from his misery.

'Maybe. Oliver – ' Perhaps this wasn't the time to mention this morning, but Tilly believed in directness, in getting things said. 'Oliver, Rufus phoned me in Paris this morning. He said you were terribly upset, that – that you felt you couldn't go through with the wedding. You can tell me to take a running jump if you like, but – well, what was that about? I mean is there some kind of connection, do you think? I'm sorry, Oliver, if I shouldn't have mentioned it, but – well, what did you – '

Oliver stared at her; he looked first startled, then wary. 'Oh,' he said quickly, 'I didn't mean anything. Not really. Just nerves, wedding-day nerves. I'm sure lots of bridegrooms say things like that.'

'Yeah,' said Tilly. 'Yeah, I'm sure they do.' But most bridegrooms don't take an overdose, she thought, don't cry for help that loudly. Well, he clearly wasn't going to tell her. There was a silence. 'It's terribly hot in here,' she said. 'Why don't we go for a walk or something? Just you and me, Oliver?

'No,' said Oliver, 'I don't think so. Nice idea, Til, but I think I ought to stay by the phone.'

There was a knock on the door. It was Mungo. 'OK, Oliver?'

'He's fine. I was just trying to persuade him to come for a walk with me, but he says he ought to stay by the phone.'

'You can take my mobile,' said Mungo. 'I think it's a really good idea. You have a chat with Tilly, and we'll ring you if there's any news at all. Anyway, you don't have to go far.'

He was clearly desperate for a break, Tilly thought. She stood up, held out her hand to Oliver.

'Come on. I'm not used to being turned down. I might get difficult.'

'God forbid,' said Oliver, and for the first time he smiled. 'OK. We'll go. Thanks, Tilly. Thanks, Mungo. For everything. You've been one hell of a best man, you know that? You too, Rufus.' He smiled at them all weakly, and followed Tilly out of the room.

As they walked out of the front door of the hotel, a Jaguar pulled into the drive.

'Christ,' said Oliver, 'it's James Forrest. I wonder if there's any news.'

'Oh God,' said Tilly. She stood quite still, staring at the car, at the shadowy figure inside it. Her heart was thudding so hard she felt it might break right through her ribs; she felt sick and very hot, and at the same time oddly clammy, as if she might faint. It had happened, finally: she was going to come face to face with this man who had wrecked her mother's life, as good as murdered her baby, greatly damaged her physical and mental health, and deprived Tilly herself of a twin sister – and had refused to make any recompense for any of it. God, how was she going to deal with it, what was she going to say?

And then he got out of the car, James Forrest, and walked towards them slowly, and she could see he recognized her, knew who she was, and was as totally thrown, as horrified as she. But any anxieties about what she might say or do were swept away as Tilly stared into his face. At a set of features so familiar to her she could scarcely believe she was looking at them on a different person, at a head of thick wavy hair that despite being more grey than fair was instantly recognizable, at a way of moving – slowly, almost carefully – that was one she knew, had studied tenderly, lovingly, at a body that was tall, narrow-hipped (despite a burgeoning paunch), but with surprisingly broad shoulders. Only the eyes were different, blue not brown, but otherwise, God, God Almighty, how could anyone not see it, the almost astonishing resemblance? Presumably it had always been there, developing so slowly no one had taken it in – and as she stood there, staring, drinking him in, her enemy, learning who he really was, she knew with a rush of sadness and something close to rage that even setting aside all her other reasons she could never ever marry Rufus now.

Chapter Twelve

Susie 2.30pm

Susie decided not to say anything to Alistair that day, about her breast, her conversation with Mr Hobson: there was enough drama, enough crisis going on. There would be plenty of time tomorrow. In any case she didn't know quite what she was going to say, not until she had spoken to James. But she longed to talk to James, more than she ever had in her life, to lay her fear and her misery on him, to ask his advice, to draw on his strength. Until she had done that, she would wait, head in sand.

Anyway, Alistair had always hated scenes, emotion, conflict. It was one of the reasons Susie had married him. Partly because she hated them too, partly because she knew he would never become overanalytical about their marriage. A marriage to someone she didn't love Susie could handle (especially when the someone was charming, rich, civilized and clever). Having that marriage and its foundations examined, queried, fretted over, she could not

Alistair had left that afternoon, just after two. 'Darling, of course you must go,' Susie said. 'No earthly point you being here in the middle of this nightmare, there's absolutely nothing you can do, and you'll be much much happier back at your desk.'

'Well, that's certainly true. I must say this has revised my view that nothing could be worse than a wedding. There not being a wedding. Where do you think the silly girl's gone?'

'God knows,' said Susie with a sigh. 'I just hope she's all right. One hears such awful things and Cressida is so trusting and sweet. I fear for her, I really do.'

'I think she's well able to take care of herself actually,' said Alistair.

'That sounds interesting. Why do you think that?'

'Oh – nothing really.'

'Alistair! You can't do this to me. What is it?'

'Well – I've never told you this. Didn't seem very important. But I was once dancing with her, you remember, that terrible New Year thing we were all at, at Hurlingham, and she came on very strong at me. Tried to dance me out of the ballroom.'

'Alistair! You must have been drunk.'

'Susie, you know I never get drunk.' That was true; he didn't. 'She was, though. Extremely.'

'And?'

'And I just gently disentangled myself. Took her back to the table.'

'Was she upset?'

'No,' said Alistair briefly. 'She was furious.'

Susie saw him out to his car. 'I expect I'll be up later, but it may not be till tomorrow. Would that be all right?'

'Yes of course. As long as you keep the children down here. I really don't want to have to worry about Annabel.'

'You don't have to worry about Annabel, I promise,' said Susie, kissing him. 'Anyway, she's still hoping to make an impression on Mungo Buchan. So she'll be more than happy to stay.'

'I hope she's not successful,' said Alistair, plainly alarmed at the prospect. 'That boy is serious trouble.'

'He isn't actually, but you don't have to worry. There's no danger of him taking any notice of Annabel. I happen to know he has a perfectly lovely girlfriend somewhere who is fortunate enough not to have been asked to this nightmare, and he can't wait to get back to her. So Rufus tells me anyway. Annabel may seem very lovely to you and me, but to Mungo she's a very immature, slightly overweight schoolgirl. Incidentally you didn't really tell her you'd buy her a car as soon as she passed her test, did you?'

'No, of course not. I wouldn't unleash that child out on the roads with a shopping trolley.'

'I thought not. Only she implied it was on the delivery truck now, just round the corner from the house, unless I was evil enough to send it away. Anyway, you get back up to London, and don't worry about anything here. And I do assure you, your family is safe from the Buchans, my darling.'

'Even my wife?'

'Alistair! Have you not studied the lovely Sasha? Sex on legs, and Theo is mad about her. And they've been married less than a year.'

'She seems very stupid,' said Alistair cheerfully, throwing his leather Gladstone into the boot of the Jaguar. 'I don't give it more than another year. At the most.'

'I fear you may be right. It would be so nice to see Theo properly settled. These bimbos are all very well, but he needs something a bit more – substantial.'

'Sasha seems quite substantial to me. Especially in the pectoral area.'

'You know I don't mean physically. I just wish he could find another Deirdre. The one real love of his life.'

'Only because she died.'

'Alistair!'

'I'm sorry, darling, but it's true. I can't help my incisive legal mind. If Deirdre had lived, Theo would have been fooling around within the year. You know he would.'

'Well – I *don't* know actually. I think I take a slightly more benign view of Theo than you do. Anyway, there's nothing we can do to help him, I'm afraid.'

'No, he's beyond help,' said Alistair. 'Well, my darling, I'm off. How will you get back to London?'

'In Rufus's car.'

'Oh yes of course. What's the superstar girlfriend like? Wish I hadn't missed her.'

'Glorious.'

'Well I know that. I've seen her pictures.'

'No, but she's intelligent and funny too. I really liked her.'

'Do you think they'll get married?'

'Oh no,' said Susie coolly, opening the car door for him. 'Definitely not. They couldn't.'

'Why not?'

'Oh – it just wouldn't work.'

'Pity. Bit of exotica in the family might have been nice. Bye, darling.'

'Bye, Alistair.'

He kissed her fondly, patted her neat, well-exercised backside and climbed into the car. Susie waved him off, smiling, and then went back rather wearily into the house. She was stunned by the swift, almost cataclysmic change the news from Mr Hobson had wrought in her feelings about everything. Including Alistair, including her marriage. Until today, she had been very clear about it all. Alistair was a dear, sweet man, whom she was extremely fond of and with whom she got along extremely well. As a marriage it had seemed very near perfect. She had always wondered why people got so worked up about being in love with the person they married. Alistair had the occasional affair – he was probably off to see his latest girlfriend now, a little bonus of time Cressida had provided him with, so some good had come of this fiasco – and she had Jamie and no harm had been done to anyone. (Not, she was fairly sure, that Alistair knew about Jamie, and certainly, most certainly, not about Rufus.) It had all worked perfectly, and she had known as surely as she had known her own name that it was an infinitely more practical arrangement than the other way, endless misery and tears and divorce.

She and Alistair would no more have thought of getting divorced than – Susie struggled for something sufficiently unlikely – than moving to the country. They would agree – had they ever discussed it, which they had not – that divorce would be disagreeable, disruptive and extremely expensive. Marriage was a business arrangement, and as long as both parties adhered to the original principles, the business thrived. The French knew that; French marriages had always been based on the principle of convenience.

But now, today, she felt completely differently. She needed Jamie, because she loved him, she needed to be with him, she needed them to be a couple, a strong united force, she needed his support, his overt support, not the rather vague intangible awareness of it buried deep within herself and her life. She needed to wake up with him and to go to sleep with him, she needed to have a home with him, to be recognized as his wife, as the woman he loved. It was the only way she could survive, survive the pain and the fear and the prospect of the awful, final separation. The children might be upset, Maggie might be deeply wounded, but they would survive. They were strong, they were whole, healthy people who were not going to die. If they didn't like it, she thought, then that was absolutely their problem. She did not, could not care. The time had come for selfishness. She wanted to be with the person she loved.

She wondered suddenly if that might have been why Cressida had run away: thinking that she didn't love Oliver enough, or that he didn't love her. I should have made an effort to spend some time with her, she thought to herself, over the past few weeks, maybe she needed a confidante, some reassurance, she was such a romantic, naive little thing. She and Cressida had always been able to talk, and enjoyed one another's company, and Maggie was so neurotic and hopeless, no use at all in such a situation.

Then she remembered what Alistair had said about Cressida making a pass at him at the dance, and she reflected that perhaps Cressida was not quite so romantic and naive after all . . .

'Susie dear,' said Janet, as she went into the kitchen. 'That was Janine on the phone. She said could you perhaps go over there, take over for a bit, she's absolutely exhausted, and Jamie's disappeared somewhere. I must say that's a bit bad of him, but – '

'He's probably gone to see the police or something,' said Susie. 'Anyway, if I was Jamie today I think I'd have disappeared by now. Yes, of course I'll go over.' God, that was all she needed, feeling as she did, having to comfort and cheer Maggie. 'Is Janine still on the phone?'

'Yes.'

'Janine, hi. How are things?'

'Not fun,' said Janine. 'Jamie has been trying to persuade Maggie to take something, just to calm her down, but she won't. She veers between hysteria and terrible deadly silence. I'm running out of smoke, I'm afraid.'

'Steam, darling, steam,' said Susie. 'All right, I'll come over. You've earned a break. I'll have to borrow a car.'

'I'll come with you.' Harriet's voice was behind her. 'I've got my car here.'

'Oh – all right, darling. Thank you. The cavalry's on its way, Janine.'

Harriet looked rotten, Susie thought. Well, it was hardly surprising. She'd taken a great deal today. Poor little thing. She was so fond of Cressida. Always been the big sister, looked after her, protected her.

'You all right to drive, poppet?' she asked as Harriet swung her Peugeot 205 away from the Beaumonts' house.

'Yes, I think so,' said Harriet. 'What a bitch of a day.'

She braked suddenly, switched off the engine and burst into tears. It was extraordinarily out of character; she never cried.

'Oh sweetie,' said Susie, putting her arm round her. 'Darling Harriet, you cry. You need that. You must feel so terrible.'

'I do,' said Harriet. 'Absolutely terrible.'

'It's so – harsh somehow. So sudden. And Cressida of all people. So well behaved, so – perfect. Everyone loving her, wanting her to be happy.'

'That's Cressida,' said Harriet. 'Well behaved. Perfect. Everyone loving her.' Her voice sounded dead, almost bitter. Susie looked at her sharply.

'Sorry,' said Harriet, lightening her voice with a clear effort. 'I'm so sorry. I'm upset, Susie, I didn't mean anything.'

'You sounded as if you did.'

'No, honestly. It's – well – I just don't know what to do.'

'Of course you don't, darling. None of us do.'

'No, but –' She slumped back in her seat and looked at Susie. Her eyes were very dark, very shadowed.

'Harriet, has something happened? Something new? That you haven't told us.'

'Oh – well, yes and no,' said Harriet with a sigh.

'Want to tell me about it? I promise not to pass it on,' she added, 'I'm very good at keeping secrets.'

'Are you?' Harriet looked at her, seemed to be trying to decide something. 'Yes, I expect you are.'

If only you knew, thought Susie, and thank God you don't.

'Tell me,' she said, 'I might be able to help.'

'I don't think so,' said Harriet, bleakly. 'Not unless you could give me a couple of million pounds.'

'Ah,' said Susie. 'Possibly not. It's the business, is it?'

'Yup,' said Harriet briefly. She sighed. 'I've got myself into the most filthy mess, Susie. Mostly through my own arrogance. Wouldn't listen, wouldn't take advice. And now – oh Susie, you can't begin to imagine.'

And Susie sat there, listening sadly, sorrowfully, to the quintessential nineties story, of overexpansion, high interest rates, lower profits. Harriet had overexpanded, mostly in France: her little shop in Passy making a fortune, she had bought the right to a lease on another – 'the most beautiful shop, in the rue du Bac, right by the Conran shop it was, and I looked at it and it was perfect. Loads of people pouring past every day, the very chic-est area, and terribly expensive. But I could just see it, my clothes in it, my name over the door, the interior all done out in my lovely silver and white, and I wanted it. I had to have it.'

'Well, it doesn't sound too silly, so far,' said Susie gently. 'Good sites are what good business is all about.'

'Yes and no,' said Harriet, blowing her nose. 'I mean you're right, but that wasn't actually what it was about. Not a shop, not a site at all, Susie, it was about my bloody fucking ego – sorry – '

'That's all right, darling.'

'I have to be so important, you know, have to have everyone looking at me. I mean what was wrong with the dear little shop in Passy? Nothing, nothing at all, except it wasn't big-time stuff. And I wanted to be big-time. To get my name on the fashion pages, be one of the in-crowd. I mean what a pathetic, pitiful ambition. God, I'm ashamed of myself. And it was so much money, that lease. You know how it works in Paris, you buy the right to rent a place. Two million francs it cost me, only it wasn't me, it was – oh shit, Susie, I'm so ashamed of myself.'

'Who was it?' asked Susie quietly.

'It was Janine. Darling Janine, who's been there for me all my life. She insisted I took it, said she wanted to help. It's a lot of money, you know, it's – '

'Yes, I know, it's two hundred thousand pounds, give or take a bit. Well I'm sure she could afford it if she offered it.'

'No she couldn't. Not easily, anyway, not so it didn't matter if she lost it. I mean of course it was a loan, and I'm paying her interst, well I was, but lower than the bank would take. But it's gone, Susie, all of it. The shop never even broke even, and then I remortgaged the shop in Covent Garden, just to keep it open, and you know how big the turnover on that one is, and even that didn't support the loan. I really, really should have listened to Rufus, he said right from the beginning – '

'Rufus?' said Sue sharply. 'What does Rufus have to do with it?'

'He told me I should get a proper business adviser, rather than just Johno – '

'Who's Johno?'

'He's my accountant. Has been right from the beginning. And he's sweet and lovely and clever, but he just isn't up to all this stuff. Rufus even had someone in mind for me, someone he knows. But no, I had to know best, had to be able to manage. I wasn't satisfied with being a good designer, I had to be a brilliant businesswoman as well, Jean Muir and Anita Roddick rolled into one. Someone actually wrote that about me in an article a few months ago, well, not quite that, but said I had the makings of one. No doubt there'll be plenty now saying that I haven't.'

'Harriet darling,' said Susie, 'you really mustn't be quite so hard on yourself. You've done so well, and everyone makes mistakes. And I can't believe that just a little bit of overextending could really bring your whole business down. I mean you have lots of shops, surely – '

'Susie, don't. Yes, there are other shops, other Harry's. But none of them are actually making real money any more. Oh, the turnover's fine, but they mostly just about break even. And this is pack-of-cards stuff. It's all going to come tumbling down very very fast. I certainly can't sustain this debt. And I'm going to look such a fool, and I have to get rid of all those lovely girls. You know Ellie, in Covent Garden, she's worked for three weeks now without money, because she believed in me, and now what do I say to her? Sorry Ellie, sweet of you. Here's your reward, one P45 and the directions to the DHSS. But it's Janine, that is absolutely the worst thing, I mean she's quite an old lady now, she's going to need that money, and – oh Susie, what am I going to do?'

'Well,' said Susie briskly. 'I don't know exactly, but sitting and sobbing and berating yourself certainly isn't going to help anyone, least of all Janine. Listen, Harriet, Janine is a very wise, very worldly woman. I can't believe she would have lent you that sort of money if she hadn't been ready to risk losing it. I'm amazed she's got it, but that's beside the point. And I'm also sure she didn't just give it to you without a second thought, I mean presumably she saw some kind of business plan – '

'Well – yes she did. But it was a bit amateurish and optimistic. I – well, I was so sure, so confident. I just made certain it was all presented in a very positive way. Rounded figures up, that sort of thing. Not much, don't look at me like that, only a few thousand here and there. But enough to be just that bit more persuasive. And then I threw my flat into the ring. As surety.'

'Well then,' said Susie, surprised to find how relieved she was, 'that's all right. You can still sell it. I don't see what you're so upset about. Of course it will be sad, it's a lovely flat, but – '

'Susie, it's worthless. In cash terms. You see before you an outstanding example of negative equity. I bought my flat at the height of the boom, knew it was desperately overpriced, but there I was, flying along, got a ninety-five per cent mortgage. It's worth about – oh, I don't know, sixty per cent of what it was.'

'Ah,' said Susie quietly. 'Ah, I see.'

'So – Harry's goes into liquidation. Tomorrow, actually. I was blocking it out of my brain, not thinking about it until after the wedding. And now there's no wedding.'

'Can't you find someone to buy the business?'

'It isn't easy. Have you noticed how many shops are empty in so many high streets at the moment? Half South Molton Street even is for sale. But yes, I have tried. I've done so many presentations, I go into my spiel in my sleep. Twice I thought I'd done it, been saved, and then at the last moment they pulled the plug on me. Trotting out the usual platitudes about return on equity, too much long-term investment needed.'

'How – how much are you prepared to give away?' said Susie, trying to sound as tactful as possible.

'A lot,' said Harriet. 'I know what you're saying, but honestly, Susie, I'd lost most of my pride. At first of course I wanted to keep control, have it all my way, but I'd long since stopped that. My only condition in the end was the final word on design, when my name was literally on the line. Which is fair enough. I mean I wasn't going to have some purple lurex number with "Harry's" stitched into it. And I'd almost got to the point where I'd have given way on that. But it still wasn't working. There was just one last hope, a guy called Cotton. You may have heard of Cotton Fields? Nice clothes. Cheap and cheerful, but nice.'

'Yes of course,' said Susie. 'Annabel buys quite a lot of them.'

'Well, there you are. I'd have gone in with him quite happily. He's American. His head office is in New York. Anyway, I really thought he was going to make me an offer – not huge, but enough. I'd been really, really honest with him, told him all the problems, but he still wanted to buy. I thought. We were down to the small print. And then he backed off. Much as the others did. Yesterday, actually. He sent me a fax saying he wasn't interested after all, and when I tried to ring him, to talk about it, right up to about midnight, his secretary just kept telling me he was in meetings.'

'Well,' said Susie, 'that does sound strange. But maybe if he was reading the small print, rather than just writing it – '

'Yes,' said Harriet. 'I know. Anyway, I can't do anything about it. That's it. Finito.' She smiled a slightly wobbly smile at Susie. 'I'm so sorry, Susie. To burden you with this. But you did ask – '

'I know, darling. And I'm glad you did. I wish to God I could help. But the only person I know with that sort of money is Theo. I suppose you couldn't – '

'No,' said Harriet quickly. 'No I couldn't. Not possibly.'

'He's very fond of you. I'm sure he'd like to help.'

'Well – I just can't. It's too – close to home. I might ask him for Janine's money, if I absolutely had to, but nothing else.'

'Oh well. That's your decision. It's nothing to do with me. Now look, I'll have a think about all this, and if you'll let me, maybe ask Alistair if he knows anyone who might be able to help. He really does know every investor in town.'

'Susie, it's sweet of you, but I honestly do think I've turned over every possible stone – '

'I bet you haven't,' said Susie, 'and it's surely worth giving it just another couple of days. Now look, we really have to get over to your mother and relieve poor Janine. She's at the end of her tether. Would you like me to drive?'

'No, I'm fine,' said Harriet. 'And thank you for listening.'

There were an awful lot of tethers being stretched that day, thought Susie, as she lay back slightly wearily in her seat. Her own felt pretty taut. Now that she knew there was a reason for her constant tiredness, she felt suddenly, sharply worse. While she had first assumed and then hoped she was simply feeling her age, and fighting it with her usual blithe determination, it had seemed merely a nuisance, a slight brake on her activities. Since it had become something different, a painful, heavy reality, she was finding it already harder to handle; her head, she acknowledged, actually ached, and so did the small of her back, and what she wanted more than anything was to close her eyes, to shut out the dazzling flashing light of the afternoon, to give in, just for a moment, to rest.

'Go on, Susie,' came Harriet's voice, half amused, half gentle. 'Take a nap. You've earned it.'

'I can't stand people who take naps,' said Susie.

'Nor can I. But you do look absolutely rotten.'

'Thanks a lot.'

'Sorry.'

'That's OK,' said Susie, smiling at her. 'I know you meant it kindly. But I'd rather chat.' She was intrigued still by Harriet's tone when

163

she'd said 'Everyone loves Cressida'; she was hoping to lead her back to that.

'How did you like Tilly?' said Harriet.

'I loved Tilly.'

'So does Rufus.'

'So I understand.'

'You know he wants to marry her?'

'Yes, I do.'

'And?

'And I think that's – fine. If it happens.'

'But you don't think it will?' Harriet's voice was gently insistent.

'Harriet, I don't know. Let's say their lives are very different. I don't want Rufus hurt.'

'Well,' said Harriet. 'I know. I know what you're saying. And I don't want him hurt either. He's just one of the loveliest people I know.'

'I think so too,' said Susie, smiling at her again. 'But then I would.'

And then she did close her eyes, remembering briefly, fiercely, how nearly Rufus had not been born at all.

★

They had agreed she should have an abortion. It was the only thing they could possibly do. There was no way Susie could bear James's child – and she knew it was his child, Alistair had been away most of the month and certainly at the time of conception, and her hormones ran with clocklike regularity – Alistair would quite possibly work it out, Maggie would come to hear of it, there would be at best dreadful recriminations, anger, ugliness, at worst divorce. They both had children already: Harriet was two, Lucy one. It was unthinkable they should put all that at risk.

James had arranged the whole thing, had booked her into a nursing home somewhere near Luton.

'Luton, Jamie, why Luton? It's the most terrible place,' Susie said, when he told her. She was hanging on, with great difficulty, to her sense of humour.

'I thought you were unlikely to know anyone there,' he said rather helplessly. 'You can't go very far out of London, and central London would be dangerous. I'm sorry. Anyway, what does it matter?'

'It doesn't,' she said, trying to smile. 'Of course it doesn't. I'll go even to Luton for you, Jamie, don't worry.'

'How do you feel?'

'I feel fine,' she said. 'Pregnancy suits me. I felt wonderful with Lucy.'

'You would,' he said morosely, 'you bloody well would feel wonderful. Maggie was sick every single day.'

164

'Yes, well, I think we'd best not talk about Maggie. Under the circumstances.'

'Sorry.'

'I'd better go now,' she said, looking at her watch. 'Bathtime beckons. Nanny's night off.'

'Good luck, darling. I love you.'

'I love you too, Jamie.'

She couldn't think how she could possibly still love him. After all he had done to her. But she did. When they had met for the first time after their respective weddings, innocently, at a drinks party, she had felt quite faint with longing for him. And hatred. He had smiled at her across the room, come over to her, and she had stood there, just staring at him, refusing even to speak.

'You look lovely,' he said, 'quite lovely.'

She was silent. 'I miss you,' he said, 'I really miss you.'

Susie raised her eyebrows, took another sip of champagne.

'How is Alistair?'

'He's very well. As you see.'

'Doing well?'

'Of course.'

'Good. Aren't you going to ask if I'm doing well?'

'No,' she said, and there was such suppressed fury in her voice that he looked round nervously, fearing Maggie, Alistair – anyone could have heard. 'No I'm not. Of course you're doing well. You would be, wouldn't you? You married to do well.'

'Susie, don't – '

'Oh fuck off,' she said quietly and turned away, went to join Alistair. She slipped her arm through his, smiled up at him, looked over her shoulder at James standing there, alone, and she wanted him so much, loved him so desperately she could scarcely believe she could feel it at the same time as the hatred.

The next day he phoned her. 'I just wanted to say I was sorry.'

'For what, James? For not marrying me? For marrying Maggie? For being such a bastard. Could you expand a little, please?'

'All of those things,' he said. 'But really for upsetting you yesterday.'

'Yes, well. Don't do it again.' But she could hear her voice lighten, ease, hating it for doing so. 'Goodbye, James.'

Three months later, they met again. At a charity ball. Fate in the form of Janet Beaumont had put them at the same table. Susie was pregnant.

'I'm pregnant,' she said to James.

'Congratulations. Alistair must be very pleased.'

'Yes he is. I hear you have a daughter.'

'Yes indeed. Sweet little thing. Would you like to dance?'

'No. No thank you.'

But later Alistair was dancing with someone else and she was alone at the table; he came over. 'Come along, one dance won't hurt you.'

But it did.

She stood in his arms, felt him, smelt him, wanted him.

'You don't feel very pregnant,' he said.

'Well I'm not very pregnant. Only five months.'

'You don't look more than five days.'

'Yes, well, I've been working at it.'

'You would,' he said.

Maggie thought she was lovely, James said; wanted to ask her to dinner.

'You mustn't let her.'

'How can I stop her?'

'We won't come.'

'Darling, I see we've been invited to the Forrests' for New Year's Eve. Might be fun. I like James.'

'Really?'

'Yes, don't you?'

'No, not much.'

'Well, I'd like to go. The Beaumonts will be there, and he was saying he had a big land-law case coming up, looking for advice. It's a field that interests me.'

'Alistair, do we have to? I feel so enormous and I'd rather stay at home.'

'I'd rather you didn't.'

When it came to his career Alistair was ruthless. Like James, she thought to herself.

She arrived at the party feeling odd. She was eight months pregnant, she was tired, she was edgy. She found it hard to sparkle.

Halfway through the evening she started having contractions. Sure they were nothing, she found a room and lay down on the floor, doing her relaxing exercises. The pain got worse.

The room happened to be James's study; he came in and found her there.

'What on earth are you doing?'

'Having a baby,' said Susie through gritted teeth.

He was concerned, professional, soothing. He felt her tummy, listened to the baby's heartbeat, timed a couple of contractions and phoned the local hospital. He drove her over himself, relaxed, cheerful, cheering. She was shivery, said she wanted to push; he told her to pant and to hang on. Alistair sat in the back of the car, panicking.

At the hospital James found a wheelchair, pushed her through reception towards the labour ward himself. 'She's in transition,' he said calmly to the nurse. 'Get a delivery room ready. The baby's premature.' Alistair had disappeared.

Through her pain, her fear, her confusion, he was there: level, steady, reassuring.

'You'll be fine,' he kept saying, 'and the baby will be fine. Just hang on. Hang on to me. Hold my hand.'

They reached the delivery room; three nurses were ready, eager to serve the great god, the consultant.

James helped them lift her onto the bed. He bent over her, smiled into her eyes. 'Yell if you want to,' he said, 'no one will mind.'

'No,' said Susie, clenching her fists. 'I don't approve of making a fuss. Just don't go away, that's all.'

'I won't,' he said, smiling down at her again, 'I won't,' and in spite of everything she saw the humour in the situation, smiled back.

And so it was that when Susie Headleigh Drayton gave birth to her first baby, James Forrest was there with her.

After that it was hopeless really. He saw her through the two desperate days after the birth when the tiny four-pound Lucy struggled to survive. He wheeled her down himself to the prem unit when the baby was out of danger, so that she might sit with her. He dried her eyes when she wept with third-day blues, and he laughed at her discomfiture when the milk arrived and leaked all over her nightie.

'Don't laugh,' she said crossly. 'It's not very pretty.'

'It's quite nice, Susie, to see you out of control just for once, even if only of your boobs.'

She scowled at him, then smiled.

'I love you,' he said gently and bent and kissed her forehead.

Alistair had gone back to London.

Two months later they were lunching regularly, a month after that they were in bed. It was wonderful. Susie thought she had never been so happy.

'A lovely baby, a sweet husband and you,' she said one afternoon after some particularly good sex. 'What more could I ask?'

James turned away from her.

'What's the matter?'

'That wasn't the most tactful thing you could have said. At such a time.'

'Jamie,' said Susie, propping herself up on her elbow, fixing her dark eyes on him, 'Jamie, I really don't think you have any right to complain about my being tactless. You've got a pretty good deal, it seems to me. Don't knock it.'

'I can't help it,' he said, 'You're so fucking – pragmatic.'

'And I can't help that,' she said, bending over, kissing his shoulder, 'it's what I'm all about, pragmatisim. Be grateful. I might just be pragmatic, without the fucking.'

And then she got pregnant. With James's baby. While Alistair had been away in the north of England.

'I don't see how it could have happened,' he said fretfully. 'You're on the pill – '

'Yes, I know, James, but I had a tummy upset that week. Quite a bad one. It must have cancelled out the pill or whatever – '

'You should have mentioned it.'

'Oh don't be ridiculous.'

'I'm not being ridiculous. What are we going to do?'

'I don't know, Jamie. You tell me.'

She drove herself to the nursing home; she had insisted on it.

'I want to be by myself, completely by myself. I'll be fine by tomorrow.'

'What have you told Alistair?'

'That I'm staying with Mummy.'

'And what have you told Mummy?'

'That I'm going to a health farm for forty-eight hours, and I don't want Alistair to know. He genuinely doesn't approve of them. Luckily.'

'And does Mummy believe you?'

'Mummy's like me. She's a pragmatist. Anyway, she's fielding phone calls. Don't worry, Jamie, it'll all be fine.'

The nursing home was a large mock-tudor house just outside Luton. The staff were polite, efficient, detached.

'Here's your room, Mrs – Henderson. Perhaps you'll get undressed for me, and then Doctor will come and examine you.'

Susie undressed, got into bed. A nurse shaved her pudenda, gave her an enema. It was horrible. She felt very odd, light-headed, slightly sick.

Doctor was an iron-grey man with a sickly manner.

'Mrs Henderson. Good morning. What a cold one. I'm Brian Miller. Now if I can just – '

He smiled rather condescendingly at her when he had finished. 'Yes. About eleven weeks. Just in time. Have you had anything by mouth this morning?'

Susie shook her head.

'Good. All over by lunchtime then. Your doctor is quite right, much too soon for you to be having another baby, you're still not fully recovered from the last one. Now you won't know anything about it, of course, you'll need a very light anaesthetic and you'll be in theatre for about twenty minutes. A simple D and C. You know what that is?'

'No,' said Susie. She did, but for some reason she wanted to hear it.

'Dilatation and curettage.' He looked a little impatient.

'I understand dilatation, but what's curettage?'

'Well – the strict definition is a scraping. To remove tissue. And – er – any growths.'

'Oh,' said Susie. She pulled the sheet up higher over her body. 'Yes I see.'

'Right then.' He picked up his notes. 'Any more questions?'

'No. No, I don't think so.'

'Good. Well, I'll pop in and see you afterwards. When it's all over. Nurse will be in to give you your pre-med in a little while.'

Susie lay there, trying not to think. The phone by her bed rang.

'Darling? It's me.'

'Oh – Jamie. Hallo.'

'Are you all right?'

'Yes. Yes, I think so.'

'He's a very, very good chap, Miller. You really don't have to worry.'

'I don't?'

'No.'

'Good.'

'I love you, Susie. I'll ring you later.'

'All right, Jamie.'

She lay there and thought about her baby. Hers and James's baby. Conceived in a moment of such fierce, flying, tearing rapture there was a physical remembrance of it; her body stirred at it even now. And it was still there, the rapture. It had become something real, something living, had not just passed away into nothingness. She had it within her, she surrounded it; it was hers.

She thought of it, what it was to her in truth: not a cluster of cells, not even the strange primeval being she knew it to be, but an embodiment of happiness, of pleasure, of love.

The nurse came in. 'Right, Mrs Henderson, ready for your pre-med?'

'Oh – yes.' She put on the hospital gown, open at the back, the paper hat, surrendered her rings.

'Just pop onto your side for me then.'

Susie rolled obediently onto her side, felt the needle jab into her buttocks. The nurse dabbed at it with a swab, smiled at her distantly.

'We'll be back for you soon then. Have a little sleep, I would.'

No you wouldn't, you silly bitch, thought Susie, you wouldn't at all, you'd lie here, like I am, thinking of what you were doing, what you were allowing them to do. To dilate you, to open you up, and then to – what was the word he had used? – oh yes, scrape, scrape away this baby, this little living thing, that she knew, she knew although she had tried not to think about it, who already had a head, eyes, hands, feet. Christ, she must stop this, stop thinking of the sweet smiling blunt foetus-face that she had seen so many pictures of, stop thinking of what she was doing to it, killing it, dragging it from the snug, safe darkness of her womb into the light and then – what? What did they do, what did they do to these babies, these little tiny half-people, how did they get rid – No, Susie, don't, you mustn't, it's only a few cells, only a dot, don't think about it, don't, don't, don't, you have to go through with this, you have to.

The door opened. A porter came in with a trolley, the nurse helped her onto it. She felt dizzy, confused, far away from them. They began to wheel her down the corridor. She felt panicky suddenly, sick, frightened of what was going to happen.

She closed her eyes; the corridor spun. Oh God, this was horrible, horrible. 'I feel sick,' she said.

'Don't worry,' said the nurse. 'It'll pass in a moment.'

She was pushed into the anteroom of the theatre; Dr Miller was there.

'Ah, Mrs Henderson. All right?'

'No,' croaked Susie. Her lips were very dry, she was having trouble framing her words.

'You will be soon.' He smiled at her, patted her hand.

Yes, she thought, I will be. But *it* won't. My baby won't. It won't be a baby any more. It won't be anything.

'Right,' he said, 'right, Nurse. Let's get this good lady into the theatre, shall we?' He had his needle poised; he was smiling at her, his awful steely sickly smile. 'Now, when I've given you this injection, Mrs Henderson, I want you to count for me.' Susie nodded feebly. She would count, and the baby would be gone. One, two, three, bye-bye, baby. Oh God, it was horrible. Horrible. Why did she have to do this? Why had she ever agreed?

'Right.' He rubbed a swab over her hand. 'Ready? Now remember, count for me, one, two – '

'No!' she screamed, managed to find the strength to sit up, thrust his hand and the needle away. 'No, no, no. Don't do it. I don't want you to do it. Stop. I forbid it. Stop.'

'Now, Mrs Henderson. Don't be silly – ' The nurse looked alarmed, tried to push her down again.

'Come along, Mrs Henderson. This isn't very sensible, is it? You wanted this, it's much for the best. Now let me – '

'No. I said no.' She was lying down now, hanging onto the sides of the trolley to try and stop the dizziness, but she was totally awake. 'Don't. Don't you dare. I shall sue if you do. I don't want you to. I forbid it. It's my body, my baby. You are not to. Take me back to my room, at once. At once.'

'Dr Miller, I think perhaps – ' The nurse was looking uncomfortable. Miller looked at her, and Susie thought she had never seen such distaste, such cold fury on any face.

'Very well. Take her back. Get her out of here quickly. Mrs Henderson, I hope you realize you are still liable for the full fee. I would be grateful for your acknowledgment of that in writing, along with your cheque.'

'You'll have your fucking cheque,' said Susie politely. 'And your fucking acknowledgment. Get me a bowl, would you?' she added to the nurse. 'Quickly. I'm going to be sick.'

The nurse wasn't quick enough. With something very close to pleasure, Susie threw up all over Dr Miller's white theatre shoes.

★

'Susie! Susie, we're here.' Harriet patted her hand gently. Susie opened her eyes, smiled at her.

'Sorry. Didn't mean to go to sleep on you.'

'That's OK. You look better.'

'I feel better.' She did. Much better. And James was walking towards them. Susie's heart lifted, as it always had, always would, at the sight of him.

'Hallo, Jamie.'

'Hallo, you two. No, no news. I've been over to see the Bergins. Josh is very upset.'

'And Julia?'

'Well she's upset too, but she seems to be what she calls handling it. She says she's quite sure Cressida will be back, as soon as she has had a little – space, I think the word was.'

'Oh God,' said Harriet. She smiled at her father. 'She is something else, as they say. What about the bank manager, Daddy?'

'He still hasn't called.'

'How's Mummy?'

171

'Asleep finally. Janine as well.'

'I'll go and make us some tea,' said Harriet.

They looked fondly after her. 'She's a glorious girl,' said Susie.

'I know. I know she is.'

'I wish – ' She looked at him and laughed. 'No I don't.'

'What?'

'I was going to say I wish Rufus wanted to marry her.'

'That would never do. One of my nightmares, actually.'

'Really? Do you know, it never occurred to me.'

'Yes, well,' he said, and his voice was heavy, almost bitter, 'bad things never do occur to you.'

And then fear and what she realized was anger hit her and her eyes filled with tears; the golden day, Jamie's face, blurred and she looked away.

He took her arm, gentle suddenly. 'What is it? Darling Susie, what is it? I'm sorry if all this has upset you.'

'No, Jamie, it's not this. Really. Can we – can we talk?'

'Yes of course. Let's go down to the bridge.'

They walked down slowly. Susie was silent for a while. Then she began to tell him. She didn't look at him, didn't touch him. When she had finished he sat down heavily on the seat, started stripping a large daisy of its petals, one by one.

'Is that my prognosis?'

'Don't be silly.'

There was a long silence; then he said, 'Have you told Alistair?'

'I haven't told anyone.'

'But you'll have to. Tomorrow.'

'Yes, I suppose so,' she said. 'I needed to tell you first.'

'Of course.'

He picked up one of her hands, turned it over, raised it to his lips. 'I'm so sorry,' he said, 'so terribly sorry.'

'I love you,' she said.

'I love you too.'

'Jamie – '

'Yes?'

'What is the prognosis?'

'Oh – I don't know. Not my field really.'

'Don't lie to me.'

'Sorry. Well, it's not great. But it does depend on what they find. It could be dealt with fairly swiftly or – '

'You mean a mastectomy?'

A long silence. Then, 'From what you've told me, possibly. And chemotherapy. But it might not come to that – '

'And it might be worse?'

'Susie, this is impossible. I haven't seen your X-rays, haven't talked to your consultant. Don't make me say things that may be wrong, irresponsible, please.'

'Sorry.'

She sat there, and looked down the years, the long, happy years, at closeness, sweetness, love, and wondered how she could have found them wanting. There had been shadows, to be sure, gentle difficulties, slight pain; they had quarrelled occasionally, longed for one another often, been forced to share one child across two sets of lives. But there had been so much good, so much joy; they had lain so often, shaken after love, smiling at one another, taking happiness for granted, pleasure as a right, and been careless of it all. And now they were to lose it, lose certainty, closeness, and she was to go alone and fearful into a new dark destiny.

'I shall need you now,' she said suddenly, before she had meant to, but the fear took her, chilled her. 'All the time, for as long as we can have. You won't leave me, will you, not any more, Jamie, you'll be there with me? I mean really with me, living with me? It's the only way I can bear it.'

She waited for him to answer and realized she had never known true fear before; she had experienced its lesser compatriots, panic, apprehension, even dread, but not this, this ugly, driving invasion of her body as well as her mind, and the fear itself frightened her.

She felt tears rising again, felt at the same time nausea, faintness; her mouth was dry, her throat closed with terror. She knew she could not have moved, could not have cried out even, no matter what might happen to her; and then he smiled at her, gently, tenderly, and as always her self-control, her courage came back to her, and she looked at him, at her love, and gripped his hand and clung to it, as she had when Lucy had been born, and said as she had then, 'Don't go away, will you? Whatever they say or do.' And he said, 'No, Susie, I won't go away. I'll stay with you now, for as long as you need me.'

And the fear receded quite quickly then, just as pain can sometimes do, leaving only a sweet weariness behind it, and she sat with her head on his shoulder, staring at the water, and trying not to wonder how short a time together they might actually have.

Chapter Thirteen

Harriet 4.30pm

The cups of tea looked horrible when she poured them out. Dark, with a floating scum on them. Harriet stared at them, amazed as always by her inability to accomplish the simplest domestic task. It was a family joke that she couldn't even make a nice jug of water. Things burnt while she watched them, remained raw however long she consigned them to the oven; any bed she made was lumpy, anything she ironed looked creased. Her only near-culinary skill was mixing martinis, which she did superbly; Merlin Reid had been her tutor and Theodore Buchan was one of her most appreciative customers. He said not even at the Ritz in Paris, or the Polo Lounge at the Beverly Hills, had he experienced such martinis. 'Not tasted, Harriet, experienced. There is a great difference. It is a rare talent in a woman.'

Harriet told him cheerfully he was a sexist pig but she liked the appreciation nonetheless.

Having made the stuff, she couldn't even find Susie or her father: how irritating. They'd probably gone for a walk: they were good friends those two. Cressida had often hinted they were more than that, but then Cressida was like that, finding intrigue, scandal where there was none. It was wishful thinking, an attempt to make them all more glamorous and interesting. Like her absurd idea that their mother was in love with Theo. 'You can laugh,' she'd said to Harriet, the first time she'd propounded it, when she was about fifteen, 'but I know I'm right. And it's so embarrassing for poor Theo. I mean Mummy's lovely, but she's hardly – sexy, is she?'

'Honestly, Cressida,' Harriet had said, 'you read too many romantic novels.' And Cressida had shrugged and told her to watch her mother next time Theo came to the house. 'She blushes a lot and sort of looks at him under her eyelashes. It's so sad.'

Harriet watched in spite of herself and could see what Cressida meant. 'But he's such a terrible old flirt himself, Mummy's only responding, and she hasn't had much practice. Anyway she's only got eyes for Daddy, you know that.'

As she grew up, Harriet had become increasingly aware of an oddness in her parents' marriage. It was not so much that her father was so extremely good-looking still, and so easy and amusing, while her mother was (despite a sweetly pretty face) so overweight and clumsy and frumpily dressed. That happened in a lot of middle-aged marriages; in the end they levelled out again. It was more that her father, against all logic, tried so much harder than her mother: he paid her compliments, teased her, kissed her, always invited her opinions, asked for her company if he was going for a walk, a drive, a drink. And her mother was cool, almost indifferent, made no effort with her appearance, no attempt to respond to him.

'I really would rather not come,' she would say to many of his invitations, or 'I really don't have an opinion' to his promptings. She was pleasant, but treated him rather as if he was a brother she was not particularly fond of, and he continued to work away at her, meeting detachment with affection, dullness with sparkle, apathy with interest. He never criticized her, either openly or behind her back, never indicated for a moment that he might deserve better. His patience with her seemed infinite, his acceptance of her without limit. It was as if, Harriet thought, he had drawn up some kind of contract and these were the terms and he had accepted them without question.

She had always adored her father; the constant acceptance by everyone when they were small that Cressida was Daddy's girl hurt her every hour of every day. Sometimes, as she watched Cressida snuggled deep into his lap, her great blue eyes sleepily contented, she hated her so much she could easily have killed her, dragged her onto the floor and pulled off her hair ribbon and wound it round and round her neck until she choked, until those eyes bulged, those cherubic features turned blue. And then he would notice, and set Cressida gently down, tell her to go to Mummy, and hold out his arms to her, and say 'Come on, Harriet, grown-up girl's time now.' But although she would flash a triumphant look at Cressida as she scrambled up, and snuggle into his arms herself, she knew it wasn't really quite a victory, that he did it out of duty, out of a sense of rightness, that he had had to notice, to remember her, whereas Cressida seemed always there first, by right.

When she was older she felt in some way she had become the son he hadn't had; she walked with him, played tennis with him, sailed with him, discussed things with him,, and that was wonderful, but it was still Cressida who charmed him and sparkled for him, flattered him, flirted with him. It was Cressida who went to official dinners with him or played hostess at home when Maggie had one of her many migraines, Cressida who jumped up and made him soup, a drink, a sandwich when he arrived at the Court House late on Friday nights, Cressida who ran up and down endlessly with trays on the rare occasions when he was ill. 'I honestly don't mind, Mummy,' she would say, 'you look tired, and I'm not. And he's such a bad-tempered old bugger when he's ill, and it just rolls off my back, and I know it upsets you.'

It was Harriet's observation that her father's bad temper had no effect on her mother either but it led to a quieter life not to argue with Cressida.

The roles intensified as they grew up and left home. 'Harriet has a career,' Cressida would say, smiling sweetly, self-deprecatingly, 'and I've got a job.' This was true, but it was certainly of her own making; she had, Harriet knew, a brain as sharp and as effective as her own. She had done modestly well in her A-levels (3 Cs) and could perfectly well have gone to university. But she had chosen to do a secretarial course and after a rather large number of run-of-the-mill jobs, had become secretary/receptionist to a large paediatric practice in Harley Street, where her charming manners, genuine fondness for children and sympathetic efficiency had made her (as more than one of them had remarked) as crucial to its success as any of the doctors themselves. The same qualities and the knowledge she had absorbed in her time there would of course equip her even more perfectly to be the wife of an upwardly mobile young medic.

She was jealous of Harriet's success, of course, but cheerfully, supportively so; and she was openly and intensely proud of her. 'She always had the brains,' she would say, 'and the drive and the energy. She's the new woman. Bit of an anachronism I am.' And she would smile at whoever was listening, and they would hasten to assure her that she was nothing of the sort, and if her audience included any of the older generation (particularly if it was male) they would frequently say something that implied it was she who had actually got it right and Harriet wrong.

Harriet could never quite remember when she decided she wanted to get into the fashion business, but she was certainly still quite small. She would wait for her mother's *Vogue* and *Harper's* to arrive each month (for a comparatively unfashionable woman, Maggie was an avid consumer of the glossy press) as eagerly as if they were a present for herself, and by the time she was eleven or twelve was making dresses for herself with astonishing skill. What was more, she made up her own patterns; she kept a store of old basic Simplicities (a dress, a skirt, a shirt) and worked on them, adding and subtracting with huge ingenuity. She raided her mother's wardrobe, the village drapery shop, jumble sales for fabric and old clothes; her greatest triumph was a party dress she made for Annabel Headleigh Drayton, aged three (when Harriet had been only fifteen herself), a gloriously simple Kate Greenaway creation, puff-sleeved and high-waisted, out of an old 1940s print dress she had found at a village sale. It had been a surprise Christmas present for Annabel, who loved it so much she wore it night and day for months. With a final touch of inspiration Harriet had used the leftover fabric to cover a pair of Annabel's dancing shoes.

Janine had been her great ally in those early days, not only having her to stay in Paris, walking her tirelessly round the shops (Harriet especially loved the stock shops on the long, dull-looking rue d'Alesia, where so many of the chic-est, most magical names, Dorothée Bis, Cacherel, Lapidus, sold their last-season's stock for a fraction of its original cost) and arranging for her to see the occasional couture show, but almost more importantly, taking an intense interest in what she was doing, happy to talk far into the night over the relative merits of Karl Lagerfeld and Vivienne Westwood, pure cotton as opposed to cotton polyester mix and the status of American couture vis-à-vis French and English. It was Janine, not Maggie or James, who had encouraged Harriet to take art at A-level, Janine who had argued with them both to let her go to St Martin's to do a foundation course, Janine who had persuaded them (with still more difficulty) that she should be allowed to go and work as a stitcher at Jean Muir, rather than carry on with a more conventional education.

From there, working long, hard, badly paid hours, learning in a week what she knew college could not teach her in a month, possibly a year, studying not only technique but the necessity for a pursuit of perfection that was unarguably religious in its fervour, she found herself by a series of extraordinary accidents answering the phone to one of the great fashion editors of her day: Caroline Baker, ex-*Nova*, then working on *Cosmopolitan*. A dress Caroline had asked to borrow for a session had not turned up; Harriet was told to take it personally in a taxi to the studio. There, relieved of the dress and her responsibilities, she stood in the back of the studio unobserved watching entranced as Caroline selected, added to, subtracted from, built on a series of garments, with shirts, jackets, sweaters, shoes, scarves, jewellery, hats, hairstyles, creating looks that were at the same time unique to her and her magazine and yet remained faithful to the spirit of the designers; and she saw too how the sparkiness of a good model, the care of a talented make-up artist, the energy of a creative photographer could intensify, bring further alive an already dazzling picture. She forgot everything, what she was meant to be doing (finishing a hem), where she was meant to be (back in the workroom); she could scarcely have told you her name. At the end of the afternoon (which was actually eight thirty in the evening), as Caroline and her two assistants were packing up the clothes and the photographer had embarked on an apparently endless conversation with a model agency in New York, she emerged timidly from her shadow and asked Caroline if she could talk to her.

Caroline smiled her rather vague, sweet smile and said of course she could; she listened to Harriet's halting explanation of her ambitions to be a designer, her slowly growing frustration with what was the painstaking discipline of couture, and her enchantment with what she had seen that day. Caroline laughed and said it wasn't always like that, but why didn't she go and talk to a girl she knew, a stylist, who was looking for a dogsbody. 'It will be just that, I warn you, trailing round London finding things like scarves and bracelets and berets, nothing glamorous, and I think she wants experience anyway, but it's worth a try, you could go and talk to her. Oh, and learn to type, then you could work for someone like me.'

The stylist took Harriet on (being more in need of cheap labour than experience). Caroline had been right: it was backbreaking, thankless work and most of the time everything Harriet contributed was discarded; but she made contacts at every manufacturer, every retail outlet in London, and on a great many magazines and several advertising agencies as well. She took Caroline's advice and taught herself to type, and on her twenty-first birthday her present from fate was a job as personal assistant to a firm called Jon Jonathan. Jon Jonathan was the pseudonym for two brothers, who designed the kind of evening dresses that fill the tables at charity balls and the social pages of the glossy magazines.

They were successful, clever and fun; Harriet had a wonderful eighteen months with them, gaining first-hand experience in running a business, made a lot more contacts, and was allowed to put a couple of dresses into a new line they were doing for the booming teenage ball market. Her dresses sold out in days, and the following season she did several more, all of which were best sellers. A year later, she got a job as a designer for a new young high street chain of upmarket leisurewear called Freetime. Working on those clothes, aiming for a line as clean-cut, as classically perfect in its own way as Jean Muir's, and yet as breezily commercial as Jon Jonathan's, Harriet felt she had established a concept that she could make her own. She turned out coordinates of shirts, sweaters, leggings, chinos, with matching hats, caps, scarves, socks. She put stinging colour with cool neutrals, outrageous detail with classic style. She finally knew where her talents fused; she knew now what she wanted to do. The Freetime studios were in Wandsworth; while she was working for them, a tiny shop became empty in the increasingly fashionable high street. With the courage, vision and refusal to look down that had characterized her working life so far, Harriet sold her car, her flat, bought the lease and opened under the name of Harry's (Mungo Buchan's childhood name for her) on her twenty-fourth birthday. For a year she lived and worked there, some weeks scarcely even leaving the four walls. She was exhausted, poor, frightened and permanently exhilarated, flying on adrenalin: cashing in shamelessly on the contacts she had made over the years. Previous customers bought from her, journalists wrote about her (she was a great story), the Jons once bailed her out when she was in a real crisis and put money into her business, in return for a ten per cent share. 'Don't ask for more,' she said coolly, the first time. 'I'd rather go under altogether than lose control of Harry's.' She refused to take money from Theo, from Merlin, from her father, even when she wanted to expand, to get another shop. Theo was particularly pressing, said he had always wanted a foot in the fashion market, that she would be doing him a favour. 'I'm sorry, Theo,' she said collectedly, sipping at the champagne over which he put to her his proposition (£1 million investment in return for a forty-nine per cent stake). 'I'm going to make it on my own.'

'Harriet, Harriet,' he said, shaking his head at her, 'it's impossible without investment. I've forgotten more about starting a company than you've even learnt yet. You'll starve from underfunding, and then you'll come back, crawling to me.' He winked at her through a cloud of cigar smoke; Harriet didn't even smile back.

'Never, Theo,' she said, 'never ever. Thank you for the offer, but it isn't even tempting.'

She was lying; it was. She was desperate for her second shop, a perfect site in the Fulham Road (where she knew her customers lived in droves), and she didn't have anything like the money. Interest rates were soaring (this was 1988), Theo's offer was as insanely generous as it was tempting. But she wouldn't take it. She went to the bank and took out a loan, and she opened the second Harry's just before she was twenty-five; she followed it with shops in Bath, Birmingham, Edinburgh and Exeter. A year after that she had her own design studio in Covent Garden, with two assistants; her turnover was £10 million. And then she looked at Paris, and saw how well shops like Laura Ashley and The Gap were doing there, and with Janine's help found a tiny shop in Passy, with a flat over it. She loved Paris, she had always loved it. She began to spend half her time there.

And still her luck held, and the economy boomed, and her clothes echoed the joyous, extravagant optimism of the era and its devotion to the fitness creed, and sold and sold, not only to the young, but to the newly young thirty- and even forty-somethings. There seemed to be no stopping her.

And then she fell in love.

It was so ridiculous when she had known him so long.

'It's so ridiculous when I've known you so long,' she said, staring at him, her heart churning, her head in turmoil, feeling her body wildly weak with longing, and shock as well that it had happened at all, looking at her hand in his across the table, as if she had never seen it, seen either of them before, feeling the hot, twisting, leaping shafts of desire between them, savouring the delicious, sweetly strange knowledge that soon, astonishingly soon, she would be in bed with him, learning of him, discovering him, feeling him, and he raised her hand and held it against his cheek, while looking at her with something that was close to amusement mixed nonetheless with love, holding her eyes with his.

'So long, all your life in fact,' he said, smiling, beginning to kiss her palm, and fronds of hot sweet excitement began to forge their way through her, and she smiled back, and said, 'What would they say to us, whatever would they say?' And he said (reaching out with the other hand, stroking her cheek, slowly, lingeringly, and then pushing her hair back, and his hand in her hair, on her head, was somehow the most sensuous thing she had ever known), 'They'd say it was dreadful, terrible, completely unsuitable,' and she said, (turning her head, leaning it on his hand, closing her eyes briefly with the effort of sitting still), 'And it is, it is terrible, it's awful, what would my father say? I can't even begin to think about it.'

'Your father,' he said simply, 'is much more of a pragmatist than you might think.' And she stared at him, arrested briefly in her delicious progress into love, and said, 'What do you mean? I don't understand,' and he said, 'I mean exactly that and don't let it trouble you.' She would have pressed him further, demanded an explanation, only he dropped her hand suddenly, and placed his hand on her thigh under the table, and she felt his fingers, his strong, thrusting fingers moving on it, stroking it, and then working upwards, slowly, inexorably, towards the tender liquid place that was yearning for him, unable to wait for him, and she forgot everything, only stood up abruptly, and said, her eyes fixed on his, 'Shit, we have to go, we have to go now, quickly,' and he threw a thousand francs onto the table (in payment for what was at the most a four-hundred franc bill) and took her elbow and guided her out of the restaurant and into the car he had waiting outside. 'My hotel,' he said briefly to the driver, then lay back and took her in his arms, and began to kiss her; hot, hungry, probing kisses. When they reached the hotel they went in quickly, through the foyer and up in the lift, and he took her hand and half dragged her out of it and into his suite.

He pushed her in impatiently, almost roughly, and slammed the door behind him, stood there leaning against it, breathing heavily, staring at her, his eyes moving all over her, her face, her breasts, her legs as if he had never seen her before, and she was panting too, staring at him, filled with excitement and fear at the same time, many fears, of what she was doing, of whether he really wanted her, of how she would be for him.

'This is bad of us,' he said, 'really bad,' (still smiling, knowing he didn't mean it, knowing she knew it too). 'Maybe even now we shouldn't, I shouldn't, not to you, you of all people.' And, 'Yes we should, we should and me of all people, it will be all right, I know it will,' and she was dragging off her shirt, fighting out of her trousers, her eyes still fixed on him.

'Yes, but he's my best friend,' he said, tearing off his tie, his shirt, struggling with his zip.

'I know, I know, and what does it matter?' she said, tearing off her tights, her pants.

'He'd be so shocked, so angry,' he said, moving forward, bending, starting to lick at her nipples, her erect, hard nipples. 'You said he was a pragmatist just now, you know you did,' she said, and her hands were in his hair, pushing at his head, pushing his mouth onto hers and he said, 'God, your breasts are so beautiful,' and then raising his head, smiling at her like a delighted child, 'I knew it, I always thought they would be.' And he pushed her down onto the bed, kissing her, his hands everywhere, on her stomach, her buttocks, her thighs, and she was writhing, moaning for him, her hands on him, too, stroking, feeling, exploring, the big firm buttocks, the surprisingly flat stomach, the soft, heavy balls, the wet, quivering penis, and then he said, 'Christ, Harriet, Christ, I can't, I can't stand it,' and it was there, his penis, in her, swiftly, impatiently, thick, heavy, reaching far far into her, urging her into sensations, hot piercing liquid sensations, and she lay back, her arms flung wide, her eyes closed, not touching him, not doing anything, just opening, opening to him and her pleasure, and there was a great white-hot brightness ahead of her, above her, and she was reaching, grasping, climbing to it, and she had never imagined, never known such strength, such power, and she thought she would tear, break with it, and then suddenly there it was, a great wild roar of joy and she realized there was indeed a great noise and it was her own voice, crying out with triumph, and for what seemed like a long long time her body gradually fell away from its climax in sweet, slow tumblings of pleasure and into peace. And then she opened her eyes, and saw him looking at her, and there was such tenderness, such love in his eyes, and she could not, would not, feel anything but triumph and joy. And 'Was that good for you?' he asked, and she smiled and said, 'Theo, you know how good it was.'

★

It had started with dinner, a perfectly ordinary dinner. He had phoned her at the shop in Passy, said he was alone in Paris staying at the Crillon while some work was done on his house, could she spare him the evening, and she had said delighted (for she had always loved him, adored him even, had grown up thinking how wonderful it must be to be the sort of woman he would want, fall in love with, had thought also that she was exactly the sort of woman he would not), had said of course she could, but he must come down to her, she had something to finish first. His car, an absurdly extended Mercedes, arrived forty minutes later, and the shop was locked; she went to the door and smiled up at him through the glass, thinking not for the first time, not even for the hundred and first, that he really was the most extraordinarily good-looking man even at the age he must be (well into his fifties), and quite absurdly sexy too, with his wild black hair, his burning, brilliant brown eyes, his permanently tanned skin. He was very tall and big, heavy even, but not fat; and he was of course, as always, beautifully dressed, not as so many middle-aged men dressed, trying to look young, but carelessly careful, in a fine lawn shirt, a silk tie, a dark jacket, perfectly cut grey trousers, and as he bent to kiss her she could smell very faintly the unmistakable scent of the Hermès Equipage he always wore.

'You look tired,' he said, half severely, 'and you've lost weight, I shall take you out and spoil you,' and she said, smiling, that that would be lovely, and he sat patiently for a while as she finished a drawing, wrote a letter, faxed them both to the studio in London, and then less patiently as she made a couple of phone calls.

'Come on, come on,' he said, 'don't you ever stop?' 'No' she said, firmly, 'not till I've finished, do you?'

'Never finish,' he said, 'actually. Can I use your phone?' And then it was her turn to wait while he called first London, then New York and Sydney, until finally, impatient herself, and irritated at his wanton and expensive use of her phone, she said, 'Theo, for Christ's sake, stop it,' and he laughed and said, 'Sorry, I'll pay for the calls,' and wrote her a cheque there and then for 500 francs.

'That's much too much,' she said, 'don't be absurd,' and he told her to shut up, it was hush money, and took her elbow and eased her out of the shop.

They ate in one of her favourite restaurants, just round the corner from her shop, classically perfect French food, the tables set with baskets of bread and jugs of wine and water, the first course brought swiftly (she had mushrooms à la Grecque, he a goat's cheese salad) and then a long wait for a shared carré d'agneau, as they talked, finished one jug of wine, and he ordered another ('Can't we have something better?' 'No, Theo, we can't and anyway, it wouldn't be'). He was slightly depressed, lonely (the fourth divorce was hitting him, he said, and he was feeling his age) and had just been trumped in a deal to buy an Australian property company. Harriet listened, politely at first, then more patiently, tenderly almost, recognizing for the first time at least with her heart what her head and her father had frequently told her: that this great ebullient, badly behaved, overindulged spoilt child of a man was in fact strangely vulnerable, oddly sad.

And then, 'How about you?' he asked, as finally the carré arrived, and he began to carve it, to put slices of it, pinkly perfect, onto her plate. 'How is it going, the great fashion empire that I'm not allowed even a smidgeon of?' And she said oh, fine, really, but it really was one long crisis after another, the latest being that the new line of cotton knits she was doing for the spring, absolutely dependent on some yarn arriving undyed from Hong Kong, had in fact gone horribly wrong because the yarn had been dyed and half the colours were totally out and she had sent them back and was battling for redress, and meanwhile time was hurtling by and she had already passed one deadline and if Benetton got what she knew was something very similar into their shops long before she did, she would lose considerable sales, and she was also in dispute with the landlord in Bristol where she was hoping to open in the spring. 'But you know,' she said, 'one fights on. It's half the – well, I was going to say fun, which of course it isn't, but it sharpens everything, I find, makes me go on caring a hundred and one per cent.'

'Absolutely right,' he said, munching through a huge mouthful of spinach. 'Of course it does. Christ, Harriet, I'm proud of you. You're a – what is it Mungo says? A star. A real star. Brave and tough and clever. I wish you were my daughter.' Harriet blushed, surprised at the praise, and dropped her fork.

'Goodness, Theo,' she said, 'praise indeed. Shit, that was my last bite of lamb.'

'Here,' he said, holding out his own fork to her mouth, a slice of succulent lamb on it, 'have mine,' and she opened her mouth to take it and, as she did so, met his eyes, and they were very strange those eyes, tender, amused and at the same time thoughtful, and distinctly sensuous, moving over her face as if for the first time, drinking her in, and it was one of the most sexually disturbing incidents she had ever known. Then she shook herself and thought that this was Theo, for Christ's sake, Theo who had been around for always, her father's best friend, an old man, and then she met his eyes again, probing hers, and she knew of course that he wasn't an old man at all, he was a vital, forceful, very sexy, oddly ageless one, and it was as if she had only just met him. She looked down and pushed what was left of the food on her plate with her knife and when she looked up again he was still staring at her, half amused, half startled, just as she was.

'Harriet?' he said gently, and it was both question and statement, and she said 'Yes, what?' quite aggressively, but he was not deceived, merely smiled rather self-confidently, called the waiter over and said, 'Do you have any champagne?'

'Theo!' said Harriet reprovingly. 'Really! At the end of the meal!'

'Why not?' he said. 'Champagne is wonderful at the end of the meal. And besides, we have something to celebrate, don't we?'

'What?' she said, deliberately misunderstanding.

'Recognizing each other,' he said simply, 'after all these years. Now then, what shall we talk about?'

'Mungo?' said Harriet hopefully, thinking that this would restore him to his rightful position as father figure, generations older.

'If you like. What shall we say about him?'

'Well – ' She was more flustered still, anxious, her pleasure gone. 'Well, I just thought – '

'I know what you thought, my darling. You thought you would remind me that Mungo is your age, and I am his father. Right?'

'No of course not,' said Harriet irritably, trying to crush the joy at being called his darling. 'Don't be silly.'

'All right. We'll talk about Mungo. Do you like Mungo?'

'Yes of course I do. I think he's lovely.'

'But you've never been in love with him?'

'No, never. I've never been in love with any of them,' she said, relaxing again, the champagne lifting, easing her.

'Any of who?'

'The three of them. Mungo, Rufus, Oliver. They all seem like – well, like brothers. Baby brothers.'

'Ah. We used to dream of you falling in love with Mungo, your father and I. I can see it's a nonsense now. That you don't like young men very much at all.'

'No,' she said, 'no I don't. I like people who've done things, know things, fought, suffered a bit.'

'Ah. Like Bill Bryant.'

'Yes,' she said, with a heavy sigh, 'yes, that's right. Daddy told you, I suppose? The whole sad story?'

'He did. And I was sorry. And sad. But you're better without him, Harriet.'

'Oh don't!' she said, angry suddenly, 'don't you start, Theo.'

'Start what?'

'Telling me he's a bad lot, that I should never have got involved, that he's famously charming, famously wicked, plays around, likes young girls – '

'Oh no,' he said, 'nothing like that. Of course he is, of course he does. But I'm like that myself, I play around, I like young girls, I certainly wouldn't criticize that. No, it's that he's a playboy, he drifts about, he's not a worker, a fighter like you, Harriet, not what you want, not what you need.'

'Yes he was,' she said, stubbornly, 'you don't understand, nobody could.' She scowled at him, angry that he dared to pronounce on her, remembering Bill Bryant, rich, hedonistic, with whom she'd had an affair the year before, with his easy lazy charm, his dazzling lifestyle, his prodigious appetite for pleasure, in and out of bed. She would have died for Bill, given up everything for him, had he asked her, but he hadn't; it had ended in horrific grief because he had not loved her, had only used her, and then moved on. But suddenly now, in a moment of pure revelation, she realized that Theo was right, that had Bill asked her to marry him (unthinkable, unimaginable) it would have been a disaster, a dreadful awful mistake, he would never have accepted her as she was, would have wanted to change her, possess her totally.

'It wouldn't have worked, would it?' she said, staring at Theo, and he said no, of course it wouldn't, and there was a long silence and then she said, 'God, I should have talked to you before,' and he said, 'Oh, you wouldn't have listened, you'd have said I was a silly old fart.' 'Quite probably,' she said, and laughed, and he patted her hand and refilled her glass.

'You seem to understand me rather well,' she said, half amused, half serious. 'I hadn't realized.'

'I think I understand you very well.'

'But not as well as Cressida?'

'Oh, there's not a lot to understand about Cressida,' he said, 'just a sweet, straightforward, nicely brought-up girl.'

'Your favourite.'

'Of course not my favourite.'

'You always acted like she was.'

'Well,' he said, 'you were always going off with Merlin. And it was awful for me. I had to settle for what was left.'

'You're a devious old bastard,' she said lightly, 'but you're lovely.'

'I wish you really thought so,' he said.

'I do.'

'No you don't.'

'Theo, I do,' said Harriet, smiling at him rather determinedly, trying desperately to keep the mood light, easy. 'And what does it matter anyway?'

'It matters,' he said, very low, very serious suddenly, 'because I care about you. I think you're glorious.'

'Theo, don't,' said Harriet, feeling within the depths of her something lurch, rise unbidden, against her will.

'Why not? Why the hell not?'

'Well, because – oh you know why not.'

'Oh for God's sake,' he said suddenly, 'this is absurd. Let's go.'

'All right,' said Harriet quietly. 'All right, Theo. It might be best.' She signalled to the waiter for the bill.

'What the hell are you doing?'

'Asking for the bill.'

'What for?'

I want to pay it. I'd like to. Please.'

'Oh for Christ's sake, Harriet.' He stood up; his hand as he drained his glass was shaking.

'Why are you so angry?' she said, startled.

'I'm angry,' he said, 'because I'm hurt. Because you so plainly think I'm a fool. Because you're so ready to dismiss me. I don't like it. I don't like it at all.'

'Theo,' said Harriet reaching out, trying to take his hand, pulling him down again, 'the last thing I think you is a fool. I was just trying to – to handle things. Badly, obviously. I was – well, I was very shaken myself just now.'

'When?'

'A little while ago. While we were still eating. I realized – '

'What?'

'I realized what – what might happen. If I let it. Let myself.'

'And you won't?'

'Theo, how can I? How can I possibly? When you're – '

'When I'm an old man?' His eyes were angry again, hurt, harsh.

'No. Not an old man. But you are practically another father to me. When you've seen me learn to walk, talk, lose my teeth – '

'Get your bosoms,' he said suddenly.

'What!' said Harriet, laughing, blushing at the same time.

'I shall never forget you getting your bosoms.'

'Theo! You really are a dirty old man.'

'I'm sorry. But I'd been away for six months, and I'd left a little girl behind, miserable, awkward – God, you were awkward, Harriet.'

'You'd have been awkward with – '

'I know, with Cressida for a sister.'

'You knew!'

'Of course I knew. Anyone would have known. Don't be absurd. Anyway, I came down for the day and went into the garden to find your parents, and there you were standing by the swimming pool, with just knickers on and two gorgeous little rosy buds, slightly uneven, they were, one bigger than the other, see how well I remember, and you didn't see me, and I stood there and got the most enormous erection, I couldn't move, and you dived into the pool and I turned away and stood there, taking deep breaths and thinking Christ Almighty, she's grown up, and then your mother appeared, and I somehow managed to talk myself down. It was one of the most profoundly moving moments of my life.'

'Literally,' said Harriet. She felt very odd, excited, touched, almost tearful.

'Literally. And ever since – '

'Don't tell me. Ever since you've been hoping to catch me by the pool again just in my knickers.'

'Or anywhere. Without them as well. If possible. Shit,' he said suddenly.

'What's the matter?'

'Same old thing,' he said, grinning slightly shamefacedly. 'Just remembering it all. Remembering you. I do have trouble with it.'

'Oh, Theo,' said Harriet helplessly, feeling herself softening, moistening, dangerously sweet. 'If only.'

'If only what?'

'If only I'd only just met you.'

'Would that be different?' he asked and his voice was odd, wary.

'Of course it would. Quite different.'

'And what would you want to do? If you'd only just met me?'

'I would want,' she said in a great surge of courage mixed with a rush of desire, 'I would want to go to bed with you.'

'Oh my God,' he said, 'dear God. Dear sweet Jesus. Look at me, Harriet, look at me.'

And she looked at him. And then she was lost.

It was so ridiculous when she had known him so long . . .

It was doomed of course; there was no way it could work. James would have been outraged, Maggie appalled, all the young horrified. 'Mungo would lynch me if he knew,' Theo said as they lay one night entwined in one another's arms, kissing lazily in the sweet aftermath of love.

'They'd all lynch us.'

'Does it matter?'

'Probably not. No. No, not at all.'

The sex was wonderful: wild, clever, original, beautiful. But it wasn't just sex, it was his very self, she told him, in all his complex, difficult, absorbed, absorbing passions. He took her to the opera in San Francisco, in Sydney, to the ballet in New York, and once in London, greatly daring, he made love to her in his box at the Opera House during a performance of *Salome*. 'Listen,' he said, as the curtain came down to great roars of applause, 'they must all have been watching us.' He took her to the races with him in Sydney and Longchamps, shouting, punching the air with excitement when the horses he had backed won, growling, scowling when they did not, and he also read aloud to her in bed, poetry usually, but sometimes from Hemingway, Tom Wolfe, Dylan Thomas, his hands moving idly over her, filling her body with longing even as his deep musical voice filled her head. Seldom was a poem, a chapter, a passage completed, the book would be dropped, flung aside, or simply lost in the bed. 'I wonder how many copies of *For Whom the Bell Tolls* have been fucked on,' Theo said one night, fishing the crushed copy from beneath him, laughing, 'and how pleased dear old Papa would have been had he only known.' They could seldom meet in London, and so she met him in a myriad different places all over the world, making long, exhausting plane journeys to Australia, to Mexico, to Barbados just to spend perhaps forty-eight hours with him. She realized again and again how vulnerable he was, even in his immense selfishness, how badly he needed people, needed affection, tenderness, how great his capacity for giving it. He cared for her as she had never been cared for, not dutifully, not mechanically, but thoughtfully, imaginatively, delightedly. 'I want to spoil you,' he said simply one night, as they shared a rare dinner in London. 'You deserve it, and you need it.'

She found that as arousing as his intense, burning sensuality, the fact that he should mind about her so much. She told him everything, trusted him with her very soul: with all her most intimate, private fears, joys, griefs, from her earliest childhood. She told him of her jealousy of Cressida, her unrequited adoration for her father, her desperate need for success. She even told him about Biggles, fearing even as she did so that he would belittle the grief and pain of that loss. He didn't. 'I had a puppy once,' he said smiling at her, wiping the tears that still flowed at the dreadful memory, 'my father sent him away, while I was at school. I just came home one day and he was gone, I never knew where. I thought I would like to kill myself.'

She could not have enough of him; she was distracted from everything, from her work, her friends, her very self. Always vain, concerned about her appearance, her style, she failed for months to go shopping, even to get her hair done. Everyone noticed, teased her about what was obviously a secret lover; she smiled, carefully vague, terrified they would guess. She had, Theo told her, accomplished the impossible and made him neglect his work too.

'I love you,' he said one night, as they sat watching the sun sink into the Mexican ocean. 'I love you as I haven't loved anyone since Deirdre. You fill my heart, Harriet, and I simply can't believe it.'

'You fill mine too,' she said, putting her hand into his. 'Absolutely and utterly.'

But things went wrong. They began to fight, angry with themselves and one another; starved of one another so much of the time, when they managed to be together they were frantic, desperate, overpossessive.

He found her youth troubling, hurtful, tormenting, she found his past, his experience worse. 'How can you wonder that I'm jealous, that I wonder where you've been, when you've had all these women, all these wives?' she would cry, when he'd been missing, hadn't phoned, hadn't been where he'd said he would be, and 'Sweet Jesus, Harriet,' he would say, 'I love you, how can you even imply I'm playing around?' And 'For Christ's sake,' he would shout at her, 'do you know how hard it is to believe you're not in bed with some boy, some beautiful young boy,' and she would cry, 'But Theo, I love you, only you, and I don't sleep around.' They agreed, after a while, that they must tell everyone, make it official, but they put it off, over and over again, afraid of ridicule, of outrage, and then fought because the fear was greater than the love.

'All right,' he said one night, as they sat seething and apart, after a dinner with Mungo and Cressida and James and Maggie, after agreeing to tell them, after totally failing, after a harrowingly complex ruse to meet later, at his house in The Boltons, 'all right, we're cowardly and feeble and pathetic and all the things you say. I'm sorry for my share in that. I'm sorry. You're not so brave either, are you? Are you, Harriet? The fault is in both of us.'

'I know, I know it is,' she said, brushing away the hot angry tears. 'I'm sorry too. I don't know why it's so hard. I can't understand it. Can't understand myself.'

'I understand it,' he said, suddenly gentle, coming over to her, wiping away the tears with his finger. 'It's because it does seem so wrong, so incestuous somehow.'

'Yes,' she said, 'yes, that's exactly right. Of course it does.'

'We've let ourselves think that. But it isn't. It isn't at all. Harriet, look at me. I love you. I love you very much.'

'I love you too,' she said, 'I really really do.'

'Perhaps we should get married,' he said suddenly, and staring at him, her eyes wide with astonishment and something close to horror, she said, 'Now that really would be awful, terrible.'

'I've never had quite such a turndown,' he said, trying to make light of it and then seeing she was deathly, deadly serious, 'Why?' he asked. 'Why so awful, why terrible? What's so wrong with it?'

'Theo, I'm not going to be Mrs Buchan the Fifth,' said Harriet with something close to distaste.

'Why not, for Christ's sake?'

'Because it's – well, it's not what I'm about. I'm not going to be Mrs anybody, and especially not Mrs Buchan the Fifth.'

'That's a filthy thing to say.'

'Well it's true.'

'I thought you loved me.'

'I do love you. But I don't want to be your wife.'

'Why the hell not?'

'Because it's – well, it's a label. Something close to absurd.'

'How very charming you are,' he said and walked out of the room, the house, and she didn't hear from him for days.

She could see why he was so hurt, so angry, but she had felt it very strongly, had had to explain. Being Theo's wife seemed to her a great deal less meaningful, less dignified than being his mistress. It seemed to her a public acceptance of submission, of selling out. When finally he took her phone call, agreed to listen, she said, 'Theo, I love you, I love you so much. I'd love to live with you. Really I would. But – shit, Theo, you've degraded marriage, it doesn't mean anything. Not in your life. I want to be your equal, not your wife,'

'Well, thanks for nothing,' he said and rang off.

Slowly, painfully, they came together again, but the rows increased. Wounded by her reaction he became obsessed with the idea of marriage; he asked her again and again, again and again she refused. She offered to live with him, but he was wounded now, savagely hurt. 'If marriage is such an awful prospect then I must be too,' he said, and try as she would, she couldn't convince or persuade him otherwise. And in the end their relationship – still new, after all, fragile, vulnerable – could not sustain the pain, and in a wretchedness of rage and misery they parted, more afraid of ridicule and outrage than of separation and grief.

'It is absurd, dreadful,' said Harriet, tears streaming down her face, her body drained, dry with hurt as they finally agreed to part, and 'That's what you said when I first told you I loved you,' said Theo, his own face ravaged with pain, and 'I know, I know,' she said, 'but it can't, it won't work, will it?' and 'No,' he said, 'no, I don't think it will.'

It was a long time before Harriet began to heal, and the agony when she heard Theo was going to marry Sasha was so frightful she seriously doubted if she could stand it; she was unable to sleep without pills for six months, and to contemplate so much as speaking to him for twelve. Indeed their first meeting after his wedding upset her so much she was physically sick. She still found herself unable to meet his eyes, or to be next to him. 'I actually now know,' she said to Tilly, who was the only person she had ever confided in about the whole wretched affair, 'how people can commit murder. I would gladly kill first him and then her, given the opportunity.'

Tilly remarked with her usual clear-sightedness that from what Harriet had told her, the break-up had been as much at her instigation as Theo's. 'I know, I know,' wailed Harriet, 'but at least I haven't married some bimbo less than a year later.'

'Maybe he's more desperate than you are,' said Tilly. 'And what's the male for bimbo?'

'Himbo?' said Harriet, and first shrieked with hysterical laughter and then burst into tears. But just the same Tilly's words had been oddly comforting.

★

She decided to go and find her father and Susie, with the tea; they'd seemed to want it so much and they couldn't be far away. She put two of the cups on a tray and went out of the back door, across the yard and into the garden, but they were not on the lawn or in the rose garden, or by the tennis court; maybe then by the bridge. Cressida was not the only person who liked to be by the bridge. She pushed open the little gate that led into the field; her thoughts (occupied with her problems, with her business, with Theo, with Cressida) distracting her so thoroughly that she had almost forgotten where she was going when she reached the bridge. And she saw then, sitting on the seat, in a position that spoke somehow most clearly of a long intimacy, Susie and her father, Susie's head on his shoulder, his arm around her, his hand in hers.

It was unmistakable, that pose; it was not one of friendship (despite its lack of passion), nor was he comforting her over the events of the day. These were two people as close, as familiar as if they had been married a long time, the image made the more forceful because her parents never sat like that, nor had she ever seen Susie and Alistair do more than exchange the briefest touch. And as she stood there, staring at them, they sensed her presence and turned round, simultaneously, and saw her, and on Susie's face at least there was some amusement mixed with her dismay, and she seemed to hear Theo's voice (and she could remember the precise words and his tone too) in the restaurant that first night. 'Your father,' he'd said,

191

'is much more of a pragmatist than you might think,' and she heard Susie's voice too, much more recently – 'I'm very good at keeping secrets' – and in a blinding, white-hot revelation she understood, saw down the years the pleasure, the happiness, the closeness between them, and understood too in the same moment the strange relationship between her parents, her father's patience, kindness, courtesy, her mother's coolness, distancing, lack of response, saw it for what it was, part of a complex, well-negotiated deal, and while she wondered exactly, precisely how she felt about it, her father spoke.

'Harriet,' he said, 'Harriet, I think we should – talk.'

'No,' she said, 'I don't think we should, I really haven't got time. I – brought you some tea. It's a bit strong, and a bit cold now. I'm sorry.' And she set the tray down on the grass and turned and walked very swiftly towards the house, wondering why it should have disturbed her so much, when she was grown-up, quite grown-up, sophisticated, experienced, that her father had a mistress (even if she was supposed to be a great family friend) and realized it was because, quite simply, all the security, the absolute knowledge of her childhood that her parents loved one another, had been faithful to one another, was lost to her, wiped out in a single moment, and that Theo, whom she'd loved so much, been so close to, had clearly known all along and had not told her.

She found it hard to see as she walked back into the kitchen; it seemed somehow dim. Maybe it was getting dark, she thought irrelevantly, looking at her watch, but that was blurred too, and she realized she was crying. Furious, she brushed the tears away, picked up the cup of tea she had made and sat down at the table, sipping at it, wondering what she should do. And then she saw that there was a letter on the table, propped against the toast rack, a white envelope with what was – couldn't be, couldn't possibly be, but yes it was, Cressida's rather neat writing on it. 'The Forrests' it said, 'Urgent.'

Harriet reached out and picked it up, cautiously, as if it might be hot, might burn her, and sat staring at it, turning it over without opening it. Then she got up and walked over to the door, called gently into the hall, 'Cress? Are you there?'

There was no answer, as she had expected, of course, nothing, so she went back to the table, sat down and with immense difficulty opened the envelope and took out the sheet of paper inside.

'Mummy, Daddy and Harriet' (it said), 'I'm very sorry about today. Please believe me. I seemed to have no choice. I'm fine, and not in any danger. I'll phone you when I can. Much love, Cressida.'

Chapter Fourteen

James 5pm

'Daddy, don't talk to me like that.' Harriet was flushed, breathing heavily. She was clearly very upset, near to frightened. 'I told you, the fucking letter wasn't there before.'

He knew why she was using language like that; it was not about the letter, it was about him and Susie, about betrayal. Just the same he hated it.

'Hariet, darling, there's no need for that.'

'Sorry,' she said, and her tone made it clear she wasn't, not in the least. 'It was horrible, you know. Like seeing – hearing – a ghost.'

'Yes of course.' James sighed; he felt terribly tired, drained of sympathy, patience, understanding. Even for Susie. He had had too much, too much of all of them. He just wanted to go away, leave them, do something nice and straightforward that he could control, like play tennis, or take out his boat or even deliver a baby. To a sensible mother who had been to all her antenatal check-ups and wanted an epidural, with a midwife in attendance who thought he was wonderful. The thought was so ridiculous he smiled in spite of himself.

'I'm glad you think it's funny,' said Harriet. She sounded extra-ordinarily angry.

'Darling, I don't think it's funny. I – well, I was thinking about something else.'

'I wish I could. Incidentally Susie thinks we should tell the police about the passport business. And I think she's right.'

'Why?'

'Well, because if she has got a duplicate passport, she can get abroad. It's obvious.'

'Yes. Yes of course you're right,' said James. He sounded very vague. 'I'll call them very soon. Let's try and get this letter business sorted first.'

'Well,' Susie said, her tone forcedly bright, 'obviously someone put it there. None of us actually believes in ghosts. Someone must have come in. It hasn't been through the post. Is it dated, Harriet?'

Harriet shook her head. 'No. But it says today.'

'It still could have been written yesterday.'

'Now that is really unbelievable,' said James. 'She couldn't have planned this, couldn't have been so deliberately – cruel.'

'Why not?' said Harriet, and her voice was even harsher. 'Why do you say that? She took her dress, she seems to have got a second passport organised – '

'I suppose so,' said James. 'I suppose so. I'm just still trying to resist the idea, that's all. And of course there was what Oliver said this morning when I – well, when I told him what had happened.'

'What did he say?' asked Harriet sharply. 'And why didn't you tell us before?'

'Because I honestly didn't – still don't – think it was important. But he said, "She hasn't actually gone, has she?" Or something like that?'

'James, how can you not think that was important?' Susie's voice was shocked. 'How could you have kept that to yourself? If Oliver knew – '

'Susie, Oliver didn't know anything. Do you think I'd have kept quiet about it if he had? But he did say that she'd had a bad panic attack about three or four days ago, and said she felt like running away. She'd been very tearful apparently. But that was all. I'm sure there aren't many brides who haven't threatened to run away, a few days before the wedding.'

He hoped he sounded convincing, as convinced as he wanted to be; he was still thoughtful about Oliver's response, but the subsequent conversation had been too distressing to allow for cross-questioning. And then there'd been the dress business and the passport –

'It sounds to me,' said Susie slowly, looking up from the letter, 'as if she was under some appalling pressure. Something she couldn't escape from.'

'Well, she has escaped,' said Harriet. 'Very nicely. As usual.'

'Darling, why are you sounding so hostile? You've never talked about Cressida like this before.'

'Yes, well, it always seemed best to keep quiet before,' said Harriet. 'It never did me any good to say anything. I just got sent away to school or out of the room.'

She sounded suddenly like the small hurt child he had left at St Madeleine's all those years ago; looked like her too, with a white face and hard, desperate eyes.

'Harriet, what are you saying?'

'Oh it doesn't matter,' said Harriet wearily. 'This isn't getting us anywhere.' She sighed, rubbed her eyes. 'I want a drink.'

'It's a little early for that, isn't it?' said James. He looked at his watch: five past five. Christ Almighty. Cressida had been missing for almost twelve hours.

'I don't care if it's early,' said Harriet. 'I want one. Just because you never drink, you never think other people might want to.' She walked over to the fridge. 'Susie, how about you? Glass of wine?'

'Yes, I think it might be nice,' said Susie.

Harriet poured two glasses of wine, handed her one. They stood there, sipping slightly awkwardly. 'This is very nice wine,' said Susie.

'Isn't it?' said Harriet. 'Lovely and fruity.'

James looked at them, thought how absurd it all was and laughed suddenly.

'You seem to be finding this whole thing very funny,' said Harriet irritably.

'It's so ridiculous, that's all. Here we are, a missing bride, a banquet for three hundred slowly going off, flowers wilting, the police alerted, a letter appearing as if from the ether, and you're suddenly discussing the merits of Californian chardonnay.'

'Yes, well, we didn't seem to be getting far discussing anything else,' said Harriet.

'Look,' said Susie suddenly, 'look, Harriet, perhaps we should – well, what you saw just now. Your father and me. It doesn't – didn't mean – '

'Susie, please. I'm not stupid,' said Harriet briskly. 'I could see what it meant. Thank you. I really don't think we should talk about it. What we have to decide is what to do about this note. Do we tell the police? Or try and find out if anyone came in? What? We can't just stand here drinking.'

'It was your idea to drink,' said James mildly.

'Oh for Christ's sake!' said Harriet. 'Can we just – '

The door opened and Maggie came in. She looked very pale and her fair hair was slightly damp around her face, but she smiled almost cheerfully at them.

'I just woke up. I feel – much calmer. I'm sorry I – well, is there any news?'

Harriet and Susie were silent; they both looked at James.

'What is it?' asked Maggie. 'What's happened?'

'Nothing – really,' said James. He felt almost inclined to hide the letter, not tell Maggie, he so dreaded the descent back into hysteria.

'Yes, it has,' said Harriet. She stared at him stony-eyed. 'Of course it has. Mummy, there's a letter. Look, from Cressida.'

Maggie sat down heavily and took the letter. She read it slowly several times, and then said, 'Where was it?'

'On the kitchen table. It just appeared.'

'It can't have just appeared. Don't be ridiculous. She must be here, Cressida must have brought it. Have you looked for her, called her – '

'Maggie, of course we have,' said James, realising suddenly that they'd done nothing of the sort, not really. 'She isn't here. Nobody's here.'

'They must be. Janine's here, for a start. Where is she? Maybe she saw Cressida – '

'She's lying down,' said Harriet. 'She's exhausted.'

'She's exhausted!' said Maggie. She sounded angry. 'I really can't imagine why Janine should be exhausted. She hasn't done anything. Anything at all.'

'Maggie, of course she has. She's lived through this whole thing with us, she's been a tower of strength, she only arrived from Paris yesterday and besides she's quite an old lady now – '

'Yes, all right, all right,' said Maggie. 'Well, we must get her up, talk to her. She might have heard, seen someone – '

'Maggie, I really don't think – '

'Jamie, I don't care what you really don't think. I really do think. Harriet, could you go and get Janine, please? And who else is in the house?'

'No one. Everyone's gone. No cars, nothing.'

'Leaving the sinking ship,' said Maggie. 'Susie, give me a glass of that wine would you? Is Alistair here?'

'No,' said Susie, quickly. 'No, he's gone back to London.'

'Ah,' said Maggie. 'Ah yes, of course.'

James looked at her sharply, but her face was blank, stony.

Harriet came in, looked at them both, went to sit near her mother. It was an oddly symbolic gesture. 'Janine's just washing her face,' she said, 'then she'll be down. But she really hasn't heard anything.'

'We should have let her be,' said James. He felt irritated, upset on Janine's behalf.

'Yes, that's what you always like to do, isn't it?' said Maggie. 'Leave things be. Carefully covered, so they aren't any trouble. To you at least.'

James felt the familiar pang of sheer, icy panic, and at the same time the equally familiar flash of hope, of relief. Christ Almighty, was she going to say something now, confront him, confront them both? All his life, all their lives, he'd been waiting for it, waiting for the confrontation, and it never came; she sat there, like a great fat cat, toying with him, with the knowledge she must surely have, and made him wait. Often he almost wanted her to face him with it, yearned for the end of the sham, the games they all had to play, wished he could start it off himself, say something, force her to say something back. But he never did and he never would. He liked to think it was his alter ego, his better self, doing that, sparing Maggie, allowing her some kind of dignity, of status at least; but he knew that actually it was nothing of the sort. James had a great talent for self-deception, but it did not extend quite this far. He played the game Maggie's way to buy her silence, her acceptance of what he had done to her; he simply could not face the ugliness of a scandal, of divorce. It was not perfect, of course, the situation; he would have been much happier married neatly, respectably to Susie, but the opportunity for that had been lost to him thirty years earlier, and in the event it had all turned out very satisfactorily. He saw Susie almost as much as he wanted to, he had plenty of freedom, he had a fair amount of money (but it was only money, only salary, not wealth, and it would diminish quite painfully, supporting two households). But now, with Susie, with the promise he had made her – Christ, how was he going to get out of that one? A great deal of very skilful talking and manoeuvring would be necessary. He had no intention of actually setting up house with her, it was an absurd, romantic notion, but she hadn't thought it through, hadn't seen that it would cause great grief and stress to herself as well as her family, would quite possibly exacerbate her condition. When she was feeling less shocked, when they had a clearer idea of what her prospects were, then he could put that to her, make her see it wasn't such a good idea. God in heaven, it was a hideous thought. He was genuinely and deeply shocked himself; he loved Susie very much, had loved her all his life. The thought of her dying, lost to him, no longer there for him was ghastly. He looked at her now, so lovely still, her face strangely serene. She had great courage, Susie, always had. Well, she was going to need it, every last final shred of it. He must not completely fail her, must do all that he possibly could.

He stared at Maggie, wondering what she might say next, feeling her hostile bitterness almost tangibly in the room; but she suddenly smiled at him with the extreme sweetness she always seemed able to summon out of somewhere and said, 'Sorry, James. I didn't mean to be cross. Ah Janine, come in, dear. Would you like a glass of wine?'

For ten, fifteen minutes they talked, argued, read and reread the letter, propounded theories as to how it had got there (paper boys, post office messengers, passing strangers), debated calling the police, the hospital, the Bergins, examined the silent afternoon behind them now for sounds of footsteps, car engines, even bicycles. 'Well, I do think we have to tell the police,' said James finally. 'We can't not, really. They're looking for Cressida, and this is a clue. Of a sort. I'll go and ring them now, tell them – Good Lord, Merlin, where have you sprung from?'

Merlin walked into the kitchen with his quick, light tread, smiling sweetly at them all. He had discarded his morning coat and was wearing a khaki safari shirt and a long white cricket cardigan over his shorts.

'Been for a walk. Felt a bit restless. Got a drink for me, Harriet? Something long, if you don't mind. A beer perhaps. That lovely creature Tilly gave me some beer in the car, and I've been dreaming of another ever since. Find the note, did you? I dropped it off on my way. I thought you'd see it if I left it on the table.'

'Merlin, did you put that note there?' said Harriet. She looked almost angry, James thought, ready to explode.

'Yes, well I couldn't find any of you. Knew you'd be back.'

'Merlin, it's from Cressida.'

'Yes, I realized that,' said Merlin impatiently. 'Know her writing perfectly well. Better than yours, Harriet, look like unravelled knitting your letters do – '

'And you just left it on the table. Merlin, how could you?'

'Harriet, calm down,' said James. 'Merlin, where did you get it from? Who gave it to you?'

'Nobody gave it to me,' said Merlin. 'I found it.'

'Yes, but where? Where was it?'

'In the lavatory,' said Merlin. He spoke as if it was the most natural place in the world to find a letter. 'Fallen on the floor, behind the cistern. Only noticed it because I dropped my compass. Can't think why I brought it today, but still. Force of habit I suppose. Anyway, just as well, wasn't it? Otherwise – '

'Yes, yes, Merlin, which lavatory?'

'The one down here,' said Merlin. 'Does it matter? Suppose the silly girl left it there on her way out. Forgot it. This is jolly good beer, Jamie. Pay a lot for it, did you?'

'Quite a bit, yes,' said James.

'Let me come with you next time. See if I can beat them down a bit. Now then – '

'Merlin,' said Maggie, her voice slightly shaky, 'I really think we have more important things to discuss than the price of beer.'

'Sorry,' said Merlin cheerfully. 'Any other news is there?'

'No, I'm afraid not,' said James. 'We were debating whether we should give that note to the police. We thought it had just arrived you see. But – '

'It must have been there all day,' said Harriet. 'She must have left it there when she went. Early. It does seem odd though – '

'Yes, but I told you, she was unwell,' said Janine. 'I heard her vomiting. The *pauvre petite*.'

'Well, there you are,' said Merlin. 'Takes it out of you, that sort of thing. Tends to happen in a rush, doesn't it? Suppose she parked the letter on the cistern while she – '

'Yes, I suppose so,' said Harriet hastily. They were all patently trying not to think too hard about the sequence of events that led to Cressida leaving her letter behind. Poor child, thought James, vomiting repeatedly, exhausted, frightened; no doubt she heard someone moving upstairs, thought she wouldn't get away and just fled. He sighed. 'Poor child,' he said aloud.' Poor little thing.'

'I still do think,' said Susie, 'that all this points to her being under some kind of intolerable strain. That there was something she was running away from. Some kind of trouble. Incidentally, has anyone phoned her flat lately?'

'We do it every hour, on the hour,' said Maggie. 'There's just no answer. I think maybe someone ought to go up there, perhaps Rufus or maybe Mungo – it seems crazy not just to check she's not there. None of us have been there for ages, anyway, you never know what clues we might find there. I know we haven't got a key, but – oh, if only she'd had a flatmate, it would have been such a help. I always said she should and now – '

'Yes, well, she could hardly have been expected to get a flatmate simply to be helpful to us in the event of her possible disappearance off the earth,' said James. He could hear the exasperation in his own voice, but he couldn't help it.

'Jamie, don't be difficult,' said Susie. 'Maggie's right, we should check the flat out. I'll ask Rufus if you like.'

'Thank you. Anyway, I don't know about strain, Susie, she seemed so happy, so calm last night. There was no sign – '

'She was a bloody good actress,' said Merlin. 'Never saw anyone turn on the tap like Cressida could.'

'Merlin!' said Maggie. 'Please!'

'Well, why not? Jolly useful attribute. I'll have another of these beers, if you don't mind, Harriet. Got her out of trouble plenty of times, I expect. And it got her things. Remember that business with the shrunken head, Harriet?'

'Merlin, not now,' said James heavily.

'Yes,' said Harriet quietly. Everyone looked at her. 'Yes, of course I do.'

'What was that?' asked Susie. She sounded genuinely interested.

'Merlin – '

'Oh, what's it matter now, James? I brought back a shrunken head for Harriet once. Knew she'd like it. Swapped it for a little transistor radio in some village in the bush. She was thrilled. Said she was going to start a collection. Only I hadn't got anything for Cressida. Well, I never saw the sort of things she liked, national dolls and all that nonsense. She didn't seem to mind too much, until her mother came in. Then she was off, weeping and wailing. Put Garbo to shame. Said I was always forgetting her, that I never brought her anything, and she wanted the head. Don't you remember, Maggie?'

'No, not really,' said Maggie. She sounded very tense. 'Merlin, do we have to – '

'Surprised. You made a bit of a scene. Told me to give her the head. Said I always brought Harriet things, and that hurt Cressida. Anyway, a week later she gave it to the dog. We saw her, didn't we, Harriet? And when she realized we'd seen her she was off again, never seen anything like it, great tears, it was giving her nightmares, she hadn't known what to do. You had to admire her. I wouldn't have minded, only it was a damn fine head.'

'I don't think this is getting us anywhere at all,' said Maggie coldly.

'No of course it isn't. I was just saying she was a fine actress, that's all.'

'I think,' said Maggie glaring at him, 'I think Susie's right. It's the only explanation really. That she was feeling so under pressure that the only way out was – escape. Poor darling,' she added. Her voice was low and slightly shaky; she looked very pale.

'Well – none of this has got us any further. Do we tell the police about the note or not?' said James. His head was aching horribly; he felt sick.

'I think we should,' said Maggie. 'I really do. And – well, maybe try the hospitals again. Especially if she was ill. She might be in terrible trouble by now.'

'I think we should talk to Oliver first,' said Harriet. 'I really don't believe he didn't even suspect there was something wrong. Can't we get him over? Or go there?'

'He was off for a walk with Tilly earlier,' said James. He tried to sound relaxed, natural, but he hated even saying the name; it made him feel uneasy.

'Well, I expect they're back now. Let's phone the hotel.'

'Tell you what,' said Merlin suddenly. 'I don't trust that mother of his. I think she might know something about it all.'

They all stared at him.

'Julia! Merlin, why?' Harriet sounded astounded, almost shocked.

'Don't like her. Damn silly fool of a woman. Always talking rubbish in that absurd language of hers.'

'Merlin, American is the same language as ours,' said Susie laughing.

'Rubbish. Ever listened to them properly? Babbling on about prioritization and fitness programmes and being in touch with themselves and all that poppycock. Do you know, she once asked me if I felt diminished as a person by never marrying. Diminished! Bloody nerve! I told her I'd be a lot more diminished if I had married, and lost my freedom and spent all my money on some bloody silly girl.'

'Merlin,' said Harriet, looking more cheerful suddenly, 'I love you. And I'd love to diminish you. But I can't see any of that is grounds for her knowing where Cressida is.'

'I didn't say that. You don't listen, Harriet. Never did. I said she might know something about it all. Someone should question her.'

James looked at Janine, remembering what she had said earlier, about not liking, not trusting Julia. It was interesting that, but they could scarcely start cross-questioning her on that basis.

'I agree with Harriet, that we should tell Oliver about the letter,' he said, 'and perhaps we should ask all the Bergins over here. It seems almost discourteous not to. Maggie, can you cope with that?'

'I suppose so,' said Maggie. Her voice was heavy, dull, but she smiled at him again, her good-wife smile. 'Yes, of course I can.'

He decided to change again; his clothes felt frowsty, over-worn. While he was upstairs the phone rang: 'James? Tony Bacon. Sorry, heavy day.'

Yes, thought James, very heavy, on the golf course. 'That's OK.'

'What can I do for you? His voice was carefully cheerful, expressionless; he knew then.

'Tell me something, Tony, if you will.'

'Will if I can.'

'Look, I'm sure you've heard. Cressida's disappeared. Early this morning.'

'Yes, James, I had. I'm sorry. No news of her then?'

'No, not yet. The police are being very helpful. But – '

'Hell of a worry for you.'

'Yes, it is rather. Look, I know this is classified information, but the circumstances are exceptional and it would help a lot if we knew. Has there been any undue activity in her bank account recently?'

'Wish there had, old boy. Yes, of course I'll tell you. It's been a bit – moribund lately. Ever since she cleared her overdraft.'

'Her overdraft?' said James. 'I didn't know she had one.'

'Well I rather assumed you didn't. It was quite big, you know, last year, bigger than I should have let her have actually, but you know how it is, you weren't going to run away, and she's always been a bit of a favourite of mine, ever since she used to come in with her pocket money every week and pay in five bob.'

'Er – how big is big?' asked James. 'A few hundred?'

'Well – rather more than that. In the end I had to take a charge on her flat. I'd actually asked her to come and have a chat. It wasn't just the overdraft, her credit card borrowing was very high, and she sold her shares as well – '

'When was this?' asked James. 'Exactly? Christ, I wish I'd known.'

'Oh – last summer. Right up to Christmas actually. Then she cleared it completely, and closed the account altogether for a while. That was when she had her windfall, came into that money – '

'What money?' said James sharply. 'I don't know anything about money – '

'You didn't? How extraordinary. Her great-aunt, leaving her all that money . . .'

'She – hasn't got a great-aunt,' said James. 'Look, Tony, I'm sorry, but I really didn't – '

'Ah,' said Tony Bacon. He was clearly embarrassed. 'Ah, I see. Well, someone must have died, or she must have broken the bank at Monte Carlo or something. A hundred thousand pounds was wired to us, on a CHAPS payment, from some solicitor. Only at the time she didn't have an account here, so we returned it to the solicitor.'

'Look,' said James, 'can we just go over that again, Tony? Someone paid Cressida a hundred thousand pounds into your bank and you returned it?'

'Yes, that's right. Because she'd just closed her bank account with us. A few weeks later she opened it again, with a small deposit, and she's hardly used it since.'

'And you have no idea where this money came from?'

'Well, I told you, she said it was a legacy. She specifically – although quite casually – asked me not to mention it since it was a bit of a sore point in the family. Her getting it, I mean.'

'It might have been,' said James, 'if we'd known about it. How extraordinary. How absolutely extraordinary. When was this, Tony? Around Christmas, you said?'

'No, a bit later than that. February, early February.'

'I see. And – and since then, nothing untoward at all?'

'No, not at all. I was slightly anxious when she came back to us, to be honest, because I thought the borrowing might start again. But it hasn't. Look, I do hope you get some news soon, and I hope I haven't made things worse.'

'Yes,' said James absently. 'Yes, thank you. I mean, no, no, of course you haven't.'

He put the phone down and sat down heavily on the bed, staring at the telephone. How in God's name, he wondered, had Cressida got hold of £100,000 and what if anything did it have to do with her disappearance? He felt suddenly and sharply as if the Cressida he had known and loved and lived with for twenty-seven years had entirely ceased to exist, had been replaced by a total stranger.

The Bergins' car pulled into the drive thirty minutes later. Oliver was driving it, with Tilly beside him. 'I thought I'd come and see Harry,' she said by way of explanation as she walked in. 'I hope that's OK.' James looked at her and felt absurdly nervous. Pull yourself together, Forrest. What can she do to you now?

'Hi, Tilly,' said Harriet, giving her a hug. 'I'm not sure if you've met my father . . .'

'Yeah, we've met,' said Tilly, smiling rather coolly at James. 'A couple of times actually.'

'Dad's still walking with Theo,' said Oliver into the slightly tense silence, 'and mother is resting. They may be over later. But thanks for inviting them.'

He looked terrible, pale and wild-eyed; he refused the drink Harriet offered, asked for tea. She filled one of the maxi-sized teacups that she kept for herself and gave it to him. 'I thought it was only the British who wanted tea in a crisis,' she said.

'I'm a Brit by marriage,' said Oliver. 'Or at least I thought I was.'

'You will be,' said Harriet cheerfully.

James led them all into the drawing room; he felt he had spent too many traumatic hours in the kitchen that day. He told Oliver about Cressida's letter, about where Merlin had found it. Oliver's reaction was dull, almost uninterested. He was clearly exhausted, unable to cope with anything more. 'It doesn't get us anywhere, does it?' was all he could say.

'Well – at least it means she wasn't abducted or has met with some horrible accident,' said Harriet. 'We found it kind of faintly comforting. The thing is, Oliver, do you think we should tell the police?'

'Oh – I don't know,' he said. 'Whatever you think.' He put his head in his hands, pushing them through his hair; Harriet went over to him, put her arms round his shoulders.

'Oliver darling, you mustn't despair. I know she'll turn up. She'll be all right. She'll just walk in here and laugh and say "you're never going to believe this" and it will all make sense.'

Oliver shook his head; He looked up at her and there was a darkness, a bleakness in his eyes that reached out to them all.

'I don't think so,' he said.

Harriet looked rather uncertainly at Tilly; she was sitting in the depths of the huge sofa, her endless legs wrapped round one another, her huge almond eyes calmly, almost lazily absorbing the scene. She was an amazing creature, James thought; quite unlike anyone he had ever known. Well, that was absurd: how many – what were they called? – Supermodels? – had he known anyway? But she had a tranquillity about her, an easiness that was highly engaging. He tried to remember her mother; she had certainly not been tranquil. But then the circumstances under which they had met had hardly been tranquil, nor the ensuing ones either. Well, she had certainly made a good job of Tilly. In the most difficult of conditions. On her own, no money. James crushed determinedly the thought of what some financial damages for the loss of Rosemary Mills's other baby might have done to make things easier for her, and smiled at Tilly rather awkwardly. She looked levelly back at him, her arched eyebrows just slightly higher. What the hell did she have in mind for him, and how was he going to handle her? Christ Almighty, what a day.

As if in response to his thoughts, Tilly suddenly stood up and walked over to him. 'I'm very interested in gardens, in growing things, Mr Forrest,' she said. 'Would you like to show me yours?'

They all looked up, startled: Maggie especially. Susie's eyes were wary, watchful. She half stood up herself. Jamie shook his head at her imperceptibly, smiled his careful consultant's smile at Tilly, trying to equate this glorious creature with the tiny scrawny baby he had laid so exhaustedly and thankfully on her mother's breast. And who now, it seemed, might quite possibly become his daughter-in-law – albeit unofficially. How the hell was he going to deal with it all?

'I would be delighted,' he said, 'there's nothing I like more than showing off my roses. Let's go.'

He stood back for her as she walked through the door; in her stack-soled boots she was at least two inches taller than he was.

'We'll be back in a minute,' he said into the room. He could see Harriet watching them both, clearly baffled.

She walked slowly, gracefully, leading the way across the lawn; she seemed to glide. He followed her, feeling like some small eager pony in the wake of some great beautiful thoroughbred. When they were out of hearing distance of the house, she turned and waited for him, pointed at the field.

'Can we go there?'

'Yes,' he said, 'and into the woods. It's a nice walk.'

'Oh good,' she said, and her tone was heavy, ironic. 'I like a nice walk.'

She was silent for a few more minutes; then as they reached the trees she turned to him again and said, 'Well, Mr Forrest. What a long time it's been.'

'Yes, I suppose it has. You're – what? Nineteen?'

'Twenty,' she said, 'as you very well know.'

'Ah. Twenty is it?'

'Twenty years. Tough ones for my mother. Very tough.'

'Yes, I'm afraid they must have been.'

'It's been OK for you,' she said, 'by the look of things.'

'In some ways yes.'

'In most ways, I would say, Mr Forrest. I mean we're talking material here. I'm not interested in any other kind of problems you might have had. Except that I hope you've had a few.'

'Miss Mills – '

'Oh, puh-leeze, Mr Forrest! Tilly. We're going to get to know one another pretty well, I think, you can't keep on calling me Miss Mills. I mean, Rufus wants to marry me. And he's family, isn't he?'

'Not quite. Not strictly speaking,' said James carefully, 'but I know what you mean.'

'The hell you know what I mean. And strictly doesn't seem to have a lot to do with it. Are you really telling me no one else in this gilded cage you all live in has noticed what Rufus looks like? Very interesting I found that. Shocking even – for a moment.'

'I – don't quite understand.' Jesus, this was worse than he'd expected.

'I think you do.'

'Miss Mills – Tilly, I assure you – '

'OK,' said Tilly, suddenly cheerful, polite even, 'let's leave that for now. I just wanted to ask you how you could possibly, possibly have done what you did to my mother. It may sound like I'm raking over old ground, but it's what I've been walking on all my life and it really does intrigue me.' She smiled at him, a great warm engulfing smile.

James stared at her, his mouth dry. 'Perhaps,' he said after a moment, 'perhaps you could clarify that question just a little. If you mean the birth, the death of your sister – '

'Yeah, I mean that. But that's not the main thing. I suppose if I was to be really really charitable, I could tell myself it was possible that my sister's death was unavoidable. I mean I don't really think so, but I could keep on telling it, and maybe in the end I'd get to believe it. I talked to Oliver about it, I thought as he was a doctor he'd know – '

'You talked to Oliver about your delivery – your birth,' said James and he felt so angry, so hot with rage he had to stop and take several deep breaths.

'No, it's OK, calm down, not mine,' said Tilly. She stopped and waited for him, smiling her odd, aloof smile. 'Just the birth of twins. I said how complicated was it, could it be, and he said these days not so difficult, but it was still tricky, still a process he hadn't liked when he'd had to do it, that often the second twin was a breech, that then there was always the danger of brain damage – '

James thanked God for any difficulties Oliver had clearly had in the delivery room during his training, and started to walk again.

'Then you can accept that there was a problem . . .'

'Yeah, I can. And I can imagine my mother might have been difficult. She can be very stubborn and she's heavily into all that natural business. With that silly cow Tamsin. And I know it kept coming up that she hadn't been for her antenatals – '

James was beginning to feel more easy; maybe she had just wanted to clear the air, maybe he could persuade her that he had acted properly, in good faith . . .

'Well then – '

'No, Mr Forrest, not well. Because you'd been drinking, hadn't you?'

'I beg your pardon!'

'I said you'd been drinking. You were drunk.'

'How dare you!' said James. 'How dare you stand there, in all your crass ignorance, and accuse me of being drunk when I was working. Of course I – '

'*I'm* not accusing you,' said Tilly easily. '*I'm* not saying it. It was the little student nurse who did that. She went to Tamsin, told her. When Tamsin was trying to get evidence together.'

'I don't recall her saying that at the inquiry,' said James smoothly. He was in control of himself again now. 'And I have to tell you that – '

'I'll do the telling, Mr Forrest. And no, she didn't say it at the inquiry. She just said you were very tired. I wonder how that happened. Not because it was her word against yours and the other medical people. No, no, of course not. She must have been wrong in the first place. Or thought she was wrong.'

'Miss Mills, you're making some very serious accusations here. I have to tell you – '

'I'm not making any accusations,' said Tilly, and her voice was icy, filled with contempt. 'Well, not yet. I can't quite decide who I'm going to talk to first about all of this: Rufus maybe. Maybe not. I can't decide. Does that lovely Susie know about it incidentally?'

'Yes, of course she does. Everyone knows. It was a widely reported case. And everyone knows also – '

'Yeah, that you were cleared absolutely. Well, bully for you. And then back to the treadmill, eh? The five-star consulting rooms and the expensive suits and the big bucks and the big career.'

'It wasn't quite that simple,' said James, fighting to keep indignation out of his voice. 'It was a considerable setback. And a very, very traumatic experience, I might add. You may find it hard to believe but I was deeply upset by the whole thing. Very deeply. It was the first and only time I ever lost a baby . . .'

'Oh, *you* lost it, did you?' said Tilly and her voice was heavy with scorn and a stony, harsh hatred. 'Do you know, I didn't realize that. I always thought it was my mother who lost it. I didn't realize it was you who went through all that pain and hell, who saw my sister born dead, dragged out of her like a rat. I didn't realize it was you who cried every night for years and years, and had nightmares and felt terrible awful guilt for not doing the right things when you were pregnant. I didn't know that it was you who needed some kind of recompense for it, for all that pain and misery, so that your life wasn't so hard. I didn't realize it was you who were made to feel irresponsible and foolish by the hospital and you who had to take the crap in that awful letter they sent. How stupid of me. How exceedingly stupid.'

'Well, I – '

'You bastard,' said Tilly. She had stopped walking now and had turned to face him, barring his way. 'You pathetic lying bastard. I wasn't sure until today what I was going to do. I thought I'd like to see what you said about it all. Now I've seen, and heard, and I feel sick.'

'How dare you!' said James. 'How dare you talk to me like this!'

'Oh quite easily,' said Tilly more cheerfully. 'I'm quite brave altogether. You'd be surprised. I expect it's in my blood. Lots of my forebears were spear-carrying warriors. Anyway, now I know exactly what I'm going to do. I'm going to tell every single person in this family of yours what you did, what really happened.'

'You can't,' said James, an icy sickness in his veins.

'Why not?'

'It would be slanderous.'

'Oh for God's sake,' said Tilly, 'what are you going to do, sue me? That would be very interesting. No Mr Forrest, you can't do that. And I'm going to make very sure they all know the truth. That poor cow of a wife of yours, I bet she thinks the sun shines out of your anus, doesn't she? I bet she'll be shocked rigid.'

'Miss Mills, I warn you – '

'And Susie? Your lovely friend? And your children? Christ, Harry idolizes you, thinks you're the next best thing to Jesus.'

'Not any more, I fear,' said James.

'Oh really? She seems pretty obsessed with you. And Rufus. What does Rufus think?'

'What I do is of little concern to Rufus,' said James, fighting for dignity.

'Oh really? What I see makes me doubt that. And that lovely old duffer, Merlin, he's your godfather, isn't he? Bet he thinks you're no end of a fine fellow.'

'Look – what do you want?' said James. He knew it was dangerous, knew he was placing himself at her mercy, appearing to be ready to do a deal, but he was desperate.

'I want justice, Mr Forrest. I want my mother convinced that it was all your fault, all of it, I want you to go and see her and tell her the truth, tell her it would have made no difference if she'd gone to her antenatal classes or not, that you were drunk and bungling and incompetent, and if you hadn't been my sister would have been alive today. And I want your family to know what a shit you are, how you lied and cheated and intimidated that poor little nurse – '

'How dare you!' James was shouting now, his rage suddenly converted into physical energy. 'How dare you say such things?'

'I dare,' she said, 'I dare quite easily. I told you – I'm quite a brave person really. And I'll tell you something else, Mr Forrest. If you don't do what I say, then you're going to be reading all about it in the tabloids. Very soon.'

'Oh for God's sake,' he said, 'why on earth do you think they'd be interested in it? After all this time.'

'Because it's me,' she said, her eyes wide, innocent as a child's. 'I have a way of making headlines, you know. I'm what's known as good copy. And so is this. I think the fact I should have been twins is a terrific story. I can see them now, all the headlines, the picture editors getting their computers to work out what she might have looked like. I think people would really love to read why there's only one of me. And about the struggle my mother's had to raise me all on my own. Don't you?'

James had never known such rage; he felt self-control leave him suddenly. He stepped forward, raised his hand to hit her. She stood there calmly, her eyes heavily contemptuous, her lips curved in a half-smile.

He pulled himself together, dropped his arm, stood looking at her.

'You're disgusting,' she said simply. 'Quite disgusting.'

And she turned and stalked off into the woods.

When he got back to the house – shaking, exhausted, fearful – Julia Bergin was standing on the back lawn. She was wearing a white polo shirt and madras bermudas; her face was porcelain-smooth, her brown hair looked freshly set.

'James! So sweet of you to ask us over. I was sent to try and find you.'

She sounded, looked even, as if she had come for drinks, or a barbecue;

her studied casualness seemed an affront to their distress, an insult to Cressida.

'Oh really?' he said, and it was difficult to speak, his tongue seemed unconnected to his brain. He felt dreadful, scarcely conscious. He had to pull himself together, work out what he was going to do. 'Any reason in particular?'

'Maggie has made some sandwiches. She thought we should all eat something.'

Bloody Maggie and her obsession with food; didn't she ever concern herself with anything else? Then he realized that he hadn't eaten all day, and was in fact something close to hungry.

He managed to smile at Julia. 'She's probably right. Is everyone still here?'

'Yes, of course. Your wonderful godfather is making everyone drinks. Such a sweetheart. Such an original. Many people would find his frankness rather rude, but I like it. I appreciate honesty, as I'm sure you do, James. It was one of the first lessons I learnt when I went into analysis, to confront the truth and then convey it.'

'Oh really?' said James. 'Good.'

She linked her arm in his, led him towards the house. 'You must try not to worry too much,' she said. 'I just know Cressida is fine. That she'll be safely back.'

'I hope you're right. And I wish I shared your optimism.'

'Well, I have feminine intuition on my side,' said Julia, 'and it tells me that there is nothing seriously wrong. I got very close to Cressida, you know. She and I were like sisters. She was a very strong, sensible girl. She wouldn't do anything stupid. I know it. Trust me.'

Nobody seemed to have moved when they went back into the drawing room. James was faintly surprised; it seemed hours, days since he had left for his walk with Tilly.

'James, are you all right? You look terrible,' said Susie.

'Yes, I'm fine.'

'Where's Tilly?' asked Harriet, surprised.

'She went for a walk,' said James briefly. 'She felt she needed the exercise.'

'She's amazing,' said Harriet fondly. 'She runs at least five miles a day you know.'

'How very energetic of her,' said James coldly.

Harriet looked at him, puzzled; he returned her stare, his face ironed blank.

Maggie came in with some large plates of sandwiches; Susie jumped up to help her.

'I say,' said Merlin, who had sat himself down next to Janine, in between Harriet and Josh, 'these are good, Maggie. Part of lunch I suppose. Well, it'll keep you going for months, that food, won't it? Needn't go to waste. Put it all in the freezer. Wonderful things, aren't they, freezers?' he said to Susie. 'I've got two. Only shop twice a year now.'

'Good heavens,' cried Julia, clearly relieved by the distraction. 'How amazing. What about fresh fruit and vegetables?'

'Never touch the stuff,' said Merlin. 'Can't stand any of it. Except for red peppers. Eat several peppers a day. Buy them fresh of course. Did you know,' he said to the room in general, 'there's more vitamin C in half a red pepper than three oranges? You'd know all about that, of course,' he added to Janine. 'Can't teach your lot anything about food. When all this nonsense is over you must let me cook you a meal one night. I do a very good ratatouille, though I say it myself.'

There was an awkward silence as everyone ignored Merlin's slightly unfortunate phraseology, then Julia spoke.

'Well, I am truly amazed you're so healthy. You could be in danger of severe tissue damage. No, not prawns, Maggie dear, I have a shellfish allergy. Just a little cucumber perhaps – '

'Tissue damage pah!' said Merlin. 'I'm eighty-four years old, woman, and a damn sight healthier than most of your compatriots. Look at them, obese, pasty-faced, mass of allergies like you, obsessed with their bowels – '

'Talking of health,' said Harriet, rather desperately, 'Oliver, we didn't tell you. We think Cressida was ill on the – God, it was this morning, wasn't it? It seems weeks ago. Well anyway, she was ill. Janine heard her – heard her being sick once or twice, and – well, sorry everyone, not a very nice topic. Did you have any idea she was ill, Ollie, or maybe it was just nerves – '

Oliver stood up suddenly. He walked over to the window and stared out for a few moments. Then he turned round and faced them.

'She wasn't ill,' he said finally, his voice shaking. 'She was perfectly well. She was pregnant, that's all. I think I'll have another drink, James, if you don't mind.'

James, looking at Oliver over the whisky bottle, wondering how many more revelations he could take about his beloved daughter, saw a very odd expression in his eyes. It wasn't embarrassment, or even bravado; it was something extraordinarily close to anger. And then thirty years of absorbing announcements of pregnancies, the near-subconscious computing of dates, symptoms, probabilities, told him something that he found almost unendurable, something he crushed hastily, ruthlessly, without even beginning to acknowledge it further. And then he looked at Harriet, who was staring at Oliver, her face very pale, and he knew she had reached the very same realization as swiftly and as certainly as he had.

Chapter Fifteen

Mungo 6.30pm

More than anything in the world, he wanted to see Alice. The events of the past twenty-four hours had been so surreal, so nightmarish that he desperately needed some of the cool common sense she brought so efficiently into his life. Maybe he could get away that evening, get to London, have dinner with her even. There was no way Cressida was going to turn up now; his role as best man had been written out of the script. And now that Tilly was here, she was looking after Oliver far more competently than he could, she and Rufus. God, it was a strange partnership, that one: nice, but totally unpredictable. Mungo thought of Tilly's two previous lovers, a wildly eccentric French film director who had recently embarked on a second career as a Formula Two racing driver, and a black bisexual interior designer who had shot to fame with a simple if slightly esoteric corner in executive jet decor. And here she was, madly in love with a beautifully behaved English lawyer, an ex-public schoolboy who was polite to his parents, held doors open for women and stood up when his elders came into the room. Oh well. Love did strange things to people: as he knew. He could have had the pick of every nubile twenty-something on several continents, and what did he do? Fall head over heels – and that was such a good expression that exactly described how he felt half the time, shaken to pieces and totally disorientated – with a woman of nearly forty with three children. Well, if nothing else, it certainly made you believe in the thing, in love. Rufus, who was a great believer in love, was always talking about it, had indeed first experienced it at the age of seventeen, had talked endlessly and tediously about it right through one summer when Mungo stayed with him and his family in France and Rufus had been forced to leave the beloved behind in London. Mungo had listened to his ramblings, impressed mainly by the fact that Rufus had insisted (shocked) that he and the beloved had not even been to bed together, that she didn't want to yet; and right up to the time that Mungo had met Alice he had thought it was a myth, a label stuck on sex, sex with possibly a bit of shared interest and background thrown in. Now he knew differently. Love, it seemed, was losing control.

He picked up the phone, dialled Alice's number. Jemima answered the phone.

'Hi, Mimi. It's Mungo.'

'Oh hi, Mungo. How was the wedding?'

'Er – interesting. Is your mother there?'

'I'll get her for you.'

Alice's low, slightly husky voice came down the line; if you could see that voice, Mungo thought, it would have a cleavage.

'Hallo, Mungo. I'm surprised you're free so soon. How did your speech go?'

'Well – it's been a funny old day. I need to see you.'

'Tonight? But Mungo, I thought – '

'Alice, it hasn't happened.'

'What hasn't?'

'The wedding. The bride ran away.'

'What!'

'Yes. Nightmare stuff. Christ, it's been awful. Anyway, I think I can get to London. There really isn't much point me being here any more. Are you free this evening?'

'Well – I could be. But – '

'Good. I'll disentangle myself and phone you when I'm on my way. It might be quite late. Does it matter?'

She hesitated slightly. Then, 'No. No of course not. But ring me first, won't you?'

'Yes of course. Bye, Alice. I love you.'

He felt instantly better: in touch with reality. He phoned the Bergins' hotel and was told they had all gone out. Great: that let him off the hook a bit. It would seem less uncaring to disappear if they'd all disappeared as well. And he could phone from Alice's, could always come back if he was needed.

Mungo showered, changed into a clean white shirt and his beloved 501s, the ones with the rip at the knee and the tear at the crotch, and put everything else into the big leather Gladstone Sasha had given him for his last birthday. Nice girl, Sasha: he hoped she'd last. For some reason, he wasn't sure what, he feared she wouldn't.

He decided he'd better at least tell his father he was leaving; as far as he knew both he and Sasha were in the bar. He went downstairs; they weren't there.

'Mr Buchan is in the pool, Sir,' said the barman, 'and Mrs Buchan has gone for a walk in the grounds.'

Mungo sighed, decided it would cause less trouble to leave a message with Sasha than his father and went to look for her.

It took a little while to find her; she was well out of sight of the hotel, sitting on a low wall beyond the tennis courts. She was talking on her mobile phone, no doubt gossiping with a girlfriend or fixing up to see some frocks, and she looked somehow different from how she usually did; Mungo, trying to analyse it, could only define it as an alertness, an air of purpose. She didn't see him coming for a while, she was engrossed in her conversation, but he didn't get near enough to hear what she was saying before she saw him, smiled, said *Ciao* – God, it was bimbo talk that – and switched the phone off.

'Hi, Mungo. How are you doing?'

'Oh – fine. You know. It's been a funny old day.'

'Certainly has. Where do you think she went?'

'Oh – God knows. The general idea seems to be she was under some kind of terrible strain and she just scarpered, couldn't take any more, but I think there's more to it than that.'

'Really? Like what?' The blue eyes were sharp, watchful suddenly, beneath the long sweeping lashes; the sugary smile just slightly set.

'I'm not sure,' said Mungo quickly. He certainly wasn't about to tell Sasha about Oliver's panic the night before, about the overdose. She was sweet, but he didn't absolutely trust her. 'What do you think?'

'I think she was certainly under a lot of strain. I talked to her yesterday. More than just normal wedding nerves, I would have said. I spoke to her briefly yesterday, in the garden here. I was quite struck by it.'

'What did she say?' asked Mungo, intrigued.

'It wasn't what she said. It was how she was. Tense, and – I don't know – odd. She had a long rambling conversation with me about make-up, and then just casually at the end she asked me if Theo was around, she wanted to ask him for something.'

'For something or just something?' said Mungo. 'There's quite a difference.'

'For. Definitely for. Anyway, he wasn't here, he'd gone into Oxford, but I said I could call him, give him a message. She said no, she'd speak to him later. But she never did. I asked him. He even rang her, but she said it was nothing, nothing at all.'

'And you've no idea what it was?'

'No idea at all. But I didn't get the impression it was nothing. At the time. I wondered if she needed money. Anyway, whatever it was all about, it's certainly a fairly drastic thing to do, run away on your wedding day. I would say she was pushed into it, that she didn't have any real choice.'

'What – you mean some kind of – well, blackmail?' Mungo was increasingly intrigued, excited even.

'Maybe not blackmail. But there has to be another element in it all somewhere, I think, some other person or factor forcing her hand. She really didn't seem to me the sort of person to just crack.'

'Oh I don't know,' said Mungo. 'She was very gentle, you know, very – well, soft, and sweet. Not a bit like Harry.'

'No, she didn't seem a bit like Harriet.'

'Now that sounded interesting,' said Mungo, grinning at her, sitting down beside her on the wall.

'What do you mean?'

'I mean it sounded as if you'd rather she had been like Harriet.'

'No. I mean I don't know either of them well,' said Sasha. 'But I like Harriet – what I've seen of her. I think she's clever and gutsy. She's got balls.'

'And you like your women with balls, do you?'

'Yes I do,' said Sasha, smiling at him.

'I'm surprised.'

'Why?'

'Oh – I don't know. You seem more of a Cressida to me. Than a Harriet.'

'Oh really? You mean you don't think I've got balls?' She was relaxed now, smiling more broadly; she was obviously enjoying herself. She seemed a rather different person suddenly. Mungo stared at her.

'Well, I – '

'I do hope, Mungo,' said Sasha gently, 'that you don't think I'm just a pretty little bimbo, with nothing in my head but getting my hands on your father's money.'

'What? No, of course not.'

'I think you do,' she said with a sigh, 'but it doesn't terribly matter.'

'Yes it does,' said Mungo, finding somewhat to his surprise that it did. 'If it matters to you, then it matters to me.'

'Oh Mungo, why?'

'Because you've been so nice to me,' said Mungo, suddenly picking up one of her hands. She had beautiful hands, very slender and delicate, the nails just a tiny bit too long (they were always a giveaway, nails, he was amazed girls never realized), longer than Susie or Alice would have worn them. She looked at him, startled, and then smiled again.

'Well, it wasn't very difficult,' she said, 'being nice to you. You were nice to me. Most people weren't.'

'Who wasn't?'

'Oh – most of your father's friends. Most of his business colleagues. All his employees. His dear son, Michael.'

'Michael sucks,' said Mungo briefly. 'You don't want to take any notice of him.'

'I try not to. Anyway, I've got used to it. But it isn't very nice. People are polite of course, but that really is all. It's a very – thin politeness, most of it.'

'I'm sure – '

'Mungo, it's inevitable. Everyone thought I was a gold-digger looking for a sugar daddy. And I suppose they were right. In a way. Although when I met him, I did genuinely fall in love with him. I found him irresistible. I suppose most women do. But of course money is very nice. Nobody could pretend it wasn't. And later, when it all began – '

'When what began?'

'Oh, you know, the patronizing, both by him and everyone else, and knowing he wasn't in love with me – '

'Sasha, I'm sure he is.' Mungo was beginning to feel uncomfortable now, felt she was telling him too much.

'Mungo, he isn't. He's only been in love twice. Once with your mother and once with – well, it doesn't matter who.'

'Tell me.'

'No. I won't. It's not my secret.'

Mungo felt a fierce curiosity. 'Did he tell you?'

'No. No of course not. I found out.'

'God. Sasha, please tell me. I won't tell anyone.'

'No, Mungo, I'm not going to. Now listen, this is getting out of hand. You look as if you're going somewhere.'

'I – well, I do want to go somewhere. Yes. To London. Do you think it would be all right?'

'And what's in London, Mungo?' She was grinning at him again, that easy, casual grin, so different from her careful neat smile. 'Love?'

'Yes. Actually. But don't tell Dad. Please.'

'I won't. As long as she's nice.'

'She's wonderful,' said Mungo simply. 'I'm going to marry her.'

'My goodness. Don't you think – ' Suddenly, sharply the phone rang; she looked at him quickly, said excuse me, turned just slightly away. 'Hallo. Yes, yes of course. Good. That's excellent. Fine. Yes, later tonight. Lovely, thanks for calling. Have to go now. Oh, Mungo, there's your father, coming now. You can tell him yourself.'

'Tell me what?' Theo's voice was good-natured, indulgent. 'Sasha darling, what on earth are you doing out here? I thought we had a tryst in the bar.'

'We did, but I got tired of waiting for you.' Sasha's voice was clear, surprisingly firm. 'And it is a lovely evening.'

Theo was silent; his face was hard to read. Then he said, clearly with an effort, 'Yes of course. Shall we have drinks out here? Mungo, will you join us?'

'Well – '

'Mungo wants to go to London,' said Sasha. 'Is there any reason why he shouldn't?'

'London? Well – I don't know. It seems a little – odd. We are in the middle of a very complex situation here, Mungo. Your friends need you; I need you. I really think it would be better if you stayed.'

'But Dad – '

'Mungo, I said I thought you should stay. All right?'

'But I don't see the point, what on earth can I do?' said Mungo. 'They've all gone out and – '

'Mungo, please. I said I'd rather you stayed.'

'Well I'm not going to stay,' said Mungo, his skin pricking with the familiar violent irritation that his father should still seek to control his actions. 'I've done my bit today. And last night. You have no idea – ' He stopped suddenly. He really didn't want to start discussing the events of the night before with his father and Sasha, didn't want to hear them start conjecturing, analysing it all.

'That's an extraordinarily selfish way of looking at it,' said Theo. 'I don't think I like that very much, Mungo.'

'Well I'm extremely sorry I can't aspire to your own high standards,' said Mungo. He knew he was sounding more and more like a spoil sulky child, but he couldn't help it. 'But I have something important to do.'

'Yes,' said Theo heavily. 'I can imagine.'

'Theo,' said Sasha suddenly. 'Theo, I really do think – '

'Sasha, this is nothing to do with you.'

Sasha got up in silence and walked over to the high fence that bordered the garden, stood looking out beyond it; Theo looked after her, seemed about to follow, then turned his attention back to Mungo.

'Right then. Are you going to have a drink with us?'

'No,' said Mungo. 'I'm not. I'm going to London.'

There was a silence, then Theo said, clearly struggling to keep his temper, 'Then perhaps I could ask why? What is so important? I do hope it's not just another poker game.'

'No, of course not. I – want to see someone.'

'Oh really? Who?'

'Do I have to tell you that as well?' said Mungo wearily.

'You don't have to, but I'd like to know.'

Theo's voice was suddenly quieter, more reasonable again. Mungo looked at him; he was half smiling, seemed genuinely interested. Go on, Mungo, go for it. You have to do it some time. Tell him, break the news.

'All right, I'll tell you. She's called Alice.'

'Pretty name. What does she do?'

'Works for a charity.'

'Oh, very debby.'

'She's – not a deb.'

'Ah. A power-suited executive then?'

'Not exactly. She – well, she's supporting her family.'

'Her family! What, you mean her parents?'

'No, her children.'

'Her children! Mungo, what are you trying to tell me? That you've got involved with some single parent? Very fashionable, very – what's the phrase – politically correct.' He was smiling now, his slightly dangerous, glittering smile.

Mungo swallowed. 'Yes,' he said, 'yes I have. Alice is divorced.'

'I see.' Theo looked genuinely nonplussed for a moment, not sure how to react. Sasha had come back to join them, was listening intently. She smiled at Mungo; it gave him courage, that smile, hope.

'How old is she, your Alice?' said Theo. 'How long has she been divorced?'

'Quite a long time. She's – she's thirty-nine.'

'Thirty-nine,' said Theo very quietly. He seemed to be thinking, processing the information. The phone still in Sasha's hand rang again; she switched it on, listened for a moment, said, 'I'll call you back.'

'Who was that?' asked Theo.

'It was Jackie.'

Jackie was their housekeeper in London; Sasha's unkinder critics had been heard to remark that she was a blonde version of Jackie.

'Oh really? Well, I'll speak to her later.'

'Theo, she called me.'

'Yes, so you said. Look, Mungo, I hope you know what you're doing with this relationship. Not getting in too deep.'

'Dad,' said Mungo, a sweep of rage, of outrage flooding through him, as he thought of how his father conducted his own private life, of the trail of misery, humiliation and chaos he left in his wake, 'Dad, I know exactly what I'm doing with the relationship. And I am getting in very deep as you put it. I'm going to marry Alice. Actually.'

'Oh really? I rather think you're not.'

'That's up to me, Dad. And I rather think I am.'

'That is a little open to debate, I would suggest,' said Theo. 'That it is up to you. Actually.' His sentences were growing shorter, as they did when he was really angry. Mungo looked at him, defiant, hoping his fear didn't show.

'Of course it's up to me. I'm twenty-seven years old. I can do what I like.'

'Is that so? Are you really? Twenty-seven, eh? Good Lord. That's hard to believe, Mungo, it really is. I mean the majority of twenty-seven year-olds are standing on their own feet, supporting themselves. I – '

'Don't start that,' said Mungo, 'don't throw that garbage at me about supporting myself. My agency is – '

'Oh Mungo, Mungo. You really are a child, aren't you? Do you realize what that office alone costs? And who's actually paying for it? Who put up the money for the lease, to pay your staff – '

'Theo, don't,' said Sasha. She sounded very upset.

'Stay out of this, Sasha. You don't know what you're talking about.'

Sasha looked at him, then at Mungo and turned and walked away towards the hotel. Mungo stood staring at his father, trying not to lose his temper, trying to be calm, rational.

'Look,' he said, his voice shaky with the effort of keeping it level. 'Look, Dad, let's start this again, shall we? I – know you're very generous. I know I'm very fortunate. But I really am making my own way now. I'd like that at least acknowledged.'

'OK,' said Theo. His voice suddenly sounded more even. 'I'll acknowledge that. You're making your own way. Tell me, how old are Alice's children?'

'Jemima's fifteen and – '

'Fifteen! For God's sake, Mungo, she's almost as old as you are. You can't be serious about this. You really can't.'

'I'm totally serious. I love Alice.'

'And I suppose she loves you?'

'Yes, she does. She's agreed to marry me.'

'Marry you! For Christ's sake, Mungo, what are you talking about? Marriage! How long have you known this woman?'

'Since the New Year.'

'Well that's a very long time. A very long time indeed. God Almighty, you're more of a child than I even thought. What are you playing at?'

'I'm not playing as a matter of fact,' said Mungo, making an immense effort not to shout. 'I'm being very serious. Trying to be responsible.'

'Look,' said Theo, sitting down gently on the wall, clearly struggling to control himself. 'Look, Mungo, what's the rush, for heaven's sake? Why do you have to marry this – person? I'm sure she's extremely nice, but six months really isn't a very long time. Can't you just – enjoy one another for a while? Why do you have to marry her? It's crazy.'

'You always do,' said Mungo. 'You always have to marry them. However crazy.'

He felt sick as he said it, knowing where it would lead. Many things made Theo angry, but being confronted by the truth about himself was the worst provocation. He had once hit Mungo when he was a little boy because he'd told his father he ate too much and that was why he was so fat. On the whole people went along with the comfortable untruths Theo managed to believe about himself.

But for some reason Theo seemed in no danger of hitting him, not even of shouting at him. He just looked at him with an infinite sadness and said, 'Yes and sometimes it's the wrong decision.'

Mungo was silent; he still felt slightly sick. Thank God Sasha had gone back to the hotel.

'And I don't mean Sasha,' said Theo, 'in case you thought I did. Now then, please, Mungo, please wait. For a while. Apart from anything else, and I'm sure you won't have thought this one through, you'll want children one day. And if your Alice is – '

'Of course I've thought it through,' said Mungo, angry again, 'and it's fine. Alice can still have children. She's checked it out. I wish you had some respect for me, for what I want, for what I'm doing. Alice is – well, she's very special. And I'm going to marry her. As soon as possible.'

There was a long, leaden silence. Then: 'Mungo,' said Theo quietly. 'Mungo, you simply can't do this. You can't.'

'Dad, I can. You can't stop me.'

'Well,' said Theo, 'maybe not. But I intend to go on trying. I cannot and will not go along with this madness.'

'It is not madness.'

'It's madness. On both your parts. And I wonder how influenced this woman – '

'Her name is Alice.'

'All right. I wonder how influenced Alice is by your situation.'

'What situation?'

'Oh Mungo, don't be so naive. You are an extremely wealthy young man. A very good catch for someone – '

'Dad,' said Mungo, 'just don't. Don't insult Alice. I'm in love with her and she's in love with me.'

'Oh really?' said Theo. He had a very odd expression on his face.

'Yes, really. I can't expect you to understand that, of course, because you're too bloody selfish and self-centred ever to have experienced it. You have to buy your wives.'

'Mungo,' said Theo, very quietly, 'Mungo, I would advise you to be careful what you say to me.'

'I won't be careful because you don't seem to understand. I don't have to buy Alice, she's going to marry me because she loves me, and just to prove it to you, I'm not going to take another penny from you as long as I live. I'm going to make my own way. With Alice's help. And I'll tell you something else, I'm glad. I've spent my whole life taking from you, being told by the whole bloody world how spoilt, how advantaged I was. Well in future that'll stop, because I'm going to be standing on my own feet, making my own way, and I can tell you that's a huge relief. You'd better remember this conversation, Dad, because it's the last one we're ever going to have. I'm going now, to London, and I won't be back.'

'Fine,' said Theo calmly. 'Absolutely fine. Bye, Mungo. Tell Sasha if you see her that I'd like her back out here, would you?'

'Deliver your own messages,' said Mungo.

He was back in reception carrying his bag when he remembered that he had no car. Well, that was all right. He could call a minicab. It was a pity, it meant a delay, but there was no real problem. On the other hand he didn't want to be hanging around the hotel waiting, quite possibly having to see his father again. Maybe he should get over to Oxford, take the train. He'd get Brian to take him to the station. Mungo was about to have Brian paged when he realized he was already doing exactly what his father had thought he would: calling on the apparently infinite resources that had been available to him all his life. Right, no Brian. He'd have to get a cab then. He picked up his bag and was about to walk out when he remembered the hotel bill. There was no way he was going to afford his father the satisfaction of picking up that one. He went over to reception, asked them to make out his share of the bill.

'Certainly, Mr Buchan.' The girl was wearing a tailored red suit and a striped shirt, the crisp neatness at odds with her wildly crinkly hair and heavily made-up face. She addressed herself to her computer with great self-importance; there was the ususal delay, the endless whirring and spewing of paper out of the machine. As Mungo stood there, trying to look calm, still shaking with emotion, with rage and something worse now, with grief, hurt, a call came in to the switchboard.

'Royal Hotel, Woodstock, how may I help you?' said the girl, passing up the bill to Mungo with a smile. (Three hundred and eighty pounds. Shit, couldn't be right, not for twenty-four hours.) 'I think he's in the grounds somewhere. I'll see if I can have him paged. What name shall I say?'

She looked up at Mungo again, said, 'Your father is still outside, isn't he, Mr Buchan?'

'Yes, I think so,' said Mungo shortly, 'by the tennis courts.'

'Miss Forrest, if you could just hold on a moment, I'll – '

'Hey, I'll take that,' said Mungo, his heart lifting at the thought of Harriet's slightly tough clear-sightedness. 'Tell her I'll take it. I need to talk to her anyway.'

'Well – Miss Forrest, Mr Buchan junior is here. Can he help you at all? Oh I see. Right. Well, then, if you'll hold, as I said I'll have him paged.' She looked up at Mungo, her face carefully, politely blank. 'I'm sorry, Mr Buchan, she said it was specifically your father she wished to speak to.'

'Oh,' said Mungo. 'Oh all right.' He felt disproportionately put out. 'Er – this bill. I don't quite see why it's so high – '

'Ah, well, let me just go through it for you,' said the girl, sweetly deadpan. 'There's the room, of course, that's a hundred and eighty. Your luncheon yesterday, for yourself and your friend, seventy pounds, that was mostly the wines of course, then the bar last night before dinner, thirty pounds, and the two bottles of champagne through room service, they came to sixty, and then – '

'Yes, yes, of course,' said Mungo, passing her his gold Amex card. 'Sorry. That's fine. Right. Well I'm off now. To Oxford,' he added, not sure why he should feel it necessary to tell her that.

'Can I call you a taxi, Mr Buchan? I can have it here in about three minutes.'

'Oh – yes. Yes, that would be very kind.'

He sat down again, picked up a copy of *The Field* and started thumbing through it. The girl was engrossed with her switchboard; taking calls, putting them through, taking messages; then he heard her saying, 'I'm sorry, Miss Forrest, we can't find him at the moment. Can I have him call you? I see. Well, all right, fine. You could try in half an hour maybe.'

What on earth was Harriet doing, refusing to speak to him, refusing to let Theo call her back? It was so unlike her. Well, they were all upset, nobody was behaving quite normally; if only Cressida would – Mungo suddenly went very cold. He stood up and walked over to the desk. 'Excuse me,' he said, 'but that call, from Miss Forrest, for my father, did she give another name? A first name? Or did she just say Miss Forrest?'

'Oh no,' said the girl, and he realized how silly he had been, that the hotel staff would surely have picked up on the drama, would have known Cressida had disappeared, would certainly have reacted to her name. 'No, just Miss Forrest.'

'And you have no idea where the call came from?'

'No, I'm afraid not. You never can now, not with direct dialling.'

'No, no, of course not. And it was a good line?'

'Yes, very good.'

'Oh. Oh, I see. Well – well, never mind. Could I just – make a call please?'

'Yes, certainly. If you go into that booth over there, I'll give you a line.'

He stood there, dialling the Court House, stood waiting, his heart thudding. It was just a chance, a very very slight chance, but he had to check up on it. It was too important not to.'

'Wedbourne 356. James Forrest speaking.'

'Oh – James. This is Mungo. Could I – could I speak to Harriet please?'

'Yes of course. I'll get her.'

'There was a long silence: then Harriet came on the line. 'Mungo, hi.'

'You're – you're speaking to me now then?' he said, trying to sound light-hearted, afraid of creating a drama before it was necessary.

'What? What are you talking about, Mungo?'

'You didn't just ring? Ask to speak to Dad?'

'No. No of course I didn't.'

'Well in that case Cressida did.'

'I don't understand.'

'A call just came through. From a Miss Forrest. I thought it must be you.'

'Shit. And she wouldn't speak to you?'

'No. And they couldn't find Dad. So she rang off. She's ringing back, though.'

'Oh God, Mungo, what do we do now?' Harriet's voice was very quiet. 'Oh how awful to have missed her. So near and yet so far. Can you find your father, talk to him? He must know something, he must.'

'Well – it might be difficult,' said Mungo. 'We just had a major fight.'

'Why? Has he gone back to London or something?'

'No. No he's here. I think. But we just had a mega fight.'

'What about?'

'Oh – I'll tell you when I see you.'

'Well, I think this has to be more important. There's some fairly staggering news this end too. I'll tell you when I see you.'

'Well – '

'Oh Mungo, really. Look, I'll come over. But I don't want to raise any hopes here. I'll make some excuse. OK?'

'Yes. Yes, OK. I was just – going to London actually.'

'Mungo, you can't. Not now. Can't it wait?'

'Yes,' he said, 'yes, of course it can.'

Alice was very sweet about it. He told her he couldn't get away after all, that there was some family conference going on about Cressida.

'Oh, and I told my father about us.'

'What about us?'

'That I intend to marry you.'

There was a long silence, then she said, 'And?'

'And he didn't take it too well, I'm afraid.'

'Well – I'm not surprised. Mungo, you shouldn't have rushed it. You should have introduced him to the idea slowly.'

'I couldn't. I wanted to tell him. I want to tell everyone. Well, I've done it now. I want us to get married very very soon.'

'Well – yes.'

'You want that too, don't you?'

'Yes. Yes, of course I do. Well, quite soon. When you say he didn't take it too well, what did you mean?'

'Oh – huge dramatics. But he's like that. He's like a child. He says I am, but he's worse. Anyway, I've told him that as far as I'm concerned we're finished. I don't ever want to see him or have anything to do with him again. Or take anything from him. He thinks I won't be able to manage, but I will. I'm sick of living in his pocket anyway, being beholden to him. This is my big chance, Alice, to prove myself. With your help. And I feel really good about it. As if I'm starting all over again.'

'Well,' said Alice, her voice soothing, 'I don't believe either of you meant it. I'm sure you'll be friends again soon.'

'Alice, I meant it and he meant it. And, like I said, I'm glad. I don't want any of his charity.'

'Hardly charity, Mungo. He is your father.'

'He sees it as charity, I can tell you. He sees it as one big handout. Which I'm just not going to take any more.'

'Well,' said Alice gently, 'well, we'll see.'

'Alice, there's nothing to see about. You seem rather concerned about all this. If – '

'Of course I'm concerned. But only for you. It seems so – sad.'

'Not sad at all. My father's a monster. And I find the thought of it all, of managing on my own, very exciting. Challenging. So what if he pays the rent on my office and lets me use his executive jet? Who needs it? I certainly don't. We can get married next weekend, if you like. In fact I think we should. Now look, I'll see you tomorrow. I really don't see myself getting up tonight, I'm afraid. But I can ring you, can't I? Any time?'

'Of course you can. Well, maybe not much after ten. I'm very tired. Tough day at the office.'

'Poor baby. Well, you'll be able to give all that up soon.'

'Yes,' said Alice. 'Yes, of course. Goodbye, Mungo.'

'Bye, darling.'

He didn't know quite what to do until Harriet arrived; he certainly didn't want to risk bumping into his father. He went into the bar, and saw Sasha sitting there alone. She was drinking champagne and flicking through *Tatler*; she had changed into a brilliant blue silk suit with a very short skirt, her tanned legs bare. She really was gorgeous, thought Mungo; if it wasn't for Alice he would quite seriously fancy her.

'Hi, Sasha.'

'Hallo, Mungo. Are you – OK?'

'Oh yes,' he said, smiling at her. 'Very much so. I'm sorry about the scene.'

'I felt so sorry for you, Mungo. But – '

'Let's not talk about it. What are your plans?'

'Long-term? Or right now?'

'Right now,' said Mungo, slightly surprised that Sasha should have anything as impressive as long-term plans.

'Oh, I think we're going to have dinner quite early. And then the idea is we go over to the Forrests. Theo feels he ought to be with them.'

'Harriet's actually on her way over here,' said Mungo. He felt Sasha stiffen slightly, and looked at her interestedly. 'You really don't like Harriet very much, do you?'

'Yes of course I do,' said Sasha briefly. 'She's fun.'

'But you prefer Cress?'

Sasha looked at him thoughtfully, clearly debating something. Then she said, 'Actually, Mungo, between you and me, I can't stand Cressida.'

'You can't stand Cressida? Why on earth not?'

'I think she's devious and manipulative. And she did something totally out of order to me.'

Mungo was so astonished he didn't notice that Sasha was sounding quite different from her usual self.

'What?'

'I can't tell you. Now. But it was malicious and very destructive. I couldn't believe it at the time. I can hardly believe it now.'

'Sasha, you can't do this,' said Mungo. 'Give me tantalizing little morsels so that I'm drooling and then declare the banquet's over for the day.'

'I'm sorry, Mungo. I really can't say any more. Maybe one day. I probably shouldn't have said that much actually. It just came out.'

'I think,' said Mungo, deciding she was after all to be trusted, thinking it might prompt further revelations, 'that she just phoned.'

'Phoned? Cressida phoned here?'

'Yes. Asked for Dad. Wouldn't speak to me. But they couldn't find him. And I didn't realize until she'd run off that it was her. Thought it was Harriet. Do you know where he is?'

'He's gone for a walk. A long walk, he said.'

'Uh-huh. No doubt reflecting upon the incompetence and ingratitude of his younger son.'

'Mungo, he loves you so much. You mustn't let it get to you. And you know he doesn't mean it.'

'Sasha, I really don't care if he means it. I mean it.'

'I'm sorry?'

'I'm absolutely determined to manage on my own. I don't want to have anything more to do with him. Or his lousy money. I don't need it.'

'Mungo – '

'And don't try telling me I do, there's a good girl.'

'Mungo,' said Sasha mildly, 'I do hate being talked to like that.'

'Like what?'

'Down to. Please don't do it.'

'Sorry,' said Mungo. Sasha was suddenly proving very unpredictable.

Theo and Harriet arrived almost simultaneously. They nodded and smiled briefly at one another; things were clearly not entirely happy between them. His father had probably been trying to tell Harriet how to run her business, thought Mungo; as if she needed that kind of advice.

Theo nodded equally curtly at Mungo. 'Thought you'd gone.'

'I was just leaving,' said Mungo, 'but there's been a development.'

'What kind of development?'

'Cressida phoned you.'

'What do you mean she phoned me? Why wasn't I told?'

'They paged you. They couldn't find you.'

'Christ,' said Theo. 'Christ Almighty. They can't have tried very hard. Why didn't you come and look for me, or Sasha?'

'We didn't realize it was her, for God's sake,' said Mungo, 'until she'd rung off. But she's phoning again. Quite soon hopefully.'

'And there's something else,' said Harriet, 'something totally unexpected, something you have to know. Apparently she's – '

'Oh Theo,' said Sasha and her expression was sweetly, carefully contrite. 'Sorry to interrupt, Harriet. I'm so sorry, Theo, I almost forgot with all the excitement. Could you call Mark? He said it was very urgent. Very urgent indeed. I tried to find you but – ' her voice trailed away.

Mungo looked at her. The coolly composed woman who had been sitting in the bar half an hour earlier reading *Tatler* and drinking champagne had not seemed too much like someone anxious to give her husband a very urgent message. The fifth Mrs Buchan had stepped sharply out of character; he wondered suddenly if it could possibly have anything to do with Cressida's disappearance.

'For Christ's sake when?' said Theo. 'When did he call? You don't have a great deal to remember, Sasha, I wish you'd – look, I'm going upstairs to call him. If Cressida phones, they can just interrupt the call, put her through. All right?'

'All right,' said Harriet. She had an odd expression on her face. Theo disappeared; they all sat picking compulsively at peanuts, not looking at one another. Not for the first time that day Mungo felt as if he was caught up in some rather strange film.

'Apparently,' Harriet said abruptly, in between munches, and Mungo never forgot that moment as long as he lived, the almost casual way she dropped her bombshell, 'apparently Cressida was pregnant.' She smiled brightly at them both, brushed some salt off her navy shorts. They stared at her.

'Well,' said Sasha finally, 'well, she won't be the first pregnant bride. Where I come from, it's considered rather posh to get married when you're not pregnant.'

Harriet smiled at her uncertainly. 'Yes of course,' she said politely. 'I mean, no of course she won't. It's just – well – '

'Not terribly like Cressida,' said Mungo.

He was, against all logic, rather shocked. He knew it was absurd, but he couldn't help it. Of course Sasha was right, of course it wasn't unusual, and not even Cressida, sweet, slightly shy, absolutely conventional Cressida would be going to the altar a virgin; but – pregnant? He thought of the drama of the night before, with Oliver, and tried to put it together with this new piece of information. It just didn't fit. None of it fitted.

'Harriet, how do you know anyway?' asked Sasha. 'Who told you and when?'

'Oliver told us,' said Harriet casually, 'about an hour ago.'

'I see,' said Sasha, her fine eyebrows arched, her voice slightly thoughtful. 'Poor Oliver. Poor, poor Oliver. It gets worse and worse, doesn't it?'

'Yes,' said Harriet. 'Yes it does. Poor Oliver,' she added dutifully, but she sounded almost impatient suddenly.

'And how did everyone take this announcement?' asked Mungo. He was trying to imagine Julia's reaction, Maggie's. 'Were they all very shocked?'

'Well, there wasn't time really,' said Harriet. 'I mean, he'd only just announced this when you phoned. I came haring over. Bit of a bombshell, though.'

'Yes,' said Mungo, 'it is a bit.'

They sat looking at one another, embarrassed without knowing why.

Then Harriet got up; it was a very decisive gesture, as if she'd just made a difficult decision and had to act on it. 'Excuse me,' she said, and walked out into reception; Mungo followed her. She went over to the desk, spoke to the girl.

'If my sister phones for Mr Buchan, could you let me speak to her first?' she said. 'It's important.'

The girl looked doubtful. 'Well, she was very emphatic last time, Miss Forrest, that she spoke to – '

'Look,' said Harriet, 'I wasn't here then. She's my sister. I need to speak to her. You can put her through to Mr Buchan after that.'

'Harry,' said Mungo. 'Harry, I don't think that's a good idea. This is such a delicate situation. Why don't you just let Cressida speak to Dad? That's what she wants.'

'Look,' said Harriet, and her face was tense, her voice shaky. 'Look, Mungo, I'm sorry, but this is nothing to do with you. Cressida will speak to me. Of couse she will. She's my sister, for God's sake. She just doesn't know I'm here, that's all. If she did, she'd ask for me.' Her face was very white, her eyes huge and dark.

Mungo hesitated, then he said, 'Harriet, I'm sorry, I'm really sorry to say this, but if she'd wanted to speak to you she'd have rung you at home. At the Court House. Don't you think?'

'No I don't,' said Harriet, and her voice was icy cold. 'Of course she wouldn't. She might have got Daddy, Mummy, anybody. Now please stay out of this, Mungo, I really don't think it has anything to do with you.'

Mungo shrugged and went back into the bar. Harriet's stubbornness, her blind pursuit of what she knew was best, was legendary. There was absolutely no point pursuing this one any further.

Sasha looked up at him, raised her eyebrows. 'Problem?'

'Not yet,' said Mungo. 'Would you like another drink, Sasha?'

'No, thank you,' said Sasha. 'I have to keep a clear head for the next couple of hours.'

Mungo, intrigued, was about to ask her what for, apart from what she might choose to wear for dinner, when Harriet came back in. She gave them a faint smile and sat down, fiddling with the gold link bracelet she always wore. She didn't say anything. Mungo looked at her, and he knew what had happened. He put his hand on her arm, patted it gently, offered her her glass. She shook her head rather feebly.

And then Theo came back into the bar. Looking surprisingly cheerful. Maybe, thought Mungo, his heart lifting, maybe Cressida had phoned back, spoken to him, told him where she was; maybe she had, after all, only been in some minor accident, been taken ill, had some personal crisis to deal with that was now over.

But: 'Nothing from Cressida then?' said Theo. 'Bloody Mark, gone out for a meal. Won't be available for another hour. We'd better all have another drink and wait for her. Why don't we all go up to our room, darling, it's nicer up there?'

Mungo was not looking at Harriet, but he felt her start forward and then withdraw again in a swift involuntary response to – what? Then he looked at Sasha and she was staring at Harriet too, a most odd expression in her big blue eyes, thoughtful, watchful and somehow compassionate. What was this? What was going on here? And then Harriet stood up, faced Theo full square, visibly braced for battle, and said, 'Theo, I'm sorry, I've made a bit of a hash of things.'

'Oh really?' he said lightly, but his voice had an edge to it. 'How unlike you, Harriet. What is it this time?'

'Cressida did ring,' said Harriet, her voice very calm. 'and I – I took the call.'

'I'm sorry?' said Theo. 'You took it? But it was for me. I gave strict instructions for it to be put through.'

'Yes I know that, Theo, but I knew – well, I thought – that Cressida would want to speak to me. You were engaged anyway,' she added, her eyes just slightly defiant, 'and she wouldn't have held on. Obviously.'

'I don't quite see that,' said Theo. 'But anyway, do go on. You took my telephone call and then what happened?'

'Well, she – she said – '

'Harriet, a few simple words should suffice here,' said Theo. He smiled at her, an icy, cold-faced smile. His voice was deathly heavy. 'Do try to put them together for us.'

'She rang off,' said Harriet. 'I said it was me and she just rang off.'

'And then?'

'Well, and then nothing.'

'Nothing at all?'

'No.'

'Nothing about where she is, how she is, what she might like us to do?'

'No.'

'You bloody fool,' said Theo quietly. 'You bloody, arrogant little fool.'

'I thought,' said Harriet, and her eyes were blank now as she faced him, 'I thought it would be better. I thought she'd want to talk to me.'

'Oh really? You thought that, did you? You thought. So you take my telephone call, override my instructions, intrude into my affairs, because you thought. Well, you didn't think, Harriet, did you? You didn't think at all. Actually.'

Christ, thought Mungo, it was foul beyond belief the way his father treated people, adult people, as if they were just mindless incompetents, but mindless incompetents who were his property, who owed him respect, obedience, allegiance. There was some slight excuse, he supposed, when those adults were in fact his own children, his employees, even to a faint, albeit arguable degree, his wives, but someone like Harriet, over whom he had no authority, no hold, that was seriously outrageous. He waited, as she stood there taking it, taking the distaste, the contempt, the – what was it? – the sheer dislike, wondering why she took it, why she didn't walk away, answer back, stop what was a most public humiliation. But she didn't.

'I'm sorry,' she said.

'Yes, well, I expect you are. Unfortunately your sorrow is not going to be a great deal of help to us. Jesus, Harriet, she could be anywhere, anywhere at all, she could be in danger, in trouble, she could be hurt, she could be ill, and she reaches out to ask for help, in her own way, and you ride in with your fucking, mindless arrogance and pull all the plugs on her. I don't understand you, I don't understand you at all.'

'I know that,' said Harriet quietly, and Mungo thought what an odd thing it was for her to say, and in such a way, then he realized, confusedly, that despite his father's rage and Harriet's defiance there was a strange intimacy between them, an undercurrent of emotion that he could not, did not want to, analyse.

'Well,' said Theo, 'well, that's that, I would imagine. She won't ring again. She'll be afraid to ring again. You'd better get back to your family, Harriet, tell them what's happened, tell them we had a chance of helping her, of knowing where she was, and that you've wrecked it. They may not be entirely pleased with you, but I think that's what you should do. I'm going back upstairs, I have other calls to make. Sasha, you'd better come up with me. Now just in case you should be passing the switchboard when any calls, any calls at all, come through for me, Harriet, would you be good enough not to take them? It might conceivably be better that way. Mungo, you can do what you like. I really don't care.'

'That's extremely good of you,' said Mungo icily.

Sasha stood up. She looked heavily, dreadfully sad. She put her hand out briefly to touch Harriet's arm, then followed Theo out of the bar. Mungo went rather helplessly towards Harriet, put his arms round her shoulder and gave her a hug.

'I'm so sorry,' he said, 'he's such a bastard. He had no right to talk to you like that.'

'Oh but he did, Mungo,' said Harriet, with a great tear-filled sigh. 'He had every right. You have no idea how much right he has. To talk to me any way he pleases.'

Chapter Sixteen

Theo 7pm

'That was a terrible way to behave,' said Sasha.

She had closed the door behind her; she stood leaning against it, staring at him. 'Really terrible. Poor Harriet.'

'I'm sorry you should think that,' said Theo. 'I personally think it was Harriet who behaved terribly as you put it. High-handed, thoughtless.'

'Yes, Theo, I heard you. We all did. The entire hotel did, I would imagine. Mindless fucking arrogance I think was your precise phrase. Not pretty.'

Theo looked at her. He was feeling disorientated already, and Sasha was hardly helping.

'I'd rather you didn't criticize me,' he said. 'What Harriet did was absolutely out of order. And, as it turns out, disastrous. You have to see that.' He went over to the drinks tray, poured himself a large whisky and started to light a cigar.

'I think disastrous is a rather strong word,' said Sasha. 'Unfortunate, maybe, but not a lot more than that.'

Theo felt a surge of irritation; he drew on his cigar, looked at her through the smoke.

'Sasha, I don't think you quite appreciate the full extent of what's happened today. I – '

'Theo, I perfectly appreciate it. Cressida has run away. She didn't want to marry Oliver, so she removed herself from the possibility. She's obviously been planning it for some time.'

'Why do you say that?'

'Well, it's so obvious. There's the pilot's licence, the letter – '

'Sasha, I don't think you know what you're talking about. Of course she wasn't planning it. Something pushed her into it at the last minute – '

'Or someone – '

'What do you mean, someone?'

'I think there was someone else,' said Sasha. 'I think she was in love with someone else. Did you know she was pregnant?'

Her words hit him like a slug in the stomach; he put down his glass, stared at her.

'Pregnant? Of course she wasn't pregnant.'

'Yes she was,' said Sasha coolly. 'Harriet told us. Just before you had your little tantrum.'

'Sasha, please don't speak to me like that.'

'Theo, I shall speak to you how I like.'

Theo looked at her. It was like being in a room with a stranger. A stranger he wasn't at all sure that he liked very much. He hung onto what was relevant with a great effort.

'OK, so she was pregnant. A lot of brides are – '

'And just suppose the baby isn't – Oliver's.'

'Oh don't be absurd. Why the hell shouldn't it be Oliver's?'

'Why the hell should it? Since she's run away from him.'

'Sasha, do you know anything about all this? You seem remarkably well informed.'

'I don't know any more than you do, Theo. But I have feminine intuition on my side.'

'Ah,' he said, 'that old thing.'

'Yes, that old thing. I happen to put quite a lot of faith in it. And I also have common sense. If you thought about it all a bit, Theo, I think you'd probably concede it was quite likely that baby is someone else's.'

'And whose do you suppose it is then?'

'Theo, I don't know. I only just heard about it a few minutes ago. Oliver had apparently only just mentioned it when Harriet came over here.'

'Pity she didn't stay there,' said Theo heavily. He had to admit that Sasha's theory made sense and he felt very shocked and very upset. Cressida, sleeping with someone else – rather seriously sleeping with them – when she was engaged to be married to Oliver. Cressida, whom he'd known all her life, since she was a tiny, unbelievably beautiful baby, lying in a frilled crib in the nursery at the Court House. And suddenly he was there, smiling down at her, his arm round Maggie's shoulders, and she had asked him to be godfather and he had said . . .

*

'I'm not a very suitable person to be anyone's godfather, Maggie,' he said. 'Immoral, amoral, you name it – '

'I'd still like it,' said Maggie. 'Very much. Besides, you'll do all the other things so well, make a fuss of her, give her lovely presents, throw parties for her . . .'

He laughed suddenly. 'You're quite pragmatic, aren't you really, Maggie?'

'Yes,' she said, 'very, actually.' And burst into tears.

'Hey,' he said, 'what's this, postnatal depression?'

'No', she said, 'just the good old-fashioned kind.' And then she looked at him and said, 'You know, Theo, don't you? About why he married me?'

'Yes,' he said, 'yes of course I do. Because he loves you. That's why.'

'No,' she said, 'no, Theo, that's not why. He married me to please my father. To get his consultancy. All that.'

'Maggie, that is nonsense,' said Theo, feeling panic clutch at his heart and his vitals at the same instant. 'Absolute nonsense. Jamie loves you. Very much. He wanted to marry you. He's very happy. Look at the pair of you. You're such a success. Two lovely little girls, a thriving career, this lovely house – '

'Yes, and no love,' said Maggie. 'No love at all. Well, I love him, but he doesn't love me. Don't, Theo, please don't. I'd rather you were honest, actually. It would make me feel better, less insulted. I feel at the moment there's a kind of conspiracy between you – '

'Oh Maggie,' said Theo, taking her in his arms, giving her a rib-crushing hug. 'Maggie, there is no conspiracy. I swear. And I certainly love you. Very much.'

'Well,' she said, 'at least that's something. It's quite hard, Theo. To know you were simply chosen for your dowry. That's what it was, you know. My dowry. The job at St Edmund's. Oh, I'm sure he's fond of me. I know he is. But he doesn't love me. Not how I love him. He didn't choose me for the – the right reasons.' Her voice shook; she tried to smile at him. 'And that's hard, Theo. It's very hard.'

'Well,' he said carefully (mindful that he must not sound dishonest, and therefore insulting), 'well, maybe there is some truth in it. But I do know his world revolves around you, Maggie. He does love you. Maybe – at the time – it wasn't an earth-moving kind of a thing. But I've known him a long time. And I can see when he's happy, the old bugger. And he's happy and he's fulfilled and for Christ's sake, Maggie, isn't that what marriage is really about?'

'Yes,' she said, with a heavy sigh. 'But you both need to be happy and fulfilled, wouldn't you say? And I'm really not.'

There was a silence. Then she said, 'But anyway, I'm not about to give up on him. On it. On the marriage. I've got what I wanted, in a way. And Cressida is a symbol of that.'

'Why?' he said, interested. 'Why do you say that?'

'Oh – I told him I knew. Just about nine and a half months ago now, actually. I told him I knew why he'd married me. And that even so I was going to make it work. And he cried and said he would make it up to me somehow. And that very night, Cressida was conceived. So you see how special she is, don't you?'

'Yes,' he said, 'yes, Maggie, I do.'

★

And a quarter of a century later, it seemed, she was indeed a symbol. A symbol of faithlessness, of manipulativeness, of sexual infidelity: of all the things her father displayed every day of his life. Theo felt sick at heart. He stared at Sasha, and his feelings obviously showed in his face for she came towards him, and kissed him quite gently on the lips.

'Poor Theo,' she said, 'you look upset. I'm so sorry.'

'Well,' he said, 'well, there's no point in conjecturing about any of it.'

'Not really.'

'And she gave you no clue yesterday when she talked to you? That she was frightened, anxious – pregnant?'

'None at all. She was jumpy, I told you that. Unsettled. But that was all.'

'Well,' said Theo with a sigh. 'No doubt we shall find out in due course. About all of it. Although – '

'I know,' said Sasha. 'We might be nearer, if Harriet hadn't done what she did. I can see why you were so angry.'

'It's just if she needs us. Needs help. And of course it would be good to know where she is.'

'You really don't think she'll ring again?'

'Not now. Not tonight. She'll be afraid of – well, of having to speak to anyone. Anyone she doesn't want to. Of having the call traced. All sorts of things.'

He finished his whisky, poured himself another, sat down and started playing with the remote control of the television. Sasha walked forward and gently removed it from him.

'I want to talk to you. What did Mark want?'

'Oh – business. Nothing for you to worry about.'

'Theo, I am growing a little tired of this,' she said.

Theo smiled up at her, put out his hand and took hers. He raised it to his lips. 'Of what, my love?'

'Of being treated like some little tart who's only fit for one thing.'

'But my darling, you're so very fit for it,' said Theo. He suddenly wanted her, wanted to be in bed with her, wanted to be taken away, however briefly, from this dreadful day. 'So beautifully, wonderfully fit. Come and sit down here. I want you to distract me.'

She looked at him and he thought for a moment she was going to refuse, then she sat down beside him and smiled at him very sweetly.

'The silly thing is,' she said thoughtfully, 'I'm really rather fond of you.'

Theo stroked her hair. 'I don't see why that's silly,' he said.

'You will,' said Sasha, 'I'm afraid.'

'Sasha, what are you talking about?' said Theo. He felt very tired and slightly drunk, and he was finding Sasha's behaviour disturbing. 'Look, let's go to bed. You look gorgeous and I need a fuck.'

'But I don't,' said Sasha.

Theo felt as if he had been hit. In the whole nine months of their marriage, Sasha had never refused him, had never even hinted that she was not one hundred and one per cent ready for him.

'What is this?' he said, trying to smile. 'What's wrong? Do I have bad breath or something? Should I have a shower?'

'No,' said Sasha coolly, 'but I should.'

She stood up, walked into the bathroom and shut the door. Theo poured himself another whisky, and sat trying to pretend that this was absolutely par for the course, that women were unpredictable, sexually quixotic, not to mention slaves to their hormones, that it had been a tough day, he should take this like a man. And the more he told himself all this, the more he knew there was something wrong. Most women were unpredictable and sexually quixotic (Harriet particularly so, her mood swings and libido fiercely, erotically interesting, and why was he thinking about Harriet and sex in one breath at this moment when, if she had walked through the door, he would have hit her?), but Sasha was not. Sasha was a constant flame, a lovely liquid, constant flame, it was the greatest source of his fondness for her, it had healed and soothed him after the pain of Harriet. And now, in his hour of great need, she was failing him. Well, she couldn't. It was unendurable.

Theo stubbed out his cigar, took a last swing of whisky and walked into the bathroom.

Sasha was in the shower; he could see the outline of her slender body against the glass door. God, she was gorgeous. The mind, the soul might not be quite there, but the body was. Theo stood staring through the glass, thinking about Sasha, about the feel of her, the look of her, the gently golden all-over tan, the firm, high breasts (there had to be a bit of silicone there, she denied it absolutely but he still suspected it), her slighly bony hips, her flat stomach, and her surprisingly thick golden-brown bush. And within the bush, behind it – Theo felt his heart beginning to beat uncomfortably hard; desire ripped through him. He tore off his belt, his trousers, his shirt, opened the shower door; and Sasha stood there, looking at him, her eyes moving thoughtfully over him, lingering contemplatively, almost amusedly on her erect cock. But she did not reach out for it, as she usually did, did not press her small, greedy body against him, onto him, but turned her back towards him, and stood there, her face raised into the thudding water.

Theo suddenly lost not just his temper but his senses. He stepped forward into the shower, pulled her round and started to kiss her, ramming his penis against her. She pulled back, startled; he went on. He knew he was being stupid, brutal even, but he couldn't help it. He had to have her, had to lose himself in her hot sweetness, had to try to forget the dreadful day.

'Theo!' said Sasha, her voice very calm, very loud against the background of the thudding water. 'Theo, stop it. Please. I don't – I don't want to. Stop it.'

But he couldn't stop; he was in the grip of a wild, angry hunger, a hunger that was totally out of control, and he was out of control with it, grasping, pushing, thrusting at her; and still she resisted, stayed closed to him. And then he was in her; and it was wrong, different, she was tight, hard, hostile, not the Sasha he knew, not fluid, not welcoming, her mouth lifeless under his, her hands hanging motionless at her sides. And still he went on, he had to, pushing into her, rising, falling, and then quite quickly it was over, he felt the rush, the flooding, the release, and felt something else too, almost at once, something rare and ugly and unfamiliar; shame he supposed it was. And he withdrew from her and stepped back out of the shower and shut the door without meeting her eyes.

He pulled on a robe, and went and lay down on the bed; he felt sick and wretched and very tired. After a long time she came in too, a towel wrapped round her sarong style, and started to rummage through the cupboard for something to wear without looking at him.

'I'm sorry,' he said suddenly, startled to hear the words. 'So sorry, Sasha. Please forgive me. I won't do it again.'

She looked at him rather distantly. 'Good,' she said. 'I'm pleased to hear it.'

'I was – upset,' he said.

'Oh dear.'

Shit, who was this? This coolly controlled woman, with no apparent desire to please, to say the right thing, to comfort him, to screw him, for God's sake.

She looked at him across the room. 'Would you like a drink?' she said, in the same distant tone. 'Because I would.'

'Yes,' said Theo, 'Yes I would. Scotch. No ice. Thank you,' he added as an afterthought.

She gave him a look of half amusement, half dislike as she handed him the glass. She sat down on a chair in the corner of the room with a glass of white wine and sipped it slowly and carefully, as if it was important what it tasted like.

'I'm sorry,' he said again. He had lit another cigar.

'That's all right,' said Sasha, 'I'll get over it. So what are you upset about?'

'Mark had news for me,' said Theo, 'quite bad news as a matter of fact. On a small scale.'

'What sort of bad news?'

'Sasha, I don't want to talk about it.'

'Theo, I do. All right?'

The same detached look, the distant coolness. For some reason it worried him. What the hell was going on? Well, it might actually help to tell her, to talk about it. Set it in perspective, clarify what he might do next.

'Oh – yes, all right. There was a company I very much wanted to get hold of.'

'Called?'

'CalVin.'

'Ah. The wine company.'

'Yes. How do you know that?'

'I know lots of things, Theo. You'd be surprised.'

'I'm beginning to be. Anyway, it was – is – in California.'

'Yes, I know. In the Napa Valley.'

'That's right,' said Theo. 'In the most beautiful spot. I'd rather fancied building a house there as a matter of fact.'

'Oh really? For whom?'

'For you and me of course.' Now what was going on? He looked at her, but her eyes were clear, wide, unreadable.

'I see. Well, so what's happened?'

'What's happened is that some other bastard has got hold of it. Well, of a lot of it. Bought a huge block of shares just today. God knows why, and it doesn't really matter, but – but – '

'It hurts,' said Sasha with that same distant look, 'doesn't it, Theo? Seeing your plans scuppered, all awry? Seeing someone playing with you, with what you want to do? It hurts.'

'Yes,' said Theo, 'it hurts. It hurts like hell. And it makes me very angry.'

'With whom?'

'With a great many people. With Mark, for letting this thing slip through his fingers. With whoever bought the fucking thing. With myself, I suppose.'

'I see,' said Sasha. 'Well, I'm sorry.'

She got up again and pulled the big leather case she had brought with her out of the clothes cupboard. She opened it, and then began taking things out of drawers and off hangers and piling them on the bed beside the case. Theo looked at her irritably.

'What the hell are you doing? I don't want to leave. We have to stay here with James.'

'You do,' said Sasha. 'I don't.' She was dressing now, pulling on some leggings and a T-shirt; she sprayed herself with perfume, brushed her hair, started checking through her handbag.

'I beg your pardon?' Theo put the cigar down in the ashtray by the bed, and stared at her.

'I don't want to stay here. I can't do anything. Sorry as I feel for everyone. So I'm going back to London.'

'You are doing nothing of the sort,' said Theo. 'I need you here with me.'

'Well, you'll have to make do without,' said Sasha sweetly.

'Sasha, you are not to go back to London. Absolutely not.'

'Theo, I'm going.'

A black, rising rage took hold of Theo. He stood up, moved across to her, took her arm in a violent grip. It was very thin, that arm, he noticed, little bigger than one of his own wrists, but it was extremely strong.

'You're staying, Sasha.'

'Theo, I'm going. For good. And let go of me. Now.'

Theo felt the ground shifting beneath him; the walls seemed to be moving before his eyes. Sasha's face, on the other hand, was quite still, gazing up at him, the eyes calm and contemptuous in the eye of the storm.

'Theo, I think I should tell you something. The – er – bastard who bought all those shares in CalVin. It was me.'

'You! Oh don't be so ridiculous.'

'I'm not,' she said. 'I bought them. They're mine.'

'But you haven't got any money.'

'Yes I have.'

'Well it's my money, if you have. And if you've used my money to do that, then the company is mine.'

'No, Theo, I think not.'

He stared at her; she was smiling gently, almost pityingly at him. He got up, refilled his glass, sat down again, without taking his eyes from her. She hadn't moved.

'I think I'd better explain.'

'I think you had.'

'You've been very generous to me, Theo. Very. Given me lots of lovely things. Lots. Except – '

238

'Except what, Sasha?'

'Except any kind of respect. Any real emotion. Just – what? – indulgence. And it wasn't very nice, Theo, actually. I didn't like it. I'm not a stupid woman, I don't enjoy being put down at dinner tables, belittled at parties, treated like some kind of pet poodle. I don't like being told I won't understand things I'm well able to understand and to stay out of things I would really enjoy being involved in. It's hurtful and humiliating. I did actually love you at first, Theo. You might find that hard to believe but it's true. I would have married you if you hadn't had any money at all actually. I thought you were lovely. Clever and charming and witty. And very very sexy of course. But it's worn out, that love. You've wrecked it, Theo, by the way you've treated me. It's not just me either, it's Mungo and Mark and – well, almost everyone. I just can't respect you. I really don't even like you any more.'

Theo wanted to speak but he couldn't. If his entire life had depended on his getting out a dozen sensible consecutive words, he would have died then and there. He just sat, taking slug after slug of whisky, staring at her.

'Anyway,' she went on more briskly, starting to put things neatly into her case. 'Anyway, I thought I'd show you that I wasn't as stupid as you thought. And do something for myself into the bargain. So I sold lots of the things you'd given me. Jewellery mostly, I had copies made, but a few clothes too, the really wonderful things, the Saint-Laurent evening dresses and the Chanel suits. Of course I didn't get very much for them, but it was enough. And I invested the money, did quite well.'

'How did you know what to – buy?' asked Theo. His voice was hoarse, rasping.

'Theo, don't be silly! I live with a master. I only had to listen and then instruct my broker. It was easy. Anyway, this was the big one, buying CalVin. Or most of CalVin. I bought that share in Tealing Mills yesterday, and sold it this morning. That's why I went out early, to find a phone. And then with that money, I bought CalVin. I'm sorry, Theo, but I really wanted it. I think I'll keep it. Of course I haven't been out there yet, to look at it, at the vineyard, but I will now. Maybe tomorrow if I can get a flight.'

Theo managed to speak again. 'I'll sue you,' he said simply, 'I'll sue you until you can't afford a drink of water.'

'Theo, what for? I haven't done anything wrong. Well, I suppose it was morally wrong, to sell the jewellery, but not legally. I don't think. It was all gifts, surely, you didn't plan on wearing any of it, or giving it to the next Mrs Buchan? And anyway, think how stupid you'd look, Theo, if you did sue me. Outwitted by your bimbo of a wife. I think you should keep very very quiet, actually. In any case' – she walked over to him,

239

kissed him gently on the forehead – 'I don't terribly mind if you do. I'm a survivor, and it will have been worth it. I'm off now. To London. Goodbye, Theo. It's been a lot of fun. Say goodbye to Mungo for me. He's a lovely boy. He's been really kind to me. Oh, and Theo, I think you should get together with Harriet again. She's obviously still in love with you, and you've never begun to get over her. Have you?'

'Did she tell you about it?' said Theo, hanging onto sanity with immense effort. 'Because if she did – '

'No, Theo, of course she didn't. Harriet would never do anything so tacky.'

'So who . . .?'

'Oh', said Sasha, and there was an expression of immense distaste on her face, 'it was Cressida, Theo. Sweet, lovely, too-good-to-be-true Cressida. She told me, very soon after we were married, actually. It wasn't very nice of her, was it? And my goodness she enjoyed it. Anyway, I must go now. I have a taxi ordered, and a train to catch. Bye, Theo. Thank you for everything.'

Chapter Seventeen

Tilly 7pm

Tilly was in the nursery bathroom, lying in the bath, her Walkman turned right up, her eyes closed, concentrating on keeping her mind blank, not thinking even about Rosenthal (she was in no state to make that sort of decision), when Mungo came in. She wouldn't have known he was there at all had he not turned off the taps and in doing so knocked one of her feet. She opened her eyes with a snap and saw him looking down at her, his black curls even wilder than usual, smiling slightly apologetically. She switched off the Walkman and smiled back.

'Hi, Mungo.'

'Hi, Til. Sorry to – er – disturb you. I came in for a pee. And you were about to flood the entire place.'

'That's OK,' said Tilly equably. 'You go ahead and have your pee. Fine by me. I should have locked the door.'

'There would certainly have been a flood in that case, and anyway you couldn't have,' said Mungo. 'One of Nanny Horrocks's rules. No locks on her bathroom doors. You'd have liked Nanny Horrocks. She was ace. Tough as old boots, terribly strict, but such fun. She could play football better than the master at my prep school, and she was brilliant at poker too. I taught her, but she was better than me in no time.'

'Really? Well, I haven't known many nannies to compare her with,' said Tilly. 'How are things, and what are you doing here anyway? Apart from having a pee?'

'I brought Harry back. From our hotel. She had a mega bust-up with Dad. She's very upset.'

'Ah,' said Tilly. 'Poor baby. What about?'

'Well, she did do something a bit unfortunate. Cress phoned for Dad and Harriet insisted on taking the call and Cress rang off. So it looks like we lost her.'

'Silly bitch,' said Tilly amiably.

'Who, Harry?'

'No, of course not. Cressida. The more I hear of her, the more I discover, the less I like her. I mean, what a way to behave. God, I must sound like Nanny whatsername. But for heaven's sake, Mungo, if she

241

didn't want to marry Oliver why couldn't she just have said so weeks ago?'

'Oh, I think there's probably a bit more to it than that,' said Mungo. He sat down on the side of the bath. 'From everything I've heard. Mind if I stay? It's not a lot of fun down there.'

'Of course not,' said Tilly.

'I've never seen you naked in the flesh before,' he said, looking at her contemplatively. 'Only shared you with millions of others in replicate.' He smiled down at her, his dark eyes flicking over what was visible of her, her boobs and her knees.

Tilly grinned back. 'I hope I don't disappoint you.'

'Not at all. You look absolutely gorgeous. If I wasn't seriously in love with someone else, I'd be in there with you.'

'Then there'd really be a flood,' said Tilly. 'And don't forget I'm seriously in love too. But it would distract them all a bit from their problems.'

'Yeah. What are you actually doing here, Til? And where's Rufus?'

'Rufus is downstairs. Doing what he does best. Being charming, and soothing. And I was desperate for a bath and that old darling Merlin showed me in here, said it was the biggest bath in the place. He's a peach.'

'Yes he is. Harry says he's working himself up for a romance with Janine. Pretty cool, eh?'

'Ah, Janine. Cressida's godmother? She's very stylish.'

'Yes she is. My dad told me she and James had a thing once, when James was very young.'

'You're kidding me!'

'Not at all. He was a virgin of eighteen and she was a worldly Parisian of thirty-five, or something.'

'Ugh,' said Tilly and shuddered.

'You don't like James, I gather?'

'I do not.'

'He's OK,' said Mungo.

'He's not OK. I may tell you why one day.'

'You know him?'

'You could say that. We have a deal on, and I'm waiting to see if he delivers.'

'Tilly, this is unfair. Exciting me like this.'

'No it's not. It's very fair actually. Let's change the subject. What's happening?'

'Well, Harriet's come back to confess, and to see what if anything needs doing, and I'm taking her car on to London.'

'I might come with you,' said Tilly, plunging her small neat head under the water, emerging and shampooing it furiously. 'Would you mind? Why are you going to London anyway?'

'I can't take much more of this. I've had a huge row with my father, and I want to see my girlfriend.'

'Your girlfriend? Is she nice?'

'She's glorious,' said Mungo simply. 'I told you, she's the only reason I'm not in that bath with you.'

'You can tell me more in the car. Pass me that towel, would you?'

'What about Rufus? Won't he want to come?'

'Maybe, maybe not,' said Tilly briefly, 'but he's not coming.'

'Why not?'

'Can't tell you. Well, partly because he knows he has to stay here and be a soothing presence. Alongside his beloved mother.

'Don't you like Susie?' said Mungo surprised.

'Yes, of course I do. Why?'

'You sounded a bit – disapproving suddenly.'

'You're imagining things,' said Tilly briefly, but Mungo, who could be surprisingly perceptive, had touched a nerve. She was in fact still to establish exactly how she felt about Susie in the light of her discovery about Rufus's undoubted parentage; more amused than shocked certainly, concerned over Rufus rather than any major moral issue, but just the same her instant liking for Susie had cooled, dimmed.

She looked at Mungo and smiled reassuringly. 'Now could you maybe go and find him and ask him to come up and see me here?'

There was a gentle knock on the door. 'Come in,' said Tilly. Only Rufus would have knocked like that.

He came in smiling, pushed the door shut behind him. 'Hallo,' he said.

'Hallo,' said Tilly, and thought how for the first time in her life the expression 'My heart turned over' meant something, meant exactly in fact what she was experiencing now.

'Nice bath? Merlin told me he'd shown you up here.'

'Very. I feel a lot better.' She put out her hand, stroked his face. He caught the hand, kissed her palm. Sensation soared through Tilly, echoing down her body. 'Shit,' she said. 'Shit, Rufus.'

'What did I do?'

'Made me want to fuck you,' she said simply.

'Now?'

'No,' she said, thinking with sorrow of the conversation they had to have, as soon as possible, 'no, not now, it wouldn't be very proper, would it?'

'Ottoline Mills, when were you concerned about being proper?' asked

Rufus, smiling. He put his hand out again, undid the towel, pulled it off, touched her breasts. 'Lovely,' he said, 'so lovely, I love those breasts so much.'

Tilly was silent. His hand moved down, over her body, smoothing her stomach, his fingers strong, rhythmic. He bypassed her bush briefly, started stroking her thighs, moved forward, started to kiss her. He kissed very skilfully, Rufus did, Tilly thought, hanging confusedly to her determination through the whirlwind of beating, throbbing sensation travelling through her; slowly, carefully, and yet with immense pleasure. 'You kiss with your cock, did you know that?' she had said the very first time he had ever kissed her and he had laughed and said how novel. He was kissing her with his cock now, it was all she could think of, his strong, pleasure-bringing, powerful cock. She felt herself begin to tremble, her invariable signal of sexual arousal, and despite her resolve, pressed very gently, tremulously even, pressed her hips against his, pulled his head harder onto hers, pushed a hand down the front of his trousers, seeking, finding, caressing his penis.

'God,' said Rufus, 'God, Tilly, come on, let's find somewhere,' and he took her hand and she pulled the towel around her again, and he led her along the corridor and up the back stairs to the big attic room, locked it behind them.

'Oh my darling, darling Tilly,' he said, 'I love you so much, so very, very much.'

Tilly said nothing, but she smiled at him and lay down instantly on the dusty floor, opening her arms; he was pulling off his clothes, dragging off shirt, jeans, shoes, pants, his eyes locked with hers, and then he lay down beside her, and very gently began to kiss her breasts again.

Tilly threw back her head, her eyes closed, feeling his tongue circling her nipples, pushing herself against him, feeling his penis growing, growing against her; she loved this moment almost best, when he was still outside her, when every atom of her energy was absorbed in reaching for him, wanting him, urging towards him, when she could think, see herself opening to him, awaiting him, and then, then he was in her, sinking in, into her fathomless wet softness, his penis reaching into her charged, innermost places, and then she turned, rose, knelt above him, riding him, wildly, almost angrily, rising and falling with her own pleasure, feeling the circles begin, the whirling, powerful circles drawing her in, faster, faster, into a vortex of sensation, and she was plunging now, pulling at him, dragging him after her, forcing his own pleasure into her, and she heard herself cry out sharply, felt herself rising finally into the bright darkness, and then the tumbling of release, endless sweet falling, and she fell on him, kissing him, stroking him, loving him and wondering how she could possibly ever have thought of leaving him.

And then she opened her eyes and looked at him, looked at James Forrest's face, and knew that that was what she had to do.

'Now listen,' she said to Harriet who was sitting tearstained in the kitchen, drinking a cup of tea with Merlin, 'you are not to let them upset you. You did what you thought you had to do, and you've taken a lot of shit today – sorry, Merlin – and if Cressida doesn't want to talk to you, frankly, that's her loss. OK?'

'Well spoken,' said Merlin. 'Couldn't have put it better myself. Don't you worry, Tilly, I'll see they don't give her a hard time. Silly little thing. Needs her bottom smacked if you ask me.'

Tilly and Harriet both smiled at him, Harriet rather weakly.

'Pity you're going,' said Merlin to Tilly, 'I would have liked to get to know you better. Another time, perhaps.'

'That'd be good,' said Tilly. 'I'd like it too.'

'And you will go to Cressida's flat, won't you?' said Harriet. 'Just to make sure. Not that you'll be able to get in. But the caretaker might – well, you could explain.'

'Sure,' said Tilly, 'I'll explain. Don't worry. And I'll call you when I get home. Sure you won't come with me?'

'I'd love to,' said Harriet wistfully, 'but it would be running away. And whatever else, I've never done that.'

'Pity you didn't run away from the awful school,' said Merlin. 'Dreadful place. Cruelty to children sending you there.'

'Janine tried to save me too,' said Harriet, blowing her nose. 'What would I have done without the pair of you? She spent hours arguing with Daddy. I heard her once. And she wrote me more letters when I was there than anybody.'

'Did she by Jove?' said Merlin, his old head lifting and almost visibly sniffing the air with pleasure. 'What a girl, eh? Can't think why I never got together with her before. Anyway, I'm taking her out to dinner tonight, what do you think about that, both of you? Your mother didn't seem too pleased, but by my reckoning Janine's earned it.'

'Oh Merlin, no, don't go out,' wailed Harriet. 'I need you here.'

'Come with us,' said Merlin.

'Darling Merlin, I wouldn't dream of playing gooseberry. But you will be back, won't you?'

'Of course. Not too late either. Got to get going in the morning.'

'Tilly,' said Harriet suddenly, 'do you know anyone at Cotton Fields? The American leisurewear chain?'

'Sure,' said Tilly, 'I did some pictures for them a few weeks ago in

245

Mexico. Nice things. A bit like yours, only not such quality. They're doing a really great catalogue.'

'So who was there from the company?'

'Guy called Ken Lazard, the head of marketing, and the chief designer, poisonous little tart called tony joel without capital letters. If he said "tony written in lower case" once he said it a hundred times. I was ready to kick him in the balls, sorry, Merlin, by the end of day one.'

'But Lazard was nice?'

'Yeah, he was a honey. Why?'

'Well, I wondered if you could do a tiny bit of research for me. Some time. Thing is, they were going to come in with me, you know – '

'Harry! What the hell are you going in with anyone for?'

'Oh – it's called salvation, I think,' said Harriet. She looked into her mug.

'You in trouble?' asked Merlin sharply.

'You could say that, Merlin, yes. Just a tad. Only please don't say anything to anyone yet, will you? Specially not Janine, I don't want her worried.'

'No, no of course not. How bad are things, though?'

'About as bad as they can be. I have to – well, I have to go into liquidation in the next forty-eight hours, I would say.'

'Shit, Harry, why didn't you say so before? That's really terrible, and it's so unfair.'

'Yes, well, life's not fair, is it?' said Harriet, determinedly calm. 'And I have to say I've been extremely stupid. I probably deserve it. 'But – '

'Nonsense,' said Merlin, 'of course you don't. Look, anything I can do, Harriet, talk to a few people, beat them down, you know I will.'

'Merlin, I do know,' said Harriet, patting his hand, 'and thank you. Anyway the Cotton people seemed really keen until a couple of days ago. Practically signing. Then they just seemed to pull the plug, wouldn't talk to me, wouldn't return my calls. I just wanted to find out why.'

'Harry,' said Tilly slowly, 'how much money do you need?'

'Oh – about a million,' said Harriet cheerfully. 'See me through. Got it on you?'

'Not exactly,' said Tilly. 'But – '

'Tilly, what on earth are you hatching?' said Harriet. 'I know you earn a bob or two, but – '

'Oh, I might be able to help,' said Tilly. 'Tell you how another time. Anyway, I'll call Ken now. No time like the present, and it's a good time, mid-afternoon there. Otherwise we'll miss them. Got the number?'

'Tilly, you will be discreet, won't you?' said Harriet, thumbing through her filofax. 'I don't want to upset them if there's even the remotest chance.'

'Yeah, yeah,' said Tilly impatiently. 'Can I use this phone, do you think?'

'No, use my mobile. It's up in my room.'

Ken Lazard was in a meeting, his secretary said, and she didn't know when he might be out, could she say who was calling and maybe have him call her back when he had the time?

'Sure, tell him Tilly Mills,' said Tilly cheerfully, 'and I'd like to speak to him pretty soon – I have a message from Patsy Torminster.' Patsy Torminster had been her co-model on the shoot: as tall as she was, ashblonde and drop-dead gorgeous.

'I really don't see him able to call you before tomorrow soonest,' said the girl, a heavy frost descending on her voice, 'he is really very busy indeed.'

'OK, OK,' said Tilly. 'Just deliver the message, would you?'

Ken Lazard was on the line inside thirty seconds; Tilly grinned into the phone.

'Hi, Ken. That must be a very important meeting.'

'It is,' said Ken. 'How are you, Tilly?'

'I'm good, thank you. How are you?'

'Fine, fine. God, that was a good week. Didn't we have fun? What's this message from Patsy?'

'Well, there isn't exactly one,' said Tilly, a rather vivid memory rising in front of her eyes of Ken Lazard and Patsy Torminster writhing around in the Mexican surf, 'but she'll be in New York next week. And I'll remind her to look you up.'

'Bitch,' said Ken Lazard amiably. 'So what do you want, Tilly?'

'I want you to do a little research for me,' said Tilly. 'And then get back to me quickly. And I really will get you the name of Patsy's hotel in return. Now this is for a friend of mine . . .'

'Ken Lazard will ring me before the end of the day,' she said to Harriet, walking back into the kitchen. 'Their day. So in around three or four hours. OK? And don't worry, he will. He's very well motivated.'

'Tilly,' said Harriet, 'I love you.'

'Tilly,' said Rufus, 'I love you. And I don't know why you have to go.'

'Because I have to work tomorrow,' said Tilly, 'and because this is family business. I did what I could for Oliver, which wasn't much. He wasn't talking.'

'He really wasn't? I thought he would to you,' said Rufus.

'No, he's scared,' said Tilly. 'Scared to start, you know? I mean he didn't even tell me Cressida was pregnant. He's a very screwed-up guy, that one.'

'Do you think so?'

'Yeah. Mind you, if I had Julia for a mother I'd be screwed-up.'

'Nothing would screw you up,' said Rufus fondly.

'You'd be surprised,' said Tilly.

Mungo talked about Alice all the way to London. Tilly was intrigued by the affair. Given Mungo's past and reputation, Alice must be one hell of a woman. Although of course it didn't exactly take Sigmund Freud to see why Mungo would be in love with someone almost old enough to be his mother. Just the same –

'What about children, Mungo?' she asked, as they began to hit the hideous outer reaches of London on the M40. 'Don't you want them?'

'Yes, of course I do,' said Mungo slightly irritably, 'but we can have them. Alice is only thirty-nine, for God's sake. She's not a menopausal old crone. Anyway, she's had it checked out.'

'Oh really? Good. Well, I can't wait to meet her.'

'You'd love her,' said Mungo, 'you really would. I've never felt so – oh, I don't know, safe before. I'd take you there with me now, but I'm surprising her, she doesn't think I'm coming and – well – '

'Of course not,' said Tilly, 'I wouldn't dream of it. Anyway, I have to get back. I'm expecting lots of calls. Including one from Mick McGrath. Fucking *Sept Jours* may want to shoot another two wedding dresses, in which case I'll have to go back tomorrow afternoon.'

'What, to Paris? Bloody hell. Pretty hectic your life, isn't it?' said Mungo.

'Tell me about it,' said Tilly. 'Now look, Mungo, I'd like you to come with me to Cressida's flat. It won't take long and it's on the way to your Alice. OK?'

'Sure. Why isn't Rufus coming up with you, as a matter of interest?'

'Because he felt he should stay down. Do his bit. You know how Rufus is about doing his bit.'

'Sure,' said Mungo. 'Are you guys going to get it properly together then?'

'Shouldn't think so,' said Tilly. She felt him look at her, fixed her eyes firmly on the architectural splendours of the Hoover factory they were passing.

'Why not? You seem pretty good together to me.'

'Yeah, well, we may be,' said Tilly, 'but that doesn't mean our lives exactly jell. Think about it. Anyway, why should we want to change things? They're OK how they are.'

'Sure.' There was a silence, then Mungo said, 'So how did you like his Mum? Now there is one nice lady.'

'Yeah,' said Tilly briefly.

Mungo looked at her again. 'But? What is it with you and her?'

'Look, Mungo,' said Tilly, 'can we drop all this? I'm tired. Let's just concentrate on getting to Cressida's flat, and then home, OK?'

'OK,' said Mungo.

Cressida's flat was in Chelsea, in a small modern block just off World's End.

'I think it's the first floor,' said Mungo, looking up at it slightly nervously. 'I've never actually been there, but it's number 2B.'

'And what do we do if we do get in? Look for clues? God, this is like that board game, what's it called, with Miss Scarlett and the Rev somebody.'

'Cluedo,' said Mungo, pulling up outside the block. 'I always rather liked it. I don't know what to do, Tilly. Let's worry about that when it happens. Shall we go up to the flat first? You never know, she might be there, and we'd look pretty silly asking the caretaker to let us in if she was.'

'Sure.'

But the door to the street was locked, with an entryphone for each flat; they tried 2B without success.

'The caretaker then,' said Mungo, ringing that bell. No answer; he rang it again without success.

'Shit. Must have gone out.'

'Excuse me,' said a girl's voice. 'Can I just – '

'Sure,' said Mungo, stepping aside to let her unlock the door; it was easy to catch it after her and let themselves in.

'Come on,' said Tilly, 'let's go up.'

The building was clean, clinical; there was a small lift. They stood in it not looking at one another; Tilly felt increasingly nervous without knowing quite why.

The landing was more of a lobby, with the doors to Flats A and B opposite one another; there was loud orchestral music coming from B, and a light showing through the small frosted-glass window in the door.

'Christ,' said Mungo, 'Christ, she's here.'

Tilly felt her heart begin to thud, her palms suddenly moist. 'You ring,' she said. 'I can't.'

Mungo looked at her. 'OK,' he said. But he didn't do anything either. 'What are we going to say to her, Tilly? What are going to do?'

'I don't know,' said Tilly. They stared at each other, frozen into stillness.

'What are we afraid of?' said Mungo. 'What is it?'

'I don't know,' said Tilly again. 'But we can't just stay here. Come on, Mungo, be a man.'

He still didn't move. Tilly sighed, raised her hand and rang the bell. It was a very ugly loud buzz; nothing happened. She did it again for longer. Still no answer.

'She must have gone out and left the radio on,' she said, relief making her weak. 'We'd better come back.'

'No, we might miss her.'

A man emerged from the lift, stood at the door of 2A, fiddling with his keys. 'Keep trying,' he said, 'she never hears anything. She's definitely there. I saw her go in with the dog.'

'The dog?' said Mungo. 'But she – she hasn't got a dog.'

'I wish,' said the man and disappeared.

Tilly started hammering on the door with her fists, in between ringing the bell. 'This is hopeless,' said Mungo, 'why don't we go and phone again?'

'No.' She rang the bell again, left her finger on it. 'Cressida!' she shouted as loudly as she could. 'Cressida, open the door.'

A dog started barking furiously. The music stopped; they heard footsteps coming towards the door, an inside key in the lock; a handle turned. Tilly swallowed, tried to ease her dry mouth. Then: 'All right, all right,' said a voice, 'just hang on a minute. Who is it?'

A rather hard voice it was, with a South London twang to it: a voice that certainly wasn't Cressida's. A face looked through the crack of the door, past the chain, a pale slightly peevish face that wasn't Cressida's either. A dog's nose thrust its way out at knee level. Tilly stood there, staring into the crack; then she said, 'I'm sorry. We're friends of Cressida Forrest's. Is she there?'

'Cressida Forrest?' said the voice. 'No, of course she's not here. She hasn't been here for over six months.'

She was a very good-natured woman actually in spite of her peevish face; she asked them in, gave them a cup of tea, told them everything she knew, which wasn't much. Her name was Sally Hawkins, she was recently divorced, and Cressida had sold the flat to her soon after Christmas, had advertised it privately in *Loot*. She had taken the phone number with her, and had given the woman the Court House as her forwarding address.

'She was a very nice girl,' said Sally Hawkins, 'a very nice girl indeed. She got on very well with Benjy,' she added, looking fondly at the dog, an extremely shaggy black mongrel. 'She said she'd always wanted a dog as a child and hadn't been allowed one.'

'Oh really?' said Mungo. 'Er – was there ever anyone here with her, when you came to see the flat and so on?'

'No. She lived alone here, as you probably know. She seemed a very lonely person.'

'Did you – that is, was the flat expensive?' asked Tilly. 'For what it was, I mean?'

'No, not really. About average, maybe a bit below. But it's hard to tell these days, with the state of the market, isn't it?'

'Yes, I guess it is. Do you think any of the neighbours might have known her?'

'Well, I don't know. This isn't a very friendly place. The guy next door moved in after me, and all he ever does is complain about Benjy and my music. And I've never got to know anyone else at all.'

'We could ask the caretaker, I suppose,' said Tilly. 'But thanks anyway. Er – here's my number. If by any chance you think of anything, remember any clues she might have given you as to where she's gone, could you ring me?'

'Yes of course,' said Sally Hawkins.

They tried the caretaker again; he was still out. Tilly looked at Mungo. He was very pale, clearly shaken.

'I need a drink,' she said.

'Me too. Let's find a pub. And then we should call Harry.'

Tilly opened her front door with a hand so weak it could hardly turn the key, and walked very slowly into her flat. She loved it, a white shell of a place, too big for her really, with very little furniture because she'd never had time to buy any, just a few couches and low glass tables, and a big iron bed, a present from Rufus ('mostly selfish' he'd said to her tenderly, 'now I want you to burn that horrible futon.') She stood there smiling round at it, feeling immediately better, and then noticed it smelt very fusty. Well, it wasn't really surprising. She hadn't been in it for three days, a hot three days; the windows were all tightly closed, the pile of dirty laundry she had meant to put into the machine before she'd left was still sitting on the bedroom floor, and the half-finished bottle of milk she'd left out on the draining board had separated into a watery rancid mess. She'd have to get a proper housekeeper or something rather than just dear Betty who came in once a week for what she called a whip-round. Tilly poured the offending milk down the sink, ran the cold tap fiercely to get rid of the smell, dumped the laundry into the washing machine and plugged in the kettle. At least she'd got some Long Life; if there was one thing she really hated it was black coffee.

She kicked off her boots, poured herself a glass of wine to go with the instant coffee and cigarette that frequently served her for a meal, and stood staring out of her small kitchen window. What a shit of a day. She couldn't ever remember one like it. It really had had the lot, that day: work, airports, hangover, sex, love, shock (several doses), new encounters, old friends, rage, confrontation – and great sadness. She wasn't sure what the deepest impression was, but it sure as hell wasn't making her feel good now. She decided that it was probably the sadness: sadness for Harriet, for her family, for Mungo, for Cressida even – but most of all for Rufus and for herself.

There could be no happy ending to their particular little story, she thought to herself, pouring the water into the mug, adding five sweeteners (God, to think that used to be three spoons of sugar), carrying it over to the white leather sofa by the window, scooping up the telephone as she went. She loved Rufus, she loved him almost beyond endurance, and he loved her as much in return; and she had to end it, end the whole thing quickly before it grew and strengthened so that there could be no hope of revival, no tender, delicate little shoots and roots left. It was the only way, she had seen that as she walked through the lovely Oxfordshire countryside with Oliver that afternoon – God, it felt like months ago – trying to concentrate on what he was saying. There was no good thinking she could live with it, avoid James, ignore Rufus's origins, turn her back on his family, because it wasn't going to work. Apart from anything else it wasn't in Rufus's nature to do that; he was in essence a family person, he adored his mother, and the man he thought was his father, he loved his home, he belonged to his background. And there was no way either she could keep her new knowledge about him, about his parentage, to herself; her intrinsic honesty would never allow it. Even if James Forrest did what she had asked – and she was very doubtful that he would, and that matters would end there – she would have to tell Rufus what she knew. And that would spread pain, misery into so many lives, and while she felt no concern for James, for Susie, she cared very very much for Harriet, and for Rufus himself. He would be upset when she told him she couldn't marry him, didn't want to see him any more, but it would be normal healthy pain, he would get over it, find some other girl to love and to marry, some suitable, well-bred blonde, who would choose pretty chintzy furniture for his pretty, smartly based house, bear him pretty blond children, and wear pretty, dull clothes at her charming important dinner parties.

It would all be much much better and she would be over it in no time, indeed be back where she wanted to be, free, untied, in charge once more. She was tough, she had a most vulgarly iron constitution, she would find some new lover, from her own world, who understood her life and whose life she understood, and in a year, probably less, she would be thinking of Rufus fondly but slightly detachedly and she would hardly be able to remember how his eyes looked when they rested upon her, how he smiled with pure childish pleasure just at her very presence, how her heart lurched and her head spun when she saw him again after some parting, however brief, how she felt somehow warmed and cared for when she was near to him, how his voice seemed to reach out and caress her, how the gentlest, most casual touch left her shaken and moved, how when she was apart from him she felt not quite whole, not quite herself: all these things, she thought, told herself, forced herself to know, would pass, would become a memory, a part of her own history. But first, first there was the pain. And she shrank from it.

She knew when she must do it, had arranged it even, there was no sense in postponing it. Every day she left it, every hour she put it off, made it worse, deeper, crueller. Rufus was coming to see her in the morning (it wasn't true that she had to work) after driving his mother back to town; she would tell him then. Not the whole truth, there would be no sense in that; she would tell him instead that they had no future with one another and their affair was best ended at once. And then she would take up the Rosenthal offer, and go to New York, quickly – and that was another thing; if she did that she could put some money into Harriet's company, that would make it seem a little more worthwhile, would ease her homesickness – it was all going to be vile; he would argue, protest, and so she would have to hurt him further, be vicious to be kind, tell him she was already half involved with someone else, some photographer, designer, spare him hope. Tilly poured herself another glass of wine, lit another cigarette, put REM onto her stero. And then the phone rang. It was Ken Lazard.

'Harry? It's Tilly. Any news? Oh, I see. Well, I have some. No, nothing about Cressida. Did you tell the police about the flat? And what did they say? That is so strange. I mean it's all so complicated. Harriet, don't sound so despairing. The more we learn, the more it's obvious that Cressida planned this whole thing. Has been planning it for months. Yes, I know it's terrible, but at least you can assume she's safe. I mean she hasn't been kidnapped or run over. Try to be positive. What? Yeah, I know you do. Now listen, Harry. Have I got news for you. As they say. Ken Lazard called me just now. Apparently – Harry, are you sitting down? Well, I really think you should – apparently your Mr Cotton, he's called Hayden by the way, Mr Cotton had dinner with – shit, Harry, I can hardly bear to tell you this – dinner with Theo Buchan three nights ago.'

There was a very long silence. Tilly could feel the shock coming down the phone; it was a physical force.

Then: 'But he can't have done. Theo was in London.'

'So was Hayden. For twenty-four hours.'

'But how does he know Theo?'

'Oh Harry, you know how all these guys link up. Theo has a textile division, for God's sake. And Theo told him not to get into bed with you. Figuratively of course.'

'What!'

'Yes, I know. I know. Harry, try to keep calm. Don't go and shoot him yet. I want to help.'

'But Tilly – oh, I can't believe it. I just can't think Theo would have been that – that unscrupulous. That evil.'

'You'd better believe it. Anyway, it fits. Think about it. The timing, everything. You said they were about to sign what? – forty-eight hours ago, that you'd agreed terms, everything.'

'But what grounds did Theo give him?'

'I don't know. Obviously it was complex and Ken couldn't find out any more. I expect he said you were incompetent – or anything really.'

'God,' said Harriet. 'Tilly, do you think he stopped the other two deals as well?'

'Don't know. Sounds possible. He's obviously been monitoring you and your plans quite closely.'

'But how – '

'Harry, it really isn't very difficult. Honestly. You know what a tiny world it is.'

'Oh my God. Tilly, thank you so much. So much. I don't know quite what I'm going to do, but – well, I'll think of something. But I tell you what. I feel an awful lot better suddenly.'

'Good. Get him by the goolies, Harry, squeeze them till he screams.'

'I couldn't bear to touch them,' said Harriet simply.

The substitute food wasn't working; Tilly decided she needed the real thing. She dialled the local pizza delivery company, but it was engaged; suddenly going out, walking a few streets seemed like a good idea.

The air was very warm still, but not close; the sky was almost dark. The streets were packed, a mass of people walking, shopping, sitting outside pubs, at pavement tables, smiling, friendly people. It was true what everyone said, Tilly thought, the weather played a huge part in the English reserve.

She walked down to the Kings Road, into the Europa supermarket, bought a basketload of vegetables and some eggs. A huge Spanish omelette was exactly what she fancied. She wandered back slowly, enjoying the evening, feeling better. It was ten o'clock: an endless day.

As she ran up the stairs to her flat, she heard the phone ringing, then stop as the answering machine took the call. She couldn't hear what the person was saying, but it was a female voice. Probably Harriet, calling to talk about Theo again.

She pressed the playback button: there were three lights flashing. The first message was from James Forrest.

'Miss Mills? This is James Forrest. I've thought over what you had to say, and I agree it would be nice if I talked to your mother. Perhaps you'd like to let me have her number some time so that I can call her. Thank you.'

'Well, well, well,' said Tilly aloud. 'You must be a very frightened man.' Even to her it seemed remarkable that he should move into action on such a day. She debated ringing her mother, then decided it would possibly upset her to get such a call, to be forced into recollection; she needed to be with her, to explain, to talk it over. She would go over at the weekend to Peckham and sit with her and tell her about it, tell her that James Forrest wanted to see her and reassure her after all this time that she had not been at fault.

The second call was from Felicity Livesey. 'Tilly, it's Felicity. Mick said you were back in London. Sorry to hound you, but I'd like to give some kind of indication at least to Meg Rosenthal on how you feel about her offer. Could you give me a ring at home? Thanks.'

Then the third message.

'Tilly? This is Cressida Forrest. When you get back, could you please just call my family and tell them I'm fine, and they are not to worry about me. Thanks.'

Chapter Eighteen

Harriet 9pm

Mr Buchan was out, they told her, in their blank, courteous way, had taken his car and gone out. No, he hadn't checked out of the hotel, but they really couldn't say when he would be back. They were so sorry. No, Mrs Buchan wasn't there either. Yes, of course they would give him a message. And yes, they would make sure he got it, not matter what time he came in.

Harriet put down the phone and wondered how on earth she was going to stand the raging mass that was centred somewhere in the area of her stomach for however long it took before she was able to confront Theo. She felt quite literally possessed; she knew now how people could kill.

She stared at the closed door of the drawing room; from behind it she could hear – what? Dear God, the television. How on earth could they watch television, all of them, when Cressida had gone missing? Then she considered the alternatives they had all been pursuing for the past two hours, and decided it was actually quite sensible. If one more person put forward a theory, she knew she would scream. She felt like screaming anyway; indeed it began to seem rather difficult to imagine that she would be able to endure many more minutes of this day without doing so.

It was almost dusk now, the sky deep brilliant turquoise, the sun sinking in a glory of orange behind the hills. The stillness was almost tangible; she felt if she went outside she would be able to put out her hand and touch it, feel it. It would be cool, she thought, slightly silken in texture; soothing, gentle. She decided to go down to the bridge and watch the sun finally settle into the night, see the stars come up. It was lovely down there in the darkness; when she and Cressida had been little they had crept out sometimes, greatly daring, and sat there, listening to the night sounds, the owls, the horses occasionally nickering, the water rats plopping into the stream. It was one of the few experiences that united them; they would snuggle together on the stone seat, holding hands, sharing a sense of courage, of adventure. They had only been caught twice (and of course she'd been blamed, being the eldest, and indubitably the instigator of the expeditions), but had gone out many times, every summer.

She went to the back door, and was about to cross the yard when she remembered Theo; she didn't want to miss his call. And they might be worried if they didn't know where she was. She went back, put her head round the drawing-room door. They all looked up slightly guiltily from what they were watching (some costume drama, she noticed confusedly, a re-run of something like *Middlemarch*). She smiled at them, as cheerfully as she could.

'I'm just going for a breath of air,' she said, 'down to the bridge. If there are any calls, any news, will you call me?'

They nodded; a heaviness had settled on them all. Since the message from Cressida there was a sense of anticlimax, a loss of adrenalin. Only Julia smiled brightly. 'I'll come and get you personally, dear,' she said. She looked marvellous, Harriet thought, as if the day had been a great success, her son safely dispatched with his bride across the Atlantic, instead of publicly humiliated, deserted almost literally at the altar.

Oliver looked at her, then at Harriet, rather uncertainly. 'Would you mind if I came with you?' he asked. 'I won't if you'd rather not – '

Harriet did mind, she minded very much, but she could scarcely say so. She forced a smile. 'No, Oliver, of course not. Really. I'm just going to get a sweater. I'll see you in the kitchen.'

She went out into the utility room; there was nothing there except Barbours and anoraks, all much too warm, and an old, rather holey cardigan of her father's that they all wore from time to time. It seemed to belong to quite a different time: when everything had been simple, straightforward, happy. A time that belonged to another age: when Cressida was engaged to Oliver and her parents had a good marriage and she had a company that might yet survive. Years and years ago that was, that other age, yet actually only yesterday.

Harriet shivered, physically chilled by what had happened to them all that day, what might happen yet; she pulled the cardigan on, noticing she ached, ached all over, and stood there patiently, waiting for Oliver.

He came out still looking slightly doubtful. 'You sure this is all right? Because you don't have to be kind – '

'Ollie,' said Harriet, slipping her arm through his, 'I think you've earned a bit of kindness. Actually. Come on, let's get the hell out of here.'

They sat on the bridge, staring up at the brightening stars. 'Does this remind you of the desert?' he said suddenly. 'You know, when Merlin took us. God, we were so happy then. Life was so straightforward. I should have marrried you, Harriet, not Cressida. Well, not that I married Cressida.'

'No,' said Harriet, 'and if this is a proposal I have to tell you I'm going to turn you down. I expect you wish right now Cressida had turned you down as well.'

There was a long silence, then he said, 'There was no question of her turning me down, Harriet. She proposed to me. And there was no question of my turning her down either.'

Harriet stared at him, trying to make out if he was joking, but his face in the near darkness was very serious.

'I don't understand,' she said. 'Why? What happened?'

'Oh God,' said Oliver, 'I shouldn't have started this. Sorry, Harriet. Forget it.'

'Ollie, don't be ridiculous. How can I forget it? You have to go on now. Why couldn't you refuse her? If you didn't want to marry her?'

'Oh Harriet,' he said, 'the oldest reason in the world. She was pregnant.'

The bridge seemed to shake under Harriet. She put out her hand, but the parapet seemed reassuringly steady.

'Oliver, I'm sorry, but you've lost me. I'm a simple soul. Could you start at the beginning please? I thought we were talking a year ago, not now – '

'Sorry, Harriet. I'm fairly lost myself. Go back a year. Nearly a year. Cressida and I had been having an affair for a while. I was very fond of her, she seemed very fond of me, she was pretty, fun – '

'Yes, all right, you don't have to go into justifications,' said Harriet impatiently.

'Sorry. Start again. Cressida and I had been having an affair. She came over for a few weeks in August, do you remember, stayed with us at Bar Harbor, sailed a lot, had a lovely time. It wasn't at all serious. We agreed it wasn't. I honestly don't think I was taking advantage of her in any way. She was twenty-six years old, for God's sake. And – she certainly wasn't a – a – '

'Virgin?' said Harriet gently. She smiled at Oliver; it was so like him, like his serious, conscientious approach to life, that he shouldn't be seen as a seducer, even of someone who had most efficiently and ruthlessly humiliated him that day.

'Yes. I mean, she wasn't. Well, anyway, in October she wrote to me, and said she had some holiday and could she maybe come over for a few days. I said of course. I was actually seeing someone else by then but not – well, you know what I mean?'

'Yes, Oliver,' said Harriet, putting her hand on his arm, 'I know what you mean.'

'So I met her at Kennedy, and I did think she seemed a bit – well, tense. But no more. That night we went out to dinner, all of us, Mother and Dad as well, and it was really good fun. When we got back we all had a nightcap and then they went on up to bed. Cressida suddenly said she had some news. She said was pregnant, that it was definitely mine, and she thought we should hurry things along and announce our engagement. Harriet, I swear to God it had never ever been mentioned, never considered an option, even in the vaguest terms. I knew I didn't really love her, and I knew I didn't really want to marry her. I – well, I kind of said that. And she was terribly upset. She started crying and carrying on, then she rushed out of the room. She came back and said she'd been sick, that she was being sick all the time, that she felt terrible. I felt so awful, Harriet, so ashamed. I sat and talked to her for a long time, and said I would do everything I could to help her, but I really didn't think we should get married, and she said didn't I care for her at all, and I said of course I did. And she said what options did I see for her, did I think she should have an abortion? I said, quite carefully, that it was certainly something we should look at, and she started crying again, and saying how could I even think of getting rid of our baby. Then she was sick again, and then she came back and started all over. Christ, Harriet, it was terrible. Whenever I read about the police interrogating witnesses and making them confess to things they haven't done, I know how they do it.'

'Oh Oliver,' said Harriet, 'oh Ollie, I'm so sorry.'

'Yes, well. Maybe out parents were right when they told us not to sleep around,' he said with an attempt at a laugh. 'It certainly doesn't make for an easy life. You can imagine the rest. I lay awake all night, thinking what a heel I was, what a lovely girl she was, how fond of her I was, what a wonderful time we'd had in the summer, what a good wife she'd make me, how happy everyone in the family would be, and about the alternative, and in the morning I went to see her in her room and said that of course I'd marry her, it was a very good idea, I'd just been a bit taken aback the night before, that was all. And she went flying down to my parents and told them, and of course they were pleased – well, Dad was pleased, Mother seemed a little reserved about it – and then she put in a call to your parents and – well, you know the rest. It's a very heavy steamroller that, Harriet, and it's very hard to get out from under it.'

'But Ollie, I don't know the rest. What happened to that – baby?'

'Oh,' he said, and his voice was heavy, infinitely sad. 'No, of course you don't. Sorry. She lost it. A couple of weeks later. She hadn't even broken the news to our parents, we were trying to decide what to do, how to handle it, whether we should get married quickly and quietly or – well, anyway, she lost it.'

'What, when she was back in London?'

'Yes.'

'Well,' said Harriet and her own voice was bitter now, 'how very convenient for her.'

'No,' he said, 'no, I know what you're thinking and you're wrong. She really was pregnant, she really was feeling terrible, she – well, she had all the symptoms. I'm a doctor, Harriet, not so easy to deceive, and she had a letter from the hospital. You don't remember her being – well, ill? Away from home? Anything like that?'

'No,' said Harriet, stifling her doubts, her suspicion that it would have been quite easy, with her connections, for this new, devious Cressida, the one they had never known, to fake a hospital letter. 'No, I don't, but then, to be fair, I'm away a lot. Last autumn I was in Paris practically all the time. But Mummy never said anything – oh for God's sake, what am I talking about? This is a girl who has just disappeared on her wedding day piloting her own plane when none of us thought she could even ride a bicycle, who sold her flat months ago and let us think she was still living in it. ('That explains the mysterious legacy at least,' James had said when she told him.) I guess a little miscarriage would hardly seem very difficult to conceal. But then, why didn't you – '

'Call it off? I couldn't, Harriet. I thought I would, of course, it was a huge relief to me, actually, but she was so miserable, so depressed. She came over the week after, and she did look awful, so thin and pale, and she was crying a lot and she said the only thing that was keeping her going now was the thought of our being married. She – well, she really did seem to love me. And need me. It's not the best time to dump someone, you must see that. And then – well, you know, I'm actually quite an easy-going guy. I had a lot to worry about, my research work, my first big job. I went along with it, and just kept telling myself how lucky I was.'

'Oh Oliver,' said Harriet. The story was making her flesh creep slightly; she felt sick. 'What a nightmare.'

'Well it was a bit. But not bad enough, you know? For me to do anything. I think I just kept hoping for a miracle. And my parents seemed so pleased, and yours were delighted, it's a tough one that, Harriet. Don't ever get into anything like it.'

'I don't think it's very likely,' said Harriet with a sigh. 'But then, here you were, getting married, and she was pregnant for real. And presumably by then it didn't matter – '

'No,' he said heavily. 'It didn't matter. Or doesn't now.'

'And when did she tell you?'

'When I arrived here,' he said briefly. 'Last week.'

Harriet looked at him, and saw on his face the same anger, the same sick distaste that had been there when he had made his announcement earlier, and the strange sense of wrongness, of disorder resurfaced, and she said, 'Oliver, forgive me, but – '

And 'Yes,' he said, 'I know what you're going to say. It doesn't make sense. I just kept trying not to think about it. The dates don't work, don't fit in with the times we were together recently. She swears they do, but they don't. She should either be quite a bit further along, or – what? – three weeks at the most. Hardly pregnant. I mean I have to believe her, well, I had to, there didn't seem to be an alternative, but – I knew it wasn't right. It just wasn't. I'm sorry, Harriet, I know she's your sister and you love her and you've always been terribly close, but – '

'I'm not sure that I do actually,' said Harriet. 'Love her. In fact,' she added in a rush of courage, 'most of the time I don't even like her very much. And we certainly aren't close. We just pretend, act out this stupid charade.'

'Well,' said Oliver, 'she's good at acting. Very good.'

'Yes. As Merlin said earlier. Dear Merlin. Oliver, you should have said something, you shouldn't have gone along with it all, you really shouldn't. It would have been so terrible.'

'Oh I know,' he said, his face pallid in the moonlight, 'and of course even now I can't imagine why I didn't, why I let things go on. But it's not an easy thing to do, Harriet, disrupt things, stop arrangements on this scale, publicly humiliate someone – '

'She has,' said Harriet. 'My God, she has.'

'Yes, well. I'm going to be grateful. I know I am. I took an overdose last night,' he added conversationally.

Harriet stared at him. She felt very sick.

'You did what?'

'I swallowed a bottle of aspirin. With some whisky. Oh, it was only a yell for help. I knew that. And Rufus and Mungo took care of me. They were fantastic.'

'Oh Oliver,' said Harriet and she suddenly burst into tears. 'Oh Oliver, I feel so ashamed for her. So sad for you.'

'Well don't be,' he said almost cheerfully, putting his arm round her, 'because it's actually going to be all right. I mean I don't have to marry her now, and when this awful day is over, I can get on a plane and fly back to New York and get on with my life, and we can tell some cosmetic lie about the whole thing. I'm very lucky I don't live here, it would be a lot more difficult. Honestly, Harriet, I *am* beginning to feel much better. Certainly better than the way I'd feel if we were on the plane en route to a honeymoon.'

'I suppose so. Oh God.' She sniffed loudly. 'What a day. What a bitch of a day. Sorry. Have you got a handkerchief?'

'Sure. Are you all right?'

'Not really,' said Harriet and burst into tears again.

'Harry, darling, don't cry. There's something else, isn't there? What is it, tell me?'

'Oh Oliver, I can't. Not all of it. It's too horrible, and too humiliating and – well, I just don't think I can face talking about it now. I'm sorry. Maybe tomorrow. Or something.'

'OK,' he said equably. 'But please do tell me if you want to. And if there's anything I can do – '

'How are you on murder?' said Harriet briefly.

When they got back to the house, James was in the kitchen making some tea.

'Your mother's gone to bed,' he said heavily. 'I'm making her this.'

'You'd better give her something to help her sleep,' said Harriet.

'I have. Your parents are moving off,' he added to Oliver, 'do you want to go with them? You're very welcome to stay here, of course.'

'No, it's kind of you, James, but I think I should go,' said Oliver. 'Harriet is that all right with you – '

'What? Oh, yes,' said Harriet. 'Yes, of course. Ring me in the morning.' She looked at her father coldly. 'What are you going to do?'

'Oh I don't know,' he said, 'wait up for a while. In case there's still some news. Merlin and Janine still aren't back, I think I should check them in,' he added with the echo of a smile. 'And I have to run Susie back to the Beaumonts', of course.'

'Of course – '

'Harriet, I think perhaps we should talk – '

'Daddy, there's nothing to talk about. I'm not stupid, I can see what's been happening. And I don't want to hear any more about it. OK? I think I'll go up and say goodnight to Mummy.'

'All right,' he said.

Maggie was lying in bed, awake but very still. She put out her hand and smiled weakly as Harriet looked round the door. She looked rather as if she had had a serious operation, Harriet thought, and went to kiss her. Maggie took her hand gently.

'You've been wonderful today,' she said, 'so good. Thank you.'

'Mummy, it was no more than anyone else did. Honestly.'

'Yes it was. You've kept me sane.' She sighed. 'Where do you think she is, Harriet, why do you think she did it? What could have happened to her, was it our fault, do you think?'

'So you do think now that she – chose to go?' said Harriet carefully.

'Yes, I do. The second message, from your friend Tilly, that really did confirm it. But I think I knew really, as soon as I heard about the plane. It's all so strange, such a nightmare. She must have been so desperate, so unhappy. And pregnant too. Oh God, who will be looking after her now?'

'Mummy, try to be calm,' said Harriet. 'The new Cressida, the one we didn't know about, she's able to look after herself I think. She'll manage.'

'Yes, but – pregnant,' said Maggie again. 'And what can she be doing for money?'

'Well, I should think she had plenty of that,' said Harriet. 'She got a hundred thousand for her flat, don't forget. That should pay for a bit of looking after.'

'Darling, don't sound so hard.'

'Sorry,' said Harriet. 'I feel a bit hard.'

'Yes, well, you always were a lot tougher than she was,' said Maggie, 'she was so easily upset always, so sensitive. She felt so bad, you know, about your puppy.'

'What puppy?' asked Harriet.

'There you are, I told her you'd forgotten all about it. Biggles. The sweet little puppy who was run over. She always felt it was her fault, you know, because she'd left the gate open. Nanny told me that night, she saw her, and of course we did speak to her about it, and she was so upset, just couldn't stop crying, begged me not to tell you. We told her we wouldn't, that it was just an accident, it could have been any of us, and of course it was much better that you didn't know, but – '

'Oh God,' said Harriet, 'oh my God. I always knew, I knew it wasn't me.'

'Now, darling, don't start getting upset about it. It wasn't anybody, I just said it was an accident.' She was getting drowsy now, her eyes closing. 'Goodnight, Harriet, thank you again. Let's hope tomorrow is a better day.'

'Poor little Biggles,' said Harriet. 'Oh God, poor sweet little Biggles.' And of all the things she had learnt about Cressida that day, this was the most shocking: that anybody, anybody at all, least of all a small child, could deliberately, cold-bloodedly, arrange things so that a round, golden, velvety-pawed and totally trusting puppy should be sent to a certain and most horrible death.

She went into Cressida's room and looked around it; she felt like smashing it up, hurling all its charming accessories, its lace-covered pillows and Victorian pin-cushions and antique scent bottles out of a broken window. And then she went into her own room and got out the photo of Biggles that she still kept, in its old leather frame in the top drawer of her desk, and he looked at her adoringly, with his squashed puppy face, his floppity ears pricked up, his fat paws hooked over the arm of the big chair he was sitting in, and even after all that time it hurt, it hurt so much, more than ever in fact, knowing now that it hadn't been an accident, need never have happened. 'Oh Biggles,' she said to the photograph, seeing it through blurred eyes, 'oh Biggles, I'm so sorry.'

It suddenly seemed very hot; she opened the window wider to air the room and then realized she was still wearing the thick cardigan. She pulled it off and started to straighten it out; it was still covered in bits of grass clippings from when her father had been cutting the grass ready for the marquee. He always cut it himself; he took an immense pride in his lawn, Cressida always said he regarded it as another child, so concerned was he over its welfare. She began to brush the grass off and as she did so saw a piece of paper in the top inside pocket. Probably nothing, she thought, pulling it out, a shopping list or a vet's bill, probably been there for years, but you never knew –

And 'Cressida,' she said aloud, staring at the note, reading and rereading it, as if the words might vanish if she looked at them long enough, 'oh Cressida. What was the matter with you, for God's sake, what were you up to?'

For it was not a shopping list or a vet's bill, it was a letter from a gynaecologist at somewhere called the Brompton Clinic, dated the previous October.

Dear Miss Forrest (it said),
This is just to confirm what I told you on the phone this morning, that although your pregnancy test showed a negative result, I see no reason to suppose there is any cause for anxiety. Many women have some difficulty in conceiving, and you are extremely healthy and have time on your side. I suggest that if after six months you are still not pregnant, you come and see me again, perhaps with your fiancé, and we can discuss whether some investigations might be appropriate then. But I really think that for the time being you should just try to relax and enjoy your forthcoming trip to New York.

Yours sincerely
Jennifer Bradman, FRCOG

Chapter Nineteen

Susie 10pm

'Jamie, I think I'd like to ring Alistair now,' said Susie.

She knew she was behaving totally out of character, that Susie Headleigh Drayton, always so serene, so in control, would never have even considered late-night panic phone calls, soul-baring sessions, ultimatums; but she didn't feel serene or in control and she didn't really feel like Susie Headleigh Drayton either, she felt like some alien creature, someone floundering in a nightmare, someone afraid.

'Ah,' said James. 'Ah, yes of course. If that's what you really want.'

'Well, yes, it is what I really want. You know that.'

She had found him in his study, sitting staring out of the window, his hand on the telephone; he had just made, he said, yet another phone call to the police. 'No news. Not from anywhere. Apparently in the morning, they can step up the search. And the Missing Persons have been very good. Tried to be soothing, reassuring. So many people do this apparently, Susie, just vanish into thin air, hundreds every year. Nobody knows why.'

'And do they return, these hundreds of people?'

'Some of them, yes.'

'Well then,' she said, 'you have some hope.'

That was when she had made her announcement, that she wanted to talk to Alistair, to tell him that she and James wanted to be together, for however long she had left.

He looked at her now, carefully, consideringly, and said, 'Susie, are you really sure about this?' and for a long, dreadful moment she thought he was going to fail her, was going to say he didn't think after all it was such a good idea, and she knew what people meant when they said their hearts stopped. But then: 'I mean, my darling,' he said, his eyes moving over her tenderly, lovingly, his hand drifting out to take hers, 'if you really want to do it now. When it's late. When you're exhausted, when I'm exhausted, when Alistair may be asleep. It's after ten. I would have thought tomorrow maybe would be better.'

'But Jamie,' she said, relief flooding her, warm and soothing, her heart starting again, steady, strong, 'Jamie, maybe it would, but I have to go in for the biopsy in the morning, and Mr Hobson wants Alistair to come with me, and I don't think I could face that, go through that sham. And besides, I'm so frightened, so afraid. I'll need you with me then. And afterwards, when I've had the biopsy, I want you to be there, I want you to be there when I wake up and have to hear the news and – ' She heard her voice quiver, shatter; she bit her lip, looked at him, willing the tears not to come.

'Susie,' said James, 'Susie darling, of course I'll come with you. Incidentally I've looked Hobson up, and he is absolutely the best man. So you're lucky there. But after that – '

'Yes,' she said, 'yes, after that? After that what? Jamie, you promised, you promised this afternoon, that from this day forward – ' she paused, realized she had unwittingly quoted from the marriage service, half smiled – 'you would be with me, would look after me.'

'Yes, and I will. Darling, don't look like that. I will. But it is bound to take a little time, the disentanglement. Nobody, nobody at all can just walk out of a marriage, a household, at a moment's notice. Or into another. What would I say to Alistair? Shove out, old chap, it's my turn now. There has to be a little space, a little room for manoeuvre, surely you can see that?'

'Yes,' she said with a sigh, 'yes, I suppose I can. But time is exactly what I haven't got. So even if we can't be physically together yet, all the time, I want everyone to know that's what's going to happen. So we do have to tell Alistair, yes.'

'Right,' said James, and there was an uncertainty in his voice that frightened her again, 'right, yes. I suppose we do. But does it really have to be tonight? Consider the ructions, darling, the implications. And I can't possibly tell Maggie, she's asleep, I've given her something very strong. And even tomorrow, do you really think she can take this news, on top of Cressida's disappearance, is it really fair?'

'Jamie, it may not be fair, but I think I do have absolutely first claim here,' said Susie. Her fear was growing. 'In a year, six months, I could be dead. I really can't wait for you, for happiness, until Maggie can handle it. I'm sorry.'

James looked at her again, and he was clearly thinking: thinking fast. She watched him in a kind of frozen fascination, fighting back the tears. What was this, what was he doing to her?

'Susie, darling, don't you think also you're being slightly premature about the whole thing? It may prove after all this to be a false alarm: just a lump, just a cyst. You don't know. Hobson doesn't know, nobody knows. Why not wait at least until tomorrow?'

'Jamie,' said Susie very quietly, 'I know. I know there's something wrong. I don't feel well, I'm terribly tired, I've lost weight. I can't allow myself to – '

The phone shrilled out sharply in the silence. James picked it up, she sat there looking at him, watched his face change from fear to a careful blank.

'Yes, Annabel, she's here. I'm about to bring her back. What? Well, in about half an hour I suppose. Oh, all right, I'll put her on. It's your daughter,' he said, handing Susie the phone. 'She says it's urgent.'

'Oh God,' said Susie, 'God, I hope it's not Tom, or Alistair. Annabel, yes, darling, what is it?'

Annabel's voice, husky, sexy, expensively educated, came down the phone. 'Mummy, some of us want to go to a club in Oxford. Is that OK?'

'What?' said Susie. She felt confused, disorientated, wrenched from fears for herself into fears for her children and husband, and thence into trivia, literally unable to believe what she was hearing. 'Annabel, what did you say?'

'I said some of us want to go to a club in Oxford,' said Annabel irritably. 'Well we have to do something to cheer ourselves up, it's been a pretty bloody awful day.'

'Annabel,' said Susie, trying to keep her voice level. 'I rather think it's been a better day for you than for most of the people concerned. Anyway, I thought you said this was urgent.'

'Yes, all right, all right,' said Annabel. 'Sorry. The thing is I haven't got any money, and my cash card's gone missing. Can you let me have some cash? Daddy said he'd give me some and then he just went off without doing it. He's so hopeless. If you hurry back now, we can go in about fifteen minutes, I don't want to hold everyone up.'

Susie carefully counted to ten. She had always found it helped enormously in the past, had enabled her to deal with her children in a calm and reasonable way, even when they were enraging her. For some reason it wasn't working.

'Annabel,' she said, and she could hear her voice rising, 'Annabel, I'm having a little trouble following this. You want to go to a club in Oxford and you haven't got any money. Is that right?'

'Yes,' said Annabel, 'I really can't see what's so complicated. If you could just – '

'What's complicated,' said Susie, settling her voice lower down the vocal range again, 'what's hard for me to believe is that you could see that as an emergency. How could you ring me up here, late, when everyone could well have been asleep, when everyone has been through the kind of day that's normally confined to nightmares, when several people are feeling literally heartbroken, and tell me it's really urgent that you have

267

some money to go to a club. You shock me, Annabel, you really do. I'm ashamed of being your mother. Now you can go to a club if you want to, I really don't care, but you'll have to get your financing from someone else. And if I find you've asked Janet or Brian Beaumont for it, I do assure you it will be a very long time before you get another penny from either your father or me. Goodnight, Annabel. I suppose I'll have to see you in the morning.'

She put down the phone, looked at James and grinned rather shakily. 'I don't usually do that sort of thing. I rather enjoyed it. You got the drift, I suppose?'

'Yes, I did. They're all the same, these children. We spoil them. I remember Cressida ringing Maggie from a party at two in the morning once when she was only a bit younger than Annabel, to tell her she'd broken the zip on her dress and could we take another one over. It was a round trip of about thirty miles.'

'And did you?'

'Well I had a lot of trouble preventing Maggie from doing it,' he said. 'She always was ridiculously indulgent with Cressida.'

'You both were,' said Susie, 'I was always telling you.'

'Yes, but it didn't seem to do her any harm.' There was a long silence. 'Well, that was a particularly bright remark,' he said, with a heavy sigh. 'Obviously it did. A lot of harm. Oh Christ. Do you think she's seriously psychologically disturbed, Susie, or just a drama queen?'

'Oh Jamie, I don't know,' said Susie, 'that is such an impossible judgment to make. Unfair to ask me.'

'I'm sorry. Bit of both, I suppose. God, where do you think she is, what can she be doing? I'm so frightened even now of hearing she's been found – beaten up somewhere, in an accident, dead even. It's such a dreadful, ghastly nightmare.'

'Jamie, she may be hurt, or worse, I suppose,' said Susie, speaking carefully, 'but I do think it's unlikely. I think actually it's far more possible that she's just run away, to escape. Taken herself off. She's sent two messages to you after all.'

'I know, I know, but they could be fakes, bluffs, she could have been forced into sending them. You just don't know, do you? The police were reassuring, but they would be. That's their job. And if she had run off, Christ, what kind of a state must she have been in? Pregnant, frightened – What did we do to her? I've made a terrible hash of parenthood, Susie. Of everything.'

'You've done pretty well with Harriet,' said Susie. 'The sort of daughter everyone dreams of. Successful, clever, nice – Jamie – '

'Yes, darling?'

'I know this is all terrible for you. But I have something terrible to deal with too. And I really can't wait. Please let me ring Alistair.'

She watched James disentangle himself from his thoughts with a great effort, turn to her. There was something in his eyes, apart from love, apart from sympathy, that troubled her. Trying to analyse, she realized that he looked trapped, cornered, almost desperate.

'Jamie, what is it? You don't have any – doubts about this, do you? You're not going to fail me. Because I don't think I could bear it if you do, don't think I could handle it.'

'No', he said smiling at her, holding out his hand, 'no, of course not. No doubts at all. Come over here. God, Susie, I love you. I love you so much.'

She went over to where he sat at his big desk, took his hand, bent down to kiss him. His mouth as always was very warm, very dry and firm.

'You taste of peppermint,' she said.

'Peppermint tea. My mainstay.'

'God,' she said, 'I don't know how Alistair would get by without his booze. Aren't you ever tempted?'

'Yes of course,' he said simply. 'Every day, almost.'

'Then why don't you ever – '

'Oh,' he said, lightly, 'it just doesn't agree with me. That's all. It just isn't worth it.'

'Tilly's lovely, isn't she?' she said. She felt him tense slightly.

'Why did you say that. Then?'

'No reason,' she said, surprised. 'I was just thinking about her. How strange it is that all our lives have intertwined. I often think about her mother, poor woman, how dreadful that must have been.'

'Yes,' he said, 'so I do. Of course.'

'Dreadful for you, too, though. But I've always hoped she does realize that it really wasn't your fault that the other little baby died. In any way. When – when Tilly asked you to show her the garden, she didn't – '

'No,' he said quickly. 'No, she didn't say anything. Of course she knows about it, knows I delivered her. But she certainly doesn't seem to hold it against me.'

'Well, she shouldn't,' said Susie, 'you were completely exonerated, at the inquiry. Just the same – '

'Susie, can we stop this please? You know its upsets me, talking about it.'

'Sorry,' she said, startled. 'Look, why don't I make us some tea – peppermint if you like – and we can sit in the drawing room and talk sensibly. I'm feeling calmer now. I'm sorry if I seemed hysterical earlier. Not like me.'

'No,' he said, 'not like you at all. It's one of the things I most love about you, Susie, your serenity. It's beautiful. It restores me. It's been restoring me today.'

'Good,' she said, and bent to kiss him, feeling in spite of everything suddenly happy, light-hearted, thinking how much she loved him, how wonderful it was that they were finally going to be together, all the time, openly, peacefully, no more concealment, no more pretence.

She went out to the kitchen, made some tea, carried it into the drawing room. 'Merlin and Janine are late.'

'He's probably arguing over the bill,' said James.

'Yes, probably.' She took a sip of her tea, waited, looking at him, willing him to take up the subject of herself and their future, wondering why she felt so nervous. Well, it was not entirely surprising: under the circumstances. She was not in any way herself.

There was a long silence: he said nothing. He didn't even look at her. Susie felt her skin begin to crawl; finally she took a deep breath, said, 'Jamie, Jamie please. Can we talk about this? Can I ring Alistair?'

'Susie, I don't know. I'm not sure.'

And now panic did hit her, hot, liquid panic, filling her head and her chest, making her limbs feel light and odd.

'Jamie, what do you mean, you're not sure? Not sure about what?'

'About the way you want to handle this.'

Well, that was better; not totally all right, but better.

'You mean we should wait till tomorrow? Well, maybe if it was really early, but – '

'Well, possibly, yes.'

'Jamie, what are you saying?' She heard an edge enter her voice, hated it, couldn't control it. 'Jamie, look at me.'

He looked at her, briefly, before she could read his eyes, then looked away again.

There was a long, frozen silence; she felt suddenly still and calm, the panic gone.

'You're not going to do it, are you?' she said finally. 'You're not going to leave her, not going to be with me.'

'Susie, there's no need to sound quite so dramatic. I'm not saying that at all. I'm just not convinced that it's actually the best thing for us to do.'

'Oh really?' she said. 'And would you like to tell me why that is, why you're lacking in this conviction?'

'Darling, I – oh for God's sake, come over here, let me hold you.'

'I think I need a little more than holding,' she said, and she could hear her voice exactly as it had been when she spoke to Annabel, oddly controlled and cold. 'I'd rather you didn't try to confuse the issue that

270

way, James. I think we have a little straight talking to do here. You promised me earlier that you would be with me, leave Maggie, and now – '

'I didn't actually,' he said. 'I said I would be with you as long as you needed me. And I will. That isn't quite the same thing as disrupting two marriages, two households at a time when – '

'At a time what? Jamie, what are you saying? I don't understand. The only time I have is now and it's possibly very short, and I need you, and as far as I'm concerned you promised me – Jamie, for Christ's sake, explain, because I – ' She stopped, biting her lip, looked at him, willing his absolute reassurance, knowing with the same icy certainty that it wasn't going to come.

'Look,' he said, and his voice was steady, level, patient, 'look, Susie, I know how frightened you must be, and I really do want to help you all I can. But you could be in for quite a tough time and I'm not entirely convinced that ripping two families apart is quite the best background for it.'

'James, I – '

'Susie, let me finish. You wanted me to explain. If you do what you say you want to do, then you're going to cause so much unhappiness, so much pain. You're such a family person, Susie, do you really want to add to your children's grief? Because that is what you'll do. They won't just be afraid of losing you, grieving for you, they'll be grieving at the break-up of their family, they'll be angry at what you've done to their father. Who incidentally they do adore. Is that really fair? Is that really going to make you feel better, stronger, more able to cope? Because I don't think so. And all right, you don't love Alistair, but do you really want to hurt him like this? Is it really the legacy you want to leave him? I can't believe it is, Susie, I can't believe it of you.'

There was a long silence; through the roar of confusion in her head, Susie dimly heard a car pull into the drive: a tiny piece of her brain thought it must be Merlin and Janine, home from their date – God, don't let them come in here – but the rest of her was still focused entirely on James and her pain.

'All right,' she said firmly, 'all right, you can't believe it. And I know it's true, what you're saying. But the thing is, James, they're strong, they'll survive. Whatever I do to them. And I can help them, I can try to explain. But I have to think of myself, because I'm not strong, I've discovered, not at all, and the only way I'm going to get through this is with you. All my life I've had to share you, James, had to live out this long charade, and OK, it's worked very nicely on the whole. I haven't exactly liked a lot of it, it's been quite hard watching you, thinking of you

271

with Maggie, however much I've smiled and known that was a charade too, I haven't liked never spending a night with you, or almost never, haven't liked a lot of the sneaking off and the lying, certainly haven't liked pretending even to myself quite a lot of the time that Rufus was nothing to do with you, haven't liked not being able to share him, enjoy him with you. But I've put up with it, because I've loved you so much it seemed worth it. Better than the alternative. Now everything's changed. I'm frightened and I feel very alone and, like I said, I need you, I need you badly.'

'But Susie, have you really thought what this means? Especially to Rufus. That you're going to tell him that he's my child, my son, that you've lied to him, to Alistair all these years? Do you think he deserves that, do you think any of them do? Please, darling, please consider terribly carefully.'

'Jamie, said Susie, and in spite of herself she felt swayed by his argument, his logic, 'Jamie, all right, I will think, I will consider. I promise. But you have to promise me something too. If I do decide I want you, that I want to be with you, will you do that, will you be there for me?'

James looked at her, and she saw it again, that expression in his eyes, the trapped, almost frightened expression, and as she waited for his answer, she knew, even as she shrank from it, what it would be: more prevarication, more equivocation, after all the loyalty, all the years, he was going to fail her when she needed him. And then she heard a sound behind her, and there in the doorway was Rufus, standing frozen still, and she could see perfectly clearly from his face that he had heard every single word.

'I'm sorry,' he said, gently polite as always, 'I'm sorry if I startled you. I came over to fetch you, I thought it would save James the trip.'

'That was – very kind,' said Susie, 'very thoughtful. Thank you. I – '

'Yes, I can see you're – busy. Stupid of me not to have phoned first. To check.'

'Rufus, I think perhaps – ' said James.

'James, it's all right. I'll just go again. Leave you in peace. No doubt you'll bring Mum back in your own good time. Is – is Harry around?'

'Well, she is somewhere,' said James. 'But I'm not quite sure where – in her room I expect – shall I – '

'No, no, she's probably asleep,' said Rufus hastily. 'Don't disturb her. Not on my account.'

There was a silence; then Susie said, 'Would you like a drink or something, darling? Or a – a sandwich?'

It was farcical, she knew, she could hear herself sounding like something in a very bad drawing-room comedy, but she had to say something, had to try to distract herself from the awful pain on Rufus's face.

'No,' he said, 'no really, I'm fine. Thanks. Er – I'll be off, I think. Probably go back to London.'

'Rufus,' said James, 'Rufus, I really don't want you to – '.

'Don't want me to what?' said Rufus and for the first time there was some emotion in his voice, he sounded alive, angry, 'tell anyone? Say anything? Well I – '

'Good Lord!' It was Merlin; he and Janine had come in, smiling, through the back door, they hadn't heard his car. 'Looks like a party in here. Pour us both a drink, Jamie, there's a good chap. No news I suppose? We've had the most marvellous evening, haven't we, Janine, absurd price they charged us for the meal, had a few words to say about that, got a few quid knocked off as a matter of fact, but otherwise, it's been – '

'Merlin, Janine,' said Susie, knowing that if she didn't do something, anything, quickly, she would scream very loudly, 'would you excuse us, Rufus and me, he's come to collect me very sweetly and he's been waiting for ages already, I really do want to get back, I'm terribly tired.' She went over and kissed them both briefly, then, not looking at James, 'Rufus, darling, let's go, we can't keep Janet up all night waiting for us.'

And amidst a blur of goodnights, of well-wishing, of admonishments to Rufus to drive carefully, of James's face, startled, almost ashamed, she walked quickly out of the room, and at last they were in the car, she could never remember afterwards getting there, and Rufus who always drove so carefully, so considerately put his foot down and screeched out of the drive, gravel flying, and up the lane. It was only when they reached the more major road that led into Woodstock that he stopped, lurched to a halt, and put his head on his arms on the steering wheel.

'Rufus,' said Susie, 'Rufus darling, I – '

'Don't,' he said, 'don't please. Say anything. I couldn't bear it. I can't bear any of it. Just let me take you back to the Beaumonts and then I'm going to London.'

'Take me with you,' said Susie, and she was surprised by how much it mattered, how much she wanted it, 'please. I want to go home. I won't say a single word all the way, but I want to go home.'

Her only fear was that Alistair wouldn't be there, but as she got out of the car, thanked Rufus, made him promise to ring her in the morning, tried to kiss him (but he turned his face away), she saw the light on in the first-floor study, saw Alistair walk over to the window and look out. She ran up the steps, fumbling with her key; by the time she had it in the lock, had managed to turn it, he was there, opening it for her, looking at her surprised, puzzled.

'Darling!' he said. 'What on earth are you doing here? And why didn't you ring me, tell me you were coming?'

'I couldn't,' said Susie, 'well, not easily.' She walked past him, into the kitchen. 'I'd love a drink, Alistair. Just some white wine or something.'

'Of course. I presume there's no news?'

'No, nothing. Well, there was apparently, on Tilly Mills's answering machine. From Cressida, saying she was fine.'

God, it seemed so long ago, all that, another lifetime, another life.

'Girl's cracked,' said Alistair cheerfully, handing her a glass. 'Needs her bottom smacked.'

'That's what Merlin said,' said Susie, and giggled; the giggle got slightly out of hand, she couldn't stop. She looked at Alistair and saw he was looking at her rather oddly.

'It's not that funny,' he said.

'No,' she said, 'no, I know,' and realized she was crying instead. She struggled back into control, sat down abruptly at the table.

'Alistair, I have to talk to you.'

'Oh dear,' he said, 'sounds heavy. Is it?'

'A bit. Yes.'

'Is it one of the children? I wondered why Rufus – '

'No,' she said, 'well, not really. It's – well, it's us.'

There was a silence. Then he said, carefully, 'Do we really have to, Susie? I mean, really have to?'

Susie stared at him. It was an extraordinary moment: for she saw in it, reading his eyes, his watchful eyes, what she had always suspected: that he had known much of it all along. Exactly how much, precisely what details, she had no idea, but certainly he had never been properly in ignorance, totally deceived. And against all odds she smiled at him, just a little, amazed, awed even, not only that their marriage could sustain such a thing, but that they could so perfectly and tacitly agree that it should.

'Well – ' she said, 'well, but you see – '

'Susie,' he said, 'Susie, let's not. I'm so very very fond of you, I've been extremely happy with you. I'd rather leave it like that if we possibly can.'

'But Alistair – '

'Susie, let me finish please. You've been very clever, I think, made a very happy family. Much happier than most. We all love you. Don't spoil it, unless you really have to. There isn't any point.'

Susie drained her glass, poured herself another. 'There is a bit of point,' she said quietly. 'Things have changed today, I'm afraid. I'm sorry.' 'It's Rufus,' she had been about to say, but decided she must go further back, explain how she had come to be behaving so out of character, so differently from herself. 'I'm ill,' she said, and her voice was steady, its old self. 'That's the thing. I possibly – probably, actually – have cancer. Breast cancer. I heard this morning. I'm so sorry, Alistair.'

She meant it; she *was* sorry. It was going to be a dreadful nuisance for everybody; she would be no use to Alistair, to any of them. All the things he relied on her for, running the house, taking care of the children, entertaining, arranging holidays, she would be able to do none of it. It was a terrible prospect; she didn't see how they would be able to bear it.

She looked at him; he was staring at her as if he had never seen her before, his face ashen, his mouth taut. He put out his hand as if to touch her, then dropped it again, sat down heavily in a chair beside her at the table.

'How – how bad is it?' he said.

'I don't know yet. Mr Hobson spoke to me this morning. I have to go in tomorrow for a biopsy, first thing. He wants to see you too. Of course. He wanted us both to go in today, but of course we couldn't. Well, it didn't seem the best day. Really. So – it's tomorrow.'

'But it might be – nothing?'

'I don't think it's nothing,' said Susie, speaking carefully, 'and he doesn't think so either. I know he doesn't. Well, he said so. He's drawn off some fluid and looked at that, I don't quite understand, and done a mammogram, and he's worried. I can tell. But we won't know for sure until tomorrow.'

'Does it – are you in pain?'

'No. No, not really. But I don't feel terribly well. I'm very tired all the time, which isn't me, and I've lost some weight. I'm sorry, I'm not trying to worry you, but it seems best to be honest. In this instance,' she added and smiled at him, wryly ironic.

'Oh God,' said Alistair, and this time he did touch her, just very gently, took her hand and stared down at it. 'Oh God, Susie, I wish you'd told me. I wish to God you'd told me.'

'But why, what good would it have done? I only found the damn thing a week ago and then it might have been nothing, and then you'd have been worried quite needlessly, and – '

'Yes, yes, I know, but you must have been so – well, so – frightened,' he said. It was not the kind of word Alistair used; he looked, she thought, quite frightened himself. And thought, even in her pain and misery, that he was actually being more thoughtful, more imaginatively caring than James had been. Well, James had had rather more on his mind. To be fair.

'I was frightened,' she said, realizing with something of a shock that that particular emotion was, briefly at any rate, in the past, 'but I'm not any more. I feel quite resigned. I'm sure it won't last though. I'm sure I'll get scared again.'

'And what did he say, your Mr Hobson, how – well, bad did he think it was, what could it entail?'

'Alistair, he didn't know, he won't know anything until he's done the biopsy. I'm sorry.'

'Oh Christ,' he said, 'oh dear Christ, Susie, I don't like this.'

He put his arms round her, cradled her head. Susie sat quite still, numb to any emotions of her own, absorbing his fear, his raw, naked terror, without being able in any way to respond to it, and realized properly and for the first time in their lives together that Alistair did actually love her.

Chapter Twenty

Harriet 11pm

Harriet was doing a cash-flow forecast for the year 2001 (with a discharged bankruptcy and with new backing, staff and premises; she was nothing, she kept telling herself, if not positive) when she heard the phone ringing. She had stayed up in her room ever since she had found the note from the gynaecologist; she couldn't face sharing it with anyone, not even Oliver, couldn't face any more emotion, recrimination, theorizing. In the morning, perhaps, she would tell them; not now. She simply wanted to get away from the whole damn thing, to concentrate on her own problems, her own future. She had been aware, but only half consciously, of the occasional car coming and going, of voices downstairs, but she ignored it all. If they wanted her, they could find her, but she had had enough of them: they had worn her out, along with the day. Only the phone call, waiting for its ring, occupied her attention, consumed her energies. The cash flow had been a good idea; it focused her mind absolutely. Reading, watching television, listening to the radio were all futile, she would just have sat there fretting, raging silently over Theo. Well, at least it was distracting her from the duller, more wretched pain of her discovery about her father; that would have to wait, until she could set aside the time to examine it, to grieve, to decide what to do. One thing at a time; one hurt at a time.

She had been half afraid Theo wouldn't ring, would continue to avoid her; she was strangely relieved to find she did not have to add cowardice at least to his list of faults.

She ran down the stairs, seized the phone in the hall. 'Harriet Forrest,' she said, hating her voice for its slight tremor, despising herself for the harsh thudding of her heart. Bloody Theo, bloody Theo, how he could –

Only it wasn't Theo; it was Tilly.

'Harry, hi. You weren't asleep, were you?'

'Asleep? I'm still waiting for that bastard to phone. I thought it was him then – '

'Sorry. Listen, something extraordinary has happened. I've found – no I haven't, let me start again. Harry, do you know anyone called Eloise Renaud?'

'No. No I don't think so. I'm sure I don't. Unless she's a supplier or something, but I can't think of anyone called that. Why?'

'Well, whoever she is, she's Cressida's double. Or – something.'

'What? Tilly, what are you on about?'

'Sorry, Harry, but this is very hard to make any sense of. In fact it's seriously strange. I – '

'Tilly, please,' said Harriet in agony, 'start at the beginning or something. What's happened, who – ?'

'OK, OK, Mick McGrath just phoned.'

'From Paris?'

'Yeah, from Paris.'

'What's that got to do with Cressida?'

'I'm trying to tell you. Just listen.'

'I'm listening.' Harriet sat down abruptly on the hall floor, cradling the phone on her lap.

'Mick went into the *Figaro* offices this evening. He had some pictures to deliver. He was waiting to see the picture editor and there was a load of stuff on his desk, you know, that hacks had brought in.'

'Yes, yes, I know. Get on with it, Tilly, for God's sake.'

'I'm trying. Well, anyway, there was one picture of a couple running down the steps of Sacré-Coeur. It was really sweet, he said, she was in a wedding dress, and laughing, and the pigeons were everywhere, and everyone round them was staring at them and smiling. Very Robert Doisneau.'

'Who?'

'Robert Doisneau. You know, the guy who did that famous picture of the boy and girl kissing in the middle of Paris, it's everywhere at the moment – '

'Tilly, what's that got to do with it?'

'Well, nothing, except the poor schmuck who took it thought that was why it might get published. Anyway, Mick suddenly realized that the girl was Cressida.'

'Cressida! In her wedding dress in Paris. But – ' The room whirled, Tilly's voice down the phone seemed to be ebbing and flowing. Hang on, Harriet, she thought, this time you really do have to be dreaming, you'll wake up in a minute. She waited, staring ahead, holding her breath, she wasn't sure why, waiting for an awakening; but only heard, still in the same strange whirling space, Tilly's voice in her head again.

'Harry, are you all right, are you there?'

'Yes,' she said, her breath coming out in a rush, 'yes I'm here. I think. Tilly, was he sure? Really sure? He wasn't on anything?'

'He was quite sure. Well, he was sure until he looked at the caption on

the back. Which said the girl was Eloise Renaud. After her wedding at
Sacré-Coeur today. It didn't give the guy's name.'

'But Tilly, it couldn't have been. It just couldn't. I mean – well, Mick
doesn't know Cressida very well. It must be a mistake.'

'Of course he knows her. Well enough to recognize her anyway. We all
had dinner a few weeks ago, for Christ's sake. Only problem is, of
course, she isn't called Eloise Renaud.'

'No,' said Harriet. 'No she isn't. Oh God. God, Tilly, I really think
we're all going mad. She's driven us mad.' She felt horribly near to tears;
she took a deep breath, tried to steady herself.

'Look, can you get somewhere where there's a fax?' said Tilly.
'Because Mick took one of the prints, he can fax it to you.'

'Well, I don't know. I could go up to London, I suppose. Bit of a long
way . . .'

'What about a hotel? They all have them now. Couldn't you bribe
someone to let you use – '

'That's a brilliant idea, Til,' said Harriet slowly. 'I'll do that.'

The Royal Hotel at Woodstock certainly contained a fax. It also
contained Theo Buchan.

She was halfway out of the kitchen when she realized she had lent her car
to Mungo. Shit. It was going to mean taking her father's, and she would
have to tell him at least. Then he'd want to know why, and – 'Oh God,'
said Harriet aloud. 'Oh God.'

'Got a problem?'

It was Merlin, his blue eyes particularly brilliant, sparkling at her. He
had a glass of whisky in his hand. 'Wanted a drop of water to put in this.
Can I help?'

'Well – ' said Harriet, 'well, you could. But I don't know if you would.
It's a huge favour.'

'Try me. Feeling pretty good as a matter of fact.'

'You look good,' said Harriet, smiling at him, distracted from her
anguish briefly by the sheer happiness radiating from him. 'What's
happened?'

'Tell you what's happened,' said Merlin, 'gone the same way as the
birds and the bees and the educated fleas, that's what.'

'Sorry, Merlin, I don't quite follow you.'

'Don't you ever listen to any decent music, Harriet? Little number by
Cole Porter. "Let's Do It", it's called. Fine song. Anyway, that's it.
Waited a bit of a time but here I am, helpless as a kitten up a tree, to quote
another one.'

'Merlin, are you trying to tell me you've – well, you've fallen in love?'

'That's it. Head over heels. Well, you can guess who with, of course. Janine. She's a wonderful girl. What an evening we've had. Could have stayed out with her forever, but didn't want to start any talk, ruin her reputation, that kind of thing.'

'No, of course not,' said Harriet, keeping her expression sober with great difficulty.

'Can't believe my luck,' he said, taking a large slug of whisky. 'She's damn fine-looking, isn't she, and extremely sharp. And a wonderful listener. But I let her talk too. Told me about her husbands, all three of them, and her life. Very interesting. One thing she's never done enough, she says, is travel. Can't wait to show her the bush. And the rain forests. Anyway, I've proposed and she's accepted. What do you think, eh?'

'Merlin, I think it's wonderful,' said Harriet, reaching up to kiss him on the cheek. 'Er – how official is it? I mean am I to keep it a secret?'

'Good Lord no. Don't want to waste any time. Don't believe in long engagements, never did. No, I'll put it in the *Telegraph* tomorrow and we'll apply for a special licence. Apparently she's got a frock she can wear, so that'll cut out a lot of messing about.'

'Good gracious,' said Harriet. 'You really are serious, aren't you?'

'Of course I am. Look, I've always said once I found the right woman I wouldn't let her get away again. She made up her mind pretty quickly too. I asked her just before they brought the pudding and by the time we'd had coffee, she'd said yes.'

'Well, I think it's lovely,' said Harriet. 'Can I say anything to her?'

'Maybe not tonight,' said Merlin. 'She seems a bit tired. All this nonsense today has taken it out of her a bit. Gone up to bed now. But in the morning, of course you can. In fact she said she'd like to tell you before anyone else.'

'Oh Merlin,' said Harriet. Tears had filled her eyes. 'Oh Merlin, I think it's so lovely. I'm so pleased for you.'

'Yes, well, I'm a fool not to have realized before,' he said, blushing slightly. 'Wasted a bit of time, I suppose. But never mind, we're not in our dotage yet, plenty of years ahead of us. Pity we can't have children, but there it is, not much chance of that I'm afraid. We could adopt I suppose,' he added suddenly. 'What would you think of that? Or do you think they'd say we were too old? The authorities, I mean?'

'Merlin,' said Harriet, kissing him again, 'I'd back you against the authorities any day. But I should wait a little while if I were you. Best to have a bit of time just the two of you on your own, don't you think?'

'I suppose so,' he said. 'Now what was this favour you wanted to ask me?'

Harriet felt absurdly happy as she drove the Lagonda down the winding lane. The pure charm of a romance between Merlin and Janine had lifted her spirits as nothing else could have done. She had longed to go and talk to Janine herself, but the door to her room had been firmly closed and no light showed under the door; she would see her in the morning. She wondered suddenly if Janine would let her design a dress, but if Merlin was in that much of a hurry, maybe it wasn't such a good idea. What a wedding it would be. She wondered who would give Janine away, and who Merlin would have as his best man. He surely couldn't have that many able-bodied surviving friends; people of his age generally spent their time attending funerals rather than weddings. Maybe, she thought, smiling fondly, he would bring over some exotic figure from his travels, some tribal chieftain. It would be exactly like him. Janine would like that, too.

Behind her in the darkness someone was flashing her, clearly someone who had no knowledge of the dangerous narrow winding lanes. 'Just you wait,' she said aloud, 'and learn some manners,' and to distract herself from the irritation started to sing 'Let's Do It', that being the first song that came into her head. Rather to her surprise she realized she knew almost all the words: 'Argentines without means do it, Down in Boston even beans do it' . . . something about English soles do it, and what came next, oh, yes, 'Goldfish in the privacy of bowls do it.' Well, it wasn't surprising, she'd been raised on those songs, Merlin had boxes full of old 78s in his dusty flat and one of her treats when she stayed with him had been playing them on his wind-up gramophone. By the time she reached the forecourt of the Royal Hotel she had moved through 'Putting on my Top Hat' and 'Isn't It a Lovely Day' to 'Just the Way You Look Tonight'; so who needed a car stereo? She had just parked the Lagonda and was patting its wooden dashboard lovingly when she saw that it was Theo Buchan's Bentley that had been following her and flashing at her; the expression on his face when he saw her, rather than Merlin, climb out made up for quite a lot of the wretchedness of her day.

Harriet walked over to the car and smiled sweetly down at him.

'Theo,' she said, 'fancy seeing you here.'

'Yes,' he said, and even allowing for the ghastly yellow lighting of the Royal Hotel car park he looked terrible, ashen-pale with great hollows under his nearly black eyes.

'It's terribly bad manners, you know, to flash endlessly at someone like that.'

'Oh for God's sake,' he said, getting rather slowly out of the car; he looked at that moment, she thought, like an old man. 'I thought you were Merlin. What on earth are you doing, driving his car?'

'Oh, I stole it,' she said, 'while he was asleep. I'm going to run away with it actually, sell it to a dealer in the Old Kent Road. Merlin lent it to me, that's what I'm doing with it. I lent my car to your son.'

'How kind,' said Theo, 'but I wish you hadn't.'

'Why not?'

'Oh – doesn't matter. Merlin must love you very much,' he added, 'he's never let me even drive it.'

'Yes, well, some of us are more deserving than others,' said Harriet, 'and I might add more trustworthy.'

'Right,' said Theo. 'Well, you must excuse me, Harriet, I'm very tired. It's been a long day. I'm going to bed.'

'No you're not,' said Harriet, 'we have things to discuss, Theo. Actually.'

'Oh really? In the nature of?'

'In the nature of business, of course. There's certainly nothing else I would wish to discuss with you.'

'Harriet, I don't know what you're talking about.'

'Yes you do,' said Harriet briefly. 'Cotton Fields.'

'I beg your pardon?'

'I think you heard. I'll say it again, though, just in case. Cotton Fields. Fashion chain. Leisurewear. Hugely successful. Any bells ringing yet?'

'I don't think so.'

'Liar,' said Harriet shortly. 'Well, anyway, I have something else to do first, and then I'll be up to your room. Or maybe we should talk in the bar, if you think Sasha might prefer that. But it could get noisy.'

'Sasha isn't here,' said Theo tersely.

'Really?'

'No. She's gone up to London.'

'I see. Without you. How enterprising.'

Theo didn't answer. He walked to the front door of the Royal, held it open for her. 'I'll see you later then. I look forward to it.'

'I wouldn't,' said Harriet.

She went over to the reception desk. The crinkly-haired girl had been replaced by a young man of immense superiority. He was dressed in a rather sharp light grey suit; he had a smooth pale face and smooth pale hair, and an extremely flashy signet ring. Harriet didn't like him.

'I wonder,' she said, struggling to overcome what she knew was prejudice, largely engendered by the suit, 'if I could ask you a huge favour.'

A chilly, half-smile crossed his face and he was clearly shaping up some bland piece of unhelpfulness when the phone rang. 'Excuse me one moment,' he said, and picked up the receiver. The call was evidently from his girlfriend; he turned away from Harriet and spoke at some length. Harriet waited, trying to hang onto her temper. Finally he turned back to her. 'Now,' he said, 'you were saying?'

'I wasn't,' said Harriet, 'actually. But what I was going to say was, could I possibly use your fax? There's something I urgently need to receive from France, and this was the nearest fax I could think of. I live at Wedbourne,' she added, anxious to impress upon him that she was not some passing tourist, 'in the Court House.'

He looked at her oddly. 'I don't know this area,' he said, 'I come from Birmingham.' He made it plain that anyone who didn't come from Birmingham was a person of very little importance.

'Yes, well, we all – ' 'have our problems' she was going to say, but bit the words back. 'That is, well, could I use the fax? Obviously I'll pay for it, but I need to phone someone in Paris and give him this number.'

'But you're not a resident of the hotel?'

'No,' said Harriet patiently, 'no, I told you, I live in Wedbourne.'

'Well in that case,' he said, 'I don't think I can possibly help you. I'm not empowered to give you access to our fax.'

'But it's there,' she said, leaning over the counter, 'I can see it. You don't have to give me access, just the number.'

'Which you would then pass on to your friend,' he said. He made it sound as if Harriet was about to do a heavy trade in drugs in the reception area.

'Yes.'

'I'm sorry, that's against management rules. The fax is for residents only,' he added carefully.

'But I'm not going to be using it all night,' said Harriet. 'I just want to receive one thing.'

'Yes, but while you're using it, a resident can't. You must see that.'

'Look,' said Harriet. 'It's eleven thirty at night. I don't see a lot of residents milling about and certainly not waving bits of paper they want to fax. It will take roughly thirty seconds to do this. Please, it's very important.'

'I'm sorry, but I really am not empowered to break management rules,' he said. 'They are very clear and – Ah, good evening, Mr Buchan, sir, can I get you anything?'

Harriet hadn't seen Theo reappear behind her; shit, he must have heard the whole humiliating episode.

'I cannot imagine that I'd want anything at all that you could get me,' said Theo in the heavy voice that made his staff the world over extremely nervous, and indeed start planning alternative employment immediately. 'Harriet, I have a fax upstairs, you can use that.'

'I'd rather use this one,' said Harriet firmly.

'Well, you're not going to be allowed to. Clearly. Some piss-pathetic management rule, I seemed to understand. So it's mine or nothing.'

Harriet looked at him. Behind the heaviness, the seriousness, there was a sparkle in the dark eyes; he had her, and he knew it. She felt furiously angry: with the young man, with herself for not handling him better, with management for having the stupid rule, but most of all with Theo for finding her at such a disadvantage and using it. 'Couldn't you – couldn't you ask him if you could use it? For me?' she said.

'Now why should I want to do that? They charge the earth, these people, for doing absolutely nothing. It would add a tenner, I daresay, to my bill, with VAT and God knows what.'

'I'll give you a tenner,' said Harriet desperately.

'Well, that would be interesting. But our young friend here would still know he was breaking his management rules. I imagine he would find that very difficult. Unethical even. No, you'd better use mine. Oh come along, Harriet, for Christ's sake. Get me a bottle of brandy sent up, would you?' he added to the young man. 'And let me have your name. I would hate to inadvertently employ you in one of my companies at some future date.'

'Poor little sod,' he said as they walked into his suite. 'Shitting bricks down there I should think.'

'How unlike you to show such concern,' said Harriet, 'and I don't know why you should either. He was horrible.'

'I agree. But it really wasn't entirely his own fault, I suppose. He had certain genetic and educational disadvantages to overcome.'

'Theo, don't be altruistic. It doesn't agree with you.'

'Oh I don't know. I think I'm being fairly altruistic, letting you use my fax machine. Now then, what it is you want so urgently? From Paris.'

'A picture,' said Harriet, giving in, 'a picture of Cressida. Well, we think it might be Cressida. I have to phone the photographer and he'll fax it over.'

'Cressida? Doing what?'

'Getting married.'

'Dear God. What's his number? I'll do it.'

Somehow, until she saw the picture, she hadn't believed it. She'd thought

Mick McGrath must have been mistaken, that it was a photograph of someone who looked very like Cressida; but there was no doubt, no doubt at all, even on the slightly smudgy fax. It was her, wearing the dress that had been hanging in the attic room for weeks, not the veil to be sure, but it was Cressida's hair, her bloody perfect blonde hair, thought Harriet, falling loosely on her shoulders, Cressida's face, smiling joyously up at the man whose hand she was holding, Cressida's pretty profile with its just turned-up nose, its neatly carved little chin, Cressida's tall, slender body, frozen forever in its joyous flight down the endless steps that led down from the great south door of Sacré-Coeur. She held not a traditional bouquet but a small bunch of what looked like sweet peas; her bridegroom (if such he was) was classically French-looking, with a darkly handsome, scrunched-up face and black curly hair, and he wore not a morning coat but a dark suit, over a white collarless shirt, open at the neck. There seemed to be no wedding guests with them, but small groups of tourists were staring at them, smiling benevolently; and around their heads, and on the steps below them, were the omnipresent, unconcerned pigeons of Paris.

'Dear God,' said Theo. 'Dear, dear God.'

'Theo,' said Harriet, 'Theo, at least try and think of something else to say.'

'I can't. I really can't. It is her, isn't it? There's no doubt at all.'

Harriet looked at him. He seemed very shaken. 'No, no doubt. It's totally nightmarish, isn't it? I feel absolutely shattered by the whole thing Apparently the name she gave the photographer was Eloise Renaud. Maybe if we went through all the directories or something.'

'Hardly an unusual name. It would take forever.'

'Well, maybe we should go over there, see the priest at Sacré-Coeur – how did they manage to arrange that, it's a huge cathedral for God's sake – get the name of the man. Who doesn't seem quite dressed for the part, I must say.'

'Yes, we could. Obviously we should. We have to. But not tonight. I'll take my plane over early in the morning.' There was a silence while he looked at her. 'I don't think we tell your parents, do you?'

'God no,' said Harriet with a shudder. 'All right, Theo, yes, that would be best. We'll wait till the morning. I'll just ring Mick McGrath, say thank you.'

'OK. Drink?'

'Coffee'd be good.'

She phoned Mick. 'Thank you. It's a nice picture. Are they going to use it?'

'No. No they're not. Look, if there's anything I can do – '

'There might be. I'll be over in the morning. I'll ring you then.'

'Yeah, OK. I tell you, Harriet, this is one weird business.'

'Oh Mick,' said Harriet, 'tell me about it.'

She put the phone down, stared at Theo. Somehow, briefly, he had ceased to be her enemy, had become divorced from any past they might have had, was simply her travelling companion in this strange new journey.

'You OK?'

'Yes. Yes I think so.'

He poured them both a coffee from the big jug that had arrived with his bottle of Martel Cordon Bleu. 'What the hell was she up to?' he said. 'What the hell?'

'Theo, I don't know. I can't make any sense of it. Any sense at all. OK, she wasn't quite the Miss Goody Two-Shoes everyone thought but – this is so – well, awful. And cruel. Wickedly cruel. She looks so happy. That's almost the worst thing. Knowing what she's done to us all – '

'Well,' he said, with a heavy sigh, 'love, if that is what she felt for this man, love does strange things. To us all.' His eyes, looking at her, were remote, brooding; she met them for as long as she could, then turned away.

'You think that's what it was then? She was in love with someone else, with this person, and finally – '

'I don't know. I really don't. I can't begin to imagine. I've done some fairly – well, unpleasant things in my life, but this is beyond even my imagining. Your parents, what they have endured today, it's unthinkable – '

'I know. I know.'

'And to think I helped her do this.'

'Theo, of course you didn't.'

'Yes I did. I paid for those flying lessons, I gave her money – '

'You gave her money? When?'

'Oh – quite often. Well, she was my goddaughter, I was very fond of her. She was hopeless with money, you know, always getting into debt, running up bills in shops and on her credit cards, in spite of her allowance and her salary and so on. Always begged me not to tell your father and of course I didn't. But it did worry me. I used to lecture her from time. Just as well Oliver had plenty of money – '

'He didn't have a lot,' said Harriet. 'I mean they're well-off, but they're not rich.'

'Oliver's going to be. Very rich.'

Harriet stared at him. 'I didn't know that.'

'Oh, you must have done,' he said, looking at her in genuine astonishment. 'Cressida certainly did. And your parents did I'm sure. But I suppose it wasn't common knowledge. Josh liked it played down. And you know how modest Oliver is, the opposite of flashy. Anyway, he was due to inherit an enormous sum from his grandfather. Julia's father. Serious money. All tied up in trusts of course, but – '

'I knew about the trust fund, but I didn't realize it was so big. I wonder why they didn't tell me. Maybe they thought – oh well.– ' She smiled rather shakily; it hurt her, hurt and humiliated her, that her parents should have thought she must be protected from the knowledge that Cressida was going to be seriously rich, that she would be jealous or upset. How much more pain was she going to have to take today? She pulled back abruptly to the present, to more immediate, more relevant questions. 'Why wasn't Julia getting it, Theo, this money? I don't understand . . .'

'Old chap didn't like Josh. Doesn't like him, rather. Never wanted Julia to marry him. Thought he was a loser.'

'I see,' said Harriet slowly. 'Well, he was wrong there, wasn't he?'

'Not really. Josh is one of my dearest friends, Harriet, but I wouldn't give him a job as my office boy. He's no real business sense. He's only held that job in the bank by the old virtues.'

'What old virtues?'

'Oh, you know, family connections, contacts, charm. They've lived off Julia's income to a large extent.'

'Which explains why Josh doesn't like talking about the money. Makes him look bad.'

'Yes, that's right.'

'Good Lord,' said Harriet. 'Oh Theo. Oh shit. This has been such a truly shocking day.'

'Yes it has.' He looked at her carefully. 'You OK?'

'Yes. Yes, I'm OK. Just. Maybe Sacré-Coeur will yield an answer tomorrow. Only I don't know if the priest or whoever will be able to help.'

'Oh he'll help,' said Theo. There was a darkness in his voice. 'I'm quite good at persuading people to – help.'

And the expression on his face, the tone of his voice, re-placed him for her, made him again the person he truly was, set him in his proper context, as tyrant, tormentor, arch-manipulator, and 'Yes,' she said, 'yes, Theo, you are, aren't you? Let's change the subject briefly, shall we? Let's talk Cotton Fields.'

'Harriet, haven't we got enough to worry about for now? I really don't know what you're talking about. Where it's leading – '

'I rather think you do, Theo. And from where I'm sitting it leads ultimately to my going absolutely and finally bust. In total humiliation. Unless of course I come crawling to you for money. Which I suspect might just be what you have in mind. Well, I can tell you, Theo, I would rather die from a thousand cuts.'

'I don't think you would,' he said, 'but still.'

'I would. Now then. Did you or did you not tell Hayden Cotton not to back me?'

There was a long silence. Then Theo said, 'Not exactly . . .'

'I see. Perhaps you could enlighten me on exactly what you did say then. It must have been fairly specific. He disappeared from the negotiating table faster than a snowflake in hell. Rather suddenly.'

'Harriet, I – '

'Yes Theo?'

'OK. I'll tell you. I told him to take a very hard look at the figures.'

'Theo, he'd *taken* a very hard look at the figures. And he seemed to be able to handle them.'

'Yes, well, I had a look at them too. He showed them to me.'

'What? Why?'

'We're old allies. He knows I know you. He wanted my advice.'

'I see. And?'

'And I thought they been massaged. A bit. And I said so.'

'They'd *what*! Massaged!' Harriet stood up. 'Theo, how dare you! How dare you even imply such a thing? There are slander laws in this country, as you very well know. I intend to use them.'

'Difficult,' he said, 'when you're bankrupt.'

'You bastard,' she said, 'you rotten, filthy bastard. What's it to you, Theo Buchan, why do you want me bankrupt? What will it do for you? Flatter your grotesque ego? Take you one step nearer your ambition to rule the world? You disgust me, Theo, you really do. I'm ashamed to have ever had anything to do with you.'

'Harriet,' he said, and there was real, raw pain at the back of his dark eyes, 'Harriet, don't say that. Please.'

'I'm afraid I have to say it, because it's true. I am ashamed. It makes me feel sick.'

'Oh God,' he said, and put his head in his hands suddenly.

'And don't,' she said, 'don't call in the throbbing strings, Theo, because they're sounding fairly badly out of tune. I find it hard to imagine that you could say anything, anything at all, that would change the way I'm feeling about you right now. Which is above all nauseated.'

He looked up at her, and his face was literally grey; he reached out for his glass and his hand was shaking so violently he had to put it down again. 'Harriet, I – '

'Theo, don't. Just don't. I've seen them all, all the routines, heard all the scripts. I'm leaving. Now.' (So why aren't you going, Harriet, why are you still standing there looking at him? Just walk out, walk away. Maybe kick him in the balls for good measure.)

'No,' he said, getting up. 'No, Harriet, don't go. I want to talk to you –'

'Well, I don't want to talk to you. Ever again. Except just possibly in court. Goodbye, Theo.' (Well, go on, Harriet, go, leave, you don't want to talk to him, you want to get out of this room, full of his bloody arrogant, manipulative presence. What's stopping you? God, Harriet, don't, don't walk forward, don't whatever you do let him touch you, take your hand away from his –)

'Oh God,' he said, and the words were a great echo of misery, 'oh God, Harriet, please, please stay, don't leave me, I'll do anything, anything at all, but don't go.'

'Theo,' she said, and she put out her other hand now, the one he wasn't holding, and to her own intense astonishment gently, tenderly touched his hair, 'Theo, we can't – ' and the words came slowly, falteringly, she had to struggle with every one, and there was something else going on now, a warmth, that bloody, dangerous, flooding warmth that he could always create in her, the prelude to something fiercer, stronger. Her body throbbed once, twice, sweetly, powerfully, and she was afraid, afraid of its betrayal, of its longing for him. 'Theo,' she said, 'Theo, we can't let it begin again. We really really can't.'

And she pulled her hand away then, hard, roughly, and looked away from him, and the effort was so intense she felt it physically, and then she turned her back on him and walked swiftly, desperately fast, to the door, wrenched it open, ran down the stairs, through the front door, across the courtyard to Merlin's car and struggled to start it, frantically fearful that he would follow her, catch her, knowing that if he did, she would be lost, helplessly, hopelessly lost, and that if he touched her once more, however lightly, she would take all her clothes off there and then, and just lie down on the hard stones and fuck him and fuck him until they were both senseless.

Chapter Twenty-One

Mungo 11.30pm

Financial reality was not something Mungo was overfamiliar with. Like most people who have grown up cushioned by apparently limitless wealth, he had really very little idea what anything cost: he had once been asked how much his weekly outgoings were and he had replied with charming naiveté that he thought about £5. His flat in Sloane Street had been bought for him out of his trust fund; its outgoings were paid for from the same source. Such food as he ate at home he had delivered from Harrods and Fortnums, on the Buchan account, his clothes were all made by the various tailors who served his father, or from establishments where a Buchan charge account had been run for decades, Harrods, Fortnums, Simpsons and Paul Smith in London, Brooks Brothers and Paul Stuart in New York, Trimingham Brothers in Bermuda. His shoes were all made by Lobb. His cars were provided and serviced by his father's garage, he bought air tickets on his father's accounts with various airlines, hired cars on his father's account with Hertz. Many of the world's great hotels welcomed him, and simply presented him with a bill to sign as he left; the same applied to a large number of restaurants. Theo had accounts with cab companies, florists, theatre ticket agencies; Berry Brothers of St James's had supplied the Buchan family with wine and spirits for three generations. For several days at a time, the only cash Mungo ever had to produce was for an evening paper or a packet of Polos. Indeed one of the more educational aspects of his affair with Alice had been discovering the cost of eating at places like McDonald's and Pizza Hut. Mungo was not stupid or even thoughtless; he knew perfectly well what an inordinate amount of money he must work his way through in the course of a year, or even a month, but there was a faceless quality to the money, it didn't mean anything, no thought went into its coming and going, it was simply part of the process by which he procured things. He thought, he chose, he signed; no decisions were necessary, no choices made, he wanted therefore he had.

And now suddenly, he could see quite a lot was going to change and there might, for a while at any rate, be a great deal he wanted and would not be able to have.

Of course, any such deprivation was not strictly necessary: when it came to Mungo, Theo's memory was famously short, his attitude notoriously liberal. Had Mungo not gone into battle so vigorously, taken Theo on so valiantly, had he told Alice that it might be politic for them to wait a while before actually getting married, had he seen his property company safely through a full financial year or maybe two, then he could have continued with his way of life more or less unthreatened. But battle, and the more vigorous the better, was Mungo's style; and having forced the confrontation, made all those brave statements, there could be no going back. Even if he'd wanted it: which he most emphatically didn't. It was going to be tough, making out on his own, but it would be very very good. There would be no more insinuations about his inadequacy, no more references to his dependency; for the first time in his twenty-seven years he would feel like an adult. And he was hardly going to be destitute: he still had a sizeable income from the capital in his trust fund, he had his flat, his car, enough clothes to see him through the next twenty years, and he had a viable – well, potentially viable – business. He would be all right.

He had spent the past hour in his office in Carlos Place, looking at business in hand, studying the cash flow, doing projections. And confronting a truth that had confronted a great many people running companies over the past thirty-six months: that his incomings simply didn't begin to match his outgoings. The costs of the offices, staff and advertising were, month on month, roughly double what they were earning. It hadn't mattered before: Theo had simply made up the shortfall. Now it mattered a lot. Mungo stared out of his window at the subtle opulence of the Connaught Hotel and realized that he would have to get rid of the office and most of the staff. He and the two Sloaney girls he had hired as negotiators (extremely effective as well as pretty) would have to run the business from his flat. It wouldn't be ideal, but it would be all right. The marketing and advertising manager, the surveyor and the interior designer would have to go; they simply weren't earning their keep. They were useful in promoting the company, but he could cope without them. He'd have to put a lot more hours in, of course, but that would be OK; he'd enjoy it. Looking through his books, his files, that night, he realized how much he loved his company, already, how much the business fascinated him, how much he wanted to develop it. And he knew he could. He might even study for a degree in estate management in his spare time: Roddy Fairfield, his rather flashy young assistant (he'd have to go too) had one, and there was no doubt he was not only very knowledgeable, he had all the jargon. People liked jargon. And it would be good to study, good to learn something again. He went off into a brief reverie, imagining himself working every night in Alice's little house while she read and did her tapestry. Well, he would get off to the little house now; it was late, but she wouldn't mind. She hardly ever went to bed before midnight, usually well after. He'd said he wouldn't be coming, so she wouldn't be expecting him of course, but that would make his arrival all the nicer, more fun.

Mungo went down the stairs and locked the heavy front door behind him; the street was deserted and very quiet. The crime wave that was theatening to engulf London, if the media were to be believed, certainly hadn't broken on Carlos Place. Now he had to get a cab; well, there were plenty outside the Connaught. He might just have a drink there, before he went to Alice. He felt he needed one suddenly; it had been a bit of a bitch of a day.

It was almost midnight when he left the Connaught, two glasses of champagne later. Maybe he should ring Alice, warn her he was coming. Then he thought that if she was asleep, the phone would wake her; he would go to the house and if all the lights were out, he would restrain himself.

'Nine, Chatto Street please,' he said to the driver and sat back.

'Lovely evening,' said the cabbie.

'Lovely,' said Mungo.

'Long day,' said the cabbie. 'Been driving tourists round since lunchtime. Can't stand them. Except the Americans of course. They're all right. Speak English as well. Mind you, why they go on coming here I can't think, the filth in the streets, and the traffic, beats me, when they've got the whole of the United States to look at. Course they haven't got the royal family, that's what brings them in, and that's a mystery too, the way they've all gone downhill, well, not the Queen herself, but the rest of them, specially the young ones, no sense of duty any more, no real class, terrible, and I'll tell you something else, I don't think she should be charging for seeing over the palace, doesn't seem right somehow, makes the whole thing too commercial, we shall be having a republic soon, I'm sure of it, and then we'll be sorry, specially when she's gone, it'll be Mrs Thatcher all over again, Lady I should say – '

Mercifully Mongo was saved from hearing how the downfall of the monarchy might be paralleled in some way with Lady Thatcher's demise; they had reached Chatto Street and he was about to pay the driver off and get out when he saw that the small house was indeed in total darkness. Shit. That was seriously irritating. Oh, well, he told himself, if he was going to be a proper businessman in future, he was going to have to get used to keeping more demanding hours. He was about to tell the cabbie to turn around and go back to Sloane Street when he realized he had only just enough money to pay the fare as it was.

'Thanks, that's fine,' he said. 'Look, I'm terribly sorry, I don't have any spare change at all, I can only give you a 5p tip, bit of an insult I'm afraid, but – '

'You keep your bloody 5p, mate,' said the cabbie, reversing viciously, preparatory to turning round, 'you must need it more than I do.'

'I'm terribly sorry,' said Mungo again. 'I thought – '

'I wouldn't try,' said the cabbie, 'thinking I mean, you might find it too much of a strain.'

And he was gone with a squeal of tyres and a blare on his horn as he reached the junction with the Kings Road.

Mungo looked after him, and sighed, and then thought he might as well just walk home. There was no point waking Alice up, she was bound to be tired, and they had all the time in the world after today. It wasn't far to Sloane Street, only about ten minutes; he would get a good night's sleep and then – His plans for the next day were gently disturbed by the quiet clunk of a door being shut. Someone leaving a dinner party, no doubt, although there was no shouted bonhomie, no 'thankyous', no 'lovely evenings'. Just the clunk.

Vaguely intrigued he turned round, and saw a figure walking away from Alice's house. A male figure. One of Jemima's friends, Mungo told himself firmly, ignoring the tiny movement, a minute curl of fear stirring somewhere in the region of his stomach; she was home for the holidays after all. Considerate of them to be so quiet: unlike Jemima that. Much of Jemima's behaviour made Annabel Headleigh Drayton appear a dead ringer for Mother Theresa by comparison. He didn't slow down, then, in order to get a better look at the person; of course he didn't. He was tired and it was very hot and he just didn't want to get any hotter, that was all. A nice gentle unwinding walk was what he wanted; the fact that the man was catching him up, about to overtake him, was neither here nor there. There really was a dinner party going on in the house he was passing now; the dining room was at street level, the light flooding out onto the dark pavement. It lit up the man's face as he passed Mungo, and he didn't look too much like one of Jemima's friends: he was at least thirty years old, extremely good-looking, his jacket was slung across his shoulders, his tie hung loosely round his neck and he was whistling 'Candle in the Wind' very quietly under his breath. 'Candle in the Wind' was one of Alice's favourite songs.

Mungo took a deep breath and walked straight back to number 9.

The house was not in total darkness any more; Alice's bedroom (front, first floor) had a light in it. Well, maybe whoever'd just left had woken her and now she was reading. She was a very light sleeper. He rang the bell gently, hardly to be heard. He wished Alice would let him have a key; he felt so foolish, having to be let in like a casual visitor. But she was very protective, possessive even, about her domain, her personal space; she told him it was on account of living alone for so long. Well, now they were definitely going to be married, she would surely agree to let him have one. Until they got a place of their own. He'd been thinking of a house, on the Kensington–Chelsea borders, maybe near The Boltons, nothing too grand, but big enough for all of them. Shit, even that would be more complicated now, he'd have to get the trustees' permission and –What on earth was she doing, why was she so long? Maybe she hadn't heard him. He rang again, a little more firmly. Ah, there were footsteps now. The door opened; Jemima's face appeared in the crack above the chain. She looked confused, embarrassed.

'Oh – Mungo. Hi. What are you doing here?'

'Visiting your mother, I hope.'

'But I thought – '

'Yes, I know, but I had to come up to town, so I just dropped by on the off-chance. Aren't you going to ask me in?'

'Oh – sorry, I wasn't thinking – but the thing is, Mungo, well, that is Mummy isn't here.'

'Isn't here? But her bedroom light's on.'

'Yes I know. I was in there myself, just – oh, you know, looking at her dresses. Seeing if there was anything I could borrow for a – a dance I'm going to.' She pushed her heavy hair back; smiled at him awkwardly.

'Well, where's your mother?'

'She's gone out to dinner. With – with a friend.'

'Oh I see.' Well, that was all right. Alice had every right to go out to dinner. With anyone really, and certainly with a girlfriend. Even if she hadn't mentioned it. It was probably a last-minute invitation.

'When do you think she'll be back? I really do want to see her.'

'Oh – I don't know. Not for ages probably. She's with her very best friend. They just talk and talk for hours.'

'Who, Anouska?' said Mungo. He didn't quite know why he said that: he wasn't really checking up, of course not, he just wanted to make sure, to be able to go home to bed with an absolutely easy mind.

'Yes,' said Jemima. 'Yes, that's right, Anouska.'

'I see,' said Mungo. Anouska was away with her husband for a long weekend in France; Alice had told him herself.

★

He stood there for a long minute, trying to convince himself that it still didn't mean anything, that Jemima was simply trying to come up with an answer, to please him, to get rid of him. He failed. 'Well, I think if you don't mind, Jemima,' he said, 'I'll come in and wait for your mother. I've got something terribly important to talk to her about. You just get off to bed and I'll sit and read or something.'

'But – '

'Jemima,' said Mungo. 'I really do want to come in. Friend of yours just leaving, was it?'

Jemima looked at him; her face in the street light was startled, guilty. 'No. Yes. Well, an old friend of the family. Of Mummy's, really.'

'I see. And you were entertaining him with all the lights out, were you?'

'Mungo, I – oh shit, I – '

She looked very scared. Mungo smiled at her suddenly, conspiratorially. 'Listen, Jemima, I'm not so much of a grown-up I'm going to tell on you. But I would like to come in.'

'Oh, all right,' said Jemima, and smiled, slightly uncertainly, back. She undid the chain and unlocked the door; Mungo wondered vaguely how Alice might have been supposed to get in, but then dismissed the thought. He had more important things on his mind.

'Thank you.' He looked at her; under her long dark lashes her eyes were knowing, defiant. She led him into the kitchen. 'Coffee? Drink?'

'I'd love a coffee. Thank you.'

She made two cups, slightly to his surprise, put them on the table, sat down on a chair opposite him. She was wearing a silk robe; her cleavage was very visible, her hair, thick, blonde, tousled, tumbled over her shoulders. One long brown leg was crossed over the other, revealed almost to the crotch. God, she was gorgeous. Talk about jail bait. Mungo concentrated very hard on his mug of coffee. 'You don't have to worry,' he said again, 'I really am not going to tell on you.'

'Thank you. Of course we weren't – '

'Of course you weren't.'

'But he's much older than me and Mummy doesn't really approve.'

'I see. Is it – quite serious?'

'Well, a bit. But only a bit. I've got another year at school yet and – '

'Three surely. Three years. With A-levels.'

'Oh, I'm not going to do A-levels,' said Jemima, with as much scorn in her voice as if he had suggested she might take up cleaning or pig farming. 'I'm going to do modelling.'

'Oh really? Well, you'll make a lot of money. If you do well.'

'Yes, I know. And it's obviously great fun. You know Ottoline, don't you? What's she like?'

'She's gorgeous,' said Mungo simply, 'and fun, and really nice. But she works like a dog.'

'Oh really? How?'

'Hours and hours on end in boiling studios. And freezing clifftops and things. And twenty-hour days in fashion showrooms, for weeks at a time. It's tough.'

'I don't call that tough,' said Jemima carelessly, 'and she gets bloody well paid for it, doesn't she?'

'Yes she does. Tell me, Jemima, what would you call tough?'

'Oh God, studying. I loathe it. And looking after kids. That's what I'm doing these holidays until we go away. It's gross. I hate it.'

'Well, I presume it's earning you a bit of money.'

'A bit. Mummy won't put my allowance up, and I just don't get enough – '

'I think it's more that she can't, Mimi, isn't it, she really doesn't have a lot of money.'

'I'm sure she could if she wanted to. She seems to have plenty of money to spend on herself. She's always buying clothes and things.'

'She seems to me to buy you quite a lot,' said Mungo, 'you and the others. So where is she then?'

He shot the question out quickly, catching her off her guard. Her voice was nervous, a bit too loud. 'I told you. She's gone out to dinner with Anouska.'

'Jemima, Anouska is in France. I happen to know. So who is your mother with?'

'Mungo, I don't know. I wasn't really listening. She's with friends, anyway.'

'Uh-huh. Look, do you want to go up and finish changing the sheets on your mother's bed? I'd hate to be responsible for your getting caught out – '

Jemima stared at him, her eyes filled with fear. 'How did you – '

'Oh Jemima, I've been fifteen too, you know. Not so long ago. You didn't invent naughty behaviour. Go on, go and get on with it.'

'OK,' she said, looking at him uncertainly, 'OK. Thanks. I won't be long.'

He sat drinking his coffee, feeling increasingly disorientated. He looked at his watch: one o'clock. Late. Well, quite late. Late for an impromptu dinner with a girlfriend. Or was it? Maybe not. Late for something Jemima was covering up anyway. Very late. He sighed, got a half-drunk bottle of wine out of the fridge and poured himself a glass. It was extremely good: expensive. Very expensive, he thought, looking at the label. Maybe one of the ones he'd bought. No, it wasn't, it was a French burgundy, he never bought French wine these days. Californian was a lot more interesting. She must have bought it herself. Maybe for a dinner party. Or maybe Jemima's friend had brought it. Yes, that was it, He drank the glass very quickly, finished the bottle, put it down under the sink. Alice was very strict about empties, taking them all to the bottle bank on Saturday mornings. There was another identical one there, plus a champagne bottle, and a bottle of red as well, a Penfold, 1989. Jemima and her friend must have had quite an evening. And he must be pretty well-heeled. Well, he'd looked well-heeled. And pleased with himself as well. Disgusting, fucking schoolgirls. Mungo felt angry suddenly, angry with all of them; he ran up the stairs and stood in the doorway of Alice's bedroom. Jemima had her back to him; she had nearly finished her task, was pulling the duvet cover finally into place. She hadn't heard him. 'Who's she with?' said Mungo. It was a dirty trick, but he couldn't help it. She jumped, spun round.

'Mungo, don't, please don't. I can't tell you. It's – it's not fair.'

He sighed. 'I suppose not. All right. Well, I'm going to wait. As long as it takes.'

'Mungo, there's not much point,' said Jemima, and for the first time that evening her large blue eyes – beautiful eyes, he noticed, irrelevantly, flecked with darker blue still – were soft, concerned.

'Why not?'

'Because – because she won't be back. Not until the morning. Oh Mungo, don't look like that. I'm so sorry.'

'That's all right, Jemima. Thank you for telling me. I think I'll still wait, though, if you don't mind. You go to bed, I'll be quite all right on the sofa.'

He was sitting there, staring into the darkness when she came in ten minutes later, bringing him a brandy and a cup of coffee. 'There you are. A nightcap.' She bent down and kissed him very gently on the cheek.

'I'm sorry, Mungo. She doesn't deserve you, she really doesn't. And you certainly don't deserve her.'

Chapter Twenty-Two

Tilly 12.30am

Considering she stood to make several hundred thousand dollars out of it herself, Felicity had been very noble about Tilly's decision. 'I really am not at all sure you should do it,' she said, when Tilly told her. 'You know how homesick you get, you know how you hate being tied down. There's more to life than money, Tilly.'

'You're kidding me,' said Tilly grinning into the phone. 'Yeah, I know. And the reason I want to do this – correction, the reason I *am* doing this – is exactly that. I have to get away, Felicity, away from London, out of this whole thing. And besides, I have plans for the money.'

'Tilly, don't get too excited about the money. It will go fast enough. Hideous tax bills, horrible expenses – '

'Yeah, outrageous commission to my agent, don't forget that. Don't fuss, Felicity, I know what I'm doing.'

'And you're sure?'

'I'm sure.'

'Can I call Meg? I mean you still won't be totally committed, not till you've signed, but she's going to start getting very wound up – '

'Sure,' said Tilly. 'Tell her. It's fine. Really.'

Felicity rang back five minutes later. 'She's so excited. She asked me to tell you she never felt more happy about anything in her life.'

'She must have had a pretty crap life,' said Tilly. Then she poured herself a very large glass of wine, and sat down to watch the last vestiges of day leave the sky.

She was woken by the entryphone ringing. She stumbled over to the door, stupid with sleep, picked it up. 'Yeah?'

'Tilly. It's Rufus.'

'I thought you were still in Wedbourne.'

'You thought wrong. Please, Tilly, let me in. I have to talk to you.'

'Rufus, I – ' God, she didn't need this. Not now. Not tonight. She needed her strength, her sleep.

'Tilly please.'

'Oh – all right.'

She pressed the entryphone, went into the bathroom. God, she looked terrible; great hollow eyes, saggy skin, and she had a spot, for Christ's sake, coming on her chin. Thank God they didn't have to reshoot any of the wedding dresses. Tilly dragged a comb through her cropped hair and cleaned her teeth. When she came out Rufus was standing in the sitting room. He had a bunch of rather tacky-looking flowers in his hand, wrapped in the lace-printed plastic garages use as substitute for wrapping paper. He was deathly pale. He tried to smile at her.

'Hallo, Tilly. These are for you.'

'Rufus, you really shouldn't have got Pulbrook and Gould out of bed at this time of night,' said Tilly, trying to sound light-hearted. She took the flowers, kissed him briefly. 'Drink?'

'Yes please. Well, if I can stay.'

Tilly took a deep breath. There was no point in postponing the agony longer than necessary. The swifter and cleaner the surgery the better.

'I – don't know. I have a six o'clock call.'

'Oh.' He looked confused. 'That never stopped you before.'

'I know, but I'm fucking tired.'

'Oh. Oh I see.' His eyes were so dark, his face so collapsed with hurt she could hardly stand it. She went into the kitchen quickly, poured two glasses of wine, handed him one. 'Here you are. I guess you could sleep on the couch.'

'Tilly! Tilly, whatever is it? What did I do?'

'Nothing. I told you, I'm just wrecked.'

'Too wrecked to talk to me?'

'No, of course not. But I have to talk to you too.'

'Oh. Well, all right. Of course. You go first.'

Oh God, he was such a nice man. Here he was, exhausted, clearly upset, desperate to talk to her, and she was treating him like some kind of pervert, and he was politely prepared to listen to her. How was she going to do this; and did she really really have to?

'No. No, you have first claim. Go ahead. I'm all yours.' She smiled at him, settled in the sofa opposite him.

'Are you, Tilly? Are you really? Because that's, at rock bottom, what I want to talk to you about. Well, there is something else, connected to it, but – before I start on that I just have to know, Tilly. Whether you'll marry me. I need you so much. More than ever now. You see – '

Right. This was it. She couldn't let this one go. Whatever else was going on. She took a deep breath, lit a cigarette, offered him one. He shook his head; he hated her smoking, she was always promising, without really meaning it, to give it up. 'Well, Rufus,' she said, not trying to be careful, tactful (for what was the point, what good would it possibly do?), 'Rufus, I've had an offer.'

'Ah.' She sensed him bracing himself, watched his eyes darken with alarm.

'What kind of offer?' he said clearly struggling to sound relaxed. 'From another man?'

God, Rufus, don't do this to me, don't try to be so nice, so brave.

'No. Well, from a whole load of men.'

'I'm sorry, Tilly, I don't follow.'

'From a cosmetics company. Called Rosenthal. I'm sure you won't have heard of them.'

'I – don't think I have. No.'

'Well, they're big. Very big. And they want to sign me up.'

'And is that what you want?'

'Yes. Yes it is.'

'Well, I should let them. If I were you. You want to get a good lawyer to look at the contract though.' He managed to smile at her; she didn't smile back.

'Yeah, I probably will. It's very big.' Might as well make herself sound as bad as possible. It would help him through it.

'How big?'

'Around two million dollars.'

Rufus whistled. 'That's a lot of dollars.'

Tilly shrugged. 'Yeah, well.'

'Tilly, what's the matter? You just don't seem yourself.'

'I'm myself,' said Tilly, beginning to believe it, 'probably more myself than I've been for a while.'

'So what does this have to do with us?' asked Rufus quietly.

'Well, I have to move to New York basically. For at least a year.'

'And?'

'And what?'

'Are you going to?'

'Yes, of course I am. Rufus, I really can't turn down two million bucks.'

'You could have talked to me about it. We could have discussed it, I would have thought.'

He looked so desperate, so bewildered, Tilly relented just a little. 'Rufus, I'm sorry. But I had to decide today. And there was rather a lot going on, it didn't seem quite the sort of thing to bother you with.'

'Tilly, anything to do with you is the sort of thing to bother me with. You know that.'

'Yes, I suppose it is. Yes of course. But – well, I do think it's for the best. In the long run.'

300

'Why?' He came over to her, took her hand, kissed it tenderly. Tilly looked at him, into his brown eyes, so full of love for her, and her heart quite literally seemed to be dying, choking to death. 'I'm sorry,' she said again, 'I'm so sorry. It just seemed – well, like I said, the best thing. To me.'

'Well,' he said, 'it doesn't to me. And I think you should have talked to me.'

'But Rufus, why?'

'Because I love you, Tilly. Because I want to marry you. To be with you. You know that.'

'Yes, Rufus, of course I do and – '

'Don't you love me? Is that what this is all about, is that what you're trying to tell me suddenly?'

'Yes,' she said, unable to lie about such an important, such a lovely thing, 'yes, Rufus, of course I love you. You know I do. But – well, love isn't everything. Is it?'

'For me it is. Everything.'

'Well, you're not very sensible, in that case,' said Tilly, getting up, fetching the wine bottle.

'No I'm not. I never thought being sensible was very important.'

'Well, I'm afraid I do. Rufus, we can't get married. I've told you so many times. It's hopeless. It would be like – I don't know. Pushing water uphill. Every day. Our lives wouldn't work together, Rufus. You'd want me to be what I'm not and I'd want you to be what you're not. It isn't practical, Rufus, I know it isn't. And in the end you'd know it too. We'd make each other so unhappy. So it's best to end it now. Before everything stops being good. And I've had this offer, and I've said I'm going. It's the right thing for both of us, Rufus, don't you see?'

'No,' he said, 'no I don't. I can't believe I'm hearing this, Tilly, I really can't. It's unbelievable.'

'I don't know why,' she said, irritated in spite of herself, in spite of her love for him. 'I've said all along that any idea of our being together, properly together, was hopeless. I think fate's come along and given us a bit of a shove.'

'And that's it, is it?' he said. 'Goodbye, baby, and amen. Just like that. You've decided it's not going to work, and so you're going. Have I got this right, Tilly?'

'Well,' she said, and she was having to drag the words out now, one by one, each more painful than the last, 'well yes, Rufus, actually, you have. I'm sorry, I'm really sorry.'

'Yes,' he said, standing up, staring down at her, 'yes I can see that. Terribly sorry. Nothing two million dollars can't fix though. Well, good.

Tilly, I think there's something more to all this. I don't know what. And I don't know that I want to hear it, but I suppose I have to ask. Good lawyer that I am, I want to examine all the facts. Has something happened today, in this bloody awful day we've all been through, that's made you feel differently about me? Apart from the prospect of being a millionaire? Like have you met someone? Or – '

And 'No,' she said, 'no of course not. Although – well, in a way, I suppose I have. I mean I've met your mother, seen how she is, what she has obviously done for your – your father. I can't do that, Rufus, and I can't be part of your world. Not ever. It's impossible.'

'And you're not prepared to try? Because,' he added, his voice infinitely heavy with sadness, 'I've tried very hard to be part of yours. And not done entirely badly, I don't think.'

'That's different,' said Tilly.

'Why? Why is it different?'

'Well, it's easier, more fluid. The people I know and work with don't wear a uniform, and talk with the same accent, and go to the same schools, and serve up the same food on the same tablecloths and talk the same fucking shorthand.'

'Yes they do,' said Rufus, 'of course they do. And I've found it quite hard, some of it. I don't even like a lot of it. I don't like people saying fuck all the time for a start. And thinking it was terribly terribly important to be wearing the right jacket and having the right haircut, and to know who did those wonderful pictures in British *Vogue* this month. But it's been worth it, to feel part of you, to feel I'm helping you. You obviously don't have the same concerns. So maybe you're right, Tilly, maybe it's better we do part. Especially if you can make a major decision like going away for twelve months without any reference to me whatsoever.'

To her horror, she realized he was going, and in spite of the heat, the flat seemed suddenly cold, deathly, horribly still and cold; and although she knew it was the right, the only thing to do, she was more afraid than she had ever been in her life. She sat there staring at him, and panic rose in her, a huge, choking panic, at the thought of life without him, without his company, his comfort, his love for her. It seemed incredible to her suddenly that she had got through nineteen of her twenty years without him, and impossible that she would get through more than another hour of the rest of her life on her own. And yet, and yet the alternative was impossible, unthinkable; and so she didn't do what she longed to, didn't explain, didn't try to tell him what she was thinking, what she knew, just sat there, willing herself to be silent, to be still.

'Well,' he said, after a very long time, 'well, I might as well leave. Goodbye then, Tilly.' He walked over to the door, turned and looked at her; she saw there were tears in his brown eyes, that one was actually rolling down his face. She clenched her fists until her long nails dug into her palms, folded her lips together, terrified that some word, some noise even, would betray her.

He opened the door, waited another moment, then walked out and shut it quietly behind him, and she heard his feet going down the stairs and knew what it must feel like to be bleeding to death, to feel life ebbing away; and still she sat motionless, enduring it. And then as she heard the outside door shut (for the night was very still now), heard his car start, heard it drive slowly away, away, she remembered that she had never heard, had never asked even, what it was he actually wanted to talk to her about.

The Next Day

Chapter Twenty-Three

Theo 5.30am

Flying, Theo Buchan had been often heard to say, was the greatest physical pleasure, next to sex. Flying yourself of course, he would add, not sitting in some godawful lorry in the sky, drinking inferior champagne; many, many parallels could be drawn, he would go on to say, the intense concentration, the surging, soaring exhilaration, the sense of absolute release – and afterwards the sweet, sweet peace. It was famously said of Theo that if he was serious about a woman, he took her flying; that was how she knew.

He was flying to Paris that morning: the physical presence beside him was that of James Forrest, but it was Harriet Forrest who filled his head and his heart and his senses, Harriet who was haunting the strange beautiful other-world he had up here, Harriet's lovely, slightly gaunt face he saw, as he had last seen it, with its extraordinary, fearful blend of hatred and desire, Harriet's voice he heard, harsh with anger, with scorn, and yet heavy with yearning, Harriet's body, its joyous, intent hunger denied him totally, and yet greedy for him still.

James had called him soon after she left, as he'd sat shaking with despair, with helplessness, said he had to talk to him, and 'Not now, James,' he'd said, 'Please not now, I'm done for.' But James had begged him, said he had to have companionship or he would go mad, and Theo had finally, wearily, agreed.

James, coming in drawn, grey-faced, had told him at once about Susie, about Rufus: 'What do I do, Theo, what the hell do I do?' and Theo, shocked himself, had counselled caution, restraint: 'Leave him to think about it, James, to come to terms with it. Don't rush in with justifications, explanations, for Christ's sake. And certainly not fatherly sentiments.'

'Christ Almighty, Theo, what do you think I am?' said James, genuinely shocked, and Theo said, not entirely seriously, an insensitive egotist with a talent for trouble.

'Do you think he'll talk to people, want his family, my family to know?' said James, draining a second jug of coffee, reaching for the phone to order a third.

'Probably not,' said Theo coolly, knowing why he asked, thinking that he should, indeed did, despise James for the question, the reasons behind it, forty years of friendship holding him loyal. 'He's not a child, and he's a very conventional young man. And sensitive. I daresay he'll tell Tilly Mills though.'

'Christ,' said James, 'dear Christ,' and added suddenly, with a look of desperation at Theo that was truly childlike, 'Theo, you'll see me through this, won't you? You won't let me down?'

And Theo said of course he would stand by him, would see him through; and the conversation had then switched to Cressida, to what she had done, was doing, where she might be, and he had listened for a while to James agonizing, theorizing, before pleading exhaustion and then suggesting he came with him next morning on his quest for Cressida, his pilgrimage to Sacré-Coeur. 'I had thought that Harriet might come, but – well, I think perhaps it would be better if it was you.'

James had not known about the photograph; he was shocked, shaken, not only by what it revealed, but because Harriet hadn't told him. 'We are not friends just at the moment, she and I,' he said, and Theo, struggling to keep emotion from his voice, said it was much the same for him.

'Oh really? Why's that, do you think?' James asked, and 'Oh, I tried to interfere in her business,' Theo said casually, thanking God that James had clearly never had the slightest shadow of suspicion that there had been anything remotely more than paternal in his love for Harriet, no inkling of the glorious, dreadful love affair that would surely and finally have shaken their friendship to death. And still might, he thought, still might. 'And of course she's angry with me about the flying lessons, I suppose. As well she should be.'

'Yes, well I'm not,' said James with a sigh. 'At first, perhaps, but after all I've learnt about Cressida today, Theo, how capable she is of such infinite deceit, I could blame no one for any of it. I'd like to come to Paris with you, like to try and find her.'

Theo had driven to the Court House to collect him at 4.30 in the morning, as another perfect day was breaking through the mists, and together they drove to the small airfield near Kidlington where Theo had had his plane taken during the night, and climbed into the plane and took off feeling, against all possible odds, strangely and cheerfully excited as if they were on some schoolboy adventure. 'Where it all started, Paris, wasn't it?' said Theo, setting the plane at a steady 90 knots and visibly relaxing for the first time. 'Our lives together, that first holiday, when we went to stay in my father's apartment and you met Janine. Do you remember eating that bad oyster?'

'Yes, and you deserted me, left me with my head down the pan.'

'Well you got the best of it in the end. Initiation in Janine's hands. Literally. You've always been a lucky bugger.'

'I think my luck's run out finally,' said James. 'Finally and forever.'

'Get any sleep?'

'Not much.'

'Poor sod,' said Theo. 'Pour me some coffee, would you, out of that flask? I feel half dead. There should be some croissants in that picnic bag. And some pains au chocolat, I hope. Myra usually organizes those as well.'

'She's some secretary,' said James. 'Yes, here they are. Want one? One of each?'

'What do you think?'

'You eat too much,' said James, looking at him. 'How much do you weigh?'

'None of your bloody business.'

'Yes it is. I don't want to lose you yet.'

'I had a fitness test only the other day,' said Theo cheerfully, 'heart, lungs, cholesterol, the lot. The guy said I was absolutely fine. It's all muscle, you know, not fat. Hit me, go on.'

'No thanks,' said James, 'I don't want the plane to crash. There's some orange juice here. Want some? Oh, and two half-bottles of bubbly. For Buck's fizz I suppose. Christ, Theo, you're spoilt. Do I detect Sasha's hand in this?'

'No you don't, said Theo briefly.

'Where is she?'

'I haven't a clue. I don't care.' He was extremely surprised to find it was true. Well, he supposed he knew why. The confrontation with love, raw, real, unarguable last night, had left Sasha already a shadow. 'She's left me,' he added, forestalling an interrogation. 'Yesterday. Taken a whole lot of goods, including a company I wanted, and scarpered. And before you say anything, I want you to know I deserved it. I treated her very badly. And not how you think either.'

'How then?' asked James.

'I put her down. Belittled her. Underrated her. Bad thing to do that, James. Don't ever do it yourself.'

'I won't get much chance, will I?' said James. His voice was heavy, full of pain.

Theo turned to look at him. 'I was wondering about you and – and Susie. If – '

'Yes?'

'If – oh I don't know, that this might be a time for honesty. So you could be together for a bit. Concentrates the mind, that sort of thing. Makes life seem more precious.'

'Good God, no,' said James, 'Susie would never want to do anything like that. Rock her beloved family. No, I just have to go on biting the bullet and taking it. Playing understudy to bloody Alistair. Hopefully she'll come through.'

'Shit,' said Theo. 'Life's a bitch, isn't it? A real bitch. I'm sorry, James. So sorry.'

'Yes, well.' James was quiet for a moment, then he said, clearly with immense difficulty, 'So – any more thoughts on Rufus?'

'Not really. Just – leave things be. For a while. I suspect he'll want to do the same. Poor little bugger. Bit of a shock.'

'Yes,' said James shortly.

'I always liked Rufus,' said Theo thoughtfully. He grinned at James. 'Chip off the old block.'

'It's not funny, Theo, for Christ's sake.'

'No, no, of course not. Sorry.'

There was a silence.

'When will you hear about – about Susie?'

'Later this morning.'

'Ah.'

Another silence. Then: 'What do you think Cressida might be up to?'

It was obviously an easier subject, horrible as it was. Theo's heart went out to James; as he'd said his luck had finally run out. 'God knows,' he said, 'but whatever it is, I really don't think we've begun to scratch the surface of it. She must be very seriously mixed up.'

'Yes,' said James, 'and Theo, what really scares me is what the hell happens if we find her? We can hardly just take her home as if nothing had happened and rearrange the wedding, can we?'

'Not really,' said Theo. 'Not now.'

They landed at a small airfield outside Paris just before six, seven French time. The admirable Myra Hartman had organized a car, a large Mercedes. 'You drive,' said Theo, 'we've hit the rush hour, it's going to be hell, and I'm bushed.'

He went to sleep almost at once, to dream not of Harriet, nor even of Sasha, but of Cressida. She was sitting on the bridge in her wedding dress, laughing at them all. He woke up angry, to realize they had arrived at the Butte, the street below Sacré-Coeur. He felt very hot and sick. James was easing the Mercedes into a spot far too small for it.

'You'll never get it in there.'

'Yes I will.'

'Arrogant bugger. Christ, I feel terrible.'

'Should we have coffee somewhere? I'm sure the priest won't be there yet.'

'No, let's go up. Someone will be there. It opens at six forty-five. Is the funicular working?'

'Doesn't seem to be. Come on, Theo, I thought you were fit.'

'I am,' he said, and ran up the first fifty steps to prove it, then sat down, fighting for breath, waiting for James who was proceeding more slowly and steadily. Theo looked round and up at the exquisite pictures behind him, the stark white domes of Sacré-Coeur carved out of the blue, blue sky. It was like a vision, like something in a children's Bible. You could see why the Church got such a hold on people: it was enough to make you believe in God. He said as much to James, who looked up at it and grinned. 'Harriet loathes it. Says it's kitsch. That's the smart view generally, I'm told.'

'Yes, well, we can't all be smart. Bloody snobbery if you ask me,' said Theo irritably and continued his climb. For some reason it eased the pain Harriet had caused, was causing him, to criticize her, however mildly.

Illogically, and without admitting it, Theo felt nervous as he walked slowly into the cathedral through the great south door: absurd, he told himself, as if Cressida might still be there, waiting for them. After the brilliance of the morning, the dimness engulfed him; he could see nothing, nothing at all, only smell the familiar cathedral blend of incense and slight mustiness and the faint smokiness of the banks of candles, already lit, and the equally familiar sounds of oddly distant organ music and muffled voices and shuffling footsteps. He looked up, into the soaring dome, and then ahead at the great mosaic above the high altar, the golden Christ figure, arms outstretched; and then glanced behind him and saw James also gazing up, an expression on his face of reluctant awe mingled with a dreadful sadness.

A young priest was walking swiftly up the main aisle, his face wearing the careful, courteous smile that seemed as crucial an appurtenance of his calling as faith, his eyes fixed several yards ahead; Theo stepped out and said, 'Bonjour, mon père. Parlez-vous anglais?'

'A little, yes.'

'Yesterday, a young girl was married here. In the afternoon. You were here, perhaps?'

The priest shook his head. 'We had no weddings here yesterday. Not at all. I am sorry.'

'Are you sure?'

'Quite sure, monsieur. No wedding.' He smiled rather blankly.

Theo fumbled in his pocket, produced the photograph of Cressida.

'Here, you see. This was taken yesterday. We know, because it was a friend.'

'No, *monsieur*. It cannot have been a wedding. There were none. I am sorry. Now if you will excuse me . . .'

He hurried away, up towards the altar; James and Theo looked at one another. 'Now what?' said Theo.

'He could have been wrong.'

'He didn't sound as if he was wrong. Let's ask someone else.'

One of the cathedral officials was standing at the back near the racks of postcards. '*Monsieur*,' said Theo, '*monsieur, parlez-vous anglais?*'

'*Non*,' said the man briefly.

Parisian charm, thought Theo, smiling at him. '*Monsieur, hier, l'après-midi, une jeune fille était mariée dans cette cathédrale . . .*'

'*Non*,' said the man, '*Il n'y a eu absolument aucun mariage.*'

Theo produced the photograph again, showed it to the man; he looked at it, shook his head, shrugged, and walked briskly away.

'Little sweetie,' said Theo. 'How I hate the French.'

They approached an old nun, who was lighting a candle, carefully, with a shaky hand; she smiled at them sweetly. '*Bonjour, ma soeur*,' said Theo. '*Est-ce que . . .*'

But she put her fingers over her lips, shook her head, sank onto her knees. Theo looked at her, wondering how it must feel to possess such faith, reflecting how greatly simplified life must be.

'Excuse me, *monsieur*.' Standing behind them was a plump, smiling old priest; he smelt of garlic and his complexion owed more than a little to a lifetime of good French wine. 'I heard what you were saying. I think perhaps I can help.'

'Oh really?' Theo held out his hand. 'How very kind. My name is Theo Buchan, and this is my friend James Forrest.'

'*Messieurs*,' said the old man courteously, with a slight bow. His robe, strained over his large somach, was threadbare, his shoes beneath it cracked and worn, but he carried with him an air of great contentment.

'We have reason to believe a young girl was married here yesterday. We have a picture of her leaving the cathedral in her wedding dress, see.'

'Yes, yes, I see. And I saw her, too. Yesterday. She was here, with her husband. A lovely girl. And a charming young man.'

'You saw them – married?' said James. His voice shook slightly.

'*Non, non*, that was not possible, I am afraid. It is not easy to be married here. They knew that, of course. But they asked me if I would give them God's blessing.'

'Oh God,' said James. His face was grey; he sat down suddenly.

'Are you all right, *monsieur*?'

312

'Yes, yes, I'm fine. Thank you. Do please go on.'

'Very well. I saw no harm in that. After all, who am I to keep God's love from a young couple? I asked them to come to one of the side chapels, this one here, and they knelt together and we said a prayer and I blessed them. That is all.' He smiled his sweet, slightly conspiratorial smile. 'There may be some here who might have felt I should have asked permission but I do not think I shall do too many extra years of purgatory for it.' He smiled again. 'They seemed very happy. She wore a wedding ring, I noticed that. Perhaps they had already been to the Bureau de l'Etat. There is not a problem, I hope.'

'No, not really,' said Theo. 'So you don't have any record of her – their name?'

'No, *monsieur*, I do not. They were gone very quickly after that. I am sorry.'

'Thank you, Father, very much. You've been most kind. And thank you for what you did for them. We are very grateful.' Theo took out his wallet, started riffling through notes. 'I would like to – for the church, of course – '

'*Merci, monsieur*. In the box, over there. Goodbye, *messieurs*. God bless you.'

'Goodbye, Father.'

Theo went over to the collection box, put a 500-franc note in it, stood looking at the bank of candles for a moment. Then he went forward and lit one. 'Cressida,' he said quietly, 'this is all I can do for you now. I hope, in spite of everything, you will be happy.'

He went back for James who was sitting absolutely still, staring ahead of him. His mouth was set.

'Come on,' Theo said gently, 'there's nothing more we can do for now. No point staying, trying to find her. She's all right, James, she's safe. That's the main thing, really. She's happy and safe. Let's go.'

James nodded, stood up and walked very slowly to the door of the cathedral. When they got outside, Theo saw that his face was wet with tears. 'I'd like to go home, Theo, please,' he said.

And all the way home, the long drive out on the nightmare of the Périphérique, and the flight back through the blue morning, Theo thought not of Cressida at all, nor of his wild and wilful son, not even of his friend and his dreadful bleak misery, but of Harriet, and how in God's name he was going to get her back.

Chapter Twenty-Four

Mungo 7am

He had slept. It seemed impossible, but he had. He woke, stiff-necked, his head aching unbearably, to hear the throbbing of a taxi outside in the street. The rest of the house was silent; Jemima and the two younger ones were clearly still asleep.

Mungo sat up, holding his aching head, pushed back his hair. He must look ghastly, he thought: unshaven, red-eyed, slightly grubby. Well, it didn't matter; he was hardly planning on seduction.

He crossed to the window, looked outside; Alice was paying off the taxi. She was wearing a light floaty dress, under a man's dinner jacket; he recognized the dress, they'd bought it together in Harvey Nichols, she'd needed something desperately, she said, for a duty party – 'Can't take you, it's business.' He had insisted on paying for it. She came to show it to him, outside the changing room, barefooted, the chiffon clinging to her slender body, her ice-blonde hair tousled with pulling things over her head. 'You look great,' he'd said, 'get that one' and 'It's terribly expensive,' she'd said, and 'You're worth it,' said Mungo, and he'd signed the slip (quite a lot for a rather insubstantial dress, even he'd thought that, £1,400, but of course she was worth it) and she'd come out and hugged him, and said 'Let's go home, I want to say thank you. Quickly.'

And they had rushed out of the shop, hailed a taxi, told the cabbie to go to Chatto Street, kissed all the way there, and when they got to the house, she'd dropped everything in the hall, and after calling the children's names briefly, to check they weren't at home, stood there, tearing off her clothes, and lay down on the stairs, quite naked, holding out her arms to him, and he came towards her laughing, pulling off his own clothes, and knelt astride her at the bottom of the stairs and started to kiss her again, slowly, very slowly and deliberately, and she raised herself up to him, her wet, greedy self, pulling herself onto him, pulling him into her, and he felt her closing round him, tightly, tuggingly, and she began to push, push, faster, faster up at him, and the familiar noisy cries began, and far far within the depths of himself Mungo felt the rising, the inexorable, rushing rise of his orgasm, and she said as she so often did, 'Wait, Mungo, wait, be still,' and as he paused somehow, forced its delay, savouring the sweet suspended pleasure, the time-stood-stillness, he had opened his eyes and looked at her, and she had looked back, and for just a moment then he had seen something watchful, wary, and then it was gone, and her head was thrown back again so that he couldn't see her face, and she was thrusting, pulling, enfolding him absolutely, and then he felt her coming, in her great powerful greedy waves, and he lay, his head on her breast, releasing his own pleasure, loving her and making himself forget what he had seen.

But he remembered it now.

'Hallo, Alice,' he said. He had opened the door, was standing smiling like a dutiful husband welcoming home his wife. 'How nice to see you.'

Alice's face was absolutely expressionless; it was a gift of hers that he had often envied, to be able to make it thus to order (except when she was in mid-orgasm). 'How do you do that?' he would say. 'Show me how to do it.' And she would laugh and say, 'you don't want to do that, Mungo, I love your face, it's so easy to read.'

'Hallo,' she said pleasantly, as if he were some neighbour, some casual friend, 'what are you doing here?'

'I came to see you last night. You'd gone out. With Anouska, I think.'

'No, not Anouska. She's away.' There she goes, he thought, bloody clever, just one jump ahead of him. 'I thought you were staying down in the country.'

'I was. But I couldn't stand it any longer. And I wanted to go to the office, and after that I came to see you.'

'And how did you get in?'

'Jemima let me in.'

'She's not supposed to,' said Alice. 'She's not supposed to let anyone in. I shall have to speak to her.'

'Don't. It wasn't her fault,' said Mungo. 'I – made her.'

'Well, that was unfair of you. But it was also naughty of her.'

'I don't think any reproaches are in order,' said Mungo, 'and I think she's very young to be left alone in the house all night. Actually.'

'Yes, well, I don't think I need advice on childcare from you,' said Alice. 'When you've spent a few years as a single parent, you'll be qualified to comment, but until then . . . Excuse me, please, I really want to make myself a cup of coffee.'

'I'll make you some coffee,' said Mungo. 'You go and sit down.'

He was surprised to find he didn't feel anything like he might have expected; he seemed to be in control, to know what to do, how to act. He was almost enjoying it. Alice went into the kitchen ahead of him and sat down. She looked very composed and orderly; her face was freshly made-up, her hair neatly done. She didn't even look tired; she had obviously had a good night's sleep.

'Nice time?' said Mungo casually, handing her the coffee.

'Yes, very nice, thank you. Mungo, this is instant. You know I don't like instant coffee.'

'It's what I've made,' he said, 'and it's what you'll have to drink, I'm afraid. I'm not messing about with that stupid grinder thing at this time in the morning. Anyway it might wake the children.'

She looked at him and though her eyes were blank there was a watchfulness behind them.

'Did you – talk to Jemima last night?'

'Oh a bit. But not about you. We were both very loyal.'

'Ah.'

'Which is more than I can say for you,' he said. Anger suddenly hit him, took him unawares. 'Where the fuck were you, and who with?'

'Don't use that horrible language in my house,' said Alice.

'I'll use what I like. Where were you?'

'I was out. With some old friends.'

'Oh really?'

'Yes, really. If you like I'll give you their number and you can ring and check. Giles and Fanny Brentwood. This is Giles's dinner jacket I'm wearing.'

'I see,' said Mungo. He was beginning to feel a little uncertain. 'Do you often stay out all night with people? Leaving your daughter on her own?'

'Yes, sometimes. She has to put the chain on the door, double-lock it, and if I want to come back I have to ring her. Last night it was so late, it seemed unfair to wake her. But you did, it seems, so I needn't have been so scrupulous.'

'Why didn't you tell her you were with these old friends? Why did she have to tell me some lie about Anouska?'

'I didn't tell her anything. Just that I was going out. She was engrossed on the phone with some boy, and had her stereo on at full blast, it was just too much hassle. No doubt she thought you'd be upset unless I was with some woman. Oh Mungo, for God's sake, you can't think – look, ring Giles. Or Fanny. They won't mind. Here's the number. Go on. I'll dial it for you – '

'No,' he said hastily. 'No, Alice, don't. I really don't want to – '

'You look worn out,' she said suddenly, 'much tireder than I am. Let's go into the drawing room. I do want to talk to you. Actually. But I'm going to make some decent coffee first.'

'All right,' he said, 'all right.'

He sat on the sofa where he had spent the night staring ahead of him; he had stopped enjoying himself, the numbness was wearing off. He wasn't sure how much of this he could take. Alice came in, sat down beside him, kissed him gently on the cheek.

'You've got it all wrong you know,' she said quite cheerfully.

'Have I? Have I really?'

'Yes. You really have. And a few other things too. Are you sitting comfortably?'

'Yes thank you,' said Mungo.

Alice looked at him. 'Then I'll begin.' There was a silence. Then: 'Mungo, I did do something you wouldn't have liked last night,' she said, 'I phoned your father.'

The sofa rocked gently under Mungo; he tightened his grip on the mug of coffee she had handed him. 'What did you say?' he said finally.

'You heard. You heard right. I phoned your father. He was extremely nice to me.'

'Yes, I expect he was,' said Mungo bitterly. 'He can be very charming when it suits him. The fact remains he's a – '

'Mungo, I can see what he is. He's manipulative, and he's immensely arrogant and possessive and he doesn't like being crossed. But he loves you, Mungo, my God he loves you.'

'Yes,' said Mungo tersely, 'when I do what he wants. I don't know how you could have done that, Alice, I really don't.'

'Well,' she said simply, 'I had to do something. There you were, falling out with him, setting yourself on the path to financial ruin, probably wrecking that extremely promising little business of yours, all because of me.'

'Alice, it isn't like that. You're not just some game or toy I'm playing with.'

'I should certainly hope not,' she said lightly.

'I love you. I want to marry you. Well, I thought I did.'

'And what's changed that? Me being out when you came to call? Really, Mungo, this certainly can't be love. Love is about trust. I thought.'

'I know but – '

Christ, she was clever. She was tying him up in knots, just as his father did

'Mungo, I give you my word, I'll swear on the Bible if you like, if I can find it, that I was simply out to dinner with my friends last night. I was not in any other man's bed, I don't have an interest in any other man. I love you. There. Does that make you feel better?'

He looked at her, and against all the odds he found himself believing her. 'Jemima seemed to think – ' he started, and then stopped.

'Seemed to think what? That I was plying a brisk trade in Piccadilly? That I was in some hotel in King's Cross with three other men?'

'No, of course not, but she – '

'Mungo, Mungo, Jemima is a very naughty, manipulative little girl. She would get on wonderfully well with your father. She has just discovered her own sexuality, and she's jealous of mine. She also has a bit of a crush on you. And what was she up to last night anyway? Entertaining a gentleman far too old for her?'

'No,' said Mungo quickly, and then wondered if he was being irresponsible, immature, taking the side of youth against the grown-ups. 'Well, that is – '

'I thought so. You're right, I shouldn't leave her alone. She's trouble, Mungo, much as I love her.'

'Don't say anything to her, will you? Not about last night specifically. She was very sweet to me, and I'd hate her to think I'd – well – '

'Sneaked on her,' said Alice tartly. 'No, I won't. Unless I find evidence on my own account. The laundry bills have gone up a lot lately, I've noticed. Lot of sheet changing going on . . . Anyway, let's not talk about Jemima. You and me is a much more agreeable subject. And I want to tell you what we talked about, your father and I.'

'What then?' said Mungo sulkily. He hated to think of the pair of them discussing him, agreeing no doubt that he was a silly, reckless child. 'I suppose you had a little laugh about it all, and then you said that of course you wouldn't marry me if he didn't want you to, that it was a crazy idea.'

'No, we didn't laugh and I didn't say I wouldn't marry you. Although we did agree it was a crazy idea. And then he said – '

'Yes?'

'He said he liked crazy ideas. That a lot of his were fairly crazy. Especially when it came to what he called entanglements. I liked that word.'

'You obviously got on very well,' said Mungo. He felt wretchedly, horribly foolish.

'Yes, I think we did. We agreed that we would meet. And – '

'Oh, well, that's great,' said Mungo, standing up. 'The two of you meeting, talking about me, the silly little boy, discussing what it would be best to do, how you could distract me.' He felt violently hurt, abused almost; he had to get out, quickly. He slammed his coffee mug down, and the contents slopped over the coffee table onto Alice's beige carpet. He looked at it, at the dark spattered stain, and he thought that was what had happened to his love for her; it had been treated roughly, spilt, become something dirty, messy, spoiling everything.

'I'm so glad you've been able to discuss our future with my father,' he said. 'What a pity it's all become irrelevant. Because I really don't want to see you again, Alice. Perhaps he'd be a better friend for you. I don't know how you could do it to me, when I loved you so much. And trusted you. Goodbye, Alice.'

He walked over to the door, then turned to look back at her. She was staring up at him, startled, shocked almost, her face concerned, no longer carefully blank. 'Mungo,' she said, 'Mungo, please. You don't understand. Please don't go.'

'I want to go,' he said, 'and I do understand, I'm afraid.'

He walked out of the front door, slammed it behind him, and then leant against it briefly, thinking of all the happiness he had had in the little house, the lovely Sundays, the golden evenings, the rapturous love-making, and for just an instant he was amazed that he could leave it, walk away. Then he thought of Alice, Alice and his father, talking, laughing indulgently about him, and he ran, ran away from her, away from both of them, as fast as he could down the street and into the Kings Road, and hailed a taxi, and told the driver to take him to the one place where he wanted to be at that moment, the one place where he was a person in his own right, the one place he felt was his own: his office in Carlos Place.

Chapter Twenty-Five

Tilly 8am

'Yeah, I'll go,' said Tilly, 'if you want me to. The sooner the better.'

'You don't sound very enthusiastic.'

'Felicity, right this minute I'd find it hard to be enthusiastic if Brad Pitt and Keanu Reeves asked me to spend a year on a desert island with them both. Sorry. I'm just gutted. I'd actually love to go to New York. Anything to get out of this place.'

'I can get you on a flight at noon. You'll have to be at Heathrow at ten. I'll send a car.'

'OK. Fine.'

'And the Rosenthal people will meet you at Kennedy. They said they'd book you into the Pierre. For three nights, I think.'

'Fine.'

'Right then. Take a couple of slightly smart outfits. You can't meet le tout New York in those torn cut-offs.'

'Felicity, as if I would . . .'

'Tilly, you know you would. Anyway, I'll confirm your flight. Call me when you get there. I hope you feel better soon. Lots of love.'

'Thanks. Bye, Felicity.'

She hauled herself out of bed: just under two hours till she had to go. Bit of careful packing. Slightly smart. What did that mean, for God's sake? The Karan probably, the black silk jersey suit, and the glorious new stuff from Claude Montana, the white linen crepe Nehru jacket and trousers. That would do for le tout New York, surely. If it didn't, they could go play with themselves. She needed some shoes, but she could get them when she got there. Fuck, it was going to be hot . . . she suddenly heard Rufus's voice saying 'I don't like people saying fuck all the time,' and a spasm of such intense pain took hold of her heart that her eyes filled with tears. Now, Tilly, don't start. It's over now, he belongs in the past. A lovely, loving, joyful past, but the past. The future's what you have to think about now. The immediate future first, just getting things into your bag, youself into the car, onto the plane – 'Shit,' she said aloud, 'shit, I have to see my mum.' That was essential; and she had to phone James too, with the phone number. She had victory in her hands; she mustn't let it go. She could call at her mother's house on her way to the airport; she would tell Felicity to send the car there. That would be good. And she could phone James Forrest right now.

She dialled the number; Harriet answered the phone. She sounded calmer than she had last night; she had called Tilly when she got back from seeing Theo. It had taken Tilly half an hour to talk her down. 'I hate him,' she kept saying, 'I hate him so much, Tilly, I can hardly bear to think about him.' And Tilly had made soothing, calming, sympathetic noises into the phone, listening, listening to the half-truth, to the anger, to the passion in Harriet's voice, and wondered how long it would be before Harriet admitted even to herself how much she still loved Theo.

'Hi, Harry, it's Tilly. How are you today?'

'OK, I think.'

'No news?'

'No. My father's gone off with Theo to Paris. They left at dawn in Theo's plane. Seem to think they'll find Cressida still sitting at Sacré-Coeur, waiting for them.'

Her voice was immensely, heavily scornful; her hostility seemed to extend to her father, as well as Theo. Tilly did not, could not pursue that one; she lacked the strength.

'Well,' she said, for want of something more intelligent to say, 'maybe they will.'

'Yeah yeah. But there is one delicious piece of news. It's not all gloom and doom here. We have an engagement to celebrate.'

'An engagement! Don't tell me Mungo – '

'No. Why should it be Mungo? Much more exciting. Merlin and Janine. Getting married by special licence, wandering round the garden holding hands like a couple of kids.'

'Now that is seriously nice,' said Tilly. 'That I like. Give him a huge hug from me.'

'I will. Mind you, I think it was a toss-up whether he proposed to you or Janine. He's very taken with you.'

'Tell him it's mutual. Next time around. No seriously, I think it's wild. Harry, I'm off to New York.'

'Now?'

'Yes, now. I'm signing with Rosenthal and they want to inspect the goods. Or something like that.'

'Tilly, are you sure it's a good idea? You know how homesick you get, and what will Rufus say?'

'Rufus is history,' said Tilly and burst into tears.

'Tilly, don't. You can't do that. Why, Tilly, why? He loves you and you love him and – '

'Yeah, and we get married and start hating each other. It isn't any good, Harriet, really it isn't.'

'Oh, Tilly, are you sure? Really sure? Couldn't you try – '

'Try what? Becoming someone else? Taking a course in legal wifehood?' Thank God she's always made a lot of the differences between her and Rufus, had said repeatedly that their lives could never work together. And anyway, it was true: they never could. 'There's nothing to try. Honestly.'

'Did you tell him?'

'Yes, I told him. Last night.'

'And?'

'And nothing really. We parted. Said goodbye. That was it.' She groped for a Kleenex, blew her nose. 'Now listen, I don't want to talk about that. I *can't* talk about that. But there's something else that I do want to talk about. If you need some money, I mean real money for your company, I can let you have it.'

'Tilly, don't be absurd.'

'I'm not being absurd. I mean it. What do you need, a million? It's yours. You can pay me back some time. OK?'

'Tilly, darling – '

'Think about it. I have to go. Oh, that's reminded me, that's why I called really. I'm leaving in a couple of hours, but I'm going to my mum's house first. Could you' – she thought fast – 'could you give her number to your dad?'

'My father? What on earth for?'

'Well, it's kind of complicated. But she has a little – female trouble, and I'm worried about her. He said he'd give me the name and number of the best person in town for her.'

'Tilly, this is the most extraordinary thing I ever heard. When on earth did you get to talk female trouble with my father?'

'When we were out in the garden yesterday, you know?'

'Oh – yes. Yes, all right.' She was clearly baffled. 'And you're going there now, you say?'

'Yes, to say hallo and goodbye. How's *your* mother?'

'Still asleep. My father gave her a mega shot of something last night.'

'And when are you seeing Mr Buchan again?'

'Never, I hope. Unless it's in hell.'

'Cool. Bye, Harry. And I meant it about the money.'

'Bye, Tilly. Thank you, but I really couldn't. And take care.'

★

322

Tilly had a shower, dressed (not in the torn cut-offs but leggings and an oversized T-shirt), called a cab, grabbed her big leather Gladstone, and her Gucci leather rucksack that was never really unpacked, just occasionally cleared out, which carried all her needs, money, credit cards, make-up, cigarettes, chewing gum, passport, keys, appointment book, set her answering machine, looked round her flat and went out, locking the door after her. She was halfway down the stairs when she heard the phone ringing; she simply couldn't go back now, she was running quite late enough already.

'Tilly, you look terrible,' said Rosemary Mills. 'I'm going to make you some camomile tea. It will calm you down.'

'Mum, I hate camomile tea. And rosehip tea and peppermint tea. They all make me want to throw up. What I need is a seriously strong cup of coffee. Do you have any real or is it all that decaff rubbish?'

'It's all decaff,' said Rosemary, 'and it will have to do.'

Tilly sat drinking the coffee, studying her mother. She really was looking good. She looked about ten years younger; she was happy, busy, her aromatherapy practice growing fast. She had had a haircut (Nicky Clarke had done it as a favour to Tilly: 'Pity you don't know what a fortune you're carrying about on your head, Mum') and although she still favoured her rather droopy ethnic clothes, they were at least new and pretty, not bought at jumbles and Oxfam shops.

'So where are you off to now?'

'New York. Midday.'

'New York! Paris yesterday, Mexico the week before. Tilly, I wish you'd settle down a bit. It's so bad for your body clock, all this.'

'Mum, my body clock's fine.'

'It doesn't look fine,' said Rosemary Mills. 'What about the boyfriend?'

'The boyfriend's finished,' said Tilly, 'and don't start, or I shall cry. It wasn't going to work, Mum, and that's all there is to it. Now listen, I have something much more important to talk to you about.'

'What's that?'

'James Forrest will be coming to see you.'

'James Forrest? What on earth for?'

'He wants to explain a few things to you,' said Tilly briefly. 'Like – '

The phone rang suddenly. 'Excuse me, dear,' said Rosemary. 'Peckham 4111. Rosemary Mills speaking. Yes, that's right. Yes, she's here. It's for you,' she said, holding the phone out to Tilly, 'a woman.'

'I expect it's Felicity,' said Tilly, 'or Harry.'

It wasn't. It was Susie Headleigh Drayton and she sounded as if she had been crying.

'Tilly? Sorry to bother you at your mother's. Your agent told me you were there. I thought you might know where Rufus is?'

'No,' said Tilly, 'no, I don't. I'm sorry. Isn't he – still in the country?'

'No,' said Susie, 'no he isn't. He brought me up to London last night. I've got to – well, have a little op this morning. Nothing serious, I'm sure. But I'm worried about Rufus. I can't find him anywhere. Not at his flat, not at Harriet's place, not in the office – well, I suppose he wouldn't have been there yet, but – '

'Oh, I'm sure he's fine,' said Tilly, trying to sound as if she meant it. 'He was fine last night.'

'So you did see him last night? When was that? I'm sorry to ask you, Tilly, but what with my going into hospital and – well, he was a bit upset about something, I'm afraid. I just wanted to speak to him, make sure he was all right before I went in.'

'If he was upset,' said Tilly, 'it was probably my fault. I – well, we – I told him I thought we shouldn't see each other any more.'

'Oh Tilly! Oh no.' Susie's voice rose on a panicky note. 'Not last night.'

'Yes, but – '

'That's not why he was upset, Tilly. Well, obviously he would have been very much more upset then. But there was something – something that happened yesterday. Earlier. Before we left Wedbourne.'

'He didn't mention it,' said Tilly slowly. No, because she hadn't let him, poor sod, hadn't listened, had just sat there dealing out body blows. Shit. *Fuck* . . . 'I don't like people saying fuck all the time.' Sorry, Rufus, sorry, sorry. For everything.

'I see. Oh dear. Well, if he does get in touch will you ask him to come and see me? I'll be in the Princess Diana Hospital. He – well, he doesn't know. I hadn't told him. I hadn't told anyone.'

'I'm so sorry,' said Tilly, and meant it. 'Is it – I mean is it serious?'

'Oh I shouldn't think so.' Susie's voice had recovered itself, was its level, slightly husky self. 'I hope not anyway. Just a little lump. You know how careful they like to be.'

'Yes,' said Tilly, 'yes of course. Well, good luck. I really will be thinking of you. I'd come and see you, but I'm going to New York.'

'Today?'

'Yes, in a little while actually. I've been signed up by Rosenthal. Their new face. You know?' Now why the hell was she telling her that? Why should Susie care? With a son gone missing and what was clearly a cancer scare? Silly self-centred bitch, Ottoline, that's what you are.

'Oh how exciting, Tilly. Congratulations.' How did she manage it, thought Tilly, how could she even sound as if she cared about something so idiotic?

'Yeah, well. It's all crazy really. I don't actually want to do it at all.' Now why had she said that, to Susie Headleigh Drayton of all people? Of course she wanted to do it. 'Er – I don't suppose you want to tell me what Rufus was upset about? Just in case I can help?'

'No. No, I don't think so. I don't want to sound rude, but it was – well, quite private. Family business.'

'Of course,' said Tilly. 'I'm sorry –' Christ! Could it be? Surely not, but maybe, maybe it could – with so much emotion flying about, truth had a way of getting out. Had Rufus been told, had James said something, was that what he wanted to tell her? Her head whirled, she felt sick.

'Mrs Headleigh Drayton –'

'Tilly, I have to go. The doctor's here. Please come and see me when you get back. And I hope you didn't make your decision too hastily. Rufus loves you very much.'

'Yeah,' said Tilly. Then, and she really hadn't meant to say it, she added, 'And I love him too. Very much. But it couldn't possibly work. Mrs Headleigh Drayton, could I just –'

'Please call me Susie. Look, I really have to go. Goodbye Tilly.'

'Now then,' said Rosemary Mills, 'what's all this James Forrest business. I don't want to see him, Tilly. I really don't. It just – reminds me, brings it back. Why is he coming anyway, after all these years?'

'I met him,' said Tilly trying to calm her own panic, to concentrate on the present. 'He's Harriet Forrest's dad. Harriet of Harry's you know? The one whose sister was getting married yesterday. Only she didn't. Well, maybe she did. Oh God.' She lit a cigarette; she suddenly felt very frightened about Rufus. Where was he, what had happened to him?

'Tilly, dear, you really aren't making any sense,' said her mother. 'Why is James Forrest coming to see me?'

'He's coming to tell you some things,' said Tilly shortly. 'About – well, you know what about. Beatrice and everything. He wants to make sure you understand that it wasn't your fault, and – '

'But Tilly, it was. To an extent. Oh, I hate going over this awful old ground. He was right – I should have gone to the antenatal clinic. And all right, maybe he was incompetent, maybe he had been drinking. I don't know. He was very kind to me at the time, which was important. He did his best. I just don't want to drag it all up again, Tilly. Beatrice died, but you lived and we've been very happy together, and you've done wonderfully well. Why can't you leave it alone, just drop this dreadful obsession? It's me that should have the obsession anyway, not you. Now please tell him that I really would rather not speak to him. I appreciate his kindness and generosity, but – '

'Oh yes,' said Tilly bitterly, 'very kind, very generous. After – what? – nearly twenty years. Bastard.'

'Tilly, don't. Don't spoil everything. You have so much, and so do I now – just let it rest.'

'Mum, you don't – ' said Tilly. There was a knock at the door; it was the car to take her to the airport. She gave her mother a hug. 'You're the best,' she said suddenly, 'the very best. Bye, Mum. I'll – I'll think about James Forrest some more – '

'It would be better,' said Rosemary Mills, 'if you stopped thinking about him altogether. And I think you've made a mistake about that boyfriend too.'

'Mum, it wouldn't have worked,' said Tilly patiently. 'I'm too fond of my independence, you know I am. And he's a white upper-class lawyer and I'm a black working-class girl. Where's the future in that?'

'In some beautiful, clever, middle-class children,' said Rosemary, giving her a hug back. 'We're in the nineties, Tilly. You're sounding very out of date. And he loves you, and I think you love him. And independence is a very lonely commodity. You shouldn't let love go. It doesn't often come back. Goodbye, Tilly. Take care of yourself. Eat something now and again, there's a good girl. And try to – '

'Yes, all right, Mum. I'll try. I'll leave them all here, look.'

Tilly tipped sixty Marlborough out of her bag onto her mother's kitchen table. 'Throw them away. I won't buy any more.'

'Promise?'

'No,' said Tilly, thinking gratefully of the two full packs in her rucksack. 'I don't make promises unless I know I can keep them. But I will try.'

'And think some more about Rufus.'

'I wish I could stop,' said Tilly.

Chapter Twenty-Six

Susie 9am

Susie thought how odd it was, how relevant, that her heart and her breast, situated so conveniently near one another, should both be aching so much. She wasn't quite sure which was worse, only that the confusion was somehow helpful. She was surprised that the breast should be so sore; she had always heard that cancer, in its early stages, was painless.

She said as much, hopefully, to Mr Hobson, as she sat up in her room at the Princess Diana Hospital; they were waiting for Alistair who had disappeared briefly to make a phone call.

'I'm afraid it doesn't really mean very much either way,' he said, if there is inflammation of any kind, the result can be discomfort. Simple as that. Or of course it could be psychosomatic. Understandable. How are you feeling?'

'Oh, wonderful,' said Susie, 'absolutely wonderful,' and burst into tears. Mr Hobson, who had never seen the serene Mrs Headleigh Drayton in any kind of disarray, but who was used to his patients becoming emotionally labile, sat down on the bed and took her hand. 'Hope Matron doesn't catch me doing this,' he said. 'Absolutely not allowed. Now you have a good cry. It always helps. I'm not going to come up with any bloody silly nonsense about not worrying and all that, because of course you're worried. You'd be a fool not to be. I'm worried, we're all worried. But the sooner we get this over and know what we're actually up against the better.' He handed her his handkerchief. 'Blow hard.'

'Yes I know,' said Susie, blowing obediently, 'thank you. It's just that I've tried so hard to be brave, but I have other problems, other worries.'

'Oh really? Want to tell me about them?'

'Um – no, I don't think I can. Well, I've lost Rufus. My son,' she added. 'I'm a bit worried.'

'And how old is Rufus?'

'Well – he's twenty-seven,' said Susie, feeling suddenly foolish.

'And where is he? In the Himalayas or wherever it is they all go these days?'

'No, no, he's in London somewhere,' said Susie, 'but I don't know where. And he's very upset about something.'

'I think,' said Mr Hobson, 'that if he's twenty-seven he can handle a bit of upsetness. Worried about you, is he?'

'No, no, he doesn't even know. There was some – some family thing yesterday – '

'What, this wedding? Dreadful things weddings, always get people churned up.'

'No, not the wedding. He – well, he found something out. And – '

'Mrs Headleigh Drayton – or may I call you Susie – ?'

'Yes of course. I'd like that.'

'I think you can let your little twenty-seven-year-old boy take care of himself, and concentrate all your energies on yourself. If he's reached that age and not been badly upset yet, he's very lucky. You could even say it's time he learnt a bit about real life. All right?'

Susie was about to argue with him, to protest, to say that Rufus really couldn't take care of himself, not in this instance, when she found that not only did she not have the strength, she felt Mr Hobson might just possibly be right. She thought of herself at twenty-seven, dealing with most complex emotional matters, quite competently; was Rufus, her son, the most like her of all her children, really so different? She blew her nose again, smiled at Mr Hobson weakly. 'Maybe.'

'That's better. Now you don't want to be crying when your husband comes in, do you? He's quite worried enough. You've very lucky to have a husband who loves you so much, after such a long marriage, you know. Quite rare. Lucky and clever I'd say you were, Susie. In equal proportions. Ah, Mr Headleigh Drayton. Good morning. Do sit down. I'd offer you coffee, but your poor wife is thirsty enough without having to watch us drinking it. Now, I just want to take you through her case as I see it thus far, so that at least we all know what we're talking about, and don't have any misconceptions . . .'

Susie looked at Alistair and wanted James so much she could hardly bear it. She closed her eyes briefly, then smiled at him and took the hand he held out to her. Lucky and clever, was she? With a son shocked into disappearance, a lover who had deserted her in her hour of great need, and a husband who knew she had been unfaithful to him for most of their marriage. Dear God. Very lucky, and very clever.

Alistair had gone now, with a tender kiss and a promise to be there when she woke up. She felt fiercely, terribly alone. And dreadfully afraid. Afraid of what they would find, what they would do, that in spite of Mr Hobson's reassurances she would wake up without her breast. And what would there be? A great wound? A cobbling together of her flesh? A mutilation, pain, ugliness. Panic rose in her, she began to sweat.

The nurse came in with the pre-med tray; suddenly, vividly she remembered the other time, all those years ago, when she had been pregnant with Rufus, when there was nearly no Rufus. Thank God, thank God there had been. Her lovely, gentle, handsome, clever son. Who had disappeared. Who no longer trusted her. No longer loved her . . .

A moan escaped Susie, a low quiet moan; the nurse was alarmed. 'I'm sorry, Mrs Headleigh Drayton. Did I hurt you?'

'No. No, it's all right. Could I – could I have the phone? I'll be quick, before this takes effect.'

'Yes of course. Here, let me dial the number.'

'No, no, it's all right.' Hang on, Susie, hang on, don't let go; just once more, that was all she asked, just to hear his voice once more, to take with her into this awful, ugly darkness . . .

'Wedbourne 240.' It was Harriet's voice.

'Harriet, it's Susie.'

'Ah. Hallo.' Hostility, polite but unmistakable.

'Harriet, could I speak to your father? I'm sorry to ask you but . . .'

'He's not here I'm afraid. He's gone to Paris. With Theo.'

'To Paris! Why?' God, she was feeling strange already: hazy, confused, dry-mouthed. Her tongue seemed thick, out of control.

'Yes. To look for Cressida.'

'Oh yes. Yes, of course. Cressida. Poor Cressida.' Her eyes were getting heavy, she felt very dizzy, even though she was lying down.

'Is mother there?' That wasn't quite right; the words weren't properly ordered.

'My mother? Yes. Susie, are you all right? Where are you?' The hostility was gone, she sounded alarmed.

'I'm hospital Harriet. In operation. Princess Diana. Good – breast.'

Somehow then the receiver was gone, taken gently from her, and she was drifting, drifting down a long, dark corridor, and the fear was gone and the pain too, just a lovely lightness, and oh God, this was what happened when people died, she had read it so often, people saw a bright light at the end of a dark tunnel, and how lovely it was, she was safe now, quite safe, safe from all of them, just her and the soothing quietness, and there was Mr Hobson smiling at her, so kindly, saying, 'Good, good, can you hear me?' And she tried to say 'yes' but she couldn't, she couldn't speak, she couldn't move, obviously she was really dying, and she suddenly thought how awful, how awful to die in this horrible green paper hat, she couldn't, what would everyone think, and suppose some of the children saw her, and she was wrenching it off, tugging it, and it hurt, it really hurt trying to do it, her hand hurt, and someone was holding it now, holding it gently, telling her to relax, and she did, falling sweetly into darkness, falling, falling, and now even the bright light was gone . . .

Chapter Twenty-Seven

Harriet 9am

'So we thought a very quiet wedding.'

'Don't talk about weddings,' said Harriet with a shudder.

'Sorry, *mon ange*. A very quiet ceremony. In Paris. Which I hope very much you will attend. And then Merlin wishes to take me to see a rain forest. Or perhaps China. What do you think?'

'I think it all sounds wonderful. So wonderful. I'm really very very happy for you, Janine.'

'*Bon*. I am happy for myself.' Janine smiled at her, her dark eyes brilliant. 'And a little surprised. It was, what do you say, an arrow from the blue – '

'Bolt, Janine. You're getting confused with Cupid.'

'And why not? Very well, a bolt from the blue. You do not think we will seem a little ridiculous?'

'Janine, really! Neither of you could ever seem that.'

'I am not so sure,' said Janine quietly. She looked troubled. 'Both of us quite old people. Very different. And to get married, to set up home together like twenty-year-olds, it seems so – I don't know, so foolish somehow.'

'Janine, not foolish at all. Lovely. Sweet and lovely. And anyway, why should you care what it seems? You're going to be terribly happy, I know you are, and that's what matters.'

'Yes,' said Janine, suddenly relaxing, smiling at her. 'Yes, I think we will be. I am sure we will be. And one should take happiness, should one not? With both arms. While one can.'

'One should,' said Harriet, with a sigh, 'with both arms. And hold onto it.'

She thought of her own difficult happiness the year before, wondering if she should have clung to it more tightly; too late now, it was gone, long, long gone.

'What a sigh, Harriet darling. You are not happy, I think?'

'Oh, I'm all right, Janine. Worried obviously. But all right. Thank you. And certainly very happy for you. Really. Where are you going to live?'

'In Paris,' said Janine firmly. 'I could not be happy living anywhere else. And Merlin doesn't mind where he lives. Besides, if he has his way we won't be there so very much. We have several continents to look at.'

Harriet was silent for a moment, smiling at the vision of Merlin and Janine looking at continents together. 'It sounds lovely,' she said, 'as if you were going to be on a magic carpet.'

'I am sure we would be,' said Janine, 'if Merlin could get one at half price.'

'Where is he now?'

'He has gone out on a mysterious errand. I have an inkling as to what it is, but we must wait and see.' She put out her hand, stroked Harriet's cheek. 'You look so tired, *chérie*. It was a terrible day yesterday, was it not?'

'It was,' said Harriet with a sigh, 'truly terrible. And I – ' She took a deep breath. She had to confess to Janine some time, had to get it over, had to tell her what had happened to her money. 'Janine, there's something else as well. You see I –'

'Just look at this!' It was Merlin, stalking into the kitchen flushed, his white hair standing up round his head like a halo. 'Hope you like it, my dear. Chap said he'd take it back if you didn't.'

With a proud beam he handed Janine a small, rather worn leather ring box. She looked at him, then opened it very carefully. Inside was a ring: a lover's knot worked in gold, with a flower of garnets and diamonds at its centre.

'Merlin, it's beautiful,' said Janine. She put it on her long slender wedding finger; amazingly it fitted. She reached up and kissed his cheek. 'Thank you. Does this make it official?'

'I should hope so. Glad you like it. Victorian. Beat the chap down a lot, ridiculous price he was asking, told him I'd – '

'Merlin,' said Harriet gently, 'you really can't tell your fiancée her engagement ring was a bargain. It just isn't done.'

'Oh really? Suppose I've got a lot to learn. Sorry, my dear. Well, it still cost a lot of money. Does that make you feel any better?'

'I did not feel bad in the first place,' said Janine. 'Isn't this a beautiful ring, Harriet? Am I not a lucky woman?'

'Yes,' said Harriet, 'you are. But you deserve it. Both of you. And I hope you'll be terribly happy.'

'Oh, no doubt about that,' said Merlin. 'Got it right, I can see it. Thank goodness I was still free, waited for the real thing . . . Nearly married a dreadful girl I met in India, just after the war . . .'

'Good gracious,' said Harriet, 'that was a narrow escape.'

'Yes, well, she wasn't really dreadful of course, but she certainly couldn't hold a candle to Janine. Isn't she lovely?' he said to Harriet, a sweet soft smile on his handsome old face. 'Isn't she fine?'

'Merlin, you speak of me as if I were a horse,' said Janine briskly.

'No, Janine, that's not fair,' said Harriet. 'That's exactly what you are, fine. A fine person. It's a good description.'

'Well, all this is making me blush,' said Janine. 'Harriet, my darling, should I go and see your mother, do you think?'

'No, she's still asleep, thank goodness,' said Harriet, 'and I honestly think when she does wake up she'll feel better. Be able to come to terms with it a bit more. Poor Mummy. She dreamed of yesterday for so long . . .'

'Lot of bloody nonsense,' said Merlin suddenly. 'Silly spoilt little girl. Needs her bottom smacking. Where's your father, Harriet?'

'Oh – he's – he's gone to see Theo,' said Harriet quickly.

'Good chap, Theo,' said Merlin. 'Always liked him. Needs the right woman, that's all. That little thing he's got with him now, very pretty, but no good for him.'

'Merlin, he isn't very nice to her,' said Harriet.

'That's what I mean. He needs someone who'll stand up to him. Give as good as she gets.'

'That's what all those wives try to do. He just sends them packing.'

'Well that's because he knows they don't really give two figs for him,' said Merlin. 'Most of 'em married him for his money. Damn shame. Must hurt, that.'

'Yes, I suppose so,' said Harriet slowly. 'I'd never thought of it like that.'

'Merlin, you have been engaged for less than twelve hours and you are already an expert on marriage,' said Janine, laughing. She stood up and gave him another kiss. 'Now, Harriet, *ma chère*, what do you think I should do? Should I stay here with your mother for a day or two longer, or would it be better if I left? I am willing to do whatever is best.'

'That's sweet of you, Janine, but I think she'll probably be best left in peace. She's so hurt, so humiliated, as well as frightened and worried – she has to come to terms with it by herself.'

'Yes, and of course Cressida may yet come back. I have heard of these things, where people go away, disappear, it is a little like a suicide. They reach the end of their rope – '

'Tether, Janine.'

'All right, tether. They cannot cope. A cry for help, that is what this might be.'

'It might, I suppose,' said Harriet, trying to sound convinced, thinking of the picture of the radiant Cressida running down the steps of Sacré-

333

Coeur in her wedding dress. 'It might indeed. Well, we must wait and see.'

'And you? What will you do?'

'Oh, I have to get back to London,' said Harriet. Her voice sounded taut, strained, even to her.

'Today?'

'Yes, I'm afraid so. My business is – well, anyway, I do have to go. I have an appointment with a man about an overdraft at two – '

'Now look, Harriet,' said Merlin, 'the offer stands. Anything I can do . . .'

'Is there a real problem?' asked Janine. Her eyes were brilliant, thoughtful.

'Yes, Janine, there is.' Harriet faced her, looked at her very levelly. 'There's something I have to tell you. I was going to do it just now, when Merlin came in. I may have to ask you to bear with me for a while before I can give you your money back. I'm so sorry. I've fought so hard to be able to save it, tried everything, but you see – '

'My darling child, I don't want my money back. It was an investment I made, and if it was a bad one, that is my problem. Well, it is yours as well of course, but anyway, I certainly do not want to hear the details now. Another time. We will go through it all and you can tell me what has happened, and what should be done. But just now, clearly you must go and see this bank manager.'

'Think young Tilly could help?' said Merlin. 'Said she would, didn't she? Lovely girl, don't you think, my dear? Just right for young Rufus. Maybe we could make it a double wedding. There's an idea now.'

'Merlin, it's a terrible idea,' said Harriet, laughing, 'and I'm afraid there won't be any wedding there, double or otherwise. Tilly is hell-bent on finishing the whole thing. Oh God, I completely forgot. Janine, did you know Susie was in hospital?'

'Susie? No, of course not. What's wrong? It must have been very sudden. She looked well yesterday. Thin, of course, but – '

'She phoned my – well, she phoned a little while ago. From the hospital. She sounded very strange. I told Rufus, he phoned about Annabel and Tom, he didn't know either.'

'Let us hope it is not serious,' said Janine. 'Such a nice woman.'

'Yes,' said Harriet shortly. Janine looked at her sharply; Harriet looked back, her eyes a careful blank. 'Well, I must go and sort out a few things. Excuse me. And congratulations to you both again. That ring is heaven, Merlin.'

She was on her way upstairs when the phone rang; it was James. 'Harriet, darling, we're almost back.'

'Back! But you've only just gone.'

'I know. Let's just say there didn't seem any future in staying.'

'No Cressida?'

'Well – no. Not really. Certainly she won't be back. Not for a while. I'll explain when we get there. There's a lot of talking to do.'

'I'm sorry,' said Harriet, 'but I may have gone. I simply have to get to town. Meeting with the bank. Obviously I'll come back tonight if I possibly can. I'll have to take Mummy's car.'

'All right,' said James with a sigh. 'Is Mummy awake?'

'Not yet. Well, she wasn't twenty minutes ago.' Don't ask me what my problem is, will you, thought Harriet, don't worry about me. There's Cressida and Mummy and Susie to think about, quite enough for one day. No wonder I'm so obsessed with success, with proving myself.

'Good. What was that, Theo? Ah, Harriet, Theo wants to know if he could have a word with you.'

'He couldn't,' said Harriet and put the phone down.

She went up to her room, repacked her briefcase, then sat down on the bed and picked up the letter from the gynaecologist she had found in the cardigan pocket.

Jennifer Bradman, FRCOG, said she could see her around midday: 'I'm sorry it can't be before. Full morning. I don't know how much I can help, but I'll certainly try.'

'Thank you,' said Harriet.

She looked in at her mother on her way down. Maggie was lying awake but calm; she gazed rather hopelessly at Harriet from her mound of pillows.

'I'll get you some tea, Mummy. Then I really have to go up to London. I'm sorry. Urgent business. I'll be back tonight if I possible can.'

'You always have urgent business,' said Maggie fretfully. 'Don't delay yourself on my account, Harriet, I'll get my own tea.'

Harriet walked out in silence, closing the door with acute care behind her. Otherwise she would have slammed it.

Chapter Twenty-Eight

James 10am

'You drive,' Theo had said, when they finally reached Kidlington, fell exhaustedly into the Bentley. 'I want to hit the phone.'

'You sound like a character in a TV drama,' said James, grinning at him.

'I am like a character in a TV drama,' said Theo rather grimly. 'Ridiculous. Absurd. Hard to believe in.' He was punching out numbers. James, aware of how tired he was, how upset, desperately trying to concentrate on the road, heard a long trail of conversations: with Myra Hartman, about faxes, letters, appointments, flowers (flowers?); with Mark Protheroe, about prices, selling, buying, markets; with Jackie the housekeeper, about arrivals, departures, guests, the weekend; and then a brief heated exchange clearly with Mungo, and another, brief as well, but coolly level, with his elder son Michael. 'I've got to do something about that boy,' he said, finally hanging up the phone.

'Which one? Mungo?'

'Oh, I can't do anything with Mungo. He's absolutely impossible. Pig-headed, arrogant, totally absurd – '

'Like a character in a TV drama,' said James mildly.

'What? Oh for God's sake, James. Mungo is nothing, nothing in the least like me. I'm talking about Michael. He's thirty-two now, you know. Got to give him something to run.'

'Well, is that a problem?'

'Yes it is. He's efficient, shrewd, conscientious, got an excellent business head.'

'So what's the problem?'

'He's got no passion. No style. None at all. Never does anything on impulse. He's all brain.'

'Isn't that a good thing in business?' asked James, genuinely intrigued.

'No of course not,' said Theo. He sounded astonished, as if James had suggested that a good businessman should possess a talent for ballet or pottery. 'Passion is what makes it all work, James. You can get other people to crunch numbers and deal with contracts and contacts, but it's what you do with your heart and your instinct that wins you the day. It's like falling in love, James, it's like sex, it's an excitement, a thud of the heart. Michael's heart doesn't thud. Ever.'

'What about Mungo's?'

'Thuds too bloody much,' said Theo and picked up the phone again.

'Can you drop me at the Bergins' hotel?' said James. 'I left my jacket there yesterday and I can see how they're coping at the same time. I hope quite honestly they go home very soon – there's no point their hanging around. Or do you think there is? Do you think she might even now come back?' he added, hearing the note of hopeful pain in his own voice as he said it, feeling foolish.

Theo looked at him. 'Honestly,' he said, 'I don't. It's a bitch of a thing to admit, but I don't.'

James was silent.

'James! Good morning. How are you?' Julia was as china-doll perfect as ever, smiling, holding out her hand as she came across the hotel lounge.

'Oh – all right,' said James wearily. He was too tired, too wretched to keep up any pretences, to try to sound positive.

'You look exhausted,' said Julia Bergin severely. 'Has there been any development?'

'Yes,' said James, and told her what it was.

He didn't look at her as he talked; he couldn't. When he finally lifted his head, met her eyes, there was a moment of appalling truth. Before shock, distress, disbelief carefully took over, for just one second Julia Bergin looked complacently, smugly self-satisfied.

Then: 'Poor Oliver,' she said quietly. 'My poor poor Oliver. And you James, and Maggie, what you must be going through. I only wish – '

'Maggie doesn't know yet,' said James briefly. What was it with Julia, was Merlin right, did she know something? No, she couldn't, she couldn't. It must have been one of those inappropriate shock reactions, like giggling when you heard that someone had died.

'Maggie doesn't know?' repeated Julia.

'No. I gave her some very heavy sedation last night. I've rung home and apparently she's only just woken. I'm going home to tell her now.'

'Oh James. How terrible. That lovely little girl – what she must have gone through.'

'That's very charitable of you,' said James. 'To take that view.'

'Well, one has to try to understand. To imagine what might have led her to do such a thing. What unhappiness, what confusion.'

'Yes, yes,' said James, 'and what selfishness, what cruelty.' He didn't want Cressida defended; had she walked into the lounge then he would have hit her.

'Well, there had to be more to it than that.'

'I don't think so. Is Oliver about?'

'He's gone for a walk. With his father.'

'I see. I really wanted to tell him myself.'

'James, I think it would be better if I told him. He's been through such a terrible time. He's very hurt. I think I would know how to break it to him – '

'Yes, all right,' said James. He found he was grateful for an escape route; telling Oliver how nearly he had married a liar and a cheat who happened to be his daughter was not a pleasant prospect.

'So if you want to get off home to Maggie, then do please feel free. She needs you more than Oliver does, James. Poor woman. As a mother, I feel for her so much. If you think I could help in any way – '

She sat down abruptly, buried her face in her hands. James stood looking down at her helplessly. 'Julia, please – I'm so sorry – '

'Oh James, don't feel – it's all right – I – ' She looked up again; her eyes were brilliant with unshed tears, her mouth taut with an attempt at control. 'Suddenly I – so silly – shock, I suppose. Please excuse me.'

She was gone, leaving James staring after her with nothing left to do now but go home and tell Maggie the horrible thing her beloved daughter had done.

Chapter Twenty-Nine

Mungo 10.30am

'Mungo! Call for you on Two.'

It was Belinda, one of the Sloaney negotiators; she was moderately pretty, extremely charming and very sexy, with good legs, long blonde hair (which Mungo swore actually grew attached to the black velvet hairband which held it off her high forehead), a hugely infectious laugh and a fine line in dirty jokes. Her pedigree was impeccable: her father worked for Lloyd's, her boyfriend at Christie's and her mother had been deb of the year. The clients all adored her; Mungo adored her too. If he hadn't been so much in love with Alice, he thought he might well have gone into battle for her with the Christie's boyfriend.

'Thanks. It's not my father, is it?'

'No, Mungo, it's not your father. It's a female. Didn't give a name.'

Wouldn't be Alice; she always rang on his mobile. 'If you think I'm giving those girls the pleasure of knowing how often I want to talk to you, you don't know me very well,' she'd said to him when he pointed out that if she used the office line she could leave messages. He picked the phone up. He felt very tired suddenly; his arms were leaden and his head ached.

'Mungo Buchan.'

It was Jemima. 'Mungo, sorry to ring you in the office. Is this all right?'

'Depends what you're going to say,' said Mungo.

'I'm going to say thank you,' said Jemima.

'What on earth for?'

'For not ratting on me to Mummy. It was really nice of you.'

'That's OK,' said Mungo wearily. 'But if you want a bit of advice from an old man, Jemima, you'll find somewhere else to conduct your love life in future. Somewhere a bit more discreet.'

'Yes, I know. I will. Promise. Um – there's something else, Mungo. I – I might have given you the wrong impression last night. About Mummy. I was – angry with her, we'd had a fight.'

'What kind of wrong impression?'

'Well, that she – you know. She – well, she isn't – she doesn't – '

'Jemima, what are you trying to say?'

'Well, that she's really really fond of you. And she – well, she wouldn't do anything to hurt you. I know she wouldn't.'

'I'm afraid, Jemima, she already has,' said Mungo and put the phone down. 'Get me some coffee, Carol, would you?' he shouted through the door. Carol was his long-suffering secretary: more conventionally pretty, but rather less well connected, than Belinda and plainly and helplessly in love with him. She came in early, worked through most of her lunch hours, left late and had more than once worked until long after Mungo had left and she had missed her last train home if there was an urgent brochure or prospectus to prepare, and then paid for a taxi back to Ealing with her own money rather than cause Mungo any more trouble. She found the things he had lost, remembered the things he had forgotten and enjoyed nothing more than performing such politically incorrect secretarial duties as sewing on his buttons and taking his clothes to the cleaners. She came in now looking slightly nervous, the coffee in a large mug and a plate of Jaffa cakes in her other hand. Mungo's devotion to Jaffa cakes was well known, and Carol made frequent pilgrimages to Selfridge's Food Hall to keep the supply topped up. It was usually worth the effort, he would smile and thank her, but this morning he simply took the mug and waved the plate away without a word.

'Er – how was the wedding, Mungo? You look tired.'

'Lousy and I am tired. Get me the file on the Bruton Lane building, Carol, and get the bank on the phone.'

'Yes, Mungo, of course.'

Mungo looked at her as she half ran out of the office; she'd have to go, he couldn't stand the sense of guilt she engendered any longer. Well, that would be easily effected; she could be part of the cost-cutting exercise. He'd talk to her at lunchtime.

'You,' said Alice, 'are a brat.'

She was standing in the doorway of the office, Belinda hovering uncertainly behind her.

Mungo looked up at her. 'Please leave,' he said coldly.

'Mungo, I have no intention of leaving.'

'Well in that case I will.'

'No you won't,' said Alice, and closed the door behind her. She leant against it, looking at him thoughtfully, then she said, 'Mungo, we have to talk.'

'There's nothing to talk about as far as I can see,' said Mungo icily. 'Now if you will excuse me, I have work to do.' He started tapping at his keyboard, calling up details of properties; then he picked up the phone and punched out a number rather too viciously. 'Mrs Packard? Mungo

Buchan. Mrs Packard, I think we might have a very interesting property for you. In – '

'Mrs Packard will have to wait, I'm afraid,' said Alice coolly. She had come over to his desk and cut him off. 'Mungo, do you have to be so rude? I thought you were supposed to love me.'

'You thought wrong, I'm afraid. Well, I suppose I did, but you've fucked it up rather neatly.'

'Mungo, the only fucking up that's being done is by you. Of just about everything. Your life, your work, your relationships, not just with me but with your father. And – '

'Please don't talk to me about my father,' said Mungo. 'What you did, phoning him like that, was absolutely unforgivable. And you're doing a pretty good job of fucking up my work yourself. Please go away. I have clients to attend to.'

'No, Mungo, I won't go. And I'd like you to tell that poor little soul out there who seems to have the misguided idea that you're some kind of a cross between Tom Cruise and the Messiah to hold all your calls for a while.'

'I'll do nothing of the sort.'

'In that case,' said Alice, starting to unbutton her dress, 'I shall scream and say you were assaulting me.'

Mungo looked at her. There was an expression in her blue eyes that he had come to know very well: one of absolute steely determination. He picked up the phone. 'Carol,' he said, 'hold all the calls for now, please. And ask Roddy Fairfield to talk to Mrs Packard urgently. If she hasn't already gone to another agent,' he added, glaring at Alice.

'Yes, Mungo. Er – would you like some more coffee in there?'

'No I wouldn't,' said Mungo.

As he put the phone down again, he heard muffled giggles; he looked up at Alice. 'How dare you,' he said, 'how dare you come in here and disrupt my business and make a fool of me in front of my staff?'

'Oh don't be so pompous,' said Alice. 'I dare, as you put it, because it's very important you hear what I have to say. I want your undivided attention. It won't take long.'

'All right. Get on with it. And then get out.'

'Mungo, do look at me please, stop sulking. It's impossible to talk to the top of someone's head.'

Mungo looked at her and scowled. She laughed. 'You really look very like your father when you do that.'

'How do you know what he looks like, Alice? If you've been to see him – '

'Oh Mungo, don't be ridiculous. Of course I haven't been to see him.

341

But he is quite famous, you know. I've seen him on things like the *Money Programme*, and he was on *Panorama* the other night.'

''Was he?' said Mungo, genuinely surprised. 'I didn't know.'

'Yes, a programme about the Third World. He was giving his views on the food surplus here and in the States. It was very interesting. You should have watched it.'

'No thanks,' said Mungo. 'I know most of his interesting views off by heart. They bore me.'

'What a little charmer you are,' said Alice lightly. 'Let's talk about you, shall we, Mungo? That will presumably interest you more.'

'Alice,' said Mungo, losing his temper suddenly, 'Alice, last night I told my father how much I loved you and that I wanted to marry you. He was foul to me. He talked to me as if I was six years old, it was patronizing to me, insulting to you, and – '

'Yes, he knows that, and he was very sorry,' said Alice.

Mungo could not have been more astonished if she had told him his father was taking up ice skating or social work.

'He was what?'

'He was sorry.'

'My father doesn't know the meaning of the word.'

'Mungo, I think he does. He sounded very sorry indeed to me. He said he wasn't very good at apologizing, but he was going to have a go at doing it to you. He's a honey. I really liked him.'

'Oh,' said Mungo, 'oh, shit.'

'What?'

'He phoned – earlier. Tried to speak to me. I told him to – well, I told him to fuck off.'

'Well,' said Alice, 'that was very charming. And it probably won't encourage him to pursue the art of contrition.'

'Sorry?'

'I don't suppose he'll try apologizing to you again.'

'Did you – did you have to point it out to him?' said Mungo.

'Point what out?'

'Well, that he's been patronizing and insulting?'

'No, of course not.'

'If you knew him,' said Mungo, 'you'd know there was no "of course" about it.'

'You may be right. I happen to think you're wrong. Anyway, I'm hoping to get to know him.'

'Oh really? Over cosy little dinners while you discuss my appalling behaviour and what you're both going to do about it?'

'Oh don't be so childish,' she said wearily.

'I'm not being childish. Maybe you should set your sights on him, rather than me. He's a lot nearer your age, and he's not exactly picky. I'm sure you could get rid of the current Mrs Buchan in no time, if you set your mind to it – '

Alice walked over to the desk and hit him; first she slapped him extremely hard across the face, and then she drew her arm back and punched him with surprising force on the nose. The room went briefly black and then a few lights danced in front of his eyes; the famous stars, he thought confusedly. He felt something warm trickling down his upper lip: blood he supposed. He sat slumped back in his chair, staring at her. He felt very odd.

'Right then', she said. She stood over him, her hands on the arms of his chair, her eyes blazing in her white face. He could feel the heat of her, could smell her, not just her perfume but something else, a hot musky smell, the smell of rage. 'Right then, Mungo, I've got a few things to tell you and then I'll go. First of all, I don't go round setting my sights on anyone. I actually thoroughly enjoy being single. It's fun and it's easy. I didn't want to fall in love with you, Mungo, I fought it very hard. For a long time. As for marrying you, it still seems the most ridiculous, the most impractical, the most appalling idea.'

'Well then,' he said, and his voice was somehow quieter than he had expected it to be, 'if it seems so appalling why did you say you would?'

There was a very long silence; he stared up at her. Her eyes, holding his, were still hostile, still furious.

'Because I couldn't help it,' she said finally. 'I simply couldn't help it. Because I do love you. I think you're spoilt and self-centred and childish and dreadful and yet you make me terribly happy. And I love you. I weakened. I just couldn't hold out any longer.'

'Oh,' said Mungo, his voice quieter still. The blood was pouring down his nose now, and onto his shirt; he reached for his handkerchief, mopped at it rather helplessly. 'I've fucked this up rather, haven't I?'

'Just a bit,' said Alice. 'But since I told your father last night I wasn't going to marry you, it doesn't really matter what you did. Or said.'

'Ah,' said Mungo, 'ah, I thought so. He did talk you out of it. Somehow or another.'

'No, Mungo, he didn't. I talked me out of it. He hardly said a word. I heard myself saying, and thinking how sensible of me it was, that I wouldn't marry you. That it was a stupid idea.'

'Appalling,' said Mungo mechanically.

'Appalling. Yes. That I must have been out of such mind as I have, agreeing to it in the first place. And I also said that if he thought it would be better for you, I would go away altogether.'

'Well, I'm very glad you consulted him so fully about our lives, rather than me,' said Mungo. 'And what did he say to that?'

'He said it was no business of his,' she said. 'Absolutely none at all.'

'He did?' said Mungo, staring up at her. 'My father said that?'

'Yes he did. He said he had absolutely no intention of telling me what I should or shouldn't do.'

'He didn't even express a view?'

'No he didn't.'

'I don't believe I'm hearing this,' said Mungo. 'My father spends his entire life telling people what to do. Expressing very strong views indeed. He was just being clever, stringing you along – '

'Mungo, I told you, he was really sorry about – about what he said to you. About us. I don't know why you can't believe it.'

'I can't believe it,' said Mungo, 'because I know him so well. I've lived with him for twenty-seven years. I tell you, Alice, every leopard on the face of this planet is more likely to change its spots to sky-blue pink than my father is to stop interfering in everyone's lives. Especially mine.'

'There are some white leopards, you know,' she said quietly.

'I'm sorry?'

'I mean some leopards have actually changed their spots. Well, lost them anyway. In response to certain situations.'

'Yes, maybe, but not overnight.'

'You're very hard on him, aren't you?'

'Yes, I am. I've learnt to be.'

'He's very proud of you, you know.'

'Yeah, yeah,' said Mungo, 'when I'm being a good boy, doing what I'm told.'

'No, not really. He told me last night how proud of you he was. Of the way you've built this business up. He said he hadn't actually thought you'd got what it takes, but he was wrong. That you've done it without any input from him at all. It was one of the things he was most sorry about, implying that you couldn't. And he also said he was very proud of the way you'd stood up to him. He said' – she smiled at what was obviously a funny memory – 'he said he knew it took some doing.'

'Good God,' said Mungo, 'this really was some conversation.'

'Yes it was. Anyway – '

'And he actually said that? That I've got what it takes?'

'Mungo, how many more times do I have to tell you? That's what he said.'

Mungo looked at her. He felt very powerful suddenly, very joyful, as if he could do anything, anything at all. And he felt something else, too, a sense of immense, heady freedom.

'Shit,' he said, 'shit.'

'Is that all you have to say?'

'No,' said Mungo, 'no it isn't.' He looked at Alice and thought how it had taken her and her clear-sightedness and courage to do this for him, to cut into the complex, cross-purposed lines that lay between him and his father and to deliver each of them safely, if a little shamefaced, back to one another.

'I love you,' he said to her, 'I really really love you.'

'And I really love you too. Like I said.'

'But you won't marry me?'

'No, Mungo, I won't marry you. I can't. I told you, It's an – '

'Yes, yes, all right, it's an appalling idea. You're going to have to work quite hard to convince me of that.'

'No,' she said, 'no, not really. I won't have to. Because what I'm going to do is go away, leave London.'

'What do you mean, you're going away? Going away where? I don't understand, you weren't going away yesterday.'

'Mungo, I know. But I did a lot of thinking yesterday. And – well, I am. I'm going to Italy.'

'Italy? What the fuck for?'

'Not fucking,' she said smiling, touching his face gently. 'Oh Mungo, your poor, poor nose.'

'Never mind my nose,' he said, rummaging in his pocket for a handkerchief, unable to find one. 'What's with this Italy business?'

'Business actually,' she said. 'Exactly that. Here, let me clean you up.' She bent over him, started tenderly wiping his face; she was very near him, he could smell the warmth of her, smell her skin, her hair. He put out his hand, gently touched one of her breasts, clearly defined beneath the white silk jersey.

'Alice,' he said, 'oh Alice – '

And 'Mungo,' she said, 'Mungo, don't. Please don't.'

'Why not?' he said and he could hear the pain deep down in his voice. 'Don't you like it? Don't you want me any more, is that it, are you tired of me, Alice, are you in love with someone else?'

'Mungo darling, I do want you, and I do love you, and I'm not tired of you. It's none of those things. That's what makes it all so difficult. That's why I'm going away.'

'Oh Alice, please. Don't be ridiculous. You can't go away. What would you do?'

'Work. My friends of last night, the ones you didn't believe in, Giles and Fanny, they've bought a big house in Tuscany and they want to turn it into a small, very luxurious hotel. They want me to run it for them. For a while at least.'

345

'You can't do that,' he said, 'you don't know anything about hotels, you don't speak Italian, it's nonsense.'

'I know quite a lot about hotels actually, Mungo, and I *can* speak Italian. I think I'll be very good at it.'

'What about the children? You can't leave them.'

'I'm not going to leave them. The little ones will come with me, go to the International School in Florence, and Jemima will come out in the holidays, practise her burgeoning sexual talents in a different language. It'll do them good, to discover there's a world beyond SW3.'

Mungo felt panic, clammy, cold, clutching at him. 'Alice, you can't. You can't do this to me.'

'I'm doing it *for* you,' she said, with a peculiarly sweet smile. She reached out, touched his cheek very gently. 'Because I love you so much. And for me, actually. It'll be wonderful.'

'Alice, please don't go. Please. I need you.'

'Mungo, I have to go. It really is the only thing to do.'

'Well then, I'll come too. I want some European business, I could be your agent, find more places to let and – '

'Mungo, no. That is really not the idea. Much as I'd love it.'

'Well, if you'd love it,' he said, feeling in spite of himself that he was losing ground, 'why don't you let me?'

'Mungo, listen to me.' She took his face between her hands, looked into his eyes. 'I can't let you because it wouldn't work. We have lives to live, you and I, and they don't go together too well. It's been lovely having you all this time, and the children have adored it and so have I, but it hasn't been about real life. You couldn't fit permanently into my life, Mungo, and, much more importantly, I couldn't fit into yours. I should never have let you think so, never have let myself think so. And I'm more sorry than I can tell you. And I do love you very, very much.'

'But I need you. I need you so much.'

'Not really. You can manage beautifully without me. You're a very special person, Mungo. Just don't forget it, that's all. Don't – er – fuck the very special person up, OK?'

'Oh God,' he said, staring at her, a clutch of misery starting at his heart, realizing she meant it. 'Oh God, Alice. I don't know if I can do this. Say goodbye to you. Live without you. And it seems so unnecessary somehow.'

'Nonsense,' she said, 'of course you can. And it isn't unnecessary, actually, Mungo. Not at all.'

'And this is it? I'm not to see you any more?'

'Not any more,' she said.

'You seem very cheerful about it.'

'Mungo, I'm not cheerful at all. I'm going to be very unhappy for quite a long time. But I'll survive. And so will you.'

'Well – can't we still be friends? At least?'

'Mungo,' she said, bending down, kissing him very gently on the lips, his sore, bloody, cracked lips; her own mouth was cool, soft. 'Mungo, I would love to be your friend. In time. But not just yet. It wouldn't work and I – ' Her voice cracked, she stood up quickly, decisively, her eyes brilliant with tears. 'I couldn't bear it,' she said quietly. 'Goodbye, Mungo. I'll see you – I'll see you maybe next year? Come and find me, then, in Italy. If you still want to.'

'Of course I'll want to,' he said slowly, staring at her. He felt as if he was seeing her for the first time, not the last, discovering her all over again, her lovely face, with its high cheekbones, its curvy mouth, her blue eyes, brilliant, tender, fixed on him, her ice-blonde hair (more dishevelled than usual) and – oh God, her perfect slender body, the body he knew so well, how it felt, smelt, how it welcomed him, loved him, wanted him; and he knew she meant what she said, that there would be no dissuading her, that he had to say goodbye to her, for a long while.

'You'd better go,' he said, 'I think you'd better go quickly. Goodbye, Alice. I love you. I love you so much.'

'I love you too,' she said, 'and I'm sorry about your face.'

'Oh,' he said, 'don't worry about that. I expect I deserved it.'

'Yes, you did,' she said, and smiled again, gaily, bravely. 'Darling Mungo. Take care. Goodbye.'

And she was gone, closing the door quietly behind her, and Mungo sat at his desk, just looking, staring at the space where she had been, thinking of the space in his life she had filled, empty of her, empty of everything about her, and he couldn't see how he was going to bear it, even while he knew he had to, and he buried his head in his arms and wept like a child.

'Mungo.' It was Belinda; she was standing in front of him, looking very tender, very concerned. 'Mungo, I've brought you some coffee. Is there anything else I can do for you, get you?'

'Yes,' said Mungo, taking a gulp of coffee, blowing his nose hard on his bloodstained handkerchief, 'Yes, Belinda, there is. Could you please get hold of my father? And tell him I'd like to buy him dinner tonight.'

Chapter Thirty

James 10.30am

James was half a mile down the lane in the cab the hotel called for him when he realized he still hadn't picked up the jacket he had left there yesterday. Bloody hell. The last thing he wanted to do was go back to that place. On the other hand, he did have to get it, and retrieving it would postpone the conversation with Maggie a little while longer. On balance probably better to turn around.

'I'm terribly sorry,' he said to the cab driver. 'I've left something behind. Could we go back please?'

'I'm sorry, Mr Forrest, the Bergins are all out. Mrs Bergin has gone for a walk with Dr Bergin and Mr Bergin has gone into Oxford. I'm sorry, sir. Is there anything we can do to help?'

'Well, yes, there is actually,' said James. 'I left my jacket in Mr Bergin's room yesterday. I do rather want it. Could one of your staff fetch it for me?'

'Certainly, sir.' He called a young man in a striped waistcoat who was standing in the hall trying to look importantly busy. 'Michael! Would you go and get Mr Forrest's jacket from Mr and Mrs Bergin's room, please? He left it there yesterday.'

'Certainly, Mr Rogers. Er – how will I know which jacket it is, Mr Forrest? Is it distinctive in any way at all, sir?'

'Oh Lord, I don't know,' said James. 'No – yes – look, I'll come up with you. All right?'

'Well, sir, I don't know – ' The young man in reception looked dubious. 'We're really not supposed – '

'Oh for God's sake,' said James, feeling nearer to a loss of control than he had for twenty-four hours. 'Mr Bergin is a very old friend of mine, his son was about to marry my daughter, my daughter's gone missing, now will you, for Christ's sake, let me go and retrieve my own jacket from his room?'

'Yes, sir. I'm sorry, sir. Michael, go along please, don't keep Mr Forrest waiting.'

James followed the unfortunate Michael into the lift and out again, along the first-floor corridor into the Bergins' room; Michael stood awkwardly silent while James walked over to the cupboard. His jacket was there, hanging neatly next to Josh's morning coat, still in its plastic cover. The sight of that, forlornly unworn, brought back more poignantly than anything what had happened, the loss of Cressida, the heartache and the grief of the day. Tears rushed to his eyes; he sank down on the bed and buried his head in his hands. To his horror and humiliation he began to cry, loud racking sobs. Michael coughed gently, discreetly.

'Oh for God's sake,' James shouted, his voice rich with tears and pain, 'for God's sake get the hell out of here. I'm not going to rob the bloody room. Get out.'

Michael withdrew and closed the door very quietly; James continued to sob. After a while he felt better, lay back exhausted, staring at the ceiling. Why had she done it, why, why? Was she really so bad, so totally devoid of morals? Was it his fault, Maggie's fault, for spoiling her, loving her too much? Was it his bad genes, his own lack of morality, passed on to her? Christ Almighty, was this his judgment, his punishment? Or was Susie's illness that, a punishment for them both? He suddenly felt filled with terror for Susie, for the danger she was in, with shame too, at what he had done to her, for failing her. Christ, he was a mess, an appalling, amoral mess. He looked at his watch: she would be out of theatre by now; maybe he could phone.

He went over to the bedside table, picked up the phone, dialled the number of the Princess Diana Hospital. 'Is Mr Hobson out of theatre, please?' he asked. 'This is James Forrest, obstetrics consultant at St Edmund's. I'm a colleague of his.'

'Just a moment, please, Mr Forrest,' said the girl. There were a few clicks, then she said, 'I'm sorry, Mr Forrest, Mr Hobson is still in theatre. Can I ask him to call you?'

'No, it's all right,' said James, 'I won't be here. I'll call back in about an hour. Will he be there?'

More clicks. 'I'm sorry, Mr Forrest, Mr Hobson won't be here in an hour, his secretary says he'll be in his consulting rooms. Can I give you the number?'

'Yes, please,' said James. He had no pen or paper on him; he rummaged in the small drawer of the bedside table, found a pad, took it out, pulling half the contents of the drawer with it. 'OK, fire away, yes, 934-2268. Thank you very much.'

He tore the piece of paper off the pad, replaced the rather florid gold-plated biro that was clearly Julia's and started picking up the papers from the floor. Lists in Julia's spidery American writing; a note from Maggie, giving the name and address of the hotel; a – James suddenly sat down on the bed staring, staring at the letter in a hand that had begun to shake, fallen from inside a leather-bound notebook of Julia's.

The writing paper was headed with an address in Palm Beach, Florida, and the letter was written in a slightly shaky but absolutely legible hand. It was dated a week earlier.

My darling girl (it said)

So very lovely to see you the other day. I wish you could come more often, but of course I know you have your duties to your husband. He is extremely fortunate to have you, to ease his path so loyally and effectively. I hope he recognizes his good fortune.

I was very distressed to hear that this girl is proving to be so unsuitable for Oliver. It seems tragic that such a brilliant and charming young man should have his future endangered by falling into the hands of someone so amoral and, if it is not too strong a word, dangerous. How foolish love makes one; even you, my darling.

Of course I am more than happy to extend what I am pleased to see you now perceive as the favour I did you, in keeping the Coleridge fortune safe from incompetent hands. I have spoken to my lawyers and changed my will. Under the new terms, Oliver is no longer a beneficiary, of either capital or income, and will not be one for so long as he remains married to this creature; should the marriage end, as I know you pray it will, then we can review the situation. I enclose a photocopy of the relevant passage; the fully revised document is now lodged, as always, with the trustees.

I have done as you advised and not writtten to Oliver myself. I trust you, in your wonderfully charming and tactful way, to break the news to him. He may be a little hurt and even angry, as you were so many years ago, my dearest, but I am sure he will come in the fullness of time to see the wisdom of what we have done. We have a duty to protect and care for our children for as long as God grants us; I thank Him daily that I have been able to do that for you.

My fondest love,
Dada

'Dear Christ,' said James aloud, putting the piece of paper down, 'dear Christ in heaven.'

He went over to the mini-bar and, for the first time in twenty years, poured himself a drink.

Chapter Thirty-One

Susie 10.30am

Maybe she hadn't died yet. The darkness was somehow softening. And the light was back, a faint pinprick now, but getting bigger. She was drifting towards it rather fast, so obviously she hadn't got long. Her arm and her breast hurt; hurt quite a lot. Well, that would be over soon, at least. You didn't feel pain if you were dead. Oh God, she was thirsty, her mouth was so dry. She wondered if you had drinks in heaven, and what they were. Would there be champagne? She wouldn't think much of a heaven without it. And would James be there? If she was going to be happy, she'd need him. But he couldn't be, because he hadn't died. And he didn't love her anyway. She knew that now. He didn't love her and he probably never had. The whole of her grown-up life had been lived on a lie. It hurt so much to think that. And all that time Alistair had loved her, and she hadn't realized it. And that hurt, too. She'd wasted him, and wasted herself on James. 'Oh God,' she said fretfully, through dry, thick lips, finding her throat was sore. 'Oh God, I'm so sorry.'

'Darling,' a voice said, very gently, 'darling Susie. Hallo.'

She hadn't expected God to use that sort of endearment; she'd thought He'd be rather gruff. Kind but gruff. The light got bigger suddenly, brighter; she braced herself to open her eyes, look at Him, look at God. And found herself looking at Alistair.

He was smiling very tenderly at her; he put out his hand and stroked her hair. Then he picked up her hand and kissed it. 'Hallo,' he said.

'Alistair,' said Susie, 'Alistair, aren't I dead?'

'Not in the least,' he said, 'I'm happy to say. Very much alive.'

'Hi, Mum,' said another voice. It was Rufus.

Susie turned her head to the other side of the bed; he was sitting there, smiling down at her with equal tenderness. He took her other hand.

'Ouch,' said Susie, 'that hurts. So does my arm.'

'Sorry. How are you feeling?'

'All right I think. Bit woozy. I – ' She remembered suddenly the fear, the awful fear that it would be gone, and tried unsuccessfully to move her good arm, her right arm, over to try to feel if it was still there, her precious, treacherous breast. It was too much of an effort; she relaxed again, biting her lip. Alistair kissed her again.

'It's all right, darling. It's still there.' He knew, had realized what she was trying to do. She was so touched by that, and by a great flood of relief, of joy, her eyes filled with tears; she closed them briefly. They stung; they hurt. Everything hurt. Maybe if she kept them closed for just a second, it would be better . . .

When she opened them again, Mr Hobson was standing at the foot of her bed; he was wearing his green gown, and he was looking rather pleased with himself. A nurse was taking her pulse. 'Good,' she said. Definitely not dead then, thought Susie, smiling at Mr Hobson.

'Your husband's popped off to make a quick phone call,' he said. 'He was getting just a tiny bit restive, watching you sleep.'

'Watching me sleep! I just woke up.'

'Half an hour ago. Then you promptly went off again.'

'No I didn't,' said Susie, indignantly.

'Yes you did, Mum.' Rufus's face was very solemn, very loving. 'Honestly.'

'Rufus, what are you doing here? How did you know? I told your father – ' She bit her lip, realizing she would never be able to say that again to Rufus without guilt, without shame. But he didn't seem to react any differently from usual. 'I told Alistair not to tell any of you.'

'Dad didn't.' Did she imagine it, or was there just a slight emphasis on the word Dad? She hoped so. 'Harriet told me.'

'Harriet! How did she know?'

'You rang her up. Don't you remember?'

'No. I'm sure I didn't. I – ' And then she did remember, struggling to speak to Harriet through the fog of her pre-med, wanting, needing to speak to James. For the last time. And failing.

'Mum, why didn't you tell me? How do you think I'd have felt if – well, if I hadn't – oh, you know what I mean.'

'I know what you mean,' said Susie, smiling rather uncertainly at him.

He bent to kiss her. 'Love you loads,' he said. He had always said that, ever since he was a tiny little boy, whenever they said hallo or goodbye.

'Love you too,' said Susie, hoping Rufus was telling the truth.

Mr Hobson cleared his throat. 'I hate to intrude on this touching family scene, but there's something I have to tell you.'

Susie braced herself; even that very tiny movement hurt. 'What?' she said, and a sickening, dreadful fear took hold of her. She gripped Rufus's hand, and realized to her immense surprise that it wasn't enough. She wanted Alistair, wanted him to be there, to hear her sentence. Maybe, she thought confusedly, through her terror, maybe this whole thing was a judgment on her, a punishment for all her wickedness.

'Mr Hobson, could you wait until my husband gets back, please? I want – ' she corrected herself – 'I need him to be here.'

'Yes, of course you do. The only thing is you're not my only patient. I should be down in theatre again now.'

'I'll go and find him,' said Rufus.

'Oh Rufus, darling, thank you. Could I have a drink of water, Mr Hobson? I'm so terribly thirsty.'

'What do you think, Nurse?'

'Should be all right,' said the nurse. 'Just a sip.'

Susie sipped. Her throat really hurt. 'What's the time?' she asked, trying to see what the nurse's upside-down watch said.

'Almost eleven.'

'Oh my God,' said Susie. She suddenly remembered everything. Tilly. The flight. Rufus. 'Oh God, where's my son?'

'Gone to find his father,' said Mr Hobson. 'What is it, what's the matter?'

'I have to tell him something urgently. Very, very urgently. Nurse, could you – please – '

She lay back on her pillows, exhausted. The nurse on a nod from Mr Hobson hurried out of the room.

'Mum, what is it? What's wrong? Dad's just coming, he – '

'It's not me, Rufus, not Dad. Listen, you have to get to Heathrow fast.'

'Why?' said Rufus.

'You have to catch Tilly.'

'Tilly won't want to catch me. Or see me,' said Rufus flatly. For the first time Susie looked at him, looked at him properly. He was very white; he looked as if he hadn't slept.

'Rufus, she will. I know she will.'

'No she won't. Last night I wanted to talk to her so badly about – well, it doesn't matter what about – '

'Me,' said Susie quietly.

'Well – yes.'

'Rufus, I'm so – '

'Mum, I really don't want to talk about it. Sorry.'

'All right, darling. Maybe another time. Well, anyway, I spoke to Tilly this morning. When I couldn't find you. She was at her mother's house. She sounded very down. And she's going to New York this morning. In – in an hour. Rufus, you've got to stop her. You've got to explain things to her.'

'Mum, I told you, she doesn't want to hear. She doesn't want to see me any more.'

'Oh, I think she does,' said Susie. 'She may not quite know it but she does. And she loves you very much. And cares about you.'

'No she doesn't. She just wants to sign this bloody stupid contract.'

'Rufus, she does care about you. She told me so, and she doesn't actually want to sign the contract. But she will if you don't stop her. Rufus, darling, please, go and catch her. You should be able to, if you break a few speed limits.'

'I want to hear what Mr Hobson has to say.'

'Well then, will you go after that? Rufus, I'm beginning to feel very upset. That's bad for people after surgery, you know.'

'All right, Mum, all right, I'll go. After that.'

Mr Hobson came in with Alistair. Alistair looked very drawn. He sat down in the chair beside the bed and took Susie's hand.

She clung to it.

'Well now,' he said, 'the news is – what can I say?'

'Please say it,' said Susie.

'The news is – fairly good. It's not excellent, but it's good. The biopsy showed that the lump was benign; but some of the surrounding tissues have undergone changes which could lead to malignancy later on. In other words, it's something we need to keep an eye on, and long term we might need to consider a subcutaneous mastectomy – ' Susie caught her breath in swiftly, felt Alistair's hold on her hand tighten – Mr Hobson smiled, patted the bedclothes. 'It's not as bad as it sounds, it means in its simplest terms a mastectomy beneath the skin. Which means inevitably that reconstruction is a great deal easier, and you'd be surprised how good you'd look again. And that would remove any possible danger. But there's no hurry, you have plenty of time to think about it. I'm sorry you had to be so worried, but – '

'Oh dear God,' said Alistair. He stared at Susie, then got up and walked over to the window, gazed out. He doesn't know what to do, thought Susie confusedly, he isn't pleased, he's turned against me. And who could blame him? She herself felt nothing, nothing at all.

'Thank God,' said Rufus. 'That is just so wonderful.' He was looking down at her, and his expression wasn't hostile or angry, just very very happy.

'Oh, Mum, I'm so pleased, so relieved. Thank God. Listen, I'll go now, try and catch Tilly. Heathrow, yes?'

'Yes. Midday flight to New York,' said Susie dully, staring at Alistair's back.

'Bye, Mum. Love you.'

'I love you too,' said Susie quietly.

'Well,' said Mr Hobson, 'I must go. I'll pop in and see you later, Susie. Goodbye. Well done. You were very brave. Let us know if you want anything for the pain. Bound to be sore. Goodbye, Mr Headleigh Drayton.'

'Goodbye,' said Alistair. He sounded very strained. 'Thank you so much.'

He still hadn't moved. Mr Hobson went out, closed the door noiselessly behind him.

'Alistair,' said Susie, 'Alistair, please do go if you want to. You must be – '

'Oh Susie,' he said, 'oh Susie, I – '

And then he turned, and there were tears, tears pouring down his face, and he came over to her and sank onto his knees by the bed and took both her hands and kissed them.

'I love you so much,' he said, 'so very much. I didn't realize it, but I do. I thought we had – well, we both had – a – a marriage of convenience. Neat, functional, highly suitable. But I know now it wasn't that at all. Not for me at any rate. I couldn't have lived without you, Susie. I really couldn't.'

'But Alistair – '

'Don't,' he said, 'please don't. Don't start on it all. As long as I've got you, Susie, I don't care. I've been able to live with it all these years, and I'm sure I still can. As long as you're alive, as long as I have you. That's what matters. That's all that matters.'

'No, Alistair,' said Susie, reaching out her good arm, stroking his hair gently, wiping away his tears with her finger. 'No, it isn't all that matters. You matter very much and I don't deserve you. And I'm going to – '

'Don't,' he said again, 'please don't.'

'Alistair,' said Susie, with an effort so immense it startled her (but she had to begin, begin now putting things right, making it up to him), 'you're what matters to me now. You and making you happy. We won't ever talk about this again, I promise, but I just have to say one thing. I – did want some – something else. As you know. But now – well, I realize what I wanted wasn't what I'd thought it was. And that what I'd got was actually better. So that's it really. I'm sorry to have been so stupid. Sorry to have made you unhappy if I did.'

'You didn't,' he said quite cheerfully. 'In fact. I'm an uncomplicated sort of chap. I'd got so absolutely used to it. Had my own little arrangements of course. As I'm sure you knew. And you were always so extremely nice to me. Give me a kiss.' He leant over, kissed her on the mouth, very, very tenderly.

'And – Rufus?' said Susie.

'Rufus?' said Alistair, deliberately vague. 'My darling Susie, Rufus is old enough and ugly enough as they say to take care of himself.'

'He's not ugly,' said Susie defensively.

'You're his mother, you would say that. Anyway, he's got your looks and my brains, as GBS so neatly encapsulated it. And both of our happy dispositions. No doubt whatsoever about his genealogy.' He met her eyes with a look that said let us leave it at that. Forever.

'Well,' said Susie, taking her cue from him, 'I just hope he catches that plane and marries that gorgeous Tilly.'

'So do I. Then I shall die a contented man.'

'Don't talk about dying,' said Susie with a shudder. She felt terribly tired suddenly, tired and still emotionally in turmoil. She meant what she said: she would remove James from her life as resolutely, as thoroughly as Mr Hobson had removed her tumour. But he would not be as neatly removed from her thinking, from her heart; it would be hard, there would be struggles and pain and much confusion. She hoped she was equal to the task.

There was a knock at the door. The nurse stood there with an enormous bunch of roses. 'For you,' she said. 'Aren't they lovely?'

Susie looked at Alistair; he had got to his feet and was picking up his coat. The knuckles on his hands were white. He didn't look at her.

She looked at the card. 'For my darling,' it said, 'with all my love.'

'I'm sorry,' she said to the nurse, 'there's been a mistake. These aren't for me. Please send them back to the florist, and make sure the person who sent them knows that. Thank you.'

'But Mrs Headleigh Drayton – '

'Nurse,' said Susie, and was surprised at the firmness in her own voice, 'please take them away. I really really don't want them.'

Chapter Thirty-Two

James, 11am

'Really, James. Do you make a habit of rifling through other people's possessions?' said Julia. She was standing in the doorway; she looked from the letter in his hand to his face, and smiled, her carefully placed, dazzling smile. 'Perhaps I see now where Cressida got some of her unfortunate genes from – '

'Please don't insult my daughter,' said James.

'James, I have every right to insult your daughter. And I am hugely relieved that in the end I was able to save my son from a marriage that even he had become deeply unhappy about.'

'What the hell do you mean?' said James. He sat down again on the bed, drained his glass. It had helped; he walked over to the bar and poured another one.

'I've never seen you drink,' said Julia.

'You've never seen me in need of a drink before,' said James. 'Now, would you like to explain what this' – he shook the letter at her – 'was all about?'

'I would have thought it was self-explanatory,' said Julia. 'My father, God bless him, was deeply worried at the prospect of Cressida getting her hands on his money. He had left it all to Oliver, as you know, although held in trust until after my death.'

'I did, but I didn't think it was so very much,' said James.

'It was an enormous amount. We – he always tried to play it down, in fact it was quite a well-kept secret, but we're talking real money. We had even kept from Oliver how much was involved until after his twenty-fifth birthday. I think it's very bad for young people to get the idea that they don't need to work, or to make their own way in the world. But Cressida did know. I'm not sure how she found out, but she certainly knew. I think perhaps your extremely overpowering friend Mr Buchan might have told her. These millionaires all know one another, know what they're worth.'

'Why are you so convinced that she knew?' asked James.

'Because she asked Oliver about it. If he was really going to inherit that much money. He told me, he seemed slightly bemused by it, and by the fact that she knew.'

'Oh really? And when was this rather strange conversation?'

'A year ago. When she was staying with us at Bar Harbor.'

'I see,' said James. He felt slightly sick. 'Well anyway, I don't quite follow –'

'Oh James, really. Cressida was marrying Oliver entirely for his money.'

'Julia, I won't – '

'James, please be quiet. She didn't love him. She certainly had a bit of a crush on him, maybe last summer when she was staying with us, but no more than that. But she decided to marry him and she manipulated him into it. I could tell, the morning they announced that they were engaged, that he was uncertain, not quite happy, but he's so loyal, Oliver, such a gentleman, he would never admit it. I tried to get him to talk about it, but he wouldn't.'

'I think,' said James, speaking with difficulty, 'he is probably old enough to make up his own mind.'

'Oh really? How very naive of you, James. But then your marriage to Maggie has been so perfectly happy, hasn't it, you probably don't understand the complexities of lesser mortals.'

Shit, thought James, does she know about that as well? He took another slug of whisky. He was beginning to feel very strange.

'Anyway, gradually I discovered it wasn't just maternal anxiety. I was right. Your daughter was – is – a tramp, James. A slut.'

'Julia, please be careful what you say.'

'I shall say what I please. She had several – what shall I say – lovers. One of them in New York, while she was staying with us.'

'This is absurd. How do you know?'

'Because I followed her. There was just something about her. I was suspicious, once I had established that she knew about the money. And every other day she went off on long shopping and sightseeing expeditions, saying very charmingly, I have to say, that she liked to be alone. And of course she was extremely hostile to me. When we were alone. To the point of rudeness.'

'I can't imagine why,' said James dryly.

Julia ignored him. 'I tried to talk to Josh about it, but he wouldn't take any notice. Of course, he'll trust anyone with a pretty face and nice manners. So I followed her one day. She went down to Gramercy Park, spent the day in some man's apartment. I saw him open the door to her, saw her kiss him, go inside.'

'Julia, this is horrible. I'm not going to listen.'

'Nobody would listen to me. I tried to tell Oliver, after she'd gone home, but he just got angry. There was another incident as well, some nonsense about an attack. Josh thought I knew nothing about it, but the hall porter mentioned it, and I put two and two together, phoned the limo hire company. It wasn't very difficult. Finally I made Oliver confront Cressida next time he saw her. She denied it, of course, wept, stormed, said I hated her, that she'd kill herself if he didn't believe her, or walked out on her. He was still unhappy, but he was completely in her thrall, you know. Even though he didn't actually love her, she had some strange influence over him, he wanted to make her happy. She was a very emotionally powerful girl, James. And very neurotic of course. Before I despaired of her, I begged her to see my analyst – '

'Oh for God's sake,' said James, 'you and your analysts.'

'She agreed actually,' said Julia quietly. 'She went a few times, then said it was too much for her.'

'So you really expect me to believe that Oliver went ahead with this marriage, knowing that Cressida was sleeping around – '

'James, he didn't actually know it. Well, not until the end. He wouldn't know it. He blinded himself to it. And don't forget they weren't seeing a lot of one another. There was a lot of pride involved by then, pride and kindness, and an innate decency. Oliver is a very trusting, straight-forward person. There was nothing I could do with him. He got angry with me, told me it was I who was obsessed. He just kept saying "Mother, I'm going to marry her, I love her, she needs me." The more I tried to tell him, the less he believed me. Although I think at the end, when he knew about this pregnancy, he must have done. But by then it was too late. It was only days before the wedding.'

'And what makes you so sure, Julia, that it wasn't Oliver's baby?'

'James, it couldn't have been. You should know that. The dates don't make any kind of sense.'

James was silent, knowing she was right; remembering his own unacknowledged certainty of the night before.

'So – I realized there was nothing I could do. Except appeal to Cressida.'

'Which you did?'

'Yes, of course I did. And she did what she does with Oliver, cried, told me I hated her, that I was crazy, jealous because I was taking Oliver away from her. And then she said, and I'll never forget it, "Julia, you can't stop it now. You just can't. He'll never back out now. Never." So then I knew I had to try and do something myself. I just wanted to hurt her, to make this marriage less what she had hoped, stop her getting her hands on what she wanted. Stop her going down the aisle feeling quite so triumphant. I did think that way the marriage would be a lot less likely to last. If I couldn't stop her marrying Oliver, I could make sure she divorced him pretty damn quick. Which I was sure she would.'

'So you told your father he had to change his will?'

'Yes. I just don't know why I didn't think of it before. I went to see him, down in Palm Beach, and I told him everything, and he agreed to do it. He's a very – amenable old man.'

'I can see that,' said James, thinking of the almost psychotic adoration that the letter had exuded.

'And I thought I would just let Cressida know.'

'On the night before the wedding? That was unspeakable. Cruel.'

'Oh really, James. You can say that still, in the light of what she did to you? How blind you all are about her. She's rotten, James, thoroughly rotten. And you're all taken in by her, by that sweet little face, those charming little ways. All of you. Except maybe that old Merlin fellow. He seemed to see through her. Anyway, when I went up to say goodnight to her – maybe you'll remember – I showed her the letter. She just read it in silence, there was no reaction whatsoever, she just threw it onto the bed. And then she said "Goodnight, Julia" and went over to the dressing table and started cleaning her face. And I picked up the letter and went out, and that was the last time, thank God, I ever saw her. But obviously she decided after all that it wasn't worth it . . . .'

'No,' said James, slowly, 'even then surely she wouldn't have decided not to go through with the wedding. Surely. It's just – oh, I can't believe it, Julia. I can't believe any of it.'

Julia shrugged. 'Well, the facts speak for themselves, I think. I can only tell you that I think this is the happiest outcome. Under the circumstances. For us all. Even you. And of course you will remain quiet about it. About what I did.'

'Of course I won't,' said James. 'Why should I? I shall make quite sure that everyone knows – '

'Yes, James? Yes? Knows what?'

And then he realized that of course he would have to remain silent; that he was trapped into silence by the possible truth of the story, and indeed by what was unarguably the truth of much that had happened anyway: that Cressida had in fact run away, on her wedding day, to marry someone else, for whatever reasons, had betrayed and savaged them all, and the more of the story that could remain in obscurity the better.

'I'm going,' he said heavily. 'Home to Maggie. To tell her – I don't know what. Does – does Josh know about all this?'

'No, of course not. He's such a fool, James. He'd just start babbling it out. And he wouldn't understand. Nor would Oliver. Oliver is so much happier this morning. Really, James, you should be grateful to me. She is no loss to any of us. I know it's painful to recognize, but if she never comes back, that will be a very, very great blessing.'

'Julia,' said James, 'Julia, I don't know how you can even think that, let alone say it. You must surely know that to a parent a child is always welcomed, always loved, whatever it has done. We forgive our children anything, anything at all. If we are human. Which I begin to doubt you are. Goodbye, Julia. I hope we never have to meet again.'

Chapter Thirty-Three

Harriet 11.30am

'How about if I slept with you?' said Harriet pleasantly.

'I beg your pardon?'

'I said how about if I slept with you. You know, went to bed with you, had sex, that kind of thing. Would that make any difference? Change your decision?'

'Miss Forrest, I do assure you – that is, I – '

'Well, would it?' She smiled sweetly at him.

He was visibly flushed, beads of sweat on his pale forehead. He shifted uneasily in his seat. 'Miss Forrest – '

'I'm told I'm not entirely without talent in that area. It wouldn't be that bad – oh, Mr Carter, don't look so frightened. I find it insulting. Of course I'm not serious. Well, I don't think I am. I suppose if you'd agreed to a further two million I might have been. But I can see you wouldn't. Sorry, Mr Carter. Bad joke. Bad.'

Geoffrey Carter visibly relaxed. He wiped his forehead with his initialled handkerchief, eased his slightly over-floral tie. He had not enjoyed the past half-hour; the past half-minute had been very bad for him indeed. The training he had been given in business banking had just about equipped him for telling highly attractive and patently emotional young women that their business futures were over for the foreseeable future; what it had not equipped him for was to deal with sexual propositioning.

Harriet smiled at him. The past half-minute had quite cheered her up. 'I understand. You're only doing your job. And throwing good money after bad is clearly not what the bank would see as doing it. Oh well. What next?'

'Well, I'm afraid I have no alternative but to appoint a receiver.'

'And what precisely will he do? This receiver?'

Geoffrey Carter cleared his throat. 'Well, he'll arrive at your company some time later today.'

'Today!' said Harriet, thinking of her staff, her beloved, loyal, self-sacrificing staff, who had taken salary cuts, worked uncomplainingly harder as she laid the less vital amongst them off, refused, in two cases, tempting offers, who had no idea that this final awful thing was to happen. 'Why today? Why so soon? It's brutal. Horrible.'

'I'm afraid this is a rather brutal world, Miss Forrest. But, well, you see, the thing is that in some cases people have been known to dispatch their employees with equipment and other assests, such as company cars. Now I'm sure you wouldn't think – '

'What a good idea,' said Harriet cheerfully. 'I'd never have thought of that. Thank you, Mr Carter. Don't look like that, it's all right, I'm only joking.'

'Yes. Yes of course. And he will also want the keys to the building. He will lock it up, to safeguard it. We will also, of course, be calling in any personal guarantees, which includes your flat, and inform your debtors and creditors.'

'I have a lot of both,' said Harriet. 'And if the debtors had behaved a bit better I wouldn't be here now. Well, I might be, but – anyway, Mr Carter, thank you for at least listening to me. How long have I got?'

'No longer at all, I'm afraid, Miss Forrest. You are legally obliged to cease trading as from now. I'm sorry.'

'Mr Carter, you don't want to go to the toilet or anything, do you?'

'I beg your pardon?' said Geoffrey Carter. The sweat broke out again, this time under the armpits of his monogrammed cotton polyester City Style shirt.

'There's a last call I really would like to make. You don't have to pay for it, I have a charge card.'

'Well, I – '

'Please Mr Carter, you've drunk all that tea. Just a few moments – '

Geoffrey Carter began to feel he really did need the lavatory; a churning was taking place somewhere in his stomach. He took a deep breath. Harriet smiled at him encouragingly. 'Mr Carter?'

He stood up. She could have sworn he almost smiled. 'Miss Forrest, I will just go and – ask my secretary to get the receiver on the phone. I won't be more than a moment.'

'Thank you, Mr Carter. You're a star. I'll take you to lunch at the Caprice if – well, I'll take you anyway.'

Geoffrey Carter hurried out of the office; Harriet rang the studio. 'Kitty? It's me. Nothing from Cotton Fields?'

'No. I'm sorry, Harry. Nothing at all. Theo Buchan rang though. He's ringing back. What shall I – '

'Just tell him to go away and leave me alone,' said Harriet. She felt totally dispirited; her emotions resembled a foot that had gone to sleep, as Nanny Horrocks used to call it. In time, no doubt, the pain would start, shooting, agonizing pain, but just now she felt nothing, only a great swollen numbness.

Geoffrey Carter came back into the room, complete with secretary, presumably, she thought, more as chaperone than anything else. He looked at her warily, clearly nervous of what she might say or do next. 'Right, Miss Forrest. I presume you have no further – observations to make?'

'No,' said Harriet, 'none at all.'

'I think that's all then. I'll call the receiver now.'

'Yes,' said Harriet, 'er – thank you.' She sat staring at him, as he lifted the phone, wondered if she was actually going to throw up all over the desk. She picked up the file on his desk: her file, labelled 'Harriet Forrest – Harry's Fashion Retail Business', and the life of Harry's began to roll before her eyes, in painfully slow motion: the tiny shop in Wandsworth, the twenty-four-hour shifts she worked all on her own, her head aching, fighting sleep; the exhilaration of her very first sale, the rapture of reading her first editorial: 'Harriet Forrest's designs show a clean-cut originality, an extraordinarily daring sense of colour. Do go and visit her small treasure trove of a shop, Harry's, in newly fashionable Wandsworth High Street for coordinated casual classics . . .'

And then there had been the next shop, and the next, full of eager customers, and the shock of excitement at realizing she really did have something to offer that people wanted; and hiring staff, doing cash flows, more sleepless nights, raising money, putting it to work, feeling the ideas burgeon, grow, more shops, bigger shops, her own small factory, the design studio, her first modest show – oh, that show, with Tilly gliding down the studio, laughing, on the catwalk that the four of them, she and Tilly and Rufus and Mungo, had built right through the night, people clapping, actually standing up and clapping.

And then moving into Paris, Paris! home of fashion, the heady wonder of girls in Paris wanting, buying her clothes. By then there had been Theo too, taking hold of her life, turning it upside-down, loving her, driving her to all kinds of new intensities, making her happy as she had never been before, and disturbed and disorientated too, and then – shit – and then overreaching herself, getting into trouble. Real trouble. And it wasn't the fault of the clothes, her lovely, witty, charming, beautifully cut, perfectly coordinating clothes, nor of Theo for distracting her, taking her mind from its total concentration; it was her fault, her fault for being vain and self-important and egotistical. She had let them all down, everyone who worked for her, who had lent her money, encouraged her, praised her, supported her; failed them through her own foolishness. She deserved this, she thought, this moment of absolute misery and humiliation, deserved it well.

She looked at Geoffrey Carter and his secretary, and they were blurred, and so was the paper as she looked down at it, and a great tear fell on her file and smudged the label. 'Sorry,' she said, groping for a tissue, blotting at the paper, and had just wiped her face with the same tissue when Geoffrey Carter's other phone rang. She stopped, froze; it might, it just might be Cotton Fields. Miracles did still happen. Even to the un-deserving.

'Geoffrey Carter. Yes. Yes, she's here. I'll just see if – ' He looked at Harriet rather uncertainly. 'It's a Mr Buchan. Mr Theodore Buchan. He wants to speak to you.'

'Tell him I'd rather die,' said Harriet firmly, putting the file down.

'Miss Forrest can't speak to you at the moment, she's – oh, I see. Ah, yes of course. Yes. Miss Forrest, Mr Buchan says he would like to put the necessary money into your company. Er – will you speak to him now?'

'Tell him I'd still rather die,' said Harriet and turned and walked out of the office, feeling that just for one moment the whole dreadful thing had been worthwhile.

Chapter Thirty-Four

Tilly 12 noon

'I hope you're good at sweet-talking,' said the cab driver to Tilly. They were sitting in a traffic jam on the A4. Heathrow was two miles away; it might as well have been two hundred.

'I am,' said Tilly, 'but how long do you reckon now?'

'Well – I could try the back doubles, go round the back of the airport. If we're lucky, fifteen minutes. But there's no telling really, you never know in this game. And that'll be only fifteen before you fly.'

'That'll be OK,' said Tilly. 'I've phoned them, and I have an instant check-in gold card, you know? They know I'm going to be late. I've no luggage, it'll be fine. Yeah, try the back doubles. And just keep going, OK? Never say die, that's my motto.'

'Wish it was never say fly,' said the cabbie and spent the next five minutes patently enjoying his own joke. Tilly smiled politely and lit a cigarette; he turned round, looking pained. 'Don't do that if you don't mind, love,' he said, 'I'm a non-smoker, there's a sign up in the cab, and it makes me feel sick. Can't concentrate, you see. And with the passive smoking and all that, I don't want to – '

'OK, OK. Sorry,' said Tilly and stubbed it out again.

She didn't really feel calm, she felt sick and her head ached. What the hell was she putting herself through this for? Why was she tearing herself away from London, which she loved so much, and Rufus, whom she loved so much, to go and sign a contract to do a lot of boring things: beauty sessions were always the least fun, and there were going to be endless in-store events and God knew what else, personal appearances everywhere, videos: hell on earth. She must be mad.

'No, I'm not actually,' said Tilly aloud. 'I'm not.'

'What's that, love?'

'Nothing,' said Tilly and spent the next ten minutes rehearsing the reasons for her lack of madness: James Forrest's treatment of her mother, her intense, almost fanatical desire to be her own mistress, unarguably in charge of her own life, her recognition of Rufus's undoubted parentage, and finally, and probably most importantly, her total unsuitability to be Mrs Rufus Headleigh Drayton. She had to go: she had no choice. And she could help Harriet, give her some money, and she'd get over Rufus much more quickly and – and – God, she didn't want to go. She just didn't want to go. 'Fuck,' she said aloud. 'Sorry, Rufus. Sorry.'

The back double way was clear; but then the tunnel was jammed. 'You sure you've got this right?' said the driver. 'Sounds funny to me. Usually Terminal Four for the States.'

'Yes, yes, it's Air America,' said Tilly irritably. 'It's OK, we'll make it. Maybe I should get out and run.'

'Don't. You'll be had up.'

It was seven minutes to twelve when she finally shot into the departures terminal, tore over to the information desk. The girl was charmingly helpful. 'That's OK, Miss Mills, we've been expecting you. Just go right over to departures and through. Gate thirty-nine. Have a good trip.'

The man at departures was slightly less helpful and a lot less charming. 'Final call ten minutes ago,' he said.

'I'm sorry,' said Tilly, handing him her boarding card. 'I'm really sorry.'

'You should be, they're practically holding the plane for you.'

'I run fast. I'll make it. Here's my boarding card and here's my – shit, where is it, where's the bloody thing? Hold on, I have it, I have it, it never leaves this bag, it's here, it has to be . . .'

She turned the leather rucksack upside-down, shook the contents out onto the man's desk; her wallet opened, coins spattered everywhere, mingling with the chewing gum, the make-up, the cigarettes, Polaroids from recent sessions, the odd battered Tampax – it would have been funny if it hadn't been so awful. But no passport. For her passport, she realized, staring at the mess on the desk, must still be in Merlin Reid's Lagonda (placed, she remembered now, on the dashboard shelf as she rummaged for his second beer) and it was two minutes to twelve and she heard her name now on the tannoy: 'Would Ottoline Mills, passenger to New York on American Airlines Flight 279, proceed immediately to gate thirty-nine.' But the man was shaking his head, saying she couldn't proceed anywhere, not without a passport, couldn't go through, no, couldn't even try, it was more than his job was worth. And so it was that as Rufus Headleigh Drayton came haring into the terminal, knocking over an elderly Asian cleaning lady and picking her up with most uncharacteristic brusqueness, as he looked up and saw the words 'Flight Closed on Air American Flight 279 to New York' on the indicator, and as he uttered a loud roar of despair that made everyone in the vicinity stare at him, and draw their baggage and their children closer to them, Tilly Mills appeared before him as if in a vision, clutching what looked like the contents of an entire rubbish bin in her arms, and said, 'Fu – I mean good gracious, Rufus, what on earth are you doing here?'

They went and rescued his Porsche from a double yellow line (no warden, the fates were famously kind to Rufus) and drove extremely fast and in complete silence out onto the hideous wastelands of the A4, rather more slowly up to the concrete mountains of what the traffic officials call the elevated section of the M4, and eventually reached the long car park that is the Cromwell Road extension, where finally Rufus spoke.

'I still can't believe you did that,' he said.

'Did what?'

'Oh for God's sake, Tilly, do I have to spell it out to you?'

'Yes you do. Traffic's moving, Rufus.'

She got out a cigarette and lit it; Rufus sighed and wound down his window. 'You know I hate you smoking in the car,' he said, 'I hate you smoking altogether, but particularly in the car.'

'First the cab driver, then you,' said Tilly. 'I think I might get out and walk.'

'If you like,' said Rufus, glaring at her. 'Shall I stop?'

'You'd better,' said Tilly, 'if you're not going to hit the car in front of you.'

'Fuck,' said Rufus and hit the brakes just in time.

'I've never seen you in a temper before,' said Tilly thoughtfully.

'I've never been angry with you before.'

'But why, Rufus, why? Why are you so angry?'

'Oh for God's sake, Tilly. I can't believe you're that stupid. There are several things actually. First you just take this decision, all on your own, without consulting me, to sign this ridiculous contract and go and live in New York. Then you're so bloody full of your own problems you don't even notice I have some that I want to talk to you about. Plus you persist in this ridiculous obsession that a marriage between us couldn't ever work, when you really ought to see that I'm the best judge of that. It's outrageous, Tilly, the way you shut me out, just go on your own sweet way, do what you think is best. I'm absolutely fucking fed up with it.'

'Rufus,' said Tilly, 'that's the second time you've used that word in five minutes. I thought you hated it. You'll be smoking next.'

'I might be driven to it,' said Rufus.

Tilly was silent. She reached out to put the radio on; Rufus pushed her hand away. 'And don't do that either. I cannot face that bloody mindless rubbish you listen to.'

'Dear, dear,' said Tilly. She was beginning to find it all rather funny.

'And don't patronize me.'

'Rufus, I'm not patronizing you.'

'Yes you are. That's what all this is about. You deciding you know best for us without even consulting me. It's horrible. It's unkind and it's insulting. I hate it.'

'All right,' said Tilly, 'I get the idea. Rufus – '

'Just shut up,' he said, 'just don't say anything.'

'Where are we going?'

'To my flat.'

'Oh.'

She sat in silence for a minute, then with a sickening thud remembered Susie, Susie sick and frightened and going to hospital. 'Shit, Rufus, I'm so sorry. I'd forgotten about your mum. Is she going to be all right?'

'Yes, thank God,' he said, sounding more normal suddenly, more himself. 'Well, we think so. The surgeon is – what shall we say? – cautiously optimistic. Anyway – '

'And she didn't say anything about it before?'

'No.'

'Brave lady.'

'Yes,' said Rufus briefly.

His jaw was very tightly clenched, his eyes fixed determinedly on the traffic ahead. Tilly put her hand tentatively on his knee.

'Don't,' he said, 'don't do that. I can't stand it.'

'Rufus, I'm not at all sure I want to go to your flat. With you in this mood.'

'You'll do what I decide,' he said. 'For once. I spend my life doing what you say, having to abide by your decisions. And I've decided we're going to my flat.'

'Oh all right,' said Tilly meekly.

Rufus's flat was in Brook Green, ten minutes' drive from Chiswick Mall. Tilly had often teased him about being tied to his mother's apron strings. It was a very nice flat, charmingly furnished by Susie, kept spick and span by Susie's cleaning lady; for the hundredth, the thousandth time, looking round at the furniture (Victorian), the pictures (water-colours), the photographs (family groups, silver-framed), the gleaming wooden floors, the flourishing plants, Tilly wondered how Rufus could possibly imagine she could be moved into this world that he inhabited so easily and unquestioningly, its tribal customs so clearly defined, its tribal members so carefully initiated; and she decided also for the hundredth, the thousandth time, that she absolutely couldn't.

'Rufus, I really must phone Felicity. She'll be so cross with me.'

'Yes, of course.' He was still tense with rage. Tilly looked at him and then went to the phone. This was proving an extremely uncomfortable morning.

Felicity was cross: so cross Tilly was quite startled. 'The Rosenthal people have a reception committee laid on for you, and an incredible programme. It's appalling, Tilly, what am I going to tell them?'

'Felicity, I don't know. Tell them I got sick or something. I'm so sorry.'

'It's so unprofessional. So unlike you, Tilly. I just can't think what's got into you.'

'Felicity, I said I'm sorry. Anyone can make a mistake.'

'People being paid two million dollars don't make mistakes, Tilly. They just don't. Look, I'll see if I can organize a flight for tomorrow. Can you get your passport back by then?'

'Yeah, I – I think so.'

'OK, I'll call you later. Where are you?'

'Um – in Rufus's flat. You have the number. I'm really really sorry, Felicity.'

Felicity had put the phone down.

'I'll make some coffee,' said Rufus, 'but first I'd like to call the hospital again.'

'Of course.'

He made the call, looked at her slightly more cheerfully. 'She's fine. I said I'd go in later. She sent her love.'

'Ah,' said Tilly. Then, 'She's great,' she said carefully, 'I really really like her. I can see why you love her so much.'

'Yes, well. I – '

'What?'

'Oh, it doesn't matter.'

'Is your dad there with her?'

'Yes,' said Rufus briefly. Then he said, 'Actually, he's not my dad.'

Tilly was silent; she didn't say anything, anything at all, just looked at him, her face carefully blank.

'Excuse me,' he said, 'I'll just get that coffee.'

He was a while; he came back looking suspiciously moist-eyed, sat down on the leather chesterfield by the window.

Tilly went over, sat down, took his hand. 'Do you want to tell me about it?'

'Yes,' he said, and for the first time that morning he looked at her without hostility, without anger. 'Yes please, Tilly, I do.'

He told her: how he had heard his mother and James Forrest talking late the evening before, how he felt, shattered, betrayed, totally bewildered.

'I just can't believe it, Tilly, you know? I can't. She's always been so lovely, so perfect – '

'Nobody's perfect,' said Tilly evenly.

'She was. For me. And now – I just feel so disorientated. As if everything I thought, everything I knew, was wrong. I think if you told me the earth was flat I'd believe you today. And my father – I mean Alistair – oh God, I don't know, Tilly: how must he feel? Such a fool, so betrayed, how has he stood it all these years? I hate it all so much, it's so different from everything I thought – oh God, I'm not making any sense, am I? I'm sorry. But, oh Tilly, I needed you so much, to tell me what to think, what to do. And you weren't there for me, and I couldn't stand it.'

He stared at her, his eyes full of such bewilderment Tilly's own filled with tears. She reached out, touched his face very gently, leant forward, kissed him lightly on the lips; and all the time her mind was racing, flailing around, trying frantically to work out what what to say, what would best help him.

'Listen,' she said carefully, finally, 'listen. This is what I think. Which is not telling you what to think. I think your mother is just great. OK, so she's been unfaithful to your dad. That's not the biggest thing in a marriage. Not really. Your dad isn't a fool, he must have known. Don't tell me he didn't, Rufus, that really is like thinking the earth's flat. He must have known and he must have decided she was worth it. Which I think she most certainly is. It hasn't made her less good to you, has it? It hasn't suddenly meant all these years she hasn't loved you and cared for you and changed your shitty nappies – although I suppose Nanny did that for you – '

'Sometimes,' said Rufus with a faint smile.

'OK, and she wiped your snotty nose and drove you to your poncey school every day, and read you bedtime stories and made sure you knew the facts of life, and laughed at your jokes and listened to your troubles, and furnished this bloody place for you and made it so perfect it scares the fuck out of me. Didn't she, Rufus? It didn't stop her being brave enough not to tell you all about her cancer, and not making a fuss yesterday when she must have been shitting herself, sorry, Rufus, and it didn't stop her being out of her head because she didn't know where you were this morning. She's still the same person, nothing's changed – '

'Yes,' he said, 'yes, it has changed, of course it has.'

'Only if you let it. Listen. This time yesterday you were the nicest, cleverest, best-adjusted most – fuck it, sorry, Rufus, but I have to say it –

most decent person I ever met. Has that changed? Has it? Not at all. You're still that person, and it was your mother made you that person. Don't be too hard on her, Rufus. You don't know what made her do what she did. But she's never let you down. You or any of the rest of that spoilt tribe of yours. Which includes your father. Yes, your father, he's your father, he raised you, as they say where I come from, not that self-important, jumped-up – '

She stopped. Rufus was looking at her oddly.

'You don't like him, do you? James?'

'No,' said Tilly flatly, 'I don't. But I like him a lot better now I know he's your dad. How's that?'

'That sounds – interesting. Oh God, Tilly, I wish I could think it was all as simple as you make it, but – ' He got up, walked round the room in silence. He seemed filled with a feverish distress. Tilly watched, wishing as she had never wished for anything that she could help him, do, say something positive, something healing. He sat down again, took her hand, sighed, looking down at it. 'Maybe I will in time. Right now – oh God, I don't know, I just can't. See it that way. I can't have it how I want it, how I thought it was, and that's that. It's so bloody hard to come to terms with. I wish I had your pragmatism. Maybe you can teach it to me.'

'I would if I knew what it meant,' said Tilly.

Rufus laughed suddenly; he looked better, the colour had come back into his face. 'Oh Tilly, Tilly, why couldn't you have done this for me last night?'

'Because I'm a self-centred bitch,' said Tilly cheerfully. 'Rufus, could we possibly go to bed?'

She fell asleep briefly afterwards, worn out with love, with care, with soaring, singing, wonderful sex. She woke to see him sitting on the bed looking at her.

'I love you,' he said.

'I love you too.'

'Tilly, what happened yesterday? What happened, for God's sake, that you suddenly felt it – us – was so impossible? You've got to tell me, we've got to talk about it. It wasn't – it wasn't the contract, was it?' He gazed at her, his dark eyes full of pain; it was clearly what he most dreaded.

'No,' said Tilly, 'no, it wasn't the contract. Honestly.'

'Well, what was it then?'

Tilly looked at him. She thought of James Forrest, of how she had hated him for as long as she had been able to understand what he had done: of what he had put her mother through, of her grief and pain, her guilt and her ruined health, and what James Forrest could have done to make their lives easier, with a little compassion and generosity and honesty. She thought of her mother, toiling in the sweatshop, sewing sequins onto dresses for twelve hours a day, and she thought of the small plaque with 'Beatrice Mills' on it, all the result of bungling, of incompetence, of dishonesty and cowardice. And she thought of Rufus being the son of this man, and she hardly knew how to bear it.

'Well, Rufus, you see, it's very complicated,' she said. 'There's something – ' And then she thought of how much he must have endured himself, making the discovery about his mother, his father and the man he had always thought to be his father, the man he adored and idolized, and how he would feel if she added to the knowledge of his beloved mother's adultery by telling him that the man who was truly his father had done this awful thing to her and her family. And she knew she could never tell him, that it would be the depths of cruelty, brutal, awful cruelty, to tell him, she must not, could not do it; she sat there, staring at him, at the bewilderment, the pain in his eyes, and love held her silent, love helped her to lie.

'I suppose,' she said carefully and truthfully, 'I suppose I panicked. You know. I'm so frightened of getting married, Rufus, of having to totally belong to anyone, it isn't just that it's you, although a lot of it is that it's you – '

'Thanks,' he said, amusement and hurt mixing on his face.

'Please, Rufus, listen, try to understand.'

'I am listening, I am trying to understand.'

'OK. I just get so scared when I think of that degree of handing over. You know?'

'No,' he said, 'I don't know.'

'Look,' she said, taking his hand, 'look. It's all right now. I love you, you love me, we have a great time, we have wonderful sex, it's all perfect. What could anyone want more than that?'

'I want to know you're there for me. Always. I want you to know I'm there for you. That's what marriage is, in my book. A commitment. A total commitment. It's saying look, everyone, we're an entity. Not just two people having a good time.'

'That's what I'm scared of.'

'But why? What can go wrong?'

'Life,' she said, 'and if it does go wrong, I want to decide how to put it right.'

'And why can't we do that together?'

'Because I want to deal with life my way. It's so important to me, Rufus, to be able to do what I think best, and not have to ask, fit in, say "would it be all right if". I need to be in control. Of everything. To be able to run my life on my terms. I suppose it's seeing my mum all those years, not in control, forced to do awful demeaning things – '

'Tilly,' said Rufus gently, 'you're not seeing this thing straight. What took your mother out of control of your life was the sort of person she was. Not her situation. If you'd been in her position, you'd have got it all sorted in no time. You wouldn't have been doing demeaning things, as you put it. Whether you'd been on your own or not, had me, had a baby to care for or not. You'd have been running the dressmaking business or whatever it was, no time at all. And I'd have been standing on the sidelines cheering.'

'No, no, you don't understand,' said Tilly. 'You're being dense, Rufus.'

'Maybe I am. Try again.'

'Listen, you might not have wanted me to run the dressmaking business. Or you might have wanted it run differently from how I was going to do it. That's what I'm scared of. Having to fit in, compromise. Surely you understand that.'

'I do understand,' said Rufus, 'and it's you being dense. Stubborn. Stupid. And besides, Tilly, where does all that leave love? If you love someone, surely you have to fit in and compromise anyway. Because you care about that person, what they think, what they need. Is it really worth being able to run the whole world your way if you're doing it on your own, with no one to turn to when things get tough, no one to talk to at the end of the day, no one to care about, to care for? I just don't see the connection.'

'Well, you wouldn't,' said Tilly crossly, 'you're in control of your life, always will be.'

'Oh really?' he said. 'You say that to me now, when I'm falling apart, when I have all this wretched situation to cope with? Do you really think I can sort all this mess out on my own? Of course I can't. Maybe I can with your help. But not on my own.'

'That's what I mean,' she said in an agony, 'I don't want to be dependent. Even emotionally. Even on you.'

'But you have to be dependent when you love someone. You can't take them out of the equation, by refusing to commit yourself to them. Not if they're there at all. You can cut them completely out of your life, but that's the only way. And where's the sense in that, the happiness, keeping them at arm's length, not letting them near you? It just doesn't work. The only way you can be independent is never to care for anyone. Where's the joy in that, Tilly? It seems pretty sterile and miserable to me.'

'You don't understand,' she said again, growing angry now. 'You just don't.'

'All right, I don't. Let's leave that one for now. Let's look at the other nonsense, shall we? About this obsession that you're not good enough for me.'

'Not not good enough,' she said indignantly, 'just terribly different.'

'Wonderfully wonderfully different. That's good, it's healthy. I don't want to marry a clone. Which is what you seem to think. I want to marry *you*, Tilly. I love you and you love me. That's what matters.'

'No, Rufus, it isn't. What matters is what you are, how you are. And however I'm going to fit into all this. You need a proper wife, Rufus, someone who'll say all the right things, in the right accent to the right people. Not a jumped-up black girl from Brixton.'

'You are amazingly bigoted,' he said, smiling at her, 'and you're sounding so terribly out of date.' (Someone else had said that to her, what seemed like years ago: who was it, who was it?) 'You're not a jumped-up black girl from Brixton, you're one of the most beautiful women in the world. No contest, as you would say. And I have somehow managed to make you fall in love with me. You could have any man you wanted, and for some inexplicable reason you've settled on me. It's me that should be feeling panicky and scared. Not you. Now get real, Tilly, as you would also say, I think, and stop talking this bloody prejudiced rubbish.'

Tilly stared at him. 'But Rufus, you don't' – she said, and then she remembered who'd said these things earlier that day, her mother: 'We're in the nineties, Tilly, you're sounding very out of date.' And she remember something else her mother had said, that she should try to drop her obsession about James Forrest and what he had done. She sat there, thinking, very carefully and clearly, thinking about what Rufus had said, knowing it was quite possibly true, all of it, that love, real love as she knew she felt for Rufus, was worth giving up her independence for (albeit not without a fight, lots of fights, probably), that love could maybe even teach her somehow to be a good, supportive wife to him, even persuade her to give a dinner party once in a while, say the right important things to the right important people; but thinking too about the greatest reason for her inability to commit herself to him, the one she hadn't even known about twenty-four hours ealier, about James Forrest, who had dominated her life for so long; and she didn't want to let that go, let him go, let him get away with it, this monster of a man. It hurt, the very thought of it, it was like giving something away that had been important to her ever since she could remember. But then, she thought, was her mother right, saying that it was no longer important, that it was in the past, that no good could come of her pursuing him? Would it really help her, help any of them, publicly to humiliate James Forrest, castigate him in the press? Wouldn't it just hurt Rufus further, and her mother, and indeed herself? But – well – maybe – if – 'Shit,' she said aloud. 'Oh shit.'

'Tilly,' said Rufus, very gently, 'Tilly, please, please, Tilly, will you marry me? I love you so very much. And I need you so much too, more than ever now. You can't not marry me. And you can go on smoking and saying fuck and listening to that dreadful music and you can stay independent, go where you like, do what you like, make all the important decisions in our lives if you really want to, and you needn't have any babies, but please, please marry me.'

Tilly looked at him, in silence; and still she couldn't quite do it, couldn't quite give it all away. And after another moment or two a terrible sadness came into his eyes and he stood up, visibly withdrawing from her.

'You'd better go,' he said, 'I really think you'd better go.'

The phone rang, sharply; Rufus answered it.

'Hallo. Yes, she's here, Felicity. Hold on. It's for you,' he said to Tilly. His voice was very heavy.

'Hi,' said Tilly. 'What? Oh I see. Well – ' She looked at Rufus, and he was picking up her clothes from the floor where she had thrown them as she had feverishly dragged them off an hour earlier; he was folding them up very carefully and neatly, and then he suddenly sighed and sat down, hugging them to him, staring at them as if he was holding her for the last time, and 'Felicity,' she said, 'Felicity, I don't know quite how you're going to take this, but I've changed my mind. I'm not going to New York. Please tell them how sorry I am, will you? And – what? Oh, I see. Well, let's just put it this way, Felicity, I'm going to get married. Rufus, for fu – for heaven's sake, Rufus, that's a Joseph T-shirt you're blowing your nose on . . .'

Chapter Thirty-Five

Harriet midday

'I'm so sorry,' said Jennifer Bradman. 'How dreadful for you.'

'Thank you,' said Harriet. The morning had taken on a surreal air; she was having difficulty in properly realizing that the rather dazzling and glamorous Mrs Bradman, who did not conform too closely to the traditional image of a gynaecologist, was referring to Cressida's disappearance rather than the death of her company. 'It was – is – terrible actually.'

'Your parents must be so upset.'

'Yes, they are. We all are. And I'm here because – well, I'm just looking for clues really. To where she might have gone. And why. I know you're not supposed to talk to me but – '

'Oh, don't worry about that,' said Jennifer Bradman. 'This is an exceptional case. Besides, I won't be giving away any secrets, or indeed helping you very much, when I say first that your sister was a very mixed-up girl, and second I'm afraid I don't have the faintest idea where she is.'

'But she was – pregnant this time?'

'Oh definitely. About fourteen weeks. And wretchedly sick, poor girl.' She looked at Harriet sharply. 'Why do you say this time?'

'Because I found a letter from you, saying that she wasn't pregnant last year. That's how I found you. Not that any of us knew anything about it.'

'I see. That was a very strange thing,' said Jennifer Bradman. 'It was a genuine phantom, if that is not a contradiction in terms. They do happen, you know. She had every symptom, her periods had stopped, her breasts were swollen, she was being terribly sick – '

'She's always had a dodgy tummy,' said Harriet. 'Ever since she was quite a little girl. Anything remotely difficult and Cressida started throwing up.'

'Yes, well, it goes with the syndrome.'

'What syndrome?'

'Of a hysterical personality. Which is what I would say she suffered from. Did she have other health problems?'

'Oh God, yes,' said Harriet. 'She was allergic to dairy products, she could only wear cotton next to her skin, you name it, she had it.'

'Ah yes. And the dysmenorrhoea – painful periods – '

'Yes,' said Harriet, thinking of the countless dinners, tennis games, picnics, cycle rides that had had to be cancelled while Cressida lay white-faced, unarguably in pain, a hot-water bottle on her tummy, Maggie sitting by her, stroking her head. 'So – um, what happened with the phantom pregnancy?'

'Well, she was desperately upset. When it proved not to be a pregnancy. She came to me, telling me she and her fiancé were about to be married anyway – '

'This was last September or thereabouts?'

'Er – October,' said Jennifer Bradman, consulting her notes. 'She was just off to New York to see him anyway. She was excited, happy, in spite of feeling so wretched. But when I examined her, I found that in spite of the other symptoms her uterus was not at all enlarged. I did a test – negative. She broke down. Became actually quite hysterical. I couldn't understand it at all. She told me there was a history of infertility in her – in your family, that your mother had had to have all kinds of treatment before becoming pregnant, and she was terrified that the same thing was going to happen to her.'

'Total garbage,' said Harriet. She felt very angry suddenly, without being sure why. 'I'm absolutely sure my mother never had to have any kind of fertility treatment, and Cressida wasn't even engaged to Oliver then. She really is – oh, I don't know – '

'I can see this is all very hard for you,' said Mrs Bradman gently. 'As I told you, she has, I believe, a very complex personality. She displayed a lot of what I think the psychiatrists would call histrionic behaviour. Even this flying is a classic indication. Of a desire for escape, for getting away from everything.' She smiled at Harriet suddenly. 'It sounds very corny, I know, but it's true.'

'So what does that mean exactly? With relation to what happened yesterday?'

'It means, I would guess, that she simply couldn't cope with life. All of it. Not just with regard to yesterday, but to everything. Running away like that – I think again the technical term is a hysterical fugue.'

'You seem to know a lot about it,' said Harriet.

'Yes, well, I'm married to a psychiatrist. It tends to rub off. Oh dear, I'm rather aware I'm not being very constructive. I do wish I could help more. I wish I could have helped your sister more. I did suggest she had some sort of help, counselling perhaps, but she refused.'

'Really?' said Harriet.

'Yes. I even suggested she came to see me with her mother, or you – she spoke about you quite a lot.'

'Really?' said Harriet again, genuinely surprised, almost startled.

'Oh yes. She's terribly fond of you. She admires you a great deal. And I would say she's very – what shall I say? – overawed by you. By your success. She feels she has a lot to live up to.'

'I can't think why,' said Harriet, 'she was always the favourite, always the perfect daughter. Never in trouble.'

'That's not the impression I got. She seemed to feel herself a failure.'

'Well, that's absurd,' said Harriet, 'of course she wasn't. And she was making this wonderful marriage, everyone was over the moon about it, and her – '

'Miss Forrest,' said Jennifer Bradman, 'whether or not we are failures depends on our own self-perception, our self-image. And I would say your sister's self-image was not very good.'

'I see,' said Harriet slowly. Cressida seemed to be falling into fragments, in front of her eyes, re-forming differently, awkwardly.

'You see,' said Jennifer Bradman, 'this kind of thing, this running away, is very often a cry for help. An alternative to suicide if you like.'

'But – ' Harriet paused. She didn't really want to get into a complex discussion with the slightly daunting Jennifer Bradman, to confess to any more perfidy on Cressida's behalf, start telling her about the photograph, the other wedding.

'I'm simply trying to help you find explanations – understandable explanations,' said Mrs Bradman. 'The human personality, Miss Forrest, even at its most healthy, is a very complex thing. And Cressida's was not entirely heathy.'

'No,' said Harriet, 'no, I can see that. But – she didn't give you any indication that there was a problem with – with this pregnancy?'

'No, not at all. She seemed very happy about it. In spite of feeling so unwell. Mind you, the approaching wedding must have been something of a strain for her. Under the circumstances. Why do you ask?'

'Oh, nothing,' said Harriet. She suddenly felt sickened by the whole thing, wanted to get away from Jennifer Bradman and her reasonable, pragmatic approach. 'I just wondered. But you did say she was happy about it – '

'Oh, very happy. And her fiancé was delighted too, I understand. Hoping for a boy!

'Oh really?' said Harriet. 'I didn't know that. I don't think he did either.'

She reached Covent Garden just before one; her studio, converted from one of the old warehouses, was on the first floor, just off the central piazza. She stood outside it looking up, thinking how much she loved it, how much it meant to her, how it was truly home to her (and she was going to mind losing it a great deal more than she would her flat), and that this was the last time she would ever come back to it as hers, that in future it would be literally barred to her, the locks changed, strangers inside, and – 'Shit,' she said aloud, recognizing the car parked on the double yellow line outside her door, recognizing the large figure at the wheel, and turned away, ready to run, but he was out of it, had grabbed her arm.

'Harriet,' he said.

'Theo, go away.'

'Harriet, I just have to talk to you.'

'Theo, there's nothing to talk about.'

'There's a great deal to talk about.'

'No, Theo, there isn't. And let go of my arm, or I shall scream and have you up for assault.'

'The way London is these days,' he said, 'no one would take the slightest notice of your screaming. I'm certainly prepared to take my chance on it. I don't think I look too much like a rapist.'

Harriet looked at him: he was immaculately dressed, as always, his huge frame oddly elegant in a grey pinstripe suit, cream shirt, silk tie – even in her rage and misery Harriet found herself noticing the print of the tie, half floral, half abstract, thinking how good it was.

'That's a very naive remark,' she said coolly. 'Rapists come in all shapes and sizes, you know.'

'Yes,' he said, suddenly subdued, 'yes, I do know.'

There was an expression on his face Harriet had not often seen there; it was wretchedness. It was unlike him. Grief, fury, despondency, but not that absolutely dispirited near-defeated look. 'Please,' he said, sensing a softening, a concern, 'please Harriet, come and have lunch with me.'

'I couldn't eat lunch, Theo, I feel as if I shall never eat again. I probably will never eat again, I won't be able to afford it.'

'Oh don't be ridiculous,' he said, 'you'll rise again from this little heap of ashes you've made for yourself, and – '

'Theo, I didn't make it,' said Harriet.

'Yes you did. You have to recognize that, it's important. You overreached yourself, Harriet, overspent. You're a brilliant designer, but you're a bad businesswoman. I've seen the figures, don't forget. I'm ready to help, but I'm not prepared to heap sympathy upon you, because you don't actually deserve it. I stand by what I said to Hayden Cotton, you did massage those figures . . . a little . . .'

Harriet looked at him, then up at the window of her studio, thought of what she had endured that morning at the bank, what she was to endure that afternoon, and a violent rage swept over her. She wanted to hurt him, really hurt him; she knew then what the expression 'beside herself with rage' meant, for she stood beside herself and watched as she drew back her fist and hit him, hard, twice, in the crotch. She saw him wince, draw back; then 'I wouldn't do that again,' he said quietly.

'I will do it again,' she said, and did.

He reached out, took hold of her, put his arms round her and pushed her into the car, then, with a speed extraordinary in so large a man, ran round to the other side, started the engine and drove off down Floral Street at some speed. He had been right, she thought, about people's reaction: most of them had hurried carefully past, a few had stopped to watch interestedly, a couple had laughed, but nobody had been even remotely near to coming to her aid.

'That was a foul, filthy thing to do,' he said. He was obviously in pain; he was white, his jaw set.

'So was what you did to me. Stop this car, Theo, I want to get out.'

'I will not stop it.'

'You have to. There's a red light ahead,' she said, looking at the traffic lights at the bottom of Bedford Street where it met the Strand.

'Fuck the red light,' he said and paused briefly to check, then drove through it, turning left up towards Fleet Street and the City. There was a screech of brakes; a van driver swerved violently to avoid him. 'Bloody wanker,' shouted the driver, his face distorted with rage, 'bloody great poofter, look where you're bloody going.' Theo ignored him, put his foot down, drove through the next lights (orange) and extremely fast round the Aldwych.

'Theo, for Christ's sake, you'll get arrested,' said Harriet.

'Oh shut up,' he said. 'Just shut up. Leave me alone.'

They had swerved back into the Strand, and were crossing Waterloo Bridge when a policeman came up behind them on a motorbike, blue light flashing, and waved them over to the side. Theo wound down his window resignedly.

'Yes?'

'Did you realize you just drove through a red light, sir?' said the policeman. He looked about sixteen years old.

'Yes, of course I did,' said Theo. 'I'm extremely sorry, I was in appalling pain and I really wasn't concentrating.'

'I'm sorry to hear that, sir. Would you mind telling me the nature of this pain, sir?'

'Yes, certainly,' said Theo. 'This young lady here had just punched me in the balls.'

Harriet looked at him in total disbelief.

'Is this true, madam?'

'No! Well – yes. Yes, I suppose so. In a way.'

'Harriet,' said Theo, 'you can't punch someone in the balls in a way. Either you do or you don't.'

'Was there a problem, madam? Was the gentleman making a nuisance of himself?'

'Er – no,' said Harriet hastily. Much as she hated Theo, she didn't actually want him had up for sexual assault.

'Not threatening you in any way?'

'No. Not really.'

'Do you know the gentleman well then, madam?'

'Yes,' said Harriet, wearily, 'very well. Too well.'

'So it was just a straightforward argument, was it, madam? Which caused you to strike the gentleman?'

'Not straightforward,' said Harriet, with dignity, 'but an argument, yes.'

'It's very dangerous to engage in physical violence with the driver of a moving vehicle, madam. I'm sure you must realize that.'

'Look,' said Harriet, seeing she was rapidly becoming the culprit rather than the victim in this exchange, 'he wasn't driving at the time.'

'He wasn't?'

'No.'

'What were you doing, sir?'

'Standing by my car. Talking to her.'

'I see, sir. So you were able to get into your car and drive it away. You were not incapacitated?'

'No, not entirely.'

'And you got into the car beside him, madam?'

'I was pushed into the car,' said Harriet, 'and driven off. Abducted, I would imagine the word would be.'

'I see,' said the policeman. He was clearly out of his depth; he looked rather less than sixteen. 'Do you have your driving licence on you, sir?'

'Yes,' said Theo gloomily. He produced his wallet, took out his licence.

The policeman got out his notebook and started filling in what seemed to be a very elaborate form. Harriet sat staring straight in front of her; the sense of total unreality the day had taken on had intensified dramatically. Surely, surely, she thought, I shall wake up in a minute, find it's all perfectly all right, that it's yesterday morning, that Cressida's in the next room, that Mummy's bringing us both a cup of tea . . .

'If I could just have your name and address as well, madam. You may be needed as a witness.'

Harriet gave him her name and address. It certainly wasn't yesterday, and she wasn't dreaming. It was today and she was very much awake . . .

'Right,' said Theo, as they pulled round onto the Embankment, 'now let's have lunch.'

'There's nowhere decent to have lunch round here,' said Harriet sulkily, 'and I don't want to have lunch with you anyway.'

'There's the Tate,' said Theo, 'restaurant there. Very good wine list. How would that be?'

'Theo, it wouldn't be at all. I'm not coming.'

'We'll have a bottle of the Bollinger,' said Theo, handing back the menu to the waiter, 'and just some smoked salmon and scrambled eggs. Thank you.'

'How do you know I just want smoked salmon and scrambled eggs?' asked Harriet irritably.

'Because I know you so terribly well. Intimately would not be an inaccurate description. Look at me.'

She looked at him. His almost black eyes were probing, intense. She felt a distraction from herself and her misery, a faint turning to him; memories stirred, physical memories. She looked resolutely away, pushed back her hair.

'I felt that,' he said, quietly, gently.

'Felt what?'

'You know.'

'Theo, I don't know. I don't know anything any more.'

'You look tired,' he said.

'I feel tired. Terribly tired. It's been a fairly shitty twenty-four hours.'

'It has indeed.' The champagne arrived; he tasted it, nodded to have it poured. 'Drink it, Harriet. It will do you good.'

She drank obediently; the champagne hit her bloodstream, lifted her awareness.

'That was terribly painful,' he said, suddenly more light-hearted, 'what you did to me back there. It's like being hit all over, you know, very hard, very deep down. Did you realize that?'

'No, but I'm glad,' she said briefly. 'That's exactly how I felt when I heard about you. Telling your friend about me massaging the figures.'

'Well,' he said, 'we'd better leave that one for now.'

'Fortunately for you,' said Harriet, 'you can. You don't know a lot about humiliation.'

'Now there you are mistaken,' said Theo, refilling her glass. 'I was well and truly humiliated about – oh, twelve hours ago. Do you want to hear about it?'

'No.'

'I think you should. Sit quietly and listen.'

'Well,' said Harriet, 'good for Sasha.' She was shovelling smoked salmon into her mouth with some relish.

'Yes, I suppose so. I suppose, too, you think I deserved it.'

'I certainly do.'

'Well,' he said with a sigh, 'I expect you're right.'

'Are you upset? That she's gone?'

'No,' he said and sounded faintly surprised, 'no, I'm not upset, I find. Not in the least.'

'Why not?'

'Because,' he said very quietly, 'because I still love you.'

'Oh Theo, stop it. Stop it, stop it.'

'Why?'

'Becasue it's pointless. And stupid. And insulting.'

'Why insulting?'

'Because if you still loved me, you shouldn't have married her.'

'I know that. But – '

'Yes?'

'I had to do something,' he said more quietly still, 'to ease the pain.'

'Oh for God's sake, I can't believe you said that. That you married someone you didn't love just to get over someone else. You're so self-centred, Theo, so appallingly, childishly, self-centred.'

'I know, I know.'

She wasn't looking at him. 'The universe revolves round you, doesn't it, Theo?'

'I'm working on making it that way.'

She looked up sharply; his eyes were amused. 'It isn't funny.'

'I didn't mean to imply it was.'

Harriet gave up.

'Sasha knew,' he said.

'Knew what?'

'About us.'

Harriet felt very odd; she stared at him, trying to take in what he had just said. 'Who told her?'

'Cressida.'

'Oh God,' she said and burst into tears.

'She was so awful,' she said, 'so awful. I can't believe how awful she was.'

They had left the restaurant and were sitting in the gallery with the Degas; Harriet was gazing determinedly at the sculpture of the little ballerina and moving determinedly away from Theo every time he tried to get closer to her.

'I've learnt so many terrible things about her. It's as if she was someone else altogether, another woman, someone none of us really knew. Living a secret life, an appalling secret life, all lies and cruelty. It's horrible. Poor Oliver, poor poor Oliver. She was pregnant, you know, but not by him – by this man in Paris, I suppose. Who knows? The one she's married to. Or isn't married to. Who knows that either? And last year she told Oliver she was pregnant and she wasn't. I don't understand it, Theo, I really don't. How could she have done all that, Theo, lied to us all, to me, to you, to Oliver, and especially to my parents, who loved her so much? The gynaecologist said she was a hysterical personality, she said even the flying was – what was it? – oh yes, symptomatic of her condition, and I was beginning to think the same, to be sorry for her, but now you've told me that, I think she was just vile.'

'Maybe a bit of both,' said Theo mildly. 'What gynaecologist?'

'Oh, the one she was seeing. I found a letter in the pocket of a cardigan. I went to see her this morning. She was very nice. Tried to make me see Cressida as sick rather than bad, but I –'

'She must be,' said Theo.

'She's not,' said Harriet fretfully, 'and don't you start feeling sorry for her. I couldn't bear it. She's done that all her life and –'

'Harriet, if she is sick, if she is psychiatrically disturbed, it does put a very different complexion on all this. Explains it to an extent.'

'Not to me,' said Harriet. The latest disclosure about Cressida had re-formed her yet again in her mind.

'How would you feel if she came back?'

'I don't know, but I hope she never does. I honestly think I'd kill her if she did. I learnt something else about her the other night, something my mother told me. You know my puppy, Biggles, remember?'

'Yes,' he said gently, 'of course I do, of course I remember.'

'It was her fault all along. She opened the gate deliberately, so he could get out, could be run over. She – '

'Harriet, I can't believe that – '

'You have to believe it,' she cried, and was startled at the anguish in her voice. 'You have to, because I always knew in my heart that that's what happened. She told my mother that it was an accident, that she just forgot, but of course it wasn't. She hated me and she wanted to hurt me. It was – '

'Harriet, Harriet, don't – '

'Don't what?' she said. 'Don't mind? Don't blame her? Don't reproach her? Theo, you don't understand, you just don't understand the

385

wickedness of her. I suppose it's not surprising really. She could twist you round her little finger more easily than anyone. Bat those long eyelashes at you – '

'Oh shut up,' he said wearily, 'don't be so bitter, Harriet. It won't help.'

'Oh really,' she said, angry again, 'how can I not be bitter? I feel so betrayed, so – oh, this is ridiculous, I don't know what I'm doing even sitting here talking to you. You of all people.'

'Harriet,' he said, and his voice was heavy with emotion, with pain. 'Harriet, I of all people probably know you best, understand you best, love you best. It is me of all people you should be talking to.'

'No, Theo, it isn't.'

She got up, walked over to the little ballerina, stood looking at her, at her awkward grace, her almost simian beauty, the stalklike neck, the hands clasped behind her back; he followed her over.

'Harriet, please – '

'No,' she cried, loudly, passionately hostile. The gallery guard looked at her, raised his eyebrows warningly; she felt herself flush. 'I have to get back,' she said, 'please take me. The man from the receiver's office will be there, impounding all my stuff. If you remember.'

'Harriet,' he said, 'let me help you at least. Let me give you the money. Sorry. Lend you the money. At very stiff terms if you like. You should be able to buy the company back from the receiver, you know. Let me do it for you. Please.'

'Theo,' she said, 'you really don't understand me at all, do you? Don't know what I want. Of course I won't take your money, of course I won't let you help me.'

'Why not?'

'Because,' she said, 'because then you'd have won. Beaten me. Forced me to do what you want. And I meant what I said to the bank manager. I really would rather die. Now please, Theo, leave me alone. I don't want you. Or anything you might possibly do for me. Is that really so beyond your comprehension?'

'Harriet,' he said, very quietly now, putting his hand out to touch her, then dropping it again in an oddly helpless gesture. 'Harriet, please don't do this. Please. I love you. I love you more even than I ever knew.'

There was a very long silence, while she stood there, staring at him, thinking, remembering love, Theo loving her; physically shaken by the force of her longing for it, yearning for it, for him.

'Please,' he said again, absolutely still, 'please, Harriet. I want you so.'

It was that word that changed it, changed everything; that one word, *want*. That was the whole thing about Theo, the key to him: he wanted, and he had to have. Houses, land, works of art; cars, planes, horses; companies, people, power; women, sex, love. And she would not, couldn not, join his catalogue of possessions, of things he wanted, and thus of things that then belonged to him.

'Theo,' said Harriet, 'you don't know anything about love, I'm afraid. Anything at all.'

She turned then and left him, ran out of the room and out of the front door, down the steps of the Tate, hailed a taxi, got into it, managed not to look back, despite a dreadful yearning just for the sight of him, until they were driving quite quickly away from the gallery, away from him, away from comfort, from help, from love. When she did, he was walking down the steps, his hands in his pockets, his head bent, utterly dispirited, looking drained, bereft of power and strength.

'Bastard,' said Harriet aloud. 'Fucking bastard.'

Then she burst into tears.

Chapter Thirty-Six

James 1pm

The house was terribly quiet, its stillness a tangible, heavy thing. Everyone had gone, even Janine and Merlin. James sat in his study, trying to recover just a little from the previous hour before going to find Maggie, to talk to her, to tell her what? That her beloved daughter was a manipulative promiscuous monster, greedy, ruthless, using her, using all of them, careless of their feelings, their love, their concern for her, heedless of their humiliation, their pain. He tried to remember her as she had been, only thirty-six hours earlier, her sweetness, her thoughtfulness to him, the way she fussed over him, so patently enjoyed his company, asked to go for walks with him, loved to hear about his work, how she would sit on the arm of his chair, chatting to him, as Maggie and Harriet never would. Remembered how proud of her he had always been, how he loved to show her off to friends and colleagues, how deep-down sad he had been at the thought of losing her to Oliver, to her new life, three thousand miles away. Remembered her charm, her lovely smiling prettiness, her grace; and yes, of course he loved Harriet too, was desperately proud of her, admired what she had done, could do, but Harriet was different – Harriet was tough, clever, ambitious, self-sufficient; she didn't need an adoring, protective father.

There was a collage of pictures of Cressida on his desk that Maggie had made for him once: a snapshot of her life, composed of many snapshots: Cressida lying in Maggie's arms in the hospital, Cressida toddling across the garden, her fair curls haloed round her face, Cressida in her school uniform, in tennis clothes, in party dresses – the frillier the better she liked them, unlike Harriet who had always chosen plainer, starker clothes – Cressida blowing out candles on her birthday cake, sitting by the Christmas tree, building sandcastles, in her first grown-up party dress, on Theo's yacht, and his favourite picture of all, the two of them together, him and her, walking arm in arm along a wintry beach somewhere, laughing, their hair blowing in the wind.

And as he looked, as he tried to equate her with the person he now knew about, he realized she was gone, gone forever and the pain in his heart was as great, greater even, than if she had truly died, if she was lying in front of him white and still. He had lost her, lost her completely; she was no longer his child, and he buried his head in his hands on the desk and started to weep.

The phone rang, sharply; he sat looking at it, lacking the strength even to reach out and pick it up. It stopped again, after a few rings. Maggie must have answered it. It was probably yet another well-meaning friend, another well-wishing enquiry. It was so kind of people to phone, so kind, and so appallingly, stupidly insensitive. Well, it looked as if Maggie would be able to cope with some of it at least today; her sleep must have done her good. Poor Maggie: poor hopeless hapless Maggie. He should be grateful she was so hopeless and so hapless, he supposed; otherwise she would be demanding her own life, revenge, recompense. As it was, she accepted it all, accepted her role, did what he needed her to do, in return for a home, security, status, and a life she managed, although God knew how, to enjoy. He supposed it was much the same for Alistair, in a totally different way: if he did know anything, suspect it even (and James felt he must, although Susie swore he didn't), he presumably preferred the status quo, the unarguable value of a beautiful charming wife who ran his home and his life, was the perfect consort and mother. Why exchange those benefits for scandal, disruption, hideous expense? He was not in love with Susie, never had been: theirs was a shining, exemplary version of the marriage of convenience. God, he hoped Susie would come back to recognizing the value of the same thing; he had been badly shaken by her demands. His mind (distracted briefly by the events of the morning) returned to the nightmare of Rufus, the new but already familiar panic rising and falling in his chest. He stared out of the window, thinking about it, about Rufus, and into his head came the memory of a survey done on inherited characteristics in Birmingham or some such place, that over half the children were fathered by men other than their mothers' husbands: they'd had to abandon the survey for that very reason. He clung to the memory, finding it oddly comforting, easing his panic. Maybe he was overreacting, maybe Rufus and his generation were overfamiliar with such things, had grown up in such knowledge that he would take it all in his stride, maybe Maggie, Alistair, Harriet, the other children would just laugh – 'Christ,' he said aloud, shocked at his own crassness, 'Christ Almighty, James, what are you thinking about – '

Suddenly, desperately, he wanted Susie, wanted to hear her voice, know how she was, tell her he loved her. He dialled the Princess Diana Hospital on his own line; he couldn't have Maggie picking it up in error, listening to him.

'Could I speak to Mrs Headleigh Drayton? In room fifteen. This is James Forrest again.'

'I'll see. One moment please, Mr Forrest.'

He waited, seeing as he waited Susie's lovely face, her soft dark eyes, heard, before she spoke, her pretty, husky voice. Christ, he was missing her already.

'Mr Forrest?' It wasn't Susie's voice. It was the receptionist again. 'Yes?'

'Mrs Headleigh Drayton says she can't speak to you, I'm afraid. She's very tired.'

'I see,' said James. He felt a slug of shock. Susie had always wanted to speak to him, however exhausted: hours after the birth of all her children, immediately after the funeral of her mother, leaving the deathbed of her father, she had been on the phone, wanting him, wanting the comfort of him. 'Are you sure?'

'I'm quite sure, Mr Forrest.'

'Did she send any message?'

'No, Mr Forrest.'

'Is Mr Hobson there?'

'Yes he is. I'll put you through.'

'Martin? James Forrest.'

'Ah, James. Good to hear from you. How's things? Surviving dear Mrs Bumley's reforms, are you?'

'Don't start me on that,' said James. 'I might get violent. Er – Martin. You operated on an old friend of mine this morning. Well, an old family friend. Susie Headleigh Drayton. I – can't get hold of Alistair and she's tired of course. I just wondered if she was OK.'

'Yes, she's absolutely fine. Well, almost, I'm happy to say. She'll give you the details, no doubt. Pretty woman, liked her. I thought the husband was with her as a matter of fact. They were holding hands like a couple of teenagers a bit earlier. Gives you hope, that sort of thing. Shall I ask him to ring you if I see him?'

'No, no, it's all right,' said James hastily. 'I'm just going out. Thanks anyway.'

'That's OK, old chap. You going to that conference in Bournemouth next month? The one on pre-malignancy? I'm presenting a paper. Try and make it. Should be quite a good bash.'

'I'm not sure,' said James. 'Thanks anyway, Martin. Goodbye.' He put the phone down: it rang again almost immediately.

'Mr Forrest? This is Crowthorne's Florists here. Mr Forrest, there seems to be some confusion about the flowers you ordered for Mrs Headleigh Drayton. At the Princess Diana Hospital. The hospital have just asked us to query the order with you. Apparently Mrs Headleigh Drayton sent the flowers back. Insisted they were not for her. We wondered if we had the right Mrs Headleigh Drayton, or even the right hospital?'

James felt very sick suddenly. 'Oh, no,' he said, 'must have been my mistake. Tell – tell the hospital to keep them anyway, put them in reception or something. Goodbye.'

The feeling of panic was increasing. Cressida, Rufus, Susie. Christ, what was happening to him, to his well-ordered life? His head was beating extremely hard; it almost hurt. The pain reached downwards, towards his churning stomach. He felt very physically shaky, and horribly near tears again. He thought how wonderful the drink he'd had earlier had been, and longed sharply, desperately for another.

'God,' he said aloud, throwing back his head, closing his eyes. 'God help me.'

Dimly in the distance he heard the phone ringing again. He could not, would not answer it. He couldn't take any more. He sat, his hands clasped tightly together, trying to stop his teeth from chattering. His legs were shaking violently. The ringing stopped: Maggie had obviously answered it. Thank God. He lit a cigarette, drew on it heavily. He didn't often smoke, maybe once a week, after dinner. It helped.

He had stubbed out the second before Maggie came into the room. She was smiling; she looked radiant. James stared at her.

'What is it?' he asked. 'What's happened?'

Maggie sat down, and just looked at him, her eyes bright, studded with tears. Happy tears. 'That was Cressida,' she said simply.

'Cressida! What do you mean it was Cressida?'

'It was Cressida. She phoned. She's in Paris. We had a long talk.'

'Oh for Christ's sake,' he said, 'what did she say? What is going on, I don't – '

'Nothing's going on,' said Maggie, 'except that she is ill and frightened and terribly terribly upset. She needed to talk. I think I helped her a little. She is desperately sorry about it all.'

'Well, I'm so glad to hear that,' said James. Rage was flooding him, hot, dangerous. 'Absolutely delighted. She walks out on a wedding and a husband and a family and terrifies us and humiliates us but she's terribly terribly sorry about it. Well, that makes it perfectly all right then, doesn't it? Let's all relax and hang out the welcome home banner.'

'James, don't. You don't understand.'

'Oh really?' he said. 'Is that right? Well, I don't think you can make me understand, Maggie. Not just now. I don't think you can even make me want to understand. As far as I'm concerned, Cressida is – '

'James, listen! Please. She's desperate.'

'All right,' he said, 'all right, I'm listening. But not exactly sympathetically. If she's desperate that's fine by me.'

'James, she's pregnant. Well, we knew that – '

'Yes, we did.'

'It – it isn't Oliver's. She – she's in love with someone else.'

'Oh, right. So far I'm not bowled over with sympathy by this story.'

'James, please. She never wanted to marry Oliver. She felt under tremendous pressure, poor darling. He was so passionately in love with her, and she thought she was with him. By the time she realized she'd made a mistake it was too late. Everything was planned, everyone was so happy, she didn't have the heart to pull out.'

'Well, bully for her.'

'James, try to understand. You know how sensitive she is, how she can't bear to hurt anyone. Well, early this year, she met this man in Paris. Fell passionately in love with him. She tried to break off with Oliver, but he was beside himself. She just didn't have the heart to do it to him.'

'Why didn't she talk to us?'

'She said she did try, again and again, but it always seemed impossible. The arrangements were going ahead so fast, we were all so excited, you'd spent so much money, and she just got deeper and deeper in the mire. I feel so dreadful, James, that she had no one to turn to, no one understood how desperate she was. What kind of a mother am I, to fail her like that? To make her think a wedding was more important that her happiness?'

'A foolish, gullible one, I should think,' said James, but a stab of hope, a faint stirring of relief was rising in him. Maybe, just maybe Cressida wasn't so bad, maybe Julia had been lying, it was possible, maybe the letter had had nothing to do with it.

'Anyway, early in May, she broke off with this man in Paris. His name was Gérard. Gérard – ' She looked down at a piece of paper in her hand; there was a name written on it, over and over again. 'Gérard Renaud. He's a writer of some kind. A journalist.'

'Really?'

'Yes. Anyway, she told him she had to do the right thing, go ahead, marry Oliver. She still didn't realize she was pregnant then, you see. She thought she would be able to cope, that it was an infatuation she was going through, a sort of last fling, that she would settle down and be happy with Oliver. Gérard was heartbroken, but he understood. He went away, on some assignment his paper sent him on, to South Africa. He was gone for weeks. She couldn't trace him.'

'Not through the paper? How extraordinary.'

'No. Oh James, I don't know. Stop putting me in the witness box. And when she discovered she was pregnant she just didn't know what to do.

She panicked, she arranged a termination but she couldn't go through with it. Oh James, why couldn't she have come to us, why couldn't we have been there for her?'

'We were there for her,' said James grimly.

'Not enough. So then she – she told Oliver the baby was his.'

'Poor old Oliver.'

'Yes. Yes, that was bad of her. Of course I agree. But she was frightened, feeling so wretchedly unwell – '

'Maggie, not even you should be falling for this garbage. And she didn't look unwell – '

'James, she was. She was so terribly pale, and tired-looking. And she has got very thin. You know the dress had to be taken in. We all thought it was exhaustion and nerves and of course all brides lose weight. I swear to you it isn't garbage as you call it. You didn't speak to her, you didn't hear her voice. She was beside herself with remorse, with guilt – and there's something else – '

'Yes?'

'Very late on the night before the wedding, this man – this Gérard – phoned her. I do remember a call. I was half asleep. He was back in Paris. He said he had to speak to her, he had something to tell her. Something dreadful, that she had to know.'

'His story wasn't going to be published? Oh all right, I'm sorry, what was it?'

'He's ill, James. I mean really ill. He has leukaemia. He'll probably be dead in three months, certainly six. He told Cressida he wanted to see her just once more. He said he could wait until after the wedding but – well, that was the last straw, she said. She had to be with him, for the time they had left, had to let him know about their child, had to care for him.'

'But Maggie – '

'She said she felt she had absolutely no choice. She had to go. She said it was as if she became someone else, watching herself. She said she felt fate had stepped in and saved her from something she knew anyway was wrong, terribly wrong.'

'So why couldn't she have come to us, talked to us, told us what she was going to do? Spared us at least some of the misery, the anguish – '

'I asked her that. She said she knew that if she even just began talking to us she'd find herself weakening, giving in. And she'd written the letter, don't forget. I know it got lost, but she thought we'd find it much earlier and we wouldn't be so worried. That wasn't her fault.'

'No,' said James. 'No, I suppose it wasn't.'

His mind was whirling. Who should he believe? He wanted to believe Maggie, Cressida; the story was so wild, so absurd it almost made sense.

Almost. On the other hand, it was very carefully constructed, perfectly designed to melt her mother's heart. But then – what of Julia's version? She surely wouldn't have made that up. It was too checkable. The opposite of carefully constructed. But then, maybe – maybe Julia herself was mad. Knocked off-balanced by a psychotically overprotective adoring father, herself overpossessive and protective of her own son. Josh had said himself she could hardly be described as well adjusted, was permanently in analysis. She might well have shown Cressida the letter and Cressida would simply have shrugged it off.

'Did she – ' his voice cracked, he cleared his throat, started again – 'did she say anything about Julia?'

'Julia? No, why should she? What did Julia have to do with it?'

'Oh,' he said, his voice as casual as he could manage, 'oh, nothing really. I just wondered. Julia said something about her seeming upset when she went up to say goodnight to her.'

'Julia is about as perceptive as a rhinoceros,' said Maggie. 'I really don't think she – '

'No, all right. So what's happened? Where is she?'

'She's at Gérard's flat. In Paris. She's alone, he's gone back into hospital for more tests. She's desperately worried, she just wanted to talk to me.'

'I'd like to talk to her,' said James grimly. 'Give me the number, would you?'

'No, James, I won't.'

'I'm sorry?' He stared at her blankly. 'Of course you must give it to me.'

'No, I'm not going to. Not yet at any rate, until she's settled down, come to terms with it all, feels a little better. I'm not having you upsetting her, making her feel worse, more guilty. She's in a bad enough state already. Poor child.'

'Maggie, she is not a child. At best she's a mixed-up woman. I actually think she is rather worse than that – '

'I knew you'd say that, think that,' said Maggie. 'That's precisely why I have no intention of giving you the number.'

'Oh for God's sake. You're crazy about that child. You always were. Could never see any harm in anything she did. Did you know she actually married this man yesterday?'

'What?'

She faltered then, her mother's faith plainly momentarily shattered.

'She married him. Does that tally with her story about rushing off to a desperately sick boyfriend?'

'James, that's ridiculous. She can't have done.'

'She did.'

'How do you know?'

'There was a photograph of her somebody saw, running down the steps of Sacré-Coeur, presumably with him, wearing her wedding dress. Oh she didn't marry him there, of course – '

'Oh that,' said Maggie. She was patently relieved. 'Oh, it was just something they decided to do. She took her dress with her, and they went to Sacré-Coeur to ask a priest for a blessing. She told me that. She wanted to do something to mark the day – '

'Oh for Christ's sake,' said James, 'this pantomime has gone on long enough – let's leave it there. I'm terribly tired, Maggie, I can't take much more of this.' Just the same, just the same, the story was beginning to sound better, more feasible. The cracks in it were being filled. It didn't excuse what Cressida had done but it made her less evil, less immoral.

'But she's not actually married,' said Maggie. 'She couldn't be. There wasn't time for them to arrange it. Anyway,' – she stared at him – 'how do you know all this?'

'A photographer friend of Tilly Mills saw the picture at some newspaper where he was delivering his own pictures. Faxed it to Harriet last night.'

'To Harriet?'

'Yes.'

'Have you seen it?'

'Yes. And I went to Paris this morning – '

'You went to Paris?' Her face was grey with shock.

'Yes, with Theo. We went in his plane. We went to Sacré-Coeur and found the priest who'd blessed them, as a matter of fact. I have to say he does confirm something of this story. He – '

'And you didn't tell me, neither of you did, that you went to Paris looking for Cressida, didn't even show me the picture – ?'

'Maggie, you were asleep. Drugged. I was going to, of course I was. I didn't know myself until about two this morning. What good would it have done to have woken you, upset you all over again? And we left here at four-thirty. I was back on English soil before you'd woken up, and then – '

'It all sounds very par for the course, I have to say,' said Maggie. She had an expression on her face James had not seen before: a hard, cool look, absolutely sure of herself, utterly in command. 'Keep Maggie in the dark. Lie and keep on lying. Keep her out of it, and she'll come to heel. Well finally, James, I won't. I'm leaving you.'

'Oh don't be absurd,' said James. He hardly took the words in, they were just another set of Maggie's histrionics.

'Yes I am. I'd decided anyway, before all this. That as soon as the wedding was over I was going.'

'Oh Maggie, really. Of course you can't go. What would I do without you, how could I – '

'James, you'll do fine without me. You'll have exactly what you wanted. Freedom to do what you want, sort yourself out. Live with Susie if she'll have you.'

'Susie?' said James. He had rehearsed this conversation in his head so often he was word-perfect. 'Susie? What has Susie got to do with it?'

'James, please. Don't insult me. Don't start play-acting.'

'But Maggie – '

'James, I know. Of course I know. And the way I feel right now, you're very welcome to each other. Do what you fucking well like. I simply don't care.'

It was the word fucking that made James realize she meant it. Maggie hated bad language, never swore; the harshest word he had ever heard on her lips had been bloody and that was only about once every five years and then under the most dire provocation. He stared at her, trying to take in what she was saying, absolutely silent. He could not have spoken if his life depended on it.

'I hate you,' she said simply. 'I really do hate you. It's a strong word, but that's what I feel. For all these years you've made a fool of me. With your mistress, God how I hate her too, bloody Susie with her perfect figure and her lovely face, taking you away from me, poor fat stupid Maggie. Of course I knew, I knew quite quickly, and presumably you either thought I didn't or I'd accept it for all the dubious benefits of having you as my husband. Well I did accept it, in a way, because I never made a fuss or threw wobblies. How could I? I'd have looked even more stupid. Everyone would have said poor old Maggie, how can she expect to keep a husband like James, behaving like that? And I had the girls to think of, and they both adored you. I couldn't have broken things up before.'

James looked at her. She had changed. Overnight she had changed. She was still Maggie, still fat, still awkward, and she was pale and tired-looking, but she had clearly washed her hair, and she had put on a nice dress, and even some make-up. She was a pretty woman, still; her plumpness had safeguarded her face, she had fewer lines, her skin was fresher and younger-looking than most of her contemporaries', and her eyes, large, black-lashed eyes, so like Cressida's, were still a clear cornflower blue. He felt an odd rush of panic at the thought of her leaving; he didn't love her but he needed her, she was important to him, to his life.

'Don't talk like this,' he said finally. 'I hate it.'

'Well, that's very unfortunate for you, James, but I'm afraid you'll just have to hate it. I need to explain, to tell you what I'm doing and why.'

'You mustn't go,' he said. 'You mustn't leave. It's a terrible idea. Go and see Cressida if you must, but come back.'

'Why, James? I really don't see why.'

'Well,' he said, 'because we're married. We've been married a long time. And we – '

'No we haven't,' said Maggie, 'not what I call married. I've run the house and looked after the children and organized our social life and seen to your laundry and so on, but we haven't been married. We haven't slept together for years – no, James, we haven't. Well, hardly ever, and when we do I hate it, because I know you think it's time and you ought to and you're thinking about Susie – '

'Maggie, please – this isn't fair.'

'It's perfectly fair. I don't even blame you for it, I'm just explaining why it's not a marriage. We don't talk, we don't ever go out on our own, not even to the cinema, we don't do anything together, except have meals, and then I know you're watching me, thinking I eat too much.'

'Maggie, I don't – '

'Yes you do. And thinking about Susie and her bloody perfect figure, and the way she takes care of herself and watches what she eats and – '

'When did you find out about her? How?' he said, curious in spite of himself.

'Oh – very early on. I suppose before Rufus was born.'

James held his breath. Did she know about that, had she suspected?

'I used to wonder about Tom, you know,' she said conversationally, 'fantasize that maybe he was yours. But he does look so exactly like Alistair, doesn't he?'

'Yes,' said James, relief flooding hard into his lungs, 'yes, of course he does. What an extraordinary idea.'

'Not really. These things do happen. And I did so long for a boy, for more children, it seemed just the kind of thing that would have happened. But I suppose if Susie had been going to have your child she would have had an abortion. Not gone ahead with it. She's hardly the maternal type, is she?'

James didn't answer. He couldn't defend Susie; it would be too dangerous.

'I tried to ignore it, to tell myself I was being neurotic, that you were just flirting with her because she was so lovely and everything I wasn't, but I could see. I watched you together, and I listened to your excuses for being away, and I went through your wallet for clues, and checked up on you both occasionally, phoned your flat or your secretary, and then her home, and you were always missing together. Or the answering machine at the flat was on when I knew you were there. I used to sit and listen to your voice saying you were out, while I knew you must be in bed with her, making love to her, and I hated you so much for a while I wanted to kill you. I actually thought about it sometimes. Well, not really of course, but I did occasionally wonder about poisoning your food. Or hers.'

'Why did you never say anything? I can't understand it.'

'Because,' she said simply, 'I knew it wouldn't do me any good. I knew you wouldn't give her up, whatever I said, and I knew I didn't want a divorce. Not when the girls were young. So I just waited. Hurt and cried and ate a lot and waited. Until now. And it's been worth it. It's been worth it just to have this conversation, James. I've really enjoyed it.'

'Oh God,' he said, 'oh Maggie, I'm so sorry.'

'What for?' she said in genuine puzzlement. 'Whatever for?'

'For hurting you so much.'

'James, really! You wouldn't have stopped it though, would you? Even if you'd known how much it hurt.'

'I don't know,' he said. 'I might have tried.'

'James, you wouldn't. You're too absolutely selfish. And too much in love with her, I suppose. Well, it doesn't hurt me any more. I don't give a toss. I really really don't. She's very welcome to you. And you'll be able to have her now. To marry her. If you want her.'

James said nothing, just stared out of the window.

'Anyway,' said Maggie brightly, 'I'm lucky. Just when I thought I was really going to be on the scrap heap, I have a role to play again. Cressida needs me, and that's wonderful.'

'What? You're going to go and live with her, in Paris, with this man? Do you really think that's a good idea?'

'No, I won't live with them, of course I won't. What a very low opinion you must have of me, James. I'm not that stupid. I shall get a little flat near London, Putney, Wimbledon, somewhere like that, I've still got friends there, and I'll rebuild my life. I've been planning it for quite a long time. Cressida wants me to go and visit, meet Gérard, so when the baby arrives I shall maybe go and stay with her, and when – well, when she's alone, she can decide where she wants to be. And where she wants me to be.'

'So you really believe this story?' said James. He had shut his mind to Maggie's announcement for a while; his consciousness had closed down, he simply couldn't cope with any more.

'Yes, I believe it. Of course I do. Why shouldn't I? I'm a truthful person, James. Unlike you. I recognize and respect it in others. Or is there something else you know that I don't?'

'No,' said James hastily, 'no, there isn't.'

'Well,' she said, 'I'm going now. I'm just sorting out a few clothes.'

'You're going today?' said James. 'Where, how?'

'I'm going to stay with an old nursing friend, in Guildford. That will be convenient for my house-hunting. Sarah Jennings, you know?' He nodded silently. 'You never liked her. She never liked you either,' she added. 'She's delighted at my decision. Anyway, she's on her own, her husband died last year, and she says I can stay as long as I like. And then, as I say, I shall be available for Cressida as and when she wants me. Don't look like that, James. She's very upset and frightened. Waiting for the results of these tests on – on Gérard. I feel I've failed her enough. Quite enough. Now then, I'll need some money from you, of course, and I think I've earned it, but I don't want either this house or the flat. I'll come and say goodbye before I go.'

And she walked out of the room and out of his life, as he had so often dreamed of her doing, longed for her to do, leaving him utterly chilled, utterly alone.

Chapter Thirty-Seven

Theo 2.30

Like Queen Victoria, Theodore Buchan was not interested in the possibilities of defeat; he was reminded of her words to Lord Balfour on the subject that afternoon as he sat in a traffic jam outside Buckingham Palace looking broodingly up at it. He was a great fan of the old Queen; he admired her stubbornness, her shrewdness, her political flair, and above all her preference for conservative principles. He often said he and she would have got on famously; there were those, Harriet amongst them, who observed that the Queen was scarcely likely to have received a man with five wives, let alone got on with him famously, but Theo was quite undeterred by this, explained that he would have won her heart Disraeli-style by making her Empress of his Scottish island and wearing a kilt in the manner of her beloved ghillie. John Brown.

'Theo,' Harriet had said, 'not a kilt. Not you.'

This coversation had led on to a subsequent one of some lewdness, on the subject of what he might have worn under the kilt, and that had led in turn to some fairly intense physical pleasure, as they contemplated together the area under discussion. All this flooded back into his bleak mind, making him first smile and then wince as he remembered Harriet's most recent assault on his person. It also made him still less interested in the possibility of defeat. He wanted her, he needed her, he loved her; and he was going to have her. It was perfectly simple: merely a matter of patience and logistics. Being strong on logistics he could not see that a great deal of patience should be called for.

He reached for his car phone, to call his office; the movement hurt his tender balls.

'Bitch,' he said aloud, 'bitch.'

'Who, me, Mr Buchan?' said Myra. 'What did I do?'

'Nothing, Myra, nothing. Sorry. I'm on my way in.'

'Where are you?'

'In the Mall. Any messages?'

'A few. Mungo called about six times, he wanted to have dinner with you. Hayden Cotton called, can you ring back soonest, he said.' Myra didn't like Americans, her clipped upper-class English voice disdainful

400

when she relayed messages, absolutely verbatim, and she spoke to them politely but slightly condescendingly; Theo teased her about it and referred to them in her presence as colonials.

'Mark Protheroe's rung several times, please ring him, most specifically about CalVin. A Mr Hennessy called, he's acting for Mrs Buchan, he says, can you call him urgently. James Forrest rang, he wants to see you, maybe this evening. Everything else can wait.'

'Fine. Tell Mungo I'm not sure about dinner, but I'd love to see him and I'll ring him the minute I'm free. I'll get the rest when I arrive.'

He rang off, found himself in another traffic jam in St James's and rang James.

'James? Theo. You OK? I can't do dinner, sorry, but – '

'Maggie's left me,' said James flatly.

'She's what?'

'Left me.'

'Why?'

'She says she hates me.'

'Well, I suppose that could be called a reason,' said Theo carefully. He eased a cigar out of his top pocket, clipped the end with some difficulty and pushed it into the lighter on the car dashboard.

'It isn't funny.'

'Of course it isn't. I'm sorry. Really sorry. Unless it's what you want, of course . . .'

'I don't know what I want,' said James, and Theo realized he was crying.

'Jamie, what is it? Not Susie?'

There was a silence; he heard James blowing his nose. 'Sorry,' he said, 'sorry, Theo. No, no, Susie's fine. False alarm.'

'Rufus?'

'No, not Rufus either.'

'Where – where is Maggie going?'

'Well, she's talking of buying a flat in London. And then spending a lot of time in Paris, looking after Cressida.'

'Cressida?' Theo almost drove into a taxi, jammed on his brakes. 'Sorry,' he shouted at the cabbie, 'sorry, mate.'

'Keep your bleeding eyes open,' said the cabbie equably.

'Theo, what is going on?' asked James.

'I'm in the car. Almost had an accident. You did say Cressida, James? Really? Have you found her?'

'No. Well, yes, I suppose. She rang Maggie. Told her some extraordinary story and – well, I won't go into it now.'

'You might as well,' said Theo, 'I'm not going anywhere.'

And he sat there in the midst of the thick Friday afternoon traffic, surrounded by hooting, swearing drivers, a light rain falling now onto the windscreen, listening as James told him Cressida's story and then, falteringly, clearly upset, Julia's story. Theo put them together in his mind with Harriet's story and not for the first time in the past thirty-six hours wondered if he was dreaming.

'Oh, and Theo, did you really ever tell Cressida the full extent of Julia's father's wealth? I really had no idea it was such serious money.'

'Yes I did,' said Theo with a sigh. 'I didn't mean to, but she was very good at wheedling information out of one. I told her I'd just seen the old bugger, at a convention in Palm Beach. He's virtually a recluse these days, but still obsessed with the heart of his business which is computer technology.'

'Well, I'm afraid that rather confirms Julia's story,' said James wearily. 'She said she thought it was you who'd told Cressida.'

'Mea culpa,' said Theo, 'I'm sorry, James.'

There was a silence. Then James said, 'Well, I don't suppose it would have made that much difference. She'd have found out somehow. If Julia's right.'

'I don't think you should assume that.'

'Maybe not. I'm trying not to.' There was another silence, then he said, 'And Maggie's gone. She wants a divorce.'

'Oh Jamie,' Theo said finally, as he eased the Bentley into the car park beneath his office, 'I'm sorry. We seem to have made a bit of a hash of things, you and I. If only we could go back to that weekend in Paris and start again – '

And as he said that he knew who he could talk to, who would advise him about Harriet.

Janine had returned to the Basil Street Hotel; she said she was delighted to hear from him, but that she was busy just at the moment and would he like to have tea with her.

'And I am not sure if you have heard the news, *chéri*. I am engaged to be married.'

'Janine, you're not, you're supposed to be keeping yourself for me. Who is the swine?'

'The swine is Merlin. Are you not happy for me?'

'Merlin! The old bugger. Janine, that's the most wonderful thing I've heard for – well, for years. Of course I'm happy for you, very happy, delirious in fact. And him. How amazingly cheering. Whenever did that happen?'

'Rather swiftly. Yesterday. Last night. Merlin took me out to dinner and in between bargaining with the waiters he asked me to marry him. You do not think we are a little old for it?'

'Janine, you are two of the youngest people I know. Give the old boy a hug from me. Will he be there at teatime?'

'No, Theo, he will not. He is going off to some unfortunate travel agency to book our honeymoon trip. We are going to China.'

'China! God, I'm jealous. Terribly jealous. But you did promise to marry me next, you know.'

'Well, I am sorry, Theo, but you are married already, are you not?'

'Not for very much longer, Janine,' said Theo soberly.

'Oh really? And what have you done to the lovely Sasha?'

'She's done it to me. Taught me a lesson.'

'Then she is a clever girl,' said Janine. 'You are not quick to learn lessons, Theo. But I am sorry if you are upset.'

'I'm not,' said Theo, 'but I do need advice.'

'Then you shall have it. For what it is worth.'

He put the phone down and sat smiling at it. Nothing, with the exception of hearing Harriet tell him she loved him, could have made him feel more cheerful.

Hayden Cotton had wanted to confirm that he was not putting any money into Harry's.

'It's not the figures. Sure, she's worked them over a bit, but nothing serious. That's not really the problem, it's just that the business is no use to me. Not big enough, and she duplicates what we do. And we're already strong in the UK. It's a lot of hassle for no real return. Pity, she's a bright girl, and a brilliant designer. She just isn't a businesswoman. I'd like to hire her, but I don't think she'd come.'

'Hire her as what?' asked Theo.

'As a designer. I'm thinking of launching a new range. More upmarket. Think of Ralph Lauren. Well, Diffusion Ralph Lauren.'

'What's Diffusion?'

'Oh, it's a kind of a budget line for the top designers. Jean Muir does Studio, Lagerfeld does KL, that sort of thing. And then think evening too. Not frocks, exactly, more tailored. Female dinner jackets.'

'Tough one to crack I'd have thought,' said Theo.

'I know. But it's there. The potential. And I think she could be my girl.'

'Mm,' said Theo thoughtfully. 'Based where?'

'Oh, over here, it would have to be here. I could put together a terrific package for her. But she's such an independent creature, I really don't think she'd come.'

'I don't think she would either,' said Theo, 'but it's exactly right for her. And she's right for you and the idea. And it could altogether – Actually, Hayden – '

'Yeah?'

'I tell you what would make her come.'

Michael Hennessy, representing Mrs Sasha Buchan, was humourless, pompous and extremely efficient. Mrs Buchan wanted a divorce, a quick, no-fault divorce, she had no desire to be vindictive, but she said that if Mr Buchan was going to contest it she would tell the press how she had acquired CalVin. Mr Buchan said he had no intention whatsoever of contesting it, and that he was very happy to go along with Mrs Buchan's request. Mr Hennessy said Mrs Buchan was prepared to be reasonable on the matter of settlement, in fact her demands were extremely modest, she would like a small London house, and a realistic income – 'The word realistic is of course open to interpretation and discussion,' said Mr Hennessy. 'Indeed,' said Theo – 'and she would also like you to give bank guarantees as and when required for the business she intends to set up, as an independent financial adviser, and she wants a flat sum, in the region of a hundred thousand pounds, with which to set up the business.'

'The hell she does,' said Theo. 'She can find her own banker.'

'She said you might say that, Mr Buchan, and in that eventuality, asked me to remind you again about the matter of the CalVin company.'

'This is blackmail,' said Theo.

'That is a very serious allegation, Mr Buchan.'

'It's a statement of fact. But – ' He paused, thinking, then grinned into the phone. 'OK. Tell her – tell her she can have all that in exchange for a ten per cent share in her company. And a directorship. Strictly non-executive, of course.'

'I will certainly tell her that, Mr Buchan. But I don't know if Mrs Buchan will agree to it.'

'I think she'll agree,' said Theo, 'she's a good businesswoman, and a good sport. And tell her I'll throw a copy of the original version of her engagement ring into the melting pot for good measure. On condition she doesn't sell this one.'

This obviously defeated Mr Hennessy; Theo bade him good afternoon and put the phone down, smiling. He loved getting the better of lawyers, however briefly.

He rang Mungo; he was out, Belinda said, showing someone round a new property.

'He'll be sorry to have missed you, Mr Buchan, he's been trying to get you all day. Shall I call him on his mobile?'

'Good God, no,' said Theo, 'what he's doing is much more important. Just ask him to call me when he gets back. Tell him I'd love to have dinner with him.'

'Certainly, Mr Buchan.'

I knew there was someone,' said Janine, 'I knew there had to be. She looked so different for a while. She was warmer, softer, she glowed. Sex is very good for the looks, all Frenchwomen know that.'

'Oh really?' said Theo. 'I don't think it's ever done a lot for mine.'

'You are not a woman, *chéri*.'

'That's true.'

'Besides, I think you are wrong. Anyone can see you are a man of great passion. It shows.'

'*Tiens!*' said Theo.

'But of course I did not think it was you. You did well. Nobody knew? Nobody at all?'

'My staff.'

'What, the terrifying Mme Hartman, she knew?'

'She did. And several others. Brian, of course. He spent a lot of time collecting Harriet, driving her to airports, that sort of thing. Various housekeepers. But nobody else – I don't think. I like running secrets. It appeals to me.'

'And Cressida?'

'Ah,' said Theo, 'yes.'

He had told Janine, because he'd wanted to, because he thought she had earned it, because he trusted her, all the Cressida stories. 'Which one do you favour, Janine?'

'I agree certainly with the doctor, that she was disturbed. A very difficult personality. She always was. A charming, difficult, disruptive child.'

'I would have thought Harriet was the disruptive one,' said Theo.

'No, no, not at all. You were all so wrong about that. Harriet suffered greatly from Cressida. She seemed difficult herself, yes, and her parents could never see anything really wrong with Cressida's behaviour, it was always, every time, a surprise, they would say oh, but she has always been so good, how strange that her teacher should say she is being naughty in the classroom and not working at school, or how can it be, when she is normally so thoughtful and sensible, that she failed to come home until almost half past three? They never put two and three together – '

405

'Two and two, Janine.'

'Oh, well, whatever. And the squabbling with Harriet, they always thought it was her fault, because Harriet was the one caught shouting, or hitting her, and Cressida would be sitting there crying. I could see Cressida very often started these things, but they would not accept it. She was very good at appearing to be the victim, indeed thinking herself the victim. But she was so loving, so sweet to them, could wrap Maggie especially right round her thumb.'

'Finger.'

'Finger then. One of the reasons I have fallen in love with Merlin, Theo, is that he never corrects my English.'

'Sorry, Janine.'

'And now she is doing it again. She could lie and lie, with those great eyes of hers wide. I often caught her out, I have sharp eyes of my own, but again her parents nearly always believed her. And if they didn't, then she could turn on the shower and win them round.'

'Oh really?' said Theo with a heavy sigh, silently translating shower into tap and thinking that Cressida's light, cosmetic tears were actually more reminiscent of a shower, and at the end of them she looked as pretty as when she started. Harriet on the other hand cried noisily, heavily and messily and ended up with red eyes, smudged mascara and a runny nose.

'I'm afraid,' he said, 'she took me in very thoroughly too. I loved her, loved her company, enjoyed taking her away with me.'

'She had – has great charm,' said Janine. 'I enjoyed her company too. In spite of everything. And remembering things you had said to her, which is always enchanting, and making small pretty gestures. She never forgot my birthday, always wrote sweet thankyou notes – she was easy to love. And Harriet – more difficult. She kept you at a distance.'

'Well, I found Harriet very easy to love,' said Theo mournfully. 'Dreadfully, dangerously easy to love. Merlin always adored her,' he added, 'never really liked Cressida.'

'Merlin is a man of great perception,' said Janine with a slight complacency.

'You sound as if you'd been married to him for years and years already,' said Theo laughing.

'I only wish we had. But I tell you, Theo, I cannot quite accept this story of the belle Julia's. I do not believe Cressida is so bad as that.'

'Well, whether it was true or not, Julia believed it. Believed Cressida could be bought off. Or at any rate a variation on that theme. James saw the letter. Oh Janine, I don't know. Poor old Jamie's in a terrible state.'

'I know it,' said Janine, 'and he has other problems as well, I think. I expect he too will be here before very long.' She smiled at Theo wryly.

'He always comes to me when things go wrong for him; when they are right, I do not hear from him. Cressida has much of that quality too, I think. But Theo, you are not here to discuss Cressida or James. What can we do to help *you*? And Harriet?'

'You don't think it's a disgraceful idea then?' said Theo cautiously.

'Absolutely disgraceful,' said Janine, smiling again. 'Unsuitable, impractical, almost incestuous. What her father will have to say I really hate to think. But I cannot think of two people better suited to loving one another. Except for me and Merlin of course. Two delightful surprises in one day. Now let us put ourselves together and think how you can overcome this little temporary problem you have run into.'

'Not so little or so temporary,' said Theo with a sigh. 'She's told me on three separate occasions in the last twenty-four hours that she hates me and never wants to see me again.'

'You cannot be surprised, I think. You have done some terrible things to her. Marrying someone else within months of the break-up, the pauvre Sasha – '

'Not so pauvre.'

'*Comment?*'

'Oh, I'll tell you another time. Let's just say the pauvre Sasha can take care of herself.'

'I'm pleased to hear it,' said Janine. 'Harriet must be able to do the same, I think. It was not nice or kind to tell your friend not to put his money into her company . . .'

'Janine, it would not be nice or kind to encourage Harriet into thinking she was a good businesswoman when in the last resort she is not. Or of allowing my friend to waste what was actually a great deal of money – '

'Well, perhaps. But it could have been done with more finesse. You lack tact, my Theo.'

'I'm afraid, Janine, you're absolutely right.'

'And how do you know that Harriet does not mean it when she says she hates you?'

'I just do,' said Theo simply. 'I know it. I feel it and I know it.'

'Then we have to help her to find out for herself. But it will not be easy. You cannot tell Harriet anything. She does not listen.'

'No. Well, she certainly doesn't listen to me.' The small phone in his pocket rang shrilly. 'Excuse me, Janine. Can I take that? It's probably Mungo.'

It wasn't Mungo, it was Mr Hennessy. 'Mrs Buchan asked me to tell you that she accepts all your terms, Mr Buchan.'

'That's very good of her,' said Theo.

'She is particularly happy with your offer of the ring. She says she will send the one she is currently wearing over to my office this afternoon in order that you may get it copied.'

'How helpful of her,' said Theo. He grinned suddenly into the phone; the irony of having a genuine diamond ring made to match a fake greatly charmed him. He suddenly remembered rather sharply why he had married Sasha in the first place: she was sexy, she was pretty, she was charming, but she was also a lot of fun. For the first time since she had walked out, he felt a pang of loss.

'Indeed. There is an additional matter, Mr Buchan. Mrs Buchan has found a house and is anxious to proceed with the purchase as soon as possible. A cheque from you is therefore required. Perhaps if you could see your way to coming to my office – '

'Mr Hennessy, I'm an extremely busy man. I really can't drop everything at a moment's notice to come and sign cheques at your office. Besides, I need to see the details of this house, I need to be sure it's a good investment and – '

'May I remind you, Mr Buchan, the house will be for Mrs Buchan, not yourself. She did ask me to remind you again that she thought the story about the CalVin deal would be very interesting – '

.'I don't give a shit about the CalVin deal,' said Theo, and then after a moment's thought realized he did. 'All right, Mr Hennessy, but I'm not prepared to come to your office. You can come to mine. In an hour. You have the address, I imagine. Dover Street. Yes, that's right. Good afternoon.'

'What was that about?' asked Janine.

'Oh – Sasha playing games. Clever games, I have to say. Clever girl. And I'm a fool not to have realized it.' He sighed. 'I'd better go, Janine. Ring me if you have any good ideas. I'll be at my office and then – '

There was a knock at the door; Janine went over and opened it. Merlin stood on the threshold beaming, holding a very large bunch of red roses.

'Merlin!' said Theo, giving him one of his bear hugs. 'Let me congratulate you. It's wonderful news. Couldn't be more delighted.'

'Thank you,' said Merlin. 'Pretty delighted myself. Can't think why I couldn't have sorted it out before. Love is blind, I suppose. These are for you, my dear. Got them just down the street on my way back from the travel agent. Terrible price, and the chap wasn't budging, but I thought you deserved them.'

'They're beautiful,' said Theo. 'Perhaps I'd better get some for Sasha. Might sweeten her up a bit. Off to meet her – ' His phone rang again. 'Sorry, Merlin. Hallo? Yes, Myra, I'm on my way. Yes, yes, of course, immediately. Merlin, I'd like to buy you both dinner, maybe tomorrow? But I have to rush now. I'll call you. I wouldn't mind coming on your honeymoon with you either. Don't look so alarmed, Merlin, I didn't mean it . . .'

Chapter Thirty-Eight

Harriet 4pm

'You all right, miss?'

Harriet looked up from where she was sitting, hunched up in the doorway of what had been her studio until three o'clock that afternoon, and found herself staring into the eyes of a policeman. Or was it a small boy dressed in policeman's uniform? No, it was a real one. God, it was true, the joke about policemen getting younger; first the one who had stopped her and Theo on the bridge, now this one. She must be getting old. She certainly felt it now. She smiled at him slightly uncertainly, struggled to her feet.

'Yes. Yes, I'm fine. Thank you.'

'Can I call you a taxi or something?'

'No, thank you. I'll be fine. Really.' Well at least the £550 she'd spent on her Nicole Fahri suit hadn't been wasted, if even a policeman could tell she wasn't actually a vagrant, could afford a taxi. Only she couldn't of course; she couldn't afford anything. She was bankrupt, she would shortly be homeless, and she was all alone in the world. She might as well settle back into her doorway and make that her home. It might be quite clever actually; it would cause the receiver a bit of trouble when he came back again to try to sell her offices. Then a cleaning lorry rumbled past, spraying a mixture of rain and dust across the pavement, and she thought perhaps there might be a better option. She realized suddenly she was very thirsty; she walked slowly down to the Strand and into McDonald's and ordered an orange juice and thence headed for Charing Cross station and the uncertain haven of the underground and finally her flat. Her car was parked outside it, returned by Mungo, with a note and a red rose tucked under the windscreen wiper. He was getting as dangerous as his father, she thought, smiling at the gesture as she read the note: 'Keys in the letterbox. Thank you for lending it. I'd love to see you soon.'

It was a very nice flat, but it was blank, anonymous, in a small purpose-built block near Kensington High Street. She had furnished it at high speed from John Lewis and Habitat; it was rather dully tasteful in all shades of beige, its only really interesting feature a dark blue gas-powered Aga which Theo had had installed for her in the kitchen at considerable cost, replacing the immensely more practical Neff wall cooker that had come with the flat. She had gone to be with him for a few days on the island near Mustique, and when she had come back it had been there, waiting for her, the ravages of installing it immaculately put to rights, with a card standing on the top that said, 'I could get jealous of this. Theo.'

She had once told him that what she most associated with love and comfort was her mother's Aga, standing in the kitchen at the Court House and never going out, summer or winter. She had grown up by that Aga, she said, warming her hands over it when she got in from school, leaning against its comfort when she had a tummyache, drying her wet clothes on its rail, opening the oven to see what was in it for dinner, watching happily as Christmas puddings bubbled on its hob, Christmas and birthday cakes went in and out of it, had sat in Purdey's basket for long hours beside it, reading (and before that, for a brief, joyous time, had cradled the tiny Biggles in her lap by it, actually slept there with him on his first night, after creeping down in the stillness of the sleeping house, hearing him, frightened, bewildered, whimpering for his mother); had brought half-dead animals to lie in soft boxes by its warmth, birds, two of the farm cat's abandoned kittens, and once even a small fox cub she had found lying by its dead mother near the bridge. She made her first disastrous forays into cooking in it (but they'd been more successful than any of her other efforts since in more sophisticated stoves.) She and Cressida had always hung their stockings on it, rather than the conventional fireplaces in the house (ignoring the fact that Santa would have had more than a little trouble negotiating its chimney), and whenever there was a family conference (sadly an increasingly rare event) it was in the kitchen, near the Aga, that it took place.

Nothing, she'd told Theo on the phone that night, half laughing, half crying, could have made her realize how much he loved her, nothing could have made her love him more. 'Next time you're here, I shall cook you a meal on it,' she said, and 'Good God, I hope not,' he said in alarm (having sampled her cooking once or twice). 'It's just to remind you of me. We could have some sex with it,' he'd added more cheerfully, 'I'd much rather that,' and sure enough, they had. She'd dragged the mattress from her bed and laid it in front of the cooker, heaped with cushions and pillows, had greeted him at the door wearing nothing but a striped cook's apron, had led him to it and then removed the apron and lain down, watching him undress, hurling his clothes onto the floor, feeling her body warming, softening, opening to him before he even touched her, seeing the pleasure ahead, his mouth on hers, his hands everywhere on her, unfolding joy, the sweet heavy settlement of him within her, the clenching, the gathering round him, the pushing, the pulling of desire, the leaping and falling of delight, and then the last slow, sure climb into orgasm, hearing the great roar of her own voice as she reached, accomplished, conquered, and then the oddly quieter cry in his own. And then much much later, as she lay beside him, her body throbbing into quietness, she looked at him and smiled and he smiled back and said, 'That's quite a cooker you have there, Miss Forrest.' And she thought, reaching out and touching the warm sides of the Aga, that she had never been so happy.

She'd intended to have it ripped out when the affair was over, as a final, painful gesture, but it proved so complicated and so expensive that she'd abandoned the attempt. It seemed to her absolutely symptomatic of Theo that he had managed to bestow upon her something that she couldn't get rid of without enormous difficulty and expense; other girls wrapped up their engagement rings, their necklaces, their bracelets and sent them back, and she had to sit, day after day, staring at a love token that weighed half a ton.

Well, it would go now, she thought, along with the flat, and it might even be a selling point, would actually have a cash value. What should have been a cheering prospect made her sit down and burst into tears. She cried for a long time; racking sobs, cathartic, almost pleasurable, and so loud they almost drowned the ring of her phone. 'Shit,' she said and decided to leave it, to let the answering machine take it; but her rush of tears once halted refused to start again and she grabbed a tea towel to wipe her eyes on and ran into the tiny bedroom she had converted into a study. A female American voice was telling her to ring Mr Hayden Cotton most urgently, and issuing an endless list of numbers which Harriet wrote down in the wrong order twice so that she made two extremely expensive calls first to a truck company in Ohio and then a health club in Miami before finally reaching the haven of Mr Cotton's office just off Delancey Street, Manhattan. Hayden Cotton insisted on remaining in Delancey Street, where he had launched his empire in a small sweatshop and where it now occupied an entire block.

'Why quadruple overheads?' he would growl whenever (as they frequently did) one of his executives suggested moving up-town, or even further down towards the Seaport area. 'Or are you offering to take a salary cut?'

They never were, and so he never moved, and never would, it was famously said, until he had to leave feet first; and it was true, he saved hundreds of thousands of dollars a year, and since all his employees, even the most humble stitcher, operated under a profit-sharing scheme, they did not argue too much about it.

Harriet, who had visited the Cotton Fields offices, would not always have agreed with him, would have protested that a good address, a glamorous image, were essential. Having been forced to see that a good address and a glamorous image had done her very little good at all, possibly very much the reverse, she would now have consented to run her company from Cardboard City had she been given the opportunity. Waiting now to be put through to Hayden Cotton, she wondered if she was to be given the opportunity, and if maybe it wasn't too late: Theo had said companies could be bought back from receivership. Perhaps . . .

'Harriet Forrest?'

'Yes, speaking.'

'Hayden Cotton. You get a backer yet?'

'No, Mr Cotton, I haven't, I'm afraid. And my company's gone into receivership today.'

'Uh-huh. That's a shame. And I'm sorry we didn't get a chance to do business together.'

'So am I, Mr Cotton.'

'However, I have another proposition for you.'

'Yes?' Could the sound of a heart thudding be heard down the phone? Did a voice strangled with excitement, with emotion, give you away?

'How would you like to come and work for me?'

'For you? In what way?'

'I'm thinking of launching a new range. Tell you more about it if and when you want to talk. I need a designer for it. A chief designer. I'd like that person to be you.'

'Oh,' said Harriet, 'Oh I see. Well, Mr Cotton, I don't know. I mean I'd love it and I'm terribly flattered to have been asked, but I've got used to working for myself, you see, and – '

'I do see and I greatly admire what you've done. But I think, with the greatest respect, Miss Forrest, your talents are ninety-nine per cent in the design field. Running a business just distracts you from that.'

'Oh,' said Harriet. 'Well, I haven't done that badly, Mr Cotton. I mean – '

'I think you've done extremely well. All you needed was a really good business manager. But even so, designing is what you were made for. And what you should do for me. I could make you a very good offer, Harriet. Very good indeed.'

'Well – I don't know. It's not something I – I ever thought of – ' Harriet started again, trying to sound more efficient, less daffy. 'Where would I work? In London?'

'No. That wouldn't be any good. You'd have to come over here. I'd want you working closely with me.'

'Oh, I see.' Her mind was racing, raking over his offer, thinking of all the implications. They were scary, they weren't what she wanted at all: but then was she really in a position to argue? A new city, a new lifestyle, a new life; it could be exactly, exactly what she needed

'The pay'd be good,' said Hayden Cotton, 'I thought quarter of a million for starters.'

Quarter of a million dollars a year! That was at least, at least £150,000. And the low tax structure in the States, the lower cost of living, would make it worth far, far more than the same sum in England. She'd be –

'With profit-sharing, of course,' said Hayden Cotton, cutting into her thoughts. 'And there'd be a lot of potential built in. Maybe a partnership one day. And naturally a car and an interest-free loan to buy an apartment or whatever. And you'd be able to get home to London often, obviously. Think about it, Harriet. At least come and talk to me.'

Harriet thought. She thought of the pleasure of designing clothes, her own collection, with none of the attendant headaches of cost, cash flow, financial forecasting, VAT returns; she thought of the heady lifestyle that would surely ensue; she thought of having more money, real money, to spend on herself, not plough endlessly back into the company, of freedom to enjoy herself, of not having to work through weekends and nights, not having to find staff, get rid of staff, find more staff. She thought of living in New York, a city she loved, of jetting backwards and forwards across the Atlantic, and she thought of getting away from England, from the pain of her discovery about her father, the nightmare of Cressida – and from Theo. Theo hated New York, visited it as rarely as he could. The opportunities for bumping into him, for being pursued by him, would undoubtedly be fewer. It was very, very attractive. And then she thought of the joy, the pure, unalloyed pleasure of having her own business, of seeing it grow, of doing what she wanted, what she thought best; and yes, she had made mistakes, but she had learnt from them, she wouldn't make the same ones again, and she would do it again, somehow, she would get hold of some more money. Owning a company was like having a garden, planting things in it, ideas, talent, skills, risk, courage, and seeing them grow in entirely your own way, and however hard, however exhausting, however at times unrewarding, the pleasure was heady, and the rewards, however meagre, were absolutely your own, absolutely personal. Working for Hayden Cotton, as his chief gardener, might be a lot easier, but the end result, however grand and splendid, would still be his.

'I really don't think I could,' she said finally. 'I have to do things my way, Mr Cotton. I've made lots of mistakes, and I'm sure I'll make lots more, but they'll be different ones. Thank you for asking me, but I have to stick it out here.'

'Oh well,' he said with a sigh, 'pity. I thought you just might. Mind you, Theo said you wouldn't, said you'd never come.'

'Theo! Theo Buchan?'

'That's the one.'

'You discussed this with Theo?'

'I mentioned it. We talk a lot, you know. We go back a long way, to when I dealt direct and bought textiles from him.'

'Yes I know,' said Harriet bitterly.

'He thought it was a great idea for you, but he told me I was wasting my time. I guess he knows you better than I thought he did.'

'Oh he does?' said Harriet. 'I think not. You can tell Theo Buchan I – ' She stopped, confused. It was hardly Hayden Cotton's fault that Theo still saw it as his prerogative to go around trying to run her life for her. It was outrageous, but –

'I'm sorry,' she said carefully. 'I didn't mean to sound rude, Mr Cotton. I really didn't.'

'That's OK, I understand. Listen, Harriet, don't rush this. Take a day or two thinking about it. It may seem better when you've slept on it. Come and talk to me, spend a few days here.'

'Well – yes, all right,' said Harriet slowly. 'Maybe I should. That'd be good.'

It still didn't feel right, but she wasn't going to give Theo the satisfaction of knowing what was best for her, what suited her. And she could do it for a year or two maybe, get some money together and then start again. Bloody, bloody overbearing, officious man; he would not, could not go on behaving as if he owned her, as if she still loved him.

'Good. Very good. You call me tomorrow and we'll fix a trip. Goodbye, Miss Forrest. You'll like New York. You'd suit it.'

'Yes,' said Harriet thoughtfully, 'yes, I think maybe I would. And I'll ring you in the morning. Goodbye, Mr Cotton.'

'Oh, and by the way,' he said suddenly, as she was about to put the phone down. 'In case you thought otherwise, I took no notice of Theo's views when I was making my decision as to whether or not I bought your company. I make my own decisions, too, you know.'

'Oh,' said Harriet, 'oh, I see.'

She ran herself a bath and lay in it, thinking; she woke up an hour later, freezing cold, to hear the phone ringing again. She dragged on her bathrobe and sat hugging the radiator, looking at her interestingly wrinkled feet and hands, feeling rather sick. It was her father.

'Darling. Can I come and see you?'

'I'd rather you didn't, if you don't mind,' said Harriet. 'Not tonight. I'm terribly tired.'

'Oh,' said James. It was a small, hurt little sound. Harriet didn't care. She felt a cold, hard hostility towards him; she didn't want to see him, didn't want either alternative, of confrontation or pretence. She supposed she might get used to the idea of his having an affair with Susie, but she would never get over it. It was too hurtful, too literally shocking.

'Surely Mummy needs you?'

'No,' he said very quietly, 'no, Harriet, she doesn't.'

'Daddy, what is it?' she said.

'Your mother's gone.'

'Gone? Gone where?'

'She's left me.'

'Oh', said Harriet. 'Oh I see.' She knew she sounded dull, absurdly uninterested, but she couldn't help it. She wasn't quite sure what she should feel, what she did feel, but whatever it was, she wasn't feeling it. Her prime emotion, she discovered, exploring her mood briefly, was admiration for her mother. Certainly not sympathy for her father.

'You don't sound very surprised.'

'I'm sorry,' she said with an effort. 'Very sorry. Er – where exactly has she gone?'

God, she hoped her mother wasn't coming to her. Sympathize with her she might, but that would truly be more than she could stand. She had had enough: enough of all of them.

'To stay with a friend,' said James. 'And quite soon, I fancy, to visit Cressida.'

'Cressida? Cressida! You mean you've found her?'

'She rang up.'

'Where from? Paris?'

'Yes.'

'Well, is she all right?'

'Yes and no,' he said.

'Can't you tell me about it?'

'Not on the phone. It's too complex, too difficult. I just need to talk to you, Harriet, so badly.'

He sounded terrible; in spite of everything, Harriet felt a pang of alarm. 'Look,' she said, 'I'm frozen, I went to sleep in the bath. Give me five minutes to get dressed, and I'll ring you back.'

'Can't I come and see you, Harriet? Please?'

'Maybe,' she said, 'but don't leave yet. I really have to sort out what I'm doing.'

★

She put the phone down feeling utterly chilled; not just physically, her heart seemed to have ice round it too, heavy grey ice, and there was ice in her veins and ice in her head. Everywhere she looked there was betrayal, loneliness, no one seemed to be there for her. She was very happy for Rufus and Tilly (who had phoned to tell her they were getting married, Tilly full of remorse that she would not after all be able to lend her any money; Harriet told her not to be crazy and she'd never have taken it anyway), very glad for Janine and Merlin (who had also phoned and asked her out to dinner, which she had rather half-heartedly refused), very sorry for Mungo (who, Rufus told her, had had his heart broken by his mysterious lady-love, but was burying himself in his work: 'Mungo!' said Harriet. 'Working!'), very sympathetic with a shattered Oliver who had rung from the airport to say goodbye, a swift careful phone call, thanking her for her help, not talking about Cressida, about what might have happened. She even now felt the stirrings of pity for her father; faint, echo-y but there. You couldn't adore someone for twenty-nine years and then feel nothing for them, just abandon them.

She went to her room, pulled out some leggings and a big sweater and some thick socks, dried her hair – God, it looked awful, wispier than ever, maybe she should have it cut off again – then went back into the kitchen and made herself a cup of tea. As she got warmer, began to come back to life, the numbness left her and she began to ache. She ached with weariness and loneliness and misery, she ached in every bone, every muscle, in her head, in her stomach and in the very heart of herself. She was very tired, she would have liked to go to sleep, but every time she closed her eyes she lived again the awful scene when the receiver, having arranged for the phones, the electricity to be cut off, having picked up all her books, all her files, all her chequebooks and bank statements, asked everyone to leave the building with him, and they filed out, her and her four girls (none of whom would go without her: 'We're all in this,' they said to her, 'we're all in this with you'), taking with them only their personal possessions, and some work folders – 'they're personal,' Harriet said defiantly, 'pictures of our own, to hang on our own walls in our own homes.' She could see he didn't believe her, but he allowed them to take the folders all the same; he was not an unreasonable man, just a very dry and precise one. But as he stood there, screwing a padlock onto the door, snapping it shut, looking up at the building with a strangely satisfied expression, as if it had somehow become his, all the work, all the love she had put into it negated by that one action, she could gladly have killed him.

The girls had asked her to go for a drink, but she refused; she said she had things to do; and that was when she had settled in the doorway and the policeman had found her.

She sat in the kitchen, drinking the tea, putting off without knowing quite why the moment when she had to phone her father again, staring out at the misty rain, wondering what was to become of her. Was she to end up one of those powerful, rich New York women who returned at night alone to empty, stylish apartments after long days of ruling companies and running lives? Or was she to stay here in England, following her instinct, picking up a myriad of untidy tangled ends, battling to get back to where she had been before? Here she was, twenty-nine years old, bankrupt – well, maybe that was an achievement in itself, at so tender an age – absolutely alone, or so it felt, her mother concerned only with her sister, her father become someone she preferred not to see, her friends scattering – 'Now don't start, Harriet,' she said aloud, feeling the treacherous tears rising, the choking sensation in her chest, 'don't start.'

The phone rang sharply; God, it must be her father again, she'd promised him five minutes and it was almost twenty-five. It was.

'Harriet – '

'Sorry, Daddy,' she said. 'Listen, you stay there. I'll come down. It'll only take me an hour or so. And I'd like to come home.'

'You would?' He sounded touchingly, frighteningly grateful.

'Yes, I really would,' she said, and found to her surprise it was true. She wanted to go home: to go home to the Court House. This flat wasn't home, even with the Aga; the only other home she had was her studio and that was barred to her, its locks changed, the heart ripped out of it. She would go home and see her father, spend a few days with him, perhaps discover why he had done what he had; and there, where she had grown up, where she had become what she was, with all the good and all the bad, she could decide what she wanted and what she should do. She felt more cheerful straight away; journeys always lifted her spirits, distracted her. She would play some really nice music, and stop on the way at a service station – Harriet was always surprised by how much people disliked service stations, they seemed to her lovely warm womblike places, faintly reminiscent of fairgrounds with all the cheerful tat and rubbish for sale, and she liked the food too, cheerful rubbishy food – and she would arrive at the Court House and her father would be waiting for her and she would at least be somewhere she belonged, where someone cared about her.

That reminded her of Janine; she ought to ring her, tell her she definitely wouldn't be going to dinner with her.

Merlin answered the phone: Janine had gone out, he said, gone shopping: 'Oh, I see. Well, look, Merlin, I'm going home. Now. To

Wedbourne, so I definitely won't be joining you for dinner. My father sounds pretty low. Thank you anyway, and I'll see you soon.'

'Quite all right, Harriet. I'll tell Janine. Your father does sound bad. He phoned here, wanted Theo – '

'Theo!' said Harriet. 'What was Theo doing there?'

'Oh, he came to see Janine. Not sure why. Anyway he's gone now, rushing off to see Sasha, apparently.'

'Sasha! Theo's gone to see Sasha? Merlin, are you sure?'

'Quite sure. He said something about buying her some roses, I'd got some for Janine you see, and – '

'Yes, I see, Merlin,' said Harriet very quietly. 'Well, send my love to Janine. Goodbye.'

'Bye, my dear. Are you all right? You sound a bit down. Not surprising really, I suppose.'

'No,' said Harriet, 'not really.'

She put the phone down, picked up her car keys and her bag, and, keeping her mind carefully blank, walked out of the door.

Harriet had had her appendix out when she'd been eleven; due to the bungling of an inefficient anaesthetist (whom her father had had removed from his hospital within the week), she came round from the anaesthetic a little too soon, before she was even out of the theatre. She had never forgotten it, the way she was hurtled from darkness into white-hot pain; she had screamed, and then was dispatched swiftly back into the darkness and awoke again hours later, safely and aware only of mild discomfort, but traumatized nonetheless. Her experience that evening was much the same: one moment she was driving automatically and dully down the Cromwell Road extension and the next she was in such emotional pain that she almost crashed the car.

Theo back with Sasha. Taking roses to Sasha, rushing to meet Sasha, only – what? – two hours after he had told her he loved her still, that he had always loved her, that he felt nothing for Sasha, never had, had only married her to ease the pain of losing her, losing Harriet. 'Christ!' she yelled aloud, throwing her head back, trying to concentrate, to keep at least most of her mind on the road, the traffic. 'Christ, Theo, how could you, how could you?'

Chapter Thirty-Nine

Theo 6.30pm

Theo sat at his desk looking at the relics of his marriage to Sasha: a large fake diamond engagement ring, her keys to the house in The Boltons, the Daimler and the Range Rover (he had never allowed her to drive the Bentley) and a rough draft of the articles of association of her new company. Mr Hennessy had proved to be younger and better-looking than he had expected, and possessed of a redoubtable legal mind, but he was more than a little out of his depth with his new client. Theo felt almost sorry for him.

Right. He would phone Mungo, fix a place for dinner, go back to the office and do some work, and then maybe try, just try phoning Harriet again.

Mungo sounded subdued but no more; he said it had been a bitch of a day but he was looking forward to seeing his father. 'Me too,' said Theo. 'Ritz, eight o'clock?'

'Fine,' said Mungo.

Theo spent two hours trying to distract himself from the thought of Harriet, and then rang her flat. No answer. The studio. No answer. He tried Rufus, Tilly, the Headleigh Drayton house: Annabel told him sulkily that everyone was at the hospital visiting her mother and she had been left to answer the phone. 'And before you ask, she's fine.'

'Good,' said Theo, 'send her my love. Harriet's not there?'

'No, I don't think so. I'm sure she's not, it's family only tonight.'

'All right, Annabel. If by chance she phones, get her to call me.'

'I will if I'm here,' said Annabel. 'I'm hoping to go out.'

'Love you too,' said Theo and rang off. He had forgotten briefly about Susie; he ordered some flowers for her, and then rang Janine again. She was out, but Merlin answered the phone.

'She rang – oh, about half an hour ago. Said she was going home to Wedbourne. I told her you'd been here, said you were off to see Sasha – '

'You what? Merlin, I wasn't.'

'But you said you were, my boy. I heard you. You said you were going to take her some roses.'

'No, Merlin, I said I was going to see Sasha's lawyer. You must have misunderstood. Sasha and I are getting divorced. It was a joke about the roses.'

'What, already? That's a pity. Quite liked Sasha. I'd have liked to have her around for a bit longer. Oh dear, well, I've given some duff information then.'

'You have a bit.'

'Even told her you were taking flowers along,' said Merlin cheerfully. 'She will be confused. Better get onto her.'

'Oh Merlin,' said Theo in agony, 'Merlin, this is terrible. And I can't get onto her. If she's on the way to Wedbourne.'

On the M40, in the pouring rain, in that bloody Peugeot of hers, that went so much too fast, that she never had serviced; upset, angry, thinking he was rushing off to see Sasha with flowers. Christ Almighty, what a mess.

'Better get after her then,' said Merlin. 'You can catch her up easily. Bit of sport. I'd come with you if I didn't have so much to do here. Very complicated, getting married. Can't think how you've managed it five times.'

Theo ran out of his office, tore down the stairs, into the car park, into the Bentley, roared out into Dover Street. It was raining; the traffic was appalling.

An hour later he was still not even on the motorway.

He rang James. 'Is Harriet there?'

'No, not yet. I'm getting worried about her actually. The weather's frightful and she's been over two hours already.'

'Can't you ring her on her mobile?'

'She doesn't seem to have it with her.'

'Oh Christ,' said Theo.

After the Beaconsfield turn-off, the traffic eased. Theo put his foot down, tried to tell himself she was all right. It wasn't dark, she was a good driver, she wasn't hysterical, she'd be fine. Probably just stopped for a coffee or something. Or run out of petrol, she was always doing that. Silly girl. Stupid girl. Why couldn't she have listened to him at lunchtime, then she'd be all right, safe, with him – His car phone rang. 'Yes?'

It was Janine. 'Theo, I am so sorry. I just heard what Merlin did. The stupid, stupid old man – '

Even in his anguish Theo was amused to hear Merlin, who was only a little more than ten years Janine's senior, described by her as an old man.

'It's all right, Janine. I remember how it happened. I was talking and my phone rang mid-sentence. He meant well.'

'He should not have meddled. We have just had our first quarrel. I have told him – '

'Janine darling, not now.' He really couldn't face the details of a lover's tiff. 'Have you spoken to James?'

'Yes, and she is still not there. He is very worried.'

'Me too,' said Theo and rang off.

It was round the next corner, between the huge white chalk cliffs near the Thame turn-off, that he hit the tailback to the crash. It was maybe half a mile ahead: he could see it, several cars and a lorry packed together, police lights flashing, two ambulances. The traffic was at a complete standstill. Theo sat there for roughly thirty seconds, thinking he was going to throw up, then got out of the Bentley, just left it in the fast lane, and ran, ran down the hard shoulder, his lungs straining, his heart bursting, until he reached the heap of cars. One of the ambulances was just pulling away; a policeman waved him back.

'Not now, sir, if you don't mind. Keep the area clear. Terrible mess.'

'I can see that,' said Theo. He walked forward slowly, peering terrified into the wreckage. Two of the cars were unrecognizable. The third was a Peugeot. Crumpled, mangled, standing almost on its tail, but still indisputably a Peugeot. A Peugeot 205. Black. Christ Almighty. A K-reg black Peugeot 205.

'Not now, sir,' said the policeman again.

Theo ignored him, went on.

'For God's sake, sir.'

'I think,' said Theo, speaking with immense difficulty, 'in fact, no, I know – that's my girlfriend's car.'

A police car took him to the hospital; he stood in the doorway of casualty while the young sergeant went up to the desk, made inquiries. He looked over his shoulder at Theo, then turned his back on him and followed a nurse into the netherland beyond the waiting room. Theo knew then; he knew that she had died. She had died, and she had died thinking he was a cheap, tacky boor who lied and fucked around and did not, as she had said so often, know the meaning of love. She was lost to him now, lost forever, and he would never get the chance to be with her again, talk to her again, hold her, care for her, love her. She was gone, in all her passionate, lovely courage, gone in a tangle of metal, crushed, brutally murdered by a mistake, by a misunderstanding. Theo felt suddenly violently sick; he rushed outside and threw up, over and over again, then walked very slowly back into casualty, into reception, sat down and put his face in his hands.

A young nurse, the one who had led the policeman off, came over to him, put her hand gently on his shoulder. 'Mr Buchan is it?'

'Yes,' said Theo, 'yes, that's right.'

Every word was an enormous struggle to get out; it was as if some huge pressure was constricting his throat.

'Would you like a cup of tea?'

They always did that, offered relatives tea. It was supposed to help, God knows why. He shook his head at her dumbly.

'Well, if you wait just a little while, someone will see you. Are you sure you're all right?'

He nodded again. The doctor, he supposed: to tell him. All the usual clichés, that they had done all they could, that she hadn't suffered, hadn't known anything about it; maybe he would even have to identify her, someone had to, he knew that. He found the thought of looking at Harriet, a suddenly dead Harriet, quite horrific. It was not death itself, Deirdre had died, she had died in his arms, he had held her for hours, and for hours after she died had sat looking at her, wondering where she had actually gone, why he could not have gone with her; but they'd said all the right things, he and she, all the things that needed to be said, had reassured, tried to comfort one another, and he'd had Mungo at least, had that much of Deirdre left to him. He'd said nothing to Harriet that was right, and he had nothing left of her, only her face, raw with misery when she told him to get out of her life and leave her alone. And now she had got out of his.

'Mr Buchan?' It was a young doctor; he looked, Theo thought, like an extra in *Casualty*, with his white coat and his stethoscope and his carefully arranged face.

'Yes?'

'Mr Buchan, if you come with me you can see Miss Forrest now.'

So he *was* going to have to identify her. How bad would she look, how badly mutilated would she be? Was he going to be able to stand it? He stood up, and felt suddenly very dizzy.

'Are you all right, Mr Buchan? Did anyone give you tea?'

'No. Yes. Well – '

'This is a terrible ordeal, I know,' said the doctor. 'Nothing can really prepare you for it. I'm so sorry. Now, I think you should be ready for a bit of a shock, but – '

Theo wasn't listening. He was standing outside the cubicle and nothing he had ever done in his life had required this kind of courage. He raised his hand to pull back the curtain, and it fell again; he simply couldn't do it. 'I'm sorry,' he mumbled to the doctor. 'I don't seem to be able to – '

'That's all right,' said the doctor. 'Let me.'

Theo looked away, hearing the curtain pulled back, knowing he must turn, look at her, what was left of her, still unable to do it.

'Just a moment,' he mumbled to the doctor. 'Just a moment. Sorry.' Go on, Theo, do it, do it, man, for Christ's sake, look at her, get it over, do it, do it –

'Theo.' It was Harriet's voice, weak, slightly slurred, but still her voice, unmistakably hers, unmistakably real. 'Theo, what on earth are you doing here?'

He drove her home next morning to Wedbourne, his car retrieved from the fast lane of the M40 and brought to the hospital by a reproachful policeman who told him he was lucky, it could well have caused another accident.

James followed in his car; he had arrived at the hospital in response to Theo's phone call, and they had sat together through the night while Harriet slept, checked on hourly for concussion and a suspected fractured skull. They all said it was a miracle she had come out alive; two people had died, three had sustained major injuries, and she had suffered only a fractured ankle (although broken in two places, possibly requiring surgery), a broken arm, two cracked ribs, a great many cuts and bruises on her face and what they were assured was a comparatively mild concussion.

The police came in the morning to question her, but there was no question of any of the blame being hers; several witnesses had seen the lorry (going in any case far too fast) swerve from the middle lane straight across the road, and go into a skid and then a spin, hitting the first car head-on, and then Harriet's. She had crashed onto the hard shoulder and into the barrier, and the car behind her had hit her tail sideways. She had been saved by her seat belt and the fact that she had been skidding so fast her brakes had been useless.

'If they'd worked, the car, and therefore you, might have been hit much nearer the centre,' said James, stroking her head tenderly.

'Oh God,' said Harriet, 'and you know what I thought? The last thing I thought? That I really should have had the car serviced, then I could have stopped.'

'Wouldn't have made any difference,' said Theo.

'What I don't understand,' said James, 'is why you were here at all, Theo. I thought you were having dinner with Mungo.'

'Oh God,' said Theo, 'he's probably still sitting at the Ritz.'

They set her up in the drawing room, made a bed for her there, since she couldn't handle the stairs. She slept a lot for the first few days, her head gave her a lot of pain, but then she became more cheerful and a great deal more demanding, wanted to be out in the garden (summer had returned), wanted a phone, wanted endless jugs of fresh iced lemonade, wanted very specific kinds of food, mainly rather spicy things, curries and chillies. They raided Maggie's freezer, then moved on to takeaways and the food department at Marks and Spencers.

James provided her with crutches, but her broken arm prevented her from using them, so he got her a wheelchair, which she rather liked but still needed help with; she couldn't propel it efficiently herself (again because of her arm) and sat crossly dependent while they wheeled her about the house and garden, and even on occasions down the lane.

Theo refused to leave her; he nursed her and cared for her with surprising sweetness, performing the most intimate tasks with a detached competence, anticipating her needs with extraordinary perception. It was only after a week of this that Harriet properly realized that the sickroom was familiar territory to him, that he had nursed Deirdre, Mungo's mother, almost single-handed during her illness. She found the thought infinitely moving, found, too, that her emotions towards him shifted, softened, found herself in those first shocked, pain-filled days dangerously near to admitting love. Then as she recovered, began to gain strength, physical and emotional, as thought took over from reaction, she struggled to put herself back into a more objective mode. Theo observing all this, recognizing the conflicts, was at once amused and touched by it.

She woke one night, hot, aching, thirsty, reached out for the glass of water by her bed, and knocked it over. 'Shit,' she said aloud, but quite quietly, her sense of helplessness adding to the blanket of misery, wondering if she felt bad enough, desperate enough to ring the little bell Theo had supplied her with to summon them. But before she'd had time to decide he was there, sleepily alert, struggling into his dressing gown, and 'What is it, Harriet?' he said. 'Is the pain bad, do you want me to get you something?' And she stared at him, so awed by his response to her need, his sensitivity to her pain that she was unable to speak, unable to do anything but smile and reach out for his hand.

'I seem to be making progress,' was all he said, smiling back at her, and was gone, to return with more iced water, her painkillers, and a quiet swift neatening of the bed; and then he sat beside her, waiting for her misery to ease.

'You're wonderful,' was the last thing she said, drifting back to sleep. 'Dear Theo. Thank you.'

In the morning her mood had changed; she was irritable, tired, and anxious too that he should not think she and her resolve were weakening. Always one jump ahead of her, he teased her, said it was all right. He wasn't going to cash in on any goodwill he might have engendered, he was going to London for the day, so she could relax.

'I'm perfectly relaxed,' said Harriet petulantly, aware of a distinct lack of such a quality in almost every area of herself.

'You don't look it,' he said mildly and bent to kiss her cheek. Harriet turned away.

Mostly he stayed at the Court House, conducted his business from there, moving Myra Harman and Mark Protheroe into the Royal Hotel for several days a week, using both the phone lines, one for his fax, as well as his own mobile and car phone.

'You must be singly responsible for most of Telecom's profits,' said James plaintively after three days of this. 'I really can't go on, Theo, having to go out to the village post office to make a call.'

'Sorry, James. It's not for long.'

He had told James on the long night at the hospital about Harriet, told him he loved her, that he wanted to marry her. James had taken the news with interesting calm.

'I can't imagine what she sees in you, and it had better be the last marriage you ever make, or I swear to God I'll kill you, but if that's what she wants – '

'She does, but she doesn't know it yet,' said Theo.

At Harriet's request, her accident was played down to Maggie. 'I know she'll want to come home and look after me, but that will be difficult for everyone and probably most of all me. I shall have to be fussed over which I hate and listen to her telling me how wonderful Cressida is being and I just shan't be able to stand it.' So Theo phoned and simply told Maggie that Harriet had had a bit of a bump in her car and hurt her arm and was taking a few days off to recuperate. Maggie was happy, he reported, with her friend and was house-hunting. Cressida, it seemed, was also happy, feeling better, coping with her situation. Maggie was probably going over for a few days in September. 'She says,' he added, his dark eyes gleaming with malice, 'that Cressida has written to Oliver, trying to explain. Your mother says she is sure Oliver will understand and see that's for the best.'

'I'm sure it is,' said Harriet, hitting her pillow viciously, 'but not for the reasons Mummy thinks. I wonder what this person is like. A sucker I should think.'

A week after the wedding day a letter arrived from Cressida for James, begging his forgiveness, hoping he would understand. 'We plan to be married in the Bureau de l'Etat (that's the registry office) as soon as he is out of hospital. I wish you could meet Gérard, but I expect you would prefer not to. He is very ill, I'm afraid, he's having treatment, transfusions, they're seeking a bone-marrow donor for him. But he's not expected to live for very long. The best we can hope is that he will survive to see his child born.'

James was clearly distressed by the letter; he went for a long walk and came back his face drawn and grey.

'Do you want to talk about it?' said Harriet.

'No,' he said, 'no, not now.'

He spent the rest of the day in his study, only emerging for supper which he ate in almost complete silence.

'It sounds a terrible thing to say but this is a perfect scenario for Cressida,' said Harriet to Theo later. 'It's got everything, romance, tragedy, mystery. She must be very happy.'

'You sound very cynical,' said Theo.

'Cressida makes me feel cynical,' said Harriet. 'I can't help it.'

Slowly, painfully, she was coming to terms with her father's long relationship with Susie.

He broached the subject one evening when Theo was in London, and oddly, after an initial resistance, she found it helped her, eased her hostility to him, to air it, to hear his halting apologies.

'I can't excuse it, can't explain it,' he said simply. 'I was in love with her. I behaved very badly for a long long time. Now I'm getting my just desserts.'

'You are.'

'Yes, I've lost them both. I'm going to be very lonely. It's a fitting punishment for me.'

Harriet was silent.

Tilly and Rufus came down to visit. Tilly was wearing a large engagement ring, a futuristic sculptured gold design, set with tiny spangled diamonds. She said she had given up swearing, and planned on giving up smoking for Rufus, but it was too much to ask her to do both things at once.

'And what are you giving up, Rufus?' asked Theo.

'I couldn't think of anything,' he said. 'I seem to be perfect already. But I've promised Tilly we won't send our sons to public school.'

'Sons? Tilly, this is a huge change of heart,' said Harriet laughing.

'Yeah, I know, I know. I think maybe, one day, with a Caesarian under a double general anaesthetic I might be able to manage something. I really am quite interested to see what we might produce between the two of us.'

'Me too,' said Rufus. He pushed back his fair hair, smiled his lovely, gentle smile at her, his dark eyes soft with love.

'Rufus, you look more and more like your mother every day,' said Harriet.

Susie was recovered, but had agreed to have the surgery Mr Hobson recommended. Another lump had appeared – still benign but none the less worrying.

'I can have a reconstruction done,' she said to Alistair, 'I hate the thought of it so much, but I think I should. And I shouldn't be so vain, it's terribly wrong of me. Anyway, no one but you will see it, and if you can cope with it then so can I.'

'Is that a promise, my darling?' said Alistair lightly. Susie looked at him; he was smiling carefully, but his eyes were unreadable.

'Yes, Alistair, it's a promise.'

Mungo came to visit too, bearing a jeroboam of champagne, a bunch of three dozen roses and a sheaf of details of studios and offices where Harriet might start up her next business. 'Special rates to you, madam, and we'd waive our usual insistence on a year's rent in advance.'

He looked vaguely different, Harriet thought; more sober, more grown-up. The wild black hair was shorter, neater-looking, he was wearing a suit (linen to be sure, but still a suit) and a tie, and he produced the studio details from a formal-looking briefcase, rather than the canvas bag he had always used before. But he looked happy, more self-confident than she could remember, and the hug he gave his father was unmistakably affectionate.

'Mungo, you're sweet,' said Harriet laughing, flicking through the papers, lingering longingly over a studio in Bloomsbury, 'but I'm an undischarged bankrupt. I can't possibly start taking on expensive new premises. If I do start again, it will have to be from the kitchen table here, I should think. I've even got to sell my flat.'

'That's ridiculous, there must be dozens of people who'd make you a loan. Dad for a start, why don't – '

'Mungo, no,' said Harriet hastily. 'Your dad is the last person I'd take money from.'

'Why?'

'Well, because – just because.'

'You're mad,' said Mungo. 'He'd like to do it and he's very fond of you, you know.'

'Yes,' said Harriet, 'yes, I know he is.'

Janine and Merlin also came to visit several times. They'd set their wedding date for the end of August. They were having a small civil ceremony in Paris, followed by a luncheon at the Meurice and a large party in London, before leaving for their journey through China. Merlin was remorseful, still convinced he had been instrumental in causing Harriet's accident. 'Darling Merlin, you weren't. Don't flatter yourself. And don't flatter Theo either. As if I'd care if he was going back to Sasha or not anyway.'

'Not what he's hoping to hear, I understand,' said Merlin, and received a sharp kick on the ankle from Janine. 'Sorry, my dear. Can't do a thing right these days,' he said to Harriet plaintively; but he winked at her and then at Janine, and took her small white hand and kissed it tenderly.

'Have you been saying things to Merlin?' said Harriet crossly to Theo that evening, as she lay in the garden on a chaise longue, drinking her way through yet another jugful of lemonade.

'I say a lot of things to Merlin.'

'You know perfectly well what I mean. About me. Us.'

'No, but Janine might have. Why don't you have some champagne in that?'

'You know I'm not allowed alcohol. Theo, you are appalling. How dare you discuss our lives with other people?'

'Well, I'm not allowed to discuss them with you.'

'There's nothing to discuss,' said Harriet.

They talked for hours, night after night, the three of them, about Cressida: whose story to believe, which explanation might be the right one, tracking backwards and forwards over the same ground, the same details, the story each of them wanted to believe, the story that to each of them seemed the most likely.

'A combination of them all, perhaps?' said Theo. 'There is no doubt she is in love with this man, that he is ill – '

'He doesn't look ill,' said Harriet sharply, 'in that photograph.'

'Harriet, you're being very hard,' said James. 'You can't tell from a photograph, and besides leukaemia patients often look comparatively normal until very near – well, for a long time. He's in hospital – '

'How do you know that?' said Harriet. 'We have Cressida's word for it. Oliver had her word that she was pregnant last year and she wasn't, we had her word she loved Oliver, was going to marry him. For God's sake, you're all obsessed with her, duped by her – ' Angry tears had filled her eyes; she struggled to stand up on her crutches, to leave the room, almost fell over.

'Harriet,' said Theo gently, easing her back into her chair, 'Harriet, don't be so hostile. It doesn't help.'

'I can't help it,' she said, 'I am hostile. I can't forgive her, I can't even think about forgiving her. How you can, Daddy, I really don't know. At best, at very best, even if we believe her wonderful, romantic story, she still hurt you so much that day. And Mummy too, who adored her so. She could have talked to you, discussed it, told you what she felt she had to do. I just don't understand you.'

'Well,' said James, 'the human psyche is very complex. And she was in crisis. Try to put yourself in her position, Harriet, desperate, pregnant, trapped. What would you have done?'

'That's an impossible question for her to answer,' said Theo quietly. 'Harriet would not, could not, have been in that kind of situation. She's too honest even to imagine it.'

Harriet stared at him, surprised as always by the depth of his knowledge of her family, the daily conflict of her feelings towards him intensifying sharply.

'Theo, don't speak for me,' she said finally. 'My brain hasn't been affected by the accident, you know.'

'No,' he said, 'I can see that. James, can I take some more of that excellent Armagnac?'

'Yes of course,' said James. He seemed distracted, scarcely aware of where he was. 'It's so odd talking about her like this, I feel somehow I don't know her at all any more, that she can in no way be my child, the one I loved and cared for and endeavoured to bring up well and did so badly with. It's as you said to your mother, Harriet, she has become another woman altogether, one we simply don't know any more. And conjecture as we may, we can't properly understand her or why she did what she did. But I – I have to share that woman's view – what was her name, Harriet, the gynaecologist – '

'Bradman,' said Harriet. 'Jennifer Bradman.'

'Yes. I have to share her view, looking at Cressida from this viewpoint, that she was – well, disturbed. With hindsight, she did display a classic personality disorder. The near compulsion to lie, the complex deceptions – those flying lessons she talked you into are classic, Theo, there was no real reason for secrecy there, after all, her constant health problems, her ineptness with money.'

'You say that,' said Harriet, 'but I've been pretty inept with it myself. No one suggests I have a personality disorder. Or perhaps you do,' she said, glaring at Theo.

'Harriet, of course we don't,' said James. 'Don't be silly. You've just made some bad business decisions. That's completely different.'

'Oh well, good,' said Harriet, her voice loaded with sarcasm. 'That's all right then, I can relax. Well, I think that selling the flat, for instance, keeping that a secret, just proves she was planning on doing something drastic.'

'Not at all,' said Theo. 'She would have had to sell her flat anyway, what use would it have been to her if she was living in New York? She could have explained it away so easily.'

'You're all obsessed with her,' said Harriet. She felt the tears rising again. 'Here we are still making excuses for her, saying poor Cressida, there must have been something wrong with her, when she was just a – a brat, a spoilt, self-centred girl, who you all adored.'

'She was indeed,' said James, his face heavy with pain, 'and it hurts me to say it, but that is another reason for not being too hard on her now. Being overindulged, the spoilt baby as she undoubtedly was, the youngest, having excuses made for her all the time, does predispose to that sort of condition. I've talked to people about it.'

'Well,' said Theo, 'as I said, I personally take the view the answer is not simple. That we have to accept an amalgam of all three explanations.'

'Not, surely not, Julia's?' said James, desolation in his voice.

'I'd say not, I'd like to think not,' said Theo, 'but it's an extraordinary lie on Julia's part, and if she did show Cressida the letter and Cressida had no interest in the money, then surely she would have told Oliver, would have laughed – or even cried about it.'

'Maybe,' said Harriet slowly, 'that was the last straw. Maybe she was desperate anyway, and Julia's hostility tipped her over into going.'

Theo was staring into his glass, his dark eyes very sombre, his face infinitely sad. 'I think,' he said, 'I think the truth is that none of us will ever really know. Only Cressida knows. And she will never tell.'

'Listen,' said Theo one evening, sitting down by Harriet, taking her hand, 'there's a lot to discuss. I don't understand you, Harriet. I love you. I know you love me – '

'Theo, I don't. Well, of course I do, but not like that. It's over. It was a lovely time, a lovely experience, but – well, it just wouldn't work. It couldn't. I know.'

'How do you know?'

'Because – because I just do. Our lives won't, can't go together. You'd start taking me over, owning me, and I won't be owned.'

'I don't want to own you.'

'Theo, you can't help owning things. It's in your very soul.'

432

'Harriet, I swear I won't even try to take you over. I won't ask you to marry me, I won't suggest I give you any money for your wretched company, I won't even suggest I give you money for anything. You can live in some hovel in Brixton or somewhere like that and I'll come and visit you sometimes and we can eat baked beans and drink bitter paid for out of your social security money. How's that? As long as I can love you, that's all I ask.'

'Oh don't be ridiculous,' said Harriet. 'And anyway, you know perfectly well I'm probably going to New York.'

'Good God,' he said. 'I'd forgotten about that. I thought you'd given the whole idea up.'

'Well I haven't. You were wrong. Wrong about the whole thing.'

'What do you mean?'

'Telling Hayden Cotton I'd never go.'

'Oh,' he said, 'oh yes. I'd forgotten that too. It seemed like a good idea at the time – and it worked, didn't it?'

'What do you mean it worked? What worked?'

'I told him to tell you I'd said you'd never go, because I knew that was the one thing that would change your mind. And I was right.'

'You what!' said Harriet. 'Theo, you are absolutely outrageous. Playing with my life as if it was some kind of a – a computer game.'

Rage swept over her, pure, sweet rage, hot, liquid. All he had done for her since her accident, all the care he had lavished on her, the thoughtfulness, the love, was blotted out, and she could have, given the strength, killed him. Her voice rose, shook with fury. 'How dare you, Theo, how could you? I'm not one of your businesses, one of your projects that you can just push around however and whenever you like. Dear God, you've made a mistake telling me that. If anything, anything could have convinced me I was right, that we could never – '

He looked at her, and saw she was actually near to tears, her face white and tense.

'Harriet I – '

'Theo, for God's sake just leave me alone. Leave me alone.' She was shouting now, her fists clenched. 'All right? Get out of my life. I keep saying it, and you won't take any notice. Get out, go back to London, go to New York, just go anywhere, but please please stop this, I can't stand it.'

'All right,' he said quietly. 'I'll stop it. I'll go. I'll go now. You win, Harriet. It's over.'

Looking after him as he left the room, seeing his great shoulders drooped in misery, hearing his voice, his deep, resonant voice, harsh with pain, she had to put her hand over her mouth to stop herself calling out, calling that she knew she was wrong, that she knew she loved him.

He was gone within the hour, everything packed into the Bentley. He didn't even say goodbye to her, just left. The house seemed bleak, bereft of him.

Harriet went to bed early; she was tired, but slept badly, and when she did sleep she had dreadful, complex dark dreams, with Theo at the heart of them. She woke late, feeling exhausted, shattered; her father helped her downstairs. She sat drinking cup after cup of coffee, staring morosely out of the window, trying not to think too much about what she had done, trying to convince herself that she'd been right, that she was actually feeling much better. It was a lovely day, rather like Cressida's wedding day, mistily golden, but summer was almost over now, the roses were drooping, dropping, and the lawn looked parched. Only a few weeks, but a whole life ago; and here she was still hurting, still angry, still lonely. Why did she have to do this, behave as she did, so sure she knew what was best for her when she didn't know at all? She suddenly wanted Theo so much, so badly, just wanted him there, near her, that she moaned aloud.

James looked up startled from the paper. 'Ankle hurting?'

'No.'

'Head hurting?'

'No. Just my heart.'

'Ah,' he said, 'that old thing.'

He paused, then said, 'You love him, don't you?'

'Yes,' she said, 'yes, I'm afraid I do. So much. So very much. But – '

'But what?'

'Oh – nothing. It could never ever work out. And it's too late, I'm afraid.'

'It's never too late.'

'It is this time. And I know it's for the best really. We could never, ever have had a life together. We'd have killed each other.'

'Well,' he said, 'it might have been fun for a while. Until you did.'

'No. No, I don't think so. The thing is, Daddy, he's got me wrong. He's never done anything really, not a single thing, that showed he properly understood me. And what I'm about. He thinks he does, but he just doesn't.'

'It isn't easy,' said James, 'understanding someone properly.'

There was a silence, then she said, 'I think I'd really like to go down and sit by the bridge. I love it there, it always makes me feel better, and I haven't been since – well, since Cressida's wedding day. Could you help me down there?'

'Yes, of course I will. Get your crutches and we'll hobble down together.'

It was very quiet at the bridge; the water was low after the summer drought, and there was a mass of weed muffling the small waterfall. But it was cool there, and comforting. She sat on the stone seat and threw bits of twig into the water, and smiled at a particularly foolish moorhen trying to walk on the weed. 'You really should know better than that,' she said.

'I could say the same to you,' said Theo.

She turned; he was standing there, on the other side of the bridge, looking at her very seriously. He looked slightly odd, slightly misshapen; he seemed to have something buttoned into his jacket.

'Theo,' she said, with an immense effort, 'Theo, I wish you'd stop prolonging the agony. How many more times do I have to say it? It really would be much better if you'd just go away.'

'It's all right,' he said, 'I've only come to say goodbye. I think we owe each other that.'

'Oh,' said Harriet uncertainly. 'Yes, yes of course we do.'

'Can I come and shake hands,' he said. 'Would that be all right?'

'Yes, yes of course,' she said, smiling brightly. 'Please do.'

He walked slowly over the bridge, stood in front of her.

She looked up at him, studying him for the last time, still carefully smiling. He looked back at her very solemnly.

Finally he said, 'I've got something for you here. A goodbye present. I can't really shake hands until I give it to you.' There was a silence as he started to undo the buttons of the jacket.

'You're always saying,' he said, 'that I don't understand you, don't know what you really want. This might make you change your mind. God, I wish you'd help me with the bloody thing.'

Harriet sat wordless, staring at the bundle, the bump wriggling inside his jacket, realizing slowly that it was moving, was wriggling slightly, that emerging from the darkness of the jacket came first a small wet black nose then a golden rumpled face, then two fat blunt paws.

'Here you are,' said Theo. 'Something I do know you really want. He comes with all my love. He's called Biggles.'

Forbidden Places

Dedication

For Paul. For a lot of nerve-steadying, and hand-holding as the going got rough and the deadline loomed, not to mention help of a more practical nature with plots, counter plots and on more than one occasion when there seemed a serious danger of there being no plot at all . . .

Acknowledgments

As always a large supporting cast helped me get this book on stage: in no particular order I would like to call them most gratefully from the wings.

Captain A. R. Simpson, R.E. TM., John Casson, O.B.E., Jill Saxton, Ronald Wilson, Mrs. Estelle Lee who worked for the WVS, Mrs. Joyce Haydn Jones, Mrs. Glenys Thomas, and Miss Pam Elson who were all in the WRNS, Mrs. Jean Proctor and Mrs. Irene Price who worked with the Women's Land Army, Monica Joyce and George Kiddle.

There were also several books which were outstandingly helpful to me: *Elizabeth's Britain* and *London at War*, both by Philip Ziegler, *MacIndoe's Army*, by Peter Williams and Ted Harrison, *Spitfire Patrol* by Group Captain Colin Gray and *The Day They Took the Children* by Ben Wicks.

No one ever had better publishers: Katie Pope and Caroleen Conquest guided the book safely into harbour (bit of a mixed metaphor here, but never mind) and tied up a thousand loose ends brilliantly, Claire Hegarty made sure it looked wonderful, Louise Page made sure everyone knew about it, and Rosie Cheetham, brilliant editor (and amazingly still good friend!) as always knew exactly how it should be and made sure I got it right.

Desmond Elliott, not so much an agent, more a delightful way of life, did much to keep me both sane and sanguine; and last, but of course not least, my family helped enormously simply by being there, listening to my frequent wails of despair and assuring me with admirable patience that it would all be all right in the end.

June 24th 1995

'I'm going to make her tell us today. She's kept that secret from us for fifty years now, and I really feel that's quite long enough.' These words, spoken in a clear, melodic and extremely well-bred voice echoed through the Palm Court of the Ritz Hotel, halting several conversations in mid-sentence, if not word and causing several more cups to rattle in their saucers; the owner of the voice, elegant and extremely stylish, dressed in a white silk suit, long shapely legs curled neatly beneath her gilt chair, became aware of the fact and smiled pleasedly at her companion. The companion, dressed more conservatively but still with considerable chic, in a black wool dress, a wide pearl choker round her long, graceful neck, looked back at her seriously for a moment and then said, 'Well I'd put my money on Grace personally, Clarissa. You've been working on her all this time with a complete lack of success. Anyway, does it really matter? As you say it's fifty years. Probably best left I'd have thought.'

'I just don't like not knowing things,' said Clarissa. 'Secrets irritate me, Florence. Fifty-year-old secrets irritate me even more. And that one of Grace's is a particularly intriguing one.'

'And I suppose you haven't got any yourself?' said Florence lightly.

'Me!' said Clarissa, her large brown eyes opening very wide, her smile sweetly frank as she looked at Florence. 'Of course not. Always tell everybody everything, I do. Can't keep anything to myself at all. You should know that Florence darling.'

'Mmm,' said Florence; she looked back at Clarissa, her grey eyes thoughtful.

'And what's that supposed to mean?'

'Nothing. Nothing at all.' She visibly brushed the question aside.

'Only that we all three of us had a fairly – well, a very – eventful war. Wouldn't you say? None of us got off exactly lightly. Lots of interesting stories all round. And secrets come to that.'

'Well yes, but you and I knew each other's,' said Clarissa. 'Grace's has remained her own. Well, the main one anyway. And I think she owes it to us – oh now look there she is, the darling, now.

She stood up and waved a graceful arm; 'Grace, over here!'

'Hallo Clarissa, Florence!' said Grace, embracing them both, settling herself into her chair, tugging at her gloves. 'Sorry to be so late. I got stuck in traffic coming through the park. And then I was thinking, as I sat there, how it was all allotments once, and your friend, whatever was she called Clarissa, oh yes, Bunty, she joined the pig club they ran from it. A pig farm, right under the Albert Memorial. Who'd believe that now?'

'Nobody I'm sure,' said Clarissa. 'Sit down darling and have some tea. Or shall we have some champagne? I think the occasion merits it don't you? Let's get that sweet waiter over and ask for some.'

'Champagne!' said Florence. 'Clarissa, it's only half past four.'

'I know, I know. But I think one of the compensations of being our immense age is being able to do exactly what we like when we like. And just at the moment I'd like some champagne.'

'Yes,' said Florence, 'and you think it might loosen Grace's tongue. I warn you Grace, she's going to get you talking today. Hell bent on it.'

'Oh really?' said Grace. 'About what I wonder.'

'You know what about,' said Clarissa, 'you know perfectly well. And I think after fifty years you really owe it to us to – '

'That is such a lovely suit Clarissa,' said Grace. 'Where did you get it?'

'Oh you are so irritating,' said Clarissa. 'I got it at Harvey Nichols. If it matters.'

'It does to me, I like to know these things. I feel I'm still catching up. I've never quite got over being the country mouse on clothing coupons while you swanned round looking dazzling in your Wrens uniform.'

'Yes, well I must say you did often look a bit dreary,' said Florence, reaching for a sandwich in a slender, beautifully manicured hand, 'quite a lot of the time anyway.'

'Thanks Florence. And you did know how to make me feel worse. Quite a lot of the time.'

'Girls, girls,' said Clarissa, 'let us not get rowdy. Not here anyway. Ah, the champagne. How lovely. Grace darling, you first.'

'Thank you,' said Grace, 'but I think I should warn you Clarissa, I have absolutely no intention of having my tongue loosened. If Florence is right and that's what you want.'

'Oh really!' said Clarissa. 'What harm could it possibly do now? For you to tell us all about it? And anyway as if we'd tell.'

'I might not tell, Clarissa,' said Florence, 'but you certainly would. Anyone and everyone who'd listen.'

'Oh, how unkind,' said Clarissa. 'Of course I wouldn't. And anyway, who'd listen to the ramblings of an old lady?'

'Everyone listens to you,' said Florence briskly, 'they have to, they don't have any choice.'

'I do hope you're more tactful when you're in the House of Commons, Florence darling,' said Clarissa, 'although I suppose it's not really a very tactful place. If I talked like that to my shareholders, I'd be in a lot of trouble. Anyway, as I said in the first place, Grace, the time has come.'

'But why?' said Grace. 'Why specially now?'

'Well because it's such a milestone. As I said. Fifty years we've been meeting here in this restaurant, every single midsummer day, such a lovely idea I must say, even though I say it myself, and never missed once, have we, no matter what happened?'

'Well except that one year when Florence was canvassing and we all went to help, and had the meeting up there,' said Grace.

'And the other year when Grace took all her pupils to play at that lovely festival in Ireland and we went to listen,' said Florence, 'and don't forget when you were in New York, opening your company there, and we all went up the Empire State together – '

'Yes, all right, all right,' said Clarissa, 'you're just proving my point. We've always had the meeting, and we've always stayed absolutely and utterly close. And supported each other. Husbands, babies, success and failure, heartaches and happiness, shared it all. And still Grace keeps this huge secret to herself. And I absolutely know for a fact there is a secret, that there was much more to it all than you ever let on. I think it's very mean of you.'

'Well I'm sorry,' said Grace, 'sorry if you think I'm mean. But I still can't tell you.'

'But – '

'Excuse me,' said Florence, 'fascinating as this is, I simply have to go and make a phone call. Check out what's happening with the European vote. I'll be back very soon. Don't tell her a thing Grace, will you?'

'Now Clarissa,' said Grace, watching Florence disappear in the direction of the foyer and the phones, and her blue eyes had a surprisingly steely expression in them suddenly. 'I wasn't the only one with a secret was I? We all had them. And you wouldn't want me to try and make you tell yours would you?'

'No, but that's quite different, said Clarissa smiling sweetly, and

3

there was a flush suddenly on her still-lovely English rose skin. 'Mine was – well – more personal. As you might say.' She looked round to make sure Florence was not yet returning. 'It could hurt still if it was told. Your story – what we know of it anyway,' she added briskly, 'was the sort they make movies about. Unbelievably exciting. A husband who – '

'Not different at all,' said Grace interrupting her, smiling equally sweetly. 'A secret is a secret. And I made a promise, all those years ago, never to tell anyone mine, and I never have. And I never will.'

Chapter One

Spring 1938

The first thing Grace Marchant did on meeting her future husband was burst into tears. This was not because he did or said anything unkind to her, rather the reverse; it was because she was in considerable physical pain, having fallen off her bicycle, and mental anguish, having tipped a box of eggs and a pound bag of sugar out of the basket and onto the road as a result.

The reason she fell off the bicycle was partly her own fault and partly that of Miss Parkin's Scottie which everyone in the village agreed – with the exception of Miss Parkin herself – should be kept on the lead, certainly in the High Street. He had seen a cat coming out of the butcher's shop and charged; Grace, who was not concentrating wholly on what she was doing, but was enjoying the feel of the late spring sunshine on her face and admiring the cherry blossom trailing over the wall of the vicarage, collided with him. The Scottie was fine, despite a lot of anguished yelping; Grace suffered two cut knees, a badly grazed elbow, and the wrath of Miss Parkin who told her she should be looking where she was going. Grace was too well brought up and too gentle to argue, and too clearsighted not to realize Miss Parkin had at least some right on her side, but as she was picking herself up, Miss Parkin hovering irritably by her, trying to recover her dignity and to suppress the pain of her stinging knees – no wonder children cried so much when they fell over – she heard a car pull up beside her and what her mother would call a dark brown voice say, 'Are you all right there?' Grace looked up into the face of an extremely handsome man (amazed afterwards at how much she took in, thick blond hair, brilliant blue eyes, very nice mouth, lightly tanned skin) and then down again at her muddy skirt, her bleeding knees and the congealing mass of egg and sugar on the road and started – to her greatly increased humiliation – to cry.

'Oh look, let me help,' he said and he got out of his car – a rather nice little MG, she noticed distractedly – picked up the bike, set it against the wall of the butcher's shop, and then took her hand and led her to the wooden seat set by it (more usually used for tying dogs to than sitting on), and sat her down. Grace looked up at him and tried to smile, groping in her pocket for a handkerchief; the young man passed her his own, and went to rescue her bike.

'It's fine,' he said, 'no lasting damage there.'

'Well of course not,' said Miss Parkin (a degree of anxiety and guilt clearly setting in), 'it was only a tumble. And I'm sorry if Mackie got in your way, Grace, but I really can't be held responsible for the butcher's cat.'

'No of course you can't,' said the young man, 'but perhaps your dog should be on the lead. In the middle of the village.'

And he smiled at her very charmingly.

'Mackie on the lead!' said Miss Parkin, in tones that implied he might as well have suggested Mackie should have been sent off to work in a travelling circus or do a little bear-baiting. 'Mackie has never been on the lead, ever, he – '

'Miss Parkin, never mind,' said Grace, fearing that Miss Parkin was about to go into one of the quivering states of umbrage for which she was famous. 'It's all right, really. I – should have been looking where I was going. You were right.'

Miss Parkin was clearly mollified by this, and offered to replace the eggs; Grace shook her head and gratefully accepted the glass of water Mr Briggs the butcher had brought her, enjoying his shop's place in the drama.

'Well now,' said the young man, coming back to the seat, sitting down beside her. 'You must let me see you home. You look quite pale. Oh, and by the way,' – he held out his hand – 'Charles Bennett. How do you do.'

'How do you do,' said Grace, taking the hand rather weakly. It was a nice hand, she thought, very firm, nice and dry – she feared her own was a bit clammy – 'Grace Marchant.'

'And do you live in Westhorne?'

'Yes, I do. Just on the edge of the village. By the green.'

'Then I insist on taking you home. Come along, I'll wheel your bicycle. You're in no state to ride it. I'll just move my car along a bit to a wider place, and then we'll go.'

Grace's conquest, as her mother insisted on describing it to her father at supper, was considerable.

'He's the son of Clifford Bennett, you know? The solicitor in Shaftesbury. And he has a share in a practice in London as well. They're very rich, they live in the most beautiful house over at Thorpe Magna. His mother is an Honourable . . .' Grace's father caught her eye and winked. 'The Honourable Muriel Saxton, she was, she was quite a well-known social figure. Her own daughter, that is Charles's sister – '

'That would quite possibly figure,' said Frank Marchant with one of his quick sweet smiles.

Mrs Marchant ignored him. 'Charles's sister, she was quite a well-known debutante, I believe. She lives in London, married a barrister. It was a very big wedding – '

'Mother,' said Grace laughing, 'who told you all this?'

'Well everyone knows, dear. It's common knowledge. And of course Charles isn't married. A bachelor gay. And rich.'

'Mother, I really don't think I'm very likely to marry Charles Bennett, if that's what you're thinking,' said Grace. 'I wouldn't get too hopeful, if I were you – '

At which point the phone rang.

Betty Marchant went to answer it. They could hear her voice from the hall, moving into its gracious extra-well-modulated mode. Frank raised his eyebrows at Grace; then Betty came in. She was flushed, and her eyes were very bright.

'It's him,' she said. Triumphant would not have been too strong a word to describe her tones.

'Who?'

'Charles Bennett of course. He's rung you up, Grace. Well, go along, dear, quickly, don't keep him waiting.'

Grace was still smiling when she picked up the phone. 'How did you get my number?' she said.

'From Mrs Boscombe of course.'

'Oh of course.'

Mrs Boscombe was the lady on the local telephone exchange. Not only did she supply anyone she approved of (a hugely necessary qualification) with anyone else's telephone number, she would deliver messages ('Your sister said to tell you she'll be here on the three o'clock bus') and pass on the information she gleaned from a devoted listening-in ('No point ringing her now, dear. She's gone for a walk and then on to see the vicar about Mrs Babbage's sister').

'I phoned to see how you were,' said Charles.

'I'm fine, thank you. And thank you for your great kindness this morning.'

'My pleasure. Look, there was something else. If your knees aren't too sore, that is. How would you like to come over on Sunday afternoon, have a game of tennis?'

'Oh,' said Grace, mild panic gripping her heart. 'Oh, well, I don't know – that is, I'm not very good I'm afraid.'

'Oh, good heavens, nor are any of us. My sister and her husband are coming down for the weekend. They're Londoners, so frightfully out of practice. But it would be nice. Do come.'

'Well, thank you,' said Grace. 'It sounds lovely.'

'Good. About three then?'

Grace walked back into the dining room and with great reluctance, trying to sound casual, told her parents what Charles had said. From that very moment she knew, until he was officially engaged to someone else, her mother would be planning the wedding.

Grace was nineteen years old. She had been educated at a small girls' day school near Salisbury, done well in her Higher School Certificate and gone on to do a secretarial course at her parents' insistence, despite having a hankering to pursue a musical career. She was a talented pianist, she sang very nicely, and she also played the violin rather beautifully; but it was a hopeless field to find work in, her parents had pointed out, and anyway she was a girl, she would be getting married before she knew it, and she could always perhaps join an amateur orchestra or operatic group. Grace hated the idea of amateur anything, she wanted to do it properly or not at all; but she also knew that if she wanted to be a musician she would have to be extremely tough and single-minded, and the fact that she had fallen at the first hurdle, that of her parents' opposition, undoubtedly meant she lacked both those qualities, and quite possibly the talent as well.

Frank Marchant was a bank manager in Shaftesbury; modestly well-off, but devoid of the kind of ambition that might have taken him much higher up his own particular ladder. This was a source of some anguish to Betty, who was very ambitious – not for herself naturally, but, as women were supposed to be, for her husband. She had worked very hard on Frank for a great many years, urging him to apply for this and that job, entertaining and being charming to his more important customers, having a considerable yearning for a bigger and grander house than the overgrown cottage in Westhorne where they lived; a slightly more impressive domestic help than Mrs Hobbs who came in daily and Mr Hobbs who helped in the garden, a husband she could boast about more, and an entrée into the kind of society where she felt (on no stronger basis than a rather ill-informed instinct) she truly belonged. She yearned to give and go to large dinner and tennis parties and be invited to the kind of dances that found their way into the pages of *Tatler*, partly on her own account and partly so that her daughter might then marry into that class and enjoy its privileges in her turn.

As it was, while being a highly respected and active member of the village, the chairwoman of countless worthy causes and having an undoubted cachet of her own as the bank manager's wife, she knew she hadn't made it, and never would now: that the best she could hope for in the way of a social life was the black-tie suppers she and Frank gave and went to, with Mrs Hobbs in a black dress and white apron waiting at table, dances at the tennis club and of course the Round Table and, her ultimate social achievement, an annual very grand dinner dance in London at the Savoy given by the bank for their more successful managers.

But she still had hopes for Grace.

Grace had a job working as junior secretary to the managing director of Stubbingtons, a haulage contractor based near Shaftesbury; she didn't like it, in fact she hated it, and so far the prospect of the escape her parents had pointed out to her in the form of marriage seemed to be nowhere in sight; but she was only nineteen, and even if three of her closest friends from school were already engaged, and one actually married, she and the rest still clearly had a little time in hand. In spite of marriage (and motherhood) being the one unarguable career for any girl, it didn't as yet appeal greatly to Grace; wifedom, as far as she could make out from observing her mother, consisted largely of performing a great many rather tedious tasks and making sure that her father's every wish and instruction was carried out.

Frank Marchant was actually a very sweet man, not in the least like some of her friends' fathers, who seemed to have their entire household in a state of feverish anxiety and expected unthinking obedience and respect, simply by virtue of being the breadwinner. Nevertheless he still got the paper to read if he wanted it, even if Grace or Betty were in the middle of it, the programme he wanted to listen to on the radio even if they were listening to something else, the last slice of cake, the best cut of meat; it was an unquestioning process, had always been thus and always surely had to be. Grace had occasionally wondered in her idler moments whether, if a wife went out to work and helped to win the bread, she would perhaps be entitled to at least the suggestion that she might like to hear the end of a concert before it was switched over to the news, and even a little help with clearing the table after supper, or her views on the rising crisis in Europe listened to, but she knew there was no point in voicing such thoughts to her mother, and even most of her own generation regarded them as

9

verging on sacrilegious. Some of the more intellectual girls at school had put such points to the debating society and had even argued them vigorously, but they were always beaten soundly. Had Grace been educated in a more intellectually vigorous environment, rather than at what was little better than a finishing school with a nod in the direction of higher education, her whole life might have turned out very differently.

Grace was extremely pretty; she had reddish-gold hair (although a little too wildly curly for her choice, and requiring a great deal of determination with the setting lotion), dark blue eyes, a straight little nose and a perfect (and fashionable) cupid's bow of a mouth. She was quite tall (almost five foot seven) and very slim, although a small bosom caused her some anguish, with nice legs and very pretty hands; she had charming manners, a sweet, biddable disposition and, beneath her shyness, a certain sharp-sightedness about both herself and others.

She was an only child; her parents were inordinately proud of her and, although they would have liked a son, 'he never came along' her mother would say with sigh, adding more cheerfully that a daughter was yours for life and that you had the great joy of grandchildren. And now Grace was well into her twentieth year and not a serious boyfriend, let alone a father for the grandchildren, in sight; and Betty Marchant was, although she would have died rather than admit it even to herself, growing a little worried.

Frank Marchant insisted on driving her over to the Bennetts' house on Sunday; Grace was perfectly happy to go on her bike, she said, but Mrs Marchant had been horrified and said whatever would the Bennetts think, that they might even assume they didn't have a car, and that of course Frank must take her.

'I wish you'd teach me to drive,' said Grace, 'then I could take myself about.' But her father answered time enough when she was twenty-one, that was the age to start driving, certainly for girls, and the roads were getting so crowded these days he'd never know a moment's peace and he never minded taking her anywhere, in fact it was a good opportunity for them to talk in peace. Grace and her father greatly enjoyed talking to each other; when Betty was present, it was rare for either of them to be able to complete a sentence.

The Priory (which had never actually been a priory but was christened thus in the mid nineteenth century by the socially ambitious businessman who had bought it) was an exquisite Queen

Anne house set on the outskirts of Thorpe Magna, behind a very high, curving brick wall.

Frank Marchant pulled up his Morris outside the gates, which were hung on tall, stone posts, and Grace got out, holding her tennis racket and feeling suddenly and helplessly shy.

She walked up the curving drive, studying the tall windows, the wide doorway, the wisteria growing beside it that drooped over the upper part of the house, looked warily at the black labrador that was loping towards her, barking half-heartedly, at the three cars parked to the side of the house, Charles's green MG, a rather dashing red Morris Tourer (presumably the town-dwelling sister's) and a heavily imposing Daimler, and at the figure bent over the flowerbed beyond the drive, presumably the gardener.

'Afternoon,' he called to her, and she nodded just slightly distantly (as one would to a gardener, she thought, especially in a house like this one, thinking too that it was hard for him to have to work on a Sunday, that the Bennetts must be very tough employers).

She tugged the bell pull, heard it jangle through the house, and he called out to her. 'They're all at the back, on the courts, they won't hear you, go on round this way.'

'Thank you,' said Grace, and started in his direction, a little worried still by the dog who was clearly not going to let her out of his sight; but the front door opened suddenly and Charles hailed her.

'Hallo! Sorry, didn't hear you. We were just having a knock-up. Magnus, come here at once. Get down. Get down I said. Bloody dog. Where's your car?'

'I came with my father,' said Grace awkwardly. 'He dropped me off.'

'Oh, I see.' He looked awkward too, anxious not to seem surprised. She liked him for it, and at the same time felt shyer still. 'Right then, follow me.'

'I was going round that way. Your gardener was just telling me – '

'Who? Not here today – Oh, you mean Dad. Come and meet him.' He laughed, slightly awkwardly again, led her over to the stooping figure.

'Father, this is Grace Marchant.'

Clifford Bennett stood up, smiling; he was very tall, taller than his son, white-haired, with the same piercing blue eyes.

'You must be the damsel in distress we've heard so much about,' he said, holding out his hand. 'Clifford Bennett. How do you do.'

'How do you do,' said Grace, flushing, appalled to think how nearly she had walked past him, dismissing him totally, praying

Charles wouldn't say anything that would reveal her lack of sophistication.

He didn't. 'You joining us, Father?'

'No, no, got to get these beds sorted out. Dreadful time of year in the garden, weeds outpace flowers ten to one. You like gardens, my dear?'

'I love them,' said Grace, 'really love them. One day I want to have a walled garden of my very own, filled with roses and wonderful climbing things – '

She flushed again, surprised at her willingness to talk to him, hoping he wouldn't find her foolish. He didn't seem to. 'We've got one here, although I don't know if it would be wonderful enough for you, bit neglected, I'm afraid. Get Charles to show it to you later. No, on second thoughts I'll show you, it's my favourite too. Come and find me when you've finished your game. Enjoy it.'

'Thank you,' said Grace.

'Right,' said Charles. 'Come and meet the folks.'

Folks didn't seem quite the right word, having a rather cosy, warm sound to it. Charles's mother, tall, thin, 'iron grey all over,' Grace said later to her father, with a low-slung voice reeking of generations of upper-class breeding, greeted her as if she was interviewing her for a job – as hired help, thought Grace desperately, trying to hang onto her sense of humour. Where exactly did she live, what did her father do? On receiving the answer to her second question, she nodded briefly and turned to her daughter as if to indicate that the interview was over.

The daughter, Florence, was marginally worse: equally tall, dark-haired, with the same gauntly good-looking face, the same good long legs and identical voice. Her nails were long and red, her mouth wide and full, painted the same brilliant colour. She clearly didn't think Grace was worth talking to at all, merely smiled at her fleetingly and began on a long description to her mother of a house she and her husband were in the process of buying near what sounded like Sloane Squaw. Only her husband seemed friendly and interested in making Grace feel welcome; his name was Robert and he was very tall and heavily built, with slicked-back dark hair, surprisingly pale skin and eyes, and a long and imposing nose which he was inclined to look down quite literally. But he seemed very nice, smiled at her warmly and was, he told her, an absolute ass at tennis – 'So I hope you are too.'

'Don't be beastly, Robert,' said Florence, her glance at Grace's just slightly worn grey tennis shoes – despite being desperately whitened by her mother that morning – making it plain that she assumed Grace must indeed be exactly that. 'Girls who live in the country are always marvellous at tennis. Play every day, I expect. Or are you a golfer, Miss Marchant?'

'Please call me Grace,' said Grace. 'And no, I don't play golf. And I'm not marvellous at tennis either, certainly don't play every day. I don't have time.'

'Oh no, of course,' said Florence. 'I forgot, Charles said you had a job.' She made it sound as if a job was a rather nasty disease.

There was a silence, then Charles said, 'Well, come on then, let's have a knock-up, shall we? Grace, are you brave enough to play with me?'

Much to her surprise she was as good a player as Florence, and a great deal better than Robert, who was indeed an absolute ass. She got the impression he was not prepared to try very hard in any case, that he saw the whole thing as mildly silly, which comforted her. She and Charles, who was really quite good and very enthusiastic, won the first set, and then Charles suggested she played with Robert. Florence, clearly irritated, started playing very hard indeed and doing some sneakily down-the-line serves; twice the ball was out when she called it in very firmly, and no one either dared or wished to contradict her. Even so, Grace and Robert only just lost.

'You're really very good,' said Charles, leading her back to the chairs by the court. 'I don't believe you don't practise lots.'

'I played a lot at school,' said Grace. That was a mistake.

'And where did you go to school?' asked Mrs Bennett. 'I think it's so wonderful the way girls go to school these days. I would have adored to go but of course I was educated at home, and actually a lot of our friends still don't believe in girls going away, although I insisted on it for Florence. So broadening to the mind, I think.'

'I went to – to St Catherine's, near Salisbury,' said Grace. 'It's only very small. Very cosy. You won't have heard of it.'

'No, I don't think so,' said Mrs Bennett carefully. 'I'm not very familiar with any of the local schools. Florence went to St Mary's Wantage, which wasn't terribly cosy. A little too academic I thought. Perhaps she would have been better at a place like yours – ' Her voice tailed off; she clearly didn't think Florence would have been anything of the sort.

'Let's have tea,' said Charles, rather too heartily.

After tea, which they ate on the terrace at the back of the house, served by the kind of properly uniformed maid Betty Marchant had fantasies about, Mr Bennett, who had clearly taken a fancy to Grace, insisted on showing her the walled garden. It was enchanting, a little closed-off world, the air filled with birdsong, climbing hydrangea pushing into flower on the walls, the beds filled with tangly shrubs, great massing clouds of dark and pale blue lobelia tumbling over onto the brick-laid paths and, set in the centre, a wonderful old stone seat.

'Oh it's lovely!' said Grace. 'So perfectly set away, a little world all of its own.'

'That's exactly why I like it,' he said, 'and I tell you what I like to do; I bring a large glass of whisky out here in the evening, and the paper, and I feel quite safe from everyone and everything.'

Grace thought that if she had to live with Muriel Bennett she would do something much the same, and she'd fit a lock on the gate as well.

Not that that was very likely. Thank God.

'Do stay for supper if you would like,' said Muriel Bennett when they returned from the walled garden. 'There isn't much, of course, it being Sunday evening, but – '

'No, really, it's very kind,' said Grace, 'but my parents are expecting me. In fact, I wonder if I might ring my father and ask him to come and collect me – '

'What a ridiculous idea,' said Charles. He had been rather quiet ever since the game of tennis had finished. 'Of course I'll take you home. Would you like to ring anyway? So they aren't worried?'

'Well, that would be very kind. If you're sure – '

'Of course. Follow me.'

He led her through some French windows into the drawing room, which, although very nicely furnished and with a fine fireplace, was rather less grand than she, and certainly her mother, would have expected, and out into the hall where the phone stood on a low table alongside a very large pile of *Country Life*.

'There you are,' he said, 'go ahead. Look' – he hesitated – 'we might even go for a drive before I take you home. If that would be all right with your parents.'

'Oh – well yes,' said Grace, more relieved that he wasn't dying to get rid of her than anything else. 'Yes, I'll ask them.'

They drove away from the house in silence, down the narrow, high-hedged lanes. It was a lovely evening. 'I thought we might go up to Old Wardour,' said Charles. 'Would you like that?'

'Yes. Yes I would.'

Old Wardour Castle was a much-revered local ruin, set high on a hill above the exquisite house built in the eighteenth century to replace it; its walls still standing, it looked austerely beautiful against the dusky sky.

'Nice old place, isn't it?' said Charles. 'I used to come up here on my pony when I got home from school every holidays, first thing I did. Did you have anywhere like that?'

'I used to head for Shaftesbury and the bright lights,' said Grace. 'On the bus,' she added and laughed.

'You mustn't mind my mother,' he said suddenly. 'She can't help being such a snob. It was how she was brought up. But she's a wonderful person really.'

'Of course I didn't mind,' said Grace untruthfully. 'I thought she was very nice. And your father. He was so sweet showing me his garden.'

'Yes, he obviously liked you. So did old Robert. Bit of a wandering eye, Robert. Florence has a rather difficult time with him, as far as I can gather.'

'Does she?' said Grace. It seemed to her it would be Robert who had a difficult time.

'Yes. Oh God, I shouldn't have told you that. There's something about you,' he said, looking at her intently, 'that invites confidences. My father obviously felt it too.'

'Is there?' said Grace. She felt herself blushing.

'Yes. You're what the Italians call *simpatico*. Ever been to Italy?'

'No. I've never been abroad. I'd love to.'

'Well, if all this nonsense in Europe gets any worse, it won't be safe to go anyway. My father thinks war's inevitable.'

'Do you?' said Grace.

'No, not really. Not inevitable anyway. I think Chamberlain might be a slightly better man than he's given credit for. What does your father think?'

'The same as yours,' said Grace. She waited for him to ask what she thought, but he didn't.

On the way home, they passed the gates of Old Wardour Cemetery, final resting place for the Arundell Estate and indeed the entire village of Wardour.

'That's my favourite place,' said Grace, looking in at it almost wistfully, the iron gates, the tangle of trees, the ghostly clusters of headstones.

'What, the cemetery? Bit of an odd place to like,' said Charles, sounding amused.

Grace flushed. 'I know. But I think it's so romantic. And beautiful.'

'Well – yes, OK. Each to their own, I suppose.' He smiled at her. 'Got time for a drink?'

'Oh, yes. That would be very nice.' They had a couple of drinks in a pub near Swallowcliffe, and then Charles drove her home.

'I would ask you in but – ' said Grace.

'No, no, of course not. I have to get back. My mother expects me and anyway I have an early start tomorrow. When you work with – for, who am I kidding? – your father there's no room for slacking. And we've got a big caseload at the moment.'

'Do you enjoy being a solicitor?' said Grace.

'Yes, it's quite good fun,' he said, 'and especially in a small town like Shaftesbury. The firm'll be mine one day, of course, and I look forward to that. Especially the London practice. That's great fun.'

'How often do you go up there?' said Grace.

'Oh, not very often, unfortunately. Father goes up for a couple of days each week, and it's my job to keep the home fires burning. But in the fullness of time I hope to spend quite a lot of time up there. I'll be making a few changes altogether.'

'What?'

'Oh good Lord, you don't want to hear about that. Look, I ought to get you back. Thank you so much for coming over today. It's been a very good afternoon.'

'Thank you for asking me,' said Grace.

He shook her hand and she got out of the car; there was no mention of another meeting. Grace let herself into the house feeling just slightly depressed.

'Before you say a word,' she said to her mother who was hovering excitedly in the hall, 'I really don't think he likes me very much, his mother is an old witch, and his sister made it clear that she saw me as so much beneath her I had no business even in the same room. Which I suppose I am. Beneath her I mean,' she added, trying to smile.

'How exceedingly rude,' said Betty Marchant. Two bright spots of colour rose in her cheeks; she was clearly upset. 'Well, I certainly don't want you marrying into that family.'

'Mother,' said Grace wearily, 'I do assure you there is absolutely no question of my marrying into it. Unless perhaps I ran away with dear old Mr Bennett.'

'Grace, you know I don't like that kind of talk,' said Betty Marchant.

★ ★ ★

Clifford Bennett was in his study listening to the nine o'clock news when the phone rang in the hall. 'I'll get that,' he called to Muriel. 'Worried client. Told him he could ring tonight.'

Five minutes later he went into the drawing room, where Muriel sat by the fire working on her latest tapestry, a design of her own, based on her father's coat of arms.

'I have to go up to London first thing, Moo my dear. Catch the milk train, I think. Just thought I'd warn you.'

'The milk train! What on earth for? And why a Monday, you never – '

'I told you I have a very worried client. Difficult case. I want to see him early and then brief Counsel.'

'Clifford, I do think it's time you eased up a little on your workload,' said Muriel. 'You're sixty next year. And you seem to be taking more and more on. You did say you were going to ease out of the London office, train Charles into it, but I haven't seen much sign of that.'

'I know, my dear, I know. But John Reeves is desperately overstretched, poor old boy. And, between you and me, a bit out of his depth, particularly on this case. It's a most interesting one, a matter of fraud, my client took out a life assurance policy two and a half years ago and – '

'Clifford, you're in my light. Well, go if you must. But I think you really must be firmer with John Reeves in future. He's taking advantage of your good nature.'

'All right, my dear. I'll try.' He paused, sipping at his whisky. 'Sweet little thing this afternoon, wasn't she?'

'What, the Marchant girl? All right, I suppose. A bit – ordinary. I wish Charles could find himself some really suitable girl and settle down. Amanda Bridgnorth for instance, she's charming, and so pretty, and she looks wonderful on horseback – '

'Moo dear, I hope and trust Charles would be looking for a little more in a future wife than her skill on horseback. And I would personally greatly prefer Grace Marchant as a daughter-in-law to Amanda Bridgnorth.'

'Oh, don't let's even think about the possibility,' said Muriel with a small careful shiver. 'I can just imagine what her mother must be like. Apparently she makes curtains for people.'

'Moo, really!' said Clifford, shaking his head even as he smiled at her. 'I'm going to do some work on this case now. I'll sleep in the dressing room tonight, so I don't disturb you in the morning. Goodnight, my dear.'

He went back into his study and phoned the London number, to confirm that he would be there in the morning.

'I don't think I want to do that again,' said Robert Grieg, putting his foot down rather hard on the accelerator as the car finally pulled onto the London road.

'Do what?'

'Come all this way, just for a weekend. It's too far, and I'm exhausted in the morning.'

'But Robert, we don't do it very often. The last time was Easter, when we could have stayed longer. And it was you who didn't want to – '

'Well, I'm afraid I find it very tedious, after a day or so. I really don't like the country – '

'Robert, you like going to the Whittakers. Or the Bedfords. They live in the country.'

'Yes, well, they have a little more to offer. They always arrange a proper dinner party, and there are plenty of people our own age. The entertainment at Thorpe is listening to your mother's views on life and watching your father in the garden.'

'That is so unfair!' said Florence. 'They often ask people to dinner, or Sunday lunch, and you can always play tennis.'

'Florence, I loathe tennis, as you ought to know. And the people on offer are hardly the most scintillating. Look at that funny little thing today.'

'She was all right.'

'You didn't behave towards her as if she was all right, if I might say so. Anyway, that's not the point. Now can we stop this please, it's extremely boring. I really don't want to spend any more weekends down there. All right?'

'What do I say if – when they ask us?'

'Well, obviously, make some excuse. They must be able to see it's a long way.'

Florence stopped arguing. She had learnt the value of silence.

Chapter Two

Summer 1938

Grace was beginning to think she might be in love.

She had done a lot of reading of romantic fiction lately, including the book everyone was talking about, *Gone with the Wind*, to try to compare how the heroines felt with what she was experiencing, and had even reread *Jane Eyre* in search of more lofty descriptions, and while she didn't think what she felt for Charles was quite the fierce passion nurtured by Scarlett O'Hara for Ashley Wilkes or by Jane for Mr Rochester, she was certainly aware of a whole new set of emotions: longing when she was going to see him, a lovely warm happiness and a feeling of rightness when they were together, and a strange, choking tenderness when he held her hand and just looked at her and didn't say anything. She liked being kissed by him too; it was an awful lot nicer than when her other boyfriends had done it, when she had, quite honestly, found it a bit disgusting, the tongue bit anyway.

With Charles it was different; his mouth was firm and strong, and she felt her own responding under it in a way that was almost unconscious, and not only her mouth, but her whole body; she felt warmed and sweet and somehow softened, it was impossible to explain, and he was clearly very moved by it too. He would lean away from her afterwards in the seat of the car or in the long grass up by the castle which had become their special place, and just look at her, his eyes probing into hers, and she would feel, even more than when he was actually kissing her, a wonderful flooding tenderness and something else, something stronger, something physically strange, a kind of moving in the depths of her. She supposed that was how you felt, only more so, when you actually Did it, as they had called it at school when they were talking about it. She thought about Doing it rather a lot these days; for the first time she could actually imagine wanting to, and her mother's rather halting and embarrassed descriptions (over more than one glass of sherry) began to make some kind of sense.

Charles hadn't actually told her he loved her, of course; she only knew that when they were together he was very romantic. But it had been from the very beginning erratic, to put it mildly. There had been the first few bleak days after the tennis game, when she had been quite sure she would never see him or hear from him again, that she was far too dull and unsophisticated for him, that he had only asked her because someone else had dropped out. Then on the Thursday evening, as she sat unpicking the hem of a dress that was beginning to look unfashionably long, the phone rang and it was him.

'Hallo,' he said, 'this is Charles Bennett' – as if she needed to be told; 'I wondered if you'd like to go and see a film on Friday.' And she had for a fraction of a second considered saying she was busy as everybody always said you should, because sounding too available scared them off, and then she knew she couldn't and she thanked him for asking her and said she'd love to.

They had sat in the cinema in Shaftesbury, surrounded by couples kissing or at least holding hands, and he had sat most politely away from her and then afterwards had driven her home, chatting about this and that, and she was just thinking despairingly that he really couldn't like her very much, and certainly didn't find her attractive, when he had stopped the car, leant forward and said, 'You're so pretty, Grace, may I kiss you?'

She hadn't said anything, just smiled uncertainly, and he had kissed her, very gently, and then said, 'What are you doing tomorrow?' and she had said, 'Nothing whatsoever!' and he had said he would like to take her out to dinner. They went to the Grosvenor in Shaftesbury, which was very expensive and grand, and where her father was taken at Christmas by really important customers but she and her mother had never been, and she had got rather drunk after a sherry and two glasses of wine, and when he had kissed her in the car that night it had been quite different for both of them.

'I hope this is all right,' he said to her tenderly, breaking off after a while, and she said it was quite all right, more than all right, and he had smiled and started again. That was the first time she had felt the strange moving in the depths of her.

And so it all began. But it was never quite the straightforward affair that her friends seemed to enjoy: daily phone calls, twice-weekly outings, the assumption that they were, informally at least, a unit. There were times when she didn't hear from him at all for up to ten days, others when he wanted to see her almost every night. He was always rather vague about his absences; very often of course they were because he had to go to London, to the legal practice up there, but there were other times when she knew he was around and he made no attempt to contact her, she would see the MG parked outside the offices in Shaftesbury day after day, and feel sick. Sick with misery and sick with jealousy. Grace was in any case very easily given to jealousy; it was, she knew, the flaw in her otherwise sweet nature. She became jealous not only when boyfriends danced and flirted with other girls, but when girlfriends excluded her – however innocently – from some outing, or she heard her boss praising one of the other secretaries at work. It was partly due to her lack of self-confidence, but also to a desire to have a special place in the hearts of everyone about her; from her earliest years she had come to recognize and dread the slightly sour hot misery that took her over, distorting her perception of things, destroying an otherwise happy occasion. And she found herself enduring it rather a lot at the moment, at Charles Bennett's rather cavalier hands.

In the early stages, she was sure that each time he had simply lost interest in her, that he was going out with someone else, probably several girls, she would think morosely; after all he was extremely eligible, free as air, there was absolutely no reason for him to launch into some kind of commitment with her, just because he had taken her out once or twice. Sometimes she got angry, swore she wouldn't see him again, would listen to her mother and her friends telling her he was playing around with her, that she should show him she wasn't prepared to put up with it, and sometimes she would defend him, to herself as well as other people, saying they enjoyed each other's company, they had a good time, why should either of them feel they had some kind of a hold on the other?

But she did like him, very much, and she liked being with him; it was hard to say no, to risk losing him just for the sake of her pride, when he always said he was sorry he hadn't contacted her, he'd been in London, or Bath, at the courts there, or just very busy. It was easier to believe him, to laugh, to perhaps tease him a bit and then say yes, she'd love to go to the cinema or whatever. And there certainly wasn't any evidence of other girls: not that she'd know, she supposed miserably when her spirits were low and she hadn't heard from him for a week or more; she was hardly in the same set as he was. She was more curious about girlfriends he might have had in the past, but he was very cagey about those, discouraged her whenever she tried to ask him, so she told herself it was nothing to do with her, and tried not to think about it.

So she settled for enjoying what she could – which was quite a lot of the time very nice and great fun – and struggled to keep her pride intact. They both liked the cinema and he took her to all the latest films; he didn't like music at all, which she found sad, but they occasionally went to the theatre in Bath, they went out in the car for drives and he had begun to give her some rudimentary lessons, which was wonderful and very generous, she felt, as she was quite likely to drive the MG into a tree. If anything was to convince her she was more than just a bit of amusement to him, it was the way he put his beloved car in her hands – literally. And they both liked sitting in pubs and just talking – she found him surprisingly easy to talk to, and he was certainly interesting to listen to; he had wonderful stories about past cases of his father's and even his own, 'but mine are pretty mundane still, most of the time,' about his childhood, which seemed to have been very happy, about his schooldays at Harrow – 'great place, a real privilege to have gone.' And then he would take her out to dinner at least once a month, somewhere expensive, and tell her she was the nicest, the prettiest, the most interesting girl he knew, and there would be a great deal of kissing in the car on the way home, and she would lie in bed afterwards thinking how lucky she was, and wondering why she had to look for more when what she had was so nice.

And Charles was not only romantic and fun and charming and attentive, but extremely gentlemanly; he clearly enjoyed kissing her, but he had never tried to do anything else, anything worrying. She was never afraid when they were alone up by the castle or in the car late at night that he would get Carried Away (an event which several of her friends and her mother had rather darkly hinted at). Sometimes, when they were especially close, she would feel his hand on her thigh, an intent probing pressure that was pleasurably and sweetly disturbing, but that was only through her dress; he had never tried to push it up, or unbutton it. Once he had started to kiss her throat, begun to move down towards the top of her dress; she had felt just faintly worried then, but was enjoying it too much to let the worry take over, when he suddenly pulled away from her and said, 'I'm sorry, Grace, sorry, it's just that you're so lovely.'

Then she wouldn't see him again for ten days or a fortnight. And however much she told herself it didn't matter, it hurt her.

She continued to worry about the difference in their social situation; and one evening, after she had had a couple of glasses of wine over dinner and he was being particularly funny and sweet and had taken her out twice in the week, and she was feeling more confident than usual: 'Charles,' she said, 'Charles, can I ask you something?'

'Yes,' he said, 'yes of course you can.'

'Well – do you ever see me as a bit different? From you?'

'What on earth do you mean?' he asked, looking at her in apparently genuine astonishment.

'Charles, you must know what I mean. Your family is much more – '

'Much what?'

Oh, God, now what did she say? All the words were so dated and stupid, things like 'well-bred' and 'higher-class'. They made her sound at best stupid and at worst neurotic. She finally settled for 'well-off' because that was unarguable.

'Yes, I know that,' he said, smiling at her sweetly. 'It's not your fault though, and it's not mine. We can just blame our fathers. I certainly never think about it, if that's what you mean. Now come and give me a kiss.'

She had a shrewd idea he had known exactly what she meant and had deliberately chosen to duck the issue, either out of cowardice or embarrassment. She tried to tell herself she should stop thinking about it, and take what he said at face value. But she couldn't. Not quite.

At the end of July it was her birthday. A very large bouquet of flowers was delivered to the house, yellow and white roses, which sent her mother into such paroxysms of excitement that Grace got the giggles; and that night he took her out to dinner, to a place they hadn't been to before, a hugely expensive place in the country, near Tisbury, and as they sat in the bar, she drinking her sherry, he his gin and Italian, he passed her a small box. 'Happy birthday, Grace,' he said, and she almost fainted, thinking it was a ring. When she opened it and saw it was a coral necklace, her first emotion was a stab of violent disappointment, but then she realized she was being ridiculous. The card said, 'For the loveliest neck I know,' which was hardly poetic, she had to admit, but the thought behind it was very romantic.

She had eaten and drunk much too much and on the way home he had to stop the car because she felt sick; she got out and walked down the road a little way and he sat watching her, and then he walked after her, took her in his arms and said, 'I really can't imagine life without you now, Grace. You're the nicest thing that's ever happened to me.'

It was all very romantic, romantic and wonderful; but even after that he disappeared again for over a week. And once again she found herself unable to believe that in the end he wasn't going to drop her in favour of one of the girls he had grown up with, carelessly confident girls with double-barrelled names and braying voices who would make wonderful wives and give grand dinner parties and in time produce extremely well-bred babies.

There was a very bad patch towards the end of the summer when he went away to the South of France for a couple of weeks 'to stay with some friends of my parents. They're already there, it's been fixed for ages.' Every hour was an agony, as she imagined him lying on the beach with a series of gorgeous girls, or even, and possibly worse, one gorgeous girl, but when he got back he came straight round to see her, looking wonderfully tanned, with a bottle of French perfume (Joy by Jean Patou), and said he'd missed her so much and had thought of her a great deal.

The other bad occasions, apart from his absences, were when she had to go to the Priory, which happened from time to time, mostly to play tennis on Sundays, or occasionally for a drink on Sunday morning; they were generally low-key occasions, with not many other people there, usually a few of the Bennetts' friends rather than people of Charles's own age, but they were still difficult to get through. She wondered sometimes why there were so seldom young people there and if Charles was deliberately keeping her away from them, his own friends, because he was in some way ashamed of her, or felt uncomfortable with her. She once broached the subject, rather bravely she thought, to Charles, and he laughed and told her she was imagining things, and that he wanted to introduce her to people slowly because she was so shy. 'All my friends who have met you think you're lovely. You do worry about silly things,' he said, kissing her.
    'I know,' said Grace humbly.

The most terrifying occasion was a big party in early August that his mother gave in a marquee in the garden for Mr Bennett's birthday. 'Please come,' Charles said as she objected at first, said she couldn't, 'it'll be fun, and I want everyone to meet you and know how lovely you are.'
    Grace spent the next three weeks alternately wilting with terror at the prospect, and telling herself it must be significant that he wanted her there at all. Surely, surely he couldn't just be whiling away a few hours with her, seeing her as some little local amusement, if she was to be at so important a family occasion.

She actually prayed for some illness to strike her down, considered sleeping in wet sheets so she would get pneumonia or eating stale cheese from the larder so she would be sick, but she lacked the courage, and in the end it was all quite all right, despite her realizing very swiftly that the simple white silk dress her mother had made for the occasion, with its little cap sleeves and handkerchief hem, was simply not grand enough, that everyone else was in slithery satin or embroidered taffeta, long, long dresses with low necklines revealing fine bosoms and bare shoulders, and a great deal of very noticeable jewellery. She walked through the house and into the marquee, a huge marquee, filled with flowers and tables and waiters in white jackets with trays of drinks, and a band playing wonderfully and people with the Voices, as she had come to think of them, marvellously, carelessly beautiful girls, gossiping and laughing, and noisily confident men, all knowing one another, all belonging to the same overprivileged, self-opinionated club; and although she was on Charles's arm she felt, she *knew*, that everyone was staring at her and asking each other if they thought Charles was serious about her, and how such a thing could be.

She would have fled then, had he not taken her straight over to his mother, who had been at least graciously polite, and dear old Mr Bennett who had been absolutely sweet to her, told her she was by far the prettiest girl there and he wanted to dance with her as soon as possible. Actually, she thought, as he led her onto the floor and swept her into a surprisingly smooth foxtrot, he didn't really look old at all, not really, just distinguished, with his thick white hair, his marvellous blue eyes and his tanned face. It was the first time she had seen him in anything other than his baggy old gardening clothes, and his dinner jacket, superbly cut, showed off a wonderfully slim figure.

'Well,' he said, 'young Charles is certainly very taken with you. We hear of nothing else these days.'

Grace half hoped that wasn't true, because she feared it would make Muriel Bennett doubly unfriendly, and half hoped it was. She actually found it a little hard to believe, even with several glasses of champagne inside her.

She and Mr Bennett danced three dances, culminating with him demonstrating a considerable skill with the new jitterbug; Grace and indeed the whole dance floor stood still to watch him. He finished, laughing, and then took her arm. 'I really am too old for that sort of thing,' he said, mopping his brow with his handkerchief, 'but I do love dancing.'

'Well, you're very, very good at it,' said Grace, 'that was just the best I've ever seen.'

'You mustn't flatter an old man.'

'I'm not flattering and you're not an old man.'

'I'm afraid I am. Fifty-nine today. I must seem like Old Father Time to you.'

'Of course you don't. It must be wonderful,' she added, as he led her back to her table, 'to be surrounded by all your friends, everyone you care about, on your birthday.' And he gave her a very odd, distant look and said, 'Oh, Grace, indeed it must,' and then smiled at her, somehow rather sad suddenly, and kissed her hand and passed her over to Charles, and told him how lucky he was to have her.

Later, briefly, she saw him all alone, standing by the tennis court, smoking a cigar; she asked Charles if they shouldn't go and see if he was all right, and Charles said no, the old boy was fine and his mother didn't like cigars, he always slipped off at parties to have one. Since half the men at the party were smoking them, Grace couldn't quite see this was necessary, but she didn't argue, especially as a slow waltz was just starting and Charles was holding her very close.

'You look lovely,' he said, 'I'm so proud of you.'

She couldn't think of anything nicer that he could have said.

Florence and Robert were very late arriving at the party. Grace was surprised; Charles had made such a big thing of how it was an annual family event, but it turned out that at the last minute Florence hadn't been well, and they almost hadn't come at all. Robert had felt she shouldn't make the journey. Grace wondered if perhaps Florence was having a baby, but didn't like to ask. Florence was very pale, and even less friendly than the last time they had met, but Robert was the reverse, came over and said how pleased he was to see her again, and later asked her to dance. It was a waltz, and he held her rather alarmingly close. She was worried that Florence might notice, but she was talking to her mother and didn't even glance at the dance floor.

'You,' said Robert, smiling down at her, his pale eyes moving over her face, lingering on her lips, 'you are the best thing that's happened to this family for a long time. If I may say so.'

Grace didn't know quite what to say, so she must smiled rather inanely at him and concentrated on her dancing. At the end of the waltz the music changed to a quickstep which he launched into with great enthusiasm, but at the end, he took her back to her table and excused himself, saying he didn't feel too well. She went into the house to find the lavatory soon after that and then, feeling hot, walked briefly into the garden to get some fresh air; Robert was hurrying towards the rose bushes, his face glassy pale in the moonlight, and although she tried not to, she heard the unmistakable sound of vomiting. It seemed to her that the only unwellness he was suffering was from a surfeit of champagne. If she was married to Florence, she thought, she would drink too much.

She had expected to find herself one of many girls invited by Charles specifically, but she was very much his chosen personal guest. He danced a great many dances with her (he had explained he had to do other duty dances, 'especially with Mother's friends') and in between she found herself, slightly to her surprise, quite in demand. Several of Charles's friends asked her to dance, saying they'd heard a lot about her; a couple of them were, although friendly, just slightly patronizing, and she couldn't think what to say to them, but one of them, introduced to her by Charles as 'my blood brother, Laurence', was really sweet, very polite and considerate, and at least made a pretence of being interested in what she had to say.

'Why blood brothers?' she asked and he said oh, they'd been at prep school together. 'Pretty grim it was too, at the end of the war, dreadful food, and masters as old as Methuselah.' One day Charles had been beaten by one of the masters and Laurence had found him sobbing in the garden, lying hidden behind a hedge. Charles had made him swear he wouldn't tell he'd been crying, and Laurence had sworn he wouldn't and had gone to fetch a bramble branch from the other side of the garden, pricked both their fingers with it and they had solemnly mingled the blood to enhance the importance of the occasion.

The party ended with everybody doing the conga round the marquee and the garden, led by Clifford and watched by an only mildly disapproving Muriel. Grace, in front of Robert in the line (recovered now, and holding her waist just a little too tightly) and behind Laurence, felt she had somehow crossed some mysterious divide and that while she would continue to be petrified of Muriel and to a lesser extent of Florence and all the rest of their kind (with the surprising exception of Charles himself), they were at least no longer an unknown terror; they seemed to have secret areas of unhappiness, to drink too much, to have had difficult childhoods, just like everyone else.

And she also found herself accepting the slightly erratic form of Charles's courtship. He obviously cared about her, was clearly not ashamed of her; it would be extremely foolish, not to mention destructive, to argue with it. In future she would simply enjoy things more.

It seemed to Grace, looking back afterwards, that that summer drew a line on what was certain, what was carefree, what was safe. Fear stalked the country; the talk everywhere was only of war. She and her mother sat at the supper table night after night and listened to Frank Marchant speaking, as men were speaking in houses and clubs and pubs the length and breadth of England, on the inevitability of war; and then they listened to the nine o'clock news and heard it again. Whenever Hitler appeared on the cinema newsreels he was booed; there was much talk of the necessity of evacuating children and old people to the country. Charles came back from London with tales of trenches being dug in the great parks, of barrage balloons being flown over London, as a deterrent against attacks from the air, of huge anti-aircraft guns being raised, of convoys of troops being moved about the country in apparently haphazard fashion. Grace came home from work one day to find her mother in tears and three gas masks lying on the hall table, hideous, obscene things, with their huge eyes and piglike snouts, somehow symbolizing the ugliness of war itself. She didn't know how to comfort her.

She was quite frightened herself. The scaremongering was considerable; she read an article in one of the papers prophesying the death by bombing in London alone of over half a million people, of looting in the streets, the breakdown of law and order and medical facilities. She showed it to Charles; he kissed her and tore it up. 'You must let us do the worrying, Grace. That's what we're here for.'

'Who?' she said irritably.

'The men,' he said in genuine surprise.

It was at moments like that that she felt she didn't know him at all.

But the turmoil was at the same time exciting; it contributed to her disturbed emotions, brought them somehow nearer the surface. If there was a war, she thought, Charles would have to go away, he would be in danger, might even be killed; the very possibility – in actual fact remote – intensified her feelings about him. Even Muriel Bennett terrified her less; in a state of war, she seemed suddenly almost unimportant.

'If only we had a decent man to lead us,' Charles said one Sunday as they strolled round the lake by the castle. 'Chamberlain's an idiot.

Hitler could have him for breakfast. Father says Churchill should be brought back, everything he said has been proved right.'

'Churchill!' said Grace. 'Surely not. He's been out of power for ages. My father says Baldwin should never have gone.'

Everyone agreed that Chamberlain was a disaster; then he stood on the aeroplane steps, waving his piece of paper from Munich, proclaiming that he and Herr Hitler had negotiated 'peace for our time', and very briefly they all agreed they must be wrong. Mrs Chamberlain was surrounded by huge crowds in the street, wanting to shake her hand; Grace's father read out an article in the *Daily Telegraph* comparing Chamberlain to Gladstone; over at the Priory a more cynical Clifford Bennett was laughing over a eulogy by the journalist Godfrey Winn comparing Chamberlain to God. 'I'm not at all sure about all this,' he said. 'Do we really want to form a pact with a racial persecutor?'

'But it does look better,' said Charles to Grace, describing this scene and laughing too. 'Do you feel calmer now, Grace darling?'

'Yes thank you,' said Grace, smiling at him, taking his hand. She found his calling her darling more exciting than anything, even more than when he kissed her. He looked back at her, very serious suddenly. 'You're lovely,' he said, 'really beautiful. I'm so proud of you.'

He often said that now; it was when she was most certain she was in love.

Florence was just checking the dinner table for what felt like the hundredth time – the candles, the flowers, the place names – was every single glass absolutely gleaming clean? It was the most crucial dinner party, Robert had stressed it again and again. God, that stupid girl had all put the fish knives the wrong way round. The doorbell rang. It was Charles. He smiled at her rather uncertainly.

'Hallo, Florence. Can I come in?'

'Oh – Charles. Goodness. Well – I suppose so. Yes.'

'You don't look terribly pleased to see me.'

'Oh, Charles, I am. Of course. But we've got a terribly important dinner party tonight, Robert's clients, you know and – '

'Florence, I'm not going to stay. Well, not now. I'm going out with some chums. But I wondered if you could give me a bed for the night.'

'For the night! Well, I don't know, Charles, you see – '

'Florence, what on earth is the matter? I'll creep in, I promise. I won't say anything unsuitable to your smart friends, in fact I won't even show my face if you don't want me to.'

'Charles, it's not that, of course – '

'Well then, for heaven's sake. You've got plenty of room, surely. And it's only one night.'

'Can't you stay at the flat?'

'No, that's why I'm here. I asked Father and he got in a terrible bait, said he was having an important meeting there. He was a bit odd, actually. He doesn't seem himself at all at the moment.'

'Oh,' said Florence.

'You don't sound very interested.'

Florence pulled herself together, smiled at him quickly. 'Sorry, Charles. I've got a lot on my mind. Look – of course you must stay. Only – well, this sounds rude, I know, but I really won't have much time to talk to you or anything. Robert gets very worked up about these dos, likes everything to be perfect. Well, they are all his clients – '

'Yes, yes, you said. Doesn't sound like Robert, he always seems such a relaxed sort of chap.'

'Yes, well, he's been working very hard,' said Florence. 'He – ' There was the sound of a car pulling up outside. 'Look, Charles, you'd better go, if you don't mind.'

'Yes, all right. Flo, are you all right? You look a bit odd.'

'Of course I'm all right. Here, I'll give you my key, then you can let yourself in. That'll be better I think . . .'

A key turned in the lock and Robert appeared. He was engrossed in some papers and didn't even look up, just shouted, 'Florence!'

'Robert, I'm here,' said Florence.

He did look up then, stared at her, his face very set, his pale eyes unblinking; then he noticed Charles and he smiled instantly, warmly, held out his hand.

'Charlie! Lovely to see you. What are you doing here?'

'Cadging a bed for the night, if that's OK. It's all right, Florence explained about your dinner party, I'll stay right out of the way.'

'Don't be absurd! Why not join us? It'll be fun. Florence, I hope you haven't been making Charles feel unwelcome. That would be dreadful of us. I would hate it. Got a dinner jacket with you, old boy? If not, doesn't matter, I can – '

'No, really, I can't join you,' said Charles. 'But thanks all the same.'

'Some wild bachelor evening I suppose,' said Robert and laughed. 'Lucky chap. Distant memory that sort of thing. Florence, is my tea ready? Please?'

'No, no, I'm sorry,' said Florence. 'I'll get it now.'

'Thank you, Florence. Not a lot to ask, is it, Charles, cup of tea at the end of a long day's work? Do you want to come upstairs to the drawing room with me, old boy? That's what I always do when I get in, sit and read the paper, have some tea. Or it's what I like to do.' He smiled at Florence.

Florence left them; as Charles went upstairs with Robert, he heard her calling to the maid to prepare Mr Grieg's tea quickly. Her voice seemed to him to sound rather strange, shaky even.

'Well done, darling,' said Robert, kissing Florence briefly as the door closed on their last guest. 'Marvellous evening. And old Forster was obviously very taken with you. You go on upstairs, I'm going to have a last drink, and read a couple of things.'

Lying awake, waiting for Robert to come up to their bedroom, hugely relieved at his pleasure and the success of her dinner party, Florence heard Charles's taxi pull up, heard the front door opening carefully, his footsteps very quiet on the stairs. It was quite late; almost two. She wondered what on earth he'd been doing. Sitting in some nightclub somewhere, getting drunk, she supposed. She was half relieved in a way he was still having nights out on the town, now that he was spending so much time with dull little Grace Marchant. Not that she wasn't very sweet, but it was a bit hard to understand what he saw in her. Still, he did seem much happier than he had been for a long time. She was very fond of him; as brothers went, he was a pretty good sample. Not that he would have got that impression from her behaviour that evening. She felt a stab of remorse at her unfriendliness; she would have to try to make it up to him in the morning. It was just so hard to explain, without saying too much. That was all.

Chapter Three

Autumn 1938

Grace's first reaction when Charles asked her to marry him was to panic. She had no idea why she was panicking, when what was happening was what she had dreamed of for months – or perhaps had tried not to dream of, not to hope for – but nevertheless panic she did. She sat there staring at him, listening to the words, those words, 'Will you marry me?' in a corner of the dining room of the Bear, where he had taken her to dinner, and instead of saying yes and throwing herself into his arms, she felt a wild, hurtling terror, a bit like being on the big dipper, a sense that life had taken hold of her and pushed her totally out of control, and she felt a violent desire to get up and run away, just as she had felt she wanted to hurl herself off the big dipper, to get it over, to escape from it, whatever the consequences.

'Grace,' he said, 'darling, are you all right? You're very pale.' And the room slowly steadied, and she felt calmer, easier, and she managed to smile at him, to tell him she would really like him to say it again (thinking how appalling, how dreadful of her to have reacted thus, and that surely, if she heard the words again, she would feel quite, quite wonderfully different), which he did, laughing at her gently, taking her hand.

'Darling Grace,' he said, 'I love you. Please will you marry me?'

And still she didn't say the right thing, still didn't say yes. 'But why?' she said instead, realizing immediately how stupid, how inappropriate it sounded; and he looked slightly hurt and said, 'I told you why, I love you.'

'Charles, what on earth did your mother say?' she said (more inappropriateness) 'when you told her. Was she furious?'

'Why should she be furious?' he said, looking genuinely puzzled. 'And anyway, I haven't told her yet, or my father. I wanted to know what you thought first. Which I still don't,' he added, taking her hand to his lips and kissing it tenderly. 'This isn't going at all the way I imagined it. I shall have to give up in a minute and go home.'

'Oh Charles, Charles,' she said, laughing and crying at the same time, knowing, recognizing how foolish she had been, how absurd, 'of course I'll marry you. I'd love to marry you. I love you.'

'Well, that means I can give you this,' he said and produced a small box from his pocket and pushed it across the table at her. 'And this – ' He waved at the waiter, who rushed across beaming with an ice bucket and a bottle of champagne which he opened with a huge flourish, and the people sitting at the next table, who mercifully they didn't know, smiled at them indulgently, and Grace opened the little box and inside was what was unarguably a very beautiful ring, a square sapphire set in tiny diamonds on a platinum band.

'It's beautiful, really beautiful,' she said, crushing hard, determinedly, just the shadow of a thought that it would have been nice to have chosen it with him, to have been asked what she wanted – which might not have been this, this slightly sombre-looking ring, but perhaps a graded row of diamonds set on a gold band, or a little round flower-like cluster of them like the one Florence had, and which she had very much admired.

'I'm so glad you like it, I bought it in Hatton Garden. I thought it was rather special, and if it doesn't fit you can have it sized. Put it on, darling, let me see.'

Grace put it on; it didn't fit, it was too big for her and actually the stone was too large for her small hand altogether, but Charles took her hand and looked at it and said 'Perfect' and she smiled again, her eyes filled with tears and she said, 'Thank you, Charles, it's lovely, really lovely' again.

Later the ring, chosen by him, not right for her, too big, overwhelming, seemed to her to epitomize their marriage.

When they got home to Bridge Cottage and told her parents, Grace really thought her mother was going to faint. She went first a very dark red and then waxy pale, and she half stood up and then sat down again, breathing heavily.

'Oh Grace,' she said finally, her voice odd, breathless, 'oh Charles. Oh, my dears.'

'She's going to cry,' said Frank, getting up, coming over to them, shaking Charles by the hand. 'I cannot tell you how delighted I am, my boy. Absolutely delighted. Give me a kiss, Grace. Congratulations, both of you.'

'Frank,' said Betty, 'you mustn't call Charles that, he's not a boy.' And she burst into tears.

'Dear oh dear,' said Frank. 'Look, I've got a bottle all ready on ice. I'll go and get it.'

'You've what!' said Grace. 'You mean you knew?'

'Well yes, of course I did,' said Frank. 'Charles did the proper thing, came and asked me for your hand. Well brought up, you see.'

'You mean you actually knew before I did!' And suddenly she was back on the big dipper again, being propelled forward, too fast, involuntarily.

'Darling, don't make it sound like a crime,' said Charles. 'It was only this afternoon and I wouldn't have dreamed of asking you without getting your father's permission.' He came over to her, put his arm round her shoulders. 'Surely you don't mind?'

'No,' said Grace. 'No, of course not.' She smiled at him carefully. 'I'm just a bit − overwhelmed, that's all.'

'Of course you are, darling, of course you are,' said Betty, blowing her nose, advancing rather nervously towards Charles. 'We all are. Er − may I kiss you, Charles? Now that you're going to be' − she hesitated, clearly almost unable to say it − 'to be part of the family.'

'You certainly may,' he said, bending down to her, 'and may I say what an extremely nice family to join. I feel very fortunate.'

Betty's eyes closed and an expression of almost beatific rapture came over her face; looking at her, Grace had the irreverent thought that she looked as if she was at the altar rails about to take Communion. She crushed the image hastily and took the glass of champagne her father had handed her. 'Thank you, Daddy.'

'Congratulations,' said Frank again, 'to you both. It's really wonderful news.'

'Do let us see the ring,' said Betty, and then her voice became just slightly careful. 'Oh, how very beautiful. Isn't it lovely, Grace?'

She doesn't like it either, thought Grace.

Later, much later, when Charles had gone, she sat with her mother in the sitting room.

'We must start making plans,' said Betty. Her face was flushed with the excitement and the champagne, her powder streaky on her cheeks where she had cried. 'When did you think the wedding might be, dear?'

'I don't think we did,' said Grace. 'Not properly. Charles said he thought quite soon, because of the situation in Europe and so on, but −'

'Well, it can't be before the spring,' said Betty determinedly.

'Whyever not? It's only October.'

'Well, dear, for one thing because I can't get everything organized, there's a great deal to be done, and anyway, short engagements aren't very – well, suitable.'

'Why on earth not?' said Grace, amused.

'Because – well, people think – might think that you – well, that you had to get married,' said Betty and blushed furiously.

'Oh Mother, really,' said Grace. She giggled. 'Goodness, what a thought. It would be worth doing just to get everyone talking.'

'Grace, really!'

'Sorry. But seriously, I don't know if we want to wait six months. Supposing the war actually came. We could have a small quiet wedding surely.'

'A small wedding!' said Betty and her voice rose at least an octave. 'Of course you can't have a small wedding. What an idea! Marrying into that family . . .'

'Mother, they're not royalty,' said Grace.

Lying wide awake in bed, far into the night, she lived and relived the evening, carefully crushing the memory of her panic, cherishing that of Charles telling her he loved her (for the very first time it had been); dreaming of the wedding; shrinking from the thought of the meeting next day with Muriel (Charles had arranged lunch, had said he would tell them over breakfast); thinking how lovely it would be to be Clifford's daughter-in-law; remembering with a stab of near panic Florence, what on earth would Florence be like about it? She fantasized about having a baby, becoming a mother; wondered where they would live; and over and over again she marvelled that Charles could have spoken to her father before he asked her, that it had been in some strange way an arrangement between them, scarcely involving her, and that her mother who had not been told about it either should have so totally accepted the fact ('Grace dear, he said if he had told me I wouldn't have been able to keep it to myself for one moment and he's quite right'). It was that last thought that occupied her more than any other until she finally fell asleep at four o'clock.

Charles came to collect her at midday to take her over to the Priory. He looked, she thought, slightly pale and heavy-eyed, but then he probably hadn't slept terribly well either.

'What – what did they say?' she asked.

'Oh, they were delighted of course,' he said quickly, smiling at her. 'My father has plans for a weekly gardening session with you.'

'And your mother?' Grace's heart felt very tight in her chest.

'Well, she's very happy of course,' he said. 'She likes you very much, you really mustn't worry so much about her. She's looking forward to seeing you today.'

'Good,' said Grace.

The Bennetts were waiting in the drawing room, standing on either side of the fireplace: like a stage play, thought Grace. They looked rather carefully styled altogether: Muriel was wearing a beige jersey dress, with diamanté clips at the neckline, and high-heeled shoes; Clifford was in a tweed jacket and flannels rather than his shapeless, shaggy gardening clothes. He came forward and gave her a bear hug. 'Delighted, my dear,' he said, 'couldn't be more pleased. Congratulations.'

'Thank you,' said Grace, returning the hug, reaching up to kiss his cheek.

'Grace, my dear – ' Muriel's voice, determinedly sweet, cut into the warmth. 'My congratulations. We are so very pleased.'

Grace withdrew reluctantly from Clifford's arms, turned to Muriel, who was smiling at her, holding out her hand; Grace went forward and took it. It was icy cold, and so, as she proffered it, was her cheek. Her hair, brushing against Grace's face, felt stiff, almost starched. It also, Grace noticed, the fact giving her some pleasure, smelt slightly stale.

'Clifford has some champagne ready, we must mark this happy occasion. Clifford, would you – '

Clifford rang the bell by the fireplace; the maid came in with a tray and glasses. She smiled cautiously at Grace.

'Right,' said Clifford, popping the cork, pouring the champagne, passing first Grace, then Muriel a glass, 'to you both. Grace, Charles, dear boy, much happiness.'

'Thank you, Father,' said Charles. He still looked strained, smiled at Grace, then rather uncertainly at his mother. She smiled back at him, but Grace looking at her was shocked at the total blankness in her eyes.

Lunch was a strain. They sat in the dining room, which was terribly cold, despite a roaring fire, and had a lengthy meal, soup, poached salmon, raspberry mousse and then cheese and biscuits. Grace had her back to the fire and began to feel sick; she found it very hard to eat, and harder to talk. Muriel asked a few gracious questions about whether they had settled on a date yet, if Charles had prepared the announcements for the column in the *Telegraph* and *The Times*, how soon Grace might be giving up her job.

'I – don't know,' said Grace to this last. 'I hadn't really thought about it. It's been a bit of a surprise,' she added, smiling, trying to lighten the atmosphere.

'For us also,' said Muriel, and then after an almost imperceptible pause, 'however delightful. But of course you will be giving it up? Your job I mean?'

'Well, I don't know. I hadn't thought.'

'My dear, of course you must. There will be so much to do, the wedding to plan, a house to find and get ready – now on that subject, Charles, the Mill House at Thorpe St Andrews is coming on the market. Very suitable I would have thought, you remember it well, I expect. You went to Geraldine's wedding, of course, I remember you saying you liked it, and you could keep a horse there, even start hunting again – '

What about me? thought Grace. What about me? 'Tell me about it,' she said to Muriel. 'This house – what is it like?'

'Oh,' said Muriel, turning briefly to her, as if to imply she was hardly worthy of consideration in the matter, 'it's a charming house, I thought you would have known it. Seventeenth-century, beautiful garden, and' – turning back to Charles – 'room for a tennis court. You'd like that, wouldn't you? Charles, I'll have a word with George Wetherby for you, say you might be interested.'

'Perhaps,' said Grace determinedly, 'we could go over and have a look at it this afternoon, Charles. After lunch. And see if we do both like it. Before your mother speaks to anyone – '

'Yes of course,' said Muriel coldly. 'What a good idea.'

Lunch finished finally; even Clifford Bennett looked relieved as they stood up.

'Got to get outside if you'll excuse me,' he said. 'Days are getting shorter, lot to do.'

'I suppose so,' said Muriel, 'if you must. Maureen, we'll have coffee in the drawing room. And please tell Cook that lunch was delicious.'

'Yes, it was, really lovely,' said Grace, smiling at Maureen. 'I'm looking forward to doing some cooking,' she said to Muriel as they sat down by the fire. 'I really enjoy it.'

'Oh do you?' said Muriel. 'Well, of course, good cooks are very hard to find these days, so you may have to manage for a while without, but I do warn you, Charles does like good food and – '

'My mother,' said Grace firmly, tiring of this, 'has always done her own cooking. She enjoys it too.'

'Really?' said Muriel, 'How very interesting.' She made it clear that doing your own cooking was tantamount to taking in washing. 'Which reminds me, Grace dear. You must bring your parents over here very soon. I am so looking forward to meeting them.'

'Yes, of course. I'm sure they'd love that,' said Grace. Her heart tumbled further within her. Of all the ordeals ahead of her, a meeting between her parents and the Bennetts looked much the worst.

'I didn't know you liked riding so much,' she said to Charles as they drove over towards Thorpe St Andrews and the Mill House that afternoon. She realized with a mild pang of alarm there was a great deal she didn't actually know about him.

'Oh – yes. I used to ride a lot. Loved hunting. But it takes a lot of time, doesn't really fit in with a full-time job. So I've let it drop. But I might get a horse again, yes. When we're married. I could teach you to ride as well.'

'Yes,' said Grace doubtfully.

The Mill House was very pretty; she had hoped she would be able to dislike it, take a stand, but she could see at once it would have been cutting off her nose to spite her face. It was set in the heart of the village of Thorpe St Andrews, the great millwheel still intact, a tall red-brick house with a beautiful garden – 'Father gets very cross about this garden, he's jealous,' said Charles laughing – and a large paddock behind it.

'Do you want to go in?' asked Charles. 'The Wetherbys are charming, I'm sure they wouldn't mind.'

'No, no,' said Grace, 'some other time. But I do like it. It's lovely.'

'Good. Well maybe – '

'Yes, maybe,' she said, reaching over to kiss him.

She would have to take a stand about something else.

The something else was the wedding itself.

At the end of a nightmare hour, when her parents sat in the drawing room at the Priory, her father trying to charm Muriel Bennett, her mother sparkling archly at Clifford Bennett over her glass of sherry, Muriel said suddenly, 'Well now, perhaps we should talk about the wedding itself. I believe April is now being discussed – providing Herr Hitler allows it, of course – I wondered where you were thinking of holding the reception, Mrs Marchant.'

'Oh, do please call me Betty. Well, we have discussed it, of course, and we were thinking perhaps the golf club – '

'The golf club,' said Muriel. 'Ah, yes, the golf club.' The words had an extraordinary venom. 'Well, that would be very nice of course. You haven't got room at home, I imagine.'

'No, not quite,' said Betty. It was clearly one of the most difficult things she had ever had to say. 'But – '

'Well, I'm sure the golf club would be very nice,' said Muriel again. There was a silence, then she went on. 'Look, do forgive me, Mrs – er, Betty – but we did wonder if perhaps you would consider having the reception here. Plenty of room, and we could have a marquee, especially if the wedding were to be moved forward to May, which would be better in any case, I would have thought – '

A surge of anger, an actual physical wave of heat, went through Grace. She stood up, so that they would all take notice of her, and said, quite quietly, 'That's very kind, Mrs Bennett, but I don't want to postpone the wedding any further. And I think the golf club would be extremely nice, don't you, Charles?'

Charles was clearly embarrassed by the whole thing.

'Grace darling, I wonder if we might consider having the reception at the Priory. Mother's quite right, there is lots of room, and it would be so much easier and – '

'Charles,' said Grace, 'you can consider it if you like. I'm not going to. I know why your mother wants to have it at the Priory and for much the same reasons I don't. If you want to marry me you can marry me at the golf club.'

She was astonished at her courage. She knew that if Charles himself had suggested the Priory she might well have agreed. She knew her mother would have been delighted once recovered from the initial humiliation. But her new status had given her courage, and she also knew that if she was not to be entirely engulfed by Muriel's crushing will she had to start resisting it at some point.

'Well,' said Charles, carefully, 'well, we'll see.'

'No,' said Grace, 'we won't see.'

They had quite a fight about it for a long time; Charles took her out in the car, they parked near the castle and Grace stood her ground, defended her parents, said she loved them and she was proud of them. Charles said that had nothing whatsoever to do with the reception and where it was held, Grace said of course it did, and she didn't believe he couldn't see that it did, that she was not going to be patronized by Muriel Bennett. Charles said his mother wasn't patronizing her, merely trying to be helpful, that he resented the implication very strongly. Grace told him he could resent it as much as he liked, she knew his mother didn't like her, that she was upset about the marriage. Charles told her she was neurotic and absurd, and Grace then burst into tears and said maybe, but if he didn't want to marry someone neurotic and absurd, then he had better find someone else.

Charles started the car at that point and drove her home without a word; she got out, walked inside and burst into fresh tears on her mother's shoulder and then after sobbing for several minutes and refusing to tell Betty what the matter was – and how could she, she asked herself, how could she say anything so hurtful, so horrible – she went upstairs and lay awake for a very long time, wondering if in fact this marriage was a mistake, if she was going to spend her entire life submitting to Charles, doing things his way, what he wanted, and if she did really love him enough – and if he loved her. She felt she had seen a new Charles that night, someone more overbearing, less sensitive than she had imagined; all her earlier doubts and anxieties revived – the long intervals between their meetings, the reluctance to talk about his past relationships, indeed the apparent absence of past relationships, the reluctance in fact to talk about himself – and she lay looking at the ring on her finger, the ring she still didn't really like, and debated very seriously if she shouldn't give it back.

In the morning she felt so dreadful she didn't go into work, got Betty to phone and say she had a sick headache; her father went to the bank, and Betty, white with what was clearly an appalling anxiety, desisting from cross-questioning her with awe-inspiring restraint, cancelled her attendance at a meeting of the Westhorne W I of which she was vice-chairwoman, and was making pastry with great determination when the doorbell rang.

'I'll go,' said Grace.

Charles stood there, with a great bunch of flowers. 'Can I come in?' he said.

'Yes,' she said, 'yes of course.'

She led him into the sitting room; he sat down in one of the wing chairs by the fire, still holding the flowers, and looked at her.

'Look,' he said, 'you really have got things all wrong.'

'Have I?' said Grace.

'Yes, you have. Terribly wrong. None of us want to hurt you, least of all me. My parents are terribly fond of you. They certainly don't wish to upset your parents. It's just a fact of life that this house' – he gestured round the sitting room – 'this house simply isn't big enough to contain a large wedding reception.'

'We could have a small wedding reception,' said Grace. She knew they couldn't, or rather that they wouldn't, but it seemed worth proposing. It wasn't.

'Darling, we can't have a small wedding reception. You know we can't. It would upset so many people.'

Grace was silent.

'So it just seemed a better idea to have the wedding at one of our homes, where it would be surely so much nicer, than somewhere like the golf club.'

'But Charles – '

'Let me finish. Please. I still think so, actually. It would be wonderful for me to have it in the house where I grew up. I hate the idea of getting married in some strange environment. But I love you, and I don't want to hurt you, and of course if it's so important to you, we'll have the wedding wherever you like, in your father's potting shed if you want to – '

'Oh Charles,' said Grace, her resolution to review their marriage, their relationship, wavering in the face of such a retreat, 'Charles, I – '

He dropped the flowers then, just dropped them on the floor, and stood up, held out his arms; she went into them, and he held her and she began to feel warmed, soothed, to think that after all he might be right: at which point Betty walked in with a coffee tray, said sorry, backed out again, still with the tray, and Charles released Grace, went over to Betty and took the tray and said, 'Please, Mrs Marchant, please come in and join us.'

'Oh,' said Betty, 'oh, but I don't want to interfere.'

'You're not,' he said, 'you never interfere. You're a model mother-in-law.'

Betty turned pink with pleasure.

'I was just saying,' said Charles carefully, 'that I do understand how Grace feels about the reception.'

In the end, of course, Charles and the Bennetts had their way; the arguments were too powerful, and Betty was halfway to being persuaded already.

'It is Charles's day too, dear,' she said to Grace, 'and our house *isn't* big enough. Oh, dear, if only we'd bought the Manor House at Norton Bradley, we were going to, you know, about ten years ago, that would have done beautifully – '

Grace agreed that it would; since they hadn't, and before a great deal more discussion had ensued, she heard herself agreeing – not only with Charles and her mother but her father as well – that it really would be much more sensible to have the wedding reception at the

41

Priory after all. And was left with the sense she had been manoeuvred with considerable skill into a corner where she wasn't sure she wanted to be.

'My sister's coming down to stay for a few days,' said Charles to Grace one evening. 'Apparently she's not terribly well. Maybe she's preggers,' he added, brightening up. 'About time, I must say. Anyway, that'll be nice, we haven't seen her since we got engaged.'

Grace tried hard to look cheerful about Florence's visit, and hoped that if Florence was indeed pregnant, it might soften her a little.

Florence arrived on a Friday evening by train; Muriel went to meet her and then insisted she went straight to bed, before announcing to Charles and Grace over supper that Florence was indeed having a baby. 'In the spring. Not very good timing, I'm afraid, for the wedding. We may have to juggle with dates a bit.'

She sounded rather stern about it; Grace's sympathies were for the first time with Florence. She could hardly be expected to have planned the conception of her child around a wedding that had not even been considered at the time.

Grace went over to the Priory again next morning. Florence was lying on a sofa in the morning room, and managed a wan smile and a half-hearted expression of pleasure to her on the engagement. 'About time he settled down anyway,' she said. 'We all thought he never would, that no one would have him.'

Grace tried not to feel as if she was the last in a very long line of girls under consideration by Charles, and smiled back at Florence. 'Thank you,' she said, 'and congratulations to you, too. How are you feeling?'

'Terrible,' said Florence, 'but thank you. I'm certainly not doing this again in a hurry.' She did look dreadful, very pale and drawn, with great shadows under her eyes; she picked miserably at her food at lunch, said she was alternately too hot and too cold, snapped endlessly at her parents, at Charles, and even down the phone at Robert.

Grace felt terribly sorry for him.

They were all sitting down to tea when there was the sound of tyres in the drive and a loud jangling on the bell; Maureen came in and said, 'It's Mr and Mrs Compton Brown, Madam.' There was a great scurry of footsteps in the hall and then the door opened wider and an extremely pretty girl appeared, swathed in fox furs and a black hat tipped rakishly over one eye, followed by a young man in a rather loud tweed suit.

'Darling Moo,' cried the girl, rushing up to Muriel and hugging her, 'and Charlie, sweetheart, and Florence, oh what luck, and you must be Grace. How lovely to meet you – '

'Clarissa, my dear!' said Muriel. 'How lovely to see you, and Jack, how are you?' She was flushed and smiling with pleasure; it was the first time Grace had ever seen her display any warmth or emotion. Charles on the other hand, she noticed, was looking rather heavy and tense; Clarissa, whoever she was, was obviously not such a favourite of his.

'We're both fine, on our way back to London. We've been visiting my darling old godmother and I said to Jack that you were only a teeny bit out of the way, didn't I, Jack, we must go and see them, and here we are. Where's my special sweetheart then?'

'I'm here,' said Clifford, coming in, giving Clarissa a hug. 'You naughty girl, why haven't you been before?'

'Oh, you know, it's a long way from London, well, Florence knows that, don't you, darling, and of course we were away when you had your lovely party, and we're so busy you wouldn't believe it, so much to do, just bought a new house, perfectly lovely, in Campden Hill Square. You must come and see it, all of you, we're going to have a huge party when it's done, I'm not taking any notice of all this war nonsense . . .'

Jack came over to Grace and held out his hand. 'How do you do. Jack Compton Brown.' She liked him; he was extremely handsome, with very dark hair and quite extraordinarily blue eyes.

'How do you do.' She couldn't think what else to say, just stood there, smiling at him.

'Congratulations,' he said, 'on your engagement. We were so pleased when we read the announcement. Clarissa meant to write, but she's – well, she's very busy.'

'Oh, that's all right,' said Grace, 'Anyway, we've been swamped with letters, I'm still answering them.'

'Jack, come and talk to me! It's so nice to see you both.' Even Florence sounded more cheerful. Whoever these people were, Grace thought, they were obviously very important to the family.

Clarissa came over to Grace, kissed her. 'You don't mind, do you? I've known Charlie so long. It's so nice to meet you.'

She was extremely and unusually pretty, with blonde hair and (rather surprisingly) brown eyes, and thick creamy skin. She had slithered out of her furs and was wearing a blue woollen dress; she was very slim, with, Grace noted miserably – oh how she would love to be like Clarissa – a full bosom and long slender legs.

'It's nice to meet you too,' she said rather feebly.

'I expect Charlie's told you all about me,' said Clarissa, settling down beside her, biting into a buttery crumpet.

'Well – a bit,' said Grace uncertainly. It seemed rather rude to say he hadn't.

'Oh,' said Clarissa. It was her turn to look uncertain, to flush even. 'Oh I see. Never mind. I just thought he would have done. Silly of me. Well, it was a long time ago, wasn't it, Florence?'

'What was?' said Florence. 'God, I feel awful. I think I might be sick again.'

'Darling, why? You're not in the club, are you? Oh what heaven. Jack, did you realize, Florence is in the pudding club, isn't it exciting? Darling, where's the gorgeous father-to-be?'

'He's in London,' said Florence. She sounded rather sulky. 'He couldn't get down.'

'Oh how thrilling. When's it due? I want to hear all about it, what names you've chosen, everything. Could I be godmother? Oh, that would be marvellous, do say I can – '

Clarissa seemed to be deliberately making a great deal of Florence's baby; Grace felt she was grateful for the change of subject from herself and whatever it was Charles might have said about her.

'You must both stay to supper,' Muriel said, 'I simply insist. Stay the night if you like, then you won't have to do any more driving.'

'Oh, sweet of you,' said Clarissa, 'but honestly we do have to get back. But may we come and stay soon? And Florence, I'm going to come and see you lots in London, knit some bootees for you, all that sort of thing.'

'Please do,' said Florence. 'I'd love it. Not the bootees so much, just the company.'

Pregnancy, Grace thought, seemed to be softening Florence, making her nicer.

They stayed for an hour or so, and then Clarissa stood up. 'Come along, Jack darling, time to hit the road, it's such a long way. Clifford dearest, I'd so adore some advice on our garden in town. It's tiny, but so sweet, not much more than a sort of courtyard really. Now what would you suggest? I've got a man coming to see me on Monday, just to talk shrubs and things, do you have any books or anything?'

'Oh, plenty,' said Clifford. 'Come along with me to my study and I'll sort a couple out. Courtyards, now let me see . . .'

He got up and went out of the room, Clarissa holding his arm. After a few minutes, Charles got up too and followed them. Grace watched him go, feeling rather miserable, and tried, without very much success, to concentrate on what Jack was saying to her, which seemed to be a lot of boring detail about their recent holiday in France.

Ten minutes later Clifford came in, smiling and shaking his head in mock despair, obviously over something Clarissa had said or done. 'What a girl!' he said, 'Mad as a hatter. Jack, you've got your marching orders, she wants to go.'

'Right,' said Jack, jumping up. 'Go we must. Goodbye, Grace, I hope to see you again soon – '

'Oh, I'll come out and say goodbye,' said Grace, and followed him out to the drive; Clarissa and Charles weren't there. She turned and walked dejectedly back into the house, through the hall, and saw them suddenly, standing in the morning room, talking intently, their backs to her, looking out of the window at the dark garden.

' – felt so awful,' Clarissa was saying, 'so stupid and tactless.'

'Well, I'm sorry,' said Charles, 'but – '

'Charlie, you really should have told her. Ages ago. I can't understand it. And what about your parents? Surely they – '

'Clarissa, I was going to. Honestly. My father said the same. But it's a bit difficult, now it's gone on so long – '

'Oh Charlie.' She sighed, reached up to him, kissed him briefly on the cheek. 'You really are so hopeless. I think that's what I first I loved – '

'Clarissa! Darling, where are you?' Jack had come into the hall, had seen Grace standing in the doorway of the morning room, saw Charles and Clarissa inside. Grace swung round, blushing furiously, moved away down the corridor into the cloakroom, hot painful tears stinging her eyes, as much at the humiliation of being caught eavesdropping as what she had heard and seen.

'Sorry, my angel,' called Clarissa, 'I'm coming. It's just that Charles and I had such a lot to talk about. Bye, Charlie darling, and Moo, thank you for tea, and dearest Clifford . . . Now, where's Grace? So lovely to have met her – '

'I don't know,' said Charles. He sounded mildly anxious. 'I really don't. Grace! Grace, darling, where are you?'

'I think she's still in the drawing room,' said Jack. 'That's where I saw her last.'

Grace, sitting on the lavatory, her head buried in her hands, thought she must repay Jack Compton Brown for his kindness if it was the last thing she did.

'Sorry,' she said to Charles, emerging from the cloakroom as they all came back into the house. 'I didn't realize they were going.'

'That's all right, darling. You all right? You look a bit pale.'

'Yes. Yes I'm fine. Well – actually, I think I'd like to go home, if you don't mind, not stay for supper. I've got an awful headache. Could I ring my father, get him to fetch me?'

'Darling, I'm so sorry. Look, go and sit down by the fire for a bit, see if it gets better. I'll get you some aspirin.'

Florence was still lying on the sofa, her eyes closed; she looked at Grace and sighed. 'I really wouldn't recommend this,' she said.

'No,' said Grace, and then, slightly desperately, 'Clarissa's very pretty.'

'Yes. Very.'

'Er – she said she expected Charles would have told me all about her. He's never mentioned her. Are they – are they old friends?'

'Good Lord,' said Florence. 'How extraordinary of him. I really can't believe that. Yes, pretty old, although not exactly friends. He was engaged to her. Oh, over two years ago now. Sorry, Grace, I really thought he'd have said.'

For the very first time Grace saw genuine friendliness in her eyes. Friendliness and sympathy.

Chapter Four

Winter–Spring 1938–1939

She told Charles she wanted to break off the engagement.

She sat in his car, outside her parents' house (aware that the curtains were moving, that her mother was behind them, looking out, not caring), and said quite calmly that if he was going to keep something of that enormity from her, then she couldn't trust him in anything, anything at all.

Charles, clearly upset, white-faced, his hands twisting round and round on the steering wheel, kept saying he was sorry, that he had always intended to tell her, that his parents had said that he must, that he should have done before he even proposed to her, but it had just become harder and harder; that it was so long ago now, almost two years, that yes, he had been in love with Clarissa, but it would never have worked, they had both realized it, had agreed mutually to end it, that they had both been upset, but it had been the right decision.

'Anyway, it was two years ago, for God's sake,' he said. 'It's over, well and truly over. Surely you can't think I'm still in love with her.'

'That's not the point, Charles,' said Grace, 'it's that you didn't tell me something so important about yourself. Anyway, you could have told me. I asked you about your past, your other girlfriends, lots of times.'

'I know you did. I'm sorry. I just couldn't bring myself to tell you. I can't explain why. What more can I say? I certainly didn't feel in the least about her as I do about you,' he added, 'you must believe that.'

'Charles,' said Grace, 'I'm beginning to find it difficult to believe anything about you. Anyway, why did you break it off?'

'I told you. It was a joint decision. We just realized it wasn't going to work.'

'I see. And having made that decision, nobody ever mentioned it again?'

'Of course they did. And my parents were very upset – '

'Yes,' said Grace slowly, 'I can see they would be. They obviously adored her. Much more suitable.' Misery, sick jealous misery consumed her; she knew she was making things worse and she couldn't help it.

'More suitable than what?'

'Me.'

'Oh Grace, don't be absurd. Please don't start that again.'

'Charles, I'm not starting anything. It's your behaviour that's finished it.'

For three days she refused to see him, to speak to him on the phone even. She felt bewildered, humiliated, totally miserable. She didn't explain to her parents, just said she and Charles had quarrelled and she didn't want to talk about it.

Betty was distraught.

She couldn't face telling anyone. Part of her misery was in the recognition that Clarissa was exactly the sort of person Charles would have been expected to marry, that she, Grace, was so clearly a second choice. If Clarissa had been plain, or if not plain at least quiet and shy, she could have coped with it better. But a dazzlingly glamorous secret ex-fiancée – her frail self-confidence simply couldn't cope with it.

She was simply glad she had found out when she did.

She was sitting in her office one afternoon later in the week when the phone rang.

'Grace? It's Clifford Bennett, my dear. I'd like to talk to you.'

'Oh,' said Grace. 'Oh, I see. I'm not sure – '

'Look,' he said, 'I know you're upset, and I'm not surprised. But Charles is desperately upset too and I thought it might help if I – well, could we meet, do you think? After you've finished work? I'm in Shaftesbury today, what about the Grosvenor, they do a splendid tea?'

'Oh – Mr Bennett, I really don't know.'

'I think it might help,' he said, 'might help you understand. Please come.'

He sounded so genuinely concerned, so kind, that it seemed churlish to refuse.

'All right,' said Grace. 'Thank you.'

Clifford was waiting by the fire in the lounge of the Grosvenor. He got up and kissed her when she came in, told her to sit down, that he had already ordered tea. Grace looked at him rather uncertainly.

'I know this isn't strictly my business,' he said, 'but I'm very fond of you, and I know Charles loves you.'

'Does he know you're here?' said Grace. 'Because – '

'Good Lord, no. But I have had a talk with him. I couldn't believe he'd been so stupid. Not to tell you something as important as this.'

'Yes,' said Grace, feeling a great weight lifting from her as she realized he did seem to understand precisely why she was so upset. 'Um – who told you? That I'd found out? Did Charles?'

'No, Florence told us. She was very upset on your behalf. And cross with Charles.'

'I see,' said Grace. She found the thought of the whole family being shocked on her behalf, sorry for her, painful rather than comforting.

'Now the thing is,' said Clifford, 'he was terribly fond of Clarissa.'

'Yes,' said Grace dully. 'I'm sure.'

'And he was desperately upset when it finished.'

'Why was it finished?' said Grace.

'Oh – nothing sinister, I assure you. They simply decided they weren't compatible. She's a town bird, you know, and he likes the country. She's so very extrovert and he's quite shy, as you also know. And,' he added, looking at her carefully, 'not perhaps quite as mature as he seems. Anyway, they were sensible enough to see it wasn't going to work. However much in love they were.'

'So they were?' said Grace.

'Oh they were. It would be silly to tell you otherwise. But I can tell you something else. He is very much in love with you too. He needs you. I suspect you see yourself as second best in some way. You're not.'

'Aren't I?' said Grace.

'No, you are not,' he said firmly, patting her knee. 'Of course you're not. Look, here's the tea. Shall I be mother? Now listen to me,' he went on, passing her a cup. 'I see you, and so does Muriel, I might tell you, as a very special young lady. Very special indeed. We are truly delighted about the engagement. And I think you can do a lot for Charles. I really do.'

'Do you?' said Grace doubtfully. 'Sometimes it feels all the other way round, as if it's just him doing a lot for me.'

'Well, that's very silly of you, if you don't mind my saying so,' said Clifford. 'Very silly. You're given Charles a lot of confidence. Clarissa, much as we love her, rather took it away.'

'Oh,' said Grace. She felt rather silly, suddenly, silly and much happier. She smiled at Clifford. 'This is very kind of you.'

'Not at all,' he said, 'very self-interested. I want you in my family. You're the best thing that's happened to it for a long time.'

'Oh,' said Grace, 'how funny you should say that.'

'Why?'

'Oh – nothing,' she said quickly, 'it sounds a bit bigheaded.'

'Not at all, your head needs to be a bit bigger. Tell me why it was funny.'

'Well, someone else said it. At your party.'

'Oh really. Who was that?'

'Robert.'

'Ah', said Clifford. There was a slightly odd note to his voice. Grace looked at him quickly, and caught a shadow of concern on his face; then it was gone. 'Very perceptive of him,' he said, 'very perceptive indeed.'

'How is Florence?'

'Oh, she's gone back now. Poor darling, she really does feel rotten. She likes you very much too, you know,' he added. 'She really does. Now then, I must go. Got a very worried client to see. Thank you for coming to meet me. Whatever you decide, I enjoyed it.'

Grace stood up and gave him a kiss. 'Thank you,' she said. 'You're so kind. A perfect father-in-law. And father too.'

'I'm afraid not,' he said and sighed, and his voice was very sober. 'I'm very much afraid not.'

Charles presented Grace with the key to the Mill House 'as a making-up present'.

'That's quite a present,' she said, laughing.

'Well, it's not exactly ours yet. But we have first refusal. The Wetherbys are away, we can go round it.'

The house was lovely: tall, sunlit rooms, glorious views from every side, and the sound of the millstream always in the background. The kitchen and the main bedroom were on the stream side of the house, and the water flowed beneath the windows; Grace opened the bedroom window, and a duck, drifting past, looked up at her, surprised, almost put out, to see her there. 'It's like being on a boat,' said Grace. 'I love it.'

'Will you live in it with me, please, Miss Marchant?'

'Yes, Charles, I will. But no more secrets? Anywhere?'

'No more secrets. Anywhere at all. Ever.' He kissed her. 'I love you.'

'I tell you what,' he said as they drove away, 'that house would be dangerous for children. We shall have to fence the stream well off. In due course.'

'Yes, we will,' said Grace. The mention of children made her feel slightly nervous. She had taken the next day off work for an appointment with the National Birth Control Clinic in Salisbury; she had told everyone she was going to look at things like china and bed linen.

She was rather impressed with herself at taking the decision to go to the clinic; it had been a conversation with Florence of all unlikely people that had propelled her there.

'For goodness sake,' Florence had said, lying on the sofa, glassy pale, 'don't you go and do this, Grace. Not straight away. Whatever Charles wants. Not a good idea.'

Her words made Grace realize that she had not really thought properly about, nor had they discussed, whether and indeed how soon she and Charles might want children; the thought of confronting the subject made her feel shy and nervous. She knew that the modern thing to do was for the woman to get contraceptive advice; even her mother had hinted at it ('Personal advice' she had called it, blushing furiously), and it really seemed a much better idea than leaving the whole thing to fate, or indeed to Charles: he might even be assuming that was what she was going to do anyway. And so she had looked up the telephone number of the clinic and phoned for an appointment from a public box, so that nobody was likely to overhear her.

The woman doctor, whose name was Phillips, was rather less cosy than Grace had expected, and after talking to her about her general health, her periods, and the wedding date, also asked her whether she had discussed birth control with her fiancé.

'No,' said Grace humbly. 'No I haven't, I'm afraid.'

'You really should,' said Dr Phillips. 'It's very important. And you certainly can't afford to be embarrassed about it. Have you talked to him about sexual relations at all?'

'No,' said Grace blushing. 'No I haven't.'

'You really should. Saves a lot of problems later on. Well, possible problems,' she added, seeing Grace's alarmed face. 'It really isn't a good idea to go into marriage without confronting these things. Are you a virgin?'

'Yes,' said Grace.

'Is he?'

'No. No, I'm sure he's not. He's well, he's thirty-two.'

'Doesn't necessarily mean anything,' said Dr Phillips, smiling slightly grimly at her, 'although I agree these days it is unlikely. Now then, the most satisfactory method of birth control all round is the Dutch cap. Know about that?'

'No,' said Grace.

'Well, it's a device that you wear, internally of course. It's undetectable in use, doesn't get in the way of love-making, very discreet indeed, about ninety-five per cent safe, and it means you can take responsibility for the whole thing. Far better than the old way. But you can't use one when you're a virgin, so you'll have to come back and see me after your honeymoon. Unless of course you want a family right away. Which is never something I recommend and certainly not in the state the world's in at the moment. I expect your fiancé will take care of things on the honeymoon, but you really can't depend on that, men are notoriously selfish and irresponsible. So I'm going to give you a douche and then – '

Grace left the clinic armed with a strange-looking rubber contraption, a bit like a small hot-water bottle with a tube attached, a booklet entitled *Married Life*, several new pieces of knowledge and a determination to talk to Charles about it all.

Charles was clearly shocked when she broached the subject when they were alone one evening in the room he called his study at the Priory and which was actually a rather untidy second sitting room.

'Darling, what a question,' he said, struggling to smile, downing a rather large Scotch in one go and pouring another. 'No, of course I'm not a virgin. Whyever did you think that?'

'Well – I didn't know,' said Grace, 'how could I? But I didn't think you could be.'

'You were right. Of course.'

He smiled and took another drink; there was a silence.

'But we've never – never even talked about it at all,' said Grace. 'I thought perhaps – '

'Grace darling, there isn't a lot to talk about. I promise you. I love you and respect you. That's all you need to know. I'm looking forward to our wedding night more than I can tell you. And you don't have to worry, I shall take care of things.'

'What do you mean?'

'Well I mean,' – he looked awkward – 'I'll see there aren't any babies. Yet. For a little while anyway. I think that would be best.'

He didn't ask her if she thought it would be best.

'I've seen to it too, Charles.'

'You've what?'

'I've been to a clinic. A birth-control clinic.'

'What on earth for?'

'What a stupid question,' said Grace, trying to look amused, as if this was a perfectly easy, matter-of-fact conversation. 'Because it's important, that's why.'

'It may be important,' said Charles, 'but I don't think it's the sort of thing you should be worrying about.'

'Charles, why on earth not?' said Grace, her courage growing as it always did when he patronized her. 'Surely it concerns me. You're not cross, are you?'

'Not cross exactly,' he said, 'but a bit taken aback. I would have thought that you would at least have asked me first.'

'Asked you what?'

'Whether I minded you going, of course. It's very, very personal, this sort of thing – '

'Charles, of course it's personal. But I don't see why you wouldn't want me to – '

'To talk about something so – so intimate to a complete stranger. Of course I don't want that.'

He was plainly very upset; Grace put her hand on his arm. He shook it off.

'Charles, please! What's the matter?'

'Oh,' he said, 'if you can't see, there's no point talking about it. Let's change the subject.'

He drove her home shortly after that, kissed her goodnight only very briefly. Grace was totally baffled by the whole incident, but decided she must have wounded his male pride and should apologize for upsetting him. He accepted, but was still clearly not happy for a day or two; he managed finally to laugh it off and say he had simply been rather shocked by her.

'You're a more modern girl than I thought,' he said, kissing her, 'and I'm a bit old-fashioned.'

The male pride, Grace thought, was evidently horribly easy to wound; she wondered if Clarissa had been the sort of girl to leave birth control to the man. She really rather doubted it.

Grace left her job at the end of November. She was actually rather reluctant to do so; it seemed quite a long time to May still, and although she could see that supervising the work on the Mill House, getting her wedding dress made (her mother had finally and regretfully abdicated the responsibility in favour of Mrs Humbolt, who made all the local dresses quite beautifully), organizing the bridesmaids, sending out the invitations, receiving the presents and writing the thank-you letters was going keep her fairly busy for five months, she would still, given the choice, have stayed on until

Christmas. But both her mother and Muriel had told her it was impossible, and she had given in gracefully. She seemed to be giving in, gracefully or otherwise, a great deal these days.

She stood in her boss's office, sipping the sweet wine he had supplied for the occasion, eating a slice of the cake one of the other girls had baked, accepting the wedding present from her colleagues (a set of table napkins with drawn thread embroidery and matching tablecloth), and listening to him making a speech about what a loss she would be, what an asset she had been, how he was sure the entire firm would crumble about his ears without her. Looking round at the smiling friendly faces, she felt very sad: at the loss not just of the friendship and all the gossip and fun, but of her own independence. She hadn't realized it mattered to her so much until she said goodbye to it. From now on, she would be dependent on someone else for everything: relying totally on Charles not just financially but for her status in life as well. Any importance she had, any position, would be dependent on his importance and position. She was longing to marry him, was looking forward to being his wife, and in due course a mother; but something deep within her still wanted to be something else as well. Herself.

She was about to set off to meet Charles at the cinema – the new musical *Love Finds Andy Hardy* with Judy Garland and Micky Rooney had finally reached Shaftesbury – when her phone went. It was Charles.

'I'm sorry, Grace, but I won't be able to see you tonight. Something awful's happened.'

Florence had had a miscarriage.

Robert had phoned sounding distraught at about five; he had arrived home to find Florence lying at the bottom of the stairs, mildly concussed and already in labour. The maid was out, it was her afternoon off; nobody had been there when it happened. Florence couldn't remember much about it, only that she had fallen from top to bottom of the flight. 'I know I felt a bit dizzy,' she said over and over again, 'after that everything's – blank.'

Muriel went straight up to London to see Florence in hospital; she came back after a few days visibly shaken.

Florence was not only desperately upset at losing the baby, she said, but was suffering from appalling headaches. She looked dreadful, a huge bruise all down one side of her face, and a badly swollen right eye. 'Poor child. I felt so sorry for her. And poor Robert was beside himself. He's hardly left her side since he found her.'

The baby had been a boy; the doctors had been encouraging, had said there was no reason why she shouldn't have another, as soon as she was better, but Florence said it was the last thing in the world she wanted.

'I expect she'll change her mind later, when she's feeling better,' said Clifford. He was also deeply upset by the whole thing and had wanted to go up and see Florence himself, but Muriel told him that Robert was finding the whole thing extremely hard to cope with and that, as the doctors had said in any case she should be kept absolutely quiet, he thought it best if there were no visitors for a few weeks.

'I can understand that,' said Grace, her heart aching with sympathy not only for Florence but for Robert too. 'I'd feel just the same, I know, I'd just want to dig a hole and crawl into it.'

Muriel wanted Florence to come to the Priory to convalesce when she left hospital, but she refused. 'Robert thinks we should be together, and I agree. Maybe later on.'

'She's lucky to have him,' said Charles. 'Good bloke, old Robert.'

Charles was worrying about the honeymoon.

'I hope it's going to be all right,' he said. 'I would have taken you somewhere abroad, of course, but I really don't think it's going to be possible now. So I thought Scotland. Not so romantic, but – '

'Scotland would be lovely,' said Grace. She found it so hard to think beyond the wedding itself that if he had suggested a honeymoon in the middle of the Sahara Desert she would have thought it was a good idea. Not that Hitler would let them get there either.

She still worried about not knowing him properly. It hadn't just been the shock over Clarissa, or even the slightly sporadic nature of their early courtship – she had tried to ask him about that from the safety of their engagement but he had laughed, made a joke of it, said nicely brought-up girls should never look too hard into their fiancés' pasts, and then grown irritable and said he didn't know what she was making such a fuss about, it was necessary for him to go to London on business from time to time, and that was all there was to it. She had tried very hard to accept that, but the fact remained that he hardly ever went now they were engaged and if he did he was usually back on the next day. So she fell back on platitudes about wild oats, and tried to stop worrying about it. Far more troubling she found was his reluctance to talk about himself, altogether; whenever the conversation became personal, when she asked him things, quite harmless they seemed to her, what made him happy, what sad, what he was afraid of, if anything, what his childhood had really been like, how he had felt when he had been sent off to school, he would become first monosyllabic and then abruptly change the subject. The nearest she got to an answer was when he told her men didn't like talking about such things; it wasn't exactly satisfactory, but it had to do. They had all their lives together to get to know each other, after all.

'I do worry occasionally a bit about that dear little soul marrying Charles,' said Clarissa suddenly.

She and Jack were sitting in the drawing room of their house in Campden Hill Square. It was a very pretty room on the first floor, overlooking the square, and designed entirely to Clarissa's taste (Jack not being overconcerned with aesthetics) by a very expensive and fashionable young man. The predominant colour was white: white walls, carpets, and a fine marble fireplace, the curtains and upholstery yellow and cream; the furniture eighteenth-century, bequeathed to them by Clarissa's mother from her own London house. Clarissa adored her drawing room and frequently said it was there she wished to die – 'On the chaise longue, Jack, now do get it right if you're around, won't you, and I want to be wearing something very elegant, not my nightie. At a pinch a satin robe of some kind, maybe.'

Clarissa's enemies (who were few) frequently said her entire life was a public performance, designed to be watched, and there was some truth in this, the fact that she was already famously stage-managing her death at the age of twenty-four seeming to support this view. But that was not altogether her intention; it was simply an expression of her love for her drawing room in particular and for agreeable surroundings in general. Clarissa was not easily depressed, but a disagreeable place could send her spirits plummeting faster than any number of disagreeable people – partly due to the fact that she possessed in such good measure the ability to transform the disagreeable people into agreeable ones.

Jack got up, refilled their glasses from the champagne bottle that stood on the sofa table and passed her one of them. 'I don't actually think you need to worry about her too much,' he said. 'I sense quite a steely little soul tucked underneath that shyness. I'm sure she'll be fine.'

'Really?' said Clarissa. She sipped thoughtfully at her champagne.

'How terribly perceptive you are, darling. I'd never have spotted that in a million years.'

'Yes, well, I spend a little more time observing people than you do,' said Jack, smiling at her, 'and less in making them observe me.'

'Jack! Is that a criticism?'

'Absolutely not. It's an observation. Another observation. Anyway, you make Charles sound as if he's some kind of a monster. Which he certainly isn't. Or are you trying to tell me with your intimate knowledge of him that he is?'

He sounded just slightly edgy; Clarissa looked at him warily. She and Jack both had pasts, as they put it; had confessed to them, early in their relationship, as a modern young couple should. She was no more concerned with Jack's former lovers than about the clothes he might have worn or the cars he might have driven, but she knew he had a most carefully stifled jealous streak within him, found it hard to set her colourful personal history entirely aside, and especially the part of it that concerned the two other men she had been engaged to. Freddy Macintosh, the first fiancé as she called him, was more easily dealt with – he lived in Scotland and they saw him seldom – but Charles was an intrinsic part of their circle, the brother of her best friend. It was a situation she watched with care.

'There really is nothing for you to be upset about, my darling,' she had said, as she drove Jack down to meet the Bennetts for the first time. 'In the first place it's over a year now since I – we – broke it off, really lost in the mists of time, and in the second I don't think I ever really loved him.'

'Then why get engaged to him?'

'Oh I don't know,' she said vaguely, 'I can't quite think now. Because he was there, I suppose. I was awfully young and silly. Not like I am these days. Not a bit.'

Now she smiled at Jack across the drawing room, and raised her glass to him.

'Here's to us, my darling, and how much we love each other. Let's not waste time and energy on those two any more.'

'You started it.'

'I know and I'm sorry. Suddenly I can't think of anything more tedious. I've got a much better idea for your consideration. Let's just go to bed. It's our favourite time, after all.'

'Let's just,' he said, smiling at her. 'We can work up an appetite for dinner.'

They went upstairs. Clarissa lay on the pillows on their huge high bed and watched Jack as he removed his clothes, gazing happily at his lean brown body, the flat stomach, the thick black pubic hair, the jutting penis that would soon – well, quite soon, he could delay things for a very long time, until she was quite literally screaming for him – be within her, working at her, bringing her to leaping, climbing, shattering orgasm. She loved him so much, and for all kinds of reasons, not least the endlessly wonderful ways he made love to her. And he was so extremely good-looking. She couldn't understand people who said looks didn't matter, weren't important; they were to her an essential part of loving, of wanting, of sex, of fulfilment, and when she had first met him, first seen him, she couldn't believe anyone so perfect could have been delivered to her.

They had met at a cocktail party; she had spotted him instantly, wanted him, known she had to have him, had carefully positioned herself in the group next to him, started kissing, laughing, talking in her highly noticeable way. And he had noticed her, of course, and had joined the group, smiled at her, held out his hand. He was dark, wonderfully, romantically dark, with dazzling blue eyes and an absurdly, classically straight nose; and even his handshake was somehow sensuous, not hearty, not hard, but firm, warm, immensely – well, immensely pleasant. She had left her own small white hand in his for a long time, it was a trick of hers, she would pretend not to have noticed, to be so engrossed with the person and what he (always he, of course) was saying, and he had said, 'How do you do, Jack Compton Brown' and smiled at her – well, it wasn't even a smile, it was a huge, heart-turning, world-stopping grin, and that had been that really, there was no question of where things would lead, what might happen to them both. Three weeks later they were in bed; three months later engaged. And after almost a year of marriage, still helplessly, hopelessly in love.

He was young, younger than he looked, only twenty-four, rich – 'Well, quite rich,' Clarissa explained carelessly to her friends, 'his father left him a few thousand, not too many, just about right really' – charming, amusing. He was a stockbroker, he lived in a small, very pretty house in Kensington, was a fine tennis player, a good horseman, and enjoyed pretty women above all other things. He and Clarissa shared a blithely uncomplicated approach to life, an appreciation of its more sensual and materialistic pleasures and a rather touching recognition that they were both extremely fortunate. All of which made them a perfect match. As her godfather had said, without too much originality, in his wedding speech, it seemed indeed to be a marriage made in heaven. 'And heavenly it will be, I know,' she had said in response, raising her glass to Jack, kissing him. And so far she had been right.

He climbed in beside her now, and didn't do anything, just lay, looking at her, his eyes moving over her, inch by inch, and even that gaze, that intense, intent gaze, made her long, lurch within herself for him.

'Perfect,' he whispered, moving his mouth down her throat, onto her breast, 'perfect, perfect love,' his lips closing tenderly, sweetly, on her nipples. Clarissa held his head, pressing it closer, harder to her, and then as he moved down, kissing her stomach, reaching further, tonguing her, as she felt the hot, liquid heart of her beginning to open, to flutter, to yearn for him, to be round him, she moaned, thrusting herself, and his tongue grew firmer, more determined, lapping, smoothing round her clitoris; tiny piercing, shooting sensations began to grow in her, and she cried out, a raw greedy sound. He moved then, turned her sideways, lay behind her, his fingers feathering, pushing, probing her buttocks, her anus, kissing her neck, her back, saying her name over and over again, telling her she was beautiful, and then he turned and lay on his back and smiled at her, just lay there, his arms flung wide; and panting, gasping with greed, with love, she climbed on top of him and lay there, legs splayed, fighting, working at him, her vagina closing onto his penis, feeling it wonderfully, savagely in her, pushing, pushing her up, up towards the hot white shaking brightness and then, then she was there, had found it, reached it, and she fell finally upon it, and there was a wild, strange sound in the room, as she called out over and over again and then at last, but so, so slowly, released herself into a reluctant, shuddering peace.

On the same Sunday evening, Grace and Charles sat in the dining room at the Priory, with Clifford and Muriel, doing the invitation list. Muriel was saying fretfully that she didn't know how they were ever going to get it under five hundred, and Grace was wishing, more fretfully still, that it could be got under five, when the phone rang. Maureen came in. 'It's your secretary, sir,' she said, 'from the London office.'

Clifford got up and pushed the chair back startlingly hard. 'Oh yes,' he said, 'that case I was telling you about, Muriel, complicated land law. The whole thing's got very complex, I really will have to – '

'Yes, yes,' said Muriel impatiently. 'Just go, Clifford, and get it over with. We don't want to hear the details.'

'Of course. Excuse me, please, all of you.'

He was gone a long time; clearly, Grace thought, it must be a very complex call.

'I'd love a glass of beer,' Charles said suddenly, putting aside his list and rubbing his eyes. 'This is a hell of a job. Can I get either of you anything?'

'Some coffee might be helpful,' said Muriel. 'Go and ask Maureen to make some, would you, Charles?'

'I'll go,' said Grace, 'I want a drink of water anyway.'

Clifford Bennett's study was off the corridor that led to the kitchen; the door was half open. As she passed it, she glanced in. He was lying back in his chair, one foot on his desk, laughing into the telephone. She had never seen him looking quite so happy and relaxed; his London secretary was clearly a very positive presence in his life.

He didn't rejoin them for a long time, and when he did it was only to say goodnight and to tell Muriel he had to go up to London early next day.

Chapter Five

Spring 1939

Grace dreamt at least once a week now that she was back on the big dipper. It was rushing her along towards May the seventeenth, and she was sitting in it surrounded by an ever-increasing pile of presents (and of letters to be written), a four-tier cake, several bales of curtain material, a couple of carpets and her wedding dress, which was a triumph on the part of Mrs Humbolt, wild silk, with a scooped-out neckline, a fitted bodice, long narrow sleeves coming into a point over the hands, a just slightly dropped waist, and a gently full skirt falling into a train at the back. Her headdress (which she was wearing in the big dipper) was a small, seed-pearl tiara lent most graciously by Muriel (the something borrowed) and a long, embroidered lace veil. She was carrying a very large bouquet of white and yellow roses and freesias, and clearly visible as the dress blew up in the wind was a pair of red camiknickers (she was actually going to wear palest blue satin lingerie, an idea of her own which was the something new and blue rolled into one). In the car behind was the vicar, the choir, all rehearsing the hymns ('Love Divine', 'Love Be in My Head' and 'Lord of All Hopefulness'), and behind that one a third containing her parents, the Bennetts and Florence – all quarrelling. Far below her on the ground was Charles, waving frantically, and (and this rather disturbed her) in the car with her was Robert, holding her hand very tightly and telling her not to worry about anything.

She told Charles about the dream (except the bit about Robert) and he told her it was simply her subconscious worrying away; she said with a sigh she felt she certainly had quite enough for her conscious to worry about without getting her subconscious involved as well.

She knew why she had dreamt the bit about Robert: there had been another incident with him which had touched her at the time, but clearly, she could see, had worried her subconsciously.

Florence and he came down to the Priory for a long weekend, in February; Florence still looked and indeed seemed extremely unwell. She was desperately thin, very pale and listless, and Robert was obviously anxious about her, fussing over her like an old woman, refusing to leave her alone for more than a minute.

He greeted Grace warmly, gave her a hug and told her she was looking very pretty: 'Engaged life obviously suits you.'

'Thank you,' said Grace. 'I'm so sorry about Florence. I'm sure she'll feel much better soon. And feel like trying again. After all, it's not as if there was something permanently wrong.'

'No, you're quite right,' he said, 'but she seems to feel rather hostile towards me. That's what's upsetting me most. It's as if she blames me in some way. Maybe because I wasn't there, looking after her. I don't know.'

'That's so sad,' said Grace, 'but I expect it's all part of the depression. My mother had a miscarriage once, she said she was depressed for a year afterwards, and felt she disliked absolutely everyone, including my father.'

'Oh really?' he said. 'Well, that's comforting in a way. Bless you for telling me that. It's the most helpful thing anyone's said to me about this whole wretched thing.' He looked at her thoughtfully. 'So there might have been another one of you, might there? How delightful for the world that would have been.'

They were walking round the garden in the crisp morning sunshine; he suddenly put his arm round her shoulders, gave her another hug. 'You're a lovely girl, Grace,' he said, 'such an asset to the family.' And he bent and kissed her, very gently, on the lips: just a brotherly kiss, nothing more, of course, Grace knew, but it still made her feel awkward. On the other hand, it also made her like him even more; he was so warm and friendly, so unlike Florence and indeed Muriel.

Betty had made her outfit herself, a raspberry silk suit, and bought a navy hat in London; her father had had a new morning suit made at his tailors. Muriel was wearing, she announced firmly, what she had worn to Florence's wedding: a rather stern-looking dark brown woollen suit, with an even darker hat.

'It's as good as new, it was absurdly expensive, and I can't stand waste. And who's going to look at me anyway?'

Grace said politely she was sure lots of people would and, try as she might, was rather hurt that Muriel should see buying something to wear for her son's wedding as wasteful, but it certainly didn't seem worth arguing about.

Laurence, the blood brother, was to be Charles's best man.

'My father's very sensibly keeping well out of everything,' said Charles to Grace, laughing, as the wedding fever mounted. 'He's spending more time in London than I can ever remember. Pressure of work, he calls it.'

'Doesn't your mother mind?' said Grace, thinking that if she was married to Muriel she would spend all her time in London.

'I think she's too busy to mind,' said Charles. 'She just says every now and again that she hopes he isn't going to cause us all a lot of inconvenience by having a heart attack before the wedding.'

'I hope so too,' said Grace, looking alarmed.

'Darling, don't be silly,' said Charles, kissing her. 'Old boy's fighting fit. Heart's sound as a bell.'

There were to be three hundred and fifty guests in the end: the Bennett seniors had invited a hundred and fifty, Charles a hundred, Grace and her parents a hundred between them.

'I wish we needed to ask more,' wailed Betty as the final list went over to the Priory. 'They'll think we don't know anyone.'

'They'll think we know a hundred people,' said Frank wearily, 'which seems quite a lot to me. Dear God, I shall be glad when this damn thing is over.'

He never swore; Grace and Betty looked at him in alarm.

Most of Frank and Betty's friends had accepted the rationale behind the wedding reception being held at the Priory, but a few clearly felt it was odd. Sometimes as Grace listened to her mother, her voice overbright, explaining how extremely sweet Muriel was, how generous of her to offer her home, how they had planned the whole thing together, and how it would give the wedding much more of a family feeling than holding it at some hotel, she felt her heart ache for her and wished passionately that she had stuck out and insisted on the golf club.

Grace had decided not to have any grown-up bridesmaids; her best friend from school had been married in February at what seemed to Grace a wonderfully uncomplicated, small and charming occasion, and there really wasn't anyone else she cared enough about, certainly none of the overconfident girls in Charles's circle, despite a certain amount of gentle pressure from him. Most of them still behaved with a rather distant politeness towards her, and displayed what she could only describe as slight surprise that the wedding was happening at all. So she had chosen the two small granddaughters of Betty's best friend,

Marion, as attendants (both of them being in possession of the obligatory blonde curls and blue eyes) to be dressed in cascading pink frills. Muriel clearly felt this showing was a little sparse, and had said surely she would like to have a couple of pageboys at least, but Grace had said no, she didn't know any little boys, and she certainly wasn't prepared to have any she didn't know for the sake of form. She was actually quite surprised to hear herself utter these words: as the wedding grew nearer, she found it increasingly hard to stand up to Muriel.

She was haunted by all the usual terrors: that Charles would not turn up, that her mother would sob so loudly throughout the service that no one would be able to hear anything else, that she herself would fall over, fluff her lines, drop her bouquet. One night she actually dreamt her knickers fell down on the way up the aisle. Charles on the other hand didn't seem to be worried about anything at all.

National nervousness echoed her own: Mr Chamberlain's pledge at the end of March that Britain would go to war to guarantee the independence of Poland was seen as tantamount to a declaration of war itself. The London *Evening Standard* asked the capital what it would do if a bomb suddenly dropped on it, and although nobody was doing much officially – apart from the crypt at Lambeth Palace being shored up as a possible shelter, and the preparation of gas and bomb-proof cellars at Buckingham Palace for the King and Queen and the little Princesses – everybody was aware of the imminent dangers, and were haunted by them. People old enough to have vivid memories of the First World War – which included the Marchants and the Bennetts – felt they were living through a nightmare, 'a film I've seen before and hated' as Betty put it, with a second run-up to war. Conscription, everyone said, would be automatic in the event of war. It was not an entirely happy atmosphere in which to be embarking on a new life.

Early in April, Grace decided to go to London. She still hadn't got a going-away hat to wear with the blue and white silk suit she had bought in Salisbury, and *Vogue* told her the place to go was Harvey Nichols, in Knightsbridge.

'It'll be probably be expensive, but I'm only getting married and going away once,' she said cheerfully to her mother.

She went on her own. Her mother was beginning to get seriously on her nerves, not only echoing all her own anxieties but finding more:

supposing it rains, what if Frank's father (who, it had been decided, could not be invited) found out and insisted on coming anyway, whatever would Mr and Mrs Bennett think of Frank's Aunt Ada, who was not refined, to put it mildly, and was quite likely to get tipsy and start singing, suppose the bridesmaids didn't behave properly in church, suppose also none of the Bennetts' friends spoke to any of their friends, what would happen if and – of course, for this was the what-if that preceded every conversation about every arrangement that spring – what if war was declared before the seventeenth of May?

Grace and her father had an unofficial pact to take it in turns to soothe Betty, but as the date got nearer and Frank's own nerves about giving his daughter away and making his speech in front of 350 people, three-quarters of them strangers, increased, his temper shortened and any panacea he was able to offer Betty became rather severely rationed.

Grace reached Waterloo at eleven o'clock and took the underground to Knightsbridge. She had half expected, from everything she had heard and read, to find London in a state of military readiness, with soldiers in uniform, tanks rolling up the streets and sandbags in doorways. What she found were shop windows full of pretty summer clothes, streets busy with well-dressed people clearly without a thought in the world beyond what they were going to buy or eat next, and a general air of carefreeness. She bought a copy of *Tatler* to read on the train and learnt that there was a large number of outstandingly pretty girls to be presented to the King and Queen at the beginning of the London season, that the forthcoming Caledonian Ball would be attended by not only the obligatory number of Titles, but possibly also the beautiful young actress Vivien Leigh, fresh from her triumph as Scarlett O'Hara in the already legendary film of *Gone with the Wind*. Everything suddenly seemed much safer than Grace had thought.

She went first to Harrods, wandered through the lush departments, gazing in awe at things she might buy if she could afford them – most notably a sable coat, a bit like Clarissa's, and the almost unimaginable magic of a radio and television receiver for twenty-nine guineas – and then walked along Knightsbridge to Harvey Nichols. The hats there were wonderful. Grace finally settled on a straw in raspberry pink, which tilted rakishly over her forehead; it was indeed appallingly expensive at two guineas, but she knew Charles would like it.

She bought herself some make-up for the day, too: Coty powder and mascara and an Elizabeth Arden lipstick in a pink just slightly lighter than the hat. All the articles she had read, from *Vogue* to

Woman's Weekly had told her not to try to look different from her usual self on her wedding day, but she told herself she could surely look more glamorously familiar. She found herself in the lingerie department, subsequently parting with another three guineas for a shell-pink satin nightdress and swansdown-trimmed bedjacket: appallingly expensive, but it would give her confidence on the honeymoon, make Charles aware that he had married someone special, someone more glamorous than he had perhaps imagined. Finally, feeling slightly shocked at herself, she decided she would have an economical lunch of soup and a sandwich and then take a stroll in Hyde Park before making her way back to Waterloo.

She sat by the Serpentine and watched people rowing past her, some of them laughing helplessly as they lost their oars and were unable to control their boats, walked along by Rotten Row, admired the horses with their superbly turned-out riders. That reminded her of Charles, and her resolve to have him riding again after the wedding; and as she walked on, thinking of him and the wedding that was now so near, she thought how lucky she was, how happy. Her nervousness, her anxiety had vanished in the sunshine, in the carefree extravagance of her day; she wished she could stay for longer, safe from reality.

She had just decided she should get back to Waterloo, catch her train home, was waiting to cross the road in fact, when she saw Florence standing outside the underground station, looking at her watch. She was wearing a very glamorous cream suit, with a fur stole round her shoulders, but she was hatless, her dark hair tumbled on her shoulders. She looked lovely, perfectly well again, though very thin. Of course, her house was quite near here, Grace thought, and was about to try to attract her attention, to wave, to get across the street when someone came up to Florence, a male someone. Grace could not see very clearly what he looked like, only that he was most assuredly not Robert, that he had very fair hair, that he was tall and slim. He took Florence's hand, lifted it to his lips and kissed it just briefly; and watching her, Grace saw Florence's face change, lighten, saw her smile, an odd, swift, radiant smile. Grace watched first intrigued, then shocked, then almost incredulous as together they crossed the road, onto her side, walked along a little way – not speaking, not touching, but still unmistakably linked, joined, bonded – and disappeared into the haven of the Hyde Park Hotel.

All the way home, Grace felt sick; not just at what she had seen, at what she had known it meant (however hard, at first, she tried to tell herself it did not), but at the implications for herself: should she tell, who should she tell, what would happen if she did? Most of all she minded for Robert, sweet, kind Robert, who had been so genuinely distraught about the miscarriage, so worried and saddened by Florence's depression, so ready to blame himself. But she thought too of the Bennetts and how shocked and unhappy they would be, of Charles, who in spite of everything loved and admired his sister, and she thought of Florence, of her arrogance, her coldness, her superiority, and reflected that if she so wished she could bring not only such behaviour, but even her marriage itself to her rich, charming, and devoted husband, to an end.

'Good day, darling?' asked Charles. He was waiting for her on the platform in Salisbury. 'How did you find the wicked city?'

'Wicked,' said Grace, smiling at him with an effort.

'And did you get yourself a hat?'

'Yes.'

'A horribly expensive, wonderfully flattering hat?'

'Yes.'

'Is it in that box? Can I see it?'

'Yes. If you really want to.'

'Of course I don't. Well I do, but I know I mustn't. Grace, are you all right? You don't seem quite yourself?'

And 'Yes' she said smiling, determinedly (having decided in that very minute there was nothing she could do or say to make things better, only worse, that it was none of her business anyway what Florence did, what harm she wrought on her life and her marriage), 'I'm quite all right. But I tell you what, Charles. I'm not really up to all that sophisticated living. It's awfully nice to be safely back in Wiltshire. I like it much better here.'

'So do I,' he said, kissing her tenderly, 'so do I. Especially if you're here.'

'Oh Charles,' said Grace, feeling simultaneously a wave of love and a sense of remorse, guilt even that she was deceiving him for however good a reason. She put down her parcels, throwing her arms round him, giving him a hug. 'Oh Charles, I'll never ever love anyone but you. Never leave you, never ever.'

'Darling Grace,' he said, looking down at her, laughing gently, tenderly, 'I'm very pleased to hear that, but there's no need to cry about it.'

'I hope there isn't,' said Grace.

They had some wonderful presents. Bed linen, table linen, china, sets of silver; more practical things too, a marvellous set of copper pans for the kitchen, a set of garden chairs, an electric mixer. Florence and Robert had given them a pair of extremely nice silver Georgian candlesticks, which Charles had been especially thrilled with; every time Grace looked at them she saw Florence's face lit up as she gave her hand to the man in Knightsbridge, and found it impossible to enthuse wholeheartedly with him.

The Bennetts had given them a very fine Queen Anne dining-room table and a large cheque and Betty and Frank had given them the deposit for the house. It was an appallingly extravagant present, and had reduced Grace to tears; but her father had kissed her and said simply that he had been putting some money by for that very purpose ever since she had been born and it would give him immense pleasure to see her living somewhere so lovely. 'And besides,' he had said, as she continued to protest, 'it makes me feel I can make a slightly larger contribution to this marriage of yours.'

That, more than anything else that had been done or said, made Grace realize how excluded her parents felt, no matter how hard they tried to disguise it.

And Clarissa and Jack had given them a ciné camera, which they had delivered themselves.

They had been to stay in Bath with Clarissa's godmother (who had been unwell and of whom Clarissa was clearly inordinately fond), and had come to Sunday lunch at the Priory on the way back. Grace, who had spent the two weeks leading up to this event feeling almost as sick with nerves as she did about her wedding, suggested that she might not be present at the lunch, that it might be awkward, but Charles had been not only horrified but plainly irritated by this.

'Of course you must come. Clarissa, and Jack for that matter, will be hurt, think it's terribly odd. Besides, nothing could be awkward with Clarissa there.'

This was perfectly true; Clarissa talked almost unceasingly through lunch, making them all laugh at her stories of a recent trip to Le Touquet – 'In someone's tiny plane, too thrilling' – of a big charity ball they had attended, where the committee's president – 'huge anyway, my dears, of course' – had split her dress and had to leave hurriedly 'before the *Tatler* photographer arrived, she was sick with misery'; of the 'frightfully grand gardener' who had come for an interview, taken one look at her 'tiny yard' and left again without even sitting down.

Charles asked her if she had been to see Florence, as she had promised, and Clarissa said yes, she had seen her lots, and she seemed very much better although still awfully thin, poor darling; and was she imagining it, Grace wondered, or was there a slightly evasive note in her voice suddenly? Quite possibly, she thought, insecurity and a helpless hostility towards Clarissa combining to form a hard, tight lump somewhere in her chest, very possibly indeed Clarissa was privy to Florence's secret, enjoying it, was helping her to deceive Robert, providing alibis. It was the kind of thing she would clearly find exciting and intriguing. Grace thought of Robert's anxious face when she had last seen him as he talked about Florence, the hug he gave her as he told her she was an asset to the family, and she felt sick.

After lunch, Clarissa asked if they could go over to the Mill House and see it: 'It sounds lovely, I feel quite ill with envy.'

'Of course we can,' said Charles, 'and we need to have another look at the main bathroom, don't we, Grace, check out what they've done to the flooring?'

'Yes, I suppose so,' said Grace and then, unable to contemplate another hour of Clarissa's sparkling, 'If you don't mind I'll stay here, I've got a terrible headache.'

'Oh, you poor, poor thing,' cried Clarissa, her voice vibrant with the sort of sympathy normally reserved for terminal illness. 'I have the most marvellous pills in my bag, I carry them always for my migraine. You must have some, Grace, they'll have you better in no time – '

'It's all right,' said Grace, 'I have some of my own. Thank you,' she added, seeing Charles's face, mildly reproachful, 'but I really will stay here. You won't be long, will you?'

'Not terribly I don't suppose,' said Charles, clearly irritated. 'And I'll check the floor myself. Anything else while we're there?'

'No, no, that's fine,' said Grace. 'Thank you. I hope you like it, Clarissa.'

Clarissa did. She came flying into the drawing room, where Grace was pretending to read *Country Life*, and flung herself beside her on the sofa.

'What heaven! Oh you are so lucky. I told Jack it was enough to turn us into country-dwellers too. You will ask us to stay lots, won't you?'

'Yes of course,' said Grace, trying not to sound short.

They were alone in the room; Clarissa looked at her rather piercingly. 'Grace, are you all right?'

'Yes,' said Grace, 'thank you.'

'You're not, are you? What is it? Darling, tell. Is it because of me and Charlie? I really, really wouldn't blame you. I was so shocked and furious when I found he hadn't told you. Men are so dense, aren't they? So thoughtless and dense.'

'Some men, yes,' said Grace. 'But no, really, Clarissa, I'm fine. Thank you.'

'Good. Because I do so want us to be friends. And I do promise you, there's been nothing between us for years. Ever since I broke it off.'

'I thought it was by mutual agreement,' said Grace. 'Breaking it off, I mean.'

'Well, yes, yes of course it was,' said Clarissa hurriedly. 'But you know,' she added with a quick little laugh, 'one has one's pride.'

Grace, looking at her, saw a flush rising on the creamy skin, a slight tension behind the lovely brown eyes. And then she said, very seriously, quite a different person suddenly, and it was the most extraordinary moment, one Grace never forgot: 'He is not an easy person to know, Grace. You must realise that.'

'Yes,' said Grace briefly (although she longed to ask her more, ask exactly what she meant, but she too had her pride), 'yes I do. Of course.'

'Good,' said Clarissa quickly, 'Well, that's all right then. Now I must go and find my darling Jack, and we must make our way back to the soot.' She stood up, smiling. 'And I'll see you at the wedding, Grace darling. You're going to look wonderful, I simply can't wait.'

Grace smiled at her rather feebly and followed her out to the hall.

She did look wonderful. Everyone said so. She could even see it herself, staring at herself in the long mirror in her bedroom, quite awed at the dazzling creature she had become, taller somehow and so slender in the drifting fall of her dress, her red–gold hair drawn up under the tiara. As she came down the stairs of Bridge Cottage in her dress, smiling at her parents, at the bridesmaids, the bridesmaids' mother who were all standing there, her mother burst into tears. 'Oh Grace,' she said, 'oh Grace. Oh my dear.'

Later when they had all gone, and she was alone in the house with her father, waiting to leave for the church, he gave her a kiss. 'I'm so proud of you,' he said, and blew his nose hard. 'So very proud.'

'Father,' said Grace gently, 'I'm very proud of you too. And Mother. And thank you for everything. Everything.'

The service was perfect: the organist had been practising for weeks the rather difficult piece to which Grace had chosen to make her entry (the March from Handel's *Judas Maccabaeus* rather than the predictable 'Here Comes the Bride'); the choir surpassed itself, even William Everton whose sublime voice was only matched by his naughtiness and who could usually be relied upon to come in at the wrong moment, or not come in at all because he was examining the contents of his pockets and had been known to release a beetle or a few worms, and once even a field mouse, into the choir stalls; the vicar gave a most moving address, saying he had known and loved Grace since she was brought to him for baptism and that Charles was truly the most fortunate of men, inspiring a great many tears and much clearing of throats by the guests.

It was a perfect day, warm for May; the sunshine streamed in a great golden rush through the windows, and Mrs Boscombe, who doubled up as the flower committee at the church when she was not working on the switchboard, had surpassed herself, with two great urns on either side of the altar steps filled with white tulips and lilies, and had knotted tiny posies of sweetheart roses onto the end of each pew.

Grace did not stumble as she came down the aisle, nor did her knickers fall down; rather, on her father's arm, sweetly composed, she seemed to float towards her Charles and the expression on her face as she looked at him prompted even Muriel Bennett to look rather stern and start feeling for her handkerchief and Clifford to dash his hand briefly across his eyes.

And as she came out of the church into the sunshine, the photographer (nice friendly Martin Fisher from Shaftesbury, insisted upon by Grace in preference to the smart firm from London proposed by Muriel) saw her turn to Charles and move into his arms, and for a brief moment there was clearly nobody else in the world for them, nobody at all.

The reception was splendid: the champagne delicious, the food wonderful, the speeches very funny (Frank Marchant's especially so, everyone said so), and there was such a feeling of happiness, of well-wishing, of bonhomie, such an absence of any kind of criticism, of a sense of opposing factors, that Grace wondered how she could ever have worried for a moment about it at all. Through the happy haze of her day, she kept seeing cameos that surprised her even as they delighted: Clarissa with her arm linked through her father's, Clifford Bennett talking, sweetly serious, to her mother, Florence (Florence!) dancing with the little bridesmaids, Laurence hugging her and telling her he was so jealous of Charles he could hardly bear to look at him, Robert most courteously escorting Aunt Ada to a chair before the speeches began, Jack carefully filming (with the wedding present camera) every word of her father's speech.

And then at last it was over; and she was actually, finally and quite unbelievably Mrs Charles Bennett.

Chapter Six

Summer 1939

And now she was really a married woman. One mind and one flesh. Only she didn't really feel one mind with Charles; her mind was actually rather distant from his, she thought, and she wasn't quite sure about the one flesh either.

It had gone on being perfect for a while; they had driven away in the MG (with tin cans and toilet paper tied onto it, and a big silver horseshoe and 'just married' painted on the window) and the last thing she had seen as the car pulled out of the drive had been her mother, crying yet again into her handkerchief. Half a mile down the road Charles had stopped and kissed her, rather violently, but then he was very drunk, and then they had driven on again, to Salisbury, which was quite a long way, and from there had got the train to London. They had had the carriage all to themselves, and Charles had pulled down the blind and started kissing her again, and at first she had responded, but then she began to feel slightly sick, with all the champagne and the excitement, and he had realized it and pulled back from her and said, 'Are you all right?' and he was clearly trying not to sound irritated.

And 'Yes' she had said, carefully, 'yes, fine, just tired,' and he had said, 'Oh I'm sorry, darling,' but he hadn't sounded terribly sorry, and then he had gone to sleep and snored, and very slowly Grace's happiness had begun to seep away from her.

They were spending the night in London, at the Dorchester Hotel; it was Clifford's personal wedding present to them, he said they deserved to start their married life in style. Grace suddenly remembered his words as she lay there, in the great bed that was obviously designed for the most spectacular love-making, and felt – what did she feel? She didn't even know. Only that what had happened between her and Charles, while perfectly satisfactory, she supposed, had hardly seemed to have a great deal to do with love.

She eased her legs over the edge of the bed and very stealthily got up and went into the bathroom. There was a chair in there; she pulled the pink satin bedjacket round her shoulders (thinking it had been something of a waste) and sat there, looking through into the bedroom and the inert heap that was Charles beneath the bedclothes. A contented, clearly satisfied Charles; well, that was all right, that was good. What wasn't quite so all right was that he was also equally clearly *self*-satisfied. And she didn't really like that very much.

They had had dinner, a dinner which Grace really hadn't wanted; she still felt sick, and she was excited and yes, all right, nervous as well. Charles ate three courses very heartily and drank a lot of red wine, and then the band began to play and they danced for a while, and then he said, 'Time for bed I think, Mrs Bennett' and kissed her and she felt happier again suddenly, the day restored to its brightness, and they had gone up to their room, and he had said, just slightly awkwardly, 'You first,' and she had gone into the bathroom and washed, cleaned her teeth, brushed her hair and sprayed on some of her Elizabeth Arden Blue Grass cologne and undressed into the pink satin, just the night-dress, and then gone into the bedroom and climbed rather quickly into bed. Charles had already undressed and was wearing some rather fiercely striped pyjamas; he disappeared into the bathroom very briefly and then came back, smiled at her, and turned the dim bedside lights abruptly off. Grace had been disappointed by that somehow; she had been looking forward to some kind of courtship, kissing and caressing and talking; told herself they had plenty of time for that, and slithered down in the bed, and into Charles's arms.

'Oh Grace,' he said, and the voice was the one she remembered from the day of the quarrel, a different voice, slightly harsh, almost impatient, 'Grace, it's been a long time.' And after that she had lain there, and he had made love to her, and when he had finished he had gone to sleep; and from beginning to end she had seemed to play no part in it at all.

She was, of course, very lucky in a way, she could see that. He had known exactly what he was doing (she thought back to her diffident, embarrassed enquiry as to whether he was a virgin and felt quite horribly foolish), had removed her nightdress with speed and skill, had kissed her for a while before turning his attention to her breasts, had kissed and stroked them most expertly, calling up piercingly loud echoes of the more muffled sensations she had experienced over the months of their courtship, had moved his hands down to her thighs, her stomach, her buttocks, smoothly, confidently, and then, just a trifle more tenderly, she had felt his hand between her legs, feeling, seeking, stroking, probing, but gently; then he had rolled away from her briefly, fumbling for something at the side of the bed (the contraceptive, she supposed) and turned back towards her, and said, nicely, but quite firmly, not lover-like at all, 'Now just relax, darling, relax.' Then he had been on top of her, and she could feel it now, his penis, pushing gently at first, then more firmly into her, into her vagina, and she had been not afraid, but slightly tentative, resistant, and he had said again, more firmly still, 'Relax, just relax,' and then went on pushing smoothly in, kissing her at the same time. And it did hurt, a little, but not as much as she had expected; it had been accomplished with such gentle competence. And then she really did begin to feel something, a slow stretching into something that was close to pleasure; he was thrusting now, but still not painfully, slowly and carefully, and then rather faster, and she was trying to follow him in some strange way, but afraid to at the same time, afraid of doing the wrong thing, and suddenly there was a deep, deep push and she wanted that to go on and on, and she felt a slightly distant throbbing, not from herself but from him, and he lay still and then, and she never forgot that moment for the rest of her life, he said, 'Good, darling, very good,' and rolled off her, kissed her briefly, asked her if she was all right, and when she said yes – for what else could she say? – he repeated 'Good' and kissed her again and fell immediately asleep.

And Grace had lain there and relived it all and wondered, since it had really been much more pleasurable and less painful than anything she could have expected from the first time, from the rather veiled hints from her mother and her married friends, and even the literature Dr Phillips had given her, why she was feeling let down, lonely, even a little sad. And then she realized that while Charles had been extremely competent, skilful even, he had said nothing throughout the whole performance about love, or even given the impression that love had anything to do with it; and that a performance was exactly what it had been, a display of almost mechanical skill, with no space in it anywhere for anything she might do or feel or wish to try and contribute.

In the morning he was immensely cheerful, smiling at her over the cup of tea they had ordered.

'Good morning, Mrs Bennett,' he said, 'I hope you slept well.'

And that was all he said.

'Oh,' said Grace quickly, 'I did. Thank you.'

He leant over and kissed her. 'Good. Me too. Pretty bedjacket, darling. Let me remove it.'

And it began again, the same expert performance, the same lack of interest in her responses and needs. It was as if, she thought, she was a rather difficult car that he had to drive carefully, or perhaps, more appropriately, an untrained horse that needed skilful handling. She tried to concentrate on her own sensations, which were stirring and moving within her, and on the fact that she should simply be grateful for the skill and the care.

And anyway, she thought, sinking into the great bath afterwards, looking down at her body which at least seemed to have a certain capacity for pleasure, however muted, it was early days. It would almost certainly get better, more personal, more tender. And it certainly seemed to please him.

Throughout their fortnight's honeymoon, the sun shone. They walked a lot, talked a little, ate a great deal, talked of the future; and every night Charles made love to her, expertly, confidently. By the time they went home she had experienced several orgasms. She could see she was extremely fortunate; at the same time, it was precisely that which troubled her. She wanted to give as well as receive, to be participant rather than passive, have her body asked what it wanted, not simply told. But Charles made it very plain that this was his territory and he was in control. He allowed no discussion, crushed any approaches; her body was his, to be handed over, without question, without comment, without request. There was no room in their bed for any approach, or indeed any rebuff, from her.

She learnt more about him therefore in those two weeks than in the whole of the previous year.

It had been the most wonderful summer. The sun shone, day after day, dispersing in some strange way the dark fears of war. Grace, generally contented, busy making the Mill House home, enjoying her garden, supposed she must be, knew she ought to be, happy, as she adjusted to married life in all its complexities: Charles's innumerable food fads, spared her before (he was almost phobic about eggs, liked his vegetables overcooked and his meat underdone, and had to have Force with prunes for breakfast every day); his near-intolerable snoring, his reluctance to discuss his work with her, his clear assumption that she wouldn't understand it, any more than she would understand the situation in Europe; Muriel's habit of arriving without warning at the Mill House and expecting meals, drinks, attention; Charles's insistence on their leading a rather fuller social life than she would have liked, certainly in those early days, when she felt so uncertain of herself and her capabilities, dinner parties, cocktail parties, people to stay; her own mother's constant exclamations as to her great good fortune (especially her domestic help, a live-in cook, a housemaid and a gardener); and her enragingly coy questions about how Grace was enjoying it all, whether Charles was happy and, worst of all, whether she was feeling quite well – a veiled allusion, Grace knew, to the possibility that she might be pregnant.

Carefully using her Dutch cap (which Charles had slightly irritably agreed was an advance on the contraceptives he used), she was sure she was not.

And the procedure by which she might become so continued to disappoint her.

Gasping, moaning, crying out with the vibrant, raw sound of triumphant orgasm, her body rippling slowly, reluctantly into a fitful peace, Florence turned her head, smiled tenderly at the face of her lover, beside her on the pillow, took his hand, kissed it, kissed the fingers one by one.

'I love you,' she said, 'I love you so very much.'

'I love you too. You're the most perfect thing that's ever happened to me.'

'Hardly perfect,' said Florence, studying him, thinking how almost unbearably beautiful he was, her archetypal Englishman, with his blond hair, his hazel eyes, his suntanned skin, his wide, perfect smile. She was not in the least beautiful, not even particularly good-looking; she knew she wasn't. She had grown up convinced she was plain, her mother had made constant allusions ever since Florence could remember to the unfortunateness of Charles getting the looks, the fair, blue-eyed looks; while she, Florence, with her dark hair, her almost sallow skin, her overlarge mouth, was the ugly sister. And she also, she knew, lacked Charles's charm, his open easy manner, so like his father's; she was shy, abrupt, slightly awkward even, much more like her mother. She often wondered why she didn't hate Charles. But she didn't, she loved him dearly.

Giles smiled. 'Well, you are. You're perfect to me. Sexy and clever and lovely and absolutely perfect.' He bent and kissed her flat, almost concave stomach, moved down, kissed her thighs, put his face into her pubic hair, kissed her there too. 'You taste delicious. The taste of love.'

'Oh God,' said Florence. 'Oh God, what are we going to do?'

'What are *you* going to do, Florence? It's your decision. I'm here, I'm waiting, I'm ready for you. It's easy for me.'

'Yes,' she said, 'yes, it's easy for you. Terribly easy for you.'

She sat up suddenly, took his head in her hands, gazed intently into his eyes. 'I keep thinking I can do it, that I'm brave enough, and then I look at him, and I know I'm not. It's so hard to understand.'

'I think I understand,' he said, 'I'm certainly trying to. But I love you so much, and I want to be with you, to have you with me – '

'I know, I know,' she said, staring out at the golden day, 'and I want to be with you. So desperately. But – oh God, it's so difficult, all of it. Especially now, with all this talk of war. I mean – oh God, I can't even say it.'

'I think I know what you mean,' he said, very serious. 'You don't have to say it. And don't think it's wicked to think that.'

'Giles, of course it's wicked, but I still can't help it.'

She paused, lay back on the pillows looking at him very soberly, reached out and stroked his cheek. 'You must, you must give me time, Giles. I need time to think, to plan it all. Time and peace.'

'Peace,' he said, deliberately misunderstanding, 'is going to be a forgotten luxury soon.'

'I'd like to have Florence and Robert down to stay,' said Charles. 'How would you feel about that darling?'

'Oh – well, that would be nice,' said Grace carefully. 'But I thought Florence said Robert was still terribly busy.'

'We can ask them at least,' said Charles. 'I'm still worried about Florence. Although she did seem very happy and jolly at our wedding.'

'Yes,' said Grace. 'Yes she did. Well, yes of course I'll ask them. Just give me a couple more weeks – '

'What on earth for?' said Charles. 'The house looks lovely, you've got plenty of help, I don't see any reason for putting it off. Perhaps I'll ask them.' He sounded irritable.

'No, no, it's all right, I'll do it. It's just that I feel it must be rather dull for them here. They lead such a terrifically busy life in London, and – '

'Oh, don't be absurd,' he said, 'we can give them a very jolly time. Plenty of tennis, and a dinner party on the Saturday. We could ask the Frasers, we owe them hospitality. It's important not to let that happen, Grace. Mother always keeps a book, not only of who came when and who they sat next to, but who she owes hospitality to.'

'Yes,' said Grace, trying to sound calm, 'yes I know, she told me.

'Right, well, let's do that. They'd all get on very well, I'm sure.'

'Yes – I'm sure they will,' said Grace. 'I'll organize it. Don't worry, Charles. It'll be fun.' And then, taking advantage of the moment, of knowing she had pleased him, 'Charles, do you think if I learnt to drive properly we could afford for me to have a car? I'd really like that, and I could come and meet you in Shaftesbury sometimes, we never seem to go to the pictures any more, or even out to the Bear, anything like that – '

'Well, we've got our own home now,' he said, sounding genuinely surprised. 'What are you saying, Grace?'

'I'm not saying anything,' she said firmly, 'just that it would be nice to be able to get around a bit more easily.'

'I don't see why you need to,' he said, 'to be honest. The tradesmen all deliver, you have plenty to do here, and we go out a fair bit. I hope you're not complaining of boredom – '

'No, of course I'm not,' said Grace, trying to keep the irritability out of her voice, 'but that's just it, I can only go out, out of the village that is, with you. Or on my bike of course. But I can hardly pedal all the way to Shaftesbury.'

'I really don't see why you should want to,' said Charles. 'Get out of the village, I mean.'

'I want to because sometimes I feel a bit lonely,' said Grace, 'I haven't got many friends in the Thorpes, Charles. I – well, I even miss my job at times.'

'I have to say,' said Charles, and there was a slight flush on his face suddenly, 'that seems a little insulting: that you should not find taking care of our home, and of me for that matter, sufficiently amusing for you.'

'Charles, don't be silly,' said Grace. 'Of course I find it amusing, as you put it. I love looking after you. But it is lonely for me, sometimes. You must see that.'

'I don't really, no,' said Charles, 'and all the more reason, if indeed it was, for you to be keen to have people to stay.'

'Yes of course, you're right,' said Grace, not wishing to antagonize him any more. 'I'm sorry, Charles, I didn't mean to upset you. But' – she hung onto her self-esteem with an effort – 'I'd still like to learn to drive. Think if there was an emergency or something – '

'Well, all right,' he said; he was always surprisingly easily soothed by an apology. 'I could give you some more lessons, I suppose. Then we can see about a car after that. They're a big expense, you know.'

Grace was surprised by his last remark; shortage of money usually seemed the last thing on his mind. Maybe it was the war. Everything was the war these days.

She sometimes felt, and crushed the thought as quickly as she could, that Charles was changing slowly but very steadily into someone she didn't entirely like. He had never been oversensitive, but he had been at least caring; now he treated her increasingly with a rather more distant affection. Echoed, she thought, in bed. He had done enough, his behaviour seemed to say, in marrying her; had given her a home, status, financial security, and she should know she was fortunate, and very little more effort was required on his part. If he felt tired, or bad-tempered, he made only the most perfunctory attempt to disguise the fact; if he wanted to be on his own, sit in his study after dinner, play a round of golf on a Saturday morning, tennis in a men's four, he would do so with only the briefest nod in the direction of considering her feelings or arrangements. If he had to go to London on business he simply announced it; if he had a business dinner he did the same, often telling her only the night before. In fact, Grace thought, as she took one of her many solitary walks in the woods one afternoon, an evening ahead of her with only the wireless for company, he behaved a great deal of the time as he behaved in bed: thoughtlessly, complacently, and – Grace struggled to find the right word – tactlessly.

On the other hand, he was still very charming most of the time, generous – she had a much more than adequate housekeeping allowance, a separate one for her clothes – he told her frequently how proud of her he was and how much he loved her, praised what she had done with the house and the garden, and in public at any rate was very fond of telling people he was the luckiest man in Wiltshire, if not in England.

Florence and Robert refused the invitation. 'Robert is terribly busy, I told you I thought he was,' said Grace, hugely relieved to have been spared the strain of knowing that Florence was having at least a romance if not a full-blown affair, while pretending for a whole weekend of close proximity to her and indeed Robert that she had no idea.

'We could have Clarissa and Jack,' she said tentatively, surprising herself with her courage, anxious to show Charles she wasn't really trying to avoid her duties as a source of entertainment and hospitality to his friends, but to her surprise Charles said rather shortly that he didn't think it was a very good idea.

'Whyever not, Charles? I thought you liked them both.'

'I do, but I don't really want them to stay,' he said. 'They're such townies, I don't feel we could amuse them very satisfactorily.'

As this was the reverse of what he had said about Robert and

Florence's visit, Grace was baffled, but as she didn't want them to come either, she left it, thankfully, at that.

As the lovely summer wore on, everyone became increasingly and openly resigned to the inevitability of war. In July the Poles began to mobilize; if the Germans crossed their border, then that was it; Chamberlain had said so. Various official preparations were now being made. Early in August, the Home Office had a trial blackout, which was something of a disappointment to the large crowds gathered in Piccadilly to watch it; not quite all the lights went out and the timing of the whole thing was far from precise, but it was felt to be an important landmark.

Other plans went into action: there were full-scale rehearsals for the evacuation of children, and in the middle of August 150 French bombers made a practice raid on the capital. Clarissa, who had been in the Open Air Theatre in Regent's Park with Jack watching *A Midsummer Night's Dream*, reported that it was 'horridly interrupted' by the searchlights and the noise of the aircraft.

Women everywhere were urged to stockpile food; Grace, who had wanted some chickens for ages and had been discouraged by Charles ('stupid messy things'), used this as an excuse to get a few. Three or four times the usual number of couples were going to registry offices to be married; police leave was cancelled and so were driving tests ('No point you learning now, darling,' said Charles), and the embryonic television service was taken off the air because, they were told, the signals coming from Alexander Palace would make things easier for Germany.

And on 24 August the military reservists were called up; the next day Britain signed a formal treaty of alliance with Poland.

Grace was sewing one darkening evening, looking at Charles as he sat peacefully reading the paper, envisaging what lay ahead of them both, and felt very frightened.

It was on Monday, 4 September that it happened.

Not the declaration of war, that had been the day before, not Chamberlain's reedy voice on the wireless, saying 'We are now at war with Germany,' not the announcement in church as Grace and Charles sat with Clifford and Muriel in their pew and the verger hurried down the aisle with a piece of paper and the vicar mounted the pulpit and said, 'My friends, we are now at war with Germany. I think we should return to our homes. God bless us all.' Not the agonizing lunch, as plans were made, dangers cited, probabilities mooted – Charles would be called up, Robert would be called up, London evacuated, thousands of children were already being taken out on every train, Florence must come to stay with them; not the report on the nine o'clock news that there had already been an air-raid warning in the capital (as the result of a stray French bomber coming over) and that people had gone into shelters and done what they were supposed to with admirable efficiency; not the knock on the door of the Mill House in the evening by Mr Larkin, the local ARP warden, to check on their blackout arrangements; not the voice of Clarissa, shakily cheerful, saying that Jack was off to join up in the morning, and had decided on the RAF; not even Charles deciding that he would join the Royal Fusiliers, his father's old regiment; and not even Charles making love to Grace that night with a tenderness and a strange sadness that she found rather moving and almost, she thought afterwards, arousing. For Grace the war seemed to begin in earnest with Muriel, phoning the following evening, her voice raw with pain, to say that Clifford had had a heart attack, that he was in St Thomas's Hospital and that he was not expected to live.

'I'll come up with you,' said Charles, 'I'll drive you. Do you want to go tonight? It'll be very difficult in the blackout but – '

'Yes, yes I do,' said Muriel. 'Of course I do. We can stay at the flat. Although it will be so dangerous up there, of course, maybe it won't be possible. We have to get him out of London, Charles, if – well, if we possibly can. At the first opportunity. Florence agrees. She's been to the hospital already, but they wouldn't let her see him.'

'Yes of course we must,' said Charles.

They had gone over to the Priory immediately; by the time they got there, Muriel was apparently calm, but very pale, and her hands, tearing compulsively at her handkerchief, were shaking. Grace, embracing her briefly, was shocked at the tension in her thin body.

'Where was he?' asked Charles. 'When he had the heart attack. In the office?'

'No,' said Muriel. 'No. In the flat in Baker Street.'

'Was he alone?'

'No,' said Muriel, 'no, apparently there was someone with him. Who called the ambulance.'

'Well, who? Someone from the London office?'

'I don't know if she was from the London office or not,' said Muriel irritably. 'I'm not familiar with all the staff names.'

'Well, what was the name? Of this person who called the ambulance.'

'Saunders,' said Muriel. 'Mrs' – the word came out with distinct difficulty – 'Mrs Mary Saunders.'

'Oh, not staff. I expect she was a client,' said Charles easily.

'Yes. Yes, I expect so,' said Muriel.

'Look, I think we should go. Grace, will you stay – '

'I want to come,' said Grace.

'Grace, of course you can't come. It will be terribly dangerous up there, you don't seem to realize, bombing will start any minute, gas attacks as well. Mother, you mustn't forget your gas mask. No, Grace, I want you to stay here. And besides, what good would it do?'

'It will do a lot of good,' said Grace. 'To me anyway. Possibly to Muriel, I don't know. If you're all going to be bombed or gassed, then I think I'd rather be with you, and anyway, I want to – well, I want to see Clifford.'

'Say goodbye to Clifford' she had been going to say: she loved him so much, her kind, gentle, perceptive father-in-law, who had been so kind to her, done so much to help. She couldn't stay safely in the country, let him go without seeing him once more.

'Grace, I'm sorry, but it's out of the question,' said Charles. 'I want you to stay safely here. Keep an eye on things.'

'What things?' said Grace. 'And I've told you I don't want to stay safely here. If you won't take me in the car, Charles, I shall follow in the train. So you might as well.'

Charles looked at her; he was clearly very angry. She was almost frightened. 'Grace,' he said and his voice was very heavy, 'Grace, I repeat – '

And then Muriel spoke. 'Oh for heaven's sake, Charles,' she said, 'if she wants to come let her. She might be able to do something useful.'

Seeing Charles's furious face quite made up for any hurt induced in Grace by Muriel's words. In any case, she was getting used to her mother-in-law's terminal tactlessness.

They reached London just after two; it had taken an endless time in the total darkness, without even a glimmer from their own headlights, with only the white-painted kerbs, once they reached the city, to guide them. The roads were practically deserted, apart from a great many army lorries; the whole experience seemed to Grace to be straight out of a nightmare. They had half expected to find barbed wire surrounding the approaches to London, to hear heavy bombing, but apart from the darkness it might have been any night in the last twenty years: exceptionally quiet and peaceful. They came into

London through Clapham, Vauxhall, Lambeth; the palace, shrouded in darkness, looked smaller, less imposing.

As they reached St Thomas's, an ARP warden stopped them at the gate, flashed a torch briefly into the car.

'My father's here,' said Charles, 'he's very ill. Which way should we go?'

'That way, sir. Leave your car over there.'

'Right. Seems pretty quiet.'

'Oh it is, sir. Don't know how long for, of course. Cunning blighters, the Germans. Just waiting, biding their time. Hope your father's all right, sir.'

'Thank you,' said Charles.

Grace got out thankfully; she had been sitting in the back the whole way, feeling terribly sick for the last couple of hours.

The Thames looked black, threatening in the darkness; she shivered, breathing in its murky smell, hoping she wasn't going to be sick, or pass out.

Muriel was standing looking up at the hospital with a strange expression on her face: it wasn't just grief or weariness, Grace thought, watching her, it was fear.

Clifford was in a small room on the first floor. They were taken up by a porter, greeted at the top of the stairs by a nurse.

'He's along here,' she said. 'Please follow me.'

'How – how is he?' said Muriel.

'I'm afraid I can't tell you that. You must see Sister. And the doctor of course.'

It was a long corridor; the silence as they walked was excruciating. Afraid of what was at the end of it, Clifford dying, dead even, of what might happen any moment, a sudden bomb attack, poison gas, Grace felt she might scream.

'You're very brave,' she said to the nurse suddenly, realizing she was about the same age as herself. 'Aren't you frightened?'

'Oh no,' she said, smiling, 'we've no time to be frightened.'

'Ah, Mrs Bennett.' The ward sister came towards them. 'You must be exhausted after your long journey. How brave of you to come into the bomb-torn capital.' Her voice was amusedly ironic; she smiled at them briefly. Grace liked her.

'It seems very quiet,' said Charles. 'We were expecting – well, I don't know what.'

'Yes, everyone's expecting I don't know what. I personally think a great deal of hysteria is going on. However, Mrs Bennett, you will be pleased to hear your husband is – stable. Very ill, but stable.'

'I see,' said Muriel, and only a twitch at the sides of her mouth revealed any emotion at all.

'Now, I cannot give you any kind of prognosis, of course,' said the sister, 'You must speak to the doctor in the morning, but I can tell you that he is no worse than when he was brought in, possibly a little better. That at least is something.'

Muriel nodded mutely. Two tears trickled out of her eyes, rolled unchecked down her cheek. Grace, amazed, took her hand suddenly, squeezed it; there was no response.

'May I see him?' Muriel said.

'For a moment, yes. You must be prepared, though, for him not to recognize you. Need I say that you must on no account worry him, try to arouse him.'

'Of course not,' said Muriel. Sister ushered her gently into the room.

Later they sat in Sister's office; she had made them a cup of tea. Muriel seemed perfectly calm.

'Er – I believe a Mrs Saunders called the ambulance,' she said.

'Yes. That is correct. She has phoned a couple of times since.'

'Do we have a number for her?' asked Muriel. 'Or an address? So that we can thank her.'

'Er – it seems not,' said Sister, 'nor an address. I'm sorry.'

Her face was absolutely impassive; it was a practised impassivity, Grace thought; she had worn the expression many times before.

'Well,' said Charles finally, 'perhaps if she phones again, Sister, you could ask her for it. So that we can thank her. And now, perhaps – well, we're all very tired, I wonder if there is any point in staying, or if we should get on to my father's flat in Baker Street. Perhaps you would advise us – '

'I really think you should get some rest,' said the sister. 'I don't think there is any immediate danger now, Mr Bennett is mercifully a very strong man, but of course if there is a change we will telephone you immediately. You can come back in the morning, see Mr Mackie, he is the cardiologist who is looking after Mr Bennett. We should have a little more news by then.'

Her voice was very firm; she clearly had no intention of allowing a distraught family to be cluttering her corridors, even if they were expensive, privately paid-for ones.

'Yes,' said Muriel. 'Yes, we should do that. If you're quite sure.' She seemed rather dazed suddenly, smaller and frailer.

'Quite sure,' said Sister. 'Now do finish your tea and then I will arrange for someone to see you out.'

As they passed the room, the door was opened and the nurse who had greeted them came out and shut it again. In that brief moment Grace looked in and saw Clifford lying quite flat on the bed, on his back. A drip was attached to his arm. She shuddered. He had looked, to her, quite horribly dead.

They got Muriel to bed, Grace made her a whisky with hot milk, took it in to her. She was lying in the bed, staring at the ceiling, but she did seem more relaxed.

Grace set the milk down by the bedside, bent over, patted her hand. 'You must try not to worry,' she said, 'I'm sure he'll be all right.'

'Yes,' said Muriel. 'I suppose he might.' There was a silence, then she said, clearly with an effort, 'Thank you for coming, Grace. I appreciate it.'

'That's all right,' said Grace.

Muriel's patent misery touched and surprised her; she had not observed between her mother-in-law and Clifford anything more than the most basic courtesy and very little else, especially on Muriel's part. Grace supposed this was where marriage led, even a less than perfect one: to a state of underlying affection and a dependency that when threatened was extremely frightening. She hoped that hers would have a little more substance to it than that.

She had never been to the Baker Street flat; it was rather grand, heavily Victorian, furnished rather as she imagined a gentleman's club would be, with a lot of mahogany and leather. If Clifford had been taken ill there, whoever had been with him had cleared up very efficiently; there was no trace at all of any human activity, the beds were freshly made up, the place immaculately tidy.

Charles showed Grace the second bedroom, asked her to make some tea while he phoned Florence. 'She'll meet us at the hospital in the morning,' he said. 'She sounded very upset. Poor Florence. She's had a bad year.'

'Yes,' said Grace, 'terribly bad.'

Charles looked at her sharply. 'That didn't sound entirely sympathetic,' he said. 'I know you don't like Florence, Grace, but I wish you'd try and make a little more effort – '

'I do like Florence,' said Grace wearily. 'If anyone doesn't like anyone, it's Florence not liking me. Oh, Charles, let's not start squabbling. I'm so tired and so sad. Your father looked terrible. Poor old darling.'

And to her great surprise she burst into tears.

Charles sat down beside her, put his arms round her. 'Darling, don't cry. I'm sorry. You've been so marvellous. I was so glad you came in the end, it was right. Mother seems very – calm though now.'

'Yes,' said Grace, 'yes, she does. Charles, who do you think Mary Saunders is?'

'Oh, I told you, a client,' said Charles easily. 'I'll track her down in the morning. Thank her.'

'Yes,' said Grace, 'yes, of course. That must be right.'

She didn't say what she had actually been wondering, all the way to London: that the mysterious Mrs Mary Saunders might mean more to Clifford Bennett than perhaps a client would. She had a shrewd idea that that was something which had been frightening Muriel as well.

Chapter Seven

Autumn 1939

Linda Lucas stood at the gates to the platform, desperately trying to control the hot tears, feeling as if her heart was being wrenched out of her, but managing to smile, wave her handkerchief to the two skinny little figures being swallowed up rapidly in the crowd. The taller of them turned, his small face taut in his effort not to cry, his dark eyes, enormous with misery, looking frantically for her. Linda jumped up and down, so that he could see her.

'Bye-bye, David. Be a good boy. Look after Daniel. We'll see you soon.'

He couldn't hear her, but he could see her, and see her smiling; it clearly cheered him. She was glad she had worn her nice coat, bothered with her hair; boys liked to be proud of their mothers, even when they were only five and three. And wanted to be like their dads.

'I won't cry,' little Daniel had said, sitting on his father's knee at breakfast that morning, 'cos you wouldn't cry, would you, Dad? Only girls cry.'

'Usually, yes,' said Ben Lucas, his own dark eyes, so like his small son's, tender, thoughtful as he looked at him, 'but mind you, girls can teach us a thing or two about being brave.'

'Course they can't,' said David. 'Anyway, I bet you never cry, Dad.'

'I have cried,' said Ben. 'I cried when my own dad died. Nothing to be ashamed of in crying. Not when it really matters. Now I've got to go. You enjoy the country, and we'll see you at Christmas.'

'Sounds a long time off,' said David, pushing aside his plate of uneaten toast.

'Not really. It'll go very fast. You'll have a great time. And have a lot to tell us. Bye, Daniel. Give me a kiss. You too, David.'

He had gone rather quickly, blowing his nose loudly as he went. His mother, who shared the small house in Acton, looked after him with only faintly disguised pride. 'Soft he is,' she said, 'always has been.'

It was Ben's softness, his gentleness that had made Linda fall in love with him in the first place. If you'd told her beforehand that she'd have abandoned Colin Banks at the dance that night, she'd have laughed out loud. She'd been angling for Colin for weeks, Colin who all the girls fancied; he had a motorbike, and slicked-back fair hair and a swaggering walk and he was a very good, rather flashy dancer. If you were on the dance floor with him everyone tended to watch you. Anyway, that night he'd finally asked Linda, and she was feeling really excited and happy, especially since during the slow number (as his hands moved expertly up and down her back, a bit lower on each trip downwards) he'd asked her what she was doing the next night, and then she was sitting waiting for him to bring her a drink, wondering if she had time to go and powder her nose, she didn't really want to risk not being there when he got back, when she saw a long tall shadow in front of her and heard a voice saying, 'Would you like to dance?' and looked up into a pair of intensely dark, almost black eyes, set rather deeply beneath some very thick eyebrows, looking at her in a mixture of nervousness and acute determination. She was just about to say no, that she was waiting for someone to come back, while absorbing the fact that he had a really lovely smile, very wide and warm, with especially nice white straight teeth, when she saw that Colin was chatting rather too busily to a girl at the bar, and was actually doing that thing of lighting two cigarettes at once and then handing the girl one. Linda certainly wasn't going to sit here looking silly while that went on, so she stood up, smiled again at the owner of the dark eyes, and said yes, that would be lovely.

'Good,' he said, sounding rather touchingly surprised. 'Ben Lucas is the name.'

'Hallo, Ben Lucas,' said Linda, taking his large bony hand and following him onto the floor. She hoped Colin had noticed; but he hadn't seemed to. 'I'm Linda.'

Ben Lucas was rather difficult to dance with since he was at least twelve inches taller than she was, and she found herself pressed rather closely into his chest, since it was a waltz and the floor was very crowded. Suddenly she felt a hand on her shoulder and heard Colin's voice saying loudly, above the music, 'I thought you were supposed to be with me.'

Which annoyed Linda quite a lot. In the first place, it just wasn't what you did in the middle of a dance, unless it was an Excuse Me, and in the second, if he hadn't been gone so long she would indeed still have been with him, both of which points she made, quite loudly and firmly herself, and the people near to them stopped dancing to listen.

Her partner was clearly embarrassed and told Colin he was very sorry; whereupon Colin told him he'd better show it, and quickly, or he'd make him sorrier, and greatly to her own surprise Linda told Colin to go and take a long walk off a short plank and stalked off the floor. She went and sat in the ladies for a bit, mentally kicking herself, and when she came out Colin was draped all over the girl at the bar. Linda sighed and was fumbling in her bag for a cigarette when she heard Ben Lucas's voice.

'You didn't have to do that,' he said.

'I know that,' she said shortly, illogically irritated with him as well as with herself. 'I don't do things cos I have to.'

'That's nice,' he said, smiling at her, the same lovely smile, 'that's really nice.'

'What is?' she said, more irritated still. 'You got a light?'

'No, sorry, I don't smoke. I'll get you one though.'

'Don't bother. I'll find my girlfriend.'

'Please don't,' he said, 'it's the least I can do.' And he was gone, leaving her more irritated than ever, while able to notice at the same time that although he wasn't exactly good-looking, there was something quite sexy about him.

He came back with a box of matches and lit her cigarette. 'You OK then?' he said.

'Yes of course I am. Why shouldn't I be?'

He shrugged. 'Don't know. Can I get you a drink?'

'Yeah,' she said, thinking she might as well make the most of him, 'yeah, port and lemon, please.'

'Right. Don't go off dancing with anyone else now, will you?' He smiled at her, and she smiled reluctantly back.

'Course not. I'm not that sort of girl.'

When he got back they found a table and Linda sat trying not to look at Colin Banks, draped now over another girl. Ben asked her where she lived and what she did. She quite liked that; most men weren't interested in anything more than your name, and not even that really, just how quickly they could get you outside the hall, or onto the dance floor during a slow number. 'Shepherd's Bush,' she said, 'with my dad. And I work at the Co-op. What about you?'

'Acton,' he said, 'and I work for an insurance company. As a clerk. I hate it,' he added.

'Well,' she said, 'no work's much fun, is it?'

'Maybe not. I don't know. I wanted to do something that might've been fun.'

'What was that then?'

'I wanted to be a teacher.'

'Oh,' she said, surprised. He was obviously brainy. 'Well, why didn't you?'

'Because I had to leave school. My father's an invalid. Got TB. I have to keep him and my mum.' He sounded very cheerful about it, not at all resentful. She liked that.

'My mum's dead,' she said, surprised to hear herself telling him. 'She died when I was born.'

'I'm sorry,' he said and it sounded as if he meant it, 'but it must be nice for your dad, to have you with him.'

'Not really. He doesn't like me much. Blames me, I s'pose.' Now why did she tell him that? She never told anyone, not till she knew them quite well. It was just that he was so easy to talk to. More like a girl, in a funny way.

'I'm sure that's not true.'

'Yeah, I think it is,' she said soberly. 'And he drinks too much.'

'Bit of a worry for you then?'

'A bit, yes,' she said.

There was a silence, then: 'Your friend's coming over,' he said, and he was, Colin Banks, cigarette in the corner of his mouth, the smoke curling up past his narrowed eyes, grinning at her confidently; obviously the other girl had gone off with someone else.

He held out his hand to Linda. 'Dance?' he said.

She hesitated just for a moment, longing to accept, thrilled that even after the rejection he was prepared to try again. She looked at Ben Lucas, staring into his drink rather intently, felt a pang of guilt, then thought he really wasn't her type at all, however nice he might be, was about to stand up when Ben said, with his sweet smile, 'You go on, don't mind me, I've got to go anyway.' And that did it really: that he liked her enough to be so thoughtful, to make it easy for her, and she turned and said to Colin, who was looking at Ben with a mixture of contempt and impatience, 'No, I'm sorry, I'm tired. Maybe next week, OK?'

Colin didn't even answer, just turned away from her, and Ben said, 'Well, if you're really tired, maybe I could see you home.' And he went on the bus with her, and walked her right to her door even though it was completely the wrong direction for him, and didn't even try to get a kiss from her in return.

But he did say he'd like to see her again; and on that occasion, sitting in the pictures, he did kiss her and with surprising expertise, and she found herself not only liking it, but responding with enormous enthusiasm.

Three weeks later he told her he loved her, and she knew without even thinking about it (having never experienced anything remotely similar in the whole of her nineteen years) that she loved him too and told him so. And a year and a half later they were married.

'I know he's different,' she told all her friends, who were surprised, shocked even, at the match, at the sheer unsuitability of the flighty, flirty Linda settling down with this quiet, shy, not even good-looking creature. 'Different and lovely. I want to be with him. All the time. And I'm not in the family way,' she added firmly, seeing the unspoken question in several pairs of eyes. 'He hasn't even tried it.'

But when he did try it, it was wonderful: almost straight away and beyond her wildest imaginings.

Life wasn't easy for them; Linda's father died and they had to live with Ben's parents, in their extremely small house, and his father succumbed to the TB and died after the first year, leaving her alone with his mother a lot of the time, a perversely difficult, hugely demanding old woman, critical, jealously hostile to Linda. She was physically tiny, only four foot eleven, with a small, sharp face, an oddly harsh voice and an unshakable conviction that she was in the right one hundred per cent of the time; initially Linda loathed her and fought with her vociferously, much to Ben's distress. It was only when Linda found Mrs Lucas alone one night in the front room, reading a letter her husband had written to her in the hospital just before he died, thanking her for everything, that they began an uneasy friendship.

Mrs Lucas had begun literally to wail with grief and Linda rather tentatively put an arm round her and Mrs Lucas had clung to her for hours; Ben had found them, uncomfortably asleep together, on the lumpy old sofa. The friendship had been greatly increased as Mrs Lucas held Linda's hand and soothed her for twenty-four long hours while she endured with considerable stoicism David's traumatic birth (he was over nine pounds, a breech, and the midwife didn't believe in pain relief), and was finally cemented eighteen months after that when she actually delivered Daniel; he had slithered out onto the living-room floor while they waited for what seemed like an eternity for Ben to get back with the doctor.

'You always were dopey,' she had said briskly as he rushed in, wild-eyed, with the news that the doctor was on another call but wouldn't be long. 'Just pull yourself together and go and get me some towels and that, and stop looking so daft. Anyone would think you'd had the bloody baby yourself.'

After that they still sparred constantly; but there was a rock-solid fondness between them that was unshakable.

Linda could never satisfactorily explain to anybody why she loved Ben so much, or why they were so happy; no two people could have been more different. He was quiet where she was noisy, thoughtful where she was impulsive, serious where she was flippant. Linda's idea of a good time was a roomful of people, Ben's a quiet time alone with her. To Ben music meant what Linda called the classics, and very boring too; to her it was Glenn Miller, crooners, anything she could dance to. Ben's ultimate ambition was still to be a teacher, Linda's to have their own house with a spare toilet and to go away for a family holiday. But together they adored the boys, endured Ben's mother, and truly admired one another. This simple fact overrode the considerable problems they had to live with – financial difficulties, claustrophobic living conditions, and frequently conflicting desires – and made them seem of little real importance. As a marriage, it worked most wonderfully.

And now they were being separated from each other, and from the boys, and it was all extremely painful.

'Stop crying,' said David. 'Stop it, Daniel, or the lady'll be up and she'll get cross again.'

'Can't,' said Daniel. 'I want Mum. I want my mum.'

'Well you can't have Mum. She's back in London. Where it's dangerous, getting bombed,' he added. This was clearly meant to cheer Daniel up. It failed; a loud wail went up.

'Shut up,' said David. 'She's coming.'

She was; there were footsteps on the ladder-like stair to the attic and the lady's face appeared; worn, irritable, flushed with the exertion.

'What's this noise about? I said you were to go to sleep.'

'Yes, miss. Sorry, miss. My brother's a bit homesick, miss.'

'Yes, well, it wouldn't do him any good to be at home. Would it? With the bombs. You're lucky to be here. Now be quiet, both of you. Or I'll have to get my husband up to see to you.'

'Yes, miss.'

When she had gone, David reached out across the attic bedroom, grasped his little brother's hand. 'We'll be all right,' he said. 'Don't cry any more. It's fun in the country. Everyone says so.'

'I don't like it,' said Daniel. But he was quieter now, exhausted with crying; he fell asleep holding David's hand. David didn't go to sleep; he lay looking out at the fading light, trying to be brave, trying to remember he was the oldest, that at five he had to set an example, trying not to think of leaving his mother at King's Cross, of hugging her desperately, trying not to cling, but not being able to tear himself away from her, from the warmth of her, the safe familiar smell of her, then having to make way so Daniel could kiss her, watching her holding his brother to her, trying not to cry, looking so pretty in her pale blue coat and her bright red lipstick, much prettier than all the other mothers. And then the fat lady in the beret had come along, the one who had earlier ticked off their names in her book, given them a carrier bag each, and said, 'Follow me, now, all of you,' and mum had said, 'Be brave now, David, be a big brave boy,' and he had swallowed the lump in his throat because he wanted her to be proud of him, and held Daniel's hand very tightly, trying to dry his tears at the same time with his dirty handkerchief, and off they had gone in a great crowd of other children, some crying, some showing off, all with their names pinned to their chests and their rucksacks on their backs, and their gas masks. He had looked back finally, as they were shepherded onto the train, to this far, far-away place called – what was it called? – York-something, and he could hardly see his mother, so lost was she in the crush, pressed against the iron gates, but he could see her pale blue arm waving, so he knew she was still there, and then he was pushed into a carriage, still holding Daniel tightly, and when he turned round all the places at the window had gone and he couldn't see her any more.

They had travelled all day, first a long train journey, followed by another, and then a bus, finally finishing up in this hall place, and they had had to wait to be chosen by their foster-mothers as they called them. Some of them had looked quite nice, but theirs had a mean, stern face, that was fat at the same time, a bit like Miss Barrington at school. David knew that they were lucky in one respect: they hadn't been separated. Two other boys had been wrenched apart peremptorily and sent off in different directions, both crying. Their lady, whose name was Mrs Harris, had taken them back to what she called their billet; it was a small, rather dirty cottage down a street she called a lane. She'd shown them where the lav was, outside at the bottom of the garden, and their room which wasn't really a room, just a space in the roof, an attic, with beds made up on the floor, and told them they would be expected to work hard for their keep. David didn't want to argue with that, but he knew she was getting seven and six a week each for them, he'd heard his dad say so, but he did say Daniel was only three, too little to work, and she'd said not too little to do things in the house he wasn't. 'And you can help in the garden, and around the place. My husband works on the farm, there's always too much to do here.'

She'd also taken the two half-crowns their father had given them that morning 'for emergencies'; David tried to explain, but she said she'd need them for all the extras she'd had to buy. That was very hard to bear; worse was when she'd taken Daniel's sucky, the old nappy he needed to get to sleep, saying it was filthy and she wasn't having it in the house until it was sterilized. At least she hadn't found the two tiny threadbare teddies they'd got in the bottom of their rucksacks, or David was sure she'd take them too.

And then she'd given them what she called tea, a couple of slices of bread and jam and mugs of tea, and sent them up to bed. It had been, he'd looked at the clock carefully, just after five . . .

Charles had gone; he was at Sandhurst, doing his basic training with the army. He would be there for two or three months before being sent to his battalion. He had joined the Royal Wiltshires as a lieutenant and had been assured that in the space of a very few months he would be promoted to captain, possibly major.

Grace was terribly proud of him even while she was sad: that he had not hesitated for a day, or at any rate not since Clifford was pronounced out of immediate danger. She had cried for a brief while in his arms in bed the night before he went, had clung to him after he made love to her, to have something to remember – although of course he would be home again, more than once probably, before he was sent anywhere remotely dangerous – and then had waved him off bravely, gaily in the morning before going back into the house and wandering round and round it in a black misery that was not only to do with Charles going away from her.

It was mid-October now; Clifford was home, in a convalescent unit created in the house by Muriel on the ground floor, with a full-time nurse to care for him. He was very weak still, but recovering steadily; Dr Hardacre had told him he was the luckiest man in England. Grace spent a long time there, reading to him, planning changes to the Mill House garden with his help, or just sitting with him sewing while he listened to the wireless. He loved music as much as she did, and she liked to pick out concerts on the Third Programme that she knew they would both enjoy, get a tray ready with tea and biscuits, make an occasion of it. It tended to make Muriel cross, but neither of them cared.

Charles had spent the morning after they had arrived in the London office trying among other things to contact the mysterious Mary Saunders, had trawled the firm's files; he had found nothing, he told his mother, but no doubt something would emerge in a day or two. 'Or the Sister at the hospital will get something more tangible for us.'

Nothing emerged and the Sister didn't; 'a mystery,' said Charles to Muriel, 'but obviously she was something to do with work, maybe a typist or something.'

He looked less cheerfully confident than he sounded; Muriel accepted the explanation, but Grace didn't.

'Charles,' she said quietly to him that evening, after Muriel had gone to bed, 'who do you think this Mary Saunders is? You don't think – well –' Her voice trailed away.

Charles glowered at her. 'I don't think what?' he said, heavily irritable. 'What are you trying to say, Grace?'

'Nothing,' she said quickly.

'Yes you are.'

'Well, I just wondered if she – well, you know, Charles, if she – '

'If you're trying to imply that there was something unsavoury going on between my father and this woman, Grace, I would urge you very strongly to reconsider.'

She had never seen him look so angry; she was quite frightened. 'No, of course not,' she said, 'of course not.'

'Good. Because not only would I find it immensely offensive that you should think that of my father, but it would greatly distress my mother.'

'Charles, all right,' said Grace, 'let's forget it. I'm sorry if that's what you thought. I mean that's what you thought I thought.'

'This is a ridiculous conversation,' said Charles shortly. 'Let's stop it at once, shall we?'

'Yes of course,' said Grace meekly.

But it didn't alter her basic suspicions.

Robert had not volunteered for the army; he had said that he would go, of course, when he was called up, but until then he would work on in London. Florence was still a little fragile, he didn't want to leave her, he was terribly busy, and – he added to Muriel to whom he was imparting this information – it required a fair amount of courage to stay in the capital at all.

Grace couldn't help feeling a slight touch of amused satisfaction at this; if Florence was still conducting her affair, she must be dying for Robert to go.

Florence did come down to stay for a few days once her father was home; Muriel said she would like to have her, and that London was dangerous. It didn't seem in the least dangerous; people were amused at their own early panic, as the bombs and the gas attacks failed to arrive, and the regulations seemed more ridiculous every day. Cinemas, closed with much drama, began to open again; masks were provided for car headlights, and the use of torches was permitted, providing their beams were muffled with two layers of tissue paper. 'Honestly,' Florence said, 'you're in more danger of being run down walking down the street at night than from a bomb.'

She looked better, Grace thought, not so thin, but she was still very jumpy, starting every time the phone rang, sitting tensely by the wireless listening to the news each night.

'What are you going to do,' Grace asked her, 'when Robert is called up? Come and stay with your mother?'

'Oh – I don't know,' said Florence vaguely. 'I might stay in London, I want to work for the Red Cross. One of my friends said she was sure they'd welcome me.'

'Florence, you are not staying in London on your own,' said Muriel firmly. 'I wouldn't know a moment's peace. You can work for the Red Cross down here, I'm sure, if you want to be useful.'

'Mother, I really don't know what I'm going to do,' said Florence. 'Clarissa said I could go and stay with her if I liked, I don't have to be alone.'

'Well, that's nonsense too,' said Muriel, 'You're not going to be any safer just because the two of you are together. What's Clarissa planning to do anyway? I imagined she'd go and be with her own mother.'

'She's talking about going in the Wrens,' said Florence, 'but Jack's a bit against it.'

'I'm not surprised,' said Muriel, 'although knowing Clarissa I can't imagine that will stop her.' As always when she was talking about Clarissa an indulgent note came into her voice.

'What I'd like to do,' said Grace tentatively, feeling herself rather left out of all this, 'is take in some evacuees.'

There was a silence, then: 'What an appalling idea,' said Muriel.

'Why?' said Grace boldly. 'There's a great deal of room at the Mill House, and there are so many of them needing homes. Poor little things,' she added. 'They looked so lost the other day. I saw a coachload arrive, really tiny some of them, clinging to their brothers and sisters, trying not to cry.'

'My dear, a lot of them come from the most appalling slums,' said Muriel. 'I heard that they all have headlice and wet their beds, and in fact Mrs Tucker was saying that the two her daughter has taken in just – well – relieve themselves on the floor. You couldn't possibly have children like that in the Mill House.'

'I dare say they could be educated quite quickly to use the lavatory,' said Grace firmly, 'and one could get rid of the headlice. It just seemed to be something I could do.'

'Well, of course, Charles might agree,' said Muriel, looking at her as if she might have headlice herself, 'but I very much doubt it.'

'I can't see that it's got a lot to do with Charles,' said Grace. 'Actually. As he won't be there.'

'Of course it has,' said Muriel. 'It's his house that you would be bringing these creatures into. And when he comes home on leave, he will need peace and quiet, not the place turned into some kind of children's hostel.'

Grace was silent. But the next day she telephoned the town hall in Shaftesbury and asked for details about the evacuee scheme.

After six weeks at Sandhurst, Charles came home on a forty-eight-hour pass; he looked tired and a bit thinner, but he was good-humoured and full of funny stories about his new life.

'I'm enjoying it,' he said to Grace, over dinner the first night, 'marvellous spirit of camaraderie, you know. I almost wish I'd thought of the army as a career.'

'Goodness,' said Grace.

'Rather see myself as a major general. How would you like that, darling? Being a lady of the regiment. No, that's not right, makes you sound like the regimental trollop.'

He was rather drunk; he would never have said anything so crude if he'd been sober. He had already got through more than a bottle of claret over dinner and two very large gin and tonics beforehand. He put out his hand and took hers, raised it to his lips. 'I've missed you,' he said, 'I've really missed you.'

'I've missed you too,' said Grace truthfully.

'Let's have some coffee, shall we, darling, and then have an early night?'

'Yes. Yes of course.'

Out in the kitchen, she sighed inwardly; sex with Charles when he was drunk was even more predictable, less sensitive than when he was sober. Maybe if he had a couple of brandies he'd just fall asleep – She crushed the thought decisively, shocked at herself. Her husband had been away for six weeks, and here she was begrudging him – what was the official name for them? – his conjugal rights. What sort of a wife was she? She carried the tray in, smiling determinedly.

'Here you are, darling. Any news yet as to where you might go?'

'No, not really. France I imagine.'

Another silence; he pulled heavily on his cigar.

'I was talking to your mother. According to Florence, there's nothing happening in London at all,' said Grace. 'All the cinemas are reopening, and the restaurants and so on. The only difference she says is that the roads are deserted, because of the petrol rationing, and the policemen are in tin hats of course, instead of their helmets. Otherwise you'd never notice anything out of the ordinary.'

'I didn't realize Florence had set herself up as a kind of unofficial war reporter,' said Charles; but he looked more cheerful again, poured himself another brandy – that must be the third, Grace thought. 'Anyway she's missed the biggest change. Buckingham Palace guard in khaki. Bit of a shame that.'

'How do you know?' said Grace. 'You haven't been to London, have you?'

'No, of course not,' said Charles. 'Every soldier knows that, Grace. Most important military change this century.' He had moved closer to her again, was massaging her thigh. 'Darling, hurry up and drink your coffee, and let's go up.'

Sex that night, as she had feared, was more mechanical, more emotionless than she could ever remember. She was beginning to worry about it, to think that she wasn't giving Charles any pleasure; she had even tried to broach the subject, but he had discouraged it, said it wasn't for her to do anything, that was his department, everything was fine. She was also finding the absolute predictability of his performances the opposite of exciting, was finding herself resenting the fact that he could make her come without apparent effort, could control his own orgasm totally, waiting until she had finished, then releasing himself moments later and promptly turning over and falling asleep. Increasingly, as she lay beneath him, responding almost unwillingly, she felt like some well-trained animal, doing what its master told it.

'I wondered,' she said, smiling brightly at Charles over the breakfast table, 'if you'd like to ask your parents over for lunch. I've got a big piece of beef, and I expect your father would like it, like to come out. He's strong enough now.'

'Why not?' he said, smiling back at her. He seemed completely unaware that she might have been anything but perfectly content the night before. 'Got a bit of a head this morning. I might go for a walk. Want to come, darling?'

'No, I think I'd better stay and do the lunch,' said Grace. 'Otherwise I would have come. I love walking. Which reminds me, Charles, I'd like to get a dog. I'd feel less alone somehow. And safer,' she added.

'Good idea. Only do get something decent, a lab or something. No point having some little runt.' The implication was very clear: that she was quite liable to buy a little runt, something rather less than aristocratic. 'Get my mother to help you choose one.'

'Yes, all right,' said Grace. She had actually longed for a cocker spaniel, and she certainly didn't want any dog that Muriel might think suitable, but she was so relieved he had agreed that she wasn't going to argue. 'I'll talk to her about it today.'

'Grace wants a dog, Mother,' said Charles, over the beef. It was slightly overdone, and Grace feared he was going to complain about it. It had been so difficult to time everything, it being Janet's day off, and the potatoes had been a bit hard so she'd had to leave it in for an extra ten minutes. But he didn't, was eating it very cheerfully, had even remarked it was nice and tender. 'I said you'd help her get one. If you don't mind, that is,' he added.

'Of course,' said Muriel. 'Good idea. You'd be best off with a lab, Grace, a black one, like Marcus. Joan Durrant's bitch is a splendid animal. She's just whelped so we could go over and have a look at the litter this week. I'll have a word with her.'

'I really would rather have a long-haired dog,' said Grace, trying to sound firm rather than defiant. 'I thought a spaniel, or maybe a setter.'

'Oh you don't want anything long-haired,' said Muriel. 'Get caught up in the undergrowth and they're always filthy. And setters are stupid creatures, and they stray. No, you have one of Joan's puppies. Ideal for your purpose, and Charles likes them too.'

'But — '

'Grace darling, if there's one thing Mother knows about it's dogs,' said Charles. 'You let her advise you. And labs are so sensible, and so easy to train. And Joan's puppies are always beauties. Never any hip problems or anything like that — '

'But I really don't terribly like black labradors,' said Grace, making a last desperate stab. 'I'd at least like a golden one if – '

'Grace darling, this will be my dog too,' said Charles, an end-of-the-subject note in his voice.

Grace told Clifford, quite casually, that she was thinking of going to London to do some shopping and asked him if there was anything he'd like her to get him while she was there. She had meant no more than that; but it occurred to her, even as she suggested it, that he might want a message delivered or even a letter posted to the mysterious Mary Saunders.

She was right: Clifford looked at her for a moment or two, then he said, 'Sweet of you, my dear, but I have everything I need. There is one thing though – I might ask you a small favour.'

'Yes?' said Grace.

'I've a letter I'd like posted. It's to – to a client of mine. If Muriel thought I was – well, doing anything remotely connected with work, she'd have me under lock and key literally, with the nurse as jailer. I wonder' – he hesitated, went slightly pink – 'I wonder if I could ask you to do that for me?'

'Yes of course,' said Grace, smiling at him. 'That would be fine. Do you want to give it to me now?'

'Yes, please. If that would be all right. Now not a word to Muriel.'

'Of course not,' said Grace. 'And Clifford, if you – well, if you wanted any urgent letters sent to you, you could always have them addressed here. That would be quite all right.'

'Sweet of you, my dear. I would try not to bother you, but of course in an emergency – well, thank you. Now here we are – all stamped, as you see.'

He gave her the letter; as she had expected, it was addressed to Mrs Mary Saunders. The address, which she really couldn't not look at, was in Hammersmith.

She felt fairly certain there was more to the relationship than a business one, but if that was the story Clifford was happy with, then she had no intention of embarrassing him by saying so. Allowing him to use her as postmistress seemed a very small return for all his kindness to her. She wondered if Mrs Saunders was a past girlfriend. Or even a present one. The thought made her giggle. If she was married to Muriel, she'd want a little light relief.

Charles was awarded a week's leave over Christmas, then he was to go to France. He had promised to be home on the day before Christmas

Eve, but he phoned that morning, saying he had to stay an extra day. 'Be back tomorrow night, darling. Along with Santa.'

'But Charles,' said Grace, aware she sounded fretful, unable to help it, 'that's nearly two extra days. Will they make it up to you at the end?'

'Grace, of course not. There's a war on. I do assure you I'm as disappointed as you are.'

She was looking forward to Christmas. Muriel had persuaded Florence and Robert to come, and had also − Grace suspected at Clifford's suggestion − invited her parents for Christmas lunch, and however fraught with tension that might be, at least she wouldn't have to worry about them on their own.

She was trimming the small tree she had bought and set up in the hall a week before Christmas when the phone rang; Janet came and said it was Mrs Grieg.

'Who? Hallo? Oh, Florence!' said Grace. She was astonished.

Florence had never rung her, never made the slightest attempt to be more than coolly friendly.

'Yes, hallo, Grace. How are you?'

'I'm fine. Absolutely fine, Florence. And you?'

'I'm all right, thanks.' She sounded rather bright and brittle, and − what ? Embarrassed. 'Look, Grace. I wondered if I − well − could ask you a bit of a favour.'

'Yes, I expect so,' said Grace carefully.

'Could I come and stay with you, at the Mill House, for a couple of days after Christmas? On my own I mean: Robert's got to get back, he's terribly busy, and I'd like to stay down for a bit longer, but I don't think I could stand too much of Mother just at the moment.'

'Oh,' said Grace. She didn't quite know how to react.

'Well, she does go on and on about my coming to live down here when Robert's gone and I really don't want to' − (No, thought Grace, I'm sure you don't) − 'and it's beginning to get on my nerves. I thought if I said I wanted to spend a bit of time with you and Charles she wouldn't mind too much. Would that be all right?'

'Yes. Yes, I suppose so,' said Grace. She was completely baffled by this request; the story sounded so unlikely, and Florence never seemed to take the slightest notice of her mother; Grace couldn't imagine her allowing Muriel to get on her nerves. On the other hand, she couldn't think of any other reason for Florence wanting to stay with them; in fact surely if she was still seeing her man-friend she'd want to get back to London.

'Thanks very much. I'll come over on Boxing evening if I may. Well, goodbye, Grace. Looking forward to seeing you,' she added, in so transparent an afterthought that Grace almost laughed.

'Yes, you too, Florence. Well, till Christmas then.'

'Yes. Oh, by the way, I may be a bit of a liability to you all. I've sprained my wrist. Fell over on the icy steps yesterday. Can't cut up my food very well. And I've got a great bruise developing on my forehead as well. So silly. Bye, Grace.'

'Goodbye, Florence. I'm sorry to hear – ' But Florence had rung off. She really did seem to have a great propensity for hurling herself down steps and stairs, thought Grace; which led her to wonder when or if Florence would find herself in the position of having to have another baby and how she might resolve what was clearly going to be a rather knotty little problem.

Charles didn't actually arrive on Christmas Eve; he phoned after midnight, as a near-hysterical Grace sat by the fire visualizing car or train crashes on icy roads or rails, a sudden military crisis necessitating his departure for France, a car turned over in a ditch in the blackout.

'Darling, it's me!' he shouted down the crackling line, 'I'm terribly sorry, but we've been delayed, and it's impossible to get anywhere now. Much too dangerous. I'll leave really early in the morning, be with you by lunchtime. As long as I don't get lost. These beastly road signs being turned round doesn't help. Sorry I didn't ring before – simply couldn't get through. What? Oh darling, don't be absurd. There is a war on, you know.'

And Grace went to bed alone, not sure whether her prime emotion was rage, relief or misery, trying to tell herself there was indeed a war on, that she had to expect these things, and at the same time wondering why it had been so impossible for him to at least phone earlier in the day. She couldn't believe he hadn't been told of this delay until after he was supposed to leave for home. She finally fell asleep at five, into a confused dream whereby she was in a bus driven by Robert down endless dark icy lanes. Florence was on the back seat with her boyfriend, kissing him, and her task was to keep Robert from turning round and seeing them. Charles didn't seem to figure in the dream at all.

Charles finally reached the Priory at half past one on Christmas Day; he looked shattered, but very cheerful, still in uniform, and hugged and kissed her most tenderly in the front drive before producing an improbably large pile of presents out of the boot of the MG. After lunch, during which he talked a great deal, he distributed them with great and rather touching pride: a silk scarf for Grace, and another for her mother, cigars for her father, perfume for Florence and Muriel, a tie for Robert and a first edition of *Bleak House* for his father.

'Charles, how extravagant!' said Clifford, examining this last with huge pleasure. 'They must be paying you very handsomely in the army. Have you been made up to brigadier already, dear boy?'

'No, but I'll be major by the time we leave for France,' said Charles. 'How do you feel about that, Grace darling? Aren't you proud of me?'

'Terribly,' said Grace. 'Charles, wherever did you get all these lovely things? I thought the shops were empty.'

'Oh,' he said vaguely, 'in London, months ago. We had to go up for a regimental dinner.'

'Good for the regiment,' said Grace, smiling at him. She had quite forgiven him. She hadn't yet told him about Florence coming, but she thought he would probably be pleased.

Florence had been quiet, but seemed cheerful; Robert was very attentive, cutting up all her food for her, enquiring constantly if her wrist hurt. The bruise on her forehead was fading to an interestingly variegated blend of green and purple; she also, Grace noticed, had a second one on her kneecap which made her limp and was obviously painful. It had obviously been a hard, bad fall.

Muriel asked Robert about his call-up; he said he hadn't yet heard, and that it was all a bit slower than everyone had thought. 'Apparently there's a shortage of uniform and arms, only no one's meant to know that, of course.' He was hoping to join the Sappers, he said, he'd always fancied himself as a bit of an engineer, but as long as he saw some active service that was all he really cared about. 'My father was killed at Mons. I'm looking forward to redressing the balance.'

It seemed to Grace a rather chilling remark, a cold-blooded determination to kill, unlike the affectionate, tactile Robert she knew. But if you had grown up without a father you probably felt pretty cold-blooded about it. She looked at Florence, to check her reaction, but she was rather determinedly reading the *Radio Times*. 'We mustn't miss the King's broadcast,' she said.

They were all sitting in the drawing room having tea when there was a ring at the front door; Clifford caught Grace's eye, winked at her and said, 'I'll get that.'

He walked slowly out of the room; there was then a lot of laughter, and a yelping sound, and he came in again with a rather wriggly bundle in his arms, covered with a blanket.

'Right,' he said, 'this has just arrived. Grace, my dear, it is for you. *She* is for you, I should say, I don't mean to insult her. Here she is, with my love, a token of my gratitude for all those concerts you arranged for me. Happy Christmas.'

And into Grace's arms he deposited a small silken copper-coloured creature; it was trembling slightly, but as she stroked it tenderly, and bent, laughing, to kiss its head, it reached up and first sniffed and then rather tentatively licked her nose.

'She's called Maplethorpe Bougainvillaea,' said Clifford, 'but I expect you might go for something rather shorter.'

'Oh,' said Grace, looking up at him through a blur of tears. She had never quite dared to hope the puppy was going to materialize. 'Oh, Clifford, she's so lovely. Thank you so much. I love her. Really, really love her. I'm going to call her' – her mind roved for something tactful, something gracious that would in some way balance out the undoubted irritation that Charles must be feeling – 'Charlotte. Yes, that's it, Charlotte, so she'll never forget her master the major, even when he is away.'

'She'll cause you a lot of trouble,' said Muriel irritably; but even her face softened into a near smile as the small creature slithered out of Grace's arms and wandered floppily towards her, and Charles, mellowed with a great deal of port, reached out for the puppy and then fell fast asleep by the fire with her in his arms, a most indulgent smile on his face.

'What a lovely Christmas,' said Betty as she and Frank prepared to leave an hour or so later. 'Thank you so much for inviting us, Muriel. Let us hope and pray that by this time next year the war will be over.'

'Amen,' said Clifford, very soberly.

Chapter Eight

Winter–Spring 1940

Charles had gone and Grace had felt genuine pain as the MG disappeared down the lane. He would be home once more before he was sent to France, but only for twenty-four hours; the war, which up to Christmas had seemed so remote, almost unbelievable, had suddenly becoming real, painful and frightening.

She went back into the house, called Charlotte, and sat cuddling her in the big chair by the drawing-room fire. She felt very alone.

'Grace! Grace, are you all right?'

It was Florence; her expression as she looked at Grace was genuinely concerned. Grace was surprised.

'Yes. Yes, I suppose so,' she said. She wasn't about to enter into a soul-baring exercise with Florence.

'Can I get you a drink? Nice cup of tea, as Maureen would say. Cigarette?'

'No. No, really,' said Grace. She straightened herself up, set Charlotte on the floor; she promptly squatted down and did a puddle.

'Oh how sweet,' said Florence rather absently. 'Shouldn't you mop it up?'

Grace fetched a cloth, mopped up the puddle and was rather ineffectively rubbing at the carpet – 'Try soda water,' Florence suggested helpfully from the sofa – when the phone rang.

'I'll get that,' said Florence, jumping up. It was the first time she had moved all morning. 'Don't worry.'

There was a brief conversation; then Florence came in looking faintly awkward. 'Grace, would you be all right if I went out for the day tomorrow? That was Clarissa – apparently her godmother isn't too well and she's asked me to go and visit her. Over at Bath. You know how fond of her she is.'

'Oh. Oh yes, of course,' said Grace, Florence's visit suddenly made perfect and utter sense to her; had she proffered this story to her mother, Muriel would have insisted on going with her, driving her there. 'Yes I do. Of course I'll be all right. I'd rather be on my own. Actually.'

'Good. Now the thing is I can't drive, with this wretched wrist, but Mrs Hartington, that's the godmother, is sending over her chauffeur. Isn't that sweet of her? Now are you sure you don't mind, don't think I'm terribly rude?'

'No of course not,' said Grace briefly. 'No, you must go. How very sweet of you, Florence.'

'Oh I don't mind,' said Florence. 'She's a wonderfully amusing old lady. I love listening to her.'

'I'm sure you do,' said Grace. Florence looked sharply at her, but Grace smiled. She was slightly tempted to ask if she could go too, just to frighten her.

There seemed little doubt that visiting the godmother was genuinely at least part of the trip; a very beautiful light grey Rolls Bentley pulled up in the Mill House drive next morning, and a uniformed chauffeur came to the door and asked for Mrs Grieg.

'Goodbye, Grace,' said Florence, kissing her briefly. 'I'll see you tonight.'

She must be very excited, Grace thought; Florence had never kissed her before.

It was after tea when the phone rang. It was Florence; she sounded strained.

'Grace, it's me. Look, Grace, I've got in a bit of a hole. The chauffeur can't bring me back tonight in the blackout, and of course there aren't any buses. So I'm staying here. Is that all right?'

'Florence, of course it's all right,' said Grace, feeling rather sick. 'You do whatever you like.'

There was a silence, while Florence was obviously digesting this, then she said, 'I don't know what you mean, Grace, it's not what I like. I can't get back.'

'No,' said Grace, 'so you said.'

Another silence, then: 'Well, goodbye then, Grace, I'll see you in the morning. Oh, and by the way, if by any chance, any chance at all Robert rings and wants me, could you explain? But I'm sure he won't. Bye, Grace.'

And the line went dead before Grace could ask her for the telephone number.

She went into the kitchen and most unusually poured herself a stiff whisky. The thought of what Florence was doing, the risks she was running, made her feel very frightened. Supposing Robert did phone, supposing he then tried to ring Mrs Hartington; it couldn't be that difficult to get her phone number. Clarissa would have it, Muriel might even have it. And then presumably Florence wouldn't be there. Surely not even a godmother of Clarissa's would lie for her to that extent? Grace spent the whole evening dreading Robert's call, the sound of the phone ringing, but it remained most conveniently and steadfastly silent.

Until the morning, when Robert did ring.

'I told him you were in Shaftesbury, shopping,' said Grace briefly, when Florence finally arrived back at lunchtime, flustered, embarrassed, dropped off, she said, at the end of the lane 'by a sweet friend of Mrs Hartington's'. 'I don't know why I should lie for you, Florence, but I did. So you'd better know that. When you speak to him.'

'Grace,' said Florence tentatively, 'Grace – '

'Look, Florence,' said Grace, 'I don't care what you do. It so happens I saw you one day in London, with – well, it wasn't Robert. But I do mind having to lie on your behalf. And most of all I mind you treating me like a fool. So please don't in future, because I'm not.'

There was a long silence; then Florence said slowly, hesitantly, as if it was hugely difficult, painful even to begin, 'Grace, please, I think I ought to try and explain – to make you understand – '

'I'd rather you didn't,' said Grace, 'and I do understand. Rather too well.'

'Grace,' said Florence, and her voice was ineffably weary and sad, her angular face softened and more fragile, 'Grace, I do assure you you don't understand. You really don't.'

She left that afternoon, without either of them mentioning the subject again.

'Are you sure we're doing the right thing?' said Ben. 'I can't see that we are, Linda, not any more. It's not dangerous at all up here, is it? Safe as houses.'

'Yeah, till the houses get bombed,' said Linda. 'Oh Ben, I really don't know. It seems all right at the moment, yes, of course it does. But once you've gone for good – ' She looked at him, laughed slightly awkwardly. 'Oh Ben, I didn't mean that. I meant once you'd gone off to France or wherever. Then what?'

'Well, I know. But I'd rather think of the three of you all together. I really would.'

'What, with the bombs raining down?'

'Linda, they're not going to rain. Specially not if I'm in France.'

'No,' said Linda, 'you'll keep them all at bay, won't you, Ben Lucas? Won't get a chance if you're there.'

Ben sighed, got up, walked over to the window, looked out at the narrow street, where David and Daniel were playing football with several other small boys. 'I hated it,' he said, 'when they first came home. They seemed so – changed. Little Dan, so jumpy. David so quiet. They've just got better, cheered up and now we're sending them back again.'

'Well, we don't have to,' said Linda, 'of course. But they looked all right. You said so yourself. Daniel's grown about three inches and never stops talking about his rabbit, and they've both got a wonderful colour. You know how kids talk, like to make up stories, get sympathy. If these people were really as bad as they said, they wouldn't look like they do.' But her voice lacked conviction; she hated them being away

'No,' said Ben suddenly, 'no, I've made up my mind. They're staying here. This is where they belong. With us. I want you to go and see the woman at the town hall, tell her they're not going back.'

'All right,' said Linda, 'if that's what you really want. You're the boss.

Ben's eyes met hers across the room. 'If you say so,' he said, grinning.

'Of course you are. Don't be daft. But if the bombs start dropping on us, don't blame me.'

'I promise I won't,' said Ben. He went over to her, took her in his arms and kissed her; there was a moment's hesitation, then she pressed herself slowly, sweetly against him, her hips moving very, very gently.

'Oh Linda,' he said, 'oh Linda, I'm going to miss you, I'm going to miss you so much.' His hands moved down her back, began to work on her small neat bottom.

'Not now, Ben,' she said, laughing, pushing his hand rather feebly away, 'not now. It's three in the afternoon.'

'So? There's not a law about it, is there, saying it can only be done in the hours of darkness? Come on, Linda, I've got to go back to camp tomorrow. You wouldn't deny a soldier what could be his last chance of a happy memory, would you?'

'You're a clever bugger, Ben Lucas,' said Linda, 'and no, I s'pose I wouldn't. Come to think of it, I could do with a few happy memories myself. It's not much fun living here just with your mum.'

An hour later, several happy memories safely secured, she eased herself up in the bed and reached for her cigarettes. She always wanted one afterwards; it was supposed to be only men that did. She looked down at Ben; he was asleep, a sweet smile on his face. God, she loved him. Her dad had said he was too good for her, and she often thought he was right; he was so clever, so patient, so – well, so good. Maybe, she thought, sitting back, blowing out a cloud of smoke, maybe after the war it might still be possible for him to achieve his ambition to be a teacher. He still wanted it so much, and if the boys were at school she could go back to work and keep them for a few years. He'd passed all those exams through night school, before they were married, after all. It would be worth it, worth the struggle to see him happy. Although why anyone could want to go back to school, having finally escaped from it, she really could not imagine. Linda had hated every minute of every day at school.

God, she was going to miss him; and she was going to miss the sex as much as anything. One of the very best things about Ben was how good he was in bed. Bloody brilliant; he somehow carried her along with him, had brought her to sensations, pleasures she'd never even dreamt of. Every single time. He just knew what she wanted and did it for her; and if he didn't know he asked, asked and listened. It was lovely that, made her feel so important and special. Which made her feel sexy. It was all part of the same thing really, he said: he loved her, and he wanted to show it, in every way he knew.

And the other awful thing about Ben being away was having to live more or less alone with his mother. They might get on all right these days, but it still wasn't exactly fun. One of the reasons she'd not minded quite so much being without the boys was that she'd been able to get out of the house a bit more. Still, she'd much rather have them with her. And if she did what she really wanted, took a factory job, at least Nan would look after them. She'd argue of course, but she'd have to; Linda intended to tell her it was her war effort if there was any real resistance.

Ben stirred, smiled up at her sleepily; she bent and kissed him quickly, then got up and dressed and went to tell the boys they hadn't got to go back to the country. David threw himself into her arms and hugged and kissed her; Daniel promptly burst into tears. 'What about me rabbit?' he said.

'Kids!' said Linda in disgust.

Grace had just come in from walking Charlotte when she heard the phone ringing: on and on insistently. As she reached it, it stopped; she picked it up anyway, spoke to Mrs Boscombe.

'Was that a local call, Mrs Boscombe?'

'Yes, dear, from Mr Bennett. He's not at home though, dear, he's at the office, in Shaftesbury. I'm sure he shouldn't be working, but there you are. Shall I get you the number?'

'Oh – yes please,' said Grace.

'Right then. And how's the major?'

Charles's second promotion had already received a great deal of publicity locally, largely via Mrs Boscombe herself.

'He's fine, thank you. He's coming home – '

'Yes, dear, I know, next weekend, isn't it? Before he's off to France? And I hear Mr Grieg's off soon too. Captain Grieg, I should say.'

'Yes, that's right,' said Grace. She sometimes thought Adolf Hitler could do a lot worse than get a direct line to Mrs Boscombe. She seemed to have in her possession the most detailed knowledge of the movements of half the British Army.

'Clifford? It's Grace.'

'Ah, Grace, yes.' He sounded awkward, ruffled. 'Just a moment, my dear, let me close the door.'

There was a pause, then he said, 'Look, there's been a bit of an upset at home. My – well, my client, Mrs Saunders, phoned me there, and Muriel was – well, she was pretty angry. So I'm going off to London for a few days. Stay at the flat. I just wanted to warn you, that's all.'

'Oh Clifford,' said Grace. So she'd been right. Obviously Mary Saunders was very much more than a client. 'I'm so sorry. Is there anything I can do?'

'Fraid not,' he said. 'But don't worry, my darling, it'll all calm down in time, I'm sure. Perhaps you could give Muriel a ring in a day or two – see how she is.'

'Of course I will,' said Grace, quailing slightly at the task.

'Well, I'll say *au revoir*. If you do come up to London, then of course you must come and see me.'

'Yes, of course,' said Grace again. 'You'll be at Baker Street, will you?'

'I will indeed. And thank you again for your sympathy. Much appreciated. Don't deserve it, I'm afraid.' Grace thought he did. She felt very depressed as she put the phone down. She would miss him badly.

Life, she reflected, as she tried to concentrate on a letter from the vicar asking for volunteers with church cleaning, was a very quiet, dull affair these days. Sometimes she felt she must have slept for twenty years rather like Rip Van Winkle and woken in her middle age.

'He's going!' said Florence. 'He's finally going. On Saturday. I can't believe it. Will you take me out to dinner? Somewhere glorious, like the Ritz. And buy me absolutely masses of champagne.'

'No,' said Giles, 'I won't.'

'Beast.'

'Not at all. I'm going to take you to bed and make love to you over and over again, and we can have masses of champagne there. One bottle per orgasm, I thought. Doesn't that sound better?'

'I suppose so,' said Florence.

'You look rotten,' he said, stroking her hair. 'So thin. Thin and pale. And how on earth did you get that bruise on your shoulder?'

'I told you. I slipped in the bath. Drunk again – '

'You're a careless old thing, aren't you? Don't you think you drink just a tiny bit too much?'

'Possibly,' said Florence vaguely. 'If you were me, you'd drink a bit too much.'

'I do anyway. Well, now I shall be able to take care of you.'

'Until you get called up,' said Florence soberly. 'Christ, I don't know what's worse, no war and Robert being at home, or a war and both of you gone.'

Chapter Nine

Spring–Early Summer 1940

Charles sat staring at Grace across the drawing room at the Mill House and his face was stonily shocked; he was home for his last leave before going to France.

'I don't believe this,' he said, 'I don't and I can't believe it.'

'You don't have to,' said Grace, 'but he's gone.'

'He's left my mother?'

'Well he's left. For now anyway. Yes, that's right.'

'If he's left he's left,' said Charles. 'I'm quite sure my mother won't tolerate his return. She certainly shouldn't. And it's over this Saunders woman, you say?'

'Sort of. Yes. Well, obviously, Charles, he was having some kind of an – an affair with her. And your mother's found out. I mean I always thought it seemed possible – '

'Why?' he said. He looked terribly angry. 'Why did you think that?'

'Well, ever since it was her he was with when he had the heart attack. I just never believed she was a client. It seemed – ' she hesitated then brought the word out bravely – 'ridiculous.'

'Oh I see,' said Charles. 'You felt yourself able to make that judgment, did you? I have to say I'm very shocked at you, Grace. Very shocked.'

'But why?' she said, genuinely baffled. 'These things happen. I'm not stupid. Your parents are hardly an ideal couple, are they?'

'And what do you mean by that?'

'What I say. They don't get on very well. Your mother isn't very nice to him – '

'Well, can you wonder?' said Charles. 'If this sort of thing goes on.'

Grace was silent; she didn't want to make him angrier by saying she thought it was the other way round, that Clifford had a mistress precisely because Muriel wasn't very nice to him.

'Well, I'm horrified,' said Charles, 'by your attitude as much as anything else, Grace.'

'Why? What's my attitude got to do with it?'

'You seem to be taking his side in some strange way. To be condoning his behaviour. I would never have thought that of you, I have to say.'

'Oh Charles, really! That is so unfair. I'm a realist, that's all. I tried to talk to you about it before and you wouldn't.'

'Yes, well,' he said, 'I'm not sure that I like that kind of realism, Grace.' He looked at her very coldly. 'Anyway, how is my mother? I must go over to see her immediately. Poor, poor woman. All I can say is, if he's gone to London they'll probably be bombed, best possible outcome in the circumstances.'

'Charles!' said Grace.

'It's true. Oh God, it's so humiliating, apart from anything else, for the poor woman.'

'Yes indeed,' said Grace.

She didn't talk about it any more. She could understand that Charles should be upset at his father's conduct; upset and shocked. What she couldn't understand was his behaviour to her over it. It was as if she had strayed into some territory that was forbidden to her. Clearly men's peccadilloes were one thing when kept quietly to themselves and quite another when women knew about them. It seemed to her an unpleasantly dishonest attitude.

And in fact, Grace thought, struggling to be fair, had it been her own father guilty of this thing, might she not have found that a great deal harder to accept? However much she loved Clifford, however helplessly she found herself on his side, it was easier to be tolerant, to forgive him when he was, after all, simply a dear friend to her, and not her flesh and blood.

She also wondered how Charles might feel to learn that his sister was conducting an adulterous affair, and reflected at times and with some amusement that the family into which she had so nervously married and regarded as so awe-inspiringly perfect were in fact proving to be rather the reverse.

Charles came back from the Priory white and heavy-eyed; he looked, Grace thought, as if he might have wept. And there was something else about him, too, which she could not quite understand; something dark, something haunted.

'I love you,' he said to her fiercely that night, turning to her in the darkness. 'I love you very much, Grace. You and only you. Remember that, always. No matter what happens.'

'I will remember it,' said Grace, 'of course I will.'

All over England, the same declarations, the same promises were being made.

The phoney war which had seemed so endless, so futile, so boring had ended and the real one had begun. Looking back, people wondered that they had ever thought there was anything to complain about, now that fear stalked every street, every house, every family; and every person's faith was pinned, above all, on Winston Churchill, who had become Prime Minister on 10 May, the day Germany marched on Belgium and Holland. Grace sat by the wireless with Muriel, and listened as he told them he could offer them nothing but 'blood, toil, tears and sweat', urged them to flight 'for victory at all costs, victory in spite of all terror, victory however long and hard the road may be'. She felt inspired and uplifted in spite of her fear.

She was really lonely now: savagely so. She missed Clifford terribly, Janet had left her to join the ATS, and Muriel was hardly a warming companion. Grace felt desperately sorry for her but was helpless in the face of Muriel's cold pride to comfort her. Her mother urged her constantly to lock up the Mill House and come home, but she steadfastly refused; that was home now, she said, and it was true, she loved it most dearly, and besides, if Charles did come home on leave, they had both agreed that was where she should be.

Most of the people she and Charles had entertained early in their marriage, neighbours, friends of his from childhood and his early single life, who had invited them back when he had been at home, to dinner parties, cocktail parties, to play tennis, ignored her for the most part; she had the occasional invitation to tea, an even more occasional one to 'family supper in the kitchen', but it was generally excuses, protestations that she must come soon, when Charles was on leave, when they had time, 'So busy with everything, and you must be too.' A shorthand, she knew, for the fact that she was not really one of them, did not belong naturally and easily to their circle, was a bore over the dinner table, a near embarrassment at drinks. She was partly relieved, because she hadn't liked many of them, had found little to say to them, but although she tried not to be, she was also very hurt. It was so blatant a piece of ostracizing, and although everyone said no one was entertaining any more she knew there was still a fair amount of it going on, albeit rather more modestly. Muriel would ask her tactlessly if she was going to such and such or so and so, and she would have to say no, she wasn't; the worst thing that happened after that was that she would occasionally get a carefully casual invitation, clearly at

Muriel's instigation. In her darker hours she would imagine the conversation, 'Do ask the poor thing, she's so lonely,' and try to force herself to hang onto her dignity and refuse, but usually she accepted because it was easier and she always thought anything would be better than another long, empty day. Only mostly it wasn't.

It didn't help that she was so much younger than most of Charles's circle; the wives were mostly in their thirties with two or three children, and that alone set them in a country very remote from her own. But more than anything she knew it was because she was who she was and what she was: an outsider, an intruder into their ranks, for whom they had been prepared to make an effort for Charles's sake, but not for her own.

Muriel, who discouraged any kind of easy relationship (for which Grace was truly grateful), issued rather stiltedly formal invitations about once a week, to join her and her friends for lunch or supper, but those again were to be avoided; she was even less friendly towards Grace these days, and Grace knew why, for she had added a suspected knowledge of, collusion even, in Clifford's defection to her earlier, lesser crime of wifely unsuitability.

Grace had tried at first: had offered to help with charity and fund-raising events, to sit on committees, but not being able to drive was genuinely something of a drawback as the meetings were often held in other villages. For some time she had continued to go to morning service, but after a few Sundays of smiling determinedly at people in church, and walking rather hesitantly past them as they chatted outside it (although they always paused to say hallo, or good morning, or most likely to ask if she had heard from Charles), she began to shrink even from that.

And so she was left mostly to her own devices, and was trying determinedly to make the best of it all; she had Charlotte for company, she was following most literally the instructions to dig for victory, she had the chickens to feed, she was planning to get a goat. She had bought a piano, and she spent long hours playing it; and she was still quietly resolved to take some evacuees, the only difficulty now being that there were none to take. Most of them had gone back to London.

Nevertheless the days were long, and the endlessly light evenings, the result of 'double summertime', made them feel longer. She would have loved to join the WRNS like Clarissa, or the WRACS, but Charles had been adamant: he wanted her at home, safe, and waiting for him. She felt she owed him obedience at least, as he risked his life for her and his country.

He was in France now, she knew not quite where; his battalion had marched briefly into Belgium, and been driven immediately back again. She woke up each morning knowing only that he was still alive, and that another day of crawling fear as well as loneliness lay ahead.

Robert was also in France: with the Royal Engineers. Giles, training on a warship in Dartmouth, had left five weeks after him. He was in no immediate danger, but Florence had suddenly a different, a dreadful fear. Her period, always so regular that she could predict not only the day but almost the hour of its arrival, had failed her. And on the morning of 29 May, as the first wave of an armada of tiny ships, fishing boats, sailing dinghies, even pleasure cruisers, accompanied the larger ships across the Channel to Dunkirk to rescue the thousands of troops stranded on the beaches of Normandy, their escape completely cut off by the German Army, she was horribly and endlessly sick.

In the flat in Baker Street, Clifford sat alone, listening to the reports of the besieged troops on the beaches, knowing his son was probably among them, knowing that he might not hear for many days that Charles was safe, or indeed that he was not, knowing that the mother of his son must be raw with terror and misery and that they really should be, needed to be, together, and wondered, not for the first time, if he had done the right thing.

Linda Lucas was in the pub. She knew she shouldn't be in the pub, that she should be sitting at home by the wireless with Nan, but the crawling fear that something might have happened to Ben, who was almost certainly on the French beaches being shelled, was so bad she could only quieten it with company and alcohol. She'd get hell when she got home, but she didn't care. Sometimes she thought she'd hit Nan as she went on and on about the boys and how they were running wild – it wasn't her fault their school had been closed and was only now opening again, and with just half the number of teachers, nor was it her fault, as far as she could see, that bread had gone up again, that sugar was rationed and butter about to be, that England had now lost all her allies and certainly not that Nan's constipation was worse than she could ever remember (although she probably should have made a bit more effort to get her senna pods from the chemist). But Nan clearly blamed her for the lot.

'I can't believe it's all happening again,' she would say, glaring at

Linda, 'history repeating itself like this. I'd have thought you'd all have learnt from the last time.'

The variation on this theme was that this war was nothing, nothing at all, they should have seen the last one, that really had been a war, there had been real hardship, and people had practically starved in the streets of London. Linda had tried protesting that surely if they weren't starving this time it had to be an improvement, but Nan said that wasn't the point, the point was that Linda and her generation didn't know what a war was, didn't know what suffering was. She usually finished by saying darkly that they soon would, which led to a short silence and then back to her repeating, she couldn't believe it was all happening again. 'Like a bloody chorus in a bloody song,' said Linda to her friend Janice in the pub that night. 'I wouldn't mind, but if I argue even just a bit, she turns on the waterworks and says I don't know how much she misses Ben. *She* misses Ben! What about me, I'd like to know! I tell you what, Jan, I can't imagine how he managed to turn out the way he did, with her for a mother.'

'Well, perhaps he's more like his dad,' said Janice reasonably.

'Yeah, he is,' said Linda, thinking sadly of Ben's sweet, gentle, clever old father, always reading, coping so nobly with the terrible wife he had so incomprehensibly married, 'exactly like his dad. And sometimes, I tell you, Jan, I have nightmares that I'm going to turn out exactly like his mum.'

'Oh for heaven's sake,' said Janice, 'you're going doolally, Linda. You ought to take that job at the munitions factory, get you out of the house. They're crying out for people. I'm going to, I've decided, I'm going along tomorrow. Maurice isn't best pleased, but I don't give a toss, and he's not here anyway. It's not bad money, and it'd be fun. My friend Heather loves it, they have a good laugh – '

'Yeah, well, I might,' said Linda. 'Could you ask for me, Jan? Only thing is the boys, who's going to look after them?'

'I thought old Ma Lucas said she would.'

'Yeah, I thought she would, but now she says she won't. Says it's not right, women gadding about when they should be at home with their families.'

'You can do shift work,' said Janice. 'What about the night shift? That'd get you right out of the old bag's way.'

'I'll think about it. But she'll write to Ben and tell him most likely, and he's not keen, I know. I don't want him upset . . .'

'Oh, I shouldn't worry,' said Janice easily, 'they're not here, and we have to make our own decisions. Want another drink, Linda? Hey, look at those two over there. Norwegians, do you think? Or Dutch?'

There's quite a lot to be said for this war, at times. Let's go and find out . . .'

'No, I think I'd best get home,' said Linda with a sigh. 'God, Jan, if Ben's on those beaches – well, he is on those beaches, he has to be, they all are. Do you think I'll ever see him again?'

'Course you will,' said Janice. 'If I know Ben he'll be well hidden under some tree or other, reading or something – '

Janice's knowledge of the beaches of Normandy was not extensive.

The worst thing, Grace thought, was the telephone ringing endlessly. Every single time she thought it was either Charles, ringing to say he was safe, or someone from Whitehall ringing to say he wasn't. It was never either. Her mother phoned almost every hour to find out if she had heard anything, Muriel at least every two, and Clifford each morning and evening. In addition, Mrs Boscombe added her own enquiries every time she put any long-distance call through, or delivered a message. Grace kept asking them not to, promising to let them know the moment she heard anything, anything at all, telling them (most untruthfully) that she had been asked to keep her line clear, but they ignored her.

By the morning of 3 June, when the rescue operation was virtually over and 338,000 men had been picked off the beaches and reported safe, when every paper carried headlines about the Dunkirk Miracle, there was still absolutely no news of Charles. Muriel had phoned Grace to tell her Robert was alive, although instead of being allowed home on leave he was being sent back to his depot in Yorkshire: 'Most unfair, Florence is so upset.'

Even Clarissa phoned: 'Just a quickie. I know there's no news, darling, I just wanted to tell you I was thinking of you. All the time.'

Rather to her surprise, Grace found that less irritating than all the other calls.

She knew by now that Charles was dead; it was just a question of getting through the time until the telegram came. She was almost looking forward to it; grief, real grief would be a welcome release from the gnawing, sickening, lonely terror.

She was out in the garden, tying up the great waterfall of tiny pink rambler roses on the paddock fence, when she heard the phone. On and on it went. She looked at her watch; it would undoubtedly be Clifford. It was nearly lunchtime, he always rang then. She tried to ignore it, to tell him by her silence there was no news, but in the end it defeated her by its insistence, and wearily pushing back her hair she went into the house and slowly, reluctantly walked into the hall and picked it up. But it wasn't Clifford, nor was it Muriel or her mother; it was Mrs Boscombe, her voice loudly, shakily excited.

'I told him you were there, dear, and I told him I'd tell you. I knew you wouldn't go out without telling me, you never do.'

'Mrs Boscombe,' said Grace, holding the table, trying to steady herself against a swirling sick faintness, 'tell who, tell me what?'

'The major, dear, he's quite safe, he's back in the country, they've sent him down to Sussex, but he'll be phoning when he gets there, sent his love. Are you all right, dear, you're not crying, are you?'

'Oh Mrs Boscombe,' said Grace, who was indeed crying, and laughing at the same time, 'I'm fine, absolutely fine. Can you ring my mother and Mrs Bennett and tell them, and say I'll ring them as soon as I can, and get me the Regent's Park number straight away, please?'

Charles phoned that night; he sounded almost euphorically cheerful. 'Bit of a battering, darling, sorry I couldn't contact you before. We were covering the evacuation, and while most of the battalion went off we got left behind, hitched a lift on a funny little pleasure cruiser and – '

'Oh Charles,' said Grace, who was crying again, weak, happy tears of relief, 'you make it sound like a Sunday outing. Oh, I've been so frightened, I knew, I knew you were dead.'

'Well, if I'd got on the sloop I probably would have been,' said Charles, sounding more sober. 'It was bombed mid-Channel. Look, darling, got to go. But I've got a forty-eight next weekend. I'll see you then. I love you.'

'I love you too, Charles,' said Grace, 'terribly, terribly much. I'm longing to see you.'

She had already decided what she was going to do when he came home.

'You look terrible, darling,' said Giles. 'Are you all right?'

'Thanks,' said Florence. 'And no, I'm not.'

He was home for a week, then he had to rejoin his ship 'and God only knows when I'll see you again.'

She had meant to be brave, not to spoil his leave, not to send him back worried, but she felt so ill, was so constantly sick, so permanently frightened, that she simply couldn't help herself. She had to tell him.

'What is it? Is Robert – '

'No, no, he's still up in Yorkshire. What on earth can they be doing up there, what use is an army in Yorkshire?'

'God knows. Training, I suppose. The whole thing's a shambles half the time, it seems to me. Only of course we're not supposed to say that.'

'No,' said Florence. She looked at him, then down at her stomach. Her flat, almost concave stomach that would quite soon now begin to arch, to burgeon, to round out, that would give her away, that would tell Robert.

'Darling, what is it? There is something, isn't there?'

'Yes,' said Florence, 'yes, there is.' She looked at Giles, took a deep breath, dreading hearing the words herself. She hadn't uttered them before. 'I'm pregnant.'

There was a long silence, then: 'Oh Jesus,' he said.

'Yes, I suppose I could try that excuse,' she said, trying to smile. 'Mary's I mean – '

'Oh darling. Darling, I'm so sorry. So terribly sorry.' He was pale himself, his eyes filled with anxiety and sympathy.

'Is that all you are?' said Florence. Her sickness was making her irritable.

'What?'

'Aren't you anything else?'

'What do you mean?'

'I mean aren't you just a bit happy, proud, pleased – all those sort of things that expectant fathers are meant to be?'

'Oh Florence, of course I am. Of course. Well, I presume I have the absolute right to be – I mean – '

'Oh yes,' said Florence, 'oh Christ, yes. Robert went almost eight weeks before you. That's what's so scary, so – well, that's why I don't know – don't know – ' She suddenly started to cry, big noisy tears, clinging to him, shaking. 'What am I going to do, Giles, what can I do?'

'Darling, don't. Don't panic. We must think this through, carefully. Now listen, Florence, listen to me – ' as her sobs became wails, neared hysteria. 'There are certain things that are important. I love you. You love me. This is our baby. We always meant to be together. It's not so terrible – I'll take care of it, of you, the baby – '

'Giles,' said Florence, taking a deep breath, struggling to speak more normally, 'Giles, there's a war on. As people are so fond of telling us. You have to go back to your ship. And then to God knows where. You can't, with the best will in the world, take care of me. It's impossible. And Robert will come home, and he will know. He's only in bloody Yorkshire. He's not going to get killed up there.'

'Oh you never know,' said Giles, 'you never know your luck – '

'Giles, don't. That's terrible.'

'I bet you've thought of it.'

'Of course I haven't,' said Florence staunchly, suppressing the memory of the long days when she'd sat by the telephone willing it to ring, to tell her that Robert was missing, was dead. 'I'm not that wicked.'

'Well,' he said, 'this isn't getting us anywhere. Have you thought of – well, you know – '

'Of course I have,' said Florence, 'quite a lot. But I don't have any money. Not that I can get at. And nor have you. And it takes a lot. A lot. Unless it's going to be a knitting needle – '

'Darling Florence, don't, don't. Promise me you won't. Promise me you won't anyway. I don't know why I even thought of it.'

'I do,' she said very soberly, 'I do. Very well.'

Ben was safe. 'Not a scratch,' he had said cheerfully on the phone. 'Just fine. Home in a couple of weeks.'

'And then?'

'Then I don't know.'

'Everyone says now there's going to be an invasion,' said Linda fearfully. 'Now that the Germans are just across the Channel.'

'They may be saying it,' said Ben firmly, 'but it won't happen. England is an island. She'll defend herself. Don't you worry, my lovely. I'll be home soon. Mum all right?'

'Yes she's fine,' said Linda.

'Good. I love you. Kiss the boys for me.'

'I love you too, Ben.'

It didn't seem the moment to tell him about her job.

'Darling!' said Charles. 'Not now surely! Not the middle of the afternoon!'

He looked slightly sheepish, embarrassed even, but he was smiling.

'Whyever not?' said Grace.

She smiled at him, hoping she looked as she sounded, a self-confident, sexy woman, dying to get into bed with her husband. Charles smiled back, stood up, held out his hand. 'What a lucky man I am,' he said.

This is the third time this weekend, thought Grace, it must surely work. She'd been lucky with her dates, it was just about the middle of her cycle; how awful if he'd come home when she'd had her period. She lay there beneath him, trying terribly hard, concentrating on every tiny flicker of feeling she had. She could feel him pushing deeper and deeper into her, hear him panting, gasping, then sensed him tense, and then, then the marvellous welcome pulsing as he finished. Please God, please please let it work, she thought, let it happen, and as he eased himself off her, kissed her, told her he loved her (he always did that, it was an intrinsic part of the routine, touching, sweet), she curled her body in on itself, pulling her legs up, towards her chest, as she had read somewhere you should, to contain them all, all the millions of sperm, help them on their way.

'Oh God,' he said, smiling at her, 'oh God, I don't want to have to leave you. You are all right, aren't you? On your own here. Without Janet and so on.'

'I'm fine,' she said, 'absolutely fine. Lonely, of course, but fine. I mean I would like to – '

'No,' he said, 'no, darling, I really don't want you to. Help at the hospital of course, do any voluntary work you like, but I don't like the idea of my wife in the forces. I can't help it, I just don't. I want you here, safe, waiting for me.'

'I know,' said Grace, sounding as acquiescent, as soothing as she could, marvelling at a selfishness (so well disguised as the opposite) that could keep her living alone, bored, feeling useless and frustrated.

But she really couldn't argue with him when he was doing so much, risking his life, enduring such horror. Dunkirk had changed him; he was quieter, less inclined to tell jokes, to shrug everything off. Which was hardly to be wondered at; he had witnessed death, bloodshed, every kind of terror, shelling, drowning, had seen his comrades killed, had been instrumental in killing himself. She had tried to encourage him to talk about it, feeling that she should, that it might help, but he had simply smiled at her rather distantly, said he wanted to forget about it, not relive it, that was the only way to cope, and she had respected that, had not pressed him in any way. But it made her feel even more than usually excluded, set aside, unable properly to share his life.

Charles had expressed his unwillingness for her to have children yet for the same kind of reason that he did not want her playing an active role in the war; had said it all again that very weekend. 'I want us to be a proper family, darling, quite apart from the dangers of bringing children into the world at the moment, and you having to cope on your own. I just don't like the idea of our children being born and growing up while I'm not here. You do understand, don't you?'

'Of course I do,' said Grace. She hadn't wanted to argue with him, in case he grew suspicious, started asking her if she had 'done the necessary' as he called the use of her cap.

He left early the next morning; Wellings, Clifford's driver, came to collect him, to drive him to Salisbury.

Grace had said she'd like to go too, to see him off, but he had said she was not to: 'I want to remember you here, in our home, not on some station platform.'

She waved him off, smiling gaily, went inside the still, empty house and cried for quite a long time; then she dried her eyes determinedly and went to phone her father. She had decided to spend the next few months, while her baby gestated, learning to drive properly.

Chapter Ten

July 1940

'I'm going to join the Wrens,' said Clarissa, 'I've decided. Here's Mr Churchill telling us we've got to fight them on the beaches and in the streets and so on, and I thought I could do my bit on the top deck. Or whatever it might be called.'

She smiled at Jack: her brightest, most dazzling smile. He smiled back.

'You wouldn't mind then? Because I really don't think I could just sit here worrying about you, not doing anything. I'd go mad.'

'Of course I wouldn't mind. I'm a very modern husband, you know.'

'Yes, I do know.'

They were sitting in the garden of their house in Campden Hill Square; it was an idyllically peaceful evening, with a deep brilliant sky, the air full of birdsong. War seemed impossibly far away.

'No, I'll be very proud of you,' said Jack, taking her hand, 'and I know you'll fight them wonderfully and efficiently. Between us we can probably have the war over by Christmas, you on the sea and me in the air.'

'Absolutely. Probably before that even.'

'And it's such a very glamorous uniform. I don't suppose that's been a factor at all.'

'Of course not,' said Clarissa indignantly, 'except I certainly wouldn't even think of joining the WRACS, that awful brown. Oh God, I can't believe you're going tomorrow. I can't bear to think about it even.'

'Well, let's not.'

'Easier said than done. Unless — well, we could just go to bed, couldn't we?'

'We certainly could.'

And they went upstairs and spent an hour, an hour and a little more cutting out most wonderfully and effectively the thought of the next day; and indeed the next, and all the other days that they would be apart and in danger.

Neither of them heard the telephone ringing interminably, on and on, in the hall two storeys below.

Grace woke up feeling sick. She could hardly believe it. Definitely, and quite nastily sick. It had happened then: she had managed it, she was pregnant.

How wonderful. She could hardly believe it: a baby. Someone of her very own – well, and Charles's of course – to love and care for; to cure her loneliness, to give her life a focus. She eased herself rather carefully out of bed, and went to the lavatory, doing sums on her fingers. July the third today. Charles had gone back on 15 June, that meant it would be born in March. A spring baby. He – or she, but she felt sure it would be he – could lie in the pram under the apple tree all through the summer, rosily brown; she could take him for walks down the lanes, Charlotte lolloping ahead of them, in the big pram, her big pram, the one her mother was always hinting about having kept for her. It was perfect.

She wondered where she would have him: at home she supposed. It must be much nicer to have your baby at home, not in some strange hospital or nursing home. And then she could have her mother there, with her. Her mother! When could she tell her? Perhaps not just yet, probably not until she'd been to the doctor, Betty would get so excited. And it was a bit soon, actually, to go to the doctor, her period was only – what? – three or four days late at the most. She was a bit surprised that she felt sick so early on, but all the books she had been reading told her that every pregnancy was different. Oh, if only she could tell Charles; maybe she could, maybe she should. He hadn't gone yet, was still based, in an agony of frustration, somewhere on the south coast. In fact he'd said he might get one more short leave before he went. He phoned her quite often; maybe if he did, in the next few days, she would tell him. On the other hand he'd be so excited – once he'd got over the shock of course, she'd have to be very careful about stressing that it had been a complete accident – and probably, as with her mother, it would be better to wait until she'd seen the doctor before telling him.

Goodness, it wasn't very nice, this sickness; she stood up and thought for a moment she was actually going to be sick. She wasn't, but she decided to go and lie down for a while longer, before she went downstairs to make herself a cup of tea. She had a driving lesson this morning; she would cancel that. You had to be very careful anyway, when you were first pregnant, keep quiet, not rush about. She was glad now she hadn't joined the ATS or the WRNS. It wouldn't have done, she'd have only had to let them down, leave again. She looked down at her body, at her neat flatness, patted her stomach tenderly, thinking of the wonders that were being worked within it; and then went back into the bedroom, opened the curtains and lay watching the birds wheeling in the blue sky, listening to the millstream and thinking about names. She thought she had never been so happy, in her whole life. Even though Charles was away.

'Ben's leave's been bloody cancelled,' said Linda. She was almost in tears. 'He won't be home till I don't know when.'

'Well, there's a war on,' said Nan. 'What do you expect? And don't swear. The British Army isn't run around you, my girl. That's what it was like last time, only much worse. Harold only came home three times the whole of the war. Ben's always going backwards and forwards. Like a holiday camp it seems to me. You ought to be grateful. It'll get worse of course – '

'Oh shut up,' said Linda, unable to control herself any longer. 'Just shut up, will you? I've been looking forward to him coming so much, I'm so disappointed, and all you can do is tell me I should be grateful.'

'Yes, well, there you are,' said Nan, 'that's what comes of starting it all over again. And don't speak to me like that, Linda, if you please. I don't know what Ben would say if – '

Linda walked out, slammed the door. If she hadn't, she knew she would have hit her mother-in-law. Stupid old bag.

She looked at her watch: only twelve o'clock. The boys wouldn't be home for hours. She knew what she was going to do. Sign on at the factory, that was what. And if Nan didn't like it, she'd tell her where to get off. She had to do something with her life. She was only twenty-five after all.

'Mrs Compton Brown!'

The two girls sitting next to Clarissa at the YMCA nudged each other, watched as she got up and walked through the door for her interview. They had been studying her for the past hour, her clothes (red and white silk dress, white gloves and shoes, red hat), her blonde hair, freshly set, her long nails, brilliantly red, her make-up, carefully applied, her reading matter (*Vogue*), her voice, oh most especially her voice; their eyes had met at the sound of that voice, their lips twitched. But that was what finally did it, hearing her name: Compton Brown. That settled it, branded her as spoilt, useless, stuck-up, joining the forces to make herself feel better, do a bit of slumming, see how the other half lived.

If Mrs Compton Brown and the two of them should just happen to find themselves in the same place, May Potter and Sandra Hardy thought, as one eighteen-year-old girl, they wouldn't half give her a hard time. She'd soon learn what real life was about. They'd see to that. Women like Mrs Compton Brown needed taking down a peg or two.

Had they known that Flight Lieutenant Compton Brown was just directing his small, hideously vulnerable plane into the skies for the fourth time since daybreak in the defence of his King and Country and had already seen two of his greatest friends and comrades shot down in flames, and that Mrs Compton Brown, beneath her gracious voice and dazzling smile, was eaten up with a dreadful, fear-filled grief, they might have felt just a little less hostile.

But only a little.

'Oh Clifford,' said Michael Whyte, QC, looking at his lifetime's friend affectionately across the dark leathery recesses of the dining room at the Reform Club. 'You really do look a shadow of yourself. The bachelor life obviously doesn't suit you.'

'Not too well,' said Clifford with a sigh, 'but it's my own fault.'

'Never a very comforting thought,' said Whyte. 'The – well, the lady in question, has she faded out of your life?'

'I'm afraid so,' said Clifford. 'Who could blame her? Actresses, especially young struggling actresses, need to keep the kind of company that will further their careers. Not old-fashioned, fuddy-duddy lawyers who are very well past their prime. No, I was a mere passing whim for Mary Saunders, I'm afraid, although she was very good to me the night of my heart attack. But I think once she realized I wasn't going to actually set her up in her own establishment in London, there really wasn't much point hanging around.'

'Was that what she was hoping for then?' asked Michael Whyte in amusement.

'Oh yes. But you know, you have to be pretty fond of someone to make that kind of investment. To be a genuine bona fide sugar daddy. I wasn't quite that enamoured of Miss Saunders. And events have proved me right.'

'So what then?' said Whyte, embarking on the somewhat tortuous routine of lighting a cigar. 'Home again, tail between your legs?'

'I fear not,' said Clifford. 'However deeply it was thrust between them, my tail and my legs would not be welcome at the Priory. Muriel does not have a forgiving nature. No, I have to stick it out here while I think of something else to do.'

'What about work?'

'Well, virtually retired of course. I have a few clients up here. And I'm lucky I can use the flat. But I can't stay there for ever. However, it's not all bad,' he said with his sudden sweet smile. 'I get to lots of concerts, I can listen to the radio whenever I want to, eat irregular meals – '

'Not too irregular I hope,' said Whyte. 'Coronary patients should look after themselves.'

'No, no, of course not. But a little smoked salmon at midnight plus champagne, after a visit to the Albert Hall, is very pleasant.'

'Hmm,' said Michael Whyte. He did not look entirely convinced. 'What about your daughter? She is in London surely, can't you spend some time with her?'

'She is indeed,' said Clifford with a sigh, 'but I fear she views me in the same dark light that her mother does. It is a source of great grief to me, that. I fancy we could comfort one another very well.'

'Why does she need comforting?'

'Her marriage is not all it should be. At least that is my suspicion.'

'Few marriages are,' said Michael Whyte.

'Sadly true. But for Florence – I pray I may be wrong and I have no real grounds for thinking so, she denies it utterly, but I somehow fear there is – well, a danger of violence.'

Grace was half asleep in the garden when she realized Charlotte was missing; she had become so good, and was so devoted to Grace, always lying at her side wherever she was, in the house or outside, that she had become rather careless about keeping an eye on the dog. She sat up in her deck chair and called her, waiting for, confident of, the rustle in the bushes, the splashing in the stream that meant Charlotte was coming. She called again and whistled, stood up slightly reluctantly – it had been so warm, so peaceful, and she had been planning the nursery in her head – looking just slightly anxiously now for the russet-coloured shadow moving towards her. No Charlotte. Perhaps she was in the house, maybe it had been too hot for her; but she was not, not in the kitchen by the Aga, not in her favourite afternoon place, the puddle of afternoon sunlight that fell on the drawing-room floor by the French windows, not even on Grace's bed.

A slight knot began to gather in Grace's stomach. Charlotte was very young, much too young really to be relied upon to stay where she was supposed to be; she could easily have spotted a rabbit and gone bolting off after it, through the fence, across the fields. She had done that a few times, but had always come back.

Grace went down to the far fence and called her again, repeatedly, with slightly less hope now; then, when Charlotte still did not come, went to the front gate which, though shut, a puppy, even quite a big one, could still crawl under and peered fearfully down the lane. Of course she was most unlikely to have been run over – of course she was – there was very little traffic about, and everyone knew her anyway, somebody would have phoned and told her. She would be fine. Only – did she have her collar on, Grace wondered, with the name tag and the telephone number, or did she not? Grace always took it off when Charlotte settled for the night, because the puppy still didn't really like it, and put it on again when it was time for her walk; only she hadn't walked her today, because of feeling so sick – she still didn't feel very well – so she was rather afraid it would be – yes, it was, in the kitchen table drawer.

Grace stood staring at it, panic rising in her throat now, thinking of her foolishly, dangerously curious puppy, thinking of her on the road, in pursuit of something, a rabbit, a cat, a car coming round a corner, a lorry – oh God, how could she have done it, gone to sleep, not seen she was safe, Charlotte, who she loved so much. She was dead, no doubt, crushed beneath an army lorry, her bright, loving light put out permanently, and it served her right, Grace thought, standing there, breathing rather fast, trying not to panic, it served her jolly well right, and now –

The phone rang sharply; she rushed to it.

'Mrs Bennett?

'Yes. Yes, this is Mrs Bennett.'

'Police station here, Mrs Bennett. Constable Johnson. At Thorpe Magna. We've got your dog here, at least Miss Parker from the post office says it's your dog. Picked her up in the road, brought her in.'

'Oh thank goodness,' said Grace, her legs shaky with relief, 'thank you so much. I've been looking for her everywhere, I'm so sorry she got out – '

'Pity she didn't have a collar on,' said Constable Johnson. 'She should, you know, Mrs Bennett.'

'I know. I do know. I'm so sorry, I took it off you see to – '

'No use to her off, is it? Anyway, the thing is, Mrs Bennett, she's hurt.'

'Hurt? How?'

'Well, she got hit by a car, I'm afraid. Now it's not serious, at least I don't think so, but her leg's hanging awkward. Broken possibly. Can you come and get her please?'

'I – I can't,' said Grace. 'Not really. You see I can't – that is I haven't got a car.' God, she must learn to drive properly, she really must, she'd need to more than ever now, now she was going to be a mother –

'Well, I don't know what to suggest,' said Constable Johnson. 'We haven't got petrol to waste on a dog, or personnel come to that, specially with half our force gone.'

'Gone?' said Grace stupidly. She had a sudden vision of half the Thorpe Magna police force – which amounted to only one other man – run away, or even in the churchyard.

'Yes, Mrs Bennett. Joined up. In the Somersets he is. And I'm in the Home Guard,' he added as if that were deeply relevant to the problem of getting Charlotte back. 'So – '

'Look,' said Grace, 'I'll ring the vet and see if he can come.' She felt terrible at the thought of Charlotte lying in pain, untended, as a result of her irresponsibility. 'I'll ring you back, Sergeant.'

'All right,' said Constable Johnson, clearly soothed by this piece of instant promotion. 'I'll look after her for now.'

John Roberts, the vet, was busy: 'He's out at Haywards, delivering a calf, Mrs Bennett, and then he's got three more calls. I'll see what I can do, but I really can't imagine that – '

The vet's wife, whose name was Audrey, made it clear that an injured puppy would come very low on any list of veterinary priorities; Grace had met her once when she had taken Charlotte for her inoculations, a leathery-faced woman who looked much older than her permanently harassed husband.

'Oh, well, look, don't worry him. I'll think of something else. Thanks anyway. If I bring her round later, would he have a look at her leg?'

'Possibly,' said Audrey Roberts grudgingly.

There was only one thing for it, Grace thought: she would have to take the car herself. Muriel was away, staying with a friend in Cornwall, so she couldn't ask her; for which she was actually, even in her distress, grateful. She would have had to listen to an endless lecture about the folly of having a setter rather than a labrador, of not keeping her kennelled, of not training her properly. She would just drive the two and a half miles into Thorpe Magna, collect Charlotte and take her to the vet. The thought made her feel very frightened, but she couldn't leave Charlotte lying injured at the police station indefinitely. Charles had given her quite a few driving lessons after all now, she knew what to do; and there was certainly enough petrol in the car. If she was very, very careful she would be perfectly all right. If only, if only she didn't feel so sick. And it wasn't so hot.

The whole thing served her right; if she'd looked after Charlotte properly none of it would have happened.

The car – the thought of how angry Charles would have been if he had known she was driving his precious car like this, and for such a reason, made her feel even sicker – was not in the garage, mercifully, but in the drive, and facing the right way. She was perfectly competent at actually driving now, her father had said so, it was only parking and reversing that was difficult. With a bit of luck she wouldn't have to do either.

Grace picked up the phone and told Mrs Boscombe she was going out and would be at least an hour – better to be on the safe side should Charles phone – and then took a deep breath, went out into the drive and got into the car. She remembered to do all the right things, checked the mirror, put it into neutral – she wished the gears were easier to change – then gingerly turned the key. The car started easily, and she managed to move it into first gear, inched it cautiously out of the drive. There was nothing coming; she took a deep breath, put her foot down a little further, let in the clutch with only a couple of rocking lurches – at least it didn't stall – and pulled out smoothly and in a mood of immense triumph into the lane.

It was easy. Really easy. The car moved along – slowly, but that didn't matter; after a few minutes she moved up into second gear. She was dimly aware of a car coming towards her, hooting companionably, then going past. It clearly saw her simply as another driver: just somebody he had passed in the lane, rather than some lethal incompetent. Grace smiled to herself, gingerly tried to get into third; that defeated her. But second was fine. It was going to take a bit of a while, but it didn't matter. She had already reached the furthest outskirts of Lower Thorpe: Magna was only two miles away now. She would make it easily. This was fun: real fun. She hadn't enjoyed herself so much for ages.

The only really bad moment was when she passed the Priory. She was so afraid that Muriel might have come home unexpectedly, could come out and see her, that she put her foot right down and shot forward and round the corner much too fast; she only just managed to avoid the postbox. But she did. And now there was just about half a mile to go, through the village, but it was mid-afternoon, everything was peaceful, and she'd have done it. There was the police station now. In sight. With the beloved Charlotte inside. She'd done it. She'd done it! She knew exactly how Lindbergh must have felt after he'd flown the Atlantic.

'Thought you hadn't got a car,' said Constable Johnson.

'Oh – well – I borrowed one,' said Grace. 'Thank you.' How is Char – the puppy?'

'She's not too bad,' said Constable Johnson, 'I've got her in the cells.'

'Oh dear,' said Grace.

A pitiful whining came from 'the cells,' which was the small square lock-up room with a barred window which served the rather light duties of criminal detention in Thorpe Magna (although the much-mooted possibility of the arrival of a large number of spies had made everyone nervous and had ensured at least another lock on the door). Grace went in, fell on her knees beside the box in which Constable Johnson had placed first a blanket and then Charlotte. Charlotte looked up at her, stopped whining immediately and tried to get out of the box. She yelped, and sank back again.

'Yes, 'tis broken,' said Constable Johnson. 'Thought so. You'd best take her to John Roberts, Mrs Bennett.'

'I'm going to,' said Grace, 'right away.' She picked the box up; Charlotte licked her face. 'Thank you for making her so comfortable, it was very kind of you.'

'I didn't do nothing,' said Constable Johnson. 'Don't have time for looking after stray animals. You get a collar for her, Mrs Bennett.'

'Yes I will, and thank you anyway,' said Grace, 'and it was so lucky you had the box and the blanket in the cell.'

She smiled at him sweetly; he blushed and looked sheepish.

'Come along Charlotte.'

It was only when she had put Charlotte in the back of the car that she realized she was going to have to do a reverse.

All might have been well had not Miss Parker come out of the post office and waved to her; so busy was Grace smiling and waving back, trying to look like someone who had been driving for years, that her foot slipped on the clutch and the car shot backwards and juddered to a halt into the lamp post. She was sitting, her head thrown back, her eyes closed, wondering what on earth she could do, who could save her now, when a voice said, 'Grace can I help? And whatever is going on?'

It was Robert.

Clarissa ran up the front steps of her house in Campden Hill Square singing under her breath; she knew she had no business to be singing, when Jack was in such deadly endless danger, when the Germans were about to bound up the beaches and march on London, but she really couldn't help it, it had been such a beautiful day. She had been told she had a fair chance of being accepted into the WRNS (which she happened to know meant she almost certainly would be), had passed the medical which had been foul, some ham-fisted old hag of a doctor mauling her about with freezing cold hands, and her interview board, at which she had admitted cheerfully to being able to do nothing at all except drive and rather unusually, she thought, to ride a motorbike ('my uncle taught me up on his estate in Scotland, such fun, you can't imagine'), had told her she would be hearing shortly about her draft if she was accepted, and given her a lot of literature none of which she had had time to read. She felt very excited about the prospect of her new life. She had also had a marvellous lunch with three old friends, caught up on a lot of gossip, and, most important of all, had managed to find a very pretty hat in Harrods, in palest blue straw, for her great friend Lily Maitland's wedding. It had been horrifically expensive, but never mind; it was going to be the last hat she bought before the end of the war. The last hat she bought ever, probably. She was just fumbling in her bag for her front door key when she saw a figure huddled by the basement steps.

Her first instinct was to hurry inside and call the police, thinking it was a tramp or some other such intruder; then, as she peered down at it (thinking its hair was very shiny for a tramp), it looked up and Florence spoke.

'Clarissa! Oh thank God you're back.'

'Florence! What on earth are you doing there? Oh, here, let me help you up, you look terrible. Florence, whatever is the matter?'

Florence did look terrible; ashen, dishevelled, exhausted. She was wearing a raincoat, and flat shoes, and clutching a small attaché case. She stared at Clarissa and burst into noisy tears.

Clarissa opened the front door, took her hand, led her into the house and through into the kitchen. 'I'm so sorry, it's Dorothy's day off, otherwise she'd have let you in. She'll be back in a minute, she can make us some supper. You look as if you need it. Sit down and I'll get us some tea. Or do you want something stronger? Like gin?'

Florence shook her head. 'Tea'd be much better.'

'Well, all right. Darling, you're shaking. Are you cold?'

'No,' said Florence, her teeth chattering.

'Here, have a ciggie. I'm not at all sure I shouldn't get the doctor. Do you feel ill?'

'Yes,' said Florence, pulling herself together with a great effort, lighting the cigarette Clarissa offered her, drawing on it thankfully, 'I do feel ill. I feel terrible. All the time. But only because I'm pregnant.'

'You're pregnant! Florence, what is this, why are you hiding at the bottom of the steps? Does Robert know?'

'No,' said Florence. 'Not yet. But when he does – well, that's why I was hiding.'

'Florence, you're not making any sense. You'll have to explain.'

There was a silence. Then: 'It's – not – Robert's,' said Florence, dragging each word out of herself very slowly.

'Ah,' said Clarissa. She looked at her friend thoughtfully. 'Well, whose – I mean you don't have to tell me, but –'

'Yes, I do have to tell you. It'll be wonderful to tell you. To tell anyone, but specially you. No one you know. He's called Giles. Giles Henry. He's a musician.'

'Darling! How very exotic.'

'Not really. He plays the piano in a nightclub.'

'Oh how thrilling! I'm sure it'll be the Albert Hall next.'

'It might be. He's very good. I mean he's had a classical training but anyway, we've been – well, you know, for a long time. About – oh, I don't know, over a year.'

'So this is what the little drama was about, with my godmother at Christmas? I thought your story about being taken ill in the hotel that night and not getting back was a little far-fetched, darling.'

'Yes. I'm sorry about that. But I thought it was best not to involve you.'

'Another time involve away. It's exciting. But tell me, darling, the other baby wasn't – ?'

'Oh God no. That was Robert's.'

'Oh Florence. What a mess. What are you going to do? Have it – seen to?'

'I can't, Clarissa. I haven't got any money. Not of my own. And of course Giles hasn't.'

'Darling, I'll lend you the money. If you like.'

'Oh Clarissa, I couldn't. I really couldn't.'

'Of course you could. You have only to ask –'

'The thing is' – Florence sighed – 'it's probably too late. I'm – well, I've missed the curse three times. And I think – '

'You must see someone tomorrow,' said Clarissa firmly, 'only I don't know who. Do you?'

'No. No I don't.'

'But I know someone who will. Bunty. Bunty Levinson. You know? She's had at least three. I'll ring her in a minute. But I still don't know why you're at the bottom of my steps.'

'It's because Robert is home,' said Florence. 'He came home last night. I was ringing and ringing you, I was desperate. Weren't you here?'

'We were here,' said Clarissa, smiling fondly at the memory, 'but we were awfully busy. And – well, I suppose we just didn't hear the phone. Oh Florence, darling, I'm so sorry. Where did you go?'

'I spent the night in some awful hotel,' said Florence, 'and then I came here this morning. I've been waiting ever since. Where have you been?'

'Oh darling, I've had such a day,' said Clarissa. 'First I signed on with the Wrens, stopped talking about it and actually did it, well, applied to anyway, there are huge waiting lists, and then I went out to lunch with some chums. It was too sad, we went to the Berkeley, and the heavenly maître d'hôtel, do you know him? – his name's Ferraro, has been got rid of in a foul hurry, just because he's Italian. As if he was going to do any harm, blow up the Berkeley or something – he's been there for donkey's years. Honestly, this whole country's going mad. Oh, and then I got a hat for Lily Maitland's wedding. Are you going?'

'I don't know,' said Florence listlessly, 'I shouldn't think so. Oh God, Clarissa, I'm so frightened. Where do you think he is?'

'You really are frightened, aren't you?' said Clarissa, looking tenderly at her shaking hands, her quivering lip. 'Poor darling. I don't know. At home I expect.'

'If he comes here, you won't tell him, will you?' Florence was crying again, clinging to Clarissa's hand. 'Swear to me you won't tell him.'

'Of course I won't. But I don't see why you're quite so frightened. Unless – ' she looked at Florence intently, almost afraid to ask the question – 'he doesn't – well – hit you, does he?'

Florence looked at her, then got up and walked over to the window, looked out at the evening sky.

'Yes,' she said finally, in a very low voice, 'yes he does. He hits me all the time. He loses his temper and knocks me about. He knocked me down the stairs when I – when I was – well, that's why I lost the baby.'

'Oh my God,' said Clarissa, 'dear God, Florence, why didn't you say? Why on earth didn't you tell someone?'

'I couldn't,' said Florence simply, 'I really couldn't. I've never told anyone. Not even Giles.'

'But why? I don't understand. Whyever not?'

'I just couldn't. You don't understand, Clarissa, no one could who hadn't gone through it. You feel so frightened all the time and so ashamed. That's the worst thing. Feeling so ashamed, as if it's somehow your fault. And he's so clever. No one would have believed me, I'm sure.'

'I would have believed you,' said Clarissa, taking her in her arms, holding her very close. 'I really would.'

'I know. I know you would. But – oh, it's so hard to explain. You feel all the time that if you don't admit it, it doesn't happen. And half the time he's so sorry, says he'll never do it again, that he loves me. But he's very, very violent. And very dangerous. I just wish I knew where he was now.'

Chapter Eleven

Summer–Autumn 1940

'This is so kind of you,' said Grace.

She smiled at Robert; he had just come in from collecting Charlotte from the vet. Her leg was in plaster, but she was otherwise in high spirits, hopping round the kitchen looking for food.

'My pleasure. Really. And the chap's coming over in the morning to collect the car, do whatever's necessary. There really isn't much harm done. I was very impressed with your driving.'

'Oh Robert, really! I'm hopeless.'

'Not at all. You get a pretty good idea, following someone. You were very competent. You should be driving without any difficulty at all soon.'

'Well, anyway. Supper's ready. I hope you like stew.'

'I adore stew. I love all that homey, kitcheney cooking. Florence is very clever at the more exotic stuff, but she doesn't produce anything that smells that good.'

'Well, I hope it tastes good as well,' said Grace. 'Sit down, Robert. Can I get you a drink? I think we've got everything.'

'I'd love a G and T. That'd be very welcome. And I'll go and wash if you don't mind.'

'Of course. I've put your bag in the room next to the bathroom.'

'Bless you. Is it really all right for me to stay? I'm totally thrown by Muriel and Florence being away. Such a silly misunderstanding.'

'It's absolutely all right. Of course.'

Grace smiled at him just slightly awkwardly. She thought it was extremely unlikely that Florence was with Muriel, but if that was what her sister-in-law had told Robert, then it certainly wasn't for her to suggest otherwise. She was infinitely grateful she didn't have a number for the friend in Cornwall, and didn't have to get involved in any way. Her dislike for Florence had increased a hundredfold that afternoon, as Robert had been so kind, so gentle, so soothing, had sorted out her problems, disentangled the car from the lamp post. And he was obviously very worried about Florence and where she might be, and distressed at not being with her in his precious seven days of leave, having driven the long, long way from London to Wiltshire to try to find her.

He came back down, smiled at her; she handed him his drink.

'Bless you, Grace. Cheers. And thank you.'

'No, thank *you*,' she said. 'I don't know what I'd have done without you.'

'My pleasure. Gosh, that looks good. Can we start? I'm famished. Ages since I had some decent food.'

'I hope it is good,' she said, ladling it onto his plate. 'Meat's not what it was, awfully tough and gristly half the time. I can't imagine why, I think the war's just an excuse.'

'Probably. You're not eating much.'

'No,' she said, 'I'm not very hungry.'

'Not ill, are you?'

'Oh no. It's just the heat.'

After supper they sat in the drawing room, Grace sewing, Robert reading the paper. It was so nice to have someone in the house; she kept looking up at him and smiling. He made a few phone calls, trying to track down Florence, 'just in case she's not in Cornwall still' but without success. He tried Clarissa's number, but the maid told him she was out.

'I'll just have to head back to London in the morning, see if I can find her. Long drive. I'm so grateful not to have to do it tonight, Grace. I hope I'm not endangering your reputation, staying here unchaperoned.'

'Oh don't be silly, Robert. Anyway, I don't have a reputation. Certainly not one worth endangering.'

'I'm sure you do.'

'No I don't,' she said and was shocked at the bitterness in her voice. 'I'm the most unpopular girl in Wiltshire. Or at any rate this bit of it.'

'Grace, I really can't believe that.'

'You don't have to believe it, Robert, it's true. I'm an outcast.'

'But why?' He looked so genuinely puzzled she felt comforted.

'Oh – well, let's say I don't belong to the tribe. And they won't let me in.'

'I still don't understand, I'm afraid.'

Grace looked at him and wondered if he meant it or was just being polite. 'Robert, it's perfectly simple. I've married above myself. A bit anyway. And it – well, it doesn't make for an easy life.'

'Grace, really, that is quite absurd – '

'No, honestly. It's sweet of you to look like that, Robert, but it's true. Charles's friends don't think I'm worth inviting to their homes without him. They were perfectly nice to me when they had to be, but now they can ignore me, they do.'

'Well,' he said, 'I'm more shocked than I can say.'

'Thank you, Robert.'

'May I say,' he added, 'that you seem to me to be worth ten of every one of them. Really.'

'It's sweet of you to say so. I appreciate it.'

He stood up, came over to her; his eyes were very gentle, very sympathetic as he looked at her. 'I think it's quite foul,' he said, 'and if there's anything I can do – '

'I'm afraid there isn't,' she said, laughing. 'I daresay when I've been a Bennett for fifty years they'll start to accept me. Till then – well – '

Robert went on looking down at her; then he bent and kissed her gently on the lips. 'I repeat,' he said, 'you're worth more than the whole damn lot of them. I think you're a very special person, Grace. Very special.'

Grace sat staring up at him, suddenly very aware of the fact that they were alone in the house, that she liked Robert tremendously, that Florence hated her, that she had already probably been deeply indiscreet. She smiled awkwardly, stood up, said, 'Goodness, I'm tired, Robert. I wonder if you'd forgive me if I went to bed. Is there anything you need? Just say, otherwise – '

'No,' he said, 'no, nothing. Just a wife.' He sighed heavily. Her heart went out to him. 'Anyway, yes, of course you must go to bed. You look all in. And thank you again. Goodnight, Grace.'

She lay awake for a long time, thinking of him, opposite her on the landing, not sure what she was feeling, but most of all desperately angry with Florence.

She woke up a couple of hours later; she couldn't think at first why, then realized with a stab of alarm that it was pain. Pain, a horribly familiar, miserable pain, in the bottom of her stomach; pulling, dragging at her. 'Oh God,' she whispered, 'oh please God, no.'

Fearful even of looking, she went on lying there; in the end she had to get up. There was a large red stain on the bed, where she had been lying; her nightdress was stained too.

Misery wrenched at Grace; she felt a genuine, huge sense of loss. She wanted to wail, to rage. It wasn't fair, her baby, the only thing in the world she had that was truly hers, was not a baby at all, not a lovely, growing, tangible thing, but a hormonal hiccup, a lateness, a mistake.

She sat down on the edge of the bed and cried for quite a long time, then went to the bathroom, found a sanitary towel and a belt, put them on. The pain was bad; not as bad as the pain in her heart, but still bad. Worse than any she could remember. Maybe she had been pregnant, maybe it was an early miscarriage; the thought made her feel worse, started her crying again. She would have to go and get a hot drink and some aspirin.

She went stealthily out onto the landing, down the stairs. Charlotte followed her, hopping on her three legs.

The kitchen was warm, comforting; she put the kettle on, found the aspirin. She was just swallowing them when the door opened, slowly, cautiously; Robert came in.

'Hallo,' he said, 'I couldn't sleep. Heard you moving about. Are you all right?'

'Yes, yes, I'm fine,' said Grace. 'Just – got a bit of a headache.'

'I'm sorry,' he said, and then she saw that he had noticed her stained nightdress. Mortified, blushing furiously, she sat down, pulled it under her. He smiled, saw her distress, came over to her, stroked her head.

'Don't be silly,' he said, 'I'm so sorry. Poor you. Woman trouble, Florence calls it. Let me make the tea. What about a hot-water bottle on your sore tummy? Would that be a good idea?'

He was so kind, so tender, as Charles never was in this situation – always slightly embarrassed, impatient – that she started to cry again.

'Now look,' he said, 'there's no need for that. Here, drink your tea.'

'There is a need,' she said, swallowing it obediently. 'I thought – I thought I was pregnant. I wanted to be pregnant so badly. With Charles gone. To have someone to keep me company. Someone of my own. And now – well, that's it, I suppose.'

'There's always next time,' he said smiling.

'If he gets any more leave. I'm not sure that he will. And I don't think that anyway I can – oh Robert, I am sorry. Making such a fool of myself. What on earth would Florence say?'

'She'd say I was doing my duty, to a kind sister-in-law,' said Robert. Now where can I find a hot-water bottle? I'm sure it would help.' He brought it to her, laid it gently on her tummy; the relief was immediate.

'Oh Robert,' said Grace, no longer embarrassed in the face of his easy kindness, 'you're so nice. Been such a wonderful help today. It's been so lovely having you here. What can I do to thank you?'

'Nothing,' he said, pouring himself another cup of tea. 'It's been a pleasure. Except, of course, tell me immediately if you find out where Florence is. You will do that, won't you? Promise?'

'I promise,' said Grace.

Bunty Levinson's private gynaecologist finished examining Florence, told her to get dressed; when she came back into his office, he looked at her dolefully from behind his desk.

'I'm very sorry Mrs – Smith,' he said, 'but there really is nothing I can do. Your pregnancy is too far advanced. You must be – what? – almost four months. The uterus is already in the abdominal cavity. And I do not do that kind of – surgery. I'm sorry.' He smiled at her, a heavily regretful, oleaginous smile. 'Now then, if you will excuse me, I have another patient – '

'Yes of course,' said Florence. 'I quite understand. But couldn't you – '

'My charges for examination and assessment are a hundred pounds,' he said. 'Perhaps you could pay the receptionist on your way out. Good morning, Mrs Smith.'

'A hundred pounds!' said Clarissa. 'For doing nothing! The bastard!'

'I'm so sorry,' said Florence.

'That's all right, darling. I don't mind. I'm just furious. What do we do now?'

'I don't know,' said Florence, 'I really, really don't.'

'Robert's rung already this morning. He got back very late last night. Went down to Wiltshire apparently. God knows how he got the petrol.'

'Robert can get anything out of anywhere,' said Florence miserably. 'He'll have told some lie, wangled some coupons out of somewhere, told the army I'm ill, anything.'

'Yes, well, it's the charm, darling. He has got lots. Of a rather creepy kind. Anyway, poor old Dorothy's been lying through her teeth, saying I've gone to stay with a friend. But I don't think we can hold him off yet another day. He said to tell me that he was on his way here. We have to get you somewhere. Somewhere safe – ' She looked at Florence thoughtfully. 'What about Grace?'

'Oh, I couldn't. I haven't really been very nice to Grace. She doesn't like me. And we had a bit of a fight at Christmas. She – well, she saw me with Giles once in London. She told me. I honestly don't think she'd take me in.'

'I think she would. Poor little soul. Goodness I feel sorry for her.

But anyway, we can't worry about her now.' She paused, looking at Florence thoughtfully. 'Flo, how about your father?'

'My father!'

'Yes. That'd be a safe house, surely.'

'Clarissa, I couldn't. You don't understand.'

'Darling, what is the matter with you? Of course I understand. He's only doing what you're doing. What's the big deal?'

'I – said some very hard things to him,' said Florence reluctantly. 'I can't ask him for help now. I just can't.'

'Of course you can. That's what fathers are for. I'd ask mine, only the old darling's in Scotland. Do you have a number for him?'

'Well I do, it's the Baker Street flat, but – '

'Give it to me,' said Clarissa determinedly, 'I'll deal with it. Florence, this is a state of emergency. You have to do whatever's necessary.'

Clifford was on the doorstep of Chiltern Court, his arms open, when Clarissa and Florence got out of the taxi. The porter shot forward, saluted, took her bag.

'My darling child,' he said, 'my darling, darling child. Come in. Florence, this is Jerome. Jerome, this is my daughter Florence and this beautiful creature is Clarissa Compton Brown. A veritable angel of mercy.'

Clarissa threw herself into his arms, kissed him rapturously. 'Oh I've missed you, you wicked old thing,' she said. 'Thank goodness you were here, thank goodness I thought of you.'

'And where is Robert? Do we know?'

'On his way to my house. We think he must have spent last night at a hotel. He's been down to Wiltshire looking for her, according to Dorothy. We got a couple of phone calls, but he didn't leave a number. Don't know why not,' she added.

'These people are very cunning,' said Clifford. 'He probably thought if you knew where he was, you could act accordingly.'

'What people?' said Florence wearily.

'Psychopaths, darling. That's what you're married to.'

'Oh no,' said Florence, her eyes very haunted and frightened suddenly. 'He is not a psychopath. I can't have him called that.'

'Oh Florence, don't start feeling sorry for him,' said Clarissa impatiently. 'He *is* a psychopath, Clifford's quite right, and if you're going to start feeling sorry for him it won't help you at all. Now look, Clifford, nobody knows this number, do they? Apart from Moo, I mean.'

'And she will have struggled hard to forget it, I'm sure,' said Clifford, 'but yes, Grace knows it. Now come along, both of you, into the lift, and Jerome, if you'd just pass me that bag – '

'Grace! Oh goodness, yes. Of course. Dear Grace,' said Clarissa absently, 'but anyway she won't know Florence is here, and as long as she doesn't, then we don't need to involve her. Robert will have to go back to his regiment in – what? – three days now. As long as we can keep Florence safely hidden till then, we'll be all right, we can think what to do. Is there really room for her, Clifford? It looks awfully safe and sort of hidden.'

'It is awfully safe,' said Clifford lightly. 'No one will get past Jerome. My excellent daily, Mrs Peterson, is hard at work even now, getting the spare room ready for you. I have been to Harrods, my darling, and bought some new sheets. At the most outrageous expense. I cannot imagine why this war should have put up the price of sheets.'

'You didn't need to,' said Florence. Embarrassment and remorse at her behaviour were making her monosyllabic.

Later, when Clarissa had gone, Clifford sat her down, offered her a drink.

'I imagine you are allowed to drink. If not I will drink yours as well as my own. I find I need a great deal of alcohol at the moment.'

'No, I'd love something,' said Florence, 'thank you. Sherry would be very nice. Um – so are you alone here, Daddy?'

'I am indeed. Fancy-free and free for anything fancy. As they say.'

'Oh – I see,' said Florence.

'You probably don't,' said Clifford easily, 'but let us not dwell on any of that. Florence, my darling, however sad the circumstances under which we meet, I cannot tell you how lovely it is to have you back. And how very much happier I feel.'

Florence looked at him and smiled; a warm, tender smile. 'It's lovely to be back,' she said, 'and I'm sorry about the things I said. So sorry.'

'Understandable and forgotten. Long forgotten.'

'No,' said Florence, 'I had no right. No right at all. Especially under the circumstances. It's just that – well –'

'I know. One's father should not have feet of clay. Well, let us not talk about it any more. We have more important things to discuss. Like yourself, and what we are to do about you.'

'Yes,' said Florence, 'and what on earth are we going to tell Mother?'

'Perhaps,' said Clifford, 'we should enlist Clarissa's help with that one.'

After Robert had gone, Grace sat down and cried for a long time. She still felt a sense of bereavement about her failed pregnancy, over and above her loneliness, and the prospect of greater loneliness ahead. Not only was she frigid, it seemed, she was barren as well. If she hadn't conceived then, she was surely never going to. She couldn't quite see how she was going to get through the next months, or even years: with no purpose in life, no companionship, nothing to look after, apart from a puppy. A puppy with a broken leg, she thought, smiling at Charlotte through her tears; and she wouldn't even have her if it hadn't been for Clifford.

Dear Clifford. She wondered how he was; she didn't dare phone him very often, in case Charles asked her why the phone bill was so big. Not that he'd be paying the phone bill for the foreseeable future, or seeing it, come to that: all these jobs had become hers, paying bills, dealing with tradesmen, getting things fixed. She was a little hazy about where the money was coming from these days, Charles had simply assured her that the housekeeping money would continue to be paid into her account, that the firm would continue to pay him. She sometimes wondered about it all, now that Clifford was no longer working for Bennett & Bennett, but when she had tried to raise the matter with Muriel, her mother-in-law had told her that as far as she was concerned she would continue to take all the money she needed, which was a great deal. Grace supposed it must be all right; anyway, she was doing what she was told and not asking any questions about it. As usual.

And she was doing all right at it, making a good job of running things: so far at any rate, she thought with a sudden stab of pride. She wasn't a total incompetent; and she had learnt to drive. The thought made her feel better; there must be something, something she could do. Something that Charles hadn't forbidden, or expressed a strong reservation about; something that Muriel wasn't going to quash or crush, or report her for doing. Heavens above, Grace, she thought suddenly, what has happened to you, whatever happened to the Pride of the Fifth, which Miss Murgatroyd had once called her when she'd got the winning goal in a hockey match? Or even to Miss Marchant, whom the managing director of Stubbingtons had proclaimed as totally indispensable. Become a wife, that was what, and to someone too good for her: and at this moment Grace would have given a great deal not to have done so.

She sighed at the despairing turn of her thoughts, and turned on the wireless; caught the end of *Music While You Work* and a request for 'All the girls doing such a splendid job with the Women's Land Army in Buckfastleigh and the surrounding farms in South Devon.' The Land Army! Perhaps that was something she could do. She had never mentioned that to Charles, had never even thought of it, so he had certainly not forbidden it and it sounded extremely suitable. She could probably work for the farm down the road, doing goodness knows what, but making butter or cheese or something. It would be companionship, fun, shared endeavour, something useful.

Her mother was coming over for lunch today; she would ask her about it. She knew all about everything like that.

Betty was not very enthusiastic.

'Darling, they work so hard, I've seen them, and they're very coarse, some of them, and it's not really a job for – well, someone like you.'

'Nor is stripping engines,' said Grace, 'which I'd be doing in the WRACS. Mother, I've got to do something. I'm going to go mad.'

Betty looked at her carefully. 'You haven't thought of – of, well, having – '

'No,' said Grace briefly, 'I haven't.'

'I see, dear.' Betty sighed. 'I wish you'd come home and live with us. You'd be so much less lonely.'

'Mother, I can't. You know I can't. This is my home. I have responsibilities here.' (To what? she thought, A few chickens and a puppy.)

'Yes, dear, of course you do. Well now, look, I'm going into Shaftesbury tomorrow on the bus, why don't you meet me there? It will make a nice day out for us, we can have lunch with your father, and we can go to the town hall and see what we can find out. Only I don't know what Charles will – '

'Charles isn't here,' said Grace firmly.

There were a lot of posters up in the town hall, in the recruitment room, extolling the virtues of the WRNS, the ATS, the WVS of course – and the Women's Land Army, a picture of a great long line of girls bursting through a cornfield, smiling radiantly. It was that above all that appealed to Grace. She wanted to be one of a long line of girls too.

She settled an anguished Betty in a waiting room and went to try to join them.

'Now have you any children?' said the recruiting officer (actually a harassed housewife, trying to cram the day's work into five hours before her own children came home from school, newly bereft as she was of her domestic help, who had left her for the more congenial and companionable work of the factories).

'No,' said Grace, trying to smile brightly. 'No I haven't.'

So far it had all gone well; she met all their requirements (not overexacting, over five foot, between the ages of seventeen and forty-one, her health good).

'Well, that's the main thing. And you don't have a husband at home?'

'No. He's – well, he's about to be sent overseas. That's why I want to help.'

'Yes, of course. You wouldn't prefer the WVS? Or the Red Cross?' said the recruiting officer carefully.

'No,' said Grace, firmly. 'I wouldn't.'

She knew about the WVS and the Red Cross, formed largely, in Wiltshire at any rate, of Charles's friends' wives and their mothers; the thought filled her with horror.

'Well, you see, I really don't know – '

'Look,' said Grace, 'just tell me what I have to do. And I'll do it. I don't mind what it is, clearing out pigsties, anything.'

'Yes, well, you'd certainly have to do that. But it's not a question of doing it here, near home.'

'Whyever not?' asked Grace in astonishment. 'It seems so obvious. All the farms near here, all with the young men going off.'

'Yes, I know that, but the regulations are that you go as far away as possible.'

'How far?' said Grace, envisaging perhaps a daily journey in the direction of Wells or Taunton, thinking how extremely foolish and time-wasting.

'Well, you would probably go to Yorkshire. For example. And the girls from Yorkshire would come down here.'

'Yorkshire! But why? How ridiculous, I don't see – '

'Those are the regulations,' said the recruiting officer briskly. 'The girls settle better. They are more wholehearted about it all. And there is less danger of them running off home when things get a little – tough.'

'But that would mean I'd have to live somewhere else.'

'Well, obviously.' The brisk voice sounded increasingly impatient. 'You would live in a hostel. With the other girls. Which is why – '

'Oh,' said Grace. She suddenly felt totally bleak. Yet another plan hopelessly scuppered. It wasn't fair. It just wasn't fair. But she couldn't do it, it was impossible, lock up the house, leave Charlotte, Charles would be furious, she couldn't do it. She looked at the recruiting officer through a blur of tears.

'I'm sorry,' she said, fumbling in her bag for a handkerchief, 'so sorry. I'm just so disappointed. I wanted to – '

'Look,' said the recruiting officer, sounding more sympathetic suddenly, 'look, there is something else you could do. For the Women's Land Army. If it appealed. And frankly, I do think it would be much more suitable for you – well, your situation in life.'

She means I'm too posh to join the real thing, thought Grace, blowing her nose, amused in spite of herself. If only, if only she knew.

'Do you drive?'

'Yes. Yes I do,' said Grace decisively.

'And you have some time, I imagine?'

'Yes. Lots of time.'

'Well now, there is a great, a crying need for reps for the WLA.'

'Reps?'

'Yes. It's unpaid work, I'm afraid, but quite crucial. And you'd get some kind of petrol allowance, although of course where possible we like you to use a bicycle.' She looked at Grace rather fiercely.

'Yes of course.'

'The reps visit the girls in the hostels and at the farms, investigate any complaints, make sure their living conditions are all right, that sort of thing.'

'Are they bad then?' Grace curiously.

'No, no, of course not. Well, only very occasionally,' said the woman hastily. 'But the girls do get homesick and imagine things, work themselves up into thinking they are worse than they are. It really is very worthwhile work keeping them happy, I do assure you. What would you think about that?'

'I'd think it would be wonderful,' said Grace simply.

'Good. Then I will put your name forward to the county secretary, and she will contact you. She has the final say, of course, in selecting the reps, she and her committee, but I really don't think she will be anything but very pleased to have you.'

'Thank you,' said Grace, 'thank you very much.'

Betty was clearly hugely relieved.

'So much more suitable, dear,' she kept saying over tea and some very plain sandwiches in King Alfred's Kitchen. 'I know Mrs – Muriel would have been most unhappy about your joining those girls – '

'Mother,' said Grace firmly, 'I don't care whether Muriel is happy or not.'

Soon after she got home, the phone rang; it was Mrs Boscombe. 'Could you ring the Regents Park number, dear? As soon as possible. And the major rang. He'll phone later. About seven. He sounds very well, dear. No need to worry about him.'

'Good,' said Grace, 'thank you.'

She asked Mrs Boscombe to get her Clifford's number. It rang for a long time; maybe he had gone out. It was only a flat; it couldn't take long to get to the phone. Finally it was picked up and a voice answered, said hallo rather hesitantly: only it wasn't Clifford and it wasn't Mary Saunders. It was Florence.

Grace put the phone down again immediately, her heart thundering. Now what did she do? What on earth was Florence doing there? She and Clifford had been totally estranged since his departure, she had said some very hard things to him, Muriel had reported with some satisfaction, and had refused to see him since. Hiding, Grace supposed, with a rush of disdain and distaste, hiding from Robert, afraid to confront him. Poor Robert, sad, gentle Robert who had been kinder to her than anyone she could remember for a long time. Whom she had promised to help. Well, she would. She had sat on the fence for quite long enough. She owed it to him to repay his kindness to her and, besides, she wanted to. Florence deserved everything she got. Everything.

The phone in Robert's house was picked up instantly; not by him, but by the maid.

No, Major Grieg wasn't there, he was out for supper with some friends, but he would be back at nine, and had said specifically that he would return any calls then. Could she ask who was calling?

'Mrs Bennett,' said Grace firmly, 'Mrs Charles Bennett. He has my number.'

'Thank you, Mrs Bennett.'

Charles phoned about half an hour later.

'Darling, how are you?'

'I'm fine, thank you,' said Grace. Wishing, wishing so desperately she could tell him she wasn't, tell him why.

'I've been missing you so much.'

'I've missed you too.'

'I've got my posting. That is to say we've got our posting.'

'Oh,' said Grace, feeling bleaker than ever.

'We're off to North Africa. In a week. Can't tell you more than that.'

'Oh. Oh Charles, no – '

'Now, darling, you've got to be brave. We've all got to be brave. Anyway, I've got a thirty-six-hour leave. Look, I can't get down there, no time, no petrol allowance, nothing. I want you to come and meet me in London. Can you manage that, do you think?'

'Yes of course I can,' said Grace, feeling slightly affronted. This was after all, the woman who had driven all the way from Thorpe St Andrews to Thorpe Magna and back again.

'Good girl. We can't go to the flat of course because my father's there, but we could stay in a hotel for the night. The Basil Street, I thought. Awfully nice. Give ourselves a bit of a treat. It is the last time for a while, after all.'

'How lovely,' said Grace, struggling to sound enthusiastic.

'I'm longing to see you, darling. Really longing.'

Captain Robert Grieg reached home at eight forty-five. The maid gave him the only message. 'Mrs Bennett phoned, sir. She said you knew the number.'

'Indeed I do. Thank you, Clarkson. I'll go to my study.'

He thumbed through his address book looking for Grace's number. There it was. He reached out his hand to pick up the phone: it beat him to it, rang sharply, harshly.

'Robert?'

'Yes. Yes, Mother.'

'Dear, I just wanted to say goodbye. I know you're going back to Yorkshire in the morning. Take care of yourself, dear, and do try to write. Have you got a proper posting yet?'

'Hoping for Gib.'

'Please let me know when you have. Will it be soon?'

'Yes, I imagine so, Mother. When I get back, probably.'

'Well, all the very best, my dear. And Robert, do please try and write to your grandmother as well. She worries about you so.'

'Yes, Mother, very well. Look, I – '

'And there's one more thing, Robert. I sent you some socks and a jersey and some books. Did you ever get them? Because I didn't hear anything – '

'Yes, Mother, I did and I'm so sorry. It's pretty hectic up there, you know.'

'I'm sure it is, dear. And we're so proud of you. Is Florence all right? I do wish she'd come and stay with us here, out of London. It must be so dangerous.'

'It's all right at the moment, Mother. Thank you. But I'll tell her. And yes, she's fine.'

'Good. Well, goodbye, dear. Do try and keep us posted. And take great care of yourself. Won't you?'

'Yes, Mother, I will. Of course. Thank you. And goodbye. Don't worry about me.'

'I'll try not to, darling. Goodbye.'

'Goodbye, Mother.'

He put the phone down thankfully. Now for Grace.

'Grace? Grace, this is Clifford. How are you, my dear?'

'I'm fine, Clifford, thank you.'

'Good, good. Now listen. I have Florence here.'

'Yes, I know. I spoke to her.'

'Grace, she is in serious trouble.'

'Oh really?' said Grace.

'Yes, she really is. Very serious. Robert is – well, let us just say that Robert is not all that he seems. I had suspected it for some time.'

'I don't understand,' said Grace.

'Well – oh dear, this is very difficult. He has been – violent towards her. Quite violent. Beaten her several times.'

'Oh Clifford! Clifford, surely not, I can't believe that.'

'Grace, it's true. You must believe me. Anyway, Florence is here, and it is crucial that he doesn't know. He has to go back to his regiment tomorrow and then she will be safe. So if by any chance he tries to contact you, asks you if you know where she is, would you – '

'You want me to lie to him?' said Grace. Her voice sounded hard even to her.

There was a silence. Then Clifford said, 'Yes. I suppose I do. I really cannot have him finding her here. It would be very dangerous for her. Please respect my wishes in this, Grace. Please.'

Grace hesitated. If anyone, anyone else in the world had made that request she would have refused. She could not refuse Clifford. She loved him too much, owed him too much.

'All right, Clifford,' she said, 'I won't. Goodbye.'

'Goodbye, my dear. And thank you.'

The phone rang again almost at once. It was Robert.

'Grace! How are you? Feeling better?'

'Yes. Yes, thank you, Robert.'

So gentle, so sweet he was; it couldn't be true, that he was violent, had beaten Florence, it was unimaginable –

'Good,' he was saying, 'and remember, there's always next time.'

'Yes. Of course.'

'I enjoyed our little interlude. It was lovely.'

'Yes, I did too. And thank you again for all you did.'

'My pleasure. Anyway, you rang?'

'Yes. Yes, I did.'

'Any particular reason?'

A long silence. Grace felt torn still, longing to help him, longing to keep her promise. But she had made a more recent, more binding one to Clifford. She couldn't do it.

'No,' she said finally, 'no. Only to wish you good luck. And to say goodbye. Send me a postcard.'

'How sweet of you.' There was another silence, then: 'That was really all, was it, Grace?'

'Yes. Yes, it really was.'

'No news from Florence?'

'No. No, I'm afraid not.'

'Well, never mind. I'm here till the morning, then I have to get the milk train. Back on duty at mid-day. So it's still not too late. I'm so worried about her, so afraid something might have happened to her, I can't sleep for worry. I love her so much, Grace, so much – '

'Robert – '

'Yes, Grace?'

Out in the hall Charlotte was yelping furiously; she had slipped on the polished floor and hurt her leg. Grace told Robert to hang on, put the phone down, went to pick her up, to comfort her. Trying to buy herself time to think. And knew she must not, could not do it, betray Clifford. She didn't believe a word of this violence nonsense. Robert might have threatened Florence, with good reason if he had discovered what was going on; but he would not, could not have hit her. It just wasn't in him. He was too good, too gentle, he loved her too much. Florence had just made it up, to make herself look less blameworthy, to excuse her behaviour. Grace would never, ever believe anything else. But – she had promised Clifford. Whom she loved more than any of them.

She went back to the phone and picked it up. 'Sorry, Robert. One hurt puppy.'

'How is she? Sweet little thing.'

'She's fine. Thank you. Look, that's all, Robert. Take care of yourself. And come and see me next time you're home. I'm sure Florence is fine. Don't worry about her.'

'All right, Grace. I'll try not to. Goodbye. God bless.'

'Darling, darling, darling. Oh, God, thank God! Where are you, what are you doing?'

Clarissa stood in the hall of her house in London and tried to digest what Jack was doing: going up alone in his tiny plane, day after day, again and again, coming down, refuelling, going up again into the skies filled with noise and fire and death, pitting himself and his plane against the enemy aircraft – 'And once you're up there, you do feel you're alone, all alone in that hellfire of a sky.' Daytime was better, he said, at least you could see what you were doing; 'And they always seem to be above us, I don't know why. But it's fine, I'm fine, I keep coming through. Worst thing is the tiredness. So that isn't very serious. I tell you what, though. I've started to pray.'

'Keep praying. Loudly. Aren't you scared?'

'Yes, I'm scared. Shit-scared. Our squadron leader says anyone who says he isn't is a bloody liar. But only before, and after. When you're up there, you don't have time, time for anything, time to think even. You just keep going.'

'Oh Jack, darling, take care of yourself. Stay safe.'

'I will, Clarissa. Honestly, I'm fine. Charmed life. Don't worry. We're keeping Jerry away. We really are the superior force. Load of tram drivers they are in those planes. Not like us.'

'Oh darling, I hope so.'

'I know so. Look, I've been promised some leave in August. You're not in the Wrens yet?'

'No, but I soon will be. But don't worry, I'll desert to be with you.'

'Christ, I've got to go. Scramble. Bye, darling, I love you.'

'I love you too.'

Charles's leave was not a success. Grace had a nightmare journey to London, and found a very different situation from the eerie peace of her last visit. There was still no immediate danger, no bombing, but there was a sense of urgency that had not been there before, an atmosphere of toughness, signs everywhere to shelters, shops empty of goods. Shop and office windows were boarded up, sandbags piled in readiness in doorways; children played in the side streets, their schools closed. The only thing that seemed to have been reversed was the exodus from London. Offices were filling up again, long stretches of houses no longer for sale; it was as if people had decided to get back to real life, to stop trying to take it with them.

She and Charles ate dinner in a slightly strained silence; it was a very good dinner, giving the lie to the reports of various shortages that were supposed to be absolutely across the board, but she couldn't think of anything to say to him. She had no news, had seen no one; his mother was a dangerous area, and so was Florence, his father was not to be mentioned, she could not discuss her plans. She tried to encourage him to talk, which he did, but the stories were endlessly tedious, about exercises and training and the comparative merits of his men, and he was undoubtedly also nervous as well as excited about the next day, conscious of how momentous a parting it was to be.

'Well, that was a lovely dinner,' said Charles, over the coffee. 'Brandy, darling? You look terribly tired.'

'I'm fine,' said Grace, forcing a quick smile. 'Really. You must be exhausted though.'

'Not too bad. As I said, we've mostly been defending the south coast which in effect has meant putting up bloody great rolls of barbed wire on the beaches and watching the dogfights overhead. The little planes, you know? Jack's up there somewhere. I hope to God he's all right. Bloody brave, those chaps.'

'Yes,' said Grace.

'Darling, are you all right? You seem awfully blue.'

'Yes, I'm all right. Honestly. Sorry.'

Quite suddenly he said, 'My mother seems to think you're in contact with my father.'

'Oh really?' said Grace, wondering, fiercely angry, how Muriel might have known, why she had told Charles, not mentioned it to her. 'Yes, it's true.'

'Why is that?'

'He rings me sometimes. To keep in touch. To see how I am,' she added. 'Not many people do that. And how you are. He worries about you so much.'

'That,' he said briefly, 'is disgraceful. Oh I don't blame you. At least not to any real extent. But he has no business to try and keep in touch with the family via you. I know you were rather a pet of his. He's playing on your good nature, Grace, and you must not allow it.'

'I'm sorry?'

'You are not to speak to him if he rings you again, to have anything to do with him in future. Is that clear?'

'I'm not sure, Charles. Actually.'

'I can't imagine why not. I repeat, I don't want you to have anything to do with my father. Anything at all. It would be the most gross disloyalty to my mother and to me, and to Florence for that matter, if you did.'

'You mean you're forbidding me?'

'Yes. Yes, I suppose I am. If it comes to it. But surely that will not be necessary. I cannot imagine you would wish to see him.'

Grace was silent; she could see a full-scale row blowing up and she simply couldn't face it. It really didn't matter; it might have mattered if Charles was going to be at home, but he wasn't.

There was a long, awkward silence, then Charles said, 'Shall we listen to the news? I noticed there was a set in our room.'

After the news, which was predictable and bleak and told of the continuing bombardment of the coast, of German warplanes sighted just about everywhere, of the bombing of a destroyer just off Dover, Charles turned it off and said, 'Well, that's it. Bed, darling?'

'Yes,' said Grace, trying to smile, wincing within herself at the thought. 'Yes, bed.'

She lay there hating it, almost hating him, hating herself. When it was over, Charles turned away from her in silence and fell straight to sleep.

She tried to talk to him the next day, to explain how lonely she felt, how useless her life seemed, but it was a pointless exercise. She said again that she would like to join one of the services (carefully not mentioning the Land Army); he sat and looked at her, his face a careful blank.

'You know my views on all this,' was all he said. 'I don't know why you are still pursuing it. I may be away, Grace, but you are still my wife. It will make things a great deal harder for me if I feel you are going against my wishes.'

'But Charles, why can't I be your wife and be useful, and do something – something to help?'

'Grace darling,' he said, 'your duty is to help me. By being at home, where I want you to be. It seems to me a little loneliness is a small price for you to pay.'

Grace gave up.

She went to see him off on the Sunday evening, at Victoria. He tried to dissuade her, but she was adamant. The station was teeming with soldiers, sweethearts and wives clinging to them; Grace watched almost in tears as a young RAF man held his wife in his arms, gazing at her with a terrible intentness as if trying to memorize every feature, every inch of her face, every hair, every eyelash. And when he left she stood staring after him, as if she would never move again.

Charles kissed Grace tenderly, held her close. 'Take care of yourself, darling. I'll write lots. And maybe next time I see you the war will be over, and we can be together, properly together. Start a family.'

'Oh Charles, I – yes. Maybe. Let's hope it is. Over I mean. Take care of yourself, Charles. I love you.'

At that moment, in spite of everything, she did.

His train was delayed. He told her to go, that he couldn't bear the thought of her hanging around, maybe for hours. 'I'll sit here, have a cup of tea, probably find one or two of the chaps. You go, darling. I'd rather.'

Grace left. She felt quite numb: not even properly unhappy. She wondered what could be the matter with her.

In the morning, on the endless journey across London by bus, she read newspaper placards that said 'Croydon Airport bombed'. It all seemed to be getting terribly close. Perhaps, Grace thought, it was just as well she wasn't having a baby. This was a terrible world to bring a child into.

As the bus trundled towards Waterloo, she saw a soldier, an officer, sitting in Sloane Square, his head buried in his arms, the epitome of dejection and despair. He seemed to her to capture the mood of the day, her own mood indeed. He also looked, what could be seen of him, rather like Charles. Which made it doubly poignant.

'Christ, it's begun!' said Linda. 'Hasn't it?'

The sirens went off, mid-afternoon; she and Nan and the boys went down into the Anderson shelter Ben had dug in the garden. She remembered his words as he had toiled: 'It's the end of my vegetables,' he said, 'but never mind. Worth it. For you.'

They were all fairly frightened. It was Saturday; a beautiful day it had been. She and Nan had been sitting just outside the back door and she had been waiting for the right moment to tell her she was going out that night with Janice when the sirens had gone off. The German aircraft had been coming up the Thames, so many of them, the warden told them afterwards, the sky had been black, hundreds of them in their square block formation, the RAF firing on them relentlessly as they came. The target was the docks; far from Acton, from where they were, but they could hear the noise easily, the endless roar of the planes and then the dreadful sound of the bombing, carried through the still, clear air.

They sat in the shelter for a long time; the noise stopped briefly at dusk, then started again. Daniel started to cry, said he wanted the toilet, and she ran into the house to fetch the chamber pot; later on Nan used it too. On and on it went for hours, stopping briefly at dusk. Linda went into the house, gazing awestruck at a great mushroom of smoke in the distance across London. She fetched some more blankets, made a thermos of tea, relieved her own throbbing bladder, then, as it started again, clambered back into the shelter. All night they sat there, dipping occasionally into sleep. Later the sound crescendoed, bombs dropping nearer as the attack reached out from the docks and the first shelling of the West End began. 'The whole bloody world's on fire,' said Linda to Nan quietly over the boys' heads; Nan gripped her hand, met her eyes in a surprisingly cheerful smile. Old bag's not all bad, thought Linda, smiling back. Nan's courage throughout the night fuelled her own. The all clear went off as dawn broke, and they climbed out, cold and stiff, thankful for some fresh air, gazing across at the great red terrifying glow of the sky on the other side of London. This time it was over; but it was going to happen again and again. And again.

'I'm sending the boys back,' said Linda, 'back to the country. Back where it's safe.'

David promptly burst into tears; Daniel said, 'Will my rabbit still be there?'

'Course it will,' said Linda. 'David, don't cry. You can't stay here, you don't want any more nights like that, do you?'

'It was all right,' said David staunchly.

'I liked it,' said Daniel.

'Well, you're not staying and that's all there is to it,' said Linda. 'I'm going to see the lady at the council tomorrow.'

The lady at the council was disdainful. 'We advised you against bringing them back,' she said. 'Now everyone wants their children safe again and there aren't the billets for them.'

'Why not?' said Linda. 'Why the bleeding hell not, if everyone brought their kids back? You've got to help.'

'There is no need for that kind of language, Mrs Lucas. We are doing our best, I do assure you.'

'Sorry,' said Linda. She was very upset; along with the rest of London she was stunned, reeling with shock. The night following the first raid, a second had followed, 200 bombers pounding the East End relentlessly. The death toll was unimaginable already. 'I've got to get them away,' she said, and was horrified to find herself beginning to cry. 'I've got to.'

'Well now, where were your children, Mrs Lucas?'

'Yorkshire,' said Linda, 'village called Patley.'

'It's really most unlikely we can place them where they were. You cannot expect people to just take them back as if nothing had happened. It was very difficult for them, you know, when the children were removed. After all their kindness. Now I'll see what I can do, let you know, but I'm not promising anything.'

'Yeah, all right,' said Linda, and then smiled as sweetly as she could. 'Sorry about earlier. Bad weekend, you know?' She needed to keep the old hag on her side. 'Thank you. Thank you ever so much.'

The image of being a Wren, Clarissa thought, as she filled her pail with hot soapy water in the dim grey dawn, had not been too much like this. She had seen herself on the deck of a destroyer, looking wonderfully chic in her navy and white, standing next to a dashing captain who would turn to her and say, 'Well done, First Officer Compton Brown, you've just helped win a great battle.'

Here she was, a Pro-Wren, in the most hideous overalls, they hadn't even got their uniforms yet, in some hideous building in North London, sleeping in a hugely uncomfortable bunk in what they called a cabin in their ridiculous way, in charge of the 4am shift. And the 4am shift was not engaged in spotting enemy warships or reading radar screens or even learning Morse code so that she could take down complex and vital signals from other ships; her particular task was scrubbing down the stairs each day. And getting all the other forty-seven girls up. That was her major duty, more irksome than anything else she had to do. The barking old harridan who had briefed them all at the end of their first two days had told Clarissa she looked like someone who could get other people organized; Clarissa had been quite pleased then, had even modestly agreed. Now, as she stood by the bunks of the soundest sleepers, first telling them, then shaking them and ordering them to get up, on the receiving end of a great deal of foul language, she would have given anything to be an organizee. Most of the girls were quite nice; a few were poison. Girls from working-class homes who saw it as their duty to give her and the others like her a hard time.

'Oh excuse me!' one May Potter had said to her (Clarissa remembered her vaguely from the interview day, sitting with a friend and whispering – the friend it seemed had not been accepted), her voice heavy with sarcasm as she had asked politely if Clarissa had finished with the rather scummy water she had left in the washbasin they were sharing the first evening, 'So sorry, madam, I expect your maid runs the water for you at home.'

'No, actually,' said Clarissa with her sweet smile. 'No, I do that. And I turn down my own bed. Well, on her night off anyway.'

She had meant it as a joke; it had misfired. From then on a small faction, led by May, nicknamed her Duchess, imitated her accent, her habit of waving her hands around when she talked, the meticulous cleanse-tone-and-nourish skin-care routine recommended by Miss Arden that she refused to abandon, even on the nights when lights out caught her unfinished and she had to do it in the dark.

'Oh may deah' would come a voice through the darkness, 'Ay cannot seem to faind my naight craim. Could you ask may maid to have a look for it' – followed by fits of giggles.

Clarissa, who had never known unkindness in her life, whose blithe disposition had carved a carefree way for her, even at school, was at first surprised then shocked and hurt by this. There were several other middle-class girls from good families in the cabin, but they were less excessive in their behaviour, and did not attract the same attention. And observing Clarissa's growing unpopularity, they tended to avoid her, lest they attracted some of it to themselves. She pretended she didn't care, told herself it wasn't for long, but it hurt a lot.

Never mind, she told herself as she started work on the top step, looking dismally down the twenty-four to the bottom, it was only for six weeks. She could stick it; she was going to stick it. If Jack could risk his life every single day, several times a day, she could cope with a bit of ragging.

'You,' the chief officer had said to the girls as they sat in the reception hall at Mill Hill the night they arrived, 'are very special and fortunate young women. The WRNS is the finest, the best women's service. It is a great privilege to serve them. You should be aware of that. It is an honour and a fine tradition you will always carry with you now, long after this war is over; once a Wren always a Wren.'

There had been a lot more in that vein; none of it seemed, Clarissa thought, wearily squeezing out her cloth, to have a great deal to do with washing stairs. The only thing she really enjoyed was learning to march and salute; that at least seemed to have some connection with the life of her imagination. She supposed she was luckier than some;

several of the girls were almost ill with homesickness, having never left home and their mothers before. The sound of muffled crying in the cabin at night was not unusual.

At least, at least Jack was safe – for now. He had come through the Battle of Britain, her hero, one of the Few, to whom, as Mr Churchill had so wonderfully said, so much was owed by so many. He had been awarded the DSO and was now briefly in a comparatively peaceful backwater, a C Squadron, providing a back-up and training resource for pilots from other commands.

They had had what seemed now an unbelievably rapturous forty-eight hours together, when they had scarcely left the great double bed in their house in Campden Hill except to fetch food or more champagne from the kitchen (the six cases Clifford had given them as a wedding present were becoming rapidly depleted), and then had parted, he for Catterick in Yorkshire, she for her new life in Mill Hill. Some of the experiences they had shared during those two days and nights were so profound, so intense in their pleasure that the mere memory of them could still stir Clarissa, disturb her physically.

Which was just as well, she thought, as she clearly wasn't going to get any more sex for a very long time.

'Oh ay'm so sorry!' It was her tormentor, May Potter; she had managed to slip and kick the bucket from the top to the bottom of the stairs. 'So sorry. Ay wish ay could help clear it up, but ay have to make the breakfast.'

Beastly girl. How on earth had she got into the WRNS anyway, Clarissa wondered, with their interminable emphasis on choosing only quality young woman, only the best? She looked at May wearily over her cloth and then smiled sweetly at her. She had had enough. 'Just fuck off will you,' she said, 'PDQ. All right?'

May looked at her, startled, and for the first time an expression of faint respect came into her pale blue eyes.

'Pardon me I'm sure,' was all she said, but Clarissa knew she had won something. Not a war, not even a battle, but a skirmish. She smiled cheerfully at the petty officer who was ordering her to get on down and clear up the mess. She had enjoyed that little interlude more than anything else since she had arrived in the place.

Florence had had to tell Muriel something of her problems in the end; she needed a refuge, at least until Robert was safely overseas. She had managed to keep her pregnancy to herself – she was still very thin, and the slightly burgeoning stomach only showed when she was naked, which Muriel was certainly not going to witness. She merely told her mother she and Robert had been having problems, that he had threatened her, and she wanted to keep out of his way until he had left the country. Muriel told her she was not a fool, that she was tired of being taken for one, and asked exactly what kind of problems; Florence told her with extreme reluctance that she had been having a relationship with someone else, but that Robert didn't know and it had nothing to do with his alarming behaviour. Muriel, icily disapproving, was nevertheless persuaded to tell him that Florence had been in Cornwall with her; he clearly didn't believe her, but there was very little he could do about it. He was being posted to Gibraltar, leaving in ten days; there was no more leave due to him. Florence spoke to him, said how desperately sorry she was to have missed him, that she was now at the Priory to stay with her mother.

Robert appeared to accept this, told her he loved her, gave her an address to write to, said he would write often, and would look forward to seeing her on his next leave. Slightly unnerved by his lack of aggression, Florence said meekly that of course she would write, and when she knew he was at least four days out at sea, left Wiltshire for London.

She felt possessed of a deathly weariness; due not only to her pregnancy, but to the relief from the immediate strain and terror, and to her grief at her separation from Giles. His ship was due to sail in a week; he had put in for leave, but married officers were being given priority. There was little hope of her seeing him for many months: if ever again, she thought in her lowest moments.

She felt not only unhappy, but as if she could not remember what happiness was like.

Three days after Charles sailed, Grace received a letter.

My dearest Grace,
This is just to tell you that I love you. Please take care of yourself, and of course Mother. She is far more vulnerable than she appears. For this reason I would reiterate that I do not wish you to have any contact with my father whatsoever.

I am aware that life must be lonely for you, and I do sympathize. However, I am more happy than I can tell you that you are not intending to join any of the services. It makes me feel very much better when I am in danger to know that you are not.

Take care of yourself, and be waiting for me when I come home to you.
Charles

This did not have quite the effect on Grace that he might have hoped for; the complacency, the lack of imagination, the high-handedness were all, in her still raw disappointment over her pregnancy, her distress over Florence and Robert, more than she could endure. 'That settles it,' she said aloud, tears of rage rather than misery welling in her eyes, blurring the lines of his letter. 'Land Army here I come. And I'm going to take in some evacuees.'

Chapter Twelve

Winter 1940

'Pregnant!' said Muriel. 'But I don't understand.'

'There isn't a lot to understand, Mother,' said Florence. She was trying to keep calm.

'I thought you and Robert were – '

'Yes, well, these things still happen.'

'Well, as long as the child is Robert's. I would not wish – '

'Of course it's Robert's,' said Florence wearily. 'Anyway, I think I should come and stay here with you, now that he's gone. If that's all right,' she added.

'Of course it's all right. I've been urging you to move down here for months. Quite apart from anything else it would be very nice for me to have some company. I don't think anyone quite realizes how lonely I have been. If they do, they haven't taken much trouble to show it, or do anything about it.'

Florence felt genuine remorse; she found her mother hard to get on with, to live with, quailed indeed at what lay ahead, but she was very fond of her, and in her more clearsighted (and depressed) moments recognized that she was not unlike Muriel. She shared her mother's considerable capacity for hard work, her rather bleak perceptiveness, her tactless, taut manner, and what everyone mistook for unfriendliness and was actually an acute shyness. Florence envied Charles and her father their ease of manner more than anything in the world. One of the things that had first made her fall in love with Giles was his saying, 'I don't know why you're so afraid of being yourself.' It summed her up so exactly, revealed such an understanding of her inability to relax, to accept herself for what she was, to believe that anyone might want to be with her, to hear what she had to say.

It was those very shortcomings and insecurities that had led her to accept Robert Grieg's proposal of marriage, when she had known she didn't love him, combined with the fact that someone was going to rescue her from the wretched state of spinsterhood at the advanced age of twenty-eight.

Had she not been pregnant, she might have stayed in London, stayed in the house; but the twin fears of Robert still, somehow, managing to turn up, from Gibraltar and of the German bombers seeking her out, demolishing her and Giles's child, drove her to the admittedly irksome sanctuary of Wiltshire. It would be boring there, achingly, numbingly boring; her mother had told her repeatedly about petrol rationing, food shortages, the lack of distraction. The thought of the long days, empty of any kind of congenial companionship and occupation, frightened Florence almost as much as the threat of Robert and the Germans. But in – what? – less than four months now she would have her baby. And for that baby, and for Giles, she could endure anything.

'Look,' said Muriel, 'if you're going to come, the sooner the better. Let me know some train times and I'll meet you in Salisbury.'

'I need a few days to lock up the house,' said Florence. 'I'll come on Monday, if that's all right.'

'I suppose so. I'll get your room ready. I don't quite know where we're going to put a baby,' she added, as if the Priory was a small bungalow rather than an eight-bedroomed house, and a baby some kind of large beast in need of stabling. 'And of course Nanny has long retired, you'll have to manage on your own.'

Florence said she thought that would be just about all right and put the phone down.

Without being quite sure why, Florence packed up as much as she could. Packing cases were an unimaginable a luxury as cream and fresh fruit, but she dragged all the empty suitcases up from the cellar and filled them with the silver, with books, with pictures, with china. When the war was over, she felt, she would like to come back to neatness and order, take repossession, in the event of the house not being bombed: increasingly unlikely these days, as the Germans bombarded the capital with relentless efficiency. It seemed to be disappearing under a mountain of rubble and flames, not just the East End and the docks, but large areas of the West End now as well, Berkeley Square, Bruton Street, a stretch of Oxford Street; Madame Tussauds, the Tower of London, even Buckingham Palace had all been hit. The wail of fire engines, the crash as unsafe walls were demolished were as familiar a sound as the air-raid sirens. And yet in between the chaos and the raids, people continued to function in the most extraordinary calm, almost casual way, picking their way through rubble, broken pavements, gazing into what shop windows were left, chatting, gossiping. It was a remarkable display of sangfroid.

Florence envied them from the bottom of her heart. She would have given anything to have a job to go to, a purpose in life, a distraction. Well, she was about to have one, she thought, patting her swelling stomach tenderly; and she had to do all she could to safeguard its arrival.

She pushed and pulled the cases into the kitchen, where they were at least not visible from the street, swathed the furniture in dustsheets, checked the blackout, pulled the curtains, pausing often, caught up in memories, surprised at how many of them were happy: the good days with Robert when he had said he was sorry, he loved her, would never hurt her again, the parties they had given, the friends who had come, the lovely London evenings, when they had sat in the window of the drawing room drinking martinis and reading, her first pregnancy, before Giles, when she had felt herself so happy. And then the hideous ones, the beatings, the fear, the day he knocked her downstairs – what had triggered that? An overlong phone call to a friend, some flowers left in a vase too long, one drink too many? She really could not remember now. And then the feverish, rapturous start of her love affair, the shaky joyous terror of the coded phone calls, the first nervy meetings, the long, stolen afternoons of love. All over, all gone, wrapped up, shrouded like her house.

On her last evening, feeling a most painful mixture of regret and relief, she settled in the basement kitchen, as safe as she could be from air raids – it was amazing how one adjusted to the constant danger, adopted an attitude of fatalism, almost carelessness. Everyone said if you survived three you stopped worrying, and it was true. She made herself a sandwich, poured herself a large whisky – she had found a store of the stuff in the cellar – and settled down to read. She tried not to listen to the news if she was on her own; it frightened her. The booming tones of Mr Churchill telling her this was her finest hour made her dismally aware that it was not.

She wondered what she would most like to be doing if she wasn't pregnant: joining the Wrens like Clarissa she supposed. She admired Clarissa so much. Underneath all that excessiveness, affectedness, she was brave, kind, determinedly cheerful. Her courage through the Battle of Britain when Jack could have been killed daily, hourly, had been extraordinary. Others thought it absurd for Clarissa to be fussing over her clothes, her hair, a party she had to attend, but Florence understood; it was a front, a dressing up of herself, a blithe game so that no one might see the raw, gut-wrenching fear that lay beneath.

Within her, she suddenly felt a strange stirring, a rippling; startled, she waited, wondering what it could be. Wind, she supposed.

Heavens above, pregnancy was unromantic. It came again and then again. 'Oh,' said Florence aloud, 'oh my God, it's the baby,' and she sat staring at her stomach, awed, touched almost beyond endurance at the thought that within it lay this little creature, made by love, tentatively stretching out its tiny limbs, biding its time most carefully until it was ready to venture forth.

And as she sat there, quite still, waiting for, willing it to start again, she heard a noise: a noise at the bottom of the basement steps. Again it came, and then a shuffling; and as she tried to believe it was a rat, a cat, there was a very faint clearing of a male throat. Fear clutched at Florence, absolute in its intensity; she gripped the arms of her chair, held her breath, sweat pricking in her armpits, bile rising in her throat. Robert! It was Robert. It had all been a trick, a lie, he wasn't in Gibraltar at all, he had come back to kill her. She stood up very slowly and carefully, picked up the marble rolling pin that was the nearest thing she could see to a weapon and began to move quietly up the steps, to the hall, the hall where there was a telephone. She could phone the police and – only, only of course she had had it cut off. And then she was really frightened; she knew what people meant about their bowels turning to water. She stood there, a hot white terror rushing through her, overtaking her body, holding the rolling pin, staring at the front door huge-eyed, biting her lips so hard she drew blood.

And then there was a gentle, a very gentle knock; she stood silent, waiting, praying for it to be nothing, no one, the wind, a visiting ARP warden, anything, cursing the ill-luck that had sent a cloudy night and no bombing to London.

But it came again, slightly louder. She put her hand over her mouth now, afraid she would scream, and then something came through the letterbox: a piece of paper, a note. How strange, thought Florence, less afraid suddenly, bending down to pick it up, still stealthily silent. It was not a piece of paper at all but a visiting card, and it said – oh God, oh God, thought Florence, weak with relief, with sheer disbelieving happiness – it said: *Giles Henry. Pianist.*

She flew at the door then, scrabbling at the bolts, the locks, sobbing, laughing with joy, opened it, stood there staring in total disbelief at him, at Giles, her darling, her love.

'Our embarkation was delayed,' he said, in between kissing her face, her hands, her hair, 'for ten days. They gave me twenty-four hours. I tried to phone, but – '

'I know, I had it cut off,' she said, taking his hand, pressing it to her mouth, her tears falling on it. 'I thought you'd gone, I was afraid of Robert ringing – '

'But he's gone.'

'Yes. I told you, to Gibraltar. But – well, never mind. Oh, darling, darling, if you'd been one day later I'd have been gone.'

'Where to?'

'To my mother. In deepest Wiltshire.'

'I'm glad you're going. And thank God,' he said, 'that I came, risked it. I couldn't be sure, you see, that he wouldn't be here. But I thought – well, it was unlikely. And I was looking for signs of life before I rang the bell.'

'I heard you. Nearly brought on a miscarriage,' said Florence.

'Oh God,' he said, 'the baby, let me, let me see.'

And she pulled up her skirt and they sat on the stairs, gazing in awe and some pride at her now uncompromisingly swollen stomach. 'He was kicking,' she said proudly, 'earlier. It was the most exciting thing I can ever remember.'

Giles put out his hand, tenderly stroked her bulge.

Later, they lay in bed; he was holding her gently, afraid to hurt her, he said, he didn't want to risk hurting the baby.

'The baby will be fine,' said Florence. 'Listen.'

She reached out to the bedside for a large book. 'During the second trimester,' she read aloud, 'sexual intercourse is permissible, providing care is taken and the mother rests afterwards.'

'What's the second trimester?'

'It's now. The middle three months.'

'And what is this book?'

'It's called *Pregnancy and Childbirth* and it's very comprehensive. I know all about labour and breastfeeding and everything. It's my nightly reading.'

'Oh darling. Are you frightened? Of having it?'

'Terrified,' said Florence cheerfully, 'but my mother will probably be there, so I won't be able to make the least fuss. Anyway, I'm not having it yet, and I want to have you.'

She lay, naked, and felt her body, starved of him for months, opening to him. Her pregnancy seemed to have made her tighter, yet more fluid; every moment, every movement of him was newly intense, newly sweet. He entered her slowly, tenderly, asking her again and again if it was all right, not hurting; again and again she told him no, no, it was wonderful, impatient and cautious herself at the same time. She felt herself gathering for him, tautly sweet, felt her juices start to flow, felt the growing, burgeoning, pushing deep within herself, felt the white, blinding lightness going further, deeper, higher, impossibly far, heard a strange shriek that she knew must be herself, and then knew the wonderful untangling, tumbling release as she fell beneath him into the sweet dark peace.

Later as they lay together, smiling, she felt the baby again, stirring; she put his hand on her stomach, hoping he could feel it too, but the movement was too small, too delicate to detect.

'He liked that,' she said, 'he approved.'

'You must lie,' he said, 'and rest, like the book says. Can I get you some tea? Milk?'

'I was drinking whisky,' she said, 'I'd love some more of that.'

'I'm not sure you should have it. In your condition.'

'Boring old prig,' she said. 'All right, I'll have some hot milk. With whisky in it. Would that make you happy?'

'Happier. Only I couldn't be happier. I love you, Florence.'

'I love you, Giles.'

He had to leave early in the morning; she sat on the stairs hugging her knees, watching him put on his coat, his hat, trying to be brave, struggling not to cry, to be a good memory for him, a happy one. He came and sat beside her as he had the night before, holding her, kissing her hair.

'When this foul thing is over,' he said, 'I will come back for you, and we will be married, and everything will be perfect. All we have to do is be patient and endure it till then.'

'Yes,' she said, 'yes of course.'

'Take care of yourself, my darling darling love. And of the baby, our baby. Let me know, somehow, when he is safely here.'

'I will,' she said, 'of course I will.'

'I have to go,' he said, and his voice was rough, unwilling. 'I have to go and I don't know how I can.'

'Yes, you can. You must. Don't miss your train. Just because of me.'

'Oh Florence,' he said, 'Florence, it's the only reason I can stand all this, just because of you. The fear and the boredom and the loneliness and the futility of it. I would do anything, brave anything, just because of you. I love you. And I will be back for you. I promise you. Somehow, I will come back. Goodbye.'

'Goodbye,' she said and stood up suddenly, pulling herself out of his arms abruptly, harshly, because otherwise she would have sat there for ever. 'Go quickly. I love you, Giles. Stay safe.'

And the door opened and she shut her eyes, because she could not bear to see him go through it, and put her fingers in her ears so that she could not hear his feet on the steps, and when he had finally vanished into the cold dark morning she went on staring, staring for a long time at the place where he had been, as if somehow she could will him back again. Only she couldn't, and time and distance took him further and further away from her, him and the warmth of him and the tenderness of him and the love of him. And then she was really alone.

'Mrs Bennett?'

'Yes.'

'Mrs Bennett, I have your name down here as a possible billet for evacuees. Is that correct?'

'Yes,' said Grace, smiling into the phone, feeling foolishly nervous immediately. 'Yes, that is correct. I can take – well, let me see, easily two. Possibly three. Would that be a help?'

'A great deal of help. Thank you. I cannot tell you how difficult all this is' – the voice sounded exasperated, as if the weight of running the entire war was on its owner's shoulders – 'so many of these women sent their children down here and then took them back again. Well, naturally people can't be expected to just drop everything and be prepared to open their homes again.'

'Well,' said Grace carefully, 'there is a war on, I suppose.'

'There is indeed, Mrs Bennett, only some people don't seem to grasp the fact.'

Grace thought that if people were sending their children back to the country they probably *had* grasped the fact, but she didn't argue.

'Anyway, I have a trainload of children arriving this afternoon. Just like that, they tell me, as if I had all the time in the world. I mean a little more notice – '

'Well,' said Grace, mindful of the news, the ceaseless bombing of the capital, the terror that must fill the streets and houses, 'I suppose the faster they leave London the better. It does sound appalling.'

'Well, yes,' said the woman slightly grudgingly. 'Perhaps. Now look, can you get into Shaftesbury late this afternoon? It's the best centre. The children will be in the town hall. You can make your selection.'

'Do you mean,' said Grace, 'that we pick the children ourselves?'

'Yes of course.'

'It sounds a bit like a cattle market. Poor little things.'

'Yes, well, as you said, Mrs Bennett, there is a war on. And the children are fortunate to be coming here.'

They stood there holding hands, watching the people coming in. Not nearly as many as last time, and not so many nice ones either, a couple with really cross faces like the last old bag. They were going to get left behind, David could see; either people wanted big boys to help on the farm, they'd learnt that now, or pretty little girls. That one with the curls, she'd gone already, and that little cow in pink, standing there smirking at everyone, she'd soon be gone too. A large stout woman came up to them and looked at them severely.

'I can't take two,' she said, 'and they don't look up to much, but the bigger one could help in the house, I suppose. I'll have him, he'll do.'

'But I want to stay with me brother miss,' said David. It was a cry of anguish; Daniel's hand gripped his tighter. 'The other lady said I could – '

'The other lady had no business to say anything of the sort. This isn't a holiday,' said the woman in charge bracingly. 'You're very lucky to be here at all, safe from the bombs. Now come along, pick up your things, say goodbye to your brother. You'll be able to see him sometimes, at school and so on – '

'But – ' The tears began to flow. David gulped, fought them back. How was he going to bear this, without his mother, his home, his friends, or Daniel?

'Now don't start crying, for goodness sake. Come along, find your things and – '

'Excuse me!' Such a nice, kind, anxious voice. David looked up and saw a much younger lady standing in front of him; she was smiling and she had lovely reddish curly hair and a pretty flowery dress. She wasn't really like his mother, but she reminded him of her.

'Excuse me. I wonder if it would help if I could take these two? I wanted two, and they could be together.'

'Well of course it wouldn't help,' said the big woman. 'I've already chosen this boy. You'll have to have two others.'

'But they're brothers. They want to stay together. And they're so tiny – '

'Look,' said the big woman, 'I've made my choice and I'm abiding by it. Tiny he is, I'll give you that, but then he won't eat much. I was hoping for a proper lad, be a bit of help, but he's better than nothing. I've got to get home, it'll be dark soon, my husband's waiting out there with the van – '

David suddenly burst into loud sobs. He wasn't sure why, but he felt it might help matters. He moved his foot, kicked Daniel sharply on the ankle. Daniel obligingly burst into noisy tears as well.

'Oh for heaven's sake,' said the woman, 'I can't be doing with this. I'll take her,' she decided, indicating a large, pasty-faced girl who was standing in the corner. 'She doesn't look like much trouble. Come on. You're welcome to these two.'

And she was gone. The pretty lady stood smiling in some triumph, looking down at them both. 'Well done,' she said. 'What's your name?'

'David, miss. David Lucas. This is me brother, Daniel.'

'And how old are you?'

'Six, miss. Daniel's just turned four.'

'Well, would you like to come with me, David?'

'Yes, miss. Can Daniel come too?'

'Well of course he can. What a question.'

The lady in charge came over. 'You really can cope with the two can you, Mrs Bennett? Because if not, Mrs Carter can take the younger one.'

'Of course I can cope with the two. They have to stay together – it's inhuman to separate them.'

'Mrs Bennett, there's a war on. Sacrifices have to be made. Even by children. Anyway, if you can cope – Now here are their ration books, and – what's your name, David Lucas, have you got your gas mask?'

'I lost it, miss. On the train, miss.'

'Oh really! Really! What will you do if there's a gas raid tonight? Eh?'

'Don't know, miss. Die I s'pose, miss.'

He met the pretty lady's eyes, hoping he had said the right thing; he could have sworn she was winking at him.

She took them both by the hand and led them outside. It was almost dark, but what David could see of the town was very nice, like something in a picture book: curvy streets and lots of old buildings. By the side of the town hall was a steep, steep street, all cobbled, with little cottages beside it.

'How would you like to have tea?' said the lady. 'We could go to that place just over there, look, on the corner. They still have some nice cakes, and there's supposed to be a ghost.'

'Yeah!' said Daniel.

'Cor,' said David.

'Crikey!' said David as they pulled rather haltingly into the drive. 'Crikey, it's a bleedin' palace.'

Grace laughed. 'Not really. It's called the Mill House. Look, there's the stream.'

'Yes, miss. What's it do, miss?'

'Well, nothing much now,' said Grace, 'but it used to drive that wheel, look, which ground corn and then made flour, I think.'

David was silent. Such refinements were rather too much for him.

'That your dog?' said Daniel, backing away.

'Yes, she's called Charlotte. She's very friendly. Come and say hallo.' But he was behind his brother, peering nervously out.

'Look, Dan, chickens. The other lady had chickens. But we weren't allowed no eggs.'

'Whyever not?'

'She said they weren't for the likes of us.'

'Well, you can have eggs here. Where was this other lady?'

'In another country, miss.'

'Another country?'

'Yes. Yorkshire it was called, miss.'

'Oh,' said Grace.

They were hungry; she gave them boiled eggs and bread and butter and apples from her own tree. It was so lovely watching someone else eating what she had cooked, she felt a lump in her throat.

'That was nice,' said Daniel, smiling at her for the first time. 'Have you got a rabbit?'

Grace smiled back at him. 'Not really. But lots come to play. I'm afraid Charlotte chases them.' He was tiny; it was hard to believe he was four. They were both beautiful, with huge brown eyes and thick silky dark hair, but very thin and pale.

'Where do you live?'

'Acton,' said David briefly.

'With your parents?'

'No. Me mum and me nan. Me dad's gone to fight bleedin' 'itler.'

'Good for him. My husband's doing the same thing. Let's hope they succeed.'

'You got any boys, miss?'

'Boys? Oh, no,' said Grace, 'no. Nor girls. But you'll be my boys, won't you now? Do you think you'll like that?'

Later she heard quiet, stifled crying coming from the little room she had put them in. She went in. Daniel was fast asleep, but David was lying, his face in his pillow, his small body heaving with sobs.

Grace went over to the bed, stroked his hair gently; he promptly put his head under the pillow.

'David! Don't cry.'

Silence.

'Do you want to come downstairs with me?'

More silence.

'Well, if you do, I'll be in the kitchen. Do you think you can find the kitchen again?'

He didn't come that night, or the next, but the tears went on. He seemed all right in the day, a little distracted, but quite happy. She thought she would leave them to settle until after the weekend before she sent them to school. They were dear little things, followed her about with Charlotte at their heels; she felt she had three puppies. The dire warnings she had received from everybody seemed quite unnecessary; they said please and thank you, knew what a knife and fork were for, used the lavatory. They made their beds carefully and neatly in the mornings, and seemed to be trying very hard to please. Daniel liked feeding the chickens, and she had told him she was going to get a goat which made him very excited. He seemed more composed, less homesick than David, who was quiet and withdrawn; however hard she tried, he didn't say very much more than was strictly necessary.

Her mother was coming over to meet them at the weekend; so far Muriel and Florence had stayed away. Muriel had expressed her opinion once again that Grace had no right to fill Charles's house with waifs and strays and she hoped she had obtained his permission before he went.

Florence she had only seen once since her arrival from London; she had come over to collect some eggs. Grace, who had been resolved to be friendly, was waiting in the kitchen when they arrived, making tea; Florence walked in, unmistakably pregnant, and it had been a shock so extreme that Grace had felt it physically. So that was the reason for her acute need to hide from Robert: not because he was going to beat her up, but because she didn't want him to know that she was pregnant. Grace stood staring at her, her eyes fixed on Florence's stomach, feeling sick; Florence stared back, her own eyes defiant. They had scarcely spoken throughout the visit; Grace had been icily polite to them both, Muriel offhandedly brusque, telling Grace the garden looked neglected, remarking that Grace herself looked too thin. 'It doesn't suit you, you know,' she said, as if Grace had been losing weight deliberately, dieting in the face of plenty. 'I should do something about it before Charles gets home. You must come over for supper one night next week,' she added graciously. 'Wednesday suit you?'

'Well, I don't know,' said Grace carefully, 'I don't know about leaving the boys.'

'The boys? Oh, they'll be all right for a few hours surely,' said Muriel. She clearly saw them as small animals who could be left perfectly safely locked up in some outhouse. 'I'll expect you about seven. There won't be much to eat, of course, perhaps you could bring something with you, a bit of cheese or some of your nice apples. Now come along, Florence, Mary Davidson is longing to see you. Everyone is so thrilled to have her back,' she added to Grace. 'Goodbye, my dear. You really should tie that dog up, you know, she's ruining Charles's lawn.'

When she had gone, Grace sat down and went into peals of hysterical laughter. She supposed that must be an improvement on crying.

On the third night after the boys' arrival, she heard the muffled crying again, and went in; David as always hid under the bedclothes and pretended to be asleep. It was very cold and she had shut the windows tightly and closed the shutters. The room, devoid of fresh air, smelt unmistakably of urine.

In the morning she sent Daniel looking for eggs, went and sat on the old sofa in the kitchen window, patted the seat beside her.

'Come and sit with me. I want to talk to you.'

'Yes, miss.'

'David – I've been meaning to say – if – well, if either of you – wet the bed, I really wouldn't mind, you know. I mean Daniel is very little and it's very upsetting for anyone having to leave home. I used to wet the bed sometimes, until I was quite a big girl, at least ten. So if you – well, if he did, or if you thought he might, the best thing would be to put a rubber sheet on the bed. I've got to strip the beds today, and when I make them up, if you think that would be a good idea, I'll put one on. Just in case. Then it won't matter. All right? Now I'll tell you what I really want to talk to you about. Your mum. Don't you think you ought to write to her? I'm sure she'd like that.'

David nodded silently; but then he slid his hand into hers. 'Thanks' was all he said.

'Tell me about your mum,' said Grace, 'and your dad.'

'Me mum's really pretty. She's called Linda. She's very good at singing. She's fun. I miss her,' he said and suddenly burst into tears.

Grace held out her arms. 'Come and have a cuddle. Come on.'

'Thing is,' said David, edging slightly awkwardly up to her, 'the other lady at the other place, she used to hit us if I – if Dan wet the bed. It was awful. She was awful.'

'Well, I won't hit either of you. So there. Just don't worry about it. It doesn't matter. What about your dad? Tell me about him.'

'What about yours?'

'Who? Oh you mean my husband. Well he's very nice, of course. Very jolly and so on. Very good at riding.'

'Have you got a horse, miss?'

'Not at the moment, no. I don't really like them very much, I'm afraid.'

'The milkman 'ad a horse,' said David, enunciating with care, 'ever so big. I used to feed 'im. What's 'e look like?'

'Who?'

'Your 'usband, miss.'

'Oh, him. Well, he's got fair hair, blue eyes. He's tall. Good-looking. I miss him a lot,' she said, with a sigh. It was true; she did.

'My dad's good-looking too,' said David, 'but 'e's got dark hair, like me. You'd like my dad,' he added, looking at her consideringly, 'you really would. And 'e'd like you.'

'The kids sound fine,' said Linda to Nan. 'Got a letter from David this morning. With another one from the woman they've fetched up with. She sounds nice. Name's Grace Bennett. She says she and Daniel are getting a goat and she's teaching David to play the piano. He says, listen: "The house is very very big and the garden is like a field."'

'Piano lessons, big houses,' said Nan. 'They'll be getting ideas soon. I should watch it if I were you, Linda. Where you going?'

'Out,' said Linda, 'and don't talk so daft, Nan. How can I watch it? They're bloody lucky if you ask me. I'm grateful to this Grace person. I'm going to write to her. Now I'm only going down the pub, and if the siren goes I'll be right back, all right?'

'I suppose so,' said Nan, scowling at her. Linda scowled back. But actually they were getting on better, united by fear, by discomfort, by hardship and a determination not to be beaten.

Linda wouldn't have liked to admit it, but she was enjoying herself. Ben had been posted to Liverpool and was perfectly safe, she did not have to worry about him; and London was full of soldiers on leave, soldiers and airmen, most of them lonely, happy to buy drinks for pretty young women who flattered them and told them how brave they were. Once a week at least she and Janice went up West; she knew it was dangerous, mad even, but as Janice said, when your number was up, your number was up, and there wasn't a thing you could do about it, might as well enjoy it while you could.

The atmosphere in the pubs and clubs up there was fantastic; everyone excited, friendly, looking for fun, in case it was the last they ever got. The girls got taken dancing, to nightclubs, cocktail bars, the cinema. Very often after a film had ended there would be a further impromptu entertainment, a recital on the theatre organ, dancing, singing. It was all very good fun. The blokes obviously were hopeful, as Janice said, but would mostly settle for a kiss and a cuddle. At first Linda felt bad about even this infidelity, but she managed to persuade herself that what Ben didn't see his heart couldn't possibly grieve over, and it was a war effort of sorts, cheering the soldiers up. She never saw much of any film, that was for sure, not even *Gone with the Wind*, which ran for three and three-quarter hours, and dancing could hardly be dignified by that name either, just necking to music, but she would no more have dreamt of going all the way with any of the soldiers, however good-looking they were, than she would of walking into the factory stark naked.

The factory was fun too; she loved it. She had passed her trade test, after several weeks of training, and now worked a ten-hour shift, alternating night and day every two weeks. The night did seem particularly long, but it was broken by the hour-long dinner break when there was very often a concert of sorts, occasionally a professional one, but always someone would play the piano, one of the girls would get up and sing, and they would all dance and fool about. The work was repetitive, but when you saw a consignment of guns leaving the factory that you had helped to make, you really felt part of the war effort. And the girls were smashing; there was a sort of competition to tell the filthiest jokes, the most intimate stories, use the raciest language. Freed from the confines of marriage, they had all become young again, young and carefree. It was a funny thing to be, when your life was in daily danger, but there it was.

When they were caught in the West End and there was an air raid, she and Janice mostly went down to the underground. That was a laugh. People said it smelt, and it did, but nothing like the big public shelters; she'd once had to go into one of those and it had been absolutely disgusting, two latrines between 300 people, set behind two hastily slung-up blankets. By the end of the raid they had overflowed, sending a putrid river over the floor. The shelters in the London underground were terrific: people organized singsongs, poker schools, there was dancing, sometimes an official concert, there were hammocks for the kids slung over the lines and people had their own spaces, where they set up deck chairs. The government had been opposed to the idea, but Mr Churchill had been all for it.

Good old Winnie; the affection people felt for him, the faith they had in him was profound, almost a love affair in its intensity. Linda saw him once, walking through the rubble of a bombed area as if he was inspecting someone's garden, bowler on his head, cigar in his mouth, his fat face rather pink, waving cheerfully at everyone who greeted him. She was surprised how small he was, she had imagined a huge man from the flowing, booming voice, but she wasn't disappointed; it seemed indeed to make him more human. She felt more than ever they were in good hands. If anyone could beat Jerry, he could.

And now she knew the boys were happy, she really could relax. Enjoy herself. What a thing to say about a war.

Clarissa and Jack had both got Christmas leave. Defying every fate, every odds, they had decided to spend it at home, in London. Jack had been recalled to the south coast, based in Kent.

'If we get bombed, that'll be all right,' said Clarissa. 'We'll go together.'

She was actually enjoying life hugely. She had been posted to Portsmouth and was a dispatch rider, haring about the country on a motorbike, dressed in breeches, riding jacket and peaked cap. She earned thirteen shillings and sixpence a week, was called Wren Compton Brown, and worked in the most difficult and dangerous conditions, often at night, struggling through the blackout delivering dispatches. She gloried in it, careless of the dangers; she was in a permanently overexcited state, often unable to sleep even after a very long trip. She felt she had some idea now how Jack had continued to fly, to risk his life hour after hour, day after day; a strange force possessed her, lifting her above fear, above weariness. One night her lights, such as they were, failed nine miles from Southampton, and she had had to find her way entirely by the light of her torch; she had heard a strange whooping sound as she finally drove into the naval barracks and realized it was herself.

The Wrennery at Portsmouth was in a large private house that had been commandeered; the cabin she slept in was much smaller than the one at Mill Hill, and now that they all had jobs to do, had shaken down, there was a feeling of immense camaraderie between them all.

Clarissa's friends in civilian life were very surprised she had not become an officer: 'It doesn't work like that,' she said patiently, 'you have to earn the right to apply. Anyway, I don't know that I want to be. It's much more fun being with the other girls. Especially May.'

She had been appalled at first to discover that May Potter had also been posted to Portsmouth, had imagined that when she left Mill Hill May and her tortures would be left safely behind her. May was a cook. 'Honestly,' Clarissa had said to one of the other girls, 'I hope she won't poison my food. Or spit in it,' she added.

May had been still hostile when they arrived at the Wrennery, but as the days went by a lot of the fight seemed to go out of her; she was pale and heavy-eyed, and twice Clarissa thought she saw her crying as she passed her on their way to the bathroom. Then one night, as she got up to go to the loo, she heard the muffled sobs she hadn't heard since Mill Hill days; following the sound, she traced it to May's bed, and a heaving lump beneath the bedclothes.

Clarissa, who was nothing if not kind, sat down on the bed and put her hand cautiously on the lump, 'Piss off' came May's voice.

'Oh May, do be sensible,' she said. 'What is it? What's wrong?'

'Nothing you'd understand,' said May.

'I might. Come on, tell me. You homesick?'

'Nah.'

'Having trouble with your work then?'

'Nah.'

'May, come on. Let me help.'

Slowly, reluctantly, May's bright blonde head emerged from the bedclothes. 'What's it to you anyway?' she said crossly, blowing her nose on the handkerchief Clarissa had offered her.

'Let's say I've developed an interest in you,' said Clarissa cheerfully, and then, as a couple of voices told them to shut up: 'Let's go out to the lav. We can't talk here.'

'OK. Got any ciggies?'

'Yes. I think so. I'll get them, and meet you there.'

May was sitting on the chair in the bathroom looking pale, clutching her stomach; she took the cigarette Clarissa passed her and pulled on it hard.

'You look a bit rough,' said Clarissa sympathetically, 'Got the curse?'

'No,' said May listlessly. 'I 'aven't. That's the problem. If you must know.'

Clarissa listened for a long time in silence as May sniffed and told her story. She had been on leave, had had what she called a high old time with her boyfriend who had promptly departed for Egypt "asn't even written,' she said, stubbing out her cigarette ferociously in the basin, 'bastard. I won't 'alf give 'im what for when 'e gets 'ome.'

'Well, that won't do you much good. It could be years. How late are you?'

'Should've come on over two weeks ago.'

'Did you – well, did you take any precautions?'

'Course we bloody did. What do you think I am?' said May indignantly. 'Used a French letter, every bloody time.'

'Feel sick?'

'No.'

'Got sore breasts?'

'No. What is this, bleedin' inquisition?'

'May, I'm trying to help.'

'Sorry,' said May.

'I bet you're not pregnant,' said Clarissa, 'I bet you've just thought yourself into stopping your periods.'

'Course I 'aven't,' said May crossly. 'How could I?'

'Very easily. Honestly. Anyway, you must have a test.'

'A what?'

'A pregnancy test. Perfectly simple. You just have to take a sample of your urine to one of the birth-control clinics and they inject it into a frog and then they know.'

'How do they know?'

'I think the frog lays eggs if you are, or something,' said Clarissa vaguely. 'Anyway, it's very accurate. Lots of my friends had it done.'

'Go on,' said May, 'I didn't think your sort did all that sort of thing.'

'May,' said Clarissa severely, 'you have a lot of very silly prejudices.'

May was not pregnant. She arrived back at the Wrennery beaming one evening a week later, having wangled an hour off to attend the clinic. 'You was right,' she said to Clarissa, 'all in me mind. And I've come on. Came on on the way home.'

'Told you,' said Clarissa. 'Good.'

May looked at her awkwardly. 'I'm very sorry,' she said. 'I was so rotten to you. I feel awful now. You've been a real friend to me and I don't deserve it.'

'Don't worry,' said Clarissa, 'no hard feelings. Honestly. You just got me wrong, that's all.'

'Yeah, well, I'm still sorry.'

From then on, she and May became best friends; May still teased her a lot and called her Duchess and she still had trouble not correcting May's grammar, but they became inseparable and had, they agreed, much more in common than most of the other girls, not least a blithe ability to enjoy whatever life threw at them.

She arrived in London on 22 December and spent the day shopping. Oxford Street and Regent Street were packed. 'It was blissfully normal,' she told Florence that night when she phoned to wish her Happy Christmas. 'Apart from the fact there was nothing to buy, of course. I actually got a turkey in Selfridge's, desperately expensive, and you wouldn't believe such a thing, some liqueur chocolates. Bit of a funny lunch, can't get any fruit to make a cake or anything, but never mind. Masses of wine. I'm off to see your darling old dad now. He's horribly lonely. He's coming to have lunch with us on Christmas Day.'

'Where's Mrs Saunders?' asked Florence, surprised.

'Oh, history as far as I can make out. He's so low, poor old darling. I sometimes wonder if – '

'Mother wouldn't hear of it,' said Florence firmly, 'and it would be awful, no one would speak to him.'

'Grace would,' said Clarissa. 'How is she?'

'Beastly,' said Florence. 'To me anyway. She's taken in two rather sweet little evacuees and she's doing some voluntary work for the Women's Land Army. Frightfully pleased with herself. I don't know why she's so high-minded, I'm sure. Bit of a prig, she always was. It's a class thing, I always think.'

'Darling, how snobbish. Which reminds me, Jack's going to the Palace in February, to get his D. S. C. Too thrilling.'

'Oh Clarissa, how wonderful. You must be so proud of him.'

'I am,' said Clarissa complacently. 'How's baba?'

'Growing. Like anything. I'm enormous.'

'Oh darling, how wonderful. I can't wait. When is it due?'

'Also February, I think. I'm a bit hazy. I'm having it in a nursing home near Shaftesbury. Rather scared, if you want to know – I'm not brave like you.'

'Oh piffle,' said Clarissa. 'Nothing brave about me. Well, darling, have a wonderful Christmas.'

'Not much chance of that. Grace's dreary parents are coming, and her, and of course Mother's had to ask the refugees as she calls them.'

'I thought they were sweet.'

'They are, but Mother treats them as if they had some kind of obscene disease and didn't speak English, only addresses them through Grace.'

'Sounds grim. Well, apart from the time your papa's with us, we're going to spend the whole of Christmas in bed.'

'Oh you're so lucky,' said Florence.

'This is very good of you,' said Clifford. 'Very good of you indeed. When you could be alone together.'

'Plenty of time for that,' said Clarissa. 'Four glorious days left yet. Anyway, we were getting sick of the sight of each other, weren't we, Jack darling?'

Jack nodded sleepily. He had had a great deal of the very good brandy Clarissa had managed to wheedle out of the manager of the wine department at Harrods. He hadn't really changed a lot, Clifford thought, for a man who had looked death in the face several times a day; he had lost some weight, and his matinée idol looks, the perfectly sculpted nose, the fine jaw, were slightly sharper, more clearly defined, but that was, if anything, an improvement, and he was just as funny, just as charming, full of funny, often outrageous stories. He and Clarissa clearly had a great deal of difficulty keeping their hands off one another; even now, she had her arm linked through his, her lovely head on his shoulder. They were the most ravishing couple, he thought, too good to be true, and had assumed a strange glamour as well, the glamour of survival, of triumph in wartime. Please God it would last for them at least. He wondered how Charles was faring; he heard only from Grace that he was safe and well, surviving the heat, the considerable traumas of life in Tunisia, but cheerful.

Christmas was a painful time for separated families – and separated lovers. Clifford wrenched his mind determinedly from his loneliness and smiled at Clarissa and Jack.

'Well, I think I'll turn in. The old bones are feeling it a bit. Bless you both for a wonderful day. I'll see you first thing, will I? Then I must be off. Perhaps I could take what's left of that excellent whisky up with me. Nightcap, you know.'

'Of course,' said Clarissa, 'whatever you like. I'll come down and make you breakfast in the morning.'

They were not arguing with the fiction that Clifford had a great deal to do on Boxing Day. He needed it, for his self-respect, and they needed more time together . . .

'For love and love and more love,' said Clarissa, throwing herself rapturously back onto the pillows. 'Jack, you are stupendously, wonderfully, miraculously brilliant in bed. And out of it,' she added, tracing the shape of his profile with her finger, smiling as she reached his mouth and he nibbled it. 'I'm so lucky, so terribly, terribly lucky to have you. To have found you. Supposing I hadn't, supposing we hadn't known each other, think what we would have missed – '

'Well, you did find me,' said Jack, turning, looking at her very seriously, 'and now you've got me. For ever and ever.'

'Don't say that,' said Clarissa quickly. 'Bad luck.'

'Clarissa my darling, if I can come through the Battle of Britain, I can come through anything. I keep telling you, charmed life I've got. No, the only thing that's going to come between us is some bloody tall, dark and handsome naval commander.'

'Oh don't be ridiculous,' said Clarissa.

Chapter Thirteen

Winter–Spring 1941

'I really find this very hard to believe,' said Mrs Lacey. She looked severely at Grace. 'These girls do – well, embroider things rather, you know.'

Grace sighed, started to count up to ten, got to six and lost her temper.

'Mrs Lacey, this is not embroidery. I went to the farm and saw it myself. They are sleeping in the barn, in the barn, well, all right, in the hayloft, and they don't have enough blankets, and they don't have any sheets. It's horrible for them. And if they want to go to the lavatory in the night they have to go outside. It's appalling. Something has to be done.'

Mrs Lacey was on the West Thorne county branch of the committee; she reminded Grace of Muriel in her blind refusal to accept the word of anyone born outside her own social class, unless it was to express gratitude or some other such suitable emotion. It was that very fact that gave Grace courage now.

'Well, I really don't know what to think. These farmers are having a very difficult time, I don't feel it is for us to tell them how to do their job – '

'Mrs Lacey, we're not telling them how to do their job. And if they're having a difficult time, which I slightly doubt, they're making more money than they ever dreamed of with all these subsidies. They need the girls to help them, and therefore they ought to be nice to them. Now what are we going to do?'

'Well,' said Mrs Lacey, 'I suppose I could suggest they move to a hostel. Although I can't imagine where.'

'I don't think that would matter. If you told him why you were thinking of moving them, I think he'd improve his treatment of them pretty quickly. So will you do that, Mrs Lacey? Please?'

'Yes, very well. I'll write to him. What's his name?'

'Mr Drummond. Here's the address.'

'Any other – complaints?'

'No, well, nothing serious, only things like long hours. But the girls have to expect that. And there's some silly girl over at Westhorne who can't get the hang of milking, but I told the farmer to put her onto an older cow to practise on, that nearly always works. Dear old things there are, at every farm, they just stand there and sort of help.'

'Yes, yes,' said Mrs Lacey, clearly having no interest in cows, helpful or otherwise. 'Is that all?'

'Yes, but I've only been able to make bicycle calls recently. I really need to get further over in the Wells direction. Could I have some petrol coupons please? I haven't had any at all since I started.'

Mrs Lacey looked at Grace as if she was asking for a fur coat or several pounds of butter, and rather reluctantly reached in her drawer for the coupons. 'Please don't waste any,' she said, 'any at all.'

'No, Mrs Lacey. I won't.'

What did the old bat think she was going to do with it, Grace wondered, drink it?

She was feeling, she realized as she drove slowly home, very much happier. She was still lonely, still constantly worried about Charles, still hurt, when she thought about it, by her lack of friends, but things had improved. She loved the Land Army work, loved hearing the girls' stories, the funny ones, about farmers getting fresh, about the one who had tried to take a crop to one of them and she had seized it and turned it on him instead, even enjoyed, perversely, comforting the girls who were homesick – and some of them were very homesick, and physically quite unsuited to the unremittingly hard work they had to do. They had been lured to the country, in preference to factory work, with a vision of collecting eggs and raking up a little hay and found themselves planting potatoes, mucking out pigs and lifting endless rows of sprouts in the freezing rain and sleet. Grace felt at least she had a purpose in life; a function beyond feeding herself and keeping her house tidy.

The little boys were a joy; she loved them both with a fierceness that quite worried her at times. She supposed it was because she had nothing else to love, apart from Charlotte. There were problems, of course, the bed-wetting hadn't improved, Daniel hated school and was constantly in trouble, fighting the other boys who took the mickey out of his London accent – in spite of his small size he was very swift with his fists – cheeking nice Miss Merton largely out of defensiveness, and he couldn't get the hang of his tables which led to further ragging on the grounds of his stupidity. David felt bound to try to defend him, and got into trouble for fighting boys younger than he was; he was very clever and got teased for being a swot. On the other hand, the other children tended to like him and when he was made book monitor nobody resented it, Miss Merton told Grace. 'And he likes music doesn't he? I caught him playing the piano really nicely the other day.'

'Yes,' said Grace, 'I've been giving him lessons.'

'You play the piano, Mrs Bennett?' asked Miss Merton.

'Yes. Yes I do.'

'Well now,' said Miss Merton, 'I'm thinking of starting dancing lessons. I studied dancing at college. It was my subject. I wanted to be a dancer only I got too tall.'

Not just too tall, thought Grace, trying not to conjure up too vivid a picture of Miss Merton's thirteen stone dancing.

'Only I can't do both, dance and play. You wouldn't like to play for me one afternoon a week, would you?'

'Oh I'd love to,' said Grace, 'I'd really love it. Thank you.'

The dancing lessons took place on Wednesday afternoons: mostly skipping about, but Miss Merton was also teaching the children the rudiments of ballroom dancing, and had told any girls who were interested she would like to start them on ballet. 'And boys, if they want to,' she said, her round, apple-rosy face slightly roguish. Miss Merton doing a vigorous *grand battement*, her huge bottom aquiver, her elasticated knickers briefly but rhythmically on view, brought the boys flocking into the ballet classes; but the novelty soon wore off and they departed again.

Muriel, who had been very dismissive about the Land Army work, and told Grace the girls were bound to be ignorant and idle and best left to the farmers to sort out, was graciously approving of the piano-playing. 'So good of you,' she said, 'to try and bring a little culture into these people's lives.'

As the nearest Muriel came to culture herself was listening to the Palm Court Orchestra on the wireless on Sunday evening, Grace found this particularly ironic, but she smiled sweetly at her mother-in-law and stayed silent.

'Well now,' said Mrs Merrow, the midwife, putting away the trumpet which she had been holding to Florence's stomach. 'Well now, baby's doing very nice. Lovely strong heartbeat, wouldn't mind betting that's a boy in there.'

'I hope so,' said Florence.

'Head's not engaged, but that's not unusual, not with a first baby. But he's lying the right way, so you shouldn't have any problems at all.' She smiled at Florence. 'Any questions?'

'Well – no. Not really. That is – well, how much longer do you think?'

'Oh, I should think at least six weeks. That was the date we worked out, wasn't it? He might come earlier, he's quite a big chap, but it's very unusual for a first baby. More likely late, I'm afraid.' She patted Florence's stomach tenderly, beamed at her.

Florence looked down at it, at her big chap. It terrified her to think of how big he was, and the extremely small area he had to get through; it hardly seemed possible indeed. She was, now it was so near, very frightened.

'And – how will I know? When it's started?'

'Oh, you'll know all right,' said Mrs Merrow, laughing. 'No doubt about that. Of course you might get your waters breaking, that'll happen in the greengrocer's or in church, somewhere really convenient, or a show, now that's a spot of blood. But most likely you'll get the pains starting.'

'Oh – yes,' said Florence, 'the pains. Um – Mrs Merrow, will I be able to have anything for the pains?'

'Yes, if you want to,' said Mrs Merrow. 'Gas and air. Wonderful stuff it is, carries you right off and over it. Don't you worry about the pains, Mrs Grieg. And I'll be here, if I possibly can, or Mrs Foster, you know her, and Doctor of course. You're worried, aren't you?' she added kindly

'Well, perhaps a bit,' said Florence.

'Quite natural you should be. But it'll be all right. And when he's here, in your arms, it'll all be worth it. Believe me.'

'Oh yes,' said Florence, 'yes, I'm sure it will.'

She found it just a little hard to believe at the moment.

Mr Jacobs, the only remaining senior partner at Bennett & Bennett, had asked Muriel and Grace to go and see him in Shaftesbury. He said he had something slightly complex to discuss with them. Grace followed Muriel into Mr Jacobs's rather grand office, feeling a little nervous.

'Do sit down, Mr Jacobs,' said Muriel graciously. 'I hope this isn't going to take too long, I'm extremely busy. As you know.'

'Yes of course,' said Mr Jacobs, who could not possibly have known whether Muriel was busy or not. 'I'm sorry to take up your time. Very sorry. But – well – '

'Yes?'

'Well, it's about the firm. You see.'

'I didn't expect it to be about the conduct of the war,' said Muriel.

Grace began to feel very sorry for Mr Jacobs. She smiled at him encouragingly.

'As you know, in your husband's absence – in both your husbands' absence – ' he cleared his throat again.

'Mr Jacobs, please come to the point.'

'In their absence,' said Mr Jacobs in a rush, clearly finding a reserve of courage, 'I have been running the firm. With some difficulty, I might add.'

'I dare say,' said Muriel, 'but there is a war on, and we all have difficulties, Mr Jacobs.'

'Of course. Well now, clients have been few and far between lately. Very little conveyancing, naturally, little financial work – our income has dropped considerably.'

'Indeed?' said Muriel. Her face was very tense.

'Yes. And I'm afraid – well, I'm afraid the drawings made in your favour, both of your favours, lately, have been a considerable drain on the firm.'

'That is very unfortunate,' said Muriel, 'but I fail to see what we can do about it.'

'Well, the thing is, Mrs Bennett, the thing is – '

'Yes, Mr Jacobs – '

'The – the standing orders can no longer be met. Well, not in such large measure anyway.'

Grace suddenly felt rather sick. The one thing she had never thought about, since Charles went away, was money; it had flowed towards her in a warm, constant supply, seeing to her needs, paying for her food, her clothes, her light and heating, Mrs Babbage, the daily woman, Mr Blackstone the gardener –

'By how much?' Muriel was saying.

'Well, Mrs Bennett, I would say by fifty per cent. Er – each.'

'Fifty per cent!' said Muriel. 'I'm afraid that is quite out of the question. Speaking for myself that is. My daughter-in-law may well, of course, be able to manage on less. But I can't. I have my daughter at home, and shortly my grandchild to support. I do assure you, Mr Jacobs, you will have to go away and think of something else to keep Bennett and Bennett solvent. Now, if you will excuse me, as I told you I am extremely busy.'

'But – Mrs Bennett, I'm afraid it isn't as simple as that,' said Mr Jacobs, clearly drawing courage and strength from her attitude. 'There simply is not the money. Whatever I – we do. The income from the firm is almost at zero. Were I not retiring myself within the year I would be extremely worried. But I have my pension and – '

'I don't think we want to hear about your arrangements,' said Muriel, 'and surely my husband has a pension fund. We – I – can draw on that presumably.'

'You can, of course, Mrs Bennett, but it is a much smaller sum again than perhaps you realize. And naturally it is outside my jurisdiction. You will have to arrange it with him.'

'I'm afraid that is quite out of the question,' said Muriel. 'I repeat, Mr Jacobs, you will have to come up with some other proposal. And now if you will excuse us – '

Mrs Jacobs stood up and looked helplessly at Grace. She smiled at him.

In the reception area, waiting for Muriel to emerge from the ladies, she said, 'I'm sorry about my – about Mrs Bennett. She doesn't quite understand the real world. Let me have a think about it, perhaps talk to my father-in-law. Have you – '

'I have tried, Mrs Bennett. He has promised to give the matter some thought. But I found him a little – what shall I say? – detached.'

That was odd, Grace thought, unlike Clifford; he was so undetached, so anxious to look after everyone. She would ring him, have a chat with him.

She couldn't help feeling, as Muriel so plainly did, that there must be some mistake.

'Clifford? Clifford, it's Grace.'

'Grace! Hallo, my dear, how are you?'

'I'm very well, thank you. And you?'

'Oh – you know. Getting a little older these days. London is not very peaceful. But I do go to a lot of concerts, Grace darling, there is a simply wonderful choice, you'd be surprised, so that keeps me pretty busy, and I read a lot and – '

'Clifford, I hate to – well, to bother you, but we saw Mr Jacobs this morning. He said that – that there was a – a money problem. The company is in trouble. Well, not trouble, but not making any money.'

'Yes, yes, he told me. Clients all gone away. Well, it's hardly surprising.'

That was funny; not the kind of reaction she'd have expected. 'Yes, but Clifford, you see, there isn't enough money for Muriel. Or for me, but that doesn't matter so much. I expect I can sort something out. But she's – well, she needs money of course and she has Florence here and the baby soon – '

'Yes, the baby. When exactly is it due? Is Florence all right?'

'She's fine. It's due next month, I think. But they do need money and I wondered if – what you thought we should do about it.'

'Well, my darling, I don't know. I really don't.'

'What about the London partnership?'

'What? Oh, not a lot here, I'm afraid. At any rate not for me. Very small fish in this particular pond now. I'm lucky to be able to use the flat. Times are quite difficult. Well, you know that of course.'

'Yes. Yes, I see. Clifford, are you really all right?' His vague, distracted state seemed to her more worrying than the financial one.

'Oh, good gracious yes. Of course I am. Don't you worry about me.'

'No, of course not. Well – goodbye, Clifford. You are looking after yourself, aren't you? Eating properly and everything?'

'Of course I am. I'm absolutely tickety-boo. Now you take care of yourself, darling, won't you?'

'Yes. Yes of course. And you.'

'You're not entirely with me, are you?' said Jack.

They were lying in bed in a rather seedy hotel in Kent; he had a forty-eight-hour leave and Clarissa had been allowed to join him for twenty-four of them.

She had looked forward to it so much, longed to be with him, longed to hold him, have him with her, safe, warm, loving; and yet something was wrong. And it wasn't with him, it was with her. She felt odd, distanced from him: loving him as she did, as much as ever, but somehow less concerned, less unquestioningly committed to him. The sex had been wonderful, as always; almost better, there was a toughness, a near desperation in Jack these days that lent an edge to the pleasure, gave it a fierce, raw sensation that was almost painful in its intensity. It had been beforehand, as they ate an indigestible dinner (tough stew, followed by watery trifle), and he talked and she found for the very first time that it was just slightly hard to concentrate, to give him her one hundred per cent attention. And now, afterwards, when he wanted simply to hold her, to be with her, and her mind, usually so rapturously blank of everything but him, what she felt for and with him, what he had done for her, and she for him, that mind was wandering, straying fretfully towards what she had left behind: to two new arrivals placed in her care, homesick and lonely, abandoned in her absence to May's rather brisker attentions; to a bike she knew she should have sent for maintenance and had not done so in her hurry to get away; to a difficult assignment the next day; and a clear need to be back in Portsmouth on duty by nine a.m. and a gnawing knowledge that she needed a very strong following wind to be able to accomplish that.

'Sorry,' she said, kissing him carefully, quickly, resettling herself against him, 'I'm sorry.'

'What are you thinking about?'

'Oh – you know.'

'No,' he said, and his voice was edgy, 'no I don't. Actually.'

'Well – you ought to.'

'Why?'

'Because you must surely be thinking of other things too. Other than me, I mean.'

'Actually, Clarissa,' he said and there was a real edge to his voice suddenly, 'I'm not. In spite of everything, all I've been through, I'm not.'

'Oh,' she said.

'And I don't like it that you are.'

'Well I'm sorry,' she said again, 'but – '

'But what?'

'Oh, it's not even worth talking about. Jack, this is silly.'

'I'm afraid I don't see it as silly,' he said. 'I see it as lots of things, inevitable perhaps, unfortunate certainly, and very sad. But not silly. I wouldn't have thought anything that threatened our relationship was silly.'

'Jack, really,' she said, smiling into his eyes, kissing him, trying to make light of it, 'you're being absurd. I'm not threatening our relationship. I'm just a bit worried about a few things. That's all.'

'What things?' he said. He sat up, reached for his cigarettes, offered her one.

She shook her head. 'Oh, just Wren business.'

'Very important,' he said, 'Wren business. I can see that. What is it you're doing at the moment, Clarissa? Delivering messages still, all over the countryside?'

'Yes,' she said, misreading his mood, anxious that he should understand, 'and tomorrow I have to – '

'I really don't want to know,' he said, stubbing out his cigarette, turning away from her. 'Tomorrow I have to get back in my plane and train yet more little boys to go out and get killed. And if I can stop thinking about that, Clarissa, I would have thought you could forget about your ridiculous messenger service.'

'Jack, please, don't, don't talk like that,' she said, shocked and shaken as always when he forced her to confront (as he seldom did) what he had to endure, live with day by day. 'I didn't mean – '

'I know what you meant,' he said, 'and I don't care for it. I'm going to sleep now. I'm incredibly tired. Goodnight.'

Later he relented, turned to her, made love to her again, gently, tenderly this time, asked her to forgive him for his outburst, and she asked him to forgive her for her distraction. But she lay sleepless the rest of the night, shocked not only at the changes that were taking place between them but at the equally great ones within herself, and her inability to stop any of it. And there was something else too: a lack of willingness even to try.

She liked the new Clarissa and she liked the new Clarissa's life, even if it was hard on Jack; it seemed to have a lot more to it than the old one.

My dear Grace,

First of all, some reassurances, which I imagine will be welcome. I am alive and extremely well. We are in Egypt. We are living in tolerably comfortable conditions, although it is of course rather warm (bit of British understatement there), under the excellent command of Wavell. Morale is high and I have a fine bunch of men, and my fellow officers are an excellent bunch. Of course it is tedious at times, nerve-racking at others (more understatement), and we don't know quite what will happen next (!) but I feel quite confident that we are a winning part of a winning team, and that we have, in Mr Churchill's own words, seen at least the end of the beginning.

I am enjoying soldiering very much; far more than I expected. The sense of comradeship, of striving for a shared goal, unquestioningly, in spite of hardship, danger and fear, is a fine thing. This might be hard, not unnaturally, for you to understand, but I can only assure you that many of us have the same feelings. Anyway, your husband is in fine fettle!

I hope you are well, darling, and not missing me too much. It is a constant comfort to me, as I have told you so many times, to think of you safely over there, keeping the home fires burning! Which brings me to the second point of my letter. Mother tells me you have taken in some evacuees. She feels this is wrong, and I have to tell you that I do agree with her. You should not have done it without consultation with me, and I dislike the thought of strangers, however young and possibly in need they may be, living in my house. Of course you feel you are acting for the best, and it is very sweet of you to want to contribute to the war effort, but I must ask you to find something else to do. If I come home on leave suddenly (unlikely but possible) I do not want to have to share my home with two ragamuffins from the East End! I am sure they are very nice boys, although one hears appalling stories about these children and their behaviour, lack of morals, etc, but it is just not right that they should be there against my wishes. Could you therefore please make arrangements as soon as possible for them to be moved somewhere else? I imagine there must be many people who would have them.

My mother also tells me that she does not see a great deal of you. Please make an effort to visit her as often as you can; with the added responsibility of Florence and her baby she needs all the support she can get.

Take care of yourself, darling, and remember I love you. Charles.

This letter clarified things for Grace in a way that she was quite sure Charles would not have altogether envisaged.

That afternoon she cycled over to the Priory and found Muriel sitting huddled by a rather ineffectual fire.

'Ah, Grace,' she said, 'I would offer you a cup of tea, but Cook is upstairs resting. I'm afraid she is rather taking advantage of the situation since Maureen left and complains all the time that she has too much to do.'

'That's perfectly all right, Muriel,' said Grace, reflecting that if every cup of tea at the Priory was still expected to arrive at the press of a bellpush, it was no wonder poor Cook needed to rest. 'I've actually come to see Florence. But I thought you'd like to know I had a letter from Charles today. He's fine and in Egypt.'

'Egypt! Such an interesting place,' said Muriel as if Charles was on some kind of foreign holiday.

'Yes, I expect so. Anyway, he seems very upset about my evacuees. He obviously agrees with you about them.'

'I expect he does,' said Muriel.

'As a matter of fact, he wants me to get rid of them, send them somewhere else,' said Grace.

'I think that's a very good idea.'

'Well, they're not going,' said Grace, 'and I would be grateful, Muriel, if you would not interfere in my affairs.'

'Had you not written and asked him about them then?'

'I wrote and told him about them, yes. After they had arrived and settled, and I could see it was all going to be all right. Before then I saw no reason to worry him. You obviously decided he needed to know rather earlier.'

'Well, I think that was wrong of you. You should have asked his permission – it is his house after all.'

'Muriel, it is *our* house, not his. I wish you could see that. And while Charles is away, I shall decide what goes on in it. Now I've actually come to see Florence. Good afternoon.'

Grace allowed herself one last satisfying glance at her mother-in-law as she closed the door; Muriel was staring fixedly after her, her mouth a round, very neat O.

'I'm going up to London to see your father,' she said to Florence.

'Why?' said Florence, hauling herself to a sitting position from where she lay on the sofa.

'He sounds very – odd. Sort of distracted and detached. He said he was all right but – '

'Clarissa saw him at Christmas,' said Florence. 'She didn't say anything. Well, except that he was terribly lonely and a bit low. It's very good of you, Grace, but isn't it awfully dangerous up there? And if Mother found out, she'd be desperately upset.'

'Apparently there's been a lull in the bombing lately. Nothing for a while. And I don't really care whether your mother is upset. I'm going. Someone has to keep an eye on him.'

She tried not to sound self-righteous, but it was difficult.

On the morning she was leaving the phone rang.

'Grace, it's Florence. I'm coming with you.'

'You can't, Florence, you're about to have a baby.'

'Not for at least five weeks, according to the doctor and the midwife. You said it was quiet up there at the moment. And he's my father and I've been thinking. You're right to be worried about him. I want to come.'

'Your mother won't let you.'

'Well, she wouldn't have, but she's not here. She's gone to see some old crony of hers who's ill, over in Wells. That's what made me decide. She's staying the night. I couldn't resist. We'll be back tomorrow, won't we? If she finds out, I'll think of something to tell her.'

'I don't know,' said Grace doubtfully.

She didn't want Florence with her; she would be a terrible responsibility and, besides, she still found it very hard to be civil to her. She wasn't at all sure she believed in all this daughterly devotion anyway. She was probably going to see the other man, the father of her baby.

'Oh Grace, please. Come and pick me up. I presume you're driving to Salisbury. I really do want to come. Besides, I'm dying of boredom here, I should so love an adventure.'

'I don't think it'll be exactly that,' said Grace tartly, 'but – oh, all right. I'll be over in about fifteen minutes. And we've got to drop the boys off with my mother.'

'That's very nice of her, to have them, I mean,' said Florence. 'Can't they be left for a day?'

She obviously saw them rather as Muriel did, as small, inconvenient animals.

The train journey up wasn't too bad; they reached Waterloo by midday. Florence sat and read *Vogue* all the way: she didn't appear to be desperately worried about her father. Grace looked out of the window and thought that if Florence had any ulterior motives she was going to find herself very heavily chaperoned.

They managed to get a bus at the station; it took a complex and unconventional route, as so many did these days, the conductor explained, ducking up side streets, avoiding the worst-hit places. Grace and Florence sat gazing stricken out of the window, shocked by the damage everywhere, the missing glass in seemingly every window, the half-demolished buildings, the determinedly cheerful signs in blasted-open shops saying 'yes, we are bleeding well open.' There was a huge crater in Hyde Park where a bomb had dropped. It looked spooky, surreal, and on the southern end of it, near Rotten Row, endless neat allotments.

'My God,' said Florence, 'what a nightmare. I can't believe anything is still standing.'

Yet when they reached the select confines of Baker Street, all was quiet and peaceful; Hitler had clearly not yet reached it.

'Are you all right?' asked Grace, as they knocked on Clifford's door.

'I'm fine,' said Florence, 'better than I've felt for weeks.'

'There was no answer to their knock; they tried three times.

'He knows I'm coming,' said Grace distractedly. 'He promised he'd be here.'

'Let's try the flat next door.'

Next door housed a tall, imposing, rather elegant-looking woman. Yes, she knew Mr Bennett, such a charming man, but he had been very low of late. She had no idea where he was, but he had been supposed to come in for bridge the night before and had knocked to say he had a bad headache, was going to have an early night. He had seemed perfectly well then.

'And you've no reason to suppose he's ill?' said Grace. 'He had a heart attack eighteen months ago, we worried about him.'

'Well, no – I don't think so,' said the woman. She looked embarrassed.

'Look,' said Florence, 'I'm his daughter. If there's something I ought to know, please tell me. It's important.'

'Well – I can only say he – he drinks rather too much. Sometimes at least,' said the woman. 'At other times, he's perfectly all right. We were wondering if there was something we should do. And if he has a heart condition – well – '

Grace's eyes met Florence's in perfect understanding and some relief; if that was the only problem, it was more containable than the breakdown which Grace had feared.

'Is there any way we could get in?' asked Florence. 'An upstairs window or something?'

The woman's eyes swept over her doubtfully. 'I don't think – ' she said.

'Oh I didn't mean me,' said Florence. 'My sister-in-law here can do it.' She sounded exactly like Muriel; Grace scowled at her.

'Well, not really,' said the woman. 'You could try telephoning, that's all I can suggest. He does sometimes sleep very late – '

At which moment, the lift cranked up to the second floor and Clifford appeared from it, heavily laden with Harrods bags. 'My darlings,' he cried, setting the bags down, holding out his arms, 'how lovely, how perfectly lovely.'

But he wasn't himself. Grace and Florence watching him with loving anxiety, noticed an enormous consumption of alcohol before and after lunch, a forgetfulness about everything – where he had put things, what he was doing, where he might have been going, a vagueness when pressed on anything at all, not least his own situation; an almost deliberate refusal to discuss anything more complex than when they might have tea, whether they should go for a walk. And in repose his face was collapsed with sadness; he made a huge effort, gossiped, chatted, laughed, but he was clearly struggling with a considerable depression.

'Daddy,' said Florence, finally, 'do you really think it's all right for you to be here? In London, in the Blitz? It's terribly dangerous.'

'I know it is,' he said, his face quite savage for a moment in its misery, 'and I don't think it matters very much. Do you?'

'Daddy, of course it does.'

'Why?'

'Well – we don't want you – killed. Do we, Grace? We love you, we care what happens to you.'

'I know, my darling,' said Clifford, 'and it's sweet of you. But my future is a little bleak, don't you think? I cannot return to Wiltshire. My working days are over. My friends are few and far between. I don't have a lot to live for. Frankly.'

He smiled again, and poured himself a very large whisky. Florence and Grace looked at each other.

'But Clifford,' said Grace, 'you have us. Florence's baby to look forward to. Charles coming home one day, the end of the war – '

'Grace darling, Charles will never, I feel sure, wish to see me or speak to me again. Well, only in the briefest terms. I shall not be able to see very much of Florence's baby, I fear. Or any of you. No, I have relinquished the greater part of my life, I'm afraid. I am not saying I regret it, I don't. But it is a sadness to me in many ways. A huge sadness. And therefore I cannot fear any of Mr Hitler's bombs too much. Oh I'm sorry,' he said, sensing their unhappiness, their anxiety, 'I didn't mean to be morbid. Listen, I have lots of fun still. Mrs Turner Andrews next door is a charming woman, we play bridge a great deal, I go to concerts almost every day, Myra Hess gives the most wonderful recitals at the National Gallery. Such a marvellous, brave woman. And as I told you, Grace, I go to my club. It is not really very terrible. But I can't leave London, all I have of life is here, and I hope very much you are not going to try and tell me to drink less. Because I really don't want to do that. Now then, what shall we do this evening? Brave the West End? There are lots of restaurants still open, you'd be surprised. Or shall we eat here? I daresay I could knock something up, I have become a great whizz with the dried egg – '

'Daddy,' said Florence carefully, 'Daddy, what about the – the money side of things? It seems there isn't very much. Do you have shares or anything, perhaps, that you could – well, sell a few of?'

'Shares, my angel? Not the time to sell! The stock exchange is not exactly booming at the moment.' He poured himself another whisky. 'Tell your mother she's welcome to my pension. I don't spend much now. Only on this stuff,' he added, indicating the bottle. 'There's no food in the shops to buy. I don't need clothes. So I can make that over to her. Pay it into her account.'

'Yes but – '

'Florence darling,' he said, and he looked very serious suddenly, very intense, 'there is a war on, you know. Even your mother must face that fact. Everyone is having to make sacrifices. Even if I were still living in Wiltshire, we would be a great deal less well-off. Now any remaining stock I have she is welcome to, I will write to Larry Jacobs and tell him that, but it won't be much. Charles had some money, Grace, of course. I don't know if you could find it in your heart to help Muriel. He was left quite a large sum of money by my father, it was invested in various gilts, I expect he told you about it – '

'No,' said Grace, surprised, 'no, he didn't. I wonder why – '

'Well, anyway, there should be some income from that. So you're all right presumably.'

'Yes. Yes of course. Don't worry about me.'

'I shall always worry about you, poppet. My little friend.' He reached out, patted her hand, looked at her with an expression of great tenderness. 'And Florence, Robert is an extremely rich man. I imagine he has made satisfactory arrangements for you, no matter what has passed between you. If not – '

'Yes,' said Florence, carefully vague, 'yes of course.'

They left him at five to visit Florence's house, promising to return at six thirty for a quiet supper. The sky was cloudy; 'We shouldn't get any raids tonight,' said Clifford.

'And can we sleep here?' asked Florence. 'I don't fancy the house, it'll be freezing.'

'Yes of course. You can have a room each and I'll get out the camp bed.'

'Clifford,' said Grace firmly, 'I'll sleep on the camp bed. I absolutely insist.'

The house in Sloane Avenue was fine; intact, unbroken into. It was a pleasant surprise. Crime in London had reached unheard-of propor-tions; even the dead were not sacred, freshly bombed houses and corpses were searched for handbags, wallets, even jewellery. Florence stood in the drawing room, looking round at the shrouded furniture, the fine fireplace, the shuttered windows. 'I was so thrilled with this house,' she said, 'when Robert bought it. Now it seems like part of a terrible dream.'

Grace didn't answer.

They went to bed early. Florence phoned Muriel purporting to be at the Priory, told her everything was fine.

Clifford had consumed two bottles of wine, the best part of a bottle of whisky, and several glasses of brandy with the devilled dried egg he had cooked. He had remained comparatively articulate, continuing to relate and demand gossip, professing great interest in what he called Grace's little boys – 'You must bring them to see me' – and her war work, fussing over Florence and her impending confinement. He managed to get to his room but there was a crash as he fell over a chair, a groan as he collapsed onto the bed. Grace went up and found him virtually unconscious in all his clothes, face downwards.

'He would never hear the air-raid siren,' she said to Florence. 'I think it's terribly dangerous.'

Florence looked at her very soberly. 'I honestly think it would be better if he didn't,' she said. 'He seems to have given up on life.'

It was two in the morning when Grace woke up, to find Florence shaking her. She was confused, disorientated.

'What is it? Air raid, what?'

'No,' said Florence, and sat down heavily on the sofa. Grace realized her teeth were chattering. 'No. I – well, Grace, I think I'm in labour.'

'What! Florence, you can't be.'

'Why can't I be?' said Florence irritably. 'That's a stupid thing to say. I'm pregnant, aren't I?'

'Yes but – '

'Look, Grace, either I've wet the bed or my waters have broken. Mrs Merrow said they'd do it at an inconvenient time and she was right.'

'Does it hurt yet?' asked Grace, struggling to sit up.

'No, not yet. My back aches a bit. But I think I'd better get to hospital. Don't you?'

Grace was impressed by her calm. 'Yes. Yes of course I do. But which one, where – ?'

'I don't know any more than you do,' said Florence. 'Couldn't you ring 999 or something?'

'Yes, that's a good idea. I'll do it. You go and get your things, Florence. Or would your father's doctor be a better idea?'

'Yes, possibly. I suppose it's not an emergency. I – ooh,' she winced.

Grace looked at her nervously. 'Pain?'

'Yes. Only a – a sort of nip. Nothing serious. Nothing like it will be, I'm sure.' She tried to smile. 'Yes, try Daddy's doctor. It's in that little book there. No use trying to wake him, I suppose.'

'No use at all,' said Grace, who had looked in already on the inert, snoring heap on Clifford's bed.

The doctor didn't answer the phone; on and on they rang.

'Must have been a consulting room,' said Florence. 'Ouch.'

Grace looked at her anxiously. 'Are you all right?'

'Yes. Yes, I'm fine. Anyway, better try 999. Or maybe the woman next door might – '

'No,' said Grace, 'let's not waste any more time.'

The ambulance service was not particularly helpful. They were very short-staffed, they said, the sky was clearing and there might be a raid, and where did they think Florence could go anyway?

'The 'ospitals are full, love, full to overflowing. If you don't have anything booked – '

'But she's in labour,' said Grace desperately. 'Prematurely.'

'Well, there's nothing much to deliverin' a baby, love. Did two meself last week, in a shelter.'

'But I can't, I mean – '

He clearly heard the terror in her voice. 'All right, love, I'll see what I can do. Give me your phone number.'

An hour later nothing had arrived. Florence was timing her pains – 'That's what it said you should do in my book' – which were coming every fifteen minutes. They weren't very bad, she said, but growing stronger every time. Grace looked at her with increasing fear. Her only knowledge of childbirth had been gleaned from books, *Gone with the Wind* being the most graphic and recent; her grasp of the procedure was not good.

She was about to go and ring the bell next door when the phone rang. It was the ambulance service – her friend from earlier. 'Someone'll be there in five minutes, love. Take her to St John's in Victoria. They've just about got room.'

'Oh,' said Grace, relief flooding her, 'oh thank you so much.'

But it was actually half an hour before the ambulance came.

Florence's calm was deserting her. 'I don't like this,' she kept saying through chattering teeth, 'I don't like it at all.' She was holding Grace's hand, and when the pain came, which it did more forcefully now, she clung onto it with both of hers.

'Right then,' said the ambulance man cheerfully. 'Let's get you into the van, love. Nice comfy bed for you, all made up, you're lucky. You coming with her?' he said to Grace.

'Well, I don't think – '

'Of course she is,' snapped Florence.

'But – '

'You'd better, love. They may be short-staffed, never know what might happen these days. You can ride in the front and I'll sit with your friend in the back. You all right, love?'

'Not really,' said Florence. She doubled over suddenly, her face wrenched with pain.

''ow often they coming?' said the man.

'Every – every fifteen minutes,' said Florence with difficulty.

'Oh, you got hours to go yet. Nothing to worry about. Come on, hop in.'

Grace got in the front feeling sick. Halfway down Park Lane Road, the air-raid siren went off.

'Christ,' said the driver. 'Jesus Christ Almighty. Hold on, miss. Race now between us and Jerry. Everything all right in the back, Fred?'

'Fine. She's doing fine, aren't you, darling?'

Grace couldn't hear Florence's reply.

The driver put his flashing light and his siren on, and his foot down. Grace, sitting there as the sky filled with thunder and fire, clinging to her seat, thought she must have died and gone to hell. Her only comfort was that they seemed at least to be going away from the raid; the noise and the light was behind them. The ambulance was going so fast it was throwing her from side to side, hurting her. God knows what it's doing to Florence, she thought.

The streets were empty of traffic; she looked at the speedometer, 60 it read. Sixty miles an hour, in this horror.

'Not long now,' said the driver, whose name he had confided to her through clenched teeth was Harry, 'couple more minutes. Christ Almighty –' This was occasioned by a bomb which seemed to Grace to have dropped right behind them, and was actually, she was told, at least five miles away. He took the next corner on what seemed to be two wheels, tyres screeching. Grace heard a scream from somewhere inside the ambulance at the same time and realized it was herself. Finally they stopped; she got out and looked at the dingy entrace to St John's Hospital in some dread.

The woman in the reception of Casualty, who seemed to be some kind of a clerk, was neither helpful nor encouraging.

'This is Casualty, we're not really equipped for maternity cases. Where was your friend booked in?'

'In the country. In a nursing home in Wiltshire,' said Florence through gritted teeth. She was sitting in a wheelchair now, white-faced, gripping the arms.

'Well, you should be there then.'

'Don't be ridiculous,' said Florence, 'I'm not, I'm here and it's certainly not through choice, I do assure you.'

'Look,' said Grace hurriedly, anxious that they would both be put out on the street if Florence really started being tactless, 'look, she's in a lot of pain, we were told we could come here, surely someone can look after her.'

'Listen to me,' said the woman with a look of great contempt. 'In the last few months we've had women in here in real pain. With their feet amputated, with their legs crushed, having lain beside their dead husbands or children for hours on end trapped in half-collapsed buildings. I really can't get too worked up about a baby, I'm afraid. Now she can go and wait in that cubicle, and I'll phone the labour ward, see what I can do. We could get some air-raid cases any minute, overflow from the Hammersmith, in which case you'll probably have to look after her yourself for a bit. There is a war on, in case you hadn't heard down there *in the country*.' She pronounced the last three words with icy contempt.

Grace pushed Florence and her wheelchair over to the cubicle, helped her onto the bed, tried to sound cheerful. 'I'm sure it won't be long,' she said, 'and they're bound to be busy.'

'I suppose so,' said Florence. 'Christ. Oh Christ.'

Her eyes in her white face were suddenly huge, frightened; her body arched in pain, her hands gripped the edge of the bed. 'It hurts,' she moaned, 'Grace, it bloody well hurts.'

Grace, not knowing what else to do, tried to smooth her hair; Florence pushed her hand away. Gradually she relaxed, breathed more easily, tried to smile. 'It's even worse than I thought,' she said, 'much worse. Mummy said it was like a bad curse pain. She must have forgotten.'

Half an hour later, no one had come near the cubicle. They could still hear the noise of bombing, ambulance bells ringing, shouting, crying. 'For Christ's sake go and find someone,' yelled Florence at the height of one of her contractions. 'I can't stand this. You're being bloody useless, Grace, absolutely bloody useless.'

Grace fled to confront the chaos; anything was better than sitting there helpless witnessing Florence's pain.

And it was chaos; casualties had been brought in, some crying, moaning, yelling, others silent, still with shock, wrapped in blankets, staring ahead of them. One man, lying quite near her, seemed to have lost an arm and was groping with the other one obviously trying to find it; a small child clung to her mother, whose head lay in a pool of blood. Everyone was dusty, dirty; every nurse, every doctor was moving with determined grimness from stretcher to stretcher, cubicle to cubicle. Grace stared in a sort of terrified horror; nothing she had read or heard about the Blitz had prepared her for any of it.

It was only a further loud yell coming from Florence's cubicle that galvanized her into action; she went up to the desk, timidly tapped the woman's arm. 'Please – so sorry – my friend – '

'What? Oh, the baby. Yes, we could do with the cubicle. I'll ring up again. We've got five up there already apparently, all in labour. Tell her to keep a bit quieter, could you? She's making more fuss than this lot put together.'

'Is there – is there anything she could have? For the pain,' said Grace. 'It's quite bad.'

'Look,' said the woman, clearly trying to be patient. 'When she gets up there they'll see to her. Right now she'll have to put up with it, I'm afraid. I'll try and get a doctor to look at her.'

Slowly, unwillingly, Grace went back to Florence. She was lying on her back, her stomach arched again, her head rolling from side to side, moaning less loudly but more pitifully. After a bit she calmed again. 'What did they say?' she said.

'They're just coming,' said Grace.

It was at least another hour before a young doctor put his head round the curtain. He grinned cheerfully at Grace.

'How's she doing? Sorry about the delay, we can't even find a spare trolley. But they're coming down for her now. Want me to have a look at her?'

'Yes – yes please,' said Grace.

She waited outside while he made his examination; there was a loud yell, she heard Florence say, 'For God's sake be careful.'

He came out grinning. 'She's fine. A good little brood mare. Got a way to go yet, though. Only about six fingers dilated. Try to get her to relax when the pains come. They'll give her something up in the labour ward I'm sure. Oh Christ – ' He looked at a new stretcher being brought in, a woman screaming, the blanket that covered her drenched with blood, 'I've got to go. Good luck.'

What seemed like a whole night but was actually only another half-hour passed; Florence alternately sweated and moaned and abused Grace, and between her pains clung to her, begged her not to go, told her she couldn't manage without her. Grace was beginning to think she couldn't stand it any longer when an orderly came down from the labour ward with a trolley.

'Got someone 'ere, 'ave you? 'ope she can wait a bit, there's dozens of 'em up there, yelling their 'eads off. Poor Sister doesn't know which way to turn.'

Grace looked at him with some foreboding.

As they reached the lift, Florence suddenly yelled again. 'God oh God,' she said, 'God, I can't stand it.'

'They all say that,' said the orderly cheerfully.

They got in the lift. Florence yelled again, very loudly, and her face distorted hideously; Grace looked at her anxiously. 'The – the doctor said you should try and relax. When the pains come,' she said.

'I'll give him bloody relax,' yelled Florence. 'Oh God, oh God – ' She suddenly tensed; she appeared to be straining violently, screaming at the same time.

'Crikey,' said the orderly, 'she's bearing down. Crikey. Better get a move on.'

'What does that mean?'

'It means she's pushing the baby out. Let me look, love – yeah, she is, oh blimey. Here, come on, 'elp me get this thing out of the lift. Come on, run, it's just down 'ere.'

Florence gripped Grace's hand. 'They've got to help me,' she said, her eyes staring wildly, 'they've got to, it's terrible, I – ' And then she contorted again, heaved, groaned, a strange primitive groan.

'Come on,' said the orderly, ' 'ang on, love, 'ere we are now. Sister, she's bearing down. Baby's crownin'.'

'Oh dear,' said Sister severely, 'we don't have a single delivery bed. You'll just have to wait,' she said to Florence, 'while I find somewhere. Pant. Pant hard. They're all making a terrible fuss tonight,' she added to the orderly. 'No self-control at all.'

'I'll give you bloody pants,' said Florence, 'and bloody self-control. Just give me something. They said gas and air, they said – oh God.'

And then there was a huge wail, a wild cry, and she heaved endlessly, violently.

'Good girl,' said Sister, suddenly more sympathetic, galvanized finally into action, 'good girl. Let's have a look. Yes, I can see baby's head now. You,' she said to Grace, 'you hold her hand, try to calm her down. Come along, dear, deep breaths, wait, wait, pant, yes, like a dog. Good, good, now push, come along, push hard, I know it hurts, but never mind, just push, and – there! Baby's head. And – wait and again and – push, come on, last time – and there you are, a lovely little girl. Well done, well done.'

And Grace, looking fearfully at the bloody mess between Florence's legs as she lay on the trolley in the darkened corridor, saw a tiny, perfect creature lying there, a huge pulsating cord attached to its tummy button, and for the rest of her life, when she heard the word miracle, she remembered that moment in all its blood and gore and pain and wonder. And as she watched, in awe and disbelief, she felt Florence's hand slide into hers, and heard Florence's voice say, 'Oh Grace, thank you, thank you. I couldn't have done it without you.'

She spent the rest of the night sleeping on a camp bed in that same corridor. Florence and her small daughter were taken away, cleaned up, pronounced as having done very well and being quite perfect in their respective ways, and put to bed in an enormous ward.

Grace was allowed to visit them once; Florence was sitting up, holding the baby in her arms, smiling radiantly. 'I'm going to call her Imogen,' she said, 'Imogen Grace. Do you think that's nice?'

'Lovely,' said Grace, who thought it was awful.

'And thank you again.'

'That's all right. It was nothing really.'

'It was a lot. I won't forget.'

'Goodnight,' said Grace. 'She's beautiful.'

Even then she couldn't bring herself to kiss Florence.

In the morning she went to the ward. Florence was giving Imogen a bottle. There were twenty-four beds filled with yelling, raucous cockney women and their yelling, raucous babies, an unthinkable environment for Florence. Grace half expected her to say something tactless, but she said, 'It's wonderful here, awfully jolly. I've made lots of friends already. Much nicer than those awful single wards. Here, Maisie, this is Grace, my sister-in-law. I told you about her, she practically delivered my baby last night.'

Maisie had blonde peroxide curls and a missing front tooth. 'Pleased to meet you,' she said to Grace.

'Maisie's going to show me how to do a nappy later,' said Florence. 'After all, I've got to learn – we certainly won't be able to get a nanny now, not even a maternity nurse I imagine.'

Grace flinched, fearing this was not overtactful conversation, but Maisie merely winked at her over Florence's head. 'She's a right one isn't she?' was all she said.

Chapter Fourteen

Spring–Summer 1941

Grace took Clifford to see Florence and the baby later next morning; Florence looked radiant.

'This is such fun,' she said, 'you can't imagine. I never want to leave. And Imogen is so good, so terribly good, really the best baby in the ward. Isn't she, Maisie?'

'Yeah,' said Maisie.

'Maisie's husband is in the Engineers,' said Florence, 'same as Robert. He's on the buses in peacetime.'

She brought this phrase out with some pride, as if she was mastering a strange new language.

'Maisie's going home tomorrow, I'm going to miss her so much. Her and Clark. That's her baby, she's named him after Clark Gable, he looks a bit like him actually, I think, Maisie – '

'Oh honestly,' said Maisie, 'the things you say.'

'Did you speak to Mummy? What did she say? Was she pleased, can she come up? I can't wait to show her Imogen. Maisie's mother is such a character, she gave me a pair of bootees for Imogen. Maisie's auntie's knitted ten pairs for Clark, and she thought she could spare – '

Grace wondered when the bright bubble Florence was sitting within would burst, how she was going to face telling Robert, whether she would tell Imogen's father. She suddenly wanted to get away from it all; it seemed rather sickening. Not to mention unfair.

She left Florence in London; it was agreed that she and Imogen should go and stay with Clifford when they came out of hospital and travel home when they were both strong enough. It felt slightly like leaving them in the care of a small, not very reliable child, but there didn't seem much option. She had to get back to her boys, and she really didn't think she could stand very much more of Florence in her role of Perfect Mother. It was a relief that Imogen had arrived safely and was clearly giving so much pleasure, but Grace's loyalties were still with Robert. She hoped fervently that she would never have to communicate with him on the subject. Delivering, or helping to deliver,

Florence's lover's baby was one thing; lying to Florence's husband – who she was so fond of – was quite another.

It took her seven hours to get home; it was freezing cold, the lights were much too dim to read by and the train was so crowded it was impossible to get out of the compartment and along the corridor to the lavatory; hell, she decided, was not after all an ambulance in a London air raid, but the Great Western Railway.

My darling Giles,

I only pray this will reach you soon. I have the most wonderful news. We have a daughter. Quite the most beautiful baby ever; with blonde hair and blue eyes, exactly like her father! She arrived early, caught me quite unawares, in the corridor of a hospital in London. In fact she was almost born in an ambulance in the middle of an air raid. One day it will make a good story to tell her. She weighed almost six pounds, which the sister said was a very good weight for an early baby. It was all absolutely fine, a bit painful of course, but so exciting and marvellous at the end, who cares? My sister-in-law Grace, who I never actually liked very much, was simply wonderful, never left me (I spent most of my labour in the Casualty Department!) and did a lot to comfort and help me. I feel I owe her a great deal.

Imogen eats a great deal and has already put on three ounces. That may not sound very much to you, but I can assure you it is very good indeed. I feel absolutely marvellous and have been told I can get out of bed tomorrow. When I am discharged, I am going to stay with my father until I can get home. I shall have to tell my mother I'm with friends. She still behaves as if Daddy didn't exist, and would I'm sure come up and remove me and the baby by force if she thought we were with him. Dear old thing, he may be very naughty, but he is so sweet, and adores the baby. I didn't realize how much I'd missed him. It's lovely to be with him again.

I don't know quite what is to become of him, he's all alone in the world now. Grace seems to feel very responsible for him, and it was because of her we were up in London when the baby was born. She says he was very kind to her when she first knew Charles. That made me feel bad too, I'm afraid I was horrid to her.

Oh darling, I wish you could see Imogen. She is so beautiful. I spend hours just gazing at her, and thinking of you, and how much I love you. I long so much to hear from you. Goodness knows when you will get this, I suppose the letters wait for you at some port or other. Anyway, now I have Imogen I can be strong and brave for however long it takes. Thank you for her.

All my love, no, all *our* love,

Florence and Imogen

Cable to Major Robert Grieg, Gibraltar
Imogen Grace born finally 14 January, weight five pounds, both well. Love Florence

Let's just hope, thought Florence, entrusting Clifford with both these missives, that Robert's memories of last spring are nice and hazy.

Grace had done some careful sums after the conversation with Mr Jacobs, decided she could manage on far less than she was getting, especially with the fifteen shillings from Daniel and David, her ever-more productive hens and, now that summer was coming, produce from her garden. She had at last acquired a goat; so far it had proved a severe burden rather than a help, eating everything in sight, including all Grace's sweet peas and a whole line of washing, and had refused to give any milk, despite having been sold to them with the promise of at least a pint a day. She was called Flossie because Daniel had said she looked like Florence; Grace had frowned at him and told him not to be cheeky, but there was something about the goat's cross expression, silky black coat and long, spindly legs that – well, she just hoped Florence wouldn't put two and two together, that was all. Probably not, she was so obsessed with Imogen it seemed unlikely; she never talked or thought about anything else. Anyway, Grace said to Mr Jacobs that what with one thing and another she had the house, and the car, she got her petrol allowance, she could manage on half her allowance if she really tried; she asked him carefully what, if anything, Muriel had done.

'Nothing as yet, Mrs Bennett. I am at my wits' end.'

'What about my father-in-law's pension?'

'I have not heard from him.'

'Oh dear,' said Grace. 'I'm afraid he's not himself at all. He promised to write to you about it. I'll jog his memory.'

She got Clifford on a bad day; he sounded actually drunk, which was very unusual. 'Don't worry, my darling, will do. Will do everything. Just don't worry,' he said and put the phone down.

He clearly wasn't going to do anything; Grace phoned Florence, who was now home, and said she must impress on Muriel the need to economize.

'She won't,' said Florence, 'she thinks economizing is giving Cook an extra afternoon off.'

'Well, you must try and make her. Otherwise she'll have to sell the Priory.'

'Good Lord,' said Florence, 'then what would Imogen and I do?'

'She's driving me mad,' said Florence, having pushed Imogen the two and a half miles down the lane to see Grace one morning and stayed for the day, alternately calling on Grace to admire Imogen and asking for endless drinks, boiled water for the bottles and even at one stage to rinse out a dirty nappy. 'I have tried, Grace, honestly I have, but she never stops railing against my father, and saying *he* must make economies, it's not up to her. I suppose she has a point. I don't know that I can stand it much longer, I might come and stay with you for a bit.'

It didn't seem to occur to her that Grace might not want her.

'Oh my Lord!' said Linda. 'Ben's been posted.'

'Where to?' said Nan.

'North Africa.'

'When's he going?'

'Just a minute, hang on, hang on. Very soon, Nan, in about a fortnight or so. He's a sergeant now. What do you think about that?'

'Only what his father was,' said Nan sternly. 'Is 'e getting home first?'

'No. He says he's asked, but all the boys are asking, and they're only letting special cases come.'

'What's a special case then?'

'Well, I don't know. Maybe a new baby, something like that. Oh, Nan, it sounds a long way. Christ, I'd like to see him. Just once more – '

'Don't talk like that,' said Nan severely. 'Anyway, there's a war on, I keep telling you, last time they didn't get 'ardly any leave at all.'

'Yeah, all right, all right.'

But later she saw Nan staring out of the window, tears rolling slowly down her white face; she went over and gave her a hug. Nan smiled absently, turned and patted her hand.

'You've been a good girl to me, Linda, while he's been away, all through the Blitz and that. Couldn't have been no better, not if you'd been me own daughter.'

'Oh give over,' said Linda.

Janice said she should go up to Liverpool and try to see Ben. 'Why not?'

'Well, I don't know,' said Linda doubtfully. 'I hadn't thought of that. What about my job?'

'You could go one weekend. Be a laugh. See what he says.'

'I can't get in touch with him that easily, Jan. But I might. I'll think about it.'

'You do that. You coming up West this weekend?'

'Might as well, I suppose,' said Linda. 'If I don't go up to Liverpool, that is.'

Clarissa had a few days' leave; she had come down to see Florence and the baby. Florence had talked to her about the problem with Muriel's finances, and she arrived at the Mill House one afternoon to see Grace. Jack was up in Scotland: 'A rest period they call it, he hates it, but at least he's safe.' She had only seen him once in five months, she said, 'and then only for twenty-four rather dodgy hours.'

Grace looked at her; she had changed, become steadier, slightly more sober with her life in the Wrens. She had had her hair cut shorter, looked older, more sophisticated, but was still dazzling, still lit up wherever she was with her charm. She was also the first woman Grace had seen for a long time who looked remotely fashionable; she was dressed in a scarlet silk dress and, although it had the obligatory short skirt and unflattering square shoulders, on Clarissa's neat, slender body it looked strangely chic. She had what looked like new white shoes, and a matching white bag tucked under her arm; a small red and white straw hat perched on the front of her head. She was beautifully made up; the only clue that there was any kind of a restriction on clothes was the fact that her legs were bare. Grace thought, studying her almost greedily, that nice clothes had become exactly like delicious food, a hazy, dreamlike memory.

'Are you enjoying the Wrens?' she asked.

'Oh so much, you can't imagine. It is so marvellous, Grace, to have a sense of shared purpose. To be working with people all to the same end. Doesn't sound too much like me, does it? Jack keeps complaining I've changed. But I can't help it. Anyway, I'm not the only one. Grumpy old thing he's turned into.' She laughed, just slightly less easily than usual, carefully changed the subject. 'Anyway, how are you, darling?'

'Oh I'm fine,' said Grace. 'A bit lonely of course – missing Charles.'

'Of course you are. I've been so lucky, Jack being in England all this time. But at least you have your little boys. Goodness they're sweet.'

'Do you really like them?' said Grace, surprised.

'Well of course I do. They're enchanting. And the older one is going to be so handsome. Whyever shouldn't I like them?'

'Muriel deeply disapproves,' said Grace, 'and I don't think Florence feels much differently and Charles has written ordering me to get rid of them – '

'He hasn't! Dear God, He is – Well, I hope you're not going to, darling.'

'No I'm not,' said Grace.

'Good. I never heard anything so pompous – well he always was that way inclined. It's absurd. When you're here, coping all on your own, managing so wonderfully.'

'Well, it's very nice of you to say so,' said Grace, realizing she had never heard Charles criticized by anyone before and rather to her shame liking it; and then quite suddenly, taking herself completely by surprise, she said, 'Clarissa, why did you break off your engagement? You and Charles.'

She was amazed at herself for asking the question at all, but she had wanted to for so long and Clarissa seemed so approachable suddenly, almost a proper friend. Grace sat back and looked at her now; she was studying the grass rather intently, her lovely face thoughtful. She took her hat off and a breeze lifted her blonde hair, blew it across her large brown eyes. She was so beautiful, Grace thought, so truly and absolutely beautiful: how could Charles have ever, ever let her go?

'Well,' said Clarissa, carefully now, 'well, you see, it just wasn't working. I told you. Surely Charles told you.'

'Yes, but why? Why? Please don't give me all that stuff about him being quiet and you liking parties and everything, I don't believe it, and anyway, it's not true, he does. And why didn't he tell me about – about you? It seems so odd.'

'Oh darling, hurt pride, I expect. You know what men are like.'

'Not really, no,' said Grace, and she knew she was sounding silly, and she longed not to, but she didn't seem able to help it. 'I don't. I've led a very sheltered life, Clarissa. I'm not very – very up on men and what they're like.'

'Darling Grace, you really shouldn't put yourself down so much. It's so silly, when you're so clever and so lovely.'

'Don't try to change the subject!' said Grace, and her voice was louder now in her exasperation. 'I want to know what happened. What went wrong.'

Clarissa stood up suddenly and walked down the garden a little way, stood gazing over the fence at the field where Flossie lived so parasitically. Then she turned and looked at Grace, very steadily.

'I can only tell you,' she said finally, carefully, 'that we seemed to be making each other miserable. It just wasn't working any more. It was wonderful at first, of course, absolutely rapturous, and then it all went rather badly wrong. We started to have a lot of rows, and I could see it was only going to get worse. And he's not a person it's easy to – well, sort things out with. He doesn't take criticism exactly kindly. You must know all his faults as well as I do. Love him as we both do. I wish I could give you a better explanation, darling, but I can't. I'm sorry.'

Grace looked at her and knew with absolute certainty that Clarissa might be telling the truth as far as it went, but that there was more to it than that, and knew moreover that she was not going to hear it. Not now at any rate. Pressing Clarissa would do her no good whatsoever; she quite clearly, from the careless, confident way she spoke about him, knew more about Charles, had been closer to him than Grace ever had, even within their marriage, and it hurt and humiliated her more than she would have believed. She had tried never to think about it before, but it suddenly became very clear to her that Clarissa had been to bed with Charles while they were engaged, and no doubt had had a most wonderful time there together; and that thought more than any other made her feel helplessly wretched. She felt suddenly even shabbier than usual, aware of her droopy, unevenly hemmed dress, her sensible walking shoes, her uncut hair. She hated Clarissa with a hot, fierce jealousy, wanted her out of her garden, with her glamour and her beauty, her intimate knowledge of Charles.

'Well,' she said finally, 'I think there's obviously a bit more to it than that. But you obviously don't intend to tell me. Yours and Charles's little secret, no doubt. Now if you'll excuse me, Clarissa, I have a lot to do.' And then, to her horror, she felt tears filling her eyes, and turned away, furious at them, that Clarissa might see, know why they were there, detect her weakness, her vulnerability.

And Clarissa of course did see them; she came over to Grace, put her arms round her, and much as Grace wanted to push her away, say something clever and self-assured, she couldn't.

'Listen,' said Clarissa gently, 'please listen, Grace. All that matters is that Charles married you, he wanted to marry you, and he's terribly happy with you.'

'You don't know that,' said Grace dully.

'Of course I know it. I can see for myself, and anyway he's told me so – lots of times.'

'He has?' said Grace.

'Yes, of course he has.'

Grace wasn't sure if she liked that, the thought of Charles and Clarissa talking about her, albeit kindly, indulgently, rather as if she was a child. And then thought she was being ungrateful, ungracious even, and 'Well,' she said, smiling a bit bleakly at Clarissa, 'I'm glad he's happy with me. I do wonder sometimes. I suppose everybody does. You probably don't,' she added.

'No, I can't say I do,' said Clarissa, 'but that comes of being a bigheaded little madam, as my nanny used to call me. Dear Nanny. She died last year, I cried more at her funeral than I did at my mother's. Isn't that awful? My mother was wonderful, frightfully glamorous and everything, the original girl who danced with the Prince of Wales, you know, but I never really felt I knew her. Now your mother's a real mother. Isn't she?'

'Yes, I suppose she is,' said Grace. She hadn't really thought about it before.

'Like Florence is going to be. Isn't that amazing, whoever would have thought it? Now listen, darling, I must go. It's a bit of a hike back to the Priory. I'm going to have a chat with Clifford when I get back to London, see if I can't persuade him to do something about the finances. And darling, you really mustn't even think of getting rid of those boys. Charles had no right to ask you.' Her voice was very serious suddenly, almost passionate. Grace looked at her, startled. 'He's – well, he's rather a taker, Charles. The tiniest bit manipulative. You must stand up for yourself, Grace. You're doing a wonderful job here. Don't let him – unsettle you.'

It seemed a strange word, but she pronounced it very definitely. There was an expression in her brown eyes that intrigued Grace: an earnestness, something close to anxiety. Then she smiled, deliberately lightening the atmosphere.

'We girls have to stick together. Against these wretched men. Not let them get the upper hand. Goodbye, darling. It's been lovely.'

'Goodbye' said Grace, returning the kiss. She felt cheered suddenly by Clarissa's friendship. She was a most unexpected ally, Grace thought; but she could clearly be a very powerful one. If she ever needed help again, she would know where to ask for it.

Ben's battalion was leaving for North Africa on 12 June. Linda had written to ask him if he wanted her to go up and see him, but there had been no reply; obviously he hadn't got the letter, but she was nonetheless disappointed, upset, sharply aware of her loneliness, of missing him, of the strain of living alone with Nan. Janice told her to take pot luck, go up anyway, but she said she didn't think she should. 'I'd never find him, and he might get into trouble. No, if he doesn't reply he doesn't, and I'll just have to put it down to fate.'

On the night of 7 June, which was particularly lovely, Janice asked Linda to go to a party with her and some other girls at Frisco's Club, near Piccadilly.

'It'll be fun, go on, lots of RAF chaps coming. Someone's twenty-first, that pilot we met last week, do you remember?'

'Yeah, he was gorgeous.'

'Well then – '

'Jan, I don't think I should,' said Linda. 'Nan's always going on about me going out all the time. I'm scared she'll write and tell Ben.'

'Evil old bag,' said Janice, 'Anyway, I'm sure she won't. What's she got to tell anyway? You haven't done anything wrong. Go on, Linda, it'll do you good. You seem a bit low. Come for a bit anyway.'

'Yeah, I am a bit. Low I mean,' said Linda. 'All right, I'll come for an hour or so. Might cheer me up.'

'Course it will.'

She got ready in the factory toilets, so she didn't have to go home, told Nan she was working an extra shift; she'd been practising a new hairstyle and she'd been dying to try it out. It fell in a huge, snaky wave over one eye, and it was called the Peek-a-boo look; Veronica Lake had made it famous and it was banned in the factories because it might get caught in the machinery. She had made herself a new blouse, Nan had given her her clothing coupons, and taken her skirt up. Oh for some stockings, she thought, slapping on leg make-up, drawing the seam up the back of her legs with a thick eyebrow pencil. All the girls did, but at least she had decent legs, and her high heels were still in good nick; she looked all right, more than all right, pretty nice really.

It was a very good party: lots of booze, lots of good music and she found herself on the receiving end of a great deal of attention. Maybe it was just the hairstyle, but she really had got the hang of the jitterbug now and at one stage the whole floor cleared to watch her and her partner, the RAF pilot. He reminded her of Ben a bit; he was dark, with the same melting brown eyes.

'I must go,' she said to Janice at ten o'clock. 'I really must. I'll miss the bus else.'

'Oh go on. Why don't you stay? You look more cheerful than you have for weeks. We can sleep down the tube, go back in the morning. This is such good fun. And there's some more blokes coming later.'

Linda hesitated; it was a huge temptation. She was having such a good time and Janice was right, she had cheered up. And she wasn't going to see Ben for so long.

But – 'No,' she said finally, 'no, I think I'd best get back. Nan'll be worried. I'll ring you in the morning.'

'You're nuts,' said Janice cheerfully.

'She's gorgeous, your friend,' said one of the pilots, watching Linda's curvy figure, her slender legs, as she made her way up the steps of the club. 'I could really get to fancy her.'

'Yeah, well don't bother. She's well spoken for,' said Janice.

That night there was the first air raid for some time: a landmine fell on Chiswick and a stick of bombs on Acton. The little house where Linda and Nan lived was hit before they had time to get to the shelter; Linda was found under a heap of rubble, still holding Nan's dressing gown.

Chapter Fifteen

Summer 1941

'Thing is, miss, they're asking me to do housework, miss. Scrubbing the kitchen floor this morning, I was. Yesterday it was washing the sheets. And then out for haymaking. It's not what I came for, miss, it's not right.'

'No, it isn't right,' said Grace with a sigh. 'What about the other two girls, is it the same for them?'

'Well it is for Edna. Dorothy's all right.'

The glare that accompanied this made it clear Dorothy was a case apart. 'No better than she should be, Dorothy isn't.'

'Now what does that mean, Madge?'

Silence. Grace sighed again. 'Madge, if you don't tell me everything I can't possibly sort things out. Or try and sort them out.'

'Dorothy's sweet on the farmer's brother, Miss,' said Madge. 'And it's mutual. Always kissing, and worse, up in the lofts, she'll get her comeuppance good and proper if she's not very careful and – '

'Yes, all right, Madge. I certainly can't do anything about that. It's quite outside my area of responsibility. But I take it Dorothy doesn't get asked to scrub floors and so on?'

'No, miss. Nor do much haymaking neither.'

'Well, look, I'll report back to the committee. I'm not supposed to talk to the farmer direct. And we'll see if we can get you two moved. That's the best thing, I should think. Anything else while I'm here?'

'I'm still waiting for my shoes, miss,' said Madge. 'Just got the wellies, and they're not a pair. Two left feet.'

'Did you say anything when they gave them to you?' said Grace wearily.

'Of course I did,' said Madge. 'The woman said I had to put up with 'em for now. For now! 'itler'll be an old man before I get a pair, this rate.'

'Well I'll see if I can sort that out as well,' said Grace, 'it can't be very comfortable. I'll be in touch. All right?'

'All right, miss. Thanks, miss.'

As she drove home along the sunlit lanes, she wondered how much longer she would be able to do this job. It was all very well when she had had plenty of time and money, but it was extremely time-consuming, especially as she was so conscientious. Mrs Lacey had told her it shouldn't take more than a couple of hours a week, but then Mrs Lacey was not too much in touch with reality.

Grace had cut down the hours the gardener spent with her, and was doing a lot more herself, and the same went for Mrs Babbage and the housework. David's relentless bed-wetting actually did make for a lot of work, and cooking seemed to take longer and longer as supplies dwindled. She had become a whizz at egg dishes (although with the meal for the hens being rationed now, she had to give up her egg coupons in return), and she was beginning to reap her vegetable harvest, but not having any butter made a lot of the cooking very difficult. She had found that if she beat milk into the butter, it went much further, increased the two ounces by about twenty-five per cent, but that took a long time. They were comparatively lucky in the country with meat; although the rations were supposed to be strictly adhered to, rabbits were fairly plentiful, although their increasing popularity made them harder to come by, and a sheep had only to look a tiny bit scrapy, as Mrs Babbage called it, and it would find itself very swiftly converted into stew. Grace, who had become something of a pet with the local farmers – for she usually managed to put their view to her girls, as well as the other way round – often got half a pound of mutton or a skinned rabbit pressed into her hands as she left.

And now she had a new source of illicit supplies. One of the pupils at Miss Merton's dancing class, a tiny, rosy-faced creature called Elspeth Dunn showed, Grace thought, extraordinary musicality; she had found her picking out a tune on the piano one day and had begun to teach her a little after each class. After a few weeks, Elspeth's father, who was a burly, rather morose-looking man who collected her in his truck from school, marched up to Grace and asked her if it was her teaching Elspeth tunes; Grace rather nervously said it was.

' 'Tisn't right,' he said, ' 'tisn't right, not really.'

'Well, I'm sorry, but she seemed so keen and she's very musical,' said Grace.

'That's as maybe, And I'm not sayin' she don't enjoy it, but 'tisn't right you doing it for nothin'. So I want you to 'ave this,' and he reached into the deep pocket of his hugely ancient, baggy tweed trousers and produced a grubby greaseproof paper parcel, wrapped around with rubber bands.

'You take this,' he said, 'You look like you could do with puttin' a bit of weight on.'

And then he was gone, looking gloomier than ever; Grace rather gingerly opened the parcel and found quite a large piece of cheese inside, a wonderful dark rich Cheddar.

'Oh,' she said rapturously to David, who was waiting patiently for her, 'we can have cauliflower cheese tonight for supper, think of that.'

'Daniel won't like it, miss.'

'Daniel can lump it.'

'Yes, miss.' He grinned up at her. 'All the more for us, miss.'

However hard she tried, she couldn't get them to call her anything but 'miss'.

'There's a telegram for you, Florence,' said Muriel.

Florence had been lying in the garden, gazing at Imogen with adoring eyes, at her fat brown arms and legs, the blonde fluff appearing on her small head, the brilliantly blue eyes fixed on a toy just out of reach, and trying to decide if the rolling motion Imogen had adopted recently when put on her tummy really showed an early attempt at crawling. Muriel's words permeated her happiness, splintered it into dark, threatening fragments. Robert had written several times about the baby, had expressed his great joy and pride, had said how he missed her, how he longed to meet his daughter, how he was living for the time when they could be together again: harmless, clever letters, designed to make her feel safe, secure, back in his thrall. It was strange, she could not explain it even to herself, but when she had not heard from him for a while her determination to leave him, to seek a divorce increased, but once he was in contact with her, however tenuously, she became frightened again, trapped, helpless.

She had tried to explain it to Clarissa, she being the only person privy to her secret, and Clarissa had said, in her cheerful clearsighted way, 'He's got you by the balls, darling, that's where.'

'I don't know what you mean,' said Florence fretfully.

'I mean he's brainwashed you. Made you believe he's in control. Whatever you do. One of the chaps here was talking about it the other day, been on some sort of course. On interrogation. Someone gets right into your head, dominates you completely like Robert did when you were first married – and you can't break out of it. Unless you resist it totally from the very beginning, which of course you didn't. Well, you wouldn't want to. It's a kind of conditioning.'

'Oh,' said Florence.

'He's taught you to think that you really can't manage without him.

Whatever he does. That you need him. Also' – she looked at Florence thoughtfully – 'you were a virgin, darling, weren't you? When you got married? Well, before Robert anyway.'

'Yes,' said Florence reluctantly.

'Well, that's pretty potent stuff, you know. First lover. Very powerful hold.'

'You're terribly clever, Clarissa,' said Florence. 'No one would think it, just meeting you, but you are.'

'Thank you, darling. For those few awfully kind words.'

'Sorry. I meant it nicely. So what do I do about it?'

'Act while he's away. You must. Your lovely heavenly Giles, would he be cited? As co-respondent?'

'Oh – yes. Yes, he would, he's often said so. But it's a bit difficult while he's at sea. If he's still at sea.' She looked at Clarissa very sombrely. 'Anyway, I mustn't start thinking about that.'

'No. You mustn't. None of us must start thinking about that. Anyway, get things going, darling. Start a divorce action. There's an awful lot of it about. Not the disgrace it was.'

'There's not a lot down here,' said Florence.

'No? Well, I expect you'll go back to London soon, won't you? The bombing does seem to be over.'

'I don't know. I feel safe here. From everything. Anyway, you're right, and I will do something about it. I'll go and see someone soon. Not Jacobs, though. Clarissa – ' Florence looked at her thoughtfully. 'Was Charles – was he – '

'My first? Darling, of course not. I'm a terribly bad girl, you know that. Tell you what though. Jack is unarguably, most definitely, absolutely my last. Now have you got anything to drink in this rather chilly old house? God, can you remember what it felt like to be warm? I can't.'

Florence took the telegram from her mother with a hand that was shaking violently, tore it open awkwardly.

'Oh my God,' she said in a whisper. 'Oh God, no.'

Muriel took the telegram from her and read it: 'Wangled week's leave. Home 14 June. All love to both, Robert.'

Grace was nearly home; she stopped the car outside the vicarage to see if the vicar wanted her for choir rehearsal the next day. The regular organist had been called up and old John Stokes was commuting between the Thorpes and really couldn't cope; Grace couldn't play the organ, but there was a piano in the church and she was much in demand for all kinds of occasions, not only choir practice but early Communion, christenings and occasionally the morning service. Muriel was deeply disapproving and had threatened to report what she called the affair to the bishop: 'What he would say if he knew that organ music had been banished from this church I cannot imagine.'

'Well, he'd have to talk either to Mr Churchill or Adolf Hitler about it,' said Grace wearily, 'they're responsible, not me.'

Muriel made the distasteful noise that was so entirely her own, halfway between a snort and a sniff, and went back to the socks she was knitting – 'for Charles. You certainly won't be making any, with those refugees taking up all your time.'

The vicar did want her for choir practice; he gave her a cup of rather strong tea and a highly indigestible Spam sandwich, asked her how the boys were, whether she had heard from Charles recently, and if she could help with the fête. By the time she escaped it was well after one.

As she got back into her car, a small army truck went past her; there was so little traffic on the roads these days, apart from farm vehicles, that you noticed everything. Now where could that be going, on this lovely day, so far from anywhere? she wondered, and drove on down the High Street, thinking not for the first time that if Charles knew she was driving his precious car about, and without even having had any proper driving lessons, he would – well, she couldn't think what he would do. Maybe she would be driven to selling it if there was no money for her to live on, and that would serve him right. The thought quite cheered her up.

She was held up in the lane outside the village by a herd of cows; she sat there patiently, smiling at them, thinking how sweet they were with their long lashes and huge, moist noses, and then started again on down the hill to the Mill House. And stiffened, in something approaching terror, terror and awe, at the sight of the army truck standing in her drive.

She got out, her legs suddenly weak; stood there leaning on the car, staring, as a man climbed down from the truck, a sergeant, she noticed confusedly. He was tall, and rather thin, with immensely dark eyes, and he reminded her of someone and she couldn't think who. He walked heavily towards her, taking off his beret, holding out his hand, and his handshake was warm, warm and very steady, and his face, narrow, angular, was drawn, strained, and although he smiled at her, it was fleeting, gone again at once, and then he spoke, and his voice was gentle, quite quiet, with a London accent, and she remembered that moment, those words for the rest of her life; time froze as she stood there, her hand in his, his dark eyes fixed almost desperately on her face, and he said, 'Mrs Bennett? Mrs – Grace Bennett?'

And 'Yes,' she said, not moving, not taking her hand away, 'yes, that's me.'

'I'm sorry to disturb you, Mrs Bennett,' he said. 'I'm Ben Lucas, David and Daniel's father. Could I come inside for a bit, please?'

Summer–Autumn 1941

He sat at the kitchen table, his long legs slightly awkwardly confined under it, blowing his nose, looking at her rather helplessly as she poured him a beer.

'I'm sorry,' he kept saying, 'I'm sorry, Mrs Bennett. I didn't mean to – '

'Mr Lucas, please don't apologize. Please.'

'It was saying it. Telling you. I haven't had to do that before.'

'Of course. I really, really don't mind. I'm glad you did. It might help. A bit.'

What a stupid, crass thing to say to a man who had just told you his wife was dead; what could you, should you say to a man who had just told you his wife was dead? Who had walked into your house and stood very stiffly as if to attention in your hall, and looked around it rather vaguely and then asked if his little boys were there, and then when she had said no, they were at school, had said when would they be back because he had to tell them something, and then when she had said very gently what, had told her their mother was dead, had been killed in an air raid, two nights earlier, and had then asked if he might sit down and had gone to the bottom of the stairs and hunched himself up on them and stared at her in silence, his dark eyes filled with tears – so exactly like David's that she felt she knew him enough to go towards him and sit beside him and put her hand just very gently on his arm while he struggled painfully, dreadfully to pull himself together, to recover his self-control.

After a while he had sighed heavily, smiled at her weakly and pulled out his handkerchief; and that was when she had suggested he came into the kitchen.

'What about your – your driver?' she said. 'Would he like a drink, do you think?'

'Oh, yes, I suppose he would. Thank you. I'd rather he wasn't – well, didn't – '

'No, it's all right,' said Grace, 'I'll take it out to him.' And he said, 'You're being very patient. Linda told me how nice you were.'

'I – well, I never met her,' said Grace, horribly aware that now she never would, was underlining the fact; but he didn't seem to mind, he said, 'No, but she said the boys reckon you. Reckon you a lot.'

'Well,' she said, smiling at him, 'I reckon them too. A lot. I love them.'

She was surprised to hear herself say that, was afraid it sounded rather excessive, rather like Clarissa, but he didn't seem to mind, smiled back at her, and when she returned from taking the driver his beer, had said carefully that she would ask him in in a minute, Ben Lucas seemed to be very much more in control, was standing up, smoothing back his hair.

'Thing is,' he said, 'I've got to tell them. And I don't know how. I don't know if I can. But I must. Mustn't I?'

'Yes,' she said, 'you must, I'm afraid. Unless' – her heart quailing, flinching from the task – 'unless you'd like me to – '

'Oh no,' he said, 'no, that wouldn't be right. No, I've got to do it. When will they be back?'

She looked at her watch. 'In about an hour. Or is it, God I hope it isn't, Wednesday?'

'No,' he said, and this time he smiled more easily, 'no, it's Tuesday. What's so bad about Wednesday?'

He had a very nice voice; it was deep, and rather slow, and although usually she didn't like the London accent, it somehow suited him, suited his carefully polite manners, his quiet awkwardness.

'Nothing,' she said and smiled again, 'except it's dancing day. At school.'

'David and Daniel do dancing?' he said; the concept was plainly astonishing.

'Well, no they don't. But I play the piano for dancing and they wait for me.'

'Yes,' he said, 'Linda said you'd been giving David lessons on the piano.'

'Yes I have.'

'That was very kind.'

'Not at all, I love doing it. He's very musical, you know.'

'Is he? Well, he might have some music in him, my dad played the violin quite nicely.'

'Did he really?' said Grace. 'Did he teach you?'

'He tried, but he didn't have much time, or strength come to that, by the time I was of an age. He got the gas, in the last war, he died when he was only forty-two.'

'How sad,' said Grace, 'and your – your mother – is she – ' and then stopped with horror, realizing that she was probably dead too, only Ben Lucas had not said so, knowing that Linda and she lived together in the little house in Acton.

'Yes,' said, understanding her silence, 'yes, she was killed too, with Linda.'

'Look,' she said, 'would you like me to go and get the boys? So you don't have to – well, it must be terrible, waiting – '

'No,' he said. 'It'd only worry them, wouldn't it, and if you don't mind having me here, I'd rather wait, get myself together a bit more, work out what I can say to them.'

'I don't mind having you here,' she said. 'Of course I don't.'

She offered him some food, 'just bread and dripping and tomatoes, I'm afraid, but there's plenty,' which he refused, but said the corporal would like some. She asked the corporal to come in; he was very, very young, didn't look more than eighteen, and was clearly completely out of his depth with the hideous human drama confronting him. He came from Derbyshire, he told her, had been drafted from Salisbury to bring Ben over; he was due to go overseas any day. 'Probably North Africa, they said.'

'Oh really?' said Grace who was trying desperately to make conversation with the poor lad. 'That's where my husband is.'

'Is it all right then, over there?' asked the corporal.

'Yes, thank you. It seems absolutely fine,' she said, anxious to sound reassuring, aware that she might have been describing a holiday resort.

David and Daniel burst into the house through the kitchen door, shouting, demanding to know what the truck was; Grace stood up as they came in, watched their faces turn to incredulity and a wild joy as they saw their father. They flew into his arms together as one small wiry creature; he encased them, kissed them, hugged them, told them they'd grown, that they looked well, and was dragged outside to see the chickens, Flossie, Charlotte. He looked back at Grace helplessly as he went; she watched with a dreadful pity as he sat down on the grass, a child on each side of him, put his arms round them, and began to talk. They had their backs to her; but she watched grief first touch them, then hit harder, saw Daniel's small, hopeful face looking up at Ben, darken, crumple, watched him hurl himself into his father's lap, his small body heave with sobs, saw David say and do nothing, nothing at all, just sit very still, staring straight ahead, and then move slightly away from Ben, hugging his knees, burying his head in his arms, watched it move from side to side, that small dark head, like an animal in a trap in terrible pain.

For a long time they sat there. The whole place seemed hushed and still; even Charlotte seemed subdued, lying a little apart from them, her head drooped between her paws. Corporal Norris asked if he could use her toilet; horrified at her lack of hospitality Grace showed him into the cloakroom, gave him a towel, went back into the kitchen, tried to think of something she could do, something appropriate that would not seem callous, careless, something that might even help Ben Lucas in his dreadful task.

It was almost evening now; the sun was lower on the hills, the birds were beginning their evening chorus, she could hear a tractor throbbing up the lane. Perhaps the chickens, yes, that was a good idea; she fetched the saucepan off the stove with the boiled-up mash, and the bag full of scraps, went out into the garden, walked past them very slowly and carefully.

'Hallo,' she said, 'I'm going to feed the chickens.'

Daniel looked at her, removed the thumb from his mouth. 'Our mum's dead,' he said.

'Yes,' said Grace, 'yes, I know. I'm so very, very sorry.'

'You couldn't be,' said David, and he was glaring at her, through eyes streaming with tears, 'you didn't know her, you couldn't be sorry.'

'David!' said Ben gently. 'David – '

'It's all right,' said Grace and sat down quite near, but not too near. 'I didn't know her, David, of course, except what you told me about her. But I'm sorry for you, so very sad and sorry. And for Daniel and your daddy.'

David looked at her and then got up and walked down to the paddock fence, ducked under it and set off across the field. Ben went to follow him, but Grace put her hand on his arm.

'Leave him. He always goes over there when life gets hard for him.'

'You know him quite well, don't you?' he said, looking at her curiously. Daniel was lying against him again, his head buried in the crook of his arm.

'Quite well. We've lived together for – goodness, eight months. We get along pretty well.'

'I think they're lucky to have you,' he said.

He had a week's compassionate leave, then he had to get back to Liverpool and his squadron, ready to sail for North Africa.

'But I've got to get to London,' he said, 'sort out the – well, the funeral and that.' He glanced down at Daniel, but he appeared not to have heard. 'I'll have to do that tomorrow.'

'Oh God,' said Grace and found tears in her own eyes at his plight, his dreadful, infinitely sad plight. She brushed them away impatiently, smiled at him awkwardly. 'Sorry,' she said.

'That's all right,' he said, 'it's nice of you to be so upset.'

'What do you want to do now?'

'Well, we're supposed to go back to the barracks at Salisbury. Me and the corporal.'

'What, tonight?' said Grace, her eyes wide with horror. 'You can't, you can't leave the boys so soon, it would be so cruel – '

'It's all cruel, Mrs Bennett. It's a cruel war. That's what my colonel said.' He looked at her and his face was harsh. 'I think he meant it helpfully. Well, I s'pose he did. Anyway, what I could do, maybe, is send the corporal back and go up to London in the morning. On the train. If I could get to the station, if you've got a bike or anything.'

'I've got a car,' said Grace, 'and I get a petrol allowance, it's for some work I do for the Land Army. I'll take you.'

'I couldn't ask you to do that,' he said.

'Of course you could. I'd like to, I want to help so much.'

'Well, it's very kind. You're very kind. Might be better,' he added, looking at the now distant figure of David across the field. 'I could stay in a pub or something maybe – '

'You can stay here,' said Grace. 'Of course you can.'

'Mrs Bennett, I don't think so,' he said, and there was a wry amusement in his eyes now. 'Whatever do you think people would think, my CO apart from anyone else, your husband – well, anyway, I couldn't do that.'

'Your CO needn't know,' said Grace firmly, 'my husband is thousands of miles away, and I really don't care about anyone else. You can tell Corporal Norris anything you like. But I want you to stay here.'

'You're very kind,' he said again, 'I can't say it wouldn't be nicer. I'm really grateful. I don't know what else to say.'

'There isn't anything to say,' said Grace briskly. 'Now I have to feed my hens.'

'I don't want to help,' said Daniel, 'I want to stay here with my dad.'

'Of course you do,' said Grace.

It was a difficult, sad evening. The boys refused to eat, David wouldn't speak. He seemed consumed by a seething, sullen anger, especially hostile to Grace. Ben, at first gently patient, became embarrassed.

'I'm sorry,' he said to Grace when David went out of the kitchen, slammed the door, ran upstairs. Daniel had fallen asleep, exhausted with crying, on the lumpy old kitchen sofa.

'Don't be,' said Grace, 'I don't mind. He can hardly be blamed for anything.'

'Maybe not. Gets it from me, I s'pose. I get angry when I'm upset.'

'Are you angry now?' said Grace gently.

'Not at the moment. I was. I wanted to smash the colonel's face in. Talking crap, telling me to be a man – sorry, Mrs Bennett, I – '

'Please stop saying you're sorry,' said Grace, 'or I shall get angry.'

'OK.' He smiled at her weakly. 'And I was angry with her, with Linda. Why couldn't she have got to the shelter, and why then? There hadn't been a raid for bloody weeks, I was bloody crazy with it all. But, I've calmed down now. Just feel – well, you know.'

'Horrible.'

'Yes. That's about it. I'd best go to him, to David.'

He came down, looking wretched, sat down heavily again on the sofa. 'He won't talk to me. Gone under the bedclothes. Poor little bugger. Sorry. Sorry! I don't know how to help him, Mrs Bennett, I really don't.'

'You can't,' said Grace, 'not yet. Nobody can. He loved her so much. He used to talk about her a lot, tell me all about her, how pretty she was, what fun – ' She looked at Ben anxiously, afraid she was saying the wrong thing, but he smiled.

'Yeah,' he said, 'yeah, she was fun. A live wire. She and my mum used to fight a bit, but they were good pals underneath. She was – she was holding Mum's dressing gown, you know, when they found her, I think she must have been waiting for her, she was slow, was Mum – ' And then he cracked, his face crumpled and he began to sob, noisy, dreadful sobs, staring ahead of him, his hands clenching and unclenching on his lap.

'Oh Ben,' said Grace tenderly, and without thinking what she was doing even, she went and put her arms round him, pulled his head onto her shoulder; he turned and clung to her, still weeping, and little Daniel stirred slightly on his other side, put out his own skinny arm and said, 'Don't cry, Dad,' and they all three sat there for a long time while the sky darkened and the moon came up.

'I'm sorry,' he said, finally, sitting back, looking at her. 'So sorry. I couldn't help it.'

'Of course you couldn't,' said Grace. 'Of course you couldn't. It doesn't matter. I'm just glad I was here, that's all.'

'I'm glad too,' he said. 'Thank you.' He blew his nose, looked down at his filthy handkerchief.

'Here,' said Grace, 'that's horrible. Let me get you a clean one.'

She went up to Charles's dressing room, opened his chest of drawers, took a couple of his handkerchiefs out, linen they were, with CB embroidered on the corner, a present from his mother.

'Here you are,' she said to Ben, handing them to him. 'Have them. Not a lot of use here. At the moment.'

He looked at them. 'Very grand handkerchiefs,' he said, 'very grand. This is quite a grand house, isn't it? Well, it seems it to me, anyway.'

'I suppose it's quite big,' said Grace carefully, 'too big really. That's why it was so lovely for me to have David and Daniel.'

'You didn't – don't have any kids of your own then? Yet?'

'No,' said Grace, 'not yet.'

'Pity. They'd be company for you, wouldn't they?'

'Yes, I suppose they would. But – well, you can't have them to order, can you?'

'We did,' he said, 'like clockwork they came. Linda fell straight away, David was a honeymoon baby, and Daniel two years later, the minute we decided it was time.'

'You were lucky,' said Grace. She heard the slight bitterness in her voice, and hated it.

He looked at her sharply. 'Is it a problem then?' he asked. 'Having them, I mean. For you.'

It was a very intimate conversation, she thought, but the events, the emotions of the day had driven them far forward, curiously close.

'I'm not sure,' she said, 'actually. We haven't – well, we haven't been married very long.'

'No?'

'No. Only two years.'

There was a long silence, then he said, 'Well, I'd best get this little chap up to bed. Where does he go?'

'I'll show you,' said Grace.

They all went to bed then; she lay awake most of the night, thinking of him there, down the corridor, hurting, suffering, wishing there was something, anything she could do to ease the pain. And knowing there wasn't.

She woke up very early, before six, went down to the kitchen; he was already there, wearing nothing but a towel wrapped round his waist.

'Oh God,' he said, 'I'm sorry, Mrs Bennett. I was going to have a quick wash, I hope that's all right, and I heard your dog crying, so I came to let her out.'

'It's all right,' she said, smiling at him. 'I really don't mind. Why don't you have a bath? There's plenty of hot water, the boiler's well stoked.'

'Are you trying to tell me I need one?' he said, grinning at her; it was the first time he had smiled, really smiled, and it was an extraordinarily engaging smile, creasing his angular face up, showing surprisingly white if slightly crooked teeth.

'Of course not,' she said, 'but – '

'I probably do. It'd be a treat. Would that really be all right?'

'Of course. I'll make some tea.'

She watched him go out of the kitchen; he was brown, very lean, very fit, and his legs were extremely long, long and muscular. He actually had needed a bath, she noticed; there was a smell of sweat in the air. Male sweat. It seemed like a rather good smell, in her spinsterish house.

'The boys are both asleep. I have to talk to you about them,' he said.

'Yes of course. You're not – you're not going to take them away, are you? I mean, to live somewhere else?' she said, hearing her own voice so alarmed that he smiled again.

'I hope I'm not. That's what I wanted to ask you, though I'm going away. For a long time, I expect, maybe – well, for a long time anyway. Would you be prepared to keep them? I mean, they've got no one else now. If anything – anything did happen, you might be stuck with them.'

'I want to keep them,' said Grace, 'I want to keep them very much.'

'They'll prob'ly be difficult,' he said, 'for a bit. I'm sorry I won't be here to help.'

'I'll manage,' said Grace, thinking rather fearfully of the grief of her two little boys, robbed not only of their mother and their home, but their father too; how was she going to comfort them, help them through it? It was a hideous prospect.

'You're so nice,' he said.

'You keep saying that,' said Grace, laughing

'I keep saying it because it's true.' His eyes were on hers, dark, thoughtful eyes. 'I couldn't have got through yesterday without you.'

'I tell you what,' said Grace, breaking the slightly embarrassed silence, 'you ought to write something.'

'What sort of something?'

'A letter. Saying you've appointed me their guardian until the end of the war or something like that.'

'Why?'

'Well – I don't know. Strange things happen. Officialdom, you know. The authorities might come along, say they had to be taken into care. I don't know. It's unlikely, but I'd feel safer – '

'Oh,' he said uncertainly, 'well, if you really think so – '

'I do. If you wouldn't mind.'

'Well fine, then.'

'I'll get you some paper.'

She was surprised, and hated herself for it, at how literate his letter was. *To whom it may concern*, it said, *I appoint Mrs Grace Bennett legal guardian of my two sons, David and Daniel Lucas, for the duration of the war. Signed Benjamin Lucas (Sgt, RE)*

'I'll put it away safely,' she said, 'in my desk.'

'What does your husband do,' he asked, 'in peacetime?'

'He's a solicitor. What about you?'

'Oh,' he said, 'nothing very grand. Just a clerk in an insurance office. But I wanted to be a teacher. I wanted that a lot.'

'What happened?'

'Had to leave school,' he said simply, 'when my dad died.'

'Oh,' said Grace. She felt rather ashamed of herself suddenly.

'But I've been going to night school, studying, taking exams. I might've got there in the end, if the war hadn't come.'

'Maybe you still will,' she said, infinitely impressed by his courage.

'No,' he said, 'not now. Too late.'

'It's never too late,' said Grace firmly.

They all went to the station to see Ben off; it didn't seem possible to send the boys to school. They sat in the car in silence, all of them, all the way. When they got to the station, Daniel clung to Ben, crying. David refused to even get out of the car.

'Well,' said Grace as the train came in, 'I hope everything is – all right. As all right as it can be. Will you be back before you go abroad?'

'I don't know. If I can. But I don't think so, I really don't. Thank you again.'

'Well,' she said, holding out her hand, 'goodbye.'

'Goodbye,' he said, taking it, taking her hand, and suddenly, unbidden, a great sadness rose in her at his going; it had, in spite of everything, been a strangely sweet interlude. The tears filled in her eyes, spilled over.

'I'm sorry,' she said, 'how stupid of me. I just – '

'Oh dear,' he said, 'it seems to be my turn. Don't cry, Mrs Bennett, please don't cry – '

'Please call me Grace,' said Grace, smiling through her tears, and he said, 'All right, then – Grace. Grace, don't cry. And don't say you're sorry, either.' And then quite suddenly he put his arms round her, held her closely, gently, and she stood there in the sunlight, feeling for the first time for as long as she could remember safe, cared for, loved.

And as she stood with Daniel, holding him against her as he cried, waving to Ben Lucas as the train carried him away, she felt she had at last what everyone else talked about, a properly happy memory to sustain her through the loneliness and the fear.

'Well, I think it's most extraordinary,' said Muriel. 'Most extraordinary.'

'Why?' asked Grace,

'That they should be foisted on you. There must be someone else who could take them in, some home – '

'There probably is,' said Grace wearily, 'but they haven't been foisted on me, and I don't want someone else to take them.'

'Well, I think it's very high-handed of you. And suppose Charles came home, then what would you do?'

'I hope very much that Charles would approve,' said Grace, 'of my caring for two very unhappy little boys who don't have anyone else in the world.'

'Yes, well, I'm afraid I find that rather hard to believe,' said Muriel. 'You know perfectly well how opposed to their being here he is. I think – '

'Oh Mother, for heaven's sake!' said Florence, 'Leave the girl alone. I think it's terrific what she's doing. Really good of her.'

'But Florence, in Charles's house.'

'It's not Charles's house at the moment,' said Grace, hearing her voice rise dangerously, 'it's mine. I have to live in it and run it all on my own, it's my house. Please stop this, Muriel.'

Muriel looked at her rather uncertainly. 'Well,' she said finally, 'I do hope you know what you're doing.'

'I think I do,' said Grace.

Muriel swept out of the room; Florence looked at Grace and smiled briefly. 'Try not to mind her,' she said.

'Thank you,' said Grace, 'for supporting me.'

'That's all right. How are the little boys? Pretty cut up, I expect.'

'Pretty cut up,' said Grace.

That was an understatement. Daniel's grief was wild, noisy, predictable, although easing slightly now with the resilience of his four years; he cried a lot, had nightmares, was rarely seen without his thumb in his mouth. David was impossible: silent, morose, hostile.

The first night Grace had heard him crying she had gone in, tentatively put her hand on his shoulder; he had shaken it off, shouting at her furiously. 'Leave me alone!' he said. 'Don't try to be her. Just don't, do you hear? You're not her, don't try to be.'

She had left him, thinking in a few days it would ease, that he would come back to her for comfort, but it was three weeks now and he was still stony-faced, uncommunicative, wouldn't even have his piano lessons.

Ben had not come back, had not been able to; by the time he had organized and attended the funeral, his troopship was due to leave. He phoned late the evening before they embarked, clearly upset, to tell her; Grace was sympathetic, cheerful, said the boys were fine, that they were coping, that he was not to worry about them. She thought it was probably a good thing he hadn't come back, so wretched were they still.

'I'll write, of course,' he said, 'to them. And to you, if that'd be all right.'

'It certainly would,' said Grace, 'and we'll all write to you.'

'OK, then. Well, goodbye – Grace.' He brought the word out with obvious difficulty; she smiled into the phone.

'Goodbye, Ben. Take care of yourself.' And then heard herself say, to her immense surprise, 'God bless.'

It wasn't at all the sort of thing she said normally. It just seemed appropriate.

Florence stood in the hall holding Imogen, her teeth chattering with fear. Any time now, any moment almost, there would be a scrunch of tyres on gravel and Robert would be out there, and she would have to open the door, go out and greet him, carrying the child he surely, surely could not believe to be his. She had never been so frightened; not even on the day when she had hidden at the bottom of Clarissa's steps.

She didn't have the beginning of an idea what she was going to do. Every time she tried to think about it, to plan some kind of action, her mind seemed to close down, into a dark, determined blank. She would have given all she had to be able to have talked to Giles, to ask him for – what? What, for God's sake, she thought, help, advice, support? Promises? Did she even know what he felt any more, what he thought they should do, what might happen to them? She had had one letter from him, two months after Imogen's birth, a letter so redolent of love, so heavy with tenderness, with delight at the news of his daughter that she had felt she could continue for years on the strength of it, but the exhilaration and the courage it had given her had ebbed quite away now, to be replaced by this desperate quailing terror in the face of Robert's return. She had no idea whether Giles was still alive event; there was certainly no basis for making any kind of shared decisions or plans.

She changed her mind daily, almost hourly: at times resolved to tell Robert everything, to ask for a divorce, at others to stay with him, endure it, to take on trust his professions of love, of remorse for what he described as their difficulties, to try to forgive. Clarissa had said she must leave him, that it was the only way, had actually offered to be with her when she talked to Robert, but Florence had said no, she must face it alone, it was her marriage, her life, her chaos.

'Well, darling, nothing is quite that simple. And a hand to hold might help. Anyway, I'll come if you want me to, if you change your mind. I should be able to get away.'

It was Imogen she feared for most; would Robert, if he knew that Imogen was not his child, vent his rage, his passion on her? Would he hit her, rather than Florence, strike at her little golden head, bruise her, kick her as she lay broken and crying at his feet? It seemed unimaginable that she should stay with him, expose her child to the risk of him; but as he drew nearer to her, in time and distance, and her fear grew, she shrank increasingly from any confrontation, any kind of revelation, and found herself, almost against her own volition, ready as always to lie, to submit to him, to placate.

She had of course been vague about Imogen's birth, the time of her conception, had stressed that she had been overdue. He must certainly never know – or not for the moment – that the baby had been premature. They might, for the time being at least, continue in the fiction that she was his. But then if Florence was to leave him anyway, what was the point in such a thing, would it not be better to confess, to confront him, as Clarissa had counselled, let truth cut deep, making a clean wound, rather than for lies to fester, gangrenously, dangerously away? And so it went on, her mind ranging round and round her dilemmas, like an animal in a deadly trap, unable to escape, unable to find any kind of solution. She could hardly sleep, falling into a late, fevered nightmare and waking in the early dawn, her mind snapping instantly open to horror; she was beginning to honestly believe she was going mad.

And there it was, the noise on the gravel, and now she was going to be sick; the bile rose in her throat, she ran down the passage to the kitchen, thrusting Imogen into Cook's arms, knelt on the floor of the lavatory, vomiting again and again, and when it was over she heard his voice, calling her from the hall, Muriel saying, 'She was here, Robert, a moment ago.'

She went out, smiling weakly, wearily at him. 'Sorry,' she said, 'excitement too much for me. How are you, Robert?'

'I'm all right,' he said, 'fine,' and he did look fine, leaner, fitter, brown, handsome even, his pale eyes unreadable as always, and he bent to kiss her and she had to fight against shrinking away from him, force herself to proffer her cheek, to take the hand he held out.

'You look lovely,' he said, 'but tired. And thin. Very thin, Florence.'

'Well,' she said, 'it's hard work, Robert, looking after a baby.'

'Ah,' he said, 'the baby, that's who I've come to see. Where is she, where is my daughter?'

'Oh,' said Florence, 'yes, Imogen, she's in the kitchen with Cook.'

'Cook's taken her into the garden,' said Muriel sniffily, 'she was crying. As usual,' she added. 'She's not a good baby, I'm afraid, Robert.'

'No, but she's beautiful,' said Florence, even in this hour of crisis resistant to any criticism of her beloved, 'and advanced for her age.'

'Of course,' said Robert, smiling, his eyes still blank.

'She can sit up,' said Florence. On safer ground now, she launched into her favourite conversation. 'And she's started to creep around, not crawling, but on her bottom. And she says Mum Mum, and she laughs, really laughs, when you tickle her. She looks exactly as I did at that age. Blonde, believe it or not. Of course most babies are blonde and blue-eyed, but then all babies have blue eyes, and – '

'Florence,' he said quite gently now, 'Florence, can I see her?'

'Oh, well – yes. Yes, of course. Sorry. Come out to the garden.'

She led him out, trying to keep her teeth from chattering. Cook had set Imogen down on the ground, and she was struggling to reach a patch of daisies that were just out of reach, grunting with the effort. The silence in the garden grew, screamed; Florence could hear a bird singing, hear the ever-present chug of a tractor, but it all seemed far away, she could only see, think, about Imogen, sitting there, so vulnerable, so infinitely dear. In spite of everything she felt terrified, felt he might suddenly reach out, hit her, hurt her. He didn't move, just stood there, staring at the baby, his face absolutely unreadable, his mouth taut, tense. It was agony; she couldn't stand it, she would tell him, tell him first before he began, tell him and then pick up Imogen and run. And 'Robert,' she said, 'Robert, I – '

'Be quiet,' he said, but very gently, and then he said, smiling at her now, gazing at her in a kind of wonderment, 'She is beautiful, Florence, really beautiful. But I really don't think she looks in the least like you. I tell you who she does look like, though.' He paused, sighed, then said, 'It's hard to believe now, when I'm such a hideous burnt-out old wreck, but she looks exactly, and I do mean exactly, like me. When I was a baby. It really is quite eerie how like me she looks.'

'Mrs Bennett, dear, I've got a message for you.'

'Yes, Mrs Boscombe?'

'Could you ring a Regent's Park number, dear, not the usual one, a Mrs Turner Andrews, on 432. Said it was important. I said I didn't know when you'd be back, that you were out on your rounds, people seem to think we've all nothing to do down here in the country.'

'Thank you, Mrs Boscombe. Could you get me the number, please?'

Grace stood in the hall, realizing suddenly how tired she was; she had been out for hours, trying to establish whether Mr Tripp at the farm over near Thorpe Magna had really told Mary Mattox and Sally Watkins to get on with salting a very large pig all on their own, which seemed unlikely, or whether they had refused to help at all, which seemed even less so. The truth, she had finally discovered, lay somewhere between the two: the girls were keen but incompetent, having only just arrived from Liverpool, and had said they'd like to help, but had then found the task not unnaturally beyond them, had made a bit of a hash of it, and Jerry Tripp had lost his temper with them and told them they were a pair of useless bloody moaning minnies, whereupon they had downed tools and told him to get on with it himself. Harsh things had been said and Mary was half tearful, half angry when Grace arrived; 'And it's not the first time, miss, it keeps happening, we're willing to work hard, of course we are, but not to be called names.'

It was hard to believe, thought Grace wearily, pedalling home on her bicycle, that she was in any way contributing to the war effort, or doing a great deal to defeat Hitler, but she had to keep telling herself so, or she would have given up altogether.

'Mrs Bennett? How good of you to call. You did stress that I should.' Mrs Turner Andrews' voice was immensely gracious; Grace felt sure that if she was rescued from a blazing house she would feel compelled to offer the firemen sherry, enquiring first whether they liked dry or medium.

'Yes, of course. Is there a problem with my father-in-law?'

There was, it seemed: Clifford had been drinking, a great deal, but worse than that had taken to not coming home, to sleeping in doorways, wherever he fell: 'Last night, he was found by one of the ARP wardens outside Selfridges,' said Mrs Turner Andrews, 'and fond of him as I am, Mrs Bennett, I don't think I can take that sort of responsibility.'

'No, of course not,' said Grace. 'Look, leave it with me. I'll try and think what's best, and ring you back. And thank you so much for all that you've done for him.'

'My dear, it's a pleasure. I am so fond of him, and he still makes such a very good bridge partner.'

Grace put the phone down, went into the kitchen. The boys were eating bread and listening to *Children's Hour*.

'Hallo,' said Daniel

'Hallo,' said Grace. 'Hallo, David. Good day?'

'Was all right,' said David briefly, reluctantly.

Sometimes, in spite of her great sympathy towards him, Grace felt an overpowering desire to shake him.

She made herself a pot of tea, sat down as close to the boiler as she could, and tried to think what on earth she could do about Clifford. Finally, with great reluctance, she rang Florence. 'We have a problem,' she said, 'can you talk?'

'Um – not just now,' said Florence and her voice was careful, tense, 'Robert's just arrived and – well, could I ring you back?'

'Yes of course,' said Grace.

'He's in the garden with Imogen. And Mother. Is it Daddy?'

'Yes.'

'All right.' She was babbling now, clearly anxious to continue the conversation. 'Do you know what Imogen did today, Grace? I put a toy deliberately out of her reach and she definitely managed to move herself forward, grab it. So clever, don't you think?'

'Goodness,' said Grace, 'very clever.'

She had to admit that her innate dislike of Florence extended most illogically towards Imogen. The blonde curls sprouting all over her small head, the wide, steady blue eyes, the fair skin, all reinforced the fact that whoever her father was, nobody, unless they were entirely insane, could have thought it was the dark-haired, olive-skinned man her mother was married to.

Florence didn't ring back; Grace wasn't surprised, she could hardly begin to imagine the kind of nightmare that must be going on at the Priory. It didn't really matter, because she had made her decision anyway: she would take Clifford on. Somebody had to, or he was going to end up under a bus, or a pile of rubble; and clearly nobody else was going to. She had no illusions as to how difficult it would be, and she knew she would be further ostracized in the community, further estranged from Muriel, and she slightly quailed at the thought of what Charles would say about it; but Charles was so far away, and such a bad correspondent, he was beginning to seem somehow unreal to her, her marriage to him something she had read or heard about, but not properly experienced. If he didn't approve, she told herself, he could come home and sort out his father's affairs for himself.

She said much the same thing to her mother, who was appalled when Grace told her her plan: 'I think it's a dreadful idea, Grace, it will be very hard on poor Mrs – on Muriel. I must say I think it's most insensitive of you, I can't imagine how you can even consider it.'

'I can consider it,' said Grace, 'because I'm very fond of him.'

'I can't think why. And what do you imagine Charles would have to say about it? Your father agrees with me, it's very wrong of you.'

'Charles is not here,' said Grace, losing her temper, 'and as for humiliating Muriel, she's done a fair bit to humiliate me over the years. I did think, Mother, that perhaps you were going to express just a little concern for me, to say that it might be rather a lot for me to take on. That would be more to the point, I'd have thought, than all this nonsense about Charles and Muriel.'

Clifford was deeply resistant to the idea when she suggested it to him; he said he wasn't coming, he wouldn't dream of it, he would be a burden on her, an embarrassment to everybody, he would far rather just be snuffed out quietly one night by a passing bomb.

'Yes, but Clifford, you aren't going to be snuffed out quietly, you're going to cause everyone a lot of worry and trouble rather noisily, especially poor Mrs Turner Andrews, and there aren't any passing bombs any more. Besides,' she added, striking well below the belt, she knew, 'I'm terribly lonely and I need the company. So you're coming and that's all there is to it. And you are not to worry about Muriel,' she added, 'you won't have to see her, she never comes to the

Mill House anyway, and as for all her friends, and Charles's for that matter, I never see them either.'

Clifford was silent for a while, then he said, 'It's their loss, Grace. Their loss entirely.'

'Well,' said Robert, 'I'm pretty tired, darling. Shall we go up?'

His eyes on her were thoughtful now. Florence tried to smile, while fear and — what? — revulsion, she supposed, clutched at her.

'I — might wait a bit longer,' she said, 'but you go, you must be exhausted. Imogen has to have a last feed, and — '

'Well, do that,' he said, 'I'll wait. I'd like to be with you both then.'

'All right,' said Florence. She went out to the kitchen to warm up the bottle; she felt violently sick again at the thought of what lay ahead.

Sitting opposite Robert, the baby on her knee, looking determinedly at the small head, the little mouth working at the teat, she thought not for the first time that day that she might run away; it had been a nightmare, as she had sat with him, or near him, watching in a combination of fascination and fear as he held, cuddled, studied Imogen, terrified of what lay behind his gentleness, his apparent devotion, his delight in her, his frequent pronouncements that she looked just like him, unable to decide whether he was speaking truthfully, or leading her with his practised skill into a deadly trap. And if he was, what would it consist of? Florence could never remember being so frightened. She wouldn't even leave Imogen with him while she went to the lavatory, or fetched Robert a drink. 'I'll take her,' she said each time he protested, 'she's so naughty, so quick, she pulls things over in a trice, you have to move like lightning. I'm used to her and so is Mother. Honestly, Robert, it's better that way — '

She could hear her voice too fast, too high in pitch, knew he was noticing it, prayed he would put it down to nervousness, to the strangeness of their situation.

'How long have you got at home?' she asked suddenly, anxious to know, desperate to relieve the tension.

'Seven days,' he said, 'but I haven't told you, I have to go up to the War Office during that time. There's a possibility I may be based up in Scotland, as a training officer. I rather distinguished myself in that direction in Gib, and there's a shortage of good people. Wouldn't that be marvellous, darling, then I could see you occasionally.'

'Yes,' said Florence. The word came out in a hoarse, strange whisper. But for some reason she was not surprised; she had always known deep within herself that he would manage to beat everything, fate, the army, the whole conduct of the war, and stay near her. He was so clever; so powerfully, dangerously clever.

They went upstairs; Imogen's small cot stood in the corner of their room.

'Oh,' he said, quite lightly, 'I didn't realize we had a – companion.'

'Well of course, Robert. She can't sleep alone.'

'I don't see why not,' he said,

'Because she's a baby.'

'Florence, when my sister had a baby, it was in a room on its own from the beginning. I really do think that would be better.'

'Robert, it wouldn't be better. Not for me, I'd worry and – '

'It would be better for me,' he said, and there was an echo suddenly, albeit faint, of the old underlying menace in his voice. 'I want you to myself, Florence. Please put her back in her own room. In the nursery, next door. I'm sure she'll be perfectly all right.'

Florence took Imogen next door.

She stood at the bedside looking at him, her robe pulled tightly round her, still desperately warding off the moment when she would have to get in beside him. He was naked; she felt stiff, and icy cold in spite of the warmth of the evening.

'Darling Florence,' he said, reaching out for her hand, 'I've missed you so.'

She tried to smile, hoping, praying he could not sense her withdrawal from him, the sense of total horror. How am I going to get through this, she thought, this next hour, how will I stand it? Slowly, carefully, she slithered out of the robe, climbed into bed beside him; he reached out, put his hand on her arm, turned her face to kiss it. She gave him her mouth, hoping he would not sense the brackish bitterness in it; his tongue probed it, his hand moved down towards her breast.

'Take your nightdress off,' he whispered. 'I want you so, Florence, I've longed for this for so long.'

She sat up abruptly, pulled away from him so that she could get the nightdress off; the reprieve, however brief, was an intense relief. Then she lay down again. He turned the light off, turned her towards him, began to kiss her again; she could feel him against her now, feel his penis jutting hard against her. His hands were on her breasts, feeling them, stroking them, working at her nipples; she was grateful he was kissing her, otherwise she would have screamed. Even so a moan escaped her; he mistook it for passion, kissed her harder.

238

'Sweet,' he whispered, 'sweet, sweet Florence.'

He began to kiss her breasts; Florence threw back her head, concentrating desperately, frantically on other things, on the trees waving outside the window, on the shapes of the furniture in the room, started saying the alphabet backwards inside her head.

'I love you,' he said, 'I love you so much. You and – our baby.'

Did she imagine it, that pause, or had he put it in carefully, to warn her, to let her know that he knew, that she had much to fear? She shuddered, trembled. 'Don't,' he said quietly, 'don't, Florence. It will be all right. All right.'

And then he was on top of her, and his penis was pushing at her, into her, hard, determined, in endless, too-fast thrusts; she could feel her vagina shrinking from it, pulling back into herself, she was dry, she knew, dry and tender, and he must, he must surely feel it.

'Relax,' he whispered, 'relax, my darling. Let me in, let me love you.'

And then quite suddenly she did relax, it was the only thing to do; she yielded to him absolutely, in an utter collapse of body and will. She felt him in her, deeply now, felt his heavy body grinding into hers; his breath was coming faster and faster, he was holding her buttocks, pulling them against him – and then horribly, appallingly, it happened. Against her will, against every effort she could make, she began to come, began to feel herself gathering, climbing towards her climax, and she actually fought it, knowing that in it, in that great tumbling tumult that he would so surely feel, that she so wanted to hold back, to deny him, was the worst danger of all, of capitulation, submission, and that it would put her back totally and dreadfully in his thrall.

Chapter Seventeen

Winter 1941–1942

'I feel like absolute shit,' said Clarissa.

'You look it,' said May.

'Thanks.'

They were walking round the large courtyard it pleased the Royal Navy to call the quarter-deck (saluting it as they passed it) on their way to commence the day's duties; Clarissa had a hangover of considerable proportions.

'What's it matter anyway,' said May, 'What you look like? Not off to some poncey cocktail party, are you?'

'No, unfortunately, and I suppose it doesn't,' said Clarissa wearily, 'although I don't think our revered first officer would agree with you, crème de la crème remember, May, and all that. I know my shoes need polishing, I know my hair needs cutting. But it does matter what I feel like. I've got to drive some chaps all the way up to bloody Greenwich and I don't know how I'm going to keep awake.'

'Why you so tired then?' asked May, looking at her sharply. 'You wasn't out last night, was you?'

'Were you,' said Clarissa automatically.

'Oh piss off. Bleedin' know-all. Was you? Out last night?'

'We – ell,' said Clarissa carefully, 'a bit.'

'Oh come on, Duchess, you can't be a bit out. Either you was or you wasn't.'

'Yes, well I was. At a – well, a party.'

'What, in the officers' mess?'

'No of course not. With me only a leading Wren! No, we – well, we went to a party at a house somewhere. A few of us. Quite a few of us,' she added firmly.

'Oh yeah? And then?'

'Then nothing,' said Clarissa irritably. 'Honestly, May.'

'OK,' said May, ''ave it yer own way. I think you like that commander of yours. That new one.'

'Well of course I like him. He's charming and fun and – '

'And really good-looking. Come on, Compton Brown, I know what a pushover you are when it comes to looks.'

'May,' said Clarissa with great dignity, 'I am a happily – very happily – married woman. Just because someone's good-looking doesn't mean I'm going to start having an affair with them.'

'No,' said May, 'but it's more likely. Anyway, where is the squadron leader at the moment?'

'He's up in Scotland, poor angel. It's what known as a rest period. Bored to sobs – I mean terribly fed up. They keep promising him action, but it never seems to happen.'

'Blimey,' said May, 'you'd think he'd be grateful. Some people are never satisfied.'

Clarissa was thinking fairly wistfully of some action herself as she walked towards the car depot. There was certainly not a great deal of novelty in what she was doing at the moment. She was now a driver, had been promoted to Leading Wren, and spent her days either driving provisions and equipment about the countryside or, more usually, officers and visiting dignitaries. She had actually preferred the early days on the bike, in spite of the physical discomfort; at least there had been constant drama and excitement and she had felt she had been doing something important. Driving VIPs about in large American cars (apart from the undoubted bonus of some of the passengers being handsome and charming men) she felt little better than a taxi driver. She missed Jack desperately, but their meetings still weren't working. He was bored and irritable, chafing at his lack of action, and talking, chatting to him was a lot less easy; he resented her life bitterly in a way she found it hard to believe.

'You're no better than Charles,' she had said once, driven to overt irritation. 'Worse actually, he refuses to let Grace do anything. You said it would be fine and now you don't back me up. It's not fair.'

'Well, maybe you should have married him after all,' said Jack shortly, and then lapsed into a morose silence which she was unable to tease him from.

She regretted it later, speaking out; told herself she should remember more often what he had endured during the Battle of Britain, how he too had become a different person and in a much harder school. But it wasn't easy. And she went back, as always, to her working life with intense relief.

But just at the moment she seemed to be at a very low ebb. There was a great deal of fun to be had as a Wren, there was no doubt about it, and the navy was certainly very good at getting hold of what May called the Grog Ration Plus; on the other hand the growing restrictions and shortages of the war, the lack of clothes, the dreary food were becoming irksome. And she missed her home terribly, her pretty house, was worried constantly that it would be bombed; she was sick to death of sleeping on a hard bunk, and even sick of wearing uniform, however charmed she had been with it and its glamour at first. You were never allowed to take it off, you had to travel in it, because of the travel warrants, and in any case it was growing shabby, the skirt shiny with endless sitting, and the jacket which she had had tailored to fit her properly was now too big for her; she had lost half a stone since joining the Wrens. And yet, beneath it all, the hardship, the shortages, the boredom, she knew she was oddly content, more properly satisfied with life than she could ever remember.

The drive to London, in one of the American Hudson cars which she hated, was actually a nightmare; it was foggy, and Clarissa, disorientated both by that and lack of sleep, kept veering too far towards the middle of the road. Twice she only avoided crashing by seconds; the first time her passengers, engrossed in conversation, didn't notice, but the second time, as she braked violently and skidded to a noisy halt, a voice barked, 'Anything wrong, Leading Wren?'

'No, sir. Nothing wrong. Just the weather, sir. It's very foggy, sir.'

'We had noticed. Taking a long time this journey. We have to be there by thirteen hundred hours. Can you press on a bit?'

'I'll try, sir.'

Stupid bastard, thought Clarissa; serve them right if we end up in a ditch. She half hoped they would.

They didn't; she pulled into the great forecourt at Greenwich just before one o'clock, got out, opened the door, saluted.

'Thank you, Leading Wren. Be here at five.'

'Yes, sir.'

Sometimes she even had fantasies about running away.

The return journey was worse; they didn't leave Greenwich till six, and she arrived back at Portsmouth, almost weeping with weariness, at ten, too tired to eat, even to think. She was lying on her bunk, half asleep, when May came in.

'Come on, Duchess. I've been sent to find you. Popular request. We're going into the town.'

'Oh May, I can't,' wailed Clarissa. 'I'm absolutely done for.'

'Course you're not. Get a couple of drinks inside you, you'll be fine. Come on, what use are you to anyone lying here? Loads of chaps, all needing comfort and cheer.'

'It's me that needs comfort and cheer,' said Clarissa.

'I'm sure that can be arranged. Oh, and there's a letter for you.'

'Oh May! Why didn't you say so before? It'll be from Jack.'

'Doesn't look like it's from Jack. Looks official.'

'Oh my God,' said Clarissa, snatching it. 'Oh my God, May. Hold my hand.'

She ripped open the envelope; the contents swam so much before her eyes she could scarcely take in the words. What it didn't seem to be was a telegram, not bad news, there was nothing of a regret-to-inform-you nature about it; just an oddly formal few lines of letters – adding up to words – adding up to sentences – adding up to – 'Oh my God, May,' said Clarissa in an awed whisper, 'they've asked me to apply for a commission. Go to Greenwich for a selection board – next week.' She giggled suddenly. 'Listen, May, it says, "Your hard work and good bearing has brought you this advancement." '

'Oh my God,' said May, 'now there'll be no 'olding you. And what am I going to do without you? I hope you're going to turn it down.'

'What'll I do without you more likely. But – oh Lord, May, this is terrible.'

'What is?'

'It's the week of my leave. With Jack. Oh God, I hope he'll be able to change it.'

'What about you changing yours?' said May

'Don't be ridiculous, May,' said Clarissa, realizing with something of a shock that she wouldn't even consider such a thing. 'This is important. Of course I can't change it. There is a war on, you know.'

'Never!' said May.

'Well, if he can't, he can't. I'm sure he'll understand. Golly, May. Me an officer!'

'Fuck me!' said May. 'It's gone to the girl's head already. Come on, Compton Brown, for God's sake, let's get some gin into you.'

Ben had written to Grace, a long letter from North Africa, reporting living conditions that sounded hellish, hot and fly-ridden: 'They arrive soon after first light,' he wrote, 'and settle wherever they can find moisture, which includes of course eyes, ears and nostrils. I won't enlarge on this!'

He thanked her again for what she had done for him and the boys, and told her to tell them to be good, and finished by saying that the physical discomfort had brought about 'a numbness which is a good cure for grieving'. It was signed, rather formally, 'Yours, Ben Lucas'.

Grace stared at the letter through a blur of tears; the courage, the raw pain in it touched her horribly, made her ashamed of complaining of her own boredom and loneliness. She wrote back straight away, telling him everything she could possibly think of: that David was less wretched (she almost wrote happier, but that sounded callous) and had begun his piano lessons again, that Daniel was doing better at school, that Flossie had got out one day, had a romance with the billy goat down the road and was now, they all hoped, an expectant mother, that Daniel had rescued a baby rabbit from Charlotte and was now raising it in a hutch he and Clifford had made together. She told him about Clifford's arrival in the household, that both boys liked Clifford very much and that his arrival seemed to have helped David. ('They started calling him "sir" and then he told them to call him Clifford, Daniel misunderstood and started calling him Sir Clifford, which has stuck; Clifford is delighted, he says he's always wanted a title!')

She told him she was putting together a small concert at the school for Christmas at which her pupils would be playing and Miss Merton's pupils dancing, and that Miss Merton was threatening to do a solo (followed by a brief description of Miss Merton, lest Ben might not realize how alarming a prospect this was). David, she said, was playing a simple Chopin waltz at the concert that Clifford had taught him, and practised it night and day ('All right at first, but driving us mad now, the piano needs tuning so badly, but it's proving impossible to get done'), and that old John Stokes the organist said he would give David a few lessons on the organ from time to time, David loved the music, it made so much noise. ('He's very excited, but I don't know that he'll be able to manage it, it's a very physical instrument as I'm sure you know.') She found such details difficult to handle; she was so unfamiliar with Ben, what he did and didn't know, was terrified of sounding patronizing and more of sounding superior.

She finished with a couple of funny stories about her land girls – one had been bidden to hold a heifer while the bull did its work, ('You put your thumb and first finger up its nose and pinch, then they stand still; anyway she was so sorry for the poor thing she let go, whereupon the bull drove the heifer into such thick mud she had to be hauled out with a tractor.') She worried that this might be a rather unseemly story to tell a man she hardly knew but decided it was more important to cheer him up. She deliberated for a long time about how to sign off, and finally settled on 'Yours, Grace', which seemed warm and friendly without being overfamiliar. She realized as she posted it (complete with enclosures from David and Daniel) how much more she had enjoyed writing it than she did her letters to Charles.

'I've never been in bed with an officer,' said Jack.

'I'm very pleased to hear it,' said Clarissa lightly. She turned and traced the outline of his profile with her finger. 'Was it different?'

'Oh yes. Much more classy.'

'I think I find that faintly insulting. Was it such a common experience before?'

'Most uncommon,' he said, smiling at her, and then sighed and said, 'It always is. Every time. Sometimes I think it's the only thing that makes sense in this whole ghastly mess I call my life.'

'Oh Jack. Are you hating it so much?'

'I am now. Boredom, futility, sending little boys off to slaughter – '

He had used that phrase before; Clarissa winced. 'Don't say that, Jack. Don't.'

'Why not? It's true.'

'You make it sound as if slaughter is inevitable. It isn't.'

'It almost is.'

'You weren't. And you won't be. I know it.'

'I wish I did,' he said with another sigh, 'God, I wish I did.'

It was Christmas again, but sadly different from the previous one. They were still together, still at home in the house they both loved, but increasingly distanced, as much by time as by Jack's depression and restlessness, and what Clarissa recognized as the growing change in her. It was not so much what she was actually doing, but the effect on her of having so clear a purpose in life, above and beyond pleasing herself, pleasing Jack, travelling along the path she had always seen so clearly and pleasurably laid out for her, that of any girl of her class: the conduct of a satisfactory marriage, the running of a home and household, the eventual bearing and raising of children. Slowly that had come to seem empty, without sufficient reward; what she delighted in daily now was the acute satisfaction of doing a job, pursuing a common end, the ability she had discovered in herself to direct and even inspire other people. She could see that the war was providing her with a highly specific and extraordinary situation, but she could not, just the same, imagine her life now without this sense of direction and achievement, and the intense pleasure of its discipline. She looked back at the Clarissa who had found fulfilment in shopping, gossiping, entertaining, amusing, and wondered at her; she still loved all those things, but they were like the baubles she had hung on the tiny tree that stood in their drawing room, pleasing, delightful, but only trivial adornments to the important thing beneath.

She had tried to explain this to Jack, to tell him about her officer selection course at Greenwich, about what it meant to her and how much, but he was morose and difficult, deliberately misunderstanding, asking if she saw the war as some kind of a game. Eventually she gave up, and tried to revert to the old Clarissa, to please him, and things improved, and she told herself that when the war was over (an unimaginable concept at that point, at the very heart of all of it) there would be plenty of time to reassess, to adjust, to examine who she had become and where she might be going. But she was aware even as she did so that she was making an effort, dissembling, that a shadow lay between them; and it was only when they made love, when she soared, flew, tumbled effortlessly, gloriously into orgasm, when afterwards she lay in Jack's arms, loving him, telling him she loved him, that she could see their marriage as the thing it had once been.

On the last evening they quarrelled yet again and he left her in the drawing room and went up to bed alone, leaving her half remorseful, half defiant. She sat for a while, waiting for him to come down again, wondering why she didn't go up herself to apologize, knowing he was waiting for her, but somehow unable to do it, had fallen asleep in her chair, woke hours later, cramped, miserable, feeling sick, had run upstairs, climbed into bed beside him, woken him, weeping with remorse, with distress at wasting their last precious hours together. He had enfolded her in his arms and made love to her, but it had been different, had lacked joy, and although more profound than she could ever remember, although he had given her experiences so extraordinary her body was disturbed, shaken for many hours, days even, afterwards, it had had a weariness, almost a despair about it. And in the morning as he packed, as they breakfasted wearily together, on stale coffee and dry toast, she looked at him and wondered if it was love itself that was leaving her and not just Jack.

Before he left, she said she was sorry, again and again, asked him to forgive her, told him she loved him, and he kissed her and said he knew and he understood; but she knew it was not quite true, not really what he meant at all.

'Oh God,' said Clarissa, sitting on the stairs, hugging her knees, watching him as he stood by the door – they always said goodbye at home, he forbade the brutal, public parting places – 'Oh God, Jack, I don't like this,' and she meant not just the parting from one another, but the way their lives had parted too, and he understood while pretending he did not, looked at her seriously, said that when it was all over it would seem like a bad dream, and they could start again, start a new life.

And she stared at him, conserving him, this picture of him, carving it into her head, her consciousness, freezing time, suspending it, to keep him there, knowing that once he had opened the door, gone through it, closed it behind him, she would be left alone, without him, and with the fear, the fear of him being killed. She was afraid as she had never been before, not only of being alone, of losing him, but of the fear itself, of what it did to her, crawling through her, probing her sleep, disturbing her work. Everyone said she was so brave, so blithely, easily optimistic; if only they knew how she suffered, choked, was haunted by fear, how hard she worked to hide it, how desperately, when she was alone, she failed.

And finally he was gone, said goodbye, hoarsely, helplessly, and shut the door; and she thought for a moment she should go after him, try once more to put things right, call him, tell him she hadn't changed, that nothing else mattered but him, but she didn't, she couldn't. She stayed there, thinking about him, calling up his image, his tall graceful body, his absurdly handsome face, his blue eyes probing hers, his deep voice, and thought that it was safer that way, she could not hurt the image, could not disappoint it, nor it her. And then, tears streaming down her face at what had happened to them, as much as at his leaving, she went slowly and painfully up the stairs, to get ready for her return to what she realized with a thud of shock was real life.

Egypt

My dear Grace,

Just a short note, to thank you for yours and to let you know that all is well here. We have been through a pretty rough time, and have been driven back within the Egyptian border, as you will know by now from the newspaper reports, but the men have been terrific, morale is surprisingly good and the spirit of comradeship is excellent. I am quite convinced that we shall very shortly be pressing forward again. The men are longing for more action; the waiting is most frustrating, and there is somehow a sense of guilt that one isn't doing more.

Conditions are not too bad, although the heat is pretty unpleasant. We are in a desert station, sleeping in tents, with mud floors; scorpions are also a hazard. Don't worry, darling, if I can survive enemy bombs and guns and tanks, I can certainly get the better of a few scorpions.

The desert is rather beautiful, your romantic little soul would be very moved. The mornings, as the sun comes up, are particularly fine, although we survey that beautiful red ball rising into the sky with some foreboding, knowing the physical discomfort it brings. The stars at night are incredible. The nights are mercifully cold. I think of you so much and hope you are as happy as can reasonably be expected. I am of course disappointed that you have persisted in keeping the evacuee boys, but I understand many of these children are returning to their homes now that the bombing of London has more or less ended. So no doubt that will sort itself out – well before I get home, I trust!

On the subject of my father I confess to feeling rather ambivalent. I was appalled initially, and felt it an almost unbearable situation for my mother, but I had a letter from Florence, setting out both your case and his, and I can see that you were genuinely acting for the best and your tender-heartedness was once again to blame. He does seem to be a considerable liability. When the war is over and I am home and can take charge of things again, I shall see about some kind of a home for him. Florence has explained that funds are limited at the moment, and that this would be rather difficult. But of course I could not consider living under the same roof as him and when the normal order of things is restored then he must go again. Meanwhile, slightly reluctantly, I am prepared to tolerate his presence at the Mill House. Desperate times and desperate measures and all that.

I think of you so much, and miss you unbelievably. Please keep writing your wonderful letters; they are all we have out here. My mother is a very good correspondent, and her letters are very amusing and informative, so I don't do too badly; oh and darling, could you send some photographs, if you have any new ones? Florence sent several of Imogen, but nothing else.

All my love, darling,

Charles

Grace felt rather odd when she finished reading this letter, with its combination of clearly genuine affection and the high-handed direction of her life, and its complete lack of grasp of the anxiety and problems she was enduring as a result of taking care of his father, his nocturnal drinking, his habit of taking a bath at three in the morning, his enormous appetite, catered for so inadequately by the official rations. The thought of Charles sitting out in his lofty position in the Middle East, telling her he was — what was it? — oh yes, prepared to tolerate his father's presence in a house thousands of miles away, to giving Clifford permission to stay until the end of the war and no longer, and insisting she dispatch her little orphaned boys to some vaguely distant relative before he arrived home, first enraged her, and then made her laugh.

She wrote back a letter which was cheerful and affectionate, but avoided the subject of any of her charges. She had no intention of agreeing to anything at all as to their futures, but neither did she wish to quarrel with Charles, albeit it only on paper, while his life was in daily danger. The least she could do while he was fighting to defend her and his country was reassure him that she loved him. Time enough to worry about everything else when the war was over and he finally came home.

Florence woke up to hear the telephone ringing. She looked at her clock: 6am. It must be important; nobody could be ringing at this hour for a chat, or with an invitation to tea. She lay for a while listening to it, praying it was a mistake, that it would stop, and then finally gave in and went to answer it. Muriel certainly wasn't going to: she slept more profoundly every night, and Cook, who was now supposed to be a member of that new species, a cook-general, become selectively deafer every day. It saved her from much, that deafness, and certainly from any general duties, from doing the washing-up (she always retired for what she called a sit-down after serving the supper and was not seen again before morning), from helping Muriel with the cleaning, or Florence with caring for Imogen, but she could always hear a quiet compliment about her cooking, a request for some particular dish, or an entreaty to make chutneys and jams which she loved to do, or her sister on the telephone.

Florence glanced in on Imogen as she passed her little room; she was sleeping peacefully, her covers kicked off, her arms flung wide, her small face sweetly serene. She never looked serene during the day; she was always laughing or screaming or raging, or concentrating fiercely on what she was doing. Florence smiled at her indulgently and ran down to the hall.

'Seven-two-four,' she said.

'Florence?'

The hall swayed round Florence; she felt the floor heave beneath her, saw the pictures on the walls come first towards her, then recede, heard a roaring in her ears, a great suffocating lump in her throat, and then: 'Yes?' she said. 'Yes, this is me.'

'Darling, I'm in England. In Harwich. London by tonight. On leave. Three weeks of it. Can you come to me? Or shall I come to you?'

'Oh my God,' said Florence, and her legs gave way beneath her, and she sat down on the floor. 'Oh dear, dear God.'

'No,' he said and there was laughter in his voice, 'no, not God. Me, Giles. Giles, who loves you.'

'Oh Giles,' whispered Florence, 'oh, this can't be true.'

'Of course it's true. Darling, you sound so odd, so strange. Is everything all right?'

'Yes,' she said, swallowing with great difficulty, 'yes, yes of course, it's just the shock, I'm fine.'

'Can you get up here? Or shall I come down to you? Might be easier – I can get a travel warrant.'

'No,' said Florence, 'no, no, don't come here. I'll come to you. But not today – I really can't. Tomorrow. At the house. In the evening. You may have to wait a while for me. I'll do what I can.'

'Darling, I've waited nearly two years. I can wait two days. Just. Are you sure you're all right? Is Imogen all right?'

'She's perfect. I may have to bring her.'

'I want you to bring her. All my love, darling.'

'Yes,' said Florence, and she could hear her voice sounding shaky, 'yes, mine too. Tomorrow then.'

She burst into tears of joy and relief. At last she could share the dreadful burden of her fear of Robert, her inability to decide what to do, she could recharge herself and her courage with Giles and his love. She had not realized how desperate she felt, how lonely, until she heard his voice. The last few months had been a nightmare; Robert was in Scotland, and hadn't been home, but the very knowledge that he could appear at any moment meant that every step on the drive, or even on the stairs in the night, every phone call, every message, made her flesh crawl. She had got through his leave, after that first dreadful day and night had relaxed a little; he had been on the face of it sweet, thoughtful, kind, continuing in his insistence that Imogen looked exactly like him, never referring to the timing of her birth or indeed anything else in a way that implied he thought there was a shadow of doubt as to her parentage. He had nursed her, fed her, played with her; Florence had still not left them alone together for a moment but by the end of the week she had become less afraid at least that he would hurt the baby.

And he had made love to her every night, with a strangely increasing fervour, as if enforcing his domination of her, and every night she both shrank from him and responded to him more. Clarissa was right: the hold he had over her was a deep and deadly thing, and the fear an intrinsic part of it. And when he had gone, driving off in his jeep, she had wondered if he had indeed done as he had promised and changed, that there was less need now for the fear; and then she remembered the menace in his voice when he had made her move Imogen out of their bedroom and knew that there wasn't.

She spent the day preparing for it, for her trip to London. She checked on trains and buses − not that it meant very much, but it gave her an idea, phoned old Nanny Baines in the village who had baby-sat for her once or twice, to see if she could have Imogen for a few days, for it would surely be better if she and Giles could be alone, together, for a while at least, he could meet Imogen later. She washed her hair, pressed her only good dress, and sponged and pressed her coat, rehearsed a careful lie for her mother (that she had to go to London, for a long-overdue check on the house that Robert had asked her to make, adding that it was months since there had been any bombs, that London was as safe as Wiltshire these days, that she might even stay on and see a few friends).

She felt remorseful that she hadn't shown more joy, more excitement at Giles's call − she hadn't told him she loved him, had missed him even − but there was time, so much time for that. Tomorrow, tomorrow she would be with him, they would be together for hours, days, weeks even; time then for reassurance, for tenderness, for promises, for pledges. Perhaps, once they had worked out, decided exactly what they would do with their lives, she could bring him down to Wiltshire to the Priory and they could even be together as a family for a short, precious time. She was excited, joyfully shaky; it was well after lunch before she realized that Imogen was being particularly awkward, crying even when she wasn't thwarted, refusing to eat even the dried-egg custard she so perversely loved.

The child seemed hot; only slightly anxious, Florence took her temperature, found to her horror it was almost 101. She phoned the doctor, who said it was probably just teeth, told her to give Imogen a lukewarm bath and keep her quiet and he'd look in later.

Later was six, by which time Imogen was worse, wailing fretfully and endlessly, her little face covered with a fine red rash.

'Let's look in her mouth,' said the doctor. 'Ah, yes, thought so. Measles. Nasty. Keep her quiet, in a darkened room, her eyes are at risk, sponge her down, the worst'll be over in a few days.'

A few days! Florence's heart lurched. How could she go to London now, how could she leave her baby, even to the undoubtedly excellent ministrations of Nanny Baines? On the other hand, she had to go: Giles would be waiting on the doorstep of the house, there was no way she could get a message to him, she had no idea where he was; there was no one in London she could entrust with such a task, or even send in her stead.

Frantic now, she phoned Nanny Baines: would it be possible for her to come to the Priory and look after Imogen there, just for twenty-four hours? She wasn't too bad, it was only measles, her meeting in London was crucial. Nanny, making it clear that Imogen would be far better in her care anyway, said she would come over first thing. Half relieved, half guilt-ridden, Florence put the phone down, went back to Imogen. She was asleep now, albeit fitfully. Children did recover so quickly, she told herself; by the morning she'd probably be fine.

By two o'clock in the morning, Imogen was not fine. Her temperature had dipped briefly and then soared to 104, and she kept sitting up in bed and shouting, her eyes wide but unseeing. Terrified, Florence phoned the doctor again; he said hallucinations in the high fever of measles were alarming but not unusual and stressed again that Imogen must be kept in the dark.

'Phone me again, if the temperature goes any higher. Otherwise just keep sponging her down.'

It was an endless night; Muriel slept mercifully on, but grateful for that as she was, alone in the darkness, with her fear and her acute anxiety about the next day, about Giles, ceaselessly sponging the dry, fevered little body, Florence thought she might go mad. Towards morning, the child slept briefly, but woke again, struggling to climb blindly out of her cot, calling out in a strange hoarse voice. Florence took her temperature again and found it was almost a hundred and five. She tried to give her water, but Imogen seemed unable to swallow, and screamed ever louder; frantic, Florence rang the doctor, who arrived in ten minutes.

'Scarlet fever,' he said briefly, 'an acute form, by the look of her, which affects the throat. I'm sorry. She must be got to the hospital immediately. I'll call an ambulance.'

Imogen was put in an isolation unit; Florence was not even allowed in. She stood on the other side of the glass, watching her suffer, hearing her screams, desperately struggling to keep calm. The nurses were sympathetic, but overworked and brisk, the hospital doctor impatient with her, with her demands for information, for attention, to be allowed to be with Imogen.

'Mrs Grieg,' he said finally, 'I would advise you very strongly to go home. It would be far better for your child as well as everyone else if you did that, rather than being here, getting in our way, distracting me and my staff from our work.'

'Go home!' said Florence, 'Go home! Of course I won't go home. I wouldn't dream of going home, I want to know what's going on, that's all, is it so much to ask? That's my baby in there, looking as if she's dying. You've got to tell me what's happening, you've simply got to.'

The doctor sighed; his face was cold and filled with dislike. He was clearly not used to articulate, voluble mothers. 'Very well. Your child has an acute form of an acute illness. It is called scarlatina cynanchica, which won't mean anything to you, but which is characterized by a seriously infected throat with the additional risk of damage to her kidneys. Now then, has knowing that really made you feel any better? I thought not. It could be days before there is any change. You cannot expect to spend that sort of time here, and in any case it is a well-known fact that children are far better without their mothers in hospital, they settle and therefore relax and do better. Now kindly leave your child to us. I do assure you we are doing all we can.'

'I'll stop interfering,' said Florence, 'but I'm not going. And you can't make me.'

'Mrs Grieg, this is my hospital and I can do what I wish.'

'And that is my child, and you can't. My father is a solicitor and I shall phone him and ask him precisely what my rights are — '

'All right, all right,' said the doctor sharply, 'I really don't have the time or the energy to argue with you. If you want to spend the next few days in the hospital waiting room, that is your prerogative. You will grow very tired and hungry, I fear, and be of no use to your child whatsoever. What I will not allow is for you to remain in this ward, where you are a physical obstacle and a barrier to its smooth running. And I do assure you that legally I am within my rights. Good day, Mrs Grieg. The waiting room is on the first floor.'

Florence turned, for a last anguished look at Imogen; she was now lying terrifyingly still in the small cot, her unseeing eyes staring into the dim ward. Florence felt desperate, as if she was wilfully abandoning the child to her death as she walked away, towards the lift and the uncertain sanctuary of the waiting room on the first floor. As she looked rather uncertainly along the corridors, she saw a sign, 'To the Chapel'. She followed it; found a small, bare room with an altar and a few chairs. There was only one thing left for her to do and she did it: she sank onto her knees and prayed. She prayed and she prayed, for what seemed like hours, and as she had done on other occasions, in other crises, she made a bargain with God. If He spared Imogen, let her live, she would stay with Robert and never see or speak to Giles again.

Muriel was at the hospital with Florence that evening, sitting in the waiting room with her in a silent agony, as Imogen's tiny frail body battled for life. At the Priory, as Cook slept peacefully under the influence of a couple of aspirin and two glasses of Muriel's sherry, the phone rang unanswered with a series of trunk calls from London. Had Mrs Boscombe been on duty she would have been able to help, to pass on the information that Mrs Grieg was at the hospital with her baby, and to take a message to the effect that Lieutenant-Commander Henry's three-week leave had been cancelled, that he had to report back to his ship the following evening. But Mrs Boscombe's husband had a touch of influenza and she had taken the week off to nurse him back to health.

By midnight, the lieutenant-commander abandoned his post on the doorstep of the house in Sloane Avenue and stopped making calls from the telephone box on the corner of the street. He walked slowly and heavily back to the naval barracks, trying to persuade himself that Florence's strange, distant response to his phone call and her failure to meet him, to get any kind of message to him, did not actually mean she no longer loved him, and failing utterly.

Chapter Eighteen

Spring–Summer 1942

It was such a tiny thing that told Florence that God had answered her prayers; not the smile the sister gave her in place of a terse anxious nod as she arrived in the ward, nor the slight but undoubted improvement in Imogen's breathing, not even the fact that her colour was better. It was the fact that she was resisting, in her own unique way, the attempts of the nurse to change her nappy. Until then she had lain listlessly, her head moving from side to side occasionally, her small body limp; now, as Florence watched, she suddenly clenched her fists, and tried – admittedly without success – to hit the arm that held up her skeletally thin legs. It was for Florence a moment of pure joy. She stood there watching her, her small tyrant, and laughed aloud. The nurse, exasperated, exhausted even, turned to look at her and managed to smile too; and when the hospital doctor arrived and told her the crisis was past, she simply said, 'I know,' and then, to her own enormous surprise (for she was not a demonstrative woman), threw her arms round his neck and hugged him.

'Yes, yes,' he said, plainly embarrassed, but he was pleased for her too, and a few days later, as Imogen's health improved and her behaviour worsened, even allowed Florence to sit with her, feed her and bathe and change her.

She was not allowed home for another fortnight; as she grew stronger and Florence was able to think, to reassess her life, she recognized, even through her joy, the new and terrible pain that lay ahead of her. And it was terrible, truly terrible: the thought that she must spend the rest of her life without Giles, never seeing or hearing from him, never touching, holding him, feeling herself safe, cared for, loved. Time without him stretched before her, empty, cold, harsh, and all she could do was go into it, bravely, and not look back. She had to believe, indeed kept telling herself, that in time her unhappiness would ease; but most of the time she didn't even want to believe it. While she suffered, while she hurt, there was still something of him in her; perversely she clung to the pain.

They both returned home. Florence was exhausted now, drained of anything but the most minimal energy. Where Imogen's recovery had been swift and easy, her own was slow and difficult; she couldn't sleep, didn't want to eat, she found life impossible, almost unendurable. Imogen was tirelessly naughty and demanding, Muriel increasingly critical and querulous, and she felt totally and horribly alone. On the other hand, if Giles himself had telephoned, she thought wearily, and asked her to walk half a mile down the road to meet him, she would have difficulty persuading herself to do so. Only there was no question of him doing so, because he thought she didn't love him any more. The short terse note that had arrived three days after she got home from the hospital made that very clear. And there had been no point in answering it, disabusing him of the notion, because of the promise she had made to God. That had been solemn, holy and binding and she was not going to break it; a primitive superstition about it possessed her, convincing her that if she did her baby would even now be snatched from her, transported back to the jaws of death.

She sat one morning, trying to persuade Imogen to eat some cereal, to get some nourishment into her emaciated body, her head aching almost intolerably, half listening to Muriel who was as usual denouncing something or other as outrageous.

'Did you hear what I said?' she asked Florence.

'No I'm afraid I didn't,' said Florence. 'Come on, darling, one more spoonful, there's a good girl. Then you can have your nice orange juice.'

Cereal was not one of Imogen's favourite foods. 'No,' she said. Florence held the spoon nearer the small closed mouth; Imogen raised her fist and hit it. The cereal spattered Florence, the wall and Cook, who was trying to clear the table. Imogen laughed.

'Imogen, that was very naughty,' said Florence feebly. 'Sorry, Mother, what is outrageous?'

'Bombing Bath,' said Muriel. 'London is one thing, it's the capital, it should be expected, but Bath – They're destroying our national heritage. It's totally out of order.'

'Mother, the whole point of war is out of order,' said Florence, 'and destroying anything they can is precisely what the Germans have in mind.' Imogen was now smearing her small fists into the cereal and then rubbing them all over her face and into her hair.

Muriel looked at her with distaste. 'Florence, that child should be in the care of a good nanny. She's absolutely out of control.'

'Oh don't be ridiculous,' said Florence. 'Of course she's not.

Anyway, I've nearly lost her once, and if you think I'm going to give her up to some antediluvian old battle-axe, you're very much mistaken.'

'Molly Baines is not a battle-axe,' said Muriel firmly, 'and she could do a great deal more for Imogen than you are managing at the moment.'

Florence looked at her mother, feeling an almost overpowering inclination to shake her, and thought that if she had the strength she would.

Robert had been home to see Imogen while she was still in the hospital, had arranged forty-eight hours' compassionate leave. Florence was intrigued as well as frightened by his visit, still unsure as to whether his apparent acceptance of the child was genuine, or a hideously cunning trap set for her. He had phoned the Priory from Scotland one evening, been told by Muriel that Florence was at the hospital with Imogen, and had arrived two days later, anxious and supportive, had stood gazing at Imogen through the glass of her small cubicle, had pressed Florence to go home and let him stay so that she could go and have some rest. She had refused, so deep was her terror of him, of his manipulative talents, of what he might manage against all odds to do: inveigle his way into the cubicle, hurt Imogen there, kidnap her even; but she had against all logic been impressed by his apparent devotion, by the long hours he spent sitting with her in the waiting room, or standing in the corridor of the isolation ward. It added to the nightmare of her fear and exhaustion, of not knowing where reality ended and delusion began; she longed to trust him, longed to believe there was hope for them all, but she could not, dared not, so great were the risks, so hideous the dangers.

Her wretchedness over Giles seemed to have little to do with her relationship with Robert, she had no kind of sense that as her love affair died so might her marriage be healed; the two things were impossibly and brutally distanced from, bore no possible relation to, one another. One day, perhaps, she would get a perspective on them; for now she could only struggle mindlessly on.

She scooped Imogen out of her high chair and carried her into the garden before she actually started to scream. She did that all too easily these days and it irritated Muriel, usually provoking yet another in their long series of rows. Life, she thought, gazing at the lyrically lovely morning, was pretty bloody awful altogether.

'Good morning, ma'am. Lovely morning, isn't it?'

'Yes it is,' said Clarissa, smiling. 'A very lovely morning.'

She liked the Americans who were filling the country now, officially allies, with their easy manners, their smiles – and their money. Overpaid, oversexed and over here was the tag bestowed upon them, and all three suited them very well. They were fun to flirt with, dine with, be with; men regarded them with well-founded dislike – jealousy really, she thought, but she had yet to meet a woman who felt that way. And at this lowest-of-the-low point of the war, when it seemed to have been going on for ever and they didn't appear to be getting anywhere at all, when it was hard even to remember how it felt to have money, clothes, decent food, when excitement and patriotism lacked any kind of novelty, to put it mildly, it was very nice to spend time with people with so much more of an upbeat attitude to life.

Which Jack hardly had at the moment; if she heard once more how fed up and bored he was, she thought she would scream. She had spoken to him the night before, and of the ten minutes they had been on the phone he had moaned for eight – she had timed him. The remaining two had been taken up with her trying to tell him she was about to be posted to Dartmouth, a fact in which he had shown outrageously little interest.

She had enjoyed her spell at Greenwich as an officer cadet; apart from anything else, the sheer beauty of the place, the grandeur, made a wonderful respite from the drabness of so much of wartime life. The Wrens dined every night in the great Painted Hall, spent their days in the fine lofty rooms and long, light corridors; the only thing she didn't like was sleeping in the cellars. They were safe from the bombs, but Clarissa found it stuffy and claustrophobic.

And life was such fun, the steady flow of naval officers into their lives, endless parties, endless flirtations; she felt much of the time (and she was not sure HM Navy would have approved of this) as if she was a young girl again, enjoying grown-up life for the first time.

She had finally, after lengthy discussions with her superior officer, settled for the administrative category; she would be posted to Dartmouth and be responsible for the practical organization of a Wrennery there. She knew she would be good at that; her talents for organization, for communication, would be very well employed. Several of the girls had put in for overseas postings; volunteers were required for Singapore, Ceylon, India.

If she wasn't a married woman, she would have applied for such a posting herself – but she was. Unfortunately, she thought irreverently, and then crushed the thought. God, who would have imagined that the joyful passion and friendship she had felt for Jack only two years earlier would have turned in the direction of weariness and near disinterest. And was that the war, or was it just the relentless progress of marriage? Clarissa wondered. Probably both. She had noticed an alarmingly increased awareness of all the attractive men around her lately, and an increasing desire to flirt with them.

She missed May, she thought, more than Jack; dear May, with her cheerful irreverence, her sharp honesty, her tireless quest for fun. Clarissa was due to meet her in a couple of weeks in London; she could hardly wait.

'I'd tell you it was bloody awful here without you,' May had written, 'if it wouldn't make your head even bigger. Oh, what the hell. It's bloody awful here without you. Only good thing is the GIs. Do I enjoy them! Now an evening with them really does make me forget about you, Duchess. And can they dance — especially the coloured ones. They're better than Fred Astaire. Anyway, I don't suppose Fred could jitterbug.'

She wondered if there was any chance she could wangle May down to Dartmouth. She was a very competent driver.

She was just leaving her little office that evening when a head came round her door.

'Evening, Third Officer Compton Brown.'

'Good evening, sir.'

They both laughed; the formality was a joke between them. Lieutenant-Commander Jerry Fortescue was based for a spell at Greenwich, champing (like Jack) to be back in action; he was amusing, she liked him. He was that rare but irresistible thing in a man, a happily married flirt; he and Clarissa suited one another very well, enjoyed a sexy, unthreatening friendship that was stimulating and fun.

'Busy this evening?'

'No. Not really.'

'Like to have a drink then? At a pub. I'd quite like to get out of here for a bit. And there's a party later, in the Officers' Mess. It'd be fun if you came.'

'Well,' said Clarissa, 'I'd love a drink, Jerry. But only a quick one. Then I must get back. I wasn't very nice to my poor darling husband last night. I must try and ring him, make amends.'

'Right-ho. I'll work on changing your mind. Meet you in five minutes – I've got a car I can use.'

If anyone had told her before the war, Clarissa thought, that she would stand in an English pub amongst representatives of half the countries in the globe, Poles, Norwegians, Canadians, Czechs. Americans (black and white), French, even the odd Brazilian, she would not have believed them. It was more like the League of Nations than a bar. She stood, holding her watery beer, smiling determinedly, trying to hear what Jerry Fortescue was shouting above the hubbub; a couple more officers joined them, friends of his, and she gave up altogether. The smoke was thick, it made her eyes sting; she was just beginning to think she had made a mistake, to plan her excuses, when someone jogged her arm violently from behind and knocked the beer from her hand all down her uniform.

'Damn,' said Clarissa loudly. She was immensely irritated; she had just had her jacket cleaned.

'Oh, I am so sorry, so terribly sorry, ma'am, here let me – '

And he was there in front of her, dabbing at her jacket with a handkerchief, clearly deeply embarrassed: Clarissa looked at him and felt her irritation draining rather swiftly away.

An American, in brand-new, perfectly pressed uniform, smooth, reddish-blond hair, freckles, blue eyes, fine features – he could have been English, she thought – he alternately smiled at her nervously and looked anxiously at the drenched jacket. He looked so upset she laughed, took the handkerchief from him, told him it didn't matter; he was also, she thought, getting dangerously near, in his dabbing, to her breast.

'Look,' he said, and even his voice was almost English, 'look, ma'am, can I give you a lift home, so that you can change? I have a truck outside, it would be no problem, it would make me feel better, I'd really like to do that – '

'No, honestly,' said Clarissa, 'it's quite all right – ' and then wondered why she was being so silly; she stank of beer, the wetness had got through to her skin, she was at least twenty minutes' walk from Greenwich, Jerry wouldn't want to leave. She smiled at him. 'Yes, why not? Thank you.'

'And then I'll bring you back here to your friends. Would that be all right?'

'Perfectly all right. Clarissa Compton Brown,' she said, holding out her hand. 'How do you do.'

'Mark Twynam. This way.'

He lived in Washington, he told her, his father was a lawyer, and indeed so was he, or had been and would be again. He was thirty-two, engaged to be married, had been educated at Yale; he was clearly, thought Clarissa, studying him interestedly, that species she had heard about: a WASP. In other words an upper-class American. He was in air-force intelligence, and based in London with the American attaché.

'Goodness,' said Clarissa, 'sounds very grand. What on earth were you doing in the Queen Victoria, Greenwich.'

'I'd been over to visit a unit at Blackheath. I rather like your British pubs, I thought I'd check a couple out on the way back to London.'

'I see,' said Clarissa. 'Well, look, here we are. I'll just go and change.'

'I'll wait,' he said, 'while you change. And then take you back.' He smiled at her. He had a beautiful smile, slightly tentative but very warm; Clarissa set great store by nice smiles. Nice smiles and nice hands. She looked at Mark Twynam's hands; they were large, but long-fingered and, she noticed, freckled. Like his face. Very nice.

'Oh, there's no – ' said Clarissa, and stopped. She had been going to say there was no need to wait, that she would stay at home, that she had to ring her husband; but the thought of an hour or so further of Mark Twynam's company seemed suddenly preferable to her own, or that of a disgruntled Jack at the end of a telephone.

'Thank you,' she said, smiling. 'Then I'll introduce you to the British navy.'

She changed into a clean shirt and her other, shabbier jacket; she sometimes longed to get into civvies, but there was no doubt you got much better service in pubs and so on in uniform. Certainly Wren's uniform. The Wrens were held in very special regard; twice she had eaten in restaurants with a group of other girls all in uniform and been told their bill had been taken care of, and the experience she knew was not unique. But the most quirkily famous fact about Wrens was that Lord Nuffield paid for all their sanitary towels; at first she had thought it was a joke, but she was assured it was the truth; it was his contribution to their war effort.

'I love the uniform,' said Mark Twynam as she got back into the truck. 'So smart. You all look wonderful.'

'Thank you,' said Clarissa. She smiled at him. She had reapplied her make-up, and (a trick May had taught her) brushed fuller's earth through her hair, to make it look fresher, bouncier, more recently washed. It really worked.

'So tell me about you.'

'Oh, not a lot to tell,' said Clarissa carelessly, 'married, frightfully happily. To a pilot – '

'Where's he based?'

'In Scotland. Praying to be moved back into some action.'

'And are you praying for that?'

'Yes and no. I worry about him all the time when he's flying. But he's bored and miserable, I can't help feeling sorry for him, poor angel.'

'And where do you live, you and your husband, when there isn't a war on?'

'In London,' said Clarissa, 'in a sweet house I miss dreadfully.'

'Family?'

'Only a father up in Scotland. No sisters or brothers. Poor little orphan Annie, that's me.'

'You don't seem too desperate,' he said, grinning at her. 'Do you have a job in peacetime?'

'No,' said Clarissa, surprised at the question. Did American girls all work? she wondered; she had heard they were very emancipated and independent. 'Does your fiancée?'

'No, she doesn't. But you seem so – oh I don't know. Organized. Competent. As if you were used to being in charge of things.'

'Well, that's the Wrens for you,' said Clarissa, 'and it's funny you should say that because actually after the war I really am quite determined to work. I plan to take a secretarial course, and then maybe run a secretarial agency, something like that. I couldn't bear to go back to doing the flowers and the table settings.'

'So you're enjoying the war?'

'Oh yes,' she said, 'I'm enjoying the war.'

She and Mark had a drink, and then another; the pub was emptier now, they managed to find a seat. They talked easily, exchanging life stories, background, war anecdotes. He was immensely impressed by her experiences as a dispatch rider.

'It sounds like a movie. You really are something, aren't you?' he said.

'Oh I don't know,' said Clarissa laughing. 'It's like everything else to do with this war, you do what you're asked and worry about it afterwards.'

'I suppose so. I haven't been it in long enough to know.'

'Are you homesick?'

'A bit.' He looked at her thoughtfully. 'Would you have dinner with me one night? Just to ease a guy's homesickness?'

'I might,' said Clarissa. 'I can probably get a pass, I'm waiting to go down to Dartmouth anyway.'

She had dinner with him two nights later; he offered to send a driver for her, but she said she wouldn't hear of it, she'd come on the tube.

'Honestly, it's as safe as houses, you have no idea. We all use it all the time. And if there's a raid, which there never are any more, you're in the best place. Where shall I meet you?'

'I don't know many places in London,' he said rather hesitantly, 'but would the Savoy be all right?'

'Just about,' said Clarissa.

The Savoy, along with most of the other luxury hotels in London, did not appear to know there was a war on: it was one of the scandals which the government had pledged to end. Clarissa and Mark dined on smoked salmon, chicken, fruit sorbet and some very fine claret. She had brought with her, in a holdall, one of her trousseau dresses from Molyneux that she had taken to Greenwich with her 'just in case', and changed in the ladies' lavatory at the Savoy. It was a slither of black velvet over emerald satin, cut very low at the back, and for the first time for months she had painted her nails, sprayed herself endlessly with her precious last bottle of Chanel No. 5; the very fact of knowing she looked and smelt beautiful and expensive again made her feel sexy. Mark wore his uniform and looked very sexy too; after dinner they danced. She felt excited, reckless suddenly; he danced well, moved easily, held her with skill.

'So important, dancing,' she said to Mark as they sat down, leaning forward so that he could both light her cigarette and get a clear view of her cleavage.

'Why important?'

'Because,' she said smiling, cupping his hand with hers, then sitting back, studying his face, 'because nobody who's bad at dancing can possibly be good at making love.'

'I find you quite extraordinary,' he said, smiling back, directly ignoring her remark.

'Why?'

'I always heard the English were so – reserved.'

'Frigid you mean,' said Clarissa lightly, 'everybody does, and no, we're not. Nothing like a lusty English maiden, Mark, nothing at all. If I wasn't a respectable married woman,' she added hastily, realizing with a slight shock how very drunk she was, 'I'd prove it to you.'

'No need,' he said and his eyes on hers were very serious now, intense, disturbing, 'no need. I can see you're not frigid, Clarissa, see it and feel it. You're a very lovely, exciting woman.'

There was a silence; Clarissa wrenched her eyes away from his with a huge effort. It was a long time since she had felt so shaken within herself, so at once emotionally and physically aroused. The band struck up again, with 'Bewitched'; he held out his hand to her, stood up. She followed him onto the dance floor and moved into his arms.

Two nights later she had dinner with him again, this time at the Deep Shelter Restaurant at Grosvenor House. It was one of the few nights of the summer when there was small raid on London and they spent the night there, albeit quite innocently with several dozen other people.

But Jack Compton Brown, phoning Greenwich endlessly until well after midnight and then first thing in the morning, trying to get a message to her, to tell her he had finally and suddenly been posted, knew only that she had not returned, and he left for North Africa without being able to say goodbye.

Grace often thought how strange it was that both Ben and Charles should be in the same place; reading between the brave lines from both of them, it was clearly utterly ghastly. Quite apart from the acute physical discomfort of the desert, it seemed to be one long defeat and retreat. Along with the rest of the country she felt that the war might not yet be lost, but it was increasingly hard to believe it would ever be won, or even end; the fall of Tobruk had been the latest and heaviest of a very large series of straws.

Looking back afterwards, she wondered at how she had grown half used to the worry, the fear, to constantly expecting that harbinger of death, the telegram from the War Office. The fear was always there, all the time, but it was like everything else now, like rationing and discomfort and boredom and loneliness, a sort of background noise, omnipresent but not unbearable. Her greatest worry indeed, which she found hard to admit even to herself, was that she wasn't more frightened, that she didn't lie awake hour after hour, night after night, dreading the bad, the worst news. She missed Charles terribly, of course she did, but it had been so long now since she had seen him, heard his voice even, he had taken on an unreal quality. Which made her feel guilty, guilty and ill-at-ease, as if she was in some way shallow, unfeeling. And then she would tell herself that if they had been married longer, perhaps if she had had a child, if their lives had become properly one, it would have been different, and she would switch her mind determinedly away from it. It would all change, she knew, when the war was over, when he came home.

She finished clearing up the breakfast things, went out to feed Flossie and her adorable, silky-haired billy-kid, and settled down to write to Ben. She loved writing to him, loved raking her mind and her life for funny stories, warming news, tales about the boys, her thoughts and feelings about them. It made her feel happy and warm, as if she was doing something important. Letters to Charles were rather more difficult, with all the restrictions on news – nothing about the boys, nothing about Clifford, not a lot about her farmers for he had told her he didn't think she should get too friendly with them as it could be awkward after the war. She sometimes felt herself confined to reports on the garden, and Imogen's growth and development. It wasn't what she would have thought of as proper communication, not how she had imagined a marriage to be.

'I feel so terrible,' said Clarissa to May.

'Oh yeah?'

'Yes. Yes I do. Don't look at me like that. I was only in a shelter, for God's sake.'

'Some shelter,' said May.

'But if there hadn't been a raid I would have been back at Greenwich. Oh May, what must he have thought, what could he have thought?'

'What he did think, I expect,' said May, and then seeing tears in Clarissa's great brown eyes put her hand out, patted Clarissa's arm rather awkwardly. 'Don't upset yourself, Duchess. You've written and explained, he knows now. It's not as if you was doing anything. Was you?' she added sternly.

'Were you,' said Clarissa automatically, 'and no, I wasn't. Of course I wasn't. I love Jack, he's my husband, I'd never be unfaithful to him.'

'Well then,' said May, 'that's all right. And anyway, if he 'adn't been such a miserable old sod the last few months you'd not've been out with this Yank chap anyway, would you?'

'No of course I wouldn't,' said Clarissa, brightening up. 'No, May, you're quite right. Absolutely right. Now look, he's asked me to have dinner with him again next week, Mark has, but I think I'd better say no, don't you? In view of what's happened.'

'Whatever for?' said May. 'Not going to do the squadron leader any good now, is it? You sitting at home feeling sorry for yourself. And what he won't know won't hurt him. I should carry on as normal, Duchess, if I was you.'

'Goodness, May,' said Clarissa, 'whatever would I do without you? Now listen, I think you should apply for a transfer to Dartmouth. And I'll support your request. How would that be?'

'Be fun I should think,' said May.

That August Robert came home on a week's leave. The day before he went back to Scotland, he phoned Grace and asked her if he might come and see her.

'I've never had a chance,' he said, 'to thank you properly for what you did for Florence that night. I want to do it in person.'

Pleased because she liked him, flattered that he should want to come and see her, Grace invited him for tea.

She was in the garden when he arrived; it was a beautiful day, golden and still. It was almost impossible to believe that all over the rest of Europe and indeed much of the world a desperate conflict was raging, that men were being slaughtered hourly, that people were being killed in their homes by great bolts of flame from the sky. The news was terrible: things seemed to get worse and worse, the whole of Europe was under Nazi domination, there was still serious talk of invasion, and the beaches of England were lined with endless rows of barbed wire. But here in Wiltshire the grass in the meadows was thick and high, the hedges filled with cow parsley and honeysuckle, the corn studded with poppies.

Somewhere far above her she could hear a lark, its song pouring and tossing through the air, and nearer her the lovely liquid sound of a thrush; she looked round and saw it, in one of the apple trees, its speckled breast thrust out importantly. Charlotte lay in a patch of the very hottest sun, panting hard. 'You silly creature,' said Grace, smiling at her fondly, 'will you never learn to look for shade?' One of the cats scuttled past her, a small, helpless field mouse dangling in its mouth. Grace had spent her entire life in the country, had grown up accepting totally the logic and rhythms of its life, the careful raising of farm animals in order that they might then be killed and eaten, the preying of one wild animal on another, the inevitable wastage and cruelty of nature, but she never failed to feel pity for the cat's victims, the long torture inflicted on them in their increasingly helpless misery.

'Hallo, Grace.' It was Robert, looking relaxed and cheerful, and really, she thought, rather handsome.

He had walked through the house; Clifford, knowing he was coming, had slightly pointedly taken both the boys out fishing. He was at a complete loss to understand Florence's continuing tolerance, her reacceptance of Robert; having witnessed her terror of him at first hand, having given her protection from him, he had told her repeatedly that she should petition for a divorce. He was unsure about Imogen's parentage; his innate fastidiousness in such matters, his own requirements for privacy, prevented him from questioning Florence about any past or indeed future relationship. But common sense, an ability to count, and the evidence of his own eyes told him that it was unlikely that Robert was indeed Imogen's father. What he did know was that he disliked him more strongly than he had ever disliked anybody, and that left alone with him, he would have felt an almost overpowering urge to hit him. On the other hand, Grace had made it plain that she wanted to see Robert. Her liking for him, her clearly conveyed disapproval of Florence's behaviour in the past, her unwillingness to believe that Robert was in truth violent, was one of the few areas she and Clifford had agreed tacitly to differ on; and thus the fishing expedition had seemed the best idea.

'Won't be long,' he had said to her uneasily, as they set off for the lake, 'back in a couple of hours. You'll be all right, will you?'

'Perfectly all right, Clifford,' said Grace firmly, knowing what was in his mind and finding it almost laughable. 'Now you enjoy your fishing, don't let Daniel fall in, and see if you can actually bring something back. There's nothing for supper except the rest of that rabbit.'

'Oh God,' said Clifford, 'I tell you, Grace, if I go to heaven, the one of God's creatures that I trust will not be there is rabbits.'

'Well, bring me back some trout then,' Grace had said, laughing.

Looking at Robert now, she thought yet again how unlikely the stories about him were. Though she had come to feel some sympathy for Florence, if not fondness, she really couldn't believe Robert actually ever hit her. And Florence had never mentioned it herself. Surely, if it was true, she wouldn't stay with him. She'd divorce him: anybody would. It was just some stupid idea that possessed the family – encouraged by Florence possibly, at a time when it suited her – and which had got out of hand. He might well have lost his temper a few times, he probably had, it was absolutely understandable if he suspected anything at all about Imogen. And he really did seem to love Florence. It must be hard for him, Grace thought, to have to see her so obsessed with Imogen. Any man would have found it hard to cope with the intensity of that obsession, even with no cause for suspicion or jealousy. There was no situation, no conversation even, that involved Florence that was not dominated by Imogen, even if she wasn't there. What she had said, what she had done, what she had accomplished; there was a constant requirement to admire, to exclaim, to listen, to watch. She could at times be a beguiling little creature, but increasingly she seemed to Grace a monster, difficult, demanding, prone to terrible tantrums; Grace found it hard not to agree with Muriel that a good strict nanny would have done wonders for her.

'Hallo, Robert,' she said now, 'how nice to see you. You look well.'

'Yes,' he said, 'I'm afraid I'm having a rather easy war now. No danger and not a lot of hardship. But I'm assured what I'm doing is useful and important, so I have to put up with it.' He smiled, then said, more seriously, 'I wouldn't blame you for feeling quite hostile to me, Grace, with Charles out there, in that godawful desert.'

'No,' she said, 'no I don't. I hadn't thought of it like that and, anyway, if you're training men to go out and fight more effectively, then you *are* doing something very important.'

'What news of Charles by the way?'

'Oh,' she said, 'he's fine. Or was last time he wrote. Of course everything is months behind. But then he said it was all right. He seems to have plenty of good friends –' Her voice tailed off; she couldn't think of anything sensible or interesting to say.

'Do you worry about him very much?"

'Yes, of course I do. But you get used to it, the worry. It's like indigestion, not very nice, but not actually dangerous.'

'You're doing a marvellous job I think,' he said suddenly. 'Terrific of you to have those little lads. It can't be easy.'

'It's very easy,' said Grace, 'in fact. They're wonderful company, and they're very interesting children. David, the older one, is extremely musical and Daniel is very intelligent. Clifford's taught him to play chess and he's really good at it.'

'Oh come on, Grace. You're just being modest. They must be jolly hard work, not all sweetness and light and chess and music. And they must be a problem to you at times. Miss their family and so on.'

'Well, they do, yes. Especially as their mother's been killed.'

'She has?'

'Yes. Didn't Florence tell you?'

'Florence doesn't tell me much,' said Robert, with a slightly grim smile. 'Unless it's about Imogen. I love that little girl, but I could begin to get weary of her. I'm afraid she's very spoilt. When the war's over and I'm at home again, there's going to have to be some discipline administered.'

'Well – I suppose with her having been so ill – ' said Grace, trying to be tactful, agreeing with him nonetheless.

'Oh, of course, and it's natural Florence should feel so protective towards her. But just the same, it's not fair on the child. No one will like her, she won't have any friends.'

'Well,' said Grace, 'I suppose you're right. Even Clifford was saying something of the sort – '

'Dear old boy! How is he? I'm sorry to have missed him today. Such a fine old chap, even if he is a bit naughty. I do think you're terrific,' he added, 'in lots of ways, of course, but especially in having the guts to take him on. Not just because of Muriel's disapproval, but Florence did say he'd been drinking rather a lot – '

'No, he's much better,' said Grace, 'much better. Well, partly because what he wants is very hard to get hold of. But he really has tried. And the boys have helped him too, they think he's wonderful and he loves them both.'

'I still think you're wonderful,' said Robert, smiling at her, 'but as I said, what I really came for was to thank you, formally and officially, for all you did to help Florence the night Imogen was born. You were clearly absolutely marvellous; she's said more than once she couldn't have got through it, survived even, without you. It was marvellous of you, Grace. I just wanted to say that. I've told you before and I'll no doubt tell you again, you're a pretty good addition to this family. You're doing such a lot and not getting a lot of support, or indeed any thanks. I think it's hard for you.'

Grace, who had thought this herself and increasingly frequently lately, felt warmed, soothed, as if someone had suddenly brought her in from a cold, desolate winter landscape, wrapped her in soft blankets and sat her down by a bright, glowing fire. She smiled at him and said, 'Oh Robert, you don't realize how nice it is to hear that. It's not that one wants thanks exactly, but – '

'I know,' he said, 'recognition perhaps? I know exactly. I have felt it a little sometimes myself. When – ' He looked at her, smiled again. 'Oh now, this is self-indulgent nonsense. What I've done is nothing compared with you.'

Grace didn't say anything, just looked at him.

'I shouldn't be talking like this, I suppose,' he said, 'but you know, Grace, it is hard for me. I love Florence so much and I can see what she feels for me in return is less. There's nothing I can do about that, of course, but just the same it hurts. Can you understand that?'

'Yes,' said Grace. Her voice was hardly a whisper; she didn't dare even look at him.

'It was always like that,' he said, 'from the beginning. I was so in love with her, and I knew she didn't feel the same. I knew she had married me without being really in love with me.'

Grace was silent.

'Now I'm not suggesting for a moment that she married me for my money, as some people have suggested, she has more self-respect, more intelligence than that. It's just that – well, it all seems a bit uneven, lopsided. I would do anything for Florence, anything, and for Imogen; I sometimes feel she doesn't return that feeling.'

'I'm sure she does,' said Grace.

'No, Grace, she doesn't. I can see it for myself, Anyway, I didn't want to burden you with my – sadness. It isn't fair.'

'Oh Robert, don't say that. I hate to think of – ' She bit her lip, terrified she was going to say too much, betray Florence. She might not like her, not trust her, but she was not going to tell her secrets.

'Hate to think of what, Grace? What do you hate to think of?'

'Nothing, Robert, nothing.'

'Grace, I'd rather know. It would make it easier for me if I knew exactly where I stand. If there was really not a lot of love for me, not a lot of hope. I mean, if I thought there was someone else, for instance, I just wouldn't want to hang around.'

Grace was beginning to feel like the mouse she had seen in the cat's jaws, trapped, tormented, with no possible means of escape. Robert was clearly looking for answers, answers that he felt she could provide. She sat, trying to look puzzled, innocent, wondering how much longer she could hold out, praying for the phone to ring, Clifford to return, anything. She realized her fists were clenched, that she was sweating.

Robert started talking again. 'Although, of course, there is Imogen now. I love her so much. In spite of what I just said about her being spoilt. Sweet-looking little thing, isn't she? So pretty. A little English rose. No one will believe me, but I was blond at that age.'

'Really?' said Grace. This was a nightmare; she didn't know what to do, debated saying she had to go to the lavatory, anything. And then he smiled suddenly and said, 'I'd love that cup of tea, Grace.'

'Oh Robert, I'm sorry,' she said, 'I'll go and get it now.'

She struggled to her feet, walked into the house; Robert followed her into the kitchen, sat and watched her while she boiled the kettle, got the cake out of the tin.

'It's not much of a cake,' she said apologetically, 'more like a loaf, really. It's very difficult, without fruit or butter or anything. But it's cake. The boys seem to enjoy it.'

'I'm sure I will too.' He sat back, smiling at her. 'You've made this house so nice,' he said, 'it has such a lovely atmosphere. You have a talent for homemaking, Grace. Lucky old Charles.' He paused, then said, 'Grace – '

'Yes, Robert?'

'Grace, you were there when Imogen was actually born, weren't you?'

'I certainly was.'

'She was – very small. Wasn't she?'

'Quite, yes. Five pounds, I think. Why?'

'Oh – nothing,' said Robert. 'I found her birth registration card last night, from the hospital, and I thought that sounded extremely little. I wondered if it was a mistake. I mean it was obviously a very hectic night and it can't have been easy for them – '

'Oh no,' said Grace, 'no, I don't think it was a mistake. In fact there was a bit of a to-do because they all said that considering she was almost a month early she was quite big really.'

'A month early,' said Robert. 'Yes, of course. I hadn't taken that into the equation. How silly of me. Thank you, Grace.'

Chapter Nineteen

Autumn–Winter 1942

Clarissa thought she had never been so happy as that autumn in Dartmouth. She had loved it from the first moment she saw it, when she had got out of the train at Kingswear, on the other side of the water, and taken the ferry across the Dart. The town was built in zigzagging layers up the hillside, the houses painted blue and cream and green and white, the red and white splendour of the Royal Naval College standing high on one side, overlooking the great natural harbour, the castle and the mouth of the Dart. The air was salty and smelt of the sea, and filled with the cries of seagulls; she was billeted at the top of the town in a Victorian gothic building called Warfleet House, charming, welcoming, with large rooms and fine fireplaces. Her room was set at the side, overlooking Warfleet Creek; she would walk up the steep streets to it in the evening, from her small office in the town, and feel for the first time since she had joined the Wrens that she was actually going to a home, rather than a billet.

Life was simply the best fun: nobody could help having a wonderful time, certainly not if they were female – the shortage of women was considerable. The college was being used as an American base, and the Americans were about the town in their thousands, with their money and their charm, and their unbelievable goodies, nylon stockings, perfume and cigarettes, Camels and Chesterfields and Lucky Strikes, and chewing gum and sweets – it was said no child in Dartmouth ever went without sweets and certainly not at their birthday parties. There were English officers living in the town, or there on leave, there were endless parties, balls at the college, and an innovation brought in by the Americans, 'Wienie roasts,' when steak – an unbelievable luxury in any case – was grilled over open fires. There were hilarious evenings at the famous Dartmouth pubs, the Dartmouth Arms and the Cherub Inn; and on days off they would catch the ferry down to the lush green of the Dittisham basin and drink beer at the Ship Inn, or ring the big bell at the end of the jetty which summoned a rowboat ferry to take you to the other side, to Greenway, perfect for picnics, or on up the narrow winding lanes to the beaches of Torbay.

May was there, billeted on the other side, in the commandeered Royal Dart Hotel, renamed HMS *Cicala*; there was immense pleasure and amusement in the town when Lord Haw-Haw, the British traitor, broadcasting regular propaganda on the German radio, announced that HMS *Cicala* had been sunk.

Clarissa loved it all, every moment of it, the work as well as the fun: and she did have to work extremely hard, responsible not only for the practical administration of Warfleet, but with the personal problems of the Wrens in her care, with their boyfriends, requests for leave, homesickness, postings. The days, often twelve, fourteen hours long, tumbled one upon the other, fast, too fast; and despite the constant danger, frequent exhaustion, missing Jack, worrying about Jack, still feeling guilty about Jack, she often thought she would have liked that time to go on for ever.

And then it stopped.

Grace was sitting in the kitchen working out which carols would be best for the nativity play – not too difficult for the little ones, not too babyish for the older ones – when she heard the phone ringing. She got up to answer it, was halfway down the passage when it stopped. Clifford, having more or less hidden from the phone for months, had suddenly rather taken to answering it. It was not an entirely happy state of affairs, as he was a great deal less efficient than Mrs Boscombe about taking messages and had also taken to making decisions on her behalf when she wasn't there, telling Miss Merton she was too busy to take on another child for music that week, or the vicar that she could easily manage choir practice. She had tried to dissuade him, but he had been so hurt, had said he wanted to help, that she had given up. That would almost undoubtedly be the vicar; she couldn't manage choir practice this week, she had to take David to the dentist and she really had to get her word in before Clifford's.

She hurried into the hall and saw Clifford replacing the receiver very slowly and carefully. He looked at her, and his face was ghastly white, his eyes haunted blue caverns within it. Her first thought was Charles, and her legs became weak, threatened to give way; but he recognized her fear and said at once, considerate for her as always, 'No, it's not – not Charles,' and then just stood there, staring at her.

'Who was it Clifford? What is it?'

'It was Florence,' he said. He was speaking with great difficulty.

Grace felt sick. 'Not Imogen?' she said. 'Surely not now? Not after – '

'No, no,' he said, 'not Imogen, she's fine. No, it was about – about

Jack. Clarissa phoned the Priory. He's been shot down. His luck's broken at last.'

'Oh God,' said Grace, 'Oh Clifford, is he dead?'

'No. At least not yet. Terribly badly injured. Burnt. That's all we know at the moment. Poor boy. Poor dear boy.' And he sat down on the chair and buried his head in his hands.

Grace looked at him helplessly, not knowing how to comfort him, what to say or do. She felt rather odd; she had hardly known Jack, and it was hard to feel grief for him, but she was shocked and horrified for Clarissa, and for Clifford himself. He loved them both so; and every death brought others nearer somehow, every death they heard of made it more impossible that Charles would escape it, would come safely home. God, she thought, looking out of the window at the clear wintry sky, the sky that only a few hundred miles away was filled with fire and danger; where would it end? How many more people would have to die before it was over, before someone said enough? She shuddered, felt cold and sick, put her arms round Clifford and hugged him very close.

'Don't,' she said, 'don't despair. It may not be so bad.'

But she knew she didn't believe it.

Clarissa sat in her office at Dartmouth, trying to work. It was very difficult, but she had to hang onto something, distract herself somehow. She was filled not only with misery and fear, but with a self-loathing that was like an evil physical presence, close, clinging to her. The memory of the intense pleasure, the work she loved, the fun she had been having over the past months intensified her remorse. She had been horrible to Jack, had failed him totally, she had been distant and distracted the last time he had been on leave, out with another man the night before he had left for North Africa, utterly engrossed in her work, her own self-important life, had not even written him many letters. And now he was lying horribly injured, possibly dying, and thinking she no longer loved him. His plane had been shot down and he had gone with it, his parachute had either failed or he had been unable to try to escape; the details in the report she had received from his squadron commander were hazy. But they had got him out, somehow, and he was still breathing, still alive; for days he had clung to life and now there was at least some hope.

But his injuries were considerable; she must prepare herself for that. When – this word rather than the deadly 'if' was used – he was well enough he would be flown home to England, to Addenbrooke's Hospital near Cambridge, to be cared for there. And then she would have to face him, her betrayed, deceived husband, face his injuries, and try to reassure him that she did still love him.

Florence had been deeply shocked by the news about Jack. She was very fond of him, and extraordinarily close to Clarissa; she had not seen her, but had spoken to her on the telephone, and had been shocked by her raw pain, and her remorse.

'How could I have done it, Florence?' she kept saying. 'How could I have not been there, the night before he went away, not said goodbye to him? I love him, I love him so much and he must have thought I didn't any more. I was out all night, Florence, all night, imagine how that must have seemed. Oh God, I wish I was dead myself. I don't know how I can bear it.'

Useless in the face of such remorse to apply logic, to point out that Jack could have thought that she was on duty, to reassure, to say that of course he knew she still loved him, that they had been together at Christmas, that it was only one night she had been out.

She tried, she said all those things, but Clarissa's voice, shaken, heavy with tears, said no, no, she didn't understand, she had been horrible to Jack at Christmas, bound up in her work, impatient with him and his grumblings before he finally went away, that he had known she was not on duty, had been told so by the duty officer. 'I failed him, Florence,' she said, 'failed him totally. And now it's too late and I can never put it right.'

Florence put the phone down finally, her heart wrenched with sympathy, thinking also of Giles and how he must perceive her behaviour towards him, also a failure, a treachery. She had never written, never tried to explain, there had semed no point; sitting now, staring at the telephone, still hearing Clarissa's pain-racked voice, thinking of Giles, of how dreadful it would be if he was killed, thinking she no longer loved him, had simply, carelessly stood him up, left him waiting for long hours on her doorstep, she decided she would write, would explain. He was far, far away again, he couldn't suddenly descend on her, try to change her mind, weaken her will; she owed him an explanation, he deserved to be told the truth.

She walked into the morning room to find some writing paper, just in time to see Imogen lifting one of Muriel's more precious Staffordshire pieces and hurling it, an expression of huge satisfaction on her small face, onto the fireplace where it fragmented most spectacularly.

'Mother, I'm sorry. What more can I say?'

275

'You could do something about that child,' said Muriel. 'Discipline her. Stop her running riot.'

'It's a difficult age,' said Florence weakly.

'Florence, all ages are difficult. You don't seem to have grasped that fact. I do assure you that thirty-two, or whatever you are, seems quite difficult at the moment,' she added tartly.

'And it isn't very sensible to leave pieces of valuable china about when a small child can get at them.'

'I was always of the opinion,' said Muriel firmly, 'that the child should be trained to accommodate the house and not the other way round. Whatever is she doing now? Oh Florence, for heaven's sake, she's got the cat by the tail and she's dragging it after her down the path. Do something about her. Or I shall.'

That afternoon, Florence went to see Nanny Baines.

Nanny Baines was not only delighted to be presented with the problem of Imogen, she felt a clear sense of vindication. She had been waiting for the call, ever since Florence had brought Imogen home, had watched in horror as she insisted she could manage on her own.

'She's not bringing that child up,' she confided to Mrs Babbage, her friend and confidante for many years, 'she's dragging it down. Poor Mrs Bennett is at her wits' end. All this nonsense about wanting to rear the child herself; it never works, and there's the proof, clear for all to see.'

Mrs Babbage agreed with her most fervently, and indeed went one step further. 'It's not natural,' she said, 'not for her sort. They've not the instinct for it, Miss Baines, that's the thing. Although young Mrs Bennett, now, she's the exception. Wonderful with those little boys, she is.'

'Well,' said Nanny Baines, 'you say that, but you have to remember they're not hers. Not her own flesh and blood. Besides,' she added darkly, 'she's not quite – well, we're not talking about quite the same type of person there. Are we? Not quite. Very sweet, of course, but I know Mrs Bennett did feel Mr Charles was marrying slightly beneath him. Slightly.'

'Well I don't agree' said Mrs Babbage staunchly.

'And anyway, Nanny, I've decided to do something myself,' said Florence, 'to help, in the war I mean. They're calling up women now, and although I wouldn't be, because of Imogen, I do feel I could do my bit.'

'What were you thinking of doing?' asked Nanny Baines. 'Not

joining the Wrens like Mrs Compton Brown? Because I don't think – '

'No, Nanny, I can't possibly join one of the services. I don't want to leave Imogen to that extent. No, I'm going to get a job in a factory.'

'A factory!' said Nanny Baines. She didn't say anything further, but she felt it was no wonder Imogen had got into the state she had, with a mother who was prepared to work in a factory.

Muriel had been interestingly encouraging about the factory work; Florence had expected to hear a great deal about keeping up standards and the sort of people she would be mixing with, but Muriel had simply said she thought it was very good of Florence, and that in these hard times one had to be prepared to do anything. Florence didn't like to point out that Muriel didn't seem prepared to do anything at all, not even part with her aluminium saucepans for the munitions factories.

Factory work proved something of a difficulty: the nearest factory was so far away, and the bus service now so sparse, that it was almost totally impracticable; Florence, easily depressed in any case, was almost in tears at this obstacle. It was Grace who suggested the WVS. 'Mrs Lacey, she's my Land Army committee person, says they're crying out for people still. I was thinking of doing it myself, but I do seem to be rather busy. It's not paid, of course, but that won't be a problem, and you could fit it round Imogen better as well.'

And so Florence presented herself to the Westhorne branch of the WVS and found herself greeted with immense enthusiasm by a very large woman wearing a Churchill-style boiler suit, and possessed of a booming voice and an impressive ability to inspire and direct the ladies come to rally to her cause.

'Anything needed done, and we do it,' she said to Florence. 'No turning your nose up at anything, of course.'

'No of course not,' said Florence humbly.

'Drive, I presume?'

'Oh – yes. Yes I do.'

'Splendid. Now then, what about canteen work? We always need people there. Got a large one at Salisbury, for the troops passing through on their way to Southampton. Can I put you down for that?' Florence nodded. 'It's hard mind, on your feet twelve hours a day sometimes, and you get sick of the sight and smell of baked beans, but still. You get petrol coupons, of course.'

Florence loved the canteen work, loved its jollity and camaraderie; naturally finicky herself, she took a perverse pleasure in boiling up huge vats of beans and a totally unappetizing fish called snoek, spreading great stacks of bread and dripping, pouring out endless mugs of dark brown tea. When she wasn't doing that she spent a lot of time making up 'bundles for Britain', parcels of clothes, mostly baby things, sent from America and forwarded to the wretched bombed-out families who found themselves not only homeless but devoid of everything except what they stood up in. The WVS were also charged with trying to find accommodation for those families: 'Not easy,' Florence reported to Muriel. 'Do you know a lot of the children have never had their vests off, they keep them on all the time, until they grow out of them.' Muriel said that was only what she would have expected.

Florence also did what she called Cupid work. Letters came in shoals to the WVS, from men at the front, requesting birthday cards be sent to families, flowers delivered to wives on anniversaries, and sometimes, heartbreakingly, finding out if loved ones were safe. 'I haven't heard from my girl for over a year,' a letter would read, 'could you get in touch with her, at number 7 Queen's Avenue, and make sure she's all right.' Very often, the girl would be more than all right, merely weary of waiting and busy with war work of a rather questionable kind; Florence would endeavour to extract a promise from her to write and keep morale high. She knew this was over and above the bounds of duty, probably not what she was supposed to do, but she found it impossible to simply walk away.

But what she liked best, and found herself doing quite frequently (being an extremely good driver and also rather brave), was driving one of the fleet of Queen's Messengers, large vans, five per depot, to any spot near an air raid – usually Southampton – and delivering on-the-spot help to the bombed-out families. It could be dangerous; they often arrived before the raid was actually over, and had to park as near as possible to the bombed area. Frequently Florence sat in her van, looking at the blazing sky and listening to the incredible noise, and wondered from minute to minute whether she would survive.

'They're incredibly precious, these vans,' said a voluntary woman (as Florence called them) in Salisbury, briefing her, 'actually donated by the Queen. They have to be looked after like – well, like the egg in a cake.' Eggs seeming quite as precious as vans at that point, it was a particularly good analogy. One van carried water, one clothing, one bedding, one food, and one a stove; they would wait for people to arrive in search of food, clothing and comfort.

'They are so desperate, so grateful,' said Florence to Grace, 'and you just don't know what to say. So mostly I don't say anything.'

Knowing Florence's capacity for saying the wrong thing, Grace thought that was probably just as well.

Jack was flown home to Addenbrooke's Hospital in early December. Clarissa took the train up to Cambridge, shaking with fear at what she might find; twice she had to fight her way through the packed corridors to the lavatory to be sick. Spectres of Jack lying frail, near to death indeed, tormented her. She visualized him swathed in bandages, drips from every orifice, angry with her, hostile, dismissing her from his room, his very presence.

She presented herself nervously at the hospital, half expecting a hostile reception even there. A pretty young nurse told her to go along to see the MO before she tried to find Jack.

'He's marvellous, your husband,' she said, 'so brave and cheerful. We all think he's terrific.'

The doctor was briskly sympathetic.

'He's in pretty good shape, in some ways. Amazingly fit, he's fought back marvellously. There's no doubt that he'll make a full recovery.'

'Oh,' said Clarissa. Her heart lifted, she smiled at the doctor; she had not expected to hear such positive news.

'However, you must prepare yourself for a shock. He has been very badly burnt. You may find it hard to accept. What is quite crucial is that you hide your feelings. Many months of painful treatment and surgery lie ahead of him. He needs every ounce of support you can give him. It would hinder his recovery to an appalling extent if he even suspected you found his appearance in any way shocking.'

'Doesn't he realize himself?' said Clarissa. 'Surely —'

The MO looked at her very intently for a moment; then he said, quite gently, 'Mrs Compton Brown, we don't allow them mirrors.'

Clarissa went slowly into the room where Jack lay. He was propped up on pillows; both his arms were swathed in dressings. One leg was slung up on a pulley.

'Darling!' he said, and his voice was surprisingly strong, 'oh darling Clarissa. Is it really you?'

Two large tears rolled down his face. Clarissa went over to him, smiled into his eyes, bent and kissed his forehead.

'It's really me,' she said, 'and I love you.'

She sat with him for over an hour. She heard about the crash: 'I was flying very low, this bastard was after me, firing away. I suddenly heard a loud rattling, got a very strong smell of petrol and I could hear my flight overseer on the radio telling me I'd got a hole in my side. Well, I wasn't going to let him get away with that. I managed to climb again, and fired, and I did get him; but by then I was in trouble. There was some kind of an explosion. I don't remember much for a bit, couldn't see or anything. Then I realized my eyes were closed. I had to prise them open with my fingers, they were stuck. Next thing I knew, more darkness, more flames – and then I came to in hospital. Fraid I wasn't very brave after that.'

'That's not – ' Clarissa's throat contracted – 'that's not what everyone has told me.'

'Well, they're not going to tell you I'm anything but a hero, are they?' said Jack. He smiled. 'Oh darling, I can't believe you're really here. First I dreamt of you, then I prayed for you. I was ready for some miracle, for you to walk into the hospital, make it bearable for me.'

'I would have,' she whispered, 'if they'd let me. I would.'

'I know,' he said and smiled again. He closed his eyes for a while, apparently exhausted. Then he said, 'Sometimes when it was very bad, I was convinced you were there. I saw you, standing there, looking so bloody beautiful. I didn't mind anything, the pain, the horror. I'd reach out for you, when they were changing my dressings, doing something hideous, and say "hold my hand" because I knew then I'd be able to bear it, and you'd hold out yours, and before I could get it, you'd gone.'

Clarissa bent her head; her own tears fell onto her hand. She swallowed hard. 'That's me all over,' she said lightly, 'never there when I'm needed.'

'You're always there when you're needed. Whenever you can be.'

'Oh, Jack, Jack, don't – ' she said.

He reached out his hand, inside its bandage, and touched her cheek gently; the bandage was rough, she hated it. She forced herself to turn and kiss it.

'And I dreamt about you,' he said, 'whenever I slept, which wasn't often, they didn't give me enough dope, they said they had, but they hadn't, they didn't know, they couldn't. Christ, it was awful.' There was a silence. Then he said, 'Yes, I dreamt about you. It was always the pre-war Clarissa, in lovely clothes, saying funny, silly things, not the sensible, clever one who was there underneath. Very often I dreamt about our wedding day, God knows why. Only I wasn't there, just you standing at the altar looking marvellous. And then the church would go up in flames and – Jesus, Clarissa, I'm sorry.'

He was really crying now, racking sobs; she tried to hold him, but the drips and the bandages got in the way. The tears flooded down his face; he blinked impatiently, tried to smile, to brush them away. 'Sorry, darling, so sorry. Could you wipe them for me? And my nose.'

'Yes of course,' said Clarissa. It was the hardest thing she had ever done.

Later she sat, while he dozed; a nurse came in to see him. 'He's still very weak,' she said quietly. 'The doctor says not too long today. Can you come back tomorrow, or do you have to go back on duty?'

'No,' said Clarissa, 'no, I've got a week's leave. I'm staying at the hotel just down the road.'

'Good. It will help him so much. He talks about you all the time.'

Later, he woke, was tired, fretful, pushing the feeding cup away when she tried to give it to him. He was still on an entirely liquid diet.

'Probably better if you go now,' said the ward sister, 'bad for him to get too tired. But he's better already than when he arrived, two days ago. He's a terrific fighter.'

'I know,' said Clarissa, 'that's always been the trouble.'

Jack got very upset, clung to her when she said she was going. 'Don't leave me, darling, I'm so afraid of losing you again.'

'I'm not leaving you,' said Clarissa, 'and I'll be back tomorrow. Don't worry, darling. I promise.'

And then, she had to say it, had to clear it, took a deep breath and said, 'Jack, the night before you went, when I wasn't there, I was only in a raid, in a shelter. I couldn't bear you to think – '

'Oh Clarissa,' he said, and his eyes were fixed on hers in an agony of love, 'I knew there was a good reason, an explanation. I was irritated, that was all. You know how irritable I can be.'

'Yes,' said Clarissa, smiling at him again through her tears, 'yes, Jack, I do know how irritable you can be.'

'You don't understand,' she said, her voice a wail of animal agony as she talked to Florence on the telephone from the noisy cold hall in the hotel, 'you don't understand, Florence, it's awful, it's terrible, I don't know how we're going to bear it. It's his face, his lovely face, he doesn't know, he doesn't realize, it's just not there any more, Florence, hardly any of it. It's all been burnt away.'

The MO talked to her for longer the next day.

'I'm sorry not to have prepared you more for it,' he said, 'but there's so little that can be said. It's still a terrible shock.'

'It's horrible,' said Clarissa, simply, 'I know if he knew he'd rather be dead.'

'Mrs Compton Brown, you'd be surprised at how people don't actually prefer death. It's a pretty tough alternative, you know. And your husband is a fighter. If he hadn't been, he would have been dead by now anyway. He's a brave and clearsighted man. He'll come through this.'

'For what?' said Clarissa. 'Tell me what he's coming through for? A life where everyone finds him repulsive. Where he won't be able to go out even, without people staring, looking, avoiding him.'

She was angry, furious with the doctor, in lieu of anyone else; she would have found it quite easy to hit him.

He was clearly used to it. 'Not repulsive, Mrs Compton Brown. I think that's going a bit far.'

'I don't,' said Clarissa. 'My husband was a desperately good-looking man. Now he is repulsive. It's perfectly simple. How can he work, even?'

'What did he do? Before the war?'

'He was a stockbroker.'

'Well, I didn't think looks were a prerequisite for stockbroking.'

'No,' said Clarissa, 'they aren't. Not exactly. But who's going to want to sit across the desk from someone they have to avert their eyes from?'

'Mrs Compton Brown,' said Major Norris, 'I wonder if you are perhaps prejudging everyone. All these people you say will find your husband repulsive. Surely we all have rather finer feelings than that? Your husband has been wounded, defending his country. He is an immensely brave man. He has won the DSO. Can't you trust people to remember that, to adjust their reactions because of it?'

'Major Norris,' said Clarissa, 'I am a very realistic woman. I think you're living in a fool's paradise. People will remember for about six months at the most that my husband has been wounded, as you put it, maimed I would call it, defending his country. After that – well, I don't know. Listen, I love him, very much. And I find him repulsive. I expect that horrifies you, but I'm trying to be honest. I want to help him and I don't know how.'

Major Norris looked at her for a while in silence. Then he said, 'I can understand how you feel. I know what a dreadful shock you have endured. And I think your honesty is – courageous. But I still think things are not as bad as you imagine. And they will be better. We are sending a lot of these chaps to Archibald MacIndoe. You've heard of him, I expect?'

'No,' said Clarissa.

'He's a plastic surgeon. Brilliant. He has virtually rebuilt faces. I would think Squadron Leader Compton Brown would certainly qualify for his attentions.'

A bolt of hope went through Clarissa, bright, strong. 'You mean – he could actually restore Jack's face? As it was?'

'Oh no,' said Major Norris, 'I don't want to mislead you. It would be a great improvement on – on what you have seen at the moment. But nothing, of course, could restore your husband's face to what it was.'

It was a very long week. Clarissa felt as if she was living in some ghastly, hideous nightmare; visiting Jack every day, smiling at him, pretending everything else was all right, forcing herself to kiss him, to tell him she loved him, when every time she looked at his face, with its dreadful, blunted parodies of features, she felt physically and violently sick. She kept hoping she would get used to it, cease to see it so vividly, mind it so much, and by the end of each day, each visit, she had begun to accept it at least a little; but then next morning, confronted by it afresh, the revulsion resurfaced. She was deeply and horribly ashamed of herself for feeling as she did; she was clearly, she thought, hideously shallow, fickle, frivolous. She felt sure that Grace would not have reacted in this way, had Charles been similarly affected, or even Florence; they would have looked calmly past the physical horror to what mattered, to the person beneath.

On the third day Jack had suddenly smiled at her, said, 'Darling, it's making me all upset, your being here with me.'

'Whatever do you mean?' she had asked lightly.

'I mean I want you. Desperately. My senses seem to be working just fine. I had the most enormous erection last night, remembering you, and how you looked and smelt when you came into the room. It was quite reassuring in a way. I don't know that I can wait until I get home. I wonder if we could – '

'Oh darling, of course we couldn't,' said Clarissa quickly. 'Sister would be in here in a trice, and what about your drips and things?'

She had to excuse herself, go out for a while, sit in the hospital garden and smoke a cigarette. The thought of lying in bed beside Jack, of him kissing her, making love to her, made her feel so desperate, so terrified, she wanted to run away. And the worst thing of course was how alone she felt in all this. How could she tell anyone, anyone at all, that she found the husband she was supposed to love so much, had professed to love so much, quite literally revolting?

She returned to Dartmouth with a sense of huge and terrible relief as if she had escaped from some room filled with vile fetid air into a fresh wind-swept landscape. Jack was upset at her going, but accepted it; he knew she could do nothing else. She was an officer in the Wrens, and a wounded husband was in no way acceptable as a reason for resigning. It was a fact of life; men were wounded every day, there was a war on, everyone had to get on and make the most of it. She threw herself back into her work gratefully, deliberately exhausting herself, taking on extra projects, extra loads, so that by the time she fell into bed she could escape into sleep for a few hours at least. Even then, there was no rest; Jack's face haunted her. Sometimes she dreamt that he was still all right, that it had all been a mistake, that he had been lying there on his pillows just as he had been, smiling at her; at other times she saw it, the new face, pressing ever closer to hers, the new face with the strange tiny eyes and the non-existent nose, the awkwardly folded lips, and would wake up sweating and more than once yelling, 'No, no, no.'

But even that was better than the other nightmare: the one that she couldn't ever wake from.

As she sank down at her desk the first morning back, her mind turning, like an alcoholic to the bottle, to more imminent, more soluble problems, May's face appeared round her door.

'Welcome back, Duchess. Someone was looking for you last night. Talk about handsome. Name of Henry. Lieutenant-Commander Giles Henry to be precise. Just arrived here. Says you've never met but you'll know who he is. If you haven't got time to make him feel at home, I certainly wouldn't mind helping out.'

'Goodness,' said Clarissa, 'how nice. Tell you what, May, we'll share him.'

'Once you've seen him,' said May, 'you won't want to share him. Not with anyone. Not knowing you, Duchess.'

Chapter Twenty

Autumn 1942

Clarissa spent a lot of time wondering if it showed. Her rottenness, her duplicity. She didn't think it did; catching sight of herself occasionally as she went about her duties, moving through her day, from her room at Warfleet to her small office, confronting crises, solving problems, she seemed to look exactly the same, indeed much of the time felt exactly the same, pretty, funny, often outrageous Clarissa, popular, admired, her advice sought both on and off duty, her opinions esteemed, her company valued.

And yet beneath it, the charming glossy exterior, behind the sweet smile, the sympathetic eyes, within the efficient, sophisticated woman lay, she knew, someone rather different. A manipulative, fraudulent someone, double-dealing, faithless, worthless, guilty of a double betrayal. She crept up on the other Clarissa, this creature, haunting her days, disturbing her nights; she would wake, sweating at three in the morning, her stomach churning, forced to confront her. She disliked her intensely, hated her at times – and yet she could not get rid of her. She needed her. She needed her to survive.

It had begun so charmingly, so sweetly: she had telephoned the officers' mess, left a message for Commander Henry, and he had invited her to have a drink with him the next evening.

And she had walked into the bar, still weary, still shocked from her week at Jack's bedside, and looked at him, and he at her, and that had been that. Not love, of course not love, but a violent, almost shocking attraction, a recognition in each of them that the other had exactly, precisely what they wanted, and moreover that the circumstances and their respective states of mind meant that they were absolutely ready to offer, to share, to enjoy it.

They had danced around it for a while, of course; had put up the pretence that they were simply being sociable, friendly, easing one another's loneliness. They sat in the mess talking for a long time, about the happy coincidence that had brought them there, their different wars, their experiences, their futures: about Florence – 'She is my dearest friend,' said Clarissa perhaps a little too firmly, but she was, she was; about Jack – 'It must be so dreadful for him,' said Giles, and yes, she said, it is, quite dreadful: so why was she even looking at this man, this beautiful man, wanting him, making the dreadfulness for Jack worse? And he was beautiful, quite extraordinarily so, not in the same way as Jack, that would have been somehow better, would have stopped her short, made her realize exactly what she was doing, but perilously, differently beautiful, fair-haired (like her), dark-eyed (like her), with the most wonderfully musical voice and a graceful lounging body.

'You know,' she said as the third gin and French slithered into her consciousness, making her feel dangerously, confidently relaxed, 'we could almost be brother and sister.'

'Really?' he said, 'What an interesting idea.'

'In what way interesting?' she said.

'Oh – it has a Shakespearean quality to it, that notion,' he said, offering her a cigarette. She took it, cupped her hand round his as he lit it, aware that he would be able to smell her perfume, feel her hair falling forward.

'I'm sorry,' she said, smiling, sitting back, blowing out the smoke, 'I'm frightfully badly educated, you'll have to explain.'

'I'm sure you're not,' he said, smiling back at her, 'but it's all those twins, you know, in all those comedies, girls dressed as their brothers, other girls falling in love with them.'

'Goodness, you make it sound so depraved,' said Clarissa, laughing now. 'All I meant was that we both have fair hair and brown, well brown-ish, eyes. It's quite unusual.'

'Indeed it is,' he said, his brown eyes resting on hers, smiling into them, 'but it looks a lot better on you than me.'

'Nonsense,' said Clarissa, 'you look quite marvellous, I think.'

The thought came to her, swiftly shocking, that it was surprising that Florence should have engaged the attentions of such a creature. Florence was very attractive, of course, with her dark hair and her pale skin, and her wide gash of a mouth, and her figure was wonderful, especially her legs, and she had a certain rather stark chic, but no one could have called her pretty, nor was she conventionally charming, with her abrupt, uncompromising honesty.

For just a moment the thought was there; then she banished it again, thrust it fiercely from her head. 'She loves you very much you know,' she said firmly, as if to do penance for it, to make it absolutely and infinitely plain that she had no possible interest in him, other than as the best friend of the woman he loved.

'I'm afraid not,' he said, and there was an infinite sadness in his voice. 'I'm afraid she has put me out of her life rather finally. And rather cruelly. Actually. You must know about it, surely.'

'Well I do,' said Clarissa, 'I mean I know what she did. Standing you up that day. It must have seemed very dreadful. But – '

'It was very dreadful,' he said, 'I have never known anything so dreadful. But – here, let me get you another drink. Or are you in a hurry?'

Clarissa shook her head rather weakly. 'No. Well I have another half-hour at least.'

She looked at him as he stood at the bar, at his tall body, his sloping shoulders, his long legs, saw him turn his head and smile at her in apology for the delay, oh God, that lovely, lovely smile, and resolved that when he got back to her she must explain about Florence, about why she had done what she had done that day. She must. Before this thing went any further.

'Listen,' she said, as he settled beside her, and she heard her voice talking fast, urgently, as if in some way to save herself from – what? 'Listen, there's something you have to know about Florence. Something important. She couldn't meet you that day. She really couldn't. Imogen was ill, very ill, in hospital – oh she's all right now – and she simply couldn't get word to you. She really, really couldn't.'

'Oh,' he said. There was a long silence while he digested this; then he said, 'So do you think she still loves me? Really?'

'Oh yes,' said Clarissa firmly, 'really. I'm sure she does.'

Right. That should have done it. That would fix it. That would deal with that look in his eye as he met hers, the acknowledgment that he was lonely and unhappy as she was, that he wanted her as she did him. Amazing what looks in eyes could do, she thought inconsequentially, waiting for the withdrawal from her, the swift excuse, the rush to the phone. She was ready with her own excuses, that she had a meeting to attend, work to catch up on (both true), that she was tired (untrue, how could you be tired with this amount of sexual desire soaring through your veins?), was looking round the bar to find someone else she knew – so that his departure would be less miserable.

But it didn't quite work out that way.

'I can't accept that,' he said, finally. 'I can't quite find that enough. Of course she couldn't have come that day. If Imogen was ill, if she was in hospital. I can see that. But she could have written to me afterwards, surely, explained, we could have found another time. All I've had from her is silence. An awful, hard silence.'

Clarissa looked at him. 'Giles,' she said, summoning all her will-power, 'Florence has had the most awful time, you know. That marriage of hers – so terrible. I'm sure – I'm absolutely sure – she loves you. Why don't you write to her? Ring her?'

There. Honour satisfied. She couldn't possibly have done any more.

But 'No,' he said, 'no, I can't. I don't want to. I'd rather leave it. I'm – well, I'm just beginning to get over it. Besides, I did write to her. She didn't even answer. Not even a line, Clarissa. So let's not talk about her any more. It just makes me wretched. Let's talk about you. You and your Jack.'

'Well, that upsets *me*,' said Clarissa lightly, 'so what about talking about something quite different? Like your life before the war. I love hearing about all that sort of thing. Theatres, auditions, first nights – '

'Seaside piers, bottom of the bill, old ladies' matinées,' said Giles, laughing. 'All right, I'll give you the lowdown. What about dinner? Or what this place calls dinner.'

Clarissa hesitated. 'Can't. Not tonight. Sorry.'

'Tomorrow? Thursday?'

'Thursday would be lovely.'

She was lost already. Quite, quite lost.

Nothing happened at first. Of course. Well, it couldn't. It wasn't going to. He was, whatever he thought, the man her best friend loved. Well, presumably still loved. She, Clarissa, was desperately in love with her husband. Who needed her desperately. There was no question of their going to bed together. They were simply cheering one another up. They didn't have long, he was leaving in a month or so, they were both lonely, both unhappy. And of course there was a war on. It would have been unkind, wrong even, not to have gone on seeing him, making him laugh, giving him happy memories. That was the creed, the philosophy everyone adhered to, worked with; you owed it to people, to give them happy memories. Those memories might be their last. It was the winter of 1942, the dark heart of the war; nobody could afford to give much attention to tomorrow, next week, next year.

She liked him, very much. He wasn't really her type, too much like herself in fact. She'd been right about the possibility of their being brother and sister, and it didn't stop at the looks. They were both amusing, a bit excessive, liked the limelight, sought, rather helplessly, the centre stage. They egged each other on, in jokes and funny stories, loved gossip, intrigue, were aware of one another's capacity to engender it. They were wildly indiscreet, so indiscreet in fact that, as Clarissa said, no one could possibly suspect them of anything, not really. 'If we had anything to hide,' she said, kissing Giles affection-ately on the cheek in the bar one night, 'we simply wouldn't be here. Behaving like this.'

'And we don't? Do we?'

'No, of course not. Not really. Well, hardly anything.'

He smiled, picked up her hand, kissed it. 'Hardly anything at all. I'm kissing you now, here, so that everyone knows I don't need to kiss you anywhere else.'

'Anywhere else on me?' said Clarissa, laughing. 'Or anywhere else in South Devon?'

'Anywhere else in the world.'

'I'd be very pleased to hear that, Commander. If it wasn't just faintly insulting.'

'Very hard to insult you, Second Officer.'

That Saturday they went down to Dittisham, and drank rather a lot of cider; they took the ferry over to Greenway and walked in the woods. Clarissa felt dizzy, reckless; she took Giles's hand suddenly. 'This has been such a lovely, lovely episode. I've adored it. Every minute of it.'

He sighed: a heavy theatrical sigh.

She looked at him, startled. 'What was that about?'

'That's all I am to you, isn't it, Clarissa? An episode. Not a lot for a man to be. An episode.'

'Giles, don't be silly I – '

'I might just hurl myself into the Dart,' he said, 'right now. End it all.'

'Oh Giles, really,' she said laughing, 'I thought you meant it.'

'I did.' He sank down onto the rather soggy ground, buried his head in his hands. She looked at him, alarmed, sat down beside him, put her arms round him.

'Giles, please. Don't be – I didn't mean to hurt you – I – '

He lifted his head, looked at her suddenly, his eyes alight with laughter. 'Haven't lost my technique quite yet then,' he said.

'Oh you – you brute,' said Clarissa, 'breaking my poor innocent girlish heart – ' She started to shake him gently, laughing at the same time. He put up his hands to ward her off and fell over backwards; she fell on top of him.

And then she looked down at him, so lovely, so desirable, and had a brief, awful vision of Jack, of his mutilated face, and Giles too had stopped laughing, and lay looking up at her; and she bent and kissed him, lightly at first, then more and more hungrily, wanting him, writhing on top of him, feeling him harden against her, even through their clothes, and he was kissing her too, as hungry, as wanting, his mouth at the same time gentle; and then: 'Christ,' he said suddenly, pulling away, 'Christ, this is awful, I'm sorry, Clarissa.'

And common sense, common sense and some sort of dignity repossessed her and she allowed herself to think that it had come from him, the first approach, for it was better that way, and she rolled off him, fighting down her desire, straightened her hair and her clothes, asked him for a cigarette.

'The trouble is,' he said, as they sat there, smoking, her head on his shoulder, 'the trouble is, I want you very much. I think you're lovely. But – '

'Yes,' she said, 'yes of course but. I'm married to someone who needs me.'

'And who you love.'

'And who I love. Yes. And your – well, Florence is my best friend. And whatever you think, it might still work out between you. So – '

'So yes, of course, it's unthinkable.'

'Yes of course.'

'Best get back perhaps?'

'Yes. Perhaps.'

He stood up, put his hand down and pulled her to her feet. 'I still don't like being called an episode,' he said, and laughed. 'Aren't I anything more than that?'

'Absolutely not,' said Clarissa firmly.

That evening he was on duty. She went to meet May.

'You look pretty pleased with yourself, Duchess,' she said. 'You getting on well with the commander then?'

'Oh – yes,' said Clarissa. 'Yes, pretty well. He's charming. Sweet. But only an episode, May. Only an episode.'

'Oh yeah,' said May.

Grace, arriving at the Priory with some eggs for Muriel and Florence, found them both in tears; she stared at them in horror, thinking, assuming that it might be Charles, that they had by some dreadful official mistake been notified before her.

'What is it?' she said. 'What's happened?'

'It's Laurence,' said Muriel. 'Dear Laurence. We've known him since he and Charles were at prep school. He's been killed. Out in

India. His mother just phoned me. Florence, for heaven's sake, do stop that child whining. I simply can't stand it.'

'I'll take her for a walk,' said Grace.

She wandered round the garden, holding Imogen's small hand, crying herself, not so much for Laurence, who she had after all scarcely known, but for all the dead and dying that the world seemed to be filled with.

Jack had seen his face. He was in a state of total despair – and something else. Something ugly, something worse.

'It's shock,' said the doctor to Clarissa. She had gone up to Cambridge for two days. 'Literally shock. It's been appalling for him. He's reacted very badly. Try to be patient with him.'

She tried. It was very difficult. He was alternately angry, hostile, noisily full of self-pity – and suddenly frantically, fearfully dependent on her.

'If you leave me,' he said, clinging to her hand, tears coursing down his face, 'I shall die. I shall kill myself. It seems that simple. Don't, don't leave me.'

'Of course I won't leave you,' said Clarissa, trying to smile, to soothe him, raising his hand to her lips, kissing it. 'Never ever.'

'Kiss me,' he said suddenly, 'kiss me. Go on. On the lips.'

'Jack, I – ' She tried; she looked at his lips, his odd half-lips, curled in, tried to look at the rest of his face, swallowed.

'Go on,' he said, 'kiss me. Kiss me, damn you.'

'Jack, I – '

Her courage failed her. He got up suddenly, turned his back, walked over to the corner of the room, stood there, his back turned to her. 'I revolt you, don't I?' he said, his voice very low. 'I disgust you. Well, I'm not surprised, I disgust myself.'

'Jack, darling – '

'Don't say that,' he said, turning round, savagery in his voice, 'don't you darling me. You can't make it right with words, Clarissa. You're disgusted, and that's all there is to it. Go away, go on, just get on back to Dartmouth. I don't want you here. Get out, get out – '

He was shouting, shaking; she sat there helpless, not knowing what to do, knowing the one thing she should do, knowing she couldn't do it.

'Get out,' he said and it was a great roar of anguish. 'Get away from me.'

She got out; went back to her hotel, lay awake nearly all night, trying to come to terms with the horror that was her life. Next day she went back to the hospital; he refused to see her.

She travelled back to Dartmouth in a state of total despair; the next night she was in bed with Giles Henry.

She hadn't meant to, of course; she had meant only to talk to him, to try to rid herself of some of the misery.

'Poor, poor you,' he said gently, reaching out, touching her cheek. They had left the town, he had walked up towards Warfleet with her, they were looking out into the lovely mouth of the Dart, beyond the creek, her creek. It was a clear night, the moon was full, the frosty air had brought out the stars.

'Look, how the floor of heaven,' he said suddenly.

'Sorry?' said Clarissa absently.

'Shakespeare, my darling. *Merchant of Venice*. Look, how the floor of heaven is thick inlaid with patines of bright gold.'

'Oh,' she said, 'oh Giles, say that again.'

'Look, how the floor of heaven is thick inlaid – '

'No, not that. Say my darling again.'

'My darling.' He smiled at her. 'I think the Shakespeare is nicer actually, but each to his own.'

'It is, it's wonderful, but – '

'I know. My darling is more relevant.'

There was a silence, then she said, 'Oh Giles, it's so awful. What am I going to do?'

Tears began to spill over from her eyes, roll down her cheeks; she brushed them back impatiently. He reached out, took a tear on his finger, then put it back on her face. 'Lovely you are,' he said quietly, 'lovely and so very, very sweet. Your Jack is lucky. In spite of everything he's lucky. To have you.'

'Oh no,' she cried, 'he's not, he's not, I'm rotten, useless to him – '

There was a silence; then he bent his head and kissed her.

Clarissa had been kissed hundreds of times by dozens of men; never had one affected her so. For there was not just passion in that kiss, not just tenderness, there was kindness, sympathy, absolute understanding. His mouth was gentle, careful, yet infinitely hungry for her at the same time; the kiss was lingering, endlessly arousing, yet comforting, calming. She responded slowly; first relief, then happiness, and finally, ripping into her, desire, harsh, desperate desire. And suddenly that was all that mattered: that she should have him. She did not forget Florence nor did she cease to think of Jack; she simply set them aside as being of no possible importance. It was Giles she wanted, Giles with his lovely face and his graceful body; and he wanted her and it was all perfectly simple.

'There's somewhere we could go,' she said very quietly, seeing that he too recognized the time had come. 'A little hut down at the creek. We use it for changing in the summer, when we want to swim. It'll be cold, but – '

'We can keep each other warm,' he said, his face intently on hers. 'Is there a key?'

There was a key: hidden under a stone. She let them in, shivering. It was quite clean, the little hut, but as she had said, freezing; he took off his coat, found some towels as well.

'This bed thy centre is,' he said, smiling at her. 'These walls thy sphere. Donne,' he added.

'What's done?' asked Clarissa.

'John Donne, you lovely, lovely ignoramus.'

'Never insult a woman when you're about to seduce her,' said Clarissa. 'You should know that, I would have – '

'For God's sake hold your tongue,' he said gently, reaching out, starting to unbutton her shirt, 'and let me love. Also Donne.'

'All right,' said Clarissa.

It was absolutely wonderful. She was starved of sex anyway, her body not just hungry, but fretful, frantic for release; beneath his skilful, probing, thoughtful hands it leapt, soared into life. He entered her quickly, sensing her need, she felt the sweet pushing heaviness within her, rose to meet it, cried out, would have come almost at once had he not said, quite sternly, 'Be still. Be quite, quite still.'

And she lay there, feeling the stirrings, the bright movements towards orgasm still pulling at her, but controlled, most wonderfully; he worked on her and in her then, drawing her slowly, slowly forwards, pushing her gently back, moving her, moulding her round him, making her his, taking possession of her depths. And finally she could stand it no longer; she rose right to the top of her pleasure, her body reached into it and then she felt herself falling, falling around it, around the endless delight, each peak higher, fiercer, and she heard a great roar and knew it was her voice. And then she felt him come, on and endlessly on, and he too cried out, and then finally they were still, lay looking into one another's faces, and at once, unbidden, she heard Jack's voice: 'The only thing that will come between us is some tall, dark and handsome naval commander.'

At least Giles was fair.

'I'm going to write to Giles,' said Florence. 'I've decided.'

She was sitting in the garden at the Mill House with Grace, gazing enraptured at Imogen who was being swung by her small arms between Daniel and David. 'They really do adore her, those two, don't they?'

'Oh they do,' said Grace automatically. 'Er – what are you going to say to Giles? That you've changed your mind?'

'I can't say that,' said Florence, 'because I haven't. I can't.'

'Then why write to him?' said Grace slightly irritably. 'There doesn't seem a lot of point.'

'Of course there's a point,' said Florence, equally irritable. 'You never seem to grasp these things, Grace. The point is he doesn't know why I didn't meet him that day. He still thinks I just stood him up. I ignored his letter as well.'

'Why did you do that?' said Grace, 'I really don't understand, Florence.'

'I thought it was best,' said Florence, 'I thought if he knew I still loved him, that I'd only given him up because – well, because of Imogen – he'd go on and on trying to persuade me. And I couldn't stand it.'

'But why did you give him up because of Imogen? And don't tell me I'm stupid, please, I don't like it.'

'All right, all right. Promise you won't – well, laugh or anything?'

'I wouldn't dare,' said Grace.

'I – well, I made a promise to God. I said if He'd let Imogen live, I'd give up Giles for ever and ever. And He did. So I didn't have any choice. You see.'

'Yes,' said Grace. The stark uncompromising courage in this simple, rather primitive bargain touched her; she had never felt nearer to liking Florence. 'Yes, I do see.'

'But lately, I've thought I should write and tell him at least that I still love him. Think if what happened to Jack, or to Laurence, happened to Giles and he – well, he thought I hadn't cared about him any more. It would be too awful. I don't think it would be breaking my promise to tell him, do you?'

'No,' said Grace, 'I don't.'

They had only two weeks; Clarissa never forget a single hour of them. She swung from joy to wretchedness, laughter to self-reproach, caution to recklessness. She and Giles made love in a number of wildly unsuitable places (the boathouse, the icy woods, her office), fear of discovery giving their pleasure a sweetened intensity; and in some suitable ones as well, a very grand hotel in Exeter, a lyrically charming inn on Dartmoor, lying, plotting, wangling to arrange time and opportunity. May knew of course; she had known, she said, from the first moment she set eyes on the commander as she continued to call him, and Giles had a fellow officer who covered for him, but for the most part they simply took the opportunities as fate offered them; and fate was kind to them, they were never discovered.

As the days went by, and they knew each other better, they liked immensely what they knew. There were no illusions about love, no question of commitment; the whole thing was about pleasure, pure, uncomplicated, selfish pleasure. And guilt. Clarissa lay in Giles's arms looking at his face, listening to his voice, fighting, struggling to blank out the other face, the other voice, and that too, that effort, increased in some perverse way her pleasure, forcing concentration on the moment and what it was offering. And it offered a great deal. After the first day, they did not mention Jack, nor Florence; they set them aside, not carelessly, not thoughtlessly, but gently, most carefully indeed, knowing that was the best, the only way that they were safe from harm, both of them, so long as silence was maintained, the secret untold.

When Giles's ship sailed out of the harbour, that would be that; the story over, the end written. There would be no promises, no agreements, no arrangements; they need never, Giles said firmly, meet again.

'This has been a feast,' he said, on their last but one evening, 'a most sumptuous feast of nectared sweets – Milton, don't ask – and I shall never forget it.'

'Nor shall I,' said Clarissa soberly. 'And I thank you for it from the bottom of my heart.'

'My darling, you're getting quite poetic.'

'I feel poetic,' said Clarissa. 'You have saved me from the most wretched time in my whole life. God knows how I'm going to get through the next fifty years or whatever, or even the next fifty days, but I feel I can now. In spite of the guilt.'

'Yes,' said Giles, 'at least I don't have any guilt.'

The next morning found him racked with it.

'Why?' he said, his eyes hollow, his voice hoarse. 'Why couldn't she have done it before? Written before? I don't understand.'

'Doesn't she give a reason?' said Clarissa, her own guilt intensified by the news of Florence's letter (telling Giles she still loved him, begging his forgiveness: 'My forgiveness?' he said wildly, pushing his hair back, 'How can I ever ask for hers?')

'Now listen, Giles,' said Clarissa firmly, realizing that here might lie danger, 'you will not be asking Florence for forgiveness, because she mustn't know there's anything to forgive.'

'But you don't understand,' he said, 'she's so honest, so straight, I couldn't have this lie between us.'

'Oh for heaven's sake,' said Clarissa impatiently, 'what lie? What does it matter? As long as she doesn't know. What we've had has been lovely, lovely wonderful fun. It's done us both lots of good, and tomorrow it will just be a gorgeous memory. Two of us have been made much happier. For heaven's sake don't make four of us miserable.'

'But you know you felt guilty too,' said Giles, looking at her reproachfully.

'Of course I did. I do. I feel horribly ashamed as well. But we can't undo it. And we'll make it a lot worse if we talk about it. Remember your poster, Giles darling. Careless talk costs lives. There now, I've managed a quotation finally. Cap that if you can.'

'All right,' he said, grinning rather weakly at her, pulling out his cigarette case. ' "A truth that's told with bad intent beats all the lies you can invent." Blake.'

'Clever old Blake,' said Clarissa. 'That's much more like it. Now, Giles, are we going to have our last evening together or not?'

'Well,' said Giles, 'no turning back now, is there? And I do feel most wonderfully, rapturously happy. She still loves me. And I'm going to get her back.'

'Good,' said Clarissa, and was interested to find not a shred of jealousy within her.

Their last evening was immensely memorable.

Clarissa cried as she watched HMS *Vigour* steam out of the Dart; and she sent up a small prayer, not only for his safety, but that he would manage to maintain a silence about their time together, whether he got Florence back or not.

Then she walked soberly down into the town to her small office, sat looking at the threadbare rug on the linoleum which had suddenly acquired rather interesting memories, and knew it was time to get back to her real life and to try once again to cross the great gulf that lay between her and her husband. Who, interestingly, she realized she did still most dearly love.

'David, I know you don't want to be Joseph but I really am stuck,' said Grace. 'Robert Goss has broken his leg, and there's no one else who can do it in the time. It's only ten days off and you know the part perfectly. Please, David, please don't be awkward.'

'Why can't Robert do it with his crutches?' said Daniel. 'It'd be good, Joseph could easily have broke his leg on the way to Bethlehem, fallen over behind the donkey or something.'

'Daniel, we can't start rewriting the gospels now,' said Grace. 'And anyway, poor Robert won't even be back at school – it was a very bad break.'

'What about Daniel then? He knows the part as well as I do.'

'I'm not doing it,' said Daniel.

'Daniel is too small, much smaller than Gwen. You can't have Joseph six inches shorter than Mary.'

'Well, have another Mary then, Gwen's hopeless anyway, she can't sing for toffee apples.'

'David, that's just not true. Gwen has a very nice voice. I know you think I should have given the part to Elspeth – ' David at this point went scarlet – 'but she had it last year, and it just wouldn't be fair.'

'Don't see why not,' said David.

'David, please! I've had enough of this.' Grace did not often lose her temper, but she was very tired, and she had heard from neither Charles nor Ben for some weeks. The Battle of El Alamein, so decisive a part of the campaign for the Western Front, had been won, and Montgomery's Eighth Army had pushed forward into French North Africa, but casualties had been considerable; she knew, common sense told her, that she would have heard if either of them had been killed, but in the absence of any real news, worry gnawed at her night and day. 'Now you're going to be Joseph and that's that. There's the postman, go and get the letters before Charlotte does.'

'I'll go,' said Daniel. He came back bearing a letter with the army postmark.

'It's from my dad,' he said.

Grace took it from him, read it quickly, then again more slowly; then she sat down rather suddenly.

'You've gone a very funny colour,' said David. 'Is dad all right?'

'Yes,' said Grace, 'he's all right. He's coming home, David. Your dad's coming home.'

'You look ever so happy,' said Daniel.

Chapter Twenty-One

Spring–Summer 1943

'So where is he now then?' asked David.

'He's about thirty miles away, in a convalescent home.'

'Is that a hospital?'

'No, it's where you go when you're nearly better.'

'I didn't like that hospital,' said Daniel. 'It was horrible. Dad didn't like it either.'

'Course he didn't,' said David, 'you wouldn't like anywhere they were cutting bullets out of your spine and hurting you all the time.'

'It was a marvellous hospital,' said Grace firmly, 'and if your father hadn't gone there he would never have got better.'

'It was horrible though, wasn't it? All those men in bandages and some of them without their legs and all.'

'Well – yes. But that was hardly the hospital's fault.'

'No,' said Daniel, 'it was bleedin' Hitler's.'

'Daniel, don't use that sort of language.'

'Why not? I bet he does.'

'Course he doesn't,' said David. 'He talks German.'

'Well I bet he says bleedin' and bloody and all that in German then.'

Grace gave up.

She did not quite share the boys' view of the Wingfield Morris Hospital near Oxford; it was forever linked in her mind with a rather guilty happiness, relief, and an entirely illogical sense that the war was virtually over.

Ben had been brought home by ship in February; he had been wounded at El Alamein and his injuries had defied the medical skills of both the field hospital and the military establishment in Cairo. 'The MO says I'm a bloody nuisance,' he had written to Grace. 'I got a bullet in my shoulder, doesn't sound very serious, but it's near my spine, the bone's splintered, and they just can't get it out. Also I've got an infection in the wound and don't feel too well.'

This was all a considerable understatement; there was, it turned out, a danger of permanent damage to his central nervous system, and the most intricate surgery was required. He had also had a raging infection in the wound for weeks. The standard treatment being localized treatment of any wound with sulphanilamide, and little more, he was not only suffering considerably, but was in risk of developing septicaemia. Grace, visiting him for the first time, ten days after he was finally pronounced well enough for visitors and out of danger, was shocked at the change in him: he was desperately thin, his flesh stretched tautly over his long bony frame, his once sunburnt skin parchment-like and jaundiced-looking, his eyes dark hollows in the stark angles of his face.

He was at the far end of the ward, his position indicated vaguely to her by a nurse. Grace walking slowly down it, peering slightly embarrassedly at each man as she passed his bed, finally found him, asleep. She was holding a bunch of flowers, picked from the garden, a spilling mass of snowdrops and early primroses; in the absence of anything else to do, she sat patiently looking at him, the flowers clasped in her lap. He was lying on his side, facing her; after about ten minutes he stirred, winced, opened his eyes slowly and saw her. There was no reaction at all for a moment; then very slowly he smiled the lovely, funny, creased-up grin she remembered so well, smiled and simply said, 'Hallo.'

'Hallo, Ben.'

There was a silence, then he said, his eyes moving over her face, studying her, 'It's nice to see you.'

'It's nice to see you,' she said, feeling awkward suddenly, and at the same time rather foolishly happy. 'How are you feeling?'

'Bloody awful,' he said, and grinned again, then, 'Sorry. Not used to female company.'

'I expect you do,' said Grace, 'feel awful, I mean. Is it – is it all right now?'

'Yeah,' he said, trying to shift his position, grimacing slightly, 'yeah, it's all right. I mean I'm not going to be paralysed, not going to die. Never going to have much use in that arm again, but that doesn't seem too serious.'

'No,' she said, 'no, I suppose not. Is it very painful?'

'Pretty bad,' he said, 'but nothing like it was. They give me plenty of dope here, for a start, and at least it's not hot, there aren't any flies.'

'No, that's true,' said Grace. 'Although actually I'm warmer now than I have been for weeks. It's a very cold winter.'

'Is it? I tell you, I'll never complain about the cold again.'

'How long were you in the hospital out there? I couldn't work it out from the letter.'

'About ten days in the field hospital, then weeks in Cairo. The worst thing was the journey down there. To Cairo, I mean. First an ambulance, real old boneshaker, then a hospital train. Sounds all right, but it was a converted cattle truck. It felt like one. No corridor, open to the elements. And the MO was in a pullman at the rear. Quaffing the best wine.' He grinned at her. 'Makes a good story now, though. And at least I got there.'

'Was it good? The hospital?'

'Yeah, it was very good. The nurses did a terrific job. Pretty, some of them, too. That helped.' He smiled again. 'Anyway, I had two ops there, both useless. And finally the big boss surgeon looked at this awful gaping hole in my back, and you know the rest.'

'Yes.'

'How are the boys?'

'They're fine. Grown so much. They've been wonderful. They wanted to come today, but I said no. Well, the doctors said no as well. Next time I come perhaps.'

'It can't have been easy,' he said, 'getting here.'

'It wasn't difficult. Bit of a long way, but I left very early. I drove. I have my little petrol allowance, for my land girl work, so I can save my ordinary coupons.'

'You drove in the little MG?'

'Yes.'

'It's nice, that car. I suppose it's your husband's.'

'Yes,' said Grace, thinking how horrified Charles would be if he knew the latest unsuitable use to which his precious car was being put.

'Is he all right?'

'As far as I know, yes. I had a letter last week. They're in Tunisia now, with Montgomery.'

'He's been lucky. Well, so have I really. Very lucky, some would say. Most probably won't be going back.'

'Ah,' said Grace. The fact touched her consciousness slowly, then settled gently into her, a piece of sweet, warm comfort. 'So was it very bad,' she said, 'out there? Before this happened, I mean.'

'Pretty bloody bad. Well, until Alexander arrived, and then everything kind of got cranked up. El Alamein was fairly good chaos as far as I was concerned. I got wounded on Day One, but it was a brilliant victory, as I understand.'

'Yes,' she said, 'turning point of the war. They say.'

'My best mate was killed,' he said soberly, and was silent for a minute. 'Saw him being blown up. With a couple more. Pretty bad, that. Hard to think victory and turning points matter for a bit.'

'Yes,' said Grace. 'Yes, it must be.'

She felt inadequate, pathetic sitting there, with no bad experiences of her own, no hardships endured; she looked down at the flowers, still clasped in her lap.

'They're pretty,' he said suddenly. 'Are they for me?'

'Yes. Yes they are. I'll go and find a vase, shall I?'

'Thank you. That was kind. Ask the nurse. She's got a cupboard for them.'

She went off down the ward, was shown the cupboard, found the only vase, a large ugly thing, in which her small spring offerings dangled pitifully. She went back to him feeling silly. His curtains were drawn, and she waited outside, uncomfortable, embarrassed, unsure what might be going on behind them. A nurse emerged, holding something that was clearly a bedpan under a cloth, pulled the curtains sharply back. Grace felt even worse. She sat down again, avoiding Ben's eyes; he was clearly embarrassed too, smiled at her awkwardly.

There was a long silence; she couldn't think of anything to say. It had been a mistake to come on her own, she thought with a sense that was almost panic, she didn't know him well enough, there was no common ground, she should have waited until she could bring the boys; it had been arrogant of her to think she could carry it off, the sort of thing Clarissa could do, but not her. She was just thinking that perhaps she should make some excuse and leave, say she would come back with the boys, when she felt a hand placed on hers, quite gently, and looked up, startled, to see Ben looking at her very seriously. He hesitated, withdrew his hand, but his voice was steady, gentle, not hesitant at all.

'It's really so nice,' he said, 'to see you. So good of you to come. I've thought about you all the time, Grace. Getting your letters helped a lot. It's been so hard. All of it. Knowing you were there, with the boys – well, it made all the difference. I just wanted to – well, say that.'

'You did say it,' she said, smiling, feeling suddenly quite different, light-hearted, easy, 'in your letters.'

'I know. But I wanted to say it to you properly. Letters are – well, sort of second-hand. Do you know what I mean?'

'I think so. Yes, yes I do.'

'Tell me about the boys,' he said, lying back a bit, 'tell me all about them, what they're doing. I want to know it all, every single little thing.'

'Well' she said, 'starting with David, he – '

She talked for a long, long time about the boys, about how clever they were, how good, the company they were for her, about the things they did, about how David lit the fires for her every day, and Daniel milked Flossie every morning and evening, about David's music, Daniel's chess, how David was going to sit the scholarship for the grammar school.

'You really love them, don't you?' he said suddenly, smiling at her. 'I can't get over how you love them.'

'Yes,' she said, 'yes, I do. They mean so much to me.'

'They're so lucky,' he said, 'so lucky to have you.'

'Well,' she said carefully, 'I'm lucky too. They're very special boys. Some of the children have never fitted in.'

'I bet they'd have fitted in with you,' said Ben. 'What does your husband think about it, does he mind?'

'No, of course he doesn't mind,' said Grace staunchly. 'Whyever should he?'

Ben said nothing, just looked at her. There was something behind the dark eyes that disturbed her: made her feel uncomfortable. Physically, almost pleasantly uncomfortable. She looked down at her hands, clasped rather too tightly in her lap.

'I can't get over what you're like,' he said finally, and smiled very sweetly at her, 'I really can't.'

There was another silence; she was just wondering whatever she could say, do, when another nurse appeared.

'Time to check your dressings, Sergeant Lucas. And then you've got to go to X-ray. I'm sorry,' she said to Grace, 'but I'll have to ask you to leave now. An hour, Sister said, and you've been here much longer than that.'

'Yes of course,' said Grace. She stood up, smiled rather uncertainly. 'Goodbye, Ben.'

'Thank you for coming,' he said. 'It's made all the difference to me, made it easier to cope with.'

All the long drive home she heard his voice, over and over again saying that, telling her what a difference she had made.

Next time she went, she took David and Daniel. Ben was looking much better; a healthier colour, had even put on some weight. The boys were shy, awkward with him, at first; then they relaxed, lolled against the bed, chatting, giggling, telling him funny stories about Clifford, about school, about Miss Merton.

'She's so fat,' said Daniel, 'she wobbles all over when she laughs. David still goes to her dancing classes,' he added. 'He's a cissy.'

'I am not a cissy,' said David, reaching out and thumping him.

'You are. And you're in love with Elspeth Dunn,' added Daniel.

'I am not,' said David, blushing furiously.

'You are.'

'I'm not.'

'Cissy.'

'Shut up.'

'Boys, be quiet,' said Grace firmly, 'or you won't be allowed to come again. Why don't you go outside for a bit? The grounds are lovely.'

'Would you mind, Dad?' said David, clearly tempted.

'Of course I wouldn't.'

They went out; Grace smiled at Ben. 'They're very hard work, I know,' she said, 'and you're looking tired.'

'I am a bit. It's lovely to see them but – oh, I'm sorry. It's wrong of me to complain.'

'Don't say sorry,' said Grace. 'And I bet it all still hurts a lot.'

'Yes it does. But I've been very lucky.'

'Yes I think you have,' she said soberly. 'A friend of my husband's – well, of mine as well I suppose – her name is Clarissa. Her husband is a pilot. He was shot down and very badly burnt. His face is horribly damaged, apparently. He's having plastic surgery, but – well, that seems so dreadful. Clarissa says she honestly thinks he'd rather be dead.'

'Poor bugger,' said Ben. 'Sorry, Grace, sorry – '

'Don't say sorry!'

'All right. Anyway, a mate of mine saw some bloke in the street, no nose, hardly any chin. He said everyone was staring at him. I know I'd rather lose an arm or a leg. Funny, isn't it, it shouldn't matter that much. I mean you're the same underneath. But your face is what you've got to show to the world. It's – well, it's the heart of you really.'

'Yes,' said Grace slowly. 'I suppose that's right. You're rather – wise, Ben, aren't you?'

'No,' he said, 'I just think a lot. By the way,' he added, grinning, 'the nurse wanted to know if you were my girlfriend.'

'And what did you say?' said Grace.

'I said chance'd be a fine thing,' he said and laughed.

He was moved, in May, to the convalescent home. It was in the Lake District. 'Why it can't be somewhere more convenient I can't think,' he said on the phone to her, 'but there it is. Nice views, they said. They better had be.'

'And after that?'

'Well, I don't know. The arm is definitely going to be no use for soldiering, they said I'd be a liability. But I'm going to apply to do a signals course. Or something like that. There's a big unit at Tidworth, near Salisbury. That's what I'm hoping for. Then I could see the boys quite often. And you,' he added carefully.

She knew he was only being tactful, but it was still very sweet.

My darling darling Florence,

I cannot tell you how wonderful it was to get your letter. I read it over and over and over again; at first I thought I was dreaming or hallucinating. Yes, I do understand what you say, and yes, I understand that you mean it, but you cannot really expect me to leave it at that and not try and change your mind. When I love you so much, when I know you love me so much, when we have a daughter, when our lives together could be so perfect. If only I could have been with you when she was so ill, helped you through it. And all I did was sit and sulk and write you a bloody awful letter.

But Florence, you have got to face facts. It's not as if you were married to someone decent and good, someone who you could still be happy with in time, if you settled down and tried to forget me. He's a bully and a sadist, Florence, and don't try and tell me he's going to change, because he isn't. And you must not believe all this nonsense about him thinking Imogen is actually his. I'm sure that's just all part of a very clever game he's playing. I hate to think he's still in England or at least where he can get at you comparatively easily. You must be careful, darling, you must take care of Imogen and yourself. Christ, I love you. I can't tell you how different I feel now that I know you still love me. I fell in love with you all over again, just reading your letter, it was as if you were in my arms for the first time, as if I was holding you, discovering you. I took out your photographs that day for the first time since I was home, and sat staring at them, remembering you, how your hair falls, all silky and sweet-smelling, how your eyes go all shadowy and soft when we're in bed together, how your mouth feels, how you feel, all of you. Like Dr Faustus I would sell my soul, but not for all knowledge, just for twenty-four hours of you. Rotten old thing that it must be anyway: my soul I mean.

I hope and indeed pray most fervently that I shall have some leave at the end of this summer. I am certainly due for some, especially as the last one was cancelled. Don't worry about me, I shall return safely; I can't do anything else now that I know that you still love me. Thank you, darling Florence, for writing, for explaining, for still loving me. Take great care of yourself and Imogen and I will be with you both again one day. Don't even think that you can get away from me again. I won't let you, I can't, I love you.

Giles

Florence had read this letter so many times she sometimes felt she would wear the paper away. She kept it beneath her pillow at night, always with her during the day.

'But I can't go to him,' she said to Clarissa, in whom she had confided. 'I do have to stay with Robert, I have to.'

'Florence,' said Clarissa firmly, 'you're completely mad.'

'I'm not. I promised God. It was a pledge. I can't break it.'

'Superstitious rubbish,' said Clarissa. 'If there is a God, which I really rather doubt, He's not going to do something terrible to some innocent little child, not that anyone could call Imogen innocent, darling, but still, just because you're in bed with your lover. And if He is, then he's not the nice benign creature I'd always rather imagined.'

'You don't understand,' said Florence.

'No I don't. But I'm glad you're happier anyway, and that you've managed to make poor Giles happier. Any news of Robert?'

'No. He threatens to come home all the time, but he never does.'

'Tactics,' said Clarissa briskly, 'designed to keep you on the edge. Florence, how many more times do I have to tell you, he's dangerous. You must get away.'

'I can't,' said Florence. 'I simply can't. So let's not talk about it. How are things with you anyway, Clarissa? I want to hear about any excitements in your life. It's so – dull here. I always imagine it down there as incredibly glamorous and dangerous.'

'Oh – well, it's all right,' said Clarissa. 'Dangerous possibly, glamorous absolutely not.'

'Lots of handsome sea captains though, I suppose, to cheer you up and hold your hand.'

'Florence, you have a very strange idea of life in the navy,' said Clarissa almost sternly. 'We work terribly hard.'

'Well, you look marvellous on it,' said Florence. 'I don't know when I last saw you looking so good. It must be the sea air.'

'Yes, I expect it is.' There was a silence: Clarissa jumped up suddenly, fetched her cigarette case, lit one. Florence looked at her curiously.

'Anything wrong?'

'Oh – no. Well – well yes, there is. Obviously. Jack.' Her voice was unusually harsh, sharp; Florence was startled.

'Oh Clarissa, I'm sorry. Not to have thought. How is he?'

'He's terribly terribly depressed. But the worst thing is, we keep quarrelling. I – well, I know it's awful Flo, but I find it so – so hideous. I can't help it. His face revolts me. And he knows that. And – well it doesn't exactly help.'

'No.'

'Anyway he's actually being moved to MacIndoe's hospital next week, to begin the plastic surgery. Marvellous man, he is, MacIndoe, I mean. I can't tell you how much he's done already – for me, at any rate. With his attitude. The men there all absoutely worship him. But what he can do with Jack's face – well – '

They had formed an uneasy truce, she and Jack; she had visited him again, determinedly honest, braver, her own morale restored by her interlude with Giles. She found it a little easier now to look at him, to smile at him; but it was still a torment. She couldn't imagine how she could possibly ever desire him again.

Jack Compton Brown was about to join what its members described as the most élite club in the world: the Guinea Pig Club, its headquarters being Ward 3 of the Queen Victoria Hospital, East Grinstead. The qualifications for joining it were straightforward: to have been badly burnt while serving in the Royal Air Force. It was presided over by the genius of Archibald MacIndoe, who not only rebuilt the men's faces to an astonishing degree, but their souls as well. The guiding principle of the place was that there was always someone worse off than yourself; the regime under which it was run was quite extraordinary.

Jack, desperately depressed, hopelessly demoralized, afraid of the present as well as the future, flinching from the sight of himself in the mirror, and from people flinching from the sight of him, convinced he was going to lose Clarissa, arrived from the rather more traditional atmosphere of Addenbrooke's and found himself living in conditions more closely resembling a university common room or a school dormitory than a hospital. The men had total freedom; all discipline was self-administered. They wore what they liked, did what they liked; hours were casual, there were no restrictions on visiting. A barrel of beer stood at the end of the ward, kept permanently filled. The men were not only allowed but encouraged to go into the town, to drink, to eat at the restaurants, to visit the cinema; and the town, in a kind of corporate effort, gave the great MacIndoe its fullest and most sensitive support in this. The good people of East Grinstead did not stare, point, recoil from the Guinea Pigs, nor did they treat them in any way as if they were different; they ignored them. It was therapy of the highest order. The men, all young, more than usually high-spirited and extrovert, were also given to some fairly riotous behaviour in Ward 3. It was not unusual to find patients pouring beer over one another, coming in late from trips to the town or to London quite noisily drunk, and generally horsing around. But if a man was new, if he was about to go on the slab, as the operating theatre was known, or his treatment was proving even more difficult than he had expected, he was treated with the utmost sensitivity, kindness and love.

The nurses were all chosen for their looks as much as for any other qualities, and one of their briefs was to restore the morale of the extremely red-blooded young men in their care; many of the patients and nurses married one another.

MacIndoe's greatest gift was his honesty; he never prevaricated, never fudged the truth. He confronted the men's fears with them, with calm, unsentimental common sense; he would discuss with them what he was going to do, insist they had at least a basic knowledge of the procedure's medical implications, encourage them to watch as he worked on other patients.

When Clarissa left Jack the first day, he sat quietly on his bed, feeling miserable and very alone, trying to adjust to his feelings, trying to assess how his injuries compared with those of the other men. He found the noise, the bonhomie hard to cope with, coming from the cloistered, cushioned atmosphere at Addenbrooke's.

He got up and walked into the bathroom; there were mirrors on the walls. It shook him. He had been spared many sightings of his face, had been able to avoid the ordeal. He felt the now familiar, never-easing revulsion and self-pity, went and sat on the lavatory for some time, his head in his hands, and then finally, because he had to face it, went back into the ward.

It was almost empty; it was a fine day, and there was some sort of nonsense going on outside, men shouting, laughing. Jack felt unbearably lonely, buried his head in his hands again.

The door pushed open and he heard a man come in.

'Hi,' he said to Jack casually. 'Welcome to Ward Three.'

'Thanks,' said Jack.

'Murray Brooks.'

'Jack Compton Brown,' said Jack. He still didn't look up, merely held out a hand. Then, puzzled not to find it taken, he turned his head. The man standing in front of him, grinning at him with immense cheerfulness, was not only missing an eye and a fair amount of his scalp; he had no hands.

It was at that moment that Jack began the long journey back to self-respect.

'Well,' said MacIndoe, 'you'll look a lot better with a new nose. No doubt about it. Feel better too. We'll start with that. Settled in all right, have you?'

'Yes. More or less.'

'Good. Watched any operations yet?'

'No, not yet.'

'Try it. It's interesting, and it would help you. Now, I'll start work on you at the end of the week.'

The night before he went on the slab, Jack couldn't sleep. He had expected to have to put up with the usual horseplay, into which he was being slightly unwillingly drawn, but had found himself left in peace, and when the others went to bed they were quiet, talked in low voices.

He lay and thought about Clarissa, how much he loved her, how he missed her; he knew, although she denied it determinedly, that she found him unsightly, repulsive even. She had never yet managed, since his accident, to kiss him properly, fully, on the mouth. He was terrified of losing her and yet in some strange way he wanted to, and then at least the fear would be gone. He felt physically odd most of the time; full of a strange energy and a suppressed sexuality. He could not imagine that he would ever lead a normal sexual life again, and at the same time found that thought unbearable. In all his miseries, that was the worst, worse even than small children staring at him, tugging at their mothers' hands to point him out, worse than old friends smiling with false enthusiasm, saying what fun it was to visit when he could see they were filled with horror and couldn't wait to get away, worse than the cheerfully misguided suggestions from people like his mother that he could find a nice home somewhere for the future, there were lots of them all over the country.

'Condemned to a future of basket-making,' he'd said savagely to Clarissa. 'What do you think about that?'

He looked at his watch: two o'clock. In twelve hours' time the work would have begun, his face would be under the knife; in spite of everything he wondered if it was worth it. What if it went wrong, if the grafts refused to take, if the reconstruction failed, the result was no better? He suddenly felt very sick and had to rush to the lavatory; when he came back one of the night nurses was waiting by his bed. She was a particularly pretty girl, with dark red hair and large green eyes, called Caroline; she reminded him of Grace.

'Throwing up?' she said sympathetically. 'Don't worry, everyone does it. Fancy a hot drink, or would your tummy chuck that out too?'

'I could try,' said Jack. 'Sounds nice.'

She came back with a mug of Horlicks. 'They're not starting till the afternoon, are they? That's OK, then, you can have this. Don't worry, Jack, this is the worst time.'

'Oh really?' he said and his voice was bitter. 'Aren't they all worst times? From now until I don't know when.'

'Oh you are feeling sorry for yourself,' she said cheerfully. 'No, of course not. You'll look so much better when the Boss finishes with you, you won't be able to believe it.'

'Oh really?' he said again. 'Do you actually think that?'

'I know that. You really aren't a very bad case, you know, Jack. You still have the whole of your facial structure – well, apart from your nose. You can see. You have your legs and arms.'

'I know, I know. Don't make me feel guilty as well as everything else. Until tonight, I was beginning to feel more positive. Now I'm just shit-scared.'

'Of course you are. Ward Three is full of the bravest men in England feeling scared. Want a sleeping pill?'

'Wouldn't mind.'

'I'll get you one.'

She sat in a chair writing reports while the pill took effect; suddenly, to his great surprise, he found himself reaching for her hand.

'Thanks. Thanks, Caroline.'

'My pleasure.'

'It's so nice to talk to a pretty girl again,' he said, rather drowsily now.

'You have an extremely pretty wife,' she said firmly.

'I know. But she's gone off me.'

'Of course she hasn't.'

'Yes she has. She can't bear me touching her.'

'Not unusual. At first,' said Caroline. 'It'll be OK. Honestly.'

'How do you know that?' he said.

'Well,' she said, looking at him thoughtfully, 'call it experience. Plus, I tell you, Jack Compton Brown, I could certainly fancy you. If you weren't married of course.'

'You're just being kind,' he said, more drowsy still, not sure even where he was any more.

'I am not being kind. I mean it. Ask Fenella if you don't believe me.' Fenella was another nurse, her best friend.

'I will. I warn you, I will. I'm not taking that sort of flirty poppycock. And talking of cocks, Caroline – '

She bent over suddenly and kissed his lips very lightly. 'I don't want any dirty talk on this ward. Go to sleep, Jack, straight away.'

Obediently, he went to sleep.

The first operation was not a success; nor the second. The grafting was proving difficult. Clarissa found him morose, sulky.

'Jack, you've got to be positive.'

'Oh yes,' he said, angry now, 'you try and be positive. Just you try it, Clarissa. Fuck off. Go and find some handsome admiral and be positive with him. Go on, get out of here.'

'Jack – '

'I said fuck off,' he said. She left, and he went and locked himself in the bathroom. When he came out, Murray Brooks was sitting on the chair by his bed.

'You,' he said, 'are an arsehole. You ought to be ashamed of yourself.'

'Thanks,' said Jack. 'When I want your opinion I'll ask for it.'

'And it'll be the same bloody one,' said Brooks. Then he grinned slightly sourly.

'Sorry. I guess I'm just jealous. At least you've got a woman.'

'Oh Christ,' said Jack. 'I'm sorry, Murray.'

Murray's wife had recently written to tell him she was leaving him.

Gradually his spirits lifted: a third operation saw the graft taking, over the reconstructed nose.

'Right,' said MacIndoe, 'we're getting somewhere. Now you need a break. I'm sending you to Marchwood Park. Do a bit of work for your living.'

Marchwood Park was a convalescent home in Hampshire; it also had a factory which produced items for aircraft navigation. The Guinea Pigs were proud of their record there; their work was said to be of a consistently higher standard than that produced by able-bodied people.

'I'll miss you,' said Caroline, the night before he left.

'Oh I'll be back,' said Jack, 'and don't you run off with any of the others.'

'I won't. But what about your wife?'

'She's very understanding,' said Jack.

He was feeling more cheerful about Clarissa; on her last visit she had found him joking and flirting with Caroline and been quite clearly irritated. When she left, she kissed him. Rather tentatively, but neverthless properly, on the mouth.

'You're a married man, Jack Compton Brown,' she said severely, 'and I don't want you forgetting it.'

'Could I really come and stay? Just for a few days?'

'Ben, I've told you you can.'

'Thank you very much. Then I'm posted to Tidworth, can't quite believe my luck. But it'd be nice to spend a few days with the boys.'

'How are you?'

'Fine. Really fine. What about Sir Clifford, he won't mind, will he?'

'Of course not.'

'I just wondered. Him being your husband's father and so on.'

'He's looking forward to meeting you. When are you coming?'

'In a couple of weeks. If that's all right. They said they'd put me on the train. Then I could get the bus maybe.'

'Maybe you could,' said Grace, 'and maybe on the other hand I'd meet you.'

'I'm being an awful nuisance, aren't I? Sorry.'

'Don't say sorry!' said Grace.

'I warn you,' said Florence, 'Mother's on the warpath. Says it's disgusting, in Charles's house. Threatening to order you up to the Priory for an explanation.'

'Oh Florence, how does she know?'

'Grace, really! How long have you lived in Thorpe? Look, I must dash, take Imogen to Nanny. Got to find billeting for about six more families by lunchtime. Two of them with pregnant women. How about you? Got any room at the Mill House left over?'

'Well, I – ' said Grace. But Florence laughed.

'Honestly, you're so slow on the uptake, Grace. You still never know when you're being teased, do you?'

No, and it still upsets me when you're rude to me, thought Grace, longing to say it but not quite brave enough. For the hundredth time, her heart went out to Robert.

'I shall have to report this to Charles,' said Muriel.

'What's that, Muriel?'

'That you are now entertaining grown men in his house. Total strangers.'

'Not men, Muriel. One man,' said Grace. 'And he's hardly a

stranger, he's David and Daniel's father. He's been very ill, you know. Badly wounded.'

'Wangled a passage home, I believe,' said Muriel, as if Ben had sailed home on the *Queen Mary* enjoying games of deck tennis on the way.

'Hardly wangled, but yes, he is home.'

'And ducked out of going back. I do think it's too bad. While brave men like Charles are still out there risking their lives.'

'Yes, well, he's been declared medically unfit,' said Grace, 'to go back.'

'It's well known how easy that sort of thing is,' said Muriel. 'Pull a few strings and anyone will say anything these days.'

'I don't think Mr Lucas is very well placed to pull strings,' said Grace, and put the phone down quickly before she lost her temper altogether.

She drove into Salisbury to meet Ben. It took her a while to find him; the station was milling with soldiers, all of them in uniform. Half afraid he wasn't there, she dispatched the boys to look for him, sat down rather disappointed on the seat.

'Hallo, Grace, I'm here.'

He was standing smiling in front of her; he looked well again, brown and no longer gaunt. She stood up, smiling back at him. She had forgotten how tall he was; the last few times she had seen him he had been lying in bed.

'Hallo,' she said, and held out her hand; then feeling silly at her formality snatched it back and laughed awkwardly. 'Sorry. I didn't mean to be so formal.'

'Don't say sorry,' he said: 'Goodness, that's becoming quite a catchphrase of ours, isn't it?'

'Yes, I suppose it is,' said Grace. She had no idea why, but the thought that they should share anything pleased, warmed her.

'Can't find him anywhere – Oh Dad, Dad – ' Daniel, a small wiry hurricane, launched himself into Ben's arms; Ben hugged him, but winced.

'Steady, Dan. Still a bit sore.'

'Sorry. David,' he called, 'he's over here. With Grace.'

'It's Grace now, is it? You boys should have some respect,' said Ben.

'We have lots of respect. Dad, can you play football with us tomorrow? Sir Clifford says he'll play too, we can have teams.'

'Yes,' said Ben, 'yes, of course, Dan, that'd be fine.'

It was a perfect summer evening; after tea, they all sat in the garden. The boys were unusually quiet, seemed happy to stay with their father. They sat one on each side of him, leaning against him, looking at him as if they couldn't quite believe it.

'Well, this is nice,' said Clifford, 'Look, Mr Lucas – '

'Ben.'

'Ben. Are you a whisky man? I've wangled a bottle out of the hotel over at Westhorne.'

'Clifford!' said Grace, 'you are naughty. How did you get it here?'

'Milkman brought it,' said Clifford.

'I'd love a whisky,' said Ben.

'Damn fine boys,' said Clifford later, when Grace had finally persuaded them to go to bed, gone up to kiss them goodnight. 'You should be proud of them.'

'I am. But a lot of the credit ought to go to Grace. And you. I haven't done much for them the last three years.'

'Well certainly to Grace, yes.'

'She's so nice, isn't she?' said Ben simply. 'A really good person. Your son is a lucky man, I think. But I'm sure he knows that.'

'I'm not sure that he does,' said Clifford, 'to be completely frank with you.' He was rather drunk with all the whisky.

'I hope he – and you, sir – don't mind me being here. It's only for a few days.'

'He's not in a position to mind,' said Clifford, 'and I can't think why the devil he should anyway.'

'I can't believe that,' said Ben.

Clifford turned to look at him. 'Well maybe. But I'm delighted to have you. And so is Grace. She's been looking forward to it for weeks.'

'Has she really?' said Ben. 'That's nice. That's really nice.'

Later still they moved indoors, into the kitchen. Clifford had gone to bed too. Grace was darning socks and said, 'Do you mind if I put the wireless on? There's a nice concert. Mozart. Do you like music, Ben? Sorry, I ought to know.'

'Don't say sorry,' he said, 'and yes I do. Very much. But how could you know? You hardly know anything about me. Or I about you, come to that.'

'No.'

'All I know is, I like what I do know. Now put the concert on. Shall I do some darning? We learnt in the army, you know.'

He took a sock and some wool and they sat together, darning to *Eine Kleine Nachtmusik*; she suddenly laughed aloud.

'What's so funny?'

'Us darning together. It's so domestic.'

'Nothing wrong with being domestic,' said Ben. 'It makes the world go round, being domestic.'

Next day he said he'd like to go for a walk. 'It's one of the things I've dreamt of, used to dream of, in the desert. An English walk.'

'Ugh,' said David.

'Double ugh,' said Daniel.

'I'll come,' said Grace. 'Clifford, want a walk?'

'No,' he said, 'no thank you, my dears. I'm tired. I think I'll just have another of those whiskies and a little snooze.'

'Only one more,' said Grace sternly. 'Come on, Charlotte, we're going for a walk.'

They walked across the field and into the spinney – 'David's refuge walk,' said Grace – and then cut along beside the stream. It was cool under the trees, the sun trickling down through the branches. Charlotte rushed ahead, barking furiously at moorhens, breeze-tossed leaves, a large log, and entirely missed a very self-confident rabbit sitting in the bracken.

'Stupid animal,' said Grace. 'Charles said I should have got a labrador, and sometimes I think he was right.'

'Do you miss him?' said Ben.

The question took her so much by surprise that she answered honestly. 'No. Not really.'

Then she flushed, horrified at herself, said, 'I don't mean that, of course I do, I miss him terribly, it's just that – '

'I know,' he said.

They walked on; Grace felt she should explain. 'Ben – '

'It's all right,' he said, 'I understand. Sorry. Shouldn't have asked.'

'Don't say sorry,' she said and they both laughed.

'I feel,' he said, 'a bit as if I've known you for a long time.'

'Well, you have.'

'I know. But properly known you. You seem sort of – familiar.'

'That's nice,' she said. 'I feel a bit the same.'

'Good. Can I ask you another question?'

'Yes. I'll be ready this time.'

'Can you remember what he's like, your husband? Really like, I mean.'

'No. Not really. Not any more.'

'That's my problem,' he said, 'I can't either. Linda, I mean. I know she was lovely, I know I loved her, I know she was everything to me, but I can't remember her. Not what she was really like. Not to – well, to be with. And it makes me feel bad.'

'Me too,' said Grace. 'Disloyal, somehow.'

'Yes.' He was silent for a minute, then he said, 'Can we go up that hill?'

'What, all the way? You must be feeling better.'

'I am. Fighting fit.'

They climbed Forest Hill. Out in the sunlight it was very hot; Grace knew her face must be going very pink, could feel the sweat on her forehead, her back, thought how unattractive she must look. Ben stalked ahead; she studied him, the long, long legs, the narrow hips, the long back, the dark head. He was – what? Not exactly graceful, but somehow very well ordered, tidy, carefully put together. He pulled his shirt off suddenly and tied it round his waist; his back was very brown and muscley. She suddenly remembered the morning in her kitchen when he had worn nothing but a towel, and smelt of sweat, and the memory was disturbing.

They reached the top of the hill and he sat down suddenly. 'Whoops. Feel a bit woozy,' he said, 'Overdone it.'

'Oh Ben. There's nowhere even we can get you some water.'

'I'll be OK. Just sit here for a bit.'

She sat beside him, watching him anxiously; after a bit he turned his head and looked at her. His dark eyes were very intent, very serious; they held hers, she couldn't look away. It was like a physical touch, that look, it drove into her, she could feel her entire body responding, a strange muffled disturbance somewhere within her depths.

He half smiled at her, and she didn't smile back, just went on staring at him, savouring the moment, exploring what she felt. He stopped smiling, put out his hand, very slowly, touched her arm, lightly, gently.

'Penny for 'em?' he said finally.

'Oh – they're not worth a penny,' she said. 'Not even a ha'penny, I'm afraid.'

His hand moved up her arm, slowly, tenderly; they both watched it, that hand, in a sort of fascination, as if it was impelled in some strange way on its own. It reached the cuff of her sleeve and stopped; his thumb moved inwards towards her armpit, began to stroke her there. It was an odd, a totally oddly erotic gesture. Grace felt first awed, then shocked by the violence of her response. 'You have lovely arms,' said Ben, 'lovely, graceful arms. I noticed them straight away, your arms.'

It was hardly lover-like, hardly romantic, but nothing Charles had ever said had stirred her so; she went on staring at him, afraid to speak, afraid of what she might do.

And then abruptly, suddenly, he stood up. 'I'm all right now,' he said. 'Best get back.'

Grace followed him down the hill, feeling ineffably foolish, rejected, fighting back heavy tears.

The boys were waiting for them, with Clifford, claiming their football match; Grace went up to her room, joined them much later for supper, and then excused herself, saying she had a headache. She lay awake for hours, staring into the darkness, hating herself for wanting to be faithless, for appearing foolish and most of all for not being Linda, whom he had loved so much and still felt so loyal to.

In the morning it was raining; she said she had work to do, had to visit a land girl over near Shaftesbury who wasn't well, that she would make a few more calls while she was in the area. 'And then I'm going to do some shopping,' she said, 'and go to the library. I'll be back at teatime.'

'All right,' said Ben. He was looking at her interestedly, as if she was in some way worthy of close study. In her misery it irritated her. 'Can I do anything while you're out?'

'You could feed the hens. The boys will show you.'

'OK.'

'There's bread and stuff for your lunch.'

'OK. Sure you'll be all right?'

'Yes, of course I'll be all right,' she said shortly. 'Whyever shouldn't I be?'

'Well, I don't quite know,' he said.

She rang the Priory, asked Florence if she could get her anything in Shaftesbury. Now that Florence had a petrol ration too, they pooled shopping expeditions.

'No thanks. I got most things on Saturday. Oh, some soap. If you see any. How's the mystery man?'

'He's not a mystery man,' said Grace irritably.

'I hear he's very good-looking. Careful, Grace!'

'Who on earth told you that?' said Grace.

'Mrs Babbage. Golly, whatever would Charles say?'

'Oh for God's sake,' said Grace.

'Can I come down and meet him?'

'He's not some kind of exhibit, Florence,' said Grace.

'Oh, don't be so touchy.'

The land girl was hostile, sullen. She said she kept being sick, it was the food, it was horrible. The farmer's wife asked Grace if she could have a word.

'She's in the family way,' she said, 'I'm not a fool. No better than she should be. And it'll be a khaki. Goes out with the Yanks. Well, she's not staying here. She can go home to the wonderful Liverpool she's always going on about.'

Grace took a deep breath, went back to the girl's room, asked if she thought she might be pregnant. The girl denied it indignantly for some time, then suddenly capitulated. 'I might be, yes.'

'Have you missed a period?' asked Grace gently.

'Well, I haven't come on yet. Not this time.'

'How late are you?'

'Three months,' said the girl and burst into tears.

The father was indeed one of the GIs. The only problem was, she didn't know which one.

She said she couldn't possibly go home, her father would beat her up. Grace managed to persuade her to see a doctor, and gave her the name of a local adoption agency who might help her. She felt it was a bleak outlook for the poor girl; as bleak as her own, she thought suddenly, and then hated herself for even thinking it, when she was so patently and ineffably more fortunate. What on earth was the matter with her? she wondered and went to do her shopping. She couldn't get anything, apart from Florence's soap, which made her cross. Trust Florence to get what she wanted. She drove home feeling depressed.

Ben was in the kitchen reading when she walked in.

'Hallo.'

'Hallo,' said Grace briefly.

'Good day?'

'Not very.'

'Why not?'

'Oh – one of my land girls is pregnant. She can't go home, she says, she's got nowhere to go.'

'Who by, the farmer?'

'No,' said Grace, illogically indignant on behalf of her farmers. 'One of three GIs it seems.'

'Oh,' he said,

There was a silence. Then, 'These are funny times, aren't they?'

'What do you mean?'

'Everything up in the air. No order in anything much. Everything out of place.'

'Yes,' said Grace. 'Yes, I suppose so.'

'It makes it hard, doesn't it? For everybody.'

'Oh I don't know.' She still felt perverse.

The boys and Clifford took him fishing; when they got back, they were all tired. They had supper early, then Clifford and the boys sat playing ludo at the kitchen table. Grace picked up her sewing basket and went into the sitting room. Ben followed her.

'What's the matter?'

'Nothing.'

'Linda used to say that,' he said, 'just exactly the same. If there was something wrong, if I'd done something she didn't like, and she'd say "nothing" just like that. Then I'd have to try and work it out.'

'Really?' said Grace, irrationally stung by this reference to Linda, by the comparison.

'Yes. So I'd better try and work it out. Trouble is, I think I know, and it's embarrassing.'

'Better leave it then,' said Grace. 'If you know.'

'No,' he said, 'I don't like leaving things. I like sorting them out.'

'Ben,' said Grace, 'there's nothing to be sorted out as you put it. So let's leave it. Whatever it is.' She was aware that this statement lacked logic, to put it mildly, felt more irritated with herself than ever.

'Oh dear,' he said, 'all right. If that's what you think.' He still sounded relaxed, cheerful even.

'I do,' said Grace and busied herself sorting out cotton reels, trying to thread a needle. She couldn't do it, sat struggling, feeling foolishly furious.

'Here,' he said, 'let me do that.'

'It won't go through,' she said, 'the needle's too fine.'

'Let me try,' he said, and took it from her. His large bony hands were deft; the thread slid through immediately.

'Thank you,' said Grace shortly, and started hemming a skirt.

He sat watching her for a bit and then said, 'I'll go and play ludo, I think. If you don't want to talk.'

'I – well, yes, that might be best,' said Grace. 'I want to listen to the *Brains Trust*.'

'Oh,' he said, 'oh, right. The *Brains Trust*. Well, I'd best get to the kitchen then.'

He smiled at her, apparently unmoved, and walked out of the room; but Grace looked after him appalled, feeling she had insulted him, implied he wouldn't like the *Brains Trust*, wouldn't appreciate it, that it was not the sort of thing he could possibly enjoy. And there was nothing she could say, nothing at all, that could put it right.

The next day Florence appeared, with Imogen in a pushchair. Ben was in the garden, shelling peas with Clifford.

'Hallo,' she said, 'hallo, Daddy.'

'Hallo, my darling. Hallo, Imogen. How's my best granddaughter?'

'Very well' said Imogen, 'thank you.'

'My goodness, what beautiful manners all of a sudden,' said Clifford.

'Yes, it's Nanny,' said Florence with a sigh. 'I have a horrible feeling Mother was right all along, that nannies are what babies need. Not their mothers at all. She's eating better too, and using the po.' She turned to Ben. 'How do you do. I'm Florence. Grace's sister-in-law.'

'Ben Lucas. Pleased to meet you,' said Ben, taking her hand. 'Pretty little girl,' he added. 'She looks like you.'

'Do you really think so?' said Florence, smiling her rather reluctant smile at him. 'How extraordinary, you're the only person who's ever said that, but you're right of course, she does, exactly.'

'Well, mostly they look like a mix,' said Ben. 'I expect she looks a bit like your husband as well.'

'No, not really,' said Florence. 'Not at all actually. He thinks so of course.'

'How old is she?'

'Two and a half.'

'She seems very grown up for two and a half,' he said.

'She is. Very. Talking tremendously well, and do you know, she can count, right up to twenty. And Daddy, I was reading to her last night and when I got the book out she said "Ponce a time." Isn't that sweet?'

'Enchanting,' said Clifford with a twinkle. 'No work today?'

'No, I've got the whole week off. I was a bit tired and making a hash of a few things and the Dragon, aka Mrs Haverford, said I'd be more use to everyone if I had a rest. Only thing I've got to do is get the Home Guard's hut ready for them on Thursday. I've been loaned out to them, isn't that a hoot? You'd think they could get their own stupid hut ready, but it's women's work apparently. Where's Grace?'

'Inside,' said Clifford.

Grace was making a salad in the kitchen; she smiled rather wanly at Florence. 'Hallo.'

'I say, Grace,' said Florence, ignoring the greeting. 'What an extremely attractive man.'

'Is he?' said Grace. 'I hadn't thought of him like that.'

'Grace, not even you could not think of him like that,' said Florence. 'You want to watch it, very Mellors I'd say.'

'Florence, what are you talking about?' said Grace wearily.

'Mellors, you know, as in Lady Chatterley. The gamekeeper. Terrifically sexy. In that sort of way.'

'What sort of way?'

'Earthy. You know. It's a class thing.'

'No, I – '

There was a sound from the hall; Grace looked at Florence, saw Ben standing behind her. He turned and walked away.

'Ben,' she said later, when Florence had gone, 'Ben, now it's my turn. Don't look like that. I'm sorry. About – what you heard.'

'It doesn't matter,' he said, 'it wasn't your fault.'

'It does matter. She's a stupid, insensitive woman. I don't like her anyway. I never did.'

'Well, I liked her,' he said, laughing.

'What!' said Grace. She was genuinely astonished.

'Yeah. I thought she was nice. Honest. And attractive too. Maybe I should go and try playing Mellors with her. I do know about Lady Chatterley and the gamekeeper by the way. Thought you might think I didn't.' He grinned at her.

'Oh Ben, don't. Don't joke about it.'

'Why not joke about it? It's funny. And it's true.'

'What's true?'

'I am – well, how can we put it? Not like you. Or her. No use fighting it really.' He grinned again. 'I learnt quite a lot this afternoon.'

'Like what?'

'Oh, that babies need nannies. Not their mothers at all. Well, not if they're to get brought up right, anyway.'

'Did Florence say that?'

'Yes, she did.'

'Silly bitch,' said Grace. Her voice was violent.

'You really don't seem to like her, do you?' he said.

'No I don't. She had a sweet, kind husband and she's – well, it doesn't matter.'

'Tell me.'

'I can't.'

'Go on. I'm good at keeping secrets,' he said.

Grace hesitated. Then she said, 'He's not the father of that revolting child. And he thinks he is.'

'Ah.'

'Well, don't you think that's terrible?'

'It depends,' said Ben.

'What do you mean?'

'On just how sweet and kind her husband is. You can't really know, can you? Nobody knows what goes on inside a marriage. You don't know about mine. I don't know about yours.'

'No. No you don't.'

'What Florence said,' he said suddenly, 'that was what Sunday was about. Partly. And partly because I don't know about your marriage.'

'What do you mean?'

'When I walked away.'

'Oh,' said Grace uncertainly.

'Listen,' he said, sitting down, taking her hands, 'it's dangerous, what's going on between us.'

'Ben – '

'No, listen. You're – well, you're lovely, I think. I'm lonely and I miss Linda, and I could – well, I could anyway. And I think you could, too. But your husband is away, he's been gone a long time, you don't know what you feel. Except you're lonely too. Aren't you?'

'Yes,' said Grace. Her voice was unlike itself, shaky, strange.

'And then I'm not like you, or your husband, or any of you. I'm – I'm like Florence says. From another background, another class. That makes it worse. More difficult. Doesn't it?'

'I don't know.' The same strange voice.

'It does, Grace, I think it does.'

'Ben, please let me try and – ' 'Explain' she had been going to say, but he put his finger suddenly on his lips.

'No, don't. Least said, soonest mended, Mum used to say. Very original.' He smiled. 'We've got a nice friendship, Grace. It's – special what we've got. It means a lot to me.'

'Yes,' said Grace. 'And to me.' She managed to smile back at him, and then walked quickly out of the room. In spite of what he had said about her being lovely, things being dangerous, she felt unhappy and foolish and for some reason totally hopeless.

Chapter Twenty-Two

Autumn 1943

Clarissa drove into the car park at the Queen Victoria Hospital and checked her appearance in the mirror. She looked all right, she thought, stroking on some lipstick, spraying on a great cloud of Joy perfume, putting her hat on out of sheer force of habit. But God, she was sick of being in uniform. The minute she got home, she would change.

She looked at her watch; it was quite late, after nine, but she had suddenly got forty-eight hours' leave, arrived in London from Dartmouth, and on an impulse decided she would go and see Jack. She phoned her friend Bunty Levinson, asked if she could borrow her car; Bunty, who was having what she called a divine war, and always seemed to have an endless supply of everything including petrol coupons, had said yes of course and Clarissa had picked it up and driven straight down to East Grinstead. Jack would be so pleased to see her, and she could put up at a bed and breakfast for the night. People could always find room for Wrens.

Jack had just completed another satisfactory course of treatment; his spirits were rising daily. Clarissa could see – and indeed he could see, had admitted he could see – that he didn't look even remotely as he had once, but the improvement was enough to make him suggest dinner with her in London, not East Grinstead, the next time he was out. The nose at least resembled a nose – nothing like the fine, aquiline one that had once been there, but a nose nonetheless, however small and stubby – and a grafting on his upper lip had helped the shape of his mouth. And then of course she had grown accustomed to it now, was ready for it; it was no longer a dreadful grisly shock each time she saw him, a shock to be read so clearly on her own face.

She was looking forward to seeing him, had actually missed him recently; it was a good feeling. The events of a year ago, the weeks in Dartmouth with Giles, seemed to have become a sweet strange dream. There were times still when guilt stabbed at her, but for the most part she viewed the episode with a detached, almost amused contentment. Her only real anxiety was that Giles would not view it in the same way.

She walked into Ward 3; it was deserted, apart from a couple of men lying quietly on their beds, reading. She left them, knowing by now they were destined for the slab next day, wanted some peace, and went in search of one of the nurses who could tell her where Jack was. As she went along the corridor, she heard a strange sound coming from one of the side rooms: a kind of rhythmic banging. She hesitated for a moment, then fearing it was one of the men in some kind of distress, opened the door.

On a hospital trolley, jammed into the small room, lay her husband. He was naked, apart from his pyjama jacket, and his body was rising and falling upon that of a nurse, also in an advanced stage of undress. Her long red hair spread across the paper-covered pillow, and her green eyes met Clarissa's in an odd blend of embarrassment and triumph.

The words Clarissa spoke at that moment never ceased to astonish her, every time she remembered them, for the rest of her life.

'Jack,' she said, 'get off that fucking bed immediately and get dressed. I'm going to take you home.'

'I don't know,' she said laughing, kissing his poor, devastated, suddenly beautiful and beloved face, arching herself contentedly, the memory of the previous hour's delight still heavy in her body, 'I don't know why I didn't walk out on you. All I knew was I wanted you, more than I ever had in my whole life. I had to have you. Instead of that poor wretched unfortunate girl.'

'She's neither wretched nor poor,' said Jack. 'She's actually got a very rich daddy, and she enjoys life on Ward Three like anything.'

'I could see that. How many times have you had her?'

'Never. Not till today.'

'Liar.'

'It's true. But she has been very – good to me.'

'I bet she has,' said Clarissa.

And thought gratefully, fondly of Lieutenant-Commander Giles Henry, who had been so good to her and, without realizing it, to Jack as well.

'You've been wonderful,' he said.

'No I haven't. I've been quite – horrid. Sometimes. I can't possibly blame you for – well, deciding to fuck her.'

'I knew how you felt. It was only when I first saw my face in a mirror I realized how brave you'd been.'

'Nothing brave about me,' said Clarissa, 'frightful coward I am. I was afraid of looking at you half the time. I tried to hide it, but – '

'It's quite normal, Caroline said.'

'Oh yes?'

'Yes,' he said firmly. 'Quite normal. You mustn't feel bad about it.'

'Well I do. Jack?'

'Yes?'

'Do it again. Please, please, will you do it again?'

It was even better this time; sweeter, slower. Her body, starved of him for so long, the first desperate hunger slaked, was able to savour him, welcome him, take him to her. She felt him enter her, tenderly, gently, felt herself opening to him like some floating, drifting flower; her climax came slowly, first a distant echo, then a growing song, rising, falling, piercing fiercely. And as she rose, rose to ride it, as her body arched, sang, soared in pleasure, a terrible grief suddenly seized her and she lay there, throbbing, clinging to Jack and weeping uncontrollably, and he buried his head in the pillow and wept too.

Much, much later they sat drinking some horrible Algerian wine she had acquired in Dartmouth. 'Oh for Clifford's champagne,' she said.

'Why did you cry?' said Jack.

'I don't know. Just – grief. For what was gone, what had been lost. Not just for us but for everyone. Why did you?'

'The same, I suppose. Christ, I love you. Clarissa – '

'Yes, Jack?'

'Clarissa, I want to go flying again.'

It would have been terribly wrong to argue, to try to stop him. It was the ultimate triumph, for him, for MacIndoe, for herself. That out of the pain, the horror, the humiliation had come the raw courage to risk it all again.

'Of course you must go,' she said.

Italy had surrendered. Grace, knowing Charles was almost certainly there, read the papers and listened to the radio reports of the invasion from Sicily, the biggest bombardment since Alamein, the heavy fighting, and wondered, fearfully, how long his luck would hold. But there was no telegram, no stark messages of any kind. She returned slowly to her customary, emotionally suspended state. It had been a big turning point, everyone said so, Italy, Europe's soft underbelly, as

Churchill had called it, fallen; the Germans to be expelled from the country; 60,000 prisoners of war released. This really was the beginning of the end, everyone was saying so; no longer (again the Churchillian phrase) the end of the beginning.

Giles was coming home. Not only on leave, but on a long-term posting, with his ship, to Southampton.

'No reasons of course,' he had written to Florence, 'but I'm coming. Three weeks' shore leave and then – well, Southampton isn't far from you. Is it? It's time, Florence, my darling, for us to at least start being together. I don't want any nonsense, any arguing. You must leave Robert and bring Imogen to be with me. I shall arrive at your house on a snow-white charger, or just possibly a naval truck, and take you away.'

Florence read this letter through, eyes blurred with tears. The longing for him, increased by the knowledge that she couldn't break her promise, was intense. There was no point writing back, he would never get it in time. She would simply have to see him when he arrived, and convince him then. She bitterly regretted ever contacting him again; she should simply have left things as they were, letting him think she no longer cared for him. All she had done was subject herself to a renewal of terrible pain. She was making a new life for herself, she loved her work with the WVS, was planning to join the Red Cross after the war, possibly even train as a nurse. A life of her own, something that gave her self-respect, courage, would equip her far better to deal with Robert. She was prepared to stay with him, to try again, but she felt strong now, no longer helpless, trapped.

All she had to do now was persuade Giles that she still meant what she'd said. However difficult it was.

19 September. Italy (Not bad, thought Grace, only a couple of months late.)

My dear Grace,
Just a few lines, because we are pretty busy here, to let you know I am safe and sound in Italy. You will have read of the invasion, no doubt, it was pretty exciting, 600 guns on Italy's toe. Some very heavy fighting, and a lot of men have been lost, but I seem to lead a charmed life, not so much as a scratch. I'll write at greater length with more news when I have time.

We are really pressing onwards now; the general mood is optimistic, morale high. I am beginning to truly believe, my darling, that I shall be home with you again – one day. Not for a while, but I do believe it. Take great care of yourself. I love you. Charles.

It was the first letter she had received that made her feel he really did love her. She worried about her lack of response to it.

Giles reached Southampton at the end of November. Florence was bathing Imogen when he phoned.

'Oh God,' she said, when she heard his voice, 'oh Giles. Giles, please, please go away, leave me alone.'

'No, Florence, I'm not going to. I'm coming to find you. Tomorrow.'

'No. No you mustn't, you can't.'

'Then you will simply have to come to me. All right?'

'No. Not all right.'

'Florence, can you honestly stand there and tell me you don't love me?'

Florence hesitated for a moment, then she said, 'No. No I can't.'

'Then I'm on my way. I've been dreaming of this for a whole year, ever since I got your letter. You can't rob me of it now.'

'No, Giles, no. I'll – I'll come to you. Tell me where to find you.'

'I'll meet you at the station. And then take you to a hotel. And love you.'

'All right. Yes, I'll be there. Not tomorrow, but the next day. Phone me tomorrow, and I'll let you know when.'

'You won't stand me up this time, will you?'

'No, Giles, I won't.'

Nanny Baines said yes, she would have Imogen for a couple of days. Florence told her she had to make one of her trips to Southampton with the Queen's Messengers to sort out some bombed-out families. Nanny was impressed by her war work, and immensely proud of her. 'I like to think that the good upbringing I gave her is paying its dividends now,' she said to Mrs Babbage. 'You can't beat a disciplined childhood.'

'No indeed,' said Mrs Babbage.

Florence managed to wangle a couple of days off from the WVS; she had earned it, Mrs Haverford said, she had been working extremely hard.

She delivered Imogen to Nanny Baines and went to catch her train. Shortly after she left, Robert phoned to say he was coming home that night on a seven-day leave. Muriel, flustered, told him what she knew: that Florence was going away on WVS business.

'But she'll be back in forty-eight hours, Robert.'

'Isn't it possible to get word to her, get her back?'

'I'm afraid it isn't,' said Muriel, her voice deeply disapproving, 'she takes her war work rather seriously, Robert, I'm afraid.'

'Well,' he said, 'I'll just have to wait for her return, won't I? I'll stop off in London, check the house, arrive tomorrow instead. If that's all right, Moo?'

'Quite all right,' said Muriel.

Ben was staying at the Mill House for forty-eight hours to see the boys; he came whenever he could, leave from his signalling course being comparatively generous. Against all logic, for she always waved him off smiling brightly but inexplicably heavy-hearted, Grace looked forward to his visits. His easy, open attitude to her, to everything in fact, had dissolved the tensions, the unhappiness of his first visit as if it had never been; as far as he was concerned, he said, they were friends – 'best friends, even, I'd like to think.' And yes, she said, that was exactly right, and she tried to think that indeed it was.

And in lots of ways it was: he was a good, a best friend, exactly the sort of person she needed in her life. It was not just that he was helpful, appreciative, used up some of the boys' formidable energy; he was companionable, interesting to talk to, he made things fun. He and Clifford got on wonderfully well, played chess (and ludo), went for walks, drank a great deal of whisky. Grace felt she could only slightly disapprove of the drinking; Clifford, lonely, starved of company for so long, was newly cheerful, energetic, was even talking of joining the church choir at St Andrews.

'Can't avoid everyone for ever,' he said to Grace, 'and I daresay a lot of them have forgotten why I disappeared in the first place.'

Grace didn't feel too sanguine about that, but she pretended to agree.

The other thing Ben could do was cook: he quite often took over in the kitchen, making wonderful concoctions out of vegetables, dried egg and Flossie-cheese, as Daniel called it. Grace would sit knitting or sewing while he worked, or writing the endless letters necessitated by her Land Army work, watching him, usually to a background of music, and entertain forbidden fantasies. Every so often he would look up at her and grin and say, 'All right?' and she would smile back and say yes, of course she was all right, repeating the words 'lovely friendship' over and over in her head like a mantra.

In any case, she told herself, as she lay in bed, always sleepless when he was in the house, helplessly aware of him down the corridor, even without all the other huge obstacles that lay between them, Linda had obviously been incredibly lovely – and incredibly sexy. It was the height of arrogance to think that she could possibly take her place, in any way whatsoever.

'I'm not staying,' said Florence, from the depths of Giles's arms, her face sore, tenderly bruised with his kisses, 'I'm not. I have to go back. Tonight.'

'No you don't. I've booked us into this lovely hotel in the New Forest. With a four-poster bed. And I'm going to make love to you until you cry for mercy.'

'No, Giles, I'm not staying. Well, only for a very little while.'

Florence's cries, wild, almost unearthly, echoed through the room all through the dark November afternoon as Giles made love to her. He looked down at her face, her thin intense face, as she settled, silenced finally, beneath him and said, 'I love you, Florence.'

'I love you too. But now I have to go home.'

'No you don't. We have hardly begun. You can't leave me now. You can't.

'Well – until the morning then. I suppose it's too late now, too dark. I'd get lost.'

'Yes,' he said, 'you'd get lost. Stay with me, and stay safe.'

That night, Nanny Baines went to her larder and looked at the Spam that had sat on the shelf for three days. It seemed all right, but it did have a slightly funny smell. Well, there was a war on, you couldn't be too fussy. She took it out and made it into a sandwich.

'I must go,' said Florence in the morning. 'I must get back.'

'You can go back later. Just for now you belong here with me. You're going to stay with me, aren't you, Florence? I love you and you belong to me.'

She looked at him curiously, intently. 'I can't believe you're still saying that, after how I treated you, that you were still there, waiting

328

for me. It would really have served me right if you'd found someone else, fallen in love with someone else.'

'I could never love anyone else,' he said with quite extraordinary fervour.

'I can trust you, you see,' she said, settling quietly now into his arms, 'that's what I love most about you. It's the most important thing of all to me, trust. Trust and honesty. Knowing exactly where I am. Feeling safe.'

'Yes of course,' he said, kissing her. 'And you are going to leave Robert and marry me.'

'Giles, I can't. You've simply got to understand. I'm only here because I wanted you to know I do still love you. But I can't ever marry you. I have to go back to Robert.'

'But why, Florence, why? I just don't understand.'

'Because he's my husband,' she said soberly, 'and I've promised to stay with him. And he needs me. In his own peculiar tortured way he needs me.'

'Grace, this is Muriel. Look, Nanny Baines is ill. Eaten some bad meat, stupid woman.'

'I'm sorry to hear that.'

'Yes, well, the thing is, she's supposed to be looking after Imogen. As Florence is away, doing her war work.'

'Oh really?' said Grace.

'Yes. Down in Southampton. Something to do with finding billets for people. At least she doesn't bring them into her own home.'

'Muriel, please – '

'Anyway, I can't possibly have Imogen, I'm far too busy, so I've told Nanny you'd collect her and keep her until Florence gets back.'

'But Muriel, I – '

'You have the other children after all, so it will be easy for you. And you're one of the few people with petrol. She's waiting for you now. Please hurry, the poor woman's extremely unwell.'

'I have to laugh,' said Grace to Ben, relating this conversation, 'or I'd cry. As Mrs Babbage is always saying.'

Robert arrived at the Priory at lunchtime, bearing a bottle of sherry for Muriel. 'Any news of Florence?'

'No, but I'm sure she'll be back in the morning as promised.'

'Yes of course. Where's Imogen then?'

'Grace is looking after her.'

'How kind.'

'Well, it's the least she could do, I would have thought.'

Robert was reading the paper when there was a ring at the door. Muriel was having her nap; he went to answer it.

A large imposing woman in WVS green stood there, smiling graciously over some blankets clutched to a benchlike bosom. 'Ah,' she said, 'I'm Joan Haverford. From the WVS. Is Mrs Grieg here?'

'No,' said Robert, 'no, she's away. On WVS business actually. She'll be back tomorrow.'

'I do assure you she's not on WVS business,' said Joan Haverford just slightly sternly. 'I have given her two days' leave. Anyway, these blankets are for her. For the evacuees that arrived from Bristol the other night. Perhaps you could give them to her. Thank you so much.' And she was gone, with a gracious wave.

Grace was in the kitchen making soup when Robert arrived; Ben was sitting by the fire reading to Imogen. Clifford and the boys were at the school, rehearsing for the Christmas concert, Grace having persuaded him, with a mixture of whisky-flavoured carrot and stick, to take her place this year. She said she simply couldn't cope with it again so soon, the last one seemed like only yesterday. Clifford told her that Christmas coming round too quickly was a sign of age, and Grace said in that case twenty-four must be at least middle-aged.

'Hallo Robert,' she said, opening the back door to his knock. 'What a lovely surprise.'

She felt uneasy, anxious, after his last visit, worried about Florence being away.

'Yes, well, I suddenly got a week's leave and thought I'd come down. Only to find that Florence wasn't at home. It's a shame, but she's doing her bit for her country, so I can't complain.'

'Um – no,' said Grace. 'Would you like a cup of tea?'

'Yes please. Where's my little daughter? I was told she was here. Bless you Grace, for having her.'

'Yes, she's here. She's in the drawing room, being read to by Ben.'

'Ben?'

'Yes, he's a – a friend of mine. Well, the father of my little evacuees actually.'

'Oh really?' Robert's eyebrows went up, in a way Grace didn't quite like, but then he smiled at her and went to find Imogen. He came back with her in his arms; she was struggling furiously, cross at being disturbed in her story by someone she didn't know. Ben followed him in.

'Well, what do you think of her then?' said Robert.

'She's lovely,' said Grace. 'And very clever,' she added dutifully.

'I know. Very bright indeed. I only wish I could see more of her, she changes so much, so fast. You don't think she's being harmed in any way, do you, by Florence leaving her with Nanny Baines?'

'Absolutely not,' said Grace, and was about to enlarge on her view, to express everyone's delight at the change Nanny Baines had wrought in Imogen, when Robert said, 'Where's this cup of tea you promised then?'

'I'll do it, Grace,' said Ben, moving forward. Robert watched him in silence as he made the tea, poured it, passed the cups round.

'Thanks,' he said briefly. A taut silence filled the room.

'Ben was out in the Western Desert. Like Charles,' said Grace slightly desperately.

'Oh really?' said Robert.

'Yes, and then he was wounded and brought home, and now he's over at Tidworth.'

'Grace, I think I can manage to speak for myself,' said Ben lightly.

'It must have been a pretty bad wound, to get you home,' said Robert. He looked at Ben coolly.

'It was,' said Ben. 'Shoulder. Shoulder and back. I was in hospital for over six months.'

'I see. And do you often come over here to stay with Grace?'

'Every now and again,' said Ben, 'to see my boys. My wife was killed, in an air raid. Grace has taken us all in.' He smiled down at Imogen; she was trying to climb back onto his knee, waving her book at him. Robert picked her up rather pointedly and tried to get her to settle on his lap.

'Daddy will read to you, darling,' he said.

'No,' said Imogen. 'Ben read.'

'Ben has to go,' said Ben into the uncomfortable silence.

'Really, Ben?' said Grace. 'So early?'

'Yeah, I'm due back on my course at six tomorrow morning. Sorry. I'll go and get my things together.'

'See you're using an army vehicle,' said Robert.

'Yes, I did a delivery of some stores on the way. I did have permission, you can ask my CO, if you want.' Grace stared at him. He was never defensive, never rude.

'Good Lord no,' said Robert. 'Just a bit surprised, that's all. Now

Imogen, you come into the drawing room with me and I'll read you this story you like so much. I'll see you in a minute, Grace.'

'Fine.' She followed Ben upstairs. 'What's the matter?'

'Nothing.'

'Ben! There is.'

'I won't waste my breath on it,' he said shortly. 'I feel funny with him anyway, knowing what you told me about Florence.'

'What about the boys?'

'I'll call in at the school on the way, say goodbye. And to Sir Clifford. I daresay they'll be ages.'

'Yes, they will.'

'Well, goodbye.' He hesitated. 'Will you be all right? I don't – like him.'

'Of course I'll be all right. And I do like him, very much, actually. He's always been very kind to me.' She sounded as she felt, defensive.

'OK. Right then. I'll be in touch. Bye, Grace. Thanks for having me again.'

'Goodbye, Ben.'

He put his head round the drawing-room door a few minutes later. 'Bye, Imogen.'

'Bye-bye, Ben. Kiss?' she added hopefully.

He moved forward, then stopped. Robert turned his back squarely on him, said, 'Don't be silly, Imogen, we're having a story.'

'Well, I'll be off then,' said Ben. He was back in uniform. 'Goodbye – sir.' The word came out like an insult.

Robert looked at him coldly over his shoulder. 'Goodbye, Sergeant.'

Ben walked out, slamming the front door, accelerated out of the drive extremely hard, shooting the gravel under his tyres.

Grace went back into the drawing room. Robert was sitting by the fire, on his own. She smiled at him rather uncertainly. 'More tea?'

'No. No thank you. Sit down, Grace, won't you?'

She sat down. 'Where's Imogen?'

'I put her upstairs. In her cot. She was obviously tired, anyway.'

'What on earth for? I don't think she was. It's not her bedtime.'

'She'll be all right. I gave her some toys to play with. Anyway, I wanted to talk to you.'

'Oh. Well, just for a minute, then I've got to go and – '

'Grace, do you know where Florence is?'

'No,' said Grace, her heart beginning to thump unpleasantly. 'No, I don't. Except that she's on WVS business.'

'I don't think she is,' said Robert.

She felt a hot flood of colour in her cheeks, her neck. She swallowed. 'Robert, of course she is.'

'No she's not. A woman from the WVS called, said she had given her some time off.'

'Oh,' said Grace. She felt rather sick. 'Well, I suppose she's gone to see someone then. I must have got it muddled. Clarissa, perhaps she's gone to see Clarissa – '

'I don't think so, do you? Grace, look at me.'

Grace looked at him, and didn't like what she saw: a new Robert, the pale eyes flint-hard, the rather full mouth folded tight. A pulse throbbed in his neck; it looked somehow obscene, like a slug writhing.

'Grace, do you know anything about Florence's boyfriend?'

'No. Of course not. I didn't know – that is, I'm sure she hasn't got a boyfriend.'

'I think you probably did know. And I think you probably knew he was Imogen's father as well, didn't you? How do you think that makes me feel, Grace? To be taken for a fool, as well as deceived.'

'Robert, I swear I don't – '

'Oh for God's sake, Grace. You were there, with Florence, when Imogen was born. Don't tell me you went through that with her and she didn't confide in you. Of course she did.'

'Robert, she didn't,' said Grace. 'I really don't know anything about Florence's private life. I've always been careful not to ask.'

'Oh I see. Well, quite suddenly, Grace, I can imagine that you might have been conniving with her. Encouraging her, egging her on, agreeing to help, to deceive me over the baby you helped to deliver. Pity you made such a big slip the last time I was here. Let the cat out of the bag.'

'What do you mean?'

'Telling me Imogen was born early. When Florence had so carefully told me she was late.'

'I – well, I must have got that the wrong way round. I – '

'Oh Grace, please! Do credit me with a little sense. I'm disappointed in you, Grace. You're not at all what I had always thought. A very good ally for Florence, I'd say.'

'What? Robert, I don't know what you mean.'

'Oh come off it. Of course you do. Little Miss Mealy-Mouth, so pure and virginal. What a joke – '

'Robert, don't.'

'And all the time you're carrying on with this – this creature. Some oick you've brought in from the back streets of London, along with his repellent sons. Who I find nursing my daughter. It made me feel sick, Grace.'

'Robert, will you please leave!'

'Still waters evidently run deep. Going upstairs with him before he leaves, having a quick one, were you? Up against the wall? That's what they do, I believe, where he comes from.'

Grace stood up. 'Get out. Get out of my house.'

'*Your* house. It's your house now, is it? Poor old Charles. Not only cuckolded, but cuckolded by a soldier. Not even an officer. Christ Almighty. What would he say? While he was fighting to defend his country.'

'You're disgusting,' said Grace.

'Well,' he said and moved over to her, took her by the wrists and pulled her suddenly up against him. 'Well, Grace, let's see how far you can spread your favours. I always rather liked you. I like the virginal type. You know what they say about still waters.'

He had hideous breath. She turned her head away, but he pushed her against the wall, pressed his mouth hard on hers. She could feel his tongue probing through her lips, her teeth; she tried to call out, but his mouth muffled hers.

Then suddenly he stood back slightly, looking at her thoughtfully, and smiled. 'Shall we go upstairs? Where you were with him? Or shall we do it down here, by the fire? I always like sex on the floor, don't you? It's so – primitive.'

'Robert, please leave. I – I don't want to – '

'Of course you do. No, we'd better stay down here, Imogen might hear us. She's had quite enough unsuitable experiences for one day. Sitting on your boyfriend's knee, him trying to kiss her. It was disgusting.'

Grace was silent.

He pulled her backwards, still holding her wrists, towards the big rug on the floor by the fire. He held her with one hand and reached out for the buttons of her dress with the other. He started fondling at one of her breasts, reaching for her nipple.

Grace turned her head and bit the wrist; he grinned at her, continued to fondle. 'Ah. The virginal worm turns. Oh Grace, this is rather fun.'

'Please,' she said, starting to cry now, 'please, Robert, leave me alone. Just go. I won't tell anyone. I swear. Just go. Listen, Imogen's crying, she – '

'All right,' he said suddenly, 'all right.' He released her, stood back looking at her. 'I'll leave you alone, if that's what you want.'

She stared at him, stunned at the abrupt change of mood.

'Just tell me where Florence is, Grace. Tell me where she is. Who she's with.'

'Robert, I can't. I've told you I don't know.'

He raised his hand and brought it down hard on the side of her head; she was so dazed, so shocked, she just stood there, staring at him. 'Tell me where she is,' he said. 'You know, don't you?'

'No, I don't know.'

He hit her again, this time harder still; it caught her eye, hurt horribly.

'I think you do. Come on, Grace, you might as well tell me.'

It was like some obscene dream; she was unable to move, to think what to do. She felt totally impotent, trapped far from anyone or anything. She could hear Imogen crying upstairs and, far away in the kitchen, music playing on the wireless, but it wasn't real, it existed far from her, outside what was happening. She looked at Robert, and he smiled suddenly, the old, gentle, friendly smile, and for a wild moment she felt perhaps she had imagined the whole thing, that she was dreaming.

'Here,' he said, and sat down, patting the sofa beside him, 'here, come and sit down. You look very pale, Grace, are you all right?'

'Yes,' she said carefully, 'yes, I'm all right.'

'Good. I'm sorry if I startled you, I just had to ask you, had to try and find her. I love her so much, you know. Come here, come and sit with me.'

Her eyes fixed on his, she moved trancelike onto the sofa, pulling her dress closed as she did so. He sat back and looked at her.

'That's better,' he said. 'I'll get you a cup of tea in a minute.'

'Thank you,' she said, very carefully, very quietly.

Perhaps, after all, it would be all right now, perhaps he would let her go, perhaps he was ashamed of himself. He was looking quite normal, quite calm. 'Robert, could I just go to the – '

'In a minute.' A pause. 'Now,' he said softly, 'where is she?'

'Honestly, I don't know.'

And then he raised his hand and hit her again, on the jaw this time; and as she recoiled he put out his hand, ripped savagely at her dress, and this time it tore, and the slip underneath it, leaving her breasts bare.

'You do know,' he said. 'Tell me. Tell me.'

'I can't.'

335

'You're lying. Little whore. Well, let's see what happens to whores, shall we? Soldiers' whores – '

He brought his hand down once more, on the side of her head, so hard that she slipped onto the floor; then he was kneeling over her, fumbling with his fly, dragging her pants down. She could feel his penis stabbing blindly at her, at her thighs; she clenched them together, tried to push him away.

'Open your legs,' he said, 'go on, open them. Or I'll hit you again.'

Her last thought, as she tried and failed to push him off, sank into a sick, heaving darkness, was how desperately sorry she was not to have believed Florence.

'You filthy bastard! Get off her. Leave her alone.'

It was Ben; he had seized Robert by the scruff of the neck with his good arm and was pulling him up, kneeing him repeatedly in the buttocks at the same time. Then he turned him round, pushed him against the wall and drove his fist into his face.

Grace, sitting on the floor, sobbing, trying to pull her skirt down, was dimly aware that the boys were standing in the doorway, gazing at her, white with shock; she could hear Clifford on the phone in the hall calling the police. And even in her pain and wretchedness knew it was the wrong thing to do.

'Clifford, don't. Please don't.'

He put the phone down, stared at her. 'Why? Whyever not?'

'Just don't. Please.'

She crawled slowly, painfully across to the sofa, sat on it, her head in her hands; she could hear David saying, 'Dad, don't hit him any more' and Daniel saying, 'Grace, don't cry, don't cry.'

Clifford came in from the hall and said, 'Ben, it's all right, I should leave him if I were you. He's a coward like all bullies. He won't do anything more now.'

Ben dropped one hand, but still held Robert by the throat.

'Let him go,' said Grace. 'Just let him go.'

Robert shook himself like a dog, pushed back his hair, mopped his bleeding nose with his handkerchief. Then he looked at Clifford.

'Do you know where she is?' he said. 'Where my wife is?'

Clifford was silent; then he said, 'Robert, either you get out of here, and never ever come near Florence or Imogen or indeed any of us ever again, or by God I swear I will have you in jail.'

Robert walked out of the room, out of the house; they heard the jeep roaring off up the drive.

Grace, still huddled on the sofa, saw Ben looking at her with an expression of quite extraordinary intensity. Not just concern, not even just outrage: something else. Something she couldn't cope with at the moment.

'I think I'll go upstairs,' she said in a whisper. 'Excuse me, please.'

'Shall I come too?' said little Daniel and 'No,' she said, 'no, Daniel, it's all right. You must go and see to Imogen, Ben. She's been crying all this time.'

'Did he hurt you?' said David.

'Not very much. No, I'm fine. Really.'

She walked heavily out of the room, shielding her bare breasts with her arms, avoiding Ben's eyes.

She lay in the bath for a long while, washing the smell, the horror off her, over and over again; then she climbed wearily out, pulled on an old nightdress and lay down on her bed, curled up, foetus-like. She felt exhausted, deathly weary, ached violently all over, not just her head where he had hit her, but every muscle, every tissue of her, as if she had walked for many days.

There was a knock on the door. 'Grace?'

'Yes?'

'It's me, Ben. Can I come in? I've got you a cup of tea.'

'Yes. Yes, do.'

She struggled to sit up; he came in, closed the door behind her. 'Are you all right?'

'Yes. Yes, I'm fine.'

'Your eye's swollen,' he said.

'Yes. He hit me.'

'I think we should get the doctor.'

'No,' she said sharply, 'no, we shouldn't. It's perfectly all right.'

'Grace – '

'I don't want the doctor. Or the police. Clifford isn't – '

'No, no, it's all right. He isn't. Yet.'

He sat down on the bed, took her hand. 'I wish I'd killed him,' he said, 'I really do. Bastard. Great filthy bastard. He should be strung up – '

Usually so gentle, he was near to violence himself. It shocked her. 'Ben, don't – '

'I just can't face it,' he said, 'thinking what might have happened then, if we hadn't come back.'

'No.'

'Did he – did he – well – ' His voice tailed off. He couldn't quite say the words, was obviously embarrassed.

'No,' said Grace flatly. 'No, he didn't. You – well, talk about the arrival of the US cavalry.' She smiled shakily.

'Thank God. Thank God, Grace.' He was pale, shaken himself. 'Here, drink your tea. I put some honey in it. Good for shock, sweetness. They kept giving me sweet tea on the journey down to Cairo.' He managed to smile at her. 'All it did was make me want to pee all the time, which made things a bit difficult.'

He supported her while she drank it; she lay back on the pillows and looked at him. 'You must,' he said, 'you must tell the police, get him locked up. He's filthy, dangerous – '

'I can't,' said Grace, in a low heavy voice that she hardly recognized, 'I can't because I feel so – horrible. So ashamed.'

'You feel ashamed? I don't see why, how – '

'I'm sure Florence felt ashamed,' she said, 'I can see that now. It's a sort of – contamination. You feel somehow responsible. As if it was your fault, as if you'd asked for it.'

'Grace, that's really stupid. We were here, we saw, nobody could think that.'

'They would,' she said, 'they would, you know. And it would be awful, terrible, for everyone, everyone in the family, the children, for – Charles.' She brought the name out hesitantly, as if it was a difficult word.

'But what about you? And you talk about Florence, what about what he might do to her, to Imogen?'

'I don't think so,' she said, 'I don't think he'll come back, not now. Poor Florence, I feel so ashamed of the things I thought and said.'

'You're crazy,' he said suddenly and he sounded angry. 'I just don't get it. I've half a mind to go and sort him out myself. I wish I'd finished him off, finished him off for good, made him so he could never – '

'Don't talk like that, Ben. Please. It makes me feel worse.'

'Sorry, but I can't help it. I feel like throwing up. And I'm scared for you. Please, Grace, please report it, please tell someone.'

'I can't. I just can't. It would be dreadful for the family. And I'd have to talk about it, over and over again, and who would believe me? He'd tell them all I – well, that it was my fault. And they'd believe him. About you and everything.'

'What about me?' said Ben.

'He said – well, he said I was obviously – oh, you know. With you.'

'Christ!' he said. 'Dear sweet Jesus.'

'Is it that terrible an idea?' said Grace and smiled. The tea and the fading of fear, of shock, had made her feel light-headed and slightly disorientated.

'No,' he said, looking away from her quickly, 'no, of course it's not. That's not what I meant.'

There was a silence: a long taut silence. Finally she said, 'Is Imogen all right? And the boys?'

'The boys are bathing her. She thinks it's grand. They're – well, they're a bit upset, I'm afraid.'

'Oh Ben, I'm so sorry,' said Grace and burst into tears. Sobs tore at her, rising in her throat in great painful thrusts; tears streamed endlessly down her face.

'Don't,' he said, 'don't say you're sorry. It wasn't your fault, of course it wasn't, you're stupid to think it.'

'But I do think it, I do – ' Her voice began to rise, she was close to hysteria. He looked at her, then suddenly moved near her, put his arm round her. 'Here, come here. It's all right, everything's all right, there's nothing, nothing to worry about any more. You just cry, it'll help. Hush, love, hush – '

He put the other arm round her then, held her close; she found herself safe, enfolded in him, her head buried in his chest. Gradually the tears eased, ceased, the horror lessened. Her head felt very heavy, hurt where Robert had hit it; she stirred, trying to place it more gently, moved in his arms just slightly, shifted more closely against him. It felt very comfortable, very easy; she began to grow sleepy.

'I think I should go to the boys for a bit,' he said, settling her back gently on the pillows. 'I think they need me.'

'Yes of course. And then don't you have to go?'

'Oh, I'll leave very early in the morning,' he said, 'I'm not going to leave you alone here tonight. Even with Sir Clifford.'

'Ben, I'll be all right.'

'No,' he said, 'I'd rather stay. I want to take care of you.'

In their four-poster bed in the New Forest hotel, Florence clung to Giles, crying. 'I can't bear it,' she said, 'I just can't bear it.'

'There's nothing to bear,' he said, 'if you would only be sensible.'

'I can't stay with you, Giles. Robert is trying so hard, he's accepted Imogen, I just have to try again, give him the benefit of the doubt. I'm his wife and I owe him that.'

'I shan't let you,' he said, 'I shan't let you go. I love you too much.'

'You have to,' said Florence, 'you have to let me go.'

It was much, much later when Ben came back. Dimly through her drowsiness, the pain of her bruising, fighting sleep, she heard Imogen giggling, Daniel and David talking, unusually quietly, Ben's voice reading to them, then him and Clifford moving about the house. Finally there was silence.

She had just given up on him, was considering going in search of some aspirin, when her door opened. No knock, it just opened.

'Grace? Can I come in?'

'Yes. Could I have some aspirin or something?'

He brought her some, and another cup of tea. She drank it slowly, looking at him thoughtfully. Something had changed, shifted between them, and she wasn't sure what it was, how it had happened.

'Everyone asleep?'

'Everyone. Even Sir Clifford.'

He put out his hand, touched her swollen eye. 'Your poor face. Does it hurt very much?'

'Quite a lot, yes.'

'It looks horrible.'

'I'll have to tell everyone Flossie did it, butted me.'

'Oh God,' he said, 'there you go again. Why not the truth?'

'I've told you why not.'

He looked at her, hesitated, then said, rather slowly and carefully, 'I don't know what I'd have done if he'd actually raped you. I couldn't have stood it. I'd have gone mad.'

And then he went out again, closing the door behind him.

Grace knew precisely what he meant; and in spite of the horrors of the day, the physical pain she was in, she fell asleep smiling.

She woke up very early: at four o'clock. She was stiff, sore, her head ached; she got up and went downstairs very quietly, made herself a hot drink and took more aspirin. And then she sat by the boiler, huddled into her dressing gown, thinking.

Something had changed profoundly for her in the past few hours; she felt a new, a different person. She wasn't quite sure how or what it was, only that she felt, against all the odds, stronger, more in control. There were two ways you could go through life, she thought: as driver or passenger, and she was by inclination and upbringing a passenger, accepting what she was told, doing the right, the proper thing, obeying rules, remaining within boundaries. But Robert's attack, with all its shock and horror, the betrayal from so totally unexpected a source, had called everything into question, not least her submission to the rules, and had given her in some strange way the courage and authority to look past those boundaries, into the forbidden places beyond.

Chapter Twenty-Three

Christmas 1943

Florence turned up the next day to collect Imogen, heavy-eyed and pale; Nanny Baines had sent her down. 'Sorry,' she said, her voice devoid of emotion, flat and dull, 'sorry you had to look after her.'

'That's all right,' said Grace.

'You look terrible,' said Florence, rather absently, 'absolutely awful. What on earth have you been doing?'

'I – well, you see, Florence, the thing is – '

How did you begin to tell someone their husband had tried to rape you, had beaten you up? Even if they didn't love him, didn't even like him any more.

Florence as usual was not listening to her. 'Imogen looks a bit odd,' she said, 'What on earth is she wearing?'

'An old jersey of Daniel's,' said Grace. 'I ran out of clean clothes.'

'Couldn't you have washed something of hers?'

'No, Florence,' said Grace, irritated in spite of herself, in spite of her rather illogical happiness, 'I couldn't.'

'Well, never mind. Grace, I want to talk to you.'

'Oh. Yes, well, I want to talk to you too. Perhaps I should go first. You see – '

Florence interrupted her. 'What I've got to say is important. So please listen. I know you think I shouldn't have – well, had the affair. With – with Giles. And you were right, you were absolutely right, I shouldn't. The only excuse I had was that I was very unhappy, but – well, running away is never an answer. The thing is, I have been with him, with Giles, these last two days.'

'Yes,' said Grace, 'yes, I know.'

'How do you know?' said Florence, staring at her.

'Florence, if you'd just let me explain – '

'In a minute. Anyway, it doesn't matter. I just wanted to tell you that I have actually given him up. Giles, I mean. I'm going back to Robert. He's been trying really hard to turn over a new leaf, all that sort of thing. And he seems very fond of Imogen. And he's been very patient and loyal. So that's what I'm going to do – well, I have done.'

She stopped and looked at Grace rather wildly, her face set, her eyes swimming with tears.

'Florence,' said Grace, putting her hand out gently, 'Florence, there's – '

'No, don't start giving me any sympathy. I don't deserve it and I can't stand it,' said Florence. 'I don't want to talk about it any more, just get on with it. I think that's what life's about, don't you? Getting on with it.' She scowled fiercely at Grace in an effort to control her tears, swallowed hard, threw back her head and closed her eyes; she looked, Grace thought, exactly as she had in the throes of childbirth.

Imogen walked towards them, clambered into her mother's lap; holding something tightly in her small fist; Florence clasped her to her as if she was some kind of lifeline.

'Oh darling, it's so lovely to see you. Even in that awful jumper. Whatever have you got there?'

'Snake,' said Imogen, smiling up at her. 'Dan's snake.'

'Yes, well, Dan can have it right back again,' said Florence. 'Whatever is it? Oh God, it's the most enormous worm.' She took it from Imogen, went over to the window and threw it out with a shudder. 'Honestly, Grace, those boys are a nightmare, I don't know how you stand them.'

'Florence – '

'You do look absolutely terrible, you know. What did you say you did to your face?'

'I didn't,' said Grace.

'Well, you should try and cover it up a bit at least. Anyway – '

'Florence,' said Grace, in desperation, 'Florence, for God's sake listen to me.'

'All right, all right, there's no need to shout. What is it? I don't suppose you've got any alcohol in the house, have you? I could even face some of that foul elderberry wine you make.'

'No,' said Grace, 'your father's drunk it all, as usual. Florence, just sit down and shut up, will you?'

Florence looked at her, startled, and sat down; Grace told her what had happened. When she had finished, Florence stood up, her eyes very bright, her pale face flushed. 'Can I use your telephone?' she said.

'Yes of course.'

Grace listened to her asking Mrs Babbage to get her a number in Southampton, and then tried not to listen as she told whoever it was at the other end that she loved him, that she wanted to be with him for ever and ever and she had no intention of having anything to do with her husband ever again. It was a very long conversation.

She was glad Florence was happy, but it would have been nice, she thought, if she had at least said she was sorry about Robert's behaviour and asked Grace if she felt all right.

Ben was coming for Christmas. Grace found herself looking forward to it as if she was a child again. She and the boys decorated the house with paper chains made out of brightly painted strips of newspapers, and she dug up a tiny conifer tree from Thorpe Wood and decorated it as best she could. She had plenty of baubles and tinsel from the school storecupboard, but although Clifford struggled for a whole evening, he couldn't get the fairy lights to work. The tree looked rather dull but then Mrs Babbage turned up with some old Christmas tree candleholders and a few tiny candles for them: 'Mr Babbage and I won't be using them, we're going to my daughter's.'

Elspeth's father came over a few days before Christmas looking gloomier than ever with a large chicken tucked into his coat.

'Died,' he said lugubriously, 'just died, three of them did. Last night. Don't know why. May be a bit tough, that's the only thing.'

'Thank you so much, Mr Dunn,' said Grace.

She had heard there had been quite a few mysterious chicken-deaths in the village the week before Christmas.

Presents were as usual a problem, but she managed to get Daniel a clockwork train and a few feet of track at the Christmas bring-and-buy. The paint was very scratched and worn, but it did work and she thought Ben would be able to smarten it up a bit. David was more of a problem; in fact she was in despair, but three days before Christmas she was rummaging through the loft looking for some blankets and came across a rather strange contraption standing on Charles's school trunk. She took it down to Clifford. 'What's this?'

'Good Lord,' he said, taking it from her as if it was some priceless treasure. 'It's an old cat's-whisker radio set. I'd forgotten he'd had one.'

'Could I give it to David, do you think?'

'Of course. Wonderful old things. I remember the year I gave that to Charles. He was so – ' He stopped abruptly, his brilliant blue eyes very sad. Grace said nothing but she gave him a hug. It must be terrible, she thought, to have a beloved son who was not only far away and in considerable danger, but who never wrote or communicated with him in any way.

She had entertained the faint thought that Charles might get leave at Christmas; she crushed the rather shocking realization that it was only a thought, rather than a hope, told herself that she felt that way because it would have been so difficult with the boys and Ben and Clifford, wondered and shied away from, for the hundredth time, how she was going to feel about Charles, about everything, when the war was over.

Two weeks before Christmas she got a letter from him: he was still in Italy, reporting on the appalling chaos there, telling her as always that he loved her, missed her, confirming that he would not be home for Christmas. 'But next year perhaps,' he finished. 'I think the end is certainly in sight.'

It was, for him, a very philosophical, almost poetic letter, thought Grace. He had clearly changed. Suppressing determinedly the sense of relief that there was absolutely no question of his suddenly arriving home, she focused her mind on Christmas and tried not to think beyond it.

Ben's leave started on 23 December; he was arriving on the train and she and the boys were going to meet him. She hadn't seen him since the day of Robert's assault, although he had phoned several times to check that she was all right, and that the boys had recovered from their own shock. The whole thing had now receded into the shadowy area of a nightmare. Aware of it lurking obscenely at the back of her mind, Grace had firmly set herself not to forget it, but to be aware of what it had done for her, what it meant to her and her life: a turning point, a watershed. It wasn't always easy, but it certainly helped to rid her of the horror.

She was physically nervous now, though, as she had never been before, afraid that he would return. Strange noises made her jump, she locked up almost obsessively, worried about the boys, and couldn't confess this to Clifford or Ben in case they insisted on after all involving the police.

The boys had been subdued for a few days; the trauma of their sudden confrontation with events they had only been aware of from sniggered reports in the school playground, the vaguest explanations from their elders, involving one of the people they loved best in the world, had been seriously upsetting for them. Ben had sat them down and talked to them gently, honestly that night, and that and Grace's apparently blithe disregard of the episode had helped them considerably, but they had nevertheless lost a degree of innocence and trust through it, and Grace knew that and it grieved and worried her.

Florence had turned up at the Mill House early in the day after her return, pushing Imogen and looking extremely shamefaced.

'I can't believe what a bitch I am,' she said. 'It suddenly hit me in the night – all you've done for me, Grace, and you tell me my husband did – did that to you, and all I do is run up your phone bill.'

'Oh don't be silly,' said Grace, trying to pretend such a thought had not even entered her head. 'I'm all right.'

'You might not have been,' said Florence, 'and I feel dreadful. I'm so sorry, Grace. So terribly sorry. Are you sure you're all right ? Are you sure you shouldn't see the doctor? Or the police, come to that.'

'No,' said Grace, 'I – well, I really don't want to. I'm fine, he didn't – well, nothing actually – happened. In the end. Thank God. I just want to – '

'Pretend it didn't happen,' said Florence soberly. 'I should know. I spent years doing that. It's the humiliation of it all, that's much the worst thing. Feeling grubby and worthless. Do you know, even now, when I've decided to divorce him, I'm going to get him to name Giles, as co-respondent. So it's quick and straightforward. I couldn't stand up in court and talk about what he did. I just couldn't.'

'You haven't – heard from him?' asked Grace.

'No. I presume he's either at the house in London, or back at the barracks. Apparently he just went back to the Priory, picked up his stuff, told my mother he couldn't wait any longer and went. She said he seemed perfectly normal. He really is mad, you know. Clarissa always said so. The worst thing is, he made me feel it was me that was mad.'

'Yes,' said Grace, 'I can see that.'

'Well, as long as you're all right,' said Florence. She looked at Grace consideringly. 'You do still look terrible, you know. The bruises are going yellow. Good thing Ben can't see you at the moment.'

'Florence,' said Grace, trying to look unconcerned, 'Ben is simply a friend. And the father of David and Daniel.'

'All right,' said Florence, with a shrug. 'Have it your own way. Pretty nice friend to have, Grace, that's all I can say.'

And now he was coming to stay for a few days, and she was feeling nervous, shy almost of the initial contact.

He was clearly feeling the same. He walked rather too casually down the platform, smiled at her and shook her hand without properly looking at her, hugged the boys with an almost excessive enthusiasm.

They drove home through the dark silent lanes without speaking. They didn't need to: David and Daniel talked non-stop, about Christmas, the school concert, the football match with the school at Westhorne which they had won by four goals, the fact that they had a chicken for Christmas dinner, that Clifford had got hold of a bottle of whisky for him and Ben, that they had all made some ginger beer, that the house looked really nice and, most exciting of all, Charlotte was having puppies. 'Any minute,' said David. 'Her stomach's huge, bursting – they'll be here for Christmas with luck.'

'I do hope they won't,' said Grace. 'I've got quite enough to do without having the kitchen turned into a labour ward.'

'Good Lord,'said Ben, 'and who's the lucky father?'

'Don't ask,' said Grace. 'She got out somehow, and Mr Tucker rang up to say he'd found her with his sheepdog in the barn, both of them looking very pleased with themselves.'

'Should be rather nice,' said Ben. 'I prefer mongrels myself. Not too keen on thoroughbreds.'

He grinned at her for the first time, and she felt better, less tense.

'I've got to go to the church after tea,' she said, 'to play at the blessing of the crib. Sorry.'

'Don't say sorry,' he said. 'Can I come?'

'Of course you can, if you want to. David's coming, aren't you, David?'

'Yeah, because Elspeth's doing some stupid solo,' said Daniel.

'Shut up,' said David and reached out and cuffed the side of his brother's head.

'Shut up yourself,' said Daniel and punched him in the side.

'Boys,' said Clifford, 'not at the table.'

Ben's eyes met Grace's. 'They seem fine,' he said.

'Yes,' she said, understanding at once, 'they seem to have come through it all right. Not too bothered.'

'Bothered by what?' said Daniel.

'Whether I'm going to give you your presents or not,' said Grace. 'Now clear the table for me, it's nearly time to go.'

The service was very sweet. Grace as always found her eyes filled with tears as the carols were sung, the lessons read and the children grouped round the crib, gazing at it, their eyes large, their imaginations seized by the simple, peaceful magic of the story.

Clifford had come with them, and stood next to Ben, singing staunchly and rather beautifully: a few people smiled at him, albeit frostily. The Christmas spirit, Grace thought, whether you believed in it all or not, really was a most potent force for the good.

Elspeth sang a verse solo of 'In the Deep Midwinter', and David listened scarlet-faced, his eyes fixed on the floor. Ben, noticing, met Grace's eyes and winked at her.

It was very dark walking home; they had their torches, but it was a freezing, cloudy night. David was ahead with Clifford, and Grace, her hands in her pockets, was walking determinedly just a little too far apart from Ben.

'Come on,' he said, 'you'll end up in the ditch. Take my arm.'

She wished the journey could have lasted for hours.

Clarissa and Jack had come down to spend Christmas with Florence. She had begged them to come, to cheer up what would otherwise have been a rather bleak occasion. Giles was not allowed leave. 'I had those three weeks,' he wrote, 'and we have the rest of our lives together. I suppose we can survive one last Christmas apart.'

'I'm not sure if I can, though,' Florence had said to Clarissa. 'You've simply got to come.'

On Christmas Eve they all came over to the Mill House for tea.

'Oh I love Christmas,' said Clarissa, sinking into a chair by the fire, 'wonderful, magical time. I really can almost believe, you know, that Father Christmas is up there somewhere in his sleigh, with the reindeer, bells ringing like anything.'

'Are you telling me he's not?' said Ben, his face a study in innocence.

Clarissa laughed.

'He is heaven, darling,' she said later, out in the kitchen, helping Grace find some more drinks. 'Absolute heaven. And so attractive!'

'Is he?' said Grace shortly.

Clarissa looked at her sharply and changed the subject.

Jack was very cheerful; he was going back on duty in January, to Rednal, in Shropshire, ostensibly training young pilots, but hoping, he said, for some action. Grace looked at his ravaged face and marvelled at his courage. And at Clarissa's; she was sitting beside him on the sofa, holding his hand, which was draped round her shoulders. She looked lovely, in a scarlet sweater and black trousers, her fair hair swept up, her full mouth painted brilliant red, to match the sweater; Grace, in a much-mended blouse and slightly droopy skirt, felt as always shabby and drab beside her. She was full of gossip, of stories about London – 'There's a plague of rats in the sewers, no, honestly, don't look at me like that, there is, it's a whole new little war up there, they say they've killed a million just in the past few weeks ... Bunty Levinson has joined a pig club in Kensington Gardens, too glorious, you pay a pound for a share in one and then you get a few chops or something when the poor thing finally rolls over … Do you know that when Suzy Renshaw got married last month, you remember her, Florence, apparently she had the sweetest little tea-cosy thing over her cake, because she couldn't get icing – '

She was talking, performing even more than usual, seemed almost frenetically determined to keep the level of entertainment high; not to let the conversation steady into anything approaching the sober or thoughtful. Grace could see Ben was very taken with her, was laughing at her more absurd remarks, swapping silly jokes with her, the sort that came out of crackers. Linda had probably been like Clarissa, she thought, sparkly and quick: and sexy too, no doubt, wonderfully clever and inventive in bed. She felt upset, the old familiar snarls of jealousy uncurling within her. The sensation made her feel more awkward, more silent still.

'You looking forward to going back then?' said Ben to Jack. He was very relaxed with them all, Grace thought, and then for the thousandth time hated herself, wondering why on earth he shouldn't be.

'Yes, hugely,' said Jack. 'I feel as if I've been in some kind of a cage for the past eighteen months. Useless, impotent.'

'Hardly that, darling, at least,' murmured Clarissa. Ben grinned at her, his dark eyes brilliant, and Grace hated her.

'Do be quiet, Clarissa, don't lower the tone,' said Jack. 'Ben was asking a serious question.'

'I'd give anything to go back,' said Ben.

Grace stared at him; she hadn't realized he felt like that.

'Really?' said Jack.

'Yeah. I feel like some woman, sitting there at Tidworth, sending and receiving bloody – sorry – stupid useless signals, while my mates are still out there, doing something.'

'Ben, women are no longer confined to useless tasks,' said Clifford firmly. 'Look at these three, all doing the most marvellous things. I'm so proud of them all.'

But only Clarissa was doing something really positive, Grace thought, something exciting. She was now engaged in that most classic of all Wren activities, the one depicted in all the films, known as plotting, monitoring the progress of ships at sea: 'It's too thrilling. We all stand there like croupiers with our long poles, pushing our little ships about the board, and every so often some scrambled eggs come down and inspect.'

'What on earth are scrambled eggs?' said Ben.

'Commanders and upwards. The ones with gold braid on their caps.'

'Ah,' he said.

'We must go,' said Florence, 'Imogen is simply dropping. Look, everyone, doesn't she look sweet? She's had her stocking up for three nights now. Poor angel, I've hardly got anything to put in it.'

'I've got some chocolate for her,' said Clarissa, 'I forgot to tell you, from the Americans. And some oranges.'

'Oranges! said David, who had been listening quietly from a corner. 'I used to like oranges, didn't I, Dad? Me and Mum used to have peeling races.'

'Then you shall have an orange,' said Clarissa. 'I'll bring some down on Boxing Day. And for your brother, and your father too. For everyone. Now, Grace darling, here are some presents for you all, and a bottle of something for lunch tomorrow.'

'Oh Clarissa, I haven't got anything for you,' said Grace miserably. She felt cast down, very much the poor relation.

'No, but you've given us the most lovely start to Christmas, set it off with a real bang,' said Clarissa. 'Come on, Jack, darling, I have stockings to hang up.'

When they had gone, Grace went into the kitchen. She was standing at the sink washing up when Ben came in.

He smiled at her. 'What a ridiculous woman,' he said.

'You seemed to like her,' said Grace. She knew it wasn't a very sensible thing to say but she couldn't help it.

'I did like her. I thought she was lovely. And obviously very clever too. But that doesn't stop her being ridiculous. I liked him too. What a man. Going through all that and coming out the other side, and then going back to flying. No nonsense, no fuss. God!'

'Yes. Yes, he's very brave.'

'What's the matter?'

'Nothing.'

'Yes there is. Come on. You can't be miserable on Christmas Eve. It's not allowed.'

'Oh – I don't know. I expect I'm just tired.'

'You look tired,' he said.

'Thanks.'

'Don't be silly. Doesn't stop you looking pretty. Very pretty. I was looking at you. Your hair looked grand in the firelight.'

'Oh,' she said. She didn't know what to say.

She looked up and he was smiling at her. 'You're a bit silly

349

sometimes, you know,' he said. 'Very silly I'd say. Well, I'm going to play with the boys for a bit. Then I'll come back and help you with the supper. All right?'

'All right.'

She was about to go to bed after filling the stockings when she heard a yelp from the kitchen; she went in and saw Charlotte, panting hard, lying on her side, one leg lifted. Something dark and moist was protruding from her nether regions.

'Oh my goodness,' said Grace, 'it's a puppy.'

The puppy emerged, still foetus-like, in its sac; Charlotte examined it, sniffed it, tore open the sack, bit through the cord, ate the afterbirth, all as if she had been most carefully trained to do so. She licked the puppy affectionately, settled it near her udders; had scarcely finished when her body heaved again, and another emerged. She didn't seem to be suffering very much, nor did she seem to have to struggle to get it out.

'Very much more efficient than we are,' said Grace, watching in awe and a kind of tenderness. She stroked Charlotte's head, made sure she had plenty of water, as the vet had told her, and settled herself for a long vigil.

By two o'clock it was over. Nine puppies, three russet-coloured, five black and white, one especially sweet, russet and white and especially small ('We'll keep you,' said Grace), lay by their mother. Grace tucked a big blanket round them, told Charlotte she loved her, and went to bed.

She went down early. Charlotte was awake, sniffing at her babies; there was a lot of noise. 'They're hungry,' said Grace sternly. 'You have to feed them.'

A few of the puppies were having trouble getting at supplies; she knelt and lifted them carefully closer. Then she noticed one was missing. The little russet and white one.

She found it in the corner of the whelping box, cold and still. She picked it up and held it in her hands; its coat was very silky, its small face very determined in death.

'Oh dear,' whispered Grace, 'oh dear. I'm so sorry.'

She moved nearer the boiler, as if the warmth might help the poor thing in its coldness, and stroked it with her finger; she was still kneeling there when the door opened and Ben came in.

'Good Lord,' he said, 'a lying-in ward. Very suitable on Christmas morning. When did this lot all arrive?'

'Last night,' said Grace.

He went over and looked at them, stood smiling down at them.

'What's that you've got there?'

'Another one. That didn't make it.'

'Ah. Let me see.' He looked at the puppy, then at her. 'You're crying!'

'Yes. It seemed so sad. Little lonely thing, here for such a short time, and then just dying, alone in the corner of a big, cold box. Sorry. It's so stupid, isn't it, when millions of people are dying, have died. Sorry, Ben.'

'Don't say sorry.' He looked at her and smiled again. 'I don't think anything you do is stupid,' he said. And then he knelt down beside her, and wiped away the tears with his finger; and then stared at her, intently, just like the day on the hill. Only this time he leant forward and kissed her. Gently, tenderly at first, little more than a touch of mouth on mouth; but then, slowly, almost stealthily, he parted her lips with his tongue, and she just knelt there, feeling it working, his mouth working, exploring hers, on and on, slowly, carefully, thoughtfully, and it was more extraordinarily powerful than anything she could ever have imagined, invading her head, herself, all her thinking, all her feeling, and still he didn't touch her. And then finally he sat back on his heels and studied her face for a long time, his eyes moving over it as if he had never seen it before, her hair, her forehead, her eyes, her nose, her mouth, her joyfully awoken mouth, and said quite cheerfully, matter-of-fact, his dark eyes alight with amusement, pleasure, tenderness. 'Well, that's that, then. I've been and gone and done it now, haven't I?'

By the evening she was beside herself: with pent-up excitement and pleasure, and a physical yearning she would not have thought she was capable of. They had not had another moment alone: she had moved through the day apart from him, hardly daring to look at him, a great undercurrent of emotion tugging at her constantly, insistent, strong. The boys had come crashing in almost as he had drawn away from her, shouting, exclaiming, overwhelmed with awe at the sight of the puppies; Clifford shortly afterwards, grumbling good-temperedly at the noise; and then there had been Flossie and the chickens to see to, a huge breakfast to organize for Charlotte – 'Thank God for Flossie's milk,' said Grace – and after that the inexorable happy ritual of Christmas, breakfast, presents – David's face when he saw the radio and Clifford's watching it was something she thought she would remember for ever – and then church, and lunch.

Betty and Frank came for lunch, Frank bearing a bottle of port given to him by a grateful customer. 'Goodness,' said Grace, 'we've got more alcohol even than usual this Christmas.'

Betty was a little quiet; helping Grace wash up after lunch, she said, 'I hope you don't have him here very often, dear.'

'Who?' said Grace.

'Mr Lucas, dear.'

'I don't, because he's posted at Tidworth, but why shouldn't I anyway? He's the boys' father, they haven't got a mother – '

'Exactly, dear. That's what I mean. What will people think, say, suppose it got back to Charles? He is your husband, Grace, and this is his house. And whatever must Muriel think?'

'I – don't know what she thinks,' said Grace.

'Well, I'm afraid I can imagine,' said Betty, 'all too well. And I think you should be a lot more – careful, Grace. For Charles's sake, if not your own.'

Grace was silent.

'I don't mean to criticize him, dear, Mr Lucas that is. He's very nice of course. Even though he is a bit of a rough diamond. Don't look at me like that, Grace, it's true. I just feel it's a rather dangerous situation. And so does your father.'

'Well,' said Grace. 'All right, Mother, I will be careful as you put it. Don't worry. Goodness, look, it's time for the King's speech.'

A few weeks ago, she thought, she would have been upset, deeply anxious; as it was, she simply found it funny, stored it up to tell Ben.

They went for a walk after the King's speech, and then played charades. Clifford, doing a gyrating-hipped Dorothy Lamour, enacting *Road to Rio*, was only bettered by Daniel being Violet Elizabeth Bott in *Just William*. 'The males certainly have it,' said Grace, wiping tears of laughter from her eyes. 'Daniel, you're a genius.'

After supper, when her parents had gone, she finally lit the precious Christmas tree candles and turned the other lights out. David played some carols on the piano, and they sat gazing at the tree and the tiny flames dancing against the darkness. Daniel came and put his arms round her and said, 'Thank you, Grace, for a lovely Christmas,' and she looked back over the day, and for the rest of her life, when she thought about happiness it was a warm, almost dark room filled with the smell of woodsmoke, lit by a Christmas tree, and in the background a small boy playing an out-of-tune piano.

At last the boys went to bed; Clifford, who had fallen asleep over his whisky, hauled himself to his feet and said, 'If you'll excuse me, my dears, I must go up. I'll take a look at those puppies on the way.'

'Yes, all right, Clifford, thank you,' said Grace.

'God bless you, my dear,' he said, bending to kiss her. 'And thank you for everything. Goodnight, Ben.'

'Goodnight, Sir Clifford.'

'Oh really! That ridiculous name,' said Clifford and went off chuckling.

Ben looked at Grace from where he was sitting on the sofa, and held out his arms. 'Come on,' he said, 'time to get on with it a bit.'

She laughed and went over to sit beside him.

After a while he said, holding her very tenderly, his face in her hair, 'Will you, Grace? Will you?' and she said, realizing and hating herself for it, that she was nervous as well as conscience-stricken, shy as much as guilty, 'I don't know. I really don't know.'

'Then we won't,' he said, 'and there's no need to start saying sorry either. We won't until you do know, until you're ready, and if that never happens, I'll still be a very happy man.'

'Will you?' she said doubtfully. 'Will you really?'

'Yes,' he said, 'yes I will. I love you, Grace.'

'Do you?' she said, scarcely daring to believe she had heard it, wanting to hear it again.

'Of course I do. I've loved you from the first minute I saw you. I can remember every minute of it, I can tell you everything about you, what you were wearing, a blue flowery dress it was, how your hair was a bit shorter than now, and all tangled up with the wind, what your face looked like, a bit pale and frightened. I can remember what you said, and how kind you were, and how you held me when I cried, and – well, it was you got me through it.' He smiled at her. 'Long speech. Been thinking it for a long time. But anyway, I do know I love you.'

'But Ben, you – '

'I know what you're going to say. Not how I loved her, of course. She was one thing and one way of loving and you're another thing and another way.'

'I don't think,' said Grace, speaking very slowly and with great difficulty, 'I don't think I ever loved Charles.'

'You shouldn't say that,' he said and he looked anxious.

'No, it's true. I've thought about it such a lot. I think I do love you, and what I felt for him was nothing like it. Nothing at all.'

'Well,' he said finally, 'he's a long way away and you haven't seen him for a long time. You've forgotten maybe.'

'I haven't forgotten,' she said, 'I haven't forgotten anything.'

'Well,' he said, 'only you know that.'

'Yes. Only me. And I do know I love you. But – '

'I know about the but,' he said. 'You're still married to him and he's still your husband, right?'

'Yes.'

'And he's out there, fighting for you, and for me, God help me, me and my boys, and all of us. And you can't turn your back on him.'

'No. No I can't. Not quite. Not yet anyway. I'm sorry.'

'Don't say you're sorry.'

They lay on the floor by the fire for a long time, and they did not make love; but Ben awoke in Grace sensations and longings just the same that she was quite unprepared for, powerful, warm, piercing in their intensity. He kissed her not as Charles had done, not with the almost detached, practised skill that was the first deliberate step in arousing her, but thoughtfully, slowly, carefully, a pleasure to be savoured in itself. Every so often he would draw back and look at her, study her face, gazing into it as if he had not seen it before and he had things to learn from it; would ask her if she was all right, how she felt, whether she was happy, would tell her again, and with an increasing depth to his voice, that he loved her. She had not known desire before, she realized now, had not known its great surging force, its joyful, all-pervading power, was not prepared for its temptations, its ability to negate thought, sense, conscience. And in spite of what she had said, what she believed, her own fear that she would prove disappointing, she would have gone along with it then in all its insistence, had not Ben himself suddenly drawn back, leant on his elbow and sighed heavily, gazed distantly into the fire.

'I think,' he said, 'I think perhaps we'd better go to bed. Alone, I mean.'

And 'Oh Ben,' she said, 'perhaps I was wrong, perhaps we are being foolish. After all – '

But he put his hand over her mouth very tenderly, traced the shape of it with his finger, and said, 'No, love, you weren't wrong, and you mustn't do it if you don't want to.'

'I do want to. More than anything in the world I want to – '

'I didn't mean quite like that,' he said, smiling, bending to kiss her,

354

'and anyway, it's not easy for me either. I never was unfaithful to Linda, we were both virgins when we married, it feels like putting her aside. Saying goodbye, I suppose.'

'Yes,' she said, shocked at her own insensitivity, that she hadn't thought of that. 'Yes of course. I hadn't really – well – '

She stopped, confused, and he bent and kissed her again. 'I don't think your mum liked me much,' he said.

'No,' said Grace. 'Well, she did I expect, but she didn't like the fact of you being here. She said I should be careful, that I was still married to Charles and what would Muriel say.'

'She's right,' he said heavily, 'quite right. I don't blame her for any of that. What my mum would have said I dread to think. My trousers would be down by now and my bottom smacked. Do you know, she still used to take the hairbrush to me when I was sixteen and out at work, if I got back late. And I used to let her do it, stand there saying, "'sorry, Mum".'

'Well, it didn't do you any harm,' said Grace smiling. 'No harm at all. Tell me about your parents, Ben. About your childhood and everything.'

And they sat in the firelight and he talked: about a 'mostly happy' childhood in the small house in Acton, his limited schooling, his tough, demanding mother – 'She didn't understand me much', the gentle father he had loved so dearly – 'Nor him neither'; the little sister who had died at five from diphtheria. 'I really loved her, Sally she was called. I can still remember them taking her off in the ambulance, all the street watching. I felt guilty it wasn't me.' And then his thwarted ambitions to become a teacher. 'I might have made it,' he said, 'if I'd got the scholarship when I was eleven. Then I'd have hung on a bit longer, maybe got my school cert. But I failed it, my elementary school was bad, and Mum just didn't feel I had the right to go on taking from them, when Dad was so ill. And I expect she was right. So I left. Went out to work.'

'And how was that?'

'Depressing,' he said, surprising her, 'really boring and depressing. All day at a desk in a big room with dozens of others. I hated it all then, living with Mum and Dad in that street – it's all right when you're a kid, you don't notice, and you're all in it together, but when I was older – well, it looked like going on for ever. Grey and dull. And then I met Linda. And she made it all – brighter. Better.'

'Tell me about her,' said Grace quietly, stifling, crushing her jealousy.

'She was lovely,' he said simply, 'and pretty, fair-haired, you know, good figure, fun, always laughing and joking. My dad loved her. Called her his sunshine.'

'Oh,' said Grace. She forced a smile.

'I loved her so much,' he said, 'and she loved me. We quarrelled now and then, but she made life good. That was her thing, making life good. Whatever went wrong. "Buck up, Ben," she used to say, "cut that long face out." '

Grace didn't say anything; she couldn't. Ben smiled, put out his hand and took hers. 'I think I know what you're thinking,' he said, 'and don't. You're quite different from her but that's good. It's good because I can love you differently. Without feeling unfaithful.'

'I see,' said Grace uncertainly. She was thinking not just about Linda, but about Ben's life, its deprivations, its lack of any kind of material richness, of physical beauty, contrasting it with Charles's golden existence, growing up in his large house, waited upon by cooks and nannies, given ponies to ride, dogs to play with, well dressed, superbly educated – and wondered what fundamental differences these things wrought upon a person, how they shaped them for good or ill. And wondered too where she fitted between these two extremes, how she could be what they both loved – or said they did – both wanted. It made her feel very odd.

'Penny for them,' he said.

He had said that before: on the hill, in the hot sun. She smiled at the memory.

'Oh,' she said quickly, 'I was thinking about Charles. How spoilt he was. How someone should have taken a hairbrush to him, like your mum did to you.'

'I expect they did,' said Ben, 'sort of thing that happens at posh schools, isn't it?'

'Yes,' said Grace, remembering Laurence's words at the wedding, 'I suppose so, yes. Only it was worse than hairbrushes. Much worse.'

'What – other boys, do you mean? That goes on a lot in those places, doesn't it?'

'Well – I don't know about that. I – I suppose there might have been. I never asked him.'

'Why not?'

'I couldn't,' she said, genuinely shocked and surprised. 'Not possibly. It's not the kind of thing I could have asked him. Too – well, too personal. Private.'

'That's strange to me,' he said, 'very strange. That you could marry someone, make love with them, and not be able to talk about some-thing to them. Linda and me – we didn't have anything like that. I can't imagine there could be anything about her I didn't know, couldn't have asked. Even all those – well, you know, women's things, and when she didn't want me and when she did, we just talked about it all.'

'Oh,' said Grace. She could hear her voice sounding bleak suddenly, bleak and distant. He reached out for her hair, pushed it back from her face.

'Now don't start being silly,' he said, smiling, 'I'd feel just the same about you, there'd be nothing I couldn't ask you, or tell you either. That was one of the first things I loved about you. The way you didn't run away from things. Listen, my lovely, we must go to bed. Or I shall start finding out more than I should. Come on, let's go and see your babies, shall we?'

She fell asleep smiling, happier than she would have believed possible, savouring the memory of his voice calling her his lovely. And woke up with a heavy, hard boulder of guilt in her heart.

Boxing Day started all right; perfectly all right. Ben had slept late and she and Clifford had gone for a long walk. When they came back, Clarissa was sitting at the kitchen table talking to Ben, talking and laughing, her lovely head bent towards him, his eyes on her face. Such was Grace's happiness that she didn't even feel the drift of a shadow over it.

'Hallo, Clarissa,' she said. 'I'm sorry, I'd forgotten you were coming.'

'I've brought the oranges, darling, and, quite honestly, to get away just for a moment or two from Moo. She is hard work, miserable old bat – oh, I'm so sorry, Clifford, my darling, I didn't think – '

'That's all right, Clarissa,' she said, 'I did live with her for over thirty years, you know.' He smiled, but his face was heavy and he excused himself and went out of the room soon afterwards, closing the door carefully behind him.

'Poor old darling,' said Clarissa, looking remorseful. 'What a stupid cow I am. I bet he still misses her in spite of everything. But honestly, she never stops, started this morning about Robert, about how sad it was he wasn't there, how much she missed him. Florence told me, Grace darling, about what happened, how absolutely frightful for you – '

'Oh it was all right,' said Grace quickly. 'And at least it cleared a few things up.'

'God, you're a saint,' said Clarissa, looking at her thoughtfully. 'I was just saying to Ben how much we all of us owe you, how we couldn't manage without you.'

'I'm certainly not,' said Grace, thinking what a dowdy quality saintliness was, promptly feeling drab and uninteresting again. Nobody, she thought, would call Clarissa a saint.

'Well anyway, darling, I suppose I'd better get back now. I left Jack being forced to admire Imogen while she counted up to seventy. And before that we had to admire her using the po. And before that, cleaning her teeth all by herself. I do hope Florence's Giles has got a good admiration quotient.'

'Yes,' said Grace. 'Yes, I'm sure he has.'

Clarissa kissed her and then looked at Ben. 'Can I kiss you too?' she said.

'If you like, yes.'

'I certainly do.'

He leant down from his considerable height to kiss her; then walked out to the car with her. As she started the engine, he leant in at the window and she said something to him; Grace watched them, carefully careless, telling herself how wonderful it was that she didn't mind in the least.

It was still all right for a while, even after that; they ate lunch, sat and listened to a concert, Ben played with Daniel and his train set. It was rather unreliable, the key didn't always work from being so worn and used; he said he could get another made in one of the workshops at Tidworth.

'Let's have one of those oranges,' said Daniel. 'She's nice, that Clarissa is. Ever so pretty.'

'She is,' said Ben, 'very nice. And very pretty?' He winked at Grace over Daniel's head; later, when Daniel had gone upstairs with David to listen to the cat's-whisker radio, he said, 'Clarissa was once engaged to Charles, then?'

'Yes,' said Grace, startled, 'yes she was. Did she tell you this morning?'

'Yeah. Yeah she did. She was telling me about him.'

'I see.' She didn't know why, but illogically it annoyed her, to think of the two of them discussing her husband.

'He sounds exactly like I thought,' said Ben.

'Oh really?'

'Yeah. Very English, very stiff-upper-lip, all that.'

'Yes, well, he is. It's not a crime, is it? And very kind and generous as well. And brave,' she added.

'Of course he is. No one's doubting that. Don't be silly, love.'

She was silent for a moment, then, 'Did she tell you why she broke off her engagement?'

'Sort of. She said it just didn't work out. That told me quite a bit about him too.'

'Oh really? What exactly did it tell you?'

'Oh – I don't know. She'd take quite a bit of living up to, Clarissa, wouldn't she?'

'And I don't. Is that what you mean?'

'Grace, of course it's not. What's the matter with you?' He reached out, stroked her hand; she pulled it back.

'Oh dear. Shall we go and sit by the fire? There's nobody about.'

'No,' she said, 'no, I don't think so.'

She suddenly didn't want to have to start stealing minutes, moments of pleasure; the thought wearied her. She had been alone for so long, lonely for so long, she wanted someone there all the time, someone to talk to, laugh with, share things with. Ben wasn't going to be that person. He couldn't be.

He shrugged. 'OK. I'm going to read for a bit. Would that be all right?' He was teasing her, she knew, but it irritated her just the same.

'Oh for heaven's sake,' she said, 'of course it would be all right.'

Much later, after a slightly strained supper, he came to find her. 'Come and have a cuddle, come on. The boys and Sir Clifford are all asleep. It'll do you good. I want to tell you I love you again. The novelty hasn't worn off yet.'

She smiled at him rather half-heartedly and took the hand he held out, followed him into the drawing room. He sat down on the battered old sofa, took her in his arms, looked at her very solemnly. 'I really do love you,' he said. 'I don't want any nonsense about it.'

'I know,' she said wearily. 'I know. I'm sorry.'

'Don't say sorry. You look so lovely, Grace. Clarissa said I must be doing you good, she'd never seen you look so pretty.'

Grace sat back. 'Clarissa said that! What did she mean? Did you tell her that you – that we – '

'No, of course not. Calm down. She just said – well, she just said that. You know what she's like, far better than I do.'

'I don't like you talking about me to her,' said Grace. 'And certainly not about Charles. All right?'

'Yes, all right. Come on, I want to give you a kiss.'

He started to kiss her, but she was distant, withdrawn: partly from genuine confusion, partly because immediately he began, so did the longing, the throbbing frustration, and quite suddenly she could see that unless she made her decision, took her stand, it wasn't going to get any better; it was going to get worse and worse, and they weren't going to have a lovely warm protracted courtship as she had had with Charles, it was impossible, she was no longer a virgin, no longer innocent, and a relationship that denied that, denied sexual knowledge, sexual pleasure, just wasn't going to be possible. Either she went with it, went forward into this new and lovely thing, this forbidden place, or she turned her back on it. She couldn't have it both ways. Either she turned her back on Charles, who loved her, who was her husband, who was out there somewhere, enduring hardship, discomfort, danger, climbed into bed, made love with another man; or she finished with Ben, before any real harm was done, told him that the whole thing was unthinkable and wrong. Either way, she had to make a decision: take charge.

And she wasn't ready to do so.

She pulled back from him, said rather quickly, 'I'm sorry, Ben, I don't feel – well, I don't feel like it. Not just now.'

He sat back, looked at her. 'Why not?'

'I just don't.'

'You're a bit mixed up really, aren't you?' he said after a pause.

'I don't think so. No. I mean you can hardly expect me to feel perfectly happy about all this. It's too complicated. Surely you can see that.'

'Of course I can.'

She was silent. Then, 'Maybe we've taken it all too fast,' she said.

'Hardly.'

She was stung. 'What's that supposed to mean?'

'It's not supposed to mean anything. Just that. I've said I'd wait, that I'd be patient. I am being. It all seems quite simple to me.'

'Well it is for you,' said Grace.

'Yes, I know that too. Come here, please, let me love you.'

'No,' said Grace, 'no. I'm sorry, Ben. I'm going to bed.'

He looked at her. 'You're being a bit silly, you know,' he said.

'Ben,' said Grace, 'don't start making judgments on me, please. Goodnight.'

'Goodnight,' he said. He had picked up a copy of *Picture Post*; he didn't even look up.

Next day he left, things still strained between them. He had hardly gone when Grace heard a crunch of tyres on the gravel outside, and sighed; she didn't want to see anybody. The back door opened. It was Clarissa. Her least of all, thought Grace.

'Darling! All alone? Where's your lovely man?'

'Gone back to barracks,' said Grace shortly. 'And he's not mine either.'

'I left my cardigan here yesterday,' said Clarissa ignoring this. 'There it is. We're about to leave.' She looked at Grace piercingly. 'Have you been crying?'

'No.'

'Yes you have,' she said. 'What's the matter?'

'Nothing,' said Grace and then increasingly loudly, 'nothing nothing nothing. Don't interfere, Clarissa, please.'

'You're in love with him, aren't you?' said Clarissa.

'No. No, of course I'm not.'

'Yes you are. And he's in love with you.'

'Did he – did he tell you that?'

'Not in so many words, no. But if ever a man was in love he is. He talks about you all the time. He watches you all the time. Darling, I'm not stupid.'

'I know you're not,' said Grace with a sigh. She felt tears welling up again, blinked them back furiously.

Clarissa put her arm round her. 'Don't,' said Grace, 'or I shall really start crying again.'

'So what exactly is the matter?' asked Clarissa, sitting down, lighting a cigarette.

'Oh Clarissa, I don't know. Feeling so bad about Charles, I suppose. Guilty, terrible.'

'Have you – well, been to bed with Ben yet?'

'No,' said Grace very quietly, too wretched to take exception to so personal a question. 'And I'm not going to. I just can't. It feels too wrong.'

'I would say, darling,' said Clarissa lightly, after a pause, 'that you should.'

'What?' said Grace. She felt genuinely shocked.

'I think you should go to bed with him. Quickly. Get it over, see it through. Listen, Grace. You're in love with Ben. You're in knots of love with him. Anyone can see. And him with you. That's what really matters. That's what is or isn't going to hurt your marriage. Whether you've actually had sex with him or not is fairly immaterial.'

'I just can't see how you can say that.'

'Well, I have said it,' said Clarissa. 'So let's not worry about how. Look – ' She hesitated. 'This is absolutely between us. But it's important. All right?'

Grace nodded.

'When – when Jack was in hospital, when he was first burnt, I couldn't stand it. I really couldn't. And do you know what cured me, made it all right?'

Grace shook her head dumbly.

'I found him in bed with a nurse. Darling, don't look so shocked. What it did was make me realize how much I loved him. It certainly didn't wreck our marriage, because that was so strong. I love Jack so much it didn't touch it. Don't you understand?'

'And what about you?' said Grace.

'What do you mean?'

'Would you ever go to bed with – with someone else?'

'Oh you know me,' said Clarissa easily, 'last of the bad girls I am. A quick little fling just might take place. Under certain circumstances. These are funny times we're all living in, after all.' She smiled at Grace; and Grace looked back at her and just for a second saw – what? Not even something, just the shadow of something, at the back of her eyes, something wary, something forbidden. And then it was gone and she dragged her mind away from it, back to what was important, what Clarissa was saying. 'It's what's underneath that matters, Grace. Who you really love. And what I'm saying is that I think you don't quite know. Now look, I must go. Jack's in an awful bait already because I've held him up.'

She gave Grace a hug. 'Lots of luck, darling. I think your Ben is heaven and I think you deserve him. Bye. Happy New Year.'

'You're very quiet,' said Jack as he swung Bunty's car onto the main London road.

'Sorry,' said Clarissa, 'I'm thinking about something. I've just been handing out some rather strong advice to Grace, bossing her about really, and I just hope it doesn't all go wrong.'

'She needs a bit of bossing,' said Jack, 'poor little thing.'

'I'm not at all sure,' said Clarissa, 'that she is quite such a poor little thing. Actually.'

Far from making life simpler, Clarissa's advice put Grace into an even worse torment. She changed her mind almost hourly: she would go to bed with Ben; she wouldn't; she would tell him what Clarissa had said and ask him what he thought; she wouldn't tell him what Clarissa had said, but ask him what he thought anyway, presenting the ideas as her own.

There was so much to be afraid of: what being unfaithful would do to her relationship with Charles, what might happen if Muriel, for instance, found out, what might happen next. And suppose she got pregnant, then what? It was a possibility after all. And was she going to commit herself to Ben permanently, or simply have a fling with him, the sort of thing Clarissa might do? But she wasn't like Clarissa, not in the least; if she went on feeling like this about Ben, she would want to stay with him for ever. And how could she? How could she possibly? She was married to Charles. And most of all, she supposed, she was afraid of being a disappointment to Ben in bed, of revealing her hopelessness, her lack of sexiness. She was sure Linda had been wonderful in bed. The more she heard about Linda, the more she sounded like Clarissa. That really frightened her.

At times, when she was feeling particularly low, she would decide to finish the whole thing; at others she knew she couldn't. Or she would decide to go to bed with him and then finish it, knowing at least they had extracted every last possible shred of joy and pleasure from it; and in her craziest moments she would decide to leave Charles, to run away with Ben, taking the boys with them.

In the end, fate made her mind up for her.

'Eat your tea, Daniel,' said Grace.

'Not hungry.'

'Now, Daniel, you said that last time we had this. Then I found you raiding the larder. Eat it up.'

'I don't want it,' he said, 'I've got a stomach ache.'

Grace looked at him. He seemed fine; he had been out playing all afternoon. 'Then you'd better go up to bed,' she said sharply. Her indecision, her anguish was having a bad effect on her temper.

'But Grace – '

'Go to bed.'

'Can't I have my Ovaltine?'

'No. Not if you won't eat your supper.'

She went to bed early herself that night; she felt permanently tired from sleeping so badly. As she passed the boys' room she heard a faint groan. She pushed the door open. Daniel was lying curled up, clutching his stomach; he managed a smile when he saw her.

'Are you feeling really bad?' asked Grace in alarm.

'A bit. It really hurts.'

'And he's hot,' said David.

She took his temperature; it was 102. Alarmed, she called the doctor; while they were waiting for him Daniel was sick.

The doctor diagnosed appendicitis, said he should be got to the hospital without delay. 'I'll get an ambulance. Get him into Salisbury General, I don't like the look of this.'

Daniel started to scream. 'I want Dad. I want Dad.'

'Daniel, don't be silly. Dad's away, you know he is.'

'I want him. I want him here. I hate it all, it hurts, I feel sick' – this accompanied by further vomiting – 'I hate you, Grace, I hate the doctor, I want Dad.'

Without a great deal of hope, Grace phoned the barracks at Tidworth; Ben was still there as far as she knew. She left a message to say that Sergeant Lucas's younger son was being taken to Salisbury Hospital, that his appendix had to come out, that there was no serious danger, but that if Sergeant Lucas could possibly get leave to come over, then she was sure it would be very helpful.

The ambulance came quite soon; they were in Salisbury by ten. The hospital doctor examined Daniel, said the appendix should come out straight away, told the young nurse who was standing by the bed to prepare Daniel for his operation. Daniel screamed on.

'I'm surprised the pain is that bad,' said the nurse to Grace, quietly. 'And I have to give him an enema. Do you think he'll be all right?'

'Oh yes,' said Grace, sounding more optimistic than she felt.

The nurse advanced on Daniel with a rubber tube and a bowl, and smiled at him uncertainly; he stopped yelling briefly. 'What's that for?'

'It's – well, it's – it's to empty out your tummy,' she said uneasily. 'How?'

She looked at Grace for support; Grace gripped Daniel's hand and attempted rather nervously to explain the mechanics of an enema.

Daniel became hysterical, fighting them off, pushing the nurse, the tube, Grace away: 'No! No, I won't let them, I won't. Leave me, leave me alone. I want my dad, I want my dad.'

'I don't know what to do,' said the nurse. 'He has to have it, they can't do the operation without. Daniel, come on, be a brave boy – '

'No,' screamed Daniel. 'No, no, no.'

'Daniel, please!' said Grace. 'It won't hurt, I promise. Not nearly as much as your tummy. Please, Daniel. For me.'

'No.'

'Daniel,' said a voice, 'behave yourself. When I was in hospital I had to have those all the time. The nurse is trying to help you.' It was Ben. Daniel promptly gave in, submitted himself to the tortures of the enema.

'Poor little boy,' said Grace much later, as they sat by his bed while he lay motionless, still unconscious. 'Poor, poor little boy. I feel so terrible, Ben. I was cross with him, sent him to bed for not eating his supper, wouldn't let him have his Ovaltine.'

'Just as well,' said Ben, 'or he'd have been even more sick. Don't blame yourself, love.'

'Thank goodness you got here. I don't know what would have happened otherwise.'

'I reckon,' said Ben quietly, indicating a hovering figure at the end of the ward, 'that she would have dealt with him.'

She was the ward sister; a lady of such proportions that Miss Merton resembled a nymph by comparison.

'Well, maybe. But he was so upset. Was it hard for you to get away?'

'No. I've got a forty-eight.'

'Oh,' she said, hoping she didn't sound as confused, as overwhelmed as she felt.

'Mr and Mrs Lucas?' It was the outsized ward sister.

'Er – yes,' said Ben. (It seemed simpler, he said to Grace later, to let her think that.)

'You can't stay here all night, you know. You shouldn't really be here at all. This is a hospital, not a hotel.'

'Yes,' said Grace humbly.

'Your little boy is perfectly all right. Perfectly. An absolutely normal appendectomy. A good night's sleep and he'll be fine. You can visit tomorrow, between two and three.'

'Yes. But what happens when he wakes up all alone?'

'Mrs Lucas, when he wakes up, he will not be alone. We will be here.'

'But he may – want me. Us.'

'In which case,' said the sister, her face extremely stern, 'he will be told you will be here between two and three. I really don't see any problem whatsoever. He is not seriously ill. Now do please go home and get to bed. It's the sensible thing to do.'

'Well – '

'Come along, Grace,' said Ben, 'you heard what Sister said. We should get to bed. It's the sensible thing to do.'

He had an army truck outside; he drove it just a little too fast through the dark lanes. He didn't say anything; neither did Grace. When they got to the Mill House, Clifford and David were waiting for them in the kitchen.

'Shit,' said Ben under his breath as they walked in, and then smiled at them. 'No need to worry. Dan's fine. We can all visit him tomorrow.'

'Excellent news,' said Clifford. 'There you are, David, I told you.'

'Honest?'

'Honest. You go on up to bed now, I'll come and tuck you up.'

'All right.'

'I'm turning in too,' said Clifford. 'Jolly tired.'

'I'll come and tuck you up too, Clifford,' said Grace, 'and bring you a hot toddy if you're very good.'

'Will you really, my dear? I would be grateful.'

It was an hour before the house was quiet. Ben looked at Grace across the kitchen and smiled.

'Here I go again,' he said, 'saying thank you.'

'It's all right,' said Grace. 'I'm just sorry it had to happen like that.'

'Don't say sorry,' he said, 'and it certainly wasn't your fault.'

There was a long silence. Then he said, 'Shall we go and sit by the fire then?'

Grace looked at him and wondered what she had been making such a fuss about. It all suddenly seemed very simple.

'No,' she said, 'no, let's go upstairs.'

'I love you,' he said, as she lay beside him, looking at his face on the pillow, her hand in his. 'I know you're scared, and I am too. But I love you. Just remember that. That's what matters. That's all that matters really.'

There were other things that mattered: that he was gentle and soothing and calming in the beginning, when she was frightened and edgy and unable to believe she could be in any way what he wanted; that he talked a lot all the way through, told he loved her, that she was beautiful, that she felt lovely; that his body was at one and the same time demanding and gentle, skilful and diffident, powerful and anxious to please; that her body, reaching, wanting, responding to him was not at all as she had ever known it; that her head and her heart seemed to be as involved in her delight as the rest of her; that she could hear all the time murmurings, then moans, then soaring cries of pleasure (stifled by his hand over her mouth, his voice in her ear saying shush), and realized it was herself; that the gathering, the enfolding, the holding and then finally the great glorious thrusting of release was of a scale and a brilliance she had not ever imagined possible; that she cried sweet, sad tears as her orgasm faded and she fell into peace; and that the last thing she heard as she fell asleep in his arms was his voice telling her he loved her.

They woke early, went downstairs and drank huge steaming mugs of tea, watched by Charlotte and her puppies who fell on their bare feet with eager tongues and tiny sharp teeth; they were big now, scurrying about, messing everywhere, tumbling over one another, a relentless loving army, driving their mother mad. 'I can't wait for them to go now,' Grace said, and 'how could you,' said Ben 'when they brought us together?'

'Thank you for last night,' he said suddenly, smiling at her, taking her hand.

And 'was it really all right?' she said. 'I was so nervous, so afraid I wasn't going to be able to – well, to do it. I think that was half the trouble really.'

'You did it fine,' he said, very serious. 'Thank God for appendicitis, that's all.'

'Clarissa told me I should,' said Grace. 'She said it was the right thing to do.'

'Thank God for Clarissa as well then,' said Ben.

Later they went to see Daniel, who was fretful and difficult and sore, full of complaints and reproaches. Guiltily grateful for the end of visiting hours, they left and drove not home, for then they would have to be with Clifford and David, but into the countryside, and went for a long walk in the New Forest. It was very cold, but they did not care, did not even notice; there was so much to talk about (released finally from inhibition, shyness, awkwardness), so much to discover, to ask, to tell. The ground was stony-hard, the trees harshly bare, but Grace felt as if she had wandered into some kind of warm, golden place filled with flowers and birdsong; she took Ben's arm, and hugged herself to him and told him again and again how much she loved him, and he smiled down at her and told her he loved her too, and there was room for nothing else at all just then, not for guilt, nor for anxiety about their future and whether they might be together in it; they were too new to happiness to feel anything else at all.

He left early in the morning, after another long sweet night, back to Tidworth and then was immediately sent to Yorkshire, leaving Grace alone, trying not to think too much about what was happening to her, resolving simply to enjoy it, feeling for the first time since her marriage valued, important, desirable even. She was even glad that

Ben was not there, so that she could study her feelings for him and the implication of him upon her life with at least a degree of detachment. She thought about him constantly, heard his voice, saw his face, felt his arms round her, his mouth on hers, his body pleasuring her with an immensely strong, physical vividness. Charles on the other hand had become a distant ghost, a shadow of someone she could scarcely remember. She would sit with his letters, his photographs, trying to summon him up, to make the comparison fairer, the scales more evenly balanced, but it was useless: he remained out of focus, a distant, hazy figure, with no real substance or quality.

The winter was exceptionally cold; London and other cities were beset by freezing fog. Life seemed particularly joyless everywhere; the drought of the summer before and now the intense frosts meant that green vegetables and even potatoes were increasingly rare. The war, with its shortages and hardship, seemed to have gone on for ever, depression was almost tangible. At the end of January, there was a spate of bombing on London and more a week later. Mr Churchill was heard to remark with his usual humour that it was just like old times. Then, as the days grew just slightly longer and the air a little warmer, a sense of almost tension grew in the country. There was talk, rumour, informed gossip that the invasion, so long awaited, was finally to happen: men recalled from the battlefields of Egypt, Tunisia and Italy were joined by raw young recruits for intensive training. Ships had been gathering in harbours all around the southern coast for many months.

Grace, as weary of it all as anyone, scarcely noticed that Clifford was increasingly depressed until she heard him moving about downstairs very late one night, and afraid he might be ill went down to investigate. He was sitting by the boiler, huddled in his threadbare dressing gown, drinking whisky; she went over to him and gave him a hug and realized to her infinite sadness that he had tears in his eyes.

'Darling Clifford, what is it? What's the matter?'

He was resistant to explanation at first, said he was just feeling a bit low, obviously afraid of hurting her feelings; then suddenly he began to talk. He was lonely, he told her; desperately and profoundly lonely. He missed his old life, his old friends, and perhaps most surprisingly of all, he missed Muriel.

'I know she's difficult, often rude and so on, and not at all nice to you, and that grieves me very much. But I was very fond of her. We lived together for over thirty years, you know, Grace, had children together, brought them up, saw them marry. That is a very close bond. Almost unbreakable, I have to say.'

'Yes,' said Grace, her voice hardly audible even to herself. She sat stony-still, listening to Clifford's tired, gentle voice as he talked, told her he regretted most horribly giving up everything and hurting Muriel so deeply.

'Given the time again, I would have been more circumspect. Honesty, grand gestures are all very well, Grace, but I am not sure they are truly appropriate. There is great value in the old order, you know; in remaining true to what you have always known, the way you have always lived. Hypocrisy may have a price, but it is sometimes worth paying.'

He smiled at her suddenly, a sweet, gentle smile. 'What I would have done without you, my darling, you and the boys, I really don't know. And, oh dear, I must sound so ungrateful. Take no notice, these are just the ramblings of a foolish old man. Very foolish. Well, I'm going up to bed. Enough nightcaps for a week, I've had. Goodnight, Grace.'

'Grace,' said Florence, 'I know it's nothing to do with me, but are you – well, are you having an affair with Ben?'

'You're right,' said Grace, anger sweeping through her, 'it isn't anything to do with you. How dare you even ask me?'

'All right, all right,' said Florence, 'I'm hardly in a position to criticize, am I? I wouldn't blame you, quite honestly.'

'Oh,' said Grace and sat down rather hard at the kitchen table.

'Well, he is very attractive,' said Florence, 'very attractive indeed. And Charles has been gone for a long time. Honestly, Grace, there's no need to look so stricken, there is a war on after all. Nothing's like it used to be.'

'No,' said Grace, 'no, Clarissa was saying something very similar. Actually.'

'Well, there you are then,' said Florence. 'I'm not going to say anything to anyone. Certainly not to Charles when he comes home.'

'Why did you – think that anyway?' said Grace.

'Oh – I just wondered,' said Florence vaguely.

'Your mother doesn't – isn't – '

'Good Lord no. It would be so unthinkable for her, it really wouldn't enter her head.'

'Why so unthinkable?' said Grace.

'Well, because – because – '

'Because he's not been to public school?' said Grace, deceptively quiet. 'Not an officer? Gamekeeper class, is that it?'

'Well yes, something like that,' said Florence. 'Not that I – '

'Oh no, Florence, not that you would think anything like that, would you? I'm sure your lover is socially very suitable, isn't he? Ben's all right to have a fling with, to sleep with, that's it, isn't it? But obviously, of course, that's all. I mean it couldn't be anything more than that, anything permanent, could it?'

'Well no,' said Florence, looking at her in genuine astonishment, 'I wouldn't have thought so. How could it? How could it work? Unless you moved right away, went to live wherever he came from, but then you wouldn't fit in there, would you? With his people? Don't look at me like that, Grace, it's true. Oh for heaven's sake, let's talk about something else.'

Grace suddenly stopped being indignant. Florence was too honest, too childishly transparent to take any real exception to. She spoke as she found, as Betty would have said, and there was, besides, quite a lot in what she said. Grace hadn't really considered that side of their relationship before; she had been entirely concerned with the emotional problems, of being unfaithful to Charles, of worrying where it might be leading. It was true: if – *if* – she made any kind of permanent commitment to Ben, and she really wasn't ready even to consider such a thing, life would be difficult in lots of ways, and they would have to find some neutral territory in which to build their lives. It was all very well at the moment, everyone being matey – or pretending to be – with everyone else, but it was a false situation, a false premise. Her own experiences of moving even slightly out of her class, of the difficulties she had encountered, were still vivid, and sometimes painful. The difficulties of the whole situation swept over her suddenly, hugely increased.

'Oh God,' said Grace, aloud, 'oh dear God, whatever is going to become of me?'

But God did not reply. And there seemed no one else she could ask, with the possible exception of Clarissa; and Clarissa was back at Dartmouth and inaccessible.

From a prison camp in south Germany, via the International Red Cross, came the news of the death of a British officer. The details in the report of the discovery of his body by Corporal Brian Meredith, himself taken prisoner near the border, were a little fudged by the time they reached the authorities, but his army identity tag revealed him to be beyond any doubt whatsoever one Major Charles Bennett.

Chapter Twenty-Four

Early Spring 1944

The worst thing was not knowing how to feel.

Shock, grief (genuine grief, thank God, she did experience, she had been so afraid she would not); guilt, terrible guilt, that she had been faithless, in love with another man, quite possibly even making love with him while Charles had died in some unimaginable horror, defending her and his country; and through it all, unbidden, unquenchable, the dreadful, treacherous tiny spring of relief.

Gradually a story of sorts was pieced together. 'Killed escaping' had been the form of words used on the telegram, together with the inevitable expression of regret. Further details were not forthcoming. The last real information was that he had been involved with his platoon in some heavy street fighting in a small Italian town, and with a handful of men had been taken prisoner, put into a truck under armed guard and driven off, presumably to a German prison camp. The chaos in Italy at that point, with the nation officially surrendered to the Allies but large sections of the army still loyal to Mussolini, the fighting fragmented but intense, and towns and villages falling slowly into Allied hands, made the garnering of definite information a near-impossible task. There was an unconfirmed report that Major Bennett had been seen escaping from the truck near the French-Italian border, but after that the trail had become fudged.

And now he was dead, he had been identified, and then buried by the German authorities. They were told they would be notified precisely where in due course.

A letter from his commanding officer told Grace he had been a brave man and a fine soldier, never flinching from anything, often putting himself in intense danger, admired by his men, popular with his fellow officers. He was a loss to the company and the regiment, and was being recommended for decoration.

Grace sat reading the letter and wondered how many others, identical in their platitudes had been wept over by other widows like herself.

Clifford was terribly upset; he tried, with a most touching courage, to be brave, but she found him several times weeping, and he would sit up far into the night, drinking, reading and rereading the few letters Charles had written to him, looking at old photographs of him. She knew the worst thing must be the estrangement, the fact that Charles had rejected him, that Clifford had lost him twice; but she could see also the loneliness for him, and the impossibility of sharing his grief, to any proper degree, was dreadful. She had rung the Priory when the news came and had gone in the morning to see Muriel. She had been shocked, withdrawn, rejecting any words of comfort herself, but oddly gentle with Grace, had taken her hand, told her how brave she must be, and then, extraordinarily, had enquired after Clifford, if he was all right.

Florence was devastated, crying intermittently, her face white and ravaged. Grace had not realized she loved Charles so much; an only child herself, she found it hard to imagine the bond between siblings.

Her parents came over later, towers of strength; her mother comforting and thoughtful, even offering to have the boys for a few days, her father sensible and practical, familiar with the grim procedures necessary to formalize Charles's death.

Everyone was very kind. The boys were painfully quiet and good, tiptoeing about the house, doing all their chores long before they were told, making her endless cups of rather nasty lukewarm tea. They also with a touching, straightforward sensitivity that reminded Grace, rawly, of their father, seemed to know that they must help Clifford, and suggested interminable games of chess, found him concerts on the wireless to listen to, insisted he came for walks with them and Charlotte and her two remaining russet puppies that no one had been prepared to take on.

Miss Merton took Grace literally to her large bosom and held her, unembarrassed, while she had the one and only fit of protracted, hysterical crying, and then quietly made sure all the children knew what had happened; when Grace came in the next time for music, there was a whole sheaf of posies on the piano, primroses, snowdrops, early pussy willow. Elspeth's father came round, white with embarrassment and agonized sympathy, a large cheese under his coat, and told her she was to ask for any help she needed around the house or garden, he'd be pleased to do it. Mrs Babbage came every day for a fortnight to clean the house and do all the washing and ironing and refused to take a penny in payment, and Mrs Boscombe told Grace any trunk calls she wanted making, any time in the next few weeks, she'd not be noting down. 'Least I can do, and I'm sure Mr Churchill would agree,' she said firmly.

The house was inundated, inevitably, with letters of sympathy from Charles's old friends and their parents, the very people who had most ignored and neglected her while he had been alive; she was amused rather than angered by this. Clarissa wrote, a letter of such sensitivity and perception it made Grace cry more than any other, finishing: 'If you need me, or if there is any kind of a service, then I will be there, no matter what, and Jack will be with me.'

Grace had no idea what to do about a funeral; a conventional affair was obviously not in order, but she felt some formalization was necessary, some open expression of grief, of acknowledgment of Charles's death, something that gave it dignity, that would bring some sense of importance to it and to his life. She talked to the vicar, who suggested a memorial service; she liked that idea, it gave her a focus, threw herself into organizing it, planning music, readings. She wanted someone to say a few words about Charles, but couldn't think who: Laurence would have been the obvious choice, but he was dead too, it was clearly quite beyond Clifford, and she had no intention of asking any of the old guard. Then she thought of Clarissa: it was an unconventional, quirky choice, and not something women were usually called upon to do, but the more she tried to set it aside, the better an idea it seemed. She wired Clarissa at Dartmouth, fearing a letter wouldn't reach her, and Clarissa wired back: 'Touched, honoured, will try to deserve it. Best love. Clarissa.'

One of the most difficult problems was that of Clifford. Clearly he must come to the service, but there was a danger of Muriel being openly hostile. In the end, after several almost sleepless nights, filled with visions of Muriel flying at Clifford's throat in the nave of St Andrews, she talked to Florence about it.

'Don't worry,' she said, 'I'll deal with her. She usually does what I say. Anyway, lots of her old cronies will be there, she won't want to do anything undignified.'

She was glad there was so much to think about, to do; it made it easier not to think about Ben. When she did, usually lying awake in the darkness, she felt violently ill, ill with guilt, with shame, and with a longing she crushed so determinedly that she became physically breathless. She had not dared to write to him.

It was a bright, windy March day when Grace sat in the front pew of the church, her parents on either side, the boys and Clifford next to them. Muriel sat opposite, with Florence and Imogen, ramrod straight, her face stonily controlled. Clarissa and Jack, both in uniform, sat behind.

There were a great many people in the little church, and the old guard had indeed turned out in force, Muriel and Clifford's generation as well as Charles's friends, mostly young women, all of them smiling graciously if slightly embarrassedly at Grace. They found themselves sitting with a rather broader cross-section of the local community than they might have expected, a large bunch of children from the village school, under the stern eye of Miss Merton, several farmers from quite far-flung villages accompanied by their wives, Elspeth Dunn's father, white-faced and more ill-at-ease even than usual in a stiffly uncomfortable suit, Mrs Lacey and several of the county committee for the Land Army, groups of the girls themselves (some arriving on bicycles, others on farm vehicles), Mrs Babbage in her Sunday best with Mr Babbage beside her, ready with not just one but three clean handkerchiefs in his hand, Mrs Boscombe from the telephone exchange, her work left in the less than tender care of a brash new young assistant she had been assigned.

All there because they loved and cared for Grace and wanted to show her so. She looked round from time to time and the sight of them gave her comfort, courage; as the vicar entered the church, and John Stokes urged the organ into the glory of 'Jesu, Joy of Man's Desiring', she stood up and reached suddenly across her mother and took Clifford's hand and gripped it very tightly, wishing to pass those things on.

It was not a very long service; they sang 'Lord of All Hopefulness', the vicar said some prayers and gave a short address, the choir sang 'Crimond' most beautifully. And then Clarissa stood up, walked to the steps of the chancel, stood there, looking at them all for a moment. She was clearly genuinely moved; there were tears in her dark eyes, she had to struggle to speak. But once she began, her voice, more musical in its task than usual, gained in power, in confidence, and Grace sat listening to her in something close to awe.

'Some of you,' she said, 'knew Charles Bennett, and some did not. You are all here to honour him, and his life, and that is what matters. I knew him very well, most of his life indeed: at one stage I was going to marry him.' She paused, the echo of a smile on her mouth. 'That we remained friends, good friends, although that did not happen, is proof of his wonderfully level, positive approach to everything. There are several people here today who knew and loved him very well: his parents, Muriel and Clifford, his sister, Florence, and of course his wife, Grace. To them must go our most heartfelt, our most tender sympathies. Others too, who knew him as a small boy, who cared for him, taught him, watched him grow up, will find his loss very hard. There is so much loss at the moment, so much pain, so many young men cut down in the prime of their lives. This does not make any individual loss easier to bear. But the quality of a life is what matters, and the quality of Charles's life was very fine. A generous friend, a loving husband, a marvellous and brave officer, an exceptionally devoted son – '

She paused here, for Muriel had stood up suddenly, her face quite transformed with grief, tender, somehow undone; she looked at Clarissa, then turned and hurried down the aisle, out of the church, her fists clenched in a clear effort to remain quiet, to retain some self-control. There was a brief pause and then, before even Florence could follow her, there was a sudden movement from Grace's pew, a resonance of footsteps, and Clifford was seen moving with extraordinary speed down the side of the church and out of the door after her. Florence half rose, but Jack put his hand out and pressed her down again; Clarissa resumed.

'There is not a great deal more to be said. But one thing I think is important. Many of you here today did not know Charles at all and are here for Grace, to give her support. I think she will draw great comfort from that and also from the knowledge that she was, in her sadly brief marriage to Charles, a most good and loving wife. He was, I know, so proud of her, and with good reason.'

Her dark eyes rested on Grace then, smiled at her with such sweetness, such absolute complicity, that some of the guilt and its pain fell away from her; and as John Stokes began to play that most lovely of funeral hymns, 'God Be in My Head', and the congregation rose to sing, she knelt, weeping tears of relief and thankfulness that Charles had never had any idea at all of her frailty. That much, through no great virtue of her own, he had been granted.

And when finally she got outside and looked anxiously for Muriel, she saw a wonderful and unexpected sight: she was standing in a corner of the graveyard, clearly still overwhelmed with grief, but the person comforting her, holding her, wiping her eyes most tenderly, was not Florence. It was Clifford.

Three days later she got a letter from Ben.

My dear Grace,
The boys wrote and told me about Charles. I know how very
unhappy you must be, and I am truly sorry. I have been thinking of
you and hoping so much you are all right. There is nothing I can
do, but you know I am here.
My love.
Ben

'Thank you for writing to your dad,' she said. 'It was very thoughtful.'

'We thought you'd want him to know,' said Daniel.

'Yes,' she said, 'yes I did.'

She wrote back, thanking him for his letter, sending him her love;
no more than that. She knew he would understand; and determinedly, carefully, then, as if packing away something for storage
through a long winter, she set him into the dark shadows at the back of
her mind and her heart, until such time as she was ready to think what
to do.

As she surfaced from her deep and genuine grief over Charles,
Florence finally decided to ask Robert for a divorce. She had no idea
why she had taken so long to make the decision, or why even going to
see the solicitor frightened her so much; and it was not Giles's loving
insistence, nor her desire to start a new life with him, nor even the
rather heavier pressure put on her by her father, but Robert's assault
on Grace that had given her the necessary courage. She went to a firm
of solicitors in Salisbury, who knew nothing of her or her family, and
certainly not of Robert; lawyers, she felt instinctively, were as
cohesive a force as doctors, and would join ranks wherever necessary,
and she was very much afraid of what Robert, probably in association
with his colleagues at the bar, would be able to do with her and a small
firm of country solicitors.

The solicitor's name was Dodds; he was grey-haired, grey-faced,
efficient and brisk, his face politely blank as she furnished him with
details.

'I want a divorce,' she said, firmly, 'on grounds of adultery.'

'On grounds of your husband's adultery?'

'No,' she said, 'my own.'

Mr Dodds passed the first test; he didn't even blink. 'I see. So it is in
fact your husband who wants the divorce?'

'No,' said Florence, 'I do.'

'But he has expressed a willingness to divorce you?'

Florence hesitated. 'Well – yes.'

'That is clearly essential, Mrs Grieg.'

'I see. Well, yes, of course he is willing.'

'And you will provide the necessary evidence?'

'Yes, I will.'

'You have someone prepared to be cited?'

'Yes I do. The father of my child. Actually.'

Mr Dodds's face became even more expressionless. 'Ah. And is there incontrovertible proof of that relationship?'

'Only visual,' said Florence. 'I mean he's not on her birth certificate.'

'I see. Well, certain procedures may need to be followed, if we are to allow that as evidence. Blood tests and so on.'

'I can prove my husband was away at the time of – of her conception.'

'That could be helpful,' said Mr Dodds.

'So what happens next?'

'I will write to Major Grieg, informing him that you have instructed me and on what basis. We will then await his response. Have you had any contact with the major during the past few months?'

'Not directly,' said Florence.

Ten days later she got a letter from Robert.

My dear Florence,

I have taken my time in communicating with you on the subject of an extraordinary letter from Mr Kenneth Dodds of Dodds & Partners in Salisbury.

I have to tell you, I have no intention of divorcing you; I care for you far too much.

Of course I know our marriage has not been ideal, and I think if we were honest we would have to admit we had both behaved less than perfectly at times, but the whole point of a marriage, it seems to me, is that it is something to be worked at, in partnership with one another. Nobody expects marriage to be easy; and if you did, my dear, then you were very naive. But I think we have the basis still for a happy life together, and I think we should go forward in pursuit of that happiness.

I would like to assure you that I do regard Imogen as my child; I love her very much and want to bring her up with you in our home together. And I would like, of course, to have more children. This war has put an appalling strain on all relationships, even the happiest; but if our separation has done anything positive for me at all, it has made me realize how much I love you.

I think we all know that the end is in sight, even if it is still a while off; another year perhaps, and we can be together in our own home again, building a future.

If you can accept and forgive my shortcomings, Florence, I can certainly accept and forgive yours.

I am hoping for some leave in the next few weeks, and then we can perhaps discuss all this together and find a way forward.

Until then I remain your loving,

Robert.

'Oh dear God,' whispered Florence, setting down the letter, staring out of the window, feeling the old constricting terror in her throat, 'dear dear God, what am I going to do?'

More than anything in the world now Grace wanted to see Ben; but more than ever she felt he was forbidden territory. Guilt still haunted her; guilt and an entirely illogical, superstitious fear that she was somehow to blame for Charles's death, that it was in some way a judgment on her. She knew also that it would be a very long time indeed before it would be considered decent, acceptable for her to see Ben, that everyone would be shocked, that she would be an outcast if she did; that added to the guilt made her more wretched still. She slept badly, was irritable and miserable during the day, and felt unable to work, not even to give music lessons at the school; boredom consequently added to her other miseries.

Miss Merton, seeing it as therapy as much as anything else, asked her to consider helping to organize a Maypole dance for the school fair on Whit Sunday; Grace said rather listlessly that she would if she had the time. Elspeth Dunn passed her Grade Two piano exam with distinction, and Grace merely told Miss Merton how pleased she was, made no attempt to see Elspeth herself. The only emotion she'd shown for weeks was when David Lucas had heard he'd got his scholarship to the grammar school; then she had burst into floods of tears and hugged him to her, saying over and over again, 'Your father will be so pleased, so terribly, terribly pleased.'

Both David and Daniel asked her constantly when Ben would be coming to see them again; she told them, trying not to sound too short, that she had no idea, that he was far away now in the north of England. She knew she was being unfair on them, that they needed affection as much as ever, but she found herself unable to give it; her resources were depleted.

Florence, clearly edgy and fractious herself, came to visit, ostensibly to cheer her up, but actually to unburden herself on the subject of her so far abortive attempt to divorce Robert. She told Grace she was looking awful.

'Thanks,' said Grace briefly.

'And that dress looks terrible, it's hanging off you. You ought to take it in or something.'

'Florence, when I want your advice about anything, anything at all, including my appearance, I'll ask you,' said Grace.

'All right. No need to be like that.'

'There is actually,' said Grace. 'It's time someone told you, Florence, to think before you speak. Rather than just opening your mouth and upsetting people. You're just like – like your mother.'

'Am I really?' said Florence. She sounded astonished, rather than upset.

'Sometimes, yes, you are.'

'How absolutely appalling,' she said. 'I'm so sorry.'

Even dear Mrs Babbage, still insistent on coming in to clean the Mill House, endeavouring to cheer Grace up with her observations that the end was in sight, irritated her almost beyond endurance.

'Got them on the run now,' she would say, or 'We'll see the whites of their eyes soon' as she scrubbed the kitchen floor, polished the dining-room table fiercely, 'although there's the invasion to be got through yet, of course, have to brace ourselves for that.' She would then move on to comment on what they had all been through, as if the Thorpes had been bombarded nightly along with London and the other great cities of England, concluding with her climactic judgment that the British had always been able to take it. In the end Grace told her, not quite gently enough, that she really thought she could manage in future, much as she appreciated what Mrs Babbage had done for her; she then spent the next hour in tears of remorse at the memory of Mrs Babbage's hurt face as she packed her apron and dusters into her bag and told her she was glad she was feeling better.

But it was David who pulled her up finally, made her realize how mean she was being. Clifford had asked her to a concert at the cathedral one Saturday; Grace told him she was sorry, she really didn't feel like going out, to take David instead.

David came to find her later. 'That was mean,' she said. 'Sir Clifford had got tickets specially. Asked Florence to get them, as a surprise for you.'

'Well, he shouldn't have done it without asking me,' said Grace.

David looked at her. 'You're not a bit like you used to be,' he said.

That afternoon she went for a long walk and thought extremely hard about herself and indeed everything else. She thought about Charles and told herself for the hundredth, the thousandth time that at least he had never known she had failed him. She thought about Ben, and how sure she was still that she loved him. And she thought about the night after Robert had attacked her, and how she had decided that she was going to take charge of her life in the future, to be less passive, more positive. The alternative, being negative, being unpleasant to everyone, was doing neither herself nor the memory of Charles any good. She stood on the hill where Ben had stroked her arm, that hot afternoon so long ago, and looked down at the house, and the happiness she had managed to find there; and resolved to take it back again.

When she got home, she sat down and wrote two letters; a brief apologetic note Mrs Babbage and a rather faltering letter to Ben.

It wasn't a long letter, but it took her a long time to write. The desk and wastepaper basket were filled with drafts before she had finished. The words wouldn't flow: she felt odd, guilty, as if Charles were watching her. And thoughts of Ben troubled her too. Was it arrogant to assume that he had been waiting, frantic with impatience, for her summons, that he would drop everything and come running to her the moment it came? Would he consider her contacting him hasty, distasteful, callous? And might he perhaps have wearied of waiting, anyway, regretted at least some of what he had said and done?

'Oh for heaven's sake,' said Grace aloud, reaching for another sheet of paper, 'pull yourself together.'

In the end she simply told him that she missed him, that she thought about him all the time, that when he had some leave and if he would like it, she would love him to come to the Mill House 'and see us all'. She signed it 'With my love to you, Grace'.

The moment she had posted it she felt better.

Florence was awoken one sunny April morning at six by her phone ringing: it was Joan Haverford.

'Florence, we need to meet some poor wretches off the train in an hour. Big block of flats hit in South London last night, latest in this new spate of bombs. I've been asked if we can meet the train, help with placing a few. Can you get over to Salisbury by nine, say?'

'Yes of course,' said Florence.

The dozen women coming off the train, children trailing behind them, were, as so often, shocked, sullen, resentful.

'They must be so grateful to you,' people said to Florence and found it hard to believe that often they were nothing of the sort, seemed indeed to blame her, in the absence of anyone else, for their misfortune.

They took them into the waiting room which had been commandeered, gave them hot drinks, warm clothes, clean nappies and milk for the babies.

''ow long we going to be 'ere?' asked one girl, clutching a small runny-nosed child to her, 'I got to get back, got me job to do.'

'I don't know,' said Florence patiently, 'but if you haven't got anywhere to live, you can't do your job, can you? Not for a bit, anyway.'

The girl looked at her, digesting her accent, her tweed suit, so clearly once expensive, and said illogically, 'Yeah, well, it's all right for you.'

'What is your job?' said Florence, ignoring this.

'Work in a factory,' said the girl.

'And where's your husband?'

''aven't got one.'

'Ah. Well, who – whose –?' said, Florence, indicating the baby.

'What's it to you?' said the girl.

'I need to know, you must see that,' said Florence briskly. 'For records and so on. If I'm to find you a billet.'

'You can tell them to stuff their records,' said the girl. She sniffed hard; she was near to tears. The baby suddenly smiled, reached out for Florence; it was pretty in spite of its disgusting nose, with enormous brown eyes and black silky curls. It was clearly one of the GI 'khaki babies', she thought, a growing army of innocent casualties of the American invasion.

'How sweet,' she said. 'How old is she?'

'Nine months.'

'She's very pretty. What's her name?'

'Mamie,' said the girl, won over immediately by this piece of admiration. 'After Mrs Eisenhower. 'er dad's a pilot. We're getting married after the war,' she added, with more hope than conviction in her voice. 'Got a big 'ouse over there 'e 'as, wiv a swimming pool and all.'

'How nice,' said Florence. She had heard this before: a lot of GI babies had been fathered on this premise. 'Well now, let me see, you want somewhere temporary, I suppose, just till you can get back to London. Is there anyone up there you can live with? For a while?'

'No, not really,' said the girl, 'me dad threw me out, when I – well, when I knew Mamie was on the way, and I was staying with me friend, only she – she copped it last night. And all 'er three kids.'

She promptly burst into tears; Mamie joined in, the congealed snot on her face blending with fresh. Florence reached for a handkerchief in her bag, wiped the small face tenderly. 'You go and sit down over there,' she said. 'I'll bring you another cup of tea and see what I can do.'

At the end of a long morning they had found billets for everybody; everybody that is except a girl with a small khaki baby.

Florence looked at the girl, and thought hard. Nanny Baines was finding Imogen increasingly hard to cope with; she complained a lot and needed a break. The Priory was dirty and unkempt, Cook had gone into more or less permanent retirement. The baby would amuse Imogen.

'How would you like,' she said, 'to come and stay with me? Just for a few weeks?'

'Dunno,' said the girl. 'What's the deal? What's it going to cost?'

'The deal is you help in the house and look after my little girl while I'm doing this job. Five days a week, that is. It won't cost you anything at all. Only I won't be able to pay you much either. You can have a nice big room, and we've got a very pretty garden – oh, and you'll have to be nice to my mother. She's a bit difficult.'

The girl looked at her and grinned suddenly; she had a very nice grin, wide and full of humour.

'She can't be worse than mine,' she said.

Putting the girl, whose name was Jeannette – 'with an *e*, Jeanette Macdonald I was named after – ' into the car with Mamie, Florence was suddenly overcome with panic. It wasn't like her to act so impulsively, she didn't know anything about Jeannette, she might have a criminal record for all she knew, Mamie might be a nightmare and cry all the time, and Muriel would undoubtedly have a fit. Well, it was too late now, she thought, she had made it very plain that it was only for a few weeks, and it would be nice for Imogen to have some company. And there was a war on after all.

'I've just got to go and see my solicitor,' she said to Jeannette, 'on the way home. It shouldn't take long.'

'We can write again,' said Mr Dodds, 'reaffirming your intent to request a divorce from him. But you see, you are asking him to divorce you. He may well continue to refuse.'

'Yes.'

'I had understood you to say, Mrs Grieg, that *he* wished to divorce *you*.'

'Yes,' said Florence, 'yes, well, I thought he did.'

'You seem to have misread the situation. Now it is clearly within his rights to refuse. If he were to be the plaintiff that would be a different matter. Is there no evidence of grounds on Major Grieg's part?'

He was looking, for him, quite animated: he was visibly gaining in enthusiasm for his task. He probably wasn't used to cases of such complexity, Florence thought; and of course his fee must be escalating nicely. She sighed and said slowly, 'No. No, not really.'

'Mrs Grieg – ' He hesitated. 'Mrs Grieg, I really must stress how important it is for you to tell me everything. It may be that with further information at my disposal I will be able to suggest another approach. And of course' – he cleared his throat – 'anything between us is totally confidential.'

He looked at her earnestly, then, as she met his gaze, blushed slightly. 'There is no need to feel embarrassed in any way, Mrs Grieg. There is very little that would surprise or shock me, anyone indeed in the legal profession, I do assure you.'

Good Lord, thought Florence, he thinks Robert's some kind of pervert. That he's queer, or dresses up in women's clothes. The thought made her smile.

Then she realized that Mr Dodds was actually right, and that Robert was indeed a pervert. But of oh so much more dangerous a kind. The kind that could come back, find her, haunt her for the rest of her life, if she spoke out, had him damned in court, wrecked his professional career. She couldn't do that; it was too dangerous. He would come and find her and take his revenge. On her and Imogen. Wherever they were.

'No,' she said, 'no, there's nothing I haven't told you.'

Muriel was appalled by the arrival of Jeannette and Mamie. 'I'm sorry,

Florence,' she said, 'I'm simply not prepared to put up with it. It's one thing Grace filling Charles's house with riffraff, and quite another for you to do it in mine. The girl can stay tonight if she has to, but she must leave in the morning.'

Imogen burst into the room, beaming, holding an indignantly struggling Mamie to her small chest. 'Baby's done a poo,' she said, 'on the floor.'

'I think I'm going to be ill,' said Muriel.

'My mother's going to have supper in her room,' said Florence. 'She's feeling very tired.'

'Doesn't want to 'ave to sit at a table with me, more likely,' said Jeannette cheerfully. 'That little girl of yours isn't 'alf bright. Fancy knowing the words of all them songs at 'er age. And being able to count – right up to eighty-four she got.'

Any qualms Florence might have had about the wisdom of taking Jeannette in were immediately banished.

She took Muriel's supper tray up, knocked gently on the door and set it by her bed.

'I really don't want it,' said Muriel, 'whatever it is. I feel much too upset.'

'It's some soup,' said Florence, 'that Jeannette made. Goodness knows what with, but she rummaged round and – well, it smells a lot better than anything Cook ever made.'

'I might have a sip,' said Muriel, 'but I'm sure it's not very nice, these people just don't know the meaning of decent food.'

'Not like Cook, you mean,' said Florence.

When she went back for the tray the soup bowl was empty.

'It was lovely,' she said to Jeannette, helping herself to more soup. 'What was in it?'

'Potatoes mostly. And some bits and pieces. Yeah, well, I like cooking. Me mum worked in the kitchen at the Savoy,' she added, 'till she got sacked.'

'What did she get sacked for?' asked Florence nervously.

'Nicking things.'

'I think it might be better,' said Florence, 'if you didn't mention that to my mother.'

Mamie didn't cry all night, she didn't cry at all, and Florence came down to breakfast to the smell of fresh bread.

'Put some to rise,' said Jeannette, 'found some yeast. Much nicer than that national loaf rubbish. Tastes like smelly feet, national loaf does.'

After three days of delicious soups, vegetable casseroles and near-miracle omelettes made from a mixture of dried and fresh egg, Muriel said rather grudgingly that Jeannette could stay until the end of the month, 'as long as Cook doesn't mind.'

Florence didn't report Cook's actual words on the subject which were to the effect that if she never saw Mrs Bennett again until Judgment Day it wouldn't be too long for her.

'Do you suppose,' said Grace to Clifford one evening, a week or so later, 'that Charles left a will? If so, I ought to see it. I don't know much about all this sort of thing, but I do know there are various things that have to be sorted out, probate and so on. I'm not a bank manager's daughter for nothing.'

'I'm quite sure he did,' said Clifford. 'Most unlike a solicitor not to leave everything in apple-pie order.'

'Well, I've looked in all the obvious places, his desk and so on. Where do you think it might be?'

'Probably at the bank, or lodged with another solicitor. Maybe even up at the Priory. I'm – well, I'm going up there tomorrow for a short while. Muriel's having a bit of trouble with the garden. I could have a look in his old files there if you like.'

His expression was carefully blank, he didn't meet her eye; Grace said how kind that would be, but fled to the phone when he went out for a walk, made Florence promise to report back the following day. Florence did: 'Sitting in the garden, like an old married couple they were. Mother looking disapproving and knitting rather pointedly, Daddy asking her help with crossword clues. Heaven, as Clarissa would say.'

'It is heaven,' said Grace, thinking that if Charles's death could accomplish what had hitherto seemed impossible, the reunion of two lonely unhappy old people, then it had not, after all, been entirely in vain.

Clifford had found the will: perfectly straightforward, everything left to Grace, the house, all his assets. She was, he told her, a woman of some substance, of independent means; Grace, trying to adjust to that thought, felt more guilty about Ben than ever. Guilty and wretchedly depressed.

She hadn't heard from him for weeks; had decided he must have been posted somewhere completely different, or worse, was uncertain himself what to do; every morning she waited, feigning disinterest, pretending even to herself, for the postman; every morning she took the letters, riffled through them, pretending her hand wasn't shaking, put them down on the hall table, went upstairs to her bedroom and gazed blankly out, every day her heart lower, heavier, out onto the drive where she had first set eyes on him, easing his long, rangy body out of the jeep, wondering if she was ever to see him there again. She told herself she was being absurd, ridiculous, there was a war on, and that war was at a stage where every shred, every atom of available human endeavour was engaged in fighting it; that letters were held up for weeks, were censored, possibly never arrived at all, but it didn't really help; the daily torture continued.

And then finally one morning, when she had given up all hope, one morning when everything went wrong, when she overslept and woke up with a headache, when David spilt tea on his homework and Daniel remembered he had football even as Flossie was observed munching her way contentedly through his shorts, when Clifford asked her three times if she felt all right, told her she was looking very peaky, when Muriel phoned and insisted she spoke to Florence about Jeannette, when Mrs Lacey wrote to say there had been three complaints about a land girl she had been staunchly defending, when she glanced in the mirror and saw that not only did her hair need washing, but she had a pimple right on the end of her nose, when Florence dropped by on her way to work to ask could she possibly take a delivery of several dozen old blankets and wash them for her, when the postman hadn't been at all, never mind bring a letter from Ben – suddenly there was a crunch of tyres in the drive and she stood up and knocked her tea all over her toast, the last slice in the loaf. 'If,' she said, 'if that is those wretched WVS blankets, arriving already, I'll – '

And then she stopped, and Clifford watching her saw her turn first glassy pale, then bright pink; and he got up, walked over to the window himself, and there in the drive was a jeep, and out of it appeared a very long leg, and then –

'Ben!' said Grace, her voice shaky, quiet, and then, more loudly, 'It's Ben!' and she was gone, flying into the hall, out of the front door, into his arms, and they stood there entangled, the pair of them, she on tiptoe, his head bent low over her, his mouth buried in her hair, her face in his chest, her body pressed against his.

'Good gracious,' said Clifford, looking at the two of them with some indulgence, 'Good gracious. So I was right.'

He greeted Ben charmingly, graciously ('And it couldn't have been easy for him,' said Grace later. 'He must have felt some jealousy and reservations about you'), then said he felt like a walk, and he would meet the boys from school, tell them the news.

'Why were you so long?' she said, looking up at him, from the depths of her happiness. 'Why didn't you ring at least? What happened? I was so frightened, so terribly worried – '

'I didn't get your letter,' he said, 'not until two days ago. I've been all over the place, and then I had to lie to get away, I said Dan was ill again. I can't stay long.'

'How long?' she said, and 'Only till tomorrow,' he said, 'but at least you'll know I love you.' And 'Yes,' she said, 'yes, I'll know you love me. And you'll know I love you too.'

She looked out of the window; the tall figure of Clifford was walking away down the lane. 'Come along,' she said, holding out her hand to him, 'we have a little while now. A little while to show you how much I love you.' And she led him upstairs without a word, into her room, and her bed.

She was never to forget that time; never again, in the whole of her life, did she fly so high, so exquisitely perfectly into pleasure, climbing, reaching, soaring into it, his hands, his mouth, his voice all taking her, carrying her towards it, his body moving through hers, a long, long journey of high brilliant peaks and sweet tumbling valleys, of great raging triumph and slow, gentle peacefulness; of strange wild progressions close, close to the brink, and then again and yet again a drawing back, a gathering towards the next, and then the next and then, yes, surely this time, yes, yes, the tumbling, final release.

'I love you,' he said, after they had lain in the stillness for a while, smiling in something close to astonishment at what they had accomplished, 'I love you so much. More than ever.'

'And I love you,' said Grace, 'more than ever.'

'It can't be very easy,' he said, looking at her consideringly. 'You must feel at least a bit – bad.'

'I do, Ben, I feel more than a bit bad. Guilty and remorseful and quite wicked, quite often. And afraid of what everyone will say, and think. But the thing is, the only person who matters, who would really have been hurt by it, is dead. Safe from it. And he never knew. Thank God. Thank God. And I keep thinking it's wicked to think that, but it's not, not really, well, it might be wicked to think it, but it's not doing him any harm.'

He lay there looking at her, reached out a hand, pushed back a tendril of hair that had fallen over her eyes. 'I think you're perfect,' he said simply, 'quite perfect.'

'Ben, I'm not,' said Grace, laughing at the absurdity of the statement. 'Of course I'm not.' I've got a spot on the end of my nose for a start and my hair needs washing and – '

'For me you are,' he said, 'that's what I meant. I love you however you are. You're perfect for me.'

'You two in love then?' said Daniel.

'Well – yes. Yes, I think we probably are,' said Ben cautiously. He smiled at Grace.

They had come in with Clifford, haring into the house, hurling themselves at him; they all had tea in the garden, for it was hot, really hot for May, and then Ben and Grace had sat on the bench, outside the French windows, his arm round her shoulders, smiling at them slightly foolishly.

'Yuk,' said Daniel. 'Like David and Elspeth. Yuk.'

David was very quiet. Grace looked at him; Ben followed her eyes, saw it too.

After a bit, he said, 'Dave, d'you want to come for a walk?'

'Not specially,' said David briefly.

'I would like it. Then we could play football.'

David looked at him rather distantly. 'OK.'

'I'll come,' said Daniel.

'You've got to come with me up to the Priory,' said Grace firmly.

'Not the Priory,' said Daniel, 'not to see Imogen!'

'Well, she might be there. But Jeannette wants some help. She rang up. Skinning a rabbit.'

Daniel brightened. Skinning rabbits was one of his proudest accomplishments. 'OK, then. Sir Clifford, what are you going to do?'

'I have an appointment up there too,' said Clifford, 'with some blackfly.' He winked at Grace.

Ben and David walked across the field in silence. Then Ben said, 'So it's the grammar school in September?'

'Yup.'

'Well done. Looking forward to it?'

He shrugged. 'S'pose so.'

'Good lad. I'm proud of you.

'Yeah, well.'

'How's the music?'

'OK.'

'Want to learn something else at school? You could probably learn the fiddle, like your granddad.'

He shrugged again. 'Dunno. Might.'

'David.'

'What?'

'David, look at me.'

David looked at him, and Ben saw hurt, deep hostility in his eyes.

'What is it? Is it Grace? Grace and me?'

'No.'

'It is, isn't it?'

There was a silence. Then he said, all in a rush, 'I don't know how you could. You were supposed to love Mum. What do you think she'd say, if she knew?'

'I think,' said Ben with great care, 'I think she'd say she was glad.'

'Why? What's there to be glad about?'

'That I'm not lonely any more.'

'Are you lonely?'

'Yes, of course I was. It's been not so bad for you, you've had Grace to love you and look after you. I didn't have anyone.'

'But you loved Mum. How could you forget her?'

'David, have you forgotten her?'

'Course not.'

'Well then, there you are. Neither have I. I haven't forgotten anything about her. I can remember how she looked, and how pretty she was, how she made us laugh, and how she used to boss us all about, and the nice meals she cooked us, and how she got cross with Nan, and with us, come to that, and how much she loved us. I haven't forgotten anything. Honest.'

David didn't say anything. His eyes, looking determinedly ahead of him, were blank.

'She was a very special person, Mum was,' said Ben. 'We were lucky to have her. But now she's gone. She's been gone a long time. We can't get her back.'

David sat down suddenly and buried his head in his skinny arms. 'I miss her,' he said, his voice muffled, 'I still miss her. I do. I want to tell her things. I wanted to tell her when I got the scholarship and when we won the football league, and I wanted to show her how I trained the puppies and taught Imogen to play "Three Blind Mice".'

'So do I,' said Ben, gently, sitting down beside him, taking him in his arms, 'I still miss her too. I don't love Grace instead of her. I love her as well. I know it seems hard to understand but it's true. And Mum would have liked Grace, wouldn't she? She'd have liked her very much.'

'Yeah,' said David, slightly reluctantly. 'I s'pose so. Yeah.'

There was a long silence, then he looked up at his father. 'You going to marry her then? Marry Grace?'

'Maybe,' said Ben. 'Maybe, one day. If that'd be all right.'

There was another silence. Then David said, 'Yeah, I s'pose so.' He grinned rather sheepishly at his father. 'Yeah, that'd be all right.'

Chapter Twenty-Five

Early Summer 1944

It was an incredibly beautiful early summer. The days grew warm and golden, and everyone said it was an omen, that the war must soon finally be over. Spirits rose, people stopped complaining about shortages and deprivation. Grace moved through the lovely days, happier than she could ever remember, her head full of half-formed plans, struggling to keep the future carefully blank. Ben was at Tidworth and did not know when he would be given leave again. In a strange way that suited her; she was almost glad not to see him. He loved her and she loved him; for the time being that must be enough. She was not ready to move forward; she was still confused, still guilty, still to her surprise grieving for Charles. They had, if nothing else, time; she had to take it and use it with care.

Happiness seemed to her to be everywhere: Clifford was noisily busy, whistling and singing through the days – 'Honestly, it's like living with the Seven Dwarfs,' said Grace, laughing, to Florence one day – and spending an increasing amount of time at the Priory. He had, as he had threatened to do, joined the church choir, was on the organ rota, and had become a rather belated and unnecessary recruit to the Home Guard. He got up early every day to do the garden at the Mill House before mounting his rickety old bicycle and pedalling over to Thorpe Magna and Muriel. He often stayed for lunch, and even once or twice for supper, although lured quite as much, Florence said, by Jeannette's cooking as Muriel's charms. And Florence herself was uncharacteristically serene, staunchly pursuing her divorce, her frequently waning courage bolstered by almost daily love letters from Giles. She – or rather Mr Dodds the solicitor – had sent yet another letter to Robert, reaffirming her wish for him to divorce her. At least this time he hadn't written to refuse. Perhaps he had finally got the idea.

She was working longer and longer hours for the WVS, her domestic responsibilities almost entirely taken over by Jeannette; Mrs Haverford frequently said she couldn't imagine how they had managed without her. She was enchanted herself, by her own newly discovered organizational skills; she now talked as endlessly and passionately about her work as she did about Imogen. She could not envisage a return to the old life, of dinner parties and domesticity; her plans for herself were varied, ranging from politics to industrial management, but ambitious in the extreme. Like Grace, she shied away from anything but the haziest thoughts about her personal future; like Grace she saw it as forbidden territory. The present was occupation enough.

Clarissa was too busy to think at all, a fact for which she was profoundly grateful. Dartmouth was a restricted area, and nobody was allowed to leave or enter it except on official naval business. The town by now was so full that it was, she said to Jack in a rare conversation one night, like being permanently on the tube in the rush hour: 'Americans are just sitting on the pavements, all over the town, waiting to embark. And thousands of bored, homesick soldiers, all desperate for something to do. One feels so sorry for them, darling.'

'Just keep it that way,' said Jack, 'I don't want you easing their homesickness.'

There had been an appalling casualty at the end of April at Slapton Sands: some American ships, on an exercise simulating the Normandy landings, were attacked by German E-boats. Hundreds of men were killed or seriously injured; in the following days pubs and dance halls in the town were hushed by a grief and shock no one could openly acknowledge. Such was the intense security that anyone revealing what had happened, even the medical staff treating the men, was subject to court-martial.

In so strangely nightmarish a world, her anxieties, her fear for Jack and his safety seemed comparatively easy to contain.

The Maypole dance at the school May Fayre, to take place at the Whitsun bank holiday was difficult and causing problems to the children. 'It's difficult but not impossible,' said Miss Merton firmly, 'and if they could do it two hundred years ago or whatever, I don't see why we can't do it now.'

Grace could, but she had agreed to find a suitable piece of music and to play for the event; it made a welcome distraction from fretful land girls and bad-tempered farmers. The more she worked with the children, the more she loved it; one of her few positive – and she felt sound – plans for the future was to start some kind of music school.

Grace and Miss Merton were near to despair. It was Wednesday, the

May Fayre was on the Saturday, only three children had really mastered the intricacies of the Maypole dance, and that was no good at all, as Miss Merton said. They all had to get it right. Miss Merton was by this stage of half a mind to cut it out of the programme altogether, but its fame had spread and the local newspaper was coming specifically to photograph it.

'We'll be a laughing stock,' moaned Miss Merton. She was sitting at her desk after the latest disastrous rehearsal, her face with its multiple chins drooping with misery. She looked like a huge bloodhound. 'We'll just have to abandon it.'

'No we won't,' said Grace firmly. 'We'll get it right. I know we can. We'll just have to pack in some extra rehearsals after school. Starting tomorrow. Don't despair, Miss Merton. Think of – well, think of Winston Churchill.'

'I think I'd rather have the Germans,' said Miss Merton. 'At least they do what Hitler tells them.'

In Scotland Major Robert Grieg had asked for an emergency interview with his CO.

'I'm sorry to ask you, sir, but I desperately need a twenty-four-hour pass. My wife is not at all well, may have to go into hospital. It's – well, it's a woman's thing, sir. I wondered if – '

'Yes, yes. I should think that could be arranged, Major Grieg. Take forty-eight if it'd help. Pretty quiet for a few days now, I should think. Before the move. You've done a fine job. Sorry to hear about your wife.'

'Thank you, sir.'

Robert arranged for a travel warrant for the next day, and then made a phone call to a friend in London. 'I need a car and some petrol tomorrow, Bertie, and I don't care how much it costs. Got to get down to Wiltshire first thing, to see my wife. Got any strings you can pull?'

'Robert! When did I not have any?'

'Jeannette,' said Florence the next morning, 'I'm going now. I won't be back till teatime, probably later. I'm on late shift at the canteen. Is that all right?'

'All the same if it's not,' said Jeannette cheerfully. 'What about you, Mrs B? You busy today?'

'I am as a matter of fact,' said Muriel coldly. She had made it very plain on several occasions to Jeannette that she didn't like being called Mrs B, but it had had little effect.

'Suits you,' Jeannette had said. 'My old gran was known to the whole street as Mrs B. You remind me of her, you know.' Muriel had closed her eyes in an expression of immense pain.

'So you'll be on your own, Jeannette,' said Florence. 'If there are any problems, any problems at all, just ring Grace, at the Mill House, all right? Oh and there's a rehearsal of the Maypole dance this afternoon, you know she's persuaded me to let Imogen be in it. So could you take her down to the school at three o'clock?'

'Yeah, OK. What you doin' then, Mrs B? Imogen, say ta if you want some more.'

'Ta,' said Imogen.

'Good girl.'

'The word is thank you, Imogen,' said Muriel. 'I'm doing the flowers at the church, Jeannette. I shall be there most of the day. Whitsun is a very important Christian festival you know,' she added, as if Jeannette was from some primitive country that news of Christianity had not yet reached.

'Yeah, I 'ad 'eard. Imogen, take Mamie outside. But not near the pond, mind.'

'Clifford,' said Grace, 'we're going to rehearse the Maypole dance this afternoon, at the school. Do you want to come? I could do with a deputy pianist and Miss Merton's going to need some help with the choreography. Jeannette's bringing the little ones down, Florence has twisted my arm to let Imogen be in it. It'll be so sweet. At least,' she added, 'if Miss Merton doesn't have a heart attack it'll be sweet.'

'What a charming idea. Yes, I'd love to.'

'Good. Perhaps we could go over early, at lunchtime, so you could run through the music.'

'Absolutely fine by me.'

'And who's going to be doing her awful drippy singing by the Maypole then? And who'll be watching her with a yukky stupid face on? Yuk!'

'Be quiet, Daniel, at once. Now go and wash your face. And you, David. You both look as if you've been dragged through a hedge backwards.'

'I have,' said Daniel, 'only because I said about Elspeth being such a – Ow! David, stop it. Ow!'

Jeannette was upstairs cleaning the bathroom when she heard the car in the drive. She looked out of the window. It was quite a big one: someone must have money.

A man got out of it, wearing uniform. Officer's uniform. He looked up at the house, then walked to the door and rang the bell. Jeannette went down and opened it.

'Good morning,' he said, taking his hat off, smiling at her. He was very good-looking in a sort of foreignish way. Bit too dark for her taste, but still.

'Mornin',' she said.

'Is Mrs Grieg here?'

'No, she isn't. Off with the WVS.'

'Oh yes of course, how stupid of me. When will she be back?'

'Not till late.'

'Oh,' he said, 'oh dear.'

'Why?'

'Well, I thought – oh well. She's obviously forgotten.'

'Forgotten what?'

'An arrangement we had. Damn. Is Mrs Bennett here? Or is she' – he looked at his watch – 'yes, she would be.'

'Would be what?'

'Resting.'

'You seem to know a lot about her,' said Jeannette.

'Yes, well, I'm her son-in-law. Major Grieg. Mrs Grieg's husband. Sorry, I should have introduced myself. And you are?'

'My name's Jeannette. Jeannette Marks. I look after Imogen and the house and that. I do recognize you,' she added, 'from the photo in Mrs B's room.'

'Oh really? Is that a new idea – you looking after Imogen? Where is Miss Baines?'

'Over at 'ers I suppose,' said Jeannette. 'She couldn't cope no more, Imogen being so into everything and that.'

'Well, this is very difficult,' said Major Grieg. 'I can't believe my wife didn't tell you.'

'Tell me what?'

'That I was to collect Imogen this afternoon. Take her to tea with my mother.'

'No, she didn't. Where is she then? Your mother?'

'Oh – not far away. She's staying with a friend, over the other side of Salisbury. Oh dear. It's her birthday, you see. It was going to be such a treat for her, seeing Imogen.'

'Yeah, well, it would be nice, I can see that.'

Imogen and Mamie suddenly appeared round the house, Mamie in

Imogen's wooden wheelbarrow. Her small brown face and arms were coated liberally in green slime; she was crying.

'Imogen!' said Jeannette. 'Imogen, what you done to 'er?'

'She fell in the pond,' said Imogen.

'Imogen, I told you not to go near the pond. Really. What will your dad think?'

'Hallo, Imogen darling,' said Robert, bending down, trying to kiss Imogen's face. She turned away. 'It's so sad,' he said. 'She's seen me about three times in three years. That's what the war's done to families. What about your husband?'

''aven't married 'im yet,' said Jeannette briefly.

'I see. Well now, look. I don't suppose you'd let me take Imogen, would you? I'd only be a couple of hours. She'd be back before Florence – before my wife gets home.'

'Well, I don't know,' said Jeannette. 'I ought to ask.'

'Oh really! I am her father. Do you want to see proof of my identity or something?'

He looked hurt, upset; then he said, 'But if you want to check – I mean, that would be quite the proper thing to do.'

'I could, I s'pose. But I don't know who with. Mrs G, she's never where I can get 'er. I'm s'posed to be taking them down to the other village, do some dance or other this afternoon. But Mamie don't look too much in the dancing mood – '

She looked at Mamie, who was still screaming. She could quite do with a couple of hours' peace, she didn't really fancy the five-mile round trip to Thorpe Magna and back. 'Tell you what,' she said, 'I'll just check with young Mrs B. She'll know if it's all right. To miss the dancing and that.'

'Oh – all right. Fine. I'll keep Imogen here, shall I, and then you can take your little one with you?'

'Yeah, OK.'

Mrs Boscombe was just telling her that everyone at the Mill House was out, they were all down at the school, when she heard the car engine start; alarmed, she ran out, but he was still sitting there, Imogen beside him, smiling. She loved cars.

'Going driving,' she said. 'Broom-broom.'

'Mrs Bennett's not there,' said Jeannette. 'They're all at the school, down at Lower Thorpe.'

'Well look,' he said, 'I tell you what, just so you're not worried. I'll go that way, check with Grace that Imogen's not needed. Then I'll take her over to my mother. And have her back by – what? – half past four? That be all right?'

'Yeah,' said Jeannette, 'yeah, fine. Mamie, do shut your face. I'm just coming.'

He moved off quite slowly, with a wave and a smile. Imogen's small blonde head appeared out of the window.

'Bye-bye' she said, 'broom-broom.'

She'll be all right, thought Jeannette. She'll be perfectly all right. He is her father after all.

'Jeannette's very late,' said Grace, 'we'll have to start without her. Well, Imogen was never going to be anything but a nuisance, I'm afraid. At least I'll have an excuse not to include her in the actual thing. She really didn't have a clue.'

The rehearsal was as much a disaster as ever; the children all went the wrong way at the wrong time, and the ribbons at the top of the pole more closely resembled a tangled skein of wool than a neatly woven plait.

'Never mind,' said Miss Merton, philosophical in her despair. 'You know what they say about bad dress rehearsals. It'll be all right on Whit Monday, I'm sure. Elspeth dear, that was lovely. David, would you help Elspeth with those ribbons please? Daniel, are you all right, dear?' Daniel was making loud being-sick noises behind the piano.

'Well-earned cup of tea, I think,' said Miss Merton. 'I'll put the kettle on in the staff room. Mr Bennett, would you join us?'

'Delighted,' said Clifford. 'Most kind. Let me help with those ribbons, David. You have a very lovely voice, my dear,' he said to Elspeth. 'A great gift. I've heard all about your musical prowess from young David here.'

David went scarlet; there were further vomit noises in the background from Daniel.

'Well, let's have this tea then,' said Grace. 'Goodness, it's almost five. And then we must get back. I wonder what did happen to Imogen. Maybe Jeannette just couldn't face the walk.'

'Where's Imogen?' said Muriel.

'With 'er gran,' said Jeannette, 'and 'er dad.'

'With whom?'

'I told you, with 'er gran.'

'Her grandmother is up in the North of England.'

'Not today she's not,' said Jeannette. 'She's in Salisbury.'

'How extraordinary. And what did you say about her father?'

''er father came to get 'er,' said Jeannette patiently, with only a slightly anxious glance at the clock, which now read 4.45, 'to 'ave tea with 'er gran.'

'But Robert's mother never comes down here,' said Muriel. 'There must be some mistake.'

'Yeah, well, 'e was very clear about it. Said she was staying with a friend. Said it was 'er birthday.'

'Oh,' said Muriel uncertainly. 'Well Florence certainly didn't know about it. I do hope – Are you sure it was her father? Major Grieg?'

'Oh yeah. I recognized 'im from the picture in your room,' said Jeannette. ''e was very nice. And Imogen definitely seemed to know 'im. Said they'd be back by four thirty.'

'It was very wrong of you,' said Muriel severely, 'to let her go. But I expect it will be perfectly all right. Perfectly all right. Major Grieg is a charming man.'

'Yeah,' said Jeannette.

The small party were halfway up the lane in the soft spring evening when Florence's car came screeching down the hill; she leapt out of it, rushed at them, clutched Grace's arm as if she was drowning.

'Grace, Grace,' she said, 'Oh Grace, have you seen Imogen?'

'No,' said Grace, 'no, we haven't. They never turned up. I'm sorry, Florence, we – '

'Robert didn't bring her down?'

'Robert! No, of course not. Florence, what on earth is it? What's happened?'

'Robert's got her,' said Florence, bursting into hysterical sobs. 'He's got her, Grace, he's taken her, and I know why, it's to stop me divorcing him, keep me with him always. What am I going to do, Grace, what am I going to do?'

'Oh God,' said Grace. 'Florence, surely, surely he wouldn't – '

'Of course he would,' said Florence. Her voice rose in a loud wail. 'It's exactly the sort of thing he'd do.'

'Well, look. Try to calm down. You're not helping Imogen like that. Come to the Mill House, we'll phone the police.'

'No no, I must get back. Just in case there's any news. Please, please ring at once, won't you, if you hear anything.'

She hurled herself back into the car, wrenching at the wheel, turned it round and roared back up the lane.

'She shouldn't be driving,' said Clifford, 'not in that state. She's not safe.'

Florence's main emotion was one of sheer disbelief that she could have been so stupid. Leaving Imogen with anyone, anyone at all, not making sure that she was safe, not at the very least warning Jeannette that there was a danger such a thing might happen. She should have stayed with her, all the time, instead of haring round Wiltshire feeling important with the WVS. What on earth would Giles say, what would everyone say, when they heard she'd been kidnapped?

And then another thought struck her, so awful, so hideous that panic rose up and literally blinded her and she had to stop the car. Why should Robert stop at kidnapping Imogen? Suppose he beat her up – or worse? It was not unlikely. He was perfectly capable of it, mad enough. He couldn't possibly believe she was really his child, he must see her as living proof of Florence's infidelity, he must quite literally loathe the sight of her. Suppose, even now, he was hitting her, hurting her; Imogen was absolutely defenceless, so tiny and vulnerable, there would be nothing at all that she would be able to do. A vision rose before Florence's eyes of Imogen's small blonde head hit, knocked from side to side, her great blue eyes wide with hopeless, helpless terror, her little body lying on the ground, broken, kicked repeatedly. She fell out of the car, vomiting repeatedly into the hedge.

'Florence? Florence, what on earth is the matter? Are you all right?' It was Robert's voice. Florence turned round, very slowly, sure she must be hallucinating, and saw him sitting at the wheel of a large car, an Austin, she thought confusedly, as if it mattered, smiling at her. He was alone.

'Robert,' screamed Florence, 'Robert, where is Imogen? What have you done with her?'

'Florence darling, do calm down. I took her to have tea with my mother and her friend. She's still with them as a matter of fact. I explained it most carefully to that ghastly woman at the house. Who I really don't think, incidentally, is a very suitable person to take charge of my daughter.'

'Where? Your mother's in Yorkshire. What friend? Where is she? I want her back now, now, Robert, at once.'

'This is ridiculous,' said Robert. He still sounded very calm, was still smiling easily at her. 'She's only in Salisbury, with two extremely respectable old ladies. You can ring them the minute we get back to the Priory. I'm sorry I was a bit late back, but Imogen was having such a nice time I thought I'd leave her there for a bit. Shall I drive you back? You look absolutely terrible.'

Florence drove very slowly back to the Priory, following Robert. She could hardly see for a thick, suffocating fear; it was exactly like being in a nightmare.

Muriel was waiting on the doorstep. 'Thank goodness he found you,' she said, 'so absurd, rushing off like that, Florence.'

'I need the phone – I want to speak to Imogen.'

'Florence, she's fine,' said Robert. 'How many more times do I have to tell you?'

'I want to speak to her.'

'You can in a minute. Come in here.' He half pushed her into the drawing room; Muriel with a rare and most unwelcome tact had disappeared. 'Sit down,' said Robert, 'You look terrible. Let me get you a drink.'

'I don't want a drink.'

Robert looked at her with an extraordinary blend of distaste and pity. 'I think you do.' He moved over to the sideboard, found a bottle of sherry, poured her a glass. 'Drink it.'

'Robert, I don't want it.'

'Drink it, Florence.'

Florence drank it. He sat watching her. 'Now,' he said, very quietly. 'Now then, Florence. We need to have a little talk.'

The familiar crawl of icy fear crept up Florence's spine. She swallowed, gripped the empty glass. 'Robert – '

'Be quiet. Listen to me. Very carefully. I do not, I repeat not, want a divorce. You are my wife, I want you to remain that way. I want this whole wretched, absurd business dropped. Do you understand?'

She was silent, staring at him.

'Once you've accepted that, everything will be very much better. Won't it? Florence, I said won't it?'

Florence nodded. 'Yes,' she said, her voice weak, croaky.

'So I want you to sit down now and write to that absurd solicitor of yours and tell him the whole matter is closed. All right?'

'Yes. Yes, all right, Robert.' She felt exhausted, deathly weary.

'I'd like you to do it now. I've put some paper and envelopes out for you. Over there. On the desk.'

Florence got up, walked over to the desk, sat down heavily.

'There are a couple more things,' said Robert.

'Yes?'

'I don't like the idea of that girl looking after my daughter. Not at all. She seems grotesquely unsuitable to me. Your mother agrees with me. I want her out of this house, within the week. All right?'

'Yes,' said Florence, hating, despising herself.

'Good. I shall look forward to hearing she's gone. Your mother has promised to let me know.'

'Can I speak to Imogen now?'

'When you've written the letter and given it to me.'

When she had finished she looked at him. 'Anything else?'

'Not really. No. I'll telephone my mother and her friend, you can speak to them and to Imogen, and then I'll go and collect her.'

'I'll collect her,' said Florence furiously. 'If you think I'm – '

'Oh no,' he said, 'I'll bring her back. What on earth do you think I'm going to do, run off with her or something? How absurd you are. No, I feel much happier about everything now. Of course if I heard anything, anything at all that might indicate you were not being entirely loyal and supportive over the next few months – well, who knows? It hasn't been very difficult, borrowing her for a few hours. I might easily want to do it again. For a bit longer even. Sweet little thing. I find myself surprisingly fond of her. Surprisingly. And I would like to think we'll have some more children, after the war. You and I.'

She spoke to Imogen; she sounded cheerful, excited even; Robert left and was back within the hour. Imogen rushed in. 'Went driving,' she said, 'went driving in Daddy's car.'

Florence sat holding her, hugging her for a long time. Then, when she had put her to bed, she sat down and wrote to Giles. She knew when she was beaten.

Chapter Twenty-Six

June 1944

Major Robert Grieg, who had been involved in a mission of the utmost secrecy and importance for many months, was finally to be granted his frequently expressed wish for a return to active service. He was to travel with his unit to the Isle of Wight for final training and to prepare for embarkation early in June for a destination unknown. The details were secret but the broad picture was well known, widely anticipated. It was truly the beginning of the end of the war, the final trouncing of Hitler's army, the Allied invasion of France on a vast scale.

Lieutenant-Commander Giles Henry was on his ship, waiting for orders for his own departure for France in an agony of impatience. His depression was such, after receiving a letter from Florence telling him she no longer loved him, wanted never to see him again, had decided finally to stay with Robert, that he could not imagine that anything fate might throw at him, death included, could be anything but welcome.

Squadron Leader Jack Compton Brown was in his beloved Spitfire again, riding the deadly skies on target support missions, paving the way for the great invasion of Normandy. He found himself in mortal danger, day after day, in the direct line of fire from German aircraft. It was all he had dreamt of, longed for, pushed himself for in the long months in hospital. He was joyfully triumphant; he had won his own war.

Clarissa, awaking on 6 June to the eerie emptiness of Dartmouth Harbour, having grown accustomed over the previous months to seeing it filled so tightly with all manner of ships and landing craft it seemed impossible that it could accommodate even a dinghy more, and hearing the endless roar of aircraft overhead, sent up a small fervent prayer for Jack, and then became caught up in a spiral of work so intense, so absorbing, she ceased to notice hunger, thirst, weariness, until waking one night on the lavatory, she realized she had been there fast asleep for over an hour. She was grateful for it, grateful for the work; it crushed the fear.

The departure of the ships had taken place over several days; people had waved them off from balconies, windows, offices, knowing where they were going, what lay ahead, not saying so to each other, to anybody. Years later, when she told an American she had been there that day, his eyes filled with tears as he told her how a group of Wrens had signalled Goodbye and Good Luck in semaphore as they left the Dart.

On the morning of the 6th, cold, windy, she heard a great roar from far out to sea. She knew what it meant. The invasion had actually begun.

Ships came in endlessly through the weeks for fresh supplies, ammunition, tanks, troops, bringing the wounded who had then to be taken on to hospitals. The casualties were legion.

The Wrens formed a cohesive part of the infrastructure of the operation: drivers, riders, cooks, telegraphers, coders, plotters, and the boatscrews, who buzzed about the packed waters delivering messages, orders and supplies to the ships. Clarissa was plotting herself some of the time, watching awestruck as the great naval invasion bore down the Channel and later sailed up from the Mediterranean.

The triumph was great, but the tragedies profound. She looked at the faces of the young men, many scarcely more than children, some filled with bravado, some with fear, on the nights before they sailed and wanted to weep. She read of the mounting casualties, of the sweep of death in the wake of victory, and wondered again and again where it would end. She only knew it was worth it: it had to be.

Grace, guiltily aware she had nothing personally to fear, felt impotent, set apart from it all. She offered Florence – a gauntly wretched Florence, dark eyes craters of misery in her white face – her help with the WVS, was told shortly that she'd be more trouble than she was worth, that it was a bit late, that she might have thought of it sooner instead of wasting her time with stupid land girls. Grace, knowing the reason for the misery, the wretchedness, having been given a brief résumé of the events of the dreadful day of the kidnapping, accepted this meekly, and busied herself instead making soup for Clifford and the other members of the Home Guard on their night watches. It was hardly vital work but it was something practical she could do.

Jeannette, spared from banishment by the information that Robert was overseas, made soup too, in huge quantities, for Florence to take to the canteen, and played her own small part in the victory effort by boosting the morale of the troops she met in the pubs and bars of Salisbury on her occasional nights off.

Robert Grieg was in Arromanches now, with his men, part of the mighty, almost unimaginable achievement of the construction of the Mulberry harbours, the great floating bridges that were to become one of the most crucial lifelines to the British Army.

Florence was busier than she could ever have imagined, working long days, and sometimes longer nights. Troops poured through the canteen endlessly, en route to Portsmouth and Southampton; trainloads of women and children arrived from London, seeking refuge from the vengeance of the Luftwaffe which it was widely anticipated would follow the invasion. Like Clarissa she became too tired to think or to feel, and was grateful for it. That Robert was actually in France, actually in danger, after being safe for so long, she found oddly disturbing; Grace was not alone in discovering she did not really know herself or her feelings. As for Giles, Florence couldn't believe he would survive: she followed the progress of the ships, on the news, in the papers, knew he must have been involved in the landings, almost certainly in the first most dreadful days when death hovered over and stalked the beaches and the seas, striking haphazardly, pitilessly, taking no hostages.

'Do you think,' said Grace, putting down the paper after reading of the great success of the invasion, of the million Allied troops in Normandy, and also of further fighting, further casualties, the desperately slow progress of the Allies through France, the inevitable claims of victory, 'do you think it's going to be all right?'

'Good Lord yes,' said Clifford. 'Got Hitler on the run now. Don't worry. I shouldn't read that stuff too much if I were you, my darling. Just be thankful you're not up in London. Nasty things, those V2s. Look, I'm going up to the Priory for a bit. Muriel's got a bit of trouble with her roses. Blackfly again. Need urgent treatment.'

He winked at her; Grace smiled back. Only Muriel, at this hour of the nation's greatest drama, could find her blackfly an urgent problem.

'Yes of course. I'll see you later.'

It was a grey, almost misty June day. A good old-fashioned English summer day, she thought, smiling. Almost cold enough to think about lighting a fire. Only there weren't any logs, and she didn't feel quite cold enough to make the effort to go out and chop some. She rummaged through the hooks in the utility room and found a very large, thick old cardigan of Clifford's and huddled into that instead, thinking rather guiltily about Ben, about how happy she was.

The phone rang suddenly; she went out to the hall. And it was Ben. 'You all right my love?' he said.

'I'm perfectly all right. So are the boys.'

'I wanted to tell you I love you. That's all.'

'That's enough,' she said.

'And to say I've got a forty-eight this weekend. I don't suppose you'd have time to see me, would you?'

'Oh no,' she said. 'No time for you, Ben. No time at all.'

He came to Salisbury by train and she met him; they went for a walk, holding hands, and he kissed her a great deal, and then they went home and had tea with the boys, and they all played ludo.

Clifford was up at the Priory, having supper with Muriel. 'He's there a lot now,' said Daniel. 'I think he's going to marry her again.'

'Do you now?' said Ben.

'Yes I do. I think it'd be good too. He's been lonely. It's not nice to be lonely.'

'Too right it isn't,' said Ben.

'Grace gets lonely, don't you, Grace?'

'Mmm – a bit. Sometimes. But not as bad as I did before I had you.'

'You should've had your own boys,' said Daniel. 'Why didn't you?'

'Oh – I don't know,' said Grace quickly. 'It – well, it seemed a bad idea, what with the war and everything.'

'Florence didn't think so.'

'No, well Florence is different from me,' said Grace.

'How? How is she different? Do you mean she likes babies more than you?'

'Dan,' said Ben firmly, 'concentrate on the board, will you? And it's rude to ask personal questions.'

Later he said, laughing, 'Would you like to have your own boys? If – well, if you were married again.'

'I might,' said Grace, 'and then again I might not.'

'Oh,' he said. He looked slightly hurt. She laughed, leant forward and kissed him tenderly. 'I might want my own girls,' she said. 'Too many boys around already.'

'I'd like to have babies with you,' said Ben. 'We can talk about it one day, maybe. But not just yet.'

'No,' said Grace. 'Not just yet.'

She was constantly amazed by how right he got everything.

Next day they climbed the hill. 'This is where I first knew I really wanted you,' she said, 'really badly. When you held my arm, do you remember?'

'Of course I remember,' he said, 'but did that really have that much of an effect on you?'

'Oh yes,' she said. 'I sat here and I could hardly contain myself, I just wanted to take all my clothes off and – well – '

'Good Lord,' he said, laughing, 'what a great bloke I must be. Move over Errol Flynn.'

'Now don't get bigheaded,' said Grace, 'or I shall go off you.'

'Oh Grace,' he said, very serious suddenly, 'as if I could get bigheaded. About someone as lovely as you.'

Just before lunch, Florence appeared in the garden with Imogen. She looked tired and pale, her hair needed washing and the hem of her dress was hanging down; she snapped at everyone, shouted at Imogen and even at one point slapped her. Then she burst into tears. 'How could I have done that?' she said.

Ben passed her his handkerchief, picked up the wailing Imogen and cuddled her. 'Do her good I expect,' he said calmly. 'They need to know grown-ups are a bit dodgy sometimes.'

'Goodness,' said Florence, blowing her nose, 'you're a clever one. As Nanny Baines would say.'

'Not really.'

'It's just that everyone's so bloody happy,' she said, 'it's not fair. You two are happy, and Clarissa and Jack are happy, and now even Mother and Daddy are happy. I can't stand it. I really can't. Grace, don't just sit there looking soppy, go and get me a drink for heaven's sake. Anything'll do, even that foul elderberry stuff you make.'

Grace looked out of the window while she struggled to open a bottle of the wine, and saw Florence talking rather intently to Ben. When she had gone, she asked him what she'd been saying.

'Oh, much the same,' he said. 'She's just bloody miserable. Who

406

could blame her? Locked up with a bastard like that. I still wish I'd cut his balls off that day.'

'Oh Ben, don't. What good would that have done?'

'A lot,' he said grimly. 'You're barmy, the pair of you.'

'You just don't understand,' said Grace. 'He's got her exactly where he wants her. Cornered. Completely cornered. I can't imagine anything worse than that. There being no escape. I think I'd run away.'

'No you wouldn't, love,' he said, reaching out, stroking her arm, 'you wouldn't do anything of the sort. You'd see it through, too. I know you.'

'Well, you may be right,' she said, 'but with luck I won't be put to the test.'

When they went to bed that night, she felt edgy, miserable, dreading his departure, perversely reluctant to make love, to do and be what she knew he wanted her to do and be. 'What's the matter, love?' he said after kissing her a few times. 'What's wrong?'

'I don't know,' she said fretfully, 'I just don't know. I think I'm tired, that's all.'

'Well you might be,' he said, 'but that's not what the problem is. Don't you – don't you want to, Grace? Make love?'

'No,' she said very quietly, 'no I don't. I don't know why, I just don't. I'm sorry.'

'Don't say sorry,' he said, smiling. 'It doesn't matter. Just tell me, next time, that's all.'

'I couldn't,' she said, shocked, 'I couldn't.'

'Why not? That's silly. You're no use to me pretending. I'll wait, I'd much rather. It's hard for you, I suppose, having to switch it on and off to order. Give me a kiss and we'll go to sleep.'

She went to sleep with him curled round the back of her, woke in the darkness wanting him desperately. He was deeply asleep, breathing heavily; cautiously she eased herself away from him, put her hand behind her, felt for him, began to fondle him, very gently. Desire pierced his sleep; he stirred, stretched a little, his penis began to harden. She turned to face him, began to kiss him softly, tenderly, and he awoke to her, began to kiss her sleepily, first her face, then her breasts.

Grace moaned quietly, the longing for him hot, liquid in her; and 'That's more like it,' he said, and she could hear the smile in his voice, 'that's much more like it.' He turned onto his back, and she lay above him, sinking, working onto him, feeling him thrusting upwards deep within her. He pushed her up gently, and she sat astride him, feeling something close to pain, so huge and deep was the pleasure.

It was growing light; she could see him now, his eyes moving over her, loving her, a slight smile on his face, his hands caressing her stomach, and she wished it could last for ever, that moment, when she felt she could actually see love, see it as a great, perfect whole, tangible and abstract, physical and emotional, momentary and eternal.

Before he left, he said, 'I love you so much, Grace, I can't believe it.'

'Nor can I,' she said. 'I mean, I feel the same.'

'That's probably enough for now, isn't it?' he said.

And 'Yes,' she said, 'that's exactly right. It is enough for now. Quite enough.'

It all seemed, she thought, joyfully, guiltily, fearfully, too perfect to be true.

It was 19 June. The most dreadful summer storm in memory, only second to the one that had wrecked the Armada, was raging in France, threatening the precious construction of the Mulberry harbours. Not only the harbours themselves but the men upon them were in deadly danger, clinging to them at times with their bare hands. Waves nine, twelve feet high lashed the bridges for three days and nights; repair work was virtually impossible, although the attempts went on. Small boats, the only ones usable in the circumstances, were run constantly alongside the harbours in the desperate conditions, rescuing the men.

Involved in this mission, displaying a calm, almost humorous courage in the darkness and the screaming wind, Robert Grieg risked his life over and over again.

Chapter Twenty-Seven

Late Summer 1944

Muriel looked at Florence across the breakfast table, her nostrils flaring just slightly in the way that indicated a particularly high level of intent, and said, 'Florence, it really is time.'

'What for, Mother?' said Florence wearily. She had a long day ahead of her and hadn't got home until eight the night before; her head ached, her eyes were sore, and her skin felt tender. She looked at herself briefly in the mirror and thought what a good thing it was that Giles didn't have to see her now, with her gaunt face, sallow, papery skin and dull, stringy hair. He'd leave her anyway.

'For that girl to go. With that child of hers. I've been very patient – '

'Mother, you have not been patient at all. You've enjoyed an enormous number of extremely nice meals, in a beautifully clean house,' said Florence.

'Possibly, yes, and had to put up with an hourly assault on my ears, and to share my home with a runny-nosed guttersnipe who calls me Big Nan,' said Muriel. 'And that's not funny, Florence.'

'I think it's funny,' said Florence, but the twitch at the corners of her mouth that she had not been able to control had gone, suddenly, and she was flushed, her eyes bright. 'I think it's pathetically funny you should think that was something to put up with. Actually. When I think of the real hardship I see every hour of every day. Jeannette is part of this family now, I'm very fond of her, and Imogen loves her. Now I've told her she's got to leave when – well, when she's found somewhere, and until then I will not turn her out onto the street.'

'Florence, that's not quite the point. Is it?'

'I don't know what you mean.'

'I think you do. Robert insists that she goes. Otherwise he threatens to remove Imogen from the house.'

'He can't,' said Florence sharply. 'He's in France in the first place, and in the second, he's got nowhere to take her.'

'His mother would take her. She has written to me and said so.'

'The old bitch!' said Florence. 'How dare she! I hope you told her to take her interfering nose out of our affairs, Mother, and if you didn't I want to know why. And why you didn't tell me this before – '

'Florence, really! It was kindly meant. And that is not the point. Robert is a powerful and strong-willed man – '

'He's a bully,' said Florence briefly.

'So you say. I have seen no evidence of that myself.'

'Mother!' said Florence. 'Mother, really. Why do you think I – '

She stopped. Disloyalty to Robert was going to serve no purpose now. She had to make a life with him for Imogen's sake; had to be positive, had to be brave. It was a bleak, if not terrifying prospect, but there was no alternative.

'Yes, all right,' she said suddenly. 'I'll talk to Jeannette today. Just let me – '

'About what?' said Jeannette, coming into the room. 'If it's them blankets, I can't get them dry in this weather. More tea, Mrs B?'

'No thank you,' said Muriel, infinite chill in her voice. 'It was rather too strong anyway, Jeannette, I do prefer it very pale. I've told you that several times.'

'Sorry,' said Jeannette, 'can't seem to get it to come out of the pot that way. Well, Florence, what was it then? And is it all right if I go out tonight? Ted Miller's asked me to the pictures – '

Ted Miller worked at the farm the other side of Thorpe Magna. He and Jeannette had been going out for over a month now (he taking his turn, albeit unknowingly, with the armed forces) and he was generally seen as a very lucky man. Jeannette was regarded by the locals as the epitome of sophistication with her peroxided curls, bright lipstick and her unrivalled ability to jitterbug, and the existence of Mamie inevitably gave rise to strong rumours of other benefits. These were encouraged by Ted Miller – who had actually been told in no uncertain terms that Jeannette was not letting anyone inside her knickers again without a wedding ring.

'Yes, that'd be fine,' said Florence, 'of course. I'll be back early, but Jeannette, actually what I was going to say was that – well, the thing is, Jeannette, I'm going to have to ask you to – '

'Imogen, give over,' said Jeannette. 'She's tired, they both are, sitting up late last night they were, waiting for you. Tell you what – I'll leave the housework till later, take 'em down to the stream near Grace's place with a picnic, they can 'ave a paddle. Always cheers 'em up, that does. Now come on, Florence, spit it out. I've left Mamie sitting on the jerry, she's got the runs after eating them strawberries, she'll be in with it any minute now – '

'Florence,' said Muriel, 'please! If you don't I will.'

'Will what?' said Jeannette.

'Jeannette,' said Florence, 'I'm going to have to ask you to – '

There was the roar of a motorbike from the lane, footsteps in the drive, a bang on the door.

'I'll go,' she said thankfully.

When she came back into the dining room a minute later, she was paler than ever, her mouth drawn and almost grey. She sat down heavily on one of the chairs, looked at Imogen in silence for a while. Then she said, 'Sorry. It's all right, Jeannette, I didn't want to say anything important. Maybe you'd better take the children straight away. I've got rather a lot to do today, I find.'

'Florence,' said Muriel, 'what on earth is the matter with you?'

'Nothing's the matter with me, Mother,' said Florence, 'but that was a telegram. Robert's been killed.'

She felt terrible; she would not have believed how terrible she felt. Guilt filled her, made her physically sick. She tried to remember the beatings, the pain and the fear, Robert's face as he knocked her head from side to side, the pain of his feet in her stomach, the dreadful grief of losing the baby, the psychological terror he had waged on her since, and she could only think of how she had deceived him, loved, made love with, another man, borne that man's child, how she had told her mother Robert was a bully, been about to say more, even as he lay dead.

And he had died a hero, displaying an unbelievable courage, it seemed, was undoubtedly to receive a decoration. He had died in the great storm; later she was to learn that he had been knocked out of the small boat he was in while rescuing his men, lost in the darkness and the waves, untraced for days until his body had been found washed up on the beach several miles away. He had been an inspiration to his men, she was told, a brilliant soldier and an instinctive leader. That made her feel worse, much, much worse, convinced that she was to blame for his behaviour to her, that beneath the flawed creature she had been married to had been a fine, good man. She wondered how he might have thought of her, as he died, this hero, as some faithless creature who had failed him, never been the wife he wanted. She got out the last letter he had written her, and read it again and again, weeping tears of remorse, of self-denigration. He loved her, he had said, he was going off happily, hopefully even, knowing that when it was over they would start again, make a new life. She wondered whether he meant these things, whether he believed them himself, and decided that he did. She had never replied to that letter, nor to any of them; she was a useless, worthless woman who had been a useless, worthless wife. She had married Robert deliberately, cold-bloodedly even, knowing she was not properly in love with him, and she had got her just deserts. She felt no sense of relief, no thought that the nightmare that had haunted her for so long was over: merely remorse and, extraordinarily, sadness.

'Florence,' said Grace, almost severely, 'you have to stop this.'

'Sorry.'

'You did your best for Robert – '

'No I didn't, I didn't – '

'Florence, you did. He beat you up, for heaven's sake. And you never betrayed him, never told anybody.'

'No, but I had an affair with someone else. Had a baby that wasn't his. That he knew wasn't his – '

'Yes, all right. No one could really blame you – '

'You did. You blamed me.'

Grace stared at her, flushed. 'Yes. Yes I know. I'm sorry. But I didn't understand. I – well, I was wrong. Anyway, you were going back to him, you'd told him, he knew that. He probably died as happy as it was possible for him to be. God only knows what that was. You've just got to stop berating yourself.'

'Yes, all right,' said Florence. 'I know you're right. I'll try. It's just so terrible the guilt. You don't know.'

'But I do,' said Grace. 'I really do know. I still feel it. Even though Charles is – is dead. Honestly.' She looked at Florence. 'I don't think I'll ever be rid of it. It haunts me.'

'But there's one huge difference,' said Florence, 'Charles never knew.'

'And another huge one, which makes me worse than you,' said Grace quietly, 'Charles wasn't cruel to me.'

There was a long silence. Then Florence said; 'I've got to go to London. To the house. Get papers and things. Will you come with me?'

'Every time I come here,' said Florence, as they stood in the ghostlike drawing room, its furniture shrouded in dustsheets, 'I'm amazed it's still standing.'

'It's a very big house,' said Grace, 'Very grand.'

'Yes. I can't wait to get rid of it. It's so full of horrible memories. Well' – she added, and sighed, remembering the night she had been there with Giles – 'well, and the occasional nice one. Anyway, it's not what I want.'

'What do you want?'

'I don't know. I really don't. What I feel I can't do is go running to Giles saying come back, come back, I do love you after all.'

'Why not,' said Grace, 'when he loves you so much, must be so unhappy?' thinking even as she spoke how horribly easy it was to sort other people's lives out, to find simple answers, how impossible to do that to your own.

'Oh, it's so hard to explain. I've done it once. I can't do it again. It seems so arrogant.'

'I don't think he'd see it that way,' said Grace, 'I think he'd just be pleased. Otherwise he'll be thinking you don't love him. That's much worse.'

'Maybe. But I keep thinking maybe he won't even care any more. I've put him through such a lot. I love you, I don't love you, I want you, I don't want you. Poor chap, what can he possibly make of it all? And it's not fair, he's always been so absolutely loyal and patient with me. I don't deserve him. Any more than I deserved – '

'Florence,' said Grace sternly, 'don't start on that one again. Please.'

'No, all right. Anyway, it's irrelevant at the moment,' said Florence, suddenly brisk, firm, 'I don't have the faintest idea where Giles is, whether's he's well, I don't know anything. Now we'd better get going. I probably won't be long. I just need to find all Robert's personal stuff, his papers, our marriage certificate, stuff like that. And I think I'll take a few of my clothes, if the moths haven't eaten them away. They'll be a bit dated, but I don't think the residents of the Thorpes will know that do you?'

'Probably not,' said Grace.

It was a hot day; the house was stuffy. London was like a ghost town; emptied of nearly all military personnel, most of the cafés and restaurants closed, empty taxis in the streets, a spirit of depression almost tangible. People had had enough; while the much-vaunted and dreaded reprisals for the D-Day landings had not been on the scale expected, there was still the ever-present fear, the misery of the attacks from the V1 flying bombs, the new damage to buildings, streets, trees that had only just begun to recover. Everyone was patently war-weary, but still resigned and immensely brave. The taxi driver who had taken Florence and Grace to Sloane Avenue was cheerfully pragmatic.

'If you're out and you can 'ear one of the doodle bugs,' he said, 'you're all right. If the noise stops, dive for cover. That's when the bleeder's coming down. Pardon my French.'

That evening they sat in the kitchen eating some rather unappetizing bread and tinned fish that Grace had managed to buy, and drinking a bottle of superb claret from Robert's cellar.

'Still a few down there,' said Florence, pouring the wine happily into two tumblers. 'Oh, Grace, I do feel better. It's coming here, remembering it all. How awful it was. Puts some reality into it all. Thank you for coming. Here's to us. Us and the future. What do you think yours will hold?'

'I don't know,' said Grace. 'I really don't. I'm frightened to think about it.'

'Why?'

'Oh because I'm so happy and yet there are so many ifs and buts – ' Her voice tailed off. She found it hard to talk to Florence; she liked her a lot better these days, but she was still wary of her.

'Do you think you might – well – stay with Ben?'

'Florence, I don't know. How can I?'

'What does he want? Have some more wine.'

'No, I don't want any. I don't like wine. And I don't know what he wants.'

'You, obviously,' said Florence. 'Only, as I said, it won't be that simple. You being so different. Don't look at me like that, Grace, it's true. It's stupid to deny it.'

'I suppose so,' said Grace, with a sigh. 'My mother would have a blue fit for a start.'

'There you are,' said Florence. 'Now come on, have another drink, you've drunk quite a lot of it already for someone who doesn't like wine.'

They went to bed quite early; Grace, unaccustomed to wine of any kind, let alone heavy claret, woke up in the middle of the night feeling terrible, with a raging headache and a churning stomach. She lay with her eyes closed, wishing the room would stop spinning about her; then rushed to the bathroom and was extremely sick.

She was kneeling on the floor by the lavatory, wondering how on earth she was going to get back to bed when Florence came in. 'You OK? I heard you moving about.'

'No,' moaned Grace, 'I feel terrible.'

'Come on. I'll help you back to bed. It's called a hangover, Grace, I don't suppose you've had many.'

'Don't make me feel like some stupid little schoolgirl,' said Grace sharply.

'Sorry. Come on. I'll get you some water. That's what you need. Lots of it.'

She sat on the bed, making Grace drink the water; Grace shivered. 'I'm cold,' she said miserably.

Florence went over to the wardrobe. 'I've got some old jackets and sweaters and things in here. I used it as an overflow from my room. God, I had a lot of clothes. I used to shop compulsively. It used to make me feel better, sort of soothed. It was the only way I could get back at Robert. Clarissa calls it retail therapy. Look at this lovely fox jacket, I hardly wore it and it costs hundreds. Good Lord – '

'What?'

'This is one of Charles's suits. I didn't realize he had anything here still. Anyway, put the fox on, Grace, that'll make you warmer.'

'Thank you,' said Grace. 'What's the suit doing here anyway?'

'Oh, he kept it here, and a couple of shirts. Just in case he wanted to change and couldn't use Baker Street. This is really old, well pre-war.'

'Oh,' said Grace.

She put the fur jacket on and lay back on her pillows. It felt rather dissolute sitting up in bed in the middle of the night in a huge London house, with a bad hangover, wearing a fur coat, even if it did smell of mothballs. It quite cheered her up. She looked at the suit, Charles's suit, still hanging in the cupboard. It made her feel odd, as if it was some kind of a ghost, hanging there, watching her.

'Did Charles often come here?' she said.

'No, because Robert discouraged it. But after Daddy got rid of Baker Street, Charles had a key, just for emergencies. I don't think he ever used it though, he knew I was awfully unkeen. Would you like a cup of tea or something?'

'Yes please,' said Grace. 'That'd be lovely.'

When Florence had gone downstairs, she walked rather unsteadily over to the cupboard, pulled the jacket of the suit off the hanger and took it back to bed with her. It too smelt of mothballs. 'How very romantic,' she said aloud and giggled.

It made her feel strange, to be holding it; a piece of his past, a piece of him. His clothes at the Mill House she had put away, in a huge tea chest, ready, when she felt strong enough, to give to Florence for her WVS hoard.

She felt in the pockets: he had always made a big performance of emptying his pockets every night, it was part of his rather obsessive neatness. Well, he hadn't done it that night: there was a half-crown in one pocket, a hanky and a tram ticket in another. And in the breast pocket a piece of paper.

The paper was folded into four, very neatly. He always did that too: like the pocket-emptying. He never screwed bills or lists up and thrust them in his pockets, or even threw them into wastepaper baskets. She opened it, feeling faintly guilty, as if she was prying. It was a very old, almost brittle piece of paper, torn in places along the folds. As long as it wasn't a love letter. She really didn't think she could cope with that.

It wasn't exactly a love letter. 'Charles darling,' it said, in Clarissa's extravagant, wildly sloping handwriting.

I don't know what more I can say. Except that we shouldn't and mustn't change our minds. I certainly haven't changed mine. I can't. Whatever, *whatever* you say, or say you'll do. I don't believe you mean that, anyway, for a moment.

It simply isn't going to work, and you've got to accept it. Just got to. I love you to pieces, but I can't marry you. Quite apart from anything else, I'm simply not worthy of you. You know that now, and it should make you feel a bit better. You can't spend the rest of your life shackled to a bad lot like me. So, my darling, no more nonsense. You'll find some sweet, lovely girl, I know you will, who'll make you happy. But it isn't me. Please, Charles, let me go. There really isn't anyone else, I swear it. Certainly not Monty – purest nonsense that was, please, please believe me. But I know if we did get married, we'd be awfully miserable. In the long run, it would be cruel of me to let us do it.
Best love,
Clarissa.

Grace sat reading and rereading the letter; she felt very confused. Charles had obviously been absolutely beside himself at the ending of his engagement to Clarissa. The carefully presented story that they had simply agreed they weren't suited didn't seem to quite make sense. Or to tie up with the rather overbearingly confident Charles she knew. And what about Clarissa being a bad lot? She was always joking about that, saying how naughty she was, but did it mean she had actually been unfaithful to Charles? While they were engaged?

She felt rather upset suddenly by the whole thing: if he had been this desperate over Clarissa, it cast her very much as second choice, understudy to a much-favoured leading lady: the – what was it? – 'the sweet, lovely girl' who would make him happy. The sweet, lovely, biddable girl, dazzled, overawed by him. Was that what he had been looking for? Was that what explained his choice of her? Rather than some other confident creature, who might, like Clarissa, turn him down, find him wanting, reject him for someone else?

When Florence came back with the tea, Grace said as casually as she could, 'Was Charles terribly upset over his broken engagement to Clarissa?'

'Pretty upset,' said Florence, 'yes, he was. But it was very much a mutual decision. They both agreed it wasn't going to work. Why?'

'Oh – I just wondered,' said Grace.

She lay awake for a long time, thinking about Charles, about herself, and about Ben. She realized she felt just slightly less guilty.

Chapter Twenty-Eight

Autumn–Winter 1944

'Clarissa, the whole point is you don't know, because you've never even met Giles,' said Florence. Her pale face was flushed with earnestness, her dark eyes brilliant. There were times, Grace thought, when she looked actually beautiful.

'No,' said Clarissa, 'no, I realize that. But – '

'So don't try and tell me what he's feeling or might be feeling, because it's pointless. I don't know why everyone thinks they know how I should conduct my personal life so much better than I do.'

'No,' said Clarissa again. She sounded quite humble. Very humble for her.

'I simply can't put him through all that again. It's not fair. Anyway, I'm not even sure that I want to,' she added, sounding cross as she always did when she was upset. 'Everything is so confused, so awful, I feel so bad about Robert. So guilty and everything. So will you just leave me alone? Both of you.'

'Yes, all right,' said Grace and Clarissa meekly and in unison.

They were all sitting in the garden at the Priory; it was a golden September day. Clarissa was on leave and had come to stay for a few days. She was very thin, clearly exhausted, but as lovely, as determinedly sparkling as ever. Grace looked at her with a mixture of resentment and admiration; the gnawing uneasy jealousy Clarissa always inspired in her had been increased by the discovery of her letter to Charles.

'How's Jack?' she asked, anxious to divert the conversation away from Florence and Giles.

'He's splendid,' said Clarissa. 'Safely back on a rest period, I'm glad to say. I didn't think lightning was going to strike him twice, but I kept a cotton reel in my pocket the entire time, so I could touch wood whenever I thought of him.'

'Clarissa, you really are ridiculous,' said Florence severely.

'Ridiculous I may be. But it worked,' said Clarissa.

'Yes, all right. Maybe Churchill should have kept some cotton reels in his boiler-suit pockets, then the whole thing would have been over a lot quicker. Oh golly, there's Jeannette with Imogen. I must go and talk to her about tomorrow, I think I might have to work.'

She scrambled up, held out her arms to Imogen who hurtled into them like a small rocket, clasped her mother round the neck and covered her face with rapturous kisses.

'She's very sweet, I must say,' said Clarissa, raising her face to the sun. 'Although she's so frightful.' She yawned. 'Oh I'm tired. My poor brain feels as if it's been wrapped in layers and layers of cotton wool, it can hardly work at all.'

'Why don't you have a nap?' said Grace. 'You've earned a bit of idleness. She's pretty too, isn't she? Imogen, I mean. She looks a bit like Charles when he was a baby.'

'Charles!' said Clarissa, smiling slightly sleepily into the golden air. 'Not really, surely? Much more like her papa, I'd have said.'

'You've never met her papa, as you call him,' said Grace, slightly irritated without knowing why.

'No of course I haven't,' said Clarissa. She sounded – what? Grace couldn't quite work it out, not cross, not irritable even, but somehow a little unsteadied. And suddenly very alert, awake again. 'But I've seen pictures. Haven't you?'

'No,' said Grace. 'No I haven't. Ever.'

'Oh well. Anyway, I suppose it's reasonable that she should look like Charles, actually. I'd just never thought of it. Now look, I can't go to sleep or I'll never wake up again. I'd better go and have a bath or something energetic like that. See you later, darling.'

'Yes of course,' said Grace.

She wanted to have a talk with Clarissa: about Charles and about the letter, but this was clearly not the moment. She needed her to be at her most clear-headed.

In HMS *Cicala*, at Kingswear, across the water from Dartmouth, May Potter was lying on her bunk, reading an article in *Woman & Beauty* about keeping your elbows smooth, when her friend Leading Wren Sally Bishop came in.

'Phone for you. Male. Very upper-crust. Sounds drunk,' she added.

'Oh Lord,' said May, 'that's all I need. You ever been worried about rough elbows, Sal?'

'Oh constantly,' said Sally, 'wrecked my war, my elbows have.'

May was still laughing when she picked up the phone. 'Petty Officer Potter,' she said.

'May, my darling, it's me.'

'Oh yeah. And this is me. You'll have to do a bit better than that.'

'May, it's me, Giles Henry. Clarissa's friend. You must remember.' He sounded plaintive.

'Oh yeah. Course I do. Sorry. You all right, are you?'

'I'm fine. Thankfully. Back here for a few days, then up to Liverpool. Look, where's Clarissa?'

'On leave. Staying with – ' She paused. Clarissa had assured her the affair was 'one hundred and one per cent over, darling, I swear' but you never knew. Not with Clarissa anyway. And the rule had been, always: no messages left anywhere, except with her.

'Staying with her mum,' she said carefully.

'Her mother? I thought her mother had died?'

'Oh I don't think so,' said May. Damn, silly mistake that, Potter, you should be able to do better. 'That's her mother-in-law. But you never know with Compton Brown anyway, do you? Wouldn't put it past her, popping up to St Peter, talking him into a brief stopover. Anyway, she's off for a fortnight.'

'Oh God. Oh God, no.' He sounded so desperate that she almost relented. Then she remembered he was a musician 'Never trust a theatrical,' her mother had said, and she never had. 'But she might ring me,' she added helpfully. 'If she does I can give her a message.'

'Oh May darling, would you? It would transform my whole life if you could.'

God, he was just like Clarissa: a male version of Clarissa.

'Well, go on, then. Let me transform it. What's the message?'

'Tell her I have to talk to her. About Florence. And get a number for her, would you? If you possibly can?'

'Yeah, OK. Where do I contact you?'

'Leave a message at the officers' mess. Till – well, till Thursday. After that I'll be gone.'

'OK.'

'Bless you, May. You're an angel from heaven.'

She looked at her watch: too late to ring Clarissa now. The morning would have to do.

She went back to her *Woman & Beauty* and another article, on home perming. She might just give that a try. The salt played havoc with your hair.

Giles had had a bad war. Well, he supposed that compared with many others he had had a good war, his life apparently charmed; he had not been wounded, had not suffered so much as a bruise himself, but he had seen countless men die, their ships sunk or torpedoed, some enemy, some not; had watched convoys leave, bearing friends and comrades, knowing they were probably never to return, had left himself, expecting never to return also, had stared his own mortality constantly in the face. He had spent three days at sea on a raft in the freezing Atlantic, his ship sunk, heard his shipmates' groans as they slipped slowly and mercifully into unconciousness and then death from hypothermia; had seen sights on the beaches of Normandy he knew he would never forget, men dying in their hundreds, even before they reached the shore, pulled and dragged by their fellow soldiers, terrified boys new to battle and desperately calling up the blind courage trained into them to go forward, and hardened, battle-scarred men equally, if not more, afraid. He had long ceased to believe in the rightness of what he had been doing, to believe in anything at all, had developed a numbness, a near inability to feel, had simply fixed his mind on the end of it all, a near-incredible but essential dream. And Florence had been part of that dream, almost the whole of it indeed, and now he had lost her, lost her, if she was to be believed, irrevocably, and that was harder to bear than any of it. Her last letter, bleak, hopeless, waiting for him as he sailed joyfully back into Dartmouth, telling him that she knew now she must stay with Robert, that Imogen would be in danger if he even tried to contact her, had nearly broken his heart. And he knew Florence: where Imogen was concerned, she would endure anything, any pain, simply to keep her child safe. This was the one thing he could not fight. A tiger defending its young paled into absolute insignificance beside her. He would not risk phoning her; Robert might be home. But Clarissa, she could, would help. Clarissa could act as their fairy godmother. A beautiful, carnal fairy godmother.

'I'm terribly sorry to have to do this to you, Clarissa,' said Florence at breakfast, 'but I've simply got to work for a couple of hours at least this morning. Will you be all right?'

'Darling, I think so. Just about. I might go down and see Grace, and those heavenly boys of hers. I love little boys.'

'You just love boys,' said Florence, 'of any size. Right then, I'll be back after lunch. Want anything from Salisbury?'

'Only about ten yards of red silk velvet, and two pairs of very high-heeled shoes. And a huge bottle of Chanel. Funny how we all used to take such things for granted.'

Clarissa borrowed Muriel's bicycle to go down to the Mill House; she arrived to see the boys and Clifford setting off with their fishing rods.

'Grace is inside,' said Clifford, 'if you want her. How lovely you look, my darling.'

'I feel lovely this morning,' said Clarissa. 'Lovely and rested. I slept and slept last night.'

'Good. We'll try and bring you some trout back for lunch. Make you feel even better.'

She kissed them all and waved them off, and then went to find Grace.

Grace was not entirely pleased to see Clarissa without being quite sure why; she supposed because she knew she ought to have the conversation with her about Charles and breaking off the engagement, and she didn't really relish it.

She made a pot of coffee and carried it out to the garden; it was quite warm, the best kind of September day. There had been a mist earlier; now the meadow was drenched in golden light. Great spangled cobwebs hung on the fence and the rose bushes; Flossie was trying to eat them, clearly frustrated at their lack of nourishment.

'Silly creature,' said Clarissa fondly. 'How are you, darling?'

'I'm fine. Thank you.'

'And lovely, lovely Ben?'

'He's fine too,' said Grace slightly shortly, 'thank you.'

'Good. Oh, this is heaven. So exactly what I need. If only Jack were here it would be quite perfect.' She looked at Grace and laughed. 'Actually it's quite perfect without him. He's still quite hard work. The minute he stops flying he starts fretting about his face again.'

'Well, I expect he – oh damn, there's the phone. Excuse me, Clarissa.'

It was a trunk call: from Dartmouth. The caller had a very cockney accent, sounded in a hurry, wanted Clarissa. 'It's for you,' called Grace through the French windows. 'May someone? Porter?'

'Potter. Fellow Wren. Oh God, I hope it's nothing urgent down there. Sorry, Grace. Thanks. Where shall I take it?'

'The study would be quieter,' said Grace, 'Mrs Babbage is about to start hoovering.'

She was on her way back through the hall with the coffee cups when she realized the phone was still off the hook; she went over to replace the receiver.

May Potter's voice was loud: loud and clear. She couldn't help hearing it. She really, really couldn't. No one could have. 'Well, Duchess,' it was saying, 'guess who's turned up? Like a bright golden penny. The commander, that's who.'

'Giles!' said Clarissa. 'My God, May, when did he arrive?'

'Yesterday I think.'

Put it down, Grace, put it down.

'Anyway, he wants to see you. Desperately. Says it will transform his life. Honestly, Duchess, he's just like you.'

'The darling,' said Clarissa absently. 'Look, May, give him this number, I'll speak to him here. Any time up to lunchtime, tell him. After that Florence will be here so he mustn't ring. OK? And give him my love.'

'Right you are.'

Grace was rinsing out the coffee cups when Clarissa came into the kitchen; she didn't dare turn round.

'Sorry, darling,' said Clarissa, 'naval business. I'm afraid someone else may ring later, I hope that's all right. Honestly, I can't even have a bath these days without being disturbed.'

'Really?' said Grace. She went on looking into the sink, scrubbing the cups.

'Yes. Are you all right, darling? You sound a bit odd.'

'Yes thank you. Fine. Clarissa, could we go back outside? I want to talk to you.'

'Yes, of course we can. Are you sure you're all right?'

'Yes, I'm quite sure.'

She led the way out to the garden; she still felt so shocked, so frightened by her discovery she could hardly function at all. She sat down rather heavily on the seat.

'So what is it you want to talk to me about?' asked Clarissa. She looked slightly uneasy now, clearly picking up on Grace's distress.

'Charles,' said Grace shortly. She couldn't face discussing Giles. Not yet.

'Charles? What about Charles?'

'Why did you break off your engagement, Clarissa? Really? And why has it always been such a secret?'

'Grace darling, please, not again. I've told you – '

'No, Clarissa, you haven't. I don't believe you've told me at all. I – well, I found a letter. At Florence's house. From you to him. There seemed to be a bit more to it than just not getting on – '

There was a long silence, then finally Clarissa said, 'Well, I suppose now it doesn't matter any more. I always promised him never to tell.'

'Tell what?' Grace felt very nervous suddenly, and she wasn't sure why.

'Oh, it's nothing dreadful. Well, a bit dreadful for him at the time, of course, but really nothing serious. It just wasn't working. That much was true. Not working at all. We weren't going to be happy. A child of three could have seen that. We'd stopped getting along, stopped enjoying one another. Anyway, I went out to dinner with someone else one night: in London while Charles was down here. Perfectly – well, almost perfectly – innocent. Just an old chum. But – well, you know me, darling, can't resist an opportunity to flirt. We got a bit drunk, we went back to my flat – and – and Charles arrived.'

'And you were in bed, I suppose?' said Grace.

'In bed! Of course we – ' Clarissa met her eyes, looked away, flushed slightly. 'Yes, all right, we were. Oh dear. Well, you might as well know the full story.'

'I might as well, yes,' said Grace.

'The thing was, I'd been trying to break it off for weeks. I really had. There were so many things wrong. But he wouldn't. He kept saying it would be all right, that we were just both under a lot of strain. I was getting a bit frantic actually. Anyway, that night did it. Sort of.'

'Yes, I would imagine it would.'

'I said surely now he wouldn't want to marry me, knowing how awful I was. And he got absolutely desperate, started crashing about, threatening me, saying he'd go and shoot Monty – that was his name, the other chap, shoot himself. It was terrible. In the end he calmed down and then he started to cry. Which was worse. He begged, implored me to marry him, said he didn't care what I did, that he'd forgive me anything – '

'But why?' said Grace. 'Why? I just don't understand. Surely, if you'd – '

'Pride, darling. Male pride. Charles has – sorry, had – a superabundance of it. And what I'd say was an almost pathological need to be highly thought of. He simply couldn't face telling everyone the engagement was off: it had been in the papers, the date had been set, about six or seven months off, but still, his best man had been chosen, everything. He was going to look a complete fool, whatever way we did it, as he saw it. If I broke it off, people would think I'd got tired of him, or found him wanting in some way, and if he broke it off – well, he'd either look a cad, or he'd have to admit he'd found me playing around. Which also made him look a fool. So I said why on earth couldn't we just say the decision had been absolutely mutual, and leave it at that? He said he'd think about it, and left. And I thought I'd done it.'

'And hadn't you?' said Grace. She was finding the story utterly enthralling.

'Not quite. In the morning a note came through the door. He said he'd been thinking and he really couldn't face the break-up. He said he loved me too much and if I didn't marry him he'd kill himself. Of course I knew that was nonsense, he'd never do such a thing, it was totally out of character. And I told him so. But it was a measure of how desperately he cared.'

'About you,' said Grace quietly.

'No, darling, you miss the point. About himself.'

'Oh. Oh, I see,' said Grace uncertainly.

'Well, I hope you do. You don't look quite convinced. But any man, Grace, who finds his fiancée in bed with someone else and still prefers marrying her to breaking it off – he's a bit odd. Don't you think?'

'Yes,' said Grace, 'a bit odd. And a bit odd of her to be in bed with someone else. Don't you think?'

She could hear the edge, the hardness in her voice; she was rather pleased by it. She didn't want Clarissa to think she was upset. 'And so then you sent him off to find me, did you?'

'Sorry, darling?'

'Find some sweet, lovely girl who'd make him happy. I think that was the phrase in your letter. Some dull, shy, sweet girl who'd never do such a thing again. Who'd never get into bed with someone else because there wouldn't be someone else who'd want her. That was it, wasn't it, Clarissa? And I fitted the bill pretty damn well. Sweet, safe Grace. Was there anyone else first, do you think, who you suggested maybe, or was I a bit hard to find?'

She was starting to cry now, tears stinging her eyes; she was afraid she was going to start sobbing noisily, look ridiculous. 'What about Jack, did he know about this, Clarissa? Did you tell him why Charles had chosen me? He must have been puzzled, knowing he'd been engaged to you. And Florence, I suppose she knew – ' She stopped suddenly; she had forgotten, briefly, about Giles, Giles and Clarissa. Her new awareness of Clarissa's sexual pragmatism made that story even more shocking; earlier she might have given her the benefit of the doubt.

'Grace, you're being silly,' said Clarissa. 'Nobody wondered why Charles chose you, they could see he loved you, that you were absolutely perfect for him.'

'Absolutely,' said Grace bitterly.

'Oh darling, stop being silly. And certainly Florence had no idea about Charles and me. About how upset he was. She believed the story, just like everyone else.'

'She seems to be good at believing things,' said Grace. 'Lucky for you, that.'

'I'm sorry?' Clarissa's eyes were brilliant suddenly, brilliant and sharp; her cheeks flushed.

'I said it was lucky for you she was good at believing things.'

'I don't know what you're talking about.'

'I heard you on the phone just now,' said Grace, 'talking to that – that person, about Giles. I couldn't believe it, not Giles, not when Florence is your best friend. It's – '

'Grace,' said Clarissa, and she was very pale now, sweat on her forehead, 'Grace, you simply don't understand – '

'Oh but I do,' said Grace, 'very, very well. It all fits together quite neatly. I knew there was something, something odd even at Christmas, you were – edgy. And then yesterday, that little slip about Imogen looking like Giles. I don't understand you, Clarissa, I really don't. Or perhaps I do. Anyway – '

'You are not to tell Florence,' said Clarissa, her voice very low.

'I'll decide that,' said Grace. 'Not you. I think I should tell her. Actually. If he came back to her now, and she was still madly in love with him, it would be – well, it would be horrible. She ought to know.'

'You're talking like a child,' said Clarissa, 'like an arrogant, self-satisfied child. You don't understand half of it. Not half – '

'I think I do,' said Grace, 'I understand that you're not much better than a tart, Clarissa. That you can't resist anything with a – a cock.'

She stopped. It was so unlike her to talk like that she had shocked herself.

Clarissa started laughing. 'Darling Grace. What a thing to say.'

'Don't patronize me,' said Grace and she stood up and hit her, hard across the face. Clarissa sank back on the seat, her eyes round with shock, her hand to her red cheek.

And then Florence arrived. 'What on earth is going on?' she said. 'Did I see you hitting Clarissa, Grace? Whatever for?'

'She was upset,' said Clarissa quickly. 'I – well, I just said something a bit hard about Ben. It was wrong of me, Grace, please forgive me.'

Grace was so taken aback by the swiftness and competence of the lie, the only one that Florence might have believed in the circumstances, that she stood silent, gazing down at Clarissa.

'Oh really?' said Florence vaguely. 'I'm always upsetting Grace about him too. Telling her how difficult it would be if they got married or anything. With their different backgrounds and all that. I don't know why you can't see it, Grace, I really don't. Is that your phone? Shall I get it?'

For a very long moment Grace and Clarissa stayed motionless, staring at one another, their eyes taking in, sending messages. Then, 'No,' said Grace, 'no, don't, I'll get it' and 'No,' said Clarissa, 'I'll go, it might be that call from Dartmouth again, from May Potter – '

But neither of them got there in time, for Mrs Babbage came out, saying it was for Mrs Compton Brown. 'A gentleman,' she said, 'trunk call. Didn't give a name, said she'd know.'

'Must be darling Jack,' said Clarissa. 'Excuse me, please, both of you.'

She came out looking very cool, smiling; she had powdered over her reddened cheek, proffered the other one to Grace.

'It was Jack. Just wanted a chat. It's been lovely, darling,' she said to Grace, 'really lovely. I'm sorry I upset you so badly. And please don't do anything rash. I'll go back with Florence now, I think. I'll see you very soon.'

And she slipped into Florence's car. The last Grace saw of her was her small, well-manicured hand waving gaily through the window.

'Grace,' said Ben, 'you haven't heard a word I've said. Have you?'

'What?' said Grace.

'I said – oh, it doesn't matter.' He sounded, for him, irritable.

'Sorry,' said Grace, 'I'm very sorry. I've got – I've got something on my mind. Something that's upsetting me. What – what did you say?'

'Forget it. Doesn't matter.'

'I'm sorry,' said Grace again.

'What's the matter anyway? Want to talk about it?'

She shook her head. 'No, honestly. It's not important.'

'It seems to be.'

'No, really. It's not.'

'OK.' There was a silence.

She struggled to realign her mind, to appear more sympathetic. Ben had troubles of his own, she knew; he was worried about what he was going to do after the war was over – now so real a prospect – and about David, who was having problems settling at the grammar school, worn out by the long journey every day and by the additional burden of homework.

'If it's David,' she said, 'I really don't think you should worry. It's early days and he's a clever boy, he'll be all right. And I got his plimsolls at last, so there won't be any more trouble about them, and – '

'Grace,' said Ben, 'do stop talking. I'm not specially interested in David's plimsolls, if you want to know. Not at the moment anyway.

'Well, you ought to be,' said Grace, stung. She had spent hours walking round the shops in Shaftesbury before finally going to Salisbury to find the white plimsolls the grammar school so arrogantly insisted on, and had had to part with some of her own coupons to get them. 'He is your son, you know – '

'I know he's my son,' said Ben, leaning forward, kissing her firmly on the mouth to stop her talking. 'That's not at issue. Now please, love, just be quiet for heaven's sake, and listen.'

'Look,' said Grace, 'I think I know what it is.'

'Oh you do, do you?'

'Yes. It's about what you're going to do after the war, isn't it? I'm sorry, Ben, and I have been thinking about it. The thing is, if you still want to try for the teaching, you can leave the boys here while you go to college or whatever. I don't mind a bit. In fact – '

'It is about after the war, yes,' he said, 'but not what I'm going to do for a job. Well, that's part of it. But what I'm trying to say is, well, you know I love you. And you love me. But we're going to have terrible problems if we stay together. Don't you think?'

'Well – I don't know,' said Grace. She suddenly felt very sick. He was going to tell her it was over, that he was leaving her.

'You *should* know. You should think about it,' he said and he sounded worried, almost angry. 'It's all very well at the moment, everyone's playing games, I come here to your big house and pretend I'm the same as you, and I'm not. And my boys aren't either, and they've spent all this time thinking they belong here, in the big house, and it's not right. And what we ought to do, well, what we've got to do, is get out and go on our way. Once the war's over, anyway.'

'Oh,' said Grace flatly, 'oh I see. Yes.'

'I'll get back to work, and they'll be fine, they're older now.'

'Yes. Yes, of course they will.'

It hurt so much she could hardly bear it; the pain seemed to be moving around in the pit of her stomach. She put her hand there, as if she could push it away.

'What my mum would say if she could see them now,' he said, 'I can't begin to think. Spoilt, she'd say they were. Getting above themselves. And it's true. She'd be shocked.'

Grace began to feel irritable. She'd worked very hard on the boys; she didn't like the feeling of being somehow criticized for it.

428

'I'm very sorry – ' she began.

'But then,' he said, 'my dad would be pleased. About the music and that. And the grammar school.'

'Good,' she said. She tried to sound bright, unconcerned. 'And what about Linda? What would she say, do you think?'

'I'm not sure,' he said, 'to tell you the truth. I was wondering about that. I think she'd be – well, a bit surprised.'

Grace had had enough of this. She stood up suddenly. 'Ben, I'm sorry but I've got to go,' she said.

'Go where?'

'To – to the church. To play the piano. I don't suppose your mum would like that either, going out, not giving you your tea – '

She couldn't finish the sentence; she turned and half ran from the kitchen, upstairs to her bedroom, slammed the door, threw herself on the bed, burying her head in the pillow in case he heard her. It was over, nothing further to come of it, the war would end and he would go away, with the boys, leaving her behind, a rather charmingly odd interlude. Only of course he wouldn't label it quite like that.

There was a knock at the door; gentle but firm. She ignored it; it came again.

'Grace! Love, let me in. I want to say something else.'

'You've said quite enough already,' she said. 'I don't think I want to hear any more.'

'You might want to hear this.'

'I won't.'

'You're being silly,' he said, and he sounded irritated. That made her cross: that he could be so insensitive as not to realize how much he had hurt her.

She got up suddenly, flung open the door. 'Look,' she said, 'look, Ben, perhaps I should just explain a few things to you. I always thought – wrongly it seems – that you were a bit more sensitive than most men.'

'I'm sorry,' he said. He stood there, looking down at her rather uncertainly, clearly nervous.

'Yes, well, for once you can say it,' she said. 'Years and years I've looked after those children, and it's been really nice, I've loved it, but it's been very hard work, and I'm afraid I didn't have the time or energy to make sure they weren't getting funny ideas along the way. I'm sorry, Ben, but I didn't actually have the time to take them along to one of the smaller streets in Salisbury at regular intervals and make sure they knew that's where they really ought to be. Silly of me, I know. And I'm extremely sorry I taught David the piano. What should it have been, Ben, the banjo or something? And as for chess, well, that was unforgivable of Clifford. You'd better talk to him about that. You seem to be very worried about them all of a sudden. So you'd better take them off now, before things get any worse. Back to your barracks for a start, maybe, they might – '

'Do stop shouting,' he said, and he put out his hand gently and stroked her face. 'Do be quiet. You've missed the point completely. I was only trying to – '

'Well, you've succeeded,' said Grace. She dashed her hand across her eyes.

Ben smiled and gave her his handkerchief. 'Here, use this,' he said. 'Your nose is running.'

'Oh – go away,' shouted Grace, and she had never felt more angry with anyone, more angry and miserable, 'Just go away. I never want to see you again.'

'Oh dear,' he said. 'I seem to have made a bit of a mess of things. I didn't mean to upset you. Honestly I didn't.'

'Well you have,' said Grace, 'and what did you think I was going to be? Happy? Grateful?'

'You might've been,' he said, 'if you'd let me finish. Well, not grateful maybe. But happy.'

'Why? What could you possibly have said that was going to make me happy? After giving me all that rubbish?'

'Well,' he said, and cleared his throat, seeming to gather himself together, physically as well as mentally, 'well, you see, I was going to – to – ask you if you'd like to think about marrying me. Only think about it, mind. Take it very steady. Because of all the things I'd been trying to say. But it did come out a bit wrong. I can see that. I'm sorry, Grace. Very sorry.'

'Oh,' said Grace. She stood there staring at him, feeling rather faint suddenly. She put her hand on the wall to steady herself. 'Oh, I see.'

'But maybe I shouldn't even have tried,' he said, 'maybe I should've seen it was an impossible idea. Anyway, sorry, Grace. Sorry for upsetting you so much. Maybe I'd better – '

'Don't say sorry,' she said slowly, reaching out, touching his face as gently as he had touched hers. 'And it's not an impossible idea. It's lovely. I'd love it. I'd love to think about it.'

'You would?' he said, and his long bony face lost its anguish suddenly, broke into its most triumphantly glorious grin. 'You really would?'

'Yes, I would. And I don't see there's that much to think about.

Actually. I think all those things you were talking about are pretty silly really. I think you're letting them matter a bit too much.'

'Well,' he said, 'not really. You see – '

'Ben,' said Grace, 'now it's my turn. Shut up, will you?' She reached up and kissed him: gently at first, then very hard, on his mouth. He responded, exploring hers, fiercely tender, with his tongue. She took his hand, pulled him back into the room, shut the door behind him, turned the key. 'Just in case,' she said, 'just in case they come back.'

'Where are they?'

'Fishing. With Clifford. Is that suitable for them or not?'

'Oh stop it,' he said. 'Just let me love you.'

It was swift, as it never usually was: as if he needed to show her, urgently, how much he loved her. He was in her almost at once; aroused sexually by the waves of raging emotion she had experienced in the past hour, she was eager, hungry for him. She felt herself clenching, reaching round him, the sweet, urgent, overlapping fronds starting to stir almost at once.

'I love you,' he said, 'I love you very much.' And even as he spoke she started climbing, rising and rising, and he was forcing her up, into, through it, through the brilliance, the pleasure, the white-hot release. She lay there, almost detached, feeling her body knowing him, loving him, feeling him part of her, taking her, following her, leading her, and as he came, as he cried out, the long, vibrant sound of love, she called out, loudly triumphant herself, 'I love you, Ben, I love you,' and thought that never as long as she lived would she feel herself so perfectly happy.

Later, they lay slightly dazed by what had passed between them, and he said, 'Feeling better now?'

'Oh yes,' she said, 'of course I am.'

'You do,' he said, and leant over and kissed her as he said it, 'you do get things wrong, you know.'

'I know,' she said, and sighed. 'I don't stop and think enough. I never have.'

'I've noticed.'

'Ben?'

'Yes.'

'Can I tell you something? Nothing to do with us. Something that's upset me.'

'Of course.'

She lay there, holding his hand, and told him about Clarissa. Giles and Clarissa. 'What do you think I should do then?' she said.

'Nothing,' he said, 'nothing at all. For God's sake, Grace, do nothing at all.'

'But – '

'Listen,' he said, 'in the first place, you don't know what really happened.'

'Yes I do.'

'Love, you don't. Well, OK, I expect she – I expect they did it.'

'Ben, of course they did. And Florence is her best friend and – '

'Grace! You're off again. So they went to bed. So what?'

'Ben, what do you mean, so what?' She was shocked.

'I mean it isn't everything. Not always.'

'Oh,' she said.

'You've got to try and see things from their point of view. Listen. What do you think it was like for Clarissa, seeing Jack like that? Horrible, awful. Christ, lots of women would've just gone. You wouldn't have seen them for dust. She stuck by him. She loves him. I think that's pretty good. Really.'

She turned and looked at him interestedly. 'You really like her, don't you?'

'Yeah. Yeah, I do. I think she's smashing. Very sexy. But I like her too. I think she's brave and kind and much more loyal than you think.'

'Loyal! Ben, she doesn't know what loyalty is.'

'Course she does. It's just not sexual loyalty, that's all. She can't help it, she fucks – sorry, love, goes to bed with – '

'Fucks is better,' said Grace grimly.

'All right, she fucks like most people kiss. She collects men, like trophies.'

'Has she tried to collect you?' asked Grace. She was so interested she didn't even feel jealous.

'Not exactly. She came on a bit strong, once. That Christmas, when you were out once and she was here alone with me. I don't mean she tried to get me upstairs, or anything, but she wanted to know she could've done.'

'Oh,' said Grace. 'Oh I see. And could she?'

'Let's say,' he said grinning, 'she'd be pretty hard to resist. Under certain circumstances. I wouldn't rate my chances.'

'Ben, how can you say that? I don't – '

'Look,' he said, 'just be quiet. Of course I wouldn't. I'm just trying to explain. I reckon they were alone down there in Dartmouth. She was upset, trying to cope with Jack. He was bloody miserable, thought he'd lost Florence, was getting sent back to sea to get killed most likely. Why the hell not, love? What harm was it going to do? Really?'

'I would have thought a lot,' said Grace. She felt rather upset again: shocked at Ben's pragmatism.

'Yes, you would. And it would matter for you. But not Clarissa. Dear oh dear, you haven't been listening at all.'

'I have.'

'No you haven't. Anyway, what would do a lot of harm is if you went rushing up to Florence and told her what Clarissa did. You mustn't, Grace. You really mustn't.'

'I wasn't going to,' she said, 'actually. But I just can't help hating Clarissa now. And not trusting her. And I feel so awkward when I'm with them both.'

'There's worse things than feeling awkward,' he said, 'much worse. I should know. Give me a kiss. And then you'd better get dressed, or I don't know what I might find myself doing.'

They didn't tell anyone: it was too soon, they agreed, too soon after Charles's death. 'It would especially hurt Clifford, I know, even in spite of everything,' said Grace. 'And there isn't a hurry, is there? I mean when did you think we might actually – well – '

'Oh, not for a long time probably,' he said, 'well, quite a long time. Next year maybe. When I've got myself sorted out a bit. But I just needed you to know that's what I want. And I needed to know if you want it too.'

'I do want it too,' she said. 'I love you, Ben.'

'I love you too, Grace.'

For the hundredth time, possibly the thousandth time, she thought it was too perfect to be true.

Clarissa telephoned Florence to let her know she would soon have an extended leave and asking her to come and stay with her in London. 'It'll do you good,' she said, 'to get away. We can have some fun.'

'Oh I don't know,' said Florence. 'I don't seem to have any energy. I'm better down here with Mother, being bored. Mother and Grace.'

'Have you seen much of Grace lately?' asked Clarissa casually.

'No,' said Florence, 'she seems to be avoiding me. I've probably said something unfortunate to her. You know how tactless I am.'

'I certainly do,' said Clarissa. 'Anyway, you're coming to stay with me, darling, whether you think you want to or not. I'll be in touch about dates. Bye for now.'

She put the phone down thoughtfully. It didn't look as if Grace was going to say anything. Clarissa hadn't really thought she would but it was still a gnawing worry. God, she was a little prig. She was very fond of Grace, but she was a prig. Clarissa had thought that Ben might sort her out a bit, but it didn't seem to be working yet. She remembered Florence's saying, years ago, that being overmoral was a class thing; and she was so right. She hoped Florence would be true to her own class, if she was put to the test. Not to mention Jack.

With that extraordinary ability to set aside disagreeable facts that made her own life so infinitely pleasant, Clarissa opened her diary and started leafing through it. Then she picked up the phone and dialled the officers' mess in Liverpool.

'Could I have a word with you, my dear?' said Clifford one evening when the boys had gone to bed. He was slightly flushed; he also looked tired. He had been wrestling with decimal points and Latin declensions with a distressed David, who was now saying daily that he wished he'd never got the rotten scholarship but was at the secondary modern with all his friends.

'Yes of course,' said Grace. 'I'll make some tea.'

He finished his tea, set the cup down, cleared his throat. Grace smiled at him encouragingly. 'What is it, Clifford? Come on, you can't fool me, there's something up.'

'Well, darling, yes, there is. I – well, that is, Muriel and I – '

'Clifford!' said Grace, going over to him, throwing her arms round his neck. 'Clifford, you're going to live together again. I'm so pleased!'

'You are? You don't think I'm making a terrible mistake?'

'Of course not. I think it's lovely. Nothing could please me more.'

'Oh Grace,' he said, and the relief in his voice was heavy, 'what a wonderful girl you are. I thought you might be opposed to it.'

'Of course I'm not opposed to it. I've been hoping for it ever since Charles's funeral when I saw you standing with her. It seemed so silly, you both being so lonely, when you could be together. I mean she's clearly forgiven you – '

'As much as Muriel ever forgives,' said Clifford with a rueful smile. 'She never mentions it precisely, and neither do I. There are quite a few references, of course, to a time when I wasn't there, wasn't seeing to things, helping her, and so on and so forth. But I can put up with that.'

'You're still really fond of her, aren't you?' said Grace.

'Oh yes,' he said, 'yes, I am. Really fond. I expect that seems funny to you. Anyway, I don't want you to think for a moment that I discount what you did for me. It was kind and immensely brave, and I owe you a huge debt. Which one day perhaps I can repay.'

'I enjoyed it,' said Grace, 'I really did.'

When Ben phoned at the weekend, she told him about Clifford. 'It's lovely, he's so happy. Why anyone should wish to live with Muriel I can't imagine, but there it is. And it means when – well, next year or whatever – we shall have the Mill House to ourselves. Us and the boys. Which will be rather nice.'

'Yes,' said Ben, 'yes, I suppose it will.' He sounded a little guarded.

'Of course it will, Ben. Don't be silly. Clifford's lovely, but – '

'Look, Grace, I've got to go. I'll see you soon,' said Ben. 'I love you,' he added carefully.

'I love you too.'

She put the phone down, feeling slightly rebuffed. Rebuffed and anxious.

Chapter Twenty-Nine

Autumn–Winter 1944

Ben and Grace had been for a walk, and were just coming back over the field from the wood: David's wood as they now called it.

'Doesn't it look lovely?' said Grace happily, looking at the Mill House sunk into its small hollow, the late sun catching its tall windows, smoke spiralling out of its double chimney. 'I love that house so much. It's a happy house. And in spite of everything, I've been happy there. Well, we all have.'

'Yes,' said Ben. He sounded odd.

Grace looked at him. 'What is it? What's the matter?'

'It is a nice house, yes,' he said, after a long pause, 'but I don't think we can stay there.'

'Whyever not?' she said, astonished. 'It's perfect. The boys see it as home, and there's no problem with money, I mean it's mine, Charles left it to me and – '

'That's exactly it,' he said, 'it's yours. Very much yours. Charles's house once, now yours. Nothing to do with me.'

'Oh Ben, don't be silly. Of course it's to do with you.'

'No,' he said, 'it isn't. And I don't want to live in it.'

'But why not?'

'Because it's not mine. It's yours. When we're married, we'll live in my house. Surely you can understand that.'

'Ben, that's absurd. You've just being perverse.'

'No,' he said, 'it's not absurd. It seems quite reasonable to me. I'm sorry, Grace, and I do like the Mill House, but I can't live in it with you. It would feel like sponging, living off you. I couldn't cope with that.'

'Oh,' said Grace. 'Well, I'll have to think about it, I suppose.'

'No,' said Ben, 'you won't have to think about it. There's nothing to think about. We'll find another house to live in.'

It was a side of him she had never seen before, the egotistical, proud male. He had always been so gentle, so easy; she was shocked. Shocked and upset. She loved the Mill House, loved it most dearly, felt attached to it almost physically. And what sort of house would he want to live in anyway? The sort he had had with Linda, small, cramped, in a town? She suddenly heard Florence's voice saying, 'It couldn't work if you lived here, and if you lived with his sort of people you wouldn't fit in there.'

For the first time, she began to think properly about the implications of marrying a man from so different a background to her own. Was it going to matter as much as Florence had said? As Ben had been trying to say, the day he had proposed to her? And was she more of a snob, more troubled by such things than she would ever have admitted? It was all very well, she thought, drawing Ben into her life; was she actually going to be able to cope with being drawn into his?

She got up early next morning and wandered round the Mill House, pausing in her favourite places, the porch, overhung with wisteria, the kitchen with its great cupboards and stone floor, the drawing room with its tall windows and shutters, the curved staircase and the long light landing with its beautifully turned banisters. The thought of turning her back on it made her feel desperately sad, almost tearful; it was only a house, she tried to tell herself, only bricks and mortar, but it wasn't, it was hers, her own place, all she had had in the world for a while, a source of comfort and strength, and she felt she belonged to it as much as it to her.

She made herself a mug of tea and went out of the back door, freezing cold as it was outside, and looked out at the sloping garden, the stream, the field beyond. Charlotte shot out after her, followed by Puppy. They had never given her a name. What would they do, in a small, towny house without a proper garden? And who would have Floss and the chickens? Absurdly, tears filled her eyes; she blinked them back, felt Ben's arm round her shoulders.

'I know what you're thinking,' he said, 'and I'm sorry. But you have to see it my way, Grace. I can't be Mr Grace Bennett. I really can't.'

'So would you want to – to move away from here?' she said. 'Go somewhere different? To a – a town or something?'

'Not a town, not necessarily. Although what I could do in the country I don't know. Yet. But yes, I would want to leave here. As long as we're here, Grace, I'm the odd man out. I can't cope with that. Not for the rest of our lives. Do you think the people round here, your friends, would really accept me?'

'I haven't got any friends round here,' she said, 'not like that. You know I haven't.'

He ignored her. 'Do you think I can stand at those parties, a glass of sherry in my hand, and feel them watching to see if I know how to behave, what to say, how to say it? Of course I can't.'

'You – never said all this before,' she said.

'I tried to. Tried to make you think about it. The day I asked you to marry me, I was trying to. We were dreaming before, love, it was all make-believe. Make-believe, in a war that had turned everything upside-down. Who cared if I was a sergeant and your husband was a major? If I'd left school at fourteen and he'd gone to Oxford? Didn't matter. But it will, Grace. If we're going to live a real life, get married, it will matter.'

'But Ben – '

'No, Grace. I'm sorry. I can't live here and have people think how nice and charming I am, "considering", as they'll put it. How amusing and brave of you to have married me. We have to go somewhere else, start a life on our own terms.'

'Yes, I can see that,' said Grace quietly. She didn't want to argue about it. She needed time to think, to get used to the idea.

Over the next few days she thought she had. Ben was right. She remembered all the times she had complained about, been upset by, Charles's friends and their ostracism of her. How much worse it would be for him. It had been totally crass of her to think he would, could, just settle down in her house and life; the Mill House was only a house, of course it was, a place, bricks and mortar, she kept saying determinedly, and she loved Ben enough to leave it, to be brave. Then she got a letter from him.

Dear Grace,

There was something else I wanted to talk to you about, but you were so upset about the house I felt I couldn't. It's what I'm going to do with my life. I really don't want to go back to being an insurance clerk. Apart from anything else, loving you has made me more ambitious. So you should be pleased about that, at least! I dreamt about being a teacher, as you know, and for a long time I thought I might try that. But it would be very hard. I'd have to go to college for years, and I just don't see it as practical. But I liked the engineering side of the army, it suits me, and I think I could make a go of it. I was talking to one of the NCOs the other night and it seems I could possibly get on a sponsored course, at one of the technical colleges. It would mean staying in the army for quite a lot longer, though. And that would mean you'd be a sergeant's wife, us

438

not knowing where we might end up a lot of the time. I'd like you to think about that, Grace, very carefully. My love to you.
Ben

She wasn't quite sure what he was saying; she only knew that she felt suddenly uneasy about things.

Florence was going to London to stay with Clarissa. Clarissa had been most insistent that she came. She had even stipulated a date, the first Friday in December, 'And I want you to stay for at least a week. You can bring Imogen if you like but it would do you good to get away. I'm sure Jeannette would cope wonderfully.'

'Well, I don't know,' said Florence, 'I really don't like being away from her that long – '

'Florence, darling, you'll like it once you're here. Now I've got lots of fun planned for us, people to see, it'll be like the old days, and you can get the house on the market, if that's what you want. And we can talk plans. I mean you don't want to stay down at the Priory for ever, do you?'

'No,' said Florence slightly doubtfully.

'Flo! You can't.'

'No, not at the Priory. But I'm not sure about being in London now. No friends I'm still in touch with, no reason for being there. I'd be a real country bumpkin.'

'You're being silly,' said Clarissa, 'and anyway, what about all those plans to rule the world?'

'Oh, I've gone off all that. I don't think the world will want me,' said Florence wearily.

'Of course it will. You must be positive, darling. You should just hear what Jack's planning on. But I'll let him tell you himself. Bye, darling. Now next Friday. Without fail.'

Florence asked Jeannette if she thought she could cope with Imogen for a week, and Jeannette said she could, easily, but not that Friday, since Ted had asked her to a dance, and she had a feeling he was going to come up with the goods. Florence told Clarissa she would come on the Saturday instead, and was rather surprised when Clarissa said that wouldn't do. 'I've got a dinner party planned, darling, everyone's dying to see you. Can't Moo cope?'

'Not with both of them. I'll come on Saturday.'

An hour later Grace phoned; she said Clarissa had rung her and she'd be very happy to have both the children on the Friday night, if

Jeannette would come and stay on the Saturday in exchange, so that she could go to a concert with Ben at the cathedral. 'Then you can go to Clarissa's dinner party.'

'I can't quite see why everyone's so keen for me to go to Clarissa's dinner party,' said Florence irritably, 'as if I needed some kind of outing. Still, if you really want to, Grace.'

'I do,' said Grace, 'I really do.'

'And bring something really nice to wear,' said Clarissa. 'It's going to be a very smart dinner party. Black tie.'

'Clarissa, who on earth goes to a black-tie dinner party these days?'

'Oh – various chums,' said Clarissa vaguely, 'my lovely American attaché, Bunty and her wicked gynae husband, Jack of course. It's going to be such fun. So don't let me down. I want you at your absolute best.'

'Clarissa, do stop going on,' said Florence. 'I'll be there, and I won't wear my WVS uniform. I can't promise more than that.'

'All right, darling. That'll do.'

She sat on the freezing cold train as it crawled its way to London, and tried to feel cheerful. She couldn't imagine what she was going to say to any of Clarissa's smart London friends. She would probably fall asleep over the soup; a deep weariness possessed her these days, a sense of total uselessness, which not even Imogen could dispel. She could not imagine ever again wanting to do anything; it was all a most dreadful effort. She had failed at everything; she had been a disastrous wife, she had made another man wretchedly unhappy, she had brought an illegitimate child into the world, she had no career, no talents, no qualifications; and she looked much older than her thirty-three years.

It was very kind of Clarissa to have her to stay, but Florence was sure she would most assuredly regret it; she wished devoutly now that she had refused. By the time she reached Waterloo, she had decided to go to Sloane Avenue and stay there, phone Clarissa and plead illness, a migraine, anything. But as she walked slowly down the platform, she saw Jack standing at the barrier, smiling at her. He still looked so very strange, with his small, blunt nose, his shiny, grafted skin, his little eyes. If he could be brave and smile, Florence thought, then surely so could she.

'You look tired,' he said, giving her a kiss, taking her case. 'Now look, don't blame me, but Clarissa's booked you into her hairdresser, says it will give you a little boost. So I'm to take you there and collect you again afterwards.'

'Oh,' said Florence, 'well, that's very kind, but surely, Jack, you have better things to do with your leave than wait around while I have my hair done.'

'It's only one afternoon,' he said, 'and it does mean I can pop into the club. Play a game of bridge.'

'I'm not going to run away you know,' said Florence, exasperated, choosing to forget she almost had. 'I'll turn up at the dinner party on time.'

'I know, but Clarissa said that's what I had to do, and you know what that means.'

'Yes, I suppose I do. Well, all right.'

She actually rather enjoyed her afternoon; she sat and read *Vogue* in the hairdresser's; it was full of wonderful pictures of the liberation of Paris, including one of General de Gaulle passing *Vogue*'s Paris office, and she learnt several interesting facts that she thought she could trot out at the dinner party: that Elsa Schiaparelli had found food cost twenty times as much as it had in 1939, that Colette was writing her memoirs, and that there was only one hairdresser in Paris, one Gervais, who could dry hair, by a most tortuous method involving teams of boys riding a stationary tandem in the basement by way of power.

After that Jack took her out to tea at the Ritz. 'This is ridiculous,' said Florence, laughing.

The sandwiches were very dull, and the cakes a little conservative, but the service was as superb as ever, and the palm court almost as lovely.

Jack told her his plans. 'I'm going to study as a plastic surgeon,' he said simply. 'I don't care how long it takes, many years of course, it means going right back to the beginning, going to medical school. But it fascinates me so much and I know I can do it; and I feel I can pass on some of the wonders that were worked for me. Clarissa says she's going out to work,' he added. 'She and her friend May are going to go into business together.'

Florence stared at him in something close to awe.

When she arrived at the house Clarissa was ecstatic. 'Your hair looks divine, darling, and what are you going to wear? Show me.'

She pronounced the wine jersey restaurant dress that Florence had bought in 1939, tucked and pleated across the bosom, as perfect: 'Not dated at all, but you must let me lend you a pair of shoes, those won't do, I'm sorry,' and sent her off to have a bath. 'And don't come down till I call you, I really can't cope if you're under my feet. Lie down with some pads on your eyes or something. Help yourself to scent, darling, off my dressing table. See you in a couple of hours.'

Florence, to whom having a bath had become no more than the briefest rather chilly dip in between getting Imogen up and leaving for the canteen, or alternatively late at night when the water was even colder, surrendered herself to pleasure.

At seven thirty she sat and looked at herself in the mirror, and actually smiled. Her hair, two inches shorter and softly waved off her forehead, softened her face; her eyes, accentuated by mascara, looked larger, and her mouth, etched sharply with deep red lipstick, wonderfully dramatic, rather than just large as she had come to see it. Even her bosom, tiny as it was these days, looked fuller beneath the layered pleats and folds of her dress. And at least her legs were still the same. Long, slender, 'racehorse legs', Giles had once called them. She pushed Giles out of her head by a huge effort of will, sprayed herself copiously with Clarissa's Arpège, and as she heard the doorbell ring went slowly down to the drawing room.

Expecting a crowd of people, she was surprised to find it empty; empty and shadowy-dim. Only one of Clarissa and Jack's beautiful Tiffany table lamps was lit, and there were candles on either end of the fireplace but otherwise the room was in darkness apart from the fire, throwing golden arched shadows on the walls.

Frowning slightly, bemused, she sat down on the sofa, not knowing quite what to do, reached out for the cigarette box. As she opened it, she heard a footstep outside, and looked up. The light outside silhouetted a man standing in the doorway. 'Oh Jack,' she said, relieved, 'Jack, I – ,' and then she stopped.

For it did not seem to be, it wasn't Jack; the figure was too tall, the hair too light, the shoulders too narrow. And she sat there, staring in absolute disbelief into the shadowy shape, which couldn't be, which seemed to be, that was, unbearably, unbelievably was, yes, was Giles, his face very serious, his eyes tenderly moving over her. There seemed an infinitely long distance between them, one that she seemed unable to travel, but he moved slowly towards her, holding out his arms, and she stood up and very, very gradually, as if easing herself out of some dreadful danger, she went forward into them, and she felt him holding her, felt his face buried in her hair, heard his voice saying her name, quite quietly, over and over again, and then she heard Clarissa, her voice strange, saying, 'We're going out now. We'll see you much, much later,' and heard the front door close, very gently, and for a long

442

time they continued to stand there, not moving, not doing anything at all, just knowing happiness and remembering what it truly meant.

Chapter Thirty

Winter 1944 – Spring 1945

'Look, said Grace, 'I've agreed to – well, sell the Mill House. I've agreed to move away from the Thorpes. Those are two big concessions. Not even concessions,' she added, seeing the warning expression in Ben's eyes, his mouth tightening in preparation for yet another clear expression of his will. 'Good, right moves. But I don't want you to stay in the army.'

'Because you don't think it's right for me?'

'Yes. I don't think it's right for you.'

'Not that you don't want to be a sergeant's wife?'

'Oh Ben, please!' said Grace. She felt the newly familiar flood of exasperation filling her. 'Give me some credit. No, actually, I don't want to be a sergeant's wife. I don't want to be an army wife. It's perfectly simple. And I don't think deep down you're an army person. Or an engineer, come to that. I think you'd be a wonderful teacher. I think that's what you ought to do.'

'Grace, we've been over this so many times,' said Ben. 'I haven't even got my school certificate. Not enough qualifications to get into teacher training college.'

'Ben, you've done all those evening classes, you could pass your school certificate tomorrow, you know you could. You're just being awkward. Laying it on with a trowel, to make me feel bad.'

He looked at her, his eyes angry; then suddenly, as it so often did, his face softened, he smiled at her. 'Yeah, well, maybe I am. So go on.'

'So you could do that this summer even. Well, maybe. You could ask. You said yourself your arm was getting worse, and the headaches. I think you could get invalided out. I think you should, actually. The country could just possibly get by without you now.' She gave him a kiss, to show him she was joking. She had to be much more careful these days.

'I don't think I could,' he said.

'Have you talked to the MO?'

'No. But if I did get out, then what?'

'Then you could apply for college.'

'And how would we live while I was at college?'

'Ben, I have some money. The – the sale of the house would provide more. You have some compensation for your house, don't you?'

'Not enough. And I won't live off you,' he said. 'I won't go into all that again. I don't know why you keep on trying.'

'But Ben, not even for three years? That is so stupid. And then you can let me live off you for the rest of our lives.'

'Well – maybe.' He seemed to genuinely be considering what she said; she felt more hopeful. 'And when would I go to college, do you think?'

'This autumn maybe. Why not? The war will be over.'

'You have information on that, do you?'

'Yes, I do. Well, I read the newspapers.'

'And I don't do that, of course. Find the words a bit long.'

'Ben, stop it. This is ridiculous.'

'Oh, I'm sorry,' he said. He held out his arms. 'Come here. I'm really sorry. It's – difficult for me, you see. Suddenly.'

'I don't understand why,' she said, moving into his arms. 'You were so easy before, so relaxed about – about everything, seemed to think it was funny almost. I don't see why it's so difficult suddenly.'

'It's because it's so near,' he said slowly, 'making it formal, official, telling people, taking you on, taking care of you, assuming responsibility for you. You and – and our children. Thinking what people will be saying, wondering how I can make it work – '

'How *we* can make it work,' said Grace firmly.

'Yes, all right. We. But I have to do most of it.'

'Ben, that's not true. I resent that.'

And they were off again. Arguing, actually quarrelling sometimes, unthinkably hostile to one another. She thought back to the soft, gentle, easy Ben of a year ago and wondered what had happened to him.

'Grace,' said Daniel, 'did I hear you saying you were going to sell this house?'

'Well – I might.'

'Why?'

'Well, you see,' – she hesitated – 'your dad wants to – to live somewhere else.'

'What, with us? Without you?' He looked frightened, panic-stricken, as if he might cry.

Grace thought very carefully. Then she said, 'No, not without me. With me.'

'Oh. You going to get married then?'

'Well – we might. We just might. You'll have to ask your dad.'

Daniel leapt up, tore up the stairs, rode down the banisters doing a war whoop. David appeared on the landing looking cross. Like Ben, thought Grace suddenly.

'What's going on?'

'Grace and Dad. They're getting married.'

'Daniel, I – '

'Yeah, I knew that,' said David coolly. 'Dad told me.'

Grace stared at him. 'When did he tell you?'

'Oh – ages ago. When he came back, after being away.'

'Oh,' said Grace, slightly uncertainly.

'Dad says we've got to move from here,' said Daniel. 'Live somewhere else.'

'Whatever for?'

'Dunno.'

'That's daft,' said David. 'I'll tell him.'

The next time Ben came home they had a monumental row. David, as he'd promised, told Ben he thought it was daft to move; Ben asked him who'd said they had to, and what had it got to do with him anyway; David said Grace had said so and if they were getting married it was a lot to do with him. Ben asked Grace what the hell she was doing, getting the boys on her side, and Grace said she wasn't, and what the hell was he doing telling David they were getting married when they'd agreed they wouldn't. Daniel burst into tears and said if they had to leave the Mill House he wasn't coming, and David went storming out of the house and didn't come back for so long they began to get seriously worried about him.

They made it up, in bed: a strange, fierce hour of love-making during which Ben seemed alternately angry and grieving, dominating her, pushing her to her climax in a frantic urgency, leaving her exhausted by its violence. But 'I love you so much,' he said afterwards, restored to tenderness, sweetness, 'you're so lovely, so everything I want. And I know that ought to be enough. But it isn't. It's got to be got right. All of it.'

He had not asked about being invalided out, said it would scupper his chances of a sponsored course. He said he hated the idea, it seemed wrong.

'But Ben, if your shoulder is genuinely more painful, you won't be able to stay in anyway.'

'Yeah, well, I think I'd rather that was left to them to decide,' he said.

'All right. Have you thought any more about what I said? About the teaching?'

'Yes. And I don't want to do it.'

'The teaching? Or being dependent on me?'

'Both.'

'I know that's not true,' said Grace and went out of the room, slamming the door.

She talked to Florence about it, thinking how extraordinary it was that she should feel so close to Florence now, that she could ask her advice on something so complex, so delicate. That worried her too: that she had changed so much, come so far. Florence was sympathetic, but cautionary.

'You've got a real problem, Grace. I always thought so. Ben is very proud. He's bound to be. It's a class thing. I know that sounds snobby and awful and all right, maybe it is. But it's something you're going to have to accept. And make all the concessions.'

It didn't help. For the first time almost since she could remember, she found herself thinking about Linda. Wondering what she had really been like. And how she, Grace, so clearly and extremely different in every way, could possibly replace her.

They seemed to be on a steep downward spiral. The slightest thing made it worse. David telling Ben he was really good at explaining things and ought to be a teacher produced a furious accusation that she had planted the idea in his head. Daniel crying because he didn't want to leave Flossie made Grace cry too, and led to a resentment so furious that she couldn't bear Ben to touch her that night. Florence flying into the Mill House to say she and Giles were getting married on his next leave and Ben, when she told him, simply saying 'Oh' rather dully, not proposing any kind of date for them. Even her starting to look at pretty little town houses in Salisbury made him angry. 'We should be doing this together,' he said, 'not you on your own, making decisions.'

Sharply, almost frighteningly then, she began to think about Charles and her marriage to him: even to miss him.

She wouldn't, couldn't, give in to Ben totally, go along with him, with what he wanted, all the way. She knew it was wrong. That was the way Charles had run their marriage and it had made her resentful and miserable. She was older and a great deal wiser and she knew there had to be compromise.

'How did you and Linda work things out?' she said carefully, casually one night, when he was home for a few days, when they were feeling closer, safer.

And 'I know why you're asking that,' he said, and she could feel him withdrawing from her, both physically and emotionally, 'and I'd really rather you didn't.'

'Why?'

'Because it's not fair. To either of us.'

'But why not, Ben?'

'Because,' he said, 'because we didn't have the same kind of problems, that's why,' and wouldn't enlarge any further. She was silent; it was what she was most afraid of.

Slowly and rather painfully she began to question seriously the wisdom of what she was doing: blinded by love, by desire, by happiness, she had turned her back on reality. She tried to think forward a few years: when the first joy of being with Ben, being his wife, would be gone. Were the differences between them greater than she had realized? Did the new qualities in him that she had discovered, the need to dominate and to be seen to dominate, not only her but her situation, the almost overbearing pride, the strong driving will, did they really all spring from the fact that his background was so different from hers? Was there more to class than accent, education, stupid things like expressions of speech?

Hurt by her own difficulties in the past, she had refused to accept that there was; Ben had seemed simply to be exactly the kind of man she warmed to, liked, wanted. She had never for a single moment felt embarrassed by him, awkward when he was with her family, minded the way he spoke. Rather the reverse: she was fiercely, happily proud of him, astonished by how right he was for her in every way. Now more crucial things were arising: she could see endless conflicts over money, friendships, her own life and independence even. Was he going to become possessive and overbearing with her, turn into some kind of stereotype of working-class manhood? Charles had been a stereotype – in a very different but equally class-ridden way, and she had hated it, had thought that in Ben she had found originality, escape. She tried to equate this new person with the sweetly liberal one who had excused Clarissa's behaviour with Giles, and wondered at the difference.

The crisis came, as crises so often do, over something very small. It was a Saturday morning and Ben had arrived late the night before; his shoulder was hurting and he was tired.

He looked out of the window and said, 'Those beds need sorting.'

'I know,' she said, 'Mr Blackstone couldn't get along this week.'

'I'd better see to it,' he said.

'No, Ben, don't, that's silly, when your shoulder's so sore. I'll do it. When I've got time.'

'No,' he said, 'I don't want you to do it.'

'Whyever not?'

He shrugged.

'Ben, why not? I'm perfectly capable.'

'You may be capable,' he said, 'but it's not what you should be doing. It's not a woman's job.'

'Oh Ben, honestly! When women have been half running this country for five years. What a stupid, old-fashioned thing to say.'

'Yes, well, I am old-fashioned,' he said, 'and I don't like to see women lugging spades and that about.'

Whereupon Grace said she had never heard anything so silly, and he said she was going to hear a lot of equally silly things in the future and she'd better get used to it.

'Any minute now,' she said, trying to make a joke of it, 'you'll start telling me women belong in the kitchen.'

'What's that supposed to mean?'

'Nothing,' said Grace quickly.

'Yes it does. You're implying that's the sort of thing working-class men say. Isn't it? Not nice liberal upper-class chaps, like Charles and Jack.'

'Charles wasn't liberal, Ben, and don't be ridiculous.'

'If I can't say something I believe in,' he said suddenly, 'without you relating it to my background, I don't know quite what we're doing together at all.'

'Ben, you're just being paranoid. It wasn't what I meant at all. And you know it wasn't. You're just picking a quarrel, finding difficulties.'

'I'm glad you can read my mind so well,' he said, and went out into the garden and slammed the door.

Grace was shaking: with fright as much as rage. She had just finished clearing the table when he came back in. She thought he was

449

going to apologize, but he said, 'Look, I think I'd best go back to Tidworth.'

'Why?'

'Because we're not going to have a good weekend. And I need to think a bit.'

Panic gripped her; she thought she was going to be sick. 'Think about what?'

'Us. What we're going to do.'

She didn't argue; she had at least too much self-respect for that. He left almost at once, giving her the briefest kiss, and she did not hear from him until Sunday evening. Then he phoned, and said he was sorry, that he needed more time to think, that although he loved her, he wasn't sure they had really faced up to the situation properly. 'I'll write to you or something,' he said. 'Sorry about this. But we've got to be sure.'

She didn't hear from him for a week, and then he came over to see her.

He sat in the study, his head bowed, and told her that much as he loved her, he thought they should postpone any decisions about their future for quite a long time, that things were even more difficult than he had first thought. Grace was not without pride; she told him she thought so too. He said he'd be over to see the boys in a couple of weeks, and until then it would be best not to have any contact with each other.

When he had gone, she went upstairs and lay awake on her bed all night, staring into the darkness, unable to believe such happiness could have arrived and left her again so swiftly. Against all odds, she expected to hear from him again within a few days, but she didn't. The phone remained stubbornly silent. As stubborn as he was.

Misery, anxiety made her physically ill. She felt nauseated a lot of the time, had headaches, was lethargic, devoid of energy. She wanted to sleep a great deal, found herself heavy-eyed after lunch, dropping off on the sofa after supper.

'You look rotten,' said Florence, who was herself radiant, shining with happiness. 'Are you all right?'

'Yes, I think so. Just worried.'

'What about?'

'Ben,' said Grace, 'Ben, and what we're going to do.' She refused to discuss it further.

'You ought to eat more,' said David, watching her push her food round her plate. 'You're awfully thin.'

'I'm not hungry,' said Grace.

'You look awful,' said Daniel, 'ever so pale. You all right?'

'Yes, I'm all right. I've just been feeling a bit sick lately, that's all.'

'You ought to go to the doctor. S'pose it's appendicitis like me.'

'Oh don't talk about appendicitis,' said Grace, remembering the happiness of that night, after the sister had told them to go home to bed.

'Why not?'

'Just don't,' she said and burst into tears, rushed away upstairs.

David looked at Daniel. 'I think she *might* have appendicitis,' he said. 'She's scared it might be, that's why she keeps crying. She was sick the other day, I heard her, just like you were.'

'Should we tell Dad?'

'Yeah. I'll write him a note.'

Ben stood in his small room in the barracks at Tidworth, reading the letter from David that said Grace wasn't well, that she kept being sick and didn't want her food, and was terribly tired all the time and kept crying, and they thought it might be appendicitis and he ought to come and see her and make her go to the doctor, and an extraordinary series of emotions went through him. He was not surprised to find that when he tried to reread the letter, the lines were slightly blurred.

He arrived at the Mill House the next evening. Grace was sitting in the kitchen, trying to concentrate on a complicated letter from one of her land girls' mothers. She looked up and flushed as he came in.

'Hallo. What are you doing here?'

'I've come to see you. That's all.'

'Oh.' He looked odd, rather worked up, different from the heavy, hostile creature he had become. She was puzzled.

'I shouldn't really be here. Get into trouble if they knew. But I – '

'Well, just let me finish this,' she said as coolly as she could, determined not to let him see how disturbed she was by his arrival. 'It's rather complicated. And then I'll get you a drink.'

'I don't want a drink,' he said.

This was clearly it; the final announcement.

'Come into the other room, will you?' he said. 'I want to talk to you.'

'All right.' She followed him through, sat on the sofa beside him, feeling terrified. She took a deep breath, forcing down the panic, looked at him steadily. She was not going to make a fool of herself; she was not.

'I had a letter from David,' he said abruptly. 'He seemed to think you might have appendicitis.'

'Oh, that's silly. Of course I haven't.'

'You sure? He said you'd not been eating, been feeling rotten.'

'Yes. Yes I have. But it's certainly not appendicitis.'

He put his hand on her belly. 'Not tender here?'

'No. No of course not.'

'He said you'd actually been sick though.'

'Yes, I have. But I'd know if it was my appendix. I'm not daft.'

'I think you might be,' he said, 'daft, I mean.' He hesitated, then said, 'Grace, when did you last have a period?'

'I don't know,' she said irritably, 'about – about – ' Her voice trailed away, she stared at him, flushed, her eyes very bright. 'Oh my God,' she said finally, her voice an awed whisper, 'it was Christmas Eve, I remember, remember thinking it was the last straw.'

'And now it's March.' He felt her belly again. 'It feels just a tiny bit swollen,' he said, 'fluid of course, that's all it is.'

'Why do you always have to be so bloody clever about everything?' she said and burst into tears.

Suddenly, magically, everything was much better. Ben said they'd have to get married quickly, that he didn't want any little bastards in the family. He smiled at her and kissed her as he said it; he was suddenly quietly, confidently happy.

He said he would still like to leave the Mill House, but he certainly didn't want to live in a town, that children were much better in the country and anyway it was cheaper, and that as David was finally happily settled at the grammar school perhaps somewhere in a village the other side of Salisbury might be a good idea. He also said he'd been doing a lot of thinking and that, for a family man, teaching did seem to be the ideal profession; if Grace was really prepared to sponsor him while he was at college, he'd take her on for the rest of his life. Grace said that would be perfectly all right.

She lay in bed and looked at him as he said all this, smiling, unable to believe her happiness. 'I love you,' she said, 'I love you so much.'

'I love you too. And I'm sorry I've been such a miserable bugger lately.'

'Don't say sorry,' she said.

He smiled, put his hand out, caressed her breasts. She winced. 'They're awfully sore.'

'Oh dear,' he said, 'what a lot of changes we're going to have to make.'

'But it's worth it, isn't it?'

'Oh yes,' he said, 'very well worth it.'

Their baby – his baby – seemed to have worked a most remarkable change in him. It was as if everything had shifted, come back into focus, restored his self-respect. She could only suppose it had its roots in something primitive; that he felt now she was carrying his child she was clearly and indisputably his, his woman. She didn't really care; whatever the explanation he was the old Ben again, gentle, caring, relaxed, and something else too, confident, because this was something he knew about, that he could tell her about. She was the novice, finding herself in unfamiliar territory, he leading the way, showing her what to do. It was at one and the same time very complicated and extremely simple; she knew only that she was perfectly happy.

'I think we should have a party,' said Grace, 'just a family one, of course. But to tell everyone. And celebrate everything. All the happy endings. Ours, and Florence and Giles, and Muriel and Clifford, and Jack, he's got into medical school – you see he's not making all this silly fuss about his wife supporting him. Oh, and Jeannette – Ted Miller has finally popped the question, apparently. And according to Daniel, Charlotte's pregnant again. I'm not much good at keeping her in, I'm afraid. I'm not sure that we ought to celebrate that, actually.'

'Of course we should,' said Ben, 'it was Charlotte's first confinement that brought us together. Yes, you go ahead and have your party if you want to. The whole country'll be partying soon, anyway.'

She was surprised she felt well enough; but suddenly, miraculously, she did. Filled with energy, no longer sick. 'I told you,' said Ben complacently, 'thirteen weeks almost to the day.'

He continued to be filled with a proprietorial happiness about her pregnancy, clearly regarding it as rather more his province than hers. She didn't mind. She didn't mind anything. 'What about Easter Monday?' she said, and started planning in earnest. They could all be there: for Clarissa, who had finally left her beloved Dartmouth and been posted back to Greenwich, leave was easy; Jack was in Norfolk but said nothing would keep him away; Giles could get down from Liverpool; Clifford said it would be delightful.

She asked her parents; Betty looked doubtful. 'Is there some special reason for it, dear?'

Grace hesitated; she knew she must do it, get it over with, it wasn't fair to spring it on them in public, but she had been dreading it nonetheless.

'Yes,' she said finally, 'yes, there is.'

They took it very well; Frank seemed genuinely pleased, said he had always liked Ben, that he was a fine young chap, and one of nature's gentlemen, and that he would be very happy to put his daughter in his care. Betty had a little cry, and said rather more doubtfully that she supposed it would be all right, and that she did like Ben, but 'it just still seems a little – well, a little – odd, dear,' she said.

Grace didn't point out that her engagement to Charles had been at least a little odd, that Charles's friends and family had certainly seen it as so; she just said she was very happy indeed, and that at long last Betty would be a grandmother. 'You've been very patient, Mother,' she said, kissing her. 'It'll be lovely, and if we moved to Salisbury, you'll be even nearer.'

'I certainly think it's very sensible to move,' said Betty unexpectedly. 'That is Charles's house and always would have been. I wouldn't have respected Ben if he'd stayed there.'

Grace said it had been Ben's idea entirely to leave the Mill House, not hers, indeed she had tried to resist it, whereupon Betty's graciousness towards Ben visibly increased.

The advance on Berlin, Hitler's increasing physical and mental instability, the public hanging from lamp posts of German deserters all too aware of the final outcome of the war, the bloody fighting the length of Germany, the appalling desecration of the northern German cities and countryside, the slow-growing perception of the full horror of the Holocaust: all seemed very far away from the sleepy charm of Shaftesbury, the peace and loveliness of Thorpe St Andrews as Grace prepared for her party that Easter weekend.

She had filled the house with flowers, had picked basketfuls of primroses and primulas and daffodils, and even a few early bluebells, cut great sheaths of forsythia and branches of apple blossom from the garden. Mrs Babbage had been in for what she called a special, 'something between a spring clean and an ordinary,' she explained, had waxed the golden wooden floors, polished the lovely windows, and scrubbed the stone flags in the kitchen. The house was full of dappled light, of pale, pure colour; the garden lush, lovely, rich with birdsong. Jeannette had come down from the Priory to bake, and the kitchen gave out wonderful warm, luscious smells, of baking bread and simmering soups, chives and parsley and garlic ('Jeannette should go down in history as the person who brought garlic to south Wiltshire,' said Florence proudly). She liked to have a musical background while she worked, and when the wireless failed her, she would create her own, warbling 'Accentuate the Positive' and 'If I Loved You' and sundry Vera Lynn classics in a surprisingly true and powerful voice.

The night before the party, Grace rang the Priory and asked to speak to Clarissa. She came onto the phone, her voice light, easy as always.

'Darling! Lovely to hear from you. Everything all right?'

'Yes. Yes, thank you. Clarissa, I'd really like to see you for a minute. Could we – well, go for a walk or something?'

'Of course. Lovely idea. I'll pop down, shall I? In about half an hour?'

'Yes, that'd be nice,' said Grace.

'I just wanted to apologize,' she said, as they wandered across the meadow, 'for being so – arrogant that day. It was wrong of me. I – well, I talked to Ben about it, and he made me see it wasn't really nearly as bad as I thought.'

'How very clever of him,' said Clarissa, her voice just slightly tart, 'especially as he didn't really know what had happened.'

'No, but he pointed out what a lot you'd been through with Jack, and that you both thought it was over with Florence, and – well, I, was a bit priggish about it. I'm sorry. And I shouldn't have hit you.'

Clarissa smiled at her, took her arm. 'Darling, don't give it another thought. Sweet of you to apologize. Anyway, it was naughty of me, whatever Ben, the darling, might find in the way of excuses. Lovely, lovely man. Ben, I mean. But no harm done, and Florence is never going to know. So let's just put it all out of our minds, and concentrate on you and your blissful baby. What did you think you might call her? It's got to be a girl, hasn't it? And you know, what I'd like best in the entire world would be to be godmother. What would you think about that?'

'I'd think it was a lovely idea,' said Grace, surprised to find she meant it. 'But I'll have to ask Ben,' she added dutifully.

Grace woke early next morning, slithered out of bed so as not to disturb Ben and decided to indulge herself by having a bath in the first and indeed only really warm water of the day. She was lying staring in some awe at her considerably enlarged veined breasts, so far the only visible signs of her pregnancy, when Ben came in rubbing his eyes sleepily.

'You look lovely,' he said.

'I wonder if you'll be saying that in five months' time,' said Grace, 'when I'm huge and hideous.'

'You won't be huge and hideous, you'll be huge and beautiful,' he said, bending to kiss her.

Jeannette arrived an hour later with Imogen and Mamie, both already hopelessly overexcited. 'Ted's comin' down for 'em in a while,' she said, 'taking 'em for a walk, to keep 'em occupied.'

'That's very kind of him,' said Grace.

'Yeah, well, I said 'e'd got to start as I mean 'im to go on,' said Jeannette cheerfully, 'otherwise it's over before it's begun.'

'Very wise,' said Ben. 'Good tactics.' Grace made a face at him.

At eleven Clarissa and Jack suddenly appeared. 'We couldn't stand it up there any longer,' said Clarissa. 'Moo's discovered blight on her early roses, and somehow it's Clifford's fault, he's in the most terrible disgrace. How he could have left this wonderful haven, Grace darling, I cannot imagine. Now do tell us what we can do, we haven't come to just sit around, have we, Jack? Ben darling, how lovely to see you, I swear you've got taller than ever. Give me a kiss. Now listen, I hear you and Jack are both going to be students, I think it's simply too wonderful –'

Grace left Clarissa, laughing, to put the glasses out and take the champagne she and Jack had brought ('Don't thank us, it was from my wicked, wicked friend Bunty,') into the larder. One of the things she was determined to have, in her new house, was a refrigerator.

Florence and Giles and Clifford and Muriel arrived together, Clifford clearly already having shipped in a fair bit of Dutch courage. Muriel passed Ben her coat and hat. 'You may put these away,' she said to him graciously, 'and I'd like a drink immediately. It has been the most dreadful morning. I am quite exhausted.'

'In what way dreadful?' asked Ben.

'Oh, to do with the garden. You probably wouldn't understand, it's very complex. Anyway, it's all Clifford's fault.'

Ben caught Clifford's eye and winked at him. 'I'll get you a drink as well,' he said.

They had agreed, Grace and Ben, to make their announcement just before lunch, when the ice was broken and everyone had had a drink or two; so perfect a day was it that everyone was in the garden. 'I wish we could freeze this moment, keep it for ever and ever,' said Grace quietly to Ben, looking at them all from where they stood by the French windows, just within the drawing room, looking at all the people she cared about, close to her, Imogen and Mamie chasing Puppy, the boys sitting on the paddock fence, Ted and Jeannette laughing together under the willow tree. Giles and Florence were sitting on the grass, his arm round her shoulders; Jack was talking earnestly to Muriel; Clarissa's arm was through Clifford's, making him laugh with some no doubt scurrilous story. 'Look,' she said, 'look, Ben. That's happiness. Happiness for all of us.'

Ben smiled down at her, took her hand. 'Give me a kiss,' he said, 'and then we'll go and tell them all.'

And then the phone rang.

It was Clarissa who saw her first, standing frozen still in the drawing room, motionless, white, her face drawn and somehow very old. Something was clearly wrong, terribly, terribly wrong, and Clarissa had just begun to take it in, to move towards the house, when she saw her crumple up as if she had not an atom, a shred of strength within her, and fall to the floor, lie there, her fan of red-gold hair heavy around her face, her eyes closed.

'What is it, Grace, what is it, whatever is it?' cried Florence, flying in through the door ahead of the others. 'Jack, quickly, call the doctor, something's happened. Giles, get some water. Where's Ben? Ben, come here, quickly, quickly.'

Grace moved then, struggled to sit up; Ben knelt behind her, his arms round her, supporting her. 'What is it?' he said. 'Is it the – '

And 'No,' she said, 'no, it's not that. I'm all right.'

'Who was it on the phone?' he said. 'Was that it? Who was it? Was it bad news?'

'It was Charles,' said Grace. 'He's alive.'

Chapter Thirty-One

Summer 1945

She lost the baby. They said it was the shock. She lay in the hospital, and she hardly noticed the physical pain, so terrible was her grief, as her baby, Ben's baby, ebbed away from her, taking happiness with it.

Apart from anything else, she was frightened, terribly frightened at the thought of Charles's coming back: a stranger, walking into her house, taking over her life, moving into her bed. In the first few terrible hours, when the strange tableau began to play, wild plans formed, established themselves, only to be rejected again, as plainly foolish, impracticable, wrong: that she would run away, just go, on her own, where no one could find her; that she would run away with Ben, Ben and the boys; that she would refuse to see Charles, tell him simply that she was leaving him; that she would go to see him, and tell him that she was leaving him. All this against a background of confusion, embarrassment, sympathy: no one knew quite what to do, what to say. Muriel, of course, was joyfully, wonderfully happy, and Clifford too, and she could understand that, could not find it in her heart to be-grudge them; Florence more torn, shocked and concerned for Grace even in her pleasure at having her brother restored to her. Clarissa was simply shocked; she came to Grace where she sat, shaking, in her room, put her arms round her and held her for a long time, then said quietly, 'I'll do anything, anything at all that might help.'

Her parents were distraught with anxiety, embarrassment, at the same time oddly practical and thoughtful. 'We'll take the boys, dear, for as long as is necessary,' said Betty as they left, half reluctant, half relieved, 'and tell Ben he can come and stay whenever he likes.'

By three everyone had gone, taking silently awkward farewells. Grace came down, shakily, to an empty house, the only visible remaining traces of the party being the flowers. David and Daniel, bored, irritated by the fuss, not comprehending it, had finally gone fishing; Ben was sitting, staring out of the window.

'Do you want to talk?' he said, and there was in his voice, along with concern, sympathy, an odd impatience, almost an anger. She understood it, it was not at her, but at fate, life, that it could throw such a thing at him.

'No,' she said, 'not yet. I – we can't. Not yet. It's too complicated.'

'Tell me again,' he said, 'where he is.'

'In an Allied base camp, somewhere in central Germany. They're going to be flown home. In a couple of weeks or so apparently. I don't know any more than that. Not at the moment. The man who phoned, someone from the War Office, don't ask me who, said he'd keep in touch.'

'But there's no doubt about it?' he said. 'It's not a mistake, not this time?'

'I'm – I'm afraid not, no.'

'You're very calm,' he said.

'I know. It won't last, I'm afraid.'

It didn't; by suppertime she was hysterical, crying, clinging to him, begging him to take her away. And then suddenly, horribly, the pain started.

Gradually a picture emerged of how the whole ghastly mistake had happened. Charles had not escaped alone; he had been with another officer when he got away from the convoy, and it had been the other officer, a Lieutenant-Colonel Barlowe, who had been shot and wounded and subsequently died. Details were still hazy, but it was clearly where the confusion over identities had arisen. Charles, totally unaware of what had officially happened to him, had made his way slowly and tortuously across southern France, but had finally been shot and captured in Vichy France, spent weeks in a German-controlled hospital and was then taken back into Germany by the retreating army to a long series of prison camps. He had written, tried to make contact, but no letters had been getting through. It was only with the arrival of the Allies in northern Germany that he had been taken to a transit camp and managed to get word home. He was now at an Allied air base, waiting to be flown to England. He had had a bad, a terrible time; Grace knew without any doubt at all that she must be there when he got home. That much at least she owed him.

She went home from hospital after a few days, pale and fragile, struggling to be brave. She had not only Charles but Ben and the boys to worry about; she couldn't allow herself to go under. She found the boys very hard to cope with: baffled by events, uneasy about their own future (despite reassurances from both her and Ben), they were noisy, restless, demanding. Ben had had to return to Tidworth, in itself a strange relief, so she was alone with them; after a few days she accepted Florence's offer to have them.

'They'll be all right here, Jeannette can feed them and they know Clifford so well – '

'What about your mother?'

'I'll deal with her,' said Florence.

And so she was alone, alone with her fear and her dread, trying not to think, to plan, to feel: just waiting.

Then he phoned; he was in Kent, in Lympne, flown there by a British bomber.

'Grace?' he said, 'Grace, darling, hallo, it's me, Charles.'

'Hallo,' she said. Her own voice was very faint, faltering, she had trouble projecting any sound at all. She stood there in the hall, gripping the phone tightly, trying to remain calm.

'Darling, are you all right?'

And 'Yes,' she said, 'I'm fine. Thank you. How about you?'

'Oh, you know, Pretty good really.'

There was a silence. What an extraordinary conversation, she thought, to be having; to be having with a ghost. The ghost of a man she had been married to, who she had thought dead, whom she had betrayed. It was very hard; any sense of reality deserted her.

'I thought you were dead,' she said. 'We all did.'

'Yes. Yes, I know that now. I'm sorry. So very sorry.'

Another silence. 'When will you be home?' she said.

'Tomorrow, I think. God, it seems so unreal. I can get a train to London and then down to Salisbury. Perhaps a taxi – '

'I'll meet you,' she said.

'How?'

'In the car,' she said, surprised he should ask; then remembered he didn't even know she could drive. So many changes; how could they begin to accommodate them?

'Darling, how clever. Right. I'll phone you when I get to London, shall I?'

'Yes. Yes, do.'

'I'm so longing to see you,' he said.

His train would be in Salisbury by four, he said. She got ready to go and meet him, brushing her hair, putting on her most respectable dress, making up her face so that it looked just a little less blanched, feeling violently sick.

The train was late of course. She sat in the car park, remembering, remembering all the times she had been there with Ben: the day he had gone away, after Linda had died, and he had stood there holding her, for the very first time; the time he had come to stay after leaving hospital, the Christmas he had told her he loved her. Memories flooded her, and she sat there, eyes tightly closed, forcing them back, crushing them. She went and bought a *Picture Post*, sat reading about the events of the past few weeks, the fall of Berlin, Hitler's death, the total capitulation of the German Army, and it was all meaningless, a jumble of letters and words, adding up to nothing at all. She heard the train come in; heard the steam, the scream of brakes; heard doors opening, slamming, tried desperately to compose herself; then got out of the car, went to the barrier, terrified even of seeing him.

There were a lot of people on the platform, many of them soldiers. She couldn't see him: a wild hope that he wasn't there, that she was to be granted at the very least a reprieve, filled her. And then she saw him: not unrecognizable, as so many people had predicted, not even almost so, but terribly changed nonetheless, thin, gauntly, hideously thin, limping, his face pallid, a different shape, the cheekbones higher in their new prominence, the jaw sharper, harder, his eyes somehow lighter. He saw her and smiled, waved, took off his hat; his hair was darker, very short. He had a deep scar right down the side of his face, running from his forehead to his jaw. She forced herself to smile back, to wave; and then he was beside her, had set down his bag, put his arms round her, hugged her very tightly.

'I can't believe you're here,' he said, and there were tears in his voice. 'I can't believe I'm really home.'

She drove back very carefully; she didn't want him worrying about his car, criticizing her driving.

'You drive quite well,' he said, his voice surprised. 'When did you start?'

'Oh – ages ago,' said Grace quickly.

'It all looks so lovely here,' he said. 'I'd forgotten how beautiful England was. I'd really forgotten.'

'Where exactly have you been?'

'Darling, what a question. Where haven't I been! You don't want to hear about that now.'

'Yes I do. Of course I do. How can I begin to understand otherwise, if you don't – '

'Grace, you can't begin to understand in any case,' he said shortly.

'Oh.'

'Sorry. Didn't mean to snap. But it's so hard to – well, anyway, a large number of godforsaken places, most recently in France, in the Ardennes and then in Germany.'

She looked at him sharply, but he was staring blankly ahead of him.

'Was it – very bad? Or don't you want to talk about it?'

'I don't want to talk about it. Not yet, anyway. And it was pretty bad, yes. The hospital was OK.'

'Your – your limp. Was that where you were shot?'

'Yes,' he said briefly.

'And the scar on your face?'

'Yes. Darling, I said I didn't want to talk about it.'

'Sorry.'

As they reached Thorpe Magna, he said, 'How's my mother?'

She had been surprised he hadn't asked before. 'She's fine. Very well. Your father's back there at the Priory with her.'

'Good Lord. She took him back. How extraordinarily generous. Well, that's one thing I don't have to worry about.'

'What?'

'Confronting him.'

'Oh, I see. No. They said they'd love to see you later, but if you were tired, tomorrow perhaps – '

'Yes of course. Well, I'll see. What about Florence? And Robert?'

She felt an intense shock at the realization of how much he didn't know. 'Robert's dead, Charles.'

'Good Lord. How terrible. Poor Florence.'

'Yes,' she said. She didn't feel able to embark on explanations, on anything.

They drove on; her terror increased. Suddenly he said, 'Those – those boys aren't at home, are they? You've got rid of them?'

'No,' she said, 'no, they're not there.'

'Well done. I was a bit anxious. About finding them there.'

'They're at the Priory actually,' she said. She couldn't help it, it should have waited, but she was so angry, so outraged on their behalf, her boys, her beloved boys; and he had to know.

'What on earth are they doing there?'

'They have to be somewhere, Charles. They don't have any other home.'

'They'll have to be found one,' he said shortly, and was silent again.

And then they were there, pulling into the drive; and he sat back, looked out at the house in silence. Then he got out, walked up to the front door, and she unlocked it and he walked in, through into the hall, the kitchen, the drawing room, exploring it, invading it, reclaiming it, her house, her refuge. And then he turned to her and smiled, said, 'It looks marvellous, darling. You've cared for it beautifully. Well done.'

Grace managed to smile back and to put the kettle on, and then she fled upstairs, into the bathroom, and sat on the edge of the bath for a long time, fists clenched, composing herself; when she went down again, he was out in the garden, wandering around.

'Bit neglected,' he said, 'but not too bad. What on earth's been going on on the lawn down there? Looks like a ploughed field.'

'It's the boys. It's where they play football.'

He didn't say anything.

Charlotte came waddling out, hugely pregnant. 'Good Lord,' he said, 'you've had her mated. Whose stud dog did you use?'

'Um – the farm collie, I think,' said Grace, smiling, hoping he would smile back. He didn't.

'Darling, really! Well, we could drown most of them, I suppose. Just keep a couple so she doesn't get milk fever. Better have her spayed, Grace, if you can't be bothered to do it properly. What on earth's that?'

'That's Puppy. From an earlier marriage.'

'Dear oh dear,' he said, trying this time to smile, 'I can see things have got a bit out of hand.'

'Just a bit,' she said.

She made supper early; the atmosphere was increasingly strained. There was so much to say, so little that could be said. She talked as brightly as she could about her work with the Land Army, about Florence and the WVS, about Clarissa and Jack, but he was distracted, clearly not interested. His only real concern appeared to be with Robert, when and how he had been killed, what Florence would do. She couldn't bring herself to tell him about Giles, the territory seemed too dangerous. He was also delighted about his mother, said several times how good of her to have taken Clifford back. 'I suppose it was just an aberration with this other woman,' he said. 'It happens of course.'

'Yes,' said Grace.

He wasn't even interested in Jack, Jack and his injuries, his plans for the future. Just Robert and Muriel: the two people least worthy of his concern.

And then it was bedtime. She had thought endlessly about what she ought to do, what she could do. The doctor at the hospital had forbidden what he called intimacy for at least a month; how did you explain, though, to a husband who had been away for four years that you had just had a miscarriage, couldn't sleep with him? In the end, she decided to endure it. Whatever happened to her didn't seem to matter very much. She climbed into bed beside him, her body clenched with dread, looking at him rather uncertainly; he leant down and kissed her, quite gently, and said, 'Oh Grace darling, it's been so long.' And then he turned out the light and started to kiss her properly. In that dreadful, mechanical, well-rehearsed way she remembered so well.

She decided to count. It never took very long: by the time she got to five hundred, she thought, it would be over. Besides, he was her husband, she had loved and wanted him once – or had at least thought she did – perhaps she could again. She lay there, feeling his hands on her, in her, probing her, feeling him harden, wanting her, trying to concentrate on her counting, on breathing deeply, on wiping her mind clear of Ben, and she couldn't do it; it was like rape, it was like Robert all over again. She felt a scream rising in her throat, knew it was going to surface if he didn't stop, if she didn't make him stop. Suddenly, sharply, she pulled away from him, sat up, hugging her knees, mumbling something about not being ready. He switched the light on, and his face was harsh, his eyes angry.

'Darling,' he said, bringing the endearment out with an obvious effort, 'darling, please! Surely I deserve more of a welcome than that!'

And 'Charles,' she said, and was shocked to hear herself saying it, she had meant to wait, to wait a while longer, 'Charles, there's something I have to tell you.'

She told him very briefly, in a few sentences; there seemed little need, rather the reverse, to elaborate. He stared at her, his face white, drawn, listening in absolute silence; when she had finished, he got out of bed, pulled on his dressing gown and went downstairs. She waited a while, then followed him. He was sitting in the drawing room, had lit a cigarette; he didn't look at her as she came in.

'Look,' she said tentatively, 'we should talk. There's – '

'I don't want to talk about it,' he said, 'not now. Just leave me alone, please.'

She left him.

She woke up very early, feeling cold, surprised she had slept at all; she got up and went to find him. He was in the spare room, fast asleep, several cigarettes in the ashtray by his bed, and an empty glass. She left him, went downstairs, tidied the house, fed the dogs and Flossie.

'Please,' she said to Charlotte, 'please don't have those puppies today. Not a good idea.'

Charlotte wagged her tail and went back to sleep.

It was dancing day, she realized, at school; she phoned Miss Merton, told her she couldn't come.

'That's quite all right, Mrs Bennett. I understand. It must be very – hectic for you,' she said, choosing her words with care, 'your husband coming home. What about next week?'

'Next week will be fine,' said Grace, and put the phone down.

'What will be fine?' said Charles. He had come downstairs; he looked terrible.

'Oh – I play the piano at the school, for dancing lessons. I cancelled it today, though. As you were here.'

'What, the village school?'

'Yes. Is there anything wrong with that? I give some of them individual lessons as well.'

'Do they come here?' he said. 'To the house?'

'A few of them, yes. There's one little girl called Elspeth Dunn, she's very – '

'I don't think I quite like that idea,' he said, 'not in the house. Keep it at the school in future perhaps.'

'Well, we can see,' said Grace.

'No, Grace, we won't see,' said Charles, and for the first time since his return he looked as she remembered him, overbearing, self-important. 'I don't want the village children overrunning this house.'

'Hardly overrunning.'

'It seems that way to me. Village children, evacuees from London slums – God help me.' He pushed his hands through his cropped hair. 'We have to talk. Urgently.'

'Yes,' she said and followed him meekly into the kitchen.

'This man,' he said, 'the business with this man – '

'Yes?' said Grace.

'Did – did everyone know about it? I mean was it common knowledge?'

'Well – yes and no.'

'Grace, either it was or it wasn't. Answer me please!'

He sounded angry; his mouth was very taut, a white line round it. For the first time she felt frightened.

'Well, everyone knew, I suppose, that we – that, well, that we were very close. I mean it was fairly obvious.'

'But possibly as friends. Is that possible?'

'I don't know. I shouldn't have thought so, not really. Does it matter?'

'It matters very much. Of course it does. It's all the difference between my being a laughing stock and not, I would say.'

Grace stared at him. 'Is that your main concern, Charles? That you might be a laughing stock?'

'It's a concern, yes. Although obviously not the only one. I would have thought you could see that.'

'Oh,' she said.

'What I'm trying to get at,' he said, 'is did everyone know you were – Christ, that you were sleeping with him?'

'I don't know,' said Grace again. 'If they'd had any common sense, I would have thought so, yes. I mean Florence knew, and Clarissa – and your father of course – '

'What? Florence knew? What the hell did she have to say about it?'

'She – she – oh, you'd better ask her yourself,' said Grace. 'All I would say is, she's been a very good friend to me. And I to her, for that matter. We've been through a lot together, Charles. If you'd let me tell you about it, I'd – '

He interrupted her. 'And Clarissa? I suppose she thought it was rather amusing, did she? Had a good laugh together, did you, the two of you?'

'Charles, please don't. You're making things worse.'

'They couldn't be much worse,' he said, 'as far as I can see. What about this – pregnancy? Was that common knowledge?'

'No,' said Grace quietly.

'Thank Christ for that.'

He was silent for a moment, staring at her, broodingly, blankly angry; she looked back at him, and thought of her baby, Ben's baby, lost to her, dismissed as something that had not been common knowledge, that could be covered up, and suddenly she stopped being sad, and became furiously, wildly angry. She stood up, hit him suddenly, hard about the head; then stood back, shocked at herself, but still feeling the same violence.

'Don't talk to me like that,' she said. 'Don't, don't. That baby was precious to me. You don't seem to understand any of it. You'd been away, Charles, for four years. I'd been alone all that time. For the last

466

year I thought you were dead. We all did. I haven't been behaving like some whore – '

'Don't use words like that.'

'I'll use any words I like,' said Grace, her voice quieter now, 'and you will listen. I am sorry, so sorry, about what has happened, sorrier than I can possibly tell you. Of course it's terrible for you. I understand. It's dreadful, horrible. But you have to think of me too. I – I loved Ben. I was going to marry him. I thought so long and so hard about it, felt such guilt, even after you were – after I thought you were dead. Think what it's like for me, too, Charles, please. Or there is no hope for either of us.'

'I'm going for a walk,' he said.

When he got back he seemed calmer, even tried to smile at her. She smiled back, warily, offered him food; he ate some toast and a couple of eggs in silence, went and had a bath and got dressed.

When he came down she said, 'Why don't you go over to the Priory? They're longing to see you. Especially your mother.'

'I don't think I can,' he said, briefly, 'not yet. I can't face them. In the knowledge of all this, and their collusion in it – '

She dug her nails into her hands, in an effort not to say anything.

'It's Florence, I think,' he said, 'that I mind most about. That she could have tolerated it. Which she obviously did. You and some – some other man. In my house.'

'You haven't listened to a word I've said,' said Grace. She felt icy calm suddenly, went upstairs, started putting a few clothes into a bag.

He followed her up, into the room. 'What are you doing? Leaving me, going to your soldier, I suppose.'

'I don't know,' said Grace, 'I haven't decided. Not yet anyway. And I'm not going to my soldier, as you call him. That's what hurts most, isn't it, Charles? A soldier, not even an officer, being in love with a soldier.'

'Where are you going then?' he said ignoring this.

'I'm not sure. To my parents, probably. Just for a few days. To think.'

'To think about what?' he said, and he looked genuinely baffled.

'About what I'm going to do.'

'You mean you might – might not stay?'

'No,' she said, 'I might not. I might not feel I can.'

'I don't understand you,' he said, 'I simply don't understand you. I can see – just how this thing has happened. But to talk of not staying now. It's – well, it's terrible, Grace. Shocking. That's it. I'm shocked.'

'How can you be shocked?' she said.

'I'm shocked because you seem to have no sense of honour. Of wanting to do the right, the decent thing. We're married, Grace. You're my wife. I've had a dreadful, a terrible, five years. And at the end of them, I think I'm coming home to a loving wife, and I find a – a – oh, Jesus. Christ Jesus, help me.'

Grace sat down suddenly on the bed. For the first time she felt genuine pity for him. Pity and remorse. She put out her hand and took his. 'I'm sorry,' she said, 'so sorry. I don't feel I've done anything wrong, but I am terribly sorry for you.'

He looked down at them, at their two clasped hands, and said dully, 'It would be very wrong of you to leave me. Wrong and dishonourable. As I said.'

A little later she heard him on the phone to his mother.

'Yes,' he was saying, quite normally, 'absolutely fine. It's marvellous to be home. What? Yes, I'd like that very much. I'm a bit tired, today, maybe tomorrow? Lunch, yes, thank you. Yes, I'm sure she'd like to come. How's Father? Good. Give him my regards. Tomorrow then. Will Florence be there? Oh, I see. No, don't worry about anything. I really am pretty fit. Yes, I agree, the house does look very nice. Bye, Mother.'

'What would I like to go to?' said Grace.

'Lunch. At the Priory. Tomorrow.'

'I can't, I'm sorry. I'm working tomorrow.'

'Can't you cancel it?'

'No, of course I can't. You should have asked me, Charles. Anyway, it'll be better for you to go on your own.'

He had moved his things into the guest room; they sat all evening, reading in silence. She found a concert to listen to, but he said he would prefer her to switch it off. Nobody phoned; the house was hideously silent.

She got back at four the next day to find him sitting in the kitchen. He looked exhausted.

'How were they all?' she asked, putting down her file. She was tired; she had cycled a long way, to a couple of farms near Westhorne. She would have taken the car, but he had simply assumed he could have it, and it certainly didn't seem worth arguing about.

'Oh – all right. Bloody chaos over there. That ghastly woman, I cannot imagine how my mother stands her. And those children, the small ones, totally undisciplined. Florence must be out of her mind, turning Imogen over to her.'

'Did you – did you meet the boys?'

'Who? Oh – yes, briefly. They didn't seem too bad. Not a lot to say for themselves.'

'No,' said Grace.

'My mother looks marvellous though. And my father seems pretty well settled again. A lot older of course.'

'Yes, poor old chap,' said Grace. 'He's had a very difficult time.'

'I really don't think,' said Charles, 'he deserves any sympathy whatsoever.' There was a silence. Then, 'What's this fellow Giles like?'

'Sweet,' said Grace, 'terribly nice. He's a musician.'

'Yes, so I gather. Plays in nightclubs, or did, is that right? Extraordinary.'

'Extraordinary,' said Grace. The irony was completely lost on him.

That night Charlotte had her puppies. Grace sat there, stroking her, talking to her, hardly able to bear the pain of remembering. There were only four this time, all black and white, all large and healthy. None to die, none to grieve over.

In the morning, Charles said shouldn't they get rid of at least two of them, and she said no, they shouldn't. He was obviously annoyed, but he didn't argue. He was struggling to accommodate her; she could see that.

The next day he arranged to go to London; he said he had an appointment at the War Office, had to try and sort a few things out. 'What do you think you might do now?' said Grace. 'Go back to the firm, or – '

'Yes, of course, back to the firm,' he said, clearly astonished that she should ask. 'I know there's not much of it left, but I think I can work it up again. Not sure about the London office, but we'll see.'

'I thought I might like to train properly as a music teacher,' she said.

'What's that, darling?' he said, slightly absently. It was the first time he had called her darling since she had told him about Ben.

'I said I wanted to train as a music teacher.'

'Whatever for?' he said.

'Because I want to do something. With my life.'

'Grace,' he said, 'you have quite a lot to do with your life. As I see it.'

He came back from London looking rather wary. He had a large bunch of flowers in his hand. 'These are for you,' he said.

'Oh. Thank you, they're lovely.' She reached up, kissed him briefly.

'I saw Clarissa while I was there.'

'Oh, did you?'

'Yes. We had quite a chat, actually. She made me feel better about everything. I' – he looked at her awkwardly – 'well, I can see it's very hard for you. I'm sorry. If I didn't seem to understand, it was – it was a bit of a shock, you know. For me. As well as for you, of course.'

'Yes of course. I do know.'

'Poor old Jack, face like that. Dreadful.'

'Yes.'

'Of course I'd seen some other cases. In the hospital.'

'Tell me,' she said carefully, later, over supper, 'tell me about the hospital. About all of it. It's still all such a muddle, such a mess.'

He still seemed reluctant to talk at any length. He had been taken prisoner in Italy, in the street fighting; the chaos was indescribable, he said. They were driven northwards for a couple of days, were fairly near the French–German border and had stopped for a break, and he and another officer, Colin Barlowe, had escaped.

'It was about two in the morning, there was some nonsense with another convoy overtaking us and somehow or other we got away. Barlowe was shot in the leg, but we still managed to get quite a way, travelled for three days and nights, practically reached the border by then, pretty bloody exhausted, and hungry and thirsty, but we thought we had at least a chance of making it. Then he began to get worse. His wound became infected, he was pretty bad. I didn't know what to do. Then some local farmer found us, hiding in a barn – '

'What, an Italian farmer?'

'Yes of course,' said Charles irritably.

'Sorry.'

'He was a good chap, and he said he'd help, fetched blankets and so on, promised to get a doctor. I left at that point, Barlowe insisted, said there was no point both of us risking recapture. Well, it was true, and he was obviously going to be OK by then. Or so I thought.'

For months Charles was on the run, travelling across southern France, sleeping in barns, haystacks, occasionally given help by sympathizers, surviving on his wits, what he was given, or could steal or beg. 'Luckily it was summer, it was warm, one farmer gave me some boots, another a jacket to wear over my uniform.' Finally he reached Vichy France, only to be captured by the German Army. 'That was when I got this,' he said, indicating his face, 'and the leg.' He was in hospital for weeks – 'hardly knowing or caring if I was alive or dead' – sent into Germany under escort to a prisoner-of-war camp, and then twice moved with the retreating army. 'There was absolute bloody chaos, it was a complete nightmare. Twice I thought they were going to shoot us just to get rid of us. There were dozens of us, always on the move, got caught up in the most ghastly heavy fighting in the Ardennes, and so on. No way I could get word to you. Absolutely no way.'

'No, of course not. I can see that,' said Grace. 'And this other man? What was his name?'

'Barlowe.'

'Obviously he did die. And they thought he was you.'

'Yes. Yes, it must have been him. No doubt at all really. It was in the right area certainly, as far as I can make out, that he was found, we'd escaped together, we weren't dissimilar to look at, and there was this strange business with the identity tags. You see he had mine – '

'I don't understand. How did that happen?'

'God knows. I thought it was lost. I was half carrying him by then, trying to help him along. It must have broken or something. Got caught in his clothing – '

'And where was his?'

'I had that. He gave it to me. We agreed I must have one in case I was captured and they thought I was a spy and shot me. Very strong on that, both sides.'

'Oh, I see,' said Grace. 'So poor Mrs Barlowe must have thought her husband was all right. Until now. Alive. Or at least she could hope.'

'I'm afraid so, yes.'

'So you've no idea what happened to him after that?'

'No, of course not. But as I say, when I left he was being looked after, he was fine, I thought. Poor chap.'

'We were just told you'd – he'd – been found dead. Killed escaping,' said Grace. 'No details or anything. I don't see how he could have been escaping, if he was in someone's care – '

'Grace, it was Germans with a jeepload of prisoners who found him, wasn't it? Well, you wouldn't expect chapter and verse. I don't think you can have the faintest idea of the chaos out there. It's not like anything you might have seen in a film, you know.'

'No, of course not,' said Grace humbly. 'But – '

'Look,' said Charles, 'can we stop this now? I'm in no mood for a bloody inquisition.'

'Sorry,' said Grace.

That night he came to her room. She had been half asleep, woke to see him standing there. The light from the landing showed him up clearly; there was an expression on his face that terrified her, half rage, half raw misery. She pulled the bedclothes round her, tried to sound calm.

'Can't you sleep?' she said.

'No,' he said, and his voice was harsh, 'no, I bloody well can't.'

He had obviously been drinking; he smelt of whisky and cigarettes. He sat down on the bed, leant over, tried to kiss her; she turned her head away.

'Jesus Christ!' he said. 'How long do I have to endure this? Well, I won't Grace, do you hear me? I've come home, and I need you.'

He dragged the bedclothes off her, pulled up her nightdress; fell on her. She could feel his penis, hard, jutting at her. 'Don't,' she said, 'please, please don't.'

'I will,' he said, and his voice was filled with a violence that frightened her. 'I will.'

It was over very quickly. He entered her, thrust a few times and climaxed; then he rolled off her and lay quietly on his side, turned away from her.

'You just don't seem to understand,' he said after a while, 'you don't seem to be trying to understand. I'm so appalled, Grace. At what you've done to me. At what I've come back to.'

'But – ' she said.

'No, don't start. I know it's not your fault. I know it's a shock for you. But you're my wife, for God's sake, don't you feel anything for me?'

She was silent.

'You shock me,' he said, 'you shock me, with your lack of feeling. You must have got very hard, in the years I've been away. And lost any sense of loyalty. Or even of honour. Goodnight.'

And he was gone, leaving her alone with her guilt.

The war was over: or at least the war in Europe. The Rhine had been crossed, Hitler was dead, Germany had surrendered; every street and village had held parties, bonfires were lit on every hill. Blackout curtains were ripped down and thrown away; the country partied and celebrated. And a quarter of a million British servicemen had died in battle, as many injured, almost a hundred thousand civilians had been killed. And many many millions more: Germans, Russians Americans, French. The cost was almost immeasurable; but the war had been won.

For Grace the days crawled painfully past. At times she felt so unhappy she thought she couldn't stand it another moment; at others a kind of peace, a dull acceptance settled on her. She was not even in a state of indecision, she could not dignify her zombie-like condition with so active a label, she had no idea what she thought and felt about her future. Still depressed from her miscarriage, she was also desperately lonely. She missed the boys; the land girls were all going home (or marrying farmers or GIs); and her only occupation, apart from running the silent house, was the dancing afternoons at school and the music lessons. Florence was spending a lot of time in London, looking at houses, at schools for Imogen. Clarissa, about to be demobbed, was full of plans for her secretarial agency. Grace was painfully aware that Florence and Clarissa probably saw a lot of one another, discussed their new futures, sorry for her but unable to help, and so putting her out of their busy agendas; she did not resent it exactly but it added to her depression. She was aware too, more painfully still, of Ben waiting, silently patient, for her decision: the decision she had neither the strength nor the ability to make.

Clarissa phoned, as if on cue: did she want to come and stay for a few days? She would be so welcome, it would do her good.

'Charles won't like it,' said Grace cautiously, feeling guilty at her grudging thoughts.

'Charles can lump it,' said Clarissa. 'You come.'

She went.

'I don't think you should stay with Charles,' said Clarissa carefully, 'if you can only offer him second best.'

'Well, at the moment that's all I can offer him,' said Grace fretfully, 'but who is to say it won't get better? I know it's what I ought to do,' she added, 'I just don't know if I can.'

'Is it right in the long run, though,' said Clarissa, 'if it stays second best?'

'Drink?' said Jack. They were sitting in the little courtyard at the back of the house, waiting for Clarissa's return: she had been looking at offices with May.

'Yes, that'd be lovely. I've taken to drink lately.' She smiled at him weakly.

'I'm not surprised. Very, very tough, what's happened to you.'

'I'm sure I'm not the only one.'

'No, probably not.'

'And think of the other poor woman, the one who thought her husband was alive, and he was actually dead.'

'Yes. indeed.' He handed her a glass. 'G and T, that all right?'

'Lovely. Nice and weak I hope. I thought I'd go and see her. Mrs Barlowe, the other man's wife. Do you think that would be nice?'

'Very nice. Quite brave of you, I'd say, but very nice.'

'Well, I think I owe it to her. I feel responsible in some peculiar way. Jack – '

'Yes?'

'Oh – it doesn't matter.'

'No, no, go on. There's obviously something worrying you.'

'Well, there is a bit. Not worrying exactly, but puzzling. I always thought the Red Cross were pretty good about informing families about prisoners. Didn't you?'

'Oh they were, very good. With the prisoners in Germany, at any rate – the Germans stuck to the Geneva Convention pretty well. Picture was a bit different in Japan, I'm afraid.'

'Yes, of course. But don't you think if they'd held Charles all those months, he could have got word to us, somehow?'

'Not necessarily, no,' said Jack easily. 'The kind of conditions Charles was held under, moved twice, army in retreat, fighting as they went, oh no, absolute bloody chaos. No puzzle there, I'd say, Grace.'

'Oh I see,' said Grace humbly.

Florence said the same as Clarissa: 'You mustn't stay with him if you don't love him.'

'Well,' said Grace, and she could hear the carefully cool note in her own voice, her unfamiliar voice, 'what's love, Florence? After a few years would I feel for Ben what I do now, do you think. In five years time? Charles is still my husband, I know I ought to stay with him. And he's had such a ghastly time.'

'He's been telling you that, I suspect.'

'Yes he has. It's true though, surely, isn't it?'

'Yes,' said Florence, 'I suppose it is.'

She went home feeling rather more cheerful, without knowing why. She supposed it had just been good to be with other people. Charles met her off the train; he kissed her slightly awkwardly on the cheek. 'You look better.'

'So do you,' she said, studying him, and it was true. He had put on a little weight since coming home, his hair had grown.

'I thought we might go out for supper,' he said, 'go to the Grosvenor, our old haunt.'

'Oh,' she said, surprised, 'yes, that would be nice.'

The dinner was really very good; not pre-war standard, but well cooked and with an unexpectedly wide selection of vegetables. Charles ordered a bottle of wine. He'd had a good day, arranged to go back to the office. 'Old Jacobs has let things slide,' he said. 'Hardly surprising. He's retired now. I can't wait to get my hands on it all. Father seems pretty pleased about that too. Well, here's to us,' he added, still rather awkward. 'New beginnings, and all that.'

'Charles, I can't – '

'No, I know. I'm sorry. We could drink to the past, perhaps, to what we had. Would that be all right?'

'Yes, that would be all right,' she said. She felt oddly touched.

'I just want to get back, you see,' he said later, 'to normality. To things being right, in order. That's what I long for.'

'Yes. Yes, I can see that.'

Suddenly she heard Clifford's voice: sad, remorseful, the night she had found him so drunk, mourning his loneliness.

'There is great value in the old order, in remaining true to what you have always known.'

When they got back, the house was cold. 'Better go straight to bed,' he said.

'Yes. I'll just see to Charlotte and the puppies. It was good of you to look after her while I was away. Thank you.'

'Oh, I know where my duty lies,' he said lightly. She looked at him sharply but he appeared to be quite relaxed, smiling pleasantly.

'I'll bring you a hot drink if you like,' she said.

'That would be nice, thank you.'

She went into the guest room; he was reading. He looked up, said, 'Grace, I'm – well, I'm sorry about the other night. Wrong of me. Won't happen again.'

'Well,' she said, 'understandable. As you – as you said.'

She lay awake almost all night; and in the morning her mind was made up. She wrote to Ben.

Chapter Thirty-Two

Summer–Autumn 1945

The letter came almost by return of post, as if he knew it must be done and done quickly.

My lovely Grace,

I find it very hard to say thank you for your letter, but I know I have to. I also find it very hard to say I understand, but I do. I think I knew this is what would happen. You are too honest, too loyal to do anything else. I just wish I'd had a bit more time with you. It has all been so lovely and so sweet. I shall never forget it, ever. I love you, Grace, and I don't love you any less for taking this decision. More if anything. It must have been so hard. I don't think I could have done it.

I will do everything I can to help you now. I won't come to the house, or try and see you. It is very good of your parents to have the boys. I have spoken to my CO and it seems I can get accommodation for us all here. It will be difficult for them, but they were going to have to move anyway, and at least the three of us will be together. I'm sure we can work something out.

I don't feel too bad yet. I know it's going to come, I'm waiting for it, it's a bit like waiting for a burn to start hurting. Just at the moment you seem still with me and that's getting me through. What you look like, what you sound and feel like.

Loving you has been such a big thing in my life, and for a long time now. It will be strange without it, like losing a leg and still thinking it's there, still feeling it. I spend a lot of time just remembering, things we said, and the first time I kissed you on Christmas morning, and the day I knew you were pregnant, and when I woke up in that hospital and you were sitting there, the flowers in your lap, and I thought I was dreaming.

I am so sorry about the baby. You were so brave. I sat there with you, watching you, and I knew I could never be as brave as you were then.

Tell Sir Clifford to look after you for me. I shall miss him a lot, and the boys will miss him too, he was such a good friend to us. It helps to think he will be there with you at least.

I can't bear to finish this letter, it feels like putting you out of my arms for the last time. Thank God I didn't know that's what I was doing.

I love you, Grace. Thank you for everything. Thank you for being you.

Ben

Clifford, come over from the Piory with some papers for Charles about the business, found her sitting at the bottom of the lawn, by the fence, gazing towards the woods, tears streaming down her face, holding the letter. She looked up at him, her face almost unrecognizable, so distorted was it by pain.

He understood at once. 'It's all right,' he said gently, 'you don't need to say any more. Here, come and let me hold you.'

He eased his stiff old body down onto the grass, took her in his arms; she clung to him, as if to life itself, sobbing, gasping with grief. Finally she stopped, said, choking, 'I couldn't do anything else, could I? Not really.'

'No,' he said, 'no, not really. You being you.'

'We don't like it here,' said Daniel.

'Shut up,' said David. 'That's rude to Grace's mother.'

'It's all right,' said Grace wearily. 'I understand. She is a bit irritating. But she does mean to be kind. And it really isn't for very long. Your father will be – will be taking care of you very soon. He's getting a house, over by the barracks.'

'Well, why can't we come home till then? Doesn't your husband like us or something?'

'Of course he likes you,' said Grace, 'but you see, it's awkward. He knew I was going to marry your dad. That I' – she swallowed – 'that I loved your dad. It would be very uncomfortable for him to have you living in his house. Surely you can understand that.'

'I suppose so,' said Daniel. Then he looked up at her, his small face working as he tried not to cry. 'But we miss you. We miss you a lot.'

'I miss you too,' said Grace, 'I miss you terribly. But we all have to be brave. All of us.'

'So what's happened?' said Daniel. 'Don't you want to marry Dad any more? Don't you love him any more?'

'I – can't marry him,' said Grace carefully, 'because I'm not free to

477

marry him. It's quite simple. I thought I was, and now I'm not. I have to stay with my husband. That's the right thing to do.'

'Do you love him then? Instead of Dad?'

'I do love him,' said Grace, speaking with great difficulty, 'but not instead of Dad, no. Not instead.'

She didn't know quite what to expect when she told Charles; she supposed in some small shred of her being was a hope that he might tell her he didn't want her back after all, that it wasn't going to work, that he had decided that it would be best to make a clean break. What seemed more likely and indeed more appropriate was that he would tell her how very happy she had made him, and that he would work very hard to make her happy too. What she didn't expect was a slightly cool nod, a quick kiss on the forehead.

'Good,' he said, retreating to his own chair – they were sitting in the drawing room after supper. 'Good.'

'Yes,' she said, totally taken aback, 'well, I thought I'd better tell you. As soon as I – as I knew.'

'Indeed. Well, I don't need to tell you how pleased I am, I'm sure. Now we can go forward together, plan our life properly. Which reminds me, darling, I have to go to London again in a couple of days. I really must get some decent clothes, and there are various other matters to deal with. My demob papers and so on.'

'Oh,' she said. She was so astounded by his calm, his detachment, she felt physically breathless. 'Oh I see.'

He looked up at her. 'You all right?'

'What? Oh – yes. Yes, I suppose so.'

'Sure?'

'Well – yes. I thought – I don't know what I thought. Quite.'

'Look, Grace,' he said, his voice determinedly level, 'this has been a bloody awful business. For us both. Now it's over, please God, and I think the least said the better, really. It'll be easier for us both to put it behind us that way.'

'But you are – pleased?'

'I said I was pleased, darling. And I know you've made the right decision, and I think you know that too. I just don't think we should make a big drama out of it now. Look, why don't you come with me to London? You could do a bit of shopping, we could even see a show. You'd like that, wouldn't you?'

'No,' she said, 'no, I don't think so. Not this time. Thank you.'

'Fine. Another occasion then.'

She cried herself to sleep that night, her head buried in her pillow, to muffle the sound.

'I'd like to get some work done on the house,' he said.

'What sort of work?'

'Oh – in the kitchen mainly. It's awfully rundown-looking in there. I'd like to take out that awful old boiler, I always meant to anyway, get a new one in, an Aga probably, take down all those shelves, have cupboards put in. And if we can get hold of some fabric, I know it's difficult, it would be nice to get the chairs and sofas covered in the drawing room, don't you think? It all looks so shabby.'

'I hadn't noticed,' she said dully, thinking of the happiness that had been contained in that shabby room, on those shabby sofas.

'Well, darling, you've lived with it for too long. And while we're on the subject of the house, Grace, I really think those dogs should go outside now. Preferably in a kennel, but at the very least in the utility room. It's absurd having them all in the kitchen.'

Mr Blackstone was set to work on the garden. The boys' football posts were pulled up, new beds made on the lawns. The tennis court was to be built. Flossie was sold to Mr Dunn. Grace, who had never thought she would live to see the day when she felt the remotest affection for Flossie, shed tears as she was driven off in Mr Dunn's trailer.

But at least the dogs stayed in the kitchen.

'Charles,' said Grace, 'don't you think it would be nice if we contacted Mrs Barlowe. She must be feeling so dreadful, and at least you could tell her what happened, as far as it went.'

'Oh, she will have been given a full report by now, I'm sure,' he said, 'and I'm not at all certain it's a good idea to keep going over things in that way. Raking things over.'

'But she won't have been given a full report, because nobody knows quite what happened. Not even you. And surely she would like to hear from you, as you were the last person to – '

'Grace,' said Charles, 'that's exactly the point. Not even I know what happened. And I personally don't think it would be at all helpful for her if I suddenly turned up. I should think it would be rather distressing, as a matter of fact. Now can we leave it please?'

Sandra Meredith was out shopping when Corporal Meredith got home. It happened a lot, men arriving home looking for a hero's welcome and finding an empty house. Unlike most of them, Brian

Meredith understood. He could quite see that with only the vaguest information about his demob, and them not having a phone, or her mother, or any of her friends, and her not being psychic, it was unreasonable for him to expect her to be there.

When she did come in, weary, laden with heavy bags, little Deirdre trailing behind her grizzling, having wet her pants in the Co-op, she found the kettle on, the table laid for tea, and Brian sitting reading the *Daily Mirror* as if he had never been away.

'Oh my God,' she said, 'oh my God – '

'No,' said Brian, smiling cheerfully, 'not God. Brian. Your husband. Hallo, San.'

Sandra dropped all her bags and flew into his arms.

'Who that man?' said Deirdre, suspicious and jealous.

'It's your dad, Deirdre,' said Sandra, crying and laughing at the same time. 'Your dad, what you've never even seen.'

Much later, as she got rather reluctantly out of bed to see to Deirdre, and to make them both a restorative cup of tea, she said, 'What's this ring doing here then, Brian? With your things.'

'Oh,' he said, 'I found some poor bloke who'd copped it. Died escaping, looked like. I thought his wife'd like it, if I ever got home, so I took it. Shouldn't have, of course, but – well, no one saw. I thought I'd try and find her, send it to her. In the fullness of time, that is.'

'How you going to find her?'

'Well, I got his name. Through the War Office I suppose. In the gunners he was.'

'You're a good-hearted bugger, aren't you?' said Sandra, smiling at him.

'Not so much of the bugger. You keep a civil tongue in your head, Mrs Meredith. Now are you coming back to bed of your own free will, or do I have to come and grab you?'

'How nice,' said Charles. 'How very nice.'

'What's that?'

'The Darby-Smiths have asked us for dinner. Big party, black tie. Celebrate Norman's return and Diana's birthday. That'll be fun, won't it?'

'Yes,' said Grace.

'I always liked Diana. Jolly pretty, and very gutsy. Did you see much of her, darling, while I was away?'

'No,' said Grace, 'nothing at all.'

She had suggested Charles came back into their bedroom. There seemed no possible reason for delaying it, and it had to be done. The sooner she got over that particular hurdle the better. She went to the family-planning clinic and got her diaphragm checked; a new young doctor prescribed her a replacement, said she was lucky not to have got pregnant before.

'Oh really?' said Grace.

'It's showing its age,' said the doctor, smiling, 'looking tired, worn out, even. Mrs Bennett, are you all right? Here, wipe your eyes on this. Is there some problem you'd like to discuss with me?'

'No,' said Grace, 'no, I'm fine. Thank you.'

She told Charles she didn't want to even think about children for quite a long time.

'No, all right, darling. I understand. Maybe next year – '

'Maybe,' said Grace.

Charles remained tersely reluctant to talk about his war. He would never discuss it with her, except in the broadest terms; he was tense, secretive about it all, it was his way of coping with it. She knew he had suffered horribly, knew it had been hard; he was often morose, silent where he had always been cheerful, bad-tempered where he had been merely irritable, given to sudden sweeping moods of depression, and suffered alternately from insomnia and nightmares. All those things she understood, sympathized with; she wished only that he would share them with her, talk about them, explain what he had been forced to endure. But he would not. And while other men told tales and swapped stories over the dinner table of battles, danger, imprisonment, escape (all carefully lightened and sanitized for the occasion and their audience), he remained silent, almost melancholy, the occasional story dragged unwillingly out of him.

One night he became the centre of attention; the talk turned to his great escape as they chose to call it, and the nightmare of being on his own and on the run for months. 'How did you stay sane?' said someone and 'With great difficulty,' said Charles shortly, and then, as the laughter faded, he said, 'It was actually not too bad. When you got used to it. Peaceful at least.'

'Why Spain though?' said one woman. 'What made you head for there? Surely Switzerland would have been nearer, easier.'

'Border terribly heavily guarded,' said a red-faced man called Mick Dunstan whose wife Grace especially disliked. 'Isn't that right, Charles?'

'Yes,' he said briefly, and then as the silence grew and they all sat listening to him, waiting for him to finish, he said, 'I was heading for the embassy in Madrid. It was – unofficially – neutral. Or so we'd heard. There was a chance of being smuggled out down to Gib on the supply trucks.'

'Yes, I knew about that one,' said Dunstan. 'Not many spare places, though. Based on rank, I heard. Colonels did pretty well, corporals left to play with themselves.'

'Absolute rubbish,' said Charles sharply. 'Nothing to do with it whatsoever. Look, it's getting late, I've got a heavy day tomorrow. Grace, perhaps we should – ' and 'Yes,' she said, standing up gratefully, sorry for him anyway, for their insensitivity when he so clearly didn't want to talk.

Days later, she asked him, gently, why he wouldn't talk about it, even to her. 'Grace,' he said, infinite weariness in his voice, 'it was pretty good hell on the whole. Don't you understand that? I don't want to keep reliving it, I'm trying to forget.'

'Yes,' she said, 'of course, but don't you think it might help you to forget if you did talk about it, get it out of your system just a bit?'

'Oh for God's sake,' he said, 'spare me that sort of claptrap, would you? You don't have the faintest idea what you're talking about, and I find it slightly offensive that you should try.'

'Sorry,' said Grace.

Sex with Charles was awful now. She never came. She didn't want to. It would seem the ultimate disloyalty, the final betrayal of Ben. In any case, she couldn't; the easy, mechanical response he had been able to produce before no longer took place. She just pretended, to keep him happy, and kept her mind blank.

Angela Barlowe was very much afraid she was cracking up. She had always assumed herself to be a strong and levelheaded person, indeed had proved herself to be so, right through the war, caring for her large house, her widowed mother and her four children, in between her voluntary work at the local hospital in Cirencester. She had remained calm and optimistic, even after hearing that her husband, Lieutenant-Colonel Barlowe, had been captured in Italy at the beginning of 1944, but the long wait at the end of the war, initially hopeful, increasingly anxious, and then finally opening the carefully regretful letter from the War Office (saying that it had not been possible to notify her earlier, due to a most unfortunate confusion of identity with another officer, but that it had now been established beyond all reasonable doubt that her husband had been killed escaping from a convoy in Italy), had almost defeated her. She was not given to bitterness, in fact she was a devout Christian and had a deep faith in the rightness of God's will; but she found herself deeply disturbed by the unsatisfactory nature of the outcome, and the lack of proper information. She was trying to come to terms with it, but the awful, gnawing doubt about exactly how her beloved Colin had died and how much he might have suffered invaded her dreams and disturbed her days.

She decided that if she did not make some investigations on her own account, she would go quietly – or even noisily – mad.

Giles and Florence had been married, very quietly, in a registry office; (it was either that or a 'big do' said Florence 'which we couldn't face') he had got a job playing the piano and singing in a West End revue. Florence, fiercely proud, invited them all to go and see it.

'You can stay here,' she wrote to Grace, 'it'll be lovely to see you. Clarissa and Jack are coming, and I've asked Mother and Daddy. All news then. Give my love to Charles.'

'Oh Lord,' said Charles, 'do we have to go? I hate that sort of show, and it'll be so embarrassing if he's no good.'

'Yes we do,' said Grace, 'if I can go to the Darby-Smiths, you can come to your brother-in-law's first night.'

'That's different. Quite different.'

'Charles,' said Grace, 'it isn't different at all.'

Clifford said he would like to go; Muriel said she couldn't possibly get away. 'Much too busy. I can't imagine how you can find the time, Grace. With Charles trying to build up his practice again.' But in the end Clifford persuaded her.

Florence and Giles had bought a very pretty house just off Walton Street. 'Isn't it nice?' said Florence, kissing Grace, when they arrived just after lunch. 'I'm so pleased to see you, Grace, but you do look absolutely awful.'

'Thanks,' said Grace laughing. 'You don't change, Florence, do you?'

Charles had business in town with Clifford, sorting out the remnants of the London office. Grace and Florence sat in the small garden, waiting for the new young nanny to bring Imogen back from school.

'I had to give in on the nanny front,' said Florence, 'I couldn't manage, not with my latest plan.'

'What's your latest plan?'

'Politics. Don't laugh.'

'I wasn't going to laugh,' said Grace.

'Well, you had that stupid half-smile on your face,' said Florence. 'Anyway, yes, I'm going to start with local politics, and then see. I know it's not going to be easy, I don't have any illusions, but I just think it's a way I can use my talents. And do something useful. The thing is, the party's going to have a real fight on its hands, to get back into power. It's hard to believe that after all Churchill has done for this country they should've thrown him out, but still. So it's a lot of hard slog, door-to-door campaigning. I can't wait.'

'It sounds wonderful,' said Grace wistfully.

'How about you?'

'Oh – you know. Early days. I'm – we're settling down. I think.'

'You don't look as if you're settling down,' said Florence.

'I don't want to talk about it,' said Grace.

Clarissa and Jack met them at the theatre. Clarissa was looking dazzling, in a black velvet dress with softly rounded shoulders and just a suggestion of a full skirt, and Florence wore a very chic, rather tight green jersey dress with swathed bodice and a wonderfully dramatic pre-war fox cape, complete with the fox's head and tail. Grace felt painfully aware that she was looking the poor relation up from the country, in her old navy-blue crepe dinner dress and woollen coat, and was upset by it until she saw people staring at Jack's face, and him smiling cheerily and determinedly back at them. She might have thought he didn't care, had she not noticed his fists clenched rather tightly in the pockets of his dinner jacket.

The show wasn't really very good, but Giles was excellent. His charm as much as his talent sang out; when he was on stage the music seemed better, the lyrics less banal, even the other actors more gifted.

They had drinks in his dressing room after the show; then they all went back to Walton Street.

'That was too wonderful,' said Clarissa. 'What a thrill in our drab lives, Giles.'

'You know me,' he said lightly, 'one long thrill.' He was very drunk; Grace felt edgy suddenly.

'Oh Clarissa, really!' said Clifford, laughing. 'As if your life could by any stretch of the imagination be called drab.'

'You have no idea,' said Clarissa. 'We spent the whole of today,

May and I, scrubbing down the walls of this pigsty we call our office. Worth it, though, it's going to be lovely.'

'Who's May?' said Charles.

'My business partner. A fellow Wren. We went through the whole war together. Hence the name of our agency: Marissa. Get it?'

'Yes thank you,' he said shortly, 'I think I can just about manage that.'

'And she brought me and Giles safely together again, don't forget,' said Florence. 'We should have asked her tonight, Clarissa. I'd have loved that.'

'Another time,' said Clarissa quickly: just a bit too quickly, Grace thought, watching her.

'I still can't get over that,' said Florence with a shudder, 'how easily we might have missed one another.'

'Oh no we wouldn't,' said Giles. 'Do you really think I'd have left you, not tried again anyway?'

'I still think it was amazing,' said Florence. 'May just meeting you out of the blue, remembering your name, thinking to ring Clarissa.'

'Hang on a minute,' said Charles, frowning slightly, 'you've lost me completely. What happened?'

'Oh, it was one of those strange coincidences,' said Giles, 'I'd docked at Dartmouth, and I just happened to meet May Potter in a pub. And we got chatting – '

'And Giles can chat!' said Florence fondly. 'Like a girl he is, like Clarissa – '

'Yes, lots of people said that,' said Giles, 'that we were like brother and sister.'

There was a sudden uneasy silence; then Florence said, rather slowly, 'Lots of people couldn't have said it surely, Giles. I mean lots of people didn't ever see you together.'

Another silence; then into it came Grace's voice, steady and clear. 'Well, I said it for one,' she said, 'I said it the minute I met Giles, didn't I? I couldn't believe it. You even look alike. And' – she looked over at Clifford, who was drooping, half asleep, into his whisky – 'Clifford said it too. Didn't you, Clifford?'

'What's that, my darling?' he said, as she knew he would. 'Oh yes, of course I did.'

'Moo, darling,' said Clarissa, startled at Grace's unexpected deftness, 'you should take the old love up to bed, he looks awfully sweet sitting there, but any minute now he'll have to be carried, and no one's sober enough. I'm quite tired myself, maybe we should hit the road, Jack. Giles, darling, it was too wonderful. Thank you again for asking us along. May I kiss you?'

And Grace, watching Florence watching Clarissa, knew that there was a darkness in her, a shadow on her happiness.

Later, as Grace was in the kitchen filling a glass of water, Florence came in. She looked tired and pale.

'Grace,' she said, 'can I ask you something?'

'Yes of course. But I'm awfully tired, may not make a lot of sense.'

'Grace, don't give me that. You always make sense,' said Florence. Her voice was heavy. 'That's why I want to talk to you.'

'Well, go on then.'

'There's something – well, I think there might be something between Giles and Clarissa. I thought I was imagining it before. But they're just a bit – funny together. And then that thing he said tonight, about lots of people saying they were alike. I mean, it is jolly strange, May knowing his name, never having met him before. And they could have, down there, you know. What do you think, Grace? Because I don't think I could bear it. I really don't. I have to trust people, it's the most important thing to me, being honest.'

'I know it is,' said Grace, who had suffered considerably from Florence's honesty. 'But – '

'The thing is, I do trust you, Grace. I think you're honest too. And I think you see things straight. So if you knew anything, anything at all – '

Grace shivered suddenly. Where had she heard that phrase before? Oh yes, on Robert's lips, when he had been trying to trick her into telling him where Florence was. Evil, awful Robert, who had made Florence so wretched. And now she was happy, very happy, and Grace realized that she held in her hands the power to make her extremely unhappy, and that only by lying, and lying hard, could she save her from that. It was true what Florence had said; Grace was a basically honest person. She would probably – well, possibly – still be with Ben otherwise. She hated deception, deviousness, she too needed to trust people. And she lacked the skills, really, to follow lies and deception through; it wasn't in her make-up. Whenever she told lies, they doubled back on her, refused to work. She could make things much, much worse with this one.

'Grace!' said Florence, 'Grace, you do know something, don't you? You've got to tell me.'

Silence: then Grace said, 'No, Florence, of course I don't. You're being silly. I answered the phone to May that morning, and she wanted Clarissa, and Clarissa hadn't arrived, she was between houses, so I took the message. And there is absolutely no doubt that she and Giles had only just met. She went on and on about the coincidence, even asked me if I knew his name, so she could check it. So there you are. Stop making yourself miserable. Enjoy Giles, and what you've got.'

As she spoke a great lump rose in her throat, at the thought of Ben, and what she had not got. She tried not to cry, but she couldn't help it; the double strain of the evening and the lie she had just told defeated her and she broke down, sat at the kitchen table and burst into tears.

'Oh God,' said Florence, 'oh God, Grace, don't, don't, I'm sorry, here, let me give you a drink, have a hanky, oh I'm so sorry.'

'You'd better not give me a drink,' said Grace, her voice cracking with tears. 'Last time you did that late at night I was puking till dawn.'

'So you were. Well, what about a cup of tea? Oh dear – '

'Don't worry,' said Grace, 'I'll be all right. I'd better get upstairs or Charles will be down. Oh God, I don't think I can face him yet.'

'Tell you what,' said Florence. 'You go and have a bath. In the nursery bathroom. And sleep up there if you like. There's a tiny little room with a bed. I'll tell Charles you've got a terrible headache and he's to leave you alone. He'll do that if I say so.'

'But Florence,' said Grace, thinking longingly of the tiny room, being alone in the bed, smiling through her tears, 'that wouldn't be true.'

'No, I know,' said Florence, 'but even I tell tiny lies sometimes. Oh Grace, thank you so much for talking to me. You've no idea how much better I feel.'

'Good,' said Grace.

Lying in the small bed, she reflected on what she had done. She had lied (with alarming competence, not once but twice), had taken control of a situation, decided what should be done. In the morning she would somehow have to brief Clarissa and Giles on the lie. And pray that Florence would ask no more questions. It was all very much out of character. Or perhaps it wasn't. The changes in her over the past few years had been profound. She really hardly knew who she was at all any more. And certainly not who she was supposed to be.

At breakfast Charles was silent; cross that she hadn't slept with him, physically miserable with a bad hangover. Florence and Giles on the other hand seemed very happy, smiling at one another across the table, occasionally reaching out for one another's hands. This made Charles patently more uncomfortable.

'What about your music, Grace?' said Giles suddenly, 'I seem to remember you telling me you wanted to do a music teacher's course.'

'That was before I came home,' said Charles. 'She won't have time now, will – '

'Yes, Giles,' said Grace, ignoring this, 'yes I do. I've applied, actually. I'm waiting to hear exactly what it entails. But there's a very good music school in Salisbury which might suit me rather well.'

'Well, that's wonderful,' said Giles. 'All that talent, much too good to waste, don't you think, Charles?'

'Yes, I suppose so,' said Charles.

He and Clifford had a meeting in Lincoln's Inn. 'Why don't you go shopping?' he said to Grace. 'Get a couple of new dresses. Your wardrobe could do with a bit of a boost.'

'Thanks,' said Grace. She felt the easy tears stinging behind her eyes.

'Now, darling, I – '

'Charles,' said Florence briskly, 'why don't you just go? I think Grace can manage to look after herself for a couple of hours. Pig,' she added when they'd gone. 'Oh Grace, do you really – '

'Shut up, Florence,' said Grace fiercely, 'I don't want to talk about it. Look, I want to go to the War Office. How do I get there?'

Chapter Thirty-Three

Winter–Spring 1945–1946

'How would you like to go and live in Australia?' said Ben.

'Australia? Blimey, yeah,' said Daniel.

'Dunno,' said David. 'Why Australia?'

Why Australia? Because it was a new beginning. Because it was so far away from Grace she would become an impossible dream. Because there would not be the faintest, slightest chance that he would bump into her somewhere. Because he wouldn't lie awake at night there, fighting a temptation to go and see her that was almost irresistible. Because it was a young country, his social background would be meaningless, because he would be accepted for what he was, what he could do. Because no one, no one at all, would be sorry for him.

In a way it was the sympathy that got him down the most. They meant well, the lads, trying to cheer him up, trying to persuade him to go out with them, pushing girls in his way. And, because they meant so well, he felt sometimes he had to go along with them, go out, get drunk, have a laugh. One evening he'd got so drunk he'd found himself in bed with some tart over a pub somewhere; another night he came to as the beaten-up old car he was driving hit a tree. It was a miracle he wasn't killed, everyone said so; he knew that was supposed to be comforting, but if it hadn't been for the boys he would have welcomed death.

The boys were alternately good and difficult; he had sat them down, when all three of them had finally moved into his temporary accommodation in Tidworth, talked to them honestly. He told them he had loved Grace very much, and she him, but the way things had turned out they had had to part. They were both very unhappy, he said, and he knew that at times he might not behave too well, he was sorry about that, he apologized in advance, but they all had to get through it somehow.

'Can't you see her sometimes, just to cheer yourself up?' Daniel had asked. No, Ben had said, he couldn't. That would only make things worse in the long run.

'Well, we'll have to cheer you up then,' said Daniel, and gave him a hug. Ben hugged him back.

Daniel was being very brave, very good; he'd had a worse time than David because he'd had to change schools and, of the two, he had been more attached to Grace. He had only been four when they first went to live with her; his mother had become a hazy memory. He missed Grace terribly, her kindness, her gentleness, her ability to know what he was thinking about, but he struggled not to show it. He thought that would make his father feel worse.

David's main emotion was exasperation. He was in the throes of pre-adolescence, wrapped up in himself, still struggling at school (more, these days, without Clifford to help); he couldn't see why the adults couldn't sort themselves out. He had disliked Charles intensely the day he had met him at the Priory, and while he accepted the fact that Grace had to stay with him, he couldn't understand how someone as nice, as sensitive as she, could have married someone so unpleasant in the first place. He also felt, while trying to crush the sensation, that his father was being a bit feeble. If it had been him, he thought, he would at least have had a go at getting Grace back. He found his father's rather negative attitude to everything these days depressing. He had asked if he was still going to train as a teacher and Ben had said no. David thought that at least he could have stuck to that idea. He might be quite old, but he had to do something for the rest of his life, he couldn't just mope around being miserable about Grace for the next however long it was he had to live. Staying in the army had been quite a good idea, David thought, but in the end they'd told him he didn't have a future there because of his shoulder.

'Would you like to go to Australia then?' Daniel asked him.

'No,' said David shortly, 'no, I wouldn't. I've just made a whole new lot of friends, I don't want to start again.'

'But it'd be good there. Sunny all the time, and we could be on the beach every day. Cheer Dad up and all.'

'Yeah, well, maybe. But I bet we won't go anyway. It'll come to nothing, like everything Dad talks about.'

'Do you miss Grace?' said Daniel.

'Yeah, course.'

'I know Dad doesn't want to see her, but could we, do you think?'

'Dunno. Not over there at Thorpe. Her horrible husband wouldn't let us.'

'No, but we could meet her in Salisbury maybe. I'm going to ask Dad.'

Ben said he supposed it would be all right, if Grace was willing.

'Why don't you write to her? That way she can think about it. But you know I can't see her, don't you?'

'Course I do.'

'And she mightn't feel she should see you, even.'

'Don't see why not,' said Daniel.

Grace recognized Daniel's writing at once; she put the letter away quickly in her pocket until Charles had left for the office. Then she read it, several times, and after a great deal of thought, wrote back, arranging to meet them for tea at the Bear in Salisbury.

'I – might be a bit late back today,' she said to Charles. 'I've got an extra music lesson.'

He looked at her and sighed. 'I hope this isn't going to happen a lot,' he said. 'When I agreed to you doing this course, you assured me it wouldn't affect our lives together.'

'Oh don't be so ridiculous,' said Grace. 'I might be on the six thirty bus rather than the six o'clock. I don't see that as having a major effect on our marriage. If it does, there's something very wrong. Anyway, if you'd only agree to my having a car – '

'Grace, we can't afford to run two cars at the moment,' said Charles, 'I told you that. When the business is up and running again, perhaps – '

Grace didn't argue. She knew it was nothing to do with economics; he didn't want her to have the freedom a car would provide. He had no idea she had never had any proper lessons, and had driven his car throughout the war largely self-taught; she was saving that up to tell him when she really wanted to shock him. Shocking Charles was one of the few pleasures she found in their relationship these days.

She had bought presents for both boys, a set of rail tracks for Daniel and a second-hand camera for David. She had also had a picture framed for Daniel of Floss and Charlotte together in the paddock.

It was over six months since she had seen them; she waited for them, her heart pounding, almost as if she was going to see Ben.

They came into the lounge of the Bear looking slightly nervous, David swaggering, hands in his pockets, pretending to whistle. She stood up, called them.

Daniel flew into her arms. 'Grace, Grace, it's so lovely to see you.'

'It's lovely to see you too. I think you've grown. Well, you have. Definitely.'

'We miss you so much,' said Daniel.

'I miss you too. So much. Hallo, David.'

'Hallo,' he said, and shook her hand solemnly.

'David,' said Grace, smiling, 'you're so grown up. How's school?'

'It's OK, thanks.'

'Second year now.'

'Yeah.'

It was awkward at first, but once they started eating tea in the dining room they relaxed, began to chat, to tell her things: David was in the under-fourteen football team, Daniel had a hamster, they were moving again soon, into a house quite near, their dad was coming out of the army, got a job in a factory for now.

'He said just to tell you he was fine,' said Daniel carefully. 'That's all. And he wants to know how you are.'

'Tell him I'm fine, too. All right?'

'Yeah.' He smiled at her.

They went through into the lounge again after tea.

'I'm doing the scholarship this year,' said Daniel, sitting next to her, cuddling up to her, big boy though he was.

'I know. Think you'll pass?'

'Dunno,' he said.

'No,' said David. Daniel punched him.

'Anyway, you won't be able to go, if we go to Australia.'

'Australia!' said Grace. The shock was so intense she thought she might faint. 'You're going to Australia?'

'We might. It's Dad's idea. We don't want to.'

'I do,' said Daniel. 'Well, except I couldn't see you any more.'

She saw them onto their bus. Daniel was ecstatic at the photograph. 'I'll never go anywhere without it, ever. Not even to Australia. Specially not to Australia.'

As she was waiting at the stop for her own bus, Charles appeared in the car. He hooted at her, leant across, told her to get in.

'Hallo,' she said.

He was silent. Then, 'What the hell do you think you're doing?'

'What do you mean?'

'Meeting those boys. I saw you seeing them onto the bus. Without telling me. Without asking me.'

'Charles!'

'I mean it. Did you see their father as well? Did you?'

'No!' she said, almost amused at his rage. 'No, of course not. I will never, ever see him again. I gave you my word.'

'For what that's worth,' he said.

'Charles, stop it. That's outrageous.'

'Why do you want to see them? For God's sake, why?'

'Because I miss them. I love them and I – '

'You love them?' he said, and there was total derision in his voice. 'Love them? Two little guttersnipes. From the East End of London. You – '

'Stop the car,' she said, her voice shaking. 'Stop it at once. Or I shall get out anyway.'

'No.'

'Charles – ' She put her hand on the door; he looked at her, screeched to a halt.

'Don't,' she said, 'don't you ever, ever talk like that about those boys again. Do you understand me? They were all I had for a very long time. I loved them dearly. I still love them.'

There was a long silence, then he said, 'I cannot believe that you can't understand why it upsets me. You can get out now if you want to.'

She hesitated, finally said, 'No, it's all right. I'll stay. Let's go home.'

By the time they reached the Mill House, she was feeling guilty again.

'I'm sorry,' she said to Charles much later that night, after they'd had supper and were sitting in the drawing room. 'I – I didn't think. Of course it would upset you. But – '

'It's all right,' he said coldly, 'let's leave it. I accept your apology.'

That night he made love to her: as always, when he was upset, more thoughtfully, more sensitively than usual. It was almost all right. Not pleasant, but at least all right. When it was over he said, 'I'm sorry if I – overreacted. It was only because I – well, I was so upset. Upset and shocked.'

'Yes of course,' she said.

Charles had tried to make her give up teaching at the school. He had said several times he didn't like it, that if she must work at a school why not St Edwin's, the prep school over at Westhorne? Grace told him firmly that she had no intention of wasting her time on children who had plenty of music in their lives already and that she would go on helping Miss Merton for as long as Miss Merton needed her.

As she was leaving one day, Miss Merton said, 'I'm a bit worried about Elspeth Dunn.'

'Why?' said Grace.

'You know she failed the scholarship?'

'Yes, I do. I was very surprised, but – '

'I wasn't,' said Miss Merton. 'All her brains go into her music. She can't spell, never learnt her tables. Anyway, she's at the secondary modern and I hear she hates it, really miserable. I thought perhaps if she could still have her lessons – '

'Of course,' said Grace. 'I'll go and see her.'

Elspeth had just got home when she arrived, and was laying the table for tea. She flushed with pleasure when she saw Grace. 'Hallo, miss.'

'Hallo, Elspeth.' She was still very small, still only looked about nine, her only concession to adolescence being a crop of spots on her nose.

'How's the new school?'

'All right.'

'You doing any music?'

'Only class music, miss. The teacher's not very nice.'

'No piano lessons?'

'No, miss.'

'Well, that's a shame. Look, I wondered if you'd like to come to my house after school once a week. I could give you a lesson. And you can always come and practise if you want to.'

'Oh, miss!' Elspeth's small face was scarlet, the spots disappeared in the general bright colour. 'That'd be lovely, miss. I'll have to ask my dad, though.'

'I'm sure your dad won't mind. You can tell him I miss the cheese as much as you miss the lessons. He'll get the idea.'

'Yes, miss.'

'How very, very nice,' said Angela Barlowe.

'What's that, dear?' asked her mother. They were having a rather early breakfast; it was Angela's day at the hospital, and the two girls had to be dropped off at their school first. The boys were both away, one at prep school, the other at Wellington. The army was paying for most of his fees.

'I've had a letter from a Grace Bennett. She's married to the officer Colin was – well the one there was the confusion of identity over. Anyway, it's such a nice letter. She says she wants to come and see me.' She looked at her mother, and tears filled her eyes; then she said, her voice very shaky as she wiped them away on her table napkin, 'If I could just know a bit more about it all, I'd feel so much better. I must write to her straight away.'

Grace and Angela Barlowe agreed that the easiest place to meet would be London; they could both get the train up, cross-country was much more difficult and Angela said she wanted to go to Daniel Neal's to get some things for Sarah, her elder daughter, who was going away to school after Christmas.

Grace was very anxious for Charles not to know she was seeing Angela Barlowe; she knew it was precisely the sort of thing that would make him angry. She told him she was going to see Florence and Imogen. 'She is my goddaughter, and I haven't seen her for ages.'

Charles said he didn't think even God could do a lot for Imogen.

Grace sat waiting for Angela at the Charing Cross Hotel. She felt rather nervous; supposing she was a fierce dragon of a woman, who would resent the fact that her husband was dead while Grace's had come safely home. Or would demand to see Charles himself, hear more about it all – then what would she do? She was just beginning to think it was a terrible mistake when she felt a gentle tap on her arm.

'Mrs Bennett?'

'Yes. Yes, that's me. And you must be Mrs Barlowe.'

'Mrs Bennett and Mrs Barlowe, it sounds like a music-hall turn,' said Angela Barlowe, smiling. 'I'm Angela.' She held out her hand. She didn't appear to be too much of a fierce dragon, being fair and sweet-faced and very weary-looking, her unfashionably long dress drooping below her coat, and a pair of rather shabby shoes on rather large feet.

'And I'm Grace. I've ordered some coffee. I do hope that's all right.'

'It's very much so. I haven't had time for anything since I got out of bed. Have you got children?'

'No,' said Grace bleakly. 'No I haven't.'

'Oh – well. They're lovely, of course, a great joy, but terribly exhausting.'

There was an awkward silence; the coffee arrived.

'I'll be mother,' said Grace and giggled weakly at the inappropriateness of the joke. 'It's so nice to meet you. I'm not at all sure what I was going to say, but I just thought it would be helpful for you if I told you everything I knew. Which isn't much, I'm afraid. Because it must all seem a bit – unsatisfactory. That's what I thought.'

'It is,' said Angela, 'more than a bit. And I'm so grateful to you. Please do, tell me everything. Whatever it is, however – well, however unpleasant, I know it will help me feel better.'

Grace told her: that Charles and Colin had escaped together, that Colin had been wounded, that Charles had been helping him, and that a kind, friendly farmer had taken him in and got medical assistance. 'I don't know much more I'm afraid. I know he was found by a British soldier, but he was – well, he was dead. And I don't even know where he was; I imagine at this farm. Maybe the man decided to turn him in or maybe he needed to be got to hospital, and that wasn't possible. The wound was quite serious, Charles said. But at least, as far as we know he was in good hands, was kindly treated at the end. I'm sorry, it doesn't sound very much now. Hardly worth coming to London for,' she added, feeling suddenly embarrassed.

'No, you're wrong,' said Angela, 'it's been very much worth it. The main thing was I could never quite be sure that it was Colin, the man they found. I mean I wondered if he had died some other awful way. Or wasn't' – she hesitated – 'wasn't dead at all.'

'No, I think – oh dear, is this really making you feel better?' said Grace.

'Yes, it is. Very much better. There's nothing worse than uncertainty.'

'Well then, yes, I'm sure it must have been him. Your husband. Especially as he had my husband's identity tag. You know about that, do you?'

'It sounded a little strange. But yes – '

'The thing was, Charles's got broken, he was helping your husband, half carrying him by then, I think, and they were struggling along. They thought it had got lost, but it must have got caught in their clothes or something. Anyway, your husband insisted Charles had his, said it would be dangerous for him not to have one, in case he was thought to be a spy.'

'Yes, I see.'

'So that proves they were together, doesn't it? That it was him with Charles. I'm so sorry. So very sorry. I feel – guilty in a way.'

'Oh, don't be ridiculous,' said Angela Barlowe, smiling rather feebly. 'Anyway, you had a year of pretty good hell, didn't you? Thinking your husband was dead?'

'Oh – oh yes,' said Grace, thinking of her year of hell, the most joyful, the happiest in her life, thinking how dreadful that Angela Barlowe, who had clearly loved her husband so much, should have lost him, of the dreadful irony that they had both lost the men they loved, because Charles had come safely home.

'And do you know who – who found him?' said Angela.

'Not really. A jeepload of Allies. Under German guard. They were also prisoners, on their way somewhere. They reported the – what they had found, and I think it must have been the International Red Cross went into action. Informed us.'

'I see,' said Angela.

'And then he was of course properly buried. By the Germans. Apparently they were really very good in that way. Kept to the Geneva Convention and so on.'

'Yes, I know. And in time, apparently, I will be notified as to where the – the grave is. So I suppose gradually the fog is clearing – '

Her rather quiet voice faded away; Grace felt desperately sorry for her. 'Charles did say the chaos was indescribable,' she said. 'It is possible to see how this sort of thing might have happened. And in particular in Italy. The street fighting, literally man to man. It sounds so ghastly.'

'Yes, when you read about it, think about it, you somehow imagine it all being rather remote and impersonal, don't you? Distant guns, bombs dropping, that sort of thing. Not two men, face to face in a street somewhere. Er – your husband didn't say exactly where this was? This farm? Where he left Colin?'

'No. No he didn't. But very near the Italian–French border.'

'Not much use, I'm afraid. I was thinking, if I could get the name of a town, or a village, I might go down there some time, in the future of course, try to find the exact place, perhaps even the farmer who helped, thank him. I expect that sounds very silly to you.'

'Not at all silly,' said Grace. 'And I'll ask my husband, but I really don't think he knows. I'm sorry.'

She did go and see Florence, and stayed the night. Florence was full of self-importance about her political work, talking in a rather proprietary way about the party. A casual listener, Grace thought, might have imagined Florence was actually in the shadow cabinet.

'Do you really think you might be an MP?' she said. 'You'd make history if you did, wouldn't you? Being a woman.'

'Not quite,' said Florence, 'there are a few precedents. Lady Astor was the first, and then there's that terrible Braddock woman, and Jennie Lee of course, but there certainly aren't many. I'd certainly like to be the first woman prime minister,' she said and grinned. 'Anyway, what about you?'

'Oh I'm fine,' said Grace.

'And how are things?'

'All right. Fine.' She never felt she could say anything really derogatory about Charles; it wasn't fair to Florence. But later she went to see Clarissa, who as always made her talk.

She had spoken to Clarissa the morning after the show, primed her on the lie she had told Florence. Since then, their relationship had shifted: Grace felt less in awe of Clarissa, more in control. She no longer disapproved of her, she just felt oddly closer to her, more able to cope with her various excesses.

Now Clarissa looked at Grace anxiously. 'You look rotten, darling.'

'It's all right, I suppose,' she said. 'I just feel totally and absolutely low all the time. As if there's no hope of being properly happy ever again. I mean of course I'm very lucky really, and Charles is being very sweet to me, which – '

'Which makes it worse,' said Clarissa briskly, 'makes you feel you've got to stay loyal.'

'Yes. Well, I *have* got to. It's what's right. You know how strong Charles is on doing the right thing.'

'And telling you about it,' said Clarissa with a slightly grim smile. 'Oh Grace, darling, I wish I could help somehow.'

'You can't,' said Grace. 'Nobody can.'

She asked Charles, carefully casual, if he knew exactly where the farm was where he had left Colin Barlowe; he was, as with any enquiry into his war, irritably vague. 'I told you I have no idea. Three days on the run, mostly in the dark. How could I possibly know exactly, as you put it? Anyway, why?'

'Oh – I just thought the – the farmer might have said something. To indicate where you were.'

'Well he didn't.'

Afterwards she did actually wonder that Charles hadn't asked the farmer: simply to find out where he was, in which direction he should go. But she didn't like to raise the question again.

'I'm sorry,' she said to Angela Barlowe, 'he really can't tell you. Doesn't know.'

'Never mind. It was so kind of you to go to so much trouble. I would really like to meet your husband, thank him for what he did do for Colin. However it turned out, he obviously tried so hard to help

498

him. Why don't you both come over – maybe for lunch one Sunday? Or I could put you up for a night, it's quite a big house.'

'That would be lovely,' said Grace carefully, 'but it's a very long way, and it might be a bit difficult at the moment, petrol still being rationed and everything. Thank you for asking us anyway, it's most kind.'

'I think a bed for the night and a meal is a very small return for what your husband did for Colin,' said Angela, 'and I would like to meet him. So if you change your mind, or if you're in the Cirencester direction, do please let me know.'

'Yes, of course I will,' said Grace.

'Did you ever get in touch with that woman?' asked Sandra Meredith.

'What woman?'

'The one whose husband you found. Dead. You know, Brian, the one whose ring you got.'

'No, I didn't,' he said, 'and it's been on my conscience. I don't quite know where to start, to tell you the truth. How to find the address and that. War Office might not like what I did.'

'No need to tell 'em,' said Sandra. 'Just say you want the address. You've got his number and all, haven't you, and his name?'

'Never forget it,' said Brian Meredith with a faint shudder. 'He – well, he'adn't just died that day. Not that week, even.'

'Oh Brian, do stop,' said Sandra. 'You're putting me off my tea.'

Brian Meredith resolved to write to the War Office that very evening.

The woman at Australia House was very nice and helpful. She said she was sure Ben and the boys would stand a good chance of being accepted as Australian citizens; they were exactly the sort of people the country would welcome. She gave them a lot of leaflets to read, and some forms to fill in; they would need references of course, she said, clean bills of health and so on, and proof that they had a bit of money behind them, but that wouldn't be a problem, would it? She said they would have considerable trouble getting a passage on a boat, and it would be better to wait until the following year, when all the stranded servicemen were home, not to mention their brides and fiancées, numbered in hundreds if not thousands. Ben said he wouldn't want to wait a year.

'Well,' she said, 'the best way for you, then, would be by air. On a short empire flying boat, one of the old Sunderlands. That would be an adventure for your boys, wouldn't it?'

'Don't know about the boys,' said Ben, 'it sounds pretty exciting to me too.'

Sydney was lovely, she said, but if they wanted somewhere that would feel more at home, they might be better choosing Melbourne; anyway, he should go home and think about it.

With a miserable Christmas behind him and the ache in his heart no better, Ben couldn't see there was an awful lot to think about. He began to fill in the forms and to line up some references.

Chapter Thirty-Four

Spring 1946

Charles had told Grace he wanted to talk to her. She knew what it meant. It meant he had something serious on his mind. She even had a fairly shrewd idea what the serious something was. And she shrank from it.

She was right.

'I think it's time,' he said carefully after dinner one evening, 'that we started our family.'

'Oh really? But – '

'Grace, I don't see any buts. We've been married almost seven years.'

'Well, not exactly,' she said.

'What do you mean?'

'I mean you were away for five of them at least.'

'You're splitting hairs,' he said, smiling just slightly grimly. 'The fact is we were married almost seven years ago, and that seems to me quite long enough to wait. I'm nearly forty, Grace, that's a little late to become a father for the first time. Now I realize that it's because of the war, and indeed at my insistence, but I really think we've put it off long enough.'

'Yes, I see,' she said. She could hear the dullness in her voice.

'Darling, do try to be a little more enthusiastic! Don't you want children?'

No, thought Grace, not your children. I don't. The thought of something that was partly Charles growing inside her, invading her body, made her feel sick. It frightened her, that sickness; she wanted to run away, not only from Charles, but from it.

'Yes, of course I do,' she said, trying to smile. 'Of course. It's just that – '

'Yes?'

'Well, you know I said I needed time and – '

'Grace, you've had a great deal of time. If you're talking about that – that business, I've been extremely patient, I think, and it's very much in the past now.'

'Charles – '

'Grace, please! You've obviously forgotten part of the marriage service.' He smiled again, the self-confident, persuasive smile this time that she most hated. 'It was designed for the procreation of children. Apart from anything else, it's beginning to look odd. People will think – well, anyway. So is that all right, darling?'

'Yes of course,' said Grace, forcing herself to smile back. She supposed she could go on putting it off herself for a bit longer. 'He never seemed to know if she had her cap in or not.

'Good. That's settled then. Oh, and there's something else. I'd like to have a really big dinner party as soon as it's feasible. I thought that would be rather nice. We've had such a lot of hospitality lately, and we never seem to get quite on top of repaying it. So would you think about that, darling? How best to organize it and so on.'

'Well, I will, but – '

'Grace,' said Charles, 'you did say that none of our friends seemed to have much time for you in the war. Can you wonder, if you don't make an effort for them? Now if you draw up a guest list, I'll have a look at it. I'm going for a walk now. Stretch my legs. Got a bit of a problem at the office, need a breath of air.'

'What sort of problem?' asked Grace.

'Oh – not the sort of thing you'd be interested in.'

'I might be. I'd like to help, to be involved in your work – '

'No, honestly, darling, it's terribly complicated, it would take much too long to explain. You get on with that guest list – the most helpful thing you can do for me is some entertaining, I'm always telling you that.'

'Yes, all right,' said Grace humbly.

Later, when she got into bed, he leant over, kissed her on the mouth. Her heart sank. He was obviously planning on putting his plans for a family into action immediately.

'I do love you,' he said unexpectedly, 'and I so want you to have our children.'

She smiled quickly.

'You do love me, don't you?' he said.

'Yes. Yes of course. You know I do.'

'Say it then.' There was a strange note in his voice. She was startled.

'You know I do.' She had not yet been able to bring herself to actually tell him she loved him: not since he came back.

'I know you never tell me you do.'

'Oh Charles – '

'Say it,' he said, and he sounded rough, angry. 'Say it, Grace. Now.'

'I – I do,' she said very quietly.

'Say you love me.'

'I love you.'

'You don't still think about him, do you?' he said, his voice still harsh. 'That – that man. It is over, isn't it? He's gone?'

'Don't be ridiculous, Charles. You know he's gone. I never, never see him, I told you, I – '

'But you still think about him, don't you? Go on, admit it. You do, I know you do. I can tell.'

'Charles, please.'

'Stop it,' he said and forced her down in the bed, pushing her legs apart, 'stop thinking about him, remembering him. I'll make you, do you understand? I'll make you. All right?'

'Yes, Charles, all right. All right.'

Sex had never been uglier; she felt Ben a physical presence in the bed, with herself betraying him. She had never felt nearer to hating Charles.

'And get rid of that cap thing, will you?' he said as he rolled off her. 'I can tell it's there. Always. Don't think I can't.'

'Yes, all right.'

She fell asleep, woke up much later to find him gone; in the morning he was in the guest room.

'I'm sorry,' he said as she went in with his cup of tea. 'Very sorry. About last night. It's only because – because I love you so much. And get upset.'

'It's all right,' she said.

'Is it? Is it really?' His eyes had a slightly desperate, pleading expression.

The ever-present guilt surfaced. 'Yes. It really is.'

'I'll feel much, much happier, I know, if we have a child. More secure. Give me a kiss.'

She gave him a kiss, quickly, and left the room. Later she went for a walk with the dogs and wondered how she was going to survive.

She decided to throw herself into the party. It wasn't exactly what she most wanted to do, but it made for a quiet life and eased her guilt. Charles had told her to hire a marquee, brief caterers; he clearly had something very grand in mind.

'Get my mother to help you with the guest list,' he said. 'I don't want to miss anyone out, any of my old friends, or someone who might have been especially kind while I was away.'

Grace didn't say no one had been especially kind; she knew it would only lead to more trouble.

'Charles, I've had an idea for the catering,' she said. 'Jeannette, you know, who helped Florence, married Ted Miller, she's a wonderful cook, and she could do a marvellous buffet. In fact she's setting herself up in business with – '

'Grace,' said Charles, and there was an expression of acute exasperation on his face, 'that woman is not what could by any stretch of the imagination be called a caterer. And I don't want her in this house. She's insolent, she's slatternly, she'd probably bring that half-caste child with her, and – '

'Clarissa had her for a party in London,' said Grace. She smiled innocently at him. 'She did supper for fifty. Apparently it was quite wonderful.'

Charles stared at her coldly. Then he said, 'Find someone else, will you?' and left for the office.

Muriel read the guest list.

'Well, there are obviously several omissions,' she said, making it plain such a thing was so predictable as to be taken for granted, 'but I can help of course. I'm glad Charles had the sense to ask me. I'll make a second one, and let him have it. Now then, tell him he mustn't forget the Hardings, or the Wilsons. Both very important.'

'Yes, all right, I will.'

Muriel looked at her. 'Are you feeling quite well? You're very pale.'

'I'm fine,' said Grace. 'A bit tired. I've got the curse,' she added.

'Oh,' said Muriel. She went rather pink; she didn't like such matters talked about. It was one of the reasons Grace had told her. The other was that she didn't want Muriel thinking she was pregnant. She knew her mother-in-law was watching her, waiting for it to happen with some impatience. She herself was filled with dread; so far she had been lucky, but it couldn't last for ever.

Just, please God, until she felt a bit better. The feeling bad couldn't last for ever either. Could it?

She spent a lot of time trying to analyse her feelings for Charles, in an attempt to come to terms with them. It didn't really help. She knew she didn't love him; but neither did she actually dislike him. She wished him no ill, at times she managed to feel quite fond of him, in spite of his faults, his arrogance, his insensitivity. It was just that he was not the person she wanted to be with; it was not him she wanted to live with, to wake in the morning with and go to sleep with at night, not him she wanted to look at across the table, not his friends she wanted to entertain, not him she wanted to make love with, not his children she wanted to bear, and the simple fact of knowing that for the rest of her life she had no option weighed on her constantly, a dreadful leaden burden, crushing her spirit, draining her courage.

'I've written to her,' said Brian Meredith, 'the lady. About the ring.'

'Oh good,' said Sandra. 'That's good. She'll be ever so pleased, I'm sure. Where's she live then?'

'Wiltshire. Near Salisbury. Thought I'd go down there with it, if she wants it. Don't want to trust it to the post.'

'You'll do no such thing, Brian Meredith,' said Sandra. 'It's a long way and think what it'd cost.'

She was pregnant, and not entirely happy about it; they were going to be very stretched, managing with another mouth to feed, and any suggestion of expenditure made her jumpy. 'Get her to come to London, I 'spect she's got plenty of money. What's the address?'

'The Mill House. Thorpe St Andrews.'

'Well, there you are then,' said Sandra, as if that settled the matter.

Grace was immensely touched by Brian's letter. 'Dear Madam,' it said:

> I hope you will forgive me for writing to you in this way. I have in my possession a ring belonging to your late husband. I am the soldier that found him. I took it, because I thought it would be nice for you to have something of his back. I hope you will not mind that, and that this will not be too much of a shock for you. I did not want to send it, in case of it getting lost in the post, but could meet you with it, London would suit me best, if that would be all right, and give it to you. You can write to me at the above address.
> Yrs truly
> Brian Meredith

'Isn't that sweet?' she said to Charlotte and Puppy, who liked to be with her when she read her post, and indeed often removed the empty envelopes and scattered them carefully round the garden. 'What a kind nice man he must be.'

She thought for a bit, and then decided it would be better if she met Mr Meredith, rather than Angela Barlowe (whose husband's ring it actually was). You never knew, some of the details might be painful for her. And at least, she realized, she would be able to find out exactly where Colin Barlowe had spent his last hours.

There was absolutely no reason, she decided, for Charles to be told about it.

Ben and the boys were booked on the flying boat, leaving for Melbourne on 27 May. They had their passports, their visas, Ben had a work permit. Initially he would do clerical work; he had decided to see what the land of opportunity could offer him once they had settled down. The boys were apprehensive, excited, the envy of their friends, particularly over the flying. The journey would be endless, almost six days, with overnight stops in Cairo, Karachi, Singapore ... every time David thought about it, he smiled.

Life, they were told with enormous authority by those in the know who had any idea at all about Australia, would consist of one long beach party, sunbathing, surfing, and drinking ice-cold beer, interspersed with the occasional deep-sea fishing trip. The girls, it was well known, were all blonde and only ever wore bikinis. On Christmas Day they would barbecue a turkey on the beach. It didn't sound too bad. David was keener than Daniel now, particularly about the bikini-clad girls. Daniel had a recurring nightmare: they were being pushed onto a great aeroplane, just him and David, along with a lot of other children, just as they had been pushed onto the train at Waterloo all those years ago, and people kept saying be brave, be brave, and he could see his dad waving, miles away behind a barrier, and he wouldn't get on, Dad wouldn't, just kept on standing there, and the plane started moving away and still his dad wasn't on it, and then right out of reach from all of them there was Grace, Grace with Charlotte and Floss, calling them. And while he tried to attract her attention, yelling, 'Grace, Grace,' and waving furiously, frantically, the plane started to lift into the air, and still she didn't hear him, nor did she see, and he would wake up, crying, sweating, and lie staring at the picture of Charlotte and Floss, and wishing they could go back to the Mill House instead of Melbourne.

Ben had heard him calling for Grace; he wondered if he ever did the same thing in his sleep.

The night before the party, Grace was running over the table plan in the marquee, thinking that everything seemed to be going very smoothly, when Charles came out and asked her where his dinner jacket was.

'At the dry-cleaners, Charles, I told you.'

'Which dry-cleaners?'

'Townsend's in Salisbury.'

'Why not the one in Shaftesbury?'

'Because I hardly ever go to Shaftesbury at the moment.'

'Well, you'll have to pick it up,' he said, 'because I certainly haven't got time.'

'Charles, I can't. Not tomorrow. Not all the way to Salisbury. Surely you can – '

'No,' he said, 'I can't. I've got meetings all day. Why didn't you get it today?'

'Because I had a lecture this afternoon, and it didn't finish until the cleaner's was closed. It's Wednesday, it's early closing day.'

'Oh God,' he said, 'so I have to make a special trip into Salisbury to fetch my dinner jacket. Because you had a lecture.'

'Charles, that's nonsense. You've got the car, you can be there in half an hour, it's not fair to blame my lecture.'

'I do blame it,' he said, 'I blame it, that course, for a lot of things. It's taking up too much of your time and your attention, it wears you out as far as I can see, and I wouldn't be at all surprised if it wasn't a factor in preventing you from becoming pregnant.'

'Oh really!' said Grace. 'That's absurd. It's no time at all since you – since we decided. I can't – '

'It's several months,' said Charles. 'And I think this course nonsense has gone on long enough. I want it to stop. You won't have time to teach, anyway, when you do have a child, the whole thing is nonsense. I agreed initially, when you – well, when I first came home. But now I'm getting extremely tired of it and the way it's used as an excuse for everything. I think you should tell them you won't be coming any more. Is that quite clear?'

'Yes,' said Grace, 'it's quite clear. Thank you. But I'm not going to do it.'

'You have to,' said Charles simply, 'I'm afraid. It's quite expensive. I can simply stop paying the fees. All right? Now then, if I have to go and get my dinner jacket, I shall have to do some work now. I'll sleep in the guest room. Goodnight, Grace.'

Sometimes, even now, she thought of leaving him.

The party went beautifully. Everyone said so. The marquee looked wonderful, the flowers were lovely, the caterer, down from London and hugely expensive, a great success. She stood on the doorstep of the Mill House looking, she knew, very pretty, in a new, almost full-

507

skirted pale blue satin dress, made by Mrs Babbage but copied from a picture in *Vogue*, her hair put up for the evening, and wearing more make-up than usual. Charles, in a stiff, awkward truce, had told her she looked very nice indeed. Clifford told her she looked beautiful; even Muriel told her she looked very pretty. People arrived, half strangers, the people who had ignored her all through the war, kissed her, told her how lovely it was to see her. She moved dreamlike from table to table through dinner, chatting to everyone, her mind only half on the evening.

'This is wonderful, darling,' said Clarissa, 'a real triumph. Charles has just been telling me how brilliantly you've organized this marvellous party. He's so proud of you, Grace.'

'Is he?'

'Yes,' she said, her face very serious, 'yes he is. He does love you, Grace. Very much. I know – well, I know it's hard. But – '

'It's so hard,' said Grace simply, 'that I still don't know how to bear it, quite a lot of the time.'

She was standing by the buffet, rather half heartedly making up a plate of desserts for Muriel, when Jack came over. He smiled at her. 'Lovely party. What a clever girl you are.'

'Not really,' said Grace, 'I just found a few clever people to do it for me.'

'That's a skill in itself,' he said, 'delegation. Not easy at all. Here, let me help you. Are you all right? You look a bit flushed?'

'I'm fine,' said Grace quickly, 'but it is quite warm isn't it? With all the people in here.'

'Look,' he said, 'you go outside for a minute, I'll bring your plate.'

'It's for Muriel,' said Grace.

'Well I'll take it to her. Off you go, find some fresh air.'

She was sitting on the swing seat, trying to keep her thoughts clear of the past, of other occasions she had sat there, when he appeared again.

'Just checking on you,' he said, 'practising my medical skills.'

'Honestly, I'm fine,' she said, 'don't worry about me, Jack.'

'But I do worry about you,' he said, 'we both do, Clarissa and I. We think you're wonderful.'

'Oh nonsense,' said Grace, but his kindness, his concern made her heart ache suddenly, fiercely, 'I'm very lucky really.'

'Well, it's all relative,' he said after a long pause, 'of course you are in lots of ways. I am in lots of ways. But I still can't help being angry sometimes. Resentful at others. We'd hardly be human otherwise, would we?'

'No,' said Grace, surprised at his suddenly letting down his guard; he was always so heartily cheerful. She realised he was actually quite drunk. 'No I suppose not.'

'If it wasn't for my work – ' he said, 'I sometimes think I'd go quite mad. Now I am lucky, being able to do that. And to have Clarissa of course. She's – well she's been magnificent. Not always easy for her either.'

'No,' said Grace. She felt slightly nervous suddenly; feeling herself with the old sensation of things being out of control, of being in dangerous territory.

'I nearly lost her you know,' he said, 'back in the beginning. It was hard for her. Terribly hard.'

'Yes.'

'You knew didn't you?' he said suddenly.

'Knew what?'

'About Giles. About Clarissa and Giles.'

'Jack I don't know what you're – '

'Dear Grace, it's all right. And of course you knew. I'm not stupid. I saw you covering up for them, that night, so very sweetly. And very competently too. I was impressed. Deception doesn't come easily to you, does it?'

'No,' she said, her voice very low.

'It's all right,' he said, 'I understand. I knew there'd been someone, and I worked out who it was quite easily. And I forgave them long ago. I know what it did for Clarissa, helped her to come to terms with me. Me and the face. That's how I think of it, you know. The face. Not my face, the face.'

'Oh Jack. Jack I'm so sorry.'

'Don't be. As long as Florence never knows that's all that really matters. And of course Clarissa and I have never mentioned it. There are places in every marriage that are best not entered don't you think? But I have wanted to thank you for a long time, for what you did that night, for all of us. I wish we could help you in return.'

'You do help me,' said Grace, leaning up impulsively, kissing him tenderly, almost lingeringly on the mouth, 'just by being there.'

'Thank you,' he said gently. 'Thank you. For the kiss I mean. It's not often a pretty woman does that, these days. Come along, we'd better get back.'

Later she was dancing with some man called Reggie she had never

509

met but who had told her three times already how lovely it was to see her again.

'Old Charles is looking a lot better,' he said, 'I haven't seen him for six months or so. Terrible war, he must have had. Those months on his own, more or less in hiding and then getting captured again, – doesn't bear thinking about.'

'No,' said Grace.

'And then being so badly wounded, and then months in prison camps – God, I don't know how he came through it at all. Without cracking up. Got a DSO I heard. For the Italian business.'

'Yes.'

'You must be very proud of him.'

'Oh I am,' said Grace mechanically.

As she lay in bed that night, accepting Charles's apologies (and a slightly ambivalent retraction of his demand that she gave up the course), his thanks for organizing the party so well, she felt she had reached some kind of a watershed: that she could at least envisage now settling down, being happy. She thought for a long time about Jack, about his courage, in accepting things, difficult, terrible things, that he could not change; if he could do it, then surely so could she. And she was not so incompetent after all, could clearly be in time, the kind of wife Charles wanted, giving parties, looking nice, saying the right thing. It might not be what she wanted, but was it really so bad?

And besides, how could she even think of leaving him, leaving her husband, her husband the hero?

Chapter Thirty-Five

Early May 1946

Charles had bought a horse. Or rather half a horse. Muriel had bought the other half, he told her. 'What, you mean the hind legs? As in the pantomime?' said Grace icily. She could never remember being so angry. First that he should have spent what she knew must be a great deal of money on a horse when she had been pleading unsuccessfully for months for a car: second that he should have liaised clearly in secret with his mother over it.

Even Clifford came as near to disloyalty to both of them as he was capable of when he said, 'Never mind, darling, I'll give you half a car if you like.'

The horse was a thoroughbred, extremely beautiful, a bright bay mare called Lara. Grace was terrified of her; she was very young and what the previous owner called feisty. 'You've got an absolute humdinger there,' he said to Charles, watching her careering round and round the paddock after she had been released from the horsebox. 'I know you're going to enjoy her. Mind you,' he added to Muriel, who had come down to witness the arrival, 'she does take a bit of riding. He'll have his work cut out with her at first.'

'Oh, he'll be able to handle her easily,' said Muriel. 'And he'll enjoy it so much. He's missed having a horse dreadfully. But ever since his marriage it's been out of the question, I'm afraid.'

'Muriel,' said Grace, finding herself quite unable to swallow this one, 'Charles hasn't had a horse because of the war. He hasn't been here.'

'Well, yes, I suppose that was a factor,' said Muriel grudgingly.

Lara was actually too much for Charles. Even Grace could see that. She was immensely strong, she had quite a nasty temper and she was very jumpy. She shied at everything: not just tractors and cars, and other large unexpected objects, but birds, rabbits, the wind in the hedges. For some reason she hated cows; getting her to walk past a field of them was almost impossible. Charles had to dismount and lead her, while she danced all over the road. She had a nasty habit of taking the bit, she had twice bolted with Charles, and she also did an extremely theatrical double buck, so that if she didn't dislodge him the first time, she almost always got him off the second.

Charles was undeterred by this; Grace came to admire his courage. He rode every day, early in the morning, refusing to give in to Lara; by the end of the first week he was covered in bruises and had a badly sprained wrist.

'You'll have to wait for that to get better, surely,' she said, when the doctor had left after strapping it up.

'Oh no,' he said, 'can't do that, she'll get even fresher, got to keep working at her.'

'Fresh!' said Grace. 'Is that what you call it?'

She had written to Brian Meredith; she said she would like to meet him in London, some time during the next month, that she was most grateful for his kindness. She suggested three dates, and said that any of them would suit her, and if he would like to write or to telephone her <u>during the day</u> (she underlined this) they could agree on the most suitable. She didn't attempt to explain that the ring had actually belonged to Colin Barlowe. It would be a lot simpler to do that when she saw him.

After ten days he still hadn't answered; she was surprised, and sent another little note, in case he hadn't got the first.

Daniel had passed the scholarship to the grammar school. He wanted to tell Grace. 'I'd never have done it without her,' he said, 'her and Sir Clifford. I want to tell them both.'

'Well, write to her,' said Ben, 'but I don't know if she'll be able to see you this time.'

Grace had written a short, sad letter to the boys saying she didn't think she would be able to meet them again for quite a long time. She said she was very busy with her music studies. They had both been rather upset; Ben had read between the lines, known what it meant and tried to explain to them.

'Her husband is jealous, I expect. It's understandable. He doesn't like her seeing you, because he thinks she might want to see me again.'

'Well, I 'spect she does,' Daniel had said, entirely reasonable, 'anyone'd want to see you.'

Ben gave him a hug. 'Yeah, well, thanks. I wish you were right.'

'You still miss her too, Dad?'

'Terribly,' said Ben, 'sometimes so much I think I can't stand it.'

Now he said again, 'Yes, you write to her, Daniel. Or maybe write to Sir Clifford, tell him to tell her, that might be better.'

'I wish I could go to the grammar school,' said Daniel wistfully, 'I wish we could stay here, and I could go.'

'I know you do, Dan. But we've gone over and over this and I still think it's the best thing. To go, I mean.'

'Course it is,' said David, looking up from his homework. 'Don't be selfish, Dan. Anyway, think of the surfing. That's better than going to any rotten old school.'

'You'll still have to go to school sometimes, David,' said Ben.

While he was sorting things out and packing, he found a book Clarissa had lent him: a book of O'Henry stories which she'd said she knew he would like. 'Clarissa,' it said on the flyleaf, 'the most fabulous story of them all. My love, Jack.'

It clearly had to go back, only he didn't know her address. He wrote her a note, and another to Clifford at the Priory, explaining that he must ask him to forward it.

A week later Clarissa wrote:

Darling Ben,
How lovely to hear from you, and thank you for the book. Sweet of you, and I had been looking for it.

I can hardly bear to think of you going so far away. But I do understand. I think it's a wonderfully clever idea. So marvellous for the children too.

Grace is doing splendidly. It is hard for her, and she is very, very brave.

Now, Ben, I see that you are leaving from Victoria. I absolutely insist you stay here the night before. It will be much easier for you than dragging up from Salisbury that day, and then we can say goodbye. Florence would like to see you too, and sends her love. She is immensely important now, a councillor; and Giles has a part in the most marvellous new musical. Second lead! Imogen is at school and between you and me greatly improved by it. I have a bit of news: I'm going to be a mama! What do you think of that? Wildly unsuitable really, don't you think? But Jack and I are both thrilled to bits. The baby will just have to come to work with me and sit quietly in a corner, as I can't possibly leave. We are absolutely snowed under with work, moving to bigger offices.

Jack is loving his medical studies, and passed his first exams with the most impossibly high flying colours.

Best love, darling Ben. The beds will be made up for you on 26 May. I will have no excuses!

Clarissa

Ben grinned rather weakly and sat down to accept Clarissa's offer.

Grace read Daniel's letter and burst into tears. She wrote him a long one by return of post and sent it, enclosing a big box of oil paints in tubes which she knew he had always wanted:

This is to go to Australia too, without fail, as well as the picture of Charlotte and Floss. And we'll have a last tea. You say you're going on the 27th. What about the 24th? That would suit me, and you won't be quite all packed up. If I don't hear from you, I'll see you both in the Bear at four.

Brian Meredith had had gastric flu. He was getting better now, but he was still feeling feak and weeble, as Sandra called it. The doctor said he should have another week off work.

'What you really need is some good country air,' he said.

'Chance'd be a fine thing,' said Brian.

But the mention of country air reminded him of Mrs Bennett and the fact that he hadn't answered her letter. One of the dates she had suggested was already gone, and the other one was only a couple of days off.

'I'd best telephone her,' he said to Sandra.

'Think what that'd cost,' said Sandra. 'You write.'

'Yeah, OK,' he said. A sudden spasm gripped his innards; he winced. An hour later he was back in bed; Mrs Bennett seemed a rather low priority.

'I'm going for a ride, darling,' said Charles, putting down the Sunday paper. 'I'll be back in an hour. Mother might phone, she's keen to see how Lara's shaping up. Perhaps she could come for lunch – Father's playing golf.'

Grace was stuffing a chicken for Sunday lunch, a very small chicken. She knew what that meant: Muriel would eat her share of it as well as her own.

'All right,' she said and sighed.

Charles heard the sigh and glared at her. When he came over to kiss her briefly, she turned her head away.

Elspeth appeared at about eleven o'clock, to do her practice. Grace listened to the scales winging through the golden morning and felt calmer; when Elspeth had finished she gave her a cup of cocoa, told her to come and sit in the garden.

'How's school going? Any better?'

'It's all right, miss.'

'Is it really? You don't sound very enthusiastic.'

'No, not really,' said Elspeth and smiled rather feebly at her. 'Most of the girls are horrible, and the work's really boring.'

'I've been thinking,' said Grace. 'There's a music scholarship offered at St Felicia's. The big school, you know, the other side of Shaftesbury. I think you ought to go in for it. If you agree, I'm going to speak to your father.'

'Oh, I don't know, miss,' said Elspeth doubtfully. 'I failed the other scholarship.'

'I know you did, but that was nothing to do with music. I think you have a really good chance of getting this one. Look, if you wait I'll write a note to him and suggest it. Only we'll have to get our skates on – it's in a fortnight. I only know about it because I heard about it at my music college. You tell him to ring me today, if he thinks it's a good idea.'

'Yes, all right, miss.'

When Elspeth had gone, she most unusually poured herself a drink and sat on the terrace trying to enjoy it. She felt edgy, she wasn't sure why. She supposed it was because Muriel was coming to lunch without Clifford. She would have to sit and listen to horsy talk for hours, and wait on them both like an exceptionally stupid maidservant.

Charles had been gone a very long time; she hoped he was all right. Sooner or later he was going to have a real fall from that horse. Break something. Well, serve him right, she thought, and then felt dreadful. In the house the phone rang sharply; she went to answer it.

It was Peter Roberts, a riding friend of Charles; Charles had dropped in for a drink, he said, and had thought she might be worried, asked him to ring. He was on his way back, shouldn't be more than half an hour longer.

'Thank you,' said Grace, and put the phone down; Charles's thoughtfulness made her feel even more remorseful.

She was just thinking she ought to go in and get on with the lunch when she saw Lara and Charles in the distance, walking admirably slowly, she thought, down Thorpe Hill. He disappeared briefly into the woods, and then she saw him on the path that cut round the edge of the wood, coming towards the paddock. It was all very lyrical, like a watercolour painting: the sun shining on Lara's gleaming coat, her tail swishing the flies away, and behind them the brilliant springtime woods. And then it happened.

Something – no one would ever know what – startled Lara; Grace saw her shy violently, then go into her well-known double buck, and when that failed to unseat Charles she began to gallop towards the paddock gate. She gathered herself, jumped it high, landed awkwardly, and pecked: had it not been for that peck, all might have been well. But it was that which sent Charles flying off her, over her head, landing with horrible awkwardness on the ground. Lara, finally calm, stood nuzzling him, clearly wondering why he didn't get up and remount her as he had so many times in the past. Or why he didn't even move at all.

Chapter Thirty-Six

Late May 1946

All Grace could think, as she raced across the paddock, careless for once of Lara and what the horse might do to her, was that the last thing she had done before Charles left was turn her face away and refuse to let him kiss her. And the last thing he had done was thoughtfully phone to tell her not to worry about him.

Well, maybe this was a judgment on her. For all her wickedness.

She stood looking down at him, lying still as stone, totally silent and wondered if he was dead, or hopelessly paralysed perhaps, would have to spend the rest of his life in a wheelchair. That would probably be worse. She didn't like to touch him; she knew it was dangerous to move anyone after an accident, she had learnt that at a first-aid course she had done, had been told so repeatedly by Florence. But she did have to know if he was actually alive. She sank to her knees and put her hand out gingerly to his neck, trying to find a pulse. She couldn't. Dear God, he was, he was dead.

She looked round wildly, wondering what to do; Lara, pleased with her morning's work, was cropping at the grass a few yards away. Over in the drive she could see Muriel's car. She waved frantically, thinking it was the first and probably the last time she would ever be pleased to see her. Muriel ducked under the rails and came running towards them.

'What is it? What's happened?'

'It's Charles, he – she – he – '

'I can see it's Charles,' said Muriel, 'but what happened? Surely even you – '

'Sorry,' said Grace, thinking as she said it that even Muriel could hardly blame her for Charles being thrown by his horse. 'She jumped the gate, stumbled and he fell. And I can't feel a pulse, I think – I think – '

Muriel knelt down by Charles, put her hand to his neck, probed about a bit. Grace watched in agony. Then: 'What the hell are you doing?' said an irritable voice.

He had broken his leg and sustained mild concussion, Dr Hardacre said. He was driven off in the ambulance, Grace and Muriel following, to have his leg set, and came home next day. Grace looked at him with some foreboding, as he was borne into the house. Charles was a terrible patient. He found the crutches difficult to manage, and most of the time he lay on his bed and railed at Grace. He didn't complain about the pain he was in, which was clearly considerable, but he did complain about everything else: boredom, discomfort, the heat, the food, the books Grace brought him, the radio programmes the BBC chose to put on, the work which was piling up, the dogs barking, Grace's inability to cope with Lara. Lara was easily dealt with, sent back to her stud farm; the rest was more difficult.

Grace had made up a bed for Charles in the drawing room, so that he could have the French windows open to the lovely summer air, but he complained that he got no peace; unsure why not, she moved the bed into his study. He said that was an improvement as there was a phone there, and he could talk to the office, but after a few days he said he got no peace from the phone and Grace had to fly to answer it at the first ring, dropping whatever she was doing. If she went to the lavatory, or even to hang out the washing, she took it off the hook first. As it was almost always for him anyway, it all seemed a complete waste of time and effort, but it obviously made him feel better to have the calls filtered.

She did her best with the food, but there was no pleasing him: he said he needed meat to build up his strength, but after the first couple of meals complained that it was too heavy, while he was so inactive; she gave him eggs and cheese instead, but he said they gave him indigestion. He demanded sweet things, but sugar was still rationed, and he had a craving for bread, which Grace made herself, and which he criticized as being too doughy.

'Get my mother to give you her recipe, much nicer.'

Grace knew Muriel had never made a loaf of bread in her life, and the recipe was Cook's, but she didn't argue. The recipe that actually came down was Jeannette's which was delicious.

He couldn't sleep, and he said reading made his head ache; Grace offered to read to him, but after the first chapter he complained the story was too slow and he couldn't stand listening to it.

After another week, she could have cheerfully throttled him with his pyjama cord.

Mr Dunn had agreed that Elspeth should try for the scholarship at St

Felicia's. It was clearly impossible for Elspeth to practise at the Mill House, while Charles was there, so Grace had asked Miss Merton if she could go to the school.

'You can go in every day when you get home,' she said to Elspeth, 'and then drop the key off at Miss Merton's when you finish.'

'Thank you, miss. What do you think I should play? The Mozart or the Haydn?'

'Both,' said Grace firmly. 'They want at least two pieces, and your scales and so on, and I think you should play the one you wrote, you know, the lullaby? It really shows off your musicality. All right? Now they'll notify me when they want you, what time and so on, as I'm your teacher. And I'll take you there. It's on the twenty-fifth of May. Don't look so frightened, Elspeth, I know you're going to do wonderfully.'

'Yes, miss.'

'Oh my lord,' said Brian Meredith, properly recovered at last, 'I still haven't been in touch with Mrs Bennett. Tomorrow's the nine-teenth, isn't it? The day I was supposed to meet her. The last one of the three she suggested. What'll I do, San?'

'S'pose you'll have to phone. Want me to do it? I've got to go out.'

'No, it's all right. I ought to really. She sounds a nice person – what must she be thinking? I'll go down the corner now I've got to go to the surgery, anyway, get my final certificate signed.'

'You really going back to work?' said Sandra. 'I'll be glad to get you out the house.'

'You don't mean that.'

'No I don't,' she said, giving him a kiss. 'I'll miss you.'

Whereupon one thing led to another and it was rather later than Brian had intended before he set off; he decided he would have to go to the surgery before he made his telephone call, otherwise he might miss the doctor and then there'd be hell to pay when he went back to work next day.

'I've got to do some shopping,' said Grace, 'we're out of everything and – '

'Can't you get it delivered?'

'No I can't, Charles. It's still difficult getting things delivered. Apart from fish, and you won't eat that. I won't be long, and if you have a problem you can just lift the phone and your mother can be down in ten minutes. I've checked that she's there. But I'll only be an hour.'

The number Brian had for Mrs Bennett was engaged for a very long time; the woman on the exchange was sympathetic.

'Been engaged all afternoon, my dear.'

'There's not a problem, is there?'

'I don't know. I'm only temporary here.'

'Oh dear,' said Brian.

'Is it urgent? I know Mrs Boscombe, she's the usual operator, takes a message if it's really urgent.'

'My Lord,' said Brian, 'that wouldn't happen up here, in London.'

'Don't s'pose it would, my dear,' said the operator. 'Look, give me your name, and I'll try once more. Can they ring you back?'

'No, they can't. The name's Meredith. Brian Meredith. I can't meet Mrs Bennett, that's the message. Oh, and I'll call again.'

'Right. I've written that down. Oh now then, wouldn't you just know, it's ringing. Hold the line, caller.'

A man answered the phone; he sounded disagreeable. 'No,' he said, 'she's not here. Who wants her?'

'This is Mr Meredith,' said Brian.

'Look, if you're from the college, or it's about some music scholarship, I really don't want to have to – '

'No I'm not,' said Brian, pushing another two pennies in. He felt rattled by the severely authoritative tone; the conditioning of five years in the army surfaced. 'Sorry about that, sir, running out of money. No, nothing to do with music, sir. I had an appointment with Mrs Bennett, and I can't keep it. I'm very sorry. I've been ill.'

'What sort of appointment? What is this?' He sounded even more bad-tempered. 'With a doctor or something?'

'No, not a doctor. It's a bit difficult to explain, sir.'

'Well, I think you'd better try. I've got better things to do than embark on some guessing game.'

'Yes, sir, of course. I've got something for her, something that belonged to her late husband. Something he – well, that he lost. In the war. That I've been keeping, sir.'

There was a silence; then the voice said, 'What regiment were you in?'

'Paras, sir.'

'How could you have anything of – of Major Bennett's?'

'Well, sir, it was me found him, you see. In France. After his – after he – '

There was a very long silence; then the man said, 'Look, what is it exactly you've got?'

The pips went again; he had only two more pennies. He pushed them in. 'I'll have to be quick, sir, haven't got no more money.'

'Give me your number, I'll ring you back.'

'You can't do that, sir, it's a public box.' Didn't these people know anything? 'Could you just tell Mrs Bennett I'll write and arrange another day?'

'Absolutely no point in that,' said the man. 'Sorry. She's gone away, for some time as a matter of fact. Hasn't been at all well. Look, just send it, whatever it is. A letter did you say?'

'No, I didn't say, sir.'

'Well, what is it?'

'A ring, sir. A signet ring.'

Another long silence; the pips went yet again. 'Christ,' said the voice, 'just send it. I can't imagine why you took it anyway. Most irregular. But don't worry Mrs Bennett any more. I'll deal with it. All right?'

'Yes, sir. Who shall I address it to, sir?'

'To me. The name's Jacobs. Michael Jacobs. At this address. And I'd like your address, and − ' The phone went dead.

He was obviously Mrs Bennett's new bloke, thought Brian, putting down the phone. None too nice either by the sound of things. He decided to take his time sending the ring. There was still a chance Mrs Bennett might get in touch herself.

'There may be some stuff for the office coming here,' said Charles that evening. 'Some of it addressed to Jacobs. I know he's retired, but he still gets mail. Just bring it all to me, won't you? I mean don't start opening it.'

'Yes of course,' said Grace. 'I wouldn't dream of opening any of your letters. You know that. And I'm sure you wouldn't open mine.'

'No. No, of course not.'

'Did John Stokes phone this afternoon by the way? About the music on Sunday?'

'No. Nobody rang.'

'I'd better ring him then. Charles, are you all right? You look a bit odd.'

'No, I'm perfectly all right. Just sick to death of lying here, bored out of my mind.'

Early next morning, the music head of St Felicia's rang up about Elspeth's scholarship.

'This is just to warn you. We're asking all the children to play a piece sight unseen. And there will also be a few extra compulsory scales, chords and so on. Can I just tell you those, so that Elspeth can work on them?'

'Yes of course,' said Grace, 'let me just get a piece of paper. Could you just hold on while I – '

'Grace!' came a roar from the study. 'Can you come here quickly? I've spilt the damn tea.'

'Oh dear,' said Grace, rustling frantically through her bag for something, anything to write on, finding the letter from Brian Meredith, turning it over, scribbling frantically. 'B sharp minor, G flat, yes, chords, yes – yes, got those. Thank you so much. See you next week. Goodbye.'

She put the letter back into her bag, went into the study; Charles was looking furious, tea dripping all over his *Times*. She tried to appear suitably sorry for him.

She looked at the date on *The Times* as she dabbed at it. The twentieth of May. Exactly a week until Ben and the boys sailed for Australia. In four days she was seeing the boys. Every time she thought about that, saying goodbye to them for the last time, she felt sick; she didn't know how she was going to get through it. She wished desperately now she had never said she would meet them. But she owed it to them; they wanted to say goodbye, it would be wrong, unkind, to refuse them. She didn't want them to remember her as someone who hadn't had time for them, who refused to see them.

She wasn't sure whether the thought of Ben going made her feel better or worse; the thought of him being on the other side of the world was horrible. On the other hand knowing he was there, quite near, but forbidden to her, was very painful; there had been times when she had been so unhappy, so desperate for him, she had found the temptation simply to go to where she knew he lived, to knock on the door, to cross over into that territory, almost overwhelming. And she was terrified of bumping into him by accident one day; she knew that if she did she wouldn't be able to stand it. She never went to Salisbury without half expecting it, never stood at her bus stop or walked through the streets without feeling he might, must one day be there.

After lunch that day, Charles fell asleep. She decided to take advantage of it, and go for a walk. She called the dogs, set out across the paddock, thinking how nice it was not to have Lara there. The horse would be back soon, she supposed; she had tried to persuade Charles to sell her, but he wouldn't hear of it.

She walked further than she had intended; on the way back she saw the school bus coming in, Elspeth getting off it. She waved at her.

'Elspeth! I had a phone call about your exam this morning. There are some scales and chords you need to practise. If you come back with me now, we can run through them. All right?'

Elspeth nodded. 'How's David?' she asked casually as they walked up the drive. 'I never hear from him. He said he'd write to me, but – '

Her voice was forlorn. Grace smiled at her. 'Oh – fine. Very grown up. Terribly busy. They're going to Australia, you know,' she added, trying to sound unconcerned. 'He'll probably send you a postcard from there.' I must tell him to do that, she thought, when I see him on the twenty-fourth.

'Australia! Oh my goodness. That's a long way. I'll never see him again then.'

'Oh I don't know,' said Grace. 'When you're a famous concert pianist you can go on a tour there.'

'Yes, miss,' said Elspeth with a grin.

Charles had hobbled into the kitchen, was sitting stony-faced, eating bread and jam. 'I was terribly hungry,' he said. 'Where on earth have you been?'

'Just walking. I've brought Elspeth back with me, she's doing her scholarship exam in a week. I just want to give her a short lesson now, Charles – '

'Well, could you make me some tea first, please? I'm absolutely parched.'

'Yes of course I will. Now, Elspeth,' said Grace, picking up her bag, 'I've made a note of these scales, you can make a start on them – That's funny. I could have sworn it was in here.'

She looked round the kitchen distractedly. 'Charles, you haven't taken an envelope out of my bag, have you?'

'No of course not. What sort of envelope?'

'A small brown one. I just scribbled some notes for Elspeth on the back.'

She hoped he hadn't, hoped he hadn't read it. It didn't exactly matter, but – She looked at him sharply; but he was sitting scowling at the paper. 'Look, Grace, I have better things to do than go through your bag. Well, slightly better.'

'Oh dear,' she said, 'I wonder – well look, Elspeth, go and run through your other scales and I'll try to find – '

'Do you have to do this now?' said Charles. 'I really want something to eat, it's after five – '

'Yes, I do,' said Grace firmly, 'and it won't take a minute. Well, about fifteen, if I can only find the wretched list.'

While she was making the tea she suddenly saw the letter; it was on the floor, under the kitchen table. It must have fallen out of her bag while she was getting out her purse or something.

When Elspeth was halfway through her practice, she heard Mr Bennett calling Mrs Bennett from the study, telling her to make him a cup of tea, that he couldn't wait any longer. She was just thinking how horrid to her he was when he hobbled in on his crutches and gave her a letter.

'Post this for me, would you?' he said. 'It's very important. It's to do with a surprise for Mrs Bennett. No need to mention it to her.'

'Yes, Mr Bennett,' said Elspeth, pushing it into her pocket. 'I mean no, Mr Bennett.'

'Oh dear,' said Brian Meredith. 'Oh Lord. I was a bit worried about something like this.'

'What's that?' said Sandra.

'I wish I hadn't said anything to that man. That man on the phone, about Mr Bennett's ring. Look at this, Sandra.'

He passed Sandra a letter; it was headed Bennett & Bennett, Solicitors, Bell Street, Shaftesbury.

'Thought Mr Bennett was dead,' said Sandra.

'Yes, well, he is, that's just the firm. Obviously. This is from that Mr Jacobs I spoke to. I told you he – '

'Shush, Deirdre,' said Sandra. 'I'm reading. You eat that egg up, there's poor people starving all over the world be glad of that egg. Oh I shouldn't take any notice of this, Brian. They can't do anything to you. You're not in the army now.'

'No, but – ' He took it back, read it again.

Dear Mr Meredith,

Following your phone call the other day, I must repeat that you should make no further contact with Mrs Bennett. Apart from distressing her, the repercussions could be most unfortunate for you. You must understand that what you did in removing any of Major Bennett's belongings was strictly illegal and you had no right to do so. It could be considered theft in a court of law.

Because I am sure you would not wish things to come to such a pass, please send the ring as instructed, to me, at the above address, with your assurance that as far as you are concerned the entire matter is closed.

Above all, I repeat, trying to make any contact with Mrs Bennett would prejudice your case.

Yours sincerely,

Michael Jacobs

'Oh dear,' said Brian Meredith again.

'Best do what he says,' said Sandra, 'but don't worry, Brian, they can't do nothing to you really.'

She hoped she sounded more convincing than she felt.

'And then every day we'll be surfing,' said Daniel, trying to sound as if he was really looking forward to it, 'and having picnics on the beach and that. And Dad says the people are really friendly and nice. And –'

'Shut up a minute, Dan,' said David. 'Grace doesn't want to hear all that.'

'Yes I do,' said Grace. But she smiled at David to show she appreciated his thoughtfulness. He was very thoughtful, very sensitive. Like – well, like she'd always known he would be.

'Well anyway. How's Sir Clifford?'

'He's very well. He sent his love. And he sent you these – one each.' She produced two packages and handed them over.

'Crikey!' said Daniel.

'Blimey!' said David.

They were two wallets, grown-up wallets, in leather; how Clifford had got hold of them Grace couldn't imagine. She smiled at the boys. 'Nice, aren't they?'

'Really nice. We did think he might come, Sir Clifford –'

'No, he's with – with my husband,' said Grace, thinking lovingly of Clifford who had, in response to her urgent request, not only come to sit with Charles for the afternoon, but had also told him that some documents had arrived from the London office needing his urgent attention.

'Been here for a few weeks actually,' he'd said, winking at Grace, 'but I really shouldn't have left them so long. Quite complex, some of them. Take a long time to go through. Give the little tykes my love.'

'We're going to stay with Clarissa,' said David, 'us and Dad. On our last night before we get the flying boat.'

'Oh really?' said Grace, trying to sound as if she didn't mind at all, as if the red-hot jealousy wasn't flooding her, as if the thought of Ben and the boys spending an evening with Clarissa, laughing, joking, chatting, being hugged and kissed by her, being called her darling, left her quite calm and unbothered. 'Well, that will be nice for you. Tell her – well, tell her I'll come and see her soon.'

'Yeah, OK.'

'And are you all packed up?'

'Nearly. Dan's not helping. Won't put half his things away,' said David.

'I will.'

'You won't.'

'I will.'

'Boys, boys. What sort of things?'

'Well, the things you gave me mostly,' said Daniel. 'The picture of Floss and Charlotte, and those paints, and – well, that's all.'

'And your old teddy,' said David.

'Yeah, well, Mum gave me that.'

'And the golliwog Grace gave you.'

'Well, you've still got the picture of you and Elspeth the last day of school.'

'Oh, that reminds me,' said Grace, feeling less jealous suddenly at this catalogue of memorabilia. 'David, will you promise me to send Elspeth a postcard from Australia. She really misses you – '

'Look at his face!' said Daniel. 'It's all red.' He clasped his hand to his heart and rolled his eyes dramatically to the ceiling.

'Be quiet, Daniel. Anyway, she's doing a scholarship exam tomorrow. A music scholarship, that is. I'm very hopeful for her, actually.'

'Yeah, OK,' said David. His face was still crimson.

'Aren't you going to send her your love?' said Daniel. 'Say good luck and that?'

'Course I'm not,' said David.

'That's not very nice,' said Grace.

Saying goodbye to them was the hardest thing she could ever remember doing. She stood in the doorway of the Bear and put her arms round Daniel and held his small skinny body, remembering, remembering the first time she had seen him, a tiny pale thing, with huge eyes in a frightened face, clinging to her hand as they left the town hall as if he would never let it go, remembering him importantly collecting eggs, feeding the chickens, playing with Floss, coming home from school always filthy, always covered in bruises, remembered him huddled against her on the old sofa, asleep, remembered

looking at him lying white and still in the hospital bed, remembering –
oh God – remembering the ward sister saying, 'Go home to bed, it's
the sensible thing to do – ' She wrenched them out of her head, the
memories, put Daniel gently out of her arms, tried to smile through
her tears and failed totally.

'I love you, Grace,' he said, 'I'll miss you so much. I wish you could
come too.'

'I can't,' she said, 'you know I can't,' and then as she stood there,
fighting not just tears now but sobs, David said quietly, gently,
'Goodbye then, Grace,' and held out his hand, very grown-up. She
took it, was about to shake it when he suddenly took a rather odd
shaky breath and put his arms round her, tightly; he was tall now, taller
than her, and now there were more memories, horribly, intensely
vivid, and she could feel other arms, another long, rangy body, see
another dark head and deep-set dark eyes, hear another quiet, gentle
voice, and it was more, she thought, than she could possibly bear.

'I have to go,' she said suddenly, fiercely. 'Now you be good. Very
good. Write a lot. And – and tell your dad I – '

'That you still love him?' said Daniel hopefully.

'No. No, you mustn't say that. Just tell him I hope it will all go very
well, Daniel, please.'

When she got home, she told Charles she had a migraine and was
going to bed and asked Clifford to get him his supper.

'You don't want anything?' he said gently, seeing her white-faced
misery, knowing, realizing why.

'No,' she said, 'no thank you, Clifford. Well, nothing you can get
me. I'm sorry.'

'Don't say sorry,' he said, and couldn't understand why her face
suddenly crumpled, and she turned and ran up the stairs without
another word.

In the morning she felt almost cheerful; she supposed because the
ordeal was over. She had said goodbye, they had gone – to all intents
and purposes – and she could truly regard them as out of her life. She
had to; she had no alternative.

Charles was fretful, difficult, annoyed she was going out yet again –
to take Elspeth to her exam – impatient with his leg which had
stopped hurting and now itched intolerably under the plaster.

'Look, Mrs Babbage is coming to look after you for the morning.
I'll tell her to bring you one of her extra-long knitting needles. To
push down the plaster,' she added.

'Right,' said Grace. 'You ready, Elspeth?'

'Yes, I think so, miss. Ready as I'll ever be.'

'Good. Now, Charles, we'll be back in a couple of hours. I'll pick up your post from the office. And Mrs Babbage will do your lunch, if you want it early. Oh heavens – '

It was the phone: Mrs Boscombe's voice. 'Mrs Bennett, dear, a message for you. Well, for Elspeth actually. From young David. Said to wish her good luck. He tried earlier, but he couldn't get through. I expect the major's very busy.'

'Oh how lovely of him,' said Grace, her eyes filling with tears. 'How kind of you, Mrs Boscombe.'

'Yes, well, I won't be doing this much longer,' said Mrs Boscombe. 'They're bringing in the automatic down here, I heard.' She sounded outraged.

'Oh dear,' said Grace, 'I'm so sorry.'

'It's not right, is it? Not round here. Oh, now that reminds me, Mrs Bennett, I found a message for you the other day, left on my day off it was. Did you ever get it, my dear? From a Mr Meredith?'

'A who?' said Grace.

'Mr Meredith, that's what it says here. Can't meet you, he'll be in touch again. Does that make sense?'

'I think so, yes,' said Grace very slowly. 'Yes, thank you, Mrs Boscombe. Er – when was your day off?'

'Last Thursday. Wish Elspeth luck from me as well, won't you?'

Grace put the phone back very gently. She forced a smile at Elspeth. 'That was a message. From David. Good luck. Isn't that nice?'

'David?' said Elspeth. 'David Lucas? Oh my good Lord!'

Grace had never seen her so excited.

She sat outside listening while Elspeth played (most beautifully), her mind racing. Thursday. When she had gone shopping, and Charles had said emphatically there had been no phone calls for her. Well, maybe he had been asleep. Or maybe Mr Meredith hadn't been able to get through. Charles's calls were endless. Yes, that was probably it. But then there had also been the slightly baffling business with the letter from Mr Meredith. Missing from her bag, and then found under the table. She had put it back so carefully, had actually zipped it into the pocket (knowing how important those details were, of Elspeth's scales and chords and so on). Letters didn't actually leap out of such places of their own free will. But then why should Charles lie about such a thing? Unless he didn't want her meeting Mr Meredith, was upset at the prospect. It was understandable, she supposed, although she wasn't quite sure why.

Anyway, she could write back to him, suggest another meeting. Probably best not to worry Charles, if it bothered him so much.

Elspeth came out beaming. 'Whether I got it or not,' she said, 'I had a nice time. She was really lovely. I had to sing, as well. She said we'd know in a couple of days.'

'A couple of long days,' said Grace, smiling at her. 'Well done. Look, Elspeth, if you don't mind we'll go back through Shaftesbury. I've got a couple of things to pick up from my husband's office.'

'No, that'd be fine,' said Elspeth.

The secretary at Bennett & Bennett had a pile of post for Charles. 'And there's this for Mr Jacobs. From London. Obviously someone doesn't know he's retired. Do you want to take it, Mrs Bennett?'

'Yes,' said Grace, 'yes, I will. Thank you.'

When she got home Mrs Babbage had gone; Charles was lying on the sofa looking pained.

'Made me some horrible salad, covered it in vinegar and didn't give me anything to drink. Honestly, Grace, I've been very patient but – '

'Sorry,' said Grace. She fled out to the kitchen, putting the pile of post down on the chair in the hall as she passed.

'And call these dogs, will you? They're driving me mad.'

'Puppy!' said Grace. 'Charlotte! Out of there.'

This was proving quite a day. At least it distracted her from her thoughts of yesterday – and of the day after tomorrow.

Much later, as Charles had his nap (having tried and failed to get his secretary three times and become even more bad-tempered), she went rather wearily out into the garden. It was a lovely day; summer had suddenly arrived, as it so often did, the sky hazily blue, the lavender bushes and the honeysuckle alive with bees, the air thick with birdsong. She thought, despite trying very hard not to, of Ben and the boys, with only forty-eight hours left in England; she tried to imagine leaving for ever, wondering what it could possibly feel like to see the country literally disappearing from view.

Puppy suddenly appeared beside her, presenting something proudly in her jaws; a half-open package. 'Oh Puppy,' said Grace sternly, 'that is naughty. You should have grown out of that sort of thing. And it's for your master. Let me have it. Oh dear – ' And then she was silent, opening the inner package carefully, very carefully. First tissue paper, then cotton wool and finally she could see what it was: a ring, a gold signet ring, with the initials CB engraved on it.

And only slightly chewed, still absolutely legible, a letter. A letter signed Brian Meredith.

> Dear Mr Jacobs,
> I am returning the ring as instructed. I am so sorry, did not mean any harm, nor intend anything illegal. I give you my assurance not to contact Mrs Bennett further and wish her better from her illness.
> Yrs truly,
> B. Meredith

'Oh God,' said Grace aloud. 'Oh my God.'

'Right,' said Ben, 'last night in the old home.'

'There's a painting called that,' said David.

'Yes, I know. You're not the only one who's been to school. Shall we have fish and chips? As a treat?'

'Yeah,' said Daniel. 'D'you think they have fish and chips in Australia?'

'Nah,' said David.

'They'd better,' said Ben.

'Oh my goodness,' said Sandra. 'It's a telegram. Oh my good Lord, I hope it's not Mum. Deirdre, turn that wireless off, there's a good girl. Oh God, I can't look. Oh, why isn't your dad here? If it's Mum I'll never forgive myself.'

She ripped open the envelope, read the telegram. 'Well, well, well,' she said, 'what do you know! Thought it was funny, that letter. No reply,' she said to the telegram boy. 'Thank you.'

She went back inside and sat down for a bit; it had given her a nasty turn. Enough to bring on the baby, that sort of thing. Well, if Mrs Bennett was coming next day, she'd better clean the house up a bit. Whatever would Brian say when she told him?

'Charles, I've got to go to Salisbury for the day tomorrow,' said Grace briskly.

'You've what?'

'I said I've got to go to Salisbury. I'm very sorry. I've got two vital lectures. Mrs Babbage is coming in again.'

'You can't,' he said, 'you really can't. It's too bad of you. I'm going crazy here, and I think for the time being at least you should give up that course.'

'Charles, I'm sorry. I'll fail my exam if I miss these lectures.'

He looked at her and his eyes were very hard in his white face. 'You're not going to see those boys again, are you?'

'No,' said Grace, 'I give you my word. I'm not going to see those boys.'

'I will not have that Babbage woman here again, Grace. She's a nightmare.'

'Then I suggest you ring your mother and ask her if she can come down and look after you,' said Grace. 'I haven't got the time to make fresh arrangements. I really am sorry, Charles. But it's very, very important.'

'Now look,' said Ben, 'our cases will have to be padlocked, ready to go on the aeroplane. You can just keep a small attaché case each, all right? So anything you need for your night with Clarissa, put it in that. Which does not mean, Daniel Lucas, large photographs of dogs and goats, all right? Put that in your trunk, is that clear?'

'Yes, Dad.'

'I hope it's all right,' said Brian Meredith.

'Course it's all right,' said Sandra. 'Read what it says, Brian.'

He read it again. 'Coming midday tomorrow 26th stop Ignore letter from Jacobs stop not correct stop, In perfect health stop Grace Bennett.'

'Does she mean it's not correct about it being illegal or not correct about her being ill?'

'Brian, I don't know. I'm not a mind-reader. But it's obvious something fishy's going on. Can you be here midday tomorrow?'

'Course not. She'll have to wait. I'm on early shift though, I'll be home about two thirty. Lucky for her, that. Oh, I do hope this is going to be all right, San. I wish I'd never started it, I really do.'

'Too late for that now,' said Sandra.

Grace sat on the train, staring out of the window, hoping she wasn't on a complete wild-goose chase. She felt rather frightened, and she didn't know why. Frightened and extremely excited. She didn't understand that either.

Brian Meredith lived in Paddington. Fifty-seven Queen's Avenue, W2. Easy from Waterloo, on the underground. Grace had always been rather pleased with her skill on the underground.

She stopped at a flower stall just outside Paddington station and bought some slightly dusty-looking wallflowers for Mrs Meredith. She presumed there was a Mrs Meredith. If there wasn't, then Mr Meredith's house might need cheering up anyway.

She reached 57 Queens Avenue just before midday and knocked at the door. A pretty little girl with blonde curls opened it.

'Hallo,' said Grace, 'is your mummy in?'

Another larger pretty girl, her curls just a little darker, appeared behind her. She was pregnant. 'Yes?' she said.

'You look just like your daughter,' said Grace, smiling and holding out her hand. 'I'm Grace Bennett, how do you do?'

'Sandra Meredith. Pleased to meet you. You come to see Brian?'

'Yes. I don't suppose he's here. I'm so stupid, I just didn't think of him being at work, but – '

'No, but he'll be back about two thirty,' said Sandra. 'On the early shift this week.'

'Oh well, shall I come back?'

'No, that's all right. You can wait here if you like.' She opened the door wider; Grace smiled, stepped inside.

The small house was rather dark, but spotlessly clean and tidy.

'What a pretty house,' said Grace. 'Oh how stupid of me – these flowers are for you.'

'Thanks,' said Sandra. 'Very kind of you.'

'Well, I do realize it's a bit of an imposition, coming here like this. But I had to clear things up.'

'My mum's been cleaning for you,' said the little girl. 'All morning and all last evening.'

'Shut up, Deirdre. I haven't.'

'Yes you have!'

'Kids!' said Sandra Meredith. 'Always let you down. You got any?'

'Um – no,' said Grace. 'Not – not yet.'

'Oh well.' There was a silence, then Sandra said, 'Would you like some tea or something?'

'That'd be lovely.'

'You go in there,' said Sandra, indicating the front room, 'I'll bring it.'

'Thank you,' said Grace. She sat down heavily; she felt suddenly rather weak. 'She's ever so pretty,' she heard Deirdre say.

'Shush,' said Sandra.

Gillian Waters from Bennett & Bennett in Shaftesbury had had a very difficult client on the phone; she'd tried to soothe him, but without too much success. She decided to check she'd said all the right things; with young Mr Bennett being away and the new young partner always seeming to be in court or with clients, she found herself increasingly left alone, which she enjoyed, but the responsibility was considerable.

'Mr Bennett?' she said, when Charles answered the phone, after a very long wait – poor Mr Bennett, where was his wife? she wondered – 'Mr Bennett, I've just had Mr Morton on the phone, worrying about his contract. I've told him there was no need to worry and I did ring Mr Rogers to make sure everything was going through, but I thought I should just check – '

Charles told her everything was going through, but she had nevertheless been right to check, and then added that he had a lot of letters to dictate, and perhaps he should give her the more urgent over the phone. 'Then next week I'm hoping to be in, and we'll have them under our belt, so to speak.'

'Fine, Mr Bennett. Oh, by the way, that package that came yesterday, addressed to Mr Jacobs. I hope you didn't mind my sending it on to you, but someone clearly doesn't know he's retired.'

'Package?' said Charles. 'What package?'

'Oh, a small one, London postmark. I gave it to your wife – she said she's give it to you. Mr Bennett, are you still there?'

The secretary at the Salisbury School of Music told Mr Bennett that she was very sorry, she couldn't possibly contact his wife, explaining with admirable patience and courtesy as Mr Bennett started shouting at her that there must be some mistake, there were no lectures today on Mrs Bennett's course.

It was a very long two hours, sitting in the Merediths' small, rather stuffy sitting room; Grace didn't like to leave, in case Brian Meredith got home early. In the event he was fifteen minutes late; he rushed in, looking nervous, shook her hand and asked her to excuse him while he had what he called a clean-up.

'It's very kind of you to go to all this trouble,' said Grace, as he finally sat down opposite her, 'I really do appreciate it.'

'I do hope there won't be any trouble about it,' he said. 'The letter from Mr Jacobs did make me anxious.'

'I assure you there won't. Mr Jacobs got it wrong. Er – how did you first come across him? Mr Jacobs, I mean?'

'I phoned the number you gave me, and he answered the phone. I – well, I did phone during the day, as you said.'

'Yes of course. It was a silly mix-up. Now the thing is, Mr Meredith, I just wanted to thank you in person. What you did was so kind. And to – well, ask you a couple of things.'

'Yes, Mrs Bennett?'

'I – wondered where it was exactly you found him. The – the person in question. You see for a long time we thought he'd been shot escaping, my husband, but – well, I'd just like to know all about it. Please.'

'Oh, I see. Well, in Italy, but it's impossible to say where exactly. We were being driven up Germany; we'd been taken prisoner, you understand. It was quite near the French border, and I do remember driving through a small town called Brianca. I know that was correct, because it's so similar to my own name.'

'Yes of course. But the village, or the hamlet, where you found – Major Bennett, you don't remember anything about that?'

'It wasn't a village, Mrs Bennett. Nothing like a village. Miles from anywhere, really.'

'Oh, I see. But there was a farm? I mean, signs of life?'

'No, nothing. It was open countryside, no buildings or anything, as I say, for miles. Well, not as far as I could see.'

'But – but, Mr Meredith, where was Major Bennett? When you found him?'

'He was – oh dear, Mrs Bennett, I don't want to upset you – '

'You're not upsetting me,' said Grace firmly, 'I've always wanted to know. Please tell me. Everything you can remember.'

'Well, he was just – just lying there, you see. In a – in a sort of a ditch.'

'Oh,' said Grace. She looked at Brian Meredith. He seemed to be rather far away from her suddenly, his voice loud and echo-y. 'Oh, I see. So – there was no evidence of anyone looking after him? Of him having been given any kind of attention?'

'No, no, there wasn't, I'm afraid. I don't see how there could have been. As I say, he was miles from anywhere.'

'Yes. Yes, I see. And why – that is how did you know it was him? Major Bennett, I mean.'

'Well, it was the identity tag, you see.'

'Was it round his neck?'

'No, not round his neck. But he was holding it. In his hand. Mrs Bennett, would you like a cup of tea? You look rather pale.'

'Yes,' said Grace, 'yes please. I would.'

'She looks shocking,' said Brian Meredith to Sandra in a low voice

534

as he came out to put the kettle on. 'I'm afraid it's very hard for people to imagine what war is really like. How terrible it is.'

'Darlings!' cried Clarissa, opening the door and flinging her arms round all three of them. 'Darlings, how wonderful to see you. My goodness, you boys have got so big. David, I can hardly tell you from your father. Now don't even look at me. I'm so hideous, this great stomach. Come along in, I've got your rooms all ready for you, Jack will be home soon. Oh, this is just the greatest treat. I've been looking forward to it for so long, I can't tell you. Now I was hoping Florence would be here, but Giles is doing some preview in Cambridge and of course she's had to go up there and see him. So you've got to make do with boring old us.'

Charles was waiting for Grace when she got home. Everything was unnaturally tidy and in order; the table was set for supper, the fire in the drawing room lit, the smell of roasting chicken filled the house.

He was hobbling into the hall on his crutches when she opened the front door. 'Hallo,' he said. 'Good day?'

'Yes thank you,' said Grace briefly.

'Good. My mother came down, she looked after me very well. Cooked supper for us even.'

'Good for her.'

'Would you like a drink?'

'Yes. Yes, I think I would. Unlike me, isn't it, Charles? But I think I need one.'

'I've got the gin out,' he said, 'and some tonic. Would that be all right?'

'Fine. I'll get it. Let's go into the drawing room.'

She sipped her drink slowly, hoping it wasn't a mistake having it: she couldn't afford to get confused.

'I haven't been to Salisbury,' she said eventually.

'No, I know. I rang the college.'

'Ah. Well, anyway, I went to see Brian Meredith.'

'Who?'

'Corporal Meredith that was. The one who found the man they thought was you. The one you tried to scare off, Charles. You know.'

He was silent.

'Bit mean that,' she said, 'such a nice little man, so kind and anxious to do the right thing. He didn't deserve a dirty trick like that being played on him. Still, I've told him there's nothing to worry about.'

'You had no right to do that – '

'I shouldn't start talking about rights, if I were you,' she said, listening to her own voice, her cool, authoritative voice in amazement. 'Now then, would you like to tell me what really happened? With poor Colonel Barlowe?'

'I've told you,' he said.

'No you haven't. You told me a lot of lies. At least I think they were lies. I think they *must* have been lies. What happened, Charles?'

'For God's sake, I've told you,' he said again. 'He'd been wounded. The wound had become infected, he was ill, running a temperature. I was helping him as best I could. We reached this farm, the farmer offered to help, took him in, said he'd get the doctor –'

'Took him in where?'

'His – well, one of his buildings.'

'Not the house?'

'No, not the house, he wouldn't risk that. That would have been dangerous. For him I mean.'

'Yes, I suppose so. But it was definitely inside, was it? Some kind of building?'

'Yes. How many times do I have to tell you?'

'I don't know. Until we get to the truth,. I suppose. So then how was it, do you think, that Colonel Barlowe was actually found in a ditch? Miles from anywhere.'

'I have no idea,' he said. 'No idea at all. Maybe he panicked, rushed off, tried to get away again –'

'I thought he couldn't walk by then? I thought you had to half carry him?'

'Well, maybe he'd had some medical attention, was better, I don't know. Christ, Grace, I wasn't there by then.'

'No,' she said, 'you weren't. You were miles away by then. Miles and miles away. With Colonel Barlowe's identity tag. I still haven't quite fathomed that one out, but I expect I will. So are you going to tell me what happened, Charles? Or shall I tell you?'

'You tell me,' he said, 'since you're so bloody clever.'

'All right,' she said, 'I will tell you. But I'm going to get your parents down first, to listen. I think they ought to hear it. What you, their heroic son, actually did. To his friend and comrade in arms. And unless you do tell me, I'm going to tell a few other people what I think, too. Your sister, and your friends round here, your marvellous friends, who were so good to me while you were away. I wonder if the local paper might get to hear of it. And then there's Colin Barlowe's poor widow. She'd be pretty upset, if she knew what I'm thinking. I mean it is only my theory, I realize that. But Mr Meredith has a very clear memory of what happened. Anyway, we'll start with your parents. I'll just ring them up and – '

'You wouldn't do that,' he said, and there was sheer panic in his eyes, his white face, 'you wouldn't tell them. You couldn't – hurt them, shock them that much.'

'I certainly wouldn't want to, no. Especially not your father. Who I love so much, who loves you so much. I don't actually remember you according much loyalty to him, when he was in disgrace and needed help. That was left to me. You forbade me to have anything to do with him. Anyway, I would tell them, if I had to. But really I just want to know. For myself, for my own satisfaction. What happened, Charles?'

'If I tell you,' he said, and his voice was weak, hoarse, 'it won't go any further? Do you give me your word?'

'Yes,' she said, 'I give you my word.'

It was exactly as she had thought, worked out on the long, painful journey home from London. Charles had found Barlowe an increasing burden, had seen the man was going to impede his progress hopelessly, if not halt it altogether; that taking him to a hospital would mean recapture. And so he had left him. 'I did make him as comfortable as I could, I got him some water from a stream. I did mean to go back but – '

'And the identity tag? How did that happen?'

'I'd lost mine.'

'Charles, don't be absurd. You hadn't lost it, Colin Barlowe was holding it. I don't – ' And then suddenly, out of the past, came the conversation at a dinner party, someone saying, what was it, oh yes, that the higher the rank the better your chances. 'Colonels did pretty well' – those had been his exact words – 'corporals were left to play with themselves.' She looked at Charles, sitting waxy pale, staring at her. 'You took it, didn't you? You took his. And gave him yours. Knowing full well you probably wouldn't be back.'

'No, no,' he said, 'no, that's not true. I didn't take it. I told you, he insisted, he insisted I'd do better if I got caught.'

'But you said you'd lost yours – '

'Well – well, he must have found it.'

It was easier to believe him; she wanted to believe him. 'Oh all right,' she said wearily, 'go on.'

And so, he told her, the hours became days, and he had found no one who would help, no one he could trust, and he had no idea where he was any more. Either someone had found Barlowe, or he would have died. There seemed little point trying to return. 'Putting yourself at risk you mean?' said Grace.

'Yes. No. Oh for Christ's sake, don't sit there looking so fucking sanctimonious.' She had never heard him really swear before; it was a measure of his panic. 'You have no right to criticize me, anything I did. You have no idea what it was like. The sheer bloody hell of it. Months, years of fighting, of violence, of terror. Losing friends, losing men, never any respite, losing sight of any kind of hope of it ending. You sat here in England, playing at war, playing Lady Bountiful to a load of land girls, filling my house with riffraff, sleeping with your soldier, and then you think you have a right to judge me.'

She was silent; then she said, 'You don't understand, Charles. I'm afraid.'

'I do understand,' he said, 'all too well. You've found this – this thing out about me. And it renders me totally black in your judgment. No shades of grey, are there, Grace, for you? Just black and white. And once I was white, in your wide, innocent little eyes, and now I'm black, black as hell. Oh I understand all right. I understand.'

'No,' she said, 'you don't. What I do judge, Charles, what I find impossible to bear, is your lying about what you did. Preaching things like honour and duty at me, when you had done – well, what you did. If you'd been honest, if you'd told me what happened, I might have been shocked, I *would* have been shocked, but I would have tried to understand. How it happened, why it happened. I know what a terrible war you'd had, I can see how you'd suffered. But you couldn't trust me with it. You never could trust me with anything, could you? Just thought I was stupid, crass, incompetent in every way. I wish I knew why you married me, Charles, I really do.'

'I wish I knew too,' he said, and his voice was full of bitterness as well as rage. 'Looking back now I really cannot imagine. Well, I hope your soldier had more pleasure out of you than I did. For his sake.'

'Charles,' said Grace, 'be careful. Be very careful.'

'What I don't understand,' said Ben, his tongue loosened by some of Jack's fine whisky, sitting with his long legs stretched out in Clarissa's drawing room after dinner, 'is why she married him. And why he married her. Come to that.'

They were alone; the boys had gone to bed, Jack was studying.

'I think I can answer both questions,' said Clarissa. 'Goodness, was that lightning? I hope it won't affect your thrilling journey, Ben darling. She married him because she was dazzled by him, hopelessly impressed. He was frightfully good-looking, you know, very charming, quite rich, much older than her. She was very young, barely twenty I think, and very, very unsophisticated. Shy, couldn't say boo to the tiniest gosling. And he swept her off her feet. And once she was on that slippery slope, she just had to stay on it.'

'Yes, I suppose so. But why did he – '

'Charles likes to dominate situations,' said Clarissa, 'that's why I didn't marry him. I should never have said I would, but he was there, and he was fun, and I was always getting engaged to people, you can't imagine. Broke off at least four. But it really almost destroyed him when I told him I wasn't going to marry him. Mostly because he can't bear failure, can't bear people thinking he's not an entirely good egg. He was much more upset at the humiliation than at my telling him I didn't love him. And I think he just couldn't risk it happening again. He thought Grace was a pushover; a sweet, innocent little thing who would do everything he told her to do. And she was incredibly pretty – well, she still is – and sweet, and charming, and the absolutely ideal wife for him – only in theory, Ben darling, don't look like that. And he knew that she wouldn't in a million years do what I did, let him down, make a fool of him, leave him. Even now.'

'I know,' said Ben. 'That's why I never tried to persuade her, never tried to make her change her mind.'

'I have decided to leave you, Charles,' said Grace, 'that's about the only thing I do feel sure about at the moment.'

'Oh don't be absurd,' he said, 'of course you're not going to leave me. Just over this.'

'No, not just over this. You haven't heard a word I've been saying, have you?'

'Well, why then?'

'Because you've got me so terribly wrong. Because you don't understand me, don't value what I am at all. We don't have a relationship. You want someone, something utterly different, and you're never going to find her – it – in me. I'm not leaving you because of what you did to Colonel Barlowe. Well, not really. It's just shown me, that's all, what you've been doing to me.'

'Grace,' he said, and there was panic in his voice now, 'Grace, please don't go. I can't manage without you, I need you – '

'No you don't,' she said, 'that's what I'm telling you. Listen to me, Charles, you might learn something. You don't need me at all. You don't need anything I can do for you. If I thought you did, I'd struggle on, and I daresay in the end we'd be quite happy. But you don't, and I can't cope with that.'

'So I suppose you're going to tell everyone, are you? You'll enjoy that, won't you? Telling them what a rat I am, how I deserted a friend in his hour of need.'

'Charles – '

'I don't know why you're so sure everyone would believe you,' he said. 'I can deny anything that fool of a corporal said.' He sounded suddenly more confident. 'Who would take his – and your – word against mine?'

'Nobody probably,' said Grace, 'that's the whole point. And it would cause so many people so much pain, if they knew, that I wouldn't dream of telling anyone the truth. In fact I shall probably write to nice Mrs Barlowe and send her the ring and tell her it was sent to me anonymously by someone who nursed him. Or something like that. Something comforting, anyway.'

'So what are you going to do?' he said. 'Just use what you know to taunt me with for the rest of my life, I suppose. Get what you want out of me. Is that it?'

'No,' said Grace, 'no, that's not it. But I can't go on living with you. I just can't.'

'Ah,' he said, 'now we come to it. You'll be going off to your soldier, no doubt.'

'I haven't even thought about that,' she said, surprise in her voice that she so genuinely had not. 'And anyway, he's going to live in Australia. He's leaving in the morning. I certainly can't go with him. And I don't know that he would even want me to.'

She sat quietly for a moment, reflecting on that fact, so confused by her day, so exhausted, she had no idea, no idea at all what was to become of her, once she had left Charles and his house. His house, she thought, always his house; never hers, never even theirs. It summed up their entire marriage, that fact, the whole sorry, wasteful, miserable affair.

'And what am I to tell people?' he said. He was looking rather more uncertain now.

'Oh for God's sake, what does it matter what you tell people?' said Grace, her voice a deep well of exasperation as well as despair. 'You can tell them whatever you like, I really don't care. They all think I'm worthless, your friends, anyway. You can just say I've gone, left you. Your mother will think it's only to be expected, will be relieved, I imagine. I shall tell your father some comforting half-truth. You really don't have to worry, Charles. You can divorce me, marry someone else, someone suitable, someone who can ride and give cocktail parties – '

'Oh don't be so bloody pathetic,' he said.

But she could see that already the idea had its attractions. 'You don't love me at all, do you?' she said. 'You never did.'

'Not really,' he said, politely surprised at the discovery, 'no, I don't think I ever did.'

Grace lay on the sofa; she felt deathly weary and terribly cold. Charles was in his study, had closed the door very firmly on her. It seemed symptomatic not only of the end of their marriage, but of his treatment of her right through it.

Every so often she had a fit of violent shivering; she supposed she was in some kind of shock. It had been a bit like that when she had first heard about Charles, that he was alive. Before she lost the baby. Ben's baby.

She looked around the room: this room that she loved so much, in this house that she loved so much, that her heart was in. In every corner of every room there was a memory, some of them happy, some of them dreadful: all of it so much more than just walls and floors, bricks and mortar.

Well, she had to leave it now; she couldn't stay. She had to walk away, bequeath it, that part of her life that had been lived in it, and start again. And not even with Ben. On her own.

If only, if only she had made this discovery earlier. There were so many ifs: if Brian Meredith hadn't been ill, if Charles hadn't broken his leg, if Elspeth's exam had been one day earlier. But it was too late now. Much too late. And anyway, she thought, was she really quite, quite sure Ben wanted her still? After this long, painful year. He hadn't written so much as the briefest note to say goodbye, hadn't even sent a message; she must not assume he missed her as much as she missed him.

'Do you still miss Grace?' said Clarissa.

'Of course I do,' he said, 'I miss her so much. What she looks like, what she sounds like, what she feels like. I don't think I'll ever get over it.'

'Oh Ben,' said Clarissa, her dark eyes bright with tears, 'oh Ben, darling, don't you think even now you might – '

'No,' he said fiercely, 'no, I don't. I can't. We promised each other. She's so – so straight, Clarissa. And brave. It would be wrong of me, it would just make things worse for her. Besides,' he said with a crooked grin, 'how do I know she still feels the same about me. It's a whole year now, she's probably settling down with her – with him.'

Clarissa looked at him, thought of Grace's voice saying, 'It's so hard that I still don't know how to bear it,' and made a decision that she hoped she wasn't going to regret for the rest of her life.

'I think you should phone and say goodbye,' she said. 'It's worth just a few more tears. You'll regret it for ever if you don't.'

Ben looked at her for a long time; then he said, 'I couldn't. I don't think I want to hear her voice. I couldn't stand it. And besides, supposing he answered the phone.'

Clarissa thought for a moment. Then she said, 'You could always use Clifford as a go-between.'

The dogs were whining; they hated to be in the kitchen on their own. Grace went in to see them, gave them a biscuit each. That made her realize, rather to her surprise, she was hungry herself; she found some bread, spread it with some of Mr Dunn's honey. It was bread she had made herself; Charles was right, it was very doughy – she'd have indigestion now to add to her miseries. She decided to go for a walk; it might help to clear her head, which was aching very nicely too. 'Come on,' she said to the dogs, 'just a little way.'

'Beddy-byes soon, I think,' said Clarissa. 'This little sprog makes me awfully sleepy. If it's a boy, I'm going to call him Benjamin. What would you think about that?'

'I'd think you were flattering me,' said Ben, smiling at her. 'But if you did, I'd like it. I'll miss you, Clarissa.'

'And I shall miss you. All of you.' She lay back on the sofa, looked at him. 'Those boys are such heaven. I just looked in on them: Daniel's fast asleep with a huge framed picture of Charlotte and Floss under his pillow. It must be terribly uncomfortable.'

'He does it every night,' said Ben.

'Well, as I said, darling, bedtime. Goodnight, sweet dreams.'

'Goodnight,' said Ben, 'and thank you for everything.'

He went out of the room; Clarissa thought she had never seen anyone look so alone. Her heart ached for him.

Grace walked into the house to find Charles standing in the kitchen. He half smiled at her; he was clearly still feeling extremely wary of her.

'My father phoned while you were out,' he said, 'said he wanted to speak to you, said it was urgent. Wouldn't tell me what it was about. Could you ring him back?'

'Yes of course,' said Grace. 'Thank you.'

Clarissa started plumping up cushions, putting away newspapers, then remembered she had to ring May. A last-minute booking had come in, and there was no one left to send: on such occasions May went to the client herself. She picked up the phone, dialled the number. The phone was dead. It was, the operator told her, due to the thunderstorm.

She would just have to go in to the office early, catch May then.

'Clifford, it's Grace. What's the matter, is there a problem?'

'No,' he said, 'no, not exactly. I just had a call from Ben.'

'Oh,' said Grace, and sat down very abruptly. 'What – what did he say?'

'He said just to say goodbye and to tell you he still loves you very much. That's all.'

'Oh Clifford,' said Grace, 'Oh dear. It's all too late,' and she burst into tears.

'Well,' said Clifford, and she could tell he was having great difficulty making up his mind quite what to say. 'He's still at Clarissa's, you know.'

So it wasn't actually too late. Not yet. Not quite. Not too late at all. She said goodbye to Clifford, put the receiver down and closed the study door.

'I'm sorry,' said the operator, 'that number is out of order. Definitely out of order. Most of the numbers on that exchange are.'

'It can't be,' said Grace stupidly.

'I'm sorry?'

'It – oh never mind.' She could ring Florence. Florence wouldn't mind. They were always up terribly late.

'Could you try Sloane 543? Please?'

'Hold the line, caller.' An endless, endless wait. 'I'm sorry, caller, there doesn't seem to be any reply.'

'Could you try again?'

Another long wait.

'I'm sorry, caller. No reply.'

Oh God. He would think she hadn't even tried. He had wanted to say goodbye, would be waiting, hoping that she would phone, and thinking she didn't care. Didn't love him. He was going off to the other side of the world, and this was her last chance, her very last chance, to tell him she still loved him too, and she couldn't do it. Well, she had to, she simply had to. Otherwise she would never forgive herself and he would never forgive her. She looked at her watch. Half past ten. She wondered wildly, briefly if she shouldn't just take the car and start driving to London; then thought that if she got the milk train in the morning she would actually get there much more quickly and safely. She could get a taxi to Clarissa's, be there by – well, by eight or so – and still catch Ben. See Ben. If only to say goodbye.

In Clarissa's house, David and Daniel slept, both restless, sharing excitement-packed dreams of planes and sunshine and sharks. Ben lay awake, staring out at the night sky, cleansed now of its thunderclouds, the half-moon covered with scudding clouds, thinking about Grace, half wishing he hadn't phoned and wishing desperately she had phoned him back. If only to say goodbye.

There were only two things Grace was really worried about as she crept downstairs at four in the morning: one was Charlotte and the other was Puppy. She thought briefly, wildly of taking them, and then rejected the idea: Clifford would look after them. He wouldn't mind. There was no way she could actually go to Australia: apart from anything else, she didn't have a ticket. She could be back to collect the dogs next day. Or later that day.

She scribbled a note to Clifford, put it in an envelope to post through the Priory door, asking him to collect the dogs later, explaining she had gone to say goodbye to Ben. Then she wrote another note to Charles, saying his car was at Salisbury station and the keys were with the stationmaster, and left it on the kitchen table. And then she left. She had been terrified he would wake and hear the car starting until she realized there would be nothing he could do about it, except watch her disappearing down the lane. The thought made her smile.

The milk train left Salisbury at five, was due to reach London at half past seven or thereabouts. Grace, finally exhausted, slept in a corner of the carriage, having extracted a promise from the guard that he would wake her at Waterloo.

'I'll do that, my dear,' he said. 'You have a nice sleep now.'

'I will,' she said. And she did.

'Now we have to leave this house at eight o'clock at the latest,' said Ben firmly to the boys. 'We have to make our own way to Victoria station to go down to the coast and we don't know the way. We'll be carrying our luggage, and we can't afford to be in a rush. All right?'

'Yeah, OK,' they said.

'So go and wash, and then come down for breakfast. Clarissa's waiting to say goodbye, she's got to go to her office.'

'She looks ever so different, all fat and that,' said Daniel.

'I think she still looks lovely,' said Ben firmly.

Clarissa cried when she said goodbye to them.

'I don't know how I'm going to bear it,' she said. 'Now I want hundreds of photographs and letters, don't forget, and when I've made my fortune as the first lady tycoon, I'll be over. I might even open a branch of Marissa in Sydney.'

'Yeah, you do that,' said Ben. He hugged her, kissed her. It reminded him perversely of kissing Grace and that upset him. She looked up at him and smiled, understanding.

'She'll be all right,' she said, 'I'll look after her.'

'Tell her I love her,' he said, 'tell her I'll always love her.'

'I will. Oh dear – oh my goodness, I must go. Jack darling, lock up when you leave, won't you?'

'Yes, Clarissa. I think I can just about remember to lock the front door.'

Grace tried the phone again at Waterloo; it was still out of order. She ran over to the taxi rank. 'Campden Hill Square, please. Quickly.'

It was already seven forty.

'Take a bit of time from here, madam. To be honest with you, you'd do better on the tube. Notting Hill Gate.'

'Oh, all right. Thank you.'

'Right,' said Ben, 'I think that's just about it. Daniel, what's the matter?'

'I've got to go to the toilet, Dad.'

'Well, be quick.'

'Yeah, OK. I've got stomach ache, though.'

Ever since his appendicitis he had been neurotic about his stomach. 'Go on then.'

Five minutes later Daniel had still not come downstairs. Ben looked at the clock. It was eight ten. 'David, go and tell him to hurry up, for God's sake.'

David came down again looking exasperated. 'He says he feels sick now.'

'Oh God,' said Ben. 'All right, I'll go up.'

The tube stuck in the tunnel; for almost fifteen minutes it sat there, making chugging noises, followed by high-pitched revving-up ones and then more chugging. Grace thought she had never in her entire life been so close to murdering anyone as the little man who sat next to her telling her his life story, which seemed to consist in its entirety of a series of journeys from his home to his office and back again on the tube, and thence to his allotment on his bicycle. He also gave her a bed-by-bed description of what the allotment managed to produce.

'Better get a taxi,' said Jack. 'I'll ring for one. The phone's just come back on.'

'I didn't know it was off,' said Ben, staring at him, feeling a great weight of misery lifting from him.

'Yes, went dead late last night,' said Jack. 'Thunderstorm apparently.'

'Good God. Yes, please could you get us one?'

'Campden Hill Square, please,' said Grace to the taxi driver.

'Hardly worth it from here, Madam.'

'I don't care. Just get me there, would you?'

'Phew,' said Ben as the taxi finally pulled away from the house. 'Nick of time. Better this way, though. At least we won't have to get to the station on the bus. And hopefully we'll get the train. Honestly, Dan, you and your stomach. Just cost me at least a pound.'

'Sorry, Dad. Hey, did you see, we nearly hit that other taxi coming down the hill.'

'Grace! What a lovely surprise,' said Jack. 'Clarissa's gone to work, I'm afraid.'

'Is – is Ben still here?'

'No, I'm sorry. He left – oh, about five minutes ago. In a taxi.'

'A taxi. Oh God. When's his plane?'

'About two. They were pretty late anyway. Hence the taxi. The train leaves the station at nine. If you want to try and catch them, I'll come with you of course, but I don't think – '

'Oh no!' said Grace. She sat down on the steps and burst into tears.

'Daniel, what on earth is the matter now?'

'The photograph, Dad. The one of Charlotte and Floss. I left it in the lav.'

'You what?'

'I left it in the lav. I had it, and then when I had to go to the toilet I took it in with me. Then you started shouting, and I forgot it. I've got to have it, Dad. I've got to.'

'You can't.'

'I've got to.'

'Daniel, I am not risking missing our flight because of a photograph. It's ridiculous. We can ask Clarissa to send it on.'

'Dad, Grace said I had to have it.'

'Daniel, no.'

Daniel started to yell; he screamed and yelled and kicked the seat. The cab driver looked in his rear mirror. 'What's wrong, guv?'

'My son's forgotten something.'

'Sounds pretty important.'

'Oh – not really.'

'You got time, you know,' said the cabbie. 'Can get you to Victoria by nine, easy.'

'No,' said Ben firmly.

Unfortunately Daniel had heard this exchange. 'Dad, I feel sick again – I'm going to be sick, it's coming, it's coming, I'm going to throw up – '

'Oh all right,' said Ben wearily to the cabbie, 'let's go back.'

'Could I use your phone, Jack?' asked Grace. She was amazed at herself for even thinking of it, but she suddenly very badly needed to know whether Elspeth had won her scholarship. It would mean that at least something had been achieved in this fruitless, desperate, dreadful morning.

'Yes of course. In there, in my study. Do go ahead.'

'Thank you. One of my pupils just put in for a scholarship and we were told the result would be through this morning – '

Grace was on the phone to St Felicia's waiting to be put through to the music department when she heard a peremptory ring at the bell. The postman, or some other tradesman, she supposed. It rang again. Maybe she should go. She'd thought Jack was still in the house, but perhaps – '

'Mrs Bennett?' said the voice of the head of music at St Felicia's.

'Yes. This is Grace Bennett.'

'Mrs Bennett, yes, I have the results here – '

The bell rang yet again. Tradespeople up here were a lot more impatient than in the country. Well, they'd just have to wait. Learn some country manners.

'Yes?' she said. 'Yes, do please go on.'

'Lovely news, Mrs Bennett. You'll be pleased to hear Elspeth has been awarded our scholarship. I have of course written to her father, but I'm sure you'd like to – '

This was really odd; she could have sworn that was Daniel's voice in the hall. It couldn't be. No, she must be hallucinating, with exhaustion and emotion. It was Jack's. She could hear it now, unmistakable, quite loud and deep, his Battle of Britain burr as Clarissa called it. She forced her mind back to Elspeth and the scholarship.

'I'm so absolutely delighted,' she said. 'Thank you – '

She heard the door opening behind her; she put her arm out, gave the thumbs-up sign without looking round, presuming it was Jack. 'Thank you,' she said again into the phone, 'and I'm sorry to – '

And then she felt a hand most surprisingly on her shoulder, moving up gently to the nape of her neck, stroking it; and as she tried to turn round then, to see who it was, knowing who it was, even while she did not dare to know, she heard a voice, filled with love, with tenderness, with amusement.

'Don't say sorry,' it said.

June 1948

It would not normally have been Grace's chosen reading of course, the *Tatler*, but it was the only thing available to her, as she waited patiently to see her doctor in Dublin – just to make sure, to her absolute satisfaction, that she and Ben were indeed about to provide the small Kate Lucas with a smaller brother or sister. She picked the magazine up and started flicking idly through it – and there it was, a whole page, with lots of pictures, reporting the recent wedding of Major Charles Bennett DSO to the Honourable Caroline Pennington, held in the grounds of the beautiful Georgian house in Somerset where the bride had grown up.

She had known about it of course, both Florence and Clarissa had written both before and after the event, and indeed Charles himself had written her a stiff little note informing her; but it was wonderfully intriguing to actually see the pictures, to study them all, to feel she had been there, an unseen almost ghostly observer. She had been truly pleased at the news, not the smallest shadow of an uncharitable thought had fallen across her consciousness; she bore Charles no ill-will whatsoever, she had been pleased to discover, and Caroline was clearly the most suitable of brides for him, pretty, vivacious, a wonderful cook, a fine horsewoman (or so Florence had said) a little young perhaps, but he would like that, it would suit his pomposity, his need to be completely in charge. So much more suitable than she had been, Grace thought, studying Caroline's radiant smile, her slightly bosomy figure (encased in a lace dress, strongly reminiscent of the one worn by Princess Elizabeth when she had married her Prince Philip Mountbatten the previous year); Caroline would do all the things at which she had failed so miserably, would ride with him, entertain for him, join charity committees, become an integral and important part of the local community – and no doubt provide him with a son and heir within the year.

Charles looked very handsome in his morning suit, she thought, in spite of his scar; and although the marriage itself had been held in a registry office, there had been a blessing in church – 'a charming ceremony' according to the reporter.

There were four small bridesmaids in frilly dresses, and four pageboys in white satin, all smiling very nicely at the camera except for one – Imogen – who was scowling vigorously; (and had later apparently according to Clarissa been seen riding a pony bareback round the paddock, her frilly skirt tucked into her knickers – 'while her mother breast fed little Cedric right in the middle of the tent, too funny, Florence is so wonderful, I expect she'll be doing it in the House of Commons next, but let's hope this one won't be quite so spoilt . . .')

There was a picture of all the parents flanking the bride and groom: Muriel looking extremely complacent, no doubt satisfied that finally Charles had married a girl who was at least nearly good enough for him, Clifford looking extremely jolly (no doubt as much as a result of drinking several glasses of champagne as at the events of the day) and Lord and Lady Pennington looking charmingly, graciously happy.

She could imagine exactly what all the guests (photographed sipping champagne in the marquee) would have been saying; how nice it was that poor Charles had found the right wife at last, how they had all known it could never last, his first marriage; that she had been very nice in her way, of course, the first Mrs Bennett, but she simply wasn't the sort of person Charles should have married, and agreeing that it been no great surprise to anyone really when she had run off like that, just to be with the other man, the father of those two boys she had taken in – against Charles's wishes incidentally, straight from the slums.

And there was Clarissa, looking ravishing in her New Look outfit, and dear Jack, standing very upright beside her, smiling his determined smile – 'War hero Jack Compton Brown' read the caption, 'shortly to complete his studies at medical school, to qualify as a plastic surgeon.' How brave he was: braver than any of them. Ben had said he would like to have them to stay, him and Clarissa; it would be so lovely to see them again.

Well, there would be three of them, of course, for there was the exquisite small Vanessa as well, and probably a uniformed nanny in tow; quite a party. But the house was just big enough, her lovely grey stone house in the small village just outside Dublin, bought for them by Clifford, dear Clifford, his handsome old face flushed with determination when he handed her the cheque: 'No need to tell anyone, my darling, anyone at all of course, not even Ben if you don't want to, small legacy, I should think wouldn't you, from that dear old great aunt of yours perhaps, the one up in Scotland, who died while all the drama was going on – '

She had been afraid Ben wouldn't believe that, would be suspicious, but he had accepted it without question: probably because he was so grateful. Their responsibilities at that point had been rather onerous, he with his teacher training course only halfway through, Kate on the way, David and Daniel both at the grammar school by then, and getting very expensive – all his savings gone on the un-used tickets to Australia. Ireland had been such a brilliant idea of Ben's: far from all the gossip and scandal, the houses so much cheaper, and the people so friendly and welcoming, the countryside so beautiful.

And there was Giles, looking wonderfully handsome: she had read all the reviews of his latest triumph, lead in the fashionable new musical, a rather daring but much praised adaptation of *As You Like It* which was touring all the major provincial cities before opening in the West End; it was rumoured to be coming to Dublin, which would be wonderful, Florence had promised to let her know definitely – 'and I'll come too, of course, canvassing permitting, but I have a real chance of getting in this time (local only of course) and of course that must come first. I can see you any time.'

Grace presumed that tact was not an essential quality in a politician.

She looked at her watch: she had been waiting a long time. She had three pupils that afternoon; if she wasn't out of here in twenty minutes she'd be late. Not that it would terribly matter, Bridget who looked after Kate while she was teaching would simply give some cake and some lemonade to whoever it was – Mary? Or Felicity – first? God, pregnancy played havoc with your brain. That was really why she was so sure she was having another one: it started long before she even felt sick, an inability to remember even her own name and address, never mind anyone else's.

'Mrs Lucas? Sorry to have kept you. Doctor will see you now. Did you want to keep that magazine Mrs Lucas, that you're holding, I'm sure it would be fine if you did.'

Grace stood up.

'Thank you. No, sorry I wasn't thinking. And don't worry about the wait. I've been quite happy.'

'Well isn't that a fine thing. So many people get annoyed. You look *very* happy, Mrs Lucas, if you don't mind my saying so.'

'Thank you,' said Grace.

She went into the surgery, leaving the magazine behind her. She had thought, briefly, of taking it home to show Ben, but on the whole it seemed a bad idea. It was all part of another life, a strangely unbelievable other life, that they both looked back on less and less. Now was what mattered, now and the future and each other and their children. The past was another place: none of it dangerous, none of it forbidden any more: but certainly best left undisturbed.

All Orion/Phoenix titles are available at your local bookshop or from the following address:

Mail Order Department
Littlehampton Book Services
FREEPOST BR535
Worthing, West Sussex, BN13 3BR
telephone 01903 828503, *facsimile* 01903 828802
e-mail MailOrders@lbsltd:co.uk
(Please ensure that you include full postal address details)

Payment can be made either by credit/debit card (Visa, Mastercard, Access and Switch accepted) or by sending a £ Sterling cheque or postal order made payable to *Littlehampton Book Services*.
DO NOT SEND CASH OR CURRENCY.

Please add the following to cover postage and packing

UK and BFPO:
£1.50 for the first book, and 50p for each additional book to a maximum of £3.50

Overseas and Eire:
£2.50 for the first book plus £1.00 for the second book and 50p for each additional book ordered

---

BLOCK CAPITALS PLEASE

name of cardholder _____   *delivery address*
                    _____   *(if different from cardholder)*
address of cardholder _____

□ I enclose my remittance for £_____

□ please debit my Mastercard/Visa/Access/Switch (delete as appropriate)

card number [ ][ ][ ][ ][ ][ ][ ][ ][ ][ ][ ][ ][ ][ ][ ][ ]

expiry date [ ][ ][ ][ ]   Switch issue no. [ ][ ]

signature _____

prices and availability are subject to change without notice